D. H. LAWRENCE

D. H. LAWRENCE

D.H. LAWRENCE

SONS AND LOVERS
ST MAWR
THE FOX
THE WHITE PEACOCK
LOVE AMONG THE HAYSTACKS
THE VIRGIN AND THE GIPSY
LADY CHATTERLEY'S LOVER

Heinemann/Octopus

Sons and Lovers first published in Great Britain in 1913
St Mawr first published in Great Britain in 1925
The Fox first published in Great Britain in 1923
The White Peacock first published in Great Britain in 1911
Love among the Haystacks first published in Great Britain in 1930
The Virgin and the Gipsy first published in Great Britain in 1930
Lady Chatterley's Lover first published in Great Britain in this
complete and unabridged text in 1960

This edition published 1979 by
Book Club Associates
by arrangement with Octopus Books Limited
This edition first published in 1976 by
William Heinemann Limited
15-16 Queen Street, London W1
in association with
Octopus Books Limited
59 Grosvenor Street, London W1
Copyright © The Estate of D. H. Lawrence 1911, 1913, 1923, 1925, 1930, 1960
ISBN 0 7064 0570 6
Printed in Great Britain by
Jarrold & Sons Ltd., Norwich

BOOK CLUB ASSOCIATES
LONDON

CN 2553

Printed in the United States of America
by R. R. Donnelley and Sons Company,

CONTENTS

Sons and Lovers 11
St Mawr 303
The Fox 403
The White Peacock 451
Love among the Haystacks 673
The Virgin and the Gipsy 703
Lady Chatterley's Lover 761

INTRODUCTION

'I was a delicate pale brat with a snuffy nose, whom most people treated quite gently as just a delicate little lad. When I was twelve I got a county council scholarship, twelve pounds a year, and went to Nottingham High School.

'After leaving school I was a clerk for three months, then had a serious pneumonia illness in my seventeenth year that damaged my health for life.

'A year later I became a school-teacher, and after three years' savage teaching of collier lads I went to take the "normal" course in Nottingham University.

'As I was glad to leave school, I was glad to leave college. It had meant mere disillusion, instead of the living contact of men. From college I went to Croydon, near London, to teach in a new elementary school at a hundred pounds a year.

'It was while I was at Croydon, when I was twenty-three, that the girl who had been the chief friend of my youth, and who was herself a school-teacher in a mining village at home, copied out some of my poems, and without telling me, sent them to the *English Review*, which had just had a glorious re-birth under Ford Madox Hueffer.

'Hueffer was most kind. He printed the poems, and asked me to come and see him. The girl had launched me so easily on my literary career, like a princess cutting a thread, launching a ship.'

David Herbert Lawrence, born at Eastwood, Nottinghamshire, on 11 September 1885, the fourth child of a miner, packed a lot of autobiography into those short paragraphs.

Learning and teaching were no substitutes for 'the living contact of men'. That statement sums up Lawrence's attitude to life and the way in which he wrote. The power of his intuition, the immediacy of his feeling and his firm grasp of the characters, the times and surroundings he is describing bring total living individuals into his novels. His people are real people and not puppets manipulated through charades of social behaviour.

His health was marked for life, as he said, when he was seventeen. He eventually became tubercular and died in 1930, his body no longer able to sustain the flame of his imagination, his invention and – to use the word that has been hurled back and forth across his memory and reputation ever since like a white-hot missile – his genius.

That word was first used about Lawrence's work to his face on a London bus. It was Ford Madox Hueffer (the novelist who wrote later as Ford Madox Ford) who had published some of Lawrence's poems, and who bawled cheerfully above the noise of the traffic 'It's got every fault that the English novel can have' of *The White Peacock*, which he had just read, 'But,' he shouted, 'you've got GENIUS.'

'This,' said Lawrence, 'made me want to laugh, it sounded so comical. In the early days they were always telling me I had got genius, as if to console me for not having their own incomparable advantages. . . . Anyway, he sent the MS of *The White Peacock* to William Heinemann, who accepted it at once. . . .'

And so, in 1911 his first novel was published. Annable, an ex-parson who had married an aristocrat, is convinced that civilised society is rotten under its veneer and, hating society and society women in particular, becomes a gamekeeper. There are themes in that first novel to which Lawrence returned again and again in later work – the conflicts between instinct and intellect, the low-born and the high-born, and between men and women.

It was in *Sons and Lovers* (1913) which is not only one of his best works but one of the great novels in the language, that he examined in depth and with passion the relationship between parents and children. Autobiographical in inspiration, he portrayed in unforgettable style his own parents, his near-illiterate and often drunken miner father and his socially 'superior' mother – the instinctive man and the spiritual woman – and the mysterious ties of blood which he both felt and communicated so strongly.

The mystery of sensual and spiritual communication, though not of kinship, is present powerfully in *The Fox* where the two Lesbian chicken farmers feel their livelihood threatened by the prowling fox and then their relationship by the young soldier who comes to stay with them.

In *Saint Mawr* it is again an animal – the stallion of that name – who acts as a catalyst in the relationships of the human beings around him, but in *The Virgin and the Gipsy*, another force of nature – water – sweeps away the social divisions and inhibitions that formerly stood between the girl and the man trapped together by the floods and linked by the fight to survive.

In fact the 'force of nature' in every sense permeates nearly the whole of Lawrence's prose and poetry. Included in that force was the beauty of nature, seen, felt and absorbed by his poet's and painter's eye. The reader immediately sees, for example, 'the haystack being built just above the hedge. It was of great size, massive, but so silvery and delicately bright in tone that it seemed not to have weight. It rose dishevelled and radiant among the steady, golden-green glare of the field.' *Love Among the Haystacks* is full of his personal impressions gained while haymaking in 1908 and was probably written in 1912, the year when Lawrence, whose life was often like one of his own novels, left for Europe with the woman he later married.

Frieda von Richthofen, aristocratic and German, was married and the mother of two children when she met Lawrence. She left her family and stayed with Lawrence through his wanderings in Germany, Italy, and New Mexico, through the difficult war years in England when, because of her origins and the couple's 'oddness' in rural settings, rumours of his being a spy were set about. Frieda was with him in the South of France during his final illness and death at Vence in 1930.

The last novel by Lawrence is probably the most notorious ever written, its title known to millions who have never read a word of Lawrence and may not in some cases even know the name of the author. Lawrence had been a victim of puritanical censorship before, when *The Rainbow* was published in 1915. It was withdrawn and was not available again until it was reissued in a slightly changed form by Martin Secker in 1926. But it was *Lady Chatterley's Lover* that unleashed a raging hurricane around the very name of D. H. Lawrence and prevented publication, except in private, pirated or expurgated editions until the famous 'trials' in the USA and England in the early 1960s freed the complete, unexpurgated edition which appears in this volume. Lawrence wrote three versions of this novel, changing and adding as he went along but it was not until 1972 that the two earlier drafts appeared in England under the titles *The First Lady Chatterley* and *John Thomas and Lady Jane*.

Here again Lawrence attacked savagely the hypocrisies and false values of civilisation, the desecration of the countryside, the artificialities of intellectual modes and the cynicism of the business world. Above all he celebrated the power and beauty of physical love in his story of Mellors (a gamekeeper, like Annable in his first novel *The White Peacock*) and Lady Connie Chatterley.

Lawrence had the first word in this introduction to his novels. Frieda Lawrence has the last in her true and moving epitaph on him:

'He died unbroken; he never lost his own wonder of life. He never did a thing he did not want to do and nothing and nobody could make him. He never wrote a word he did not mean at the time he wrote it. He never compromised with the little powers that be; if ever there lived a free, proud man, Lawrence was that man.'

D.H. LAWRENCE

SONS AND LOVERS

PART I

I

THE EARLY MARRIED LIFE OF THE MORELS

'The Bottoms' succeeded to 'Hell Row'. Hell Row was a block of thatched, bulging cottages that stood by the brookside on Greenhill Lane. There lived the colliers who worked in the little gin-pits two fields away. The brook ran under the alder-trees, scarcely soiled by these small mines, whose coal was drawn to the surface by donkeys that plodded wearily in a circle round a gin. And all over the countryside were these same pits, some of which had been worked in the time of Charles II, the few colliers and the donkeys burrowing down like ants into the earth, making queer mounds and little black places among the corn-fields and the meadows. And the cottages of these coalminers, in blocks and pairs here and there, together with odd farms and homes of the stockingers, straying over the parish, formed the village of Bestwood.

Then, some sixty years ago, a sudden change took place. The gin-pits were elbowed aside by the large mines of the financiers. The coal and iron field of Nottinghamshire and Derbyshire was discovered. Carston, Waite and Co appeared. Amid tremendous excitement, Lord Palmerston formally opened the company's first mine at Spinney Park, on the edge of Sherwood Forest.

About this time the notorious Hell Row, which through growing old had acquired an evil reputation, was burned down, and much dirt was cleansed away.

Carston, Waite and Co found they had struck on a good thing, so, down the valleys of the brooks from Selby and Nuttall, new mines were sunk, until soon there were six pits working. From Nuttall, high up on the sandstone among the woods, the railway ran, past the ruined priory of the Carthusians and past Robin Hood's Well, down to Spinney Park, then on to Minton, a large mine among corn-fields; from Minton across the farm-lands of the valleyside to Bunker's Hill, branching off there, and running north to Beggarlee and Selby, that looks over at Crich and the hills of Derbyshire; six mines like black studs on the countryside, linked by a loop of fine chain, the railway.

To accommodate the regiments of miners, Carston, Waite and Co built the Squares, great quadrangles of dwellings on the hillside of Bestwood, and then, in the brook valley, on the site of Hell Row, they erected the Bottoms.

The Bottoms consisted of six blocks of miners' dwellings, two rows of three, like the dots on a blank-six domino, and twelve houses in a block. This double row of dwellings sat at the foot of the rather sharp slope from Bestwood, and looked out, from the attic windows at least, on the slow climb of the valley towards Selby.

The houses themselves were substantial and very decent. One could walk all round, seeing little front gardens with auriculas and saxifrage in the shadow of the bottom block, sweet-williams and pinks in the sunny top block; seeing neat front windows, little porches, little privet hedges, and dormer windows for the attics. But that was outside; that was the view on to the uninhabited parlours of all the colliers' wives. The dwelling-room, the kitchen, was at the back of the house, facing inward between the blocks, looking at a scrubby back garden, and then at the ash-pits. And between the rows, between the long lines of ash-pits, went the alley, where the children played and the women gossiped and the men smoked. So, the actual conditions of living in the Bottoms, that was so well built and that looked so nice, were quite unsavoury because people must live in the kitchen, and the kitchens opened on to that nasty alley of ash-pits.

Mrs Morel was not anxious to move into the Bottoms, which was already twelve years old and on the downward path, when she descended to it from Bestwood. But it was the best she could do. Moreover, she had an end house in one of the top blocks, and thus had only one neighbour; on the other side an extra strip of garden. And, having an end house, she enjoyed a kind of aristocracy among the other women of the 'between' houses, because her rent was five shillings and sixpence instead of five shillings a week. But this superiority in station was not much consolation to Mrs Morel.

She was thirty-one years old, and had been married eight years. A rather small woman, of delicate mould but resolute bearing, she shrank a little from the first contact with the Bottoms women. She came down in the July, and in the September expected her third baby.

Her husband was a miner. They had only been in their new home three weeks when the wakes, or fair, began. Morel, she knew, was sure to make a holiday of it. He went off early on the Monday morning, the day of the fair. The two children were highly excited. William, a boy of seven, fled off immediately after breakfast, to prowl round the wakes ground, leaving Annie, who was only five, to whine all morning to go also. Mrs Morel did her work. She scarcely knew her neighbours yet, and knew no one with whom to trust the little girl. So she promised to take her to the wakes after dinner.

William appeared at half-past twelve. He was a very active lad, fair-haired, freckled, with a touch of the Dane or Norwegian about him.

'Can I have my dinner, mother?' he cried, rushing in with his cap on. ''Cause it begins at half-past one, the man says so.'

'You can have your dinner as soon as it's done,' replied the mother.

'Isn't it done?' he cried, his blue eyes staring at her in indignation. 'Then I'm goin' be-out it.'

'You'll do nothing of the sort. It will be done in five minutes. It is only half-past twelve.'

'They'll be beginnin',' the boy half cried, half shouted.

'You won't die if they do,' said the mother. 'Besides, it's only half-past twelve, so you've a full hour.'

The lad began hastily to lay the table, and directly the three sat down. They were eating batter-pudding and jam, when the boy jumped off his chair and stood perfectly still. Some distance away could be heard the first small braying of a merry-go-round, and the tooting of a horn. His face quivered as he looked at his mother.

'I told you!' he said, running to the dresser for his cap.

'Take your pudding in your hand—and it's only five past one, so you were wrong—you haven't got your twopence,' cried the mother in a breath.

The boy came back, bitterly disappointed, for his twopence; then went off without a word.

'I want to go, I want to go,' said Annie, beginning to cry.

'Well, and you shall go, whining, wizzening little stick!' said the mother. And later in the afternoon she trudged up the hill under the tall hedge with her child. The hay was gathered from the fields, and cattle were turned on to the eddish. It was warm, peaceful.

Mrs Morel did not like the wakes. There were two sets of horses, one going by steam, one pulled round by a pony; three organs were grinding, and there came odd cracks of pistol-shots, fearful screeching of the coconut man's rattle, shouts of the Aunt Sally man, screeches from the peep-show lady. The mother perceived her son gazing enraptured outside the Lion Wallace booth, at the pictures of this famous lion that had killed a negro and maimed for life two white men. She left him alone, and went to get Annie a spin of toffee. Presently the lad stood in front of her, wildly excited.

'You never said you was coming—isn't the' a lot of things?—that lion's killed three men—I've spent my tuppence—an' look here.'

He pulled from his pocket two egg-cups, with pink moss-roses on them.

'I got these from that stall where y'ave ter get them marbles in them holes. An' I got these two in two goes—'aepenny a go—they've got moss-roses on, look here. I wanted these.'

She knew he wanted them for her.

'H'm!' she said, pleased. 'They *are* pretty!'

'Shall you carry 'em, 'cause I'm frightened o' breakin' 'em?'

He was tipful of excitement now she had come, led her about the ground, showed her everything. Then, at the peepshow, she explained the pictures, in a sort of story, to which he listened as if spellbound. He would not leave her. All the time he stuck close to her, bristling with a small boy's pride of her. For no other woman looked such a lady as she did, in her little black bonnet and her cloak. She smiled when she saw women she knew. When she was tired she said to her son:

'Well, are you coming now, or later?'

'Are you goin' a'ready?' he cried, his face full of reproach.

'Already? It is past four, *I* know.'

'What are you goin' a'ready for?' he lamented.

'You needn't come if you don't want,' she said.

And she went slowly away with her little girl, whilst her son stood watching her, cut to the heart to let her go, and yet unable to leave the wakes. As she crossed the open ground in front of the Moon and Stars she heard men shouting, and smelled the beer, and hurried a little, thinking her husband was probably in the bar.

At about half-past six her son came home, tired now, rather pale, and somewhat wretched. He was miserable, though he did not know it, because he had let her go alone. Since she had gone, he had not enjoyed his wakes.

'Has my dad been?' he asked.

'No,' said the mother.

'He's helping to wait at the Moon and Stars. I see him through that black tin stuff wi' holes in, on the window, wi' his sleeves rolled up.'

'Ha!' exclaimed the mother shortly. 'He's got no money. An' he'll be satisfied if he gets his 'lowance, whether they give him more or not.'

When the light was fading, and Mrs Morel could see no more to sew, she rose and went to the door. Everywhere was the sound of excitement, the restlessness of the holiday, that at last infected her. She went out into the side garden. Women were coming home from the wakes, the children hugging a white lamb with green legs, or a wooden horse. Occasionally a man lurched past, almost as full as he could carry. Sometimes a good husband came along with his family, peacefully. But usually the women and children were alone. The stay-at-home mothers stood gossiping at the corners of the alley, as the twilight sank, folding their arms under their white aprons.

Mrs Morel was alone but she was used to it. Her son and her little girl slept upstairs; so, it seemed, her home was there behind her, fixed and stable. But she felt wretched with the coming child. The world seemed a dreary place, where nothing else would happen for her–at least until William grew up. But for herself, nothing but this dreary endurance–till the children grew up. And the children! She could not afford to have this third. She did not want it. The father serving beer in a public-house, swilling himself drunk. She despised him, and was tied to him. This coming child was too much for her. If it were not for William and Annie, she was sick of it, the struggle with poverty and ugliness and meanness.

She went into the front garden, feeling too heavy to take herself out, yet unable to stay indoors. The heat suffocated her. And looking ahead, the prospect of her life made her feel as if she were buried alive.

The front garden was a small square with a privet hedge. There she stood, trying to soothe herself with the scent of flowers and the fading, beautiful evening. Opposite her small gate was the stile that led uphill, under the tall hedge, between the burning glow of the cut pastures. The sky overhead throbbed and pulsed with light. The glow sank quickly off the field; the earth and the hedges smoked dusk. As it grew dark, a ruddy glare came out on the hill-top, and out of the glare the diminished commotion of the fair.

Sometimes, down the trough of darkness formed by the path under the hedges, men came lurching home. One young man lapsed into a run down the steep bit that ended the hill, and went with a crash into the stile. Mrs Morel shuddered. He picked himself up, swearing viciously, rather pathetically, as if he thought the stile had wanted to hurt him.

She went indoors, wondering if things were never going to alter. She was beginning by now to realize that they would not. She seemed so far away from her girlhood, she wondered if it were the same person walking heavily up the back garden at the Bottoms as had run so lightly on the breakwater at Sheerness ten years before.

'What have *I* to do with it?' she said to herself. 'What have I to do with all this? Even the child I am going to have! It doesn't seem as if *I* were taken into account.'

Sometimes life takes hold of one, carries the body along, accomplishes one's history, and yet is not real, but leaves oneself as it were slurred over.

'I wait,' Mrs Morel said to herself–'I wait, and what I wait for can never come.'

Then she straightened the kitchen, lit the lamp, mended the fire, looked out the washing for the next day, and put it to soak. After which she sat down to her sewing. Through the long hours her needle flashed regularly through the stuff. Occasionally she sighed, moving to relieve herself. And all the time she was thinking how to make the most of what she had, for the children's sakes.

At half-past eleven her husband came. His cheeks were very red and very shiny above his black moustache. His head nodded slightly. He was pleased with himself.

'Oh! Oh! waitin' for me, lass? I've bin 'elpin' Anthony, an' what's think he's gen me? Nowt b'r a lousy hae'f-crown, an' that's ivry penny–'

'He thinks you've made the rest up in beer,' she said shortly.

'An' I 'aven't–that I 'aven't. You b'lieve me. I've 'ad very little this day, I have an' all.' His voice went tender. 'Here, an' I browt thee a bit o' brandysnap, an' a coconut for th' children.' He laid the gingerbread and the coconut, a hairy object, on the table. 'Nay, tha niver said thankyer for nowt i' thy life, did ter?'

As a compromise, she picked up the coconut and shook it, to see if it had any milk.

'It's a good 'un, you may back yer life o' that. I got it fra' Bill Hodgkisson. "Bill," I says, "tha non wants them three nuts, does ter? Arena ter for gi'ein' me one for my bit of a lad an' wench?" "I ham, Walter, my lad," 'e says; "ta'e which on 'em ter's a mind." An' so I took one, an' thanked 'im. I didn't like ter shake it afore 'is eyes, but 'e says, "Tha'd better ma'e sure it's a good un, Walt." An' so, yer see, I knowed it was. He's a nice chap, is Bill Hodgkisson, 'e's a nice chap!'

'A man will part with anything so long as he's drunk, and you're drunk along with him,' said Mrs Morel.

'Eh, tha mucky little 'ussy, who's drunk, I sh'd like ter know?' said Morel. He was extraordinarily pleased with himself, because of his day's helping to wait in the Moon and Stars. He chattered on.

Mrs Morel, very tired, and sick of his babble, went to bed as quickly as possible, while he raked the fire.

Mrs Morel came of a good old burgher family, famous independents who had fought with Colonel Hutchinson, and who remained stout Congregationalists. Her grandfather had gone bankrupt in the lace-market at a time when so many lace-manufacturers were ruined in Nottingham. Her father, George Coppard, was an engineer–a large, handsome, haughty man, proud of his fair skin and blue eyes, but more proud still of his integrity. Gertrude resembled her mother in her small build. But her temper, proud and unyielding, she had from the Coppards.

George Coppard was bitterly galled by his own poverty. He became foreman of the engineers in the dockyard at Sheerness. Mrs Morel–Gertrude–was the second daughter. She favoured her mother, loved her mother best of all; but she had the Coppards' clear, defiant blue eyes and their broad brow. She remembered to have hated her father's overbearing manner towards her gentle, humorous, kindly souled mother. She remembered running over the breakwater at Sheerness and finding the boat. She remembered to have been petted and flattered by all the men when she had gone to the dockyard, for she was a delicate, rather proud child. She remembered the funny old mistress, whose assistant she had become, whom she had loved to help in the private school. And she still had the Bible that John Field had given her. She used to walk home from chapel with John Field when she was nineteen. He was the son of a well-to-do tradesman, had been to college in London, and was to devote himself to business.

She could always recall in detail a September Sunday afternoon, when they had sat under the vine at the back of her father's house. The sun came through the chinks in the vineleaves and made beautiful patterns, like a lace scarf, falling on her and on him. Some of the leaves were clean yellow, like yellow flat flowers.

'Now sit still,' he had cried. 'Now your hair, I don't know what it *is* like! It's as bright as copper and gold, as red as burnt copper, and it has gold threads where the sun shines on it. Fancy their saying it's brown. Your mother calls it mouse-colour.'

She had met his brilliant eyes, but her clear face scarcely showed the elation which rose within her.

'But you say you don't like business,' she pursued.

'I don't. I hate it!' he cried hotly.

'And you would like to go into the ministry,' she half implored.

'I should. I should love it, if I thought I could make a first-rate preacher.'

'Then why don't you—why *don't* you?' Her voice rang with defiance. 'If *I* were a man, nothing would stop me.'

She held her head erect. He was rather timid before her.

'But my father's so stiff-necked. He means to put me into the business, and I know he'll do it.'

'But if you're a *man*?' she had cried.

'Being a man isn't everything,' he replied, frowning with puzzled helplessness.

Now, as she moved about her work at the Bottoms, with some experience of what being a man meant, she knew that it was *not* everything.

At twenty, owing to her health, she had left Sheerness. Her father had retired home to Nottingham. John Field's father had been ruined; the son had gone as a teacher in Norwood. She did not hear of him until, two years later, she made determined inquiry. He had married his landlady, a woman of forty, a widow with property.

And still Mrs Morel preserved John Field's Bible. She did not now believe him to be—Well, she understood pretty well what he might or might not have been. So she preserved his Bible and kept his memory intact in her heart, for her own sake. To her dying day, for thirty-five years, she did not speak of him.

When she was twenty-three years old, she met, at a Christmas party, a young man from the Erewash Valley. Morel was then twenty-seven years old. He was well set-up, erect, and very smart. He had wavy black hair that shone again, and a vigorous black beard that had never been shaved. His cheeks were ruddy, and his red, moist mouth was noticeable because he laughed so often and so heartily. He had that rare thing, a rich, ringing laugh. Gertrude Coppard had watched him, fascinated. He was so full of colour and animation, his voice ran so easily into comic grotesque, he was so ready and so pleasant with everybody. Her own father had a rich fund of humour, but it was satiric. This man's was different: soft, non-intellectual, warm, a kind of gambolling.

She herself was opposite. She had a curious, receptive mind, which found much pleasure and amusement in listening to other folk. She was clever in leading folk on to talk. She loved ideas, and was considered very intellectual. What she liked most of all was an argument on religion or philosophy or politics with some educated man. This she did not often enjoy. So she always had people tell her about themselves, finding her pleasure so.

In her person she was rather small and delicate, with a large brow, and dropping bunches of brown silk curls. Her blue eyes were very straight, honest, and searching. She had the beautiful hands of the Coppards. Her dress was always subdued. She wore dark blue silk, with a peculiar silver chain of silver scallops. This, and a heavy brooch of twisted gold, was her only ornament. She was still perfectly intact, deeply religious, and full of beautiful candour.

Walter Morel seemed melted away before her. She was to the miner that thing of mystery and fascination, a lady. When she spoke to him, it was with a southern pronunciation and a purity of English which thrilled him to hear. She watched him. He danced well, as if it were natural and joyous in him to dance. His grandfather was a French refugee who had married an English barmaid–if it had been a marriage. Gertrude Coppard watched the young miner as he danced, a certain subtle exultation like glamour in his movement, and his face the flower of his body, ruddy, with tumbled black hair, and laughing alike whatever partner he bowed above. She thought him rather wonderful, never having met anyone like him. Her father was to her the type of all men. And George Coppard, proud in his bearing, handsome, and rather bitter; who preferred theology in reading, and who drew near in sympathy only to one man, the Apostle Paul; who was harsh in government, and in familiarity ironic; who ignored all sensuous pleasure;–he was very different from the miner. Gertrude herself was rather contemptuous of dancing; she had not the slightest inclination towards that accomplishment, and had never learned even a Roger de Coverley. She was a puritan, like her father, high-minded, and really stern. Therefore the dusky, golden softness of this man's sensuous flame of life, that flowed off his flesh like the flame from a candle, not baffled and gripped into incandescence by thought and spirit as her life was, seemed to her something wonderful, beyond her.

He came and bowed above her. A warmth radiated through her as if she had drunk wine.

'Now do come and have this one wi' me,' he said caressively. 'It's easy, you know. I'm pining to see you dance.'

She had told him before she could not dance. She glanced at his humility and smiled. Her smile was very beautiful. It moved the man so that he forgot everything.

'No, I won't dance,' she said softly. Her words came clean and ringing.

Not knowing what he was doing–he often did the right thing by instinct–he sat beside her, inclining reverentially.

'But you mustn't miss your dance,' she reproved.

'Nay, I don't want to dance that–it's not one as I care about.'

'Yet you invited me to it.'

He laughed very heartily at this.

'I never thought o' that. Tha'rt not long in taking the curl out of me.'

It was her turn to laugh quickly.

'You don't look as if you'd come much uncurled,' she said.

'I'm like a pig's tail, I curl because I canna help it,' he laughed, rather boisterously.

'And you are a miner!' she exclaimed in surprise.

'Yes. I went down when I was ten.'

She looked at him in wondering dismay.

'When you were ten! And wasn't it very hard?' she asked.

'You soon get used to it. You live like th' mice, an' you pop out at night to see what's going on.'

'It makes me feel blind,' she frowned.

'Like a moudiwarp!' he laughed. 'Yi, an' there's some chaps as does go round like moudiwarps.' He thrust his face forward in the blind, snout-like way of a

mole, seeming to sniff and peer for direction. 'They dun though!' he protested
naïvely. 'Tha niver seen such a way they get in. But tha mun let me ta'e thee
down some time, an' tha can see for thysen.'

She looked at him, startled. This was a new tract of life suddenly opened
before her. She realized the life of the miners, hundreds of them toiling below
earth and coming up at evening. He seemed to her noble. He risked his life
daily, and with gaiety. She looked at him, with a touch of appeal in her pure
humility.

'Shouldn't ter like it?' he asked tenderly. ''Appen not, it 'ud dirty thee.'

She had never been 'thee'd' and 'thou'd' before.

The next Christmas they were married, and for three months she was
perfectly happy: for six months she was very happy.

He had signed the pledge, and wore the blue ribbon of a teetotaller: he was
nothing if not showy. They lived, she thought, in his own house. It was small,
but convenient enough, and quite nicely furnished, with solid, worthy stuff
that suited her honest soul. The women, her neighbours, were rather foreign to
her, and Morel's mother and sisters were apt to sneer at her lady-like ways. But
she could perfectly well live by herself, so long as she had her husband close.

Sometimes, when she herself wearied of love-talk, she tried to open her heart
seriously to him. She saw him listen deferentially, but without understanding.
This killed her efforts at a finer intimacy, and she had flashes of fear.
Sometimes he was restless of an evening: it was not enough for him just to be
near her, she realized. She was glad when he set himself to little jobs.

He was a remarkably handy man—could make or mend anything. So she
would say:

'I do like that coal-rake of your mother's—it is small and natty.'

'Does ter, my wench? Well, I made that, so I can make thee one.'

'What! why, it's a steel one!'

'An' what if it is! Tha s'lt ha'e one very similar, if not exactly same.'

She did not mind the mess, nor the hammering and noise. He was busy and
happy.

But in the seventh month, when she was brushing his Sunday coat, she felt
papers in the breast-pocket, and, seized with a sudden curiosity, took them out
to read. He very rarely wore the frock-coat he was married in: and it had not
occurred to her before to feel curious concerning the papers. They were the
bills of the household furniture, still unpaid.

'Look here,' she said at night, after he was washed and had had his dinner. 'I
found these in the pocket of your wedding-coat. Haven't you settled the bills
yet?'

'No. I haven't had a chance.'

'But you told me all was paid. I had better go into Nottingham on Saturday
and settle them. I don't like sitting on another man's chairs and eating from an
unpaid table.'

He did not answer.

'I can have your bank-book, can't I?'

'Tha can ha'e it, for what good it'll be to thee.'

'I thought–' she began. He had told her he had a good bit of money left
over. But she realized it was no use asking questions. She sat rigid with
bitterness and indignation.

The next day she went down to see his mother.

'Didn't you buy the furniture for Walter?' she asked.

'Yes, I did,' tartly retorted the elder woman.

'And how much did he give you to pay for it?'

The elder woman was stung with fine indignation.

'Eighty pound, if you're so keen on knowin',' she replied.

'Eighty pounds! But there are forty-two pounds still owing!'

'I can't help that.'

'But where has it all gone?'

'You'll find all the papers, I think, if you look—beside ten pound as he owed me, an' six pound as the wedding cost down here.'

'Six pounds!' echoed Gertrude Morel. It seemed to her monstrous that, after her own father had paid so heavily for her wedding, six pounds more should have been squandered in eating and drinking at Walter's parents' house, at his expense.

'And how much has he sunk in his houses?' she asked.

'His houses—which houses?'

Gertrude Morel went white to the lips. He had told her the house he lived in, and the next one, was his own.

'I thought the house we live in—' she began.

'They're my houses, those two,' said the mother-in-law. 'And not clear either. It's as much as I can do to keep the mortgage interest paid.'

Gertrude sat white and silent. She was her father now.

'Then we ought to be paying you rent,' she said coldly.

'Walter is paying me rent,' replied the mother.

'And what rent?' asked Gertrude.

'Six-and-six a week,' retorted the mother.

It was more than the house was worth. Gertrude held her head erect, looked straight before her.

'It is lucky to be you,' said the elder woman, bitingly, 'to have a husband as takes all the worry of the money, and leaves you a free hand.'

The young wife was silent.

She said very little to her husband, but her manner had changed towards him. Something in her proud, honourable soul had crystallized out hard as rock.

When October came in, she thought only of Christmas. Two years ago, at Christmas, she had met him. Last Christmas she had married him. This Christmas she would bear him a child.

'You don't dance yourself, do you, missis?' asked her nearest neighbour, in October, when there was great talk of opening a dancing-class over the Brick and Tile Inn at Bestwood.

'No—I never had the least inclination to,' Mrs Morel replied.

'Fancy! An' how funny as you should ha' married your Mester. You know he's quite a famous one for dancing.'

'I didn't know he was famous,' laughed Mrs Morel.

'Yea, he is though! Why, he run that dancing-class in the Miners' Arms club-room for over five year.'

'Did he?'

'Yes, he did.' The other woman was defiant. 'An' it was thronged every Tuesday, and Thursday, an' Sat'day—an' there *was* carryin's-on, accordin' to all accounts.'

This kind of thing was gall and bitterness to Mrs Morel, and she had a fair share of it. The women did not spare her, at first; for she was superior, though she could not help it.

He began to be rather late in coming home.

'They're working very late now, aren't they?' she said to her washer-woman.

'No later than they allers do, I don't think. But they stop to have their pint at Ellen's, an' they get talkin', an' there you are! Dinner stone cold–an' it serves 'em right.'

'But Mr Morel does not take any drink.'

The woman dropped the clothes, looked at Mrs Morel, then went on with her work, saying nothing.

Gertrude Morel was very ill when the boy was born. Morel was good to her, as good as gold. But she felt very lonely, miles away from her own people. She felt lonely with him now, and his presence only made it more intense.

The boy was small and frail at first, but he came on quickly. He was a beautiful child, with dark gold ringlets, and dark-blue eyes which changed gradually to a clear grey. His mother loved him passionately. He came just when her own bitterness of disillusion was hardest to bear; when her faith in life was shaken, and her soul felt dreary and lonely. She made much of the child, and the father was jealous.

At last Mrs Morel despised her husband. She turned to the child; she turned from the father. He had begun to neglect her; the novelty of his own home was gone. He had no grit, she said bitterly to herself. What he felt just at the minute, that was all to him. He could not abide by anything. There was nothing at the back of all his show.

There began a battle between the husband and wife–a fearful, bloody battle that ended only with the death of one. She fought to make him undertake his own responsibilities, to make him fulfil his obligations. But he was too different from her. His nature was purely sensuous, and she strove to make him moral, religious. She tried to force him to face things. He could not endure it–it drove him out of his mind.

While the baby was still tiny, the father's temper had become so irritable that it was not to be trusted. The child had only to give a little trouble when the man began to bully. A little more, and the hard hands of the collier hit the baby. Then Mrs Morel loathed her husband, loathed him for days; and he went out and drank; and she cared very little what he did. Only, on his return, she scathed him with her satire.

The estrangement between them caused him, knowingly or unknowingly, grossly to offend her where he would not have done.

William was only one year old, and his mother was proud of him, he was so pretty. She was not well off now, but her sisters kept the boy in clothes. Then, with his little white hat curled with an ostrich feather, and his white coat, he was a joy to her, the twining wisps of hair clustering round his head. Mrs Morel lay listening, one Sunday morning, to the chatter of the father and child downstairs. Then she dozed off. When she came downstairs, a great fire glowed in the grate, the room was hot, the breakfast was roughly laid, and seated in his armchair, against the chimney-piece, sat Morel, rather timid; and standing between his legs, the child–cropped like a sheep, with such an odd round poll–looking, wondering at her; and on a newspaper spread out upon the hearthrug, a myriad of crescent-shaped curls, like the petals of a marigold scattered in the reddening firelight.

Mrs Morel stood still. It was her first baby. She went very white, and was unable to speak.

'What dost think o' 'im?' Morel laughed uneasily.

She gripped her two fists, lifted them, and came forward. Morel shrank back. 'I could kill you, I could!' she said. She choked with rage, her two fists uplifted.

'Yer non want ter make a wench on 'im,' Morel said, in a frightened tone, bending his head to shield his eyes from hers. His attempt at laughter had vanished.

The mother looked down at the jagged, close-clipped head of her child. She put her hands on his hair, and stroked and fondled his head.

'Oh–my boy!' she faltered. Her lips trembled, her face broke, and, snatching up the child, she buried her face in his shoulder and cried painfully. She was one of those women who cannot cry; whom it hurts as it hurts a man. It was like ripping something out of her, her sobbing.

Morel sat with his elbows on his knees, his hands gripped together till the knuckles were white. He gazed in the fire, feeling almost stunned, as if he could not breathe.

Presently she came to an end, soothed the child and cleared away the breakfast-table. She left the newspaper, littered with curls, spread upon the hearthrug. At last her husband gathered it up and put it at the back of the fire. She went about her work with closed mouth and very quiet. Morel was subdued. He crept about wretchedly, and his meals were a misery that day. She spoke to him civilly, and never alluded to what he had done. But he felt something final had happened.

Afterwards she said she had been silly, that the boy's hair would have had to be cut, sooner or later. In the end, she even brought herself to say to her husband it was just as well he had played barber when he did. But she knew, and Morel knew, that that act had caused something momentous to take place in her soul. She remembered the scene all her life, as one in which she had suffered the most intensely.

This act of masculine clumsiness was the spear through the side of her love for Morel. Before, while she had striven against him bitterly, she had fretted after him, as if he had gone astray from her. Now she ceased to fret for his love: he was an outsider to her. This made life much more bearable.

Nevertheless, she still continued to strive with him. She still had her high moral sense, inherited from generations of Puritans. It was now a religious instinct, and she was almost a fanatic with him, because she loved him, or had loved him. If he sinned, she tortured him. If he drank, and lied, was often a poltroon, sometimes a knave, she wielded the lash unmercifully.

The pity was, she was too much his opposite. She could not be content with the little he might be; she would have him the much that he ought to be. So, in seeking to make him nobler than he could be, she destroyed him. She injured and hurt and scarred herself, but she lost none of her worth. She also had the children.

He drank rather heavily, though not more than many miners, and always beer, so that whilst his health was affected, it was never injured. The week-end was his chief carouse. He sat in the Miners' Arms until turning-out time every Friday, every Saturday, and every Sunday evening. On Monday and Tuesday he had to get up and reluctantly leave towards ten o'clock. Sometimes he stayed at home on Wednesday and Thursday evenings, or was only out for an hour. He practically never had to miss work owing to his drinking.

But although he was very steady at work his wages fell off. He was blab-mouthed, a tongue-wagger. Authority was hateful to him, therefore he could

only abuse the pit-managers. He would say, in the Palmerston:
'Th' gaffer come down to our stall this morning, an' 'e says, "You know,
Walter, this 'ere'll not do. What about these props?" An' I says to him, "Why,
what art talkin' about? What d'st mean about th' props?" "It'll never do, this
'ere," 'e says. "You'll be havin' th' roof in, one o' these days." An' I says,
"Tha'd better stan' on a bit o' clunch, then, an' hold it up wi' thy 'ead." So 'e
wor that mad, 'e cossed an' 'e swore, an' t'other chaps they did laugh.' Morel
was a good mimic. He imitated the manager's fat, squeaky voice, with its
attempt at good English.

'"I shan't have it, Walter. Who knows more about it, me or you?" So I says,
"I've niver fun out how much tha' knows, Alfred. It'll 'appen carry thee ter bed
an' back."'

So Morel would go on to the amusement of his boon companions. And some
of this would be true. The pit-manager was not an educated man. He had been a
boy along with Morel, so that, while the two disliked each other, they more or
less took each other for granted. But Alfred Charlesworth did not forgive the
butty these public-house sayings. Consequently, although Morel was a good
miner, sometimes earning as much as five pounds a week when he married, he
came gradually to have worse and worse stalls, where the coal was thin, and
hard to get, and unprofitable.

Also, in summer, the pits are slack. Often, on bright sunny mornings, the
men are seen trooping home again at ten, eleven or twelve o'clock. No empty
trucks stand at the pit-mouth. The women on the hillside look across as they
shake the hearthrug against the fence, and count the waggons the engine is
taking along the line up the valley. And the children, as they come from school
at dinner-time, looking down the fields and seeing the wheels on the headstocks
standing, say:

'Minton's knocked off. My dad'll be at home.'

And there is a sort of shadow over all, women and children and men, because
money will be short at the end of the week.

Morel was supposed to give his wife thirty shillings a week, to provide
everything–rent, food, clothes, clubs, insurance, doctors. Occasionally, if he
were flush, he gave her thirty-five. But these occasions by no means balanced
those when he gave her twenty-five. In winter, with a decent stall, the miner
might earn fifty or fifty-five shillings a week. Then he was happy. On Friday
night, Saturday, and Sunday, he spent royally, getting rid of his sovereign or
thereabouts. And out of so much, he scarcely spared the children an extra
penny or bought them a pound of apples. It all went in drink. In the bad times,
matters were more worrying, but he was not so often drunk, so that Mrs Morel
used to say:

'I'm not sure I wouldn't rather be short, for when he's flush, there isn't a
minute of peace.'

If he earned forty shillings he kept ten; from thirty-five he kept five; from
thirty-two he kept four; from twenty-eight he kept three; from twenty-four he
kept two; from twenty he kept one-and-six; from eighteen he kept a shilling;
from sixteen he kept sixpence. He never saved a penny, and he gave his wife no
opportunity of saving; instead, she had occasionally to pay his debts; not
public-house debts, for those never were passed on to the women, but debts
when he had bought a canary, or a fancy walking-stick.

At the wakes time, Morel was working badly, and Mrs Morel was trying to
save against her confinement. So it galled her bitterly to think he should be out

taking his pleasure and spending money, whilst she remained at home, harassed. There were two days' holiday. On the Tuesday morning Morel rose early. He was in good spirits. Quite early, before six o'clock, she heard him whistling away to himself downstairs. He had a pleasant way of whistling, lively and musical. He nearly always whistled hymns. He had been a choir-boy with a beautiful voice, and had taken solos in Southwell Cathedral. His morning whistling alone betrayed it.

His wife lay listening to him tinkering away in the garden, his whistling ringing out as he sawed and hammered away. It always gave her a sense of warmth and peace to hear him thus as she lay in bed, the children not yet awake, in the bright early morning, happy in his man's fashion.

At nine o'clock, while the children with bare legs and feet were sitting playing on the sofa, and the mother was washing up, he came in from his carpentry, his sleeves rolled up, his waistcoat hanging open. He was still a good-looking man, with black, wavy-hair, and a large black moustache. His face was perhaps too much inflamed, and there was about him a look almost of peevishness. But now he was jolly. He went straight to the sink where his wife was washing up.

'What, are thee there!' he said boisterously. 'Sluther off an' let me wesh mysen.'

'You may wait till I've finished,' said his wife.

'Oh, mun I? An' what if I shonna?'

This good-humoured threat amused Mrs Morel.

'Then you can go and wash yourself in the soft-water tub.'

'Ha! I can an' a', tha mucky little 'ussy.'

With which he stood watching her a moment, then went away to wait for her.

When he chose he could still make himself again a real gallant. Usually he preferred to go out with a scarf round his neck. Now, however, he made a toilet. There seemed so much gusto in the way he puffed and swilled as he washed himself, so much alacrity with which he hurried to the mirror in the kitchen, and, bending because it was too low for him, scrupulously parted his wet black hair, that it irritated Mrs Morel. He put on a turn-down collar, a black bow, and wore his Sunday tail-coat. As such, he looked spruce, and what his clothes would not do, his instinct for making the most of his good looks would.

At half-past nine Jerry Purdy came to call for his pal. Jerry was Morel's bosom friend, and Mrs Morel disliked him. He was a tall, thin man, with a rather foxy face, the kind of face that seems to lack eyelashes. He walked with a stiff, brittle dignity, as if his head were on a wooden spring. His nature was cold and shrewd. Generous where he intended to be generous, he seemed to be very fond of Morel, and more or less to take charge of him. Mrs Morel hated him. She had known his wife, who had died of consumption, and who had, at the end, conceived such a violent dislike of her husband, that if he came into her room it caused her haemorrhage. None of which Jerry had seemed to mind. And now his eldest daughter, a girl of fifteen, kept a poor house for him, and looked after the two younger children.

'A mean, wizzen-hearted stick!' Mrs Morel said of him.

'I've never known Jerry mean in *my* life,' protested Morel. 'A opener-handed and more freer chap you couldn't find anywhere, accordin' to my knowledge.'

'Open-handed to you,' retorted Mrs Morel. 'But his fist is shut tight enough to his children, poor things.'

'Poor things! And what for are they poor things, I should like to know?'
But Mrs Morel would not be appeased on Jerry's score.

The subject of argument was seen, craning his thin neck over the scullery curtain. He caught Mrs Morel's eye.

'Mornin', missis! Mester in?'

'Yes—he is.'

Jerry entered unasked, and stood by the kitchen doorway. He was not invited to sit down, but stood there, coolly asserting the rights of men and husbands.

'A nice day,' he said to Mrs Morel.

'Yes.'

'Grand out this morning—grand for a walk.'

'Do you mean *you're* going for a walk?' she asked.

'Yes. We mean walkin' to Nottingham,' he replied.

'H'm!'

The two men greeted each other, both glad: Jerry, however, full of assurance, Morel rather subdued, afraid to seem too jubilant in presence of his wife. But he laced his boots quickly, with spirit. They were going for a ten-mile walk across the fields to Nottingham. Climbing the hillside from the Bottoms, they mounted gaily into the morning. At the Moon and Stars they had their first drink, then on to the Old Spot. Then a long five miles of drought to carry them into Bulwell to a glorious pint of bitter. But they stayed in a field with some haymakers whose gallon bottle was full, so that, when they came in sight of the city, Morel was sleepy. The town spread upwards before them, smoking vaguely in the midday glare, fringing the crest away to the south with spires and factory bulks and chimneys. In the last field Morel lay down under an oak-tree and slept soundly for over an hour. When he rose to go forward he felt queer.

The two had dinner in the Meadows, with Jerry's sister, then repaired to the Punch Bowl, where they mixed in the excitement of pigeon-racing. Morel never in his life played cards, considering them as having some occult, malevolent power—'the devil's pictures,' he called them! But he was a master of skittles and of dominoes. He took a challenge from a Newark man, on skittles. All the men in the old, long bar took sides, betting either one way or the other. Morel took off his coat. Jerry held the hat containing the money. The men at the tables watched. Some stood with their mugs in their hands. Morel felt his big wooden ball carefully, then launched it. He played havoc among the nine-pins, and won half-a-crown, which restored him to solvency.

By seven o'clock the two were in good condition. They caught the 7.30 train home.

In the afternoon the Bottoms was intolerable. Every inhabitant remaining was out of doors. The women, in twos and threes, bare-headed and in white aprons, gossiped in the alley between the blocks. Men, having a rest between drinks, sat on their heels and talked. The place smelled stale; the slate roofs glistered in the arid heat.

Mrs Morel took the little girl down to the brook in the meadows, which were not more than two hundred yards away. The water ran quickly over stones and broken pots. Mother and child leaned on the rail of the old sheep-bridge, watching. Up at the dipping-hole, at the other end of the meadows, Mrs Morel could see the naked forms of boys flashing round the deep yellow water, or an occasional bright figure dart glittering over the blackish stagnant meadow. She knew William was at the dipping-hole, and it was the dread of her life lest he should get drowned. Annie played under the tall old hedge, picking up alder cones, that she called currants. The child required much attention, and the flies were teasing.

The children were put to bed at seven o'clock. Then she worked awhile.

When Walter Morel and Jerry arrived at Bestwood they felt a load off their minds; a railway journey no longer impended, so they could put the finishing touches to a glorious day. They entered the Nelson with the satisfaction of returned travellers.

The next day was a work-day, and the thought of it put a damper on the men's spirits. Most of them, moreover, had spent their money. Some were already rolling dismally home, to sleep in preparation for the morrow. Mrs Morel, listening to their mournful singing, went indoors. Nine o'clock passed, and ten, and still 'the pair' had not returned. On a doorstep somewhere a man was singing loudly, in a drawl, 'Lead, kindly Light'. Mrs Morel was always indignant with the drunken men that they must sing that hymn when they got maudlin.

'As if "Genevieve" weren't good enough,' she said.

The kitchen was full of the scent of boiled herbs and hops. On the hob a large black saucepan steamed slowly. Mrs Morel took a panchion, a great bowl of thick red earth, streamed a heap of white sugar into the bottom, and then, straining herself to the weight, was pouring in the liquor.

Just then Morel came in. He had been very jolly in the Nelson, but coming home had grown irritable. He had not quite got over the feeling of irritability and pain, after having slept on the ground when he was so hot; and a bad conscience afflicted him as he neared the house. He did not know he was angry. But when the garden-gate resisted his attempts to open it, he kicked it and broke the latch. He entered just as Mrs Morel was pouring the infusion of herbs out of the saucepan. Swaying slightly, he lurched against the table. The boiling liquor pitched. Mrs Morel started back.

'Good gracious,' she cried, 'coming home in his drunkenness!'

'Comin' home in his what?' he snarled, his hat over his eye.

Suddenly her blood rose in a jet.

'Say you're *not* drunk!' she flashed.

She had put down her saucepan, and was stirring the sugar into the beer. He dropped his two hands heavily on the table, and thrust his face forward at her.

'"Say you're not drunk,"' he repeated. 'Why, nobody but a nasty little bitch like you 'ud 'ave such a thought.'

He thrust his face forward at her.

'There's money to bezzle with, if there's money for nothing else.'

'I've not spent a two-shillin' bit this day,' he said.

'You don't get as drunk as a lord on nothing,' she replied. 'And,' she cried, flashing into sudden fury, 'if you've been sponging on your beloved Jerry, why, let him look after his children, for they need it.'

'It's a lie, it's a lie. Shut your face, woman.'

They were now at battle-pitch. Each forgot everything save the hatred of the other and the battle between them. She was fiery and furious as he. They went on till he called her a liar.

'No,' she cried, starting up, scarce able to breathe. 'Don't call me that–you, the most despicable liar that ever walked in shoe-leather.' She forced the last words out of suffocated lungs.

'You're a liar!' he yelled, banging the table with his fist. 'You're a liar, you're a liar.'

She stiffened herself with clenched fists.

'The house is filthy with you,' she cried.

'Then get out on it–it's mine. Get out on it!' he shouted. 'It's me as brings th' money whoam, not thee. It's my house, not thine. Then get out on't–get out on't!'

'And I would,' she cried, suddenly shaken into tears of impotence. 'Ah, wouldn't I, wouldn't I have gone long ago, but for those children. Ay, haven't I repented not going years ago, when I'd only the one'–suddenly drying into rage. 'Do you think it's for *you* I stop–do you think I'd stop one minute for *you?*'

'Go, then,' he shouted, beside himself. 'Go!'

'No!' she faced round. 'No,' she cried loudly, 'you shan't have it *all* your own way; you shan't do *all* you like. I've got those children to see to. My word,' she laughed, 'I should look well to leave them to you.'

'Go,' he cried thickly, lifting his fist. He was afraid of her. 'Go!'

'I should be only too glad. I should laugh, laugh, my lord, if I could get away from you,' she replied.

He came up to her, his red face, with its bloodshot eyes, thrust forward, and gripped her arms. She cried in fear of him, struggled to be free. Coming slightly to himself, panting, he pushed her roughly to the outer door, and thrust her forth, slotting the bolt behind her with a bang. Then he went back into the kitchen, dropped into his armchair, his head, bursting full of blood, sinking between his knees. Thus he dipped gradually into a stupor, from exhaustion and intoxication.

The moon was high and magnificent in the August night. Mrs Morel, seared with passion, shivered to find herself out there in a great white light, that fell cold on her, and gave a shock to her inflamed soul. She stood for a few moments helplessly staring at the glistening great rhubarb leaves near the door. Then she got the air into her breast. She walked down the garden path, trembling in every limb, while the child boiled within her. For a while she could not control her consciousness; mechanically she went over the last scene, then over it again, certain phrases, certain moments coming each time like a brand red-hot down on her soul; and each time she enacted again the past hour, each time the brand came down at the same points, till the mark was burnt in, and the pain burnt out, and at last she came to herself. She must have been half an hour in this delirious condition. Then the presence of the night came again to her. She glanced round in fear. She had wandered to the side garden, where she was walking up and down the path beside the currant bushes under the long wall. The garden was a narrow strip, bounded from the road, that cut transversely between the blocks, by a thick thorn hedge.

She hurried out of the side garden to the front, where she could stand as if in an immense gulf of white light, the moon streaming high in face of her, the moonlight standing up from the hills in front, and filling the valley where the Bottoms crouched, almost blindingly. There panting and half weeping in reaction from the stress, she murmured to herself over and over again: 'The nuisance! the nuisance!'

She became aware of something about her. With an effort she roused herself to see what it was that penetrated her consciousness. The tall white lilies were reeling in the moonlight, and the air was charged with their perfume, as with a presence. Mrs Morel gasped slightly in fear. She touched the big, pallid flowers on their petals, then shivered. They seemed to be stretching in the moonlight.

She put her hand into one white bin: the gold scarcely showed on her fingers by moonlight. She bent down to look at the binful of yellow pollen; but it only appeared dusky. Then she drank a deep draught of the scent. It almost made her dizzy.

Mrs Morel leaned on the garden gate, looking out, and she lost herself awhile. She did not know what she thought. Except for a slight feeling of sickness, and her consciousness in the child, herself melted out like scent into the shiny, pale air. After a time the child, too, melted with her in the mixing-pot of moonlight, and she rested with the hills and lilies and houses, all swum together in a kind of swoon.

When she came to herself she was tired for sleep. Languidly she looked about her; the clumps of white phlox seemed like bushes spread with linen; a moth ricocheted over them, and right across the garden. Following it with her eye roused her. A few whiffs of the raw, strong scent of phlox invigorated her. She passed along the path, hesitating at the white rosebush. It smelled sweet and simple. She touched the white ruffles of the roses. Their fresh scent and cool, soft leaves reminded her of the morning-time and sunshine. She was very fond of them. But she was tired, and wanted to sleep. In the mysterious out-of-doors she felt forlorn.

There was no noise anywhere. Evidently the children had not been wakened, or had gone to sleep again. A train, three miles away, roared across the valley. The night was very large, and very strange, stretching its hoary distances infinitely. And out of the silver-grey fog of darkness came sounds vague and hoarse: a corncrake not far off, sound of a train like a sigh, and distant shouts of men.

Her quietened heart beginning to beat quickly again, she hurried down the side garden to the back of the house. Softly she lifted the latch; the door was still bolted, shut hard against her. She rapped gently, waited, then rapped again. She must not rouse the children, nor the neighbours. He must be asleep, and he would not wake easily. Her heart began to burn to be indoors. She clung to the door-handle. Now it was cold; she would take a chill, and in her present condition!

Putting her apron over her head and her arms, she hurried again to the side garden, to the window of the kitchen. Leaning on the sill, she could just see, under the blind, her husband's arms spread out on the table, and his black head on the board. He was sleeping with his face lying on the table. Something in his attitude made her feel tired of things. The lamp was burning smokily; she could tell by the copper colour of the light. She tapped at the window more and more noisily. Almost it seemed as if the glass would break. Still he did not wake up.

After vain efforts, she began to shiver, partly from contact with the stone, and from exhaustion. Fearful always for the unborn child, she wondered what she could do for warmth. She went down to the coal-house, where was an old hearthrug she had carried out for the rag-man the day before. This she wrapped over her shoulders. It was warm, if grimy. Then she walked up and down the garden path, peeping every now and then under the blind, knocking, and telling herself that in the end the very strain of his position must wake him.

At last, after about an hour, she rapped long and low at the window. Gradually the sound penetrated to him. When, in despair, she had ceased to tap, she saw him stir, then lift his face blindly. The labouring of his heart hurt him into consciousness. She rapped imperatively at the window. He started awake. Instantly she saw his fists set and his eyes glare. He had not a grain of physical fear. If it had been twenty burglars, he would have gone blindly for them. He glared round, bewildered, but prepared to fight.

'Open the door, Walter,' she said coldly.

His hands relaxed. It dawned on him what he had done. His head dropped, sullen and dogged. She saw him hurry to the door, heard the bolt chock. He tried the latch. It opened – and there stood the silver-grey night, fearful to him, after the tawny light of the lamp. He hurried back.

When Mrs Morel entered, she saw him almost running through the door to the stairs. He had ripped his collar off his neck in his haste to be gone ere she came in, and there it lay with bursten button-holes. It made her angry.

She warmed and soothed herself. In her weariness forgetting everything, she moved about at the little tasks that remained to be done, set his breakfast, rinsed his pit-bottle, put his pit-clothes on the hearth to warm, set his pit-boots beside them, put him out a clean scarf and snap-bag and two apples, raked the fire, and went to bed. He was already dead asleep. His narrow black eyebrows were drawn up in a sort of peevish misery into his forehead, while his cheeks' downstrokes, and his sulky mouth, seemed to be saying: 'I don't care who you are or what you are, I *shall* have my own way.'

Mrs Morel knew him too well to look at him. As she unfastened her brooch at the mirror, she smiled faintly to see her face all smeared with the yellow dust of lilies. She brushed it off, and at last lay down. For some time her mind continued snapping and jetting sparks, but she was asleep before her husband awoke from the first sleep of his drunkenness.

2

THE BIRTH OF PAUL, AND ANOTHER BATTLE

After such a scene as the last, Walter Morel was for some days abashed and ashamed, but he soon regained his old bullying indifference. Yet there was a slight shrinking, a diminishing in his assurance. Physically even, he shrank, and his fine full presence waned. He never grew in the least stout, so that, as he sank from his erect, assertive bearing, his physique seemed to contract along with his pride and moral strength.

But now he realized how hard it was for his wife to drag about at her work, and, his sympathy quickened by penitence, hastened forward with his help. He came straight home from the pit, and stayed in at evening till Friday, and then he could not remain at home. But he was back again by ten o'clock, almost quite sober.

He always made his own breakfast. Being a man who rose early and had plenty of time he did not, as some miners do, drag his wife out of bed at six o'clock. At five, sometimes earlier, he woke, got straight out of bed, and went downstairs. When she could not sleep, his wife lay waiting for this time, as for a period of peace. The only real rest seemed to be when he was out of the house.

He went downstairs in his shirt and then struggled into the pit-trousers, which were left on the hearth to warm all night. There was always a fire, because Mrs Morel raked. And the first sound in the house was the bang, bang of the poker against the raker, as Morel smashed the remainder of the coal to make the kettle, which was filled and left on the hob, finally boil. His cup and knife and fork, all he wanted except just the food, was laid ready on the table on a newspaper. Then he got his breakfast, made the tea, packed the bottom of the doors with rugs to shut out the draught, piled a big fire, and sat down to an hour of joy. He toasted his bacon on a fork and caught the drops of fat on his bread; then he put the rasher on his thick slice of bread, and cut off chunks with a clasp-knife, poured his tea into his saucer, and was happy. With his family about, meals were never so pleasant. He loathed a fork; it is a modern introduction which has still scarcely reached common people. What Morel preferred was a clasp-knife. Then, in solitude, he ate and drank, often sitting, in cold weather, on a little stool with his back to the warm chimney-piece, his food on the fender, his cup on the hearth. And then he read the last night's newspaper—what of it he could—spelling it over laboriously. He preferred to keep the blinds down and the candle lit even when it was daylight; it was the habit of the mine.

At a quarter to six he rose, cut two thick slices of bread-and-butter, and put them in the white calico snap-bag. He filled his tin bottle with tea. Cold tea without milk or sugar was the drink he preferred for the pit. Then he pulled off his shirt, and put on his pit-singlet, a vest of thick flannel cut low round the neck, and with short sleeves like a chemise.

Then he went upstairs to his wife with a cup of tea because she was ill, and because it occurred to him.

'I've brought thee a cup o' tea, lass,' he said.

'Well, you needn't, for you know I don't like it,' she replied.

'Drink it up; it'll pop thee off to sleep again.'

She accepted the tea. It pleased him to see her take it and sip it.

'I'll back my life there's no sugar in,' she said.

'Yi—theres one big un,' he replied, injured.

'It's a wonder,' she said, sipping again.

She had a winsome face when her hair was loose. He loved her to grumble at him in this manner. He looked at her again, and went, without any sort of leave-taking. He never took more than two slices of bread and butter to eat in the pit, so an apple or an orange was a treat to him. He always liked it when she put one out for him. He tied a scarf round his neck, put on his great, heavy boots, his coat, with the big pocket, that carried his snap-bag and his bottle of tea, and went forth into the fresh morning air, closing, without locking, the door behind him. He loved the early morning, and the walk across the fields. So he appeared at the pit-top, often with a stalk from the hedge between his teeth, which he chewed all day to keep his mouth moist, down the mine, feeling quite as happy as when he was in the field.

Later, when the time for the baby grew nearer, he would bustle round in his slovenly fashion, poking out the ashes, rubbing the fireplace, sweeping the house before he went to work. Then, feeling very self-righteous, he went upstairs.

'Now I'm cleaned up for thee; tha's no 'casions ter stir a peg all day, but sit and read thy books.'

Which made her laugh, in spite of her indignation.

'And the dinner cooks itself?' she answered.

'Eh, I know nowt about th' dinner.'

'You'd know if there weren't any.'

'Ay, 'appen so,' he answered, departing.

When she got downstairs, she would find the house tidy, but dirty. She could not rest until she had thoroughly cleaned; so she went down to the ash-pit with her dust-pan. Mrs Kirk, spying her, would contrive to have to go to her own coalplace at that minute. Then, across the wooden fence, she would call:

'So you keep wagging on, then?'

'Ay,' answered Mrs Morel deprecatingly. 'There's nothing else for it.'

'Have you seen Hose?' called a very small woman from across the road. It was Mrs Anthony, a black-haired, strange little body, who always wore a brown velvet dress, tight fitting.

'I haven't,' said Mrs Morel.

'Eh, I wish he'd come. I've got a copperful of clothes, an' I'm sure I heered his bell.'

'Hark! He's at the end.'

The two women looked down the alley. At the end of the Bottoms a man stood in a sort of old-fashioned trap, bending over bundles of cream-coloured stuff; while a cluster of women held up their arms to him, some with bundles. Mrs Anthony herself had a heap of creamy, undyed stockings hanging over her arm.

'I've done ten dozen this week,' she said proudly to Mrs Morel.

'T-t-t!' went the other. 'I don't know how you can find time.'

'Eh!' said Mrs Anthony. 'You can find time if you make time.'

'I don't know how you do it,' said Mrs Morel. 'And how much shall you get for those many?'

'Tuppence-ha'penny a dozen,' replied the other.

'Well,' said Mrs Morel, 'I'd starve before I'd sit down and seam twenty-four stockings for twopence ha'penny.'

'Oh, I don't know,' said Mrs Anthony. 'You can rip along with 'em.'

Hose was coming along, ringing his bell. Women were waiting at the yard-ends with their seamed stockings hanging over their arms. The man, a common fellow, made jokes with them, tried to swindle them, and bullied them. Mrs Morel went up her yard disdainfully.

It was an understood thing that if one woman wanted her neighbour, she should put the poker in the fire and bang at the back of the fireplace, which, as the fires were back to back, would make a great noise in the adjoining house. One morning Mrs Kirk, mixing a pudding, nearly started out of her skin as she heard the thud, thud in her grate. With her hands all floury, she rushed to the fence.

'Did you knock, Mrs Morel?'

'If you wouldn't mind, Mrs Kirk.'

Mrs Kirk climbed on to her copper, got over the wall on to Mrs Morel's copper, and ran in to her neighbour.

'Eh, dear, how are you feeling?' she cried in concern.

'You might fetch Mrs Bower,' said Mrs Morel.

Mrs Kirk went into the yard, lifted up her strong, shrill voice, and called:

'Ag-gie–Ag-gie!'

The sound was heard from one end of the Bottoms to the other. At last Aggie came running up, and was sent for Mrs Bower, whilst Mrs Kirk left her pudding and stayed with her neighbour.

Mrs Morel went to bed. Mrs Kirk had Annie and William for dinner. Mrs Bower, fat and waddling, bossed the house.

'Hash some cold meat up for the master's dinner, and make him an apple-charlotte pudding,' said Mrs Morel.

'He may go without pudding *this* day,' said Mrs Bower.

Morel was not as a rule one of the first to appear at the bottom of the pit, ready to come up. Some men were there before four o'clock, when the whistle blew loose-all; but Morel, whose stall, a poor one, was at this time about a mile and a half away from the bottom, worked usually till the first mate stopped, then he finished also. This day, however, the minér was sick of the work. At two o'clock he looked at his watch, by the light of the green candle—he was in a safe working—and again at half-past two. He was hewing at a piece of rock that was in the way for the next day's work. As he sat on his heels, or kneeled, giving hard blows with his pick, 'Uszza—uszza!' he went.

'Shall ter finish, Sorry?'* cried Barker, his fellow butty.

'Finish? Niver while the world stands!' growled Morel.

And he went on striking. He was tired.

'It's a heart-breaking job,' said Barker.

But Morel was too exasperated, at the end of his tether, to answer. Still he struck and hacked with all his might.

'Tha might as well leave it, Walter,' said Barker. 'It'll do to-morrow, without thee hackin' thy guts out.'

'I'll lay no b— finger on this to-morrow, Isr'el!' cried Morel.

'Oh, well, if tha wunna, someb'dy else 'll ha'e to,' said Israel.

Then Morel continued to strike.

'Hey-up there—*loose-a'!*' cried the men, leaving the next stall.

Morel continued to strike.

'Tha'll happen catch me up,' said Barker, departing.

When he had gone, Morel, left alone, felt savage. He had not finished his job. He had overworked himself into a frenzy. Rising, wet with sweat, he threw his tool down, pulled on his coat, blew out his candle, took his lamp, and went. Down the main road the lights of the other men went swinging. There was a hollow sound of many voices. It was a long, heavy tramp underground.

He sat at the bottom of the pit, where the great drops of water fell plash. Many colliers were waiting their turns to go up, talking noisily. Morel gave his answers short and disagreeable.

'It's rainin', Sorry,' said old Giles, who had had the news from the top.

Morel found one comfort. He had his old umbrella, which he loved, in the lamp cabin. At last he took his stand on the chair, and was at the top in a moment. Then he handed in his lamp and got his umbrella, which he had bought at an auction for one-and-six. He stood on the edge of the pit-bank for a moment, looking out over the fields; grey rain was falling. The trucks stood full of wet, bright coal. Water ran down the sides of the waggons, over the white 'C.W. and Co.' Colliers, walking indifferent to the rain, were streaming down the line and up the field, a grey, dismal host. Morel put up his umbrella, and took pleasure from the peppering of the drops thereon.

All along the road to Bestwood the miners tramped, wet and grey and dirty, but their red mouths talking with animation. Morel also walked with a gang, but he said nothing. He frowned peevishly as he went. Many men passed into the Prince of Wales or into Ellen's. Morel, feeling sufficiently disagreeable to resist temptation, trudged along under the dripping trees that overhung the park wall, and down the mud of Greenhill Lane.

Mrs Morel lay in bed, listening to the rain, and the feet of the colliers from

---

* 'Sorry' is a common form of address. It is, perhaps, a corruption of 'sirrah'.

Minton, their voices, and the bang, bang of the gates as they went through the stile up the field.

'There's some herb beer behind the pantry-door,' she said. 'Th' master'll want a drink, if he doesn't stop.'

But he was late, so she concluded he had called for a drink, since it was raining. What did he care about the child or her?

She was very ill when her children were born.

'What is it?' she asked, feeling sick to death.

'A boy.'

And she took consolation in that. The thought of being the mother of men was warming to her heart. She looked at the child. It had blue eyes, and a lot of fair hair, and was bonny. Her love came up hot, in spite of everything. She had it in bed with her.

Morel, thinking nothing, dragged his way up the garden path, wearily and angrily. He closed his umbrella, and stood it in the sink; then he sluthered his heavy boots into the kitchen. Mrs Bowers appeared in the inner doorway.

'Well,' she said, 'she's about as bad as she can be. It's a boy child.'

The miner grunted, put his empty snap-bag and his tin bottle on the dresser, went back into the scullery and hung up his coat, then came and dropped into his chair.

'Han yer got a drink?' he asked.

The woman went into the pantry. There was heard the oop of a cork. She set the mug, with a little, disgusted rap, on the table before Morel. He drank, gasped, wiped his big moustache on the end of his scarf, drank, gasped, and lay back in his chair. The woman would not speak to him again. She set his dinner before him, and went upstairs.

'Was that the master?' asked Mrs Morel.

'I've gave him his dinner,' replied Mrs Bower.

After he had sat with his arms on the table—he resented the fact that Mrs Bower put no cloth on for him, and gave him a little plate instead of a full-sized dinner-plate—he began to eat. The fact that his wife was ill, that he had another boy, was nothing to him at that moment. He was too tired; he wanted his dinner; he wanted to sit with his arms lying on the board; he did not like having Mrs Bower about. The fire was too small to please him.

After he had finished his meal, he sat for twenty minutes; then he stoked up a big fire. Then, in his stockinged feet, he went reluctantly upstairs. It was a struggle to face his wife at this moment and he was tired. His face was black, and smeared with sweat. His singlet had dried again, soaking the dirt in. He had a dirty woollen scarf round his throat. So he stood at the foot of the bed.

'Well, how are ter, then?' he asked.

'I s'll be all right,' she answered.

'H'm!'

He stood at a loss what to say next. He was tired, and this bother was rather a nuisance to him, and he didn't quite know where he was.

'A lad, tha says,' he stammered.

She turned down the sheet and showed the child.

'Bless him!' he murmured. Which made her laugh, because he blessed by rote—pretending paternal emotion, which he did not feel just then.

'Go now,' she said.

'I will, my lass,' he answered, turning away.

Dismissed, he wanted to kiss her, but he dared not. She half wanted him to kiss her, but could not bring herself to give any sign. She only breathed freely when he was gone out of the room again, leaving behind him a faint smell of pit-dirt.

Mrs Morel had a visit every day from the Congregational clergyman. Mr Heaton was young, and very poor. His wife had died at the birth of his first baby, so he remained alone in the manse. He was a Bachelor of Arts of Cambridge, very shy and no preacher. Mrs Morel was fond of him, and he depended on her. For hours he talked to her, when she was well. He became the god-parent of the child.

Occasionally, the minister stayed to tea with Mrs Morel. Then she laid the cloth early, got out her best cups, with a little green rim, and hoped Morel would not come too soon; indeed, if he stayed for a pint, she would not mind this day. She had always two dinners to cook, because she believed children should have their chief meal at midday, whereas Morel needed his at five o'clock. So Mr Heaton would hold the baby, whilst Mrs Morel beat up a batter-pudding or peeled the potatoes, and he, watching her all the time, would discuss his next sermon. His ideas were quaint and fantastic. She brought him judiciously to earth. It was a discussion of the wedding at Cana.

'When He changed the water into wine at Cana,' he said, 'that is a symbol that the ordinary life, even the blood, of the married husband and wife, which had before been uninspired, like water, became filled with the Spirit, and was as wine, because, when love enters, the whole spiritual constitution of a man changes, is filled with the Holy Ghost, and almost his form is altered.'

Mrs Morel thought to herself:

'Yes, poor fellow, his young wife is dead; that is why he makes his love into the Holy Ghost.'

They were halfway down their first cup of tea when they heard the sluther of pit-boots.

'Good gracious!' exclaimed Mrs Morel, in spite of herself. The minister looked rather scared. Morel entered. He was feeling rather savage. He nodded a 'How d'yer do' to the clergyman, who rose to shake hands with him.

'Nay,' said Morel, showing his hand, 'look thee at it! Tha niver wants ter shake hands wi' a hand like that, does ter? There's too much pick-halft and shovel-dirt on it.'

The minister flushed with confusion, and sat down again. Mrs Morel rose, carried out the steaming saucepan. Morel took off his coat, dragged his armchair to table and sat down, heavily.

'Are you tired?' asked the clergyman.

'Tired? I ham that,' replied Morel. '*You* don't know what it is to be tired, as *I'm* tired.'

'No,' replied the clergyman.

'Why, look yer 'ere,' said the miner, showing the shoulders of his singlet. 'It's a bit dry now, but it's wet as a clout with sweat even yet. Feel it.'

'Goodness!' cried Mrs Morel. 'Mr Heaton doesn't want to feel your nasty singlet.'

The clergyman put out his hand gingerly.

'No, perhaps he doesn't,' said Morel; 'But it's all come out of *me* whether or not. An' iv'ry day alike my singlet's wringin' wet. 'Aven't you got a drink, Missis, for a man when he comes home barkled up from the pit?'

'You know you drank all the beer,' said Mrs Morel, pouring out his tea.

'An' was there no more to be got?' Turning to the clergyman–'A man gets that caked up wi' th' dust, you know–that clogged up down a coalmine, he *needs* a drink when he comes home.'

'I am sure he does,' said the clergyman.

'But it's ten to one if there's owt for him.'

'There's water–and there's tea,' said Mrs Morel.

'Water! It's not water as'll clear his throat.'

He poured out a saucerful of tea, blew it, and sucked it up through his great black moustache, sighing afterwards. Then he poured out another saucerful, and stood his cup on the table.

'My cloth!' said Mrs Morel, putting it on a plate.

'A man as comes home as I do's too tired to care about cloths,' said Morel.

'Pity!' exclaimed his wife, sarcastically.

The room was full of the smell of meat and vegetables and pit-clothes.

He leaned over to the minister, his great moustache thrust forward, his mouth very red in his black face.

'Mr Heaton,' he said, 'a man as has been down the black hole all day, dingin' away at a coal face, yi, a sight harder than that wall–'

'Needn't make a moan of it,' put in Mrs Morel.

She hated her husband because, whenever he had an audience, he whined and played for sympathy. William, sitting nursing the baby, hated him, with a boy's hatred for false sentiment, and for the stupid treatment of his mother. Annie had never liked him; she merely avoided him.

When the minister had gone, Mrs Morel looked at her cloth.

'A fine mess!' she said.

'Dos't think I'm going' to sit wi' my arms danglin', cos tha's got a parson for tea wi' thee?' he bawled.

They were both angry, but she said nothing. The baby began to cry, and Mrs Morel, picking up a saucepan from the hearth, accidentally knocked Annie on the head, whereupon the girl began to whine, and Morel to shout at her. In the midst of this pandemonium, William looked up at the big glazed text over the mantelpiece and read distinctly:

'God Bless Our Home!'

Whereupon Mrs Morel, trying to soothe the baby, jumped up, rushed at him, boxed his ears, saying:

'What are *you* putting in for?'

And then she sat down and laughed, till tears ran over her cheeks, while William kicked the stool he had been sitting on, and Morel growled:

'I canna see what there is so much to laugh at.'

One evening, directly after the parson's visit, feeling unable to bear herself after another display from her husband, she took Annie and the baby and went out. Morel had kicked William, and the mother would never forgive him.

She went over the sheep-bridge and across a corner of the meadow to the cricket-ground. The meadows seemed one space of ripe, evening light, whispering with the distant mill-race. She sat on a seat under the alders in the cricket-ground, and fronted the evening. Before her, level and solid, spread the big green cricket-field, like the bed of a sea of light. Children played in the bluish shadow of the pavilion. Many rooks, high up, came cawing home across the softly-woven sky. They stooped in a long curve down into the golden glow, concentrating, cawing, wheeling, like black flakes on a slow vortex, over a tree-clump that made a dark boss among the pasture.

A few gentlemen were practising, and Mrs Morel could hear the chock of the ball, and the voices of men suddenly roused; could see the white forms of men shifting silently over the green, upon which already the under shadows were smouldering. Away at the grange, one side of the hay-stacks was lit up, the other sides blue-grey. A waggon of sheaves rocked small across the melting yellow light.

The sun was going down. Every open evening, the hills of Derbyshire were blazed over with red sunset. Mrs Morel watched the sun sink from the glistening sky, leaving a soft flower-blue overhead, while the western space went red, as if all the fire had swum down there, leaving the bell cast flawless blue. The mountain-ash berries across the field stood fierily out from the dark leaves, for a moment. A few shocks of corn in a corner of the fallow stood up as if alive; she imagined them bowing; perhaps her son would be a Joseph. In the east, a mirrored sunset floated pink opposite the west's scarlet. The big haystacks on the hillside, that butted into the glare, went cold.

With Mrs Morel it was one of those still moments when the small frets vanish, and the beauty of things stands out, and she had the peace and the strength to see herself. Now and again, a swallow cut close to her. Now and again, Annie came up with a handful of alder-currants. The baby was restless on his mother's knee, clambering with his hands at the light.

Mrs Morel looked down at him. She had dreaded this baby like a catastrophe, because of her feeling for her husband. And now she felt strangely towards the infant. Her heart was heavy because of the child, almost as if it were unhealthy, or malformed. Yet it seemed quite well. But she noticed the peculiar knitting of the baby's brows, and the peculiar heaviness of its eyes, as if it were trying to understand something that was pain. She felt, when she looked at her child's dark, brooding pupils, as if a burden were on her heart.

'He looks as if he was thinking about something–quite sorrowful,' said Mrs Kirk.

Suddenly, looking at him, the heavy feeling at the mother's heart melted into passionate grief. She bowed over him, and a few tears shook swiftly out of her very heart. The baby lifted his fingers.

'My lamb!' she cried softly.

And at that moment she felt, in some far inner place of her soul, that she and her husband were guilty.

The baby was looking up at her. It had blue eyes like her own, but its look was heavy, steady, as if it had realized something that had stunned some point of its soul.

In her arms lay the delicate baby. Its deep blue eyes, always looking up at her unblinking, seemed to draw her innermost thoughts out of her. She no longer loved her husband; she had not wanted this child to come, and there it lay in her arms and pulled at her heart. She felt as if the navel string that had connected its frail little body with hers had not been broken. A wave of hot love went over her to the infant. She held it close to her face and breast. With all her force, with all her soul she would make up to it for having brought it into the world unloved. She would love it all the more now it was here; carry it in her love. Its clear, knowing eyes gave her pain and fear. Did it know all about her? When it lay under her heart, had it been listening then? Was there a reproach in the look? She felt the marrow melt in her bones, with fear and pain.

Once more she was aware of the sun lying red on the rim of the hill opposite. She suddenly held up the child in her hands.

'Look!' she said. 'Look, my pretty!'

She thrust the infant forward to the crimson, throbbing sun, almost with relief. She saw him lift his little fist. Then she put him to her bosom again, ashamed of her impulse to give him back again whence he came.

'If he lives,' she thought to herself, 'what will become of him—what will he be?'

Her heart was anxious.

'I will call him "Paul",' she said suddenly; she knew not why.

After a while she went home. A fine shadow was flung over the deep green meadow, darkening all.

As she expected, she found the house empty. But Morel was home by ten o'clock, and that day, at least, ended peacefully.

Walter Morel was, at this time, exceedingly irritable. His work seemed to exhaust him. When he came home he did not speak civilly to anybody. If the fire were rather low he bullied about that; he grumbled about his dinner; if the children made a chatter he shouted at them in a way that made their mother's blood boil, and made them hate him.

On the Friday, he was not home by eleven o'clock. The baby was unwell, and was restless, crying if he were put down. Mrs Morel, tired to death, and still weak, was scarcely under control.

'I wish the nuisance would come,' she said wearily to herself.

The child at last sank down to sleep in her arms. She was too tired to carry him to the cradle.

'But I'll say nothing, whatever time he comes,' she said. 'It only works me up: I won't say anything. But I know if he does anything it'll make my blood boil,' she added to herself.

She sighed, hearing him coming, as if it were something she could not bear. He, taking his revenge, was nearly drunk. She kept her head bent over the child as he entered, not wishing to see him. But it went through her like a flash of hot fire when, in passing, he lurched against the dresser, setting the tins rattling, and clutched at the white pot knobs for support. He hung up his hat and coat, then returned, stood glowering from a distance at her, as she sat bowed over the child.

'Is there nothing to eat in the house?' he asked, insolently, as if to a servant. In certain stages of his intoxication he affected the clipped, mincing speech of the towns. Mrs Morel hated him most in this condition.

'You know what there is in the house,' she said, so coldly it sounded impersonal.

He stood and glared at her without moving a muscle.

'I asked a civil question, and I expect a civil answer,' he said affectedly.

'And you got it,' she said, still ignoring him.

He glowered again. Then he came unsteadily forward. He leaned on the table with one hand, and with the other jerked at the table drawer to get a knife to cut bread. The drawer stuck because he pulled sideways. In a temper he dragged it, so that it flew out bodily, and spoons, forks, knives, a hundred metallic things, splashed with a clatter and a clang upon the brick floor. The baby gave a little convulsed start.

'What are you doing, clumsy, drunken fool?' the mother cried.

'Then tha should get the flamin' thing thysen. Tha should get up, like other women have to, an' wait on a man.'

'Wait on you—wait on you?' she cried. 'Yes, I see myself.'

'Yis, an' I'll learn thee tha's got to. Wait on *me*, yes, tha sh'lt wait on me—'

'Never, milord. I'd wait on a dog at the door first.'

'What—what?'

He was trying to fit in the drawer. At her last speech he turned round. His face was crimson, his eyes bloodshot. He stared at her one silent second in threat.

'P-h!' she went quickly, in contempt.

He jerked at the drawer in his excitement. It fell, cut sharply on his shin, and on the reflex he flung it at her.

One of the corners caught her brow as the shallow drawer crashed into the fireplace. She swayed, almost fell stunned from her chair. To her very soul she was sick; she clasped the child tightly to her bosom. A few moments elapsed; then, with an effort, she brought herself to. The baby was crying plaintively. Her left brow was bleeding rather profusely. As she glanced down at the child, her brain reeling, some drops of blood soaked into its white shawl; but the baby was at least not hurt. She balanced her head to keep equilibrium, so that the blood ran into her eye.

Walter Morel remained as he had stood, leaning on the table with one hand, looking blank. When he was sufficiently sure of his balance, he went across to her, swayed, caught hold of the back of her rocking-chair, almost tipping her out; then, leaning forward over her, and swaying as he spoke, he said, in a tone of wondering concern:

'Did it catch thee?'

He swayed again, as if he would pitch on to the child. With the catastrophe he had lost all balance.

'Go away,' she said, struggling to keep her presence of mind.

He hiccoughed. 'Let's—let's look at it,' he said, hiccoughing again.

'Go away!' she cried.

'Lemme—lemme look at it, lass.'

She smelled him of drink, felt the unequal pull of his swaying grasp on the back of her rocking-chair.

'Go away,' she said, and weakly she pushed him off.

He stood, uncertain in balance, gazing upon her. Summoning all her strength she rose, the baby on one arm. By a cruel effort of will, moving as if in sleep, she went across to the scullery, where she bathed her eye for a minute in cold water; but she was too dizzy. Afraid lest she should swoon, she returned to her rocking-chair, trembling in every fibre. By instinct, she kept the baby clasped.

Morel, bothered, had succeeded in pushing the drawer back into its cavity, and was on his knees, groping, with numb paws, for the scattered spoons.

Her brow was still bleeding. Presently Morel got up and came craning his neck towards her.

'What has it done to thee, lass?' he asked, in a very wretched, humble tone.

'You can see what it's done,' she answered.

He stood, bending forward, supported on his hands, which grasped his legs just above the knee. He peered to look at the wound. She drew away from the thrust of his face with its great moustache, averting her own face as much as possible. As he looked at her, who was cold and impassive as stone, with mouth shut tight, he sickened with feebleness and hopelessness of spirit. He was turning drearily away, when he saw a drop of blood fall from the averted wound into the baby's fragile, glistening hair. Fascinated he watched the heavy dark drop hang in the glistening cloud, and pull down the gossamer. Another drop fell. It would soak through to the baby's scalp. He watched, fascinated, feeling it soak in; then, finally, his manhood broke.

'What of this child?' was all his wife said to him. But her low, intense tones brought his head lower. She softened: 'Get me some wadding out of the middle drawer,' she said.

He stumbled away very obediently, presently returning with a pad, which she singed before the fire, then put on her forehead, as she sat with the baby on her lap.

'Now that clean pit-scarf.'

Again he rummaged and fumbled in the drawer, returning presently with a red, narrow scarf. She took it, and with trembling fingers proceeded to bind it round her head.

'Let me tie it for thee,' he said humbly.

'I can do it myself,' she replied. When it was done she went upstairs, telling him to rake the fire and lock the door.

In the morning Mrs Morel said:

'I knocked against the latch of the coal-place, when I was getting a raker in the dark, because the candle blew out.' Her two small children looked up at her with wide, dismayed eyes. They said nothing, but their parted lips seemed to express the unconscious tragedy they felt.

Walter Morel lay in bed next day until nearly dinner-time. He did not think of the previous evening's work. He scarcely thought of anything, but he would not think of that. He lay and suffered like a sulking dog. He had hurt himself most; and he was the more damaged because he would never say a word to her, or express his sorrow. He tried to wriggle out of it. 'It was her own fault,' he said to himself. Nothing, however, could prevent his inner consciousness inflicting on him the punishment which ate into his spirit like rust, and which he could only alleviate by drinking.

He felt as if he had not the initiative to get up, or to say a word, or to move, but could only lie like a log. Moreover, he had himself violent pains in the head. It was Saturday. Towards noon he rose, cut himself food in the pantry, ate it with his head dropped, then pulled on his boots, and went out, to return at three o'clock slightly tipsy and relieved; then once more straight to bed. He rose again at six in the evening, had tea and went straight out.

Sunday was the same: bed till noon, the Palmerston Arms till 2.30, dinner, and bed; scarcely a word spoken. When Mrs Morel went upstairs, towards four o'clock, to put on her Sunday dress, he was fast asleep. She would have felt sorry for him, if he had once said, 'Wife, I'm sorry.' But no; he insisted to himself it was her fault. And so he broke himself. So she merely left him alone. There was this deadlock of passion between them, and she was stronger.

The family began tea. Sunday was the only day when all sat down to meals together.

'Isn't my father going to get up?' asked William.

'Let him lie,' the mother replied.

There was a feeling of misery over all the house. The children breathed the air that was poisoned, and they felt dreary. They were rather disconsolate, did not know what to do, what to play at.

Immediately Morel woke he got straight out of bed. That was characteristic of him all his life. He was all for activity. The prostrated inactivity of two mornings was stifling him.

It was near six o'clock when he got down. This time he entered without hesitation, his wincing sensitiveness having hardened again. He did not care any longer what the family thought or felt.

The tea-things were on the table. William was reading aloud from 'The Child's Own', Annie listening and asking eternally 'Why?' Both children hushed into silence as they heard the approaching thud of their father's stockinged feet, and shrank as he entered. Yet he was usually indulgent to them.

Morel made the meal alone, brutally. He ate and drank more noisily than he had need. No one spoke to him. The family life withdrew, shrank away, and became hushed as he entered. But he cared no longer about his alienation.

Immediately he had finished tea he rose with alacrity to go out. It was this alacrity, this haste to be gone, which so sickened Mrs Morel. As she heard him sousing heartily in cold water, heard the eager scratch of the steel comb on the side of the bowl, as he wetted his hair, she closed her eyes in disgust. As he bent over, lacing his boots, there was a certain vulgar gusto in his movement that divided him from the reserved, watchful rest of the family. He always ran away from the battle with himself. Even in his own heart's privacy, he excused himself, saying, 'If she hadn't said so-and-so, it would never have happened. She asked for what she's got.' The children waited in restraint during his preparations. When he had gone, they sighed with relief.

He closed the door behind him, and was glad. It was a rainy evening. The Palmerston would be the cosier. He hastened forward in anticipation. All the slate roofs of the Bottoms shone black with wet. The roads, always dark with coal-dust, were full of blackish mud. He hastened along. The Palmerston windows were steamed over. The passage was paddled with wet feet. But the air was warm, if foul, and full of the sound of voices and the smell of beer and smoke.

'What shollt ha'e, Walter?' cried a voice, as soon as Morel appeared in the doorway.

'Oh, Jim, my lad, wheriver has thee sprung frae?'

The men made a seat for him, and took him in warmly. He was glad. In a minute or two they had thawed all responsibility out of him, all shame, all trouble, and he was clear as a bell for a jolly night.

On the Wednesday following, Morel was penniless. He dreaded his wife. Having hurt her, he hated her. He did not know what to do with himself that evening, having not even twopence with which to go to the Palmerston, and being already rather deeply in debt. So, while his wife was down the garden with the child, he hunted in the top drawer of the dresser where she kept her purse, found it, and looked inside. It contained a half-crown, two half-pennies, and a sixpence. So he took the sixpence, put the purse carefully back, and went out.

The next day, when she wanted to pay the greengrocer, she looked in the purse for her sixpence, and her heart sank to her shoes. Then she sat down and thought: '*Was* there a sixpence? I hadn't spent it, had I? And I hadn't left it anywhere else?'

She was much put about. She hunted round everywhere for it. And, as she thought, the conviction came into her heart that her husband had taken it. What she had in her purse was all the money she possessed. But that he should sneak it from her thus was unbearable. He had done so twice before. The first time she had not accused him, and at the week-end he had put the shilling again into her purse. So that was how she had known he had taken it. The second time he had not paid back.

This time she felt it was too much. When he had had his dinner–he came home early that day–she said to him coldly:

'Did you take sixpence out of my purse last night?'

'Me!' he said, looking up in an offended way. 'No, I didna! I niver clapped eyes on your purse.'

But she could detect the lie.

'Why, you know you did,' she said quietly.

'I tell you I didna,' he shouted. 'Yer at me again, are yer? I've had about enough on't.'

'So you filch sixpence out of my purse while I'm taking the clothes in.'

'I'll make yer pay for this,' he said, pushing back his chair in desperation. He bustled and got washed, then went determinedly upstairs. Presently he came down dressed, and with a big bundle in a blue-checked, enormous handkerchief.

'And now,' he said, 'you'll see me again when you do.'

'It'll be before I want to,' she replied; and at that he marched out of the house with his bundle. She sat trembling slightly, but her heart brimming with contempt. What would she do if he went to some other pit, obtained work, and got in with another woman? But she knew him too well–he couldn't. She was dead sure of him. Nevertheless her heart was gnawed inside her.

'Where's my dad?' said William, coming in from school.

'He says he's run away,' replied the mother.

'Where to?'

'Eh, I don't know. He's taken a bundle in the blue handkerchief, and says he's not coming back.'

'What shall we do?' cried the boy.

'Eh, never trouble, he won't go far.'

'But if he doesn't come back,' wailed Annie.

And she and William retired to the sofa and wept. Mrs Morel sat and laughed.

'You pair of gabeys!' she exclaimed. 'You'll see him before the night's out.'

But the children were not to be consoled. Twilight came on. Mrs Morel grew anxious from very weariness. One part of her said, it would be a relief to see the last of him; another part fretted because of keeping the children; and inside her, as yet, she could not quite let him go. At the bottom, she knew very well he could *not* go.

When she went down to the coal-place at the end of the garden, however, she felt something behind the door. So she looked. And there in the dark lay the big blue bundle. She sat on a piece of coal in front of the bundle and laughed. Every time she saw it, so fat and yet so ignominious, slunk into its corner in the dark, with its ends flopping like dejected ears from the knots, she laughed again. She was relieved.

Mrs Morel was waiting. He had not any money, she knew, so if he stopped he was running up a hill. She was very tired of him–tired to death. He had not even the courage to carry his bundle beyond the yard-end.

As she meditated, at about nine o'clock, he opened the door and came in, slinking, and yet sulky. She said not a word. He took off his coat, and slunk to his armchair, where he began to take off his boots.

'You'd better fetch your bundle before you take your boots off,' she said quietly.

'You may thank your stars I've come back to-night,' he said, looking up from under his drooped head, sulkily, trying to be impressive.

'Why, where should you have gone? You daren't even get your parcel through the yard-end,' she said.

He looked such a fool she was not even angry with him. He continued to take his boots off and prepare for bed.

'I don't know what's in your blue handkerchief,' she said. 'But if you leave it the children shall fetch it in the morning.'

Whereupon he got up and went out of the house, returning presently and crossing the kitchen with averted face, hurrying upstairs. As Mrs Morel saw him slink quickly through the inner doorway, holding his bundle, she laughed to herself; but her heart was bitter, because she had loved him.

3

THE CASTING OFF OF MOREL–THE TAKING ON OF WILLIAM

During the next week Morel's temper was almost unbearable. Like all miners, he was a great lover of medicines, which, strangely enough, he would often pay for himself.

'You mun get me a drop o' laxy vitral,' he said. 'It's a winder as we canna ha'e a sup i' th' 'ouse.'

So Mrs Morel bought him elixir of vitriol, his favourite first medicine. And he made himself a jug of wormwood tea. He had hanging in the attic great bunches of dried herbs: wormwood, rue, horehound, elder-flowers, parsley-purt, marshmallow, hyssop, dandelion, and centaury. Usually there was a jug of one or other decoction standing on the hob, from which he drank largely.

'Grand!' he said, smacking his lips after wormwood. 'Grand!' And he exhorted the children to try.

'It's better than any of your tea or your cocoa stews,' he vowed. But they were not to be tempted.

This time, however, neither pills nor vitriol nor all his herbs would shift the 'nasty peens in his head.' He was sickening for an attack of an inflammation of the brain. He had never been well since his sleeping on the ground when he went with Jerry to Nottingham. Since then he had drunk and stormed. Now he felt seriously ill, and Mrs Morel had him to nurse. He was one of the worst patients imaginable. But, in spite of all, and putting aside the fact that he was bread-winner, she never quite wanted him to die. Still there was one part of her wanted him for herself.

The neighbours were very good to her: occasionally some had the children in to meals, occasionally some would do the downstairs work for her, one would mind the baby for a day. But it was a great drag, nevertheless. It was not every day the neighbours helped. Then she had nursing of baby and husband, cleaning and cooking, everything to do. She was quite worn out, but she did what was wanted of her.

And the money was just sufficient. She had seventeen shillings a week from clubs, and every Friday, Barker and the other butty put by a portion of the stall's profits for Morel's wife. And the neighbours made broths, and gave eggs, and such invalids' trifles. If they had not helped her so generously in those times, Mrs Morel would never have pulled through without incurring debts that would have dragged her down.

The weeks passed. Morel, almost against hope, grew better. He had a fine constitution, so that, once on the mend, he went straight forward to recovery. Soon he was pottering about downstairs. During his illness his wife had spoilt him a little. Now he wanted her to continue. He often put his hand to his head, pulled down the corners of his mouth, and shammed pains he did not feel. But there was no deceiving her. At first she merely smiled to herself. Then she scolded him sharply.

'Goodness, man, don't be so lachrymose.'

That wounded him slightly, but still he continued to feign sickness.

'I wouldn't be such a mardy baby,' said his wife shortly.

Then he was indignant, and cursed under his breath, like a boy. He was forced to resume a normal tone, and to cease to whine.

Nevertheless, there was a state of peace in the house for some time. Mrs Morel was more tolerant of him, and he, depending on her almost like a child, was rather happy. Neither knew that she was more tolerant because she loved him less. Up till this time, in spite of all, he had been her husband and her man. She had felt that, more or less, what he did to himself he did to her. Her living depended on him. There were many stages in the ebbing of her love for him, but it was always ebbing.

Now, with the birth of this third baby, her self no longer set towards him, helplessly, but was like a tide that scarcely rose, standing off from him. After this she scarcely desired him. And, standing more aloof from him, not feeling him so much part of herself, but merely part of her circumstances, she did not mind so much what he did, could leave him alone.

There was the halt, the wistfulness about the ensuing year, which is like autumn in a man's life. His wife was casting him off, half regretfully, but relentlessly; casting him off and turning now for love and life to the children. Henceforward he was more or less a husk. And he half acquiesced, as so many men do, yielding their place to their children.

During his recuperation, when it was really over between them, both made an effort to come back somewhat to the old relationship of the first months of their marriage. He sat at home and, when the children were in bed, and she was sewing–she did all her sewing by hand, made all shirts and children's clothing–he would read to her from the newspaper, slowly pronouncing and delivering the words like a man pitching quoits. Often she hurried him on, giving him a phrase in anticipation. And then he took her words humbly.

The silences between them were peculiar. There would be the swift, slight 'cluck' of her needle, the sharp 'pop' of his lips as he let out the smoke, the warmth, the sizzle on the bars as he spat in the fire. Then her thoughts turned to William. Already he was getting a big boy. Already he was top of the class, and the master said he was the smartest lad in the school. She saw him a man, young, full of vigour, making the world glow again for her.

And Morel sitting there, quite alone, and having nothing to think about, would be feeling vaguely uncomfortable. His soul would reach out in its blind way to her and find her gone. He felt a sort of emptiness, almost like a vacuum in his soul. He was unsettled and restless. Soon he could not live in that atmosphere, and he affected his wife. Both felt an oppression on their breathing when they were left together for some time. Then he went to bed and she settled down to enjoy herself alone, working, thinking, living.

Meanwhile another infant was coming, fruit of this little peace and tenderness between the separating parents. Paul was seventeen months old when the new baby was born. He was then a plump, pale child, quiet, with heavy blue eyes, and still the peculiar slight knitting of the brows. The last child was also a boy, fair and bonny. Mrs Morel was sorry when she knew she was with child for economic reasons and because she did not love her husband; but not for the sake of the infant.

They called the baby Arthur. He was very pretty, with a mop of gold curls, and he loved his father from the first. Mrs Morel was glad this child loved the father. Hearing the miner's footsteps, the baby would put up his arms and crow. And if Morel were in a good temper, he called back immediately, in his hearty, mellow voice:

'What then, my beauty? I sh'll come to thee in a minute.'

And as soon as he had taken off his pit-coat, Mrs Morel would put an apron round the child, and give him to his father.

'What a sight the lad looks!' she would exclaim sometimes, taking back the baby, that was smutted on the face from his father's kisses and play. Then Morel laughed joyfully.

'He's a little collier, bless his bit o' mutton!' he exclaimed.

And these were the happy moments of her life now, when the child included the father in her heart.

Meanwhile William grew bigger and stronger and more active, while Paul, always rather delicate and quiet, got slimmer, and trotted after his mother like her shadow. He was usually active and interested, but sometimes he would have fits of depression. Then the mother would find the boy of three or four crying on the sofa.

'What's the matter?' she asked, and got no answer.

'What's the matter?' she insisted, getting cross.

'I don't know,' sobbed the child.

So she tried to reason him out of it, or to amuse him, but without effect. It made her feel beside herself. Then the father, always impatient, would jump from his chair and shout:

'If he doesn't stop, I'll smack him till he does.'

'You'll do nothing of the sort,' said the mother coldly. And then she carried the child into the yard, plumped him into his little chair, and said: 'Now cry there, Misery!'

And then a butterfly on the rhubarb-leaves perhaps caught his eye, or at last he cried himself to sleep. These fits were not often, but they caused a shadow in Mrs Morel's heart, and her treatment of Paul was different from that of the other children.

Suddenly one morning as she was looking down the valley of the Bottoms for the barm-man, she heard a voice calling her. It was the thin little Mrs Anthony in brown velvet.

'Here, Mrs Morel, I want to tell you about your Willie.'

'Oh, do you?' replied Mrs Morel. 'Why, what's the matter?'

'A lad as gets 'old of another an' rips his clothes off'n 'is back,' Mrs Anthony said, 'wants showing something.'

'Your Alfred's as old as my William,' said Mrs Morel.

''Appen 'e is, but that doesn't give him a right to get hold of the boy's collar, an' fair rip it clean off his back.'

'Well,' said Mrs Morel. 'I don't thrash my children, and even if I did, I should want to hear their side of the tale.'

'They'd happen be a bit better if they did get a good hiding,' retorted Mrs Anthony. 'When it comes ter rippin' a lad's clean collar off'n 'is back a-purpose—'

'I'm sure he didn't do it on purpose,' said Mrs Morel.

'Make me a liar!' shouted Mrs Anthony'

Mrs Morel moved away and closed her gate. Her hand trembled as she held her mug of barm.

'But I s'll let your mester know,' Mrs Anthony cried after her.

At dinner-time, when William had finished his meal and wanted to be off again—he was then eleven years old—his mother said to him:

'What did you tear Alfred Anthony's collar for?'

'When did I tear his collar?'

'I don't know when, but his mother says you did.'

'Why—it was yesterday—an' it was torn a'ready.'

'But you tore it more.'

'Well, I'd got a cobbler as 'ad licked seventeen—an' Alfy Ant'ny 'e says:

> '"Adam an' Eve an' pinch-me,
>> Went down to a river to bade.
> Adam an' Eve got drownded,
>> Who do yer think got saved?"

An' so I says, "Oh, Pinch-*you*," an' so I pinched 'im, an' 'e was mad, an' so he snatched my cobbler an' run off with it. An' so I run after 'im, an' when I was getting hold of him, 'e dodged, an' it ripped 'is collar. But I got my cobbler—'

He pulled from his pocket a black old horse-chestnut hanging on a string. This old cobbler had 'cobbled'—hit and smashed—seventeen other cobblers on similar strings. So the boy was proud of his veteran.

'Well,' said Mrs Morel, 'you know you've got no right to rip his collar.'

'Well, our mother!' he answered. 'I never meant tr'a done it—an' it was on'y an old indiarubber collar as was torn a'ready.'

'Next time,' said his mother, '*you* be more careful I shouldn't like it if you came home with *your* collar torn off.'

'I don't care, our mother; I never did it a-purpose.'

The boy was rather miserable at being reprimanded.

'No—well, you be more careful.'

William fled away, glad to be exonerated. And Mrs Morel, who hated any bother with the neighbours, thought she would explain to Mrs Anthony, and the business would be over.

But that evening Morel came in from the pit looking very sour. He stood in the kitchen and glared round, but did not speak for some minutes. Then:

'Wheer's that Willy?' he asked.

'What do you want *him* for?' asked Mrs Morel, who had guessed.

'I'll let 'im know when I get him,' said Morel, banging his pit-bottle on to the dresser.

'I suppose Mrs Anthony's got hold of you and been yarning to you about their Alfy's collar,' said Mrs Morel, rather sneering.

'Niver mind who's got hold of me,' said Morel. 'When I get hold of '*im* I'll make his bones rattle.'

'It's a poor tale,' said Mrs Morel, 'that you're so ready to side with any snipey vixen who likes to come telling tales against your own children.'

'I'll learn 'im!' said Morel. 'It none matters to me whose lad 'e is; 'e's none goin' rippin' an' tearin' about just as he's a mind.'

' "Ripping and tearing about!" ' repeated Mrs Morel. 'He was running after that Alfy, who'd taken his cobbler, and he accidentally got hold of his collar, because the other dodged—as an Anthony would.'

'I know!' shouted Morel threateningly.

'You would, before you're told,' replied his wife bitingly.

'Niver you mind,' stormed Morel. 'I know my business.'

'That's more than doubtful,' said Mrs Morel, 'supposing some loud mouthed creature had been getting you to thrash your own children.'

'I know,' repeated Morel.

And he said no more, but sat and nursed his bad temper. Suddenly William ran in, saying:

'Can I have my tea, mother?'

'Tha can ha'e more than that!' shouted Morel.

'Hold your noise, man,' said Mrs Morel; 'and don't look so ridiculous.'

'He'll look ridiculous before I've done wi' him!' shouted Morel, rising from his chair and glaring at his son.

William, who was a tall lad for his years, but very sensitive, had gone pale, and was looking in a sort of horror at his father.

'Go out!' Mrs Morel commanded her son.

William had not the wit to move. Suddenly Morel clenched his fist, and crouched.

'I'll *gi'e* him "go out"!' he shouted like an insane thing.

'What!' cried Mrs Morel, panting with rage. 'You shall not touch him for *her* telling, you shall not!'

'Shonna I?' shouted Morel. 'Shonna I?'

And, glaring at the boy, he ran forward. Mrs Morel sprang in between them, with her fist lifted.

'Don't you *dare*!' she cried.

'What!' he shouted, baffled for the moment. 'What!'

She spun round to her son.

'*Go* out of the house!' she commanded him in fury.

The boy, as if hypnotized by her, turned suddenly and was gone. Morel rushed to the door, but was too late. He returned, pale under his pit-dirt with fury. But now his wife was fully roused.

'Only dare!' she said in a loud, ringing voice. 'Only dare, milord, to lay a finger on that child! You'll regret it for ever.'

He was afraid of her. In a towering rage, he sat down.

When the children were old enough to be left, Mrs Morel joined the Women's Guild. It was a little club of women attached to the Co-operative Wholesale Society, which met on Monday night in the long room over the grocery shop of the Bestwood 'Co-op'. The women were supposed to discuss the benefits to be derived from co-operation, and other social questions. Sometimes Mrs Morel read a paper. It seemed queer to the children to see their mother, who was always busy about the house, sitting writing in her rapid fashion, thinking, referring to books, and writing again. They felt for her on such occasions the deepest respect.

But they loved the Guild. It was the only thing to which they did not grudge their mother—and that partly because she enjoyed it, partly because of the treats they derived from it. The Guild was called by some hostile husbands, who found their wives getting too independent, the 'clat-fart' shop–that is, the gossip-shop. It is true, from off the basis of the Guild, the women could look at their homes, at the conditions of their own lives, and find fault. So the colliers found their women had a new standard of their own, rather disconcerting. And also, Mrs Morel always had a lot of news on Monday nights, so that the children liked William to be in when their mother came home, because she told him things.

Then, when the lad was thirteen, she got him a job in the 'Co-op' office. He was a very clever boy, frank, with rather rough features and real viking blue eyes.

'What dost want ter ma'e a stool-harsed Jack on 'im for?' said Morel. 'All he'll do is to wear his britches behind out, an' earn nowt. What's 'e startin' wi?'

'It doesn't matter what he's starting with,' said Mrs Morel.

'It wouldna! Put 'im i' th' pit wi' me, an' e'll earn a easy ten shillin' a wik from th' start. But six shillin' wearin' his truck-end out on a stool's better than ten shillin' i' th' pit wi' me, I know.'

'He is *not* going in the pit,' said Mrs Morel, 'and there's an end of it.'

'It wor good enough for me, but it's non good enough for 'im.'

'If your mother put you in the pit at twelve, it's no reason why I should do the same with my lad.'

'Twelve! It wor a sight afore that!'

'Whenever it was,' said Mrs Morel.

She was very proud of her son. He went to the night-school, and learned shorthand, so that by the time he was sixteen he was the best shorthand clerk and book-keeper on the place, except one. Then he taught in the night-schools. But he was so fiery that only his good-nature and his size protected him.

All the things that men do–the decent things–William did. He could run like the wind. When he was twelve he won a first prize in a race; an inkstand of glass, shaped like an anvil. It stood proudly on the dresser, and gave Mrs Morel a keen pleasure. The boy only ran for her. He flew home with his anvil, breathless, with a 'Look, mother!' That was the first real tribute to herself. She took it like a queen.

'How pretty!' she exclaimed.

Then he began to get ambitious. He gave all his money to his mother. When he earned fourteen shillings a week, she gave him back two for himself, and, as he never drank, he felt himself rich. He went about with the bourgeois of Bestwood. The townlet contained nothing higher than the clergyman. Then came the bank manager, then the doctors, then the tradespeople, and after that the hosts of colliers. William began to consort with the sons of the chemist, the schoolmaster, and the tradesmen. He played billiards in the Mechanics Hall. Also he danced–this in spite of his mother. All the life that Bestwood offered he enjoyed, from the sixpenny-hops down Church Street, to sports and billiards.

Paul was treated to dazzling descriptions of all kinds of flower-like ladies, most of whom lived like cut blooms in William's heart for a brief fortnight.

Occasionally some flame would come in pursuit of her errant swain. Mrs Morel would find a strange girl at the door, and immediately she sniffed the air.

'Is Mr Morel in?' the damsel would ask appealingly.

'My husband is at home,' Mrs Morel replied.

'I–I mean *young* Mr Morel,' repeated the maiden painfully.

'Which one? There are several.'

Whereupon much blushing and stammering from the fair one.

'I–I met Mr Morel–at Ripley,' she explained.

'Oh–at a dance?'

'Yes.'

'I don't approve of the girls my son meets at dances. And he is *not* at home.'

Then he came home angry with his mother for having turned the girl away so rudely. He was a careless, yet eager-looking fellow, who walked with long strides, sometimes frowning, often with his cap pushed jollily to the back of his head. Now he came in frowning. He threw his cap on to the sofa, and took his strong jaw in his hand, and glared down at his mother. She was small, with her hair taken straight back from her forehead. She had a quiet air of authority, and yet of rare warmth. Knowing her son was angry, she trembled inwardly.

'Did a lady call for me yesterday, mother?' he asked.

'I don't know about a lady. There was a girl came.'

'And why didn't you tell me?'

'Because I forgot, simply.'

He fumed a little.

'A good-looking girl–seemed a lady.'

'I didn't look at her.'

'Big brown eyes?'

'I did *not* look. And tell your girls, my son, that when they're running after you, they're not to come and ask your mother for you. Tell them that–brazen baggages you meet at dancing-classes.'

'I'm sure she was a nice girl.'

'And I'm sure she wasn't.'

There ended the altercation. Over the dancing there was a great strife between the mother and the son. The grievance reached its height when William said he was going to Hucknall Torkard–considered a low town–to a fancy-dress ball. He was to be a Highlander. There was a dress he could hire, which one of his friends had had, and which fitted him perfectly. The Highland suit came home. Mrs Morel received it coldly and would not unpack it.

'My suit come?' cried William.

'There's a parcel in the front-room.'

He rushed in and cut the string.

'How do you fancy your son in this!' he said, enraptured, showing her the suit.

'You know I don't want to fancy you in it.'

On the evening of the dance, when he had come home to dress, Mrs Morel put on her coat and bonnet.

'Aren't you going to stop and see me, mother?' he asked.

'No; I don't want to see you,' she replied.

She was rather pale, and her face was closed and hard. She was afraid of her son's going the same way as his father. He hesitated a moment, and his heart stood still with anxiety. Then he caught sight of the Highland bonnet with its ribbons. He picked it up gleefully, forgetting her. She went out.

When he was nineteen he suddenly left the Co-op office and got a situation in Nottingham. In his new place he had thirty shillings a week instead of eighteen. This was indeed a rise. His mother and his father were brimmed up with pride. Everybody praised William. It seemed he was going to get on rapidly. Mrs Morel hoped, with his aid, to help her younger sons. Annie was now studying to be a teacher. Paul, also very clever, was getting on well, having lessons in French and German from his godfather, the clergyman who was still a friend to Mrs Morel. Arthur, a spoilt and very good-looking boy, was at the Board-school, but there was talk of his trying to get a scholarship for the High School in Nottingham.

William remained a year at his new post in Nottingham. He was studying hard, and growing serious. Something seemed to be fretting him. Still he went out to the dances and the river parties. He did not drink. The children were all rabid teetotallers. He came home very late at night, and sat yet longer studying. His mother implored him to take more care, to do one thing or another.

'Dance, if you want to dance, my son; but don't think you can work in the office, and then amuse yourself, and *then* study on top of all. You can't; the human frame won't stand it. Do one thing or the other–amuse yourself or learn Latin; but don't try to do both.'

Then he got a place in London, at a hundred and twenty a year. This seemed a fabulous sum. His mother doubted almost whether to rejoice or to grieve.

'They want me in Lime Street on Monday week, mother,' he cried, his eyes blazing as he read the letter. Mrs Morel felt everything go silent inside her. He read the letter: '"And will you reply by Thursday whether you accept. Yours faithfully–" They want me, mother, at a hundred and twenty a year, and don't even ask to see me. Didn't I tell you I could do it! Think of me in London! And I can give you twenty pounds a year, mater. We s'll all be rolling in money.'

'We shall, my son,' she answered sadly.

It never occurred to him that she might be more hurt at his going away than glad of his success. Indeed, as the days drew near for his departure, her heart began to close and grow dreary with despair. She loved him so much! More than that, she hoped in him so much. Almost she lived by him. She liked to do things for him: she liked to put a cup for his tea and iron his collars, of which he was so proud. It was a joy to her to have him proud of his collars. There was no laundry. So she used to rub away at them with her little convex iron, to polish them, till they shone from the sheer pressure of her arm. Now she would not do it for him. Now he was going away. She felt almost as if he were going as well out of her heart. He did not seem to leave her inhabited with himself. That was the grief and the pain to her. He took nearly all himself away.

A few days before his departure–he was just twenty–he burned his love-letters. They had hung on a file at the top of the kitchen cupboard. From some of them he had read extracts to his mother. Some of them she had taken the trouble to read herself. But most were too trivial.

Now, on the Saturday morning he said:

'Come on, Postle, let's go through my letters, and you can have the birds and flowers.'

Mrs Morel had done her Saturday's work on the Friday, because he was having a last day's holiday. She was making him a rice cake, which he loved, to take with him. He was scarcely conscious that she was so miserable.

He took the first letter off the file. It was mauve-tinted, and had purple and green thistles. William sniffed the page.

'Nice scent! Smell.'

And he thrust the sheet under Paul's nose.

'Um!' said Paul, breathing in. 'What d'you call it? Smell, mother.'

His mother ducked her small, fine nose down to the paper.

'*I* don't want to smell their rubbish,' she said, sniffing.

'This girl's father,' said William, 'is as rich as Croesus. He owns property without end. She calls me Lafayette, because I know French. "You will see, I've forgiven you"–I like *her* forgiving me. "I told mother about you this morning, and she will have much pleasure if you come to tea on Sunday, but she will have to get father's consent also. I sincerely hope he will agree. I will let you know how it transpires. If, however, you–"'

' "Let you know how it" what?' interrupted Mrs Morel.

'"Transpires"–oh, yes!'

'"Transpires!"' repeated Mrs Morel mockingly. 'I thought she was so well educated!'

William felt slightly uncomfortable, and abandoned this maiden, giving Paul the corner with the thistles. He continued to read extracts from his letters, some of which amused his mother, some of which saddened her and made her anxious for him.

'My lad,' she said, 'they're very wise. They know they've only got to flatter your vanity, and you press up to them like a dog that has its head scratched.'

'Well, they can't go on scratching for ever,' he replied. 'And when they've done, I trot away.'

'But one day you'll find a string round your neck that you can't pull off,' she answered.

'Not me! I'm equal to any of 'em, mater, they needn't flatter themselves.'

'You flatter *yourself*,' she said quietly.

Soon there was a heap of twisted black pages, all that remained of the file of scented letters, except that Paul had thirty or forty pretty tickets from the corners of the notepaper–swallows and forget-me-nots and ivy sprays. And William went to London to start a new life.

4

THE YOUNG LIFE OF PAUL

Paul would be built like his mother, slightly and rather small. His fair hair went reddish, and then dark brown; his eyes were grey. He was a pale, quiet child, with eyes that seemed to listen, and with a full, dropping underlip.

As a rule he seemed old for his years. He was so conscious of what other people felt, particularly his mother. When she fretted he understood, and could have no peace. His soul seemed always attentive to her.

As he grew older he became stronger. William was too far removed from him to accept him as a companion. So the smaller boy belonged at first almost entirely to Annie. She was a tomboy and a 'flybie-skybie', as her mother called her. But she was intensely fond of her second brother. So Paul was towed round at the heels of Annie, sharing her game. She raced wildly at lerky with the other young wild-cats of the Bottoms. And always Paul flew beside her, living her share of the game, having as yet no part of his own. He was quiet and not noticeable. But his sister adored him. He always seemed to care for things if she wanted him to.

She had a big doll of which she was fearfully proud, though not so fond. So she laid the doll on the sofa, and covered it with an antimacassar, to sleep. Then she forgot it. Meantime Paul must practise jumping off the sofa arm. So he jumped crash into the face of the hidden doll. Annie rushed up, uttered a loud wail, and sat down to weep a dirge. Paul remained quite still. 'You couldn't tell it was there, mother; you couldn't tell it was there,' he repeated over and over. So long as Annie wept for the doll he sat helpless with misery. Her grief wore itself out. She forgave her brother–he was so much upset. But a day or two afterwards she was shocked

'Let's make a sacrifice of Arabella,' he said. 'Let's burn her.'

She was horrified, yet rather fascinated. She wanted to see what the boy would do. He made an altar of bricks, pulled some of the shavings out of Arabella's body, poured on a little paraffin, and set the whole thing alight. He watched with wicked satisfaction the drops of wax melt off the broken forehead of Arabella, and drop like sweat into the flame. So long as the stupid big doll burned he rejoiced in silence. At the end he poked among the embers with a stick, fished out the arms and legs, all blackened, and smashed them under stones.

'That's the sacrifice of Missis Arabella,' he said. 'An' I'm glad there's nothing left of her.'

Which disturbed Annie inwardly, although she could say nothing. He seemed to hate the doll so intensely, because he had broken it.

All the children, but particularly Paul, were peculiarly *against* their father, along with their mother. Morel continued to bully and to drink. He had periods, months at a time, when he made the whole life of the family a misery. Paul never forgot coming home from the Band of Hope one Monday evening and finding his mother with her eye swollen and discoloured, his father standing on the hearthrug, feet astride, his head down, and William, just home from work, glaring at his father. There was a silence as the young children entered, but none of the elders looked round.

William was white to the lips, and his fists were clenched. He waited until the children were silent, watching with children's rage and hate; then he said:

'You coward, you daren't do it when I was in.'

But Morel's blood was up. He swung round on his son. William was bigger, but Morel was hard-muscled, and mad with fury.

'Dossn't I?' he shouted. 'Dossn't I? Ha'e much more o' thy chelp, my young jockey, an' I'll rattle my fist about thee. Ay, an' I sholl that, dost see.'

Morel crouched at the knees and showed his fist in an ugly, almost beast-like fashion. William was white with rage.

'Will yer?' he said, quiet and intense. 'It 'ud be the last time, though.'

Morel danced a little nearer, crouching, drawing back his fist to strike. William put his fists ready. A light came into his blue eyes, almost like a laugh. He watched his father. Another word, and the men would have begun to fight. Paul hoped they would. The three children sat pale on the sofa.

'Stop it, both of you,' cried Mrs Morel in a hard voice. 'We've had enough for *one* night. And *you,*' she said, turning on to her husband, 'look at your children!'

Morel glanced at the sofa.

'Look at the children, you nasty little bitch!' he sneered. 'Why, what have *I* done to the children, I should like to know? But they're like yourself; you've put 'em up to your own tricks and nasty ways–you've learned 'em in it, you 'ave.'

She refused to answer him. No one spoke. After a while he threw his boots under the table and went to bed.

'Why didn't you let me have a go at him?' said William, when his father was upstairs. 'I could easily have beaten him.'

'A nice thing—your own father,' she replied.

'*"Father!"*' repeated William. 'Call *him my* father!'

'Well, he is—and so—'

'But why don't you let me settle him? I could do, easily.'

'The idea!' she cried. 'It hasn't come to *that* yet.'

'No,' he said, 'it's come to worse. Look at yourself. *Why* didn't you let me give it him?'

'Because I couldn't bear it, so never think of it,' she cried quickly.

And the children went to bed, miserably.

When William was growing up, the family moved from the Bottoms to a house on the brow of the hill, commanding a view of the valley, which spread out like a convex cockleshell, or a clamp-shell, before it. In front of the house was a huge old ash-tree. The west wind, sweeping from Derbyshire, caught the houses with full force, and the tree shrieked again. Morel liked it.

'It's music,' he said. 'It sends me to sleep.'

But Paul and Arthur and Annie hated it. To Paul it became almost a demoniacal noise. The winter of their first year in the new house their father was very bad. The children played in the street, on the brim of the wide, dark valley, until eight o'clock. Then they went to bed. Their mother sat sewing below. Having such a great space in front of the house gave the children a feeling of night, of vastness, and of terror. This terror came in from the shrieking of the tree and the anguish of the home discord. Often Paul would wake up, after he had been asleep a long time, aware of thuds downstairs. Instantly he was wide awake. Then he heard the booming shouts of his father, come home nearly drunk, then the sharp replies of his mother, then the bang, bang of his father's fist on the table, and the nasty snarling shout as the man's voice got higher. And then the whole was drowned in a piercing medley of shrieks and cries from the great, windswept ash-tree. The children lay silent in suspense, waiting for a lull in the wind to hear what their father was doing. He might hit their mother again. There was a feeling of horror, a kind of bristling in the darkness, and a sense of blood. They lay with their hearts in the grip of an intense anguish. The wind came through the tree fiercer and fiercer. All the cords of the great harp hummed, whistled, and shrieked. And then came the horror of the sudden silence, silence everywhere, outside and downstairs. What was it? Was it a silence of blood? What had he done?

The children lay and breathed the darkness. And then, at last, they heard their father throw down his boots and tramp upstairs in his stockinged feet. Still they listened. Then at last, if the wind allowed, they heard the water of the tap drumming into the kettle, which their mother was filling for morning, and they could go to sleep in peace.

So they were happy in the morning—happy, very happy playing, dancing at night round the lonely lamp-post in the midst of the darkness. But they had one tight place of anxiety in their hearts, one darkness in their eyes, which showed all their lives.

Paul hated his father. As a boy he had a fervent private religion.

'Make him stop drinking,' he prayed every night. 'Lord let my father die,' he prayed very often. 'Let him not be killed at pit,' he prayed when, after tea, the father did not come home from work.

That was another time when the family suffered intensely. The children came from school and had their teas. On the hob the big black saucepan was simmering, the stew-jack was in the oven, ready for Morel's dinner. He was expected at five o'clock. But for months he would stop and drink every night on his way from work.

In the winter nights, when it was cold, and grew dark early, Mrs Morel would put a brass candlestick on the table, light a tallow candle to save the gas. The children finished their bread-and-butter, or dripping, and were ready to go out to play. But if Morel had not come they faltered. The sense of his sitting in all his pit-dirt, drinking, after a long day's work, not coming home and eating and washing, but sitting, getting drunk, on an empty stomach, made Mrs Morel unable to bear herself. From her the feeling was transmitted to the other children. She never suffered alone any more: the children suffered with her.

Paul went out to play with the rest. Down in the great trough of twilight, tiny clusters of lights burned where the pits were. A few last colliers struggled up the dim field-path. The lamplighter came along. No more colliers came. Darkness shut down over the valley; work was gone. It was night.

Then Paul ran anxiously into the kitchen. The one candle still burned on the table, the big fire glowed red. Mrs Morel sat alone. On the hob the saucepan steamed; the dinner-plate lay waiting on the table. All the room was full of the sense of waiting, waiting for the man who was sitting in his pit-dirt, dinnerless, some mile away from home, across the darkness, drinking himself drunk. Paul stood in the doorway.

'Has my dad come?' he asked.

'You can see he hasn't,' said Mrs Morel, cross with the futility of the question.

Then the boy dawdled about near his mother. They shared the same anxiety. Presently Mrs Morel went out and strained the potatoes.

'They're ruined and black,' she said; 'but what do I care?'

Not many words were spoken. Paul almost hated his mother for suffering because his father did not come home from work.

'What do you bother yourself for?' he said. 'If he wants to stop and get drunk, why don't you let him?'

'Let him!' flashed Mrs Morel. 'You may well say "let him".'

She knew that the man who stops on the way home from work is on a quick way to ruining himself and his home. The children were yet young, and depended on the breadwinner. William gave her the sense of relief, providing her at last with someone to turn to if Morel failed. But the tense atmosphere of the room on these waiting evenings was the same.

The minutes ticked away. At six o'clock still the cloth lay on the table, still the dinner stood waiting, still the same sense of anxiety and expectation in the room. The boy could not stand it any longer. He could not go out and play. So he ran in to Mrs Inger, next door but one, for her to talk to him. She had no children. Her husband was good to her, but was in a shop, and came home late. So, when she saw the lad at the door, she called:

'Come in, Paul.'

The two sat talking for some time, when suddenly the boy rose, saying:

'Well, I'll be going and seeing if my mother wants an errand doing.'

He pretended to be perfectly cheerful, and did not tell his friend what ailed him. Then he ran indoors.

Morel at these times came in churlish and hateful.

'This is a nice time to come home,' said Mrs Morel.

"Wha's it matter to yo' what time I come whoam?' he shouted.

And everybody in the house was still, because he was dangerous. He ate his food in the most brutal manner possible and, when he had done, pushed all the pots in a heap away from him, to lay his arms on the table. Then he went to sleep.

Paul hated his father so. The collier's small, mean head, with its black hair slightly soiled with grey, lay on the bare arms, and the face, dirty and inflamed, with a fleshy nose and thin, paltry brows, was turned sideways, asleep with beer and weariness and nasty temper. If anyone entered suddenly, or a noise were made, the man looked up and shouted:

'I'll lay my fist about thy y'ead, I'm tellin' thee, if tha doesna stop that clatter! Dost hear?'

And the two last words, shouted in a bullying fashion, usually at Annie, made the family writhe with hate of the man.

He was shut out from all family affairs. No one told him anything. The children, alone with their mother, told her all about the day's happenings, everything. Nothing had really taken place in them until it was told to their mother. But as soon as the father came in, everything stopped. He was like the scotch in the smooth, happy machinery of the home. And he was always aware of this fall of silence on his entry, the shutting off of life, the unwelcome. But now it was gone too far to alter.

He would dearly have liked the children to talk to him, but they could not. Sometimes Mrs Morel would say:

'You ought to tell your father.'

Paul won a prize in a competition in a child's paper. Everybody was highly jubilant.

'Now you'd better tell your father when he comes in,' said Mrs Morel. 'You know how he carries on and says he's never told anything.'

'All right,' said Paul. But he would almost rather have forfeited the prize than have to tell his father.

'I've won a prize in a competition, dad,' he said.

Morel turned round to him.

'Have you, my boy? What sort of a competition?'

'Oh, nothing–about famous women.'

'And how much is the prize, then, as you've got?'

'It's a book.'

'Oh, indeed!'

'About birds.'

'Hm–hm!'

And that was all. Conversation was impossible between the father and any other member of the family. He was an outsider. He had denied the God in him.

The only times when he entered again into the life of his own people was when he worked, and was happy at work. Sometimes, in the evening, he cobbled the boots or mended the kettle or his pit-bottle. Then he always wanted several attendants, and the children enjoyed it. They united with him in the work, in the actual doing of something, when he was his real self again.

He was a good workman, dexterous, and one who, when he was in a good humour, always sang. He had whole periods, months, almost years, of friction and nasty temper. Then sometimes he was jolly again. It was nice to see him run with a piece of red-hot iron into the scullery, crying:

'Out of my road–out of my road!'

Then he hammered the soft, red-glowing stuff on his iron goose, and made the shape he wanted. Or he sat absorbed for a moment, soldering. Then the children watched with joy as the metal sank suddenly molten, and was shoved about against the nose of the soldering-iron, while the room was full of a scent of burnt resin and hot tin, and Morel was silent and intent for a minute. He always sang when he mended boots because of the jolly sound of hammering. And he was rather happy when he sat putting great patches on his moleskin pit trousers, which he would often do, considering them too dirty, and the stuff too hard, for his wife to mend.

But the best time for the young children was when he made fuses. Morel fetched a sheaf of long sound wheat-straws from the attic. These he cleaned with his hand, till each one gleamed like a stalk of gold, after which he cut the straws into lengths of about six inches, leaving, if he could, a notch at the bottom of each piece. He always had a beautifully sharp knife that could cut a straw clean without hurting it. Then he set in the middle of the table a heap of gunpowder, a little pile of black grains upon the white-scrubbed board. He made and trimmed the straws while Paul and Annie filled and plugged them. Paul loved to see the black grains trickle down a crack in his palm into the mouth of the straw, peppering jollily downwards till the straw was full. Then he bunged up the mouth with a bit of soap—which he got in his thumb-nail from a pat in a saucer—and the straw was finished.

'Look, dad!' he said.

'That's right, my beauty,' replied Morel, who was peculiarly lavish of endearments to his second son. Paul popped the fuse into the powder-tin, ready for the morning, when Morel would take it to the pit, and use it to fire a shot what would blast the coal down.

Meantime Arthur, still fond of his father, would lean on the arm of Morel's chair, and say:

'Tell us about down pit, daddy.'

This Morel loved to do.

'Well, there's one little 'oss—we call 'im Taffy,' he would begin. 'An he's a fawce un!'

Morel had a warm way of telling a story. He made one feel Taffy's cunning.

'He's a brown un,' he would answer, 'an' not very high. Well, he comes i' th' stall wi' a rattle, an' then yo' 'ear 'im sneeze. "'Ello, Taff," you say, "what art sneezin' for? Bin ta' ein' some snuff?"

'An' 'e sneezes again. Then he slives up an' shoves 'is 'ead·on yer, that cadin'.

'"What's want, Taff?" yo' say.'

'And what does he?' Arthur always asked.

'He wants a bit o' bacca, my duckey.'

This story of Taffy would go on interminably, and everybody loved it.

Or sometimes it was a new tale.

'An' what dost think, my darlin'? When I went to put my coat on at snap-time, what should go runnin' up my arm but a mouse.'

'"Hey up, theer!" I shouts.'

'An' I wor just in time ter get 'im by th' tail.'

'And did you kill it?'

'I did, for they're a nuisance. The place is fair snied wi' 'em.'

'An' what do they live on?'

'The corn as the 'osses drops—and they'll get in your pocket an' eat your snap, if you'll let 'em—no matter where yo' hing your coat—the slivin', nibblin' little nuisances, for they are.'

These happy evenings could not take place unless Morel had some job to do. And then he always went to bed very early, often before the children. There was nothing remaining for him to stay up for, when he had finished tinkering, and had skimmed the headlines of the newspaper.

And the children felt secure when their father was in bed. They lay and talked softly awhile. Then they started as the lights went suddenly sprawling over the ceiling from the lamps that swung in the hands of the colliers tramping by outside, going to take the nine o'clock shift. They listened to the voices of the men, imagined them dipping down into the dark valley. Sometimes they went to the window and watched the three or four lamps growing tinier and tinier, swaying down the fields in the darkness. Then it was a joy to rush back to bed and cuddle closely in the warmth.

Paul was rather a delicate boy, subject to bronchitis. The others were all quite strong; so this was another reason for his mother's difference in feeling for him. One day he came home at dinner-time feeling ill. But it was not a family to make any fuss.

'What's the matter with *you*?' his mother asked sharply.

'Nothing,' he replied.

But he ate no dinner.

'If you eat no dinner, you're not going to school,' she said.

'Why?' he asked.

'That's why.'

So after dinner he lay down on the sofa, on the warm chintz cushions the children loved. Then he fell into a kind of doze. That afternoon Mrs Morel was ironing. She listened to the small, restless noise the boy made in his throat as she worked. Again rose in her heart the old, almost weary feeling towards him. She had never expected him to live. And yet he had a great vitality in his young body. Perhaps it would have been a little relief to her if he had died. She always felt a mixture of anguish in her love for him.

He, in his semi-conscious sleep, was vaguely aware of the clatter of the iron on the iron-stand, of the faint thud, thud of the ironing-board. Once roused, he opened his eyes to see his mother standing on the hearthrug with the hot iron near her cheek, listening, as it were, to the heat. Her still face, with the mouth closed tight from suffering and disillusion and self-denial, and her nose, the smallest bit on one side, and her blue eyes so young, quick, and warm, made his heart contract with love. When she was quiet, so, she looked brave and rich with life, but as if she had been done out of her rights. It hurt the boy keenly, this feeling about her that she had never had her life's fulfilment: and his own incapability to make up to her hurt him with a sense of impotence, yet made him patiently dogged inside. It was his childish aim.

She spat on the iron, and a little ball of spit bounded, raced off the dark, glossy surface. Then, kneeling, she rubbed the iron on the sack lining of the hearthrug vigorously. She was warm in the ruddy firelight. Paul loved the way she crouched and put her head on one side. Her movements were light and quick. It was always a pleasure to watch her. Nothing she ever did, no movement she ever made, could have been found fault with by her children. The room was warm and full of the scent of hot linen. Later on the clergyman came and talked softly with her.

Paul was laid up with an attack of bronchitis. He did not mind much. What happened happened, and it was no good kicking against the pricks. He loved the evenings, after eight o'clock, when the light was put out, and he could watch the fire-flames spring over the darkness of the walls and ceiling; could watch huge shadows waving and tossing, till the room seemed full of men who battled silently.

On retiring to bed, the father would come into the sickroom. He was always very gentle if anyone were ill. But he disturbed the atmosphere for the boy.

'Are ter asleep, my darlin'?' Morel asked softly.

'No; is my mother comin'?'

'She's just finishin' foldin' the clothes. Do you want anything?' Morel rarely 'thee'd' his son.

'I don't want nothing. But how long will she be?'

'Not long, my duckie.'

The father waited undecidedly on the hearthrug for a moment or two. He felt his son did not want him. Then he went to the top of the stairs and said to his wife:

'This childt's axin' for thee; how long art goin' to be?'

'Until I've finished, good gracious! Tell him to go to sleep.'

'She says you're to go to sleep,' the father repeated gently to Paul.

'Well, I want *her* to come,' insisted the boy.

'He says he can't go off till you come,' Morel called downstairs.

'Eh, dear! I shan't be long. And do stop shouting downstairs. There's the other children—'

Then Morel came again, and crouched before the bedroom fire. He loved a fire dearly.

'She says she won't be long,' he said.

He loitered about indefinitely. The boy began to get feverish with irritation. His father's presence seemed to aggravate all his sick impatience. At last Morel, after having stood looking at his son awhile, said softly:

'Good-night, my darling.'

'Good-night,' Paul replied, turning round in relief to be alone.

Paul loved to sleep with his mother. Sleep is still most perfect, in spite of hygienists, when it is shared with a beloved. The warmth, the security and peace of soul, the utter comfort from the touch of the other, knits the sleep, so that it takes the body and soul completely in its healing. Paul lay against her and slept, and got better; whilst she, always a bad sleeper, fell later on into a profound sleep that seemed to give her faith.

In convalescence he would sit up in bed, see the fluffy horses feeding at the troughs in the field, scattering their hay on the trodden yellow snow; watch the miners troop home—small, black figures trailing slowly in gangs across the white field. Then the night came up in dark blue vapour from the snow.

In convalescence everything was wonderful. The snowflakes suddenly arriving on the window-pane, clung there a moment like swallows, then were gone, and a drop of water was crawling down the glass. The snowflakes whirled round the corner of the house, like pigeons dashing by. Away across the valley the little black train crawled doubtfully over the great whiteness.

While they were so poor, the children were delighted if they could do anything to help economically. Annie and Paul and Arthur went out early in the morning, in summer, looking for mushrooms, hunting through the wet grass, from which the larks were rising, for the white-skinned, wonderful naked bodies crouched secretly in the green. And if they got half a pound they felt exceedingly happy: there was the joy of finding something, the joy of accepting something straight from the hand of Nature, and the joy of contributing to the family exchequer.

But the most important harvest, after gleaning for frumenty, was the blackberries. Mrs Morel must buy fruit for puddings on the Saturdays; also she liked blackberries. So Paul and Arthur scoured the coppices and woods and old quarries, so long as a blackberry was to be found, every weekend going on their search. In that region of mining villages blackberries became a comparative rarity. But Paul hunted far and wide. He loved being out in the country, among the bushes. But he also could not bear to go home to his mother empty. That, he felt, would disappoint her, and he would have died rather.

'Good gracious!' she would exclaim as the lads came in, late, and tired to death, and hungry, 'wherever have you been?'

'Well,' replied Paul, 'there wasn't any, so we went over Misk Hills. And look here, our mother!'

She peeped into the basket.

'Now, those are fine ones!' she exclaimed.

'And there's over two pounds—isn't there over two pounds?'

She tried the basket.

'Yes,' she answered doubtfully.

Then Paul fished out a little spray. He always brought her one spray, the best he could find.

'Pretty!' she said, in a curious tone, of a woman accepting a love-token.

The boy walked all day, went miles and miles, rather than own himself beaten and come home to her empty-handed. She never realized this, whilst he was young. She was a woman who waited for her children to grow up. And William occupied her chiefly.

But when William went to Nottingham, and was not so much at home, the mother made a companion of Paul. The latter was unconsciously jealous of his brother, and William was jealous of him. At the same time, they were good friends.

Mrs Morel's intimacy with her second son was more subtle and fine, perhaps not so passionate as with her eldest. It was the rule that Paul should fetch the money on Friday afternoons. The colliers of the five pits were paid on Fridays, but not individually. All the earnings of each stall were put down to the chief butty, as contractor, and he divided the wages again, either in the public-house or in his own home. So that the children could fetch the money, school closed early on Friday afternoons. Each of the Morel children—William, then Annie, then Paul—had fetched the money on Friday afternoons, until they went themselves to work. Paul used to set off at half-past three, with a little calico bag in his pocket. Down all the paths, women, girls, children, and men were seen trooping to the offices.

These offices were quite handsome: a new, red-brick building, almost like a mansion, standing in its own well-kept grounds at the end of Greenhill Lane. The waiting-room was the hall, a long, bare room paved with blue brick, and having a seat all round, against the wall. Here sat the colliers in their pit-dirt. They had come up early. The women and children usually loitered about on the red gravel paths. Paul always examined the grass border, and the big grass bank, because in it grew tiny pansies and tiny forget-me-nots. There was a sound of many voices. The women had on their Sunday hats. The girls chattered loudly. Little dogs ran here and there. The green shrubs were silent all around.

Then from inside came the cry 'Spinney Park–Spinney Park'. All the folk for Spinney Park trooped inside. When it was time for Bretty to be paid, Paul went in among the crowd. The pay-room was quite small. A counter went across, dividing it into half. Behind the counter stood two men–Mr Braithwaite and his clerk, Mr Winterbottom. Mr Braithwaite was large, somewhat of the stern patriarch in appearance, having a rather thin white beard. He was usually muffled in an enormous silk neckerchief, and right up to the hot summer a huge fire burned in the open grate. No window was open. Sometimes in winter the air scorched the throats of the people, coming in from the freshness. Mr Winterbottom was rather small and fat, and very bald. He made remarks that were not witty, whilst his chief launched forth patriarchal admonitions against the colliers.

The room was crowded with miners in their pit-dirt, men who had been home and changed, and women, and one or two children, and usually a dog. Paul was quite small, so it was often his fate to be jammed behind the legs of the men, near the fire which scorched him. He knew the order of the names–they went according to stall number.

'Holliday,' came the ringing voice of Mr Braithwaite. Then Mrs Holliday stepped silently forward, was paid, drew aside.

'Bower–John Bower.'

A boy stepped to the counter. Mr Braithwaite, large and irascible, glowered at him over his spectacles.

'John Bower!' he repeated.

'It's me,' said the boy.

'Why, you used to 'ave a different nose than that,' said glossy Mr Winterbottom, peering over the counter. The people tittered thinking of John Bower senior.

'How is it your father's not come?' said Mr Braithwaite, in a large and magisterial voice.

'He's badly,' piped the boy.

'You should tell him to keep off the drink,' pronounced the great cashier.

'An' niver mind if he puts his foot through yer,' said a mocking voice from behind.

All the men laughed. The large and important cashier looked down at his next sheet.

'Fred Pilkington!' he called, quite indifferent.

Mr Braithwaite was an important shareholder in the firm.

Paul knew his turn was next but one, and his heart began to beat. He was pushed against the chimney-piece. His calves were burning. But he did not hope to get through the wall of men.

'Walter Morel!' came the ringing voice.

'Here!' piped Paul, small and inadequate.

'Morel–Walter Morel!' the cashier repeated, his finger and thumb on the invoice, ready to pass on.

Paul was suffering convulsions of self-consciousness, and could not or would not shout. The backs of the men obliterated him. Then Mr Winterbottom came to the rescue.

'He's here. Where is he? Morel's lad?'

The fat, red, bald little man peered round with keen eyes. He pointed at the fireplace. The colliers looked round, moved aside, and disclosed the boy.

'Here he is!' said Mr Winterbottom.

Paul went to the counter.

'Seventeen pounds eleven and fivepence. Why don't you shout up when you're called?' said Mr Braithwaite. He banged on to the invoice a five-pound bag of silver, then in a delicate and pretty movement, picked up a little ten-pound column of gold, and plumped it beside the silver. The gold slid in a bright stream over the paper. The cashier finished counting off the money; the boy dragged the whole down the counter to Mr Winterbottom, to whom the stoppages for rent and tools must be paid. Here he suffered again.

'Sixteen an' six,' said Mr Winterbottom.

The lad was too much upset to count. He pushed forward some loose silver and half a sovereign.

'How much do you think you've given me?' asked Mr Winterbottom.

The boy looked at him, but said nothing. He had not the faintest notion.

'Haven't you got a tongue in your head?'

Paul bit his lip, and pushed forward some more silver.

'Don't they teach you to count at the Board-school?' he asked.

'Nowt but Algebra an' French,' said a collier.

'An' cheek an' impidence,' said another.

Paul was keeping someone waiting. With trembling fingers he got his money into the bag and slid out. He suffered the tortures of the damned on these occasions.

His relief, when he got outside, and was walking along the Mansfield Road, was infinite. On the park wall the mosses were green. There were some gold and some white fowls pecking under the apple-trees of an orchard. The colliers were walking home in a stream. The boy went near the wall, selfconsciously. He knew many of the men, but could not recognize them in their dirt. And this was a new torture to him.

When he got down to the New Inn, at Bretty, his father was not yet come. Mrs Wharmby, the landlady, knew him. His grandmother, Morel's mother, had been Mrs Wharmby's friend.

'Your father's not come yet,' said the landlady, in the peculiar half-scornful, half-patronizing voice of a woman who talks chiefly to grown men. 'Sit you down.'

Paul sat down on the edge of the bench in the bar. Some colliers were reckoning–sharing out their money–in a corner; others came in. They all glanced at the boy without speaking. At last Morel came; brisk, and with something of an air, even in his blackness.

'Hello!' he said rather tenderly to his son. 'Have you bested me? Shall you have a drink of something?'

Paul and all the children were bred up fierce anti-alcoholists, and he would have suffered more in drinking a lemonade before all the men than in having a tooth drawn.

The landlady looked at him *de haut en bas*, rather pitying, and at the same time, resenting his clear, fierce morality. Paul went home, glowering. He entered the house silently. Friday was baking day, and there was usually a hot bun. His mother put it before him.

Suddenly he turned on her in a fury, his eyes flashing:

'I'm *not* going to the office any more,' he said.

'Why, what's the matter?' his mother asked in surprise. His sudden rages rather amused her.

'I'm *not* going any more,' he declared.

'Oh, very well, tell your father so.'

He chewed his bun as if he hated it.

'I'm not–I'm not going to fetch the money.'

'Then one of Carlin's children can go; they'd be glad enough of the sixpence,' said Mrs Morel.

This sixpence was Paul's only income. It mostly went in buying birthday presents; but it *was* an income, and he treasured it. But–!

'They can have it, then!' he said. 'I don't want it.'

'Oh, very well,' said his mother. 'But you needn't bully *me* about it.'

'They're hateful, and common, and hateful, they are, and I'm not going any more. Mr Braithwaite drops his "h's", an' Mr Winterbottom says "You was".'

'And is that why you won't go any more?' smiled Mrs Morel.

The boy was silent for some time. His face was pale, his eyes dark and furious. His mother moved about at her work, taking no notice of him.

'They always stan' in front of me, so's I can't get out,' he said.

'Well, my lad, you've only to *ask* them,' she replied.

'An' then Alfred Winterbottom says, "What do they teach you at the Board-school"?'

'They never taught *him* much,' said Mrs Morel, 'that is a fact–neither manners nor wit–and his cunning he was born with.'

So, in her own way, she soothed him. His ridiculous hyper-sensitiveness made her heart ache. And sometimes the fury in his eyes roused her, made her sleeping soul lift up its head a moment, surprised.

'What was the cheque?' she asked.

'Seventeen pounds eleven and fivepence, and sixteen and six stoppages,' replied the boy. 'It's a good week; and only five shillings stoppages for my father.'

So she was able to calculate how much her husband had earned, and could call him to account if he gave her short money. Morel always kept to himself the secret of the week's amount.

Friday was the baking night and market night. It was the rule that Paul should stay at home and bake. He loved to stop in and draw or read; he was very fond of drawing. Annie always 'gallivanted' on Friday nights; Arthur was enjoying himself as usual. So the boy remained alone.

Mrs Morel loved her marketing. In the tiny market-place on the top of the hill, where four roads from Nottingham and Derby, Ilkeston and Mansfield, meet, many stalls were erected. Brakes ran in from surrounding villages. The market-place was full of women, the streets packed with men. It was amazing to see so many men everywhere in the streets. Mrs Morel usually quarrelled with her lace woman, sympathized with her fruit man–who was a gabey, but his wife was a bad un–laughed with the fish man–who was a scamp but so droll–put the linoleum man in his place, was cold with the odd-wares man, and only went to the crockery man when she was driven–or drawn by the cornflowers on a little dish; then she was coldly polite.

'I wondered how much that little dish was,' she said.

'Sevenpence to you.'

'Thank you.'

She put the dish down and walked away; but she could not leave the market-place without it. Again she went by where the pots lay coldly on the floor, and she glanced at the dish furtively, pretending not to.

She was a little woman, in a bonnet and a black costume. Her bonnet was in its third year; it was a great grievance to Annie.

'Mother!' the girl implored, 'don't wear that nubbly little bonnet.'

'Then what else shall I wear?' replied the mother tartly. 'And I'm sure it's right enough.'

It had started with a tip; then had had flowers; now was reduced to black lace and a bit of jet.

'It looks rather come down,' said Paul. 'Couldn't you give it a pick-me-up?'

'I'll jowl your head for impudence,' said Mrs Morel, and she tied the strings of the black bonnet valiantly under her chin.

She glanced at the dish again. Both she and her enemy, the pot man, had an uncomfortable feeling, as if there were something between them. Suddenly he shouted:

'Do you want it for fivepence?'

She started. Her heart hardened; but then she stopped and took up her dish. 'I'll have it,' she said.

'Yer'll do me the favour, like?' he said. 'Yer'd better spit in it, like yer do when y'ave something give yer.'

Mrs Morel paid him the fivepence in a cold manner.

'I don't see you give it me,' she said. 'You wouldn't let me have it for fivepence if you didn't want to.'

'In this flamin', scrattlin' place you may count yerself lucky if you can give your things away,' he growled.

'Yes; there are bad times, and good,' said Mrs Morel.

But she had forgiven the pot man. They were friends. She dare now finger his pots. So she was happy.

Paul was waiting for her. He loved her home-coming. She was always her best so–triumphant, tired, laden with parcels, feeling rich in spirit. He heard her quick, light step in the entry and looked up from his drawing.

'Oh!' she sighed, smiling at him from the doorway.

'My word, you *are* loaded!' he exclaimed, putting down his brush.

'I am!' she gasped. 'That brazen Annie said she'd meet me. *Such* a weight!'

She dropped her string bag and her packages on the table.

'Is the bread done?' she asked, going to the oven.

'The last one is soaking,' he replied. 'You needn't look, I've not forgotten it.'

'Oh, that pot man!' she said, closing the oven door. 'You know what a wretch I've said he was? Well, I don't think he's quite so bad.'

'Don't you?'

The boy was attentive to her. She took off her little black bonnet.

'No. I think he can't make any money–well, it's everybody's cry alike nowadays–and it makes him disagreeable.'

'It would *me*,' said Paul.

'Well, one can't wonder at it. And he let me have–how much do you think he let me have *this* for?'

She took the dish out of its rag of newspaper, and stood looking on it with joy.

'Show me!' said Paul.

The two stood together gloating over the dish.

'I *love* cornflowers on things,' said Paul.

'Yes, and I thought of the teapot you bought me–'

'One and three,' said Paul.

'Fivepence!'

'It's not enough, mother.'

'No. Do you know, I fairly sneaked off with it. But I'd been extravagant, I couldn't afford any more. And he needn't have let me have it if he hadn't wanted to.'

'No, he needn't, need he,' said Paul, and the two comforted each other from the fear of having robbed the pot man.

'We c'n have stewed fruit in it,' said Paul.

'Or custard, or a jelly,' said his mother.

'Or radishes and lettuce,' said he.

'Don't forget that bread,' she said, her voice bright with glee.

Paul looked in the oven; tapped the loaf on the base.

'It's done,' he said, giving it to her.

She tapped it also.

'Yes,' she replied, going to unpack her bag. 'Oh, and I'm a wicked, extravagant woman. I know I s'll come to want.'

He hopped to her side eagerly, to see her latest extravagance. She unfolded another lump of newspaper and disclosed some roots of pansies and of crimson daisies.

'Four penn'orth!' she moaned.

'How *cheap*!' he cried.

'Yes, but I couldn't afford it *this* week of all weeks.'

'But lovely!' he cried.

'Aren't they!' she exclaimed, giving way to pure joy. 'Paul, look at this yellow one, isn't it—and a face just like an old man!'

'Just!' cried Paul, stooping to sniff. 'And smells that nice! But he's a bit splashed.'

He ran in the scullery, came back with the flannel, and carefully washed the pansy.

'*Now* look at him now he's wet!' he said.

'Yes!' she exclaimed, brimful of satisfaction.

The children of Scargill Street felt quite select. At the end where the Morels lived there were not many young things. So the few were more united. Boys and girls played together, the girls joining in the fights and the rough games, the boys taking part in the dancing games and rings and make-belief of the girls.

Annie and Paul and Arthur loved the winter evenings, when it was not wet. They stayed indoors till the colliers were all gone home, till it was thick dark, and the street would be deserted. Then they tied their scarves round their necks, for they scorned overcoats, as all the colliers' children did, and went out. The entry was very dark, and at the end the whole great night opened out, in a hollow, with a little tangle of lights below where Minton pit lay, and another far away opposite for Selby. The farthest tiny lights seemed to stretch out the darkness for ever. The children looked anxiously down the road at the one lamp-post, which stood at the end of the field path. If the little, luminous space were deserted, the two boys felt genuine desolation. They stood with their hands in their pockets under the lamp, turning their backs on the night, quite miserable, watching the dark houses. Suddenly a pinafore under a short coat was seen, and a long-legged girl came flying up.

'Where's Billy Pillins an' your Annie an' Eddie Dakin?'

'I don't know.'

But it did not matter so much–there were three now. They set up a game round the lamp-post, till the others rushed up, yelling. Then the play went fast and furious.

There was only this one lamp-post. Behind was the great scoop of darkness, as if all the night were there. In front, another wide, dark way opened over the hill brow. Occasionally somebody came out of his way and went into the field down the path. In a dozen yards the night had swallowed them. The children played on.

They were brought exceedingly close together owing to their isolation. If a quarrel took place, the whole play was spoilt. Arthur was very touchy, and Billy Pillins–really Philips–was worse. Then Paul had to side with Arthur, and on Paul's side went Alice, while Billy Pillins always had Emmie Limb and Eddie Dakin to back him up. Then the six would fight, hate with a fury of hatred, and flee home in terror. Paul never forgot, after one of these fierce internecine fights, seeing a big red moon lift itself up, slowly, between the waste road over the hill-top, steadily, like a great bird. And he thought of the Bible, that the moon should be turned to blood. And the next day he made haste to be friends with Billy Pillins, and then the wild, intense games went on again under the lamp-post, surrounded by so much darkness. Mrs Morel, going into her parlour, would hear the children singing away:

'My shoes are made of Spanish leather,
My socks are made of silk;
I wear a ring on every finger,
I wash myself in milk.'

They sounded so perfectly absorbed in the game as their voices came out of the night, that they had the feel of wild creatures singing. It stirred the mother; and she understood when they came in at eight o'clock, ruddy, with brilliant eyes, and quick, passionate speech.

They all loved the Scargill Street house for its openness, for the great scallop of the world it had in view. On summer evenings the women would stand against the field fence, gossiping, facing the west, watching the sunsets flare quickly out, till the Derbyshire hills ridged across the crimson far away, like the black crest of a newt.

In this summer season the pits never turned full time, particularly the soft coal. Mrs Dakin, who lived next door to Mrs Morel, going to the field fence to shake her hearthrug, would spy men coming slowly up the hill. She saw at once they were colliers. Then she waited, a tall, thin, shrew-faced woman, standing on the hill brow, almost like a menace to the poor colliers who were toiling up. It was only eleven o'clock. From the far-off wooded hills the haze that hangs like fine black crape at the back of a summer morning had not yet dissipated. The first man came to the stile. 'Chock-chock!' went the gate under his thrust.

'What, han' yer knocked off?' cried Mrs Dakin.

'We han, missis.'

'It's a pity as they letn yer goo,' she said sarcastically.

'It is that,' replied the man.

'Nay, you know you're flig to come up again,' she said.

And the man went on. Mrs Dakin, going up her yard, spied Mrs Morel taking the ashes to the ash-pit.

'I reckon Minton's knocked off, missis,' she cried.

'Isn't it sickenin'!' exclaimed Mrs Morel in wrath.

'Ha! But I'n just seed Jont Hutchby.'

'They might as well have saved their shoe-leather,' said Mrs Morel. And both women went indoors disgusted.

The colliers, their faces scarcely blackened, were trooping home again. Morel hated to go back. He loved the sunny morning. But he had gone to pit to work, and to be sent home again spoilt his temper.

'Good gracious, at this time!' exclaimed his wife, as he entered.

'Can I help it, woman?' he shouted.

'And I've not done half enough dinner.'

'Then I'll eat my bit o' snap as I took with me,' he bawled pathetically. He felt ignominious and sore.

And the children, coming home from school, would wonder to see their father eating with his dinner the two thick slices of rather dry and dirty bread-and-butter that had been to pit and back.

'What's my dad eating his snap for now?' asked Arthur.

'I should ha'e it holled at me if I didna,' snorted Morel.

'What a story!' exclaimed his wife.

'An' is it goin' to be wasted?' said Morel. 'I'm not such a extravagant mortal as you lot, with your waste. If I drop a bit of bread at pit, in all the dust an' dirt, I pick it up an' eat it.'

'The mice would eat it,' said Paul. 'It wouldn't be wasted.'

'Good bread-an'-butter's not for mice, either,' said Morel. 'Dirty or not dirty, I'd eat it rather than it should be wasted.'

'You might leave it for the mice and pay for it out of your next pint,' said Mrs Morel.

'Oh, might I?' he exclaimed.

They were very poor that autumn. William had just gone away to London, and his mother missed his money. He sent ten shillings once or twice, but he had many things to pay for at first. His letters came regularly once a week. He wrote a good deal to his mother, telling her all his life, how he made friends, and was exchanging lessons with a Frenchman, how he enjoyed London. His mother felt again he was remaining to her just as when he was at home. She wrote to him every week her direct, rather witty letters. All day long, as she cleaned the house, she thought of him. He was in London: he would do well. Almost, he was like her knight who wore *her* favour in the battle.

He was coming at Christmas for five days. There had never been such preparations. Paul and Arthur scoured the land for holly and evergreens. Annie made the pretty paper hoops in the old-fashioned way. And there was unheard-of-extravagance in the larder. Mrs Morel made a big and magnificent cake. Then, feeling queenly, she showed Paul how to blanch almonds. He skinned the long nuts reverently, counting them all, to see not one was lost. It was said that eggs whisked better in a cold place. So the boy stood in the scullery, where the temperature was nearly at freezing-point, and whisked and whisked, and flew in excitement to his mother as the white of egg grew stiffer and more snowy.

'Just look, mother! Isn't it lovely?'

And he balanced a bit on his nose, then blew it in the air.

'Now, don't waste it,' said the mother.

Everybody was mad with excitement. William was coming on Christmas Eve. Mrs Morel surveyed the pantry. There was a big plum cake, and a rice cake, jam tarts, lemon tarts, and mince-pies—two enormous dishes. She was finishing cooking–Spanish tarts and cheese-cakes. Everywhere was decorated. The kissing bunch of berried holly hung with bright and glittering things spun slowly over Mrs Morel's head as she trimmed her little tarts in the kitchen. A great fire roared. There was a scent of cooked pastry. He was due at seven o'clock, but he would be late. The three children had gone to meet him. She was alone. But at a quarter to seven Morel came in again. Neither wife nor husband spoke. He sat in his armchair, quite awkward with excitement, and she quietly went on with her baking. Only by the careful way in which she did things could it be told how much moved she was. The clock ticked on.

'What time dost say he's coming?' Morel asked for the fifth time.

'The train gets in at half past six,' she replied emphatically.

'Then he'll be here at ten past seven.'

'Eh, bless you, it'll be hours late on the Midland,' she said indifferently. But she hoped, by expecting him late, to bring him early. Morel went down the entry to look for him. Then he came back.

'Goodness, man!' she said. 'You're like an ill-sitting hen.'

'Hadna you better be gettin' him summat t'eat ready?' asked the father.

'There's plenty of time,' she answered.

'There's not much as I can see on,' he answered, turning crossly in his chair. She began to clear the table. The kettle was singing. They waited and waited.

Meantime the three children were on the platform at Sethley Bridge, on the Midland main line, two miles from home. They waited one hour. A train came–he was not there. Down the line the red and green lights shone. It was very dark and very cold.

'Ask him if the London train's come,' said Paul to Annie, when they saw a man in a tip cap.

'I'm not,' said Annie. 'You be quiet–he might send us off.'

But Paul was dying for the man to know they were expecting someone by the London train: it sounded so grand. Yet he was much too much scared of broaching any man, let alone one in a peaked cap, to dare to ask. The three children could scarcely go into the waiting-room for fear of being sent away, and for fear something should happen whilst they were off the platform. Still they waited in the dark and cold.

'It's an hour an' a half late,' said Arthur pathetically.

'Well,' said Annie, 'it's Christmas Eve.'

They all grew silent. He wasn't coming. They looked down the darkness of the railway. There was London! It seemed the uttermost of distance. They thought anything might happen if one came from London. They were all too troubled to talk. Cold and unhappy, and silent, they huddled together on the platform.

At last, after more than two hours, they saw the lights of an engine peering round, away down the darkness. A porter ran out. The children drew back with beating hearts. A great train bound for Manchester drew up. Two doors opened, and from one of them, William. They flew to him. He handed parcels to them cheerily, and immediately began to explain that this great train had stopped for *his* sake at such a small station as Sethley Bridge: it was not booked to stop.

Meanwhile the parents were getting anxious. The table was set, the chop was cooked, everything was ready. Mrs Morel put on her black apron. She was wearing her best dress. Then she sat, pretending to read. The minutes were a torture to her.

'H'm!' said Morel. 'It's an hour an' a ha'ef.'

'And those children waiting!' she said.

'Th' train canna ha' come in yet,' he said.

'I tell you, on Christmas Eve they're *hours* wrong.'

They were both a bit cross with each other, so gnawed with anxiety. The ash-tree moaned outside in a cold, raw wind. And all that space of night from London home! Mrs Morel suffered. The slight click of the works inside the clock irritated her. It was getting so late; it was getting unbearable.

At last there was a sound of voices, and a footstep in the entry.

'Ha's here!' cried Morel, jumping up.

Then he stood back. The mother ran a few steps towards the door and waited. There was a rush and a patter of feet, the door burst open. William was there. He dropped his Gladstone bag and took his mother in his arms.

'Mater!' he said.

'My boy!' she cried.

And for two seconds, no longer, she clasped him and kissed him. Then she withdrew and said, trying to be quite normal:

'But how late you are!'

'Aren't I!' he cried, turning to his father. 'Well, dad!'

The two men shook hands.

'Well, my lad!'

Morel's eyes were wet.

'We thought tha'd niver be commin',' he said.

'Oh, I'd come!' exclaimed William.

Then the son turned round to his mother.

'But you look well,' she said proudly, laughing.

'Well!' he exclaimed. 'I should think so–coming home!'

He was a fine fellow, big, straight, and fearless-looking. He looked round at the evergreens and the kissing bunch, and the little tarts that lay in their tins on the hearth.

'By jove! mother, it's not different!' he said, as if in relief.

Everybody was still for a second. Then he suddenly sprang forward, picked a tart from the hearth, and pushed it whole into his mouth.

'Well, did iver you see such a parish oven!' the father exclaimed.

He had brought them endless presents. Every penny he had he had spent on them. There was a sense of luxury overflowing in the house. For his mother there was an umbrella with gold on the pale handle. She kept it to her dying day, and would have lost anything rather than that. Everybody had something gorgeous, and besides, there were pounds of unknown sweets: Turkish delight, crystallized pineapple, and such-like things which, the children thought, only the splendour of London could provide. And Paul boasted of these sweets among his friends.

'Real pineapple, cut off in slices, and then turned into crystal–fair grand!'

Everybody was mad with happiness in the family. Home was home, and they loved it with a passion of love, whatever the suffering had been. There were parties, there were rejoicings. People came in to see William, to see what difference London had made to him. And they all found him 'such a gentleman, and *such* a fine fellow, my word!'

When he went away again the children retired to various places to weep alone. Morel went to bed in misery, and Mrs Morel felt as if she were numbed by some drug, as if her feelings were paralysed. She loved him passionately.

He was in the office of a lawyer connected with a large shipping firm, and at the midsummer his chief offered him a trip in the Mediterranean on one of the boats, for quite a small cost. Mrs Morel wrote: 'Go, go, my boy. You may never have a chance again, and I should love to think of you cruising there in the Mediterranean almost better than to have you at home.' But William came home for his fortnight's holiday. Not even the Mediterranean, which pulled at all his young man's desire to travel, and at his poor man's wonder at the glamorous south, could take him away when he might come home. That compensated his mother for much.

5

PAUL LAUNCHES INTO LIFE

Morel was rather a heedless man, careless of danger. So he had endless accidents. Now, when Mrs Morel heard the rattle of an empty coal-cart cease at her entry-end, she ran into the parlour to look, expecting almost to see her husband seated in the waggon, his face grey under his dirt, his body limp and sick with some hurt or other. If it were he, she would run out to help.

About a year after William went to London, and just after Paul had left school before he got work, Mrs Morel was upstairs and her son was painting in the kitchen—he was very clever with his brush—when there came a knock at the door. Crossly he put down his brush to go. At the same moment his mother opened a window upstairs and looked down.

A pit-lad in his dirt stood on the threshold.

'Is this Walter Morel's?' he asked.

'Yes,' said Mrs Morel. 'What is it?'

But she had guessed already.

'Your mester's got hurt,' he said.

'Eh, dear me!' she exclaimed. 'It's a wonder if he hadn't, lad. And what's he done this time?'

'I don't know for sure, but it's 'is leg somewhere. They ta'ein' 'im ter th' 'ospital.'

'Good gracious me!' she exclaimed. 'Eh, dear, what a one he is! There's not five minutes of peace. I'll be hanged if there is! His thumb's nearly better, and now—Did you see him?'

'I seed him at th' bottom. An' I seed 'em bring 'im up in a tub, an' 'e wor in a dead faint. But he shouted like anythink when Doctor Fraser examined him i' th' lamp cabin—an' cossed an' swore, an' said as 'e wor goin' to be ta'en whoam—'e worn't goin' ter th' 'ospital.'

The boy faltered to an end.

'He *would* want to come home, so that I can have all the bother. Thank you, my lad. Eh, dear, if I'm not sick—sick and surfeited, I am!'

She came downstairs. Paul had mechanically resumed his painting.

'And it must be pretty bad if they've taken him to the hospital,' she went on. 'But what a *careless* creature he is! *Other* men don't have all these accidents. Yes, he *would* want to put all the burden on me. Eh, dear, just as we *were* getting easy a bit at last. Put those things away, there's no time to be painting now.

What time is there a train? I know I s'll have to go trailing to Keston. I s'll have to leave that bedroom.'

'I can finish it,' said Paul.

'You needn't. I shall catch the seven o'clock back, I should think. Oh, my blessed heart, the fuss and commotion he'll make! And those granite setts at Tinder Hill—he might well call them kidney pebbles—they'll jolt him almost to bits. I wonder why they can't mend them, the state they're in, an' all the men as go across in that ambulance. You'd think they'd have a hospital here. The men bought the ground, and, my sirs, there'd be accidents enough to keep it going. But no, they must trail them ten miles in a slow ambulance to Nottingham. It's a crying shame! Oh, and the fuss he'll make! I know he will! I wonder who's with him. Barker, I s'd think. Poor beggar, he'll wish himself anywhere rather. But he'll look after him, I know. Now there's no telling how long he'll be stuck in that hospital—and *won't* he hate it! But if it's only his leg it's not so bad.'

All the time she was getting ready. Hurriedly taking off her bodice, she crouched at the boiler while the water ran slowly into her lading-can.

'I wish this boiler was at the bottom of the sea!' she exclaimed, wriggling the handle impatiently. She had very handsome, strong arms, rather surprising on a smallish woman.

Paul cleared away, put on the kettle, and set the table.

'There isn't a train till four-twenty,' he said. 'You've time enough.'

'Oh no I haven't!' she cried, blinking at him over the towel as she wiped her face.

'Yes you have. You must drink a cup of tea at any rate. Should I come with you to Keston?'

'Come with me? What for, I should like to know? Now, what have I to take him? Eh, dear! His clean shirt—and it's a blessing it *is* clean. But it had better be aired. And stockings—he won't want them—and a towel, I suppose; and handkerchiefs. Now what else?'

'A comb, a knife and fork and spoon,' said Paul. His father had been in the hospital before.

'Goodness knows what sort of state his feet were in,' continued Mrs Morel, as she combed her long brown hair, that was fine as silk, and was touched now with grey. 'He's very particular to wash himself to the waist, but below he thinks doesn't matter. But there, I suppose they see plenty like it.'

Paul had laid the table. He cut his mother one or two pieces of very thin bread-and-butter.

'Here you are,' he said, putting her cup of tea in her place.

'I can't be bothered!' she exclaimed crossly.

'Well, you've got to, so there, now it's put out ready,' he insisted.

So she sat down and sipped her tea, and ate a little, in silence. She was thinking.

In a few minutes she was gone, to walk the two and a half miles to Keston Station. All the things she was taking him she had in her bulging string bag. Paul watched her go up the road between the hedges—a little, quick-stepping figure, and his heart ached for her, that she was thrust forward again into pain and trouble. And she, tripping so quickly in her anxiety, felt at the back of her, her son's heart waiting on her, felt him bearing what part of the burden he could, even supporting her. And when she was at the hospital, she thought: 'It *will* upset that lad when I tell him how bad it is. I'd better be careful.' And when she was trudging home again, she felt he was coming to share her burden.

'Is it bad?' asked Paul, as soon as she entered the house.

'It's bad enough,' she replied.

'What?'

She sighed and sat down, undoing her bonnet-strings. Her son watched her face as it was lifted, and her small, work-hardened hands fingering at the bow under her chin.

'Well,' she answered, 'it's not really dangerous, but the nurse says it's a dreadful smash. You see, a great piece of rock fell on his leg–here–and it's a compound fracture. There are pieces of bone sticking through–'

'Ugh–how horrid!' exclaimed the children.

'And,' she continued, 'of course he says he's going to die–it wouldn't be him if he didn't. "I'm done for, my lass!" he said, looking at me. "Don't be so silly," I said to him. "You're not going to die of a broken leg, however badly it's smashed." "I s'll niver come out of 'ere but in a wooden box," he groaned. "Well," I said, "if you want them to carry you into the garden in a wooden box, when you're better, I've no doubt they will." "If we think it's good for him," said the Sister. She's an awfully nice Sister, but rather strict.'

Mrs Morel took off her bonnet. The children waited in silence.

'Of course, he *is* bad,' she continued, 'and he will be. It's a great shock, and he's lost a lot of blood; and, of course, it *is* a very dangerous smash. It's not at all sure that it will mend so easily. And then there's the fever and the mortification–if it took bad ways he'd quickly be gone. But there, he's a clean-blooded man, with wonderful healing flesh, and so I see no reason why it *should* take bad ways. Of course there's a wound–'

She was pale now with emotion and anxiety. The three children realized that it was very bad for their father, and the house was silent, anxious.

'But he always gets better,' said Paul after a while.

'That's what I tell him,' said the mother.

Everybody moved about in silence.

'And he really looked nearly done for,' she said. 'But the Sister says that is the pain.'

Annie took away her mother's coat and bonnet.

'And he looked at me when I came away! I said: "I s'll have to go now, Walter, because of the train–and the children." And he looked at me. It seems hard.'

Paul took up his brush again and went on painting. Arthur went outside for some coal. Annie sat looking dismal. And Mrs Morel, in her little rocking-chair that her husband had made for her when the first baby was coming, remained motionless, brooding. She was grieved, and bitterly sorry for the man who was hurt so much. But still, in her heart of hearts, where the love should have burned, there was a blank. Now, when all her woman's pity was roused to its full extent, when she would have slaved herself to death to nurse him and to save him, when she would have taken the pain herself, if she could, somewhere far away inside her, she felt indifferent to him and his suffering. It hurt her most of all, this failure to love him, even when he roused her strong emotions. She brooded awhile.

'And there,' she said suddenly, 'when I'd got half-way to Keston, I found I'd come out in my working-boots–and *look* at them.' They were an old pair of Paul's, brown and rubbed through the toes. 'I didn't know what to do with myself, for shame,' she added.

In the morning, when Annie and Arthur were at school, Mrs Morel talked again to her son, who was helping her with her housework.

'I found Barker at the hospital. He did look bad, poor little fellow! "Well," I said to him, "what sort of a journey did you have with him?" "Dunna ax me, missis!" he said. "Ay," I said, "I know what he'd be." "But it *wor* bad for him, Mrs Morel, it *wor* that!" he said. "I know," I said. "At ivry jolt I thought my 'eart would ha' flown clean out o' my mouth," he said. "An' the scream 'e gives sometimes! Missis, not for a fortune would I go through wi' it again." "I can quite understand it," I said. "It's a nasty job, though," he said, "an' one as 'll be a long while afore it's right again." "I'm afraid it will," I said. I like Mr Barker—I *do* like him. There's something so manly about him.'

Paul resumed his task silently.

'And of course,' Mrs Morel continued, 'for a man like your father, the hospital *is* hard. He *can't* understand rules and regulations. And he won't let anybody else touch him, not if he can help it. When he smashed the muscles of his thigh, and it had to be dressed four times a day, *would* he let anybody but me or his mother do it? He wouldn't. So, of course, he'll suffer in there with the nurses. And I didn't like leaving him. I'm sure, when I kissed him an' came away, it seemed a shame.'

So she talked to her son, almost as if she were thinking aloud to him, and he took it in as best he could, by sharing her trouble to lighten it. And in the end she shared almost everything with him without knowing.

Morel had a very bad time. For a week he was in a critical condition. Then he began to mend. And then, knowing he was going to get better, the whole family sighed with relief, and proceeded to live happily.

They were not badly off whilst Morel was in the hospital. There were fourteen shillings a week from the pit, ten shillings from the sick club, and five shillings from the Disability Fund; and then every week the butties had something for Mrs Morel—five or seven shillings—so that she was quite well to do. And whilst Morel was progressing favourably in the hospital, the family was extraordinarily happy and peaceful. On Saturdays and Wednesdays Mrs Morel went to Nottingham to see her husband. Then she always brought back some little thing: a small tube of paint for Paul, or some thick paper; a couple of postcards for Annie, that the whole family rejoiced over for days before the girl was allowed to send them away; or a fret-saw for Arthur, or a bit of pretty wood. She described her adventures into the big shops with joy. Soon the folk in the picture-shop knew her, and knew about Paul. The girl in the book-shop took a keen interest in her. Mrs Morel was full of information when she got home from Nottingham. The three sat round till bed-time, listening, putting in, arguing. Then Paul often raked the fire.

'I'm the man in the house now,' he used to say to his mother with joy. They learned how perfectly peaceful the home could be. And they almost regretted—though none of them would have owned to such callousness—that their father was soon coming back.

Paul was now fourteen, and was looking for work. He was a rather small and rather finely-made boy, with dark brown hair and light blue eyes. His face had already lost its youthful chubbiness, and was becoming somewhat like William's—rough-featured, almost rugged—and it was extraordinarily mobile. Usually he looked as if he saw things, was full of life, and warm; then his smile, like his mother's, came suddenly and was very lovable; and then, when there was any clog in his soul's quick running, his face went stupid and ugly. He was the sort of boy that becomes a clown and a lout as soon as he is not understood, or feels himself held cheap; and, again, is adorable at the first touch of warmth.

He suffered very much from the first contact with anything. When he was seven, the starting school had been a nightmare and a torture to him. But afterwards he liked it. And now that he felt he had to go out into life, he went through agonies of shrinking self-consciousness. He was quite a clever painter for a boy of his years, and he knew some French and German and mathematics that Mr Heaton had taught him. But nothing he had was of any commercial value. He was not strong enough for heavy manual work, his mother said. He did not care for making things with his hands, preferred racing about or making excursions into the country, or reading, or painting.

'What do you want to be?' his mother asked.

'Anything.'

'That is no answer,' said Mrs Morel.

But it was quite truthfully the only answer he could give. His ambition, as far as this world's gear went, was quietly to earn his thirty or thirty-five shillings a week somewhere near home, and then, when his father died, have a cottage with his mother, paint and go out as he liked, and live happy ever after. That was his programme as far as doing things went. But he was proud within himself, measuring people against himself, and placing them, inexorably. And he thought that *perhaps* he might also make a painter, the real thing. But that he left alone.

'Then,' said his mother, 'you must look in the paper for the advertisements.'

He looked at her. It seemed to him a bitter humiliation and an anguish to go through. But he said nothing. When he got up in the morning, his whole being was knotted up over this one thought:

'I've got to go and look for advertisements for a job.'

It stood in front of the morning, that thought, killing all joy and even life, for him. His heart felt like a tight knot.

And then, at ten o'clock, he set off. He was supposed to be a queer, quiet child. Going up the sunny streets of the little town, he felt as if all the folk he met said to themselves: 'He's going to the Co-op reading-room to look in the papers for a place. He can't get a job. I suppose he's living on his mother.' Then he crept up the stone stairs behind the drapery shop at the Co-op, and peeped in the reading-room. Usually one or two men were there, either old, useless fellows, or colliers 'on the club'. So he entered, full of shrinking and suffering when they looked up, seated himself at the table, and pretended to scan the news. He knew they would think, 'What does a lad of thirteen want in a reading-room with a newspaper?' and he suffered.

Then he looked wistfully out of the window. Already he was a prisoner of industrialism. Large sunflowers stared over the old red wall of the garden opposite, looking in their jolly way down on the women who were hurrying with something for dinner. The valley was full of corn, brightening in the sun. Two collieries, among the fields, waved their small white plumes of steam. Far off on the hills were the woods of Annesley, dark and fascinating. Already his heart went down. He was being taken into bondage. His freedom in the beloved home valley was going now.

The brewers' waggons came rolling from Keston with enormous barrels, four a side, like beans in a burst bean-pod. The waggoner, throned aloft, rolling massively in his seat, was not much below Paul's eye. The man's hair, on his small, bullet head, was bleached almost white by the sun, and on his thick red arms, rocking idly on his sack apron, the white hairs glistened. His red face shone and was almost asleep with sunshine. The horses, handsome and brown, went on by themselves, looking by far the master of the show.

Paul wished he were stupid. 'I wish,' he thought to himself, 'I was fat like him, and like a dog in the sun. I wish I was a pig and a brewer's waggoner.'

Then, the room being at last empty, he would hastily copy an advertisement on a scrap of paper, then another, and slip out in immense relief. His mother would scan over his copies.

'Yes,' she said, 'you may try.'

William had written out a letter of application, couched in admirable business language, which Paul copied, with variations. The boy's handwriting was execrable, so that William, who did all things well, got into a fever of impatience.

The elder brother was becoming quite swanky. In London he found that he could associate with men far above his Bestwood friends in station. Some of the clerks in the office had studied for the law, and were more or less going through a kind of apprenticeship. William always made friends among men wherever he went, he was so jolly. Therefore he was soon visiting and staying in houses of men who, in Bestwood, would have looked down on the unapproachable bank manager, and would merely have called indifferently on the Rector. So he began to fancy himself as a great gun. He was, indeed, rather surprised at the ease with which he became a gentleman.

His mother was glad, he seemed so pleased. And his lodging in Walthamstow was so dreary. But now there seemed to come a kind of fever into the young man's letter. He was unsettled by all the change, he did not stand firm on his own feet, but seemed to spin rather giddily on the quick current of the new life. His mother was anxious for him. She could feel him losing himself. He had danced and gone to the theatre, boated on the river, been out with friends; and she knew he sat up afterwards in his cold bedroom grinding away at Latin, because he intended to get on in his office, and in the law as much as he could. He never sent his mother any money now. It was all taken, the little he had, for his own life. And she did not want any, except sometimes, when she was in a tight corner, and when ten shillings would have saved her much worry. She still dreamed of William, and of what he would do, with herself behind him. Never for a minute would she admit to herself how heavy and anxious her heart was because of him.

Also he talked a good deal now of a girl he had met at a dance, a handsome brunette, quite young, and a lady, after whom the men were running thick and fast.

'I wonder if you would run, my boy,' his mother wrote to him, 'unless you saw all the other men chasing her too. You feel safe enough and vain enough in a crowd. But take care, and see how you feel when you find yourself alone, and in triumph.'

William resented these things, and continued the chase. He had taken the girl on the river. 'If you saw her, mother, you would know how I feel. Tall and elegant, with the clearest of clear, transparent olive complexions, hair as black as jet, and such grey eyes—bright, mocking, like lights on water at night. It is all very well to be a bit satirical till you see her. And she dresses as well as any woman in London. I tell you, your son doesn't half put his head up when she goes walking down Piccadilly with him.'

Mrs Morel wondered, in her heart, if her son did not go walking down Piccadilly with an elegant figure and fine clothes, rather than with a woman who was near to him. But she congratulated him in her doubtful fashion. And, as she stood over the washing-tub, the mother brooded over her son. She saw him saddled with an elegant and expensive wife, earning little money, dragging along and getting draggled in some small, ugly house in a suburb. 'But there,' she told herself, 'I am very likely a silly–meeting trouble half-way.' Nevertheless, the load of anxiety scarcely ever left her heart, lest William should do the wrong thing by himself.

Presently, Paul was bidden call upon Thomas Jordan, Manufacturer of Surgical Appliances, at 21 Spaniel Row, Nottingham. Mrs Morel was all joy.

'There, you see!' she cried, her eyes shining. 'You've only written four letters, and the third is answered. You're lucky, my boy, as I always said you were.'

Paul looked at the picture of a wooden leg, adorned with elastic stockings and other appliances, that figured on Mr Jordan's notepaper, and he felt alarmed. He had not known that elastic stockings existed. And he seemed to feel the business world, with its regulated system of values, and its impersonality, and he dreaded it. It seemed monstrous also that a business could be run on wooden legs.

Mother and son set off together one Tuesday morning. It was August and blazing hot. Paul walked with something screwed up tight inside him. He would have suffered much physical pain rather than this unreasonable suffering at being exposed to strangers, to be accepted or rejected. Yet he chattered away with his mother. He would never have confessed to her how he suffered over these things, and she only partly guessed. She was gay, like a sweetheart. She stood in front of the ticket-office at Bestwood, and Paul watched her take from her purse the money for the tickets. As he saw her hands in their old black kid gloves getting the silver out of the worn purse, his heart contracted with pain of love of her.

She was quite excited, and quite gay. He suffered because she *would* talk aloud in presence of the other travellers.

'Now look at that silly cow!' she said, 'careering round as if it thought it was a circus.'

'It's most likely a bottfly,' he said very low.

'A what?' she asked brightly and unashamed.

They thought a while. He was sensible all the time of having her opposite him. Suddenly their eyes met, and she smiled to him–a rare, intimate smile, beautiful with brightness and love. Then each looked out of the window.

The sixteen slow miles of railway journey passed. The mother and son walked down Station Street, feeling the excitement of lovers having an adventure together. In Carrington Street they stopped to hang over the parapet and look at the barges on the canal below.

'It's just like Venice,' he said, seeing the sunshine on the water that lay between high factory walls.

'Perhaps,' she answered smiling.

They enjoyed the shops immensely.

'Now you see that blouse,' she would say, 'wouldn't that just suit our Annie? And for one-and-eleven-three. Isn't that cheap?'

'And made of needlework as well,' he said.

'Yes.'

They had plenty of time, so they did not hurry. The town was strange and delightful to them. But the boy was tied up inside in a knot of apprehension. He dreaded the interview with Thomas Jordan.

It was nearly eleven o'clock by St Peter's Church. They turned up a narrow street that led to the Castle. It was gloomy and old-fashioned, having low dark shops and dark green house-doors with brass knockers, and yellow-ochred doorsteps projecting on to the pavement; then another old shop whose small window looked like a cunning, half-shut eye. Mother and son went cautiously, looking everywhere for 'Thomas Jordan and Son'. It was like hunting in some wild place. They were on tiptoe of excitement.

Suddenly they spied a big, dark archway, in which were names of various firms, Thomas Jordan among them.

'Here it is!' said Mrs Morel. 'But now *where* is it?'

They looked round. On one side was a queer, dark, cardboard factory, on the other a Commercial Hotel.

'It's up the entry,' said Paul.

And they ventured under the archway, as into the jaws of the dragon. They emerged into a wide yard, like a well, with buildings all round. It was littered with straw and boxes, and cardboard. The sunshine actually caught one crate whose straw was streaming on to the yard like gold. But elsewhere the place was like a pit. There were several doors, and two flights of steps. Straight in front, on a dirty glass door at the top of a staircase, loomed the ominous words 'Thomas Jordan and Son – Surgical Appliances'. Mrs Morel went first, her son followed her. Charles I mounted his scaffold with a lighter heart than had Paul Morel as he followed his mother up the dirty steps to the dirty door.

She pushed open the door, and stood in pleased surprise. In front of her was a big warehouse, with creamy paper parcels everywhere, and clerks, with their shirt-sleeves rolled back, were going about in an at-home sort of way. The light was subdued, the glossy cream parcels seemed luminous, the counters were of dark brown wood. All was quiet and very homely. Mrs Morel took two steps forward, then waited. Paul stood behind her. She had on her Sunday bonnet and a black veil; he wore a boy's broad white collar and a Norfolk suit.

One of the clerks looked up. He was thin and tall, with a small face. His way of looking was alert. Then he glanced round to the other end of the room, where was a glass office. And then he came forward. He did not say anything, but leaned in a gentle, inquiring fashion towards Mrs Morel.

'Can I see Mr Jordan?' she asked.

'I'll fetch him,' answered the young man.

He went down to the glass office. A red-faced, white-whiskered old man looked up. He reminded Paul of a pomeranian dog. Then the same little man came up the room. He had short legs, was rather stout, and wore an alpaca jacket. So, with one ear up, as it were, he came stoutly and inquiringly down the room.

'Good-morning!' he said, hesitating before Mrs Morel, in doubt as to whether she were a customer or not.

'Good-morning. I came with my son, Paul Morel. You asked him to call this morning.'

'Come this way,' said Mr Jordan, in a rather snappy little manner intended to be businesslike.

They followed the manufacturer into a grubby little room, upholstered in black American leather, glossy with the rubbing of many customers. On the table was a pile of trusses, yellow wash-leather hoops tangled together. They looked new and living. Paul sniffed the odour of new wash-leather. He wondered what the things were. By this time he was so much stunned that he only noticed the outside things.

'Sit down!' said Mr Jordan, irritably pointing Mrs Morel to a horse-hair chair. She sat on the edge in an uncertain fashion. Then the little old man fidgeted and found a paper.

'Did you write this letter?' he snapped, thrusting what Paul recognized as his own notepaper in front of him.

'Yes,' he answered.

At that moment he was occupied in two ways: first, on feeling guilty for telling a lie, since William had composed the letter; second, in wondering why his letter seemed so strange and different, in the fat, red hand of the man, from what it had been when it lay on the kitchen table. It was like part of himself, gone astray. He resented the way the man held it.

'Where did you learn to write?' said the old man crossly.

Paul merely looked at him shamedly, and did not answer.

'He *is* a bad writer,' put in Mrs Morel apologetically. Then she pushed up her veil. Paul hated her for not being prouder with this common little man, and he loved her face clear of the veil.

'And did you say you know French?' inquired the little man, still sharply.

'Yes,' said Paul.

'What school did you go to?'

'The Board-school.'

'And did you learn it there?'

'No—I—' The boy went crimson and got no further.

'His godfather gave him lessons,' said Mrs Morel, half-pleading and rather distant.

Mr Jordan hesitated. Then, in his irritable manner—he always seemed to keep his hands ready for action—he pulled another sheet of paper from his pocket, unfolded it. The paper made a crackling noise. He handed it to Paul.

'Read that,' he said.

It was a note in French, in thin, flimsy foreign handwriting that the boy could not decipher. He stared blankly at the paper.

'"Monsieur,"' he began; then he looked in great confusion at Mr Jordan. 'Its the—it's the—'

He wanted to say 'handwriting', but his wits would no longer work even sufficiently to supply him with the word. Feeling an utter fool, and hating Mr Jordan, he turned desperately to the paper again.

'"Sir—Please send me"—er—er—I can't tell the—er—"two pairs—*gris fil bas*—grey thread stockings" —er—er—"*sans*—without"—er—I can't tell the words—er—"*doigts*—fingers"—er—I can't tell the—'

He wanted to say 'handwriting', but the word still refused to come. Seeing him stuck, Mr Jordan snatched the paper from him.

'"Please send by return two pairs grey thread stockings without *toes*."'

'Well,' flashed Paul, '"*doigts*" means "fingers"—as well—as a rul—e—'

The little man looked at him. He did not know whether '*doigts*' meant 'fingers'; he knew that for all *his* purposes it meant 'toes'.

'Fingers to stockings!' he snapped.

'Well, it *does* mean fingers,' the boy persisted.

He hated the little man, who made such a clod of him. Mr Jordan looked at the pale, stupid, defiant boy, then at the mother, who sat quiet and with that peculiar shut-off look of the poor who have to depend on the favour of others.

'And when could he come?' he asked.

'Well,' said Mrs Morel, 'as soon as you wish. He has finished school now.'

'He would live in Bestwood?'

'Yes; but he could be in–at the station–at quarter to eight.'

'H'm!'

It ended by Paul's being engaged as junior spiral clerk at eight shillings a week. The boy did not open his mouth to say another word, after having insisted that '*doigts*' meant 'fingers'. He followed his mother down the stairs. She looked at him with her bright blue eyes full of love and joy.

'I think you'll like it,' she said.

'"*Doigts*" does mean "fingers", mother, and it was the writing. I couldn't read the writing.'

'Never mind, my boy. I'm sure he'll be all right, and you won't see much of him. Wasn't that first young fellow nice? I'm sure you'll like them.'

'But wasn't Mr Jordan common, mother? Does he own it all?'

'I suppose he was a workman who has got on,' she said. 'You mustn't mind people so much. They're not being disagreeable to *you*–it's their way. You always think people are meaning things for you. But they don't.'

It was very sunny. Over the big desolate space of the market-place the blue sky shimmered, and the granite cobbles of the paving glistened. Shops down the Long Row were deep in obscurity, and the shadow was full of colour. Just where the horse trams trundled across the market was a row of fruit stalls, with fruit blazing in the sun–apples and piles of reddish oranges, small greengage plums and bananas. There was a warm scent of fruit as mother and son passed. Gradually his feeling of ignominy and of rage sank.

'Where should we go for dinner?' asked the mother.

It was felt to be a reckless extravagance. Paul had only been in an eating-house once or twice in his life, and then only to have a cup of tea and a bun. Most of the people of Bestwood considered that tea and bread-and-butter, and perhaps potted beef, was all they could afford to eat in Nottingham. Real cooked dinner was considered great extravagance. Paul felt rather guilty.

They found a place that looked quite cheap. But when Mrs Morel scanned the bill of fare, her heart was heavy, things were so dear. So she ordered kidney pies and potatoes as the cheapest available dish.

'We oughtn't to have come here, mother,' said Paul.

'Never mind,' she said. 'We won't come again.'

She insisted on his having a small currant tart, because he liked sweets.

'I don't want it, mother,' he pleaded.

'Yes,' she insisted, 'you'll have it.'

And she looked round for the waitress. But the waitress was busy, and Mrs Morel did not like to bother her then. So the mother and son waited for the girl's pleasure, whilst she flirted among the men.

'Brazen hussy!' said Mrs Morel to Paul. 'Look now, she's taking that man *his* pudding, and he came long after us.'

'It doesn't matter, mother,' said Paul.

Mrs Morel was angry. But she was too poor, and her orders were too meagre, so that she had not the courage to insist on her rights just then. They waited and waited.

'Should we go, mother?' he said.

Then Mrs Morel stood up. The girl was passing near.

'Will you bring one currant tart?' said Mrs Morel clearly.

The girl looked round insolently.

'Directly,' she said.

'We have waited quite long enough,' said Mrs Morel.

In a moment the girl came back with the tart. Mrs Morel asked coldly for the bill. Paul wanted to sink through the floor. He marvelled at his mother's hardness. He knew that only years of battling had taught her to insist even so little on her rights. She shrank as much as he.

'It's the last time I go *there* for anything!' she declared, when they were outside the place, thankful to be clear.

'We'll go,' she said, 'and look at Keep's and Boot's, and one or two places, shall we?'

They had discussions over the pictures, and Mrs Morel wanted to buy him a little sable brush that he hankered for. But this indulgence he refused. He stood in front of milliners' shops and drapers' shops almost bored, but content for her to be interested. They wandered on.

'Now, just look at those black grapes!' she said. 'They make your mouth water. I've wanted some of those for years, but I s'll have to wait a bit before I get them.'

Then she rejoiced in the florists, standing in the doorway sniffing.

'Oh! oh! Isn't it simply lovely!'

Paul saw, in the darkness of the shop, an elegant young lady in black peering over the counter curiously.

'They're looking at you,' he said, trying to draw his mother away.

'But what *is* it!' she exclaimed, refusing to be moved.

'Stocks!' he answered, sniffing hastily. 'Look, there's a tubful.'

'So there is—red and white. But really, I never knew stocks to smell like it!' And, to his great relief, she moved out of the doorway, but only to stand in front of the window.

'Paul!' she cried to him, who was trying to get out of sight of the elegant young lady in black—the shop-girl. 'Paul! Just look here!'

He came reluctantly back.

'Now, just look at that fuchsia!' she exclaimed, pointing.

'H'm!' He made a curious, interested sound. 'You'd think every second as the flowers were going to fall off, they hang so big an' heavy.'

'And such an abundance!' she cried.

'And the way they drop downwards with their threads, and knots!'

'Yes!' she exclaimed. 'Lovely!'

'I wonder who'll buy it!' he said.

'I wonder!' she answered. 'Not us.'

'It would die in our parlour.'

'Yes, beastly cold, sunless hole; it kills every bit of a plant you put in, and the kitchen chokes them to death.'

They bought a few things, and set off towards the station. Looking up the canal, through the dark pass of the buildings, they saw the Castle on its bluff of brown, green-bushed rock, in a positive miracle of delicate sunshine.

'Won't it be nice for me to come out at dinner-times?' said Paul. 'I can go all round here and see everything. I s'll love it.'

'You will,' assented his mother.

He had spent a perfect afternoon with his mother. They arrived home in the mellow evening, happy, and glowing, and tired.

In the morning he filled in the form for his season-ticket and took it to the station. When he got back, his mother was just beginning to wash the floor. He sat crouched up on the sofa.

'He says it'll be here by Saturday,' he said.

'And how much will it be?'

'About one pound eleven,' he said.

She went on washing her floor in silence.

'Is it a lot?' he asked.

'It's no more than I thought,' she answered.

'An' I s'll earn eight shillings a week,' he said.

She did not answer, but went on with her work. At last she said:

'That William promised me, when he went to London, as he'd give me a pound a month. He has given me ten shillings–twice; and now I know he hasn't a farthing if I asked him. Not that I want it. Only just now you'd think he might be able to help with this ticket, which I'd never expected.'

'He earns a lot,' said Paul.

'He earns a hundred and thirty pounds. But they're all alike. They're large in promises, but it's precious little fulfilment you get.'

'He spends over fifty shillings a week on himself,' said Paul.

'And I keep this house on less than thirty,' she replied; 'and am supposed to find money for extras. But they don't care about helping you, once they've gone. He'd rather spend it on that dressed-up creature.'

'She should have her own money, if she's so grand,' said Paul.

'She should, but she hasn't. I asked him. And *I* know he doesn't buy her a gold bangle for nothing. I wonder whoever bought *me* a gold bangle.'

William was succeeding with his 'Gypsy', as he called her. He asked the girl–her name was Louisa Lily Denys Western–for a photograph to send to his mother. The photo came–a handsome brunette, taken in profile, smirking slightly–and, it might be, quite naked, for on the photograph not a scrap of clothing was to be seen, only a naked bust.

'Yes,' wrote Mrs Morel to her son, 'the photograph of Louie is very striking, and I can see she must be attractive. But do you think, my boy, it was very good taste of a girl to give her young man that photo to send to his mother–the first? Certainly the shoulders are beautiful, as you say. But I hardly expected to see so much of them at the first view.'

Morel found the photograph standing on the chiffonier in the parlour. He came out with it between his thick thumb and finger.

'Who dost reckon this is?' he asked of his wife.

'It's the girl our William is going with,' replied Mrs Morel.

'H'm! 'Er's a bright spark, from th' look on 'er, an' one as wunna do him owermuch good neither. Who is she?'

'Her name is Louisa Lily Denys Western.'

'An' come again to-morrer!' exclaimed the miner. 'An' is 'er an actress?'

'She is not. She's supposed to be a lady.'

'I'll bet!' he exclaimed, still staring at the photo. 'A lady, is she? An' how much does she reckon ter keep up this sort o' game on?'

'On nothing. She lives with an old aunt, whom she hates, and takes what bit of money's given her.'

'H'm!' said Morel, laying down the photograph. 'Then he's a fool to ha' ta'en up wi' such a one as that.'

'Dear Mater,' William replied. 'I'm sorry you didn't like the photograph. It never occurred to me when I sent it, that you mightn't think it decent. However, I told Gyp that it didn't quite suit your prim and proper notions, so she's going to send you another, that I hope will please you better. She's always being photographed; in fact the photographers *ask* her if they may take her for nothing.'

Presently the new photograph came, with a little silly note from the girl. This time the young lady was seen in a black satin evening bodice, cut square, with little puff sleeves, and black lace hanging down her beautiful arms.

'I wonder if she ever wears anything except evening clothes,' said Mrs Morel sarcastically. 'I'm sure I *ought* to be impressed.'

'You are disagreeable, mother,' said Paul. 'I think the first one with bare shoulders is lovely.'

'Do you?' answered his mother. 'Well, I don't.'

On the Monday morning the boy got up at six to start work. He had the season-ticket, which had cost such bitterness, in his waistcoat pocket. He loved it with its bars of yellow across. His mother packed his dinner in a small, shut-up basket, and he set off at a quarter to seven to catch the 7.15 train. Mrs Morel came to the entry-end to see him off.

It was a perfect morning. From the ash-tree the slender green fruits that the children call 'pigeons' were twinkling gaily down on a little breeze, into the front gardens of the houses. The valley was full of a lustrous dark haze, through which the ripe corn shimmered, and in which the steam from Minton pit melted swiftly. Puffs of wind came. Paul looked over the high woods of Aldersley, where the country gleamed, and home had never pulled at him so powerfully.

'Good morning, mother,' he said, smiling, but feeling very unhappy.

'Good morning,' she replied cheerfully and tenderly.

She stood in her white apron on the open road, watching him as he crossed the field. He had a small, compact body that looked full of life. She felt, as she saw him trudging over the field, that where he determined to go he would get. She thought of William. He would have leaped the fence instead of going round to the stile. He was away in London, doing well. Paul would be working in Nottingham. Now she had two sons in the world. She could think of two places, great centres of industry, and feel that she had put a man into each of them, that these men would work out what *she* wanted; they were derived from her, they were of her, and their works also would be hers. All the morning long she thought of Paul.

At eight o'clock he climbed the dismal stairs of Jordan's Surgical Appliance Factory, and stood helplessly against the first great parcel-rack, waiting for somebody to pick him up. The place was still not awake. Over the counters were great dust sheets. Two men only had arrived, and were heard talking in a corner, as they took off their coats and rolled up their shirtsleeves. It was ten past eight. Evidently there was no rush of punctuality. Paul listened to the voices of the two clerks. Then he heard someone cough, and saw in the office at the end of the room an old, decaying clerk, in a round smoking-cap of black velvet embroidered with red and green, opening letters. He waited and waited. One of the junior clerks went to the old man, greeted him cheerily and loudly. Evidently the old 'chief' was deaf. Then the young fellow came striding importantly down to his counter. He spied Paul.

'Hello!' he said. 'You the new lad?'

'Yes,' said Paul.

'H'm! What's your name?'

'Paul Morel.'

'Paul Morel? All right, you come on round here.'

Paul followed him round the rectangle of counters. The room was second storey. It had a great hole in the middle of the floor, fenced as with a wall of counters, and down this wide shaft the lifts went, and the light for the bottom storey. Also there was a corresponding big, oblong hole in the ceiling, and one would see above, over the fence of the top floor, some machinery; and right away overhead was the glass roof, and all light for the three storeys came downwards, getting dimmer, so that it was always night on the ground floor and rather gloomy on the second floor. The factory was the top floor, the warehouse the second, the storehouse the ground floor. It was an insanitary, ancient place.

Paul was led round to a very dark corner.

'This is the "Spiral" corner,' said the clerk. 'You're Spiral, with Pappleworth. He's your boss, but he's not come yet. He doesn't get here till half-past eight. So you can fetch the letters, if you like, from Mr Melling down there.'

The young man pointed to the old clerk in the office.

'All right,' said Paul.

'Here's a peg to hang your cap on. Here are your entry ledgers. Mr Pappleworth won't be long.'

And the thin young man stalked away with long, busy strides over the hollow wooden floor.

After a minute or two Paul went down and stood in the door of the glass office. The old clerk in the smoking-cap looked down over the rim of his spectacles.

'Good morning,' he said, kindly and impressively. 'You want the letters for the Spiral department, Thomas?'

Paul resented being called 'Thomas'. But he took the letters and returned to his dark place, where the counter made an angle, where the great parcel-rack came to an end, and where there were three doors in the corner. He sat on a high stool and read the letters–those whose handwriting was not too difficult. They ran as follows:

'Will you please send me at once a pair of lady's silk spiral thigh-hose, without feet, such as I had from you last year; length, thigh to knee, etc.' Or 'Major Chamberlain wishes to repeat his previous order for a silk non-elastic suspensory bandage.'

Many of the letters, some of them in French or Norwegian, were a great puzzle to the boy. He sat on his stool nervously awaiting the arrival of his 'boss'. He suffered tortures of shyness when, at half-past eight, the factory girls for upstairs trooped past him.

Mr Pappleworth arrived, chewing a chlorodyne gum, at about twenty to nine, when all the other men were at work. He was a thin, sallow man with a red nose, quick, staccato, and smartly but stiffly dressed. He was about thirty-six years old. There was something rather 'doggy', rather smart, rather 'cute and shrewd, and something warm, and something slightly contemptible about him.

'You my new lad?' he said.

Paul stood up and said he was.

'Fetched the letters?'

Mr Pappleworth gave a chew to his gum.

'Yes.'

'Copied 'em?'

'No.'

'Well, come on then, let's look slippy. Changed your coat?'

'No.'

'You want to bring an old coat and leave it here.' He pronounced the last words with the chlorodyne gum between his side teeth. He vanished into darkness behind the great parcel-rack, reappeared coatless, turning up a smart striped shirt-cuff over a thin and hairy arm. Then he slipped into his coat. Paul noticed how thin he was, and that his trousers were in folds behind. He seized a stool, dragged 'it beside the boy's, and sat down.

'Sit down,' he said.

Paul took a seat.

Mr Pappleworth was very close to him. The man seized the letters, snatched a long entry-book out of a rack in front of him, flung it open, seized a pen, and said:

'Now look here. You want to copy these letters in here.' He sniffed twice, gave a quick chew at his gum, stared fixedly at a letter, then went very still and absorbed, and wrote the entry rapidly, in a beautiful flourishing hand. He glanced quickly at Paul.

'See that?'

'Yes.'

'Think you can do it all right?'

'Yes.'

'All right then, let's see you.'

He sprang off his stool Paul took a pen. Mr Pappleworth disappeared. Paul rather liked copying the letters, but he wrote slowly, laboriously, and exceedingly badly. He was doing the fourth letter, and feeling quite busy and happy, when Mr Pappleworth reappeared.

'Now then, how'r yer getting on? Done 'em?'

He leaned over the boy's shoulder, chewing, and smelling of chlorodyne.

'Strike my bob, lad, but you're a beautiful writer!' he exclaimed satirically. 'Ne'er mind, how many h'yer done? Only three! I'd a eaten 'em. Get on, my lad, an' put numbers on 'em. Here, look! Get on!'

Paul ground away at the letters, while Mr Pappleworth fussed over various jobs. Suddenly the boy started as a shrill whistle sounded near his ear. Mr Pappleworth came, took a plug out of a pipe, and said, in an amazingly cross and bossy voice:

'Yes?'

Paul heard a faint voice, like a woman's, out of the mouth of the tube. He gazed in wonder, never having seen a speaking-tube before.

'Well,' said Mr Pappleworth disagreeably into the tube, 'you'd better get some of your back work done, then.'

Again the woman's tiny voice was heard, sounding pretty and cross.

'I've not time to stand here while you talk,' said Mr Pappleworth, and he pushed the plug into the tube.

'Come, my lad,' he said imploringly to Paul, 'there's Polly crying out for them orders. Can't you buck up a bit? Here, come out!'

He took the book, to Paul's immense chagrin, and began the copying himself. He worked quickly and well. This done, he seized some strips of long yellow paper, about three inches wide, and made out the day's orders for the work-girls.

'You'd better watch me,' he said to Paul, working all the while rapidly. Paul watched the weird little drawings of legs, and thighs, and ankles, with the strokes across and the numbers, and the few brief directions which his chief made upon the yellow paper. Then Mr Pappleworth finished and jumped up.

'Come on with me,' he said, and the yellow papers flying in his hands, he dashed through a door and down some stairs, into the basement where the gas was burning. They crossed the cold, damp storeroom, then a long, dreary room with a long table on trestles, into a smaller, cosy apartment, not very high, which had been built on to the main building. In this room a small woman with a red serge blouse, and her black hair done on top of her head, was waiting like a proud little bantam.

'Here y'are!' said Pappleworth.

'I think it is "here you are!"' exclaimed Polly. 'The girls have been here nearly half an hour waiting. Just think of the time wasted!'

'*You* think of getting your work done and not talking so much,' said Mr Pappleworth. 'You could ha' been finishing off.'

'You know quite well we finished everything off on Saturday!' cried Polly, flying at him, her dark eyes flashing.

'Tu-tu-tu-tu-terterter!' he mocked. 'Here's your new lad. Don't ruin him as you did the last.'

'"As we did the last!"' repeated Polly. 'Yes, *we* do a lot of ruining, we do. My word, a lad would *take* some ruining after he'd been with you.'

'It's time for work now, not for talk,' said Mr Pappleworth severely and coldly.

'It was time for work some time back,' said Polly, marching away with her head in the air. She was an erect little body of forty.

In that room were two round spiral machines on the bench under the window. Through the inner doorway was another longer room, with six more machines. A little group of girls, nicely dressed and in white aprons, stood talking together.

'Have you nothing else to do but talk?' said Mr Pappleworth.

'Only wait for you,' said one handsome girl, laughing.

'Well, get on, get on,' he said. 'Come on, my lad. You'll know your road down here again.'

And Paul ran upstairs after his chief. He was given some checking and invoicing to do. He stood at the desk, labouring in his execrable handwriting. Presently Mr Jordan came strutting down from the glass office and stood behind him, to the boy's great discomfort. Suddenly a red and fat finger was thrust on the form he was filling in.

'*Mr J. A. Bates, Esquire!*' exclaimed the cross voice just behind his ear.

Paul looked at 'Mr J. A. Bates, Esquire' in his own vile writing, and wondered what was the matter now.

'Didn't they teach you any better than *that* while they were at it? If you put "Mr" you don't put "Esquire"—a man can't be both at once.'

The boy regretted his too-much generosity in disposing of honours, hesitated, and with trembling fingers, scratched out the 'Mr'. Then all at once Mr Jordan snatched away the invoice.

'Make another! Are you going to send *that* to a gentleman?' And he tore up the blue form irritably.

Paul, his ears red with shame, began again. Still Mr Jordan watched.

'I don't know what they *do* teach in school. You'll have to write better than that. Lads learn nothing nowadays, but how to recite poetry and play the fiddle. Have you seen his writing?' he asked of Mr Pappleworth.

'Yes; prime, isn't it?' replied Mr Pappleworth, indifferently.

Mr Jordan gave a little grunt, not unamiable. Paul divined that his master's bark was worse than his bite. Indeed, the little manufacturer, although he spoke bad English, was quite gentleman enough to leave his men alone and to take no notice of trifles. But he knew he did not look like the boss and owner of the show, so he had to play his role of proprietor at first, to put things on a right footing.

'Let's see, *what's* your name?' asked Mr Pappleworth of the boy.

'Paul Morel.'

It is curious that children suffer so much at having to pronounce their own names.

'Paul Morel, is it? All right, you Paul-Morel through them things there, and then—'

Mr Pappleworth subsided on to a stool, and began writing. A girl came up from out of a door just behind, put some newly pressed elastic web appliances on the counter, and returned. Mr Pappleworth picked up the whitey-blue knee-band, examined it and its yellow order-paper quickly, and put it on one side. Next was a flesh-pink 'leg'. He went through the few things, wrote out a couple of orders, and called to Paul to accompany him. This time they went through the door whence the girl had emerged. There Paul found himself at the top of a little wooden flight of steps, and below him saw a room with windows round two sides, and at the farther end half a dozen girls sitting bending over the benches in the light from the window, sewing. They were singing together 'Two Little Girls in Blue'. Hearing the door opened, they all turned round, to see Mr Pappleworth and Paul looking down on them from the far end of the room. They stopped singing.

'Can't you make a bit less row?' said Mr Pappleworth. 'Folk'll think we keep cats.'

A hunchback woman on a high stool turned her long, rather heavy face towards Mr Pappleworth, and said, in a contralto voice:

'They're all tom-cats then.'

In vain Mr Pappleworth tried to be impressive for Paul's benefit. He descended the steps into the finishing-off room, and went to the hunchback Fanny. She had such a short body on her high stool that her head, with its great bands of bright brown hair, seemed over large, as did her pale, heavy face. She wore a dress of green-black cashmere, and her wrists, coming out of the narrow cuffs, were thin and flat, as she put down her work nervously. He showed her something that was wrong with a knee-cap.

'Well,' she said, 'you needn't come blaming it on to me. It's not my fault.' Her colour mounted to her cheek.

'I never said it *was* your fault. Will you do as I tell you?' replied Mr Pappleworth shortly.

'You don't say it's my fault, but you'd like to make out as it was,' the hunchback woman cried, almost in tears. Then she snatched the knee-cap from her 'boss', saying: 'Yes, I'll do it for you, but you needn't be snappy.'

'Here's your new lad,' said Mr Pappleworth.

Fanny turned, smiling very gently·on Paul.

'Oh!' she said.

'Yes; don't make a softy of him between you.'

'It's not us as 'ud make a softy of him,' she said indignantly.

'Come on then, Paul,' said Mr Pappleworth.

'*Au revoy*, Paul,' said one of the girls.

There was a titter of laughter. Paul went out, blushing deeply, not having spoken a word.

The day was very long. All morning the work-people were coming to speak to Mr Pappleworth. Paul was writing or learning to make up parcels, ready for the midday post. At one o'clock, or, rather, at a quarter to one, Mr Pappleworth disappeared to catch his train: he lived in the suburbs. At one o'clock, Paul, feeling very lost, took his dinner-basket down into the stockroom in the basement, that had the long table on trestles, and ate his meal hurriedly, alone in that cellar of gloom and desolation. Then he went out of doors. The brightness and the freedom of the streets made him feel adventurous and happy. But at two o'clock he was back in the corner of the big room. Soon the work-girls went trooping past, making remarks. It was the commoner girls who worked upstairs at the heavy tasks of truss-making and the finishing of artificial limbs. He waited for Mr Pappleworth, not knowing what to do, sitting scribbling on the yellow order-paper. Mr Pappleworth came at twenty minutes to three. Then he sat and gossiped with Paul, treating the boy entirely as an equal, even in age.

In the afternoon there was never very much to do, unless it were near the week-end, and the accounts had to be made up. At five o'clock all the men went down into the dungeon with the table on trestles, and there they had tea, eating bread-and-butter on the bare, dirty boards, talking with the same kind of ugly haste and slovenliness with which they ate their meal. And yet upstairs the atmosphere among them was always jolly and clear. The cellar and the trestles affected them.

After tea, when all the gases were lighted, *work* went more briskly. There was the big evening post to get off. The hose came up warm and newly pressed from the workrooms. Paul had made out the invoices. Now he had the packing up and addressing to do, then he had to weigh his stock of parcels on the scales. Everywhere voices were calling weights, there was the chink of metal, the rapid snapping of string, the hurrying to old Mr Melling for stamps. And at last the postman came with his sack, laughing and jolly. Then everything slacked off, and Paul took his dinner-basket and ran to the station to catch the eight-twenty train. The day in the factory was just twelve hours long.

His mother sat waiting for him rather anxiously. He had to walk from Keston, so he was not home until about twenty past nine. And he left the house before seven in the morning, Mrs Morel was rather anxious about his health. But she herself had had to put up with so much that she expected her children to take the same odds. They must go through with what came. And Paul stayed at Jordan's, although all the time he was there his health suffered from the darkness and lack of air and the long hours.

He came in pale and tired. His mother looked at him. She saw he was rather pleased, and her anxiety all went.

'Well, and how was it?' she asked.

'Ever so funny, mother,' he replied. 'You don't have to work a bit hard, and they're nice with you.'

'And did you get on all right?'

'Yes; they only say my writing's bad. But Mr Pappleworth–he's my man–said to Mr Jordan I should be all right. I'm Spiral, mother; you just come and see. It's ever so nice.'

Soon he liked Jordan's Mr Pappleworth, who had a certain 'saloon bar' flavour about him, was always natural, and treated him as if he had been a comrade. Sometimes the 'Spiral boss' was irritable, and chewed more lozenges than ever. Even then, however, he was not offensive, but one of those people who hurt themselves by their own irritability more than they hurt other people.

'Haven't you done that *yet?*' he would cry. 'Go on, be a month of Sundays.'

Again, and Paul could understand him least then, he was jocular and in high spirits.

'I'm going to bring my little Yorkshire terrier bitch tomorrow,' he said jubilantly to Paul.

'What's a Yorkshire terrier?'

'*Don't* know what a Yorkshire terrier is? *Don't know a Yorkshire—*' Mr Pappleworth was aghast.

'Is it a little silky one—colours of iron and rusty silver?'

'*That's* it, my lad. She's a gem. She's had five pounds worth of pups already, and she's worth over seven pounds herself; and she doesn't weigh twenty ounces.'

The next day the bitch came. She was a shivering, miserable morsel. Paul did not care for her; she seemed so like a wet rag that would never dry. Then a man called for her, and began to make coarse jokes. But Mr Pappleworth nodded his head in the direction of the boy, and the talk went on *sotto voce*.

Mr Jordan only made one more excursion to watch Paul, and then the only fault he found was seeing the boy lay his pen on the counter.

'Put your pen in your ear, if you're going to be a clerk. Pen in your ear!' And one day he said to the lad, 'Why don't you hold your shoulders straighter? Come down here,' when he took him into the glass office and fitted him with special braces for keeping the shoulders square.

But Paul liked the girls best. The men seemed common and rather dull. He liked them all, but they were uninteresting. Polly, the little brisk overseer downstairs, finding Paul eating in the cellar, asked him if she could cook him anything on her little stove. Next day his mother gave him a dish that could be heated up. He took it into the pleasant, clean room to Polly. And very soon it grew to be an established custom that he should have dinner with her. When he came in at eight in the morning he took his basket to her, and when he came down at one o'clock she had his dinner ready.

He was not very tall, and pale, with thick chestnut hair, irregular features, and a wide, full mouth. She was like a small bird. He often called her a 'robinet'. Though naturally rather quiet, he would sit and chatter with her for hours telling her about his home. The girls all liked to hear him talk. They often gathered in a little circle while he sat on a bench, and held forth to them, laughing. Some of them regarded him as a curious little creature, so serious, yet so bright and jolly, and always so delicate in his way with them. They all liked him, and he adored them. Polly he felt he belonged to. Then Connie, with her mane of red hair, her face of apple-blossom, her murmuring voice, such a lady in her shabby black frock, appealed to his romantic side.

'When you sit winding,' he said, 'it looks as if you were spinning at a spinning-wheel—it looks ever so nice. You remind me of Elaine in the "Idylls of the King". I'd draw you if I could.'

And she glanced at him blushing shyly. And later on he had a sketch he prized very much: Connie sitting on the stool before the wheel, her flowing mane of red hair on her rusty black frock, her red mouth shut and serious, running the scarlet thread off the hank on to the reel.

With Louie, handsome and brazen, who always seemed to thrust her lip at him, he usually joked.

Emma was rather plain, rather old, and condescending. But to condescend to him made her happy, and he did not mind.

'How do you put needles in?' he asked.

'Go away and don't bother.'

'But I ought to know how to put needles in.'

She ground at her machine all the while steadily.

'There are many things you ought to know,' she replied.

'Tell me, then, how to stick needles in the machine.'

'Oh, the boy, what a nuisance he is! Why, *this* is how you do it.'

He watched her attentively. Suddenly a whistle piped. Then Polly appeared, and said in a clear voice:

'Mr Pappleworth wants to know how much longer you're going to be down here playing with the girls, Paul.'

Paul flew upstairs, calling 'Good-bye!' and Emma drew herself up.

'It wasn't *me* who wanted him to play with the machine,' she said.

As a rule, when all the girls came back at two o'clock, he ran upstairs to Fanny, the hunchback, in the finishing-off room. Mr Pappleworth did not appear till twenty to three, and he often found his boy sitting beside Fanny, talking, or drawing, or singing with the girls.

Often, after a minute's hesitation, Fanny would begin to sing. She had a fine contralto voice. Everybody joined in the chorus, and it went well. Paul was not at all embarrassed, after a while, sitting in the room with the half a dozen workgirls.

At the end of the song Fanny would say:

'I know you've been laughing at me.'

'Don't be so soft, Fanny!' cried one of the girls.

Once there was mention of Connie's red hair.

'Fanny's is better, to my fancy,' said Emma.

'You needn't try to make a fool of me,' said Fanny, flushing deeply.

'No, but she has, Paul; she's got beautiful hair.'

'It's a treat of a colour,' said he. 'That coldish colour like earth, and yet shiny. It's like bog-water.'

'Goodness me!' exclaimed one girl, laughing.

'How I do but get criticized,' said Fanny.

'But you should see it down, Paul,' said Emma earnestly. 'It's simply beautiful. Put it down for him, Fanny, if he wants something to paint.'

Fanny would not, and yet she wanted to.

'Then I'll take it down myself,' said the lad.

'Well, you can if you like,' said Fanny.

And he carefully took the pins out of the knot, and the rush of hair, of uniform dark brown, slid over the humped back.

'What a lovely lot!' he exclaimed.

The girls watched. There was silence. The youth shook the hair loose from the coil.

'It's splendid!' he said, smelling its perfume. 'I'll bet it's worth pounds.'

'I'll leave it to you when I die, Paul,' said Fanny, half joking.

'You look just like anybody else, sitting drying their hair,' said one of the girls to the long-legged hunchback.

Poor Fanny was morbidly sensitive, always imagining insults. Polly was curt and businesslike. The two departments were for ever at war, and Paul was always finding Fanny in tears. Then he was made the recipient of all her woes, and he had to plead her cause with Polly.

So the time went along happily enough. The factory had a homely feel. No one was rushed or driven. Paul always enjoyed it when the work got faster, towards post-time, and all the men united in labour. He liked to watch his fellow-clerks at work. The man was the work and the work was the man, one thing, for the time being. It was different with the girls. The real woman never seemed to be there at the task, but as if left out, waiting.

From the train going home at night he used to watch the lights of the town, sprinkled thick on the hills, fusing together in a blaze in the valleys. He felt rich in life and happy. Drawing farther off, there was a patch of lights at Bulwell like myriad petals shaken to the ground from the shed stars; and beyond was the red glare of the furnaces, playing like hot breath on the clouds.

He had to walk two and more miles from Keston home, up two long hills, down two short hills. He was often tired, and he counted the lamps climbing the hill above him, how many more to pass. And from the hilltop, on pitch-dark nights, he looked round on the villages five or six miles away, that shone like swarms of glittering living things, almost a heaven against his feet. Marlpool and Heanor scattered the far-off darkness with brilliance. And occasionally the black valley space between was traced, violated by a great train rushing south to London or north to Scotland. The trains roared by like projectiles level on the darkness, fuming and burning, making the valley clang with their passage. They were gone, and the lights of the towns and villages glittered in silence.

And then he came to the corner at home, which faced the other side of the night. The ash-tree seemed a friend now. His mother rose with gladness as he entered. He put his eight shillings proudly on the table.

'It'll help, mother?' he asked wistfully.

'There's precious little left,' she answered, 'after your ticket and dinners and such are taken off.'

Then he told her the budget of the day. His life-story, like an Arabian Nights, was told night after night to his mother. It was almost as if it were her own life.

6

DEATH IN THE FAMILY

Arthur Morel was growing up. He was a quick, careless, impulsive boy, a good deal like his father. He hated study, made a great moan if he had to work and escaped as soon as possible to his sport again.

In appearance he remained the flower of the family, being well made, graceful, and full of life. His dark brown hair and fresh colouring, and his exquisite dark blue eyes shaded with long lashes, together with his generous manner and fiery temper, made him a favourite. But as he grew older his temper became uncertain. He flew into rages over nothing, seemed unbearably raw and irritable.

His mother, whom he loved, wearied of him sometimes. He thought only of himself. When he wanted amusement, all that stood in his way he hated, even if it were she. When he was in trouble he moaned to her ceaselessly.

'Goodness, boy!' she said, when he groaned about a master who, he said, hated him, 'if you don't like it, alter it, and if you can't alter it, put up with it.'

And his father, whom he had loved and who had worshipped him, he came to detest. As he grew older Morel fell into a slow ruin. His body, which had been beautiful in movement and in being, shrank, did not seem to ripen with the years, but to get mean and rather despicable. There came over him a look of meanness and of paltriness. And when the mean-looking elderly man bullied or ordered the boy about, Arthur was furious. Moreover, Morel's manners got worse and worse, his habits somewhat disgusting. When the children were growing up and in the crucial stage of adolescence, the father was like some ugly irritant to their souls. His manners in the house were the same as he used among the colliers down pit.

'Dirty nuisance!' Arthur would cry, jumping up and going straight out of the house when his father disgusted him. And Morel persisted the more because his children hated it. He seemed to take a kind of satisfaction in disgusting them, and driving them nearly mad, while they were so irritably sensitive at the age of fourteen or fifteen. So that Arthur, who was growing up when his father was degenerate and elderly, hated him worst of all.

Then, sometimes, the father would seem to feel the contemptuous hatred of his children.

'There's not a man tries harder for his family!' he would shout. 'He does his best for them, and then gets treated like a dog. But I'm not going to stand it, I tell you!'

But for the threat and the fact that he did not try so hard as he imagined, they would have felt sorry. As it was, the battle now went on nearly all between father and children, he persisting in his dirty and disgusting ways, just to assert his independence. They loathed him.

Arthur was so inflamed and irritable at last, that when he won a scholarship for the Grammar School in Nottingham, his mother decided to let him live in town, with one of her sisters, and only come home at week-ends.

Annie was still a junior teacher in the Board-school, earning about four shillings a week. But soon she would have fifteen shillings, since she had passed her examination, and there would be financial peace in the house.

Mrs Morel clung now to Paul. He was quiet and not brilliant. But still he stuck to his painting, and still he stuck to his mother. Everything he did was for her. She waited for his coming home in the evening, and then she unburdened herself of all she had pondered, or of all that had occurred to her during the day. He sat and listened with his earnestness. The two shared lives.

William was engaged now to his brunette, and had bought her an engagement ring that cost eight guineas. The children gasped at such a fabulous price.

'Eight guineas!' said Morel. 'More fool him! If he'd gen me some on't, it'ud ha' looked better on 'im.'

'Given *you* some of it!' cried Mrs Morel. 'Why give *you* some of it!'

She remembered *he* had bought no engagement ring at all, and she preferred William, who was not mean, if he were foolish. But now the young man talked only of the dances to which he went with his betrothed, and the different resplendent clothes she wore; or he told his mother with glee how they went to the theatre like great swells.

He wanted to bring the girl home. Mrs Morel said she should come at the Christmas. This time William arrived with a lady, but with no presents. Mrs Morel had prepared supper. Hearing footsteps, she rose and went to the door. William entered.

'Hello, mother!' He kissed her hastily, then stood aside to present a tall, handsome girl, who was wearing a costume of fine black-and-white check, and furs.

'Here's Gyp!'

Miss Western held out her hand and showed her teeth in a small smile.

'Oh, how do you do, Mrs Morel!' she exclaimed.

'I am afraid you will be hungry,' said Mrs Morel.

'Oh, no, we had dinner in the train. Have you got my gloves, Chubby?'

William Morel, big and raw-boned, looked at her quickly.

'How should I?' he said.

'Then I've lost them. Don't be cross with me.'

A frown went over his face, but he said nothing. She glanced round the kitchen. It was small and curious to her, with its glittering kissing-bunch, its evergreens behind the pictures, its wooden chairs and little deal table. At that moment Morel came in.

'Hello, dad!'

'Hello, my son! Tha's let on me!'

The two shook hands, and William presented the lady. She gave the same smile that showed her teeth.

'How do you do, Mr Morel?'

Morel bowed obsequiously.

'I'm very well, and I hope so are you. You must make yourself very welcome.'

'Oh, thank you,' she replied, rather amused.

'You will like to go upstairs,' said Mrs Morel.

'If you don't mind; but not if it is any trouble to you.'

'It is no trouble. Annie will take you. Walter, carry up this box.'

'And don't be an hour dressing yourself up,' said William to his betrothed.

Annie took a brass candlestick, and, too shy almost to speak, preceded the young lady to the front bedroom, which Mr and Mrs Morel had vacated for her. It, too, was small and cold by candlelight. The colliers' wives only lit fires in bedrooms in case of extreme illness.

'Shall I unstrap the box?' asked Annie.

'Oh, thank you very much!'

Annie played the part of maid, then went downstairs for hot water.

'I think she's rather tired, mother,' said William. 'It's a beastly journey, and we had such a rush.'

'Is there anything I can give her?' asked Mrs Morel.

'Oh no, she'll be all right.'

But there was a chill in the atmosphere. After half an hour Miss Western came down, having put on a purplish-coloured dress, very fine for the collier's kitchen.

'I told you you'd no need to change,' said William to her.

'Oh, Chubby!' Then she turned with that sweetish smile to Mrs Morel. 'Don't you think he's always grumbling, Mrs Morel?'

'Is he?' said Mrs Morel. 'That's not very nice of him.'

'It isn't, really!'

'You are cold,' said the mother. 'Won't you come near the fire?'

Morel jumped out of his arm-chair.

'Come and sit you here!' he said. 'Come and sit you here!'

'No, dad, keep your own chair. Sit on the sofa, Gyp,' said William.

'No, no!' cried Morel. 'This cheer's warmest. Come and sit here, Miss Wesson.'

'Thank you *so* much,' said the girl, seating herself in the collier's arm-chair, the place of honour. She shivered, feeling the warmth of the kitchen penetrate her.

'Fetch me a hanky, Chubby dear!' she said, putting up her mouth to him, and using the same intimate tones as if they were alone; which made the rest of the family feel as if they ought not to be present. The young lady evidently did not realize them as people; they were creatures to her for the present. William winced.

In such a household, in Streatham, Miss Western would have been a lady condescending to her inferiors. These people were, to her, certainly clownish—in short, the working classes. How was she to adjust herself?

'I'll go,' said Annie.

Miss Western took no notice, as if a servant had spoken. But when the girl came downstairs again with the handkerchief, she said, 'Oh, thank you!' in a gracious way.

She sat and talked about the dinner on the train, which had been so poor; about London, about dances. She was really very nervous and chattered from fear. Morel sat all the time smoking his thick twist tobacco, watching her, and listening to her glib London speech, as he puffed. Mrs Morel, dressed up in her best black silk blouse, answered quietly and rather briefly. The three children sat round in silence and admiration. Miss Western was the princess. Everything of the best was got out for her; the best cups, the best spoons, the best tablecloth, the best coffee-jug. The children thought she must find it quite grand. She felt strange, not able to realize the people, not knowing how to treat them. William joked, and was slightly uncomfortable.

At about ten o'clock he said to her:

'Aren't you tired, Gyp?'

'Rather, Chubby,' she answered, at once in the intimate tones and putting her head slightly on one side.

'I'll light her candle, mother,' he said.

'Very well,' replied the mother.

Miss Western stood up, held out her hand to Mrs Morel.

'Good night, Mrs Morel,' she said.

Paul sat at the boiler, letting the water run from the tap into a stone beer-bottle. Annie swathed the bottle in an old flannel pit-singlet, and kissed her mother good night. She was to share the room with the lady, because the house was full.

'You wait a minute,' said Mrs Morel to Annie. And Annie sat nursing the hot-water bottle. Miss Western shook hands all round, to everybody's discomfort, and took her departure, preceded by William. In five minutes he was downstairs again. His heart was rather sore: he did not know why. He talked very little till everybody had gone to bed, but himself and his mother. Then he stood with his legs apart, in his old attitude on the hearthrug, and said hesitatingly:

'Well, mother?'

'Well, my son?'

She sat in the rocking-chair, feeling somehow hurt and humiliated, for his sake.

'Do you like her?'

'Yes,' came the slow answer.

'She's shy yet, mother. She's not used to it. It's different from her aunt's house, you know.'

'Of course it is, my boy; and she must find it difficult.'

'She does.' Then he frowned swiftly. 'If only she wouldn't put on her *blessed* airs!'

'It's only her first awkwardness, my boy. She'll be all right.'

'That's it, mother,' he replied gratefully. But his brow was gloomy. 'You know, she's not like you, mother. She's not serious, and she can't think.'

'She's young, my boy.'

'Yes; and she's had no sort of show. Her mother died when she was a child. Since then she's lived with her aunt, whom she can't bear. And her father was a rake. She's had no love.'

'No! Well, you must make up to her.'

'And so—you have to forgive her a lot of things.'

'*What* do you have to forgive her, my boy?'

'I dunno. When she seems shallow, you have to remember she's never had anybody to bring her deeper side out. And she's *fearfully* fond of me.'

'Anybody can see that.'

'But you know, mother—she's—she's different from us. Those sort of people, like those she lives amongst, they don't seem to have the same principles.'

'You mustn't judge too hastily,' said Mrs Morel.

But he seemed uneasy within himself.

In the morning, however, he was up singing and larking round the house.

'Hello!' he called, sitting on the stairs. 'Are you getting up?'

'Yes,' her voice called faintly.

'Merry Christmas!' he shouted to her.

Her laugh, pretty and tinkling, was heard in the bedroom. She did not come down in half an hour.

'Was she *really* getting up when she said she was?' he asked of Annie.

'Yes, she was,' replied Annie.

He waited awhile, then went to the stairs again.

'Happy New Year,' he called.

'Thank you, Chubby dear!' came the laughing voice, far away.

'Buck up!' he implored.

It was nearly an hour, and still he was waiting for her. Morel, who always rose before six, looked at the clock.

'Well, it's a winder!' he exclaimed.

The family had breakfast, all but William. He went to the foot of the stairs.

'Shall I have to send you an Easter egg up there?' he called, rather crossly. She only laughed. The family expected, after that time of preparation, something like magic. At last she came, looking very nice in a blouse and skirt.

'Have you *really* been all this time getting ready?' he asked.

'Chubby dear! That question is not permitted, is it, Mrs Morel?'

She played the grand lady at first. When she went with William to chapel, he in his frock coat and silk hat, she in her furs and London-made costume, Paul and Arthur and Annie expected everybody to bow to the ground in admiration. And Morel, standing in his Sunday suit at the end of the road, watching the gallant pair go, felt he was the father of princes and princesses.

And yet she was not so grand. For a year now she had been a sort of secretary or clerk in a London office. But while she was with the Morels she queened it. She sat and let Annie or Paul wait on her as if they were her servants. She treated Mrs Morel with a certain glibness and Morel with patronage. But after a day or so she began to change her tune.

William always wanted Paul or Annie to go along with them on their walks. It was so much more interesting. And Paul really *did* admire 'Gypsy' whole-heartedly; in fact, his mother scarcely forgave the boy for the adulation with which he treated the girl.

On the second day, when Lily said, 'Oh, Annie, do you know where I left my muff?' William replied:

'You know it is in your bedroom. Why do you ask Annie?'

And Lily went upstairs with a cross, shut mouth. But it angered the young man that she made a servant of his sister.

On the third evening William and Lily were sitting together in the parlour by the fire in the dark. At a quarter to eleven Mrs Morel was heard raking the fire. William came out to the kitchen, followed by his beloved.

'Is it as late as that, mother?' he said. She had been sitting alone.

'It is not *late*, my boy, but it is as late as I usually sit up.'

'Won't you go to bed, then?' he asked.

'And leave you two? No, my boy, I don't believe in it.'

'Can't you trust us, mother?'

'Whether I can or not, I won't do it. You can stay till eleven if you like, and I can read.'

'Go to bed, Gyp,' he said to his girl. 'We won't keep mater waiting.'

'Annie has left the candle burning, Lily,' said Mrs Morel; 'I think you will see.'

'Yes, thank you. Good night, Mrs Morel.'

William kissed his sweetheart at the foot of the stairs, and she went. He returned to the kitchen.

'Can't you trust us, mother?' he repeated, rather offended.

'My boy, I tell you I don't *believe* in leaving two young things like you alone downstairs when everyone else is in bed.'

And he was forced to take this answer. He kissed his mother good night.

At Easter he came over alone. And then he discussed his sweetheart endlessly with his mother.

'You know, mother, when I'm away from her I don't care for her a bit. I shouldn't care if I never saw her again. But, then, when I'm with her in the evenings I am awfully fond of her.'

'It's a queer sort of love to marry on,' said Mrs Morel, 'if she holds you no more than that!'

'It *is* funny!' he exclaimed. It worried and perplexed him. 'But yet—there's so much between us now I couldn't give her up.'

'You know best,' said Mrs Morel. 'But if it is as you say, I wouldn't call it *love*—at any rate, it doesn't look much like it.'

'Oh, I don't know, mother. She's an orphan, and—'

They never came to any sort of conclusion. He seemed puzzled and rather fretted. She was rather reserved. All his strength and money went in keeping this girl. He could scarcely afford to take his mother to Nottingham when he came over.

Paul's wages had been raised at Christmas to ten shillings, to his great joy. He was quite happy at Jordan's, but his health suffered from the long hours and the confinement. His mother, to whom he became more and more significant, thought how to help.

His half-day holiday was on Monday afternoon. On a Monday morning in May, as the two sat alone at breakfast, she said:

'I think it will be a fine day.'

He looked up in surprise. This meant something.

'You know Mr Leivers has gone to live on a new farm. Well, he asked me last week if I wouldn't go and see Mrs Leivers, and I promised to bring you on Monday if it's fine. Shall we go?'

'I say, little woman, how lovely!' he cried. 'And we'll go this afternoon?'

Paul hurried off to the station jubilant. Down Derby Road was a cherry-tree that glistened. The old brick wall by the Statutes ground burned scarlet, spring was a very flame of green. And the steep sweep of highroad lay, in its cool morning dust, splendid with patterns of sunshine and shadow, perfectly still. The trees sloped their great green shoulders proudly; and inside the warehouse all the morning, the boy had a vision of spring outside.

When he came home at dinner-time his mother was rather excited.

'Are we going?' he asked.

'When I'm ready,' she replied.

Presently he got up.

'Go and get dressed while I wash up,' he said.

She did so. He washed the pots, straightened, and then took her boots. They were quite clean. Mrs Morel was one of those naturally exquisite people who can walk in mud without dirtying their shoes. But Paul had to clean them for her. They were kid boots at eight shillings a pair. He, however, thought them the most dainty boots in the world, and he cleaned them with as much reverence as if they had been flowers.

Suddenly she appeared in the inner doorway rather shyly. She had got a new cotton blouse on. Paul jumped up and went forward.

'Oh, my stars!' he exclaimed. 'What a bobby-dazzler!'

She sniffed in a little haughty way, and put her head up.

'It's not a bobby-dazzler at all!' she replied. 'It's very quiet.'

She walked forward, whilst he hovered round her.

'Well,' she asked, quite shy, but pretending to be high and mighty, 'do you like it?'

'Awfully! You *are* a fine little woman to go jaunting out with!'

He went and surveyed her from the back.

'Well,' he said, 'if I was walking down the street behind you, I should say, "Doesn't *that* little person fancy herself!"'

'Well, she doesn't,' replied Mrs Morel. 'She's not sure it suits her.'

'Oh no! she wants to be in dirty black, looking as if she was wrapped in burnt paper. It *does* suit you, and *I* say you look nice.'

She sniffed in her little way, pleased, but pretending to know better.

'Well,' she said, 'it's cost me just three shillings. You couldn't have got it ready-made for that price, could you?'

'I should think you couldn't,' he replied.

'And, you know, it's good stuff.'

'Awfully pretty,' he said.

The blouse was white, with a little sprig of heliotrope and black.

'Too young for me, though, I'm afraid,' she said.

'Too young for you!' he exclaimed in disgust. 'Why don't you buy some false white hair and stick it on your head?'

'I s'll soon have no need,' she replied. 'I'm going white fast enough.'

'Well, you've no business to,' he said. 'What do I want with a white-haired mother?'

'I'm afraid you'll have to put up with one, my lad,' she said rather strangely.

They set off in great style, she carrying the umbrella William had given her, because of the sun. Paul was considerably taller than she, though he was not big. He fancied himself.

On the fallow land the young wheat shone silkily. Minton pit waved its plumes of white steam, coughed, and rattled hoarsely.

'Now look at that!' said Mrs Morel. Mother and son stood on the road to watch. Along the ridge of the great pit-hill crawled a little group in silhouette against the sky, a horse, a small truck, and a man. They climbed the incline against the heavens. At the end the man tipped the waggon. There was an undue rattle as the waste fell down the sheer slope of the enormous bank.

'You sit a minute, mother,' he said, and she took a seat on a bank, whilst he sketched rapidly. She was silent whilst he worked, looking round at the afternoon, the red cottages shining among their greenness.

'The world is a wonderful place,' she said, 'and wonderfully beautiful.'

'And so's the pit,' he said. 'Look how it heaps together, like something alive almost–a big creature that you don't know.'

'Yes,' she said. 'Perhaps.'

'And all the trucks standing waiting, like a string of beasts to be fed,' he said.

'And very thankful I am they *are* standing,' she said, 'for that means they'll turn middling time this week.'

'But I like the feel of *men* on things, while they're alive. There's a feel of men about trucks, because they've been handled with men's hands, all of them.'

'Yes,' said Mrs Morel.

They went along under the trees of the highroad. He was constantly informing her, but she was interested. They passed the end of Nethermere, that was tossing its sunshine like petals lightly in its lap. Then they turned on a private road, and in some trepidation approached a big farm. A dog barked furiously. A woman came out to see.

'Is this the way to Willey Farm?' Mrs Morel asked.

Paul hung behind in terror of being sent back. But the woman was amiable, and directed them. The mother and son went through the wheat and oats, over a little bridge into a wild meadow. Peewits, with their white breasts glistening, wheeled and screamed about them. The lake was still and blue. High overhead a heron floated. Opposite, the wood heaped on the hill, green and still.

'It's a wild road, mother,' said Paul. 'Just like Canada.'

'Isn't it beautiful!' said Mrs Morel, looking round.

'See that heron–see–see her legs?'

He directed his mother, what she must see and what not. And she was quite content.

'But now,' she said, 'which way? He told me through the wood.'

The wood, fenced and dark, lay on their left.

'I can feel a bit of a path on this road,' said Paul. 'You've got town feet, somehow or other, you have.'

They found a little gate, and soon were in a broad green alley of the wood, with a new thicket of fir and pine on one hand, an old oak glade dipping down on the other. And among the oaks, the bluebells stood in pools of azure, under the new green hazels, upon a pale fawn floor of oak-leaves. He found flowers for her.

'Here's a bit of new-mown hay,' he said; then, again, he brought her forget-me-nots. And, again, his heart hurt with love, seeing her hand, used with work, holding the little bunch of flowers he gave her. She was perfectly happy.

But at the end of the riding was a fence to climb. Paul was over in a second.

'Come,' he said, 'let me help you.'

'No, go away. I will do it in my own way.'

He stood below with his hands up ready to help her. She climbed cautiously.

'What a way to climb!' he exclaimed scornfully, when she was safely to earth again.

'Hateful stiles!' she cried.

'Duffer of a little woman,' he replied, 'who can't get over 'em.'

In front, along the edge of the wood, was a cluster of low red farm buildings. The two hastened forward. Flush with the wood was the apple orchard, where blossom was falling on the grindstone. The pond was deep under a hedge and over-hanging oak-trees. Some cows stood in the shade. The farm and buildings, three sides of a quadrangle, embraced the sunshine towards the wood. It was very still.

Mother and son went into the small railed garden, where was a scent of red gillivers. By the open door were some floury loaves, put out to cool. A hen was just coming to peck them. Then, in the doorway suddenly appeared a girl in a dirty apron. She was about fourteen years old, had a rosy dark face, a bunch of short black curls, very fine and free, and dark eyes; shy, questioning, a little resentful of the strangers, she disappeared. In a minute another figure appeared, a small, frail woman, rosy, with great dark brown eyes.

'Oh!' she exclaimed, smiling with a little glow, 'you've come, then. I *am* glad to see you.' Her voice was intimate and rather sad.

The two women shook hands.

'Now are you sure we're not a bother to you?' said Mrs Morel. 'I know what a farming life is.'

'Oh no! We're only too thankful to see a new face, it's so lost up here.'

'I suppose so,' said Mrs Morel.

They were taken through into the parlour—a long, low room, with a great bunch of guelder-roses in the fireplace. There the women talked, whilst Paul went out to survey the land. He was in the garden smelling the gillivers and looking at the plants, when the girl came out quickly to the heap of coal which stood by the fence.

'I suppose these are cabbage-roses?' he said to her, pointing to the bushes along the fence.

She looked at him with startled, big brown eyes.

'I suppose they are cabbage-roses when they come out?' he said.

'I don't know,' she faltered. 'They're white with pink middles.'

'Then they're maiden-blush.'

Miriam flushed. She had a beautiful warm colouring.

'I don't know,' she said.

'You don't have *much* in your garden,' he said.

'This is our first year here,' she answered, in a distant, rather superior way, drawing back and going indoors. He did not notice, but went his round of exploration. Presently his mother came out, and they went through the buildings. Paul was hugely delighted.

'And I suppose you have the fowls and calves and pigs to look after?' said Mrs Morel to Mrs Leivers.

'No,' replied the little woman. 'I can't find time to look after cattle, and I'm not used to it. It's as much as I can do to keep going in the house.'

'Well, I suppose it is,' said Mrs Morel.

Presently the girl came out.

'Tea is ready, mother,' she said in a musical, quiet voice.

'Oh, thank you, Miriam, then we'll come,' replied her mother, almost ingratiatingly. 'Would you *care* to have tea now, Mrs Morel?'

'Of course,' said Mrs Morel. 'Whenever it's ready.'

Paul and his mother and Mrs Leivers had tea together. Then they went out into the wood that was flooded with bluebells, while fumy forget-me-nots were in the paths. The mother and son were in ecstasy together.

When they got back to the house, Mr Leivers and Edgar, the eldest son, were in the kitchen. Edgar was about eighteen. Then Geoffrey and Maurice, big lads of twelve and thirteen, were in from school. Mr Leivers was a good-looking man in the prime of life, with a golden-brown moustache, and blue eyes screwed up against the weather.

The boys were condescending, but Paul scarcely observed it. They went round for eggs, scrambling into all sorts of places. As they were feeding the fowls Miriam came out. The boys took no notice of her. One hen, with her yellow chickens, was in a coop. Maurice took his hand full of corn and let the hen peck from it.

'Durst you do it?' he asked Paul.

'Let's see,' said Paul.

He had a small hand, warm, and rather capable-looking. Miriam watched. He held the corn to the hen. The bird eyed it with her hard, bright eye, and suddenly made a peck into his hand. He started, and laughed. 'Rap, rap, rap!' went the bird's beak in his palm. He laughed again, and the other boys joined.

'She knocks you, and nips you, but never hurts,' said Paul, when the last corn had gone.

'Now, Miriam,' said Maurice, 'you come an' 'ave a go.'

'No,' she cried, shrinking back.

'Ha! baby. The mardy-kid!' said her brothers.

'It doesn't hurt a bit,' said Paul. 'It only just nips rather nicely.'

'No,' she still cried, shaking her black curls and shrinking.

'She dursn't,' said Geoffrey. 'She niver durst do anything except recite poitry.'

'Dursn't jump off a gate, dursn't tweedle, dursn't go on a slide, dursn't stop a girl hittin' her. She can do nowt but go about thinkin' herself somebody. "The Lady of the Lake". Yah!' cried Maurice.

Miriam was crimson with shame and misery.

'I dare do more than you,' she cried. 'You're never anything but cowards and bullies.'

'Oh, cowards and bullies!' they repeated, mincingly, mocking her speech.

'Not such a clown shall anger me,
A boor is answered silently,'

he quoted against her, shouting with laughter.

She went indoors. Paul went with the boys into the orchard, where they had rigged up a parallel bar. They did feats of strength. He was more agile than strong, but it served. He fingered a piece of apple-blossom that hung low on a swinging bough.

'I wouldn't get the apple-blossom,' said Edgar, the eldest brother. 'There'll be no apples next year.'

'I wasn't going to get it,' replied Paul, going away.

The boys felt hostile to him; they were more interested in their own pursuits. He wandered back to the house to look for his mother. As he went round the back, he saw Miriam kneeling in front of the hen-coop, some maize in her hand, biting her lip, and crouching in an intense attitude. The hen was eyeing her wickedly. Very gingerly she put forward her hand. The hen bobbed for her. She drew back quickly with a cry, half of fear, half of chagrin.

'It won't hurt you,' said Paul.

She flushed crimson and started up.

'I only wanted to try,' she said in a low voice.

'See, it doesn't hurt,' he said, and, putting only two corns in his palm, he let the hen peck, peck, peck at his bare hand. 'It only makes you laugh,' he said.

She put her hand forward, and dragged it away, tried again, and started back with a cry. He frowned.

'Why, I'd let her take corn from my face,' said Paul, 'only she bumps a bit. She's ever so neat. If she wasn't, look how much ground she'd peck up every day.'

He waited grimly, and watched. At last Miriam let the bird peck from her hand. She gave a little cry–fear, and pain because of fear–rather pathetic. But she had done it, and she did it again.

'There, you see,' said the boy. 'It doesn't hurt, does it?'

She looked at him with dilated dark eyes.

'No,' she laughed, trembling.

Then she rose and went indoors. She seemed to be in some way resentful of the boy.

'He thinks I'm only a common girl,' she thought, and she wanted to prove she was a grand person like the 'Lady of the Lake'.

Paul found his mother ready to go home. She smiled on her son. He took the great bunch of flowers. Mr and Mrs Leivers walked down the fields with them. The hills were golden with evening; deep in the wood showed the darkening purple of bluebells. It was everywhere perfectly still, save for the rustling of leaves and birds.

'But it is a beautiful place,' said Mrs Morel.

'Yes,' answered Mr Leivers; 'it's a nice little place, if only it weren't for the rabbits. The pasture's bitten down to nothing. I dunno if ever I s'll get the rent off it.'

He clapped his hands, and the field broke into motion near the woods, brown rabbits hopping everywhere.

'Would you believe it!' exclaimed Mrs Morel.

She and Paul went on alone together.

'Wasn't it lovely, mother?' he said quietly.

A thin moon was coming out. His heart was full of happiness till it hurt. His mother had to chatter because she, too, wanted to cry, with happiness.

'Now *wouldn't* I help that man!' she said. '*Wouldn't* I see to the fowls and the young stock! And *I'd* learn to milk, and *I'd* talk with him, and *I'd* plan with him. My word, if I were his wife, the farm would be run, I know! But there, she hasn't the strength–she simply hasn't the strength. She ought never to have been burdened like it, you know. I'm sorry for her, and I'm sorry for him too. My word, if *I'd* had him, I shouldn't have thought him a bad husband! Not that she does either; and she's very lovable.'

William came home again with his sweetheart at the Whitsuntide. He had one week of his holidays then. It was beautiful weather. As a rule, William and Lily and Paul went out in the morning together for a walk. William did not talk to his beloved much, except to tell her things from his boyhood. Paul talked endlessly to both of them. They lay down, all three, in a meadow by Minton Church. On one side, by the Castle Farm, was a beautiful quivering screen of poplars. Hawthorn was dropping from the hedges; penny daisies and ragged robin were in the field, like laughter. William a big fellow of twenty-three, thinner now and even a bit gaunt, lay back in the sunshine and dreamed, while she fingered with his hair. Paul went gathering the big daisies. She had taken off her hat; her hair was black as a horse's mane. Paul came back and threaded daisies in her jet-black hair–big spangles of white and yellow, and just a pink touch of ragged robin.

'Now you look like a young witch-woman,' the boy said to her. 'Doesn't she, William?'

Lily laughed. William opened his eyes and looked at her. In his gaze was a certain baffled look of misery and fierce appreciation.

'Has he made a sight of me?' she asked, laughing down on her lover.

'That he has!' said William, smiling.

He looked at her. Her beauty seemed to hurt him. He glanced at her flower-decked head and frowned.

'You look nice enough, if that's what you want to know,' he said.

And she walked without her hat. In a little while William recovered and was rather tender to her. Coming to a bridge, he carved her initials and his in a heart.

L. L. W.

W. M.

She watched his strong, nervous hand, with its glistening hairs and freckles, as he carved, and she seemed fascinated by it.

All the time there was a feeling of sadness and warmth, and a certain tenderness in the house, whilst William and Lily were at home. But often he got irritable. She had brought, for an eight-days' stay, five dresses and six blouses.

'Oh, would you mind,' she said to Annie, 'washing me these two blouses, and these things?'

And Annie stood washing when William and Lily went out the next morning. Mrs Morel was furious. And sometimes the young man, catching a glimpse of his sweetheart's attitude towards his sister, hated her.

On Sunday morning she looked very beautiful in a dress of foulard, silky and sweeping, and blue as a jay-bird's feather, and in a large cream hat covered with many roses, mostly crimson. Nobody could admire her enough. But in the evening, when she was going out, she asked again:

'Chubby, have you got my gloves?'

'Which?' asked William.

'My new black *suede.*'

'No.'

There was a hunt. She had lost them.

'Look here, mother,' said William, 'that's the fourth pair she's lost since Christmas—at five shillings a pair!'

'You only gave me *two* of them,' she remonstrated.

And in the evening, after supper, he stood on the hearthrug whilst she sat on the sofa, and he seemed to hate her. In the afternoon he had left her whilst he went to see some old friend. She had sat looking at a book. After supper William wanted to write a letter.

'Here is your book, Lily,' said Mrs Morel. 'Would you care to go on with it for a few minutes?'

'No, thank you,' said the girl. 'I will sit still.'

'But it is so dull.'

William scribbled irritably at a great rate. As he sealed the envelope he said: 'Read a book! Why, she's never read a book in her life.'

'Oh, go along!' said Mrs Morel, cross with the exaggeration.

'It's true, mother—she hasn't,' he cried, jumping up and taking his old position on the hearthrug. 'She's never read a book in her life.'

''Er's like me,' chimed in Morel. ''Er canna see what there is i' books, ter sit borin' your nose in 'em for, nor more can I.'

'But you shouldn't say these things,' said Mrs Morel to her son.

'But it's true, mother—she *can't* read. What did you give her?'

'Well, I gave her a little thing of Annie Swan's. Nobody wants to read dry stuff on Sunday afternoon.'

'Well, I'll bet she didn't read ten lines of it.'

'You are mistaken,' said his mother.

All the time Lily sat miserably on the sofa. He turned to her swiftly.

'*Did* you read any?' he asked.

'Yes, I did,' she replied.

'How much?'

'I don't know how many pages.'

'Tell me *one* thing you read.'

She could not.

She never got beyond the second page. He read a great deal, and had a quick, active intelligence. She could understand nothing but love-making and chatter. He was accustomed to having all his thoughts sifted through his mother's mind; so, when he wanted companionship, and was asked in reply to be the billing and twittering lover, he hated his betrothed.

'You know, mother,' he said, when he was alone with her at night, 'she's no idea of money, she's so wessel-brained. When she's paid, she'll suddenly buy such rot as *marrons glacés*, and then *I* have to buy her season-ticket, and her extras, even her underclothing. And she wants to get married, and I think myself we might as well get married next year. But at this rate—'

'A fine mess of a marriage it would be,' replied his mother. 'I should consider it again, my boy.'

'Oh, well, I've gone too far to break off now,' he said, 'and so I shall get married as soon as I can.'

'Very well, my boy. If you will, you will, and there's no stopping you; and I tell you, *I* can't sleep when I think about it.'

'Oh, she'll be all right, mother. We shall manage.'

'And she lets you buy her underclothing?' asked the mother.

'Well,' he began apologetically, 'she didn't ask me; but one morning—and it *was* cold—I found her on the station shivering, not able to keep still; so I asked her if she was well wrapped up. She said: "I think so." So I said: "Have you got warm underthings on?" and she said No, they were cotton. I asked her why on earth she hadn't got something thicker on in weather like that, and she said because she *had* nothing. And there she is—a bronchial subject. I *had* to take her and get some warm things. Well, mother, I shouldn't mind the money if we had any. And, you know, she *ought* to keep enough to pay for her season-ticket; but no, she comes to me about that, and I have to find the money.'

'It's a poor lookout,' said Mrs Morel bitterly.

He was pale, and his rugged face, that used to be so perfectly careless and laughing, was stamped with conflict and despair.

'But I can't give her up now; it's gone too far,' he said. 'And, besides, for *some* things I couldn't do without her.'

'My boy, remember you're taking your life in your hands,' said Mrs Morel. '*Nothing* is as bad as a marriage that's a hopeless failure. Mine was bad enough, God knows, and ought to teach you something; but it might have been worse by a long chalk.'

He leaned with his back against the side of the chimney-piece, his hands in his pockets. He was a big, raw-boned man, who looked as if he would go to the world's end if he wanted to. But she saw the despair on his face.

'I couldn't give her up now,' he said.

'Well,' she said, 'remember there are worse wrongs than breaking off an engagement.'

'I can't give her up *now*,' he said.

The clock ticked on; mother and son remained in silence, a conflict between them; but he would say no more. At last she said:

'Well, go to bed, my son. You'll feel better in the morning, and perhaps you'll know better.'

He kissed her, and went. She raked the fire. Her heart was heavy now as it had never been. Before, with her husband, things had seemed to be breaking down in her, but they did not destroy her power to live. Now her soul felt lamed in itself. It was her hope that was struck.

And so often William manifested the same hatred towards his betrothed. On the last evening at home he was railing against her.

'Well,' he said, 'if you don't believe me, what she's like, would you believe she has been confirmed three times?'

'Nonsense!' laughed Mrs Morel.

'Nonsense or not, she *has*! That's what confirmation means for her—a bit of a theatrical show where she can cut a figure.'

'I haven't, Mrs Morel!' cried the girl—'I haven't! It is not true!'

'What!' he cried, flashing round on her. 'Once in Bromley, once in Beckenham, and once somewhere else.'

'Nowhere else!' she said, in tears—'nowhere else!'

'It *was*! And, if it wasn't, why were you confirmed *twice*?'

'Once I was only fourteen, Mrs Morel,' she pleaded, tears in her eyes.

'Yes,' said Mrs Morel; 'I can quite understand it, child. Take no notice of him. You ought to be ashamed, William, saying such things.'

'But it's true. She's religious—she had blue velvet Prayer-Books—and she's not as much religion, or anything else, in her than that table-leg. Gets confirmed three times for show to show herself off, and that's how she is in *everything–everything!*'

The girl sat on the sofa, crying. She was not strong.

'As for *love!*' he cried, 'you might as well ask a fly to love you! It'll love settling on you–'

'Now, say no more,' commanded Mrs Morel. 'If you want to say these things, you must find another place than this. I am ashamed of you, William! Why don't you be more manly. To do nothing but to find fault with a girl, and then pretend you're engaged to her!'

Mrs Morel subsided in wrath and indignation.

William was silent, and later he repented, kissed and comforted the girl. Yet it was true, what he had said. He hated her.

When they were going away, Mrs Morel accompanied them as far as Nottingham. It was a long way to Keston station.

'You know, mother,' he said to her, 'Gyp's shallow. Nothing goes deep with her.'

'William, I *wish* you wouldn't say these things,' said Mrs Morel, very uncomfortable for the girl who walked beside her.

'But it doesn't, mother. She's very much in love with me *now*, but if I died she'd have forgotten me in three months.'

Mrs Morel was afraid. Her heart beat furiously, hearing the quiet bitterness of her son's last speech.

'How do you know?' she replied. 'You *don't* know, and therefore you've no right to say such a thing.'

'He's always saying these things!' cried the girl.

'In three months after I was buried, you'd have somebody else, and I should be forgotten,' he said. 'And that's your love!'

Mrs Morel saw them into the train in Nottingham, then she returned home.

'There's one comfort,' she said to Paul–'he'll never have any money to marry on, that I *am* sure of. And so she'll save him that way.'

So she took cheer. Matters were not yet very desperate. She firmly believed William would never marry his Gypsy. She waited, and she kept Paul near to her.

All summer long, William's letters had a feverish tone; he seemed unnatural and intense. Sometimes he was exaggeratedly jolly, usually he was flat and bitter in his letter.

'Ay,' his mother said, 'I'm afraid he's ruining himself against that creature, who isn't worthy of his love–no, no more than a rag doll.'

He wanted to come home. The midsummer holiday was gone; it was a long while to Christmas. He wrote in wild excitement, saying he could come for Saturday and Sunday at Goose Fair, the first week in October.

'You are not well, my boy,' said his mother, when she saw him.

She was almost in tears at having him to herself again.

'No, I've not been well,' he said. 'I've seemed to have a dragging cold all the last month, but it's going, I think.'

It was sunny October weather. He seemed wild with joy, like a schoolboy escaped; then again he was silent and reserved. He was more gaunt than ever, and there was a haggard look in his eyes.

'You are doing too much,' said his mother to him.

He was doing extra work, trying to make some money to marry on, he said.

He only talked to his mother once on the Saturday night; then he was sad and tender about his beloved.

'And yet, you know, mother, for all that, if I died she'd be broken-hearted for two months, and then she'd start to forget me. You'd see, she'd never come home here to look at my grave, not even once.'

'Why, William,' said his mother, 'you're not going to die, so why talk about it?'

'But whether or not—' he replied.

'And she can't help it. She is like that, and if you choose her—well, you can't grumble,' said his mother.

On the Sunday morning, as he was putting his collar on:

'Look,' he said to his mother, holding up his chin, 'what a rash my collar's made under my chin!'

Just at the junction of chin and throat was a big red inflammation.

'It ought not to do that,' said his mother. 'Here, put a bit of this soothing ointment on. You should wear different collars.'

He went away on Sunday midnight, seeming better and more solid for his two days at home.

On Tuesday morning came a telegram from London that he was ill. Mrs Morel got off her knees from washing the floor, read the telegram, called a neighbour, went to her landlady and borrowed a sovereign, put on her things, and set off. She hurried to Keston, caught an express for London in Nottingham. She had to wait in Nottingham nearly an hour. A small figure in her black bonnet, she was anxiously asking the porters if they knew how to get to Elmers End. The journey was three hours. She sat in her corner in a kind of stupor, never moving. At King's Cross still no one could tell her how to get to Elmers End. Carrying her string bag, that contained her nightdress, comb and brush, she went from person to person. At last they sent her underground to Cannon Street.

It was six o'clock when she arrived at William's lodging. The blinds were not down.

'How is he?' she asked.

'No better,' said the landlady.

She followed the woman upstairs. William lay on the bed, with bloodshot eyes, his face rather discoloured. The clothes were tossed about, there was no fire in the room, a glass of milk stood on the stand at his bedside. No one had been with him.

'Why, my son!' said the mother bravely.

He did not answer. He looked at her, but did not see her. Then he began to say, in a dull voice, as if repeating a letter from dictation: 'Owing to a leakage in the hold of this vessel, the sugar had set, and become converted into rock. It needed hacking—'

He was quite unconscious. It had been his business to examine some such cargo of sugar in the Port of London.

'How long has he been like this?' the mother asked the landlady.

'He got home at six o'clock on Monday morning, and he seemed to sleep all day; then in the night we heard him talking, and this morning he asked for you. So I wired, and we fetched the doctor.'

'Will you have a fire made?'

Mrs Morel tried to soothe her son, to keep him still.

The doctor came. It was pneumonia, and, he said, a peculiar erysipelas, which had started under the chin where the collar chafed, and was spreading over the face. He hoped it would not get to the brain.

Mrs Morel settled down to nurse. She prayed for William, prayed that he would recognize her. But the young man's face grew more discoloured. In the night she struggled with him. He raved, and raved, and would not come to consciousness. At two o'clock, in a dreadful paroxysm, he died.

Mrs Morel sat perfectly still for an hour in the lodging bedroom; then she roused the household.

At six o'clock, with the aid of the charwoman, she laid him out; then she went round the dreary London village to the registrar and the doctor.

At nine o'clock to the cottage on Scargill Street came another wire:

'William died last night. Let father come, bring money.'

Annie, Paul, and Arthur were at home; Mr Morel was gone to work. The three children said not a word. Annie began to whimper with fear; Paul set off for his father.

It was a beautiful day. At Brinsley pit the white steam melted slowly in the sunshine of a soft blue sky; the wheels of the headstocks twinkled high up; the screen, shuffling its coal into the trucks, made a busy noise.

'I want my father; he's got to go to London,' said the boy to the first man he met on the bank.

'Tha wants Walter Morel? Go in theer an' tell Joe Ward.'

Paul went into the little top office.

'I want my father; he's got to go to London.'

'Thy feyther? Is he down? What's his name?'

'Mr Morel.'

'What, Walter? Is owt amiss?'

'He's got to go to London.'

The man went to the telephone and rang up the bottom office.

'Walter Morel's wanted. Number 42, Hard. Summat's amiss; there's his lad here.'

Then he turned round to Paul.

'He'll be up in a few minutes,' he said.

Paul wandered out to the pit-top. He watched the chair come up, with its waggon of coal. The great iron cage sank back on its rest, a full carfle was hauled off, an empty tram run on to the chair, a bell ting'ed somewhere, the chair heaved, then dropped like a stone.

Paul did not realize William was dead; it was impossible, with such a bustle going on. The puller-off swung the small truck on to the turn-table, another man ran with it along the bank down the curving lines.

'And William is dead, and my mother's in London, and what will she be doing?' the boy asked himself, as if it were a conundrum.

He watched chair after chair come up, and still no father. At last, standing beside a waggon, a man's form! The chair sank on its rests, Morel stepped off. He was slightly lame from an accident.

'Is it thee, Paul? Is 'e worse?'

'You've got to go to London.'

The two walked off the pit-bank, where men were watching curiously. As they came out and went along the railway, with the sunny autumn field on one side and a wall of trucks on the other, Morel said in a frightened voice:

''E's niver gone, child?'

'Yes.'

'When wor't?'

The miner's voice was terrified.

'Last night. We had a telegram from my mother.'

Morel walked on a few strides, then leaned up against a truck side, his hand over his eyes. He was not crying. Paul stood looking round, waiting. On the weighing-machine a truck trundled slowly. Paul saw everything, except his father leaning against the truck as if he were tired.

Morel had only once before been to London. He set off, scared and peaked, to help his wife. That was on Tuesday. The children were left alone in the house. Paul went to work, Arthur went to school, and Annie had in a friend to be with her.

On Saturday night, as Paul was turning the corner, coming home from Keston, he saw his mother and father, who had come to Sethley Bridge Station. They were walking in silence in the dark, tired, straggling apart. The boy waited.

'Mother!' he said, in the darkness.

Mrs Morel's small figure seemed not to observe. He spoke again.

'Paul!' she said, uninterestedly.

She let him kiss her, but she seemed unaware of him.

In the house she was the same—small, white, and mute. She noticed nothing, she said nothing, only:

'The coffin will be here to-night, Walter. You'd better see about some help.' Then turning to the children: 'We're bringing him home.'

Then she relapsed into the same mute looking into space, her hands folded on her lap. Paul, looking at her, felt he could not breathe. The house was dead silent.

'I went to work, mother,' he said, plaintively.

'Did you?' she answered dully.

After half an hour Morel, troubled and bewildered, came in again.

'Wheer s'll we ha'e him when he *does* come?' he asked his wife.

'In the front room.'

'Then I'd better shift th' table?'

'Yes.'

'An' ha'e him across th' chairs?'

'You know there—Yes, I suppose so.'

Morel and Paul went, with a candle, into the parlour. There was no gas there. The father unscrewed the top of the big mahogany oval table, and cleared the middle of the room; then he arranged six chairs opposite each other, so that the coffin could stand on their beds.

'You niver seed such a length as he is!' said the miner, and watching anxiously as he worked.

Paul went to the bay window and looked out. The ash-tree stood monstrous and black in front of the wide darkness. It was a faintly luminous night. Paul went back to his mother.

At ten o'clock Morel called:

'He's here!'

Everyone started. There was a noise of unbarring and unlocking the front door, which opened straight from the night into the room.

'Bring another candle,' called Morel.

Annie and Arthur went. Paul followed with his mother. He stood with his arm round her waist in the inner doorway. Down the middle of the cleared room waited six chairs, face to face. In the window, against the lace curtains, Arthur held up one candle, and by the open door, against the night, Annie stood leaning forward, her brass candlestick glittering.

There was the noise of wheels. Outside in the darkness of the street below Paul could see horses and a black vehicle, one lamp and a few pale faces; then some men, miners, all in their shirtsleeves, seemed to struggle in the obscurity. Presently two men appeared, bowed beneath a great weight. It was Morel and his neighbour.

'Steady!' called Morel, out of breath.

He and his fellow mounted the steep garden step, heaved into the candle-light with their gleaming coffin-end. Limbs of other men were seen struggling behind. Morel and Burns, in front, staggered; the great dark weight swayed.

'Steady, steady!' cried Morel, as if in pain.

All the six bearers were up in the small garden, holding the great coffin aloft. There were three more steps to the door. The yellow lamp of the carriage shone alone down in the black road.

'Now then!' said Morel.

The coffin swayed, the men began to mount the three steps, with their load. Annie's candle flickered, and she whimpered as the first men appeared, and the limbs and bowed heads of six men struggled to climb into the room, bearing the coffin that rode like sorrow on their living flesh.

'Oh, my son—my son!' Mrs Morel sang softly, and each time the coffin swung to the unequal climbing of the men: 'Oh, my son—my son—my son!'

'Mother!' Paul whimpered, his hand round her waist. 'Mother!'

She did not hear.

'Oh, my son—my son!' she repeated.

Paul saw drops of sweat fall from his father's brow. Six men were in the room—six coatless men, with yielding, struggling limbs, filling the room and knocking against the furniture. The coffin veered, and was gently lowered on to the chairs. The sweat fell from Morel's face on its boards.

'My word, he's a weight!' said a man, and the five miners sighed, bowed, and, trembling with the struggle, descended the steps again, closing the door behind them.

The family was alone in the parlour with the great polished box. William, when laid out, was six feet four inches long. Like a monument lay the bright brown, ponderous coffin. Paul thought it would never be got out of the room again. His mother was stroking the polished wood.

They buried him on the Monday in the little cemetery on the hillside that looks over the fields at the big church and the houses. It was sunny, and the white chrysanthemums frilled themselves in the warmth.

Mrs Morel could not be persuaded, after this, to talk and take her old bright interest in life. She remained shut off. All the way home in the train she had said to herself: 'If only it would have been me!'

When Paul came home at night he found his mother sitting, her day's work done, with hands folded in her lap upon her coarse apron. She always used to have changed her dress and put on a black apron, before. Now Annie set his supper, and his mother sat looking blankly in front of her, her mouth shut tight. Then he beat his brains for news to tell her.

'Mother, Miss Jordan was down to-day, and she said my sketch of a colliery at work was beautiful.'

But Mrs Morel took no notice. Night after night he forced himself to tell her things, although she did not listen. It drove him almost insane to have her thus. At last:

'What's a-matter, mother?' he asked.

She did not hear.

'What's a-matter?' he persisted. 'Mother, what's a-matter?'

'You know what's the matter,' she said irritably, turning away.

The lad–he was sixteen years old–went to bed drearily. He was cut off and wretched through October, November, and December. His mother tried, but she could not rouse herself. She could only brood on her dead son; he had been let to die so cruelly.

At last, on December 23, with his five shillings Christmas-box in his pocket, Paul wandered blindly home. His mother looked at him, and her heart stood still.

'What's the matter?' she asked.

'I'm badly, mother!' he replied. 'Mr Jordan gave me five shillings for a Christmas-box!'

He handed it to her with trembling hands. She put it on the table.

'You aren't glad!' he reproached her; but he trembled violently.

'Where hurts you?' she said, unbuttoning his overcoat.

It was the old question.

'I feel badly, mother.'

She undressed him and put him to bed. He had pneumonia dangerously, the doctor said.

'Might he never have had it if I'd kept him at home, not let him go to Nottingham?' was one of the first things she asked.

'He might not have been so bad,' said the doctor.

Mrs Morel stood condemned on her own ground.

I should have watched the living, not the dead,' she told herself.

Paul was very ill. His mother lay in bed at nights with him; they could not afford a nurse. He grew worse, and the crisis approached. One night he tossed into consciousness in the ghastly, sickly feeling of dissolution,when all the cells in the body seem in intense irritability to be breaking down, and consciousness makes a last flare of struggle, like madness.

'I s'll die, mother!' he cried, heaving for breath on the pillow.

She lifted him up, crying in a small voice:

'Oh, my son–my son!'

That brought him to. He realized her. His whole will rose up and arrested him. He put his head on her breast, and took ease of her for love.

'For some things,' said his aunt, 'it was a good thing Paul was ill that Christmas. I believed it saved his mother.'

Paul was in bed for seven weeks. He got up white and fragile. His father had bought him a pot of scarlet and gold tulips. They used to flame in the window in the March sunshine as he sat on the sofa chattering to his mother. The two knitted together in perfect intimacy. Mrs Morel's life now rooted itself in Paul.

William had been a prophet. Mrs Morel had a little present and a letter from Lily at Christmas. Mrs Morel's sister had a letter at the New Year.

'I was at a ball last night. Some delightful people were there, and I enjoyed myself thoroughly,' said the letter. 'I had every dance–did not sit out one.'

Mrs Morel never heard any more of her.

Morel and his wife were gentle with each other for some time after the death of their son. He would go into a kind of daze, staring wide-eyed and blank across the room. Then he got up suddenly and hurried out to the Three Spots, returning in his normal state. But never in his life would he go for a walk up Shepstone, past the office where his son had worked, and he always avoided the cemetery.

PART II

7

LAD-AND-GIRL LOVE

Paul had been many times up to Willey Farm during the autumn. He was friends with the two youngest boys. Edgar, the eldest, would not condescend at first. And Miriam also refused to be approached. She was afraid of being set at nought, as by her own brothers. The girl was romantic in her soul. Everywhere was a Walter Scott heroine being loved by men with helmets or with plumes in their caps. She herself was something of a princess turned into a swine-girl in her own imagination. And she was afraid lest this boy, who, nevertheless, looked something like a Walter Scott hero, who could paint and speak French, and knew what algebra meant, and who went by train to Nottingham every day, might consider her simply as the swine-girl, unable to perceive the princess beneath; so she held aloof.

Her great companion was her mother. They were both brown-eyed, and inclined to be mystical, such women as treasure religion inside them, breathe it in their nostrils, and see the whole of life in a mist thereof. So to Miriam, Christ and God made one great figure, which she loved tremblingly and passionately when a tremendous sunset burned out the western sky, and Ediths, and Lucys, and Rowenas, Brian de Bois Guilberts, Rob Roys, and Guy Mannerings, rustled the sunny leaves in the morning, or sat in her bedroom aloft, alone, when it snowed. That was life to her. For the rest, she drudged in the house, which work she would not have minded had not her clean red floor been mucked up immediately by the trampling farm-boots of her brothers. She madly wanted her little brother of four to let her swathe him and stifle him in her love; she went to church reverently, with bowed head, and quivered in anguish from the vulgarity of the other choir-girls and from the common-sounding voice of the curate; she fought with her brothers, whom she considered brutal louts; and she held not her father in too high esteem because he did not carry any mystical ideals cherished in his heart but only wanted to have as easy a time as he could, and his meals when he was ready for them.

She hated her position as swine-girl. She wanted to be considered. She wanted to learn, thinking that if she could read, as Paul said he could read, 'Colomba', or the 'Voyage autour de ma Chambre' the world would have a different face for her and a deepened respect. She could not be princess by wealth or standing. So she was mad to have learning whereon to pride herself. For she was different from other folk, and must not be scooped up among the common fry. Learning was the only distinction to which she thought to aspire.

Her beauty–that of a shy, wild, quiveringly sensitive thing–seemed nothing to her. Even her soul, so strong for rhapsody, was not enough. She must have something to reinforce her pride, because she felt different from other people. Paul she eyed rather wistfully. On the whole, she scorned the male sex. But here was a new specimen, quick, light, graceful, who could be gentle and who could be sad, and who was clever, and who knew a lot, and who had a death in the family. The boy's poor morsel of learning exalted him almost sky-high in her esteem. Yet she tried hard to scorn him, because he would not see in her the princess but only the swine-girl! And he scarcely observed her.

Then he was so ill, and she felt he would be weak. Then she would be stronger than he. Then she could love him. If she could be mistress of him in his weakness, take care of him, if he could depend on her, if she could, as it were, have him in her arms, how she could love him!

As soon as the skies brightened and plum-blossom was out, Paul drove off in the milkman's heavy float up to Willey Farm. Mr Leivers shouted in a kindly fashion at the boy, then clicked to the horses as they climbed the hill slowly, in the freshness of the morning. White clouds went on their way, crowding to the back of the hills that were rousing in the spring-time. The water of Nethermere lay below, very blue against the seared meadows and the thorn-trees.

It was four and a half miles' drive. Tiny buds on the hedges, vivid as copper-green, were opening into rosettes; and thrushes called, and blackbirds shrieked and scolded. It was a new, glamorous world.

Miriam, peeping through the kitchen window, saw the horse walk through the big white gate into the farmyard that was backed by the oak-wood, still bare. Then a youth in a heavy overcoat climbed down. He put up his hands for the whip and the rug that the good-looking, ruddy farmer handed down to him.

Miriam appeared in the doorway. She was nearly sixteen, very beautiful, with her warm colouring, her gravity, her eyes dilating suddenly like an ecstasy.

'I say,' said Paul, turning shyly aside, 'your daffodils are nearly out. Isn't it early? But don't they look cold?'

'Cold!' said Miriam, in her musical, caressing voice.

'The green on their buds—' and he faltered into silence timidly.

'Let me take the rug,' said Miriam over-gently.

'I can carry it,' he answered, rather injured. But he yielded it to her.

Then Mrs Leivers appeared.

'I'm sure you're tired and cold,' she said. 'Let me take your coat. It *is* heavy. You mustn't walk far in it.'

She helped him off with his coat. He was quite unused to such attention. She was almost smothered under its weight.

'Why, mother,' laughed the farmer as he passed through the kitchen, swinging the great-milk churns, 'you've got almost more than you can manage there.'

She beat up the sofa cushions for the youth.

The kitchen was very small and irregular. The farm had been originally a labourer's cottage. And the furniture was old and battered. But Paul loved it—loved the sack-bag that formed the hearthrug, and the funny little corner under the stairs, and the small window deep in the corner, through which, bending a little, he could see the plum-trees in the back-garden and the lovely round hills beyond.

'Won't you lie down?' said Mrs Leivers.

'Oh no; I'm not tired,' he said. 'Isn't it lovely coming out, don't you think? I saw a sloe-bush in blossom and a lot of celandines. I'm glad it's sunny.'

'Can I give you anything to eat or to drink?'

'No, thank you.'

'How's your mother?'

'I think she's tired now. I think she's had too much to do. Perhaps in a little while she'll go to Skegness with me. Then she'll be able to rest. I s'll be glad if she can.'

'Yes,' replied Mrs Leivers. 'It's a wonder she isn't ill herself.'

Miriam was moving about preparing dinner. Paul watched everything that happened. His face was pale and thin, but his eyes were quick and bright with life as ever. He watched the strange, almost rhapsodic way in which the girl moved about, carrying a great stew-jar to the oven, or looking in the saucepan. The atmosphere was different from that of his own home, where everything seemed so ordinary. When Mr Leivers called loudly outside to the horse, that was reaching over to feed on the rose-bushes in the garden, the girl started, looked round with dark eyes, as if something had come breaking in on her world. There was a sense of silence inside the house and out. Miriam seemed as in some dreamy tale, a maiden in bondage, her spirit dreaming in a land far away and magical. And her discoloured, old blue frock and her broken boots seemed only like the romantic rags of King Cophetua's beggar-maid.

She suddenly became aware of his keen blue eyes upon her, taking her all in. Instantly her broken boots and her frayed old frock hurt her. She resented his seeing everything. Even he knew that her stocking was not pulled up. She went into the scullery, blushing deeply. And afterwards her hands trembled slightly at her work. She nearly dropped all she handled. When her inside dream was shaken, her body quivered with trepidation. She resented that he saw so much.

Mrs Leivers sat for some time talking to the boy, although she was needed at her work. She was too polite to leave him. Presently she excused herself and rose. After a while she looked into the tin saucepan.

'Oh *dear*, Miriam,' she cried, 'these potatoes have boiled dry!'

Miriam started as if she had been stung.

'*Have* they, mother?' she cried.

'I shouldn't care, Miriam,' said the mother, 'if I hadn't trusted them to you.' She peered into the pan.

The girl stiffened as if from a blow. Her dark eyes dilated; she remained standing in the same spot.

'Well,' she answered, gripped tight in self-conscious shame, 'I'm sure I looked at them five minutes since.'

'Yes,' said the mother. 'I know it's easily done.'

'They're not much burned,' said Paul. 'It doesn't matter, does it?'

Mrs Leivers looked at the youth with her brown, hurt eyes.

'It wouldn't matter but for the boys,' she said to him. 'Only Miriam knows what a trouble they make if the potatoes are "caught".'

'Then,' thought Paul to himself, 'you shouldn't let them make a trouble.'

After a while Edgar came in. He wore leggings, and his boots were covered with earth. He was rather small, rather formal, for a farmer. He glanced at Paul, nodded to him distantly, and said:

'Dinner ready?'

'Nearly, Edgar,' replied the mother apologetically.

'I'm ready for mine,' said the young man, taking up the newspaper and reading. Presently the rest of the family trooped in. Dinner was served. The meal went rather brutally. The over-gentleness and apologetic tone of the mother brought out all the brutality of manner in the sons. Edgar tasted the potatoes, moved his mouth quickly like a rabbit, looked indignantly at his mother, and said:

'These potatoes are burnt, mother.'

'Yes, Edgar. I forgot them for a minute. Perhaps you'll have bread if you can't eat them.'

Edgar looked in anger across at Miriam.

'What was Miriam doing that she couldn't attend to them?' he said.

Miriam looked up. Her mouth opened, her dark eyes blazed and winced, but she said nothing. She swallowed her anger and her shame, bowing her dark head.

'I'm sure she was trying hard,' said the mother.

'She hasn't got sense even to boil the potatoes,' said Edgar. 'What is she kept at home for?'

'On'y for eating everything that's left in th' pantry,' said Maurice.

'They don't forget that potato-pie against our Miriam,' laughed the father.

She was utterly humiliated. The mother sat in silence, suffering, like some saint out of place at the brutal board.

It puzzled Paul. He wondered vaguely why all this intense feeling went running because of a few burnt potatoes. The mother exalted everything–even a bit of housework–to the plane of a religious trust. The sons resented this; they felt themselves cut away underneath, and they answered with brutality and also with a sneering superciliousness.

Paul was just opening out from childhood into manhood. This atmosphere, where everything took a religious value, came with a subtle fascination to him. There was something in the air. His own mother was logical. Here there was something different, something he loved, something that at times he hated.

Miriam quarrelled with her brother fiercely. Later in the afternoon, when they had gone away again, her mother said:

'You disappointed me at dinner-time, Miriam.'

The girl dropped her head.

'They are such *brutes!*' she suddenly cried, looking up with flashing eyes.

'But hadn't you promised not to answer them?' said the mother. 'And I believed in you. I *can't* stand it when you wrangle.'

'But they're so hateful!' cried Miriam, 'and–and *low.*'

'Yes, dear. But how often have I asked you not to answer Edgar back? Can't you let him say what he likes?'

'But why should he say what he likes?'

'Aren't you strong enough to bear it, Miriam, if even for my sake? Are you so weak that you must wrangle with them?'

Mrs Leivers stuck unflinchingly to this doctrine of 'the other cheek'. She could not instil it at all into the boys. With the girls she succeeded better, and Miriam was the child of her heart. The boys loathed the other cheek when it was presented to them. Miriam was often sufficiently lofty to turn it. Then they spat on her and hated her. But she walked in her proud humility, living within herself.

There was always this feeling of jangle and discord in the Leivers family. Although the boys resented so bitterly this eternal appeal to their deeper feelings of resignation and proud humility, yet it had its effect on them. They could not establish between themselves and an outsider just the ordinary human feeling and unexaggerated friendship; they were always restless for the something deeper. Ordinary folk seemed shallow to them, trivial and inconsiderable. And so they were unaccustomed, painfully uncouth in the simplest social intercourse, suffering, and yet insolent in their superiority. Then beneath was the yearning for the soul-intimacy to which they could not attain because they were too dumb, and every approach to close connexion was blocked by their clumsy contempt of other people. They wanted genuine intimacy, but they could not get even normally near to anyone, because they scorned to take the first steps, they scorned the triviality which forms common human intercourse.

Paul fell under Mrs Leivers' spell. Everything had a religious and intensified meaning when he was with her. His soul, hurt, highly developed, sought her as if for nourishment. Together they seemed to sift the vital fact from an experience.

Miriam was her mother's daughter. In the sunshine of the afternoon mother and daughter went down the fields with him. They looked for nests. There was a jenny wren's in the hedge by the orchard.

'I *do* want you to see this,' said Mrs Leivers.

He crouched down and carefully put his finger through the thorns into the round door of the nest.

'It's almost as if you were feeling inside the live body of the bird,' he said, 'it's so warm. They say a bird makes its nest round like a cup with pressing its breast on it. Then how did it make the ceiling round, I wonder?'

The nest seemed to start to life for the two women. After that, Miriam came to see it every day. It seemed so close to her. Again, going down the hedgeside with the girl, he noticed the celandines, scalloped splashes of gold, on the side of the ditch.

'I like them,' he said, 'when their petals go flat back with the sunshine. They seem to be pressing themselves at the sun.'

And then the celandines ever after drew her with a little spell. Anthropomorphic as she was, she stimulated him into appreciating things thus, and then they lived for her. She seemed to need things kindling in her imagination or in her soul before she felt she had them. And she was cut off from ordinary life by her religious intensity which made the world for her either a nunnery garden or a paradise, where sin and knowledge were not, or else an ugly, cruel thing.

So it was in this atmosphere of subtle intimacy, this meeting in their common feeling for something in Nature, that their love started.

Personally, he was a long time before he realized her. For ten months he had to stay at home after his illness. For a while he went to Skegness with his mother, and was perfectly happy. But even from the seaside he wrote long letters to Mrs Leivers about the shore and the sea. And he brought back his beloved sketches of the flat Lincoln coast, anxious for them to see. Almost they would interest the Leivers more than they interested his mother. It was not his art Mrs Morel cared about; it was himself and his achievement. But Mrs Leivers and her children were almost his disciples. They kindled him and made him glow to his work, whereas his mother's influence was to make him quietly determined, patient, dogged, unwearied.

He soon was friends with the boys, whose rudeness was only superficial. They had all, when they could trust themselves, a strange gentleness and lovableness.

'Will you come with me on to the fallow?' asked Edgar, rather hesitatingly. Paul went joyfully, and spent the afternoon helping to hoe or to single turnips with his friend. He used to lie with the three brothers in the hay piled up in the barn and tell them about Nottingham and about Jordan's. In return, they taught him to milk, and let him do little jobs—chopping hay or pulping turnips—just as much as he liked. At midsummer he worked all through hay-harvest with them, and then he loved them. The family was so cut off from the world actually. They seemed, somehow, like 'les derniers fils d'une race épuisée'. Though the lads were strong and healthy, yet they had all that over-sensitiveness and hanging-back which made them so lonely, yet also such close, delicate friends once their intimacy was won. Paul loved them dearly, and they him.

Miriam came later. But he had come into her life before she made any mark on his. One dull afternoon, when the men were on the land and the rest at school, only Miriam and her mother at home, the girl said to him, after having hesitated for some time:

'Have you seen the swing?'

'No,' he answered. 'Where?'

'In the cowshed,' she replied.

She always hesitated to offer or to show him anything. Men have such different standards of worth from women, and her dear things—the valuable things to her—her brothers had so often mocked or flouted.

'Come on, then,' he replied, jumping up.

There were two cowsheds, one on either side of the barn. In the lower, darker shed there was standing for four cows. Hens flew scolding over the manger-wall as the youth and girl went forward for the great thick rope which hung from the beam in the darkness overhead, and was pushed back over a peg in the wall.

'It's something like a rope!' he exclaimed appreciatively; and he sat down on it, anxious to try it. Then immediately he rose.

'Come on, then, and have first go,' he said to the girl.

'See,' she answered, going into the barn, 'we put some bags on the seat'; and she made the swing comfortable for him. That gave her pleasure. He held the rope.

'Come on, then' he said to her.

'No, I won't go first,' she answered.

She stood aside in her still, aloof fashion.

'Why?'

'You go,' she pleaded.

Almost for the first time in her life she had the pleasure of giving up to a man, of spoiling him. Paul looked at her.

'All right,' he said, sitting down. 'Mind out!'

He set off with a spring, and in a moment was flying through the air, almost out of the door of the shed, the upper half of which was open, showing outside the drizzling rain, the filthy yard, the cattle standing disconsolate against the black cart-shed, and at the back of all the grey-green wall of the wood. She stood below in her crimson tam-o'-shanter and watched. He looked down at her, and she saw his blue eyes sparkling.

'It's a treat of a swing,' he said.

'Yes.'

He was swinging through the air, every bit of him swinging, like a bird that swoops for joy of movement. And he looked down at her. Her crimson cap hung over her dark curls, her beautiful warm face, so still in a kind of brooding, was lifted towards him. It was dark and rather cold in the shed. Suddenly a swallow came down from the high roof and darted out of the door.

'I didn't know a bird was watching,' he called.

He swung negligently. She could feel him falling and lifting through the air, as if he were lying on some force.

'Now I'll die,' he said, in a detached, dreamy voice, as though he were the dying motion of the swing. She watched him, fascinated. Suddenly he put on the brake and jumped out.

'I've had a long turn,' he said. 'But it's a treat of a swing–it's a real treat of a swing!'

Miriam was amused that he took a swing so seriously and felt so warmly over it.

'No; you go on,' she said.

'Why, don't you want one?' he asked, astonished.

'Well, not much. I'll have just a little.'

She sat down, whilst he kept the bags in place for her.

'It's so ripping!' he said, setting her in motion. 'Keep your heels up, or they'll bang the manger-wall.'

She felt the accuracy with which he caught her, exactly at the right moment, and the exactly proportionate strength of his thrust, and she was afraid. Down to her bowels went the hot wave of fear. She was in his hands. Again, firm and inevitable came the thrust at the right moment. She gripped the rope, almost swooning.

'Ha!' she laughed in fear. 'No higher!'

'But you're not a *bit* high,' he remonstrated.

'But no higher.'

He heard the fear in her voice, and desisted. Her heart melted in hot pain when the moment came for him to thrust her forward again. But he left her alone. She began to breathe.

'Won't you really go any farther?' he asked. 'Should I keep you there?'

'No; let me go by myself,' she answered.

He moved aside and watched her.

'Why, you're scarcely moving,' he said.

She laughed slightly with shame, and in a moment got down.

'They say if you can swing you won't be sea-sick,' he said, as he mounted again. 'I don't believe I should ever be sea-sick.'

Away he went. There was something fascinating to her in him. For the moment he was nothing but a piece of swinging stuff; not a particle of him that did not swing. She could never lose herself, so, nor could her brothers. It roused a warmth in her. It were almost as if he were a flame that had lit a warmth in her whilst he swung in the middle air.

And gradually the intimacy with the family concentrated for Paul on three persons–the mother, Edgar, and Miriam. To the mother he went for that sympathy and that appeal which seemed to draw him out. Edgar was his very close friend. And to Miriam he more or less condescended, because she seemed so humble.

But the girl gradually sought him out. If he brought up his sketch-book, it was she who pondered longest over the last picture. Then she would look up at him. Suddenly, her dark eyes alight like water that shakes with a stream of gold in the dark, she would ask:

'Why do I like this so?'

Always something in her breast shrank from these close, intimate, dazzled looks of hers.

'Why *do* you?' he asked.

'I don't know. It seems so true.'

'It's because–it's because there is scarcely any shadow in it; it's more shimmery, as if I'd painted the shimmering protoplasm in the leaves and everywhere, and not the stiffness of the shape. That seems dead to me. Only this shimmeriness is the real living. The shape is a dead crust. The shimmer is inside really.'

And she, with her little finger in her mouth, would ponder these sayings. They gave her a feeling of life again, and vivified things which had meant nothing to her. She managed to find some meaning in his struggling, abstract speeches. And they were the medium through which she came distinctly at her beloved objects.

Another day she sat at sunset whilst he was painting some pine-trees which caught the red glare from the west. He had been quiet.

'There you are!' he said suddenly. 'I wanted that. Now, look at them and tell me, are they pine-trunks or are they red coals, standing-up pieces of fire in that darkness? There's God's burning bush for you, that burned not away.'

Miriam looked, and was frightened. But the pine-trunks were wonderful to her, and distinct. He packed his box and rose. Suddenly he looked at her.

'Why are you always sad?' he asked her.

'Sad!' she exclaimed, looking up at him with startled, wonderful brown eyes.

'Yes,' he replied. 'You are always, always sad.'

'I am not–oh, not a bit!' she cried.

'But even your joy is like a flame coming off of sadness,' he persisted. 'You're never jolly, or even just all right.'

'No,' she pondered. 'I wonder–why.'

'Because you're not; because you're different inside, like a pine-tree, and then you flare up; but you're not just like an ordinary tree, with fidgety leaves and jolly–'

He got tangled up in his own speech; but she brooded on it, and he had a strange, roused sensation, as if his feelings were new. She got so near him. It was a strange stimulant.

Then sometimes he hated her. Her youngest brother was only five. He was a frail lad, with immense brown eyes in his quaint fragile face–one of Reynolds's 'Choir of Angels', with a touch of elf. Often Miriam knelt to the child and drew him to her.

'Eh, my Hubert!' she sang, in a voice heavy and surcharged with love. 'Eh, my Hubert!'

And, folding him in her arms, she swayed slightly from side to side with love, her face half lifted, her eyes half closed, her voice drenched with love.

'Don't!' said the child, uneasy–'don't, Miriam!'

'Yes; you love me, don't you?' she murmured deep in her throat, almost as if she were in a trance, and swaying also as if she were swooned in an ecstasy of love.

'Don't!' repeated the child, a frown on his clear brow.

'You love me, don't you?' she murmured.

'What do you make such a *fuss* for?' cried Paul, all in suffering because of her extreme emotion. 'Why can't you be ordinary with him?'

She let the child go, and rose, and said nothing. Her intensity, which would leave no emotion on a normal plane, irritated the youth into a frenzy. And this fearful, naked contact of her on small occasions shocked him. He was used to his mother's reserve. And on such occasions he was thankful in his heart and soul that he had his mother, so sane and wholesome.

All the life of Miriam's body was in her eyes, which were usually dark as a dark church, but could flame with light like a conflagration. Her face scarcely even altered from its look of brooding. She might have been one of the women who went with Mary when Jesus was dead. Her body was not flexible and living. She walked with a swing, rather heavily, her head bowed forward, pondering. She was not clumsy, and yet none of her movements seemed quite *the* movement. Often, when wiping the dishes, she would stand in bewilderment and chagrin because she had pulled in two halves a cup or a tumbler. It was as if, in her fear and self-mistrust, she put too much strength into the effort. There was no looseness or abandon about her. Everything was gripped stiff with intensity, and her effort, overcharged, closed in on itself.

She rarely varied from her swinging, forward, intense walk. Occasionally she ran with Paul down the fields. Then her eyes blazed naked in a kind of ecstasy that frightened him. But she was physically afraid. If she were getting over a stile, she gripped his hands in a little hard anguish, and began to lose her presence of mind. And he could not persuade her to jump from even a small height. Her eyes dilated, became exposed and palpitating.

'No!' she cried, half laughing in terror—'no!'

'You shall!' he cried once, and jerking her forward, he brought her falling from the fence. But her wild 'Ah!' of pain, as if she were losing consciousness, cut him. She landed on her feet safely, and afterwards had courage in this respect.

She was very much dissatisfied with her lot.

'Don't you like being at home?' Paul asked her, surprised.

'Who would?' she answered, low and intense. 'What is it? I'm all day cleaning what the boys make just as bad in five minutes. I don't *want* to be at home.'

'What do you want, then?'

'I want to do something. I want a chance like anybody else. Why should I, because I'm a girl, be kept at home and not allowed to be anything? What chance *have* I?'

'Chance of what?'

'Of knowing anything—of learning, of doing anything. It's not fair, because I'm a woman.'

She seemed very bitter. Paul wondered. In his own home Annie was almost glad to be a girl. She had not so much responsibility; things were lighter for her. She never wanted to be other than a girl. But Miriam almost fiercely wished she were a man. And yet she hated men at the same time.

'But it's as well to be a woman as a man,' he said, frowning.

'Ha! Is it! Men have everything.'

'I should think women ought to be as glad to be women as men are to be men,' he answered.

'No!' she shook her head—'no! Everything the men have.'

'But what do you want?' he asked.

'I want to learn. Why *should* it be that I know nothing?'

'What! such as mathematics and French?'

'Why *shouldn't* I know mathematics? Yes!' she cried, her eye expanding in a kind of defiance.

'Well, you can learn as much as I know,' he said. 'I'll teach you, if you like.' Her eyes dilated. She mistrusted him as a teacher.

'Would you?' he asked.

Her head had dropped, and she was sucking her finger broodingly.

'Yes,' she said hesitatingly.

He used to tell his mother all these things.

'I'm going to teach Miriam algebra,' he said.

'Well,' replied Mrs Morel, 'I hope she'll get fat on it.'

When he went up to the farm on the Monday evening, it was drawing twilight. Miriam was just sweeping up the kitchen, and was kneeling at the hearth when he entered. Everyone was out but her. She looked round at him, flushed, her dark eyes shining, her fine hair falling about her face.

'Hello!' she said, soft and musical. 'I knew it was you.'

'How?'

'I knew your step. Nobody treads so quick and firm.'

He sat down, sighing.

'Ready to do some algebra?' he asked, drawing a little book from his pocket.

'But–'

He could feel her backing away.

'You said you wanted,' he insisted.

'To-night, though?' she faltered.

'But I came on purpose. And if you want to learn it, you must begin.'

She took up her ashes in the dustpan and looked at him, half tremulously, laughing.

'Yes, but to-night! You see, I haven't thought of it.'

'Well, my goodness! Take the ashes and come.'

He went and sat on the stone bench in the back-yard, where the big milk-cans were standing, tipped up, to air. The men were in the cowsheds. He could hear the little sing-song of the milk spurting into the pails. Presently she came, bringing some big greenish apples.

'You know you like them,' she said.

He took a bite.

'Sit down,' he said, with his mouth full.

She was short-sighted, and peering over his shoulder. It irritated him. He gave her the book quickly.

'Here,' he said. 'It's only letters for figures. You put down "a" instead of "2" or "6".'

They worked, he talking, she with her head down on the book. He was quick and hasty. She never answered. Occasionally, when he demanded of her, 'Do you see?' she looked up at him, her eyes wide with the half-laugh that comes of fear. 'Don't you?' he cried.

He had been too fast. But she said nothing. He questioned her more, then got hot. It made his blood rouse to see her there, as it were, at his mercy, her mouth open, her eyes dilated with laughter that was afraid, apologetic, ashamed. Then Edgar came along with two buckets of milk.

'Hello!' he said. 'What are you doing?'

'Algebra,' replied Paul.

'Algebra!' repeated Edgar curiously. Then he passed on with a laugh. Paul took a bite at his forgotten apple, looked at the miserable cabbages in the garden, pecked into lace by the fowls, and he wanted to pull them up. Then he glanced at Miriam. She was poring over the book, seemed absorbed in it, yet trembling lest she could not get at it. It made him cross. She was ruddy and beautiful. Yet her soul seemed to be intensely supplicating. The algebra-book she closed, shrinking, knowing he was angered; and at the same instant he grew gentle, seeing her hurt because she did not understand.

But things came slowly to her. And when she held herself in a grip, seemed so utterly humble before the lesson, it made his blood rouse. He stormed at her, got ashamed, continued the lesson, and grew furious again, abusing her. She listened in silence. Occasionally, very rarely, she defended herself. Her liquid dark eyes blazed at him.

'You don't give me time to learn it,' she said.

'All right,' he answered, throwing the book on the table and lighting a cigarette. Then, after a while, he went back to her repentant. So the lessons went. He was always either in a rage or very gentle.

'What do you tremble your *soul* before it for?' he cried. 'You don't learn algebra with your blessed soul. Can't you look at it with your clear simple wits?'

Often, when he went again into the kitchen, Mrs Leivers would look at him reproachfully, saying:

'Paul, don't be so hard on Miriam. She may not be quick, but I'm sure she tries.'

'I can't help it,' he said rather pitiably. 'I go off like it.'

'You don't mind me, Miriam, do you?' he asked of the girl later.

'No,' she reassured him in her beautiful deep tones—'no, I don't mind.'

'Don't mind me; it's my fault.'

But, in spite of himself, his blood began to boil with her. It was strange that no one else made him in such fury. He flared against her. Once he threw the pencil in her face. There was a silence. She turned her face slightly aside.

'I didn't—' he began, but got no further, feeling weak in all his bones. She never reproached him or was angry with him. He was often cruelly ashamed. But still again his anger burst like a bubble surcharged and still, when he saw her eager, silent, as it were, blind face, he felt he wanted to throw the pencil in it; and still, when he saw her hand trembling and her mouth parted with suffering, his heart was scalded with pain for her. And because of the intensity to which she roused him, he sought her.

Then he often avoided her and went with Edgar. Miriam and her brother were naturally antagonistic. Edgar was a rationalist, who was curious, and had a sort of scientific interest in life. It was a great bitterness to Miriam to see herself deserted by Paul for Edgar, who seemed so much lower. But the youth was very happy with her elder brother. The two men spent afternoons together on the land or in the loft doing carpentry, when it rained. And they talked together, or Paul taught Edgar the songs he himself had learned from Annie at the piano. And often all the men, Mr Leivers as well, had bitter debates on the nationalizing of the land and similar problems. Paul had already heard his mother's views, and as these were as yet his own, he argued for her. Miriam attended and took part, but was all the time waiting until it should be over and a personal communication might begin.

'After all,' she said within herself, 'if the land were nationalized, Edgar and Paul and I would be just the same.' So she waited for the youth to come back to her.

He was studying for his painting. He loved to sit at home, alone with his mother, at night, working and working. She sewed or read. Then, looking up from his task, he would rest his eyes for a moment on her face, that was bright with living warmth, and he returned gladly to his work.

'I can do my best things when you sit there in your rocking-chair, mother,' he said.

'I'm sure!' she exclaimed, sniffing with mock scepticism. But she felt it was so, and her heart quivered with brightness. For many hours she sat still, slightly conscious of him labouring away, whilst she worked or read her book. And he, with all his soul's intensity directing his pencil, could feel her warmth inside him like strength. They were both very happy so, and both unconscious of it. These times, that meant so much, and which were real living, they almost ignored.

He was conscious only when stimulated. A sketch finished, he always wanted to take it to Miriam. Then he was stimulated into knowledge of the work he had produced unconsciously. In contact with Miriam he gained insight; his vision went deeper. From his mother he drew the life-warmth, the strength to produce; Miriam urged this warmth into intensity like a white light.

When he returned to the factory the conditions of work were better. He had Wednesday afternoon off to go to the Art school—Miss Jordan's provision—returning in the evening. Then the factory closed at six instead of at eight on Thursday and Friday evenings.

One evening in the summer Miriam and he went over the fields by Herod's Farm on their way from the library home. So it was only three miles to Willey Farm. There was a yellow glow over the mowing-grass, and the sorrel-heads burned crimson. Gradually, as they walked along the high land, the gold in the west sank down to red, the red to crimson, and then the chill blue crept up against the glow.

They came out upon the high road to Alfreton, which ran white between the darkening fields. There Paul hesitated. It was two miles home for him, one mile forward for Miriam. They both looked up the road that ran in shadow right under the glow of the north-west sky. On the crest of the hill, Selby, with its stark houses and the up-pricked headstocks of the pit, stood in black silhouette small against the sky.

He looked at his watch.

'Nine o'clock!' he said.

The pair stood, loth to part, hugging their books.

'The wood is so lovely now,' she said. 'I wanted you to see it.'

He followed her slowly across the road to the white gate.

'They grumble so if I'm late,' he said.

'But you're not doing anything wrong,' she answered impatiently.

He followed her across the nibbled pasture in the dusk. There was a coolness in the wood, a scent of leaves, of honeysuckle, and a twilight. The two walked in silence. Night came wonderfully there, among the throng of dark-trunks. He looked round, expectant.

She wanted to show him a certain wild-rose bush she had discovered. She knew it was wonderful. And yet, till he had seen it, she felt it had not come into her soul. Only he could make it her own, immortal. She was dissatisfied.

Dew was already on the paths. In the old oak-wood a mist was rising, and he hesitated, wondering whether one whiteness were a strand of fog or only campion-flowers pallid in a cloud.

By the time they came to the pine-trees Miriam was getting very eager and very intense. Her bush might be gone. She might not be able to find it; and she wanted it so much. Almost passionately she wanted to be with him when he stood before the flowers. They were going to have a communion together–something that thrilled her, something holy. He was walking beside her in silence. They were very near to each other. She trembled, and he listened, vaguely anxious.

Coming to the edge of the wood, they saw the sky in front, like mother-of-pearl, and the earth growing dark. Somewhere on the outermost branches of the pine-wood the honeysuckle was streaming scent.

'Where?' he asked.

'Down the middle path,' she murmured, quivering.

When they turned the corner of the path she stood still. In the wide walk between the pines, gazing rather frightened, she could distinguish nothing for some moments; the greying light robbed things of their colour. Then she saw her bush.

'Ah!' she cried, hastening forward.

It was very still. The tree was tall and straggling. It had thrown its briers over a hawthorn-bush, and its long streamers trailed thick right down to the grass, splashing the darkness everywhere with great split stars, pure white. In bosses of ivory and in large splashed stars the roses gleamed on the darkness of foliage and stems and grass. Paul and Miriam stood close together, silent, and watched. Point after point the steady roses shone out of them, seeming to kindle something in their souls. The dusk came like smoke around, and still did not put out the roses.

Paul looked into Miriam's eyes. She was pale and expectant with wonder, her lips were parted, and her dark eyes lay open to him. His look seemed to travel down into her. Her soul quivered. It was the communion she wanted. He turned aside, as if pained. He turned to the bush.

'They seems as if they walk like butterflies, and shake themselves,' he said.

She looked at her roses. They were white, some incurved and holy, others expanded in an ecstasy. The tree was dark as a shadow. She lifted her hand impulsively to the flowers; she went forward and touched them in worship.

'Let us go,' he said.

There was a cool scent of ivory roses–a white, virgin scent. Something made him feel anxious and imprisoned. The two walked in silence.

'Till Sunday,' he said quietly, and left her; and she walked home slowly, feeling her soul satisfied with the holiness of the night. He stumbled down the path. And as soon as he was out of the wood, in the free open meadow, where he could breathe, he started to run as fast as he could. It was like a delicious delirium in his veins.

Always when he went with Miriam, and it grew rather late, he knew his mother was fretting and getting angry about him–why, he could not understand. As he went into the house, flinging down his cap, his mother looked up at the clock. She had been sitting thinking, because a chill to her eyes prevented her reading. She could feel Paul being drawn away by this girl. And she did not care for Miriam. 'She is one of those who will want to suck a man's soul out till he had none of his own left,' she said to herself; 'and he is just such a gaby as to let himself be absorbed. She will never let him become a man; she never will.' So, while he was away with Miriam, Mrs Morel grew more and more worked up.

She glanced at the clock, and said, coldly and rather tired: 'You have been far enough to-night.'

His soul, warm and exposed from contact with the girl, shrank.

'You must have been right home with her,' his mother continued.

He would not answer. Mrs Morel, looking at him quickly, saw his hair was damp on his forehead with haste, saw him frowning in his heavy fashion, resentfully.

'She must be wonderfully fascinating, that you can't get away from her, but must go trailing eight miles at this time of night.'

He was hurt between the past glamour with Miriam and the knowledge that his mother fretted. He had meant not to say anything, to refuse to answer. But he could not harden his heart or ignore his mother.

'I *do* like to talk to her,' he answered irritably.

'Is there nobody else to talk to?'

'You wouldn't say anything if I went with Edgar.'

'You know I should. You know, whoever you went with, I should say it was too far for you to go trailing, late at night, when you've been to Nottingham. Besides'–her voice suddenly flashed into anger and contempt–'it is disgusting–bits of lads and girls courting.'

'It is *not* courting,' he cried.

'I don't know what else you call it.'

'It's not! Do you think we *spoon* and do? We only talk.'

'Till goodness knows what time and distance,' was the sarcastic rejoinder.

Paul snapped at the laces of his boots angrily.

'What are you so mad about?' he asked. 'Because you don't like her.'

'I don't say I don't like her. But I don't hold with children keeping company, and never did.'

'But you don't mind our Annie going out with Jim Inger.'

'They've more sense than you two.'

'Why?'

'Our Annie's not one of the deep sort.'

He failed to see the meaning of this remark. But his mother looked tired. She was never so strong after William's death; and her eyes hurt her.

'Well,' he said, 'it's so pretty in the country. Mr Sleath asked about you. He said he'd missed you. Are you a bit better?'

'I ought to have been in bed a long time ago,' she replied.

'Why, mother, you know you wouldn't have gone before quarter-past ten.'

'Oh yes, I should!'

'Oh, little woman, you'd say anything now you're disagreeable with me, wouldn't you?'

He kissed her forehead that he knew so well: the deep marks between the brows, the rising of the fine hair, greying now, and the proud setting of the temples. His hand lingered on her shoulder after his kiss. Then he went slowly to bed. He had forgotten Miriam; he only saw how his mother's hair was lifted back from her warm, broad brow. And somehow, she was hurt.

Then the next time he saw Miriam he said to her:

'Don't let me be late to-night–not later than ten o'clock. My mother gets so upset.'

Miriam dropped her head, brooding.

'Why does she get upset?' she asked.

'Because she says I oughtn't to be out late when I have to get up early.'

'Very well!' said Miriam, rather quietly, with just a touch of a sneer. He resented that. And he was usually late again.

That there was any love growing between him and Miriam neither of them would have acknowledged. He thought he was too sane for such sentimentality, and she thought herself too lofty. They both were late in coming to maturity, and psychical ripeness was much behind even the physical. Miriam was exceedingly sensitive, as her mother had always been. The slightest grossness made her recoil almost in anguish. Her brothers were brutal, but never coarse in speech. The men did all the discussing of farm matters outside. But, perhaps, because of the continual business of birth and of begetting which goes on upon every farm, Miriam was the more hypersensitive to the matter, and her blood was chastened almost to disgust of the faintest suggestion of such intercourse. Paul took his pitch from her, and their intimacy went on in an utterly blanched and chaste fashion. It could never be mentioned that the mare was in foal.

When he was nineteen, he was earning only twenty shillings a week, but he was happy. His painting went well, and life went well enough. On the Good Friday he organized a walk to the Hemlock Stone. There were three lads of his own age, then Annie and Arthur, Miriam and Geoffrey. Arthur, apprenticed as an electrician in Nottingham, was home for the holiday. Morel, as usual, was up early, whistling and sawing in the yard. At seven o'clock the family heard him buy threepennyworth of hot-cross buns, he talked with gusto to the little girl who brought them, calling her 'my darling'. He turned away several boys who came with more buns, telling them they had been 'kested' by a little lass. Then Mrs Morel got up, and the family straggled down. It was an immense luxury to everybody, this lying in bed just beyond the ordinary time on a weekday. And Paul and Arthur read before breakfast, and had the meal unwashed, sitting in their shirtsleeves. This was another holiday luxury. The room was warm. Everything felt free of care and anxiety. There was a sense of plenty in the house.

While the boys were reading, Mrs Morel went into the garden. They were now in another house, an old one, near the Scargill Street home, which had been left soon after William had died. Directly came an excited cry from the garden:

'Paul, Paul! come and look!'

It was his mother's voice. He threw down his book and went out. There was a long garden that ran to a field. It was a grey, cold day, with a sharp wind blowing out of Derbyshire. Two fields away Bestwood began, with a jumble of roofs and red house-ends, out of which rose the church tower and the spire of the Congregational Chapel. And beyond went woods and hills, right away to the pale grey heights of the Pennine Chain. Paul looked down the garden for his mother. Her head appeared among the young currant-bushes.

'Come here!' she cried.

'What for?' he answered.

'Come and see.'

She had been looking at the buds on the currant-trees. Paul went up.

'To think,' she said, 'that here I might never have seen them!'

Her son went to her side. Under the fence, in a little bed, was a ravel of poor grassy leaves, such as come from very immature bulbs, and three scyllas in bloom. Mrs Morel pointed to the deep blue flowers.

'Now, just see those!' she exclaimed. 'I was looking at the currant-bushes, when, thinks I to myself, "There's something very blue; is it a bit of sugar-bag?" and there, behold you! Sugar-bag! Three glories of the snow, and *such* beauties! But where on earth did they come from?'

'I don't know,' said Paul.

'Well, that's a marvel, now! I *thought* I knew every weed and blade in this garden. But *haven't* they done well? You see, that gooseberry-bush just shelters them. Not nipped, not touched!'

He crouched down and turned up the bells of the little blue flowers.

They're a glorious colour!' he said.

'Aren't they!' she cried. 'I guess they come from Switzerland, where they say they have such lovely things. Fancy them against the snow! But where have they come from? They can't have *blown* here, can they?'

Then he remembered having set here a lot of little trash of bulbs to mature.

'And you never told me,' she said.

'No; I thought I'd leave it till they might flower.'

'And now, you see! I might have missed them. And I've never had a glory of the snow in my garden in my life.'

She was full of excitement and elation. The garden was an endless joy to her. Paul was thankful for her sake at last to be in a house with a long garden that went down to a field. Every morning after breakfast she went out and was happy pottering about in it. And it was true, she knew every weed and blade.

Everybody turned up for the walk. Food was packed, and they set off, a merry, delighted party. They hung over the wall of the mill-race, dropped paper in the water on one side of the tunnel and watched it shoot out on the other. They stood on the footbridge over Boathouse Station and looked at the metals gleaming coldly.

'You should see the Flying Scotchman come through at half-past six!' said Leonard, whose father was a signalman. 'Lad, but she doesn't half buzz!' and the little party looked up the lines one way, to London, and the other way, to Scotland, and they felt the touch of these two magical places.

In Ilkeston the colliers were waiting in gangs for the public-houses to open. It was a town of idleness and lounging. At Stanton Gate the iron foundry blazed. Over everything there was great discussions. At Trowell they crossed again from Derbyshire into Nottinghamshire. They came to the Hemlock Stone at dinner-time. Its field was crowded with folk from Nottingham and Ilkeston.

They had expected a venerable and dignified monument. They found a little, gnarled, twisted stump of rock, something like a decayed mushroom, standing out pathetically on the side of a field. Leonard and Dick immediately proceeded to carve their initials, 'L.W.' and 'R.P.', in the old red sandstone; but Paul desisted, because he had read in the newspaper satirical remarks about initial-carvers, who could find no other road to immortality. Then all the lads climbed to the top of the rock to look round.

Everywhere in the field below, factory girls and lads were eating lunch or sporting about. Beyond was the garden of an old manor. It had yew-hedges and thick clumps and borders of yellow crocuses round the lawn.

'See,' said Paul to Miriam, 'what a quiet garden!'

She saw the dark yews and the golden crocuses, then she looked at him gratefully. He had not seemed to belong to her among all these others; he was different then—not her Paul, who understood the slightest quiver of her innermost soul, but something else speaking another language than hers. How it hurt her, and deadened her very perceptions. Only when he came right back to her, leaving his other, his lesser self, as she thought, would she feel alive again. And now he asked her to look at this garden, wanting the contact with her again. Impatient of the set in the field, she turned to the quiet lawn, surrounded by sheaves of shut-up crocuses. A feeling of stillness, almost of ecstasy, came over her. It felt almost as if she were alone with him in this garden.

Then he left her again and joined the others. Soon they started home. Miriam loitered behind, alone. She did not fit in with the others; she could very rarely get into human relations with anyone: so her friend, her companion, her lover, was Nature. She saw the sun declining wanly. In the dusky, cold hedgerows were some red leaves. She lingered to gather them, tenderly, passionately. The love in her finger-tips caressed the leaves; the passion in her heart came to a glow upon the leaves.

Suddenly she realized she was alone in a strange road, and she hurried forward. Turning a corner in the lane, she came upon Paul, who stood bent over something, his mind fixed on it, working away steadily, patiently, a little hopelessly. She hesitated in her approach, to watch.

He remained concentrated in the middle of the road. Beyond, one rift of rich gold in that colourless grey evening seemed to make him stand out in dark relief. She saw him, slender and firm, as if the setting sun had given him to her. A deep pain took hold of her, and she knew she must love him. And she had discovered him, discovered in him a rare potentiality, discovered his loneliness. Quivering as at some 'annunciation', she went slowly forward.

At last he looked up.

'Why,' he exclaimed gratefully, 'have you waited for me!'

She saw a deep shadow in his eyes.

'What is it?' she asked.

'The spring broken here'; and he showed her where his umbrella was injured.

Instantly, with some shame, she knew he had not done the damage himself, but that Geoffrey was responsible.

'It is only an old umbrella isn't it?' she asked.

She wondered why he, who did not usually trouble over trifles, made such a mountain of this molehill.

'But it was William's, an' my mother can't help but know,' he said quietly, still patiently working the umbrella.

The words went through Miriam like a blade. This, then, was the confirmation of her vision of him! She looked at him. But there was about him a certain reserve, and she dared not comfort him, not even speak softly to him.

'Come on,' he said. 'I can't do it'; and they went in silence along the road.

That same evening they were walking along under the trees by Nether Green. He was talking to her fretfully, seemed to be struggling to convince himself.

'You know,' he said, with an effort, 'if one person loves, the other does.'

'Ah!' she answered. 'Like mother said to me when I was little, "Love begets love."'

'Yes, something like that, I think it *must* be.'

'I hope so, because if it were not, love might be a very terrible thing,' she said.

'Yes, but it *is*—at least with most people,' he answered.

And Miriam, thinking he had assured himself, felt strong in herself. She always regarded that sudden coming upon him in the lane as a revelation. And this conversation remained graven in her mind as one of the letters of the law. Now she stood with him and for him. When, about this time, he outraged the family feeling at Willey Farm by some overbearing insult, she stuck to him, and believed he was right. And at this time she dreamed dreams of him, vivid, unforgettable. These dreams came again later on, developed to a more subtle psychological stage.

On the Easter Monday the same party took an excursion to Wingfield Manor. It was great excitement to Miriam to catch a train at Sethley Bridge, amid all the bustle of the Bank Holiday crowd. They left the train at Alfreton. Paul was interested in the street and in the colliers with their dogs. Here was a new race of miners. Miriam did not live till they came to the church. They were all rather timid of entering, with their bags of food, for fear of being turned out. Leonard, a comic, thin fellow, went first; Paul, who would have died rather than be sent back, went last. The place was decorated for Easter. In the font hundreds of white narcissi seemed to be growing. The air was dim and coloured from the windows, and thrilled with a subtle scent of lilies and narcissi. In that atmosphere Miriam's soul came into a glow. Paul was afraid of the things he mustn't do; and he was sensitive to the feel of the place. Miriam turned to him. He answered. They were together. He would not go beyond the Communion-rail. She loved him for that. Her soul expanded into prayer beside him. He felt the strange fascination of shadowy religious places. All his latent mysticism quivered into life. She was drawn to him. He was a prayer along with her.

Miriam very rarely talked to the other lads. They at once became awkward in conversation with her. So usually she was silent.

It was past midday when they climbed the steep path to the manor. All things shone softly in the sun, which was wonderfully warm and enlivening. Celandines and violets were out. Everybody was tip-top full with happiness. The glitter of the ivy, the soft, atmospheric grey of the castle walls, the gentleness of everything near the ruin, was perfect.

The manor is of hard, pale grey stone, and the outer walls are blank and calm. The younger folk were in raptures. They went in trepidation, almost afraid that the delight of exploring this ruin might be denied them. In the first courtyard, within the high broken walls, were farm-carts, with their shafts lying idle on the ground, the tyres of the wheels brilliant with gold-red rust. It was very still.

All eagerly paid their sixpences, and went timidly through the fine clean arch of the inner courtyard. They were shy. Here on the pavement, where the hall had been, an old thorn-tree was budding. All kinds of strange openings and broken rooms were in the shadow around them.

After lunch they set off once more to explore the ruin. This time the girls went with the boys, who could act as guides and expositors. There was one tall tower in a corner, rather tottering, where they say Mary Queen of Scots was imprisoned.

'Think of the Queen going up here!' said Miriam in a low voice, as she climbed the hollow stairs.

'If she could get up,' said Paul, 'for she had rheumatism like anything. I reckon they treated her rottenly.'

'You don't think she deserved it?' asked Miriam.

'No, I don't. She was only lively.'

They continued to mount the winding staircase. A high wind, blowing through the loopholes, went rushing up the shaft, and filled the girl's skirts like a balloon, so that she was ashamed, until he took the hem of her dress and held it down for her. He did it perfectly simply, as he would have picked up her glove. She remembered this always.

Round the broken top of the tower the ivy bushed out, old and handsome. Also, there were a few chill gillivers, in pale cold bud. Miriam wanted to lean over for some ivy, but he would not let her. Instead, she had to wait behind him, and take from him each spray as he gathered it and held it to her, each one separately, in the purest manner of chivalry. The tower seemed to rock in the wind. They looked over miles and miles of wooded country, and country with gleams of pasture.

The crypt underneath the manor was beautiful, and in perfect preservation. Paul made a drawing: Miriam stayed with him. She was thinking of Mary Queen of Scots looking with her strained, hopeless eyes, that could not understand misery, over the hills whence no help came, or sitting in this crypt, being told of a God as cold as the place she sat in.

They set off again gaily, looking round on their beloved manor that stood so clean and big on its hill.

'Supposing you could have *that* farm,' said Paul to Miriam.

'Yes!'

'Wouldn't it be lovely to come and see you!'

They were now in the bare country of stone walls, which he loved, and which, though only ten miles from home, seemed so foreign to Miriam. The party was straggling. As they were crossing a large meadow that sloped away from the sun, along a path embedded with innumerable tiny glittering points, Paul, walking alongside, laced his fingers in the strings of the bag Miriam was carrying, and instantly she felt Annie behind, watchful and jealous. But the meadow was bathed in a glory of sunshine, and the path was jewelled, and it was seldom that he gave her any sign. She held her fingers very still among the strings of the bag, his fingers touching; and the place was golden as a vision.

At last they came into the straggling grey village of Crich, that lies high. Beyond the village was the famous Crich Stand that Paul could see from the garden at home. The party pushed on. Great expanse of country spread around and below. The lads were eager to get to the top of the hill. It was capped by a round knoll, half of which was by now cut away, and on the top of which stood an ancient monument, sturdy and squat, for signalling in old days far down into the level lands of Nottinghamshire and Leicestershire.

It was blowing so hard, high up there in the exposed place, that the only way to be safe was to stand nailed by the wind to the wall of the tower. At their feet fell the precipice where the limestone was quarried away. Below was a jumble of hills and tiny villages—Matlock, Ambergate, Stoney Middleton. The lads were eager to spy out the church of Bestwood, far away among the rather crowded country on the left. They were disgusted that it seemed to stand on a plane. They saw the hills of Derbyshire fall into the monotony of the Midlands that swept away South.

Miriam was somewhat scared by the wind, but the lads enjoyed it. They went on, miles and miles, to Whatstandwell. All the food was eaten, everybody was hungry, and there was very little money to get home with. But they managed to procure a loaf and a currant-loaf, which they hacked into pieces with shut-knives, and ate sitting on the wall near the bridge, watching the bright Derwent rushing by, and the brakes from Matlock pulling up at the inn.

Paul was now pale with weariness. He had been responsible for the party all day, and now he was done. Miriam understood, and kept close to him, and he left himself in her hands.

They had an hour to wait at Ambergate Station. Trains came, crowded with excursionists returning to Manchester, Birmingham and London.

'We might be going there—folk easily might think we're going that far,' said Paul.

They got back rather late. Miriam, walking home with Geoffrey, watched the moon rise big and red and misty. She felt something was fulfilled in her.

She had an elder sister, Agatha, who was a school-teacher. Between the two girls was a feud. Miriam considered Agatha worldly. And she wanted herself to be a school-teacher.

One Saturday afternoon Agatha and Miriam were upstairs dressing. Their bedroom was over the stable. It was a low room, not very large, and bare. Miriam had nailed on the wall a reproduction of Veronese's 'St Catherine'. She loved the woman who sat in the window, dreaming. Her own windows were too small to sit in. But the front one was dripped over with honeysuckle and virginia creeper, and looked upon the tree-tops of the oak-wood across the yard, while the little back window, no bigger than a handkerchief, was a loophole to the east, to the dawn beating up against the beloved round hills.

The two sisters did not talk much to each other. Agatha, who was fair and small and determined, had rebelled against the home atmosphere, against the doctrine of 'the other cheek'. She was out in the world now, in a fair way to be independent. And she insisted on worldly values, on appearance, on manners, on position, which Miriam would fain have ignored.

Both girls liked to be upstairs, out of the way, when Paul came. They preferred to come running down, open the stair-foot door, and see him watching, expectant of them. Miriam stood painfully pulling over her head a rosary he had given her. It caught in the fine mesh of her hair. But at last she had it on, and the red-brown wooden beads looked well against her cool brown neck. She was a well-developed girl, and very handsome. But in the little looking-glass nailed against the whitewashed wall she could only see a fragment of herself at a time. Agatha had bought a little mirror of her own which she propped up to suit herself. Miriam was near the window. Suddenly she heard the well-known click of the chain, and she saw Paul fling open the gate, push his bicycle into the yard. She saw him look at the house, and she shrank away. He walked in a nonchalant fashion, and his bicycle went with him as if it were a live thing.

'Paul's come!' she exlaimed.

'Aren't you glad?' said Agatha cuttingly.

Miriam stood still in amazement and bewilderment.

'Well, aren't you?' she asked.

'Yes, but I'm not going to let him see it, and think I wanted him.'

Miriam was startled. She heard him putting his bicycle in the stable underneath, and talking to Jimmy, who had been a pit-horse and who was seedy.

'Well, Jimmy my lad, how are ter? Nobbut sick an' sadly, like? Why, then, it's a shame, my owd lad.'

She heard the rope run through the hole as the horse lifted its head from the lad's caress. How she loved to listen when he thought only the horse could hear. But there was a serpent in her Eden. She searched earnestly in herself to see if she wanted Paul Morel. She felt there would be some disgrace in it. Full of twisted feeling, she was afraid she did want him. She stood self-convicted. Then came an agony of new shame. She shrank within herself in a coil of torture. Did she want Paul Morel, and did he know she wanted him? What a subtle infamy upon her! She felt as if her whole soul coiled into knots of shame.

Agatha was dressed first, and ran downstairs. Miriam heard her greet the lad gaily, knew exactly how brilliant her grey eyes became with that tone. She herself would have felt it bold to have greeted him in such wise. Yet there she stood under the self-accusation of wanting him, tied to that stake of torture. In bitter perplexity she kneeled down and prayed:

'O Lord, let me not love Paul Morel. Keep me from loving him, if I ought not to love him.'

Something anomalous in the prayer arrested her. She lifted her head and pondered. How could it be wrong to love him? Love was God's gift. And yet it caused her shame. That was because of him, Paul Morel. But, then, it was not his affair, it was her own, between herself and God. She was to be a sacrifice. But it was God's sacrifice, not Paul Morel's or her own. After a few minutes she hid her face in the pillow again, and said:

'But, Lord, if it is Thy will that I should love him, make me love him—as Christ would, who died for the souls of men. Make me love him splendidly, because he is Thy son.'

She remained kneeling for some time, quite still, and deeply moved, her black hair against the red squares and the lavender-sprigged squares of the patchwork-quilt. Prayer was almost essential to her. Then she fell into that rapture of self-sacrifice, identifying herself with a God who was sacrificed, which gives to so many human souls their deepest bliss.

When she went downstairs Paul was lying back in an armchair, holding forth with much vehemence to Agatha, who was scorning a little painting he had brought to show her. Miriam glanced at the two, and avoided their levity. She went into the parlour to be alone.

It was tea-time before she was able to speak to Paul, and then her manner was so distant he thought he had offended her.

Miriam discontinued her practice of going each Thursday evening to the library in Bestwood. After calling for Paul regularly during the whole spring, a number of trifling incidents and tiny insults from his family awakened her to their attitude towards her, and she decided to go no more. So she announced to Paul one evening she would not call at his house again for him on Thursday nights.

'Why? he asked, very short.

'Nothing. Only I'd rather not.'

'Very well.'

'But,' she faltered, 'if you'd care to meet me, we could still go together.'

'Meet you where?'

'Somewhere—where you like.'

'I shan't meet you anywhere. I don't see why you shouldn't keep calling for me. But if you won't, I don't want to meet you.'

So the Thursday evenings which had been so precious to her, and to him, were dropped. He worked instead. Mrs Morel sniffed with satisfaction at this arrangement.

He would not have it that they were lovers. The intimacy between them had been kept so abstract, such a matter of the soul, all thought and weary struggle into consciousness, that he saw it only as a platonic friendship. He stoutly denied there was anything else between them. Miriam was silent, or else she very quietly agreed. He was a fool who did not know what was happening to himself; by tacit agreement they ignored the remarks and insinuations of their acquaintances.

'We aren't lovers, we are friends,' he said to her. '*We* know it. Let them talk. What does it matter what they say?'

Sometimes, as they were walking together, she slipped her arm timidly into his. But he always resented it, and she knew it. It caused a violent conflict in him. With Miriam he was always on the high plane of abstraction, when his natural fire of love was transmitted into the fine stream of thought. She would have it so. If he were jolly and, as she put it, flippant, she waited till he came back to her, till the change had taken place in him again, and he was wrestling with his own soul, frowning, passionate in his desire for understanding. And in this passion for understanding her soul lay close to his; she had him all to herself. But he must be made abstract first.

Then, if she put her arm in his, it caused him almost torture. His consciousness seemed to split. The place where she was touching him ran hot with friction. He was one internecine battle, and he became cruel to her because of it.

One evening in midsummer Miriam called at the house, warm from climbing. Paul was alone in the kitchen; his mother could be heard moving about upstairs.

'Come and look at the sweet-peas,' he said to the girl.

They went into the garden. The sky behind the townlet and the church was orange-red; the flower-garden was flooded with a strange warm light that lifted every leaf into significance. Paul passed along a fine row of sweet-peas, gathering a blossom here and there, all cream and pale blue. Miriam followed, breathing the fragrance. To her, flowers appeared with such strength she felt she must make them part of herself. When she bent and breathed a flower, it was as if she and the flower were loving each other. Paul hated her for it. There seemed a sort of exposure about the action, something too intimate.

When he had got a fair bunch, they returned to the house. He listened for a moment to his mother's quiet movements upstairs, then he said:

'Come here, and let me pin them in for you.' He arranged them two or three at a time in the bosom of her dress, stepping back now and then to see the effect. 'You know,' he said, taking the pin out of his mouth, 'a woman ought always to arrange her flowers before her glass.'

Miriam laughed. She thought flowers ought to be pinned in one's dress without any care. That Paul should take pains to fix her flowers for her was his whim.

He was rather offended at her laughter.

'Some women do—those who look decent,' he said.

Miriam laughed again, but mirthlessly, to hear him thus mix her up with women in a general way. From most men she would have ignored it. But from him it hurt her.

He had nearly finished arranging the flowers when he heard his mother's footsteps on the stairs. Hurriedly he pushed in the last pin and turned away.

'Don't let mater know,' he said.

Miriam picked up her books and stood in the doorway looking with chagrin at the beautiful sunset. She would call for Paul no more, she said.

'Good evening, Mrs Morel,' she said, in a deferential way. She sounded as if she had no right to be there.

'Oh, is it you, Miriam?' replied Mrs Morel coolly.

But Paul insisted on everybody's accepting his friendship with the girl, and Mrs Morel was too wise to have any open rupture.

It was not till he was twenty years old that the family could ever afford to go away for a holiday. Mrs Morel had never been away for a holiday, except to see her sister, since she had been married. Now at last Paul had saved enough money, and they were all going. There was to be a party: some of Annie's friends, one friend of Paul's, a young man in the same office where William had previously been, and Miriam.

It was great excitement writing for rooms. Paul and his mother debated it endlessly between them. They wanted a furnished cottage for two weeks. She thought one week would be enough, but he insisted on two.

At last they got an answer from Mablethorpe, a cottage such as they wished for thirty shillings a week. There was immense jubilation. Paul was wild with joy for his mother's sake. She would have a real holiday now. He and she sat at evening picturing what it would be like. Annie came in, and Leonard, and Alice, and Kitty. There was wild rejoicing and anticipation. Paul told Miriam. She seemed to brood with joy over it. But the Morel's house rang with excitement.

They were to go on Saturday morning by the seven train. Paul suggested that Miriam should sleep at his house, because it was so far for her to walk. She came down for supper. Everybody was so excited that even Miriam was accepted with warmth. But almost as soon as she entered the feeling in the family became close and tight. He had discovered a poem by Jean Ingelow which mentioned Mablethorpe, and so he must read it to Miriam. He would never have got so far in the direction of sentimentality as to read poetry to his own family. But now they condescended to listen. Miriam sat on the sofa absorbed in him. She always seemed absorbed in him, and by him, when he was present. Mrs Morel sat jealously on her own chair. She was going to hear also. And even Annie, and the father attended, Morel with his head cocked on one side like somebody listening to a sermon and feeling conscious of the fact. Paul ducked his head over the book. He had got now all the audience he cared for. And Mrs Morel and Annie almost contested with Miriam who should listen best and win his favour. He was in very high feather.

'But,' interrupted Mrs Morel, 'what *is* the "Bride of Enderby" that the bells are supposed to ring?'

'It's an old tune they used to play on the fells for a warning against water. I suppose the Bride of Enderby was drowned in a flood,' he replied. He had not the faintest knowledge what it really was, but he would never have sunk so low as to confess that to his womenfolk. They listened and believed him. He believed himself.

'And the people knew what that tune meant?' said his mother.

'Yes, just like the Scotch when they heard "The Flowers o' the Forest"—and when they used to ring the bells backward for alarm.'

'How?' said Annie. 'A bell sounds the same whether it's rung backwards or forwards.'

But,' he said, 'if you start with the deep bell and ring up to the high one—der—der—der—der—der—der—der—der!'

He ran up the scale. Everybody thought it clever. He thought so too. Then, waiting a minute, he continued the poem.

'H'm!' said Mrs Morel curiously, when he finished. 'But I wish everything that's written weren't so sad.'

'*I* canna see what they want drownin' theirselves for,' said Morel.

There was a pause. Annie got up to clear the table. Miriam rose to help with the pots.

'Let *me* help to wash up,' she said.

'Certainly not,' cried Annie. 'You sit down again. There aren't many.'

And Miriam, who could not be familiar and insist, sat down again to look at the book with Paul.

He was master of the party; his father was no good. And great tortures he suffered lest the tin box should be put out at Firsby instead of at Mablethorpe. And he wasn't equal to getting a carriage. His bold little mother did that.

'Here!' she cried to a man. 'Here!'

Paul and Annie got behind the rest, convulsed with shamed laughter.

'How much will it be to drive to Brook Cottage?' said Mrs Morel.

'Two shillings.'

'Why, how far is it?'

'A good way.'

'I don't believe it,' she said.

But she scrambled in. There were eight crowded in one old seaside carriage.

'You see,' said Mrs Morel, 'it's only threepence each, and if it were a tram car—'

They drove along. Each cottage they came to, Mrs Morel cried:

'Is it this? Now, this is it!'

Everybody sat breathless. They drove past. There was a universal sigh.

'I'm thankful it wasn't that brute,' said Mrs Morel. 'I *was* frightened.' They drove on and on.

At last they descended at a house that stood alone over the dyke by the highroad. There was wild excitement because they had to cross a little bridge to get into the front garden. But they loved the house that lay so solitary, with a sea-meadow on one side, and immense expanse of land patched in white barley, yellow oats, red wheat, and green root-crops, flat and stretching level to the sky.

Paul kept accounts. He and his mother ran the show. The total expenses—lodging, food, everything—was sixteen shillings a week per person. He and Leonard went bathing in the morning. Morel was wandering abroad quite early.

'You, Paul,' his mother called from the bedroom, 'eat a piece of bread-and-butter.'

'All right,' he answered.

And when he got back he saw his mother presiding in state at the breakfast-table. The woman of the house was young. Her husband was blind, and she did laundry work. So Mrs Morel always washed the pots in the kitchen and made the beds.

'But you said you'd have a real holiday,' said Paul, 'and now you work.'

'Work!' she exclaimed. 'What are you talking about!'

He loved to go with her across the fields to the village and the sea. She was afraid of the plank bridges, and he abused her for being a baby. On the whole he stuck to her as if he were *her* man.

Miriam did not get much of him, except, perhaps, when all the others went to the 'Coons'. Coons were insufferably stupid to Miriam, so he thought they were to himself also, and he preached priggishly to Annie about the fatuity of listening to them. Yet he, too, knew all their songs, and sang them along the roads roisterously. And if he found himself listening, the stupidity pleased him very much. Yet to Annie he said:

'Such rot! there isn't a grain of intelligence in it. Nobody with more gumption than a grasshopper could go and sit and listen.' And to Miriam he said, with much scorn of Annie and the others: 'I suppose they're at the "Coons".'

It was queer to see Miriam singing coon songs. She had a straight chin that went in a perpendicular line from the lower lip to the turn. She always reminded Paul of some sad Botticelli angel when she sang, even when it was:

> 'Come down lover's lane
> For a walk with me, talk with me.'

Only when he sketched, or at evening when the others were at the 'Coons', she had him to herself. He talked to her endlessly about his love of horizontals: how they, the great levels of sky and land in Lincolnshire, meant to him the eternality of the will, just as the bowed Norman arches of the church, repeating themselves, meant the dogged leaping forward of the persistent human soul, on and on, nobody knows where; in contradiction to the perpendicular lines and to the Gothic arch, which, he said, leapt up at heaven and touched the ecstasy and lost itself in the divine. Himself, he said, was Norman, Miriam was Gothic. She bowed in consent even to that.

One evening he and she went up the great sweeping shore of sand towards Theddlethorpe. The long breakers plunged and ran in a hiss of foam along the coast. It was a warm evening. There was not a figure but themselves on the far reaches of sand, no noise but the sound of the sea. Paul loved to see it clanging at the land. He loved to feel himself between the noise of it and the silence of the sandy shore. Miriam was with him. Everything grew very intense. It was quite dark when they turned again. The way home was through a gap in the sandhills, and then along a raised grass road between two dykes. The country was black and still. From behind the sandhills came the whisper of the sea. Paul and Miriam walked in silence. Suddenly he started. The whole of his blood seemed to burst into flame, and he could scarcely breathe. An enormous orange moon was staring at them from the rim of the sandhills. He stood still, looking at it.

'Ah!' cried Miriam, when she saw it.

He remained perfectly still, staring at the immense and ruddy moon, the only thing in the far-reaching darkness of the level. His heart beat heavily, the muscles of his arms contracted.

'What is it?' murmured Miriam, waiting for him.

He turned and looked at her. She stood beside him, for ever in shadow. Her face, covered with the darkness of her hat, was watching him unseen. But she was brooding. She was slightly afraid–deeply moved and religious. That was her best state. He was impotent against it. His blood was concentrated like a flame in his chest. But he could not get across to her. There were flashes in his blood. But somehow she ignored them. She was expecting some religious state in him. Still yearning she was half aware of his passion, and gazed at him, troubled.

'What is it?' she murmured again.

'It's the moon,' he answered, frowning.

'Yes,' she assented. 'Isn't it wonderful?' She was curious about him. The crisis was past.

He did not know himself what was the matter. He was naturally so young, and their intimacy was so abstract, he did not know he wanted to crush her to on his breast to ease the ache there. He was afraid of her. The fact that he might want her as a man wants a woman had in him been suppressed into a shame. When she shrank in her convulsed, coiled torture from the thought of such a thing, he had winced to the depths of his soul. And now this 'purity' prevented even their first love-kiss. It was as if she could scarcely stand the shock of physical love, even a passionate kiss, and then he was too shrinking and sensitive to give it.

As they walked along the dark fen-meadow he watched the moon and did not speak. She plodded beside him. He hated her, for she seemed in some way to make him despise himself. Looking ahead – he saw the one light in the darkness, the window of their lamp-lit cottage.

He loved to think of his mother, and the other jolly people.

'Well, everybody else has been in long ago!' said his mother as they entered.

'What does that matter!' he cried irritably. 'I can go a walk if I like, can't I?'

'And I should have thought you could get in to supper with the rest,' said Mrs Morel.

'I shall please myself,' he retorted. 'It's not *late*. I shall do as I like.'

'Very well,' said his mother cuttingly, 'then *do* as you like.'

And she took no further notice of him that evening. Which he pretended neither to notice nor to care about, but sat reading. Miriam read also, obliterating herself. Mrs Morel hated her for making her son like this. She watched Paul growing irritable, priggish, and melancholic. For this she put the blame on Miriam. Annie and all her friends joined against the girl. Miriam had no friend of her own, only Paul. But she did not suffer so much, because she despised the triviality of these other people.

And Paul hated her because, somehow, she spoilt his ease and naturalness. And he writhed himself with a feeling of humiliation.

8

STRIFE IN LOVE

Arthur finished his apprenticeship, and got a job on the electrical plant at Minton Pit. He earned very little, but had a good chance of getting on. But he was wild and restless. He did not drink nor gamble. Yet he somehow contrived to get into endless scrapes, always through some hot-headed thoughtlessness. Either he went rabbiting in the woods, like a poacher, or he stayed in Nottingham all night instead of coming home, or he miscalculated his dive into the canal at Bestwood, and scored his chest into one mass of wounds on the raw stones and tins at the bottom.

He had not been at his work many months when again he did not come home one night.

'Do you know where Arthur is?' asked Paul at breakfast.

'I do not,' replied his mother.

'He is a fool,' said Paul. 'And if he *did* anything I shouldn't mind. But no, he simply can't come away from a game of whist, or else he must see a girl home from the skating-rink–quite proprietously–and so can't get home. He's a fool.'

'I don't know that it would make it any better if he did something to make us all ashamed,' said Mrs Morel.

'Well, *I* should respect him more,' said Paul.

'I very much doubt it,' said his mother coldly.

They went on with breakfast.

'Are you fearfully fond of him?' Paul asked his mother.

'What do you ask that for?'

'Because they say a woman always like the youngest best.'

'She may do–but I don't. No, he wearies me.'

'And you'd actually rather he was good?'

'I'd rather he showed some of a man's common sense.'

Paul was raw and irritable. He also wearied his mother very often. She saw the sunshine going out of him, and she resented it.

As they were finishing breakfast came the postman with a letter from Derby. Mrs Morel screwed up her eyes to look at the address.

'Give it here, blind eye!' exclaimed her son, snatching it away from her.

She started, and almost boxed his ears.

'It's from your son, Arthur,' he said.

'What now–!' cried Mrs Morel.

'"My dearest Mother,"' Paul read, '"I don't know what made me such a fool. I want you to come and fetch me back from here. I came with Jack Bredon yesterday, instead of going to work, and enlisted. He said he was sick of wearing the seat of a stool out, and, like the idiot you know I am, I came away with him.

'"I have taken the King's shilling, but perhaps if you came for me they would let me go back with you, I was a fool when I did it. I don't want to be in the army. My dear mother, I am nothing but a trouble to you. But if you get me out of this, I promise I will have more sense and consideration. . . ."'

Mrs Morel sat down in her rocking-chair.

'Well, *now,*' she cried, 'let him stop!'

'Yes,' said Paul, 'let him stop.'

There was silence. The mother sat with her hands folded in her apron, her face set, thinking.

'If I'm not *sick*!' she cried suddenly. 'Sick!'

'Now,' said Paul, beginning to frown, 'you're not going to worry your soul out about this, do you hear.'

'I suppose I'm to take it as a blessing,' she flashed, turning on her son.

'You're not going to mount it up to a tragedy, so there,' he retorted.

'The *fool*!–the young fool!' she cried.

'He'll look well in uniform,' said Paul irritatingly.

His mother turned on him like a fury.

'Oh, will he!' she cried. 'Not in my eyes!'

'He should get in a cavalry regiment; he'll have the time of his life, and will look an awful swell.'

'Swell–*swell*!–a mighty swell indeed!–a common soldier!'

'Well,' said Paul, 'what am I but a common clerk?'

'A good deal, my boy!' cried his mother, stung.

'What?'

'At any rate, a *man,* and not a thing in a red coat.'

'I shouldn't mind being in a red coat—or dark blue, that would suit me better—if they didn't boss me about too much.'

But his mother had ceased to listen.

'Just as he was getting on, or might have been getting on, at his job—a young nuisance—here he goes and ruins himself for life. What good will he be, do you think, after *this*?'

'It may lick him into shape beautifully,' said Paul.

'Lick him into shape!—lick what marrow there *was* out of his bones. A *soldier*!—a common *soldier*!—nothing but a body that makes movements when it hears a shout! It's a fine thing!'

'I can't understand why it upsets you,' said Paul.

'No, perhaps you can't. But *I* understand'; and she sat back in her chair, her chin in one hand, holding her elbow with the other, brimmed up with wrath and chagrin.

'And shall you go to Derby?' asked Paul.

'Yes.'

'It's no good.'

'I'll see for myself.'

'And why on earth don't you let him stop? It's just what he wants.'

'Of course,' cried the mother, '*you* know what he wants!'

She got ready and went by the first train to Derby, where she saw her son and the sergeant. It was, however, no good.

When Morel was having his dinner in the evening, she said suddenly:

'I've had to go to Derby to-day.'

The miner turned up his eyes, showing the whites in his black face.

'Has ter, lass. What took thee there?'

'That Arthur!'

'Oh—an' what's agate now?'

'He's only enlisted.'

Morel put down his knife and leaned back in his chair.

'Nay,' he said, 'that he niver 'as!'

'And is going down to Aldershot to-morrow.'

'Well!' exclaimed the miner. 'That's a winder.' He considered it a moment, said 'H'm!' and proceeded with his dinner. Suddenly his face contracted with wrath. 'I hope he may never set foot i' my house again,' he said.

'The idea!' cried Mrs Morel. 'Saying such a thing!'

'I do,' repeated Morel. 'A fool as runs away for a soldier let 'im look after 'issen; I s'll do no more for 'im.'

'A fat sight you have done as it is,' she said.

And Morel was almost ashamed to go to his public-house that evening.

'Well, did you go?' said Paul to his mother when he came home.

'I did.'

'And could you see him?'

'Yes.'

'And what did he say?'

'He blubbered when I came away.'

'H'm!'

'And so did I, so you needn't "h'm!"'

Mrs Morel fretted after her son. She knew he would not like the army. He did not. The discipline was intolerable to him.

'But the doctor,' she said with some pride to Paul, 'said he was perfectly proportioned—almost exactly: all his measurements were correct. He *is* good-looking, you know.'

'He's awfully nice-looking. But he doesn't fetch the girls like William, does he?'

'No; it's a different character. He's a good deal like his father, irresponsible.'

To console his mother, Paul did not go much to Willey Farm at this time. And in the autumn exhibition of students' work in the Castle he had two studies, a landscape in water-colour and a still life in oil, both of which had first-prize awards. He was highly excited.

'What do you think I've got for my pictures, mother?' he asked, coming home one evening. She saw by his eyes he was glad. Her face flushed.

'Now, how should I know, my boy!'

'A first prize for those glass jars—'

'H'm!'

'And a first prize for that sketch up at Willey Farm.'

'Both first?'

'Yes.'

'H'm!'

There was a rosy, bright look about her, though she said nothing.

'It's nice,' he said, 'isn't it?'

'It is.'

'Why don't you praise me up to the skies?'

She laughed.

'I should have the trouble of dragging you down again,' she said.

But she was full of joy, nevertheless. William had brought her his sporting trophies. She kept them still, and she did not forgive his death. Arthur was handsome—at least, a good specimen—and warm and generous, and probably would do well in the end. But Paul was going to distinguish himself. She had a great belief in him, the more because he was unaware of his own powers. There was so much to come out of him. Life for her was rich with promise. She was to see herself fulfilled. Not for nothing had been her struggle.

Several times during the exhibition Mrs Morel went to the Castle unknown to Paul. She wandered down the long room looking at the other exhibits. Yes, they were good. But they had not in them a certain something which she demanded for her satisfaction. Some made her jealous, they were so good. She looked at them a long time trying to find fault with them. Then suddenly she had a shock that made her heart beat. There hung Paul's picture! She knew it as if it were printed on her heart.

'Name—Paul Morel—First Prize.'

It looked so strange, there in public, on the walls of the Castle gallery, where in her lifetime she had seen so many pictures. And she glanced round to see if anyone had noticed her again in front of the same sketch.

But she felt a proud woman. When she met well-dressed ladies going home to the Park, she thought to herself:

'Yes, you look very well—but I wonder if *your* son has two first prizes in the Castle.'

And she walked on, as proud a little woman as any in Nottingham. And Paul felt he had done something for her, if only a trifle. All his work was hers.

One day, as he was going up Castle Gate, he met Miriam. He had seen her on the Sunday, and had not expected to meet her in town. She was walking with a rather striking woman, blonde, with a sullen expression, and a defiant carriage.

It was strange how Miriam in her bowed, meditative bearing, looked dwarfed beside this woman with the handsome shoulders. Miriam watched Paul searchingly. His gaze was on the stranger, who ignored him. The girl saw his masculine spirit rear its head.

'Hello!' he said, 'you didn't tell me you were coming to town.'

'No,' replied Miriam, half apologetically. 'I drove in to Cattle Market with father.'

He looked at her companion.

'I've told you about Mrs Dawes,' said Miriam huskily; she was nervous. 'Clara, do you know Paul?'

'I think I've seen him before,' replied Mrs Dawes indifferently, as she shook hands with him. She had scornful grey eyes, a skin like white honey, and a full mouth, with a slightly lifted upper lip that did not know whether it was raised in scorn of all men or out of eagerness to be kissed, but which believed the former. She carried her head back, as if she had drawn away in contempt, perhaps from men also. She wore a large, dowdy hat of black beaver, and a sort of slightly affected simple dress that made her look rather sack-like. She was evidently poor, and had not much taste. Miriam usually looked nice.

'Where have you seen me?' Paul asked of the woman.

She looked at him as if she would not trouble to answer. Then:

'Walking with Louie Travers,' she said.

Louie was one of the 'spiral' girls.

'Why, do you know her?' he asked.

She did not answer. He turned to Miriam.

'Where are you going?' he asked.

'To the Castle.'

'What train are you going home by?'

'I am driving with father. I wish you could come too. What time are you free?'

'You know not till eight to-night, damn it!'

And directly the two women moved on.

Paul remembered that Clara Dawes was the daughter of an old friend of Mrs Leivers. Miriam had sought her out because she had once been spiral overseer at Jordan's, and because her husband, Baxter Dawes, was smith for the factory, making the irons for cripple instruments, and so on. Through her Miriam felt she got into direct contact with Jordan's, and could estimate better Paul's position. But Mrs Dawes was separated from her husband, and had taken up Women's Rights. She was supposed to be clever. It interested Paul.

Baxter Dawes he knew and disliked. The smith was a man of thirty-one or thirty-two. He came occasionally through Paul's corner–a big, well-set man, also striking to look at, and handsome. There was a peculiar similarity between himself and his wife. He had the same white skin, with a clear, golden tinge. His hair was of soft brown, his moustache was golden. And he had a similar defiance in his bearing and manner. But then came the difference. His eyes, dark brown and quick-shifting, were dissolute. They protruded very slightly, and his eyelids hung over them in a way that was half hate. His mouth, too, was sensual. His whole manner was of cowed defiance, as if he were ready to knock anybody down who disapproved of him–perhaps because he really disapproved of himself.

From the first day he had hated Paul. Finding the lad's impersonal, deliberate gaze of an artist on his face, he got into a fury.

'What are yer lookin' at?' he sneered, bullying.

The boy glanced away. But the smith used to stand behind the counter and talk to Mr Pappleworth. His speech was dirty, with a kind of rottenness. Again he found the youth with his cool, critical gaze fixed on his face. The smith started round as if he had been stung.

'What'r yer lookin' at, three hap'orth o' pap?' he snarled.

The boy shrugged his shoulders slightly.

'Why yer–!' shouted Dawes.

'Leave him alone,' said Mr Pappleworth, in that insinuating voice which means, 'he's only one of your good little sops who can't help it.'

Since that time the boy used to look at the man every time he came through with the same curious criticism, glancing away before he met the smith's eye. It made Dawes furious. They hated each other in silence.

Clara Dawes had no children. When she had left her husband the home had been broken up, and she had gone to live with her mother. Dawes lodged with his sister. In the same house was a sister-in-law, and somehow Paul knew that this girl, Louie Travers, was now Dawes's woman. She was a handsome, insolent hussy who mocked at the youth, and yet flushed if he walked along to the station with her as she went home.

The next time he went to see Miriam it was Saturday evening. She had a fire in the parlour, and was waiting for him. The others, except her father and mother and the young children, had gone out, so the two had the parlour together. It was a long, low, warm room. There were three of Paul's small sketches on the wall, and his photo was on the mantelpiece. On the table and on the high old rose-wood piano were bowls of coloured leaves. He sat in the armchair, she crouched on the hearthrug near his feet. The glow was warm on her handsome, pensive face as she kneeled there like a devotee.

'What did you think of Mrs Dawes?' she asked quietly.

'She doesn't look very amiable,' he replied.

'No, but don't you think she's a fine woman?' she said, in a deep tone.

'Yes–in stature. But without a grain of taste. I like her for some things. *Is* she disagreeable?'

'I don't think so. I think she's dissatisfied.'

'What with?'

'Well–how would *you* like to be tied for life to a man like that?'

'Why did she marry him, then, if she was to have revulsions so soon?'

'Ay, why did she!' repeated Miriam bitterly.

'And I should have thought she had enough fight in her to match him,' he said.

Miriam bowed her head.

'Ay?' she queried satirically. 'What makes you think so?'

'Look at her mouth–made for passion–and the very set-back of her throat–' He threw his head back in Clara's defiant manner.

Miriam bowed a little lower.

'Yes,' she said.

There was a silence for some moments, while he thought of Clara.

'And what were the things you liked about her?' she asked.

'I don't know–her skin and the texture of her–and her–I don't know–there's a sort of fierceness somewhere in her. I appreciate her as an artist, that's all.'

'Yes.'

He wondered why Miriam crouched there brooding in that strange way. It irritated him.

'You don't really like her, do you?' he asked the girl.

She looked at him with her great, dazzled dark eyes.

'I do,' she said.

'You don't–you can't–not really.'

'Then what?' she asked slowly.

'Eh, I don't know–perhaps you like her because she's got a grudge against men.'

That was more probably one of his own reasons for liking Mrs Dawes, but this did not occur to him. They were silent. There had come into his forehead a knitting of the brows which was becoming habitual with him, particularly when he was with Miriam. She longed to smooth it away, and she was afraid of it. It seemed the stamp of a man who was not her man in Paul Morel.

There were some crimson berries among the leaves in the bowl. He reached over and pulled out a bunch.

'If you put red berries in your hair,' he said, 'why would you look like some witch or priestess, and never like a reveller?'

She laughed with a naked, painful sound.

'I don't know,' she said.

His vigorous warm hands were playing excitedly with the berries.

'Why can't you laugh?' he said. 'You never laugh laughter. You only laugh when something is odd or incongruous and then it almost seems to hurt you.'

She bowed her head as if he were scolding her.

'I wish you could laugh at me just for one minute–just for one minute. I feel as if it would set something free.'

'But'–and she looked up at him with eyes frightened and struggling–'I do laugh at you–I *do.*'

'Never! There's always a kind of intensity. When you laugh I could always cry; it seems as if it shows up your suffering. Oh, you make me knit the brows of my very soul and cogitate.'

Slowly she shook her head despairingly.

'I'm sure I don't want to,' she said.

'I'm so damned spiritual with *you* always!' he cried.

She remained silent, thinking. 'Then why don't you be otherwise?' But he saw her crouching, brooding figure, and it seemed to tear him in two.

'But, there, it's autumn,' he said, 'and everybody feels like a disembodied spirit then.'

There was still another silence. This peculiar sadness between them thrilled her soul. He seemed so beautiful with his eyes gone dark, and looking as if they were deep as the deepest well.

'You make me so spiritual!' he lamented. 'And I don't want to be spiritual.'

She took her finger from her mouth with a little pop, and looked up at him almost challenging. But still her soul was naked in her great dark eyes, and there was the same yearning appeal upon her. If he could have kissed her in abstract purity he would have done so. But he could not kiss her thus–and she seemed to leave no other way. And she yearned to him.

He gave a brief laugh.

'Well,' he said, 'get that French and we'll do some–some Verlaine.'

'Yes,' she said in a deep tone, almost of resignation. And she rose and got the books. And her rather red, nervous hands looked so pitiful, he was mad to comfort her and kiss her. But then he dared not–or could not. There was something prevented him. His kisses were wrong for her. They continued the reading till ten o'clock, when they went into the kitchen, and Paul was natural and jolly again with the father and mother. His eyes were dark and shining; there was a kind of fascination about him.

When he went into the barn for his bicycle he found the front wheel punctured.

'Fetch me a drop of water in a bowl,' he said to her. 'I shall be late, and then I s'll catch it.'

He lighted the hurricane lamp, took off his coat, turned up the bicycle, and set speedily to work. Miriam came with the bowl of water and stood close to him, watching. She loved to see his hands doing things. He was slim and vigorous, with a kind of easiness even in his most hasty movements. And busy at his work he seemed to forget her. She loved him absorbedly. She wanted to run her hands down his sides. She always wanted to embrace him, so long as he did not want her.

'There!' he said, rising suddenly. 'Now, could you have done it quicker?'

'No!' she laughed.

He straightened himself. His back was towards her. She put her two hands on his sides, and ran them quickly down.

'You are so *fine*!' she said.

He laughed, hating her voice, but his blood roused to a wave of flame by her hands. She did not seem to realize *him* in all this. He might have been an object. She never realized the male he was.

He lighted his bicycle-lamp, bounced the machine on the barn floor to see that the tyres were sound, and buttoned his coat.

'That's all right!' he said.

She was trying the brakes, that she knew were broken.

'Did you have them mended?' she asked.

'No!'

'But why didn't you?'

'The back one goes on a bit.'

'But it's not safe.'

'I can use my toe.'

'I wish you'd had them mended,' she murmured.

'Don't worry–come to tea to-morrow, with Edgar.'

'Shall we?'

'Do–about four. I'll come to meet you.'

'Very well.'

She was pleased. They went across the dark yard to the gate. Looking across, he saw through the uncurtained window of the kitchen the heads of Mr and Mrs Leivers in the warm glow. It looked very cosy. The road, with pine-trees, was quite black in front.

'Till to-morrow,' he said, jumping on his bicycle.

'You'll take care, won't you?' she pleaded.

'Yes.'

His voice already came out of the darkness. She stood a moment watching the light from his lamp race into obscurity along the ground. She turned very slowly indoors. Orion was wheeling up over the wood, his dog twinkling after him, half smothered. For the rest of the world was full of darkness, and silent, save for the breathing of cattle in their stalls. She prayed earnestly for his safety that night. When he left her, she often lay in anxiety, wondering if he had got home safely.

He dropped down the hills on his bicycle. The roads were greasy, so he had to let it go. He felt a pleasure as the machine plunged over the second, steeper drop in the hill. 'Here goes!' he said. It was risky, because of the curve in the darkness at the bottom, and because of the brewers' waggons with drunken waggoners asleep. His bicycle seemed to fall beneath him, and he loved it. Recklessness is almost a man's revenge on his woman. He feels he is not valued, so he will risk destroying himself to deprive her altogether.

The stars on the lake seemed to leap like grasshoppers, silver upon the blackness, as he spun past. Then there was the long climb home.

'See, mother!' he said, as he threw her the berries and leaves on the table.

'H'm!' she said, glancing at them, then away again. She sat reading, alone, as she always did.

'Aren't they pretty?'

'Yes.'

He knew she was cross with him. After a few minutes he said:

'Edgar and Miriam are coming to tea to-morrow.'

She did not answer.

'You don't mind?'

Still she did not answer.

'Do you?' he asked.

'You know whether I mind or not.'

'I don't see why you should. I have plenty of meals there.'

'You do?'

'Then why do you grudge them tea?'

'I begrudge whom tea?'

'What are you so horrid for?'

'Oh, say no more! You've asked her to tea, it's quite sufficient. She'll come.'

He was very angry with his mother. He knew it was merely Miriam she objected to. He flung off his boots and went to bed.

Paul went to meet his friends the next afternoon. He was glad to see them coming. They arrived home at about four o'clock. Everywhere was clean and still for Sunday afternoon. Mrs Morel sat in her black dress and black apron. She rose to meet the visitors. With Edgar she was cordial, but with Miriam cold and rather grudging. Yet Paul thought the girl looked so nice in her brown cashmere frock.

He helped his mother to get the tea ready. Miriam would have gladly proffered, but was afraid. He was rather proud of his home. There was about it now, he thought, a certain distinction. The chairs were only wooden, and the sofa was old. But the hearthrug and cushions were cosy; the pictures were prints in good taste; there was a simplicity in everything, and plenty of books. He was never ashamed in the least of his home, nor was Miriam of hers, because both were what they should be, and warm. And then he was proud of the table; the china was pretty, the cloth was fine. It did not matter that the spoons were not silver nor the knives ivory-handled; everything looked nice. Mrs Morel had managed wonderfully while her children were growing up, so that nothing was out of place.

Miriam talked books a little. That was her unfailing topic. But Mrs Morel was not cordial, and turned soon to Edgar.

At first Edgar and Miriam used to go into Mrs Morel's pew. Morel never went to chapel, preferring the public-house. Mrs Morel, like a little champion, sat at the head of her pew, Paul at the other end; and at first Miriam sat next to him. Then the chapel was like home. It was a pretty place, with dark pews and slim, elegant pillars, and flowers. And the same people had sat in the same places ever since he was a boy. It was wonderfully sweet and soothing to sit there for an hour and a half, next to Miriam, and near to his mother, uniting his two loves under the spell of the place of worship. Then he felt warm and happy and religious at once. And after chapel he walked home with Miriam, whilst Mrs Morel spent the rest of the evening with her old friend, Mrs Burns. He was keenly alive on his walks on Sunday nights with Edgar and Miriam. He never went past the pits at night, by the lighted lamp-house, the tall black headstocks and lines of trucks, past the fans spinning slowly like shadows, without the feeling of Miriam returning to him, keen and almost unbearable.

She did not very long occupy the Morels' pew. Her father took one for themselves once more. It was under the little gallery, opposite the Morels'. When Paul and his mother came in the chapel the Leivers' pew was always empty. He was anxious for fear she would not come: it was so far, and there were so many rainy Sundays. Then, often very late indeed, she came in, with her long stride, her head bowed, her face hidden under her hat of dark green velvet. Her face, as she sat opposite, was always in shadow. But it gave him a very keen feeling, as if all his soul stirred within him, to see her there. It was not the same glow, happiness, and pride, that he felt in having his mother in charge: something more wonderful, less human, and tinged to intensity by a pain, as if there were something he could not get to.

At this time he was beginning to question the orthodox creed. He was twenty-one, and she was twenty. She was beginning to dread the spring: he became so wild, and hurt her so much. All the way he went cruelly smashing her beliefs. Edgar enjoyed it. He was by nature critical and rather dispassionate. But Miriam suffered exquisite pain, as, with an intellect like a knife, the man she loved examined her religion in which she lived and moved and had her being. But he did not spare her. He was cruel. And when they went alone he was even more fierce, as if he would kill her soul. He bled her beliefs till she almost lost consciousness.

'She exults – she exults as she carries him off from me,' Mrs Morel cried in her heart when Paul had gone. 'She's not like an ordinary woman, who can leave me my share in him. She wants to absorb him. She wants to draw him out and absorb him till there is nothing left of him, even for himself. He will never be a man on his own feet – she will suck him up.' So the mother sat, and battled and brooded bitterly.

And he, coming home from his walks with Mirian, was wild with torture. He walked biting his lips and with clenched fists, going at a great rate. Then, brought up against a stile, he stood for some minutes, and did not move. There was a great hollow of darkness fronting him, and on the black up-slopes patches of tiny lights, and in the lowest trough of the night, a flare of the pit. It was all weird and dreadful. Why was he torn so, almost bewildered, and unable to move? Why did his mother sit at home and suffer? He knew she suffered badly. But why should she? And why did he hate Miriam, and feel so cruel towards her, at the thought of his mother? If Miriam caused his mother suffering, then he hated her – and he easily hated her. Why did she make him feel as if he were uncertain of himself, insecure, an indefinite thing, as if he had not sufficient sheathing to prevent the night and the space breaking into him? How he hated her! And then, what a rush of tenderness and humility!

Suddenly he plunged on again, running home. His mother saw on him the marks of some agony, and she said nothing. But he had to make her talk to him. Then she was angry with him for going so far with Miriam.

'Why don't you like her, mother?' he cried in despair.

'I don't know, my boy,' she replied piteously. 'I'm sure I've tried to like her. I've tried and tried, but I can't—I can't!'

And he felt dreary and hopeless between the two.

Spring was the worst time. He was changeable, and intense and cruel. So he decided to stay away from her. Then came the hours when he knew Miriam was expecting him. His mother watched him growing restless. He could not go on with his work. He could do nothing. It was as if something were drawing his soul out towards Willey Farm. Then he put on his hat and went, saying nothing. And his mother knew he was gone. And as soon as he was on the way he sighed with relief. And when he was with her he was cruel again.

One day in March he lay on the bank of Nethermere, with Miriam sitting beside him. It was a glistening, white-and-blue day. Big clouds, so brilliant, went by overhead, while shadows stole along on the water. The clear spaces in the sky were of clean, cold blue. Paul lay on his back in the old grass, looking up. He could not bear to look at Miriam. She seemed to want him, and he resisted. He resisted all the time. He wanted now to give her passion and tenderness, and he could not. He felt that she wanted the soul out of his body, and not him. All his strength and energy she drew into herself through some channel which united them. She did not want to meet him, so that there were two of them, man and woman together. She wanted to draw all of him into her. It urged him to an intensity like madness, which fascinated him, as drug-taking might.

He was discussing Michelangelo. It felt to her as if she were fingering the very quivering tissue, the very protoplasm of life, as she heard him. It gave her her deepest satisfaction. And in the end it frightened her. There he lay in the white intensity of his search, and his voice gradually filled her with fear, so level it was, almost inhuman, as if in a trance.

'Don't talk any more,' she pleaded softly, laying her hand on his forehead.

He lay quite still, almost unable to move. His body was somewhere discarded.

'Why not? Are you tired?'

'Yes, and it wears you out.'

He laughed shortly, realizing.

'Yet you always make me like it,' he said.

'I don't wish to,' she said, very low.

'Not when you've gone too far, and you feel you can't bear it. But your unconscious self always asks it of me. And I suppose I want it.'

He went on, in his dead fashion:

'If only you could want *me*, and not want what I can reel off for you!'

'I!' she cried bitterly—'I! Why, when would you let me take you?'

'Then it's my fault,' he said, and, gathering himself together, he got up and began to talk trivialities. He felt insubstantial. In a vague way he hated her for it. And he knew he was as much to blame himself. This, however, did not prevent his hating her.

One evening about this time he had walked along the home road with her. They stood by the pasture leading down to the wood, unable to part. As the stars came out the clouds closed. They had glimpses of their own constellation,

Orion, towards the west. His jewels glimmered for a moment, his dog ran low, struggling with difficulty through the spume of cloud.

Orion was for them chief in significance among the constellations. They gazed at him in their strange, surcharged hours of feeling, until they seemed themselves to live in every one of his stars. This evening Paul had been moody and perverse. Orion had seemed just an ordinary constellation to him. He had fought against his glamour and fascination. Miriam was watching her lover's mood carefully. But he said nothing that gave him away, till the moment came to part, when he stood frowning gloomily at the gathered clouds, behind which the great constellation must be striding still.

There was to be a little party at his house the next day, at which she was to attend.

'I shan't come and meet you,' he said.

'Oh, very well; it's not very nice,' she replied slowly.

'It's not that—only they don't like me to. They say I care more for you than for them. And you understand, don't you? You know it's only friendship.'

Miriam was astonished and hurt for him. It had cost him an effort. She left him, wanting to spare him any further humiliation. A fine rain blew in her face as she walked along the road. She was hurt deep down; and she despised him for being blown about by any wind of authority. And in her heart of hearts, unconsciously, she felt that he was trying to get away from her. This she would never have acknowledged. She pitied him.

At this time Paul became an important factor in Jordan's warehouse. Mr Pappleworth left to set up a business of his own, and Paul remained with Mr Jordan as spiral overseer. His wages were to be raised to thirty shillings at the year-end, if things went well.

Still on Friday night Miriam often came down for her French lesson. Paul did not go so frequently to Willey Farm, and she grieved at the thought of her education's coming to an end; moreover, they both loved to be together, in spite of discords. So they read Balzac, and did compositions, and felt highly cultured.

Friday night was reckoning night for the miners. Morel 'reckoned'—shared up the money of the stall—either in the New Inn at Bretty or in his own house, according as his fellow-butties wished. Barker had turned a non-drinker, so now the men reckoned at Morel's house.

Annie, who had been teaching away, was at home again. She was still a tomboy; and she was engaged to be married. Paul was studying design.

Morel was always in good spirits on Friday evening, unless the week's earnings were small. He bustled immediately after his dinner, prepared to get washed. It was decorum for the women to absent themselves while the men reckoned. Women were not supposed to spy into such a masculine privacy as the butties' reckoning, nor were they to know the exact amount of the week's earnings. So, whilst her father was spluttering in the scullery, Annie went out to spend an hour with a neighbour. Mrs Morel attended to her baking.

'Shut that doo-er!' bawled Morel furiously.

Annie banged it behind her, and was gone.

'If tha oppens it again while I'm weshin' me, I'll ma'e thy jaw rattle,' he threatened from the midst of his soapsuds. Paul and the mother frowned to hear him.

Presently he came running out of the scullery, with the soapy water dripping from him, dithering with cold.

'Oh, my sirs!' he said, 'Wheer's my towel?'

It was hung on a chair to warm before the fire, otherwise he would have bullied and blustered. He squatted on his heels before the hot baking-fire to dry himself.

'F-ff-f!' he went, pretending to shudder with cold.

'Goodness, man, don't be such a kid!' said Mrs Morel. 'It's *not* cold.'

'Thee strip thysen stark nak'd to wesh thy flesh i' that scullery,' said the miner, as he rubbed his hair; 'nowt b'r a ice-'ouse!'

'And I shouldn't make that fuss,' replied his wife.

'No, tha'd drop down stiff, as dead as a door-knob, wi' thy nesh sides.'

'Why is a door-knob deader than anything else?' asked Paul, curious.

'Eh, I dunno; that's what they say,' replied his father. 'But there's that much draught i' yon scullery, as it blows through your ribs like through a five-barred gate.'

'It would have some difficulty in blowing through yours,' said Mrs Morel.

Morel looked down ruefully at his sides.

'Me!' he exclaimed. 'I'm nowt b'r a skinned rabbit. My bones fair juts out on me.'

'I should like to know where,' retorted his wife.

'Iv'ry-wheer! I'm nobbut a sack o' faggots.'

Mrs Morel laughed. He had still a wonderfully young body, muscular, without any fat. His skin was smooth and clear. It might have been the body of a man of twenty-eight, except that there were, perhaps, too many blue scars, like tattoo marks, where the coal-dust remained under the skin, and that his chest was too hairy. But he put his hand on his sides ruefully. It was his fixed belief that, because he did not get fat, he was as thin as a starved rat.

Paul looked at his father's thick, brownish hands all scarred, with broken nails rubbing the fine smoothness of his sides, and the incongruity struck him. It seemed strange they were the same flesh.

'I suppose,' he said to his father, 'you had a good figure once.'

'Eh!' exclaimed the miner, glancing round, startled and timid, like a child.

'He had,' exclaimed Mrs Morel, 'if he didn't hurtle himself up as if he was trying to get in the smallest space he could.'

'Me!' exclaimed Morel—'me a good figure! I wor niver much more n'r a skeleton.'

'Man!' cried his wife, 'don't be such a pulamiter!'

''Strewth!' he said. 'Tha's niver knowed me but what I looked as if I wor goin' off in a rapid decline.'

She sat and laughed.

'You've had a constitution like iron,' she said, 'and never a man had a better start, if it was body that counted. You should have seen him as a young man,' she cried suddenly to Paul, drawing herself up to imitate her husband's once handsome bearing.

Morel watched her shyly. He saw again the passion she had had for him. It blazed upon her for a moment. He was shy, rather scared, and humble. Yet again he felt his old glow. And then immediately he felt the ruin he had made during these years. He wanted to bustle about, to run away from it.

'Gi'e my back a bit of a wesh,' he asked her.

His wife brought a well-soaped flannel and clapped it on his shoulders. He gave a jump.

'Eh, tha mucky little 'ussy!' he cried. 'Cowd as death!'

'You ought to have been a salamander,' she laughed, washing his back. It was very rarely she would do anything so personal for him. The children did those things.

'The next world won't be half hot enough for you,' she added.

'No,' he said; 'tha'lt see as it's draughty for me.'

But she had finished. She wiped him in a desultory fashion, and went upstairs, returning immediately with his shifting-trousers. When he was dried he struggled into his shirt. Then, ruddy and shiny, with hair on end, and his flannelette shirt hanging over his pit-trousers, he stood warming the garments he was going to put on. He turned them, he pulled them inside out, he scorched them.

'Goodness, man!' cried Mrs Morel; 'get dressed!'

'Should thee like to clap thysen into britches as cowd as a tub o' water?' he said.

At last he took off his pit-trousers and donned decent black. He did all this on the hearthrug, as he would have done if Annie and her familiar friends had been present.

Mrs Morel turned the bread in the oven. Then from the red earthenware panchion of dough that stood in a corner she took another handful of paste, worked it to the proper shape, and dropped it into a tin. As she was doing so Barker knocked and entered. He was a quiet, compact little man, who looked as if he would go through a stone wall. His black hair was cropped short, his head was bony. Like most miners, he was pale, but healthy and taut.

'Evenin', missis,' he nodded to Mrs Morel, and he seated himself with a sigh.

'Good evening,' she replied cordially.

'Tha's made thy heels crack,' said Morel.   'I dunno as I have,' said Barker.

He sat, as the men always did in Mrs Morel's kitchen, effacing himself rather.

'How's missis?' she asked of him.

He had told her some time back:

'We're expectin' us third just now, you see.'

'Well,' he answered, rubbing his head, 'she keeps pretty middlin', I think.'

'Let's see–when?' asked Mrs Morel.

'Well, I shouldn't be surprised any time now.'

'Ah! And she's kept fairly?'

'Yes, tidy.'

'That's a blessing, for she's none too strong.'

'No. An' I've done another silly trick.'

'What's that?'

Mrs Morel knew Barker wouldn't do anything very silly.

'I'm come be-out th' market-bag.'

'You can have mine.'

'Nay, you'll be wantin' that yourself.'

'I shan't. I take a string bag always.'

She saw the determined little collier buying in the week's groceries and meat on the Friday nights, and she admired him. 'Barker's little, but he's ten times the man you are,' she said to her husband.

Just then Wesson entered. He was thin, rather frail-looking, with a boyish ingenuousness and a slightly foolish smile, despite his seven children. But his wife was a passionate woman.

'I see you've kested me,' he said, smiling rather vapidly.

'Yes,' replied Barker.

The newcomer took off his cap and his big woollen muffler. His nose was pointed and red.

'I'm afraid you're cold, Mr Wesson,' said Mrs Morel.

'It's a bit nippy,' he replied.

'Then come to the fire.'

'Nay, I s'll do where I am.'

Both colliers sat away back. They could not be induced to come on the hearth. The hearth is sacred to the family.

'Go thy ways i' th' arm-chair,' cried Morel cheerily.

'Nay, thank yer; I'm very nicely here.'

'Yes, come, of course,' insisted Mrs Morel.

He rose and went awkwardly. He sat in Morel's arm-chair awkwardly. It was too great a familiarity. But the fire made him blissfully happy.

'And how's that chest of yours?' demanded Mrs Morel.

He smiled again, with his blue eyes rather sunny.

'Oh, it's very middlin',' he said.

'Wi' a rattle in it like a kettle drum,' said Barker shortly.

'T-t-t-t!' went Mrs Morel rapidly with her tongue. 'Did you have that flannel singlet made?'

'Not yet,' he smiled.

'Then, why didn't you?' she cried.

'It'll come,' he smiled.

'Ah, an' Doomsday!' exclaimed Barker.

Barker and Morel were both impatient of Wesson. But, then, they were both as hard as nails, physically.

When Morel was nearly ready he pushed the bag of money to Paul.

'Count it, boy,' he asked humbly.

Paul impatiently turned from his books and pencil, tipped the bag upside down on the table. There was a five-pound bag of silver, sovereigns and loose money. He counted quickly, referred to the checks—the written papers giving amount of coal—put the money in order. Then Barker glanced at the checks.

Mrs Morel went upstairs, and the three men came to table, Morel, as master of the house, sat in his arm-chair, with his back to the hot fire. The two butties had cooler seats. None of them counted the money.

'What did we say Simpson's was?' asked Morel; and the butties cavilled for a minute over the dayman's earnings. Then the amount was put aside.

'An' Bill Naylor's?'

This money also was taken from the pack.

Then, because Wesson lived in one of the company's houses, and his rent had been deducted, Morel and Barker took four-and-six each. And because Morel's coals had come, and the leading was stopped, Barker and Wesson took four shillings each. Then it was plain sailing. Morel gave each of them a sovereign till there were no more sovereigns; each half a crown till there were no more half-crowns; each a shilling till there were no more shillings. If there was anything at the end that wouldn't split, Morel took it and stood drinks.

Then the three men rose and went. Morel scuttled out of the house before his wife came down. She heard the door close, and descended. She looked hastily at the bread in the oven. Then, glancing on the table, she saw her money lying. Paul had been working all the time. But now he felt his mother counting the week's money and her wrath rising.

'T-t-t-t!' went her tongue.

He frowned. He could not work when she was cross. She counted again.

'A measly twenty-five shillings!' she exclaimed. 'How much was the cheque?'

'Ten pounds eleven,' said Paul irritably. He dreaded what was coming.

'And he gives me a scrattlin' twenty-five, an' his club this week! But I know him. He thinks because *you're* earning he needn't keep the house any longer. No, all he has to do with his money is to guttle it. But I'll show him!'

'Oh, mother, don't!' cried Paul.

'Don't what, I should like to know?' she exclaimed.

'Don't carry on again, I can't work.'

She went very quiet.

'Yes, it's all very well,' she said; 'but how do you think I'm going to manage?'

'Well, it won't make it any better to whittle about it.'

'I should like to know what you'd do if you had it to put up with.'

'It won't be long. You can have my money. Let him go to hell.'

He went back to his work and she tied her bonnet-strings grimly. When she was fretted he could not bear it. But now he began to insist on her recognizing him.

'The two loaves at the top,' she said, 'will be done in twenty minutes. Don't forget them.'

'All right,' he answered; and she went to the market.

He remained alone working. But his usual intense concentration became unsettled. He listened for the yard-gate. At a quarter-past seven came a low knock, and Miriam entered.

'All alone?' she said.

'Yes.'

As if at home, she took off her tam-o'-shanter and her long coat, hanging them up. It gave him a thrill. This might be their own house, his and hers. Then she came back and peered over his work.

'What is it?' she asked.

'Still design, for decorating stuffs, and for embroidery.'

She bent short-sightedly over the drawings.

It irritated him that she peered so into everything that was his, searching him out. He went into the parlour and returned with a bundle of brownish linen. Carefully unfolding it, he spread it on the floor. It proved to be a curtain or *portière*, beautifully stencilled with a design on roses.

'Ah, how beautiful!' she cried.

The spread cloth, with its wonderful reddish roses and dark green stems, all so simple, and somehow so wicked-looking, lay at her feet. She went on her knees before it, her dark curls dropping. He saw her crouched voluptuously before his work, and his heart beat quickly. Suddenly she looked up at him.

'Why does it seem cruel?' she cried.

'What?'

'There seems a feeling of cruelty about it,' she said.

'It's jolly good, whether or not,' he replied, folding up his work with a lover's hands.

She rose slowly, pondering.

'And what will you do with it?' she asked.

'Send it to Liberty's. I did it for my mother, but I think she'd rather have the money.'

'Yes,' said Miriam. He had spoken with a touch of bitterness, and Miriam sympathized. Money would have been nothing to *her*.

He took the cloth back into the parlour. When he returned, he threw to Miriam a smaller piece. It was a cushion-cover with the same design.

'I did that for you,' he said.

She fingered the work with trembling hands, and did not speak. He became embarrassed.

'By Jove, the bread!' he cried.

He took the top loaves out, tapped them vigorously. They were done. He put them on the hearth to cool. Then he went to the scullery, wetted his hands, scooped the last white dough out of the punchion, and dropped it into a baking-tin. Miriam was still bent over her painted cloth. He stood rubbing the bits of dough from his hands.

'You do like it?' he asked.

She looked up at him, with her dark eyes one flame of love. He laughed uncomfortably. Then he began to talk about the design. There was for him the most intense pleasure in talking about his work to Miriam. All his passion, all his wild blood, went into this intercourse with her, when he talked and conceived his work. She brought forth to him his imaginations. She did not understand, any more than a woman understands when she conceives a child in her womb. But this was life for her and for him.

While they were talking, a young woman of about twenty-two, small and pale, hollow-eyed, yet with a relentless look about her, entered the room. She was a friend at the Morels'.

'Take your things off,' said Paul.

'No, I'm not stopping.'

She sat down in the arm-chair opposite Paul and Miriam, who were on the sofa. Miriam moved a little farther from him. The room was hot, with a scent of new bread. Brown, crisp loaves stood on the hearth.

'I shouldn't have expected to see you here to-night, Miriam Leivers,' said Beatrice wickedly.

'Why not?' murmured Miriam huskily.

'Why, let's look at your shoes.'

Miriam remained uncomfortably still.

'If tha doesna tha durs'na,' laughed Beatrice.

Miriam put her feet from under her dress. Her boots had that queer, irresolute, rather pathetic look about them, which showed how self-conscious and self-mistrustful she was. And they were covered with mud.

'Glory! You're a positive muck-heap,' exclaimed Beatrice. 'Who cleans your boots?'

'I clean them myself.'

'Then you wanted a job,' said Beatrice. 'It would ha' taken a lot of men to ha' brought me down here to-night. But love laughs at sludge, doesn't it, 'Postle, my duck?'

'*Inter alia,*' he said.

'Oh, Lord! are you going to spout foreign languages? What does it mean, Miriam?'

There was a fine sarcasm in the last question, but Miriam did not see it.

'"Among other things," I believe,' she said humbly.

Beatrice put her tongue between her teeth and laughed wickedly.

'"Among other things," 'Postle?' she repeated. 'Do you mean love laughs at mothers, and fathers, and sisters, and brothers, and men friends, and lady friends, and even at the b'loved himself?'

She affected a great innocence.

'In fact, it's one big smile,' he replied.

'Up its sleeve, 'Postle Morel—you believe me,' she said; and she went off into another burst of wicked, silent laughter.

Miriam sat silent, withdrawn into herself. Everyone of Paul's friends delighted in taking sides against her, and he left her in the lurch—seemed almost to take a sort of revenge upon her then.

'Are you still at school?' asked Miriam of Beatrice.

'Yes.'

'You've not had your notice then?'

'I expect it at Easter.'

'Isn't it an awful shame, to turn you off merely because you didn't pass the exam?'

'I don't know,' said Beatrice coldly.

'Agatha says you're as good as any teacher anywhere. It seems to me ridiculous. I wonder why you didn't pass.'

'Shorts of brains, eh, 'Postle?' said Beatrice briefly.

'Only brains to bite with,' replied Paul, laughing.

'Nuisance!' she cried; and, springing from her seat, she rushed and boxed his ears. She had beautiful small hands. He held her wrists while she wrestled with him. At last she broke free, and seized two handfuls of his thick, dark brown hair, which she shook.

'Beat!' he said, as he pulled his hair straight with his fingers. 'I hate you!'

She laughed with glee.

'Mind!' she said. 'I want to sit next to you.'

'I'd as lief be neighbours with a vixen,' he said, nevertheless making place for her between him and Miriam.

'Did it ruffle his pretty hair, then!' she cried; and, with her haircomb, she combed him straight. 'And his nice little moustache!' she exclaimed. She tilted his head back and combed his young moustache. 'It's a wicked moustache, 'Postle,' she said. 'It's a red for danger. Have you got any of those cigarettes?'

He pulled his cigarette-case from his pocket. Beatrice looked inside it.

'And fancy me having Connie's last cig,' said Beatrice, putting the thing between her teeth. He held a lit match to her, and she puffed daintily.

'Thanks so much, darling,' she said mockingly.

It gave her a wicked delight.

'Don't you think he does it nicely, Miriam?' she asked.

'Oh very!' said Miriam.

He took a cigarette for himself.

'Light, old boy?' said Beatrice, tilting her cigarette at him.

He bent forward to her to light his cigarette at hers. She was winking at him as he did so. Miriam saw his eyes trembling with mischief, and his full, almost sensual, mouth quivering. He was not himself and she could not bear it. As he was now, she had no connexion with him; she might as well not have existed. She saw the cigarette dancing on his full red lips. She hated his thick hair for being tumbled loose on his forehead.

'Sweet boy!' said Beatrice, tipping up his chin and giving him a little kiss on the cheek.

'I s'll kiss thee back, Beat,' he said.

'Tha wunna!' she giggled, jumping up and going away. 'Isn't he shameless, Miriam?'

'Quite,' said Miriam. 'By the way, aren't you forgetting the bread?'

'By Jove!' he cried, flinging open the oven-door.

Out puffed the bluish smoke and a smell of burned bread.

'Oh, golly!' cried Beatrice, coming to his side. He crouched before the oven, she peered over his shoulder. 'This is what comes of the oblivion of love, my boy.'

Paul was ruefully removing the loaves. One was burnt black on the hot side; another was hard as a brick.

'Poor Mater!' said Paul.

'You want to grate it,' said Beatrice. 'Fetch me the nutmeg-grater.'

She arranged the bread in the oven. He brought the grater, and she grated the bread on to a newspaper on the table. He set the doors open to blow away the smell of burned bread. Beatrice grated away, puffing her cigarette, knocking the charcoal off the poor loaf.

'My word, Miriam! You're in for it this time,' said Beatrice.

'I!' exclaimed Miriam in amazement.

'You'd better be gone when his mother comes in. *I* know why King Alfred burned the cakes. Now I see it! 'Postle would fix up a tale about his work making him forget, if he thought it would wash. If that old woman had come in a bit sooner, she'd have boxed the brazen thing's ears who made the oblivion, instead of poor Alfred's.'

She giggled as she scraped the loaf. Even Miriam laughed in spite of herself. Paul mended the fire ruefully.

The garden-gate was heard to bang.

'Quick!' cried Beatrice, giving Paul the scraped loaf. 'Wrap it up in a damp towel.'

Paul disappeared into the scullery. Beatrice hastily blew her scrapings into the fire, and sat down innocently. Annie came bursting in. She was an abrupt, quite smart young woman. She blinked in the strong light.

'Smell of burning!' she exclaimed.

'It's the cigarettes,' replied Beatrice demurely.

'Where's Paul?'

Leonard had followed Annie. He had a long comic face and blue eyes, very sad.

'I suppose he's left you to settle it between you,' he said. He nodded sympathetically to Miriam, and became gently sarcastic to Beatrice.

'No,' said Beatrice, 'he's gone off with number nine.'

'I just met number five inquiring for him,' said Leonard.

'Yes—we're going to share him up like Solomon's baby,' said Beatrice. Annie laughed.

'Oh, ay,' said Leonard. 'And which bit should you have?'

'I don't know,' said Beatrice. 'I'll let all the others pick first.'

'An' you'd have the leavings, like?' said Leonard, twisting up a comic face. Annie was looking in the oven. Miriam sat ignored. Paul entered.

'This bread's a fine sight, our Paul,' said Annie.

'Then you should stop an' look after it,' said Paul.

'You mean *you* should do what you're reckoning to do,' replied Annie.

'He should, shouldn't he!' cried Beatrice.

'I s'd think he'd got plenty on hand,' said Leonard.

'You had a nasty walk, didn't you, Miriam?' said Annie.

'Yes–but I'd been in all week–'

'And you wanted a bit of a change, like,' insinuated Leonard kindly.

'Well, you can't be stuck in the house for ever,' Annie agreed. She was quite amiable. Beatrice pulled on her coat, and went out with Leonard and Annie. She would meet her own boy.

'Don't forget that bread, our Paul,' cried Annie. 'Good night, Miriam. I don't think it will rain.'

When they had all gone, Paul fetched the swathed loaf, unwrapped it, and surveyed it sadly.

'It's a mess!' he said.

'But,' answered Miriam impatiently, 'what is it, after all–twopence ha'penny.'

'Yes, but–it's the mater's precious baking, and she'll take it to heart. However, it's no good bothering.'

He took the loaf back into the scullery. There was a little distance between him and Miriam. He stood balanced opposite her for some moments considering, thinking of his behaviour with Beatrice. He felt guilty inside himself, and yet glad. For some inscrutable reason it served Miriam right. He was not going to repent. She wondered what he was thinking of as he stood suspended. His thick hair was tumbled over his forehead. Why might she not push it back for him, and remove the marks of Beatrice's comb? Why might she not press his body with her two hands? It looked so firm and every whit living. And he would let other girls, why not her?

Suddenly he started into life. It made her quiver almost with terror as he quickly pushed the hair off his forehead and came towards her.

'Half-past eight!' he said. 'We'd better buck up. Where's your French?'

Miriam shyly and rather bitterly produced her exercise-book. Every week she wrote for him a sort of diary of her inner life, in her own French. He had found this was the only way to get her to do compositions. And her diary was mostly a love-letter. He would read it now; she felt as if her soul's history were going to be desecrated by him in his present mood. He sat beside her. She watched his hand, firm and warm, rigorously scoring her work. He was reading only the French, ignoring her soul that was there. But gradually his hand forgot its work. He read in silence, motionless. She quivered.

'"*Ce matin les oiseaux m'ont éveillé,*"' he read. '"*Il faisait encore un crépuscule. Mais la petite fenêtre de ma chambre était blême, et puis jaune, et tous les oiseaux de bois éclatèrent dans un chanson vif et résonnant. Tout l'aube tressaillit. J'avais rêvé de vous. Est-ce que vous voyez aussi l'aube? Les oiseaux m'éveillent presque tous les matins et toujours il y a quelque chose de terreur dans le cri des grives. Il est si clair–*"'

Miriam sat tremulous, half ashamed. He remained quite still, trying to understand. He only knew she loved him. He was afraid of her love for him. It was too good for him, and he was inadequate. His own love was at fault, not hers. Ashamed, he corrected her work humbly writing above her words.

'Look,' he said quietly, 'the past participle conjugated with *avoir* agrees with the direct object when it precedes.'

She bent forward, trying to see and to understand. Her free, fine curls tickled his face. He started as if they had been red hot, shuddering. He saw her peering forward at the page, her red lips parted piteously, the black hair springing in fine strands across her tawny, ruddy cheek. She was coloured like a pomegranate for richness. His breath came short as he watched her. Suddenly she looked up at him. Her dark eyes were naked with their love, afraid, and yearning. His eyes, too, were dark, and they hurt her. They seemed to master her. She lost all her self-control, was exposed in fear. And he knew, before he could kiss her, he must drive something out of himself. And a touch of hate for her crept back again into his heart. He returned to her exercise.

Suddenly he flung down the pencil, and was at the oven in a leap, turning the bread. For Miriam he was too quick. She started violently, and it hurt her with real pain. Even the way he crouched before the oven hurt her. There seemed to be something cruel in it, something cruel in the swift way he pitched the bread out of the tins, caught it up again. If only he had been gentle in his movements she would have felt so rich and warm. As it was, she was hurt.

He returned and finished the exercise.

'You've done well this week,' he said.

She saw he was flattered by her diary. It did not repay her entirely.

'You really do blossom out sometimes,' he said. 'You ought to write poetry.'

She lifted her head with joy, then she shook it mistrustfully. 'I don't trust myself,' she said.

'You should try!'

Again she shook her head.

'Shall we read or is it too late?' he asked.

'It is late—but we can read just a little,' she pleaded.

She was really getting now the food for her life during the next week. He made her copy Baudelaire's 'Le Balcon'. Then he read it for her. His voice was soft and caressing, but growing almost brutal. He had a way of lifting his lips and showing his teeth, passionately and bitterly, when he was much moved. This he did now. It made Miriam feel as if he were trampling on her. She dared not look at him, but sat with her head bowed. She could not understand why he got into such a tumult and fury. It made her wretched. She did not like Baudelaire, on the whole—nor Verlaine.

'Behold her singing in the field
Yon solitary highland lass.'

That nourished her heart. So did 'Fair Ines'. And—

'It is a beauteous evening, calm and free,
The holy time is quiet as a nun.'

These were like herself. And there was he, saying in his throat bitterly:

'*Tu te rappelleras la beauté des caresses.*'

The poem was finished; he took the bread out of the oven, arranging the burnt loaves at the bottom of the panchion, the good ones at the top. The desiccated loaf remained swathed up in the scullery.

'Mater needn't know till morning,' he said. 'It won't upset her so much then as at night.'

Miriam looked in the bookcase, saw what postcards and letters he had received, saw what books were there. She took one that interested him. Then he turned down the gas and they set off. He did not trouble to lock the door.

He was not home again until a quarter to eleven. His mother was seated in the rocking-chair. Annie, with a rope of hair hanging down her back, remained sitting on a low stool before the fire, her elbows on her knees, gloomily. On the table stood the offending loaf unswathed. Paul entered rather breathless. No one spoke. His mother was reading the little local newspaper. He took off his coat, and went to sit down on the sofa. His mother moved curtly aside to let him pass. No one spoke. He was very uncomfortable. For some minutes he sat pretending to read a piece of paper he found on the table. Then—

'I forgot that bread mother,' he said.

There was no answer from either woman.

'Well,' he said, 'it's only twopence ha'penny. I can pay you for that.'

Being angry he put three pennies on the table, and slid them towards his mother. She turned away her head. Her mouth was shut tightly.

'Yes,' said Annie, 'you don't know how badly my mother is!'

The girl sat staring into the fire.

'Why is she badly?' asked Paul, in his overbearing way.

'Well!' said Annie. 'She could scarcely get home.'

He looked closely at his mother. She looked ill.

'*Why* could she scarcely get home?' he asked her, still sharply. She would not answer.

'I found her as white as a sheet sitting here,' said Annie, with a suggestion of tears in her voice.

'Well, why?' insisted Paul. His brows were knitting, his eyes dilating passionately.

'It was enough to upset anybody,' said Mrs Morel, 'hugging those parcels—meat, and greengroceries, and a pair of curtains—'

'Well, why *did* you hug them; you needn't have done.'

'Then who would?'

'Let Annie fetch the meat.'

'Yes, and I *would* fetch the meat, but how was I to know? You were off with Miriam, instead of being in when my mother came.'

'And what was the matter with you?' asked Paul of his mother.

'I suppose it's my heart,' she replied. Certainly she looked bluish round the mouth.

'And have you felt it before?'

'Yes—often enough.'

'Then why haven't you told me?—and why haven't you seen a doctor?'

Mrs Morel shifted in her chair, angry with him for his hectoring.

'You'd never notice anything,' said Annie. 'You're too eager to be off with Miriam.'

'Oh, am I—and any worse than you with Leonard?'

'*I* was in at a quarter to ten.'

There was silence in the room for a time.

'I should have thought,' said Mrs Morel bitterly, 'that she wouldn't have occupied you so entirely as to burn a whole ovenful of bread.'

'Beatrice was here as well as she.'

'Very likely. But we know why the bread is spoilt.'

'Why?' he flashed.

'Because you were engrossed with Miriam,' replied Mrs Morel hotly.

'Oh, very well—then it was *not*!' he replied angrily.

He was distressed and wretched. Seizing a paper, he began to read. Annie, her blouse unfastened, her long ropes of hair twisted into a plait, went up to bed, bidding him a very curt good night.

Paul sat pretending to read. He knew his mother wanted to upbraid him. He also wanted to know what had made her ill, for he was troubled. So, instead of running away to bed, as he would have liked to do, he sat and waited. There was a tense silence. The clock ticked loudly.

'You'd better go to bed before your father comes in,' said the mother harshly. 'And if you're going to have anything to eat, you'd better get it.'

'I don't want anything.'

It was his mother's custom to bring in some trifle for supper on Friday night, the night of luxury for the colliers. He was too angry to go and find it in the pantry this night. This insulted her.

'If I *wanted* you to go to Selby on Friday night, I can imagine the scene,' said Mrs Morel. 'But you're never too tired to go if *she* will come for you. Nay, but you neither want to eat nor drink then.'

'I can't let her go alone.'

'Can't you? And why does she come?'

'Not because I ask her.'

'She doesn't come without you want her—'

'Well, what if I *do* want her—' he replied.

'Why, nothing, if it was sensible or reasonable. But to go trapesing up there miles and miles in the mud, coming home at midnight, and got to go to Nottingham in the morning—'

'If I hadn't, you'd be just the same.'

'Yes, I should, because there's no sense in it. Is she *so* fascinating that you must follow her all that way?' Mrs Morel was bitterly sarcastic. She sat still, with averted face, stroking, with a rhythmic, jerked movement, the black sateen of her apron. It was a movement that hurt Paul to see.

'I do like her,' he said, 'but—'

'*Like* her!' said Mrs Morel, in the same biting tones. 'It seems to me you like nothing and nobody else. There's neither Annie, nor me, nor anyone now for you.'

'What nonsense, Mother—you know I don't love her—I—I tell you I *don't* love her—she doesn't even walk with my arm, because I don't want her to.'

'Then why do you fly to her so often!'

'I *do* like to talk to her—I never said I didn't. But I *don't* love her.'

'Is there nobody else to talk to?'

'Not about the things we talk of. There's lots of things that you're not interested in, that—'

'What things?'

Mrs Morel was so intense that Paul began to pant.

'Why—painting—and books. *You* don't care about Herbert Spencer.'

'No,' was the sad reply. 'And *you* won't at my age.'

'Well, but I do now—and Miriam does—'

'And how do you know,' Mrs Morel flashed defiantly, 'that *I* shouldn't? Do you ever try me?'

'But you don't, Mother, you know you don't care whether a picture's decorative or not; you don't care what *manner* it is in.'

'How do you know I don't care? Do you ever try me? Do you ever talk to me about these things, to try?'

'But it's not that that matters to you, Mother, you know it's not.'

'What is it, then—what is it, then, that matters to me?' she flashed. He knitted his brows with pain.

'You're old, Mother, and we're young.'

He only meant that the interests of *her* age were not the interests of his. But he realized the moment he had spoken that he had said the wrong thing.

'Yes, I know it well–I am old. And therefore I may stand aside; I have nothing more to do with you. You only want me to wait on you–the rest is for Miriam.'

He could not bear it. Instinctively he realized that he was life to her. And, after all, she was the chief thing to him, the only supreme thing.

'You know it isn't, Mother, you know it isn't!'

She was moved to pity by his cry.

'It looks a great deal like it,' she said, half putting aside her despair.

'No, mother–I really *don't* love her. I talk to her, but I want to come home to you.'

He had taken off his collar and tie, and rose, bare-throated to go to bed. As he stooped to kiss his mother, she threw her arms round his neck, hid her face on his shoulder, and cried, in a whimpering voice, so unlike her own that he writhed in agony:

'I can't bear it. I could let another woman–but not her. She'd leave me no room, not a bit of room–'

And immediately he hated Miriam bitterly.

'And I've never–you know, Paul–I've never had a husband–not really–'

He stroked his mother's hair, and his mouth was on her throat.

'And she exults so in taking you from me–she's not like ordinary girls.'

'Well, I don't love her, Mother,' he murmured, bowing his head and hiding his eyes on her shoulder in misery. His mother kissed him a long, fervent kiss.

'My boy!' she said, in a voice trembling with passionate love.

Without knowing, he gently stroked her face.

'There,' said his mother, 'now go to bed. You'll be *so* tired in the morning.' As she was speaking she heard her husband coming. 'There's your father–now go.' Suddenly she looked at him almost as if in fear. 'Perhaps I'm selfish. If you want her, take her, my boy.'

His mother looked so strange. Paul kissed her, trembling, 'Ha–Mother!' he said softly.

Morel came in, walking unevenly. His hat was over one corner of his eye. He balanced in the doorway.

'At your mischief again?' he said venomously.

Mrs Morel's emotion turned into sudden hate of the drunkard who had come in thus upon her.

'At any rate, it is sober,' she said.

'H'm–h'm! H'm–h'm!' he sneered. He went into the passage, hung up his hat and coat. Then they heard him go down three steps to the pantry. He returned with a piece of pork-pie in his fist. It was what Mrs Morel had bought for her son.

'Nor was that bought for you. If you can give me no more than twenty-five shillings, I'm sure I'm not going to buy you pork-pie to stuff, after you've swilled a bellyful of beer.'

'Wha-at–wha-at!' snarled Morel, toppling in his balance.

'Wha-at–not for me?' He looked at the piece of meat and crust, and suddenly, in a vicious spurt of temper, flung it into the fire.

Paul started to his feet.

'Waste your own stuff!' he cried.

'What—what!' suddenly shouted Morel, jumping up and clenching his fist. 'I'll show yer, yer young jockey!'

'All right!' said Paul viciously, putting his head on one side. 'Show me!'

He would at that moment dearly have loved to have a smack at something. Morel was half crouching, fists up, ready to spring. The young man stood, smiling with his lips.

'Ussha!' hissed the father, swiping round with a great stroke just past his son's face. He dared not, even though so close, really touch the young man, but swerved an inch away.

'Right!' said Paul, his eyes upon the side of his father's mouth, where in another instant his fist would have hit. He ached for that stroke. But he heard a faint moan from behind. His mother was deadly pale, and dark at the mouth. Morel was dancing up to deliver another blow.

'Father!' said Paul, so that the word rang.

Morel started, and stood at attention.

'Mother!' moaned the boy, 'Mother!'

She began to struggle with herself. Her open eyes watched him, although she could not move. Gradually she was coming to herself. He laid her down on the sofa, and ran upstairs for little whisky, which at last she could sip. The tears were hopping down his face. As he kneeled in front of her he did not cry, but the tears ran down his face quietly. Morel, on the opposite side of the room, sat with his elbows on his knees glaring across.

'What's a-matter with 'er?' he asked.

'Faint!' replied Paul.

'H'm!'

The elderly man began to unlace his boots. He stumbled off to bed. His last fight was fought in that home.

Paul kneeled there, stroking his mother's hand.

'Don't be poorly, Mother—don't be poorly!' he said time after time.

'It's nothing, my boy,' she murmured.

At last he rose, fetched in a large piece of coal, and raked the fire. Then he cleared the room, put everything straight, laid the things for breakfast, and brought his mother's candle.

'Can you go to bed, Mother?'

'Yes, I'll come.'

'Sleep with Annie, Mother, not with him.'

'No, I'll sleep in my own bed.'

'Don't sleep with him, Mother.'

'I'll sleep in my own bed.'

She rose, and he turned out the gas, then followed her closely upstairs, carrying her candle. On the landing he kissed her close.

'Good night, Mother.'

'Good night!' she said.

He pressed his face upon the pillow in a fury of misery. And yet, somewhere in his soul, he was at peace because he still loved his mother best. It was the bitter peace of resignation.

The efforts of his father to conciliate him next day were a great humiliation to him.

Everybody tried to forget the scene.

9

DEFEAT OF MIRIAM

Paul was dissatisfied with himself and with everything. The deepest of his love belonged to his mother. When he felt he had hurt her, or wounded his love for her, he could not bear it. Now it was spring, and there was battle between him and Miriam. This year he had a good deal against her. She was vaguely aware of it. The old feeling that she was to be a sacrifice to this love, which she had had when she prayed, was mingled in all her emotions. She did not at the bottom believe she ever would have him. She did not believe in herself primarily; doubted whether she could ever be what he would demand of her. Certainly she never saw herself living happily through a lifetime with him. She saw tragedy, sorrow, and sacrifice ahead. And in sacrifice she was proud, in renunciation she was strong, for she did not trust herself to support everyday life. She was prepared for the big things and the deep things, like tragedy. It was the sufficiency of the small day-life she could not trust.

The Easter holidays began happily. Paul was his own frank self. Yet she felt it would go wrong. On the Sunday afternoon she stood at her bedroom window, looking across at the oak-trees of the wood, in whose branches a twilight was tangled, below the bright sky of the afternoon. Grey-green rosettes of honeysuckle leaves hung before the window, some already, she fancied, showing bud. It was spring, which she loved and dreaded.

Hearing the clack of the gate she stood in suspense. It was a bright grey day, Paul came into the yard with his bicycle, which glittered as he walked. Usually he rang his bell and laughed towards the house. To-day he walked with shut lips and cold, cruel bearing, that had something of a slouch and a sneer in it. She knew him well by now, and could tell from that keen-looking, aloof young body of his what was happening inside him. There was a cold correctness in the way he put his bicycle in its place, that made her heart sink.

She came downstairs nervously. She was wearing a new net blouse that she thought became her. It had a high collar with a tiny ruff, reminding her of Mary Queen of Scots, and making her, she thought, look wonderfully a woman, and dignified. At twenty she was full-breasted and luxuriously formed. Her face was still like a soft rich mask, unchangeable. But her eyes, once fitted, were wonderful. She was afraid of him. He would notice her new blouse.

He, being in a hard, ironical mood, was entertaining the family to a description of a service given in the Primitive Methodist Chapel, conducted by one of the well-known preachers of the sect. He sat at the head of the table, his mobile face, with eyes that could be so beautiful, shining with tenderness or dancing with laughter, now taking on one expression and then another, in imitation of various people he was mocking. His mockery always hurt her; it was too near the reality. He was too clever and cruel. She felt that when his eyes were like this, hard with mocking hate, he would spare neither himself nor anybody else. But Mrs Leivers was wiping her eyes with laughter, and Mr Leivers, just awake from his Sunday nap, was rubbing his head in amusement. The three brothers sat with ruffled, sleepy appearance in their shirtsleeves, giving a guffaw from time to time. The whole family loved a 'take-off' more than anything.

He took no notice of Miriam. Later, she saw him remark her new blouse, saw that the artist approved, but it won from him not a spark of warmth. She was nervous, could hardly reach the teacups from the shelves.

When the men went out to milk, she ventured to address him personally.

'You were late,' she said.

'Was I?' he answered.

There was silence for a while.

'Was it rough riding?' she asked.

'I didn't notice it.'

She continued quickly to lay the table. When she had finished—

'Tea won't be for a few minutes. Will you come and look at the daffodils?' she said.

He rose without answering. They went out into the back garden under the budding damson-trees. The hills and the sky were clean and cold. Everything looked washed, rather hard. Miriam glanced at Paul. He was pale and impassive. It seemed cruel to her that his eyes and brows, which she loved, could look so hurting.

'Has the wind made you tired?' she asked. She detected an underneath feeling of weariness about him.

'No, I think not,' he answered.

'It must be rough on the road—the wood moans so.'

'You can see by the clouds it's a south-west wind; that helps me here.'

'You see, I don't cycle, so I don't understand,' she murmured.

'Is there need to cycle to know that?' he said.

She thought his sarcasms were unnecessary. They went forward in silence. Round the wild, tussocky lawn at the back of the house was a thorn hedge, under which daffodils were craning forward from among their sheaves of grey-green blades. The cheeks of the flowers were greenish with cold. But still some had burst, and their gold ruffled and glowed. Miriam went on her knees before one cluster, took a wild-looking daffodil between her hands, turned up its face of gold to her, and bowed down, caressing it with her mouth and cheeks and brows. He stood aside, with his hands in his pockets watching her. One after another she turned up to him the faces of the yellow, bursten flowers appealingly, fondling them lavishly all the while.

'Aren't they magnificent?' she murmured.

'Magnificent! it's a bit thick—they're pretty!'

She bowed again to her flowers at his censure of her praise. He watched her crouching, sipping the flowers with fervid kisses.

'Why must you always be fondling things!' he said irritably.

'But I love to touch them,' she replied, hurt.

'Can you never like things without clutching them as if you wanted to pull the heart out of them? Why don't you have a bit more restraint, or reserve, or something?'

She looked up at him full of pain, then continued slowly to stroke her lips against a ruffled flower. Their scent, as she smelled it, was much kinder than he; it almost made her cry.

'You wheedle the soul out of things,' he said. 'I would never wheedle—at any rate, I'd go straight.'

He scarcely knew what he was saying. These things came from him mechanically. She looked at him. His body seemed one weapon, firm and hard against her.

'You're always begging for things to love you,' he said, 'as if you were a beggar for love. Even the flowers, you have to fawn on them—'

Rhythmically, Miriam was swaying and stroking the flower with her mouth, inhaling the scent which ever after made her shudder as it came to her nostrils.

'You don't want to love—your eternal and abnormal craving is to be loved. You aren't positive, you're negative. You absorb, absorb, as if you must fill yourself up with love, because you've got a shortage somewhere.'

She was stunned by his cruelty, and did not hear. He had not the faintest notion of what he was saying. It was as if his fretted, tortured soul, run hot by thwarted passion, jetted off these sayings like sparks from electricity. She did not grasp anything he said. She only sat crouched beneath his cruelty and his hatred of her. She never realized in a flash. Over everything she brooded and brooded.

After tea he stayed with Edgar and the brother, taking no notice of Miriam. She, extremely unhappy on this looked-for holiday, waited for him. And at last he yielded and came to her. She was determined to track this mood of his to its origin. She counted it not much more than a mood.

'Shall we go through the wood a little way?' she asked him, knowing he never refused a direct request.

They went down to the warren. On the middle path they passed a trap, a narrow horseshoe hedge of small fir-boughs, baited with the guts of a rabbit. Paul glanced at it frowning. She caught his eye.

'Isn't it dreadful?' she asked.

'I don't know? Is it worse than a weasel with its teeth in a rabbit's throat? One weasel or many rabbits? One or the other must go!'

He was taking the bitterness of life badly. She was rather sorry for him.

'We will go back to the house,' he said. 'I don't want to walk out.'

They went past the lilac-tree, whose bronze leaf-buds were coming unfastened. Just a fragment remained of the haystack, a monument squared and brown, like a pillar of stone. There was a little bed of hay from the last cutting.

'Let us sit here a minute,' said Miriam.

He sat down against his will, resting his back against the hard wall of hay. They faced the amphitheatre of round hills that glowed with sunset, tiny white farms standing out, the meadows golden, the woods dark and yet luminous, tree-tops folded over tree-tops, distinct in the distance. The evening had cleared, and the east was tender with a magenta flush under which the land lay still and rich.

'Isn't it beautiful?' she pleaded.

But he only scowled. He would rather have had it ugly just then.

At that moment a big bull-terrier came rushing up, open-mouthed, pranced his two paws on the youth's shoulders, licking his face. Paul drew back, laughing. Bill was a great relief to him. He pushed the dog aside, but it came leaping back.

'Get out,' said the lad, 'or I'll dot thee one.'

But the dog would not be pushed away. So Paul had a little battle with the creature, pitching poor Bill away from him, who, however, only floundered tumultuously back again, wild with joy. The two fought together, the man laughing grudgingly, the dog grinning all over. Miriam watched them. There was something pathetic about the man. He wanted so badly to love, to be tender. The tough way he bowled the dog over was really loving. Bill got up, panting with happiness, his brown eyes rolling in his white face, and lumbered back again. He adored Paul. The lad frowned.

'Bill, I've had enough o' thee,' he said.

But the dog only stood with two heavy paws, that quivered with love, upon his thigh, and flicked a red tongue at him. He drew back.

'No,' he said–'no–I've had enough.'

And in a minute the dog trotted off happily, to vary the fun.

He remained staring miserably across at the hills, whose still beauty he begrudged. He wanted to go and cycle with Edgar. Yet he had not the courage to leave Miriam.

'Why are you sad?' she asked humbly.

'I'm not sad; why should I be?' he answered. 'I'm only normal.'

She wondered why he always claimed to be normal when he was disagreeable.

'But what is the matter?' she pleaded, coaxing him soothingly.

'Nothing!'

'Nay!' she murmured.

He picked up a stick and began to stab the earth with it.

'You'd far better not talk,' he said.

'But I wish to know–' she replied.

He laughed resentfully.

'You always do,' he said.

'It's not fair to me,' she murmured.

He thrust, thrust, thrust at the ground with the pointed stick, digging up little clods of earth as if he were in a fever of irritation. She gently and firmly laid her hand on his wrist.

'Don't!' she said. 'Put it away.'

He flung the stick into the currant-bushes, and leaned back. Now he was bottled up.

'What is it?' she pleaded softly.

He lay perfectly still, only his eyes alive, and they full of torment.

'You know,' he said at length, rather wearily–'you know–we'd better break it off.'

It was what she dreaded. Swiftly everything seemed to darken before her eyes.

'Why?' she murmured. 'What has happened?'

'Nothing has happened. We only realize where we are. It's no good–'

She waited in silence, sadly, patiently. It was no good being impatient with him. At any rate, he would tell her now what ailed him.

'We agreed on friendship,' he went on in a dull, monotonous voice. 'How often *have* we agreed for friendship! And yet–it neither stops there, nor gets anywhere else.'

He was silent again. She brooded. What did he mean? He was so wearying. There was something he would not yield. Yet she must be patient with him.

'I can only give friendship–it's all I'm capable of–it's a flaw in my make-up.

The thing overbalances to one side–I hate a toppling balance. Let us have done.'

There was warmth of fury in his last phrases. He meant she loved him more than he her. Perhaps he could not love her. Perhaps she had not in herself that which he wanted. It was the deepest motive of her soul, this self-mistrust. It was so deep she dared neither realize nor acknowledge it. Perhaps she was deficient. Like an infinitely subtle shame, it kept her always back. If it were so, she would do without him. She would never let herself want him. She would merely see.

'But what has happened?' she said.

'Nothing–it's all myself–it only comes out just now. We're always like this towards Easter-time.'

He grovelled so helplessly, she pitied him. At least she never floundered in such a pitiable way. After all, it was he who was chiefly humiliated.

'What do you want?' she asked.

'Why–I mustn't come often–that's all. Why should I monopolize you when I'm not–You see, I'm deficient in something with regard to you–'

He was telling her he did not love her, and so sought to leave her a chance with another man. How foolish and blind and shamefully clumsy he was! What were other men to her! What were men to her at all! But he, ah! she loved his soul. Was *he* deficient in something? Perhaps he was.

'But I don't understand,' she said huskily. 'Yesterday–'

The night was turning jangled and hateful to him as the twilight faded. And she bowed under her suffering.

'I know,' he cried, 'you never will! You'll never believe that I can't–can't physically, any more than I can fly up like a skylark–'

'What?' she murmured. Now she dreaded.

'Love you.'

He hated her bitterly at that moment because he made her suffer. Love her! She knew he loved her. He really belonged to her. This about not loving her, physically, bodily, was a mere perversity on his part, because he knew she loved him. He was stupid like a child. He belonged to her. His soul wanted her. She guessed somebody had been influencing him. She felt upon him the hardness, the foreignness of another influence.

'What have they been saying at home?' she asked.

'It's not that,' he answered.

And then she knew it was. She despised them for their commonness, his people. They did not know what things were really worth.

He and she talked very little more that night. After all he left her to cycle with Edgar.

He had come back to his mother. Hers was the strongest tie in his life. When he thought round, Miriam shrank away. There was a vague, unreal feel about her. And nobody else mattered. There was one place in the world that stood solid and did not melt into unreality: the place where his mother was. Everybody else could grow shadowy, almost non-existent to him, but she could not. It was as if the pivot and pole of his life, from which he could not escape, was his mother.

And in the same way she waited for him. In him was established her life now. After all, the life beyond offered very little to Mrs Morel. She saw that our chance for *doing* is here, and doing counted with her. Paul was going to prove that she had been right; he was going to make a man whom nothing should shift off his feet; he was going to alter the face of the earth in some way which mattered. Wherever he went she felt her soul went with him. Whatever he did she felt her soul stood by him, ready, as it were, to hand him his tools. She could not bear it when he was with Miriam. William was dead. She would fight to keep Paul.

And he came back to her. And in his soul was a feeling of the satisfaction of self-sacrifice because he was faithful to her. She loved him first; he loved her first. And yet it was not enough. His new young life, so strong and imperious, was urged towards something else. It made him mad with restlessness. She saw this, and wished bitterly that Miriam had been a woman who could take this new life of his, and leave her the roots. He fought against his mother almost as he fought against Miriam.

It was a week before he went again to Willey Farm. Miriam had suffered a great deal, and was afraid to see him again. Was she now to endure the ignominy of his abandoning her? That would only be superficial and temporary. He would come back. She held the keys to his soul. But meanwhile, how he would torture her with his battle against her. She shrank from it.

However, the Sunday after Easter he came to tea. Mrs Leivers was glad to see him. She gathered something was fretting him, that he found things hard. He seemed to drift to her for comfort. And she was good to him. She did him that great kindness of treating him almost with reverence.

He met her with the young children in the front garden.

'I'm glad you've come,' said the mother, looking at him with her great appealing brown eyes. 'It is such a sunny day. I was just going down to the fields for the first time this year.

He felt she would like him to come. That soothed him. They went, talked simply, he gentle and humble. He could have wept with gratitude that she was deferential to him. He was feeling humiliated.

At the bottom of the Mow Close they found a thrush's nest.

'Shall I show you the eggs?' he said.

'Do!' replied Mrs Leivers. 'They seem *such* a sign of spring, and so hopeful.'

He put aside the thorns, and took out the eggs, holding them in the palm of his hand.

'They are quite hot—I think we frightened her off them,' he said.

'Ay, poor thing!' said Mrs Leivers.

Miriam could not help touching the eggs, and his hand which, it seemed to her, cradled them so well.

'Isn't it a strange warmth!' she murmured, to get near him.

'Blood heat,' he answered.

She watched him putting them back, his body pressed against the hedge, his arm reaching slowly through the thorns, his hand folded carefully over the eggs. He was concentrated on the act. Seeing him so, she loved him; he seemed so simple and sufficient to himself. And she could not get to him.

After tea she stood hesitating at the bookshelf. He took 'Tartarin de Tarascon'. Again they sat on the bank of hay at the foot of the stack. He read a couple of pages, but without any heart for it. Again the dog came racing up to repeat the fun of the other day. He shoved his muzzle in the man's chest. Paul fingered his ear for a moment. Then he pushed him away.

'Go away, Bill,' he said. 'I don't want you!'

Bill slunk off, and Miriam wondered and dreaded what was coming. There was a silence about the youth that made her still with apprehension. It was not his furies, but his quiet resolutions that she feared.

Turning his face a little to one side, so that she could not see him, he began, speaking slowly and painfully:

'Do you think–if I didn't come up so much–you might get to like somebody else–another man?'

So this was what he was still harping on.

'But I don't know any other men. Why do you ask?' she replied, in a low tone that should have been a reproach to him.

'Why,' he blurted, 'because they say I've no right to come up like this–without we mean to marry–'

Miriam was indignant at anybody's forcing the issues between them. She had been furious with her own father for suggesting to Paul, laughingly, that he knew why he came so much.

'Who says?' she asked, wondering if her people had anything to do with it. They had not.

'Mother–and the others. They say at this rate everybody will consider me engaged, and I ought to consider myself so, because it's not fair to you. And I've tried to find out–and I don't think I love you as a man ought to love his wife. What do *you* think about it?'

Miriam bowed her head moodily. She was angry at having this struggle. People should leave him and her alone.

'I don't know,' she murmured.

'Do you think we love each other enough to marry?' he asked definitely. It made her tremble.

'No,' she answered truthfully. 'I don't think so–we're too young.'

'I thought perhaps,' he went on miserably, 'that you, with your intensity in things, might have given me more–than I could ever make up to you. And even now–if you think it better–we'll get engaged.'

Now Miriam wanted to cry. And she was angry, too. He was always such a child for people to do as they liked with.

'No, I don't think so,' she said firmly.

He pondered a minute.

'You see,' he said, 'with me–I don't think one person would ever monopolize me–be everything to me–I think never.'

This she did not consider.

'No,' she murmured. Then, after a pause, she looked at him, and her dark eyes flashed.

'This is your mother,' she said. 'I know she never liked me.'

'No, no, it isn't,' he said hastily. 'It was for your sake she spoke this time. She only said, if I was going on, I ought to consider myself engaged.' There was a silence. 'And if I ask you to come down any time, you won't stop away, will you?'

She did not answer. By this time she was very angry.

'Well, what shall we do?' she said shortly. 'I suppose I'd better drop French. I was just beginning to get on with it. But I suppose I can go on alone.'

'I don't see that we need,' he said. 'I can give you a French lesson, surely.'

'Well–and there are Sunday nights. I shan't stop coming to chapel, because I enjoy it, and it's all the social life I get. But you've no need to come home with me. I can go alone.'

'All right,' he answered, rather taken aback. 'But if I ask Edgar, he'll always come with us, and then they can say nothing.'

There was silence. After all, then, she would not lose much. For all their talk down at his home there would not be much difference. She wished they would mind their own business.

'And you won't think about it, and let it trouble you, will you?' he asked.

'Oh no,' replied Miriam, without looking at him.

He was silent. She thought him unstable. He had no fixity of purpose, no anchor of righteousness that held him.

'Because,' he continued, 'a man gets across his bicycle–and goes to work–and does all sorts of things. But a woman broods.'

'No, I shan't bother,' said Miriam. And she meant it.

It had gone rather chilly. They went indoors.

'How white Paul looks!' Mrs Leivers exclaimed. 'Miriam, you shouldn't have let him sit out of doors. Do you think you've taken cold, Paul?'

'Oh, no!' he laughed.

But he felt done up. It wore him out, the conflict in himself. Miriam pitied him now. But quite early, before nine o'clock, he rose to go.

'You're not going home, are you?' asked Mrs Leivers anxiously.

'Yes,' he replied, 'I said I'd be early.' He was very awkward.

'But this *is* early,' said Mr Leivers.

Miriam sat in the rocking-chair, and did not speak. He hesitated, expecting her to rise and go with him to the barn as usual for his bicycle. She remained as she was. He was at a loss.

'Well–good night all!' he faltered.

She spoke her good night along with all the others. But as he went past the window he looked in. She saw him pale, his brows knit slightly in a way that had become constant with him, his eyes dark with pain.

She rose and went to the doorway to wave good-bye to him as he passed through the gate. He rode slowly under the pine-trees, feeling a cur and a miserable wretch. His bicycle went tilting down the hills at random. He thought it would be a relief to break one's neck.

Two days later he sent up a book and a little note, urging her to read and to be busy.

At this time he gave all his friendship to Edgar. He loved the family so much, he loved the farm so much; it was the dearest place on earth to him. His home was not so lovable. It was his mother. But then he would have been just as happy with his mother anywhere. Whereas Willey Farm he loved passionately. He loved the little pokey kitchen, where men's boots tramped, and the dog slept with one eye open for fear of being trodden on; where the lamp hung over the table at night, and everything was so silent. He loved Miriam's long, low parlour, with its atmosphere of romance, its flowers, its books, its high rosewood piano. He loved the gardens and the buildings that stood with their scarlet roofs on the naked edges of the fields, crept towards the wood as if for cosiness, the wild country scooping down a valley and up the uncultured hills of the other side. Only to be there was an exhilaration and a joy to him. He loved Mrs Leivers, with her unworldliness and her quaint cynicism; he loved Mr Leivers, so warm and young and lovable; he loved Edgar, who lit up when he came, and the boys and the children and Bill–even the sow Circe and the Indian game-cock called Tippoo. All this besides Miriam. He could not give it up.

So he went as often, but he was usually with Edgar. Only all the family, including the father, joined in charades and games at evening. And later,

Miriam drew them together, and they read 'Macbeth' out of penny books, taking parts. It was great excitement. Miriam was glad, and Mrs Leivers was glad, and Mr Leivers enjoyed it. Then they all learned songs together from tonic solfa, singing in a circle round the fire. But now Paul was very rarely alone with Miriam. She waited. When she and Edgar and he walked home together from chapel or from the literary society in Bestwood, she knew this talk, so passionate and so unorthodox nowadays, was for her. She did envy Edgar, however, his cycling with Paul, his Friday nights, his days working in the fields. For her Friday nights and her French lessons were gone. She was nearly always alone, walking, pondering in the wood, reading, studying, dreaming, waiting. And he wrote to her frequently.

One Sunday evening they attained to their old rare harmony. Edgar had stayed to Communion—he wondered what it was like—with Mrs Morel. So Paul came on alone with Miriam to his home. He was more or less under her spell again. As usual, they were discussing the sermon. He was setting now full sail towards Agnosticism, but such a religious Agnosticism that Miriam did not suffer so badly. They were at the Renan 'Vie de Jésus' stage. Miriam was the threshing-floor on which he threshed out all his beliefs. While he trampled his ideas upon her soul, the truth came out for him. She alone was his threshing floor. She alone helped him towards realization. Almost impassive, she submitted to his argument and expounding. And somehow, because of her, he gradually realized where he was wrong. And what he realized, she realized. She felt he could not do without her.

They came to the silent house. He took the key out of the scullery window, and they entered. All the time he went on with his discussion. He lit the gas, mended the fire, and brought her some cakes from the pantry. She sat on the sofa, quietly, with a plate on her knee. She wore a large white hat with some pinkish flowers. It was a cheap hat, but he liked it. Her face beneath was still and pensive, golden-brown and ruddy. Always her ears were hid in her short curls. She watched him.

She liked him on Sundays. Then he wore a dark suit that showed the lithe movement of his body. There was a clean, clear-cut look about him. He went on with his thinking to her. Suddenly he reached for a Bible. Miriam liked the way he reached up—so sharp, straight to the mark. He turned the pages quickly, and read her a chapter of St John. As he sat in the arm-chair reading, intent, his voice only thinking, she felt as if he were using her unconsciously as a man uses his tools at some work he is bent on. She loved it. And the wistfulness of his voice was like a reaching to something, and it was as if she were what he reached with. She sat back on the sofa away from him, and yet feeling herself the very instrument his hand grasped. It gave her great pleasure.

Then he began to falter and to get self-conscious. And when he came to the verse, 'A woman, when she is in travail, hath sorrow because her hour is come', he missed it out. Miriam had felt him growing uncomfortable. She shrank when the well-known words did not follow. He went on reading, but she did not hear. A grief and shame made her bend her head. Six months ago he would have read it simply. Now there was a scotch in his running with her. Now she felt there was really something hostile between them, something of which they were ashamed.

She ate her cake mechanically. He tried to go on with his argument, but could not get back the right note. Soon Edgar came in. Mrs Morel had gone to the friends'. The three set off to Willey Farm.

Miriam brooded over his split with her. There was something else he wanted. He could not be satisfied; he could give her no peace. There was between them now always a ground for strife. She wanted to prove him. She believed that his chief need in life was herself. If she could prove it, both to herself and to him, the rest might go; she could simply trust to the future.

So in May she asked him to come to Willey Farm and meet Mrs Dawes. There was something he hankered after. She saw him, whenever they spoke of Clara Dawes, rouse and get slightly angry. He said he did not like her. Yet he was keen to know about her. Well, he should put himself to the test. She believed that there were in him desires for higher things, and desires for lower, and that the desire for the higher would conquer. At any rate, he should try. She forgot that her 'higher' and 'lower' were arbitrary.

He was rather excited at the idea of meeting Clara at Willey Farm. Mrs Dawes came for the day. Her heavy, dun-coloured hair was coiled on top of her head. She wore a white blouse and navy skirt, and somehow, wherever she was, seemed to make things look paltry and insignificant. When she was in the room, the kitchen seemed too small and mean altogether. Miriam's beautiful twilightly parlour looked stiff and stupid. All the Leivers were eclipsed like candles. They found her rather hard to put up with. Yet she was perfectly amiable, but indifferent, and rather hard.

Paul did not come till afternoon. He was early. As he swung off his bicycle, Miriam saw him look round at the house eagerly. He would be disappointed if the visitor had not come. Miriam went out to meet him, bowing her head because of the sunshine. Nasturtiums were coming out crimson under the cool green shadow of their leaves. The girl stood, dark-haired, glad to see him.

'Hasn't Clara come?' he asked.

'Yes,' replied Miriam in her musical tone. 'She's reading.'

He wheeled his bicycle into the barn. He had put on a handsome tie, of which he was rather proud, and socks to match.

'She came this morning?' he asked.

'Yes,' replied Miriam, as she walked at his side. 'You said you'd bring me that letter from the man at Liberty's. Have you remembered?'

'Oh dash, no!' he said. 'But nag at me till you get it.'

'I don't like to nag at you.'

'Do it whether or not. And is she any more agreeable?' he continued.

'You know I always think she is quite agreeable.'

He was silent. Evidently his eagerness to be early to-day had been the newcomer. Miriam already began to suffer. They went together towards the house. He took the clips off his trousers, but was too lazy to brush the dust from his shoes, in spite of the socks and tie.

Clara sat in the cool parlour reading. He saw the nape of her white neck, and the fine hair lifted from it. She rose, looking at him indifferently. To shake hands she lifted her arm straight, in a manner that seemed at once to keep him at a distance, and yet to fling something to him. He noticed how her breasts swelled inside her blouse, and how her shoulder curved handsomely under the thin muslin at the top of her arm.

'You have chosen a fine day,' he said.

'It happens so,' she said.

'Yes,' he said; 'I am glad.'

She sat down, not thanking him for his politeness.

'What have you been doing all morning?' asked Paul of Miriam.

'Well, you see,' said Miriam, coughing huskily, 'Clara only came with father—and so—she's not been here very long.'

Clara sat leaning on the table, holding aloof. He noticed her hands were large, but well kept. And the skin on them seemed almost coarse, opaque, and white, with find golden hairs. She did not mind if he observed her hands. She intended to scorn him. Her heavy arm lay negligently on the table. Her mouth was closed as if she were offended, and she kept her face slightly averted.

'You were at Margaret Bonford's meeting the other evening,' he said to her.

Miriam did not know this courteous Paul. Clara glanced at him.

'Yes,' she said.

'Why,' asked Miriam, 'how do you know?'

'I went in for a few minutes before the train came,' he answered.

Clara turned away again rather disdainfully.

'I think she's a lovable little woman,' said Paul.

'Margaret Bonford!' exclaimed Clara. 'She's a great deal cleverer than most men.'

'Well, I didn't say she wasn't,' he said, deprecating. 'She's lovable for all that.'

'And of course, that is all that matters,' said Clara witheringly.

He rubbed his head, rather perplexed, rather annoyed.

'I suppose it matters more than her cleverness,' he said: 'which after all, would never get her to heaven.'

'It's not heaven she wants to get—it's her fair share on earth,' retorted Clara. She spoke as if he were responsible for some deprivation which Miss Bonford suffered.

'Well,' he said, 'I thought she was warm, and awfully nice—only too frail. I wished she was sitting comfortably in peace—'

'"Darning her husband's stockings,"' said Clara scathingly.

'I'm sure she wouldn't mind darning even my stockings,' he said. 'And I'm sure she'd do them well. Just as I wouldn't mind blacking her boots if she wanted me to.'

But Clara refused to answer this sally of his. He talked to Miriam for a little while. The other woman held aloof.

'Well,' he said, 'I think I'll go and see Edgar. Is he on the land?'

'I believe,' said Miriam, 'he's gone for a load of coal. He should be back directly.'

'Then,' he said, 'I'll go and meet him.'

Miriam dared not propose anything for the three of them. He rose and left.

On the top road, where the gorse was out, he saw Edgar walking lazily beside the mare, who nodded her white-starred forehead as she dragged the clanking load of coal. The young farmer's face lighted up as he saw his friend. Edgar was good-looking, with dark, warm eyes. His clothes were old and rather disreputable, and he walked with considerable pride.

'Hello!' he said, seeing Paul bareheaded. 'Where are you going?'

'Came to meet you. Can't stand "Nevermore".'

Edgar's teeth flashed in a laugh of amusement.

'Who is "Nevermore"?' he asked.

'The lady—Mrs Dawes—it ought to be Mrs The Raven that quoted "Nevermore".'

Edgar laughed with glee.

'Don't you like her?' he asked.

'Not a fat lot,' said Paul. 'Why, do you?'

'No!' The answer came with a deep ring of conviction. 'No!' Edgar pursed up his lips. 'I can't say she's much in my line.' He mused a little. Then: 'But why do you call her "Nevermore"?' he asked.

'Well,' said Paul, 'if she looks at a man she says haughtily "Nevermore", and if she looks at herself in the looking-glass she says disdainfully "Nevermore", and if she thinks back she says it in disgust, and if she looks forward she says it cynically.'

Edgar considered this speech, failed to make much out of it, and said, laughingly,

'You think she's a man-hater?'

'*She* thinks she is,' replied Paul.

'But you don't think so?'

'No,' replied Paul.

'Wasn't she nice with you, then?'

'Could you imagine her *nice* with anybody?' asked the young man.

Edgar laughed. Together they unloaded the coal in the yard. Paul was rather self-conscious, because he knew Clara could see if she looked out of the window. She didn't look.

On Saturday afternoons the horses were brushed down and groomed. Paul and Edgar worked together, sneezing with the dust that came from the pelts of Jimmy and Flower.

'Do you know a new song to teach me?' said Edgar.

He continued to work all the time. The back of his neck was sun-red when he bent down, and his fingers that held the brush were thick. Paul watched him sometimes.

'"Mary Morrison"?' suggested the younger.

Edgar agreed. He had a good tenor voice, and he loved to learn all the songs his friend could teach him, so that he could sing whilst he was carting. Paul had a very indifferent baritone voice, but a good ear. However, he sang softly, for fear of Clara. Edgar repeated the line in a clear tenor. At times they both broke off to sneeze, and first one, then the other, abused his horse.

Miriam was impatient of men. It took so little to amuse them—even Paul. She thought it anomalous in him that he could be so thoroughly absorbed in a triviality.

It was tea-time when they had finished.

'What song was that?' asked Miriam.

Edgar told her. The conversation turned to singing.

'We have such jolly times,' Miriam said to Clara.

Mrs Dawes ate her meal in a slow dignified way. Whenever the men were present she grew distant.

'Do you like singing?' Miriam asked her.

'If it is good,' she said.

Paul, of course, coloured.

'You mean if it is high class and trained?' he said.

'I think a voice needs training before the singing is anything,' she said.

'You might as well insist on having people's voices trained before you allow them to talk,' he replied. 'Really, people sing for their own pleasure, as a rule.'

'And it may be for other people's discomfort.'

'Then the other people should have flaps on their ears,' he replied.

The boys laughed. There was a silence. He flushed deeply, and ate in silence.

After tea, when all the men had gone but Paul, Mrs Leivers said to Clara:
'And you find life happier now?'

'Infinitely.'

'And you are satisfied?'

'So long as I can be free and independent.'

'And you don't *miss* anything in your life?' asked Mrs Leivers gently.

'I've put all that behind me.'

Paul had been feeling uncomfortable during this discourse. He got up.

'You'll find you're always tumbling over things you've put behind you,' he said. Then he took his departure to the cowsheds. He felt he had been witty, and his manly pride was high. He whistled as he went down the brick track.

Miriam came for him a little later to know if he would go with Clara and her for a walk. They set off down to Strelley Mill Farm. As they were going beside the brook, on the Willey Water side, looking through the break at the edge of the wood, where pink campions glowed under a few sunbeams, they saw, beyond the tree-trunks and the thin hazel bushes, a man leading a great bay horse through the gullies. The big red beast seemed to dance romantically through that dimness of green hazel drift, away there where the air was shadowy, as if it were in the past, among the fading bluebells that might have bloomed for Deirdre or Iseult.

The three stood charmed.

'What a treat to be a knight,' he said, 'and to have a pavilion here.'

'And to have us shut up safely?' replied Clara.

'Yes,' he answered, 'singing with your maids at your broidery. I would carry your banner of white and green and heliotrope. I would have "W.S.P.U." emblazoned on my shield, beneath a woman rampant.'

'I have no doubt,' said Clara, 'that you would much rather fight for a woman than let her fight for herself.'

'I would. When she fights for herself she seems like a dog before a looking-glass, gone into a mad fury with its own shadow.'

'And *you* are the looking-glass?' she asked, with a curl of the lip.

'Or the shadow,' he replied.

'I am afraid,' she said, 'that you are too clever.'

'Well, I leave it to you to be *good*," he retorted, laughing. 'Be good, sweet maid, and just let *me* be clever.'

But Clara wearied of his flippancy. Suddenly, looking at her, he saw that the upward lifting of her face was misery and not scorn. His heart grew tender for everybody. He turned and was gentle with Miriam, whom he had neglected till then.

At the wood's edge they met Limb, a thin, swarthy man of forty, tenant of Strelley Mill, which he ran as a cattle-raising farm. He held the halter of the powerful stallion indifferently, as if he were tired. The three stood to let him pass over the stepping-stones of the first brook. Paul admired that so large an animal should walk on such springy toes, with an endless excess of vigour. Limb pulled up before them.

'Tell your father, Miss Leivers,' he said, in a peculiar piping voice, 'that his young beas'es' as broke that bottom fence three days an' runnin'.'

'Which?' asked Miriam, tremulous.

The great horse breathed heavily, shifting round its red flanks, and looking suspiciously with its wonderful big eyes upwards from under its lowered head and falling mane.

'Come along a bit,' replied Limb, 'an' I'll show you.'

The man and the stallion went forward. It danced sideways, shaking its white fetlocks and looking frightened, as it felt itself in the brook.

'No hanky-pankyin',' said the man affectionately to the beast.

It went up the bank in little leaps, then splashed finely through the second brook. Clara, walking with a kind of sulky abandon, watched it half-fascinated, half-contemptuous. Limb stopped and pointed to the fence under some willows.

'There, you see where they got through,' he said. 'My man's druv'em back three times.'

'Yes,' answered Miriam, colouring as if she were at fault.

'Are you comin' in?' asked the man.

'No, thanks, but we should like to go by the pond.'

'Well, just as you've a mind,' he said.

The horse gave little whinneys of pleasure at being so near home.

'He is glad to be back,' said Clara, who was interested in the creature.

'Yes—'e's been a tidy step to-day.'

They went through the gate, and saw approaching them from the big farmhouse a smallish, dark, excitable-looking woman of about thirty-five. Her hair was touched with grey, her dark eyes looked wild. She walked with her hands behind her back. Her brother went forward. As it saw her, the big bay stallion whinneyed again. She came up excitedly.

'Are you home again, my boy!' she said tenderly to the horse, not to the man. The great beast shifted round to her, ducking his head. She smuggled into his mouth the wrinkled yellow apple she had been hiding behind her back, then she kissed him near the eyes. He gave a big sigh of pleasure. She held his head in her arms against her breast.

'Isn't he splendid!' said Miriam to her.

Miss Limb looked up. Her dark eyes glanced straight at Paul.

'Oh, good evening, Miss Leivers,' she said. 'It's ages since you've been down.'

Miriam introduced her friends.

'Your horse *is* a fine fellow!' said Clara.

'Isn't he!' Again she kissed him. 'As loving as any man!'

'More loving than most men, I should think,' replied Clara.

'He's a nice boy!' cried the woman, again embracing the horse.

Clara, fascinated by the big beast, went up to stroke his neck.

'He's quite gentle,' said Miss Limb. 'Don't you think big fellows are?'

'He's a beauty!' replied Clara.

She wanted to look in his eyes. She wanted him to look at her.

'It's a pity he can't talk,' she said.

'Oh, but he can—all but,' replied the other woman.

Then her brother moved on with the horse.

'Are you coming in? *Do* come in, Mr—I didn't catch it.'

'Morel,' said Miriam. 'No, we won't come in, but we should like to go by the mill-pond.'

'Yes—yes, do. Do you fish, Mr Morel?'

'No,' said Paul.

'Because if you do you might come and fish any time,' said Miss Limb. 'We scarcely see a soul from week's end to week's end. I should be thankful.'

'What fish are there in the pond?' he asked.

They went through the front garden, over the sluice, and up the steep bank to the pond, which lay in shadow, with its two wooded islets. Paul walked with Miss Limb.

'I shouldn't mind swimming here,' he said.

'Do,' she replied. 'Come when you like. My brother will be awfully pleased to talk with you. He is so quiet, because there is no one to talk to. Do come and swim.'

Clara came up.

'It's a fine depth,' she said, 'and so clear.'

'Yes,' said Miss Limb.

'Do you swim?' said Paul. 'Miss Limb was just saying we could come when we liked.'

'Of course there's the farm hands,' said Miss Limb.

They talked a few moments, then went on up the wild hill, leaving the lonely, haggard-eyed woman on the bank.

The hillside was all ripe with sunshine. It was wild and tussocky, given over to rabbits. The three walked in silence. Then:

'She makes me feel uncomfortable,' said Paul.

'You mean Miss Limb?' asked Miriam. 'Yes.'

'What's a matter with her? Is she going dotty with being too lonely?'

'Yes,' said Miriam. 'It's not the right sort of life for her. I think it's cruel to bury her there. *I* really ought to go and see her more. But—she upsets me.'

'She makes me feel sorry for her—yes, and she bothers me,' she said.

'I suppose,' blurted Clara suddenly, 'she wants a man.'

The other two were silent for a few moments.

'But it's the loneliness sends her cracked,' said Paul.

Clara did not answer, but strode on uphill. She was walking with her head hanging, her legs swinging as she kicked through the dead thistles and the tussocky grass, her arms hanging loose. Rather than walking, her handsome body seemed to be blundering up the hill. A hot wave went over Paul. He was curious about her. Perhaps life had been cruel to her. He forgot Miriam, who was walking beside him talking to him. She glanced at him, finding he did not answer her. His eyes were fixed ahead on Clara.

'Do you still think she is disagreeable?' she asked.

He did not notice that the question was sudden. It ran with his thoughts.

'Something's the matter with her,' he said.

'Yes,' answered Miriam.

They found at the top of the hill a hidden wild field, two sides of which were backed by the wood, the other sides by high loose hedges of hawthorn and elder-bushes. Between these overgrown bushes were gaps that the cattle might have walked through had there been any cattle now. There the turf was smooth as velveteen, padded and holed by the rabbits. The field itself was coarse, and crowded with tall, big cowslips that had never been cut. Clusters of strong flowers rose everywhere above the coarse tussocks of bent. It was like a roadstead crowded with tall, fairy shipping.

'Ah!' cried Miriam, and she looked at Paul, her dark eyes dilating. He smiled. Together they enjoyed the field of flowers. Clara, a little way off, was looking at the cowslips disconsolately. Paul and Miriam stayed close together, talking in subdued tones. He kneeled on one knee, quickly gathering the best blossoms, moving from tuft to tuft restlessly, talking softly all the time. Miriam plucked the flowers lovingly, lingering over them. He always seemed to her too quick, and almost scientific. Yet his bunches had a natural beauty more than hers. He loved them, but as if they were his and he had a right to them. She had more reverence for them: they held something she had not.

The flowers were very fresh and sweet. He wanted to drink them. As he gathered them, he ate the little yellow trumpets. Clara was still wandering about disconsolately. Going towards her, he said:

'Why don't you get some?'

'I don't believe in it. They look better growing.'

'But you'd like some?'

'They want to be left.'

'I don't believe they do.'

'I don't want the corpses of flowers about me,' she said.

'That's a stiff, artificial notion,' he said. 'They don't die any quicker in water than on their roots. And besides, the *look* nice in a bowl–they look jolly. And you only call a thing a corpse because it looks corpse-like.'

'Whether it is one or not?' she argued.

'It isn't one to me. A dead flower isn't a corpse of a flower.' Clara now ignored him.

'And even so–what right have you to pull them?' she asked.

'Because I like them, and want them–and there's plenty of them.'

'And that is sufficient?'

'Yes. Why not? I'm sure they'd smell nice in your room in Nottingham.'

'And I should have the pleasure of watching them die.'

'But then–it does not matter if they do die.'

Whereupon he left her, and went stooping over the clumps of tangled flowers which thickly sprinkled the field like pale, luminous foam-clots. Miriam had come close. Clara was kneeling, breathing some scent from the cowslips.

'I think,' said Miriam, 'if you treat them with reverence you don't do them any harm. It is the spirit you pluck them in that matters.'

'Yes,' he said. 'But no, you get 'em because you want 'em and that's all.' He held out his bunch.

Miriam was silent. He picked some more.

'Look at these!' he continued; 'sturdy and lusty like little trees and like boys with fat legs.'

Clara's hat lay on the grass not far off. She was kneeling, bending forward still to smell the flowers. Her neck gave him a sharp pang, such a beautiful thing, yet not proud of itself just now. Her breasts swung slightly in her blouse. The arching curve of her back was beautiful and strong; she wore no stays. Suddenly, without knowing, he was scattering a handful of cowslips over her hair and neck saying:

> 'Ashes to ashes, and dust to dust,
> If the Lord won't have you the devil must.'

The chill flowers fell on her neck. She looked up at him, with almost pitiful, scared grey eyes, wondering what he was doing. Flowers fell on her face, and she shut her eyes.

Suddenly, standing there above her, he felt awkward.

'I thought you wanted a funeral,' he said, ill at ease.

Clara laughed strangely, and rose, picking the cowslips from her hair. She took up her hat and pinned it on. One flower had remained tangled in her hair.

He saw, but would not tell her. He gathered up the flowers he had sprinkled over her.

At the edge of the wood the bluebells had flowed over into the field and stood there like flood-water. But they were fading now. Clara strayed up to them. He wandered after her. The bluebells pleased him.

'Look how they've come out of the wood!' he said.

Then she turned with a flash of warmth and of gratitude.

'Yes,' she smiled.

His blood beat up.

'It makes me think of the wild men of the woods, how terrified they would be when they got breast to breast with the open space.'

'Do you think they were?' she asked.

'I wonder which was more frightened among old tribes–those bursting out of their darkness of woods upon all the space of light, or those from the open tiptoeing into the forests.'

'I should think the second,' she answered.

'Yes, you *do* feel like one of the open space sort, trying to force yourself into the dark, don't you?'

'How should I know?' she answered queerly.

The conversation ended there.

The evening was deepening over the earth. Already the valley was full of shadow. One tiny space of light stood opposite at Crossleigh Bank Farm. Brightness was swimming on the top of the hills. Miriam came up slowly, her face in her big, loose bunch of flowers, walking ankle-deep through the scattered froth of the cowslips. Beyond her the trees were coming into shape, all shadow.

'Shall we go?' she asked.

And the three turned away. They were all silent. Going down the path they could see the light of home right across, and on the ridge of the hill a thin dark outline with little lights, where the colliery village touched the sky.

'It has been nice, hasn't it?' he asked.

Miriam murmured assent, Clara was silent.

'Don't you think so?' he persisted.

But she walked with her head up, and still did not answer. He could tell by the way she moved, as if she didn't care, that she suffered.

At this time Paul took his mother to Lincoln. She was bright and enthusiastic as ever, but as he sat opposite her in the railway carriage, she seemed to look frail. He had a momentary sensation as if she were slipping away from him. Then he wanted to get hold of her, to fasten her, almost to chain her. He felt he must keep hold of her with his hand.

They drew near to the city. Both were at the window looking at the cathedral.

'There she is, mother!' he cried.

They saw the great cathedral lying couchant above the plain.

'Ah!' she exclaimed. 'So she is!'

He looked at his mother. Her blue eyes were watching the cathedral quietly. She seemed again to be beyond him. Something in the eternal repose of the uplifted cathedral, blue and noble against the sky, was reflected in her, something of the fatality. What was, *was*. With all his young will he could not alter it. He saw her face, the skin still fresh and pink and downy, but crow's-feet near her eyes, her eyelids steady, sinking a little, her mouth always closed with disillusion; and there was on her the same eternal look, as if she knew fate at last.

He beat against it with all the strength of his soul.

'Look mother, how big she is above the town! Think, there are streets and streets below her! She looks bigger than the city altogether.'

'So she does!' exclaimed his mother, breaking bright into life again. But he had seen her sitting, looking steady out of the window at the cathedral, her face and eyes fixed, reflecting the relentlessness of life. And the crow's-feet near her eyes, and her mouth shut so hard, made him feel he would go mad.

They ate a meal that she considered wildly extravagant.

'Don't imagine I like it,' she said, as she ate her cutlet. 'I *don't* like it, I really don't! Just *think* of your money wasted!'

'You never mind my money,' he said. 'You forget I'm a fellow taking his girl for an outing.'

And he bought her some blue violets.

'Stop it at once, sir!' she commanded. 'How can I do it?'

'You've got nothing to do. Stand still!'

And in the middle of High Street he stuck the flowers in her coat.

'An old thing like me!' she said, sniffing.

'You see,' he said, 'I want people to think we're awful swells. So look ikey.'

'I'll jowl your head,' she laughed.

'Strut!' he commanded. 'Be a fantail pigeon.'

It took him an hour to get her through the street. She stood above Glory Hole, she stood before Stone Bow, she stood everywhere, and exclaimed.

A man came up, took off his hat, and bowed to her.

'Can I show you the town, madam?'

'No, thank you,' she answered. 'I've got my son.'

Then Paul was cross with her for not answering with more dignity.

'You go away with you!' she exclaimed. 'Ha! that's the Jew's House. Now, do you remember that lecture, Paul—?'

But she could scarcely climb the cathedral hill. He did not notice. Then suddenly he found her unable to speak. He took her into a little public-house, where she rested.

'It's nothing,' she said. 'My heart is only a bit old; one must expect it.'

He did not answer, but looked at her. Again his heart was crushed in a hot grip. He wanted to cry, he wanted to smash things in fury.

They set off again, pace by pace, so slowly. And every step seemed like a weight on his chest. He felt as if his heart would burst. At last they came to the top. She stood enchanted, looking at the castle gate, looking at the cathedral front. She had quite forgotten herself.

'Now *this* is better than I thought it could be!' she cried.

But he hated it. Everywhere he followed her, brooding. They sat together in the cathedral. They attended a little service in the choir. She was timid.

'I suppose it is open to anybody?' she asked him.

'Yes,' he replied. 'Do you think they'd have the damn cheek to send us away?'

'Well, I'm sure,' she exclaimed, 'they would if they heard your language.'

Her face seemed to shine again with joy and peace during the service. And all the time he was wanting to rage and smash things and cry.

Afterwards, when they were leaning over the wall, looking at the town below, he blurted suddenly:

'Why can't a man have a *young* mother? What is the old for?'

'Well,' his mother laughed, 'she can scarcely help it.'

'And why wasn't I the oldest son? Look—they say the young ones have the advantage–but look, *they* had the young mother. You should have had me for your eldest son.'

'*I* didn't arrange it,' she remonstrated. 'Come to consider, you're as much to blame as me.'

He turned on her, white, his eyes furious.

'What are you old for?' he said, mad with his impotence. '*Why* can't you walk? *Why* can't you come with me to places?'

'At one time,' she replied, 'I could have run up that hill a good deal better than you.'

'What's the good of that to *me*?' he cried, hitting his fist on the wall. Then he became plaintive. 'It's too bad of you to be ill. Little, it is–'

'Ill!' she cried. 'I'm a bit old, and you'll have to put up with it, that's all.'

They were quiet. But it was as much as they could bear. They got jolly again over tea. As they sat by Brayford, watching the boats, he told her about Clara. His mother asked him innumerable questions.

'Then who does she live with?'

'With her mother, on Bluebell Hill.'

'And they have enough to keep them?'

'I don't think so. I think they do lace work.'

'And wherein lies her charm, my boy?'

'I don't know that she's charming, mother. But she's nice. And she seems straight, you know–not a bit deep, not a bit.'

'But she's a good deal older than you.'

'She's thirty, I'm going on twenty-three.'

'You haven't told me what you like her for.'

'Because I don't know–a sort of defiant way she's got–a sort of angry way.'

Mrs Morel considered. She would have been glad now for her son to fall in love with some woman who would–she did not know what. But he fretted so, got so furious suddenly, and again was melancholic. She wished he knew some nice woman–She did not know what she wished, but left it vague. At any rate she was not hostile to the idea of Clara.

Annie, too, was getting married. Leonard had gone away to work in Birmingham. One week-end when he was home she had said to him:

'You don't look very well, my lad.'

'I dunno,' he said. 'I feel anyhow or nohow, ma.'   He called her 'ma' already in his boyish fashion.

'Are you sure they're good lodgings?' she asked.

'Yes–yes. Only–it's a winder when you have to pour your own tea out–an' nobody to grouse if you teem it in your saucer and sup it up. It somehow takes a' the taste out of it.'

Mrs Morel laughed.

'And so it knocks you up?' she said.

'I dunno. I want to get married,' he blurted, twisting his fingers and looking down at his boots. There was a silence.

'But,' she exclaimed, 'I thought you said you'd wait another year.'

'Yes, I did say so,' he replied stubbornly.

Again she considered.

'And you know,' she said, 'Annie's a bit of a spendthrift. She's saved no more than eleven pounds. And I know, lad, you haven't had much chance.'

He coloured up to his ears.

'I've got thirty-four quid,' he said.

'It doesn't go far,' she answered.

He said nothing but twisted his fingers.

'And you know,' she said, 'I've nothing—'

'I didn't want, ma!' he cried, very red, suffering and remonstrating.

'No my lad, I know. I was only wishing I had. And take away five pounds for the wedding and things—it leaves twenty-nine pounds. You won't do much on that.'

He twisted still, impotent, stubborn, not looking up.

'But do you really want to get married?' she asked. 'Do you feel as if you ought?'

He gave her one straight look from his blue eyes.

'Yes,' he said.

'Then,' she replied, 'we must all do the best we can for it, lad.'

The next time he looked up there were tears in his eyes.

'I don't want Annie to feel handicapped,' he said, struggling.

'My lad,' she said, 'you're steady—you've got a decent place. If a man had *needed* me I'd have married him on his last week's wages. She may find it a bit hard to start humbly. Young girls *are* like that. They look forward to the fine home they think they'll have. But *I* had expensive furniture. It's not everything.'

So the wedding took place almost immediately. Arthur came home, and was splendid in uniform. Annie looked nice in a dove-grey dress that she could take for Sundays. Morel called her a fool for getting married, and was cool with his son-in-law. Mrs Morel had white tips in her bonnet, and some white on her blouse, and was teased by both her sons for fancying herself so grand. Leonard was jolly and cordial, and felt a fearful fool. Paul could not quite see what Annie wanted to get married for. He was fond of her, and she of him. Still, he hoped rather lugubriously that it would turn out all right. Arthur was astonishingly handsome in his scarlet and yellow, and he knew it well, but was secretly ashamed of the uniform. Annie cried her eyes out in the kitchen, on leaving her mother. Mrs Morel cried a little, then patted her on the back and said:

'But don't cry, child, he'll be good to you.'

Morel stamped and said she was a fool to go and tie herself up. Leonard looked white and overwrought. Mrs Morel said to him:

'I s'll trust her to you, my lad, and hold you responsible for her.'

'You can,' he said, nearly dead with the ordeal. And it was all over.

When Morel and Arthur were in bed, Paul sat talking, as he often did, with his mother.

'You're not sorry she's married, mother, are you?' he asked.

'I'm not sorry she's married—but—it seems strange that she should go from me. It even seems to me hard that she can prefer to go with Leonard. That's how mothers are—I know it's silly.'

'And shall you be miserable about her?'

'When I think of my own wedding day,' his mother answered, 'I can only hope her life will be different.'

'But you can trust him to be good to her?'

'Yes, yes. They say he's not good enough for her. But I say if a man is *genuine*, as he is, and a girl is fond of him—then—it should be all right. He's as good as she.'

'So you don't mind?'

'I would *never* have let a daughter of mine marry a man I didn't *feel* to be genuine through and through. And yet, there's a gap now she's gone.'

They were both miserable, and wanted her back again. It seemed to Paul his mother looked lonely, in her new black silk blouse with its bit of white trimming.

'At any rate, mother, I s'll never marry,' he said.

'Ay, they all say that, my lad. You've not met the one yet. Only wait a year or two.'

'But I shan't marry, mother. I shall live with you, and we'll have a servant.'

'Ah, my lad, it's easy to talk. We'll see when the time comes.'

'What time? I'm nearly twenty-three.'

'Yes, you're not one that would marry young. But in three years' time—'

'I shall be with you just the same.'

'We'll see, my boy, we'll see.'

'But you don't want me to marry?'

'I shouldn't like to think of you going through your life without anybody to care for you and do—no.'

'And you think I ought to marry?'

'Sooner or later every man ought.'

'But you'd rather it were later.'

'It would be hard—and very hard. It's as they say:

> "A son's my son till he takes him a wife,
> But my daughter's my daughter the whole of her life".'

'And you think I'd let a wife take me from you?'

'Well, you wouldn't ask her to marry your mother as well as you,' Mrs Morel smiled.

'She could do what she liked; she wouldn't have to interfere.'

'She wouldn't—till she'd got you—and then you'd see.'

'I never will see. I'll never marry while I've got you—I won't.'

'But I shouldn't like to leave you with nobody, my boy,' she cried.

'You're not going to leave me. What are you? Fifty-three! I'll give you till seventy-five. There you are, I'm fat and forty-four. Then I'll marry a staid body. See!'

His mother sat and laughed

'Go to bed,' she said—'go to bed.'

'And we'll have a pretty house, you and me, and a servant, and it'll be just all right. I s'll perhaps be rich with my painting.'

'Will you go to bed!'

'And then you s'll have a pony-carriage. See yourself—a little Queen Victoria trotting round.'

'I tell you to go to bed,' she laughed.

He kissed her and went. His plans for the future were always the same.

Mrs Morel sat brooding—about her daughter, about Paul, about Arthur. She fretted at losing Annie. The family was very closely bound. And she felt she *must* live now, to be with her children. Life was so rich for her. Paul wanted her, and so did Arthur. Arthur never knew how deeply he loved her. He was a creature of the moment. Never yet had he been forced to realize himself. The army had disciplined his body, but not his soul. He was in perfect health and very handsome. His dark, vigorous hair sat close to his smallish head. There was something childish about his nose, something almost girlish about his dark blue eyes. But he had the full red mouth of a man under his brown moustache, and his jaw was strong. It was his father's mouth; it was the nose and eyes of her own mother's people–good-looking, weak-principled folk. Mrs Morel was anxious about him. Once he had really run the rig he was safe. But how far would he go?

The army had not really done him any good. He resented bitterly the authority of the petty officers. He hated having to obey as if he were an animal. But he had too much sense to kick. So he turned his attention to getting the best out of it. He could sing, he was a boon-companion. Often he got into scrapes, but they were the manly scrapes that are easily condoned. So he made a good time out of it, whilst his self-respect was in suppression. He trusted to his good looks and handsome figure, his refinement, his decent education to get him most of what he wanted, and he was not disappointed. Yet he was restless. Something seemed to gnaw him inside. He was never still, he was never alone. With his mother he was rather humble. Paul he admired and loved and despised slightly. And Paul admired and loved and despised him, slightly.

Mrs Morel had had a few pounds left to her by her father, and she decided to buy her son out of the army. He was wild with joy. Now he was like a lad taking a holiday.

He had always been fond of Beatrice Wyld, and during his furlough he picked up with her again. She was stronger and better in health. The two often went long walks together, Arthur taking her arm in soldier's fashion, rather stiffly. And she came to play the piano whilst he sang. Then Arthur would unhook his tunic collar. He grew flushed, his eyes were bright, he sang in a manly tenor. Afterwards they sat together on the sofa. He seemed to flaunt his body: she was aware of him so–the strong chest, the sides, the thighs in their close-fitting trousers.

He liked to lapse into the dialect when he talked to her. She would sometimes smoke with him. Occasionally she would only take a few whiffs at his cigarette.

'Nay,' he said to her one evening, when she reached for his cigarette. 'Nay, tha doesna. I'll gi'e thee a smoke kiss if ter's a mind.'

'I want a whiff, no kiss at all,' she answered.

'Well, an' tha s'lt ha'e a whiff,' he said, 'along wi' t' kiss.'

'I want a draw at thy fag,' she cried, snatching for the cigarette between his lips.

He was sitting with his shoulder touching her. She was small and quick as lightning. He just escaped.

'I'll gi'e thee a smoke kiss,' he said.

'Tha'rt a knivey nuisance, Arty Morel,' she said, sitting back.

'Ha'e a smoke kiss?'

The soldier leaned forward to her, smiling. His face was near hers.

'Shonna!' she replied, turning away her head.

He took a draw at his cigarette, and pursed up his mouth, and put his lips close to her. His dark-brown cropped moustache stood out like a brush. She looked at the puckered crimson lips, then suddenly snatched the cigarette from his fingers and darted away. He, leaping after her, seized the comb from her back hair. She turned, threw the cigarette at him. He picked it up, put it in his mouth, and sat down.

'Nuisance!' she cried. 'Give me my comb!'

She was afraid that her hair, specially done for him, would come down. She stood with her hands to her head. He hid the comb between his knees.

'I've non got it,' he said.

The cigarette trembled between his lips with laughter as he spoke.

'Liar!' she said.

''S true as I'm here!' he laughed, showing his hands.

'You brazen imp!' she exclaimed, rushing and scuffling for the comb, which he had under his knees. As she wrestled with him, pulling at his smooth, tight-covered knees, he laughed till he lay back on the sofa shaking with laughter. The cigarette fell from his mouth, almost singeing his throat. Under his delicate tan the blood flushed up, and he laughed till his blue eyes were blinded, his throat swollen almost to choking. Then he sat up. Beatrice was putting in her comb.

'Tha tickled me, Beat,' he said thickly.

Like a flash her small white hand went out and smacked his face. He started up, glaring at her. They stared at each other. Slowly the flush mounted her cheek, she dropped her eyes, then her head. He sat down sulkily. She went into the scullery to adjust her hair. In private there she shed a few tears, she did not know what for.

When she returned she was pursed up close. But it was only a film over her fire. He, with ruffled hair, was sulking upon the sofa. She sat down opposite, in the arm-chair, and neither spoke. The clock ticked in the silence like blows.

'You are a little cat,' he said at length, half apologetically.

'Well, you shouldn't be brazen,' she replied.

There was again a long silence. He whistled to himself, like a man much agitated but defiant. Suddenly she went across to him and kissed him.

'Did it, pore fing!' she mocked.

He lifted his face, smiling curiously.

'Kiss?' he invited her.

'Daren't I?' she asked.

'Go on!' he challenged, his mouth lifted to her.

Deliberately, and with a peculiar quivering smile that seemed to overspread her whole body, she put her mouth on his. Immediately his arms folded round her. As soon as the long kiss was finished she drew back her head from him, put her delicate fingers on his neck, through the open collar. Then she closed her eyes, giving herself up again in a kiss.

She acted of her own free will. What she would do she did, and made nobody responsible.

Paul felt life changing around him. The conditions of youth were gone. Now it was a home of grown-up people. Annie was a married woman, Arthur was following his own pleasure in a way unknown to his folk. For so long they had all lived at home, and gone out to pass their time. But now, for Annie and Arthur, life lay outside their mother's house. They came home for holiday and for rest. So there was that strange, half-empty feeling about the house, as if the birds had flown. Paul became more and more unsettled. Annie and Arthur had gone. He was restless to follow. Yet home was for him beside his mother. And still there was something else, something outside, something he wanted.

He grew more and more restless. Miriam did not satisfy him. His old mad desire to be with her grew weaker. Sometimes he met Clara in Nottingham, sometimes he went to meetings with her, sometimes he saw her at Willey Farm. But on these last occasions the situation became strained. There was a triangle of antagonism between Paul and Clara and Miriam. With Clara he took on a smart, worldly, mocking tone very antagonistic to Miriam. It did not matter what went before. She might be intimate and sit with him. Then as soon as Clara appeared, it all vanished, and he played to the newcomer.

Miriam had one beautiful evening with him in the hay. He had been on the horse-rake, and, having finished, came to help her to put the hay in cocks. Then he talked to her of his hopes and despairs, and his whole soul seemed to lie bare before her. She felt as if she watched the very quivering stuff of life in him. The moon came out: they walked home together: he seemed to have come to her because he needed her so badly, and she listened to him, gave him all her love and her faith. It seemed to her he brought her the best of himself to keep, and that she would guard it all her life. Nay, the sky did not cherish the stars more surely and eternally than she would guard the good in the soul of Paul Morel. She went on home alone, feeling exalted, glad in her faith.

And then, the next day, Clara came. They were to have tea in the hayfield. Miriam watched the evening drawing to gold and shadow. And all the time Paul was sporting with Clara. He made higher and higher heaps of hay that they were jumping over. Miriam did not care for the game, and stood aside. Edgar and Geoffrey and Maurice and Clara and Paul jumped. Paul won, because he was light. Clara's blood was roused. She could run like an Amazon. Paul loved the determined way she rushed at the haycock and leaped, landed on the other side, her breasts shaken, her thick hair coming undone.

'You touched!' he cried. 'You touched!'

'No!' she flashed, turning to Edgar. 'I didn't touch, did I? Wasn't I clear?'

'I couldn't say,' laughed Edgar.

None of them could say.

'But you touched,' said Paul. 'You're beaten.'

'I did *not* touch!' she cried.

'As plain as anything,' said Paul.

'Box his ears for me!' she cried to Edgar.

'Nay,' Edgar laughed. 'I daren't. You must do it yourself.'

'And nothing can alter the fact that you touched,' laughed Paul.

She was furious with him. Her little triumph before these lads and men was gone. She had forgotten herself in the game. Now he was to humble her.

'I think you are despicable!' she said.

And again he laughed, in a way that tortured Miriam.

'And I *knew* you couldn't jump that heap,' he teased.

She turned her back on him. Yet everybody could see that the only person she listened to, or was conscious of, was he, and he of her. It pleased the men to see this battle between them. But Miriam was tortured.

Paul could choose the lesser in place of the higher, she saw. He could be unfaithful to himself, unfaithful to the real, deep Paul Morel. There was a danger of his becoming frivolous, of his running after his satisfactions like any Arthur, or like his father. It made Miriam bitter to think that he should throw away his soul for this flippant traffic of triviality with Clara. She walked in bitterness and silence, while the other two rallied each other, and Paul sported.

And afterwards, he would not own it, but he was rather ashamed of himself, and prostrated himself before Miriam. Then again he rebelled.

'It's not religious to be religious,' he said. 'I reckon a crow is religious when it sails across the sky. But it only does it because it feels itself carried to where it's going, not because it thinks it is being eternal.'

But Miriam knew that one should be religious in everything, have God, whatever God might be, present in everything.

'I don't believe God knows such a lot about Himself,' he cried. 'God doesn't *know* things, He *is* things. And I'm sure He's not soulful.'

And then it seemed to her that Paul was arguing God on to his own side, because he wanted his own way and his own pleasure. There was a long battle between him and her. He was utterly unfaithful to her even in her own presence; then he was ashamed, then repentant; then he hated her, and went off again. Those were the ever-recurring conditions.

She fretted him to the bottom of his soul. There she remained–sad, pensive, a worshipper. And he caused her sorrow. Half the time he grieved for her, half the time he hated her. She was his conscience; and he felt, somehow, he had got a conscience that was too much for him. He could not leave her, because in one way she did hold the best of him. He could not stay with her because she did not take the rest of him, which was three-quarters. So he chafed himself into rawness over her.

When she was twenty-one he wrote her a letter which could only have been written to her.

'May I speak of our old, worn love, this last time. It, too, is changing, is it not? Say, has not the body of that love died, and left you its invulnerable soul? You see, I can give you a spirit love, I have given it you this long, long time; but not embodied passion. See, you are a nun. I have given you what I would give a holy nun–as a mystic monk to a mystic nun. Surely you esteem it best. Yet you regret–no, have regretted–the other. In all our relations no body enters. I do not talk to you through the senses–rather through the spirit. That is why we cannot love in the common sense. Ours is not an everyday affection. As yet we are mortal, and to live side by side with one another would be dreadful, for somehow with you I cannot long be trivial, and, you know, to be always beyond this mortal state would be to lose it. If people marry, they must live together as affectionate humans, who may be commonplace with each other without feeling awkward–not as two souls. So I feel it.

'Ought I to send this letter–I doubt it. But there–it is best to understand. Au revoir.'

Miriam read this letter twice, after which she sealed it up. A year later she broke the seal to show her mother the letter.

'You are a nun–you are a nun.' The words went into her heart again and again. Nothing he ever had said had gone into her so deeply, fixedly, like a mortal wound.

She answered him two days after the party.

'"Our intimacy would have been all-beautiful but for one little mistake,"' she quoted. 'Was the mistake mine?'

Almost immediately he replied to her from Nottingham, sending her at the same time a little 'Omar Khayyam'.

'I am glad you answered; you are so calm and natural you put me to shame. What a ranter I am! We are often out of sympathy. But in fundamentals we may always be together I think.

'I must thank you for your sympathy with my painting and drawing. Many a sketch is dedicated to you. I do look forward to your criticisms, which, to my shame and glory, are always grand appreciations. It is a lovely joke, that. Au revoir.'

This was the end of the first phase of Paul's love-affair. He was now about twenty-three years old, and, though still virgin, the sex instinct that Miriam had over-refined for so long now grew particularly strong. Often, as he talked to

Clara Dawes, came that thickening and quickening of his blood, that peculiar concentration in the breast, as if something were alive there, a new self or a new centre of consciousness, warning him that sooner or later, he would have to ask one woman or another. But he belonged to Miriam. Of that she was so fixedly sure that she allowed her right.

10

CLARA

When he was twenty-three years old Paul sent in a landscape to the winter exhibition at Nottingham Castle. Miss Jordan had taken a good deal of interest in him, had invited him to her house, where he met other artists. He was beginning to grow ambitious.

One morning the postman came just as he was washing in the scullery. Suddenly he heard a wild noise from his mother. Rushing into the kitchen, he found her standing on the hearthrug wildly waving a letter and crying 'Hurrah!' as if she had gone mad. He was shocked and frightened.

'Why, mother!' he exclaimed.

She flew to him, flung her arms round him for a moment, then waved the letter crying:

'Hurrah, my boy! I knew we should do it!'

He was afraid of her–the small, severe woman with greying hair suddenly bursting out in such frenzy. The postman came running back, afraid something had happened. They saw his tipped cap over the short curtain. Mrs Morel rushed to the door.

'His picture's got first prize, Fred,' she cried, 'and is sold for twenty guineas.'

'My word, that's something like!' said the young postman, whom they had known all his life.

'And Major Moreton has bought it!' she cried.

'It looks like meanin' something, that does, Mrs Morel,' said the postman, his blue eyes bright. He was glad to have brought such a lucky letter. Mrs Morel went indoors and sat down, trembling. Paul was afraid lest she might have misread the letter, and might be disappointed after all. He scrutinized it once, twice. Yes, he became convinced it was true. Then he sat down, his heart beating with joy.

'Mother!' he exclaimed.

'Didn't I *say* we should do it!' she said, pretending she was not crying.

He took the kettle off the fire and mashed the tea.

'You didn't think, mother–' he began tentatively.

'No, my son–not so much–but I expected a good deal.'

'But not so much,' he said.

'No–no–but I knew we should do it.'

And then she recovered her composure, apparently at least. He sat with his shirt turned back, showing his young throat almost like a girl's, and the towel in his hand, his hair sticking up wet.

'Twenty guineas, mother! That's just what you wanted to buy Arthur out. Now you needn't borrow any. It'll just do.'

'Indeed, I shan't take it all,' she said.

'But why?'

'Because I shan't.'

'Well–you have twelve pounds, I'll have nine.'

They cavilled about sharing the twenty guineas. She wanted to take only the five pounds she needed. He would not hear of it. So they got over the stress of emotion by quarrelling.

Morel came home at night from the pit, saying:

'They tell me Paul's got first prize for his picture, and sold it to Lord Henry Bentley for fifty pound.'

'Oh, what stories people do tell!' she cried.

'Ha!' he answered. 'I said I wor sure it wor a lie. But they said tha'd told Fred Hodgkisson.'

'As if I would tell him such stuff!'

'Ha!' assented the miner.

But he was disappointed nevertheless.

'It's true he has got the first prize,' said Mrs Morel.

The miner sat heavily in his chair.

'Has he, beguy!' he exclaimed.

He stared across the room fixedly.

'But as for fifty pounds–such nonsense!' She was silent awhile. 'Major Moreton bought it for twenty guineas, that's true.'

'Twenty guineas! Tha niver says!' exclaimed Morel.

'Yes, and it was worth it.'

'Ay!' he said. 'I don't misdoubt it. But twenty guineas for a bit of a paintin' as he knocked off in an hour or two!'

He was silent with conceit of his son. Mrs Morel sniffed, as if it were nothing.

'And when does he handle th' money?' asked the collier.

'That I couldn't tell you. When the picture is sent home, I suppose.'

There was silence. Morel stared at the sugar-basin instead of eating his dinner. His black arm, with the hand all gnarled with work, lay on the table. His wife pretended not to see him rub the back of his hand across his eyes, nor the smear in the coal-dust on his black face.

'Yes, an' that other lad 'ud 'a done as much if they hadna ha' killed 'im,' he said quietly.

The thought of William went through Mrs Morel like a cold blade. It left her feeling she was tired, and wanted rest.

Paul was invited to dinner at Mr Jordan's. Afterwards he said:

'Mother, I want an evening suit.'

'Yes, I was afraid you would,' she said. She was glad. There was a moment or two of silence. 'There's that one of William's,' she continued, 'that I know cost four pounds ten and which he'd only worn three times.'

'Should you like me to wear it, mother?' he asked.

'Yes, I think it would fit you–at least the coat. The trousers would want shortening.'

He went upstairs and put on the coat and vest. Coming down, he looked strange in a flannel collar and a flannel shirt-front, with an evening coat and vest. It was rather large.

'The tailor can make it right,' she said, smoothing her hand over his shoulder. 'It's beautiful stuff. I never could find in my heart to let your father wear the trousers, and very glad I am now.'

And as she smoothed her hand over the silk collar she thought of her eldest son. But this son was living enough inside the clothes. She passed her hand down his back to feel him. He was alive and hers. The other was dead.

He went out to dinner several times in his evening suit that had been William's. Each time his mother's heart was firm with pride and joy. He was started now. The studs she and the children had bought for William were in his shirt-front; he wore one of William's dress shirts. But he had an elegant figure. His face was rough, but warm-looking and rather pleasing. He did not look particularly a gentleman, but she thought he looked quite a man.

He told her everything that took place, everything that was said. It was as if she had been there. And he was dying to introduce her to these friends who had dinner at seven-thirty in the evening.

'Go along with you!' she said. 'What do they want to know me for?'

'They do!' he cried indignantly. 'If they want to know me—and they say they do—then they want to know you, because you are quite as clever as I am.'

'Go along with you, child!' she laughed.

But she began to spare her hands. They, too, were work-gnarled now. The skin was shiny with so much hot water, the knuckles rather swollen. But she began to be careful to keep them out of soda. She regretted what they had been—so small and exquisite. And when Annie insisted on her having more stylish blouses to suit her age, she submitted. She even went so far as to allow a black velvet bow to be placed on her hair. Then she sniffed in her sarcastic manner, and was sure she looked a sight. But she looked a lady, Paul declared, as much as Mrs Major Moreton, and far, far nicer. The family was coming on. Only Morel remained unchanged, or rather, lapsed slowly.

Paul and his mother now had long discussions about life. Religion was fading into the background. He had shovelled away all the beliefs that would hamper him, had cleared the ground, and come more or less to the bedrock of belief that one should feel inside oneself for right and wrong, and should have the patience to gradually realize one's God. Now life interested him more.

'You know,' he said to his mother, 'I don't want to belong to the well-to-do middle class. I like my common people best. I belong to the common people.'

'But if anyone else said so, my son, wouldn't you be in a tear. *You* know you consider yourself equal to any gentleman.'

'In myself,' he answered, 'not in my class or my education or my manners. But in myself I am.'

'Very well, then. Then why talk about the common people?'

'Because—the difference between people isn't in their class, but in themselves. Only from the middle classes one gets ideas, and from the common people—life itself, warmth. You feel their hates and loves.'

'It's all very well, my boy. But, then, why don't you go and talk to your father's pals?'

'But they're rather different.'

'Not at all. They're the common people. After all, whom do you mix with now—among the common people? Those that exchange ideas, like the middle class. The rest don't interest you.'

'But—there's the life—'

'I don't believe there's a lot more life from Miriam than you could get from any educated girl—say Miss Moreton. It is *you* who are snobbish about class.'

She frankly *wanted* him to climb into the middle class, a thing not very difficult, she knew. And she wanted him in the end to marry a lady.

Now she began to combat him in his restless fretting. He still kept up his connexion with Miriam, could neither break free nor go the whole length of engagement. And this indecision seemed to bleed him of his energy. Moreover, his mother suspected him of an unrecognized leaning towards Clara, and, since the latter was a married woman, she wished he would fall in love with one of the girls in a better station of life. But he was stupid, and would refuse to love or even to admire a girl much, just because she was his social superior.

'My boy,' said his mother to him, 'all your cleverness, your breaking away from old things, and taking life in your own hands, doesn't seem to bring you much happiness.'

'What is happiness!' he cried. 'It's nothing to me! How *am* I to be happy?'

The plump question disturbed her.

'That's for you to judge, my lad. But if you could meet some *good* woman who would *make* you happy—and you began to think of settling your life—when you have the means—so that you could work without all this fretting—it would be much better for you.'

He frowned. His mother caught him on the raw of his wound of Miriam. He pushed the tumbled hair off his forehead, his eyes full of pain and fire.

'You mean easy, mother,' he cried. 'That's a woman's whole doctrine for life—ease of soul and physical comfort. And I do despise it.'

'Oh, do you!' replied his mother. 'And do you call yours a divine discontent?'

'Yes, I don't care about its divinity. But damn your happiness! So long as life's full, it doesn't matter whether it's happy or not. I'm afraid your happiness would bore me.'

'You never give it a chance,' she said. Then suddenly all her passion of grief over him broke out. 'But it does matter!' she cried. 'And you *ought* to be happy, you ought to try to be happy, to live to be happy. How could I bear to think your life wouldn't be a happy one!'

'Your own's been bad enough, mater, but it hasn't left you so much worse off than the folk who've been happier. I reckon you've done well. And I am the same. Aren't I well enough off?'

'You're not, my son. Battle—battle—and suffer. It's about all you do, as far as I can see.'

'But why not, my dear? I tell you it's the best—'

'It isn't. And one *ought* to be happy, one *ought*.'

By this time Mrs Morel was trembling violently. Struggles of this kind often took place between her and her son, when she seemed to fight for his very life against his own will to die. He took her in his arms. She was ill and pitiful.

'Never mind, Little,' he murmured. 'So long as you don't feel life's paltry and a miserable business, the rest doesn't matter, happiness or unhappiness.'

She pressed him to her.

'But I want you to be happy,' she said pathetically.

'Eh, my dear—say rather you want me to live.'

Mrs Morel felt as if her heart would break for him. At this rate she knew he would not live. He had that poignant carelessness about himself, his own suffering, his own life, which is a form of slow suicide. It almost broke her heart. With all the passion of her strong nature she hated Miriam for having in this subtle way undermined his joy. It did not matter to her that Miriam could not help it. Miriam did it, and she hated her.

She wished so much he would fall in love with a girl equal to be his mate—educated and strong. But he would not look at anybody above him in station. He seemed to like Mrs Dawes. At any rate that feeling was wholesome. His mother prayed and prayed for him, that he might not be wasted. That was all her prayer—not for his soul or his righteousness, but that he might not be wasted. And while he slept, for hours and hours she thought and prayed for him.

He drifted away from Miriam imperceptibly, without knowing he was going. Arthur only left the army to be married. The baby was born six months after his wedding. Mrs Morel got him a job under the firm again, at twenty-one shillings a week. She furnished for him, with the help of Beatrice's mother, a little cottage of two rooms. He was caught now. It did not matter how he kicked and struggled, he was fast. For a time he chafed, was irritable with his young wife, who loved him; he went almost distracted when the baby, which was delicate, cried or gave trouble. He grumbled for hours to his mother. She only said, 'Well, my lad, you did it yourself, now you must make the best of it.' And then the grit came out in him. He buckled to work, undertook his responsibilities, acknowledged that he belonged to his wife and child, and did make a good best of it. He had never been very closely inbound into the family. Now he was gone altogether.

The months went slowly along. Paul had more or less got into connexion with the Socialist, Suffragette, Unitarian people in Nottingham, owing to his acquaintance with Clara. One day a friend of his and of Clara's, in Bestwood, asked him to take a message to Mrs Dawes. He went in the evening across Sneinton Market to Bluebell Hill. He found the house in a mean little street paved with granite cobbles and having causeways of dark blue, grooved bricks. The front door went up a step from off this rough pavement, where the feet of the passers-by rasped and clattered. The brown paint on the door was so old that the naked wood showed between the rents. He stood on the street below and knocked. There came a heavy footstep; a large, stout woman of about sixty towered above him. He looked up at her from the pavement. She had a rather severe face.

She admitted him into the parlour, which opened on to the street. It was a small, stuffy, defunct room, of mahogany, and deathly enlargements of photographs of departed people done in carbon. Mrs Radford left him. She was stately, almost martial. In a moment Clara appeared. She flushed deeply, and he was covered with confusion. It seemed as if she did not like being discovered in her home circumstances.

'I thought it couldn't be your voice,' she said.

But she might as well be hung for a sheep as for a lamb. She invited him out of the mausoleum of a parlour into the kitchen.

That was a little, darkish room too, but it was smothered in white lace. The mother had seated herself again by the cupboard, and was drawing thread from a vast web of lace. A clump of fluff and ravelled cotton was at her right hand, a heap of three-quarter-inch lace lay on her left, whilst in front of her was the mountain of the lace web, piling the hearthrug. Threads of curly cotton, pulled out from between the lengths of lace, strewed over the fender and the fireplace. Paul dared not go forward, for fear of treading on piles of white stuff.

On the table was a jenny for carding the lace. There was a pack of brown cardboard squares, a pack of cards of lace, a little box of pins, and on the sofa lay a heap of drawn lace.

The room was all lace, and it was so dark and warm that the white, snowy stuff seemed the more distinct.

'If you're coming in you won't have to mind the work,' said Mrs Radford. 'I know we're about blocked up. But sit you down.'

Clara, much embarrassed, gave him a chair against the wall opposite the white heaps. Then she herself took her place on the sofa, shamedly.

'Will you drink a bottle of stout?' Mrs Radford asked. 'Clara, get him a bottle of stout.'

He protested, but Mrs Radford insisted.

'You look as if you could do with it,' she said. 'Haven't you never any more colour than that?'

'It's only a thick skin I've got that doesn't show the blood through,' he answered.

Clara, ashamed and chagrined, brought him a bottle of stout and a glass. He poured out some of the black stuff.

'Well,' he said, lifting the glass, 'here's health!'

'And thank you,' said Mrs Radford.

He took a drink of stout.

'And light yourself a cigarette, so long as you don't set the house on fire,' said Mrs Radford.

'Thank you,' he replied.

'Nay, you needn't thank me,' she answered. 'I s'll be glad to smell a bit of smoke in th' 'ouse again. A house o' women is as dead as a house wi' no fire, to my thinkin'. I'm not a spider as likes a corner to myself. I like a man about, if he's only something to snap at.'

Clara began to work. Her jenny spun with a subdued buzz; the white lace hopped from between her fingers on to the card. It was filled; she snipped off the length and pinned the end down to the banded lace. Then she put a new card in her jenny. Paul watcher her. She sat square and magnificent. Her throat and arms were bare. The blood still mantled below her ears; she bent her head in shame of her humility. Her face was set on her work. Her arms were creamy and full of life beside the white lace; her large, well-kept hands worked with a balanced movement, as if nothing would hurry them. He, not knowing, watched her all the time. He saw the arch of her neck from the shoulder, as she bent her head; he saw the coil of dun hair; he watched her moving, gleaming arms.

'I've heard a bit about you from Clara,' continued the mother. 'You're in Jordan's, aren't you?' She drew her lace unceasing.

'Yes.'

'Ay, well, and I can remember when Thomas Jordan used to ask *me* for one of my toffies.'

'Did he?' laughed Paul. 'And did he get it?'

'Sometimes he did, sometimes he didn't—which was latterly. For he's the sort that takes all and gives naught, he is—or used to be.'

'I think he's very decent,' said Paul.

'Yes; well, I'm glad to hear it.'

Mrs Radford looked across at him steadily. There was something determined about her that he liked. Her face was falling loose, but her eyes were calm, and there was something strong in her that made it seem she was not old; merely her wrinkles and loose cheeks were an anachronism. She had the strength and sang-froid of a woman in the prime of life. She continued drawing the lace with slow, dignified movements. The big web came up inevitably over her apron; the length of lace fell away at her side. Her arms were finely shapen, but glossy and yellow as old ivory. They had not the peculiar dull gleam that made Clara's so fascinating to him.

'And you've been going with Miriam Leivers!' the mother asked him.

'Well—' he answered.

'Yes, she's a nice girl,' she continued. 'She's very nice, but she's a bit too much above this world to suit my fancy.'

'She is a bit like that,' he agreed.

'She'll never be satisfied till she's got wings and can fly over everybody's head, she won't,' she said.

Clara broke in, and he told her his message. She spoke humbly to him. He had surprised her in her drudgery. To have her humble made him feel as if he were lifting his head in expectation.

'Do you like jennying?' he asked.

'What can a woman do!' she replied bitterly.

'Is it sweated?'

'More or less. Isn't *all* woman's work? That's another trick the men have played, since we force ourselves into the labour market.'

'Now then, you shut up about the men,' said her mother. 'If the women wasn't fools, the men wouldn't be bad uns, that's what I say. No man was ever that bad wi' me but what he got it back again. Not but what they're a lousy lot, there's no denying it.'

'But they're all right really, aren't they?' he asked.

'Well, they're a bit different from women,' she answered.

'Would you care to be back at Jordan's?' he asked Clara.

'I don't think so,' she replied.

'Yes, she would!' cried her mother; 'thank her stars if she could get back. Don't you listen to her. She's for ever on that 'igh horse of hers, an' its back's that thin an' starved it'll cut her i' two one of these days.'

Clara suffered badly from her mother. Paul felt as if his eyes were coming very wide open. Wasn't he to take Clara's fulminations so seriously, after all? She spun steadily at her work. He experienced a thrill of joy, thinking she might need his help. She seemed denied and deprived of so much. And her arm moved mechanically, that should never have been subdued to a mechanism, and her head was bowed to the lace, that never should have been bowed. She seemed to be stranded there among the refuse that life has thrown away, doing her jennying. It was a bitter thing to her to be put aside by life, as if it had no use for her. No wonder she protested.

She came with him to the door. He stood below in the mean street, looking up at her. So fine she was in her stature and her bearing, she reminded him of Juno dethroned. As she stood in the doorway, she winced from the street, from her surroundings.

'And you will go with Mrs Hodgkisson to Hucknall?'

He was talking quite meaninglessly, only watching her. Her grey eyes at last met his. They looked dumb with humiliation, pleading with a kind of captive misery. He was shaken and at a loss. He had thought her high and mighty.

When he left her, he wanted to run. He went to the station in a sort of dream, and was at home without realizing he had moved out of her street.

He had an idea that Susan, the overseer of the spiral girls, was about to be married. He asked her the next day.

'I say, Susan, I heard a whisper of your getting married. What about it?'

Susan flushed red.

'Who's been talking to you?' she replied.

'Nobody. I merely heard a whisper that you *were* thinking—'

'Well, I am, though you needn't tell anybody. What's more, I wish I wasn't!'

'Nay, Susan, you won't make me believe that.'

'Shan't I? You *can* believe it, though. I'd rather stop here a thousand times.'

Paul was perturbed.

'Why, Susan?'

The girl's colour was high, and her eyes flashed.

'That's why!'

'And must you?'

For answer, she looked at him. There was about him a candour and gentleness which made the women trust him. He understood.

'Ah, I'm sorry,' he said.

Tears came to her eyes.

'But you'll see it'll turn out all right. You'll make the best of it,' he continued rather wistfully.

'There's nothing else for it.'

'Yes, there's making the worst of it. Try and make it all right.'

He soon made occasion to call again on Clara.

'Would you,' he said, 'care to come back to Jordan's?'

She put down her work, laid her beautiful arms on the table, and looked at him for some moments without answering. Gradually the flush mounted her cheek.

'Why?' she asked.

Paul felt rather awkward.

'Well, because Susan is thinking of leaving,' he said.

Clara went on with her jennying. The white lace leaped in little jumps and bounds on to the card. He waited for her. Without raising her head, she said at last, in a peculiar low voice:

'Have you said anything about it?'

'Except to you, not a word.'

There was again a long silence.

'I will apply when the advertisement is out,' she said.

'You will apply before that. I will let you know exactly when.'

She went on spinning her little machine, and did not contradict him.

Clara came to Jordan's. Some of the older hands, Fanny among them, remembered her earlier rule, and cordially disliked the memory. Clara had always been 'ikey', reserved, and superior. She had never mixed with the girls as one of themselves. If she had occasion to find fault, she did it coolly and with perfect politeness, which the defaulter felt to be a bigger insult than crossness. Towards Fanny, the poor, over-strung hunchback, Clara was unfailingly compassionate and gentle, as a result of which Fanny shed more bitter tears than ever the rough tongues of the other overseers had caused her.

There was something in Clara that Paul disliked, and much that piqued him. If she were about, he always watched her strong throat or her neck, upon which the blonde hair grew low and fluffy. There was a fine down, almost invisible, upon the skin of her face and arms, and when once he had perceived it, he saw it always.

When he was at his work, painting in the afternoon, she would come and stand near to him, perfectly motionless. Then he felt her, though she neither spoke nor touched him. Although she stood a yard away he felt as if he were in contact with her. Then he could paint no more. He flung down the brushes, and turned to talk to her.

Sometimes she praised his work; sometimes she was critical and cold. 'You are affected in that piece,' she would say; and, as there was an element of truth in her condemnation, his blood boiled with anger.

Again: 'What of this?' he would ask enthusiastically.

'H'm!' She made a small doubtful sound. 'It doesn't interest me much.'

'Because you don't understand it,' he retorted.

'Then why ask me about it?'

'Because I thought you would understand.'

She would shrug her shoulders in scorn of his work. She maddened him. He was furious. Then he abused her, and went into passionate exposition of his stuff. This amused and stimulated her. But she never owned that she had been wrong.

During the ten years that she had belonged to the women's movement she had acquired a fair amount of education, and, having had some of Miriam's passion to be instructed, had taught herself French, and could read in that language with a struggle. She considered herself as a woman apart, and particularly apart, from her class. The girls in the spiral department were all of good homes. It was a small, special industry, and had a certain distinction. There was an air of refinement in both rooms. But Clara was aloof also from her fellow-workers.

None of these things, however, did she reveal to Paul. She was not the one to give herself away. There was a sense of mystery about her. She was so reserved, he felt she had much to reserve. Her history was open on the surface, but its inner meaning was hidden from everybody. It was exciting. And then sometimes he caught her looking at him from under her brows with an almost furtive, sullen scrutiny, which made him move quickly. Often she met his eyes. But then her own were, as it were, covered over, revealing nothing. She gave him a little, lenient smile. She was to him extraordinarily provocative, because of the knowledge she seemed to possess, and gathered fruit of experience he could not attain.

One day he picked up a copy of 'Lettres de mon Moulin' from her workbench.

'You read French, do you?' he cried.

Clara glanced round negligently. She was making an elastic stocking of heliotrope silk, turning the spiral machine with slow, balanced regularity, occasionally bending down to see her work or to adjust the needles; then her magnificent neck, with its down and fine pencils of hair, shone white against the lavender, lustrous silk. She turned a few more rounds, and stopped.

'What did you say?' she asked, smiling sweetly.

Paul's eyes glittered at her insolent indifference to him.

'I did not know you read French,' he said, very polite.

'Did you not?' she replied, with a faint, sarcastic smile.

'Rotten swank!' he said, but scarcely loud enough to be heard.

He shut his mouth angrily as he watched her. She seemed to scorn the work she mechanically produced; yet the hose she made were as nearly perfect as possible.

'You don't like spiral work,' he said.

'Oh, well, all work is work,' she answered, as if she knew all about it.

He marvelled at her coldness. He had to do everything hotly. She must be something special.

'What would you prefer to do?' he asked.

She laughed at him indulgently, as she said:

'There is so little likelihood of my ever being given a choice, that I haven't wasted time considering.'

'Pah!' he said, contemptuous on his side now. 'You only say that because you're too proud to own up what you want and can't get.'

'You know me very well,' she replied coldly.

'I know you think you're terrific great shakes, and that you live under the eternal insult of working in a factory.'

He was very angry and very rude. She merely turned away from him in disdain. He walked whistling down the room, flirted and laughed with Hilda.

Later on he said to himself:

'What was I so impudent to Clara for?' He was rather annoyed with himself, at the same time glad. 'Serve her right; she stinks with silent pride,' he said to himself angrily.

In the afternoon he came down. There was a certain weight on his heart which he wanted to remove. He thought to do it by offering her chocolates.

'Have one?' he said. 'I bought a handful to sweeten me up.'

To his great relief, she accepted. He sat on the work-bench beside her machine, twisting a piece of silk round his finger. She loved him for his quick, unexpected movements, like a young animal. His feet swung as he pondered. The sweets lay strewn on the bench. She bent over her machine, grinding rhythmically, then stooping to see the stocking that hung beneath, pulled down by the weight. He watched the handsome crouching of her back, and the apron-strings curling on the floor.

'There is always about you,' he said, 'a sort of waiting. Whatever I see you doing, you're not really there: you are waiting—like Penelope when she did her weaving.' He could not help a spurt of wickedness. 'I'll call you Penelope,' he said.

'Would it make any difference?' she said, carefully removing one of her needles.

'That doesn't matter, so long as it pleases me. Here, I say, you seem to forget I'm your boss. It just occurs to me.'

'And what does that mean?' she asked coolly.

'It means I've got a right to boss you.'

'Is there anything you want to complain about?'

'Oh, I say, you needn't be nasty,' he said angrily.

'I don't know what you want,' she said, continuing her task.

'I want you to treat me nicely and respectfully.'

'Call you "sir", perhaps?' she asked quietly.

'Yes, call me "sir". I should love it.'

'Then I wish you would go upstairs, sir.'

His mouth closed, and a frown came on his face. He jumped suddenly down.

'You're too blessed superior for anything,' he said.

And he went away to the other girls. He felt he was being angrier than he had any need to be. In fact, he doubted slightly that he was showing off. But if he were, then he would. Clara heard him laughing, in a way she hated, with the girls down the next room.

When at evening he went through the department after the girls had gone, he saw his chocolates lying untouched in front of Clara's machine. He left them. In the morning they were still there, and Clara was at her work. Later on Minnie, a little brunette they called Pussy, called to him:

'Hey, haven't you got a chocolate for anybody?'

'Sorry, Pussy,' he replied. 'I meant to have offered them; then I went and forgot 'em.'

'I think you did,' she answered.

'I'll bring you some this afternoon. You don't want them after they've been lying about, do you?'

'Oh, I'm not particular,' smiled Pussy.

'Oh no,' he said. 'They'll be dusty.'

He went up to Clara's bench.

'Sorry I left these things littering about,' he said.

She flushed scarlet. He gathered them together in his fist.

'They'll be dirty now,' he said. 'You should have taken them. I wonder why you didn't. I meant to have told you I wanted you to.'

He flung them out of the window into the yard below. He just glanced at her. She winced from his eyes.

In the afternoon he brought another packet.

'Will you take some?' he said, offering them first to Clara. 'These are fresh.'

She accepted one, and put put it on to the bench.

'Oh, take several–for luck,' he said.

She took a couple more, and put them on the bench also. Then she turned in confusion to her work. He went on up the room.

'Here you are, Pussy,' he said. 'Don't be greedy!'

'Are they all for her?' cried the others, rushing up.

'Of course they're not,' he said.

The girls clamoured round. Pussy drew back from her mates.

'Come out!' she cried. 'I can have first pick, can't I, Paul?'

'Be nice with 'em,' he said, and went away.

'You *are* a dear,' the girls cried.

'Tenpence,' he answered.

He went past Clara without speaking. She felt the three chocolate creams would burn her if she touched them. It needed all her courage to slip them into the pocket of her apron.

The girls loved him and were afraid of him. He was so nice while he was nice, but if he was offended, so distant, treating them as if they scarcely existed, or not more than the bobbins of thread. And then, if they were impudent, he said quietly: 'Do you mind going on with your work,' and stood and watched.

When he celebrated his twenty-third birthday, the house was in trouble. Arthur was just going to be married. His mother was not well. His father, getting an old man, and lame from his accidents, was given a paltry, poor job. Miriam was an eternal reproach. He felt he owed himself to her, yet could not give himself. The house, moreover, needed his support. He was pulled in all directions. He was not glad it was his birthday. It made him bitter.

He got to work at eight o'clock. Most of the clerks had not turned up. The girls were not due till 8.30. As he was changing his coat he heard a voice behind him say:

'Paul, Paul, I want you.'

It was Fanny, the hunchback, standing at the top of her stairs, her face radiant with a secret. Paul looked at her in astonishment.

'I want you,' she said.

He stood, at a loss.

'Come on,' she coaxed. 'Come before you begin on the letters.'

He went down the half-dozen steps into her dry, narrow, 'finishing-off' room. Fanny walked before him: her black bodice was short–the waist was under her armpits–and her green-black cashmere skirt seemed very long, as she strode with big strides before the young man, himself so graceful. She went to her seat at the narrow end of the room, where the window opened on to chimney-pots. Paul watched her thin hands and her flat red wrists as she excitedly twitched her white apron, which was spread on the bench in front of her.

She hesitated.

'You didn't think we'd forget you?' she asked reproachful.

'Why?' he asked. He had forgotten his birthday himself.

'"Why", he says! "Why!" Why, look here!' She pointed to the calendar, and he saw, surrounding the big black number '21', hundreds of little crosses in blacklead.

'Oh, kisses for my birthday,' he laughed. 'How did you know?'

'Yes, you want to know, don't you?' Fanny mocked, hugely delighted. 'There's one from everybody–except Lady Clara–and two from some. But I shan't tell you how many I put.'

'Oh, I know, you're spooney,' he said.

'There you *are* mistaken!' she cried indignant. 'I could never be so soft.' Her voice was strong and contralto.

'You always pretend to be such a hard-hearted hussy,' he laughed. 'And you know you're as sentimental–'

'I'd rather be called sentimental than frozen meat,' Fanny blurted. Paul knew she referred to Clara, and he smiled.

'Do you say such nasty things about me?' he laughed.

'No, my duck,' the hunchback woman answered, lavishly tender. She was thirty-nine. 'No, my duck, because you don't think yourself a fine figure in marble and us nothing but dirt. I'm as good as you, aren't I, Paul?' and the question delighted her.

'Why, we're not better than one another, are we?' he replied.

'But I'm as good as you, aren't I, Paul?' she persisted daringly.

'Of course you are. If it comes to goodness, you're better.'

She was rather afraid of the situation. She might get hysterical.

'I thought I'd get here before the others–won't they say I'm deep! Now shut your eyes–' she said.

'And open your mouth, and see what God sends you,' he continued, suiting action to words, and expecting a piece of chocolate. He heard the rustle of the apron, and a faint clink of metal. 'I'm going to look,' he said.

He opened his eyes. Fanny, her long cheeks flushed, her blue eyes shining, was gazing at him. There was a little bundle of paint-tubes on the bench before him. He turned pale.

'No, Fanny,' he said quickly.

'From us all,' she answered hastily.

'No, but–'

'Are they the right sort?' she asked, rocking herself with delight.

'Jove! they're the best in the catalogue.'

'But they're the right sorts?' she cried.

'They're off the little list I'd made to get when my ship came in.' He bit his lip.

Fanny was overcome with emotion. She must turn the conversation.

'They was all on thorns to do it; they all paid their shares, all except the Queen of Sheba.'

The Queen of Sheba was Clara.

'And wouldn't she join?' Paul asked.

'She didn't get the chance; we never told her; we wasn't going to have *her* bossing *this* show. We didn't *want* her to join.'

Paul laughed at the woman. He was much moved. At last he must go. She was very close to him. Suddenly she flung her arms round his neck and kissed him vehemently.

'I can give you a kiss to-day,' she said apologetically. 'You've looked so white, it's made my heart ache.'

Paul kissed her, and left her. Her arms were so pitifully thin that his heart ached also.

That day he met Clara as he ran downstairs to wash his hands at dinner-time.

'You have stayed to dinner!' he exclaimed. It was unusual for her.

'Yes; and I seem to have dined an old surgical-appliance stock. I *must* go out now, or I shall feel stale india-rubber right through.'

She lingered. He instantly caught at her wish.

'You are going anywhere?' he asked.

They went together up to the Castle. Outdoors she dressed very plainly, down to ugliness; indoors she always looked nice. She walked with hesitating steps alongside Paul, bowing and turning away from him. Dowdy in dress, and drooping, she showed to great disadvantage. He could scarcely recognize her strong form, that seemed to slumber with power. She appeared almost insignificant, drowning her stature in her stoop, as she shrank from the public gaze.

The Castle grounds were very green and fresh. Climbing the precipitous ascent, he laughed and chattered, but she was silent, seeming to brood over something. There was scarcely time to go inside the squat, square building that crowns the bluff rock. They leaned upon the wall where the cliff runs sheer down to the Park. Below them, in their holes in the sandstone, pigeons preened themselves and cooed softly. Away down upon the boulevard at the foot of the rock, tiny trees stood in their own pools of shadow, and tiny people went scurrying about in almost ludicrous importance.

'You feel as if you could scoop up the folk like tadpoles, and have a handful of them,' he said.

She laughed, answering:

'Yes; it is necessary to get far off in order to see us proportionately. The trees are much more significant.'

'Bulk only,' he said.

She laughed cynically.

Away beyond the boulevard the thin stripes of the metals showed upon the railway track, whose margin was crowded with little stacks of timber, beside which smoking toy engines fussed. Then the silver string of the canal lay at random among the black heaps. Beyond, the dwellings, very dense on the river flat, looked like black, poisonous herbage, in thick rows and crowded beds, stretching right away, broken now and then by taller plants, right to where the river glistened in a hieroglyph across the country. The steep scarp cliffs across the river looked puny. Great stretches of country darkened with trees and faintly brightened with corn-land, spread towards the haze, where the hills rose blue beyond grey.

'It is comforting,' said Mrs Dawes, 'to think the town goes no farther. It is only a *little* sore upon the country yet.'

'A little scab,' Paul said.

She shivered. She loathed the town. Looking drearily across at the country which was forbidden her, her impassive face, pale and hostile, she reminded Paul of one of the bitter, remorseful angels.

'But the town's all right,' he said; 'it's only temporary. This is the crude, clumsy make-shift we've practised on, till we find out what the idea is. The town will come all right.'

The pigeons in the pockets of rock, among the perched bushes, cooed comfortably. To the left the large church of St Mary rose into space, to keep close company with the Castle, above the heaped rubble of the town. Mrs Dawes smiled brightly as she look across the country.

'I feel better,' she said.

'Thank you,' he replied. 'Great compliment!'

'Oh, my brother!' she laughed.

'H'm! that's snatching back with the left hand what you gave with the right, and no mistake,' he said.

She laughed in amusement at him.

'But what was the matter with you?' he asked. 'I know you were brooding something special. I can see the stamp of it on your face yet.'

'I think I will not tell you,' she said.

'All right, hug it,' he answered.

She flushed and bit her lip.

'No,' she said, 'it was the girls.'

'What about 'em?' Paul asked.

'They have been plotting something for a week now, and to-day they seem particularly full of it. All alike; they insult me with their secrecy.'

'Do they?' he asked in concern.

'I do not mind,' she went on, in the metallic, angry tone, 'if they did not thrust it into my face – the fact that they have a secret.'

'Just like women,' said he.

'It is hateful, their mean gloating,' she said tensely.

Paul was silent. He knew what the girls gloated over. He was sorry to be the cause of this new dissension.

'They can have all the secrets in the world,' she went on, brooding bitterly; 'but they might refrain from glorying in them, and making me feel more out of it than ever. It is – it is almost unbearable.'

Paul thought for a few moments. He was much perturbed.

'I will tell you what it's all about,' he said, pale and nervous. 'It's my birthday, and they've bought me a fine lot of paints, all the girls. They're jealous of you'– he felt her stiffen coldly at the word 'jealous'–'merely because I sometimes bring you a book,' he added slowly. 'But, you see, it's only a trifle. Don't bother about it, will you–because'–he laughed quickly–'well, what would they say if they saw us here now, in spite of their victory?'

She was angry with him for his clumsy reference to their present intimacy. It was almost insolent of him. Yet he was so quiet, she forgave him, although it cost her an effort.

Their two hands lay on the rough stone parapet of the Castle wall. He had inherited from his mother a fineness of mould, so that his hands were small and vigorous. Hers were large, to match her large limbs, but white and powerful looking. As Paul looked at them he knew her. 'She is wanting somebody to take her hands—for all she is so contemptuous of us,' he said to himself. And she saw nothing but his two hands, so warm and alive, which seemed to live for her. He was brooding now, staring out over the country from under sullen brows. The little, interesting diversity of shapes had vanished from the scene; all that remained was a vast, dark matrix of sorrow and tragedy, the same in all the houses and the river-flats and the people and the birds; they were only shapen differently. And now that the forms seemed to have melted away, there remained the mass from which all the landscape was composed, a dark mass of struggle and pain. The factory, the girls, his mother, the large, uplifted church, the thicket of the town, merged into one atmosphere—dark, brooding, and sorrowful, every bit.

'Is that two o'clock striking?' Mrs Dawes said in surprise.

Paul started, and everything sprang into form, regained its individuality, its forgetfulness, and its cheerfulness.

They hurried back to work.

When he was in a rush of preparing for the night's post, examining the work up from Fanny's room, which smelt of ironing, the evening postman came in.

'"Mr Paul Morel",' he said, smiling, handing Paul a package. 'A lady's handwriting! Don't let the girls see it.'

The postman, himself a favourite, was pleased to make fun of the girls' affection for Paul.

It was a volume of verse with a brief note: 'You will allow me to send you this, and so spare me my isolation. I also sympathize and wish you well.—C. D.' Paul flushed hot.

'Good Lord! Mrs Dawes. She can't afford it. Good Lord, who ever'd have thought it!'

He was suddenly intensely moved. He was filled with the warmth of her. In the glow he could almost feel her as if she were present—her arms, her shoulders, her bosom, see them, feel them, almost contain them.

This move on the part of Clara brought them into closer intimacy. The other girls noticed that when Paul met Mrs Dawes his eyes lifted and gave that peculiar bright greeting which they could interpret. Knowing he was unaware, Clara made no sign, save that occasionally she turned aside her face from him when she came upon her.

They walked out together very often at dinner-time; it was quite open, quite frank. Everybody seemed to feel that he was quite unaware of the state of his own feeling, and that nothing was wrong. He talked to her now with some of the old fervour with which he had talked to Miriam, but he cared less about the talk; he did not bother about his conclusions.

One day in October they went out to Lambley for tea. Suddenly they came to a halt on the top of the hill. He climbed and sat on a gate, she sat on the stile. The afternoon was perfectly still, with a dim haze, and yellow sheaves glowing through. They were quiet.

'How old were you when you married?' he asked quietly.

'Twenty-two.'

Her voice was subdued, almost submissive. She would tell him now.

'It is eight years ago?'

Sons and Lovers

'Yes.'
'And when did you leave him?'
'Three years ago.'
'Five years! Did you love him when you married him?'
She was silent for some time; then she said slowly:
'I thought I did—more or less. I didn't think much about it. And he wanted me. I was very prudish then.'
'And you sort of walked into it without thinking?'
'Yes. I seemed to have been asleep nearly all my life.'
'Somnambule? But—when did you wake up?'
'I don't know that I ever did, or ever have—since I was a child.'
'You went to sleep as you grew to be a woman? How queer! And he didn't wake you?'
'No, he never got there,' she replied, in a monotone.
The brown birds dashed over the hedges where the rose-hips stood naked and scarlet.
'Got where?' he asked.
'At me. He never really mattered to me.'
The afternoon was so gently warm and dim. Red roofs of the cottages burned among the blue haze. He loved the day. He could feel, but he could not understand, what Clara was saying.
'But why did you leave him? Was he horrid to you?'
She shuddered lightly.
'He—he sort of degraded me. He wanted to bully me because he hadn't got me. And then I felt as if I wanted to run, as if I was fastened and bound up. And he seemed dirty.'
'I see.'
He did not at all see.
'And was he always dirty?' he asked.
'A bit,' she replied slowly. 'And then he seemed as if he couldn't get *at* me, really. And then he got brutal—he *was* brutal!'
'And why did you leave him, finally?'
'Because—because he was unfaithful to me—'
They were both silent for some time. Her hand lay on the gate-post as she balanced. He put his own over it. His heart beat quickly.
'But did you—were you ever—did you ever give him a chance?'
'Chance? How?'
'To come near to you.'
'I married him—and I was willing—'
They both strove to keep their voices steady.
'I believes he loves you,' he said.
'It looks like it,' she replied.
He wanted to take his hand away, and could not. She saved him by removing her own. After a silence, he began again:
'Did you leave him out of count all along?'
'He left me,' she said.
'And I suppose he couldn't *make* himself mean everything to you?'
'He tried to bully me into it.'
But the conversation had got them both out of their depth. Suddenly Paul jumped down.
'Come on,' he said. 'Let's go and get some tea.'

They found a cottage, where they sat in the cold parlour. She poured out his tea. She was very quiet. He felt she had withdrawn again from him. After tea, she stared broodingly into her teacup, twisting her wedding ring all the time. In her abstraction she took the ring off her finger, stood it up, and spun it upon the table. The gold became a diaphanous glittering globe. It fell, and the ring was quivering upon the table. She spun it again and again. Paul watched, fascinated.

But she was a married woman, and he believed in simple friendship. And he considered that he was perfectly honourable with regard to her. It was only friendship between man and woman, such as any civilized persons might have.

He was like so many young men of his own age. Sex had become so complicated in him that he would have denied that he ever could want Clara or Miriam or any woman whom he *knew.* Sex desire was a sort of detached thing, that did not belong to a woman. He loved Miriam with his soul. He grew warm at the thought of Clara, he battled with her, he knew the curves of her breast and shoulders as if they had been moulded inside him; and yet he did not positively desire her. He would have denied it for ever. He believed himself really bound to Miriam. If ever he should marry, some time in the far future, it would be his duty to marry Miriam. That he gave Clara to understand, and she said nothing, but left him to his courses. He came to her, Mrs Dawes, whenever he could. Then he wrote frequently to Miriam, and visited the girl occasionally. So he went on through the winter; but he seemed not so fretted. His mother was easier about him. She thought he was getting away from Miriam.

Miriam knew now how strong was the attraction of Clara for him; but still she was certain that the best in him would triumph. His feeling for Mrs Dawes–who, moreover, was a married woman–was shallow and temporal, compared with his love for herself. He would come back to her, she was sure; with some of his young freshness gone, perhaps, but cured of his desire for the lesser things which other women than herself could give him. She could bear all if he were inwardly true to her and must come back.

He saw none of the anomaly of his position. Miriam was his old friend, lover, and she belonged to Bestwood and home and his youth. Clara was a newer friend, and she belonged to Nottingham, to life, to the world. It seemed to him quite plain.

Mrs Dawes and he had many periods of coolness, when they saw little of each other; but they always came together again.

'Were you horrid with Baxter Dawes?' he asked her. It was a thing that seemed to trouble him.

'In what way?'

'Oh, I don't know. But weren't you horrid with him? Didn't you do something that knocked him to pieces?'

'What, pray?'

'Making him feel as if he were nothing–*I* know,' Paul declared.

'You are so clever, my friend,' she said coolly.

The conversation broke off there. But it made her cool with him for some time.

She very rarely saw Miriam now. The friendship between the two women was not broken off, but considerably weakened.

'Will you come in to the concert on Sunday afternoon?' Clara asked him just after Christmas.

'I promised to go up to Willey Farm,' he replied.

'Oh, very well.'

'You don't mind, do you?' he asked.

'Why should I?' she answered.

Which almost annoyed him.

'You know,' he said, 'Miriam and I have been a lot to each other ever since I was sixteen–that's seven years now.'

'It's a long time,' Clara replied.

'Yes; but somehow she–it doesn't go right–'

'How?' asked Clara.

'She seems to draw me and draw me, and she wouldn't leave a single hair of me free to fall out and blow away–she'd keep it.'

'But you like to be kept.'

'No,' he said, 'I don't. I wish it could be normal, give and take–like me and you. I want a woman to keep me, but not in her pocket.'

'But if you love her, it couldn't be normal, like me and you.'

'Yes; I should love her better then. She sort of wants me so much that I can't give myself.'

'Wants you how?'

'Wants the soul out of my body. I can't help shrinking back from her.'

'And yet you love her!'

'No, I don't love her. I never even kiss her.'

'Why not?' Clara asked.

'I don't know.'

'I suppose you're afraid,' she said.

'I'm not. Something in me shrinks from her like hell–she's so good, when I'm not good.'

'How do you know what she is?'

'I do! I know she wants a sort of soul union.'

'But how do you know what she wants?'

'I've been with her for seven years.'

'And you haven't found out the very first thing about her.'

'What's that?'

'That she doesn't want any of your soul communion. That's your own imagination. She wants you.'

He pondered over this. Perhaps he was wrong.

'But she seems–' he began.

'You've never tried,' she answered.

I I

THE TEST ON MIRIAM

With the spring came again the old madness and battle. Now he knew he would have to go to Miriam. But what was his reluctance? He told himself it was only a sort of overstrong virginity in her and him which neither could break through. He might have married her; but his circumstances at home made it difficult, and, moreover, he did not want to marry. Marriage was for life, and because they had become close companions, he and she, he did not see that it should inevitably follow they should be man and wife. He did not feel that he wanted marriage with Miriam. He wished he did. He would have given his head to have felt a joyous desire to marry her and to have her. Then why couldn't he bring it off? There was some obstacle; and what was the obstacle? It lay in the physical bondage. He shrank from the physical contact. But why? With her he felt bound up inside himself. He could not go out to her. Something struggled in him, but he could not get to her. Why? She loved him. Clara said she even wanted him; then why couldn't he go to her, make love to her, kiss her? Why, when she put her arm in his, timidly, as they walked did he feel he would burst forth in brutality and recoil? He owed himself to her; he wanted to belong to her. Perhaps the recoil and the shrinking from her was love in its first fierce modesty. He had no aversion for her. No, it was the opposite; it was a strong desire battling with a still stronger shyness and virginity. It seemed as if virginity were a positive force, which fought and won in both of them. And with her he felt it so hard to overcome; yet he was nearest to her, and with her alone could he deliberately break through. And he owed himself to her. Then, if they could get things right, they would marry; but he would not marry unless he could feel strong in the joy of it—never. He could not have faced his mother. It seemed to him that to sacrifice himself in a marriage he did not want would be degrading, and would undo all his life, make it a nullity. He would try what he *could* do.

And he had a great tenderness for Miriam. Always, she was sad, dreaming her religion; and he was nearly a religion to her. He could not bear to fail her. It would all come right if they tried.

He looked round. A good many of the nicest men he knew were like himself, bound in by their own virginity, which they could not break out of. They were so sensitive to their women that they would go without them for ever rather than do them a hurt, an injustice. Being the sons of mothers whose husbands had blundered rather brutally through their feminine sanctities, they were themselves too diffident and shy. They could easier deny themselves than incur any reproach from a woman; for a woman was like their mother, and they were full of the sense of their mother. They preferred themselves to suffer the misery of celibacy, rather than risk the other person.

He went back to her. Something in her, when he looked at her, brought the tears almost to his eyes. One day he stood behind her as she sang. Annie was playing a song on the piano. As Miriam sang her mouth seemed hopeless. She sang like a nun singing to heaven. It reminded him so much of the mouth and eyes of one who sings beside a Botticelli Madonna, so spiritual. Again, hot as steel, came up the pain in him. Why must he ask her for the other thing? Why was there his blood battling with her? If only he could have been always gentle, tender with her, breathing with her the atmosphere of reverie and religious dreams, he would give his right hand. It was not fair to hurt her. There seemed an eternal maidenhood about her; and when he thought of her mother, he saw the great brown eyes of a maiden who was nearly scared and shocked out of her virgin maidenhood, but not quite, in spite of her seven children. They had been born almost leaving her out of count, not of her, but upon her. So she could never let them go, because she never had possessed them.

Mrs Morel saw him going again frequently to Miriam, and was astonished. He said nothing to his mother. He did not explain nor excuse himself. If he came home late, and she reproached him, he frowned and turned on her in an overbearing way.

'I shall come home when I like,' he said: 'I am old enough.'

'Must she keep you till this time?'

'It is I who stay,' he answered.

'And she lets you? But very well,' she said.

And she went to bed, leaving the door unlocked for him; but she lay listening until he came, often long after. It was a great bitterness to her that he had gone back to Miriam. She recognized, however, the uselessness of any further interference. He went to Willey Farm as a man now, not as a youth. She had no right over him. There was a coldness between him and her. He hardly told her anything. Discarded, she waited on him, cooked for him still, and loved to slave for him; but her face closed again like a mask. There was nothing for her to do now but the housework; for all the rest he had gone to Miriam. She could not forgive him. Miriam killed the joy and the warmth in him. He had been such a jolly lad, and full of the warmest affection; now he grew colder, more and more irritable and gloomy. It reminded her of William; but Paul was worse. He did things with more intensity, and more realization of what he was about. His mother knew how he was suffering for want of a woman, and she saw him going to Miriam. If he had made up his mind, nothing on earth would alter him. Mrs Morel was tired. She began to give up at last; she had finished. She was in the way.

He went on determinedly. He realized more or less what his mother felt. It only hardened his soul. He made himself callous towards her; but it was like being callous to his own health. It undermined him quickly; yet he persisted.

He lay back in the rocking-chair at Willey Farm one evening. He had been talking to Miriam for some weeks, but had not come to the point. Now he said suddenly:

'I am twenty-four, almost.'

She had been brooding. She looked up at him suddenly in surprise.

'Yes. What makes you say it?'

There was something in the charged atmosphere that she dreaded.

'Sir Thomas More says one can marry at twenty-four.'

She laughed quaintly, saying:

'Does it need Sir Thomas More's sanction?'

'No; but one ought to marry about then.'

'Ay,' she answered broodingly; and she waited.

'I can't marry you,' he continued slowly, 'not now, because we've no money, and they depend on me at home.'

She sat half-guessing what was coming.

'But I want to marry now—'

'You want to marry?' she repeated.

'A woman—you know what I mean.'

She was silent.

'Now, at last, I must,' he said.

'Ay,' she answered.

'And you love me?'

She laughed bitterly.

'Why are you ashamed of it?' he answered. 'You wouldn't be ashamed before your God, why are you before people?'

'Nay,' she answered deeply, 'I am not ashamed.'

'You are,' he replied bitterly; 'and it's my fault. But you know I can't help being—as I am—don't you?'

'I know you can't help it,' she replied.

'I love you an awful lot–then there is something short.'

'Where?' she answered, looking at him.

'Oh, in me! It is I who ought to be ashamed–like a spiritual cripple. And I am ashamed. It is misery. Why is it?'

'I don't know,' replied Miriam.

'And I don't know,' he repeated. 'Don't you think we have been too fierce in our what they call purity? Don't you think that to be so much afraid and averse is a sort of dirtiness?'

She looked at him with startled dark eyes.

'You recoiled away from anything of the sort, and I took the motion from you, and recoiled also, perhaps worse.'

There was silence in the room for some time.

'Yes,' she said, 'it is so.'

'There is between us,' he said 'all these years of intimacy. I feel naked enough before you. Do you understand?'

'I think so,' she answered.

'And you love me?'

She laughed.

'Don't be bitter,' he pleaded.

She looked at him and was sorry for him; his eyes were dark with torture. She was sorry for him; it was worse for him to have this deflected love than for herself, who could never be properly mated. He was restless, for ever urging forward and trying to find a way out. He might do as he liked, and have what he liked of her.

'Nay,' she said softly, 'I am not bitter.'

She felt she could bear anything for him; she would suffer for him. She put her hand on his knee as he leaned forward in his chair. He took it and kissed it; but it hurt to do so. He felt he was putting himself aside. He sat there sacrificed to her purity, which felt more like nullity. How could he kiss her hand passionately, when it would drive her away, and leave nothing but pain? Yet slowly he drew her to him and kissed her.

They knew each other too well to pretend anything. As she kissed him, she watched his eyes; they were staring across the room, with a peculiar dark blaze in them that fascinated her. He was perfectly still. She could feel his heart throbbing heavily in his breast.

'What are you thinking about?' she asked.

The blaze in his eyes shuddered, became uncertain.

'I was thinking, all the while, I love you. I have been obstinate.'

She sank her head on his breast.

'Yes,' she answered.

'That's all,' he said, and his voice seemed sure, and his mouth was kissing her throat.

Then she raised her head and looked into his eyes with her full gaze of love. The blaze struggled, seemed to try to get away from her, and then was quenched. He turned his head quickly aside. It was a moment of anguish.

'Kiss me,' she whispered.

He shut his eyes, and kissed her, and his arms folded her closer and closer.

When she walked home with him over the fields, he said:

'I am glad I came back to you. I feel so simple with you–as if there was nothing to hide. We will be happy?'

'Yes,' she murmured, and the tears came to her eyes.

'Some sort of perversity in our souls,' he said, 'makes us not want, get away from, the very thing we want. We have to fight against that.'

'Yes,' she said, and she felt stunned.

As she stood under the drooping thorn-tree, in the darkness by the roadside, he kissed her, and his fingers wandered over her face. In the darkness, where he could not see her but only feel her, his passion flooded him. He clasped her very close.

'Sometime you will have me?' he murmured, hiding his face on her shoulder. It was so difficult.

'Not now,' she said.

His hopes and his heart sank. A dreariness came over him.

'No,' he said.

His clasp of her slackened.

'I love to feel your arm *there!*' she said, pressing his arm against her back, where it went round her waist. 'It rests me so.'

He tightened the pressure of his arm upon the small of her back to rest her.

'We belong to each other,' he said.

'Yes.'

'Then why shouldn't we belong to each other altogether?'

'But–' she faltered.

'I know it's a lot to ask,' he said; 'but there's not much risk for you really–not in the Gretchen way. You can trust me there?'

'Oh, I can trust you,' the answer came quick and strong. 'It's not that–it's not that at all–but–'

'What?'

She hid her face in his neck with a little cry of misery.

'I don't know!' she cried.

She seemed slightly hysterical, but with a sort of horror. His heart died in him.

'You don't think it ugly?' he asked.

'No, not now. You have *taught* me it isn't.'

'You are afraid?'

She calmed herself hastily.

'Yes, I am only afraid,' she said.

He kissed her tenderly.

'Never mind,' he said. 'You shall please yourself.'

Suddenly she gripped his arms round her, and clenched her body stiff.

'You *shall* have me,' she said, through her shut teeth.

His heart beat up again like fire. He folded her close, and his mouth was on her throat. She could not bear it. She drew away. He disengaged her.

'Won't you be late?' she asked gently.

He sighed, scarcely hearing what she said. She waited, wishing he would go. At last he kissed her quickly and climbed the fence. Looking round he saw the pale blotch of her face down in the darkness under the hanging tree. There was no more of her but this pale blotch.

'Good-bye!' he called softly. She had no body, only a voice and a dim face. He turned away and ran down the road, his fists clenched; and when he came to the wall over the lake he leaned there, almost stunned, looking up the black water.

Miriam plunged home over the meadows. She was not afraid of people, what they might say; but she dreaded the issue with him. Yes, she would let him have her if he insisted; and then, when she thought of it afterwards, her heart went down. He would be disappointed, he would find no satisfaction, and then he would go away. Yet he was so insistent; and over this, which did not seem so all-important to her, was their love to break down. After all, he was only like other men, seeking his satisfaction. Oh, but there was someting more in him, something deeper! She could trust to it, in spite of all desires. He said that possession was a great moment in life. All strong emotions concentrated there. Perhaps it was so. There was something divine in it; then she would submit, religiously, to the sacrifice. He should have her. And at the thought her whole body clenched itself involuntarily, hard, as if against something; but Life forced her through this gate of suffering, too, and she would submit. At any rate, it would give him what he wanted, which was her deepest wish. She brooded and brooded and brooded herself towards accepting him.

He courted her now like a lover. Often, when he grew hot, she put his face from her, held it between her hands, and looked in his eyes. He could not meet her gaze. Her dark eyes, full of love, earnest and searching, made him turn away. Not for an instant would she let him forget. Back again he had to torture himself into a sense of his responsibility and hers. Never any relaxing, never any leaving himself to the great hunger and impersonality of passion; he must be brought back to a deliberate, reflective creature. As if from a swoon of passion she called him back to the littleness, the personal relationship. He could not bear it. 'Leave me alone–leave me alone!' he wanted to cry; but she wanted him to look at her with eyes full of love. His eyes, full of the dark, impersonal fire of desire, did not belong to her.

There was a great crop of cherries at the farm. The trees at the back of the house, very large and tall, hung thick with scarlet and crimson drops, under the dark leaves. Paul and Edgar were gathering the fruit one evening. It had been a hot day, and now the clouds were rolling in the sky, dark and warm. Paul climbed high in the tree, above the scarlet roofs of the buildings. The wind, moaning steadily, made the whole tree rock with a subtle, thrilling motion that stirred the blood. The young man, perched insecurely in the slender branches, rocked till he felt slightly drunk, reached down the boughs where the scarlet beady cherries hung thick underneath, and tore off handful after handful of the sleek, cool-fleshed fruit. Cherries touched his ears and his neck as he stretched forward, their chill finger-tips sending a flash down his blood. All shades of red, from a golden vermilion to a rich crimson, glowed and met his eyes under a darkness of leaves.

The sun, going down, suddenly caught the broken clouds. Immense piles of gold flared out of the south-east, heaped in soft, glowing yellow right up the sky. The world, till now dusk and grey, reflected the gold glow, astonished. Everywhere the trees, and the grass, and the far-off water, seemed roused from the twilight and shining.

Miriam came out wondering.

'Oh!' Paul heard her mellow voice call, 'isn't it wonderful?'

He looked down. There was a faint glimmer on her face, that looked very soft, turned up at him.

'How high you are!' she said.

Beside her, on the rhubarb leaves, were four dead birds, thieves that had been shot. Paul saw some cherry-stones hanging quite bleached, like skeletons, picked clear of flesh. He looked down again to Miriam.

'Clouds are on fire,' he said.

'Beautiful!' she cried.

She seemed so small, so soft, so tender, down there. He threw a handful of cherries at her. She was startled and frightened. He laughed with a low, chuckling sound, and pelted her. She ran for shelter, picking up some cherries. Two fine pairs she hung over her ears; then she looked up again.

'Haven't you got enough?' she asked.

'Nearly. It is like being on a ship up here.'

'And how long will you stay?'

'While the sunset lasts.'

She went to the fence and sat there, watching the gold clouds fall to pieces, and go in immense, rose-coloured ruin towards the darkness. Gold flamed to scarlet, like pain in its intense brightness. Then the scarlet sank to rose, and rose to crimson, and quickly the passion went out of the sky. All the world was dark grey. Paul scrambled quickly down with his basket, tearing his shirt-sleeve as he did so.

'They are lovely,' said Miriam, fingering the cherries.

'I've torn my sleeve,' he answered.

She took the three-cornered rip, saying:

'I shall have to mend it.' It was near the shoulder. She put her fingers through the tear. 'How warm!' she said.

He laughed. There was a new strange note in his voice, one that made her pant.

'Shall we stay out?' he said.

'Won't it rain?' she asked.

'No, let us walk a little way.'

They went down the fields and into the thick plantation of fir-trees and pines.

'Shall we go in among the trees?' he asked.

'Do you want to?'

'Yes.'

It was very dark among the firs, and the sharp spines pricked her face. She was afraid. Paul was silent and strange.

'I like the darkness,' he said. 'I wish it were thicker–good, thick darkness.'

He seemed to be almost unaware of her as a person: she was only to him then a woman. She was afraid.

He stood against a pine-tree trunk and took her in his arms. She relinquished herself to him, but it was a sacrifice in which she felt something of horror. This thick-voiced, oblivious man was a stranger to her.

Later it began to rain. The pine-trees smelled very strong. Paul lay with his head on the ground, on the dead pine-needles, listening to the sharp hiss of the rain–a steady, keen noise. His heart was down, very heavy. Now he realized that she had not been with him all the time, that her soul had stood apart, in a sort of horror. He was physically at rest, but no more. Very dreary at heart, very sad, and very tender, his fingers wandered over her face pitifully. Now again she loved him deeply. He was tender and beautiful.

'The rain!' he said.

'Yes–it is coming on you?'

She put her hands over him, on his hair, on his shoulders, to feel if the raindrops fell on him. She loved him dearly. He, as he lay with his face on the dead pine-leaves, felt extraordinarily quiet. He did not mind if the raindrops came on him; he would have lain and got wet through; he felt as if nothing mattered, as if his living were smeared away into the beyond, near and quite lovable. This strange, gentle reaching-out to death was new to him.

'We must go,' said Miriam.

'Yes,' he answered, but did not move.

To him now, life seemed a shadow, day a white shadow; night, and death, and stillness, and inaction, this seemed like *being*. To be alive, to be urgent and insistent—that was *not-to-be*. The highest of all was to melt out into the darkness and sway there, identified with the great Being.

'The rain is coming in on us,' said Miriam.

He rose, and assisted her.

'It is a pity,' he said.

'What?'

'To have to go. I feel so still.'

'Still!' she repeated.

'Stiller than I have ever been in my life.'

He was walking with his hand in hers. She pressed his fingers, feeling a slight fear. Now he seemed beyond her; she had a fear lest she should lose him.

'The fir-trees are like presences on the darkness: each one only a presence.'

She was afraid, and said nothing.

'A sort of hush: the whole night wondering and asleep: I suppose that's what we do in death—sleep in wonder.'

She had been afraid before of the brute in him: now of the mystic. She trod beside him in silence. The rain fell with a heavy 'Hush!' on the trees. At last they gained the cart-shed.

'Let us stay here awhile,' he said.

There was a sound of rain everywhere, smothering everything.

'I feel so strange and still,' he said; 'along with everything.'

'Ay,' she answered patiently.

He seemed again unaware of her, though he held her hand close.

'To be rid of our individuality, which is our will, which is our effort—to live effortless, a kind of conscious sleep—that is very beautiful, I think that is our after-life—our immortality.'

'Yes?'

'Yes—and very beautiful to have.'

'You don't usually say that.'

'No.'

In a while they went indoors. Everybody looked at them curiously. He still kept the quiet, heavy look in his eyes, the stillness of his voice. Instinctively, they all left him alone.

About this time Miriam's grandmother, who lived in a tiny cottage in Woodlinton, fell ill, and the girl was sent to keep house. It was a beautiful little place. The cottage had a big garden in front, with red brick walls, against which the plum-trees were nailed. At the back another garden was separated from the fields by a tall old hedge. It was very pretty. Miriam had not much to do, so she found time for her beloved reading, and for writing introspective pieces which interested her.

At the holiday-time her grandmother, being better, was driven to Derby to stay with her daughter for a day or two. She was a crotchety old lady, and might return the second day or the third; so Miriam stayed alone in the cottage, which also pleased her.

Paul used often to cycle over, and they had as a rule peaceful and happy times. He did not embarrass her much; but then on the Monday of the holiday he was to spend a whole day with her.

It was perfect weather. He left his mother, telling her where he was going. She would be alone all the day. It cast a shadow over him; but he had three days that were all his own, when he was going to do as he liked. It was sweet to rush through the morning lanes on his bicycle.

He got to the cottage at about eleven o'clock. Miriam was busy preparing dinner. She looked so perfectly in keeping with the little kitchen, ruddy and busy. He kissed her and sat down to watch. The room was small and cosy. The sofa was covered all over with a sort of linen in squares of red and pale blue, old, much washed, but pretty. There was a stuffed owl in a case over a corner cupboard. The sunlight came through the leaves of the scented geraniums in the window. She was cooking a chicken in his honour. It was their cottage for the day, and they were man and wife. He beat the eggs for her and peeled the potatoes. He thought she gave a feeling of home almost like his mother; and no one could look more beautiful, with her tumbled curls, when she was flushed from the fire.

The dinner was a great success. Like a young husband, he carved. They talked all the time with unflagging zest. Then he wiped the dishes she had washed, and they went out down the fields. There was a bright little brook that ran into a bog at the foot of a very steep bank. Here they wandered, picking still a few marsh-marigolds and many big blue forget-me-nots. Then she sat on the bank with her hands full of flowers, mostly golden water-blobs. As she put her face down into the marigolds, it was all overcast with a yellow shine.

'Your face is bright,' he said, 'like a transfiguration.'

She looked at him, questioning. He laughed pleadingly to her, laying his hand on hers. Then he kissed her fingers, then her face.

The world was all steeped in sunshine, and quite still, yet not asleep, but quivering with a kind of expectancy.

'I have never seen anything more beautiful than this,' he said. He held her hand fast all the time.

'And the water singing to itself as it runs—do you love it?' She looked at him full of love. His eyes were very dark, very bright.

'Don't you think it's a great day?' he asked.

She murmured her assent. She *was* happy, and he saw it.

'And our day—just between us,' he said.

They lingered a little while. Then they stood up upon the sweet thyme, and he looked down at her simply.

'Will you come?' he asked.

They went back to the house, hand-in-hand, in silence. The chickens came scampering down the path to her. He locked the door, and they had the little house to themselves.

He never forgot seeing her as she lay on the bed, when he was unfastening his collar. First he saw only her beauty, and was blind with it. She had the most beautiful body he had ever imagined. He stood unable to move or speak, looking at her, his face half smiling with wonder. And then he wanted her, but as he went forward to her, her hands lifted in a little pleading movement, and he looked at her face, and stopped. Her big brown eyes were watching him, still and resigned and loving; she lay as if she had given herself up to sacrifice: there was her body for him; but the look at the back of her eyes, like a creature awaiting immolation, arrested him, and all his blood fell back.

'You are sure you want me?' he asked, as if a cold shadow had come over him.
'Yes, quite sure.'

She was very quiet, very calm. She only realized that she was doing
something for him. He could hardly bear it. She lay to be sacrificed for him
because she loved him so much. And he had to sacrifice her. For a second, he
wished he were sexless or dead. Then he shut his eyes again to her, and his
blood beat back again.

And afterwards he loved her–loved her to the last fibre of his being. He loved
her. But he wanted, somehow, to cry. There was something he could not bear
for her sake. He stayed with her till quite late at night. As he rode home he felt
that he was finally initiated. He was a youth no longer. But why had he the dull
pain in his soul? Why did the thought of death, the after-life, seem so sweet and
consoling?

He spent the week with Miriam, and wore her out with his passion before it
was gone. He had always, almost wilfully, to put her out of count, and act from
the brute strength of his own feelings. And he could not do it often, and there
remained afterwards always the sense of failure and of death. If he were really
with her, he had to put aside himself and his desire. If he would have her, he had
to put her aside.

'When I come to you,' he asked her, his eyes dark with pain and shame, 'you
don't really want me, do you?'

'Ah, yes!' she replied quickly.

He looked at her.

'Nay,' he said.

She began to tremble.

'You see,' she said, taking his face and shutting it out against her
shoulder–'you see–as we are–how can I get used to you? It would come all
right if we were married.'

He lifted her head and looked at her.

'You mean, now, it is always too much shock?'

'Yes–and–'

'You are always clenched against me.'

She was trembling with agitation.

'You see,' she said, 'I'm not used to the thought–'

'You are lately,' he said.

'But all my life. Mother said to me, "There is one thing in marriage that is
always dreadful, but you have to bear it." And I believed it.'

'And still believe,' he said.

'No!' she cried hastily. 'I believe, as you do, that loving, even in *that* way, is
the high-water mark of living.'

'That doesn't alter the fact that you never *want* it.'

'No,' she said, taking his head in her arms and rocking in despair. 'Don't say
so! You don't understand.' She rocked with pain. 'Don't I want your children?'

'But not me.'

'How can you say so? But we must be married to have children–'

'Shall we be married, then? *I* want you to have my children.' He kissed her
hand reverently. She pondered sadly, watching him.

'We are too young,' she said at length.

'Twenty-four and twenty-three–'

'Not yet,' she pleaded, as she rocked herself in distress.

'When you will,' he said.

She bowed her head gravely. The tone of hopelessness in which he said these things grieved her deeply. It had always been a failure between them. Tacitly, she acquiesced in what he felt.

And after a week of love he said to his mother suddenly one Sunday night, just as they were going to bed:

'I shan't go so much to Miriam's mother.'

She was surprised, but she would not ask him anything.

'You please yourself,' she said.

So he went to bed. But there was a new quietness about him which she had wondered at. She almost guessed. She would leave him alone, however. Precipitation might spoil things. She watched him in his loneliness, wondering where he would end. He was sick, and much too quiet for him. There was a perpetual little knitting of his brows, such as she had seen when he was a small baby, and which had been gone for many years. Now it was the same again. And she could do nothing for him. He had to go on alone, make his own way.

He continued faithful to Miriam. For one day he had loved her utterly. But it never came again. The sense of failure grew stronger. At first it was only a sadness. Then he began to feel he could not go on. He wanted to run, to go abroad, anything. Gradually he ceased to ask her to have him. Instead of drawing them together, it put them apart. And then he realized, consciously, that it was no good. It was useless trying: it would never be a success between them.

For some months he had seen very little of Clara. They had occasionally walked out for half an hour at dinner-time. But he always reserved himself for Miriam. With Clara, however, his brow cleared, and he was gay again. She treated him indulgently, as if he were a child. He thought he did not mind. But deep below the surface it piqued him.

Sometimes Miriam said:

'What about Clara? I hear nothing of her lately.'

'I walked with her about twenty minutes yesterday,' he replied.

'And what did she talk about?'

'I don't know. I suppose I did all the jawing—I usually do. I think I was telling her about the strike, and how the women took it.'

'Yes.'

So he gave the account of himself.

But insidiously, without his knowing it, the warmth he felt for Clara drew him away from Miriam, for whom he felt responsible, and to whom he felt he belonged. He thought he was being quite faithful to her. It is not easy to estimate exactly the strength and warmth of one's feelings for a woman till they have run away with one.

He began to give more time to his friends. There was Jessop, at the Art School; Swain, who was chemistry demonstrator at the University; Newton, who was a teacher; besides Edgar and Miriam's younger brothers. Pleading work, he sketched and studied with Jessop. He called in the University for Swain, and the two went 'down town' together. Having come home in the train with Newton, he called and had a game of billiards with him in the Moon and Stars. If he gave to Miriam the excuse of his men friends, he felt quite justified. His mother began to be relieved. He always told her where he had been.

During the summer, Clara wore sometimes a dress of soft cotton stuff with loose sleeves. When she lifted her hands, her sleeves fell back, and her beautiful strong arms shone out.

'Half a minute,' he cried. 'Hold your arm still.'

He made sketches of her hand and arm, and the drawings contained some of the fascination the real thing had for him. Miriam, who always went scrupulously through his books and papers, saw the drawings.

'I think Clara has such beautiful arms,' he said.

'Yes! When did you draw them?'

'On Tuesday, in the work-room. You know, I've got a corner where I can work. Often I can do every single thing they need in the department, before dinner. Then I work for myself in the afternoon, and just see to things at night.'

'Yes,' she said, turning the leaves of his sketch-book.

Frequently he hated Miriam. He hated her as she bent forward and pored over his things. He hated her way of patiently casting him up, as if he were an endless psychological account. When he was with her, he hated her for having got him, and yet not got him, and he tortured her. She took all and gave nothing, he said. At least, she gave no living warmth. She was never alive, and giving off life. Looking for her was like looking for something which did not exist. She was only his conscience, not his mate. He hated her violently, and was more cruel to her. They dragged on till the next summer. He saw more and more of Clara.

At last he spoke. He had been sitting working at home one evening. There was between him and his mother a peculiar condition of people frankly finding fault with each other. Mrs Morel was strong on her feet again. He was not going to stick to Miriam. Very well; then she would stand aloof till he said something. It had been coming a long time, this bursting of the storm in him, when he would come back to her. This evening there was between them a peculiar condition of suspense. He worked feverishly and mechanically, so that he could escape from himself. It grew late. Through the open door, stealthily, came the scent of madonna lilies, almost as if it were prowling abroad. Suddenly he got up and went out of doors.

The beauty of the night made him want to shout. A half-moon, dusky gold, was sinking behind the black sycamore at the end of the garden, making the sky dull purple with its glow. Nearer, a dim white fence of lilies went across the garden, and the air all round seemed to stir with scent, as if it were alive. He went across the bed of pinks, whose keen perfume came sharply across the rocking, heavy scent of the lilies, and stood alongside the white barrier of flowers. They flagged all loose, as if they were panting. The scent made him drunk. He went down to the field to watch the moon sink under.

A corncrake in the hay-close called insistently. The moon slid quite quickly downwards, growing more flushed. Behind him the great flowers leaned as if they were calling. And then, like a shock, he caught another perfume, something raw and coarse. Hunting round, he found the purple iris, touched their fleshy throats and their dark, grasping hands. At any rate, he had found something. They stood stiff in the darkness. Their scent was brutal. The moon was melting down upon the crest of the hill. It was gone; all was dark. The corncrake called still.

Breaking off a pink, he suddenly went indoors.

'Come, my boy,' said his mother. 'I'm sure it's time you went to bed.'

He stood with the pink against his lips.

'I shall break off with Miriam, mother,' he answered calmly.

She looked up at him over her spectacles. He was staring back at her, unswerving. She met his eyes for a moment, then took off her glasses. He was white. The male was up in him, dominant. She did not want to see him too clearly.

'But I thought–' she began.

'Well,' he answered, 'I don't love her. I don't want to marry her–so I shall have done.'

'But,' exclaimed his mother, amazed, 'I thought lately you had made up your mind to have her, and so I said nothing.'

'I had–I wanted to–but now I don't want. It's no good. I shall break off on Sunday. I ought to, oughtn't I?'

'You know best. You know I said so long ago.'

'I can't help that now. I shall break off on Sunday.'

'Well,' said his mother. 'I think it will be best. But lately I decided you had made up your mind to have her, so I said nothing, and should have said nothing. But I say as I have always said, I *don't* think she is suited to you.'

'On Sunday I break off,' he said, smelling the pink. He put the flower in his mouth. Unthinking, he bared his teeth, closed them on the blossom slowly, and had a mouthful of petals. These he spat into the fire, kissed his mother, and went to bed.

On Sunday he went up to the farm in the early afternoon. He had written Miriam that they would walk over the fields to Hucknall. His mother was very tender with him. He said nothing. But she saw the effort it was costing. The peculiar set look on his face stilled her.

'Never mind, my son,' she said. 'You will be so much better, when it is all over.'

Paul glanced swiftly at his mother in surprise and resentment. He did not want sympathy.

Miriam met him at the lane-end. She was wearing a new dress of figured muslin that had short sleeves. Those short sleeves, and Miriam's brown-skinned arms beneath them–such pitiful, resigned arms–gave him so much pain that they helped to make him cruel. She had made herself look so beautiful and fresh for him. She seemed to blossom for him alone. Every time he looked at her–a mature young woman now, and beautiful in her new dress–it hurt so much that his heart seemed almost to be bursting with the restraint he put on it. But he had decided, and it was irrevocable.

On the hills they sat down, and he lay with his head in her lap, whilst she fingered his hair. She knew that 'he was not there', as she put it. Often, when she had him with her, she looked for him, and could not find him. But this afternoon she was not prepared.

It was nearly five o'clock when he told her. They were sitting on the bank of a stream, where the lip of turf hung over a hollow bank of yellow earth, and he was hacking away with a stick, as he did when he was perturbed and cruel.

'I have been thinking,' he said, 'we ought to break off.'

'Why?' she cried in surprise.

'Because it's no good going on.'

'Why is it no good?'

'It isn't. I don't want to marry. I don't want ever to marry. And if we're not going to marry, it's no good going on.'

'But why do you say this now?'

'Because I've made up my mind.'

'And what about these last months, and the things you told me then?'

'I can't help it; I don't want to go on.'

'You don't want any more of me?'

'I want us to break off–you be free of me, I free of you.'

'And what about these last months?'

'I don't know. I've not told you anything but what I thought was true.'

'Then why are you different now?'

'I'm not–I'm the same–only I know it's no good going on.'

'You haven't told me why it's no good.'

'Because I don't want to go on–and I don't want to marry.'

'How many times have you offered to marry me, and I wouldn't?'

'I know; but I want us to break off.'

There was silence for a moment or two, while he dug viciously at the earth. She bent her head, pondering. He was an unreasonable child. He was like an infant which, when it has drunk its fill, throws away and smashes the cup. She looked at him, feeling she could get hold of him and *wring* some consistency out of him. But she was helpless. Then she cried.

'I have said you were only fourteen–you are only *four*!'

He still dug at the earth viciously. He heard.

'You are a child of four,' she repeated in her anger.

He did not answer, but said in his heart: 'All right; if I'm a child of four, what do you want me for? *I* don't want another mother.' But he said nothing to her, and there was silence.

'And have you told your people?' she asked.

'I have told my mother.'

There was another long interval of silence.

'Then what do you *want*?' she asked.

'Why, I want us to separate. We have lived on each other all these years; now let us stop. I will go my own way without you, and you will go your way without me. You will have an independent life of your own then.'

There was in it some truth that, in spite of her bitterness, she could not help registering. She knew she felt in a sort of bondage to him, which she hated because she could not control it. She had hated her love for him from the moment it grew too strong for her. And, deep down, she had hated him because she loved him and he dominated her. She had resisted his domination. She had fought to keep herself free of him in the last issue. And she *was* free of him, even more than he of her.

'And,' he continued, 'we shall always be more or less each other's work. You have done a lot for me, I for you. Now let us start and live by ourselves.'

'What do you want to do?' she asked.

'Nothing–only be free,' he answered.

She, however, knew in her heart that Clara's influence was over him to liberate him. But she said nothing.

'And what have I to tell my mother?' she asked.

'I told my mother,' he answered, 'that I was breaking off–clean and altogether.'

'I shall not tell them at home,' she said.

Frowning, 'You please yourself,' he said.

He knew he had landed her in a nasty hole, and was leaving her in the lurch. It angered him.

'Tell them you wouldn't and won't marry me, and have broken off,' he said. 'It's true enough.'

She bit her finger moodily. She thought over their whole affair. She had known it would come to this; she had seen it all along. It chimed with her bitter expectation.

'Always–it has always been so!' she cried. 'It has been one long battle between us–you fighting away from me.'

It came from her unawares, like a flash of lightning. The man's heart stood still. Was this how she saw it?

'But we've had *some* perfect hours, *some* perfect times, when we were together!' he pleaded.

'Never!' she cried, 'never! It has always been you fighting me off.'

'Not always–not at first!' he pleaded.

'Always, from the very beginning–always the same!'

She had finished, but she had done enough. He sat aghast. He had wanted to say, 'It has been good, but it is at an end.' And she–she whose love he had believed in when he had despised himself–denied that their love had ever been love. 'He had always fought away from her?' Then it had been monstrous. There had never been anything really between them; all the time he had been imagining something where there was nothing. And she had known. She had known so much, and had told him so little. She had known all the time. All the time this was at the bottom of her!

He sat silent in bitterness. At last the whole affair appeared in a cynical aspect to him. She had really played with him, not he with her. She had hidden all her condemnation from him, had flattered him, and despised him. She despised him now. He grew intellectual and cruel.

'You ought to marry a man who worships you,' he said; 'then you could do as you liked with him. Plenty of men will worship you, if you get on the private side of their natures. You ought to marry one such. They would never fight you off.'

'Thank you!' she said. 'But don't advise me to marry someone else any more. You've done it before.'

'Very well,' he said; 'I will say no more.'

He sat still, feeling as if he had had a blow, instead of giving one. Their eight years of friendship and love, *the* eight years of his life, were nullified.

'When did you think of this?' she asked.

'I thought definitely on Thursday night.'

'I knew it was coming,' she said.

That pleased him bitterly. 'Oh, very well! If she knew then it doesn't come as a surprise to her,' he thought.

'And have you said anything to Clara?' she asked.

'No; but I shall tell her now.'

There was a silence.

'Do you remember the things you said this time last year, in my grandmother's house–nay last month even?'

'Yes,' he said; 'I do! And I meant them! I can't help that it's failed.'

'It has failed because you want something else.'

'It would have failed whether or not. *You* never believed in me.'

She laughed strangely.

He sat in silence. He was full of a feeling that she had deceived him. She had despised him when he thought she worshipped him. She had let him say wrong things, and had not contradicted him. She had let him fight alone. But it stuck in his throat that she had despised him whilst he thought she worshipped him.

She should have told him when she found fault with him. She had not played fair. He hated her. All these years she had treated him as if he were a hero, and thought of him secretly as an infant, a foolish child. Then why had she left the foolish child to his folly? His heart was hard against her.

She sat full of bitterness. She had known–oh, well she had known! All the time he was away from her she had summed him up, seen his littleness, his meanness, and his folly. Even she had guarded her soul against him. She was not overthrown, nor prostrated, not even much hurt. She had known. Only why, as he sat there, had he still this strange dominance over her? His very movements fascinated her as if she were hypnotized by him. Yet he was despicable, false, inconsistent, and mean. Why this bondage for her? Why was it the movement of his arm stirred her as nothing else the world could? Why was she fastened to him? Why, even now, if he looked at her and commanded her, would she have to obey? She would obey him in his trifling commands. But once he was obeyed, then she had him in her power, she knew, to lead him where she would. She was sure of herself. Only, this new influence! Ah, he was not a man! He was a baby that cries for the newest toy. And all the attachment of his soul would not keep him. Very well, he would have to go. But he would come back when he had tired of his new sensation.

He hacked at the earth till she was fretted to death. She rose. He sat flinging lumps of earth in the stream.

'We will go and have tea here?' he asked.

'Yes,' she answered.

They chattered over irrelevant subjects during tea. He held forth on the love of ornament–the cottage parlour moved him thereto–and its connexion with aesthetics. She was cold and quiet. As they walked home, she asked:

'And we shall not see each other?'

'No–or rarely,' he answered.

'Nor write?' she asked, almost sarcastically.

'As you will,' he answered. 'We're not strangers–never should be, whatever happened. I will write to you now and again. You please yourself.'

'I see!' she answered cuttingly.

But he was at that stage at which nothing else hurts. He had made a great cleavage in his life. He had had a great shock when she had told him their love had been always a conflict. Nothing more mattered. If it had never been much, there was no need to make a fuss that it was ended.

He left her at the lane-end. As she went home, solitary, in her new frock, having her people to face at the other end, he stood still with shame and pain in the highroad, thinking of the suffering he caused her.

In the reaction towards restoring his self-esteem, he went into the Willow Tree for a drink. There were four girls who had been out for the day, drinking a modest glass of port. They had some chocolates on the table. Paul sat near with his whisky. He noticed the girls whispering and nudging. Presently one, a bonny dark hussy, leaned to him and said:

'Have a chocolate?'

The others laughed loudly at her impudence.

'All right,' said Paul. 'Give me a hard one–nut, I don't like creams.'

'Here you are, then,' said the girl; 'here's an almond for you.'

She held the sweet between her fingers. He opened his mouth. She popped it in, and blushed.

'You *are* nice!' he said.

'Well,' she answered, 'we thought you looked overcast, and they dared me offer you a chocolate.'

'I don't mind if I have another–another sort,' he said.

And presently they were all laughing together.

It was nine o'clock when he got home, falling dark. He entered the house in silence. His mother, who had been waiting, rose anxiously.

'I told her,' he said.

'I'm glad,' replied the mother, with great relief.

He hung up his cap wearily.

'I said we'd have done altogether,' he said.

'That's right, my son,' said the mother. 'It's hard for her now, but best in the long run. I know. You weren't suited for her.'

He laughed shakily as he sat down.

'I've had such a lark with some girls in a pub,' he said.

His mother looked at him. He had forgotten Miriam now. He told her about the girls in the Willow Tree. Mrs Morel looked at him. It seemed unreal, his gaiety. At the back of it was too much horror and misery.

'Now have some supper,' she said very gently.

Afterwards he said wistfully:

'She never thought she'd have me, Mother, not from the first, and so she's not disappointed.'

'I'm afraid,' said his mother, 'she doesn't give up hopes of you yet.'

'No,' he said, 'perhaps not.'

'You'll find it's better to have done,' she said.

'*I* don't know,' he said desperately.

'Well, leave her alone,' replied his mother.

So he left her, and she was alone. Very few people cared for her, and she for very few people. She remained alone with herself, waiting.

12

PASSION

He was gradually making it possible to earn a livelihood by his art. Liberty's had taken several of his painted designs on various stuffs, and he could sell designs for embroideries, for altar-cloths, and similar things, in one or two places. It was not very much he made at present, but he might extend it. He had also made friends with the designer for a pottery firm, and was gaining some knowledge of his new acquaintance's art. The applied arts interested him very much. At the same time he laboured slowly at his pictures. He loved to paint large figures, full of light, but not merely made up of lights and cast shadows, like the Impressionists; rather definite figures that had a certain luminous quality, like some of Michelangelo's people. And these he fitted into a landscape, in what he thought true proportion. He worked a great deal from memory, using everybody he knew. He believed firmly in his work, that it was good and valuable. In spite of fits of depression, shrinking, everything, he believed in his work.

He was twenty-four when he said his first confident thing to his mother.

'Mother,' he said, I s'll make a painter that they'll attend to.'

She sniffed in her quaint fashion. It was like a half-pleased shrug of the shoulders.

'Very well, my boy, we'll see,' she said.

'You shall see, my pigeon! You see if you're not swanky one of these days!'

'I'm quite content, my boy,' she smiled.

'But you'll have to alter. Look at you with Minnie!'

Minnie was the small servant, a girl of fourteen.

'And what about Minnie?' asked Mrs Morel, with dignity.

'I heard her this morning: "Eh, Mrs Morel! I was going to do that," when you went out in the rain for some coal,' he said. 'That looks a lot like your being able to manage servants!'

'Well, it was only the child's niceness,' said Mrs Morel.

'And you apologizing to her: "You can't do two things at once, can you?"'

'She *was* busy washing up,' replied Mrs Morel.

'And what did she say? "It could easy have waited a bit. Now look how your feet paddle!"'

'Yes—brazen young baggage!' said Mrs Morel, smiling.

He looked at his mother, laughing. She was quite warm and rosy again with love of him. It seemed as if all the sunshine were on her for a moment. He continued his work gladly. She seemed so well when she was happy that he forgot her grey hair.

And that year she went with him to the Isle of Wight for a holiday. It was too exciting for them both, and too beautiful. Mrs Morel was full of joy and wonder. But he would have her walk with him more than she was able. She had a bad fainting bout. So grey her face was, so blue her mouth! It was agony to him. He felt as if someone were pushing a knife in his chest. Then she was better again, and he forgot. But the anxiety remained inside him, like a wound that did not close.

After leaving Miriam he went almost straight to Clara. On the Monday following the day of the rupture he went down to the workroom. She looked up at him and smiled. They had grown very intimate unawares. She saw a new brightness about him.

'Well, Queen of Sheba!' he said, laughing.

'But why?' she asked.

'I think it suits you. You've got a new frock on.'

She flushed, asking:

'And what of it?'

'Suits you—awfully! *I* could design you a dress.'

'How would it be?'

He stood in front of her, his eyes glittering as he expounded. He kept her eyes fixed with his. Then suddenly he took hold of her. She half started back. He drew the stuff of her blouse tighter, smoothed it over her breast.

'More *so!*' he explained.

But they were both of them flaming with blushes, and immediately he ran away. He had touched her. His whole body was quivering with the sensation.

There was already a sort of secret understanding between them. The next evening he went into the cinematograph with her for a few minutes before train-time. As they sat, he saw her hand lying near him. For some moments he dared not touch it. The pictures danced and dithered. Then he took her hand in his. It was large and firm; it filled his grasp. He held it fast. She neither moved nor made any sign. When they came out his train was due. He hesitated.

'Good night,' she said. He darted away across the road.

The next day he came again, talking to her. She was rather superior with him.

'Shall we go a walk on Monday?' he asked.

She turned her face aside.

'Shall you tell Miriam?' she replied sarcastically.

'I have broken with her,' he said.

'When?'

'Last Sunday.'

'You quarrelled?'

'No! I had made up my mind. I told her quite definitely I should consider myself free.'

Clara did not answer, and he returned to his work. She was so quiet and so superb!

On the Saturday evening he asked her to come and drink coffee with him in a restaurant, meeting him after work was over. She came, looking very reserved and very distant. He had three-quarters of an hour to train-time.

'We will walk a little while,' he said.

She agreed, and they went past the Castle into the Park. He was afraid of her. She walked moodily at his side, with a kind of resentful, reluctant, angry walk. He was afraid to take her hand.

'Which way shall we go?' he asked as they walked in darkness.

'I don't mind.'

'Then we'll go up the steps.'

He suddenly turned round. They had passed the Park steps. She stood still in resentment at his suddenly abandoning her. He looked for her. She stood aloof. He caught her suddenly in his arms, held her strained for a moment, kissed her. Then he let her go.

'Come along,' he said, penitent..

She followed him. He took her hand and kissed her fingertips. They went in silence. When they came to the light, he let go her hand. Neither spoke till they reached the station. Then they looked each other in the eyes.

'Good night,' she said.

And he went for his train. His body acted mechanically. People talked to him. He heard faint echoes answering them. He was in a delirium. He felt that he would go mad if Monday did not come at once. On Monday he would see her again. All himself was pitched there, ahead. Sunday intervened. He could not bear it. He could not see her till Monday. And Sunday intervened–hour after hour of tension. He wanted to beat his head against the door of the carriage. But he sat still. He drank some whisky on the way home, but it only made it worse. His mother must not be upset, that was all. He dissembled, and got quickly to bed. There he sat, dressed, with his chin on his knees, staring out of the window at the far hill, with its few lights. He neither thought nor slept, but sat perfectly still, staring. And when at last he was so cold that he came to himself, he found his watch had stopped at half-past two. It was after three o'clock. He was exhausted, but still there was the torment of knowing it was only Sunday morning. He went to bed and slept. Then he cycled all day long, till he was fagged out. And he scarcely knew where he had been. But the day after was Monday. He slept till four o'clock. Then he lay and thought. He was coming nearer to himself–he could see himself, real, somewhere in front. She would go a walk with him in the afternoon. Afternoon! It seemed years ahead.

Slowly the hours crawled. His father got up; he heard him pottering about. Then the miner set off to the pit, his heavy boots scraping the yard. Cocks were still crowing. A cart went down the road. His mother got up. She knocked the fire. Presently she called him softly. He answered as if he were asleep. This shell of himself did well.

He was walking to the station – another mile! The train was near Nottingham. Would it stop before the tunnels? But it did not matter; it would get there before dinner-time. He was at Jordan's. She would come in half an hour. At any rate, she would be near. He had done the letters. She would be there. Perhaps she had not come. He ran downstairs. Ah! he saw her through the glass door. Her shoulders stooping a little to her work made him feel he could not go forward; he could not stand. He went in. He was pale, nervous, awkward, and quite cold. Would she misunderstand him? He could not write his real self with this shell.

'And this afternoon,' he struggled to say. 'You will come?'

'I think so,' she replied, murmuring.

He stood before her, unable to say a word. She hid her face from him. Again came over him the feeling that he would lose consciousness. He set his teeth and went upstairs. He had done everything correctly yet, and he would do so. All the morning things seemed a long way off, as they do to a man under chloroform. He himself seemed under a tight band of constraint. Then there was his other self, in the distance, doing things, entering stuff in a ledger, and he watched that far-off him carefully to see he made no mistake.

But the ache and strain of it could not go on much longer. He worked incessantly. Still it was only twelve o'clock. As if he had nailed his clothing against the desk, he stood there and worked, forcing every stroke out of himself. It was a quarter to one; he could clear away. Then he ran downstairs.

'You will meet me at the Fountain at two o'clock,' he said.

'I can't be there till half past.'

'Yes!' he said.

She saw his dark, mad eyes.

'I will try at a quarter past.'

And he had to be content. He went and got some dinner. All the time he was still under chloroform, and every minute was stretched out indefinitely. He walked miles of street. Then he thought he would be late at the meeting-place. He was at the Fountain at five past two. The torture of the next quarter of an hour was refined beyond expression. It was the anguish of combining the living self with the shell. Then he saw her. She came! And he was there.

'You are late,' he said.

'Only five minutes,' she answered.

'I'd never have done it to you,' he laughed.

She was in a dark blue costume. He looked at her beautiful figure.

'You want some flowers,' he said, going to the nearest florists.

She followed him in silence. He bought her a bunch of scarlet, brick-red carnations. She put them in her coat, flushing.

'That's a fine colour!' he said.

'I'd rather have had something softer,' she said.

He laughed.

'Do you feel like a blot of vermilion walking down the street?' he said.

She hung her head, afraid of the people they met. He looked sideways at her as they walked. There was a wonderful close down on her face near the ear that he wanted to touch. And a certain heaviness, the heaviness of a very full ear of corn that dips slightly in the wind, that there was about her, made his brain spin. He seemed to be spinning down the street, everything going round.

As they sat in the tramcar, she leaned her heavy shoulder against him, and he took her hand. He felt himself coming round from the anaesthetic, beginning to breathe. Her ear, half hidden among her blonde hair, was near to him. The temptation to kiss it was almost too great. But there were other people on top of the car. It still remained to him to kiss it. After all, he was not himself, he was some attribute of her, like the sunshine that fell on her.

He looked quickly away. It had been raining. The big bluff of the Castle rock was streaked with rain, as it reared above the flat of the town. They crossed the wide, black space of the Midland Railway, and passed the cattle enclosure that stood out white. Then they ran down sordid Wilford Road.

She rocked slightly to the tram's motion, and as she leaned against him, rocked upon him. He was a vigorous, slender man, with exhaustless energy. His face was rough, with rough-hewn features, like the common people's; but his eyes under the deep brows were so full of life that they fascinated her. They seemed to dance, and yet they were still, trembling on the finest balance of laughter. His mouth, the same, was just going to spring into a laugh of triumph, yet did not. There was a sharp suspense about him. She bit her lip moodily. His hand was hard clenched over hers.

They paid their two halfpennies at the turnstile and crossed the bridge. The Trent was very full. It swept silent and insidious under the bridge, travelling in a soft body. There had been a great deal of rain. On the river levels were flat gleams of flood water. The sky was grey, with glisten of silver here and there. In Wilford Churchyard the dahlias were sodden with rain—wet black-crimson balls. No one was on the path that went along the green river meadow, along the elm-tree colonnade.

There was the faintest haze over the silvery-dark water and the green meadow-banks, and the elm-trees that were spangled with gold. The river slid by in a body, utterly silent and swift, intertwining among itself like some subtle, complex creature. Clara walked moodily beside him.

'Why,' she asked at length, in rather a jarring tone, 'did you leave Miriam?'

He frowned.

'Because I *wanted* to leave her,' he said.

'Why?'

'Because I didn't want to go on with her. And I didn't want to marry.'

She was silent for a moment. They picked their way down the muddy path. Drops of water fell from the elm-trees.

'You didn't want to marry Miriam, or you didn't want to marry at all?' she asked.

'Both,' he answered—'both!'

They had to manœuvre to get to the stile, because of the pools of water.

'And what did she say?' Clara asked.

'Miriam? She said I was a baby of four, and that I always *had* battled her off.'

Clara pondered over this for a time.

'But you have really been going with her for some time?' she asked.

'Yes.'

'And now you don't want any more of her?'

'No. I know it's no good.'

She pondered again.

'Don't you think you've treated her rather badly?' she asked.

'Yes; I ought to have dropped it years back. But it would have been no good going on. Two wrongs don't make a right.'

'How old *are* you?' Clara asked.

'Twenty-five.'

'And I am thirty,' she said.

'I know you are.'

'I shall be thirty-one—or *am* I thirty-one?'

'I neither know nor care. What does it matter!'

They were at the entrance to the Grove. The wet, red track, already sticky with fallen leaves, went up the steep bank between the grass. On either side stood the elm-trees like pillars along a great aisle, arching over and making high up a roof from which the dead leaves fell. All was empty and silent and wet. She stood on top of the stile, and he held both her hands. Laughing, she looked down into his eyes. Then she leaped. Her breast came against his; he held her, and covered her face with kisses.

They went on up the slippery, steep red path. Presently she released his hand and put it round her waist.

'You press the vein in my arm, holding it so tightly,' she said.

They walked along. His finger-tips felt the rocking of her breast. All was silent and deserted. On the left the red wet plough-land showed through the doorways between the elm-boles and their branches. On the right, looking down, they could see the tree-tops of elms growing far beneath them, hear occasionally the gurgle of the river. Sometimes there below they caught glimpses of the full, soft-sliding Trent, and of water-meadows dotted with small cattle.

'It has scarcely altered since little Kirke White used to come,' he said.

But he was watching her throat below the ear, where the flush was fusing into the honey-white, and her mouth that pouted disconsolate. She stirred against him as she walked, and his body was like a taut string.

Half-way up the big colonnade of elms, where the Grove rose highest above the river, their forward movement faltered to an end. He led her across to the grass, under the trees at the edge of the path. The cliff of red earth sloped swiftly down, through trees and bushes, to the river that glimmered and was dark between the foliage. The far-below water-meadows were very green. He and she stood leaning against one another, silent, afraid, their bodies touching all along. There came a quick gurgle from the river below.

'Why', he asked at length, 'did you hate Baxter Dawes?'

She turned to him with a splendid movement. Her mouth was offered him, and her throat; her eyes were half shut; her breast was tilted as if it asked for him. He flashed with a small laugh, shut his eyes, and met her in a long, whole kiss. Her mouth fused with his; their bodies were sealed and annealed. It was some minutes before they withdrew. They were standing beside the public path.

'Will you go down to the river?' he asked.

She looked at him, leaving herself in his hands. He went over the brim of the declivity and began to climb down.

'It is slippery,' he said.

'Never mind,' she replied.

The red clay went down almost sheer. He slid, went from one tuft of grass to the next, hanging on to the bushes, making for a little platform at the foot of a tree. There he waited for her, laughing with excitement. Her shoes were clogged with red earth. It was hard for her. He frowned. At last he caught her hand, and she stood beside him. The cliff rose above them and fell away below. Her colour was up, her eyes flashed. He looked at the big drop below them.

'It's risky,' he said; 'or messy, at any rate. Shall we go back?'

'Not for my sake,' she said quickly.

'All right. You see, I can't help you; I should only hinder. Give me that little parcel and your gloves. Your poor shoes!'

They stood perched on the face of the declivity, under the trees.

'Well, I'll go again,' he said.

Away he went, slipping, staggering, sliding to the next tree, into which he fell with a slam that nearly shook the breath out of him. She came after cautiously, hanging on to the twigs and grasses. So they descended, stage by stage, to the river's brink. There, to his disgust, the flood had eaten away the path, and the red decline ran straight into the water. He dug in his heels and brought himself up violently. The string of the parcel broke with a snap; the brown parcel bounded down, leaped into the water, and sailed smoothly away. He hung on to his tree.

'Well, I'll be damned!' he cried crossly. Then he laughed. She was coming perilously down.

'Mind!' he warned her. He stood with his back to the tree, waiting. 'Come now,' he called, opening his arms.

She let herself run. He caught her, and together they stood watching the dark water scoop at the raw edge of the bank. The parcel had sailed out of sight.

'It doesn't matter,' she said.

He held her close and kissed her. There was only room for their four feet.

'It's a swindle!' he said. 'But there's a rut where a man has been, so if we go on I guess we shall find the path again.'

The river slid and twined its great volume. On the other bank cattle were feeding on the desolate flats. The cliff rose high above'Paul and Clara on their right hand. They stood against the tree in the watery silence.

'Let us try going forward,' he said; and they struggled in the red clay along the groove a man's nailed boots had made. They were hot and flushed. Their barkled shoes hung heavy on their steps. At last they found the broken path. It was littered with rubble from the water, but at any rate it was easier. They cleaned their boots with twigs. His heart was beating thick and fast.

Suddenly, coming on to the little level, he saw two figures of men standing silent at the water's edge. His heart leaped. They were fishing. He turned and put his hand up warningly to Clara. She hesitated, buttoned her coat. The two went on together.

The fishermen turned curiously to watch the two intruders on their privacy and solitude. They had had a fire, but it was nearly out. All kept perfectly still. The men turned again to their fishing, stood over the grey glinting river like statues. Clara went with bowed head, flushing; he was laughing to himself. Directly they passed out of sight behind the willows.

'Now, they ought to be drowned,' said Paul softly.

Clara did not answer. They toiled forward along a tiny path on the river's lip. Suddenly it vanished. The bank was sheer red solid clay in front of them, sloping straight into the river. He stood and cursed beneath his breath, setting his teeth.

'It is impossible!' said Clara.

He stood erect, looking round. Just ahead were two islets in the stream, covered with osiers. But they were unattainable. The cliff came down like a sloping wall from far above their heads. Behind, not far back, were the fishermen. Across the river the distant cattle fed silently in the desolate afternoon. He cursed again deeply under his breath. He gazed up the great steep bank. Was there no hope but to scale back to the public path?

'Stop a minute,' he said, and, digging his heels sideways into the steep bank of red clay, he began nimbly to mount. He looked across at every tree-foot. At last he found what he wanted. Two beech-trees side by side on the hill held a little level on the upper face between their roots. It was littered with damp leaves, but it would do. The fishermen were perhaps sufficiently out of sight. He threw down his rainproof and waved to her to come.

She toiled to his side. Arriving there, she looked at him heavily, dumbly, and laid her head on his shoulder. He held her fast as he looked round. They were safe enough from all but the small, lonely cows over the river. He sunk his mouth on her throat, where he felt her heavy pulse beat under his lips. Everything was perfectly still. There was nothing in the afternoon but themselves.

When she arose, he, looking on the ground all the time, saw suddenly sprinkled on the black wet beech-roots many scarlet carnation petals, like splashed drops of blood; and red, small splashes fell from her bosom, streaming down her dress to her feet.

'Your flowers are smashed,' he said.

She looked at him heavily as she put back her hair. Suddenly he put his finger-tips on her cheek.

'Why dost look so heavy?' he reproached her.

She smiled sadly, as if she felt alone in herself. He caressed her cheek with his fingers, and kissed her.

'Nay!' he said. 'Never thee bother!'

She gripped his fingers tight, and laughed shakily. Then she dropped her hand. He put the hair back from her brows, stroking her temples, kissing them lightly.

'But tha shouldna worrit!' he said softly, pleading.

'No, I don't worry!' she laughed tenderly and resigned.

'Yea, tha does! Dunna thee worrit,' he implored, caressing.

'No!' she consoled him, kissing him.

They had a stiff climb to get to the top again. It took them a quarter of an hour. When he got on to the level grass, he threw off his cap, wiped the sweat from his forehead, and sighed.

'Now we're back at the ordinary level,' he said.

She sat down, panting, on the tussocky grass. Her cheeks were flushed pink. He kissed her, and she gave way to joy.

'And now I'll clean thy boots and make thee fit for respectable folk,' he said.

He kneeled at her feet, worked away with a stick and tufts of grass. She put her fingers in his hair, drew his head to her, and kissed it.

'What am I supposed to be doing,' he said, looking at her laughing; 'cleaning shoes or dibbling with love? Answer me that!'

'Just whichever I please,' she replied.

'I'm your boot-boy for the time being, and nothing else!' But they remained looking into each other's eyes and laughing. Then they kissed with little nibbling kisses.

'T-t-t-t!' he went with his tongue, like his mother. 'I tell you, nothing gets done when there's a woman about.'

And he returned to his boot-cleaning, singing softly. She touched his thick hair, and he kissed her fingers. He worked away at her shoes. At last they were quite presentable.

'There you are, you see!' he said. 'Aren't I a great hand at restoring you to respectability? Stand up! There, you look as irreproachable as Britannia herself!'

He cleaned his own boots a little, washed his hands in a puddle, and sang. They went on into Clifton village. He was madly in love with her; every movement she made, every crease in her garments, sent a hot flush through him and seemed adorable.

The old lady at whose house they had tea was roused into gaiety by them.

'I could wish you'd had something of a better day,' she said, hovering round.

'Nay!' he laughed. 'We've been saying how nice it is.'

The old lady looked at him curiously. There was a peculiar glow and charm about him. His eyes were dark and laughing. He rubbed his moustache with a glad movement.

'Have you been saying *so!*' she exclaimed, a light rousing in her old eyes.

'Truly!' he laughed.

'Then I'm sure the day's good enough,' said the old lady.

She fussed about, and did not want to leave them.

'I don't know whether you'd like some radishes as well,' she said to Clara; 'but I've got some in the garden–*and* a cucumber.'

Clara flushed. She looked very handsome.

'I should like some radishes,' she answered.

And the old lady pottered off gleefully.

'If she knew!' said Clara quietly to him.

'Well, she doesn't know; and it shows we're nice in ourselves, at any rate. You look quite enough to satisfy an archangel, and I'm sure I feel harmless–so–if it makes you look nice, and makes folk happy when they have us, and makes us happy–why, we're not cheating them out of much!'

They went on with the meal. When they were going away, the old lady came timidly with three tiny dahlias in full blow, neat as bees, and speckled scarlet and white. She stood before Clara, pleased with herself, saying:

'I don't know whether–' and holding the flowers forward in her old hand.

'Oh, how pretty!' cried Clara, accepting the flowers.

'Shall she have them all?' asked Paul reproachfully of the old woman.

'Yes, she shall have them all,' she replied, beaming with joy. 'You have got enough for your share.'

'Ah, but I shall ask her to give me one!' he teased.

'Then she does as she pleases,' said the old lady, smiling. And she bobbed a little curtsey of delight.

Clara was rather quiet and uncomfortable. As they walked along, he said:

'You don't feel criminal, do you?'

She looked at him with startled grey eyes.

'Criminal!' she said. 'No.'

'But you seem to feel you have done a wrong?'

'No,' she said. 'I only think, "If they knew!"'

'If they knew, they'd cease to understand. As it is, they do understand, and they like it. What do they matter? Here, with only the trees and me, you don't feel not the least bit wrong, do you?'

He took her by the arm, held her facing him, holding her eyes with his. Something fretted him.

'Not sinners, are we?' he said, with an uneasy little frown.

'No,' she replied.

He kissed her, laughing.

'You like your little bit of guiltiness, I believe,' he said. 'I believe Eve enjoyed it, when she went cowering out of Paradise.'

But there was a certain glow and quietness about her that made him glad. When he was alone in the railway-carriage, he found himself tumultuously happy, and the people exceedingly nice, and the night lovely, and everything good.

Mrs Morel was sitting reading when he got home. Her health was not good now, and there had come that ivory pallor into her face when he never noticed, and which afterwards he never forgot. She did not mention her own ill-health to him. After all, she thought, it was not much.

'You are late!' she said, looking at him.

His eyes were shining; his face seemed to glow. He smiled to her.

'Yes; I've been down Clifton Grove with Clara.'

His mother looked at him again.

'But won't people talk?' she said.

'Why? They know she's a suffragette, and so on. And what if they do talk.'

'Of course, there may be nothing wrong in it,' said his mother. 'But you know what folk are, and if once she gets talked about—'

'Well, I can't help it. Their jaw isn't so almighty important, after all.'

'I think you ought to consider *her*.'

'So I *do*! What can people say?—that we take a walk together. I believe you're jealous.'

'You know I should be *glad* if she weren't a married woman.'

'Well, my dear, she lives separate from her husband, and talks on platforms; so she's already singled out from the sheep, and, as far as I can see, hasn't much to lose. No; her life's nothing to her, so what's the worth of nothing? She goes with me—it becomes something. Then she must pay—we both must pay! Folk are so frightened of paying; they'd rather starve and die.'

'Very well, my son. We'll see how it will end.'

'Very well, my mother. I'll abide by the end.'

'We'll see!'

'And she's—she's *awfully* nice, mother; she is really! You don't know!'

'That's not the same as marrying her.'

'It's perhaps better.'

There was a silence for a while. He wanted to ask his mother something, but was afraid.

'Should you like to know her?' he hesitated.

'Yes,' said Mrs Morel, coolly. 'I should like to know what she's like.'

'But she's nice, mother, she is! And not a bit common!'

'I never suggested she was.'

'But you seem to think she's—not as good as—She's better than ninety-nine folk out of a hundred, I tell you! She's *better*, she is! She's fair, she's honest, she's straight! There isn't anything underhand or superior about her. Don't be mean about her!'

Mrs Morel flushed.

'I am sure I am not mean about her. She may be quite as you say, but–'

'You don't approve,' he finished.

'And do you expect me to?' she answered coldly.

'Yes!–yes!–if you'd anything about you, you'd be glad! Do you *want* to see her?'

'I said I did.'

'Then I'll bring her–shall I bring her here?'

'You please yourself.'

'Then I *will* bring her here–one Sunday–to tea. If you think a horrid thing about her, I shan't forgive you.'

His mother laughed.

'As if it would make any difference!' she said. He knew he had won.

'Oh, but it feels so fine, mother, when she's there! She's such a queen in her way.'

Occasionally he still walked a little way from chapel with Miriam and Edgar. He did not go up to the farm. She, however, was very much the same with him, and he did not feel embarrassed in her presence. One evening she was alone when he accompanied her. They began by talking books: it was their unfailing topic. Mrs Morel had said that his and Miriam's affair was like a fire fed on books–if there were no more volumes it would die out. Miriam, for her part, boasted that she could read him like a book, could place her finger any minute on the chapter and the line. He, easily taken in, believed that Miriam knew more about him than anyone else. So it pleased him to talk to her about himself, like the simplest egoist. Very soon the conversation drifted to his own doings. It flattered him immensely that he was of such supreme interest.

'And what have you been doing lately?'

'I–oh, not much! I made a sketch of Bestwood from the garden, that is nearly right at last. It's the hundredth try.'

So they went on. Then she said:

'You've not been out, then, lately?'

'Yes; I went up Clifton Grove on Monday afternoon with Clara.'

'It was not very nice weather,' said Miriam, 'was it?'

'But I wanted to go out, and it was all right. The Trent *is* full.'

'And did you go to Barton?' she asked.

'No, we had tea in Clifton.'

'*Did* you! That would be nice.'

'It was! The jolliest old woman! She gave us several pom-pom dahlias, as pretty as you like.'

Miriam bowed her head and brooded. He was quite unconscious of concealing anything from her.

'What made her give them you?' she asked.

He laughed.

'Because she liked us–because we were jolly, I should think.'

Miriam put her finger in her mouth.

'Were you late home?' she asked.

At last he resented her tone.

'I caught the seven-thirty.'

'Ha!'

They walked on in silence, and he was angry.

'And how *is* Clara?' asked Miriam.

'Quite all right, I think.'

'That's good!' she said, with a tinge of irony. 'By the way, what of her husband? One never hears anything of him.'

'He's got some other woman, and is also quite all right,' he replied. 'At least, so I think.'

'I see—you don't know for certain. Don't you think a position like that is hard on a woman?'

'Rottenly hard!'

'It's so unjust!' said Miriam. 'The man does as he likes—'

'Then let the woman also,' he said.

'How can she? And if she does, look at her position!'

'What of it?'

'Why, it's impossible! You don't understand what a woman forfeits—'

'No, I don't. But if a woman's got nothing but her fair fame to feed on, why, it's thin tack, and a donkey would die of it!'

So she understood his moral attitude, at least, and she knew he would act accordingly.

She never asked him anything direct, but she got to know enough.

Another day, when he saw Miriam, the conversation turned to marriage, then to Clara's marriage with Dawes.

'You see,' he said, 'she never knew the fearful importance of marriage. She thought it was all in the day's march—it would have to come—and Dawes—well, a good many women would have given their souls to get him; so why not him? Then she developed into the *femme incomprise*, and treated him badly, I'll bet my boots.'

'And she left him because he didn't understand her?'

'I suppose so. I suppose she had to. It isn't altogether a question of understanding; it's a question of living. With him, she was only half alive; the rest was dormant, deadened. And the dormant woman was the *femme incomprise*, and she *had* to be awakened.'

'And what about him?'

'I don't know. I rather think he loves her as much as he can, but he's a fool.'

'It was something like your mother and father,' said Miriam.

'Yes; but my mother, I believe, got *real* joy and satisfaction out of my father at first. I believe she had a passion for him; that's why she stayed with him. After all, they were bound to each other.'

'Yes,' said Miriam.

'That's what one *must have*, I think,' he continued—'the real, real flame of feeling through another person—once, only once, if it only lasts three months. See, my mother looks as if she'd *had* everything that was necessary for her living and developing. There's not a tiny bit of feeling of sterility about her.'

'No,' said Miriam.

'And with my father, at first, I'm sure she had the real thing. She knows; she has been there. You can feel it about her, and about him, and about hundreds of people you meet every day; and, once it has happened to you, you can go on with anything and ripen.'

'What has happened, exactly?' asked Miriam.

'It's so hard to say, but the something big and intense that changes you when you really come together with somebody else. It almost seems to fertilize your soul and make it that you can go on and mature.'

'And you think your mother had it with your father?'

'Yes; and at the bottom she feels grateful to him for giving it her, even now, though they are miles apart.'

'And you think Clara never had it?'

'I'm sure.'

Miriam pondered this. She saw what he was seeking–a sort of baptism of fire in passion, it seemed to her. She realized that he would never be satisfied till he had it. Perhaps it was essential to him, as to some men, to sow wild oats; and afterwards, when he was satisfied, he would not rage with restlessness any more, but could settle down and give her his life into her hands. Well, then, if he must go, let him go and have his fill–something big and intense, he called it. At any rate, when he had got it, he would not want it–that he said himself; he would want the other thing that she could give him. He would want to be owned, so that he could work. It seemed to her a bitter thing that he must go, but she could let him go into an inn for a glass of whisky, so she could let him go to Clara, so long as it was something that would satisfy a need in him, and leave him free for herself to possess.

'Have you told your mother about Clara?' she asked.

She knew this would be a test of the seriousness of his feeling for the other woman; she knew he was going to Clara for something vital, not as a man goes for pleasure to a prostitute, if he told his mother.

'Yes,' he said, 'and she is coming to tea on Sunday.'

'To your house?'

'Yes; I want mater to see her.'

'Ah!'

There was a silence. Things had gone quicker than she thought. She felt a sudden bitterness that he could leave her so soon and so entirely. And was Clara to be accepted by his people, who had been so hostile to herself?

'I may call in as I go to chapel,' she said. 'It is a long time since I saw Clara.'

'Very well,' he said, astonished, and unconsciously angry.

On the Sunday afternoon he went to Keston to meet Clara at the station. As he stood on the platform he was trying to examine in himself if he had a premonition.

'Do I *feel* as if she'd come?' he said to himself, and he tried to find out. His heart felt queer and contracted. That seemed like foreboding. Then he *had* a foreboding she would not come! Then she would not come, and instead of taking her over the fields home, as he had imagined, he would have to go alone. The train was late; the afternoon would be wasted, and the evening. He hated her for not coming. Why had she promised, then, if she could not keep her promise? Perhaps she had missed her train–he himself was always missing trains–but that was no reason why she should miss this particular one. He was angry with her; he was furious.

Suddenly he saw the train crawling, sneaking round the corner. Here, then, was the train, but of course she had not come. The green engine hissed along the platform, the row of brown carriages drew up, several doors opened. No; she had not come! No! Yes; ah, there she was! She had a big black hat on! He was at her side in a moment.

'I thought you weren't coming,' he said.

She was laughing rather breathlessly as she put out her hand to him; their eyes met. He took her quickly along the platform, talking at a great rate to hide his feelings. She looked beautiful. In her hat were large silk roses, coloured like tarnished gold. Her costume of dark cloth fitted so beautifully over her breast and shoulders. His pride went up as he walked with her. He felt the station people, who knew him, eyed her with awe and admiration.

'I was sure you weren't coming,' he laughed shakily..

She laughed in answer, almost with a little cry.

'And I wondered, when I was in the train, what*ever* I should do if you weren't there!' she said.

He caught her hand impulsively, and they went along the narrow twitchel. They took the road into Nuttall and over the Reckoning House Farm. It was a blue, mild day. Everywhere the brown leaves lay scattered; many scarlet hips stood upon the hedge beside the wood. He gathered a few for her to wear.

'Though, really,' he said, as he fitted them into the breast of her coat, 'you ought to object to my getting them, because of the birds. But they don't care much for rose-hips in this part, where they can get plenty of stuff. You often find the berries going rotten in the springtime.'

So he chattered, scarcely aware of what he said, only knowing he was putting berries in the bosom of her coat, while she stood patiently for him. And she watched his quick hands, so full of life, and it seemed to her she had never *seen* anything before. Till now, everything had been indistinct.

They came near to the colliery. It stood quite still and black among the corn-fields, its immense heap of slag seen rising almost from the oats.

'What a pity there is a coal-pit here where it is so pretty!' said Clara.

'Do you think so?' he answered. 'You see, I am so used to it I should miss it. No; and I like the pits here and there. I like the rows of trucks, and the headstocks, and the steam in the daytime, and the lights at night. When I was a boy, I always thought a pillar of cloud by day and a pillar of fire by night was a pit, with its steam, and its lights, and the burning bank—and I thought the Lord was always at the pit-top.'

As they drew near home she walked in silence, and seemed to hang back. He pressed her fingers in his own. She flushed, but gave no response.

'Don't you want to come home?' he asked.

'Yes, I want to come,' she replied.

It did not occur to him that her position in his home would be rather a peculiar and difficult one. To him it seemed just as if one of his men friends were going to be introduced to his mother, only nicer.

The Morels lived in a house in an ugly street that ran down a steep hill. The street itself was hideous. The house was rather superior to most. It was old, grimy, with a big bay window, and it was semi-detached, but it looked gloomy. Then Paul opened the door to the garden, and all was different. The sunny afternoon was there, like another land. By the path grew tansy and little trees. In front of the window was a plot of sunny grass, with old lilacs round it. And away went the garden, with heaps of dishevelled chrysanthemums in the sunshine, down to the sycamore-tree, and the field, and beyond one looked over a few red-roofed cottages to the hills with all the glow of the autumn afternoon.

Mrs Morel sat in her rocking-chair, wearing her black silk blouse. Her grey-brown hair was taken smooth back from her brow and high temples; her face was rather pale. Clara, suffering, followed Paul into the kitchen. Mrs Morel rose. Clara thought her a lady, even rather stiff. The young woman was very nervous. She had almost a wistful look, almost resigned.

'Mother—Clara,' said Paul.

Mrs Morel held out her hand and smiled.

'He has told me a good deal about you,' she said.

The blood flamed in Clara's cheek.

'I hope you don't mind my coming,' she faltered.

'I was pleased when he said he would bring you,' replied Mrs Morel.

Paul, watching, felt his heart contract with pain. His mother looked so small, and sallow, and done-for beside the luxuriant Clara.

'It's such a pretty day, mother!' he said. 'And we saw a jay.'

His mother looked at him; he had turned to her. She thought what a man he seemed, in his dark, well-made clothes. He was pale and detached-looking; it would be hard for any woman to keep him. Her heart glowed; then she was sorry for Clara.

'Perhaps you'll leave your things in the parlour,' said Mrs Morel nicely to the young woman.

'Oh, thank you,' she replied.

'Come on,' said Paul, and he led the way into the little front-room, with its old piano, its mahogany furniture, its yellowing marble mantelpiece. A fire was burning; the place was littered with books and drawing-boards. 'I leave my things lying about,' he said. 'It's so much easier.'

She loved his artist's paraphernalia, and the books, and the photos of people. Soon he was telling her: this was William, this was William's young lady in the evening dress, this was Annie and her husband, this was Arthur and his wife and the baby. She felt as if she were being taken into the family. He showed her photos, books, sketches, and they talked a little while. Then they returned to the kitchen. Mrs Morel put aside her book. Clara wore a blouse of fine silk chiffon, with narrow black-and-white stripes; her hair was done simply, coiled on top of her head. She looked rather stately and reserved.

'You have gone to live down Sneinton Boulevard!' said Mrs Morel. 'When I was a girl–girl, I say!–when I was a young woman *we* lived in Minerva Terrace.'

'Oh, did you!' said Clara. 'I have a friend in Number 6.'

And the conversation had started. They talked Nottingham and Nottingham people; it interested them both. Clara was still rather nervous; Mrs Morel was still somewhat on her dignity. She clipped her language very clear and precise. But they were going to get on well together, Paul saw.

Mrs Morel measured herself against the younger woman, and found herself easily stronger. Clara was deferential. She knew Paul's surprising regard for his mother, and she had dreaded the meeting, expecting someone rather hard and cold. She was surprised to find this little interested woman chatting with such readiness; and then she felt, as she felt with Paul, that she would not care to stand in Mrs Morel's way. There was something so hard and certain in his mother, as if she never had a misgiving in her life.

Presently Morel came down, ruffled and yawning, from his afternoon sleep. He scratched his grizzled head, he plodded in his stockinged feet, his waistcoat hung open over his shirt. He seemed incongruous.

'This is Mrs Dawes, father,' said Paul.

Then Morel pulled himself together. Clara saw Paul's manner of bowing and shaking hands.

'Oh, indeed!' exclaimed Morel. 'I am very glad to see you–I am, I assure you. But don't disturb yourself. No, no, make yourself quite comfortable, and be very welcome.'

Clara was astonished at this flood of hospitality from the old collier. He was so courteous, so gallant! She thought him most delightful.

'And may you have come far?' he asked.

'Only from Nottingham,' she said.

'From Nottingham! Then you have had a beautiful day for your journey.' Then he strayed into the scullery to wash his hands and face, and from force of habit came on to the hearth with the towel to dry himself.

At tea Clara felt the refinement and sang-froid of the household. Mrs Morel was perfectly at her ease. The pouring out of tea and attending to the people went on unconsciously, without interrupting her in her talk. There was a lot of room at the oval table; the china of dark blue willow-pattern looked pretty on the glossy cloth. There was a little bowl of small, yellow chrysanthemums. Clara felt she completed the circle, and it was a pleasure to her. But she was rather afraid of the self-possession of the Morels, father and all. She took their tone; there was a feeling of balance. It was a cool, clear atmosphere, where everyone was himself, and in harmony. Clara enjoyed it, but there was a fear deep at the bottom of her.

Paul cleared the table whilst his mother and Clara talked. Clara was conscious of his quick, vigorous body as it came and went, seeming blown quickly by a wind at its work. It was almost like the hither and thither of a leaf that comes unexpected. Most of herself went with him. By the way she leaned forward, as if listening, Mrs Morel could see she was possessed elsewhere as she talked, and again the elder woman was sorry for her.

Having finished, he strolled down the garden, leaving the two women to talk. It was a hazy, sunny afternoon, mild and soft. Clara glanced through the window after him as he loitered among the chrysanthemums. She felt as if something almost tangible fastened her to him; yet he seemed so easy in his graceful, indolent movement, so detached as he tied up the too-heavy flower-branches to their stakes, that she wanted to shriek in her helplessness.

Mrs Morel rose.

'You will let me help you wash up,' said Clara.

'Eh, there are so few, it will only take me a minute,' said the other.

Clara, however, dried the tea-things, and was glad to be on such good terms with his mother; but it was torture not to be able to follow him down the garden. At last she allowed herself to go; she felt as if a rope were taken off her ankle.

The afternoon was golden over the hills of Derbyshire. He stood across in the other garden, beside a bush of pale Michaelmas daisies, watching the last bees crawl into the hive. Hearing her coming, he turned to her with an easy motion, saying:

'It's the end of the run with these chaps.'

Clara stood near him. Over the low red wall in front was the country and the far-off hills, all golden dim.

At that moment Miriam was entering through the garden-door. She saw Clara go up to him, saw him turn, and saw them come to rest together. Something in their perfect isolation together made her know that it was accomplished between them, that they were, as she put it, married. She walked very slowly down the cinder-track of the long garden.

Clara had pulled a button from a hollyhock spire, and was breaking it to get the seeds. Above her bowed head the pink flowers stared, as if defending her. The last bees were falling down to the hive.

'Count your money,' laughed Paul, as she broke the flat seeds one by one from the roll of coin. She looked at him.

'I'm well off,' she said, smiling.
'How much? Pf!' He snapped his fingers. 'Can I turn them into gold?'
'I'm afraid not,' she laughed.
They looked into each other's eyes, laughing. At that moment they became aware of Miriam. There was a click, and everything had altered.
'Hello, Miriam!' he exclaimed. 'You said you'd come!'
'Yes. Had you forgotten?'
She shook hands with Clara, saying:
'It seems strange to see you here.'
'Yes,' replied the other; 'it seems strange to be here.'
There was a hesitation.
'It is pretty, isn't it?' said Miriam.
'I like it very much,' replied Clara.
Then Miriam realized that Clara was accepted as she had never been.
'Have you come down alone?' asked Paul.
'Yes; I went to Agatha's to tea. We are going to chapel. I only called in for a moment to see Clara.'
'You should have come in here to tea,' he said.
Miriam laughed shortly, and Clara turned impatiently aside.
'Do you like the chrysanthemums?' he asked.
'Yes; they are very fine,' replied Miriam.
'Which sort do you like best?' he asked.
'I don't know. The bronze, I think.'
'I don't think you've seen all the sorts. Come and look. Come and see which are *your* favourites, Clara.'
He led the two women back to his own garden, where the towzled bushes of flowers of all colours stood raggedly along the path down to the field. The situation did not embarrass him, to his knowledge.
'Look, Miriam; these are the white ones that came from your garden. They aren't so fine here, are they?'
'No,' said Miriam.
'But they're hardier. You're so sheltered; things grow big and tender, and then die. These little yellow ones I like. Will you have some?'
While they were out there the bells began to ring in the church, sounding loud across the town and the field. Miriam looked at the tower, proud among the clustering roofs, and remembered the sketches he had brought her. It had been different then, but he had not left her even yet. She asked him for a book to read. He ran indoors.
'What! Is that Miriam?' asked his mother coldly.
'Yes; she said she'd call and see Clara.'
'You told her, then?' came the sarcastic answer.
'Yes; why shouldn't I?'
'There's certainly no reason why you shouldn't,' said Mrs Morel, and she returned to her book. He winced from his mother's irony, frowned irritably, thinking: 'Why can't I do as I like?'
'You've not seen Mrs Morel before?' Miriam was saying to Clara.
'No; but she's *so* nice!'
'Yes,' said Miriam, dropping her head; 'in some ways she's very fine.'
'I should think so.'
'Had Paul told you much about her?'
'He had talked a good deal.'

'Ha!'

There was silence until he returned with the book.

'When will you want it back?' Miriam asked.

'When you like,' he answered.

Clara turned to go indoors, whilst he accompanied Miriam to the gate.

'When will you come up to Willey Farm?' the latter asked.

'I couldn't say,' replied Clara.

'Mother asked me to say she'd be pleased to see you any time, if you cared to come.'

'Thank you; I should like to, but I can't say when.'

'Oh, very well!' exclaimed Miriam rather bitterly, turning away. She went down the path with her mouth to the flowers he had given her.

'You're sure you won't come in?' he said.

'No, thanks.'

'We are going to chapel.'

'Ha, I shall see you, then!' Miriam was very bitter.

'Yes.'

They parted. He felt guilty towards her. She was bitter, and she scorned him. He still belonged to herself, she believed; yet he could have Clara, take her home, sit with her next his mother in chapel, give her the same hymn-book he had given herself years before. She heard him running quickly indoors.

But he did not go straight in. Halting on the plot of grass he heard his mother's voice, then Clara's answer:

'What I hate is the bloodhound quality in Miriam.'

'Yes,' said his mother quickly, 'yes; *doesn't* it make you hate her, now!'

His heart went hot, and he was angry with them for talking about the girl. What right had they to say that? Something in the speech itself stung him into a flame of hate against Miriam. Then his own heart rebelled furiously at Clara's taking the liberty of speaking so about Miriam. After all, the girl was the better woman of the two, he thought, if it came to goodness. He went indoors. His mother looked excited. She was beating with her hand rhythmically on the sofa-arm, as women do who are wearing out. He could never bear to see the movement. There was a silence; then he began to talk.

In chapel Miriam saw him find the place in the hymn-book for Clara, in exactly the same way as he used for herself. And during the sermon he could see the girl across the chapel, her hat throwing a dark shadow over her face. What did she think, seeing Clara with him? He did not stop to consider. He felt himself cruel towards Miriam.

After chapel he went over Pentrich with Clara. It was a dark autumn night. They had said good-bye to Miriam, and his heart had smitten him as he left the girl alone. 'But it serves her right,' he said inside himself, and it almost gave him pleasure to go off under her eyes with this other handsome woman.

There was a scent of damp leaves in the darkness. Clara's hand lay warm and inert in his own as they walked. He was full of conflict. The battle that raged inside him made him feel desperate.

Up Pentrich Hill Clara leaned against him as he went. He slid his arm round her waist. Feeling the strong motion of her body under his arm as she walked, the tightness in his chest because of Miriam relaxed, and the hot blood bathed him. He held her closer and closer.

Then: 'You still keep on with Miriam,' she said quietly.

'Only talk. There never *was* a great deal more than talk between us,' he said bitterly.

'Your mother doesn't care for her,' said Clara.

'No, or I might have married her. But it's all up, really!'

Suddenly his voice went passionate with hate.

'If I was with her now, we should be jawing about the "Christian Mystery", or some such tack. Thank God, I'm not!'

They walked on in silence for some time.

'But you can't really give her up,' said Clara.

'I don't give her up, because there's nothing to give,' he said.

'There is for her.'

'I don't know why she and I shouldn't be friends as long as we live,' he said. 'But it'll only be friends.'

Clara drew away from him, leaning away from contact with him.

'What are you drawing away for?' he asked.

She did not answer, but drew farther from him.

'Why do you want to walk alone?' he asked.

Still there was no answer. She walked resentfully, hanging her head.

'Because I said I would be friends with Miriam!' he exclaimed.

She would not answer him anything.

'I tell you it's only words that go between us,' he persisted, trying to take her again.

She resisted. Suddenly he strode across in front of her, barring her way.

'Damn it!' he said. 'What do you want now?'

'You'd better run after Miriam,' mocked Clara.

The blood flamed up in him. He stood showing his teeth. She drooped sulkily. The lane was dark, quite lonely. He suddenly caught her in his arms, stretched forward, and put his mouth on her face in a kiss of rage. She turned frantically to avoid him. He held her fast. Hard and relentless his mouth came for her. Her breasts hurt against the wall of his chest. Helpless, she went loose in his arms, and he kissed her, and kissed her.

He heard people coming down the hill.

'Stand up! Stand up!' he said thickly, gripping her arm till it hurt. If he had let go, she would have sunk to the ground.

She sighed and walked dizzily beside him. They went on in silence.

'We will go over the fields,' he said; and then she woke up.

But she let herself be helped over the stile, and she walked in silence with him over the first dark field. It was the way to Nottingham and to the station, she knew. He seemed to be looking about. They came out on a bare hilltop where stood the dark figure of the ruined windmill. There he halted. They stood together high up on the darkness, looking at the lights scattered on the night before them, handfuls of glittering points, villages lying high and low on the dark, here and there.

'Like treading among the stars,' he said, with a quaky laugh.

Then he took her in his arms, and held her fast. She moved aside her mouth to ask, dogged and low:

'What time is it?'

'It doesn't matter,' he pleaded thickly.

'Yes it does–yes! I must go!'

'It's early yet,' he said.

'What time is it?' she insisted.

All round lay the black night, speckled and spangled with lights.

'I don't know.'

She put her hand on his chest, feeling for his watch. He felt the joints fuse into fire. She groped in his waistcoat pocket, while he stood panting. In the darkness she could see the round pale face of the watch, but not the figures. She stooped over it. He was panting till he could take her in his arms again.

'I can't see,' she said.

'Then don't bother.'

'Yes; I'm going!' she said, turning away.

'Wait! I'll look!' But he could not see. 'I'll strike a match.'

He secretly hoped it was to late to catch the train. She saw the glowing lantern of his hands as he cradled the light; then his face lit up, his eyes fixed on the watch. Instantly all was dark again. All was black before her eyes; only a glowing match was red near her feet. Where was he?

'What is it?' she asked, afraid.

'You can't do it,' his voice answered out of the darkness.

There was a pause. She felt in his power. She had heard the ring in his voice. It frightened her.

'What time is it?' she asked, quiet, definite, hopeless.

'Two minutes to nine,' he replied, telling the truth with a struggle.

'And can I get from here to the station in fourteen minutes?'

'No. At any rate—'

She could distinguish his dark form again a yard or so away. She wanted to escape.

'But can't I do it?' she pleaded.

'If you hurry,' he said brusquely. 'But you could easily walk it, Clara; it's only seven miles to the tram. I'll come with you.'

'No; I want to catch the train.'

'But why?'

'I do—I want to catch the train.'

Suddenly his voice altered.

'Very well,' he said, dry and hard. 'Come along then.'

And he plunged ahead into the darkness. She ran after him, wanting to cry. Now he was hard and cruel to her. She ran over the rough, dark fields behind him, out of breath, ready to drop. But the double row of lights at the station drew nearer. Suddenly:

'There she is!' he cried, breaking into a run.

There was a faint rattling noise. Away to the right the train, like a luminous caterpillar, was threading across the night. The rattling ceased.

'She's over the viaduct. You'll just do it.'

Clara ran, quite out of breath, and fell at last into the train. The whistle blew. He was gone. Gone!—and she was in a carriage full of people. She felt the cruelty of it.

He turned round and plunged home. Before he knew where he was he was in the kitchen at home. He was very pale. His eyes were dark and dangerous-looking, as if he were drunk. His mother looked at him.

'Well, I must say your boots are in a nice state!' she said.

He looked at his feet. Then he tore off his overcoat. His mother wondered if he were drunk.

'She caught the train then?' she said.

'Yes.'

'I hope *her* feet weren't so filthy. Where on earth you dragged her I don't know!'

He was silent and motionless for some time.

'Did you like her?' he asked grudgingly at last.

'Yes, I liked her. But you'll tire of her, my son; you know you will.'

He did not answer. She noticed how he laboured in his breathing.

'Have you been running?' she asked.

'We had to run for the train.'

'You'll go and knock yourself up. You'd better drink hot milk.'

It was as good a stimulant as he could have, but he refused and went to bed. There he lay face down on the counterpane, and shed tears of rage and pain. There was a physical pain that made him bite his lips till they bled, and the chaos inside him left him unable to think, almost to feel.

'This is how she serves me, is it?' he said in his heart, over and over, pressing his face in the quilt. And he hated her. Again he went over the scene, and again he hated her.

The next day there was a new aloofness about him. Clara was very gentle, almost loving. But he treated her distantly, with a touch of contempt. She sighed, continuing to be gentle. He came round.

One evening of that week Sarah Bernhardt was at the Theatre Royal in Nottingham, giving 'La Dame aux Camélias'. Paul wanted to see this old and famous actress, and he asked Clara to accompany him. He told his mother to leave the key in the window for him.

'Shall I book seats?' he asked Clara.

'Yes. And put on an evening suit, will you! I've never seen you in it.'

'But, good Lord, Clara! Think of *me* in evening suit at the theatre!' he remonstrated.

'Would you rather not?' she asked.

'I will if you *want* me to: but I s'll feel a fool.'

She laughed at him.

'Then feel a fool for my sake, won't you?'

The request made his blood flush up.

'I suppose I s'll have to.'

'What are you taking a suit-case for?' his mother asked.

He blushed furiously.

'Clara asked me,' he began.

'And what seats are you going in?'

'Circle—three-and-six each!'

'Well, I'm sure!' exclaimed his mother sarcastically.

'It's only once in the bluest of blue moons,' he said.

He dressed at Jordan's, put on an overcoat and a cap, and met Clara in a café. She was with one of her suffragette friends. She wore an old long coat, which did not suit her, and had a little wrap over her head, which he hated. The three went to the theatre together.

Clara took off her coat on the stairs, and he discovered she was in a sort of semi-evening dress, that left her arms and neck and part of her breast bare. Her hair was done fashionably. The dress, a simple thing of green crape, suited her. She looked quite grand, he thought. He could see her figure inside the frock, as if that were wrapped closely round her. The firmness and softness of her upright body could almost be felt as he looked at her. He clenched his fists.

And he was to sit all the evening beside her beautiful naked arm, watching the strong throat rise from the strong chest, watching the breasts under the green stuff, the curve of her limbs in the tight dress. Something in him hated her again for submitting him to this torture of nearness. And he loved her as she balanced her head and stared straight in front of her, pouting, wistful, immobile, as if she yielded herself to her fate because it was too strong for her. She could not help herself; she was in the grip of something bigger than herself. A kind of eternal look about her, as if she were a wistful sphinx, made it necessary for him to kiss her. He dropped his programme, and crouched down on the floor to get it, so that he could kiss her hand and wrist. Her beauty was a torture to him. She sat immobile. Only, when the lights went down, she sank a little against him, and he caressed her hand and arm with his fingers. He could smell her faint perfume. All the time his blood kept sweeping up in great white-hot waves that killed his consciousness momentarily.

The drama continued. He saw it all in the distance, going on somewhere; he did not know where, but it seemed far away inside him. He was Clara's white heavy arms, her throat, her moving bosom. That seemed to be himself. Then away somewhere the play went on, and he was identified with that also. There was no himself. The grey and black eyes of Clara, her bosom coming down on his, her arm that he held gripped between his hands, were all that existed. Then he felt himself small and helpless, her towering in her force above him.

Only the intervals, when the lights came up, hurt him expressibly. He wanted to run anywhere, so long as it would be dark again. In a maze, he wandered out for a drink. Then the lights were out, and the strange, insane reality of Clara and the drama took hold of him again.

The play went on. But he was obsessed by the desire to kiss the tiny blue vein that nestled in the bend of her arm. He could feel it. His whole life seemed suspended till he had put his lips there. It must be done. And the other people! At last he bent quickly forward and touched it with his lips. His moustache brushed the sensitive flesh. Clara shivered, drew away her arm.

When all was over, the lights up, the people clapping, he came to himself and looked at his watch. His train was gone.

'I s'll have to walk home!' he said.

Clara looked at him.

'Is it too late?' she asked.

He nodded. Then he helped her on with her coat.

'I love you! You look beautiful in that dress,' he murmured over her shoulder, among the throng of bustling people.

She remained quiet. Together they went out of the theatre. He saw the cabs waiting, the people passing. It seemed he met a pair of brown eyes which hated him. But he did not know. He and Clara turned away, mechanically taking the direction to the station.

The train had gone. He would have to walk the ten miles home.

'It doesn't matter,' he said. 'I shall enjoy it.'

'Won't you,' she said, flushing, 'come home for the night? I can sleep with mother.'

He looked at her. Their eyes met.

'What will your mother say?' he asked.

'She won't mind.'

'You're sure?'

'Quite!'

'*Shall* I come?'

'If you will.'

'Very well.'

And they turned away. At the first stopping-place they took the car. The wind blew fresh in their faces. The town was dark; the tram tipped in its haste. He sat with her hand fast in his.

'Will your mother be gone to bed?' he asked.

'She may be. I hope not.'

They hurried along the silent, dark little street, the only people out of doors. Clara quickly entered the house. He hesitated.

'Come in,' she said.

He leaped up the step and was in the room. Her mother appeared in the inner doorway, large and hostile.

'Who have you got here?' she asked.

'It's Mr Morel; he missed his train. I thought we might put him up for the night, and save him a ten-mile walk.'

'H'm!' exclaimed Mrs Radford. 'That's *your* look-out! If you've invited him, he's very welcome as far as I'm concerned. *You* keep the house!'

'If you don't like me, I'll go away again,' he said.

'Nay, nay, you needn't! Come along in! I dunno what you'll think of the supper I'd got her.'

It was a little dish of chip potatoes and a piece of bacon. The table was roughly laid for one.

'You can have some more bacon,' continued Mrs Radford. 'More chips you can't have.'

'It's a shame to bother you,' he said.

'Oh, don't you be apologetic! It doesn't *do* wi' me! You treated her to the theatre, didn't you?' There was a sarcasm in the last question.

'Well?' laughed Paul uncomfortably.

'Well, and what's an inch of bacon! Take your coat off.'

The big, straight-standing woman was trying to estimate the situation. She moved about the cupboard. Clara took his coat. The room was very warm and cosy in the lamplight.

'My sirs!' exclaimed Mrs Radford, 'but you two's a pair of bright beauties, I must say! What's all that get-up for?'

'I believe we don't know,' he said, feeling a victim.

'There isn't room in *this* house for two such bobby-dazzlers, if you fly your kites *that* high!' she rallied them. It was a nasty thrust.

He in his dinner jacket, and Clara in her green dress and bare arms, were confused. They felt they must shelter each other in that little kitchen.

'And look at *that* blossom!' continued Mrs Radford, pointing to Clara. 'What does she reckon she did it for?'

Paul looked at Clara. She was rosy; her neck was warm with blushes. There was a moment of silence.

'You like to see it, don't you?' he asked.

The mother had them in her power. All the time his heart was beating hard, and he was tight with anxiety. But he would fight her.

'Me like to see it!' exclaimed the old woman. 'What should I like to see her make a fool of herself for?'

'I've seen people look bigger fools,' he said. Clara was under his protection now.

'Oh, ay! And when was that?' came the sarcastic rejoinder.

'When they made frights of themselves,' he answered.

Mrs Radford, large and threatening, stood suspended on the hearthrug, holding her fork.

'They're fools either road,' she answered at length, turning to the Dutch oven.

'No,' he said, fighting stoutly. 'Folk ought to look as well as they can.'

'And do you call *that* looking nice!' cried the mother, pointing a scornful fork at Clara. 'That—that looks as if it wasn't properly dressed!'

'I believe you're jealous that you can't swank as well,' he said laughing.

'Me! I could have worn evening dress with anybody, if I'd wanted to!' came the scornful answer.

'And why didn't you want to?' he asked pertinently. 'Or *did* you wear it?'

There was a long pause. Mrs Radford readjusted the bacon in the Dutch oven. His heart beat fast, for fear he had offended her.

'Me!' she exclaimed at last. 'No, I didn't! And when I was in service, I knew as soon as one of the maids came out in bare shoulders what sort *she* was, going to her sixpenny hop!'

'Were you too good to go to a sixpenny hop?' he said.

Clara sat with bowed head. His eyes were dark and glittering. Mrs Radford took the Dutch oven from the fire, and stood near him, putting bits of bacon on his plate.

'*There's* a nice crozzly bit!' she said.

'Don't give me the best!' he said.

'*She's* got what *she* wants,' was the answer.

There was a sort of scornful forbearance in the woman's tone that made Paul know she was mollified.

'But *do* have some!' he said to Clara.

She looked up at him with her grey eyes, humiliated and lonely.

'No thanks!' she said.

'Why won't you?' he answered caressively.

The blood was beating up like fire in his veins. Mrs Radford sat down again, large and impressive and aloof. He left Clara altogether to attend to the mother.

'They say Sarah Bernhardt's fifty,' he said.

'Fifty! She's turned sixty!' came the answer.

'Well,' he said, 'you'd never think it! She made me want to howl even now.'

'I should like to see myself howling at *that* bad old baggage!' said Mrs Radford. 'It's time she began to think herself a grandmother, not a shrieking catamaran—'

He laughed.

'A catamaran is a boat the Malays use,' he said.

'And it's a word as *I* use,' she retorted.

'My mother does sometimes, and it's no good my telling her,' he said.

'I s'd think she boxes your ears,' said Mrs Radford, good-humouredly.

'She'd like to, and she says she will, so I give her a little stool to stand on.'

'That's the worst of my mother,' said Clara. 'She never wants a stool for anything.'

'But she often can't touch *that* lady with a long prop,' retorted Mrs Radford to Paul.

'I s'd think she doesn't want touching with a prop,' he laughed. '*I* shouldn't.'

'It might do the pair of you good to give you a crack on the head with one,' said the mother, laughing suddenly.

'Why are you so vindictive towards me?' he said. 'I've not stolen anything from you.'

'No; I'll watch that,' laughed the older woman.

Soon the supper was finished. Mrs Radford sat in her chair. Paul lit a cigarette. Clara went upstairs, returning with a sleeping-suit, which she spread on the fender to air.

'Why, I'd forgot all about *them*,' said Mrs Radford. 'Where have they sprung from?'

'Out of my drawer.'

'H'm! You bought 'em for Baxter, an' he wouldn't wear 'em, would he?'—laughing. 'Said he reckoned to do wi'out trousers i' bed.' She turned confidentially to Paul saying:

'He couldn't *bear* 'em, them pyjama things.'

The young man sat making rings of smoke.

'Well, it's everyone to his taste,' he laughed.

Then followed a little discussion of the merits of pyjamas.

'My mother loves me in them,' he said. 'She says I'm a pierrot.'

'I can imagine they'd suit you,' said Mrs Radford.

After a while he glanced at the little clock that was ticking on the mantelpiece. It was half-past twelve.

'It is funny,' he said, 'but it takes hours to settle down to sleep after the theatre.'

'It's about time you did,' said Mrs Radford, clearing the table.

'Are *you* tired?' he asked Clara.

'Not the least bit,' she answered, avoiding his eyes.

'Shall we have a game at cribbage?' he said.

'I've forgotten it.'

'Well, I'll teach you again. May we play crib, Mrs Radford?' he asked.

'You'll please yourselves,' she said, 'but it's pretty late.'

'A game or so will make us sleepy,' he answered.

Clara brought the cards, and sat spinning her wedding-ring whilst he shuffled them. Mrs Radford was washing up in the scullery. As it grew later Paul felt the situation getting more and more tense.

'Fifteen two, fifteen four, fifteen six, and two's eight–!'

The clock struck one. Still the game continued. Mrs Radford had done all the little jobs preparatory to going to bed, had locked the door and filled the kettle. Still Paul went on dealing and counting. He was obsessed by Clara's arms and throat. He believed he could see where the division was just beginning for her breasts. He could not leave her. She watched his hands, and felt her joints melt as they moved quickly. She was so near; it was almost as if he touched her, and yet not quite. His mettle was aroused. He hated Mrs Radford. She sat on, nearly dropping asleep, but determined and obstinate on her chair. Paul glanced at her, then at Clara. She met his eyes, that were angry, mocking, and hard as steel. Her own answered him in shame. He knew *she*, at any rate, was of his mind. He played on.

At last Mrs Radford roused herself stiffly, and said:

'Isn't it nigh on time you two was thinking o' bed?'

Paul played on without answering. He hated her sufficiently to murder her.

'Half a minute,' he said.

The elder woman rose and sailed stubbornly into the scullery, returning with his candle, which she put on the mantelpiece. Then she sat down again. The hatred of her went so hot down his veins, he dropped his cards.

'We'll stop, then,' he said, but his voice was still a challenge.

Clara saw his mouth shut hard. Again he glanced at her. It seemed like an agreement. She bent over the cards, coughing, to clear her throat.

'Well, I'm glad you've finished,' said Mrs Radford. 'Here, take your things'–she thrust the warm suit in his hand–'and this is your candle. Your room's over this; there's only two, so you can't go far wrong. Well, good night. I hope you'll rest well.'

'I'm sure I shall: I always do,' he said.

'Yes; and so you ought at your age,' she replied.

He bade good night to Clara, and went. The twisting stairs of white, scrubbed wood creaked and clanged at every step. He went doggedly. The two doors faced each other. He went in his room, pushed the door to, without fastening the latch.

It was a small room with a large bed. Some of Clara's hairpins were on the dressing-table–her hair brush. Her clothes and some skirts hung under a cloth in a corner. There was actually a pair of stockings over a chair. He explored the room. Two books of his own were there on the shelf. He undressed, folded his suit, and sat on the bed, listening. Then he blew out the candle, lay down, and in two minutes was almost asleep. Then click!–he was wide awake and writhing in torment. It was as if, when he had nearly got to sleep, something had bitten him suddenly and sent him mad. He sat up and looked at the room in the darkness, his feet doubled under him, perfectly motionless, listening. He heard a cat somewhere away outside; then the heavy, poised tread of the mother; then Clara's distinct voice:

'Will you unfasten my dress?'

There was silence for some time. At last the mother said:

'Now then! Aren't you coming up?'

'No, not yet,' replied the daughter calmly.

'Oh, very well then! If it's not late enough, stop a bit longer. Only you needn't come waking me up when I've got to sleep.'

'I shan't be long,' said Clara.

Immediately afterwards Paul heard the mother slowly mounting the stairs. The candle-light flashed through the cracks in his door. Her dress brushed the door, and his heart jumped. Then it was dark, and he heard the clatter of her latch. She was very leisurely indeed in her preparations for sleep. After a long time it was quite still. He sat strung up on the bed, shivering slightly. His door was an inch open. As Clara came upstairs, he would intercept her. He waited. All was dead silence. The clock struck two. Then he heard a slight scrape of the fender downstairs. Now he could not help himself. His shivering was uncontrollable. He felt he must go or die.

He stepped off the bed, and stood a moment, shuddering. Then he went straight to the door. He tried to step lightly. The first stair cracked like a shot. He listened. The old woman stirred in her bed. The staircase was dark. There was a slit of light under the stair-foot door, which opened into the kitchen. He stood a moment. Then he went on, mechanically. Every step creaked, and his back was creeping, lest the old woman's door should open behind him up above. He fumbled with the door at the bottom. The latch opened with a loud click. He went through into the kitchen, and shut the door noisily behind him. The old woman daren't come now.

Then he stood, arrested. Clara was kneeling on a pile of white underclothing, on the hearthrug, her back towards him, warming herself. She did not look around, but sat crouching on her heels, and her rounded, beautiful back was towards him, and her face was hidden. She was warming her body at the fire for consolation. The glow was rosy on one side, the shadow was dark and warm on the other. Her arms hung slack.

He shuddered violently, clenching his teeth and fists hard to keep control. Then he went forward to her. He put one hand on her shoulder, the fingers of the other hand under the chin to raise her face. A convulsed shiver ran through her, once, twice, at his touch. She kept her head bent.

'Sorry!' he murmured, realizing that his hands were very cold.

Then she looked up at him, frightened, like a thing that is afraid of death.

'My hands are so cold,' he murmured.

'I like it,' she whispered, closing her eyes.

The breath of her words was on his mouth. Her arms clasped his knees. The cord of his sleeping-suit dangled against her and made her shiver. As the warmth went into him, his shuddering became less.

At length, unable to stand so any more, he raised her, and she buried her head on his shoulder. His hands went over her slowly with an infinite tenderness of caress. She clung close to him, trying to hide herself against him. He clasped her very fast. Then at last she looked at him, mute, imploring, looking to see if she must be ashamed.

His eyes were dark, very deep, and very quiet. It was as if her beauty and his taking it hurt him, made him sorrowful. He looked at her with a little pain, and was afraid. He was so humble before her. She kissed him fervently on the eyes, first one, then the other, and she folded herself to him. She gave herself. He held her fast. It was a moment intense almost to agony.

She stood letting him adore her and tremble with joy of her. It healed her hurt pride. It healed her; it made her glad. It made her feel erect and proud again. Her pride had been wounded inside her. She had been cheapened. Now she radiated with joy and pride again. It was her restoration and her recognition.

Then he looked at her, his face radiant. They laughed to each other, and he strained her to his chest. The seconds ticked off, the minutes passed, and still the two stood clasped rigid together, mouth to mouth, like a statue in one block.

But again his fingers went seeking over her, restless, wandering, dissatisfied. The hot blood came up wave upon wave. She laid her head on his shoulder.

'Come you to my room,' he murmured.

She looked at him and shook her head, her mouth pouting disconsolately, her eyes heavy with passion. He watched her fixedly.

'Yes!' he said.

Again she shook her head.

'Why not?' he asked.

She looked at him still heavily, sorrowfully, and again she shook her head. His eyes hardened, and he gave way.

When, later on, he was back in bed, he wondered why she had refused to come to him openly, so that her mother would know. At any rate, then things would have been definite. And she could have stayed with him the night, without having to go, as she was, to her mother's bed. It was strange, and he could not understand it. And almost immediately he fell asleep.

He awoke in the morning with someone speaking to him. Opening his eyes, he saw Mrs Radford, big and stately, looking down on him. She held a cup of tea in her hand.

'Do you think you're going to sleep till Doomsday?' she said.

He laughed at once.

'It ought only to be about five o'clock,' he said.

'Well,' she answered, 'it's half-past seven, whether or not. Here, I've brought you a cup of tea.'

He rubbed his face, pushed the tumbled hair off his forehead, and roused himself.

'What's it so late for!' he grumbled.

He resented being awakened. It amused her. She saw his neck in the flannel sleeping-jacket, as white and round as a girl's. He rubbed his hair crossly.

'It's not good your scratching your head,' she said. 'It won't make it no earlier. Here, an' how long d'you think I'm going to stand waiting wi' this here cup?'

'Oh, dash the cup!' he said.

'You should go to bed earlier,' said the woman.

He looked up at her, laughing with impudence.

'I went to bed before *you* did,' he said.

'Yes, my Guyney, you did!' she exclaimed.

'Fancy,' he said, stirring his tea, 'having tea brought to bed to me! My mother'd think I'm ruined for life.'

'Don't she never do it?' asked Mrs Radford.

'She'd as leave think of flying.'

'Ah, I always spoilt my lot! That's why they've turned out such bad uns,' said the elderly woman.

'You'd only Clara,' he said. 'And Mr Radford's in heaven. So I suppose there's only you left to be the bad un.'

'I'm not bad; I'm only soft,' she said, as she went out of the bedroom. 'I'm only a fool, I am!'

Clara was very quiet at breakfast, but she had a sort of air of proprietorship over him that pleased him infinitely. Mrs Radford was evidently fond of him. He began to talk of his painting.

'What's the good,' exclaimed the mother, 'of your whittling and worrying and twistin' and too-in' at that painting of yours? What *good* does it do you, I should like to know? You'd better be enjoyin' yourself.'

'Oh, but,' exclaimed Paul, 'I made over thirty guineas last year.'

'Did you! Well, that's a consideration, but it's nothing to the time you put in.'

'And I've got four pounds owing. A man said he'd give me five pounds if I'd paint him and his missis and the dog and the cottage. And I went and put the fowls in instead of the dog, and he was waxy, so I had to knock a quid off. I was sick of it, and I didn't like the dog. I made a picture of it. What shall I do when he pays me the four pounds?'

'Nay! You know your own uses for your money,' said Mrs Radford.

'But I'm going to bust this four pounds. Should we go to the seaside for a day or two?'

'Who?'

'You and Clara and me.'

'What, on your money!' she exclaimed, half wrathful.

'Why not?'

'*You* wouldn't be long in breaking your neck at a hurdle race,' she said.
'So long as I get a good run for my money! Will you?'
'Nay; you may settle that between you.'
'And you're willing?' he asked, amazed and rejoicing.
'You'll do as you like,' said Mrs Radford, 'whether I'm willing or not.'

13

BAXTER DAWES

Soon after Paul had been to the theatre with Clara, he was drinking in the Punch Bowl with some friends of his when Dawes came in. Clara's husband was growing stout; his eye-lids were getting slack over his brown eyes; he was losing his healthy firmness of flesh. He was very evidently on the downward track. Having quarrelled with his sister, he had gone into cheap lodgings. His mistress had left him for a man who would marry her. He had been in prison one night for fighting when he was drunk, and there was a shady betting episode in which he was concerned.

Paul and he were confirmed enemies, and yet there was between them that peculiar feeling of intimacy, as if they were secretly near to each other, which sometimes exists between two people, although they never speak to one another. Paul often thought of Baxter Dawes, often wanted to get at him and be friends with him. He knew Dawes often thought about him, and that the man was drawn to him by some bond or other. And yet the two never looked at each other save in hostility.

Since he was a superior employee at Jordan's, it was the thing for Paul to offer Dawes a drink.

'What'll you have?' he asked of him.

'Nowt wi' a bleeder like you!' replied the man.

Paul turned away with a slight disdainful movement of the shoulders, very irritating.

'The aristocracy,' he continued, 'is a really military institution. Take Germany, now. She's got thousands of aristocrats whose only means of existence is the army. They're deadly poor, and life's deadly slow. So they hope for war. They look for war as a chance of getting on. Till there's a war they are idle good-for-nothings. When there's a war, they are leaders and commanders. There you are then—they *want* war!'

He was not a favourite debater in the public-house, being too quick and overbearing. He irritated the older men by his assertive manner, and his cocksureness. They listened in silence, and were not sorry when he finished.

Dawes interrupted the young man's flow of eloquence by asking, in a loud sneer:

'Did you learn all that at th' theatre th' other night?'

Paul looked at him; their eyes met. Then he knew Dawes had seen him coming out of the theatre with Clara.

'Why, what about th' theatre?' asked one of Paul's associates, glad to get a dig at the young fellow, and sniffing something tasty.

'Oh, him in a bob-tailed evening suit, on the lardy-da!' sneered Dawes, jerking his head contemptuously at Paul.

'That's comin' it strong,' said the mutual friend. 'Tart an' all?'

'Tart, begod!' said Dawes.

'Go on; let's have it!' cried the mutual friend.

'You've got it,' said Dawes, 'an' I reckon Morelly had it an' all.'

'Well, I'll be jiggered!' said the mutual friend. 'An' was it a proper tart?'

'Tart, God blimey—yes!'

'How do you know?'

'Oh,' said Dawes, 'I reckon he spent th' night—'

There was a good deal of laughter at Paul's expense.

'But who *was* she? D'you know her?' asked the mutual friend.

'I should *shay sho*,' said Dawes.

This brought another burst of laughter.

'Then spit it out,' said the mutual friend.

Dawes shook his head, and took a gulp of beer.

'It's a wonder he hasn't let on himself,' he said. 'He'll be braggin' of it in a bit.'

'Come on, Paul,' said his friend: 'it's no good. You might just as well own up.'

'Own up what? That I happened to take a friend to the theatre?'

'Oh well, if it was all right, tell us who she was, lad,' said the friend.

'She *was* all right,' said Dawes.

Paul was furious. Dawes wiped his golden moustache with his fingers, sneering.

'Strike me—! One o' that sort?' said the mutual friend. 'Paul, boy, I'm surprised at you. And do you know her, Baxter?'

'Just a bit, like!'

He winked at the other men.

'Oh, well,' said Paul, 'I'll be going!'

The mutual friend laid a detaining hand on his shoulder.

'Nay,' he said, 'you don't get off as easy as that, my lad. We've got to have a full account of this business.'

'Then get it from Dawes,' he said.

'You shouldn't funk your own deeds, man,' remonstrated the friend.

Then Dawes made a remark which caused Paul to throw half a glass of beer in his face.

'Oh, Mr Morel!' cried the barmaid, and she rang the bell for the 'chucker-out'.

Dawes spat and rushed for the young man. At that minute a brawny fellow with his shirtsleeves rolled up and his trousers tight over his haunches intervened.

'Now, then!' he said, pushing his chest in front of Dawes.

'Come out!' cried Dawes.

Paul was leaning, white and quivering, against the brass rail of the bar. He hated Dawes, wished something could exterminate him at that moment; and at the same time, seeing the wet hair on the man's forehead, he thought he looked pathetic. He did not move.

'Come out, you—' said Dawes.

'That's enough, Dawes,' cried the barmaid.

'Come on,' said the 'chucker-out', with kindly insistence, 'you'd better be getting on.'

And, by making Dawes edge away from his own close proximity, he worked him to the door.

'*That's* the little sod as started it!' cried Dawes, half cowed, pointing to Paul Morel.

'Why, what a story, Mr Dawes!' said the barmaid. 'You know it was you all the time.'

Still the 'chucker-out' kept thrusting his chest forward at him, still he kept edging back, until he was in the doorway and on the steps outside; then he turned round.

'All right,' he said, nodding straight at his rival.

Paul had a curious sensation of pity, almost of affection, mingled with a violent hate, for the man. The coloured door swung to; there was silence in the bar.

'Serve him jolly well right!' said the barmaid.

'But it's a nasty thing to get a glass of beer in your eyes,' said the mutual friend.

'I tell you *I* was glad he did,' said the barmaid. 'Will you have another, Mr Morel?'

She held up Paul's glass questioningly. He nodded.

'He's a man as doesn't care for anything, is Baxter Dawes,' said one.

'Pooh! Is he?' said the barmaid. 'He's a loud-mouthed one, he is, and they're never much good. Give me a pleasant-spoken chap, if you want a devil!'

'Well, Paul, my lad,' said the friend, 'you'll have to take care of yourself now for a while.'

'You won't have to give him a chance over you, that's all,' said the barmaid.

'Can you box?' asked a friend.

'Not a bit,' he answered, still very white.

'I might give you a turn or two,' said the friend.

'Thanks, I haven't time.'

And presently he took his departure.

'Go along with him, Mr Jenkinson,' whispered the barmaid, tipping Mr Jenkinson the wink.

The man nodded, took his hat, said 'Good night all!' very heartily, and followed Paul calling:

'Half a minute, old man. You an' me's going the same road, I believe.'

'Mr Morel doesn't like it,' said the barmaid. 'You'll see, we shan't have him in much more. I'm sorry; he's good company. And Baxter Dawes wants locking up, that's what he wants.'

Paul would have died rather than his mother should get to know of this affair. He suffered tortures of humiliation and self-consciousness. There was now a good deal of his life of which necessarily he could not speak to his mother. He had a life apart from her–his sexual life. The rest she still kept. But he felt he had to conceal something from her, and it irked him. There was a certain silence between them, and he felt he had, in that silence, to defend himself against her; he felt condemned by her. Then sometimes he hated her, and pulled at her bondage. His life wanted to free itself of her. It was like a circle where life turned back on itself, and got no farther. She bore him, loved him, kept him, and his love turned back into her, so that he could not be free to go forward with his own life, really love another woman. At this period, unknowingly, he resisted his mother's influence. He did not tell her things; there was a distance between them.

Clara was happy, almost sure of him. She felt she had at last got him for herself; and then again came the uncertainty. He told her jestingly of the affair with her husband. Her colour came up, her grey eyes flashed.

'That's him to a "T",' she cried—'like a navvy! He's not fit for mixing with decent folk.'

'Yet you married him,' he said.

It made her furious that he reminded her.

'I did!' she cried. 'But how was I to know!'

'I think he might have been rather nice,' he said.

'You think *I* made him what he is!' she exclaimed.

'Oh no! He made himself. But there's something about him—'

Clara looked at her lover closely. There was something in him she hated, a sort of detached criticism of herself, a coldness which made her woman's soul harden against him.

'And what are you going to do?' she asked.

'How?'

'About Baxter.'

'There's nothing to do, is there?' he replied.

'You can fight him if you have to, I suppose?' she said.

'No; I haven't the least sense of the "fist". It's funny. With most men there's the instinct to clench the fist and hit. It's not so with me. I should want a knife or a pistol or something to fight with.'

'Then you'd better carry something,' she said.

'Nay,' he laughed; 'I'm not daggeroso.'

'But he'll do something to you. You don't know him.'

'All right,' he said, 'we'll see.'

'And you'll let him?'

'Perhaps, if I can't help it.'

'And if he kills you?' she said.

'I should be sorry, for his sake and mine.'

Clara was silent for a moment.

'You *do* make me angry!' she exclaimed.

'That's nothing afresh,' he laughed.

'But why are you so silly? You don't know him.'

'And don't want.'

'Yes, but you're not going to let a man do as he likes with you?'

'What must I do?' he replied, laughing.

'*I* should carry a revolver,' she said. 'I'm sure he's dangerous.'

'I might blow my fingers off,' he said.

'No; but won't you?' she pleaded.

'No.'

'Not anything?'

'No.'

'And you leave him to—?'

'Yes.'

'You are a fool!'

'Fact!'

She set her teeth with anger.

'I could *shake* you!' she cried, trembling with passion.

'Why?'

'Let a man like *him* do as he likes with you.'

'You can go back to him if he triumphs,' he said.

'Do you want me to hate you?' she asked.

'Well, I only tell you,' he said.

'And *you* say you *love* me!' she exclaimed, low and indignant.

'Ought I to slay him to please you?' he said. 'But if I did, see what a hold he'd have over me.'

'Do you think I'm a fool!' she exclaimed.

'Not at all. But you don't understand me, my dear.'

There was a pause between them.

'But you ought *not* to expose yourself,' she pleaded.

He shrugged his shoulders.

> 'The man in righteousness arrayed,
>   The pure and blameless liver,
> Needs not the keen Toledo blade,
>   Nor venom-freighted quiver,'

he quoted.

She looked at him searchingly.

'I wish I could understand you,' she said.

'There's simply nothing to understand,' he laughed.

She bowed her head, brooding.

He did not see Dawes for several days; then one morning as he ran upstairs from the spiral room he almost collided with the burly metal-worker.

'What the–!' cried the smith.

'Sorry!' said Paul, and passed on.

'*Sorry!*' sneered Dawes.

Paul whistled lightly, 'Put Me among the Girls.'

'I'll stop your whistle, my jockey!' he said.

The other took no notice.

'You're goin' to answer for that job of the other night.'

Paul went to his desk in his corner, and turned over the leaves of the ledger.

'Go and tell Fanny I want order 097, quick!' he said to his boy.

Dawes stood in the doorway, tall and threatening, looking at the top of the young man's head.

'Six and five's eleven and seven's one-and-six,' Paul added aloud.

'An' you hear, do you!' said Dawes.

'*Five and ninepence!*' He wrote a figure. 'What's that?' he said.

'I'm going to show you what it is,' said the smith.

The other went on adding the figures aloud.

'Yer crawlin' little–yer daresn't face me proper!'

Paul quickly snatched the heavy ruler. Dawes started. The young man ruled some lines in his ledger. The elder man was infuriated.

'But wait till I light on you, no matter where it is, I'll settle your hash for a bit, yer little swine!'

'All right,' said Paul.

At that the smith started heavily from the doorway. Just then a whistle piped shrilly. Paul went to the speaking-tube.

'Yes!' he said, and he listened. 'Er–yes!' He listened, then he laughed. 'I'll come down directly. I've got a visitor just now.'

Dawes knew from his tone that he had been speaking to Clara. He stepped forward.

'Yer little devil!' he said. 'I'll visitor you, inside of two minutes! Think I'm goin' ter have *you* whipperty-snappin' round?'

The other clerks in the warehouse looked up. Paul's office-boy appeared, holding some white article.

'Fanny says you could have had it last night if you'd let her know,' he said. 'All right,' answered Paul, looking at the stocking. 'Get it off.'

Dawes stood frustrated, helpless with rage. Morel turned round.

'Excuse me a minute,' he said to Dawes, and he would have run downstairs.

'By God, I'll stop your gallop!' shouted the smith, seizing him by the arm. He turned quickly.

'Hey! Hey!' cried the office-boy, alarmed.

Thomas Jordan started out of his little glass office, and came running down the room.

'What's a-matter, what's a-matter?' he said, in his old man's sharp voice.

'I'm just goin' ter settle this little–, that' all,' said Dawes desperately.

'What do you mean?' snapped Thomas Jordan.

'What I say,' said Dawes, but he hung fire.

Morel was leaning against the counter, ashamed, half grinning.

'What's it all about?' snapped Thomas Jordan.

'Couldn't say,' said Paul, shaking his head and shrugging his shoulders.

'Couldn't yer, couldn't yer!' cried Dawes, thrusting forward his handsome, furious face, and squaring his fist.

'Have you finished?' cried the old man, strutting. 'Get off about your business, and don't come here tipsy in the morning.'

Dawes turned his big frame slowly upon him.

'Tipsy!' he said. 'Who's tipsy? I'm no more tipsy than *you* are!'

'We've heard that song before,' snapped the old man. 'Now you get off, and don't be long about it. Comin' *here* with your rowdying.'

The smith looked down contemptuously on his employer. His hands, large and grimy, and yet well shaped for his labour, worked restlessly. Paul remembered they were the hands of Clara's husband, and a flash of hate went through him.

'Get out before you're turned out!' snapped Thomas Jordan.

'Why, who'll turn me out?' said Dawes, beginning to sneer.

Mr Jordan started, marched up to the smith, waving him off, thrusting his stout little figure at the man, saying:

'Get off my premises–get off!'

He seized and twitched Dawes' arm.

'Come off!' said the smith, and with a jerk of the elbow he sent the little manufacturer staggering backwards.

Before anyone could help him, Thomas Jordan had collided with the flimsy spring-door. It had given way, and let him crash down the half-dozen steps into Fanny's room. There was a second of amazement; then men and girls were running. Dawes stood a moment looking bitterly on the scene, then he took his departure.

Thomas Jordan was shaken and bruised, not otherwise hurt. He was, however, beside himself with rage. He dismissed Dawes from his employment, and summoned him for assault.

At the trial Paul Morel had to give evidence. Asked how the trouble began, he said:

'Dawes took occasion to insult Mrs Dawes and me because I accompanied her to the theatre one evening; then I threw some beer at him, and he wanted his revenge.'

'Cherchez la femme!' smiled the magistrate.

The case was dismissed after the magistrate had told Dawes he thought him a skunk.

'You gave the case away,' snapped Mr Jordan to Paul.

'I don't think I did,' replied the latter. 'Besides, you didn't really want a conviction, did you?'

'What do you think I took the case up for?'

'Well,' said Paul, 'I'm sorry if I said the wrong thing.' Clara was also very angry.

'Why need *my* name have been dragged in?' she said.

'Better speak it openly than leave it to be whispered.'

'There was no need for anything at all,' she declared.

'We are none the poorer,' he said indifferently.

'*You* may not be,' she said.

'And you?' he asked.

'I need never have been mentioned.'

'I'm sorry,' he said; but he did not sound sorry.

He told himself easily: 'She will come round.' And she did.

He told his mother about the fall of Mr Jordan and the trial of Dawes. Mrs Morel watched him closely.

'And what do you think of it all?' she asked him.

'I think he's a fool,' he said.

But he was very uncomfortable, nevertheless.

'Have you ever considered where it will end?' his mother said.

'No,' he answered; 'things work out of themselves.'

'They do, in a way one doesn't like, as a rule,' said his mother.

'And then one has to put up with them,' he said.

'You'll find you're not as good at "putting up" as you imagine,' she said.

He went on working rapidly at his design.

'Do you ever ask *her* opinion?' she said at length.

'What of?'

'Of you, and the whole thing.'

'I don't care what her opinion of me is. She's fearfully in love with me, but it's not very deep.'

'But quite as deep as your feeling for her.'

He looked up at his mother curiously.

'Yes,' he said. 'You know, mother. I think there must be something the matter with me, that I *can't* love. When she's there, as a rule, I *do* love her. Sometimes, when I see her just as *the woman*, I love her, mother; but then, when she talks and criticizes, I often don't listen to her.'

'Yet she's as much sense as Miriam.'

'Perhaps; and I love her better than Miriam. But *why* don't they hold me?'

The last question was almost a lamentation. His mother turned away her face, sat looking across the room, very quiet, grave, with something of renunciation.

'But you wouldn't want to marry Clara?' she said.

'No; at first perhaps I would. But why—why don't I want to marry her or anybody? I feel sometimes as if I wronged my women, mother.'

'How wronged them, my son?'

'I don't know.'

He went on painting rather despairingly; he had touched the quick of the trouble.

'And as for wanting to marry,' said his mother, 'there's plenty of time yet.'

'But no, mother. I even love Clara, and I did Miriam; but to *give* myself to them in marriage I couldn't. I couldn't belong to them. They seem to want *me*, and I can't ever give it them.'

'You haven't met the right woman.'

'And I never shall meet the right woman while you live,' he said.

She was very quiet. Now she began to feel again tired, as if she were done.

'We'll see, my son,' she answered.

The feeling that things were going in a circle made him mad.

Clara was, indeed, passionately in love with him, and he with her, as far as passion went. In the daytime he forgot her a good deal. She was working in the same building, but he was not aware of it. He was busy, and her existence was of no matter to him. But all the time she was in her spiral room she had a sense that he was upstairs, a physical sense of his person in the same building. Every second she expected him to come through the door, and when he came it was a shock to her. But he was often short and offhand with her. He gave her his directions in an official manner, keeping her at bay. With what wits she had left she listened to him. She dared not misunderstand or fail to remember, but it was a cruelty to her. She wanted to touch his chest. She knew exactly how his breast was shapen under the waistcoat, and she wanted to touch it. It maddened her to hear his mechanical voice giving orders about the work. She wanted to break through the sham of it, smash the trivial coating of business which covered him with hardness, get at the man again; but she was afraid, and before she could feel one touch of his warmth he was gone, and she ached again.

He knew that she was dreary every evening she did not see him, so he gave her a good deal of his time. The days were often a misery to her, but the evenings and the nights were usually a bliss to them both. Then they were silent. For hours they sat together, or walked together in the dark, and talked only a few, almost meaningless words. But he had her hand in his, and her bosom left its warmth in his chest, making him feel whole.

One evening they were walking down by the canal, and something was troubling him. She knew she had not got him. All the time he whistled softly and persistently to himself. She listened, feeling she could learn more from his whistling than from his speech. It was a sad dissatisfied tune–a tune that made her feel he would not stay with her. She walked on in silence. When they came to the swing bridge he sat down on the great pole, looking at the stars in the water. He was a long way from her. She had been thinking.

'Will you always stay at Jordan's?' she asked.

'No,' he answered without reflecting. 'No; I s'll leave Nottingham and go abroad–soon.'

'Go abroad! What for?'

'I dunno! I feel restless.'

'But what shall you do?'

'I shall have to get some steady designing work, and some sort of sale for my pictures first,' he said. 'I am gradually making my way. I know I am.'

'And when do you think you'll go?'

'I don't know. I shall hardly go for long, while there's my mother.'

'You couldn't leave her?'

'Not for long.'

She looked at the stars in the black water. They lay very white and staring. It was an agony to know he would leave her, but it was almost an agony to have him near her.

'And if you made a nice lot of money, what would you do?' she asked.

'Go somewhere in a pretty house near London with my mother.'

'I see.'

There was a long pause.

'I could still come and see you,' he said, 'I don't know. Don't ask me what I should do; I don't know.'

There was a silence. The stars shuddered and broke upon the water. There came a breath of wind. He went suddenly to her, and put his hand on her shoulder.

'Don't ask me anything about the future,' he said miserably. 'I don't know anything. Be with me now, will you, no matter what it is?'

And she took him in her arms. After all, she was a married woman, and she had no right even to what he gave her. He needed her badly. She had him in her arms, and he was miserable. With her warmth she folded him over, consoled him, loved him. She would let the moment stand for itself.

After a moment he lifted his head as if he wanted to speak.

'Clara,' he said, struggling.

She caught him passionately to her, pressed his head down on her breast with her hand. She could not bear the suffering in his voice. She was afraid in her soul. He might have anything of her–anything; but she did not want to *know*. She felt she could not bear it. She wanted him to be soothed upon her–soothed. She stood clasping him and caressing him, and he was something unknown to her–something almost uncanny. She wanted to soothe him into forgetfulness.

And soon the struggle went down in his soul, and he forgot. But then Clara was not there for him, only a woman, warm, something he loved and almost worshipped, there in the dark. But it was not Clara, and she submitted to him. The naked hunger and inevitability of his loving her, something strong and blind and ruthless in its primitiveness, made the hour almost terrible to her. She knew how stark and alone he was, and she felt it was great that he came to her; and she took him simply because his need was bigger either than her or him, and her soul was still within her. She did this for him in his need, even if he left her, for she loved him.

All the while the peewits were screaming in the field. When he came to, he wondered what was near his eyes, curving and strong with life in the dark, and what voice it was speaking. Then he realized it was the grass, and the peewit was calling. The warmth was Clara's breathing heaving. He lifted his head, and looked into her eyes. They were dark and shining and strange, life wild at the source staring into his life, stranger to him, yet meeting him; and he put his face down on her throat, afraid. What was she? A strong, strange, wild life, that breathed with his in the darkness through this hour. It was all so much bigger than themselves that he was hushed. They had met, and included in their meeting the thrust of the manifold grass-stems, the cry of the peewit, the wheel of the stars.

When they stood up they saw other lovers stealing down the opposite hedge. It seemed natural they were there; the night contained them.

And after such an evening they both were very still, having known the immensity of passion. They felt small, half afraid, childish, and wondering, like

Adam and Eve when they lost their innocence and realized the magnificence of the power which drove them out of Paradise and across the great night and the great day of humanity. It was for each of them an initiation and a satisfaction. To know their own nothingness, to know the tremendous living flood which carried them always, gave them rest within themselves. If so great a magnificent power could overwhelm them, identify them altogether with itself, so that they knew they were only grains in the tremendous heave that lifted every grass-blade its little height, and every tree, and living thing, then why fret about themselves? They could let themselves be carried by life, and they felt a sort of peace each in the other. There was a verification which they had had together. Nothing could nullify it, nothing could take it away; it was almost their belief in life.

But Clara was not satisfied. Something great was there, she knew; something great enveloped her. But it did not keep her. In the morning it was not the same. They had *known*, but she could not keep the moment. She wanted it again; she wanted something permanent. She had not realized fully. She thought it was he whom she wanted. He was not safe to her. This that had been between them might never be again; he might leave her. She had not got him; she was not satisfied. She had been there, but she had not gripped the–the something–she knew not what–which she was mad to have.

In the morning he had considerable peace, and was happy in himself. It seemed almost as if he had known the baptism of fire in passion, and it left him at rest. But it was not Clara. It was something that happened because of her, but it was not her. They were scarcely any nearer each other. It was as if they had been blind agents of a great force.

When she saw him that day at the factory her heart melted like a drop of fire. It was his body, his brows. The drop of fire grew more intense in her breast; she must hold him. But he, very quiet, very subdued this morning, went on giving his instructions. She followed him into the dark, ugly basement, and lifted her arms to him. He kissed her, and the intensity of passion began to burn him again. Somebody was at the door. He ran upstairs; she returned to her room, moving as if in a trance.

After that the fire slowly went down. He felt more and more that his experience had been impersonal, and not Clara. He loved her. There was a big tenderness, as after a strong emotion they had known together; but it was not she who could keep his soul steady. He had wanted her to be something she could not be.

And she was mad with desire of him. She could not see him without touching him. In the factory, as he talked to her about spiral hose, she ran her hand secretly along his side. She followed him out into the basement for a quick kiss; her eyes, always mute and yearning, full of unrestrained passion, she kept fixed on his. He was afraid of her, lest she should too flagrantly give herself away before the other girls. She invariably waited for him at dinner-time for him to embrace her before she went. He felt as if she were helpless, almost a burden to him, and it irritated him.

'But what do you always want to be kissing and embracing for?' he said. 'Surely there's a time for everything.'

She looked up at him, and the hate came into her eyes.

'*Do* I always want to be kissing you?' she said.

'Always, even if I come to ask you about the work. I don't want anything to do with love when I'm at work. Work's work–'

'And what is love?' she asked. 'Has it to have special hours?'

'Yes; out of work hours.'

'And you'll regulate it according to Mr Jordan's closing time?'

'Yes; and according to the freedom from business of any sort.'

'It is only to exist in spare time?'

'That's all, and not always then–not the kissing sort of love.'

'And that's all you think of it?'

'It's quite enough.'

'I'm glad you think so.'

And she was cold to him for some time–she hated him; and while she was cold and contemptuous, he was uneasy till she had forgiven him again. But when they started afresh they were not any nearer. He kept her because he never satisfied her.

In the spring they went together to the seaside. They had rooms at a little cottage near Theddlethorpe, and lived as man and wife. Mrs Radford sometimes went with them.

It was known in Nottingham that Paul Morel and Mrs Dawes were going together, but as nothing was very obvious, and Clara was always a solitary person, and he seemed so simple and innocent, it did not make much difference.

He loved the Lincolnshire coast, and she loved the sea. In the early morning they often went out together to bathe. The grey of the dawn, the far, desolate reaches of the fenland smitten with winter, the sea-meadows rank with herbage, were stark enough to rejoice his soul. As they stepped on to the highroad from their plank bridge, and looked round at the endless monotony of levels, the land a little darker than the sky, the sea sounding small beyond the sandhills, his heart filled strong with the sweeping relentlessness of life. She loved him then. He was solitary and strong, and his eyes had a beautiful light.

They shuddered with cold; then he raced her down the road to the green turf bridge. She could run well. Her colour soon came, her throat was bare, her eyes shone. He loved her for being so luxuriously heavy, and yet so quick. Himself was light; she went with a beautiful rush. They grew warm, and walked hand in hand.

A flush came into the sky, the wan moon, half-way down the west, sank into insignificance. On the shadowy land things began to take life, plants with great leaves became distinct. They came through a pass in the big, cold sandhills on to the beach. The long waste of foreshore lay moaning under the dawn and the sea; the ocean was a flat dark strip with a white edge. Over the gloomy sea the sky was red. Quickly the fire spread among the clouds and scattered them. Crimson burned to orange, orange to dull gold, and in a golden glitter the sun came up, dribbling fierily over the waves in little splashes, as if someone had gone along and the light had spilled from her pail as she walked.

The breakers ran down the shore in long, hoarse strokes. Tiny seagulls, like specks of spray, wheeled above the line of surf. Their crying seemed larger than they. Far away the coast reached out, and melted into the morning, the tussocky sandhills seeming to sink to a level with the beach. Mablethorpe was tiny on their right. They had alone the space of all this level shore, the sea, and the upcoming sun, the faint noise of the waters, the sharp crying of the gulls.

They had a warm hollow in the sandhills where the wind did not come. He stood looking out to sea.

'It's very fine,' he said.

'Now don't get sentimental,' she said.

It irritated her to see him standing gazing at the sea, like a solitary and poetic person. He laughed. She quickly undressed.

'There are some fine waves this morning,' she said triumphantly. She was a better swimmer than he; he stood idly watching her.

'Aren't you coming?' she said.

'In a minute,' he answered.

She was white and velvet skinned, with heavy shoulders. A little wind, coming from the sea, blew across her body and ruffled her hair.

The morning was of a lovely limpid gold colour. Veils of shadow seemed to be drifting away on the north and the south. Clara stood shrinking slightly from the touch of the wind, twisting her hair. The sea-grass rose behind the white stripped woman. She glanced at the sea, then looked at him. He was watching her with dark eyes which she loved and could not understand. She hugged her breasts between her arms, cringing, laughing:

'Oo, it will be so cold!' she said.

He bent forward and kissed her, held her suddenly close, and kissed her again. She stood waiting. He looked into her eyes, then away at the pale sands.

'Go, then!' he said quietly.

She flung her arms round his neck, drew him against her, kissed him passionately, and went, saying:

'But you'll come in?'

'In a minute.'

She went plodding heavily over the sand that was soft as velvet. He, on the sandhills, watched the great pale coast envelop her. She grew smaller, lost proportion, seemed only like a large white bird toiling forward.

'Not much more than a big white pebble on the beach, not much more than a slot of foam being blown and rolled over the sand,' he said to himself.

She seemed to move very slowly across the vast sounding shore. As he watched, he lost her. She was dazzled out of sight by the sunshine. Again he saw her, the merest white speck moving against the white, muttering sea-edge.

'Look how little she is!' he said to himself. 'She's lost like a grain of sand in the beach—just a concentrated speck blown along, a tiny white foam-bubble, almost nothing among the morning. Why does she absorb me?'

The morning was altogether interrupted: she was gone in the water. Far and wide the beach, the sandhills with their blue marrain, the shining water, glowed together in immense, unbroken solitude.

'What is she, after all?' he said to himself. 'Here's the seacoast morning, big and permanent and beautiful; there is she, fretting, always unsatisfied, and temporary as a bubble of foam. What does she mean to me, after all? She represents something, like a bubble of foam represents the sea. But what is *she*? It's not her I care for.'

Then, startled by his own unconscious thoughts, that seemed to speak so distinctly that all the morning could hear, he undressed and ran quickly down the sands. She was watching for him. Her arm flashed up to him, she heaved on a wave, subsided, her shoulders in a pool of liquid silver. He jumped through the breakers, and in a moment her hand was on his shoulder.

He was a poor swimmer, and could not stay long in the water. She played round him in triumph, sporting with her superiority, which he begrudged her. The sunshine stood deep and fine on the water. They laughed in the sea for a minute or two, then raced each other back to the sandhills.

When they were drying themselves, panting heavily, he watched her laughing, breathless face, her bright shoulders, her breasts that swayed and made him frightened as she rubbed them, and he thought again:

'But she is magnificent, and even bigger than the morning and the sea. Is she–? Is she–?'

She, seeing his dark eyes fixed on her, broke off from her drying with a laugh.

'What are you looking at?' she said.

'You,' he answered, laughing.

Her eyes met his, and in a moment he was kissing her white 'goose-fleshed' shoulder, and thinking:

'What is she? What is she?

She loved him in the morning. There was something detached, hard, and elemental about his kisses then, as if he were only conscious of his own will, not in the least of her and her wanting him.

Later in the day he went out sketching.

'You,' he said to her, 'go with your mother to Sutton. I am so dull.'

She stood and looked at him. He knew she wanted to come with him, but he preferred to be alone. She made him feel imprisoned when she was there, as if he could not get a free deep breath, as if there were something on top of him. She felt his desire to be free of her.

In the evening he came back to her. They walked down the shore in the darkness, then sat for awhile in the shelter of the sandhills.

'It seems,' she said, as they stared over the darkness of the sea, where no light was to be seen–'it seems as if you only loved me at night–as if you didn't love me in the daytime.'

He ran the cold sand through his fingers, feeling guilty under the accusation.

'The night is free to you,' he replied. 'In the daytime I want to be by myself.'

'But why?' she said. 'Why, even now, when we are on this short holiday?'

'I don't know. Love-making stifles me in the daytime.'

'But it needn't be always love-making,' she said.

'It always is,' he answered, 'when you and I are together.'

She sat feeling very bitter.

'Do you ever want to marry me?' he asked curiously.

'Do you me?' she replied.

'Yes, yes; I should like us to have children,' he answered slowly.

She sat with her head bent, fingering the sand.

'But you don't really want a divorce from Baxter, do you?' he said.

It was some minutes before she replied.

'No,' she said, very deliberately; 'I don't think I do.'

'Why?'

'I don't know.'

'Do you feel as if you belonged to him?'

'No; I don't think so.'

'What, then?'

'I think he belongs to me,' she replied.

He was silent for some minutes, listening to the wind blowing over the hoarse, dark sea.

'And you never really intended to belong to *me*?' he said.

'Yes, I do belong to you,' she answered.

'No,' he said; 'because you don't want to be divorced.'

It was a knot they could not untie, so they left it, took what they could get, and what they could not attain they ignored.

'I consider you treated Baxter rottenly,' he said another time.

He half expected Clara to answer him, as his mother would: 'You consider your own affairs, and don't know so much about other people's.' But she took him seriously, almost to his own surprise.

'Why?' she said.

'I suppose you thought he was a lily of the valley, and so you put him in an appropriate pot, and tended him according. You made up your mind he was a lily of the valley, and it was no good his being a cow-parsnip. You wouldn't have it.'

'I certainly never imagined him a lily of the valley.'

'You imagined him something he wasn't. That's just what a woman is. She thinks she knows what's good for a man, and she's going to see he gets it; and no matter if he's starving, he may sit and whistle for what he needs, while she's got him, and is giving him what's good for him.'

'And what are you doing?' she asked.

'I'm thinking what tune I shall whistle,' he laughed.

And instead of boxing his ears, she considered him in earnest.

'You think I want to give you what's good for you?' she asked.

'I hope so; but love should give a sense of freedom, not of prison. Miriam made me feel tied up like a donkey to a stake. I must feed on her patch, and nowhere else. It's sickening!'

'And would *you* let a *woman* do as she likes?'

'Yes; I'll see that she *likes* to love me. If she doesn't–well, I don't hold her.'

'If you were as wonderful as you say–' replied Clara.

'I should be the marvel I am,' he laughed.

There was a silence in which they hated each other, though they laughed.

'Love's a dog in the manger,' he said.

'And which of us is the dog?' she asked.

'Oh well, you, of course.'

So there went on a battle between them. She knew she never fully had him. Some part, big and vital in him, she had no hold over; nor did she ever try to get it, or even to realize what it was. And he knew in some way that she held herself still as Mrs Dawes. She did not love Dawes, never had loved him; but she believed he loved her, at least depended on her. She felt a certain surety about him that she never felt with Paul Morel. Her passion for the young man had filled her soul, given her a certain satisfaction, eased her of her self-mistrust, her doubt. Whatever else she was, she was inwardly assured. It was almost as if she had gained *herself,* and stood now distinct and complete. She had received her confirmation; but she never believed that her life belonged to Paul Morel, nor his to her. They would separate in the end, and the rest of her life would be an ache after him. But at any rate, she *knew* now, she was sure of herself. And the same could almost be said of him. Together they had received the baptism of life, each through the other; but now their missions were separate. Where he wanted to go she could not come with him. They would have to part sooner or later. Even if they married, and were faithful to each other, still he would have to leave her, go on alone, and she would only have to attend to him when he came home. But it was not possible. Each wanted a mate to go side by side with.

Clara had gone to live with her mother upon Mapperley Plains. One evening, as Paul and she were walking along Woodborough Road, they met Dawes.

Morel knew something about the bearing of the man approaching, but he was absorbed in his thinking at the moment, so that only his artist's eye watched the form of the stranger. Then he suddenly turned to Clara with a laugh, and put his hand on her shoulder, saying, laughing:

'But we walk side by side, and yet I'm in London arguing with an imaginary Orpen; and where are you?'

At that instant Dawes passed, almost touching Morel. The young man glanced, saw the dark brown eyes burning, full of hate and yet tired.

'Who was that?' he asked of Clara.

'It was Baxter,' she replied.

Paul took his hand from her shoulder and glanced round; then he saw again distinctly the man's form as it approached him. Dawes still walked erect, with his fine shoulders flung back, and his face lifted; but there was a furtive look in his eyes that gave one the impression he was trying to get unnoticed past every person he met, glancing suspiciously to see what they thought of him. And his hands seemed to be wanting to hide. He wore old clothes, the trousers were torn at the knee, and the handkerchief tied round his throat was dirty; but his cap was still defiantly over one eye. As she saw him, Clara felt guilty. There was a tiredness and despair on his face that made her hate him, because it hurt her.

'He looks shady,' said Paul.

But the note of pity in his voice reproached her, and made her feel hard.

'His true commonness comes out,' she answered.

'Do you hate him?' he asked.

'You talk,' she said, 'about the cruelty of women; I wish you knew the cruelty of men in their brute force. They simply don't know that the woman exists.'

'Don't *I*?' he said.

'No,' she answered.

'Don't I know you exist?'

'About *me* you know nothing,' she said bitterly–'about *me!*'

'Not more than Baxter knew?' he asked.

'Perhaps not as much.'

He felt puzzled, and helpless, and angry. There she walked unknown to him, though they had been through such experience together.

'But you know *me* pretty well,' he said.

She did not answer.

'Did you know Baxter as well as you know me?' he asked.   'He wouldn't let me,' she said.

'And I have let you know me?'

'It's what men *won't* let you do. They won't let you get really near to them,' she said.

'And haven't I let you?'

'Yes,' she answered slowly; 'but you've never come near to me. You can't come out of yourself, you can't. Baxter could do that better than you.'

He walked on pondering. He was angry with her for preferring Baxter to him.

'You begin to value Baxter now you've not got him,' he said.

'No; I can only see where he was different from you.'

But he felt she had a grudge against him.

One evening, as they were coming home over the fields, she startled him by asking:

'Do you think it's worth it–the–the sex part?'

'The act of loving, itself?'

'Yes; is it worth anything to you?'

'But how can you separate it?' he said. 'It's the culmination of everything. All our intimacy culminates then.'

'Not for me,' she said.

He was silent. A flash of hate for her came up. After all, she was dissatisfied with him, even there, where he thought they fulfilled each other. But he believed her too implicitly.

'I feel,' she continued slowly, 'as if I hadn't got you, as if all you weren't there, and as if it weren't *me* you were taking–'

'Who, then?'

'Something just for yourself. It has been fine, so that I daren't think of it. But is it *me* you want, or is it *It*?'

He again felt guilty. Did he leave Clara out of count, and take simply woman? But he thought that was splitting a hair.

'When I had Baxter, actually had him, then I *did* feel as if I had all of him,' she said.

'And it was better?' he asked.

'Yes, yes; it was more whole. I don't say you haven't given me more than he ever gave me.'

'Or could give you.'

'Yes, perhaps; but you've never given me yourself.'

He knitted his brows angrily.

'If I start to make love to you,' he said, 'I just go like a leaf down the wind.'

'And leave me out of count,' she said.

'And then it is nothing to you?' he asked, almost rigid with chagrin.

'It's something; and sometimes you have carried me away–right away–I know–and–I reverence you for it–but–'

'Don't ''but'' me,' he said, kissing her quickly, as a fire ran through him.

She submitted, and was silent.

It was true as he said. As a rule, when he started love-making, the emotion was strong enough to carry with it everything–reason, soul, blood–in a great sweep, like the Trent carries bodily its back-swirls and intertwinings, noiselessly. Gradually the little criticism, the little sensations, were lost, thought also went, everything borne along in one flood. He became, not a man with a mind, but a great instinct. His hands were like creatures, living; his limbs, his body, were all life and consciousness, subject to no will of his, but living in themselves. Just as he was, so it seemed the vigorous, wintry stars were strong also with life. He and they struck with the same pulse of fire, and the same joy of strength which held the bracken-frond stiff near his eyes held his own body firm. It was as if he, and the stars, and the dark herbage, and Clara were licked up in an immense tongue of flame, which tore onwards and upwards. Everything rushed along in living beside him; everything was still, perfect in itself, along with him. This wonderful stillness in each thing in itself, while it was being borne along in a very ecstasy of living, seemed the highest point of bliss.

And Clara knew this held him to her, so she trusted altogether to the passion. It, however, failed her very often. They did not often reach again the height of that once when the peewits had called. Gradually, some mechanical effort spoilt their loving, or, when they had splendid moments, they had them separately, and not so satisfactorily. So often he seemed merely to be running on alone; often they realized it had been a failure, not what they had wanted. He left her, knowing *that* evening had only made a little split between them. Their loving grew more mechanical, without the marvellous glamour. Gradually they began to introduce novelties, to get back some of the feeling of satisfaction. They would be very near, almost dangerously near to the river, so that the black water ran not far from his face, and it gave a little thrill; or they loved sometimes in a little hollow below the fence of the path where people were passing occasionally, on the edge of the town, and they heard footsteps coming, almost felt the vibration of the tread, and they heard what the passers-by said – strange little things that were never intended to be heard. And afterwards each of them was rather ashamed, and these things caused a distance between the two of them. He began to despise her a little, as if she had merited it!

One night he left her to go to Daybrook Station over the fields. It was very dark, with an attempt at snow, although the spring was so far advanced. Morel had not much time; he plunged forward. The town ceases almost abruptly on the edge of a steep hollow; there the houses with their yellow lights stand up against the darkness. He went over the stile, and dropped quickly into the hollow of the fields. Under the orchard one warm window shone in Swineshead Farm. Paul glanced round. Behind, the houses stood on the brim of the dip, black against the sky, like wild beasts glaring curiously with yellow eyes down into the darkness. It was the town that seemed savage and uncouth, glaring on the clouds at the back of him. Some creature stirred under the willows of the farm pond. It was too dark to distinguish anything.

He was close up to the next stile before he·saw a dark shape leaning against it. The man moved aside.

'Good evening!' he said.

'Good evening!' Morel answered, not noticing.

'Paul Morel?' said the man.

Then he knew it was Dawes. The man stopped his way.

'I've got yer, have I?' he said awkwardly.

'I shall miss my train,' said Paul.

He could see nothing of Dawes's face. The man's teeth seemed to chatter as he talked.

'You're going to get it from me now,' said Dawes.

Morel attempted to move forward; the other man stepped in front of him.

'Are yer goin' to take that top-coat off,' he said, 'or are you goin' to lie down to it?'

Paul was afraid the man was mad.

'But,' he said, 'I don't know how to fight.'

'All right, then,' answered Dawes, and before the younger man knew where he was he was staggering backwards from a blow across the face.

The whole night went black. He tore off his overcoat and coat, dodging a blow, and flung the garments over Dawes. The latter swore savagely. Morel, in his shirtsleeves, was now alert and furious. He felt his whole body unsheath itself like a claw. He could not fight, so he would use his wits. The other man became more distinct to him; he could see particularly the shirt-breast. Dawes stumbled over Paul's coats, then came rushing forward. The young man's mouth was bleeding. It was the other man's mouth he was dying to get at, and the desire was anguish in its strength. He stepped quickly through the stile, and as Dawes was coming through after him, like a flash he got a blow in over the other's mouth. He shivered with pleasure. Dawes advanced slowly, spitting.

Paul was afraid; he moved round to get to the stile again. Suddenly, from out of nowhere, came a great blow against his ear, that sent him falling helpless backwards. He heard Dawes's heavy panting, like a wild beast's; then came a kick on the knee, giving him such agony that he got up and, quite blind, leapt clean under his enemy's guard. He felt blows and kicks, but they did not hurt. He hung on to the bigger man like a wild cat, till at last Dawes fell with a crash, losing his presence of mind. Paul went down with him. Pure instinct brought his hands to the man's neck, and before Dawes, in frenzy and agony, could wrench him free, he had got his fists twisted in the scarf and his knuckles dug in the throat of the other man. He was a pure instinct, without reason or feeling. His body, hard and wonderful in itself, cleaved against the struggling body of the other man; not a muscle in him relaxed. He was quite unconscious, only his body had taken upon itself to kill this other man. For himself, he had neither feeling nor reason. He lay pressed hard against his adversary, his body adjusting itself to its one pure purpose of choking the other man, resisting exactly at the right moment, with exactly the right amount of strength, the struggles of the other, silent, intent, unchanging, gradually pressing its knuckles deeper, feeling the struggles of the other body become wilder and more frenzied. Tighter and tighter grew his body, like a screw that is gradually increasing in pressure, till something breaks.

Then suddenly he relaxed, full of wonder and misgiving. Dawes had been yielding. Morel felt his body flame with pain, as he realized what he was doing; he was all bewildered. Dawes's struggles suddenly renewed themselves in a furious spasm. Paul's hands were wrenched, torn out of the scarf in which they were knotted, and he was flung away, helpless. He heard the horrid sound of the other's gasping, but he lay stunned; then, still dazed, he felt the blows of the other's feet, and lost consciousness.

Dawes, grunting with pain like a beast, was kicking the prostrate body of his rival. Suddenly the whistle of the train shrieked two fields away. He turned round and glared suspiciously. What was coming? He saw the lights of the train draw across his vision. It seemed to him people were approaching. He made off across the field into Nottingham, and dimly in his consciousness as he went, he felt on his foot the place where his boot had knocked against one of the lad's bones. The knock seemed to re-echo inside him; he hurried to get away from it.

Morel gradually came to himself. He knew where he was and what had happened, but he did not want to move. He lay still, with tiny bits of snow tickling his face. It was pleasant to lie quite, quite still. The time passed. It was the bits of snow that kept rousing him when he did not want to be roused. At last his will clicked into action.

'I mustn't lie here,' he said; 'it's silly.'

But still he did not move.

'I said I was going to get up,' he repeated. 'Why don't I?'

And still it was some time before he had sufficiently pulled himself together to stir; then gradually he got up. Pain made him sick and dazed, but his brain was clear. Reeling, he groped for his coats and got them on, buttoning his overcoat up to his ears. It was some time before he found his cap. He did not know whether his face was still bleeding. Walking blindly, every step making him sick with pain, he went back to the pond and washed his face and hands. The icy water hurt, but helped to bring him back to himself. He crawled back up the hill to the tram. He wanted to get to his mother—he must get to his mother—that was his blind intention. He covered his face as much as he could, and struggled sickly along. Continually the ground seemed to fall away from him as he walked, and he felt himself dropping with a sickening feeling into space; so, like a nightmare, he got through with the journey home.

Everybody was in bed. He looked at himself. His face was discoloured and smeared with blood, almost like a dead man's face. He washed it, and went to bed. The night went by in delirium. In the morning he found his mother looking at him. Her blue eyes – they were all he wanted to see. She was there; he was in her hands.

'It's not much, mother,' he said. 'It was Baxter Dawes.'

'Tell me where it hurts you,' she said quietly.

'I don't know – my shoulder. Say it was a bicycle accident, mother.'

He could not move his arm. Presently Minnie, the little servant, came upstairs with some tea.

'Your mother's nearly frightened me out of my wits – fainted away,' she said.

He felt he could not bear it. His mother nursed him; he told her about it.

'And now I should have done with them all,' she said quietly.

'I will, mother.'

She covered him up.

'And don't think about it,' she said – 'only try to go to sleep. The doctor won't be here till eleven.'

He had a dislocated shoulder, and the second day acute bronchitis set in. His mother was pale as death now, and very thin. She would sit and look at him, then away into space. There was something between them that neither dared mention. Clara came to see him. Afterwards he said to his mother:

'She makes me tired, mother.'

'Yes; I wish she wouldn't come,' Mrs Morel replied.

Another day Miriam came, but she seemed almost like a stranger to him.

'You know, I don't care about them, mother,' he said.

'I'm afraid you don't, my son,' she replied sadly.

It was given out everywhere that it was a bicycle accident. Soon he was able to go to work again, but now there was a constant sickness and gnawing at his heart. He went to Clara, but there seemed, as it were, nobody there. He could not work. He and his mother seemed almost to avoid each other. There was some secret between them which they could not bear. He was not aware of it. He only knew that his life seemed unbalanced, as if it were going to smash into pieces.

Clara did not know what was the matter with him. She realized that he seemed unaware of her. Even when he came to her he seemed unaware of her; always he was somewhere else. She felt she was clutching for him, and he was somewhere else. It tortured her, and so she tortured him. For a month at a time she kept him at arm's length. He almost hated her, and was driven to her in spite of himself. He went mostly into the company of men, was always at the George or the White Horse. His mother was ill, distant, quiet, shadowy. He was terrified of something; he dared not look at her. Her eyes seemed to grow darker, her face more waxen; still she dragged about at her work.

At Whitsuntide he said he would go to Blackpool for four days with his friend Newton. The latter was a big, jolly fellow, with a touch of the bounder about him. Paul said his mother must go to Sheffield to stay a week with Annie, who lived there. Perhaps the change would do her good. Mrs Morel was attending a woman's doctor in Nottingham. He said her heart and her digestion were wrong. She consented to go to Sheffield, though she did not want to; but now she would do everything her son wished of her. Paul said he would come for her on the fifth day, and stay also in Sheffield till the holiday was up. It was agreed.

The two young men set off gaily for Blackpool. Mrs Morel was quite lively as Paul kissed her and left her. Once at the station, he forgot everything. Four days were clear—not an anxiety, not a thought. The two young men simply enjoyed themselves. Paul was like another man. None of himself remained—no Clara, no Miriam, no mother that fretted him. He wrote to them all, and long letters to his mother; but they were jolly letters that made her laugh. He was having a good time, as young fellows will in a place like Blackpool. And underneath it all was a shadow for her.

Paul was very gay, excited at the thought of staying with his mother in Sheffield. Newton was to spend the day with them. Their train was late. Joking, laughing, with their pipes between their teeth, the young men swung their bags on to the tram-car. Paul had bought his mother a little collar of real lace that he wanted to see her wear, so that he could tease her about it.

Annie lived in a nice house, and had a little maid. Paul ran gaily up the steps. He expected his mother laughing in the hall, but it was Annie who opened to him. She seemed distant to him. He stood a second in dismay. Annie let him kiss her cheek.

'Is my mother ill?' he said.

'Yes; she's not very well. Don't upset her.'

'Is she in bed?'

'Yes.'

And then the queer feeling went over him, as if all the sunshine had gone out of him, and it was all shadow. He dropped the bag and ran upstairs. Hesitating, he opened the door. His mother sat up in bed, wearing a dressing-gown of old rose colour. She looked at him almost as if she were ashamed of herself, pleading to him, humble. He saw the ashy look about her.

'Mother!' he said.

'I thought you were never coming,' she answered gaily.

But he only fell on his knees at the bedside, and buried his face in the bedclothes, crying in agony, and saying:

'Mother—mother—mother!'

She stroked his hair slowly with her thin hand.

'Don't cry,' she said. 'Don't cry—it's nothing.'

But he felt as if his blood was melting into tears, and he cried in terror and pain.

'Don't—don't cry,' his mother faltered.

Slowly she stroked his hair. Shocked out of himself, he cried, and the tears hurt in every fibre of his body. Suddenly he stopped, but he dared not lift his face out of the bedclothes.

'You *are* late. Where have you been?' his mother asked.

'The train was late,' he replied, muffled in the sheet.

'Yes; that miserable Central! Is Newton come?'

'Yes.'

'I'm sure you must be hungry, and they've kept dinner waiting.'

With a wrench he looked up at her.

'What is it, mother?' he asked brutally.

She averted her eyes as she answered:

'Only a bit of a tumour, my boy. You needn't trouble. It's been there—the lump has—a long time.'

Up came the tears again. His mind was clear and hard, but his body was crying.

'Where?' he said.

She put her hand on her side.

'Here. But you know they can sweal a tumour away.'

He stood feeling dazed and helpless, like a child. He thought perhaps it was as she said. Yes; he reassured himself it was so. But all the while his blood and his body knew definitely what it was. He sat down on the bed, and took her hand. She had never had but the one ring–her wedding ring.

'When were you poorly?' he asked.

'It was yesterday it began,' she answered submissively.

'Pains!'

'Yes; but not more than I've often had at home. I believe Dr Ansell is an alarmist.'

'You ought not to have travelled alone,' he said, to himself more than to her.

'As if that had anything to do with it!' she answered quickly.

They were silent for a while.

'Now go and have your dinner,' she said. 'You *must* be hungry.'

'Have you had yours?'

'Yes; a beautiful sole I had. Annie *is* good to me.'

They talked a little while, then he went downstairs. He was very white and strained. Newton sat in miserable sympathy.

After dinner he went into the scullery to help Annie to wash up. The little maid had gone on an errand.

'Is it really a tumour?' he asked.

Annie began to cry again.

'The pain she had yesterday–I never saw anybody suffer like it!' she cried. 'Leonard ran like a madman for Dr Ansell, and when she'd got to bed she said to me: "Annie, look at this lump on my side. I wonder what it is?" And there I looked, and I thought I should have dropped. Paul, as true as I'm here, it's a lump as big as my double fist. I said: "Good gracious, mother, whenever did that come?" "Why, child," she said, "it's been there a long time." I thought I should have died, our Paul, I did. She's been having these pains for months at home, and nobody looking after her.'

The tears came to his eyes, then dried suddenly.

'But she's been attending the doctor in Nottingham–and she never told me,' he said.

'If I'd have been at home,' said Annie, 'I should have seen for myself.'

He felt like a man walking in unrealities. In the afternoon he went to see the doctor. The latter was a shrewd, lovable man.

'But what is it?' he said.

The doctor looked at the young man, then knitted his fingers.

'It may be a large tumour which has formed in the membrane,' he said slowly, 'and which we *may* be able to make go away.'

'Can't you operate?' asked Paul.

'Not there,' replied the doctor.

'Are you sure?'

'*Quite!*'

Paul meditated a while.

'Are you sure it's a tumour?' he asked. 'Why did Dr Jameson in Nottingham never find out anything about it? She's been going to him for weeks, and he's treated her for heart and indigestion.'

'Mrs Morel never told Dr Jameson about the lump,' said the doctor.

'And do you *know* it's a tumour?'

'No, I am not sure.'

'What else *might* it be? You asked my sister if there was cancer in the family. Might it be cancer?'

'I don't know.'

'And what shall you do?'

'I should like an examination, with Dr Jameson.'

'Then have one.'

'You must arrange about that. His fee wouldn't be less than ten guineas to come here from Nottingham.'

'When would you like him to come?'

'I will call in this evening, and we will talk it over.'

Paul went away, biting his lip.

His mother could come downstairs for tea, the doctor said. Her son went upstairs to help her. She wore the old-rose dressing-gown that Leonard had given Annie, and, with a little colour in her face, was quite young again.

'But you look quite pretty in that,' he said.

'Yes; they make me so fine, I hardly know myself,' she answered.

But when she stood up to walk, the colour went. Paul helped her, half carrying her. At the top of the stairs she was gone. He lifted her up and carried her quickly downstairs; laid her on the couch. She was light and frail. Her face looked as if she were dead, with the blue lips shut tight. Her eyes opened—her blue, unfailing eyes—and she looked at him pleadingly, almost wanting him to forgive her. He held brandy to her lips, but her mouth would not open. All the time she watched him lovingly. She was only sorry for him. The tears ran down his face without ceasing, but not a muscle moved. He was intent on getting a little brandy between her lips. Soon she was able to swallow a teaspoonful. She lay back so tired. The tears continued to run down his face.

'But,' she panted, 'it'll go off. Don't cry!'

'I'm not doing,' he said.

After a while she was better again. He was kneeling beside the couch. They looked into each other's eyes.

'I don't want you to make a trouble of it,' she said.

'No, mother. You'll have to be quite still, and then you'll get better soon.'

But he was white to the lips, and their eyes as they looked at each other understood. Her eyes were so blue—such a wonderful forget-me-not blue! He felt if only they had been of a different colour he could have borne it better. His heart seemed to be ripping slowly in his breast. He kneeled there, holding her hand, and neither said anything. Then Annie came in.

'Are you all right?' she murmured timidly to her mother.

'Of course,' said Mrs Morel.

Paul sat down and told her about Blackpool. She was curious.

A day or two after, he went to see Dr Jameson in Nottingham, to arrange for a consultation. Paul had practically no money in the world. But he could borrow.

His mother had been used to go to the public consultation on Saturday morning, when she could see the doctor for only a nominal sum. Her son went on the same day. The waiting-room was full of poor women, who sat patiently on a bench around the wall. Paul thought of his mother, in her little black costume, sitting waiting likewise. The doctor was late. The women all looked rather frightened. Paul asked the nurse in attendance if he could see the doctor immediately he came. It was arranged so. The women sitting patiently round the walls of the room eyed the young man curiously.

At last the doctor came. He was about forty, good-looking, brown-skinned. His wife had died, and he, who had loved her, had specialized on women's ailments. Paul told his name and his mother's. The doctor did not remember.

'Number forty-six M,' said the nurse; and the doctor looked up the case in his book.

'There is a big lump that may be a tumour,' said Paul. 'But Dr Ansell was going to write you a letter.'

'Ah, yes!' replied the doctor, drawing the letter from his pocket. He was very friendly, affable, busy, kind. He would come to Sheffield the next day.

'What is your father?' he asked.

'He is a coal-miner,' replied Paul.

'Not very well off, I suppose?'

'This—I see after this,' said Paul.

'And you?' smiled the doctor.

'I am a clerk in Jordan's Appliance Factory.'

The doctor smiled at him.

'Er—to go to Sheffield!' he said, putting the tips of his fingers together, and smiling with his eyes. 'Eight guineas?'

'Thank you!' said Paul, flushing and rising. 'And you'll come to-morrow?'

'To-morrow—Sunday? Yes! Can you tell me about what time there is a train in the afternoon?'

'There is a Central gets in at four-fifteen.'

'And will there be any way of getting up to the house? Shall I have to walk?' The doctor smiled.

'There is the tram,' said Paul; 'the Western Park tram.'

The doctor made a note of it.

'Thank you!' he said, and shook hands.

Then Paul went on home to see his father, who was left in the charge of Minnie. Walter Morel was getting very grey now. Paul found him digging in the garden. He had written him a letter. He shook hands with his father.

'Hello, son! Tha has landed, then?' said the father.

'Yes,' replied the son. 'But I'm going back to-night.'

'Are ter, beguy!' exclaimed the collier. 'An' has ter eaten owt?'

'No.'

'That's just like thee,' said Morel. 'Come thy ways in.'

The father was afraid of the mention of his wife. The two went indoors. Paul ate in silence; his father, with earthy hands, and sleeves rolled up, sat in the arm-chair opposite and looked at him.

'Well, an' how is she?' asked the miner at length, in a little voice.

'She can sit up; she can be carried down for tea,' said Paul.

'That's a blessin'!' exclaimed Morel. 'I hope we s'll soon be havin' her whoam, then. An' what's that Nottingham doctor say?'

'He's going to-morrow to have an examination of her.'

'Is he beguy! That's a tidy penny, I'm thinkin'!'

'Eight guineas.'

'Eight guineas!' The miner spoke breathlessly. 'Well, we mun find it from somewhere.'

'I can pay that,' said Paul.

There was a silence between them for some time.

'She says she hopes you're getting on all right with Minnie,' Paul said.

'Yes, I'm all right, an' I wish as she was,' answered Morel. 'But Minnie's a good little wench, bless 'er heart!' He sat looking dismal.

'I s'll have to be going at half-past three,' said Paul.

'It's a trapse for thee, lad! Eight guineas! An' when dost think she'll be able to get as far as this?'

'We must see what the doctors say to-morrow,' Paul said.

Morel sighed deeply. The house seemed strangely empty, and Paul thought his father looked lost, forlorn, and old.

'You'll have to go and see her next week, father,' he said.

'I hope she'll be a-whoam by that time,' said Morel.

'If she's not,' said Paul, 'then you must come.'

'I dunno wheer I s'll find th' money,' said Morel.

'And I'll write to you what the doctor says,' said Paul.

'But tha writes i' such a fashion, I canna ma'e it out,' said Morel.

'Well, I'll write plain.'

It was no good asking Morel to answer, for he could scarcely do more than write his own name.

The doctor came. Leonard felt it his duty to meet him with a cab. The examination did not take long. Annie, Arthur, Paul, and Leonard were waiting in the parlour anxiously. The doctors came down. Paul glanced at them. He had never had any hope, except when he had deceived himself.

'It *may* be a tumour; we must wait and see,' said Dr Jameson.

'And if it is,' said Annie, 'can you sweal it away?'

'Probably,' said the doctor.

Paul put eight sovereigns and half a sovereign on the table. The doctor counted them, took a florin out of his purse, and put that down.

'Thank you!' he said. 'I'm sorry Mrs Morel is so ill. But we must see what we can do.'

'There can't be an operation?' said Paul.

The doctor shook his head.

'No,' he said; 'and even if there could, her heart wouldn't stand it.'

'Is her heart risky?' asked Paul.

'Yes; you must be careful with her.'

'Very risky?'

'No–er–no, no! Just take care.'

And the doctor was gone.

Then Paul carried his mother downstairs. She lay simply, like a child. But when he was on the stairs, she put her arms round his neck, clinging.

'I'm so frightened of these beastly stairs,' she said.

And he was frightened, too. He would let Leonard do it another time. He felt he could not carry her.

'He thinks it's only a tumour!' cried Annie to her mother. 'And he can sweal it away.'

'I *knew* he could,' protested Mrs Morel scornfully.

She pretended not to notice that Paul had gone out of the room. He sat in the kitchen, smoking. Then he tried to brush some grey ash off his coat. He looked again. It was one of his mother's grey hairs. It was so long! He held it up, and it drifted into the chimney. He let go. The long grey hair floated and was gone in the blackness of the chimney.

The next day he kissed her before going back to work. It was very early in the morning, and they were alone.

'You won't fret, my boy! she said.

'No, mother.'

'No; it would be silly. And take care of yourself.'

'Yes,' he answered. Then, after a while: 'And I shall come next Saturday, and shall bring my father?'

'I suppose he wants to come,' she replied. 'At any rate, if he does you'll have to let him.'

He kissed her again, and stroked the hair from her temples, gently, tenderly, as if she were a lover.

'Shan't you be late?' she murmured.

'I'm going,' he said, very low.

Still he sat a few minutes, stroking the brown and grey hair from her temples.

'And you won't be any worse, mother?'

'No, my son.'

'You promise me?'

'Yes; I won't be any worse.'

He kissed her, held her in his arms for a moment, and was gone. In the early sunny morning he ran to the station, crying all the way; he did not know what for. And her blue eyes were wide and staring as she thought of him.

In the afternoon he went a walk with Clara. They sat in the little wood where bluebells were standing. He took her hand.

'You'll see,' he said to Clara, 'she'll never be better.'

'Oh, you don't know!' replied the other.

'I do,' he said.

She caught him impulsively to her breast.

'Try and forget it, dear,' she said; 'try and forget it.'

'I will,' he answered.

Her breast was there, warm for him; her hands were in his hair. It was comforting and he held his arms round her. But he did not forget. He only talked to Clara of something else. And it was always so. When she felt it coming, the agony, she cried to him:

'Don't think of it, Paul! Don't think of it, Paul! Don't think of it, my darling!'

And she pressed him to her breast, rocked him, soothed him like a child. So he put the trouble aside for her sake, to take it up again immediately he was alone. All the time, as he went about, he cried mechanically. His mind and hands were busy. He cried, he did not know why. It was his blood weeping. He was just as much alone whether he was with Clara or with the men in the White Horse. Just himself and this pressure inside him, that was all that existed. He read sometimes. He had to keep his mind occupied. And Clara was a way of occupying his mind.

On the Saturday Walter Morel went to Sheffield. He was a forlorn figure, looking rather as if nobody owned him. Paul ran upstairs.

'My father's come,' he said, kissing his mother.

'Has he?' she answered wearily.

The old collier came rather frightened into the bedroom.

'How dun I find thee, lass?' he said, going forward and kissing her in a hasty, timid fashion.

'Well, I'm middlin',' she replied.

'I see tha art,' he said. He stood looking down on her. Then he wiped his eyes with his handkerchief. Helpless, and as if nobody owned him, he looked.

'Have you gone on all right?' asked the wife, rather wearily, as if it were an effort to talk to him.

'Yis,' he answered. ''Er's a bit behint-hand now and again, as yer might expect.'

'Does she have your dinner ready?' asked Mrs Morel.

'Well, I've 'ad to shout at 'er once or twice,' he said.

'And you *must* shout at her if she's not ready. She *will* leave things to the last minute.'

She gave him a few instructions. He sat looking at her as if she were almost a stranger to him, before whom he was awkward and humble, and also as if he had lost his presence of mind, and wanted to run. This feeling that he wanted to run away, that he was on thorns to be gone from so trying a situation, and yet must linger because it looked better, made his presence so trying. He put up his eyebrows for misery, and clenched his fists on his knees, feeling so awkward in presence of a big trouble.

Mrs Morel did not change much. She stayed in Sheffield for two months. If anything, at the end she was rather worse. But she wanted to go home. Annie had her children. Mrs Morel wanted to go home. So they got a motor-car from Nottingham—for she was too ill to go by train—and she was driven through the sunshine. It was just August; everything was bright and warm. Under the blue sky they could all see she was dying. Yet she was jollier than she had been for weeks. They all laughed and talked.

'Annie,' she exclaimed, 'I saw a lizard dart on that rock!'

Her eyes were so quick; she was still so full of life.

Morel knew she was coming. He had the front-door open. Everybody was on tiptoe. Half the street turned out. They heard the sound of the great motor-car. Mrs Morel, smiling, drove home down the street.

'And just look at them all come out to see me!' she said. 'But there, I suppose I should have done the same. How do you do, Mrs Matthews? How are you, Mrs Harrison?'

They none of them could hear, but they saw her smile and nod. And they all saw death on her face, they said. It was a great event in the street.

Morel wanted to carry her indoors, but he was too old. Arthur took her as if she were a child. They had set her a big, deep chair by the hearth where her rocking-chair used to stand. When she was unwrapped and seated, and had drunk a little brandy, she looked round the room.

'Don't think I didn't like your house, Annie,' she said; 'but it's nice to be in my own home again.'

And Morel answered huskily:

'It is, lass, it is.'

And Minnie, the little quaint maid, said:

'An' we glad t' 'ave yer.'

There was a lovely yellow ravel of sunflowers in the garden. He looked out of the window.

'There are my sunflowers!' she said.

14

THE RELEASE

'By the way,' said Dr Ansell one evening when Morel was in Sheffield, 'we've got a man in the fever hospital here who comes from Nottingam–Dawes. He doesn't seem to have many belongings in this world.'

'Baxter Dawes!' Paul exclaimed.

'That's the man–has been a fine fellow, physically, I should think. Been in a bit of a mess lately. You know him?'

'He used to work at the place where I am.'

'Did he? Do you know anything about him? He's just sulking, or he'd be a lot better than he is by now.'

'I don't know anything of his home circumstances, except that he's separated from his wife and has been a bit down, I believe. But tell him about me, will you? Tell him I'll come and see him.'

The next time Morel saw the doctor he said:

'And what about Dawes?'

'I said to him,' answered the other, '"Do you know a man from Nottingham named Morel?" and he looked at me as if he'd jump at my throat. So I said, "I see you know the name; it's Paul Morel." Then I told him about your saying you would go and see him. "What does he want?" he said, as if you were a policeman.'

'And did he say he would see me?' asked Paul.

'He wouldn't say anything–good, bad, or indifferent,' replied the doctor.

'Why not?'

'That's what I want to know. There he lies and sulks, day in, day out. Can't get a word of information out of him.'

'Do you think I might go?' asked Paul.

'You might.'

There was a feeling of connexion between the rival men, more than ever since they had fought. In a way Morel felt guilty towards the other, and more or less responsible. And being in such a state of soul himself, he felt an almost painful nearness to Dawes, who was suffering and despairing, too. Besides, they had met in a naked extremity of hate, and it was a bond. At any rate, the elemental man in each had met.

He went down to the isolation hospital, with Dr Ansell's card. The sister, a healthy young Irishwoman, led him down the ward.

'A visitor to see you, Jim Crow,' she said.

Dawes turned suddenly over with a startled grunt.

'Eh?'

'Caw!' she mocked. 'He can only say "Caw!" I have brought you a gentleman to see you. Now say "Thank you," and show some manners.'

Dawes looked swiftly with his dark, startled eyes beyond the sister at Paul. His look was full of fear, mistrust, hate, and misery. Morel met the swift, dark eyes, and hesitated. The two men were afraid of the naked selves they had been.

'Dr Ansell told me you were here,' said Morel, holding out his hand.

Dawes mechanically shook hands.

'So I thought I'd come in,' continued Paul.

There was no answer. Dawes lay staring at the opposite wall.

'Say "Caw!"' mocked the nurse. 'Say "Caw!" Jim Crow.'

'He is getting on all right?' said Paul to her.

'Oh yes! He lies and imagines he's going to die,' said the nurse, 'and it frightens every word out of his mouth.'

'And you *must* have somebody to talk to,' laughed Morel.

'That's it!' laughed the nurse. 'Only two old men and a boy who always cries. It *is* hard lines! Here am I dying to hear Jim Crow's voice, and nothing but an odd "Caw!" will he give!'

'So rough on you!' said Morel.

'Isn't it?' said the nurse.

'I suppose I am a godsend,' he laughed.

'Oh, dropped straight from heaven!' laughed the nurse.

Presently she left the two men alone. Dawes was thinner, and handsome again, but life seemed low in him. As the doctor said, he was lying sulking, and would not move forward towards convalescence. He seemed to grudge every beat of his heart.

'Have you had a bad time?' asked Paul.

Suddenly again Dawes looked at him.

'What are you doing in Sheffield?' he asked.

'My mother was taken ill at my sister's in Thurston Street. What are you doing here?'

There was no answer.

'How long have you been in?' Morel asked.

'I couldn't say for sure,' Dawes answered grudgingly.

He lay staring across at the wall opposite, as if trying to believe Morel was not there. Paul felt his heart go hard and angry.

'Dr Ansell told me you were here,' he said coldly.

The other man did not answer.

'Typhoid's pretty bad, I know,' Morel persisted.

Suddenly Dawes said:

'What did you come for?'

'Because Dr Ansell said you didn't know anybody here. Do you?'

'I know nobody nowhere,' said Dawes.

'Well,' said Paul, 'it's because you don't choose to, then.'

There was another silence.

'We s'll be taking my mother home as soon as we can,' said Paul.

'What's a-matter with her?' asked Dawes, with a sick man's interest in illness.

'She's got a cancer.'

There was another silence.

'But we want to get her home,' said Paul. We s'll have to get a motor-car.'

Dawes lay thinking.

'Why don't you ask Thomas Jordan to lend you his?' said Dawes.

'It's not big enough,' Morel answered.

Dawes blinked his dark eyes as he lay thinking.

'Then ask Jack Pilkington; he'd lend it you. You know him.'

'I think I s'll hire one,' said Paul.

'You're a fool if you do,' said Dawes.

The sick man was gaunt and handsome again. Paul was sorry for him because his eyes looked so tired.

'Did you get a job here?' he asked.

'I was only here a day or two before I was taken bad,' Dawes replied.

'You want to get in a convalescent home,' said Paul.

The other's face clouded again.

'I'm goin' in no convalescent home,' he said.

'My father's been in the one at Seathorpe, an' he liked it. Dr Ansell would get you a recommend.'

Dawes lay thinking. It was evident he dared not face the world again.

'The seaside would be all right just now,' Morel said. 'Sun on those sandhills, and the waves not far out.'

The other did not answer.

'By Gad!' Paul concluded, too miserable to bother much; 'it's all right when you know you're going to walk again, and swim!'

Dawes glanced at him quickly. The man's dark eyes were afraid to meet any other eyes in the world. But the real misery and helplessness in Paul's tone gave him a feeling of relief.

'Is she far gone?' he asked.

'She's going like wax,' Paul answered; 'but cheerful—lively!'

He bit his lip. After a minute he rose.

'Well, I'll be going,' he said. 'I'll leave you this half-crown.'

'I don't want it,' Dawes muttered.

Morel did not answer, but left the coin on the table.

'Well,' he said, 'I'll try and run in when I'm back in Sheffield. Happen you might like to see my brother-in-law? He works in Pyecrofts.'

'I don't know him,' said Dawes.

'He's all right. Should I tell him to come? He might bring you some papers to look at.'

The other man did not answer. Paul went. The strong emotion that Dawes aroused in him, repressed, made him shiver.

He did not tell his mother, but next day he spoke to Clara about this interview. It was in the dinner-hour. The two did not often go out together now, but this day he asked her to go with him to the Castle grounds. There they sat while the scarlet geraniums and the yellow calceolarias blazed in the sunlight. She was now always rather protective, and rather resentful towards him.

'Did you know Baxter was in Sheffield hospital with typhoid?' he asked.

She looked at him with startled grey eyes, and her face went pale.

'No,' she said, frightened.

'He's getting better. I went to see him yesterday—the doctor told me.'

Clara seemed stricken by the news.

'Is he very bad?' she asked guiltily.

'He has been. He's mending now.'

'What did he say to you?'

'Oh, nothing! He seems to be sulking.'

There was a distance between the two of them. He gave her more information.

She went about shut up and silent. The next time they took a walk together, she disengaged herself from his arm, and walked at a distance from him. He was wanting her comfort badly.

'Won't you be nice with me?' he asked.

She did not answer.

'What's the matter?' he said, putting his arm across her shoulder.

'Don't!' she said, disengaging herself.

He left her alone, and returned to his own brooding.

'Is it Baxter that upsets you?' he asked at length.

'I *have* been *vile* to him!' she said.

'I've said many a time you haven't treated him well,' he replied.

And there was a hostility between them. Each pursued his own train of thought.

'I've treated him—no, I've treated him badly,' she said. 'And now you treat *me* badly. It serves me right.'

'How do I treat you badly?' he said.

'It serves me right,' she repeated. 'I never considered him worth having, and now you don't consider *me*. But it serves me right. He loved me a thousand times better than you ever did.'

'He didn't!' protested Paul.

'He did! At any rate, he did respect me, and that's what you don't do.'

'It looked as if he respected you!' he said.

'He did! And I *made* him horrid—I know I did! You've taught me that. And he loved me a thousand times better than ever you do.'

'All right,' said Paul.

He only wanted to be left alone now. He had his own trouble, which was almost too much to bear. Clara only tormented him and made him tired. He was not sorry when he left her.

She went on the first opportunity to Sheffield to see her husband. The meeting was not a success. But she left him roses and fruit and money. She wanted to make restitution. It was not that she loved him. As she looked at him lying there her heart did not warm with love. Only she wanted to humble herself to him, to kneel before him. She wanted now to be self-sacrificial. After all, she had failed to make Morel really love her. She was morally frightened. She wanted to do penance. So she kneeled to Dawes, and it gave him a subtle pleasure. But the distance between them was still very great—too great. It frightened the man. It almost pleased the woman. She liked to feel she was serving him across an insuperable distance. She was proud now.

Morel went to see Dawes once or twice. There was a sort of friendship between the two men, who were all the while deadly rivals. But they never mentioned the woman who was between them.

Mrs Morel got gradually worse. At first they used to carry her downstairs, sometimes even into the garden. She sat propped in her chair, smiling, and so pretty. The gold wedding-ring shone on her white hand; her hair was carefully brushed. And she watched the tangled sunflowers dying, the chrysanthemums coming out, and the dahlias.

Paul and she were afraid of each other. He knew, and she knew, that she was dying. But they kept up a pretence of cheerfulness. Every morning, when he got up, he went into her room in his pyjamas.

'Did you sleep, my dear?' he asked.

'Yes,' she answered.

'Not very well?'

'Well, yes!'

Then he knew she had lain awake. He saw her hand under the bedclothes, pressing the place on her side where the pain was.

'Has it been bad?' he asked.

'No. It hurt a bit, but nothing to mention.'

And she sniffed in her old scornful way. As she lay she looked like a girl. And all the while her blue eyes watched him. But there were the dark pain-circles beneath that made him ache again.

'It's a sunny day,' he said.

'It's a beautiful day.'

'Do you think you'll be carried down?'

'I shall see.'

Then he went away to get her breakfast. All day long he was conscious of nothing but her. It was a long ache that made him feverish. Then, when he got home in the early evening, he glanced through the kitchen window. She was not there; she had not got up.

He ran straight upstairs and kissed her. He was almost afraid to ask:

'Didn't you get up, pigeon?'

'No,' she said. 'It was that morphia; it made me tired.'

'I think he gives you too much,' he said.

'I think he does,' she answered.

He sat down by the bed, miserably. She had a way of curling and lying on her side, like a child. The grey and brown hair was loose over her ear.

'Doesn't it tickle you?' he said, gently putting it back.

'It does,' she replied.

His face was near hers. Her blue eyes smiled straight into his, like a girl's—warm, laughing with tender love. It made him pant with terror, agony and love.

'You want your hair doing in a plait,' he said. 'Lie still.'

And going behind her, he carefully loosened her hair, brushed it out. It was like fine long silk of brown and grey. Her head was snuggled between her shoulders. As he lightly brushed and plaited her hair, he bit his lip and felt dazed. It all seemed unreal, he could not understand it.

At night he often worked in her room, looking up from time to time. And so often he found her blue eyes fixed on him. And when their eyes met, she smiled. He worked away again mechanically, producing good stuff without knowing what he was doing.

Sometimes he came in, very pale and still, with watchful, sudden eyes, like a man who is drunk almost to death. They were both afraid of the veils that were ripping between them.

Then she pretended to be better, chattered to him gaily, made a great fuss over some scraps of news. For they had both come to the condition when they had to make much of the trifles, lest they should give in to the big thing, and their human independence would go smash. They were afraid, so they made light of things and were gay.

Sometimes as she lay he knew she was thinking of the past. Her mouth gradually shut hard in a line. She was holding herself rigid, so that she might die without ever uttering the great cry that was tearing from her. He never forgot that hard, utterly lonely and stubborn clenching of her mouth, which persisted for weeks. Sometimes, when it was lighter, she talked about her husband. Now she hated him. She did not forgive him. She could not bear him to be in the room. And a few things, the things that had been most bitter to her, came up again so strongly that they broke from her, and she told her son.

He felt as if his life were being destroyed, piece by piece, within him. Often the tears came suddenly. He ran to the station, the tear-drops falling on the pavement. Often he could not go on with his work. The pen stopped writing. He sat staring, quite unconscious. And when he came round again he felt sick, and trembled in his limbs. He never questioned what it was. His mind did not try to analyse or understand. He merely submitted, and kept his eyes shut; let the thing go over him.

His mother did the same. She thought of the pain, of the morphia, of the next day; hardly ever of the death. That was coming, she knew. She had to submit to it. But she would never entreat it or make friends with it. Blind, with her face shut hard and blind, she was pushed towards the door. The days passed, the weeks, the months.

Sometimes, in the sunny afternoons, she seemed almost happy.

'I try to think of the nice times—when we went to Mablethorpe, and Robin Hood's Bay, and Shanklin,' she said. 'After all, not everybody has seen those beautiful places. And wasn't it beautiful! I try to think of that, not of the other things.'

Then, again, for a whole evening she spoke not a word; neither did he. They were together, rigid, stubborn, silent. He went into his room at last to go to bed, and leaned against the doorway as if paralysed, unable to go any farther. His consciousness went. A furious storm, he knew not what, seemed to ravage inside him. He stood leaning there, submitting, never questioning.

In the morning they were both normal again, though her face was grey with the morphia, and her body felt like ash. But they were bright again, nevertheless. Often, especially if Annie or Arthur were at home, he neglected her. He did not see much of Clara. Usually he was with men. He was quick and active and lively; but when his friends saw him go white to the gills, his eyes dark and glittering, they had a certain mistrust of him. Sometimes he went to Clara, but she was almost cold to him.

'Take me!' he said simply.

Occasionally she would. But she was afraid. When he had her then, there was something in it that made her shrink away from him—something unnatural. She grew to dread him. He was so quiet, yet so strange. She was afraid of the man who was not there with her, whom she could feel behind this make-belief lover; somebody sinister, that filled her with horror. She began to have a kind of horror of him. It was almost as if he were a criminal. He wanted her—he had her—and it made her feel as if death itself had her in its grip. She lay in horror. There was no man there loving her. She almost hated him. Then came little bouts of tenderness. But she dared not pity him.

Dawes had come to Colonel Seely's Home near Nottingham. There Paul visited him sometimes, Clara very occasionally. Between the two men the friendship had developed peculiarly. Dawes, who mended very slowly and seemed very feeble, seemed to leave himself in the hands of Morel.

In the beginning of November Clara reminded Paul that it was her birthday.

'I'd nearly forgotten,' he said.

'I thought quite,' she replied.

'No. Shall we go to the seaside for the week-end?'

They went. It was cold and rather dismal. She waited for him to be warm and tender with her, instead of which he seemed hardly aware of her. He sat in the railway-carriage, looking out, and was startled when she spoke to him. He was not definitely thinking. Things seemed as if they did not exist. She went across to him.

'What is it, dear?' she asked.

'Nothing!' he said. 'Don't those windmill sails look monotonous?'

He sat holding her hand. He could not talk nor think. It was a comfort, however, to sit holding her hand. She was dissatisfied and miserable. He was not with her; she was nothing.

And in the evening they sat among the sandhills, looking at the black, heavy sea.

'She will never give in,' he said quietly.

Clara's heart sank.

'No,' she replied.

'There are different ways of dying. My father's people are frightened, and have to be hauled out of life into death like cattle into a slaughter-house, pulled by the neck; but my mother's people are pushed from behind, inch by inch. They are stubborn people, and won't die.'

'Yes,' said Clara.

'And she won't die. She can't. Mr Renshaw, the parson, was in the other day. "Think!" he said to her; "you will have your mother and father, and your sisters, and your son, in the Other Land." And she said: "I have done without them for a long time, and *can* do without them now. It is the living I want, not the dead." She wants to live even now.'

'Oh, how horrible!' said Clara, too frightened to speak.

'And she looks at me, and she wants to stay with me,' he went on monotonously. 'She's got such a will, it seems as if she would never go—never!'

'Don't think of it!' cried Clara.

'And she was religious—she is religious now—but it is no good. She simply won't give in. And do you know, I said to her on Thursday, "Mother, if I had to die, I'd die. I'd *will* to die." And she said to me, sharp: "Do you think I haven't? Do you think you can die when you like?"'

His voice ceased. He did not cry, only went on speaking monotonously. Clara wanted to run. She looked round. There was the black, re-echoing shore, the dark sky down on her. She got up terrified. She wanted to be where there was light, where there were other people. She wanted to be away from him. He sat with his head dropped, not moving a muscle.

'And I don't want her to eat,' he said, 'and she knows it. When I ask her, "Shall you have anything?" she's almost afraid to say "Yes." "I'll have a cup of Benger's," she says. "It'll only keep your strength up," I said to her. "Yes"—and she almost cried—"but there's such a gnawing when I eat nothing. I can't bear it." So I went and made her the food. It's the cancer that gnaws like that at her. I wish she'd die.'

'Come!' said Clara roughly. 'I'm going.'

He followed her down the darkness of the sands. He did not come to her. He seemed scarcely aware of her existence. And she was afraid of him, and disliked him.

In the same acute daze they went back to Nottingham. He was always busy, always doing something, always going from one to the other of his friends.

On the Monday he went to see Baxter Dawes. Listless and pale, the man rose to greet the other, clinging to his chair as he held out his hand.

'You shouldn't get up,' said Paul.

Dawes sat down heavily, eyeing Morel with a sort of suspicion.

'Don't you waste your time on me,' he said, 'if you've owt better to do.'

'I wanted to come,' said Paul. 'Here! I brought you some sweets.'

The invalid put them aside.

'It's not been much of a week-end,' said Morel.

'How's your mother?' asked the other.

'Hardly any different.'

'I thought she was perhaps worse, being as you didn't come on Sunday.'

'I was at Skegness,' said Paul. 'I wanted a change.'

The other looked at him with dark eyes. He seemed to be waiting, not quite daring to ask, trusting to be told.

'I went with Clara,' said Paul.

'I knew as much,' said Dawes quietly.

'It was an old promise,' said Paul.

'You have it your own way,' said Dawes.

This was the first time Clara had been definitely mentioned between them.

'Nay,' said Morel slowly; 'she's tired of me.'

Again Dawes looked at him.

'Since August she's been getting tired of me,' Morel repeated.

The two men were very quiet together. Paul suggested a game of draughts. They played in silence.

'I s'll go abroad when my mother's dead,' said Paul.

'Abroad!' repeated Dawes.

'Yes; I don't care what I do.'

They continued the game. Dawes was winning.

'I s'll have to begin a new start of some sort,' said Paul; 'and you as well, I suppose.'

He took one of Dawes's pieces.

'I dunno where,' said the other.

'Things have to happen,' Morel said. 'It's no good doing anything—at least—no, I don't know. Give me some toffee.'

The two men ate sweets, and began another game of draughts.

'What made that scar on your mouth?' asked Dawes.

Paul put his hand hastily to his lips, and looked over the garden.

'I had a bicycle accident,' he said.

Dawes's hand trembled as he moved the piece.

'You shouldn't ha' laughed at me,' he said very low.

'When?'

'That night on Woodborough Road, when you and her passed me—you with your hand on her shoulder.'

'I never laughed at you,' said Paul.

Dawes kept his fingers on the draught-piece.

'I never knew you were there till the very second when you passed,' said Morel.

'It was that as did me,' he said, very low.

Paul took another sweet.

'I never laughed,' he said, 'except as I'm always laughing.'

They finished the game.

That night Morel walked home from Nottingham, in order to have something to do. The furnaces flared in a red blotch over Bulwell; the black clouds were like a low ceiling. As he went along the ten miles of highroad, he felt as if he were walking out of life, between the black levels of the sky and the earth. But at the end was only the sick-room. If he walked and walked for ever, there was only that place to come to.

He was not tired when he got near home, or he did not know it. Across the field he could see the red firelight leaping in her bedroom window.

'When she's dead,' he said to himself, 'that fire will go out.'

He took off his boots quietly and crept upstairs. His mother's door was wide open, because she slept alone still. The red firelight dashed its glow on the landing. Soft as a shadow, he peeped in her doorway.

'Paul!' she murmured.

His heart seemed to break again. He went in and sat by the bed.

'How late you are!' she murmured.

'Not very,' he said.

'Why, what time is it?' The murmur came plaintive and helpless.

'It's only just gone eleven.'

That was not true; it was nearly one o'clock.

'Oh!' she said; 'I thought it was later.'

And he knew the unutterable misery of her nights that would not go.

'Can't you sleep, my pigeon?' he said.

'No, I can't,' she wailed.

'Never mind, Little!' he said, crooning. 'Never mind, my love. I'll stop with you half an hour, my pigeon; then perhaps it will be better.'

And he sat by the bedside, slowly, rhythmically stroking her brows with his finger-tips, stroking her eyes shut, soothing her, holding her fingers in his free hand. They could hear the sleepers' breathing in the other rooms.

'Now go to bed,' she murmured, lying quite still under his fingers and his love.

'Will you sleep?' he asked.

'Yes, I think so.'

'You feel better, my Little, don't you?'

'Yes,' she said, like a fretful, half-soothed child.

Still the days and the weeks went by. He hardly ever went to see Clara now. But he wandered restlessly from one person to another for some help, and there was none anywhere. Miriam had written to him tenderly. He went to see her. Her heart was very sore when she saw him, white, gaunt, with his eyes dark and bewildered. Her pity came up, hurting her till she could not bear it.

'How is she?' she asked.

'The same—the same!' he said. 'The doctors says she can't last, but I know she will. She'll be here at Christmas.'

Miriam shuddered. She drew him to her; she pressed him to her bosom; she kissed him and kissed him. He submitted, but it was torture. She could not kiss his agony. That remained alone and apart. She kissed his face, and roused his blood, while his soul was apart, writhing with the agony of death. And she kissed him and fingered his body, till at last, feeling he would go mad, he got away from her. It was not that he wanted just then—not that. And she thought she had soothed him and done him good.

December came, and some snow. He stayed at home all the while now. They could not afford a nurse. Annie came to look after her mother; the parish nurse, whom they loved, came in morning and evening. Paul shared the nursing with Annie. Often, in the evenings, when friends were in the kitchen with them, they all laughed together and shook with laughter. It was reaction. Paul was so comical. Annie was so quaint. The whole party laughed till they cried, trying to subdue the sound. And Mrs Morel, lying alone in the darkness heard them, and among her bitterness was a feeling of relief.

Then Paul would go upstairs gingerly, guiltily, to see if she had heard.

'Shall I give you some milk?' he asked.

'A little,' she replied plaintively.

And he would put some water with it, so that it should not nourish her. Yet he loved her more than his own life.

She had morphia every night, and her heart got fitful. Annie slept beside her. Paul would go in in the early morning, when his sister got up. His mother was wasted and almost ashen in the morning with the morphia. Darker and darker grew her eyes, all pupil, with the torture. In the mornings the weariness and ache was too much to bear. Yet she could not—would not—weep, or even complain much.

'You slept a bit later this morning, little one,' he would say to her.

'Did I?' she answered, with fretful weariness.

'Yes; it's nearly eight o'clock.'

He stood looking out of the window. The whole country was bleak and pallid under the snow. Then he felt her pulse. There was a strong stroke and a weak one, like a sound and its echo. That was supposed to betoken the end. She let him feel her wrist, knowing what he wanted.

Sometimes they looked in each other's eyes. Then they almost seemed to make an agreement. It was almost as if he were agreeing to die also. But she did not consent to die; she would not. Her body was wasted to a fragment of ash. Her eyes were dark and full of torture.

'Can't you give her something to put an end to it?' he asked the doctor at last.

But the doctor shook his head.

'She can't last many days now, Mr Morel,' he said.

Paul went indoors.

'I can't bear it much longer; we shall all go mad,' said Annie.

The two sat down to breakfast.

'Go and sit with her while we have breakfast, Minnie,' said Annie. But the girl was frightened.

Paul went through the country, through the woods, over the snow. He saw the marks of rabbits and birds in the white snow. He wandered miles and miles. A smoky red sunset came on slowly, painfully, lingering. He thought she would die that day. There was a donkey that came up to him over the snow by the wood's edge, and put its head against him, and walked with him alongside. He put his arms round the donkey's neck, and stroked his cheeks against his ears.

His mother, silent, was still alive, with her hard mouth gripped grimly, her eyes of dark torture only living.

It was nearing Christmas; there was more snow. Annie and he felt as if they could go on no more. Still her dark eyes were alive. Morel, silent and frightened, obliterated himself. Sometimes he would go into the sick-room and look at her. Then he backed out, bewildered.

She kept her hold on life still. The miners had been out on strike, and returned a fortnight or so before Christmas. Minnie went upstairs with the feeding-cup. It was two days after the men had been in.

'Have the men been saying their hands are sore, Minnie?' she asked, in the faint, querulous voice that would not give in. Minnie stood surprised.

'Not as I know of, Mrs Morel,' she answered.

'But I'll bet they are sore,' said the dying woman, as she moved her head with a sigh of weariness. 'But, at any rate, there'll be something to buy in with this week.'

Not a thing did she let slip.

'Your father's pit things will want well airing, Annie,' she said, when the men were going back to work.

'Don't you bother about that, my dear,' said Annie.

One night Annie and Paul were alone. Nurse was upstairs.

'She'll live over Christmas,' said Annie. They were both full of horror.

'She won't,' he replied grimly. 'I s'll give her morphia.'

'Which?' said Annie.

'All that came from Sheffield,' said Paul.

'Ay–do!' said Annie.

The next day he was painting in the bedroom. She seemed to be asleep. He stepped softly backwards and forwards at his painting. Suddenly her small voice wailed:

'Don't walk about, Paul.'

He looked round. Her eyes, like dark bubbles in her face, were looking at him.

'No, my dear,' he said gently. Another fibre seemed to snap in his heart.

That evening he got all the morphia pills there were, and took them downstairs. Carefully he crushed them to powder.

'What are you doing?' said Annie.

'I s'll put 'em in her night milk.'

Then they both laughed together like two conspiring children. On top of all their horror flickered this little sanity.

Nurse did not come that night to settle Mrs Morel down. Paul went up with the hot milk in a feeding-cup. It was nine o'clock.

She was reared up in bed, and he put the feeding-cup between her lips that he would have died to save from any hurt. She took a sip, then put the spout of the cup away and looked at him with her dark, wondering eyes. He looked at her.

'Oh, it *is* bitter, Paul!' she said, making a little grimace.

'It's a new sleeping draught the doctor gave me for you,' he said. 'He thought it wouldn't leave you in such a state in the morning.'

'And I hope it won't,' she said, like a child.

She drank some more of the milk.

'But it *is* horrid!' she said.

He saw her frail fingers over the cup, her lips making a little move.

'I know–I tasted it,' he said. 'But I'll give you some clean milk afterwards.'

'I think so,' she said, and she went on with the draught. She was obedient to him like a child. He wondered if she knew. He saw her poor wasted throat moving as she drank with difficulty. Then he ran downstairs for more milk. There were no grains in the bottom of the cup.

'Has she had it?' whispered Annie.

'Yes–and she said it was bitter.'

'Oh!' laughed Annie, putting her under lip between her teeth.

'And I told her it was a new draught. Where's that milk?'

They both went upstairs.

'I wonder why nurse didn't come to settle me down?' complained the mother, like a child, wistfully.

'She said she was going to a concert, my love,' replied Annie.

'Did she?'

They were silent a minute. Mrs Morel gulped the little clean milk.

'Annie, that draught *was* horrid!' she said plaintively.

'Was it, my love? Well, never mind.'

The mother sighed again with weariness. Her pulse was very irregular.

'Let *us* settle you down,' said Annie. 'Perhaps nurse will be so late.'

'Ay,' said the mother–'try.'

They turned the clothes back. Paul saw his mother like a girl curled up in her flannel nightdress. Quickly they made one half the bed, moved her, made the other, straightened her nightgown over her small feet, and covered her up.

'There,' said Paul, stroking her softly. 'There!–now you'll sleep.'

'Yes,' she said. 'I didn't think you could do the bed so nicely,' she added, almost gaily. Then she curled up, with her cheek on her hand, her head snugged between her shoulders. Paul put the long thin plait of grey hair over her shoulder and kissed her.

'You'll sleep, my love,' he said.

'Yes,' she answered trustfully. 'Good night.'

They put out the light, and it was still.

Morel was in bed. Nurse did not come. Annie and Paul came to look at her about eleven. She seemed to be sleeping as usual after her draught. Her mouth had come a bit open.

'Shall we sit up?' said Paul.

'I s'll lie with her as I always do,' said Annie. 'She might wake up.'

'All right. And call me if you see any difference.'

'Yes.'

They lingered before the bedroom fire, feeling the night big and black and snowy outside, their two selves alone in the world. At last he went into the next room and went to bed.

He slept almost immediately, but kept waking every now and again. Then he went sound asleep. He started awake at Annie's whispered, 'Paul, Paul!' He saw his sister in her white nightdress, with her long plait of hair down her back, standing in the darkness.

'Yes?' he whispered, sitting up.

'Come and look at her.'

He slipped out of bed. A bud of gas was burning in the sick chamber. His mother lay with her cheek on her hand, curled up as she had gone to sleep. But her mouth had fallen open, and she breathed with great hoarse breaths, like snoring, and there were long intervals between.

'She's going!' he whispered.

'Yes,' said Annie.

'How long has she been like it?'

'I only just woke up.'

Annie huddled into the dressing-gown, Paul wrapped himself in a brown blanket. It was three o'clock. He mended the fire. Then the two sat waiting. The great, snoring breath was taken–held awhile–then given back. There was a space–a long space. Then they started. The great, snoring breath was taken again. He bent close down and looked at her.

'Isn't it awful!' whispered Annie.

He nodded. They sat down again helplessly. Again came the great, snoring breath. Again they hung suspended. Again it was given back, long and harsh. The sound, so irregular, at such wide intervals, sounded through the house.

Morel, in his room, slept on. Paul and Annie sat crouched, huddled, motionless. The great, snoring sound began again–there was a painful pause while the breath was held–back came the rasping breath. Minute after minute passed. Paul looked at her again, bending low over her.

'She may last like this,' he said.

They were both silent. He looked out of the window, and could faintly discern the snow on the garden.

'You go to my bed,' he said to Annie. 'I'll sit up.'

'No,' she said, 'I'll stop with you.'

'I'd rather you didn't,' he said.

At last Annie crept out of the room, and he was alone. He hugged himself in his brown blanket, crouched in front of his mother, watching. She looked dreadful, with the bottom jaw fallen back. He watched. Sometimes he thought the great breath would never begin again. He could not bear it–the waiting. Then suddenly, startling him, came the great harsh sound. He mended the fire again, noiselessly. She must not be disturbed. The minutes went by. The night was going, breath by breath. Each time the sound came he felt it wring him, till at last he could not feel so much.

His father got up. Paul heard the miner drawing his stocking on, yawning. Then Morel, in shirt and stockings, entered.

'Hush!' said Paul.

Morel stood watching. Then he looked at his son, helplessly, and in horror.

'Had I better stop a-whoam?' he whispered.

'No. Go to work. She'll last through to-morrow.'

'I don't think so.'

'Yes. Go to work.'

The miner looked at her again, in fear, and went obediently out of the room. Paul saw the tape of his garters swinging against his legs.

After another half-hour Paul went downstairs and drank a cup of tea, then returned. Morel, dressed for the pit, came upstairs again.

'Am I to go?' he said.

'Yes.'

And in a few minutes Paul heard his father's heavy steps go thudding over the deadening snow. Miners called in the street as they tramped in gangs to work. The terrible, long-drawn breaths continued–heave–heave–heave; then a long pause–then ah–ah-h-h-h-h! as it came back. Far away over the snow sounded the hooters of the ironworks. One after another they crowed and boomed, some small and far away, some near, the blowers of the collieries and the other works. Then there was silence. He mended the fire. The great breaths broke the silence–she looked just the same. He put back the blind and peered out. Still it was dark. Perhaps there was a lighter tinge. Perhaps the snow was bluer. He drew up the blind and got dressed. Then, shuddering, he drank brandy from the bottle on the washstand. The snow *was* growing blue. He heard a cart clanking down the street. Yes, it was seven o'clock and it was coming a little bit light. He heard some people calling. The world was waking. A grey, deathly dawn crept over the snow. Yes, he could see the houses. He put out the gas. It seemed very dark. The breathing came still, but he was almost used to it. He could see her. She was just the same. He wondered if he piled heavy clothes on top of her it would make it heavier and the horrible breathing would stop. He looked at her. That was not her–not her a bit. If he piled the blanket and heavy coats on her–

Suddenly the door opened, and Annie entered. She looked at him questioningly.

'Just the same,' he said calmly.

They whispered together a minute, then he went downstairs to get breakfast. It was twenty to eight. Soon Annie came down.

'Isn't it awful! Doesn't she look awful!' she whispered, dazed with horror. He nodded.

'If she looks like that!' said Annie.

'Drink some tea,' he said.

They went upstairs again. Soon the neighbours came with their frightened question:

'How is she?'

It went on just the same. She lay with her cheek in her hand, her mouth fallen open, and the great, ghastly snores came and went.

At ten o'clock nurse came. She looked strange and woebegone.

'Nurse,' cried Paul, 'she'll last like this for days?'

'She can't, Mr Morel,' said nurse. 'She can't.'

There was a silence.

'Isn't it dreadful!' wailed the nurse. 'Who would have thought she could stand it? Go down now, Mr Morel, go down.'

At last, at about eleven o'clock, he went downstairs and sat in the neighbour's house. Annie was downstairs also. Nurse and Arthur were upstairs. Paul sat with his head in his hands. Suddenly Annie came flying across the yard crying, half mad:

'Paul—Paul—she's gone!'

In a second he was back in his own house and upstairs. She lay curled up and still, with her face on her hand, and nurse was wiping her mouth. They all stood back. He kneeled down, and put his face to hers and his arms round her:

'My love—my love—oh, my love!' he whispered again and again. 'My love—oh, my love!'

Then he heard the nurse behind him, crying, saying:

'She's better, Mr Morel, she's better.'

When he took his face up from his warm, dead mother he went straight downstairs and began blacking his boots.

There was a good deal to do, letters to write, and so on. The doctor came and glanced at her, and sighed.

'Ay—poor thing!' he said, then turned away. 'Well, call at the surgery about six for the certificate.'

The father came home from work at about four o'clock. He dragged silently into the house and sat down. Minnie bustled to give him his dinner. Tired, he laid his black arms on the table. There were swede turnips for his dinner, which he liked. Paul wondered if he knew. It was some time, and nobody had spoken. At last the son said:

'You noticed the blinds were down?'

Morel looked up.

'No,' he said. 'Why—has she gone?'

'Yes.'

'When wor that?'

'About twelve this morning.'

'H'm!'

The miner sat still for a moment, then began his dinner. It was as if nothing had happened. He ate his turnips in silence. Afterwards he washed and went upstairs to dress. The door of her room was shut.

'Have you seen her?' Annie asked of him when he came down.

'No,' he said.

In a little while he went out. Annie went away, and Paul called on the undertaker, the clergyman, the doctor, the registrar. It was a long business. He got back at nearly eight o'clock. The undertaker was coming soon to measure for the coffin. The house was empty except for her. He took a candle and went upstairs.

The room was cold, that had been warm for so long. Flowers, bottles, plates, all sick-room litter was taken away; everything was harsh and austere. She lay raised on the bed, the sweep of the sheet from the raised feet was like a clean curve of snow, so silent. She lay like a maiden asleep. With his candle in his hand, he bent over her. She lay like a girl asleep and dreaming of her love. The mouth was a little open, as if wondering from the suffering, but her face was young, her brow clear and white as if life had never touched it. He looked again at the eyebrows, at the small, winsome nose a bit on one side. She was young again. Only the hair as it arched so beautifully from her temples was mixed with silver, and the two simple plaits that lay on her shoulders were filigree of silver and brown. She would wake up. She would lift her eyelids. She was with him still. He bent and kissed her passionately. But there was coldness against his mouth. He bit his lip with horror. Looking at her, he felt he could never, never let her go. No! He stroked the hair from her temples. That, too, was cold. He saw the mouth so dumb and wondering at the hurt. Then he crouched on the floor, whispering to her:

'Mother, mother!'

He was still with her when the undertakers came, young men who had been to school with him. They touched her reverently, and in a quiet, businesslike fashion. They did not look at her. He watched jealously. He and Annie guarded her fiercely. They would not let anybody come to see her, and the neighbours were offended.

After a while Paul went out of the house, and played cards at a friend's. It was midnight when he got back. His father rose from the couch as he entered, saying in a plaintive way:

'I thought tha wor niver comin', lad.'

'I didn't think you'd sit up,' said Paul.

His father looked so forlorn. Morel had been a man without fear—simply nothing frightened him. Paul realized with a start that he had been afraid to go to bed, alone in the house with his dead. He was sorry.

'I forgot you'd be alone, father,' he said.

'Dost want owt to eat?' asked Morel.

'No.'

'Sithee—I made thee a drop o' hot milk. Get it down thee; it's cold enough for owt.'

Paul drank it.

'I must go to Nottingham to-morrow,' he said.

After a while Morel went to bed. He hurried past the closed door, and left his own door open. Soon the son came upstairs also. He went in to kiss her good night, as usual. It was cold and dark. He wished they had kept her fire burning. Still she dreamed her young dream. But she would be cold.

'My dear!' he whispered. 'My dear!'

And he did not kiss her, for fear she should be cold and strange to him. It eased him she slept so beautifully. He shut the door softly, not to wake her, and went to bed.

In the morning Morel summoned his courage, hearing Annie downstairs and Paul coughing in his room across the landing. He opened her door, and went into the darkened room. He saw the white uplifted form in the twilight, but her he dared not see. Bewildered, too frightened to possess any of his faculties, he got out of the room again and left her. He never looked at her again. He had not seen her for months, because he had not dared to look. And she looked like his young wife again.

'Have you seen her?' Annie asked of him sharply after breakfast.

'Yes,' he said.

'And don't you think she looks nice?'

'Yes.'

He went out of the house soon after. And all the time he seemed to be creeping aside to avoid it.

Paul went about from place to place, doing the business of the death. He met Clara in Nottingham, and they had tea together in a café, when they were quite jolly again. She was infinitely relieved to find he did not take it tragically.

Later, when the relatives began to come for the funeral, the affair became public, and the children became social beings. They put themselves aside. They buried her in a furious storm of rain and wind. The wet clay glistened, all the white flowers were soaked. Annie gripped his arms and leaned forward. Down below she saw a dark corner of William's coffin. The oak box sank steadily. She was gone. The rain poured in the grave. The procession of black, with its umbrellas glistening, turned away. The cemetery was deserted under the drenching cold rain.

Paul went home and busied himself supplying the guests with drinks. His father sat in the kitchen with Mrs Morel's relatives, 'superior' people, and wept, and said what a good lass she'd been, and how he'd tried to do everything he could for her—everything. He had striven all his life to do what he could for her, and he'd nothing to reproach himself with. She was gone, but he'd done his best for her. He wiped his eyes with his white handkerchief. He'd nothing to reproach himself for, he repeated. All his life he'd done his best for her.

And that was how he tried to dismiss her. He never thought of her personally. Everything deep in him he denied. Paul hated his father for sitting sentimentalizing over her. He knew he would do it in the public-houses. For the real tragedy went on in Morel in spite of himself. Sometimes, later, he came down from his afternoon sleep, white and cowering.

'I *have* been dreaming of thy mother,' he said in a small voice.

'Have you, father? When I dream of her it's always just as she was when she was well. I dream of her often, but it seems quite nice and natural, as if nothing had altered.'

But Morel crouched in front of the fire in terror.

The weeks passed half real, not much pain, not much of anything, perhaps a little relief, mostly a *nuit blanche*. Paul went restlessly from place to place. For some months, since his mother had been worse, he had not made love to Clara. She was, as it were, dumb to him, rather distant. Dawes saw her very occasionally, but the two could not get an inch across the great distance between them. The three of them were drifting forward.

Dawes mended very slowly. He was in the convalescent home at Skegness at

Christmas, nearly well again. Paul went to the seaside for a few days. His father was with Annie in Sheffield. Dawes came to Paul's lodgings. His time in the home was up. The two men, between whom was such a big reserve, seemed faithful to each other. Dawes depended on Morel now. He knew Paul and Clara had practically separated.

Two days after Christmas Paul was to go back to Nottingham. The evening before he sat with Dawes smoking before the fire.

'You know Clara's coming down for the day to-morrow?' he said.

The other man glanced at him.

'Yes, you told me,' he replied.

Paul drank the remainder of his glass of whisky.

'I told the landlady your wife was coming,' he said.

'Did you?' said Dawes, shrinking, but almost leaving himself in the other's hands. He got up rather stiffly, and reached for Morel's glass.

'Let me fill you up,' he said.

Paul jumped up.

'You sit still,' he said.

But Dawes, with rather shaky hand, continued to mix the drink. 'Say when,' he said.

'Thanks!' replied the other. 'But you've no business to get up.'

'It does me good, lad,' replied Dawes. 'I began to think I'm right again, then.'

'You are about right, you know.'

'I am, certainly I am,' said Dawes, nodding to him.

'And Len says he can get you on in Sheffield.'

Dawes glanced at him again, with dark eyes that agreed with everything the other would say, perhaps a trifle dominated by him.

'It's funny,' said Paul, 'starting again. I feel in a lot bigger mess than you.'

'In what way, lad?'

'I don't know. I don't know. It's as if I was in a tangled sort of hole, rather dark and dreary, and no road anywhere.'

'I know—I understand it,' Dawes said, nodding. But you'll find it'll come all right.'

He spoke caressingly.

'I suppose so,' said Paul.

Dawes knocked his pipe in a hopeless fashion.

'You've not done for yourself like I have,' he said.

Morel saw the wrist and the white hand of the other man gripping the stem of the pipe and knocking out the ash, as if he had given up.

'How old are you?' Paul asked.

'Thirty-nine,' replied Dawes, glancing at him.

Those brown eyes, full of the consciousness of failure, almost pleading for reassurance, for someone to re-establish the man in himself, to warm him, to set him up firm again, troubled Paul.

'You'll just be in your prime,' said Morel. 'You don't look as if much life had gone out of you.'

The brown eyes of the other flashed suddenly.

'It hasn't,' he said. 'The go is there.'

Paul looked up and laughed.

'We've both got plenty of life in us yet to make things fly,' he said.

The eyes of the two men met. They exchanged one look. Having recognized the stress of passion each in the other, they both drank their whisky.

'Yes, begod!' said Dawes, breathless.

There was a pause.

'And I don't see,' said Paul, 'why you shouldn't go on where you left off.'

'What—' said Dawes, suggestively.

'Yes—fit your old home together again.'

Dawes hid his face, and shook his head.

'Couldn't be done,' he said, and he looked up with an ironic smile.

'Why? Because you don't want?'

'Perhaps.'

They smoked in silence. Dawes showed his teeth as he bit his pipe stem.

'You mean you don't want her?' asked Paul.

Dawes stared up at the picture with a caustic expression on his face.

'I hardly know,' he said.

The smoke floated softly up.

'I believe she wants you,' said Paul.

'Do you?' replied the other, soft, satirical, abstract.

'Yes. She never really hitched on to me—you were always there in the background. That's why she wouldn't get a divorce.'

Dawes continued to stare in a satirical fashion at the picture over the mantelpiece.

'That's how women are with me,' said Paul. 'They want me like mad, but they don't want to belong to me. And she *belonged* to you all the time. I knew.'

The triumphant male came up in Dawes. He showed his teeth more distinctly.

'Perhaps I was a fool,' he said.

'You were a big fool,' said Morel.

'But perhaps even *then* you were a bigger fool,' said Dawes. There was a touch of triumph and malice in it.

'Do you think so?' said Paul.

They were silent for some time.

'At any rate, I'm clearing out to-morrow,' said Morel.

'I see,' answered Dawes.

Then they did not talk any more. The instinct to murder each other had returned. They almost avoided each other.

They shared the same bedroom. When they retired Dawes seemed abstract, thinking of something. He sat on the side of the bed in his shirt, looking at his legs.

'Aren't you getting cold?' asked Morel.

'I was lookin' at these legs,' replied the other.

'What's up with 'em? They look all right,' replied Paul, from his bed.

'They look all right. But there's some water in 'em yet.'

'And what about it?'

'Come and look.'

Paul reluctantly got out of bed and went to look at the rather handsome legs of the other man that were covered with glistening, dark gold hair.

'Look here,' said Dawes, pointing to his shin. 'Look at the water under here.'

'Where?' said Paul.

The man pressed his finger-tips. They left little dents that filled up slowly.

'It's nothing,' said Paul.

'You feel,' said Dawes.

Paul tried with his fingers. It made little dents.

'H'm!' he said.

'Rotten, isn't it?' said Dawes.

'Why? It's nothing much.'

'You're not much of a man with water in your legs.'

'I can't see as it makes any difference,' said Morel. 'I've got a weak chest.'
He returned to his own bed.

'I suppose the rest of me's all right,' said Dawes, and he put out the light.

In the morning it was raining. Morel packed his bag. The sea was grey and
shaggy and dismal. He seemed to be cutting himself off from life more and
more. It gave him a wicked pleasure to do it.

The two men were at the station. Clara stepped out of the train, and came
along the platform, very erect and coldly composed. She wore a long coat and a
tweed hat. Both men hated her for her composure. Paul shook hands with her at
the barrier. Dawes was leaning against the bookstall, watching. His black
overcoat was buttoned up to the chin because of the rain. He was pale, with
almost a touch of nobility in his quietness. He came forward, limping slightly.

'You ought to look better than this,' she said.

'Oh, I'm all right now.'

The three stood at a loss. She kept the two men hesitating near her.

'Shall we go to the lodging straight off,' said Paul, 'or somewhere else?'

'We may as well go home,' said Dawes.

Paul walked on the outside of the pavement, then Dawes, then Clara. They
made polite conversation. The sitting-room faced the sea, whose tide, grey and
shaggy, hissed not far off.

Morel swung up the big arm-chair.

'Sit down, Jack,' he said.

'I don't want the chair,' said Dawes.

'Sit down!' Morel repeated.

Clara took off her things and laid them on the couch. She had a slight air of
resentment. Lifting her hair with her fingers, she sat down, rather aloof and
composed. Paul ran downstairs to speak to the landlady.

'I should think you're cold,' said Dawes to his wife. 'Come nearer to the fire.'

'Thank you, I'm quite warm,' she answered.
She looked out of the window at the rain and at the sea.

'When are you going back?' she asked.

'Well, the rooms are taken until to-morrow, so he wants me to stop. He's
going back to-night.'

'And then you're thinking of going to Sheffield?'

'Yes.'

'Are you fit to start work?'

'I'm going to start.'

'You've really got a place?'

'Yes–begin on Monday.'

'You don't look fit.'

'Why don't I?'

She looked again out of the window instead of answering.

'And have you got lodgings in Sheffield?'

'Yes.'

Again she looked away out of the window. The panes were blurred with
streaming rain.

'And can you manage all right?' she asked.

'I s'd think so. I s'll have to!'

They were silent when Morel returned.

'I shall go by the four-twenty,' he said as he entered.

Nobody answered.

'I wish you'd take your boots off,' he said to Clara. 'There's a pair of slippers of mine.'

'Thank you,' she said. 'They aren't wet.'

He put the slippers near her feet. She left them there.

Morel sat down. Both the men seemed helpless, and each of them had a rather hunted look. But Dawes now carried himself quietly, seemed to yield himself, while Paul seemed to screw himself up. Clara thought she had never seen him look so small and mean. He was as if trying to get himself into the smallest possible compass. And as he went about arranging, and as he sat talking, there seemed something false about him and out of tune. Watching him unknown, she said to herself there was no stability about him. He was fine in his way, passionate, and able to give her drinks of pure life when he was in one mood. And now he looked paltry and insignificant. There was nothing stable about him. Her husband had more manly dignity. At any rate *he* did not waft about with any wind. There was something evanescent about Morel, she thought, something shifting and false. He would never make sure ground for any woman to stand on. She despised him rather for his shrinking together, getting smaller. Her husband at least was manly, and when he was beaten gave in. But this other would never own to being beaten. He would shift round and round, prowl, get smaller. She despised him. And yet she watched him rather than Dawes, and it seemed as if their three fates lay in his hands. She hated him for it.

She seemed to understand better now about men, and what they could or would do. She was less afraid of them, more sure of herself. That they were not the small egoists she had imagined them made her more comfortable. She had learned a good deal–almost as much as she wanted to learn. Her cup had been full. It was still as full as she could carry. On the whole, she would not be sorry when he was gone.

They had dinner, and sat eating nuts and drinking by the fire. Not a serious word had been spoken. Yet Clara realized that Morel was withdrawing from the circle, leaving her the option to stay with her husband. It angered her. He was a mean fellow, after all, to take what he wanted and then give her back. She did not remember that she herself had had what she wanted, and really, at the bottom of her heart, wished to be given back.

Paul felt crumpled up and lonely. His mother had really supported his life. He had loved her; they two had, in fact, faced the world together. Now she was gone, and for ever behind him was the gap in life, the tear in the veil, through which his life seemed to drift slowly, as if he were drawn towards death. He wanted someone of their own free initiative to help him. The lesser things he began to let go from him, for fear of this big thing, the lapse towards death, following in the wake of his beloved. Clara could not stand for him to hold on to. She wanted him, but not to understand him. He felt she wanted the man on top, not the real him that was in trouble. That would be too much trouble to her; he dared not give it her. She could not cope with him. It made him ashamed. So, secretly ashamed because he was in such a mess, because his own hold on life was so unsure, because nobody held him, feeling unsubstantial, shadowy, as if he did not count for much in this concrete world, he drew himself together smaller and smaller. He did not want to die; he would not give in. But he was not afraid of death. If nobody would help, he would go on alone.

Dawes had been driven to the extremity of life, until he was afraid. He could go to the brink of death, he could lie on the edge and look in. Then, cowed, afraid, he had to crawl back, and like a beggar take what offered. There was a certain nobility in it. As Clara saw, he owned himself beaten, and he wanted to be taken back whether or not. That she could do for him.

It was three o'clock.

'I am going by the four-twenty,' said Paul again to Clara. 'Are you coming then or later?'

'I don't know,' she said.

'I'm meeting my father in Nottingham at seven-fifteen,' he said.

'Then,' she answered. 'I'll come later.'

Dawes jerked suddenly, as if he had been held on a strain. He looked out over the sea, but he saw nothing.

'There are one or two books in the corner,' said Morel. 'I've done with 'em.'

At about four o'clock he went.

'I shall see you both later,' he said, as he shook hands.

'I suppose so,' said Dawes. 'An' perhaps—one day—I s'll be able to pay you back the money as—'

'I shall come for it, you'll see,' laughed Paul. 'I s'll be on the rocks before I'm very much older.'

'Ay—well—' said Dawes.

'Good-bye,' he said to Clara.

'Good-bye,' she said, giving him her hand. Then she glanced at him for the last time, dumb and humble.

He was gone. Dawes and his wife sat down again.

'It's a nasty day for travelling,' said the man.

'Yes,' she answered.

They talked in a desultory fashion until it grew dark. The landlady brought in the tea. Dawes drew up his chair to the table without being invited, like a husband. Then he sat humbly waiting for his cup. She served him as she would, like a wife, not consulting his wish.

After tea, as it drew near to six o'clock, he went to the window. All was dark outside. The sea was roaring.

'It's raining yet,' he said.

'Is it?' she answered.

'You won't go to-night, shall you?' he said, hesitating.

She did not answer. He waited.

'I shouldn't go in this rain,' he said.

'Do you *want* me to stay?' she asked.

His hand as he held the dark curtain trembled.

'Yes,' he said.

He remained with his back to her. She rose and went slowly to him. He let go the curtain, turned, hesitating, towards her. She stood with her hands behind her back, looking up at him in a heavy, inscrutable fashion.

'Do you want me, Baxter?' she asked.

His voice was hoarse as he answered:

'Do you want to come back to me?'

She made a moaning noise, lifted her arms, and put them round his neck,

drawing him to her. He hid his face on her shoulder, holding her clasped.
'Take me back!' she whispered, ecstatic. 'Take me back, take me back!' And
she put her fingers through his fine, thin dark hair, as if she were only semi-
conscious. He tightened his grasp on her.

'Do you want me again?' he murmured, broken.

15

DERELICT

Clara went with her husband to Sheffield, and Paul scarcely saw her again.
Walter Morel seemed to have let all the trouble go over him, and there he was,
crawling about on the mud of it, just the same. There was scarcely any bond
between father and son, save that each felt he must not let the other go in any
actual want. As there was no one to keep on the home, and as they could neither
of them bear the emptiness of the house, Paul took lodgings in Nottingham,
and Morel went to live with a friendly family in Bestwood.

Everything seemed to have gone smash for the young man. He could not
paint. The picture he finished on the day of his mother's death—one that
satisfied him—was the last thing he did. At work there was no Clara. When
he came home he could not take up his brushes again. There was nothing
left.

So he was always in the town at one place or another, drinking, knocking
about with the men he knew. It really wearied him. He talked to barmaids, to
almost any woman, but there was that dark, strained look in his eyes, as if he
were hunting something.

Everything seemed so different, so unreal. There seemed no reason why
people would go along the street, and houses pile up in the daylight. There
seemed no reason why these things should occupy the space, instead of leaving
it empty. His friends talked to him; he heard the sounds, and he answered. But
why there should be the noise of speech he could not understand.

He was most himself when he was alone, or working hard and mechanically
at the factory. In the latter case there was pure forgetfulness, when he lapsed
from consciousness. But it had to come to an end. It hurt him so, that things had
lost their reality. The first snowdrops came. He saw the tiny drop-pearls among
the grey. They would have given him the liveliest emotion at one time. Now
they were there, but they did not seem to mean anything. In a few moments
they would cease to occupy that place, and just the space would be, where they
had been. Tall, brilliant tram-cars ran along the street at night. It seemed
almost a wonder they should trouble to rustle backwards and forwards. 'Why
trouble to go tilting down to Trent Bridges?' he asked of the big trams. It
seemed they just as well might *not* be as be.

The realest thing was the thick darkness at night. That seemed to him whole
and comprehensible and restful. He could leave himself to it. Suddenly a piece
of paper started near his feet and blew along down the pavement. He stood still,
rigid, with clenched fists, a flame of agony going over him. And he saw again the
sick-room, his mother, her eyes. Unconsciously he had been with her, in her
company. The swift hop of the paper reminded him she was gone. But he had

been with her. He wanted everything to stand still, so that he could be with her again.

The days passed, the weeks. But everything seemed to have fused, gone into a conglomerated mass. He could not tell one day from another, one week from another, hardly one place from another. Nothing was distinct or distinguishable. Often he lost himself for an hour at a time, could not remember what he had done.

One evening he came home late to his lodging. The fire was burning low; everybody was in bed. He threw on some more coal, glanced at the table, and decided he wanted no supper. Then he sat down in the arm-chair. It was perfectly still. He did not know anything, yet he saw the dim smoke wavering up the chimney. Presently two mice came out, cautiously, nibbling the fallen crumbs. He watched them as it were from a long way off. The church clock struck two. Far away he could hear the sharp clinking of the trucks on the railway. No, it was not they that were far away. They were there in their places. But where was he himself?

The time passed. The two mice, careering wildly, scampered cheekily over his slippers. He had not moved a muscle. He did not want to move. He was not thinking of anything. It was easier so. There was no wrench of knowing anything. Then, from time to time, some other consciousness, working mechanically, flashed into sharp phrases.

'What am I doing?'

And out of the semi-intoxicated trance came the answer:

'Destroying myself.'

Then a dull, live feeling, gone in an instant, told him that it was wrong. After a while, suddenly came the question:

'Why wrong?'

Again there was no answer, but a stroke of hot stubbornness inside his chest resisted his own annihilation.

There was a sound of a heavy cart clanking down the road. Suddenly the electric light went out; there was a bruising thud in the penny-in-the-slot meter. He did not stir, but sat gazing in front of him. Only the mice had scuttled, and the fire glowed red in the dark room.

Then, quite mechanically and more distinctly, the conversation began again inside him.

'She's dead. What was it all for—her struggle?'

That was his despair wanting to go after her.

'You're alive.'

'She's not.'

'She is—in you.'

Suddenly he felt tired with the burden of it.

'You've got to keep alive for her sake,' said his will in him.

Something felt sulky, as if it would not rouse.

'You've got to carry forward her living, and what she had done, go on with it.'

But he did not want to. He wanted to give up.

'But you can go on with your painting,' said the will in him. 'Or else you can beget children. They both carry on her effort.'

'Painting is not living.'

'Then live.'

'Marry whom?' came the sulky question.

'As best you can.'

'Miriam?'

But he did not trust that.

He rose suddenly, went straight to bed. When he got inside his bedroom and closed the door, he stood with clenched fists.

'Mater, my dear–' he began, with the whole force of his soul. Then he stopped. He would not say it. He would not admit that he wanted to die, to have done. He would not own that life had beaten him, or that death had beaten him.

Going straight to sleep, he slept at once, abandoning himself to the sleep.

So the weeks went on. Always alone, his soul oscillated, first on the side of death, then on the side of life, doggedly. The real agony was that he had nowhere to go, nothing to do, nothing to say, and *was* nothing himself. Sometimes he ran down the streets as if he were mad: sometimes he was mad; things weren't there, things were there. It made him pant. Sometimes he stood before the bar of the public-house where he had called for a drink. Everything suddenly stood back away from him. He saw the face of the barmaid, the gabbling drinkers, his own glass on the slopped, mahogany board, in the distance. There was something between him and them. He could not get into touch. He did not want them; he did not want his drink. Turning abruptly, he went out. On the threshold he stood and looked at the lighted street. But he was not of it or in it. Something separated him. Everything went on there below those lamps, shut away from him. He could not get at them. He felt he couldn't touch the lamp-posts, not if he reached. Where could he go? There was nowhere to go, neither back into the inn, or forward anywhere. He felt stifled. There was nowhere for him. The stress grew inside him; he felt he should smash.

'I mustn't,' he said; and, turning blindly, he went in and drank. Sometimes the drink did him good; sometimes it made him worse. He ran down the road. For ever restless, he went here, there, everywhere. He determined to work. But when he had made six strokes, he loathed the pencil violently, got up, and went away, hurried off to a club where he could play cards or billiards, to a place where he could flirt with a barmaid who was no more to him than the brass pump-handle she drew.

He was very thin and lantern-jawed. He dared not meet his own eyes in the mirror; he never looked at himself. He wanted to get away from himself, but there was nothing to get hold of. In despair he thought of Miriam. Perhaps–perhaps–?

Then, happening to go into the Unitarian Church one Sunday evening, when they stood up to sing the second hymn he saw her before him. The light glistened on her lower lip as she sang. She looked as if she had got something, at any rate; some hope in heaven, if not in earth. Her comfort and her life seemed in the after-world. A warm, strong feeling for her came up. She seemed to yearn, as she sang, for the mystery and comfort. He put his hope in her. He longed for the sermon to be over, to speak to her.

The throng carried her out just before him. He could nearly touch her. She did not know he was there. He saw the brown humble nape of her neck under its black curls. He would leave himself to her. She was better and bigger than he. He would depend on her.

She went wandering, in her blind way, through the little throng of people outside the church. She always looked so lost and out of place among people. He went forward and put his hand on her arm. She started violently. Her great brown eyes dilated with fear, then went questioning at the sight of him. He shrank slightly from her.

'I didn't know—' she faltered.

'Nor I,' he said.

He looked away. His sudden, flaring hope shrank again.

'What are you doing in town?' he asked.

'I'm staying at Cousin Annie's.'

'Ha! For long?'

'No; only till to-morrow.'

'Must you go straight home?'

She looked at him, then hid her face under her hat-brim.

'No,' she said—'no: it's not necessary.'

He turned away, and she went with him. They threaded through the throng of church-people. The organ was still sounding in St Mary's. Dark figures came through the lighted doors; people were coming down the steps. The large coloured windows glowed up in the night. The church was like a great lantern suspended. They went down Hollow Stone, and he took the car for the Bridges.

'You will just have supper with me,' he said; 'then I'll bring you back.'

'Very well,' she replied, low and husky.

They scarcely spoke while they were on the car. The Trent ran dark and full under the bridge. Away towards Colwick all was black night. He lived down Holme Road, on the naked edge of the town, facing across the river meadows towards Sneinton Hermitage and the steep scarp of Colwick Wood. The floods were out. The silent water and the darkness spread away on their left. Almost afraid, they hurried along by the houses.

Supper was laid. He swung the curtain over the window. There was a bowl of freesias and scarlet anemones on the table. She bent to them. Still touching them with her finger-tips, she looked at him, saying:

'Aren't they beautiful?'

'Yes,' he said. 'What will you drink—coffee?'

'I should like it,' she said.

'Then excuse me a moment.'

He went out to the kitchen.

Miriam took off her things and looked round. It was a bare, severe room. Her photo, Clara's, Annie's, were on the wall. She looked on the drawing-board to see what he was doing. There were only a few meaningless lines. She looked to see what book he was reading. Evidently just an ordinary novel. The letters in the rack she saw were from Annie, Arthur, and from some men or other she did not know. Everything he had touched, everything that was in the least personal to him, she examined with lingering absorption. He had been gone from her for so long, she wanted to rediscover him, his position, what he was now. But there was not much in the room to help her. It only made her feel rather sad, it was so hard and comfortless.

She was curiously examining a sketch-book when he returned with the coffee.

'There's nothing new in it,' he said, 'and nothing very interesting.'

He put down the tray, and went to look over her shoulder. She turned the pages slowly, intent on examining everything.

'H'm!' he said, as she paused at a sketch. 'I'd forgotten that. It's not bad, is it?'

'No,' she said. 'I don't quite understand it.'

He took the book from her and went through it. Again he made a curious sound of surprise and pleasure.

'There's some not bad stuff in there,' he said.

'Not at all bad,' she answered gravely.

He felt again her interest in his work. Or was it for himself? Why was she always most interested in him as he appeared in his work?

They sat down to supper.

'By the way,' he said, 'didn't I hear something about your earning your own living?'

'Yes,' she replied, bowing her dark head over her cup.

'And what of it?'

'I'm merely going to the farming college at Broughton for three months, and I shall probably be kept on as a teacher there.'

'I say—that sounds all right for you! You always wanted to be independent.'

'Yes.'

'Why didn't you tell me?'

'I only knew last week.'

'But I heard a month ago,' he said.

'Yes, but nothing was settled then.'

'I should have thought,' he said, 'you'd have told me you were trying.'

She ate her food in the deliberate, constrained way, almost as if she recoiled a little from doing anything so publicly, that he knew so well.

'I suppose you're glad,' he said.

'Very glad.'

'Yes—it will be something.'

He was rather disappointed.

'I think it will be a great deal,' she said, almost haughtily, resentfully.

He laughed shortly.

'Why do you think it won't?' she asked.

'Oh, I don't think it won't be a great deal. Only you'll find earning your own living isn't everything.'

'No,' she said, swallowing with difficulty; 'I don't suppose it is.'

'I suppose work *can* be nearly everything to a man,' he said, 'though it isn't to me. But a woman only works with a part of herself. The real and vital part is covered up.'

'But a man can give *all* himself to a work?' she asked.

'Yes, practically.'

'And a woman only the unimportant part of herself?'

'That's it.'

She looked up at him, and her eyes dilated with anger.

'Then,' she said, 'if it's true, it's a great shame.'

'It is. But I don't know everything,' he answered.

After supper they drew up to the fire. He swung her a chair facing him, and they sat down. She was wearing a dress of dark claret colour, that suited her dark complexion and her large features. Still, the curls were fine and free, but her face was much older, the grown throat much thinner. She seemed old to him, older than Clara. Her bloom of youth had quickly gone. A sort of stiffness, of woodenness, had come upon her. She meditated a little while, then looked at him.

'And how are things with you?' she asked.

'About all right,' he answered.

She looked at him, waiting.

'Nay,' she said, very low.

Her brown, nervous hands were clasped over her knee. They had still the lack of confidence or repose, the almost hysterical look. He winced as he saw them. Then he laughed mirthlessly. She put her fingers between her lips. His slim, black, tortured body lay quite still in the chair. She suddenly took her finger out of her mouth and looked at him.

'And you have broken off with Clara?'

'Yes.'

His body lay like an abandoned thing, strewn in the chair.

'You know,' she said, 'I think we ought to get married.'

He opened his eyes for the first time since many months, and attended to her with respect.

'Why?' he said.

'See,' she said, 'how you waste yourself! You might be ill, you might die, and I never know—be no more then than if I had never known you.'

'And if we married?' he asked.

'At any rate, I could prevent you wasting yourself and being a prey to other women—like—like Clara.'

'A prey?' he repeated smiling.

She bowed her head in silence. He lay feeling his despair come up again.

'I'm not sure,' he said slowly, 'that marriage would be much good.'

'I only think of you,' she replied.

'I know you do. But—you love me so much, you want to put me in your pocket. And I should die there smothered.'

She bent her head, put her finger between her lips, while the bitterness surged up in her heart.

'And what will you do otherwise?' she asked.

'I don't know—go on, I suppose. Perhaps I shall soon go abroad.'

The despairing doggedness in his tone made her go on her knees on the rug before the fire, very near to him. There she crouched as if she were crushed by something, and could not raise her head. His hands lay quite inert on the arms of his chair. She was aware of them. She felt that now he lay at her mercy. If she could rise, take him, put her arms round him, and say, 'You are mine,' then he would leave himself to her. But dare she? She could easily sacrifice herself. But dare she assert herself? She was aware of his dark-clothed, slender body, that seemed one stroke of life, sprawled in the chair close to her. But no she dared not put her arms round it, take it up, and say, 'It is mine, this body. Leave it to me.' And she wanted to. It called to all her woman's instinct. But she crouched, and dared not. She was afraid he would not let her. She was afraid it was too much. It lay there, his body, abandoned. She knew she ought to take it up and claim it, and claim every right to it. But—could she do it? Her impotence before him, before the strong demand of some unknown thing in him, was her extremity. Her hands fluttered; she half lifted her head. Her eyes, shuddering, appealing, gone almost distracted, pleaded to him suddenly. His heart caught with pity. He took her hands, drew her to him, and comforted her.

'Will you have me, to marry me?' he said, very low.

Oh, why did not he take her? Her very soul belonged to him. Why should he not take what was his? She had borne so long the cruelty of belonging to him and not being claimed by him. Now he was straining her again. It was too much for her. She drew back her head, held his face between her hands, and looked him in the eyes. No, he was hard. He wanted something else. She pleaded to him with all her love not to make it *her* choice. She could not cope with it, with him, she knew not with what. But it strained her till she felt she would break.

'Do you want it?' she asked, very gravely.

'Not much,' he replied, with pain.

She turned her face aside; then, raising herself with dignity, she took his head to her bosom, and rocked him softly. She was not to have him, then! So she could comfort him. She put her fingers through his hair. For her, the anguished sweetness of self-sacrifice. For him, the hate and misery of another failure. He could not bear it—that breast which was warm and which cradled him without taking the burden of him. So much he wanted to rest on her that the feint of rest only tortured him. He drew away.

'And without marriage we can do nothing?' he asked.

His mouth was lifted from his teeth with pain. She put her little finger between her lips.

'No,' she said, low and like the toll of a bell. 'No, I think not.'

It was the end then between them. She could not take him and relieve him of the responsibility of himself. She could only sacrifice herself to him—sacrifice herself every day, gladly. And that he did not want. He wanted her to hold him and say, with joy and authority: 'Stop all this restlessness and beating against death. You are mine for a mate.' She had not the strength. Or was it a mate she wanted? or did she want a Christ in him?

He felt, in leaving her, he was defrauding her of life. But he knew that, in staying, stifling the inner, desperate man, he was denying his own life. And he did not hope to give life to her by denying his own.

She sat very quiet. He lit a cigarette. The smoke went up from it, wavering. He was thinking of his mother, and had forgotten Miriam. She suddenly looked at him. Her bitterness came surging up. Her sacrifice, then, was useless. He lay there aloof, careless about her. Suddenly she saw again his lack of religion, his restless instability. He would destroy himself like a perverse child. Well, then, he would!

'I think I must go,' she said, softly.

By her tone he knew she was despising him. He rose quietly.

'I'll come with you,' he answered.

She stood before the mirror pinning on her hat. How bitter, how unutterably bitter, it made her that he rejected her sacrifice! Life ahead looked dead, as if the glow were gone out. She bowed her face over the flowers—the freesias so sweet and spring-like, the scarlet anemones flaunting over the table. It was like him to have those flowers.

He moved about the room with a certain sureness of touch, swift and relentless and quiet. She knew she could not cope with him. He would escape like a weasel out of her hands. Yet without him her life would trail on lifeless. Brooding, she touched the flowers.

'Have them!' he said; and he took them out of the jar, dripping as they were, and went quickly into the kitchen. She waited for him, took the flowers, and they went out together, he talking, she feeling dead.

She was going from him now. In her misery she leaned against him as they sat on the car. He was unresponsive. Where would he go? What would be the end of him? She could not bear it, the vacant feeling where he should be. He was so foolish, so wasteful, never at peace with himself. And now where would he go?

And what did he care that he wasted her? He had no religion; it was all for the moment's attraction that he cared, nothing else, nothing deeper. Well, she would wait and see how it turned out with him. When he had had enough he would give in and come to her.

He shook hands and left her at the door of her cousin's house. When he turned away he felt the last hold for him had gone. The town, as he sat upon the car, stretched away over the bay of railway, a level fume of lights. Beyond the town the country, little smouldering spots for more towns—the sea—the night—on and on! And he had no place in it! Whatever spot he stood in, there he stood alone. From his breast, from his mouth, sprang the endless space, and it was there behind him, everywhere. The people hurrying along the streets offered no obstruction to the void in which he found himself. They were small shadows whose footsteps and voices could be heard, but in each of them the same night, the same silence. He got off the car. In the country all was dead still. Little stars shone high up; little stars spread far away in the flood-waters, a firmament below. Everywhere the vastness and terror of the immense night which is roused and stirred for a brief while by the day, but which returns, and will remain at last eternal, holding everything in its silence and its living gloom. There was no Time, only Space. Who could say his mother had lived and did not live? She had been in one place, and was in another; that was all. And his soul could not leave her, wherever she was. Now she was gone abroad into the night, and he was with her still. They were together. But yet there was his body, his chest, that leaned against the stile, his hands on the wooden bar. They seemed something. Where was he?—one tiny upright speck of flesh, less than an ear of wheat lost in the field. He could not bear it. On every side the immense dark silence seemed pressing him, so tiny a spark, into extinction, and yet, almost nothing, he could not be extinct. Night, in which everything was lost, went reaching out, beyond stars and sun. Stars and sun, a few bright grains, went spinning round for terror, and holding each other in embrace, there in a darkness that outpassed them all, and left them tiny and daunted. So much, and himself, infinitesimal, at the core a nothingness, and yet not nothing.

'Mother!' he whispered—'mother!'

She was the only thing that held him up, himself, amid all this. And she was gone, intermingled herself. He wanted her to touch him, have him alongside with her.

But no, he would not give in. Turning sharply, he walked towards the city's gold phosphorescence. His fists were shut, his mouth set fast. He would not take that direction, to the darkness, to follow her. He walked towards the faintly humming, glowing town, quickly.

D.H. LAWRENCE

ST MAWR

Lou Witt had had her own way so long, that by the age of twenty-five she didn't know where she was. Having one's own way landed one completely at sea.

To be sure for a while she had failed in her grand love affair with Rico. And then she had had something really to despair about. But even that had worked out as she wanted. Rico had come back to her, and was dutifully married to her. And now, when she was twenty-five and he was three months older, they were a charming married couple. He flirted with other women still, to be sure. He wouldn't be the handsome Rico if he didn't. But she had 'got' him. Oh yes! You had only to see the uneasy backward glance at her, from his big blue eyes: just like a horse that is edging away from its master: to know how completely he was mastered.

She, with her odd little *museau*, not exactly pretty, but very attractive; and her quaint air of playing at being well bred, in a sort of charade game; and her queer familiarity with foreign cities and foreign languages; and the lurking sense of being an outsider everywhere, like a sort of gipsy, who is at home anywhere and nowhere: all this made up her charm and her failure. She didn't quite belong.

Of course she was American: Louisiana family, moved down to Texas. And she was moderately rich, with no close relation except her mother. But she had been sent to school in France when she was twelve, and since she had finished school, she had drifted from Paris to Palermo, Biarritz to Vienna and back via Munich to London, then down again to Rome. Only fleeting trips to her America.

So what sort of American was she, after all?

And what sort of European was she either? She didn't 'belong' anywhere. Perhaps most of all in Rome, among the artists and the Embassy people.

It was in Rome she had met Rico. He was an Australian, son of a government official in Melbourne, who had been made a baronet. So one day Rico would be Sir Henry, as he was the only son. Meanwhile he floated round Europe on a very small allowance—his father wasn't rich in capital—and was being an artist.

They met in Rome when they were twenty-two, and had a love affair in Capri. Rico was handsome, elegant, but mostly he had spots of paint on his trousers and he ruined a neck-tie pulling it off. He behaved in a most floridly elegant fashion, fascinating to the Italians. But at the same time he was canny and shrewd and sensible as any young poser could be and, on principle, good-hearted, anxious. He was anxious for his future, and anxious for his place in the world, he was poor, and suddenly wasteful in spite of all his tension of economy, and suddenly spiteful in spite of all his ingratiating efforts, and suddenly ungrateful in spite of all his burden of gratitude, and suddenly rude in spite of all his good manners, and suddenly detestable in spite of all his suave, courtier-like amiability.

He was fascinated by Lou's quaint aplomb, her experiences, her 'knowledge', her *gamine* knowingness, her aloneness, her pretty clothes that were sometimes an utter failure, and her southern 'drawl' that was sometimes so irritating. That sing-song which was so American. Yet she used no Americanisms at all, except when she lapsed into her odd spasms of acid irony, when she was very American indeed!

And she was fascinated by Rico. They played to each other like two butterflies at one flower. They pretended to be very poor in Rome–he *was* poor: and very rich in Naples. Everybody stared their eyes out at them. And they had that love affair in Capri.

But they reacted badly on each other's nerves. She became ill. Her mother appeared. He couldn't stand Mrs Witt, and Mrs Witt couldn't stand him. There was a terrible fortnight. Then Lou was popped into a convent nursing-home in Umbria, and Rico dashed off to Paris. Nothing would stop him. He must go back to Australia.

He went to Melbourne, and while there his father died, leaving him a baronet's title and an income still very moderate. Lou visited America once more, as the strangest of strange lands to her. She came away disheartened, panting for Europe, and, of course, doomed to meet Rico again.

They couldn't get away from one another, even though in the course of their rather restrained correspondence he informed her that he was 'probably' marrying a very dear girl, friend of his childhood, only daughter of one of the oldest families in Victoria. Not saying much.

He didn't commit the probability, but reappeared in Paris, wanting to paint his head off, terribly inspired by Cézanne and by old Renoir. He dined at the Rotonde with Lou and Mrs Witt, who, with her queer democratic New Orleans sort of conceit, looked round the drinking-hall with savage contempt, and at Rico as part of his show. 'Certainly,' she said, 'when these people here have got any money, they fall in love on a full stomach. And when they've got no money, they fall in love with a full pocket. I never was in a more disgusting place. They take their love like some people take after-dinner pills.'

She would watch with her arching, full, strong grey eyes, sitting there erect and silent in her well-bought American clothes. And then she would deliver some such charge of grape-shot. Rico always writhed.

Mrs Witt hated Paris: 'this sordid, unlucky city,' she called it. 'Something unlucky is bound to happen to me in this sinister, unclean town,' she said. 'I feel *contagion* in the air of this place. For heaven's sake, Louise, let us go to Morocco or somewhere.'

'No, mother dear, I can't now. Rico has proposed to me, and I have accepted him. Let us think about a wedding, shall we?'

'There!' said Mrs Witt. 'I said it was an unlucky city!'

And the peculiar look of extreme New Orleans annoyance came round her sharp nose. But Lou and Rico were both twenty-four years old, and beyond management. And, anyhow, Lou would be Lady Carrington. But Mrs Witt was exasperated beyond exasperation. She would almost rather have preferred Lou to elope with one of the great, evil porters at Les Halles. Mrs Witt was at the age when the malevolent male in man, the old Adam, begins to loom above all the social tailoring. And yet–and yet–it was better to have Lady Carrington for a daughter, seeing Lou was that sort.

There was a marriage, after which Mrs Witt departed to America, Lou and Rico leased a little old house in Westminster, and began to settle into a certain layer of English society. Rico was becoming an almost fashionable portrait-painter. At least, *he* was almost fashionable, whether his portraits were or not. And Lou, too, was almost fashionable: almost a hit. There was some flaw somewhere. In spite of their appearances, both Rico and she would never quite go down in any society. They were the drifting artist sort. Yet neither of them was content to be of the drifting artist sort. They wanted to fit in, to make good.

Hence the little house in Westminster, the portraits, the dinners, the friends, and the visits. Mrs Witt came and sardonically established herself in a suite in a quiet but good-class hotel not far off. Being on the spot. And her terrible grey eyes with the touch of a leer looked on at the hollow mockery of things. As if *she* knew of anything better!

Lou and Rico had a curious exhausting effect on one another: neither knew why. They were fond of one another. Some inscrutable bond held them together. But it was a strange vibration of the nerves, rather than of the blood. A nervous attachment, rather than a sexual love. A curious tension of will, rather than a spontaneous passion. Each was curiously under the domination of the other. They were a pair—they had to be together. Yet quite soon they shrank from one another. This attachment of the will and the nerves was destructive. As soon as one felt strong, the other felt ill. As soon as the ill one recovered strength, down went the one who had been well.

And soon, tacitly, the marriage became more like a friendship, platonic. It was a marriage, but without sex. Sex was shattering and exhausting, they shrank from it, and became like brother and sister. But still they were husband and wife. And the lack of physical relation was a secret source of uneasiness and chagrin to both of them. They would neither of them accept it. Rico looked with contemplative, anxious eyes at other women.

Mrs Witt kept track of everything, watching, as it were, from outside the fence, like a potent well-dressed demon, full of uncanny energy and a shattering sort of sense. She said little: but her small, occasionally biting remarks revealed her attitude of contempt for the *ménage*.

Rico entertained clever and well-known people. Mrs Witt would appear, in her New York gowns and few good jewels. She was handsome, with her vigorous grey hair. But her heavy-lidded grey eyes were the despair of any hostess. They looked too many shattering things. And it was but too obvious that these clever, well-known English people got on her nerves terribly, with their finickiness and their fine-drawn discriminations. She wanted to put her foot through all these fine-drawn distinctions. She thought continually of the house of her girlhood, the plantation, the negroes, the planters: the sardonic grimness that underlay all the big, shiftless life. And she wanted to cleave with some of this grimness of the big, dangerous America, into the safe, finicky drawing-rooms of London. So naturally she was not popular.

But being a woman of energy, she had to do *something*. During the latter part of the war she had worked in the American Red Cross in France, nursing. She loved men—real men. But, on close contact, it was difficult to define what she meant by 'real' men. She never met any.

Out of the *débâcle* of the war she had emerged with an odd piece of débris, in the shape of Gerónimo Trujillo. He was an American, son of a Mexican father and a Navajo Indian mother, from Arizona. When you knew him well, you recognised the real half-breed, though at a glance he might pass as a sunburnt citizen of any nation, particularly of France. He looked like a certain sort of Frenchman, with his curiously-set dark eyes, his straight black hair, his thin black moustache, his rather long cheeks, and his almost slouching, diffident, sardonic bearing. Only when you knew him, and looked right into his eyes, you saw that unforgettable glint of the Indian.

He had been badly shell-shocked, and was for a time a wreck. Mrs Witt, having nursed him into convalescence, asked him where he was going next. He didn't know. His father and mother were dead, and he had nothing to take him back to Phœnix, Arizona. Having had an education in one of the Indian high schools, the unhappy fellow had now no place in life at all. Another of the many misfits.

There was something of the Paris *Apache* in his appearance: but he was all the time withheld, and nervously shut inside himself. Mrs Witt was intrigued by him.

'Very well, Phœnix,' she said, refusing to adopt his Spanish name, 'I'll see what I can do.'

What she did was to get him a place on a sort of manor farm, with some acquaintances of hers. He was very good with horses, and had a curious success with turkeys and geese and fowls.

Some time after Lou's marriage, Mrs Witt reappeared in London, from the country, with Phœnix in tow, and a couple of horses. She had decided that she would ride in the Park in the morning, and see the world that way, Phœnix was to be her groom.

So, to the great misgiving of Rico, behold Mrs Witt in splendidly tailored habit and perfect boots, a smart black hat on her smart grey hair, riding a grey gelding as smart as she was, and looking down her conceited, inquisitive, scornful, aristocratic-democratic Louisiana nose at the people in Piccadilly, as she crossed to the Row, followed by the taciturn shadow of Phœnix, who sat on a chestnut with three white feet as if he had grown there.

Mrs Witt, like many other people, always expected to find the real *beau monde* and the real *grand monde* somewhere or other. She didn't quite give in to what she saw in the Bois de Boulogne, or in Monte Carlo, or on the Pincio: all a bit shoddy, and not very *beau* and not at all *grand*. There she was, with her grey eagle eye, her splendid complexion and her weapon-like health of a woman of fifty, dropping her eyelids a little, very slightly nervous, but completely prepared to despise the *monde* she was entering in Rotten Row.

In she sailed, and up and down that regatta-canal of horsemen and horsewomen under the trees of the Park. And yes, there were lovely girls with fair hair down their backs, on happy ponies. And awfully well-groomed papas, and tight mamas who looked as if they were going to pour tea between the ears of their horses, and converse with banal skill, one eye on the teapot, one on the visitor with whom she was talking, and all the rest of her hostess's argus eyes upon everybody in sight. That alert argus capability of the English matron was startling and a bit horrifying. Mrs Witt would at once think of the old negro mammies, away in Louisiana. And her eyes became dagger-like as she watched the clipped, shorn, mincing young Englishmen. She refused to look at the prosperous Jews.

It was still the days before motor-cars were allowed in the Park, but Rico and Lou, sliding round Hyde Park Corner and up Park Lane in their car, would watch the steely horsewoman and the saturnine groom with a sort of dismay. Mrs Witt seemed to be pointing a pistol at the bosom of every other horseman or horsewoman and announcing: '*Your virility or your life! Your femininity or your life!*' She didn't know herself what she really wanted them to be: but it was something as democratic as Abraham Lincoln and as aristocratic as a Russian czar, as highbrow as Arthur Balfour, and as taciturn and unideal as Phœnix. Everything at once.

There was nothing for it: Lou had to buy herself a horse and ride at her mother's side, for very decency's sake. Mrs Witt was *so* like a smooth, levelled, gunmetal pistol, Lou had to be a sort of sheath. And she really looked pretty, with her clusters of dark, curly, New Orleans hair, like grapes, and her quaint brown eyes that didn't quite match, and that looked a bit sleepy and vague, and at the same time quick as a squirrel's. She was slight and elegant, and a tiny bit rakish, and somebody suggested she might be on the movies.

Nevertheless, they were in the society columns next morning—*two new and striking figures in the Row this morning were Lady Henry Carrington and her mother, Mrs Witt*, etc. And Mrs Witt liked it, let her say what she might. So did Lou. Lou liked it immensely. She simply luxuriated in the sun of publicity.

'Rico dear, you must get a horse.'

The tone was soft and southern and drawling, but the overtone had a decisive finality. In vain Rico squirmed—he had a way of writhing and squirming which perhaps he had caught at Oxford. In vain he protested that he couldn't ride, and that he didn't care for riding. He got quite angry, and his handsome arched nose tilted and his upper lip lifted from his teeth, like a dog that is going to bite. Yet daren't quite bite.

And that was Rico. He daren't quite bite. Not that he was really afraid of the others. He was afraid of himself, once he let himself go. He might rip up in an eruption of life-long anger all this pretty-pretty picture of a charming young wife and a delightful little home and a fascinating success as a painter of fashionable, and at the same time 'great' portraits: with colour, wonderful colour, and at the same time, form, marvellous form. He had composed this little *tableau vivant* with great effort. He didn't want to erupt like some suddenly wicked horse—Rico was really more like a horse than a dog, a horse that might go nasty any moment. For the time, he was good, very good, dangerously good.

'Why, Rico dear, I thought you used to ride so much, in Australia, when you were young? Didn't you tell me all about it, hm?'—and as she ended on that slow, singing *hm?*, which acted on him like an irritant and a drug, he knew he was beaten.

Lou kept the sorrel mare in a mews just behind the house in Westminster, and she was always slipping round to the stables. She had a funny little nostalgia for the place: something that really surprised her. She had never had the faintest notion that she cared for horses and stables and grooms. But she did. She was fascinated. Perhaps it was her childhood's Texas associations come back. Whatever it was, her life with Rico in the elegant little house, and all her social engagements seemed like a dream, the substantial reality of which was those mews in Westminster, her sorrel mare, the owner of the mews, Mr Saintsbury, and the grooms he employed. Mr Saintsbury was a horsey, elderly man like an old maid, and he loved the sound of titles.

'Lady Carrington!—well I never! You've come to us for a bit of company again, I see. I don't know whatever we shall do if you go away, we shall be that lonely!' and he flashed his old-maid's smile at her. 'No matter how grey the morning, your ladyship would make a beam of sunshine. Poppy is all right, I think. . . .'

Poppy was the sorrel mare with the no white feet and the startled eye, and she was all right. And Mr Saintsbury was smiling with his old-maid's mouth, and showing all his teeth.

'Come across with me, Lady Carrington, and look at a new horse just up from the country. I think he's worth a look, and I believe you have a moment to spare, your Ladyship.'

Her Ladyship had too many moments to spare. She followed the sprightly, elderly, clean-shaven man across the yard to a loose-box, and waited while he opened the door.

In the inner dark she saw a handsome bay horse with his clean ears pricked like daggers from his naked head as he swung handsomely round to stare at the open doorway. He had big, black, brilliant eyes, with a sharp questioning glint, and that air of tense, alert quietness which betrays an animal that can be dangerous.

'Is he quiet?' Lou asked.

'Why—yes—my Lady! He's quiet, with those that know how to handle him. *Cup! my boy! Cup, my beauty! Cup then! St Mawr!*'

Loquacious even with the animals, he went softly forward and laid his hand on the horse's shoulder, soft and quiet as a fly settling. Lou saw the brilliant skin of the horse crinkle a little in apprehensive anticipation, like the shadow of the descending hand on a bright red-gold liquid. But then the animal relaxed again.

'Quiet with those that know how to handle him, and a bit of a ruffian with those that don't. Isn't that the ticket, eh, St Mawr?'

'What is his name?' Lou asked.

The man repeated it, with a slight Welsh twist—'He's from the Welsh borders, belonging to a Welsh gentleman, Mr Griffith Edwards. But they're wanting to sell him.'

'How old is he?' asked Lou.

'About seven years—seven years and five months,' said Mr Saintsbury, dropping his voice as if it were a secret.

'Could one ride him in the Park?'

'Well—yes! I should say a gentleman who knew how to handle him could ride him very well and make a very handsome figure in the Park.'

Lou at once decided that this handsome figure should be Rico's. For she was already half in love with St Mawr. He was of such a lovely red-gold colour, and a dark, invisible fire seemed to come out of him. But in his big black eyes there was a lurking afterthought. Something told her that the horse was not quite happy: that somewhere deep in his animal consciousness lived a dangerous, half-revealed resentment, a diffused sense of hostility. She realised that he was sensitive, in spite of his flaming, healthy strength, and nervous with a touchy uneasiness that might make him vindictive.

'Has he got any tricks?' she asked.

'Not that I know of, my Lady: not tricks exactly. But he's one of these temperamental creatures, as they say. Though *I* say, every horse is temperamental, when you come down to it. But this one, it is as if he was a trifle raw somewhere. Touch this raw spot, and there's no answering for him.'

'Where is he raw?' asked Lou, somewhat mystified. She thought he might really have some physical sore.

'Why, that's hard to say, my Lady. If he was a human being, you'd say something had gone wrong in his life. But with a horse it's not that, exactly. A high-bred animal like St Mawr needs understanding, and I don't know as anybody has quite got the hang of him. I confess I haven't myself. But I do realise that he is a special animal and needs a special sort of touch, and I'm willing he should have it, did I but know exactly what it is.'

She looked at the glowing bay horse that stood there with his ears back, his face averted, but attending as if he were some lightning-conductor. He was a stallion. When she realised this, she became more afraid of him.

'Why does Mr Griffith Edwards want to sell him?' she asked.

'Well–my Lady–they raised him for stud purposes–but he didn't answer. There are horses like that: don't seem to fancy the mares for some reason. Well, anyway, they couldn't keep him for the stud. And as you see, he's a powerful, beautiful hackney, clean as a whistle, and eaten up with his own power. But there's no putting him between the shafts. He won't stand it. He's a fine saddle-horse, beautiful action, and lovely to ride. But he's got to be handled, and there you are.'

Lou felt there was something behind the man's reticence.

'Has he ever made a break?' she asked, apprehensive.

'Made a break?' replied the man. 'Well, if I must admit it, he's had two accidents. Mr Griffith Edwards's son rode him a bit wild, away there in the Forest of Dean, and the young fellow had his skull smashed in against a low oak bough. Last autumn, that was. And some time back, he crushed a groom against the side of the stall–injured him fatally. But they were both accidents, my Lady. Things will happen.'

The man spoke in a melancholy, fatalistic way. The horse, with his ears laid back, seemed to be listening tensely, his face averted. He looked like something finely bred and passionate that has been judged and condemned.

'May I say *how do you do*?' she said to the horse, drawing a little nearer in her white, summery dress and lifting her hand that glittered with emeralds and diamonds.

He drifted away from her, as if some wind blew him. Then he ducked his head and looked sideway at her from his black, full eye.

'I think I'm all right,' she said, edging nearer, while he watched her.

She laid her hand on his side and gently stroked him. Then she stroked his shoulder, and then the hard, tense arch of his neck. And she was startled to feel the vivid heat of his life come through to her, through the lacquer of red-gold gloss. So slippery with vivid, hot life!

She paused, as if thinking, while her hand rested on the horse's sun-arched neck. Dimly, in her weary young woman's soul, an ancient understanding seemed to flood in.

She wanted to buy St Mawr.

'I think,' she said to Saintsbury, 'if I can, I will buy him.'

The man looked at her long and shrewdly.

'Well, my Lady,' he said at last, 'there shall be nothing kept from you. But what would your Ladyship do with him, if I may make so bold?'

'I don't know,' she replied vaguely. 'I might take him to America.'

The man paused once more, then said:

'They say it's been the making of some horses, to take them over the water, to Australia or such places. It might repay you–you never know.'

She wanted to buy St Mawr. She wanted him to belong to her. For some reason the sight of him, his power, his alive, alert intensity, his unyieldingness, made her want to cry.

She never did cry: except sometimes with vexation, or to get her own way. As far as weeping went, her heart felt as dry as a Christmas walnut. What was the good of tears, anyhow? You had to keep on holding on in this life, never give way, and never give in. Tears only left one weakened and ragged.

But now, as if that mysterious fire of the horse's body had split some rock in her, she went home and hid herself in her room, and just cried. The wild, brilliant, alert head of St Mawr seemed to look at her out of another world. It was as if she had had a vision, as if the walls of her own world had suddenly melted away, leaving her in a great darkness, in the midst of which the large, brilliant eyes of that horse looked at her with demonish question, while his naked ears stood up like daggers from the naked lines of his inhuman head, and his great body glowed red with power.

What was it? Almost like a god looking at her terribly out of the everlasting dark, she had felt the eyes of that horse; great, glowing, fearsome eyes, arched with a question and containing a white blade of light like a threat. What was his non-human question, and his uncanny threat? She didn't know. He was some splendid demon, and she must worship him.

She hid herself away from Rico. She could not bear the triviality and superficiality of her human relationships. Looming like some god out of the darkness was the head of that horse, with the wide, terrible, questioning eyes. And she felt that it forbade her to be her ordinary, commonplace self. It forbade her to be just Rico's wife, young Lady Carrington, and all that.

It haunted her, the horse. It had looked at her as she had never been looked at before: terrible, gleaming, questioning eyes arching out of darkness, and backed by all the fire of that great ruddy body. What did it mean, and what ban did it put upon her? She felt it put a ban on her heart: wielded some uncanny authority over her, that she dared not, could not understand.

No matter where she was, what she was doing, at the back of her consciousness loomed a great, over-aweing figure out of a dark background: St Mawr, looking at her without really seeing her, yet gleaming a question at her, from his wide, terrible eyes, and gleaming a sort of menace, doom. Master of doom, he seemed to be!

'You are thinking about something, Lou dear!' Rico said to her that evening.

He was so quick and sensitive to detect her moods–so exciting in this respect. And his big, slightly prominent blue eyes, with the whites a little bloodshot, glanced at her quickly, with searching and anxiety, and a touch of fear, as if his conscience were always uneasy. He, too, was rather like a horse–but forever quivering with a sort of cold, dangerous mistrust, which he covered with anxious love.

At the middle of his eyes was a central powerlessness that left him anxious. It used to touch her to pity, that central look of powerlessness in him. But now, since she had seen the full, dark, passionate blaze of power and of different life in the eyes of the thwarted horse, the anxious powerlessness of the man drove her mad. Rico was so handsome, and he was so self-controlled, he had a gallant sort of kindness and a real worldly shrewdness. One had to admire him: at least *she* had to.

But after all, and after all, it was a bluff, an attitude. He kept it all working in himself deliberately. It was an attitude. She read psychologists who said that everything was an attitude. Even the best of everything. But now she realised that, with men and women, everything is an attitude only when something else is lacking. Something is lacking and they are thrown back on their own devices. That black fiery flow in the eyes of the horse was not 'attitude'. It was something much more terrifying, and real, the only thing that was real. Gushing from the darkness in menace and question, and blazing out in the splendid body of the horse.

'Was I thinking about something?' she replied in her slow, amused, casual fashion. As if everything was so casual and easy to her. And so it was, from the hard, polished side of herself. But that wasn't the whole story.

'I think you were, Loulina. May we offer the penny?'

'Don't trouble,' she said. 'I was thinking, if I was thinking of anything, about a bay horse called St Mawr.'–Her secret *almost* crept into her eyes.

'The name is awfully attractive,' he said with a laugh.

'Not so attractive as the creature himself. I'm going to buy him.'

'Not really!' he said. 'But why?'

'He *is* so attractive. I'm going to buy him for you.'

'For *me*? *Darling*? how you do take me for granted. He may not be in the least attractive to me. As you know, I have hardly any feeling for horses at all.–Besides, how much does he cost?'

'That I don't know, Rico dear. But I'm sure you'll love him, for my sake.'–She felt, now, she was merely playing for her own ends.

'Lou dearest, *don't* spend a fortune on a horse for me, which I *don't* want. Honestly, I prefer a car.'

'Won't you ride with me in the Park, Rico?'

'Honestly, dear Lou, I don't want to.'

'Why not, dear boy? You look so beautiful. I wish you would.–And, anyhow, come with me to look at St Mawr.'

Rico was divided. He had a certain uneasy feeling about horses. At the same time, he *would* like to cut a handsome figure in the Park.

They went across to the mews. A little Welsh groom was watering the brilliant horse.

'Yes, dear, he certainly *is* beautiful: such a marvellous colour! Almost orange! But rather large, I should say, to ride in the Park.'

'No, for you he's perfect. You are so tall.'

'He'd be marvellous in a Composition. The colour!'

And all Rico could do was to gaze with the artist's eye at the horse, with a glance at the groom.

'Don't you think the man is rather fascinating too?' he said, nursing his chin artistically and penetratingly.

The groom, Lewis, was a little, quick, rather bow-legged, loosely-built fellow of indeterminate age, with a mop of black hair and a little black beard. He was grooming the brilliant St Mawr out in the open. The horse was really glorious: like a marigold, with a pure golden sheen, a shimmer of green-gold lacquer upon a burning red-orange. There on the shoulder you saw the yellow lacquer glisten. Lewis, a little scrub of a fellow, worked absorbedly, unheedingly at the horse, with an absorption that was almost ritualistic. He seemed the attendant shadow of the ruddy animal.

'He goes with the horse,' said Lou. 'If we buy St Mawr we get the man thrown in.'

'They'd be *so* amusing to paint; such an extraordinary contrast! But darling, I *hope* you won't insist on buying the horse. It's so frightfully expensive.'

'Mother will help me.–You'd look so well on him, Rico.'

'If ever I dared take the liberty of getting on his back–!'

'Why not?' She went quickly across the cobbled yard.

'Good morning, Lewis. How is St Mawr?'

Lewis straightened himself and looked at her from under the falling mop of his black hair.

'All right,' he said.

He peered straight at her from under his overhanging black hair. He had pale grey eyes, that looked phosphorescent, and suggested the eyes of a wild cat peering intent from under the darkness of some bush where it lies unseen. Lou, with her brown, unmatched, oddly perplexed eyes, felt herself found out.—'He's a common little fellow,' she thought to herself. 'But he knows a woman and a horse at sight.'—Aloud she said, in her Southern drawl:

'How do you think he'd be with Sir Henry?'

Lewis turned his remote, coldly watchful eyes on the young baronet. Rico was tall and handsome and balanced on his hips. His face was long and well-defined, and with the hair taken straight back from the brow. It seemed as well-made as his clothing, and as perpetually presentable. You could not imagine his face dirty, or scrubby and unshaven, or bearded, or even moustached. It was perfectly prepared for social purposes. If his head had been cut off, like John the Baptist's, it would have been a thing complete in itself, would not have missed the body in the least. The body was perfectly tailored. The head was one of the famous 'talking heads' of modern youth, with eyebrows a trifle Mephistophelian, large blue eyes a trifle bold, and curved mouth thrilling to death to kiss.

Lewis, the groom, staring from between his bush of hair and his beard, watched like an animal from the underbrush. And Rico was still sufficiently a colonial to be uneasily aware of the underbrush, uneasy under the watchfulness of the pale grey eyes, and uneasy in that man-to-man exposure which is characteristic of the democratic colonies and of America. He knew he must ultimately be judged on his merits as a man, alone without a background: an ungarnished colonial.

This lack of background, this defenceless man-to-man business which left him at the mercy of every servant, was bad for his nerves. For he was *also* an artist. He bore up against it in a kind of desperation, and was easily moved to rancorous resentment. At the same time he was free of the Englishman's water-tight *suffisance*. He really was aware that he would have to hold his own all alone, thrown alone on his own defences in the universe. The extreme democracy of the Colonies had taught him this.

And this, the little aboriginal Lewis recognised in him. He recognised also Rico's curious hollow misgiving, fear of some deficiency in himself, beneath all his handsome, young-hero appearance.

'He'd be all right with anybody as would meet him half-way,' said Lewis, in the quick Welsh manner of speech, impersonal.

'You hear, Rico!' said Lou in her sing-song, turning to her husband.

'Perfectly, darling!'

'Would you be willing to meet St Mawr half-way, hm?'

'All the way, darling! Mahomet would go *all* the way to that mountain. Who would dare do otherwise?'

He spoke with a laughing, yet piqued sarcasm.

'Why, I think St Mawr would understand perfectly,' she said in the soft voice of a woman haunted by love. And she went and laid her hand on the slippery, life-smooth shoulder of the horse. He, with his strange equine head lowered, its exquisite fine lines reaching a little snake-like forward, and his ears a little back, was watching her sideways from the corner of his eye. He was in a state of absolute mistrust, like a cat crouching to spring.

'St Mawr!' she said. 'St Mawr! What is the matter? Surely you and I are all right!'

And she spoke softly, dreamily stroked the animal's neck. She could feel a response gradually coming from him. But he would not lift up his head. And when Rico suddenly moved nearer, he sprang with a sudden jerk backwards, as if lightning exploded in his four hoofs.

The groom spoke a few low words in Welsh. Lou, frightened, stood with lifted hand arrested. She had been going to stroke him.

'Why did he do that?' she said.

'They gave him a beating once or twice,' said the groom in a neutral voice, 'and he doesn't forget.'

She could hear a neutral sort of judgment in Lewis's voice. And she thought of the 'raw spot'.

Not any raw spot at all. A battle between two worlds. She realised that St Mawr drew his hot breaths in another world from Rico's, from our world. Perhaps the old Greek horses had lived in St Mawr's world. And the old Greek heroes, even Hippolytus, had known it.

With their strangely naked equine heads, and something of a snake in their way of looking round, and lifting their sensitive, dangerous muzzles, they moved in a prehistoric twilight where all things loomed phantasmagoric, all on one plane, sudden presences suddenly jutting out of the matrix. It was another world, an older, heavily potent world. And in this world the horse was swift and fierce and supreme, undominated and unsurpassed. – 'Meet him half-way,' Lewis said. But half-way across from our human world to that terrific equine twilight was not a small step. It was a step, she knew, that Rico could never take. She knew it. But she was prepared to sacrifice Rico.

St Mawr was bought, and Lewis was hired along with him. At first, Lewis rode him behind Lou, in the Row, to get him going. He behaved perfectly.

Phœnix, the half Indian, was very jealous when he saw the black-bearded Welsh groom on St Mawr.

'What horse you got there?' he asked, looking at the other man with the curious unseeing stare in his hard, Navajo eyes, in which the Indian glint moved like a spark upon a dark chaos. In Phœnix's high-boned face there was all the race misery of the dispossessed Indian, with an added blankness left by shell-shock. But at the same time, there was that unyielding, save to death, which is characteristic of his tribe; his mother's tribe. Difficult to say what subtle thread bound him to the Navajo, and made his destiny a Red Man's destiny still.

They were a curious pair of grooms, following the correct, and yet extraordinary, pair of American mistresses. Mrs Witt and Phœnix both rode with long stirrups and straight leg, sitting close to the saddle, without posting. Phœnix looked as if he and the horse were all one piece, he never seemed to rise in the saddle at all, neither trotting nor galloping, but sat like a man riding bareback. And all the time he stared around at the riders in the Row, at the people grouped outside the rail, chatting, at the children walking with their nurses, as if he were looking at a mirage, in whose actuality he never believed for a moment. London was all a sort of dark mirage to him. His wide, nervous-looking brown eyes with a smallish brown pupil, that showed the white all round, seemed to be focused on the far distance, as if he could not see things too near. He was watching the pale deserts of Arizona shimmer with moving light, the long mirage of a shallow lake ripple, the great pallid concave of earth and sky expanding with inter-changed light. And a horse-shape loom large and portentous in the mirage, like some prehistoric beast.

That was real to him: the phantasm of Arizona. But this London was something his eye passed over as a false mirage.

He looked too smart in his well-tailored groom's clothes, so smart, he might have been one of the satirised new rich. Perhaps it was a sort of half-breed physical assertion that came through his clothing, the savage's physical assertion of himself. Anyhow, he looked 'common', rather horsey and loud.

Except his face. In the golden suavity of his high-boned Indian face, that was hairless, with hardly any eyebrows, there was a blank, lost look that was almost touching. The same startled blank look was in his eyes. But in the smallish dark pupils the dagger-point of light still gleamed unbroken.

He was a good groom, watchful, quick, and on the spot in an instant if anything went wrong. He had a curious quiet power over the horses, unemotional, unsympathetic, but silently potent. In the same way, watching the traffic of Piccadilly with his blank, glinting eye, he would calculate everything instinctively, as if it were an enemy, and pilot Mrs Witt by the strength of his silent will. He threw around her the tense watchfulness of her own America, and made her feel at home.

'Phœnix,' she said, turning abruptly in her saddle as they walked the horses past the sheltering policeman at Hyde Park Corner, 'I can't tell you how glad I am to have something a hundred per cent American at the back of me when I go through these gates.'

She looked at him from dangerous grey eyes as if she meant it indeed, in vindictive earnest. A ghost of a smile went up to his high cheek-bones, but he did not answer.

'Why, mother?' said Lou, sing-song. 'It feels to me so friendly—!'

'Yes, Louise, it does. So friendly! That's why I mistrust it so entirely—'

And she set off at a canter up the Row, under the green trees, her face like the face of Medusa at fifty, a weapon in itself. She stared at everything and everybody, with that stare of cold dynamite waiting to explode them all. Lou posted trotting at her side, graceful and elegant, and faintly amused. Behind came Phœnix, like a shadow, with his yellowish, high-boned face still looking sick. And at his side, on the big brilliant bay horse, the smallish, black-bearded Welshman.

Between Phœnix and Lewis there was a latent, but unspoken and wary sympathy. Phœnix was terribly impressed by St Mawr, he could not leave off staring at him. And Lewis rode the brilliant, handsome-moving stallion so very quietly, like an insinuation.

Of the two men, Lewis looked the darker, with his black beard coming up to his thick black eyebrows. He was swarthy, with a rather short nose, and the uncanny pale-grey eyes that watched everything and cared about nothing. He cared about nothing in the world, except, at the present, St Mawr. People did not matter to him. He rode his horse and watched the world from the vantage ground of St Mawr, with a final indifference.

'You have been with that horse long?' asked Phœnix.

'Since he was born.'

Phœnix watched the action of St Mawr as they went. The bay moved proud and springy, but with perfect good sense, among the stream of riders. It was a beautiful June morning, the leaves overhead were thick and green; there came the first whiff of lime tree scent. To Phœnix, however, the city was a sort of nightmare mirage, and to Lewis, it was a sort of prison. The presence of people he felt as a prison around him.

Mrs Witt and Lou were turning at the end of the Row, bowing to some acquaintances. The grooms pulled aside. Mrs Witt looked at Lewis with a cold eye.

'It seems an extraordinary thing to me, Louise,' she said, 'to see a groom with a beard.'

'It isn't usual, mother,' said Lou. 'Do you mind?'

'Not at all. At least, I think I don't. I get very tired of modern, bare-faced young men, *very!* The clean, pure boy, don't you know! Doesn't it make you tired?–No, I think a groom with a beard is quite attractive.'

She gazed into the crowd defiantly, perching her finely-shod toe with war-like firmness on the stirrup-iron. Then suddenly she reined in, and turned her horse towards the grooms.

'Lewis!' she said, 'I want to ask you a question. Supposing, now, that Lady Carrington wanted you to shave off that beard, what should you say?'

Lewis instinctively put up his hand to the said beard.

'They've wanted me to shave it off, Mam,' he said. 'But I've never done it.'

'But why? Tell me why?'

'It's part of me, Mam.'

Mrs Witt pulled on again.

'Isn't that extraordinary, Louise?' she said. 'Don't you like the way he says *Mam*? It sounds so impossible to me. Could any woman think of herself as Mam? Never!–Since Queen Victoria. But, do you know it hadn't occurred to me that a man's beard was really part of him. It always seemed to me that men wore their beards, like they wear their neckties, for show. I shall always remember Lewis for saying his beard was part of him. Isn't it curious, the way he rides? He seems to sink himself in the horse. When I speak to him, I'm not sure whether I'm speaking to a man or to a horse.'

A few days later, Rico himself appeared on St Mawr for the morning ride. He rode self-consciously, as he did everything, and he was just a little nervous. But his mother-in-law was benevolent. She made him ride between her and Lou, like three ships slowly sailing abreast.

And that very day, who should come driving in an open carriage through the Park but the Queen Mother! Dear old Queen Alexandra, there was a flutter everywhere. And she bowed expressly to Rico, mistaking him, no doubt, for somebody else.

'Do you know,' said Rico as they sat at lunch, he and Lou and Mrs Witt, in Mrs Witt's sitting-room in the dark, quiet hotel in Mayfair, 'I really like riding St Mawr *so* much. He really is a noble animal.–If ever I am made a lord–which heaven forbid!–I shall be Lord St Mawr.'

'You mean,' said Mrs Witt, 'his real lordship would be the horse?'

'Very possible, I admit,' said Rico, with a curl of his long upper lip.

'Don't you think, mother,' said Lou, 'there *is* something quite noble about St Mawr? He strikes me as the first noble thing I have ever seen.'

'Certainly I've not seen any *man* that could compare with him. Because these English noblemen–well! I'd rather look at a negro Pullman-boy, if I was looking for what *I* call nobility.'

Poor Rico was getting crosser and crosser. There was a devil in Mrs Witt.

She had a hard, bright devil inside her that she seemed to be able to let loose at will.

She let it loose the next day, when Rico and Lou joined her in the Row. She was silent but deadly with the horses, balking them in every way. She suddenly crowded over against the rail in front of St Mawr, so that the stallion had to rear to pull himself up. Then, having a clear track, she suddenly set off at a gallop, like an explosion, and the stallion, all on edge, set off after her.

It seemed as if the whole Park, that morning, were in a state of nervous tension. Perhaps there was thunder in the air. But St Mawr kept on dancing and pulling at the bit and wheeling sideways up against the railing, to the terror of the children and the onlookers, who squealed and jumped back suddenly, sending the nerves of the stallion into a rush like rockets. He reared and fought as Rico pulled him round.

Then he went on: dancing, pulling, springily progressing sideways, possessed with all the demons of perversity. Poor Rico's face grew longer and angrier. A fury rose in him, which he could hardly control. He hated his horse, and viciously tried to force him to a quiet, straight trot. Up went St Mawr on his hind legs, to the terror of the Row. He got the bit in his teeth and began to fight.

But Phœnix, cleverly, was in front of him.

'You get off, Rico!' called Mrs Witt's voice, with all the calm of her wicked exultance.

And almost before he knew what he was doing, Rico had sprung lightly to the ground, and was hanging on to the bridle of the rearing stallion.

Phœnix also lightly jumped down, and ran to St Mawr, handing his bridle to Rico. Then began a dancing and a splashing, a rearing and a plunging. St Mawr was being wicked. But Phœnix, the indifference of conflict in his face, sat tight and immovable, without any emotion, only the heaviness of his impersonal will settling down like a weight, all the time, on the horse. There was, perhaps, a curious barbaric exultance in bare, dark will devoid of emotion or personal feeling.

So they had a little display in the Row for almost five minutes, the brilliant horse rearing and fighting. Rico, with a stiff, long face, scrambled on to Phœnix's horse and withdrew to a safe distance. Policemen came, and an officious mounted policeman rode up to save the situation. But it was obvious that Phœnix, detached and apparently unconcerned, but barbarically potent in his will, would bring the horse to order.

Which he did, and rode the creature home. Rico was requested not to ride St Mawr in the Row any more, as the stallion was dangerous to public safety. The authorities knew all about him.

Where ended the first fiasco of St Mawr.

'We didn't get on very well with his lordship this morning,' said Mrs Witt triumphantly.

'No, he didn't like his company *at all!*' Rico snarled back.

He wanted Lou to sell the horse again.

'I doubt if anyone would buy him, dear,' she said. 'He's a known character.'

'Then make a gift of him–to your mother,' said Rico with venom.

'Why to mother?' asked Lou innocently.

'She might be able to cope with him–or he with her!' The last phrase was deadly. Having delivered it, Rico departed.

Lou remained at a loss. She felt almost always a little bit dazed, as if she could not see clear nor feel clear. A curious deadness upon her, like the first touch of death. And through this cloud of numbness, or deadness, came all her muted experiences.

Why was it? She did not know. But she felt that in some way it came from a battle of wills. Her mother, Rico, herself, it was always an unspoken, unconscious battle of wills, which was gradually numbing and paralysing her. She knew Rico meant nothing but kindness by her. She knew her mother only wanted to watch over her. Yet always there was this tension of will, that was no numbing. As if at the depths of him, Rico were always angry, though he seemed so 'happy' on top. And Mrs Witt was organically angry. So they were like a couple of bombs, timed to explode some day, but ticking on like two ordinary timepieces, in the meanwhile.

She had come definitely to realise this: that Rico's anger was wound up tight at the bottom of him, like a steel spring that kept his works going, while he himself was 'charming', like a bomb-clock with Sèvres paintings or Dresden figures on the outside. But his very charm was a sort of anger, and his love was a destruction in itself. He just couldn't help it.

And she? Perhaps she was a good deal the same herself. Wound up tight inside, and enjoying herself being 'lovely'. But wound up tight on some tension that, she realised now with wonder, was really a sort of anger. This, the mainspring that drove her on the round of 'joys'.

She used really to enjoy the tension, and the *élan* it gave her. While she knew nothing about it. So long as she felt it really was life and happiness, this *élan*, this tension and excitement of 'enjoying oneself'.

Now suddenly she doubted the whole show. She attributed to it the curious numbness that was overcoming her, as if she couldn't feel any more.

She wanted to come unwound. She wanted to escape this battle of wills.

Only St Mawr gave her some hint of the possibility. He was so powerful, and so dangerous. But in his dark eye, that looked, with its cloudy brown pupil, a cloud within a dark fire, like a world beyond our world, there was a dark vitality glowing, and within the fire another sort of wisdom. She felt sure of it: even when he put his ears back, and bared his teeth, and his great eyes came bolting out of his naked horse's head, and she saw demons upon demons in the chaos of his horrid eyes.

Why did he seem to her like some living background, into which she wanted to retreat? When he reared his head and neighed from his deep chest, like deep wind-bells resounding, she seemed to hear the echoes of another darker, more spacious, more dangerous, more splendid world than ours, that was beyond her. And there she wanted to go.

She kept it utterly a secret to herself. Because Rico would just have lifted his long upper lip, in his bare face, in a condescending sort of 'understanding'. And her mother would, as usual, have suspected her of side-stepping. People, all the people she knew, seemed so entirely contained within their cardboard let's-be-happy world. Their wills were fixed like machines on happiness, or fun, or the-best-ever. This ghastly cheery-o! touch, that made all her blood go numb.

Since she had really seen St Mawr looming fiery and terrible in an outer darkness, she could not believe the world she lived in. She could not believe it was actually happening, when she was dancing in the afternoon at Claridge's, or in the evening at the Carlton, sliding about with some suave young man who wasn't like a man at all to her. Or down in Sussex for the week-end with the Enderleys: the talk, the eating and drinking, the flirtation, the endless dancing:

it all seemed far more bodiless and, in a strange way, wraith-like, than any fairy story. She seemed to be eating Barmecide food, that had been conjured up out of thin air, by the power of words. She seemed to be talking to handsome, young, bare-faced unrealities, not men at all: as she slid about with them, in the perpetual dance, they too seemed to have been conjured up out of air, merely for this soaring, slithering dance business. And she could not believe that, when the lights went out, they wouldn't melt back into thin air again and complete nonentity. The strange nonentity of it all! Everything just conjured up, and nothing real. '*Isn't this the best ever!*' they would beamingly assert, like wraiths of enjoyment, without any genuine substance. And she would beam back: '*Lots of fun!*'

She was thankful the season was over, and everybody was leaving London. She and Rico were due to go to Scotland, but not till August. In the meantime they would go to her mother.

Mrs Witt had taken a cottage in Shropshire, on the Welsh border, and had moved down there with Phœnix and her horses. The open, heather-and-bilberry-covered hills were splendid for riding.

Rico consented to spend the month in Shropshire, because for near neighbours Mrs Witt had the Manbys, at Corrabach Hall. The Manbys were rich Australians returned to the old country and set up as squires, all in full blow. Rico had known them in Victoria: they were of good family: and the girls made a great fuss of him.

So down went Lou and Rico, Lewis, Poppy and St Mawr, to Shrewsbury, then out into the country. Mrs Witt's 'cottage' was a tall red-brick Georgian house looking straight on to the churchyard, and the dark, looming big church.

'I never knew what a comfort it would be,' said Mrs Witt, 'to have gravestones under my drawing-room windows, and funerals for lunch.'

She really did take a strange pleasure in sitting in her panelled room, that was painted grey, and watching the Dean or one of the curates officiating at the graveside, among a group of black country mourners with black-bordered handkerchiefs luxuriantly in use.

'Mother!' said Lou. 'I think it's gruesome!'

She had a room at the back, looking over the walled garden and the stables. Nevertheless, there was the *boom! boom!* of the passing-bell, and the chiming and pealing on Sundays. The shadow of the church, indeed! A very audible shadow, making itself heard insistently.

The Dean was a big, burly, fat man with a pleasant manner. He was a gentleman, and a man of learning in his own line. But he let Mrs Witt know that he looked down on her just a trifle—as a parvenu American, a Yankee—though she never was a Yankee: and at the same time he had a sincere respect for her, as a rich woman. Yes, a sincere respect for her, as a rich woman.

Lou knew that every Englishman, especially of the upper classes, has a wholesome respect for riches. But then, who hasn't?

The Dean was more *impressed* by Mrs Witt than by little Lou. But to Lady Carrington he was charming: she was *almost* 'one of us', you know. And he was very gracious to Rico: 'your father's splendid colonial service.'

Mrs Witt had now a new pantomime to amuse her: the Georgian house, her own pew in church—it went with the old house: a village of thatched cottages—some of them with corrugated iron over the thatch: the cottage people, farm labourers and their families, with a few, very few, outsiders: the wicked little group of cottagers down at Mile End, famous for ill-living. The

Mile-Enders were all Allisons and Jephsons, and in-bred, the Dean said: result of working through the centuries at the Quarry, and living isolated there at Mile End.

Isolated! Imagine it! A mile and a half from the railway station, ten miles from Shrewsbury. Mrs Witt thought of Texas, and said:

'Yes, they are *very* isolated, away down there!'

And the Dean never for a moment suspected sarcasm.

But there she had the whole thing staged complete for her: English village life. Even miners breaking in to shatter the rather stuffy, unwholesome harmony. – All the men touched their caps to her, all the women did a bit of reverence, the children stood aside for her, if she appeared in the street.

They were all poor again: the labourers could no longer afford even a glass of beer in the evenings, since the Glorious War.

'Now I think that *is* terrible,' said Mrs Witt. 'Not to be able to get away from those stuffy, squalid, picturesque cottages for an hour in the evening, to drink a glass of beer.'

'It's a pity, I do agree with you, Mrs Witt. But Mr Watson has organised a men's reading-room, where the men can smoke and play dominoes, and read if they wish.'

'But that,' said Mrs Witt, 'is not the same as that cosy parlour in the "Moon and Stars".'

'I quite agree,' said the Dean. 'It isn't.'

Mrs Witt marched to the landlord of the 'Moon and Stars' and asked for a glass of cider.

'I want,' she said, in her American accent, 'these poor labourers to have their glass of beer in the evenings.'

'They want it themselves,' said Harvey.

'Then they must have it–'

The upshot was, she decided to supply one large barrel of beer per week and the landlord was to sell it to the labourers at a penny a glass.

'My own country has gone dry,' she asserted. 'But not because we can't *afford* it.'

By the time Lou and Rico appeared, she was deep in. She actually interfered very little: the barrel of beer was her one public act. But she *did* know everybody by sight, already, and she *did* know everybody's circumstances. And she had attended one prayer-meeting, one mothers' meeting, one sewing-bee, one 'social', one Sunday School meeting, one Band of Hope meeting, and one Sunday School treat. She ignored the poky little Wesleyan and Baptist chapels, and was true-blue Episcopalian.

'How strange these picturesque old villages are, Louise!' she said, with a duskiness around her sharp, well-bred nose. 'How *easy* it all seems, all on a definite pattern. And how false! And underneath, *how corrupt!*'

She gave that queer, triumphant leer from her grey eyes, and queer demonish wrinkles seemed to twitter on her face.

Lou shrank away. She was beginning to be afraid of her mother's insatiable curiosity, that always looked for the snake under the flowers. Or rather, for the maggots.

Always this same morbid interest in other people and their doings, their privacies, their dirty linen. Always this air of alertness for personal happenings, personalities, personalities, personalities. Always this subtle criticism and appraisal of other people, this analysis of other people's motives. If anatomy presupposes a corpse, then psychology presupposes a world of corpses. Personalities, which means personal criticism and analysis, presupposes a whole world laboratory of human psyches waiting to be vivisected. If you cut a thing up, of course it will smell. Hence, nothing raises such an infernal stink, at last, as human psychology.

Mrs Witt was a pure psychologist, a fiendish psychologist. And Rico, in his way, was a psychologist too. But he had a formula. 'Let's *know* the worst, dear! But let's look on the bright side, and believe the best.'

'Isn't the Dean a priceless old darling!' said Rico at breakfast.

And it had begun. Work had started in the psychic vivisection laboratory.

'Isn't he wonderful!' said Lou vaguely.

'So delightfully worldly!–*Some of us are not born to make money, dear boy. Luckily for us, we can marry it.*'–Rico made a priceless face.

'Is Mrs Vyner so rich?' asked Lou.

'She is quite a wealthy woman–in coal,' replied Mrs Witt. 'But the Dean is surely worth his weight even in gold. And he's a massive figure. I can imagine there would be great satisfaction in having him for a husband.'

'Why, mother?' asked Lou.

'Oh, such a presence! One of these old Englishmen that nobody can put in their pocket. You can't imagine his wife asking him to thread her needle. Something after all so *robust!* So different from *young* Englishmen, who all seem to me like ladies, perfect ladies.'

'*Somebody* has to keep up the tradition of the perfect lady,' said Rico.

'I know it,' said Mrs Witt. 'And if the women won't do it, the young gentlemen take on the burden. They bear it very well.'

It was in full swing, the cut and thrust. And poor Lou, who had reached the point of stupefaction in the game, felt she did not know what to do with herself.

Rico and Mrs Witt were deadly enemies, yet neither could keep clear of the other. It might have been they who were married to one another, their duel and their duet were so relentless.

But Rico immediately started the social round: first the Manbys: then motor twenty miles to luncheon at Lady Tewkesbury's: then young Mr Burns came flying down in his aeroplane from Chester: then they must motor to the sea to Sir Edward Edwards's place, where there was a moonlight bathing party. Everything intensely thrilling, and so innerly wearisome, Lou felt.

But back of it all was St Mawr, looming like a bonfire in the dark. He really was a tiresome horse to own. He worried the mares, if they were in the same paddock with him, always driving them round. And with any other horse he just fought with definite intent to kill. So he had to stay alone.

'That St Mawr, he's a bad horse,' said Phœnix.

'Maybe!' said Lewis.

'You don't like quiet horses?' said Phœnix.

'Most horses *is* quiet,' said Lewis. 'St Mawr, he's different.'

'Why don't he never get any foals?'

'Doesn't want to, I should think. Same as me.'

'What good is a horse like that? Better shoot him, before he kill somebody.'

'What good'll they get, shooting St Mawr?' said Lewis.

'If he kills somebody!' said Phœnix.

But there was no answer.

The two grooms both lived over the stables, and Lou, from her window, saw a good deal of them. They were two quiet men, yet she was very much aware of their presence, aware of Phœnix's rather high square shoulders and his fine, straight, vigorous black hair that tended to stand up assertively on his head, as he went quietly drifting about his various jobs. He was not lazy, but he did everything with a sort of diffidence, as if from a distance, and handled his horses carefully, cautiously, and cleverly, but without sympathy. He seemed to be holding something back all the time, unconsciously, as if in his very being there was some secret. But it was a secret of *will*. His quiet, reluctant movements, as if he never really wanted to do anything; his long, flat-stepping stride; the permanent challenge in his high cheek-bones, the Indian glint in his eyes, and his peculiar stare, watchful and yet unseeing, made him unpopular with the women servants.

Nevertheless, women had a certain fascination for him: he would stare at the pretty young maids with an intent blank stare when they were not looking. Yet he was rather over-bearing, domineering with them, and they resented him. It was evident to Lou that he looked upon himself as belonging to the master, not to the servant class. When he flirted with the maids, as he very often did, for he had a certain crude ostentatiousness, he seemed to let them feel that he despised them as inferiors, servants, while he admired their pretty charms, as fresh, country maids.

'I'm fair nervous of that Phœnix,' said Fanny, the fair-haired girl. 'He makes you feel what he'd do to you if he could.'

'He'd better not try with me,' said Mabel. 'I'd scratch his cheeky eyes out. Cheek!–for it's nothing else! He's nobody–common as they're made!'

'He makes you feel you was there for him to trample on,' said Fanny.

'Mercy, you *are* soft! If anybody's that it's him. Oh, my, Fanny, you've no right to let a fellow make you feel like *that!* Make *them* feel that *they're* dirt, for you to trample on: which they are!'

Fanny, however, being a shy little blonde thing, wasn't good at assuming the trampling role. She was definitely nervous of Phœnix. And he enjoyed it. An invisible smile seemed to creep up his cheek-bones, and the glint moved in his eyes as he teased her. He tormented her by his very presence, as he knew.

He would come silently up when she was busy, and stand behind her perfectly still, so that she was unaware of his presence. Then, silently, he would *make* her aware. Till she glanced nervously round, and with a scream saw him.

One day Lou watched the little play. Fanny had been picking over a bowl of blackcurrants, sitting on the bench under the maple tree in a corner of the yard. She didn't look round till she had picked up her bowl to go to the kitchen. Then there was a scream and a crash.

When Lou came out, Phœnix was crouching down silently gathering up the currants, which the little maid, scarlet and trembling, was collecting into another bowl. Phœnix seemed to be smiling down his back.

'Phœnix!' said Lou. 'I wish you wouldn't startle Fanny!'

He looked up and she saw the glint of ridicule in his eyes.

'Who, me?' he said.

'Yes, you. You go up behind Fanny to startle her. You're not to do it.'

He slowly stood erect and lapsed into his peculiar invisible silence. Only for a second his eyes glanced at Lou's, and then she saw the cold anger, the gleam of malevolence and contempt. He could not bear being commanded, or reprimanded, by a woman.

Yet it was even worse with a man.

'What's that, Lou?' said Rico, appearing all handsome and in the picture, in white flannels with an apricot silk shirt.

'I'm telling Phœnix he's not to torment Fanny!'

'Oh!'—and Rico's voice immediately became his father's, the important government official's. 'Certainly *not!* Most certainly *not!*' He looked at the scattered currants and the broken bowl. Fanny melted into tears. 'This, I suppose, is some of the results! Now look here, Phœnix, you're to leave the maids strictly alone. I shall ask them to report to me whenever, or *if* ever, you interfere with them. But I hope you *won't* interfere with them—in any way. You understand?'

As Rico became more and more Sir Harry and the government official, Lou's bones melted more and more into discomfort. Phœnix stood in his peculiar silence, the invisible smile on his cheek-bones.

'You understand what I'm saying to you?' Rico demanded, in intensified acid tones.

But Phœnix only stood there, as it were behind a cover of his own will, and looked back at Rico with a faint smile on his face and the glint moving in his eyes.

'Do you intend to answer?' Rico's upper lip lifted nastily.

'Mrs Witt is my boss,' came from Phœnix.

The scarlet flew up Rico's throat and flushed his face, his eyes went glaucous. Then quickly his face turned yellow.

Lou looked at the two men: her husband, whose rages, over-controlled, were organically terrible: the half-breed, whose dark-coloured lips were widened in a faint smile of derision, but in whose eyes caution and hate were playing against one another. She realised that Phœnix would accept *her* reprimand, or her mother's, because he could despise the two of them as mere women. But Rico's business aroused murder pure and simple.

She took her husband's arm.

'Come, dear!' she said in her half-plaintive way. 'I'm sure Phœnix understands. Go to the kitchen, Fanny, never mind the currants. There are plenty more in the garden.'

Rico was always thankful to be drawn quickly, submissively away from his own rage. He was afraid of it. He was afraid lest he should fly at the groom in some horrible fashion. The very thought horrified him. But in actuality he came very near to it.

He walked stiffly, feeling paralysed by his own fury. And those words, *Mrs Witt is my boss*, were like hot acid in his brain. An insult!

'By the way, Belle-Mère!' he said when they joined Mrs Witt—she hated being called Belle-Mère, and once said: 'If I'm the bell-mare, are you one of the colts?'—She also hated his voice of smothered fury—'I had to speak to Phœnix about persecuting the maids. He took the liberty of informing me that you were his boss, so perhaps you had better speak to him.'

'I certainly will. I believe they're my maids, and nobody else's, so it's my duty to look after them. Who was he persecuting?'

'I'm the responsible one, mother,' said Lou.

Rico disappeared in a moment. He must get out: get away from the house. How? Something was wrong with the car. Yet he must get away, away. He would go over to Corrabach. He would ride St Mawr. He had been talking about the horse, and Flora Manby was dying to see him. She had said: 'Oh, I can't *wait* to see that marvellous horse of yours.'

He would ride him over. It was only seven miles. He found Lou's maid

Elena, and sent her to tell Lewis. Meanwhile, to soothe himself, he dressed himself most carefully in white riding-breeches and a shirt of purple silk crêpe, with a flowing black tie spotted red like a ladybird, and black riding-boots. Then he took a *chic* little white hat with a black band.

St Mawr was saddled and waiting, and Lewis had saddled a second horse.

'Thanks, Lewis, I'm going alone!' said Rico.

This was the first time he had ridden St Mawr in the country, and he was nervous. But he was also in the hell of a smothered fury. All his careful dressing had not really soothed him. So his fury consumed his nervousness.

He mounted with a swing, blind and rough. St Mawr reared.

'Stop that!' snarled Rico, and put him to the gate.

Once out in the village street, the horse went dancing sideways. He insisted on dancing at the sidewalk, to the exaggerated terror of the children. Rico, exasperated, pulled him across. But no, he wouldn't go down the centre of the village street. He began dancing and edging on to the other sidewalk, so the foot-passengers fled into the shops in terror.

The devil was in him. He would turn down every turning where he was not meant to go. He reared with panic at a furniture van. He *insisted* on going down the wrong side of the road. Rico was riding him with a martingale, and he could see the rolling, bloodshot eye.

'Damn you, *go!*' said Rico, giving him a dig with the spurs.

And away they went, down the high-road, in a thunder-bolt. It was a hot day, with thunder threatening, so Rico was soon in a flame of heat. He held on tight, with fixed eyes, trying all the time to rein in the horse. What he really was afraid of was that the brute would shy suddenly as he galloped. Watching for this, he didn't care when they sailed past the turning to Corrabach.

St Mawr flew on, in a sort of *élan*. Marvellous the power and life in the creature. There was really a great joy in the motion. If only he wouldn't take the corners at a gallop, nearly swerving Rico off! Luckily the road was clear. To ride, to ride at this terrific gallop, on into eternity!

After several miles, the horse slowed down, and Rico managed to pull him into a lane that might lead to Corrabach. When all was said and done, it was a wonderful ride. St Mawr could go like the wind, but with that luxurious heavy ripple of life which is like nothing else on earth. It seemed to carry one at once into another world, away from the life of the nerves.

So Rico arrived, after all, something of a conqueror at Corrabach. To be sure, he was perspiring, and so was his horse. But he was a hero from another, heroic world.

'Oh, such a hot ride!' he said, as he walked on to the lawn at Corrabach Hall. 'Between the sun and the horse, really!–between two fires!'

'Don't you trouble, you're looking dandy, a bit hot and flushed like,' said Flora Manby. 'Let's go and see your horse.'

And her exclamation was: 'Oh, he's *lovely!* He's fine! I'd love to try him once–'

Rico decided to accept the invitation to stay overnight at Corrabach. Usually he was very careful, and refused to stay, unless Lou was with him. But they telephoned to the post office at Chomesbury, would Mr Jones please send a message to Lady Carrington that Sir Henry was staying the night at Corrabach Hall, but would be home next day. Mr Jones received the request with unction, and said he would go over himself to give the message to Lady Carrington.

Lady Carrington was in the walled garden. The peculiarity of Mrs Witt's house was that, for grounds proper, it had the churchyard.

'I never thought, Louise, that one day I should have an old English churchyard for my lawns and shrubbery and park, and funeral mourners for my herds of deer. It's curious. For the first time in my life a funeral has become a real thing to me. I feel I could write a book on them.'

But Louise only felt intimidated.

At the back of the house was a flagged courtyard, with stables and a maple tree in a corner, and big doors opening on to the village street. But at the side was a walled garden, with fruit trees and currant bushes and a great bed of rhubarb, and some tufts of flowers, peonies, pink roses, sweet williams. Phœnix, who had a certain taste for gardening, would be out there thinning the carrots or tying up the lettuce. He was not lazy. Only he would not take work seriously, as a job. He would be quite amused tying up lettuces, and would tie up head after head, quite prettily. Then, becoming bored, he would abandon his task, light a cigarette, and go and stand on the threshold of the big doors, in full view of the street, watching, and yet completely indifferent.

After Rico's departure on St Mawr, Lou went into the garden. And there she saw Phœnix working in the onion-bed. He was bending over, in his own silence, busy with nimble, amused fingers among the grassy young onions. She thought he had not seen her, so she went down another path to where a swing bed hung under the apple tree. There she sat with a book and a bundle of magazines. But she did not read.

She was musing vaguely. Vaguely, she was glad that Rico was away for a while. Vaguely, she felt a sense of bitterness, of complete futility: the complete futility of her living. This left her drifting in a sea of utter chagrin. And Rico seemed to her the symbol of the futility. Vaguely, she was aware that something else existed, but she didn't know where it was or what it was.

In the distance she could see Phœnix's dark, rather tall-built head, with its black, fine, intensely-living hair tending to stand on end, like a brush with long, very fine black bristles. His hair, she thought, betrayed him as an animal of a different species. He was growing a little bored by weeding onions: that also she could tell. Soon he would want some other amusement.

Presently Lewis appeared. He was small, energetic, a little bit bow-legged, and he walked with a slight strut. He wore khaki riding-breeches, leather gaiters, and a blue shirt. And, like Phœnix, he rarely had any cap or hat on his head. His thick black hair was parted at the side and brushed over heavily sideways, dropping on his forehead at the right. It was very long, a real mop, under which his eyebrows were dark and steady.

'Seen Lady Carrington?' he asked of Phœnix.

'Yes, she's sitting on that swing over there—she's been there quite a while.' The wretch—he had seen her from the very first!

Lewis came striding over, looking towards her with his pale-grey eyes, from under his mop of hair.

'Mr Jones from the post office wants to see you, my Lady, with a message from Sir Henry.'

Instantly alarm took possession of Lou's soul.

'Oh!—Does he want to see me personally?—What message? Is anything wrong?'—And her voice trailed out over the last word, with a sort of anxious nonchalance.

'I don't think it's anything amiss,' said Lewis reassuringly.

'Oh! You don't,' the relief came into her voice. Then she looked at Lewis with a slight, winning smile in her unmatched eyes. 'I'm so afraid of St Mawr, you know.' Her voice was soft and cajoling. Phœnix was listening in the distance.

'St Mawr's all right, if you don't do nothing to him,' Lewis replied.

'I'm sure he is!–But how is one to know when one is doing something to him?–Tell Mr Jones to come here, please,' she concluded, on a changed tone.

Mr Jones, a man of forty-five, thick-set, with a fresh complexion and rather foolish brown eyes, and a big brown moustache, came prancing down the path, smiling rather fatuously, and doffing his straw hat with a gorgeous bow the moment he saw Lou sitting in her slim white frock on the coloured swing bed under the trees with their hard green apples.

'Good-morning, Mr Jones!'

'Good-morning, Lady Carrington.– If I may say so, what a picture you make–a beautiful picture–'

He beamed under his big brown moustache like the greatest lady-killer.

'Do I!–Did Sir Henry say he was all right?'

'He didn't *say* exactly, but I should expect he is all right–' and Mr Jones delivered his message, in the mayonnaise of his own unction.

'Thank you so much, Mr Jones. It's awfully good of you to come and tell me. Now I shan't worry about Sir Henry *at all*.'

'It's a great pleasure to come and deliver a satisfactory message to Lady Carrington. But it won't be kind to Sir Henry if you don't worry about him *at all* in his absence. We all enjoy being worried about by those we love–so long as there is nothing to worry about, of course!'

'Quite!' said Lou. 'Now won't you take a glass of port and a biscuit, or a whisky and soda? And thank you ever so much.'

'Thank *you*, my Lady. I might drink a whisky and soda, since you are so good.'

And he beamed fatuously.

'Let Mr Jones mix himself a whisky and soda, Lewis,' said Lou.

'Heavens!' she thought, as the postmaster retreated a little uncomfortably down the garden path, his bald spot passing in and out of the sun, under the trees: 'How ridiculous everything is, how ridiculous, ridiculous!' Yet she didn't really dislike Mr Jones and his interlude.

Phœnix was melting away out of the garden. He had to follow the fun.

'Phœnix!' Lou called. 'Bring me a glass of water, will you? Or send somebody with it.'

He stood in the path looking round at her.

'All right!' he said.

And he turned away again.

She did not like being alone in the garden. She liked to have the men working somewhere near. Curious how pleasant it was to sit there in the garden when Phœnix was about, or Lewis. It made her feel she could never be lonely or jumpy. But when Rico was there, she was all aching nerve.

Phœnix came back with a glass of water, lemon juice, sugar, and a small bottle of brandy. He knew Lou liked a spoonful of brandy in her iced lemonade.

'How thoughtful of you, Phœnix!' she said. 'Did Mr Jones get his whisky?'

'He was just getting it.'

'That's right.–By the way, Phœnix, I wish you wouldn't get mad if Sir Henry speaks to you. He is *really* so kind.'

She looked up at the man. He stood there watching her in silence, the invisible smile on his face, and the inscrutable Indian glint moving in his eyes. What was he thinking? There was something passive and almost submissive about him, but underneath this, an unyielding resistance and cruelty: yes, even cruelty. She felt that, on top, he was submissive and attentive, bringing her her lemonade as she liked it, without being told: thinking for her quite subtly. But underneath there was an unchanging hatred. He submitted circumstantially, he worked for a wage. And even circumstantially, he *liked* his mistress—*la patrona*—and her daughter. But much deeper than any circumstance or any circumstantial liking, was the categorical hatred upon which he was founded, and with which he was powerless. His liking for Lou and for Mrs Witt, his serving them and working for a wage, was all side-tracking his own nature, which was grounded on hatred of their very existence. But what was he to do? He had to live. Therefore he had to serve, to work for a wage, and even to be faithful.

And yet *their* existence made his own existence negative. If he was to exist, positively, they would have to cease to exist. At the same time, a fatal sort of tolerance made him serve these women, and go on serving.

'Sir Henry is *so* kind to everybody,' Lou insisted.

The half-breed met her eyes, and smiled uncomfortably.

'Yes, he's a kind man,' he replied, as if sincerely.

'Then why do you mind if he speaks to you?'

'I don't mind,' said Phœnix glibly.

'But you do. Or else you wouldn't make him so angry.'

'Was he angry? I don't know,' said Phœnix.

'He was very angry. And you *do* know.'

'No, I don't know if he's angry. I don't know,' the fellow persisted. And there was a glib sort of satisfaction in his tone.

'That's awfully unkind of you, Phœnix,' she said, growing offended in her turn.

'No, I don't know if he's angry. I don't want to make him angry. I don't know—'

He had taken on a tone of naïve ignorance, which at once gratified her pride as a woman, and deceived her.

'Well, you believe me when I tell you you *did* make him angry, don't you?'

'Yes, I believe when you tell me.'

'And you promise me, won't you, not to do it again? It's *so* bad for him—so bad for his nerves, and for his eyes. It makes them inflamed, and injures his eyesight. And you know, as an artist, it's terrible if anything happens to his eyesight—'

Phœnix was watching her closely, to take it in. He still was not good at understanding continuous, logical statement. Logical connection in speech seemed to stupefy him, make him stupid. He understood in disconnected assertions of fact. But he had gathered what she said. 'He gets mad at you. When he gets mad, it hurts his eyes. His eyes hurt him. He can't see, because his eyes hurt him. He wants to paint a picture, he can't. He can't paint a picture, he can't see clear—'

Yes, he had understood. She saw he had understood. The bright glint of satisfaction moved in his eyes.

'So now promise me, won't you, you won't make him mad again: you won't make him angry?'

'No, I won't make him angry. I don't do anything to make him angry,' Phœnix answered, rather glibly.

'And you do understand, don't you? You do know how kind he is: how he'd do a good turn to anybody?'

'Yes, he's a kind man,' said Phœnix.

'I'm so glad you realise. There, that's luncheon! How nice it is to sit here in the garden, when everybody is nice to you! No, I can carry the tray, don't you bother.'

But he took the tray from her hand and followed her to the house. And as he walked behind her, he watched the slim white nape of her neck, beneath the clustering of her bobbed hair, something as a stoat watches a rabbit he is following.

In the afternoon Lou retreated once more to her place in the garden. There she lay, sitting with a bunch of pillows behind her, neither reading nor working, just musing. She had learned the new joy: to do absolutely nothing, but to lie and let the sunshine filter through the leaves, to see the bunch of red-hot-poker flowers pierce scarlet into the afternoon, beside the comparative neutrality of some foxgloves. The mere colour of hard red, like the big Oriental poppies that had fallen, and these poker flowers, lingered in her consciousness like a communication.

Into this peaceful indolence, when even the big, dark-grey tower of the church beyond the wall and the yew trees was keeping its bells in silence, advanced Mrs Witt, in a broad Panama hat and a white dress.

'Don't you want to ride, or do something, Louise?' she asked ominously.

'Don't you want to be peaceful, mother?' retorted Louise.

'Yes—an *active* peace.—I can't *believe* that my daughter can be content to lie on a hammock and do nothing, not even read or improve her mind, the greater part of the day.'

'Well, your daughter *is* content to do that. It's her greatest pleasure.'

'I know it. I can see it. And it surprises me *very* much. When I was your age, I was never still. I had so much *go*—'

> 'Those maids, thank God,
> Are 'neath the sod,
> And all the generation.'

'No, but, mother, I only take life differently. Perhaps you used up that sort of *go*. I'm the harem type, mother: only I never want the men inside the lattice.'

'Are you really my daughter?—Well! A woman never knows what will happen to her. I'm an *American* woman, and I suppose I've got to remain one, no matter where I am.—What did you want, Lewis?'

The groom had approached down the path.

'If I am to saddle Poppy?' said Lewis.

'No, apparently *not*!' replied Mrs Witt. 'Your mistress prefers the hammock to the saddle.'

'Thank you, Lewis. What mother says is true this afternoon, at least.' And she gave him a peculiar little cross-eyed smile.

'Who,' said Mrs Witt to the man, 'has been cutting at your hair?'

There was a moment of silent resentment.

'I did it myself, Mam! Sir Henry said it was too long.'

'He certainly spoke the truth. But I believe there's a barber in the village on Saturdays—or you could ride over to Shrewsbury. Just turn round, and let me look at the back. Is it the money?'

'No, Mam. I don't like these fellows touching my head.'

He spoke coldly, with a certain hostile reserve that at once piqued Mrs Witt. 'Don't you really!' she said. 'But it's quite *impossible* for you to go about as you are. It gives you a half-witted appearance. Go now into the yard and get a chair and a dust-sheet. I'll cut your hair.'

The man hesitated, hostile.

'Don't be afraid, I know how it's done. I've cut the hair of many a poor wounded boy in hospital: and shaved them too. *You've got such a touch, nurse!* Poor fellow, he was dying, though none of us knew it.—Those are the compliments I value, Louise.—Get that chair now, and a dust-sheet. I'll borrow your hair-scissors from Elena, Louise.'

Mrs Witt, happily on the war-path, was herself again. She didn't care for work, actual work. But she loved trimming. She loved arranging unnatural and pretty salads, devising new and piquant-looking ice-creams, having a turkey stuffed exactly as she knew a stuffed turkey in Louisana, with chestnuts and butter and stuff, or showing a servant how to turn waffles on a waffle-iron, or to bake a ham with brown sugar and cloves and a moistening of rum. She liked pruning rose trees, or beginning to cut a yew hedge into shape. She liked ordering her own and Louise's shoes, with an exactitude and a knowledge of shoe-making that sent the salesmen crazy. She was a demon in shoes. Reappearing from America, she would pounce on her daughter. 'Louise, throw those shoes away. Give them to one of the maids.'—'But, mother, they are some of the best French shoes. I like them.'—'Throw them away. A shoe has only two excuses for existing: perfect comfort or perfect appearance. Those have neither. I have brought you some shoes.'—Yes, she had brought ten pairs of shoes from New York. She knew her daughter's foot as she knew her own.

So now she was in her element, looming behind Lewis as he sat in the middle of the yard swathed in a dust-sheet. She had on an overall and a pair of wash-leather gloves, and she poised a pair of long scissors like one of the Fates. In her big hat she looked curiously young, but with the youth of a bygone generation. Her heavy-lidded, laconic grey eyes were alert, studying the groom's black mop of hair. Her eyebrows made thin, uptilting black arches on her brow. Her fresh skin was slightly powdered, and she was really handsome in a bold, bygone, eighteenth-century style. Some of the curious, adventurous stoicism of the eighteenth century: and then a certain blatant American efficiency.

Lou, who had strayed into the yard to see, looked so much younger and so many thousand of years older than her mother, as she stood in her wisp-like diffidence, the clusters of grape-like bobbed hair hanging beside her face, with its fresh colouring and its ancient weariness, her slightly squinting eyes, that were so disillusioned they were becoming faun-like.

'Not too short, mother, not too short!' she remonstrated, as Mrs Witt, with a terrific flourish of efficiency, darted at the man's black hair, and the thick flakes fell like black snow.

'Now, Louise, I'm right in this job, please don't interfere. Two things I hate to see: a man with his wool in his neck and ears: and a bare-faced young man who looks as if he'd bought his face as well as his hair from a men's beauty-specialist.'

And efficiently she bent down, clip—clip—clipping! while Lewis sat utterly immobile, with sunken head, in a sort of despair.

Phœnix stood against the stable door, with his restless, eternal cigarette. And in the kitchen doorway the maids appeared and fled, appeared and fled in delight. The old gardener, a fixture who went with the house, creaked in and stood with his legs apart, silent in intense condemnation.

'First time I ever see such a thing!' he muttered to himself, as he creaked on into the garden. He was a bad-tempered old soul, who thoroughly disapproved of the household, and would have given notice, but that he knew which side his bread was buttered: and there was butter unstinted on his bread in Mrs Witt's kitchen.

Mrs Witt stood back to survey her handiwork, holding those terrifying shears with their beak erect. Lewis lifted his head and looked stealthily round, like a creature in a trap.

'Keep still!' she said. 'I haven't finished.'

And she went for his front hair, with vigour, lifting up long layers and snipping off the ends artistically: till at last he sat with a black aureole upon the floor, and his ears standing out with curious new alertness from the sides of his clean-clipped head.

'Stand up,' she said, 'and let me look.'

He stood up, looking absurdly young, with the hair all cut away from his neck and ears, left thick only on top. She surveyed her work with satisfaction.

'You look so much younger,' she said, 'you would be surprised. Sit down again.'

She clipped the back of his neck with the shears, and then, with a very slight hesitation, she said:

'Now about the beard!'

But the man rose suddenly from the chair, pulling the dust-cloth from his neck with desperation.

'No, I'll do that myself,' he said, looking her in the eyes with a cold light in his pale-grey, uncanny eyes.

She hesitated in a kind of wonder at his queer male rebellion.

'Now, listen, I shall do it much better than you—and besides,' she added hurriedly, snatching at the dust-cloth he was flinging on the chair—'I haven't quite finished round the ears.'

'I think I shall do,' he said, again looking her in the eyes, with a cold, white gleam of finality. 'Thank you for what you've done.'

And he walked away to the stable.

'You'd better sweep up here,' Mrs Witt called.

'Yes, Mam,' he replied, looking round at her again with an odd resentment, but continuing to walk away.

'However!' said Mrs Witt, 'I suppose he'll do.'

And she divested herself of gloves and overall and walked indoors to wash and to change. Lou went indoors too.

'It is extraordinary what hair that man has!' said Mrs Witt. 'Did I tell you when I was in Paris, I saw a woman's face in the hotel that I thought I knew? I couldn't place her, till she was coming towards me. "Aren't you Rachel Fannière?" she said. "Aren't you Janette Leroy?" We hadn't seen each other since we were girls of twelve and thirteen, at school in New Orleans. "Oh!" she said to me. "Is every illusion doomed to perish? You had such wonderful golden curls! All my life I've said, Oh, if only I had such lovely hair as Rachel Fannière! I've seen those beautiful golden curls of yours all my life. And now I meet you, you're grey!" Wasn't that terrible, Louise? Well, that man's hair made me think of it—so thick and curious. It's strange what a difference there is in hair; I suppose it's because he's just an animal—no mind! There's nothing I admire in a man like a good *mind*. Your father was a very clever man, and all the men I've admired have been clever. But isn't it curious now, I've never cared much to touch their hair. How strange life is! If it gives one thing, it takes away another.–And even those poor boys in hospital: I have shaved them, or cut their hair, like a mother, never thinking anything of it. Lovely, intelligent, clean boys, most of them were. Yet it never did anything to me. I never knew before that something could happen to one from a person's *hair*! Like to Janette Leroy from my curls when I was a child. And now I'm grey, as she says.–I wonder how old a man Lewis is, Louise! Didn't he look absurdly young with his ears pricking up?'

'I think Rico said he was forty or forty-one.'

'And never been married?'

'No–not as far as I know.'

'Isn't that curious now!–just an animal! No mind! A man with no mind! I've always thought that the *most* despicable thing. Yet such wonderful hair to touch. Your Henry has quite a good mind, yet I would simply shrink from touching his hair. I suppose one likes stroking a cat's fur, just the same. Just the animal in man. Curious that I never seem to have met it, Louise. Now I come to think of it, he has the eyes of a human cat: a human tom-cat. Would you call him stupid? Yes, he's very stupid.'

'No, mother, he's not stupid. He only doesn't care about most things.'

'Like an animal! But what a strange look he has in his eyes! A strange sort of intelligence! and a confidence in himself. Isn't that curious, Louise, in a man with as little mind as he has? Do you know, I should say he could see through a woman pretty well.'

'Why, mother!' said Lou impatiently. 'I think one gets so tired of your men with mind, as you call it. There are so many of that sort of clever men. And there are lots of men who aren't very clever, but are rather nice: and lots are stupid. It seems to me there's something else besides mind and cleverness, or niceness or cleanness. Perhaps it is the animal. Just think of St Mawr! I've thought so much about him. We call him an animal, but we never know what it means. He seems a far greater mystery to me than a clever man. He's a horse. Why can't one say in the same way of a man: "He's a man?" There seems no mystery in being a man. But there's a terrible mystery in St Mawr.'

Mrs Witt watched her daughter quizzically.

'Louise,' she said, 'you won't tell me that the mere animal is all that counts in a man. I will never believe it. Man is wonderful because he is able to *think*.'

'But is he?' cried Lou, with sudden exasperation. 'Their thinking seems to me all so childish: like stringing the same beads over and over again. Ah, men! They and their thinking are all so *paltry*. How can you be impressed?'

Mrs Witt raised her eyebrows sardonically.

'Perhaps I'm not–any more,' she said with a grim smile.

'But,' she added, 'I still can't see that I am to be impressed by the mere animal in man. The animals are the same as we are. It seems to me they have the same feelings and wants as we do in a commonplace way. The only difference is that they have no minds: no human minds, at least. And no matter what you say, Louise, lack of minds makes the commonplace.'

Lou knitted her brows nervously.

'I suppose it does, mother.–But men's minds *are* so commonplace: look at Dean Vyner and his mind! Or look at Arthur Balfour, as a shining example.

Isn't *that* commonplace, that cleverness? I would hate St Mawr to be spoilt by such a mind.'

'Yes, Louise, so would I. Because the men you mention are really old women, knitting the same pattern over and over again. Nevertheless, I shall never alter my belief that real mind is all that matters in a man, and it's *that* that we women love.'

'Yes, mother!–But what *is* real mind? The old woman who knits the most complicated pattern? Oh, I can hear all their needles clicking, the clever men! As a matter of fact, mother, I believe Lewis has far more real mind than Dean Vyner or any of the clever ones. He has a good intuitive mind, he knows things without thinking them.'

'That may be, Louise! But he is a servant. He is *under*. A real man should never be under. And then you could never be intimate with a man like Lewis.'

'I don't want intimacy, mother. I'm too tired of it all. I love St Mawr because he isn't intimate. He stands where one can't get at him. And he burns with life. And where does his life come from, to him? That's the mystery. That great burning life in him, which never is dead. Most men have a deadness in them, that frightens me so, because of my own deadness. Why can't men get their life straight, like St Mawr, and then think? Why can't they think quick, mother: quick as a woman: only farther than we do? Why isn't men's thinking quick like fire, mother? Why is it so slow, so dead, so deadly dull?'

'I can't tell you, Louise. My own opinion of the men of to-day has grown very small. But I can live in spite of it.'

'No, mother. We seemed to be living off old fuel, like the camel when he lives off his hump. Life doesn't rush into us, as it does even into St Mawr, and he's a dependent animal. I can't live, mother. I just can't.'

'I don't see why not! *I'm* full of life.'

'I know you are, mother. But I'm not, and I'm your daughter.–And don't misunderstand me, mother! I don't want to be an animal like a horse or a cat or a lioness, though they all fascinate me, the way they get their life *straight*, not from a lot of old tanks, as we do. I don't admire the cave man, and that sort of thing. But think, mother, if we could get our lives straight from the source, as the animals do, and still be ourselves. You don't like men yourself. But you've no idea how men just tire me out: even the very thought of them. You say they are too animal. But they're not, mother. It's the animal in them has gone perverse, or cringing, or humble, or domesticated, like dogs. I don't know one single man who is a proud living animal. I know they've left off really thinking. But then men always do leave off really thinking when the last bit of wild animal dies in them.'

'Because we have minds–'

'We have no minds once we are tame, mother. Men are all women, knitting and crochetting words together.'

'I can't altogether agree, you know, Louise.'

'I know you don't.–You like clever men. But clever men are mostly such unpleasant *animals*. As animals, so very unpleasant. And in men like Rico, the animal has gone queer and wrong. And in those nice clean boys you liked so much in the war,–there is no wild animal left in them. They're all tame dogs, even when they're brave and well-bred. They're all tame dogs, mother, with human masters. There's no mystery in them.'

'What do you want, Louise? You *do* want the cave man, who'll knock you on the head with a club.'

'Don't be silly, mother. That's much more your subconscious line, you admirer of Mind–I don't consider the cave man is a real human animal at all. He's a brute, a degenerate. A pure animal man would be as lovely as a deer or a leopard, burning like a flame fed straight from underneath. And he'd be part of the unseen, like a mouse is, even. And he'd never cease to wonder, he'd breathe silence and unseen wonder, as the partridges do, running in the stubble. He'd be all the animals in turn, instead of one, fixed, automatic thing, which he is now, grinding on the nerves.–Ah, no, mother, I want the wonder back again, or I shall die. I don't want to be like you, just criticising and annihilating these dreary people, and enjoying it.'

'My dear daughter, whatever else the human animal might be, he'd be a dangerous commodity.'

'I wish he would, mother. I'm dying of these empty dangerless men, who are only sentimental and spiteful.'

'Nonsense, you're not dying.'

'I am, mother. And I should be dead if there weren't St Mawr and Phoenix and Lewis in the world.'

'St Mawr and Phoenix and Lewis! I thought you said they were servants.'

'That's the worst of it. If only they were masters! If only there were some men with as much natural life as they have, and their brave, quick minds that commanded instead of serving!'

'There are no such men,' said Mrs Witt, with a certain grim satisfaction.

'I know it. But I'm young, and I've got to live. And the thing that is offered me as life just starves me, starves me to death, mother. What am I to do? You enjoy shattering people like Dean Vyner. But I am young, I can't live that way!'

'That may be.'

It had long ago struck Lou how much more her mother realised and understood than ever Rico did. Rico was afraid, always afraid of realising. Rico, with his good manners and his habitual kindness, and that peculiar imprisoned sneer of his.

He arrived home next morning on St Mawr, rather flushed and gaudy, and over-kind, with an *empressé* anxiety about Lou's welfare which spoke too many volumes. Especially as he was accompanied by Flora Manby, and by Flora's sister Elsie, and Elsie's husband, Frederick Edwards. They all came on horseback.

'Such awful ages since I saw you!' said Flora to Lou. 'Sorry if we burst in on you. We're only just saying "How do you do!" and going on to the inn. They've got rooms all ready for us there. We thought we'd stay just one night over here, and ride to-morrow to the Devil's Chair. Won't you come? Lots of fun! Isn't Mrs Witt at home?'

Mrs Witt was out for the moment. When she returned she had on her curious stiff face, yet she greeted the newcomers with a certain cordiality: she felt it would be diplomatic, no doubt.

'There *are* two rooms here,' she said, 'and if you care to poke into them, why, we shall be *delighted* to have you. But I'll show them to you first, because they are poor, inconvenient rooms, with no running water and *miles* from the baths.'

Flora and Elsie declared that they were 'perfectly darling sweet rooms–not overcrowded.'

'Well,' said Mrs Witt, 'the conveniences certainly don't fill up much space. But if you like to take them for what they are–'

'Why, we feel absolutely overwhelmed, don't we, Elsie?–But we've no clothes–!'

Suddenly the silence had turned into a house-party. The Manby girls appeared to lunch in fine muslin dresses, bought in Paris, fresh as daisies. Women's clothing takes up so little space, especially in summer! Fred Edwards was one of those blond Englishmen with a little brush moustache and those strong blue eyes which were always attempting the sentimental, but which Lou, in her prejudice, considered cruel: upon what grounds she never analysed. However, he took a gallant tone with her at once, and she had to seem to simper. Rico, watching her, was so relieved when he saw the simper coming. It had begun again, the whole clockwork of 'lots of fun'!

'Isn't Fred flirting perfectly outrageously with Lady Carrington!–She looks so *sweet!*' cried Flora, over her coffee-cup. 'Don't you mind, Harry!'

They called Rico 'Harry'! His boy-name.

'Only a very little,' said Harry. '*L'uomo è cacciatore.*'

'Oh, now, what does that mean?' cried Flora, who always thrilled to Rico's bits of affectation.

'It means,' said Mrs Witt, leaning forward and speaking in her most suave voice, 'that man is a hunter'.

Even Flora shrank under the smooth acid of the irony.

'Oh, well now!' she cried. 'If he is, then what is woman?'

'The hunted,' said Mrs Witt, in a still smoother acid.

'At least,' said Rico, 'she is always *game!*'

'Ah, is she though!' came Fred's manly, well-bred tones. 'I'm not so sure.'

Mrs Witt looked from one man to the other, as if she were dropping them down the bottomless pit.

Lou escaped to look at St Mawr. He was still moist where the saddle had been. And he seemed a little bit extinguished, as if virtue had gone out of him.

But when he lifted his lovely naked head, like a bunch of flames, to see who it was had entered she saw he was still himself. Forever sensitive and alert, his head lifted like the summit of a fountain. And within him the clean bones striking to the earth, his hoofs intervening between him and the ground like lesser jewels.

He knew her and did not resent her. But he took no notice of her. He would never 'respond'. At first she had resented it. Now she was glad. He would never be intimate, thank heaven.

She hid herself away till tea-time, but she could not hide from the sound of voices. Dinner was early, at seven. Dean Vyner came–Mrs Vyner was an invalid–and also an artist who had a studio in the village and did etchings. He was a man of about thirty-eight, and poor, just beginning to accept himself as a failure, as far as making money goes. But he worked at his etchings and studied esoteric matters like astrology and alchemy. Rico patronised him, and was a little afraid of him. Lou could not quite make him out. After knocking about Paris and London and Munich, he was trying to become staid, and to persuade himself that English village life, with squire and dean in the background, humble artist in the middle and labourer in the common foreground, was a genuine life. His self-persuasion was only moderately successful. This was betrayed by the curious arrest in his body: he seemed to have to force himself into movements: and by the curious duplicity in his yellow-grey, twinkling eyes, that twinkled and expanded like a goat's, with mockery, irony, and frustration.

'Your face is curiously like Pan's,' said Lou to him at dinner.

It was true, in a commonplace sense. He had the tilted eyebrows, the twinkling goaty look, and the pointed ears of a goat-Pan.

'People have said so,' he replied. 'But I'm afraid it's not the face of the Great God Pan. Isn't it rather the Great Goat Pan!'

'I say, that's good!' cried Rico. 'The Great Goat Pan!'

'I have always found it difficult,' said the Dean, 'to see the Great God Pan in that goat-legged old father of satyrs. He may have a good deal of influence – the world will always be full of goaty old satyrs. But we find them somewhat vulgar. The goaty old satyrs are too comprehensible to me to be venerable, and I fail to see a Great God in the father of them all.'

'Your ears should be getting red,' said Lou to Cartwright. She, too, had an odd squinting smile that suggested nymphs, so irresponsible and unbelieving.

'Oh no, nothing personal!' cried the Dean.

'I am not sure,' said Cartwright, with a small smile. 'But don't you imagine Pan once *was* a great god before the anthropomorphic Greeks turned him into half a man?'

'Ah!–maybe. This is very possible. But–I have noticed the limitation in myself–my mind has no grasp whatsoever of Europe before the Greeks arose. Mr Well's Outline does not help me there, either,' the Dean added with a smile.

'But what was Pan before he was a man with goat legs?' asked Lou.

'Before he looked like me!' said Cartwright, with a faint grin. 'I should say he was the god that is hidden in everything. In those days you saw the thing, you never saw the god in it: I mean in the tree or the fountain or the animal. If you ever saw the God instead of the thing, you died. If you saw it with the naked eye, that is. But in the night you might see the God. And you knew it was there.'

'The modern pantheist not only sees the God in everything, he takes photographs of it,' said the Dean.

'Oh, and the divine pictures he paints!' cried Rico.

'Quite!' said Cartwright.

'But if they never *saw* the God in the thing, the old ones, how did they know he was there? How did they have any Pan at all?' said Lou.

'Pan was the hidden mystery–the hidden cause. That's how it was a Great God. Pan wasn't *he* at all: not even a great God. He was Pan. All: what you see when you see in full. In the day-time you see the thing. But if your third eye is open, which sees only the things that can't be seen, you may see Pan within the thing, hidden: you may see with your third eye, which is darkness.'

'Do you think I might see Pan in a horse, for example?'

'Easily. In St Mawr!'–Cartwright gave her a knowing look.

'But,' said Mrs Witt, 'it would be difficult, I should say, to open the third eye and see Pan in a man.'

'Probably,' said Cartwright, smiling. 'In man he is over-visible: the old satyr: the fallen Pan.'

'Exactly!' said Mrs Witt. And she fell into a muse. 'The fallen Pan!' she re-echoed. 'Wouldn't a man be wonderful in whom Pan hadn't fallen!'

Over the coffee in the grey drawing-room she suddenly asked:

'Supposing, Mr Cartwright, one *did* open the third eye and see Pan in an actual man–I wonder what it would be like?'

She half lowered her eyelids and tilted her face in a strange way, as if she were tasting something, and not quite sure.

'I wonder!' he said, smiling his enigmatic smile. But she could see he did not understand.

'Louise!' said Mrs Witt at bed-time. 'Come into my room for a moment, I want to ask you something.'

'What is it, mother?'

'You, you *get* something from what Mr Cartwright said about seeing Pan with the third eye? Seeing Pan in something?'

Mrs Witt came rather close and tilted her face with strange insinuating question at her daughter.

'I think I do, mother.'

'In what?'–The question came as a pistol-shot.

'I think, mother,' said Lou reluctantly, 'in St Mawr.'

'In a horse!'–Mrs Witt contracted her eyes slightly. 'Yes, I can see that. I know what you mean. It *is* in St Mawr. It *is*! But in St Mawr it makes me *afraid*–' she dragged out the word. Then she came a step closer. 'But, Louise, did you ever see it in a man?'

'What, mother?'

'Pan. Did you ever see Pan in a man, as you see Pan in St Mawr?'

Louise hesitated.

'No, mother, I don't think I did. When I look at men with my third eye, as you call it–I think I see–mostly–a sort of–pancake.' She uttered the last word with a despairing grin, not knowing quite what to say.

'Oh, Louise, isn't that it! Doesn't one always see a pancake! Now listen, Louise. Have you ever been in love?'

'Yes, as far as I understand it.'

'Listen, now. Did you ever see Pan in the man you loved? Tell me if you did.'

'As I see Pan in St Mawr?–no, mother!' And suddenly her lips began to tremble and the tears came to her eyes.

'Listen, Louise. I've been in love innumerable times–and *really* in love twice. Twice!–yet for fifteen years I've left off wanting to have anything to do with a man, really. For fifteen years! And why? Do you know? Because I couldn't see that peculiar hidden Pan in any of them. And I became that I needed to. I needed it. But it wasn't there. Not in any man. Even when I was in love with a man, it was for other things: because I *understood* him so well, or he understood me, or we had such sympathy. Never the hidden Pan. Do you understand what I mean? Unfallen Pan!'

'More or less, mother.'

'But now my third eye is coming open, I believe. I am tired of all these men like breakfast cakes, with a teaspoonful of mind or a teaspoonful of spirit in them, for baking-powder. Isn't it extraordinary: that young man Cartwright talks about Pan, but he knows nothing of it at all. He knows nothing of the unfallen Pan: only the fallen Pan with goat legs and a leer–and that sort of power, don't you know.'

'But what do you know of the unfallen Pan, mother?'

'Don't ask me, Louise! I feel all of a tremble, as if I was just on the verge.' She flashed a little look of incipient triumph, and said good-night.

An excursion on horseback had been arranged for the next day, to two old groups of rocks, called the Angel's Chair and the Devil's Chair, which crowned the moor-like hills looking into Wales, ten miles away. Everybody was going–they were to start early in the morning, and Lewis would be the guide, since no one exactly knew the way.

Lou got up soon after sunrise. There was a summer scent in the trees of early morning, and monkshood flowers stood up dark and tall, with shadows. She dressed in the green linen riding-skirt her maid had put ready for her, with a close bluish smock.

'Are you going out already, dear?' called Rico from his room.

'Just to smell the roses before we start, Rico.'

He appeared in the doorway in his yellow silk pyjamas. His large blue eyes had that rolling, irritable look and the slightly bloodshot whites which made her want to escape.

'Booted and spurred!–the *energy*!' he cried.

'It's a lovely day to ride,' she said.

'A lovely day to do anything *except* ride!' he said. 'Why spoil the day riding!'–A curious bitter acid escaped into his tone. It was evident he hated the excursion.

'Why, we needn't go if you don't want to, Rico.'

'Oh, I'm sure I shall love it, once I get started. It's all this business of *starting*, with horses and paraphernalia–'

Lou went into the yard. The horses were drinking at the trough under the pump, their colours strong and rich in the shadow of the tree.

'You're not coming with us, Phœnix?' she said.

'Lewis, he's riding my horse.'

She could tell Phœnix did not like being left behind.

By half-past seven everybody was ready. The sun was in the yard, the horses were saddled. They came swishing their tails. Lewis brought out St Mawr from his separate box, speaking to him very quietly in Welsh: a murmuring, soothing little speech. Lou, alert, could see that he was uneasy.

'How is St Mawr this morning?' she asked.

'He's all right. He doesn't like so many people. He'll be all right once he's started.'

The strangers were in the saddle: they moved out to the deep shade of the village road outside. Rico came to his horse to mount. St Mawr jumped away as if he had seen the devil.

'Steady, fool!' cried Rico.

The bay stood with his four feet spread, his neck arched, his big dark eye glancing sideways with that watchful, frightening look.

'You shouldn't be irritable with him, Rico!' said Lou. 'Steady then, St Mawr! Be steady.'

But a certain anger rose also in her. The creature was so big, so brilliant, and so stupid, standing there with his hind legs spread, ready to jump aside or to rear terrifically, and his great eye glancing with a sort of suspicious frenzy. What was there to be suspicious of, after all?–Rico would do him no harm.

'No one will harm you St Mawr,' she reasoned, a bit exasperated.

The groom was talking quietly, murmuringly, in Welsh. Rico was slowly advancing again to put his foot in the stirrup. The stallion was watching from the corner of his eye, a strange glare of suspicious frenzy burning stupidly. Any moment his immense physical force might be let loose in a frenzy of panic–or malice. He was really very irritating.

'Probably he doesn't like that apricot shirt,' said Mrs Witt, 'although it tones into him wonderfully well.'

She pronounced it *ap*—ricot, and it irritated Rico terribly.

'Ought we to have *asked* him before we put it on?' he flashed, his upper lip lifting venomously.

'I should say you should,' replied Mrs Witt coolly.

Rico turned with a sudden rush to the horse. Back went the great animal, with a sudden splashing crash of hoofs on the cobble-stones, and Lewis hanging on like a shadow. Up went the forefeet, showing the belly.

'The thing is accursed,' said Rico, who had dropped the reins in sudden shock, and stood marooned. His rage overwhelmed him like a black flood.

'Nothing in the world is so irritating as a horse that is acting up,' thought Lou.

'Say, Harry!' called Flora from the road. 'Come out here into the road to mount him.'

Lewis looked at Rico and nodded. Then soothing the big, quivering animal, he led him springily out to the road under the trees, where the three friends were waiting. Lou and her mother got quickly into the saddle to follow. And in another moment Rico was mounted and bouncing down the road in the wrong direction, Lewis following on the chestnut. It was some time before Rico could get St Mawr round. Watching him from behind, those waiting could judge how the young baronet hated it.

But at last they set off—Rico ahead, unevenly but quietly, with the two Manby girls, Lou following with the fair young man who had been in a cavalry regiment and who kept looking round for Mrs Witt.

'Don't look round for me,' she called. 'I'm riding behind, out of the dust.'

Just behind Mrs Witt came Lewis. It was a whole cavalcade trotting in the morning sun past the cottages and the cottage gardens, round the field that was the recreation-ground, into the deep hedges of the lane.

'Why is St Mawr so bad at starting? Can't you get him into better shape?' she asked over her shoulder.

'Beg your pardon, Mam!'

Lewis trotted a little nearer. She glanced over her shoulder at him, at his dark, unmoved face, his cool little figure.

'I think *Mam* is so ugly. Why not leave it out!' she said. Then she repeated her question.

'St Mawr doesn't trust anybody,' Lewis replied.

'Not you?'

'Yes, he trusts me—mostly.'

'Then why not other people?'

'They're different.'

'All of them?'

'About all of them.'

'How are they different?'

He looked at her with his remote, uncanny grey eyes.

'Different,' he said, not knowing how else to put it.

They rode on slowly, up the steep rise of the wood, then down into a glade where ran a little railway built for hauling some mysterious mineral out of the hill in war-time, and now already abandoned. Even on this countryside the dead hand of the war lay like a corpse decomposing.

They rode up again, past the foxgloves under the trees. Ahead the brilliant St Mawr and the sorrel and grey horses were swimming like butterflies through the sea of bracken, glittering from sun to shade, shade to sun. Then once more they were on a crest, and through the thinning trees could see the slopes of the moors beyond the next dip.

Soon they were in the open, rolling hills, golden in the morning and empty save for a couple of distant bilberry-pickers, whitish figures pick–pick–picking with curious, rather disgusting assiduity. The horses were on an old trail which climbed through the pinky tips of heather and ling, across patches of green bilberry. Here and there were tufts of harebells blue as bubbles.

They were out, high on the hills. And there to west lay Wales, folded in crumpled folds, goldish in the morning light, with its moor-like slopes and patches of corn uncannily distinct. Between was a hollow, wide valley of summer haze, showing white farms among trees, and grey slate roofs.

'Ride beside me,' she said to Lewis. 'Nothing makes me want to go back to America like the old look of these little villages.—You have never been to America?'

'No, Mam.'

'Don't you ever want to go?'

'I wouldn't mind going.'

'But you're not just crazy to go?'

'No, Mam.'

'Quite content as you are?'

He looked at her, and his pale, remote eyes met hers.

'I don't fret myself,' he replied.

'Not about anything at all–ever?'

His eyes glanced ahead, at the other riders.

'No, Mam!' he replied, without looking at her.

She rode a few moments in silence.

'What is that over there?' she asked, pointing across the valley. 'What is it called?'

'Yon's Montgomery.'

'Montgomery! And is that *Wales*–?' she trailed the ending curiously.

'Yes, Mam.'

'Where you come from?'

'No Mam! I come from Merioneth.'

'Not from Wales? I thought you were Welsh?'

'Yes, Mam. Merioneth *is* Wales.'

'And you are Welsh?'

'Yes, Mam.'

'I had a Welsh grandmother. But I come from Louisiana, and when I go back home, the negroes still call me Miss Rachel. "Oh, my, it's little Miss Rachel come back home! Why, ain't I mighty glad to see you—u, Miss Rachel!" That gives me such a strange feeling, you know.'

The man glanced at her curiously, especially when she imitated the negroes.

'Do you feel strange when you go home?' she asked.

'I was brought up by an aunt and uncle,' he said. 'I never want to see them.'

'And you don't have any home?'

'No, Mam.'

'No wife nor anything?'

'No, Mam.'

'But what do you do with your life?'

'I keep to myself.'

'And care about nothing?'

'I mind St Mawr.'

'But you've not always had St Mawr–and you won't always have him.–Were you in the war?'

'Yes, Mam.'

'At the front?'

'Yes, Mam–but I was a groom.'

'And you came out all right?'

'I lost my little finger from a bullet.'

He held up his small, dark left hand, from which the little finger was missing.

'And did you like the war–or didn't you?'

'I didn't like it.'

Again his pale grey eyes met hers, and they looked so non-human and uncommunicative, so without connection, and inaccessible, she was troubled.

'Tell me,' she said. 'Did you never want a wife and a home and children, like other men?'

'No, Mam. I never wanted a home of my own.'

'Nor a wife of your own?'

'No, Mam.'

'Nor children of your own?'

'No, Mam.'

She reined in her horse.

'Now wait a minute,' she said. 'Now tell me why.'

His horse came to standstill, and the two riders faced one another.

'Tell me why–I must know why you never wanted a wife and children and a home. I must know why you're not like other men.'

'I never felt like it,' he said. 'I made my life with horses.'

'Did you hate people very much? Did you have a very unhappy time as a child?'

'My aunt and uncle didn't like me, and I didn't like them.'

'So you've never liked anybody?'

'Maybe not,' he said. 'Not to get as far as marrying them.'

She touched her horse and moved on.

'Isn't that curious!' she said. 'I've loved people, at various times. But I don't believe *I've* ever liked anybody, except a few of our negroes. I don't like Louise, though she's my daughter and I love her. But I don't really *like* her.–I think you're the first person I've ever liked since I was on our plantation, and we had some *very fine* negroes.–And I think that's very curious.–Now I want to know if you like *me*.'

She looked at him searchingly but he did not answer.

'Tell me,' she said. 'I don't mind if you say no. But tell me if you like me. I feel I must know.'

The flicker of a smile went over his face–a very rare thing with him.

'Maybe I do,' he said. He was thinking that she put him on a level with a negro slave on a plantation: in his idea, negroes were still slaves. But he did not care where she put him.

'Well, I'm glad–I'm glad if you like me. Because you *don't* like most people, I know that.'

They had passed the hollow where the old Aldecar Chapel hid in damp isolation, beside the ruined mill, over the stream that came down from the moors. Climbing the sharp slope, they saw the folded hills like great shut fingers, with steep, deep clefts between. On the near skyline was a bunch of rocks: and away to the right another bunch.

'Yon's the Angel's Chair,' said Lewis, pointing to the nearer rocks. 'And yon's the Devil's Chair, where we're going.'

'Oh!' said Mrs Witt. 'And aren't we going to the Angel's Chair?'

'No, Mam.'

'Why not?'

'There's nothing to see there. The other's higher, and bigger, and that's where folks mostly go.'

'Is that so!—They give the Devil the higher seat in this country, do they? I think they're right.' And as she got no answer, she added: 'You believe in the Devil, don't you?'

'I never met him,' he answered evasively.

Ahead, they could see the other horses twinkling in a cavalcade up the slope, the black, the bay, the two greys and the sorrel, sometimes bunching, sometimes straggling. At a gate all waited for Mrs Witt. The fair young man fell in beside her, and talked hunting at her. He had hunted the fox over these hills, and was vigorously excited locating the spot where the hounds first gave cry, etc.

'Really!' said Mrs Witt. '*Really!* Is that so!'

If irony could have been condensed to prussic acid, the fair young man would have ended his life's history with his reminiscences.

They came at last, trotting in file along a narrow track between heather, along the saddle of a hill, to where the knot of pale granite suddenly cropped out. It was one of those places where the spirit of aboriginal England still lingers, the old savage England, whose last blood flows still in a few Englishmen, Welshmen, Cornishmen. The rocks, whitish with weather of all the ages, jutted against the blue August sky, heavy with age-moulded roundness.

Lewis stayed below with the horses, the party scrambled rather awkwardly, in their riding-boots, up the foot-worn boulders. At length they stood in the place called the Chair, looking west, west towards Wales, that rolled in golden folds upwards. It was neither impressive nor a very picturesque landscape: the hollow valley with farms, and then the rather bare upheaval of hills, slopes with corn and moor and pasture, rising like a barricade, seemingly high, slantingly. Yet it had a strange effect on the imagination.

'Oh, mother,' said Lou, 'doesn't it make you feel old, old, older than anything ever was?'

'It certainly does seem aged,' said Mrs Witt.

'It makes me want to die,' said Lou. 'I feel we've lasted almost too long.'

'Don't say that, Lady Carrington. Why, you're a spring chicken yet: or shall I say an unopened rose-bud,' remarked the fair young man.

'No,' said Lou. 'All these millions of ancestors have used all the life up. We're not really alive, in the sense that they were alive.'

'But who?' said Rico. 'Who are *they*?'

'The people who lived on these hills in the days gone by.'

'But the same people still live on the hills, darling. It's just the same stock.'

'No, Rico. That old fighting stock that worshipped devils among these stones—I'm sure they did—'

'But look here, do you mean they were any better than we are?' asked the fair young man.

Lou looked at him quizzically.

'We don't exist,' she said, squinting at him oddly.

'I jolly well know *I* do,' said the fair young man.

'I consider these days are the best ever, especially for girls,' said Flora Manby. 'And, anyhow, they're our own days, so I don't jolly well see the use of crying them down.'

They were all silent, with the last echoes of emphatic *joie de vivre* trumpeting on the air, across the hills of Wales.

'Spoken like a brick, Flora,' said Rico. 'Say it again, we may not have the Devil's Chair for a pulpit next time.'

'I do,' reiterated Flora. 'I think this is the best age there ever was for a girl to have a good time in. I read all through H. G. Wells's History, and I shut it up and thanked my stars I live in nineteen-twenty odd, not in some other beastly date when a woman had to cringe before mouldy, domineering men.'

After this they turned to scramble to another part of the rocks, to the famous Needle's Eye.

'Thank you so much, I am really better without help,' said Mrs Witt to the fair young man, as she slid downwards till a piece of grey silk stocking showed above her tall boot. But she got her toe in a safe place, and in a moment stood beside him, while he caught her arm protectingly. He might as well have caught the paw of a mountain lion protectingly.

'I should like *so* much to know,' she said suavely, looking into his eyes with a demonish straight look, 'what makes you so certain that you exist?'

He looked back at her, and his jaunty blue eyes went baffled. Then a slow, hot, salmon-coloured flush stole over his face, and he turned abruptly round.

The Needle's Eye was a hole in the ancient grey rock, like a window, looking to England; England at the moment in shadow. A stream wound and glinted in the flat shadow, and beyond that the flat, insignificant hills heaped in mounds of shade. Cloud was coming–the English side was in shadow. Wales was still in the sun, but the shadow was spreading. The day was going to disappoint them. Lou was a tiny bit chilled already.

Luncheon was still several miles away. The party hastened down to the horses. Lou picked a few sprigs of ling, and some harebells, and some straggling yellow flowers: not because she wanted them, but to distract herself. The atmosphere of 'enjoying ourselves' was becoming cruel to her: it sapped all the life out of her. 'Oh, if only I needn't enjoy myself,' she moaned inwardly. But the Manby girls were enjoying themselves so much. 'I think it's frantically lovely up here,' said the other one–not Flora–Elsie.

'It *is* beautiful, isn't it! I'm *so* glad you like it,' replied Rico. And he was really relieved and gratified, because the other one said she was enjoying it so frightfully. He dared not say to Lou, as he wanted to: 'I'm afraid, Lou, darling, you don't love it as much as we do.'–He was afraid of her answer: 'No, dear, I don't love it at all! I want to be away from these people.'

Slightly piqued, he rode on with the Manby group, and Lou came behind with her mother. Cloud was covering the sky with grey. There was a cold wind. Everybody was anxious to get to the farm for luncheon, and be safely home before rain came.

They were riding along one of the narrow little foot-tracks, mere grooves of grass between heather and bright green bilberry. The blond young man was ahead, then his wife, then Flora, then Rico. Lou, from a little distance, watched the glossy, powerful haunches of St Mawr swaying with life, always too much life, like a menace. The fair young man was whistling a new dance tune.

'That's an awfully attractive tune,' Rico called. 'Do whistle it again, Fred, I should like to memorise it.'

Fred began to whistle it again.

At that moment St Mawr exploded again, shied sideways as if a bomb had gone off, and kept backing through the heather.

'Fool!' cried Rico, thoroughly unnerved: he had been terribly sideways in the saddle, Lou had feared he was going to fall. But he got his seat, and pulled the reins viciously, to bring the horse to order, and put him on the track again. St Mawr began to rear: his favourite trick. Rico got him forward a few yards, when up he went again.

'Fool!' yelled Rico, hanging in the air.

He pulled the horse over backwards on top of him.

Lou gave a loud, unnatural, horrible scream: she heard it herself, at the same time as she heard the crash of the falling horse. Then she saw a pale gold belly, and hoofs that worked and flashed in the air, and St Mawr writhing, straining his head terrifically upwards, his great eyes starting from the naked lines of his nose. With a great neck arching cruelly from the ground, he was pulling frantically at the reins, which Rico still held tight. — Yes, Rico, lying strangely sideways, his eyes also starting from his yellow-white face, among the heather, still clutched the reins.

Young Edwards was rushing forward, and circling round the writhing, immense horse, whose pale-gold, inverted bulk seemed to fill the universe.

'Let him get up, Carrington! Let him get up!' he was yelling, darting warily near to get the reins. — Another spasmodic convulsion of the horse.

Horror! The young man reeled backwards with his face in his hands. He had got a kick in the face. Red blood running down his chin!

Lewis was there, on the ground, getting the reins out of Rico's hands. St Mawr gave a great curve like a fish, spread his forefeet on the earth and reared his head, looking round in a ghastly fashion. His eyes were arched, his nostrils wide, his face ghastly in a sort of panic. He rested thus, seated with his forefeet planted and his face in panic, almost like some terrible lizard, for several moments. Then he heaved sickeningly to his feet, and stood convulsed, trembling.

There lay Rico, crumpled and rather sideways, staring at the heavens from a yellow, dead-looking face. Lewis, glancing round in a sort of horror, looked in dread at St Mawr again. Flora had been hovering. — She now rushed screeching to the prostrate Rico:

'Harry! Harry! you're not dead! Oh, Harry! Harry! Harry!'

Lou had dismounted. — She didn't know when. She stood a little way off, as if spellbound, while Flora cried: *Harry! Harry! Harry!*

Suddenly Rico sat up.

'Where is the horse?' he said.

At the same time an added whiteness came on his face, and he bit his lip with pain, and he fell prostrate again in a faint. Flora rushed to put her arm round him.

Where was the horse? He had backed slowly away, in an agony of suspicion, while Lewis murmured to him in vain. His head was raised again, the eyes still starting from their sockets, and a terrible guilty, ghost-like look on his face. When Lewis drew a little nearer he twitched and shrank like a shaken steel spring, away — not to be touched. He seemed to be seeing legions of ghosts, down the dark avenues of all the centuries that have lapsed since the horse became subject to man.

And the other young man? He was still standing, at a little distance, with his face in his hands, motionless, the blood falling on his white shirt, and his wife at his side, pleading, distracted.

Mrs Witt, too, was there, as if cast in steel, watching. She made no sound and did not move, only from a fixed, impassive face, watched each thing.

'Do tell me what you think is the matter,' Lou pleaded, distracted, to Flora, who was supporting Rico and weeping torrents of unknown tears.

Then Mrs Witt came forward and began in a very practical manner to unclose the shirt-neck and feel the young man's heart. Rico opened his eyes again, said '*Really!*' and closed his eyes once more.

'It's fainting!' said Mrs Witt. 'We have no brandy.'

Lou, too weary to be able to feel anything, said:

'I'll go and get some.'

She went to her alarmed horse, who stood among the others with her head down, in suspense. Almost unconsciously Lou mounted, set her face ahead, and was riding away.

Then Poppy shied too, with a sudden start, and Lou pulled up. 'Why?' she said to her horse. 'Why did you do that?'

She looked round, and saw in the heather a glimpse of yellow and black.

'A snake!' she said wonderingly.

And she looked closer.

It was a dead adder that had been drinking at a reedy pool in a little depression just off the road, and had been killed with stones. There it lay, also crumpled, its head crushed, its gold-and-yellow back still glittering dully, and a bit of pale-blue showing, killed that morning.

Lou rode on, her face set towards the farm. An unspeakable weariness had overcome her. She could not even suffer. Weariness of spirit left her in a sort of apathy.

And she had a vision, a vision of evil. Or not strictly a vision. She became aware of evil, evil, evil, rolling in great waves over the earth. Always she had thought there was no such thing—only a mere negation of good. Now, like an ocean to whose surface she had risen, she saw the dark-grey waves of evil rearing in a great tide.

And it had swept mankind away without mankind's knowing. It had caught up the nations as the rising ocean might lift the fishes, and was sweeping them on in a great tide of evil. They did not know. The people did not know. They did not even wish it. They wanted to be good and to have everything joyful and enjoyable. Everything joyful and enjoyable: for everybody. This was what they wanted, if you asked them.

But at the same time, they had fallen under the spell of evil. It was a soft, subtle thing, soft as water, and its motion was soft and imperceptible, as the running of a tide is invisible to one who is out on the ocean. And they were all out on the ocean, being borne along in the current of the mysterious evil, creatures of the evil principle, as fishes are creatures of the sea.

There was no relief. The whole world was enveloped in one great flood. All the nations, the white, the brown, the black, the yellow, all were immersed in the strange tide of evil that was subtly, irresistibly rising. No one, perhaps, deliberately wished it. Nearly every individual wanted peace and a good time all round: everybody to have a good time.

But some strange thing had happened, and the vast mysterious force of positive evil was let loose. She felt that from the core of Asia the evil welled up, as from some strange pole, and slowly was drowning earth.

It was something horrifying, something you could not escape from. It had come to her as in a vision, when she saw the pale gold belly of the stallion upturned, the hoofs working wildly, the wicked curved hams of the horse, and then the evil straining of that arched, fish-like neck, with the dilated eyes of the head. Thrown backwards, and working its hoofs in the air. Reversed, and purely evil.

She saw the same in people. They were thrown backwards, and writhing with evil. And the rider, crushed, was still reining them down.

What did it mean? Evil, evil, and a rapid return to the sordid chaos. Which was wrong, the horse or the rider? Or both?

She thought with horror of St Mawr, and of the look on his face. But she thought with horror, a colder horror, of Rico's face as he snarled *Fool!* His fear, his impotence as a master, as a rider, his presumption. And she thought with horror of those other people, so glib, so glibly evil.

What did they want to do, those Manby girls? Undermine, undermine, undermine. They wanted to undermine Rico, just as that fair young man would have liked to undermine her. Believe in nothing, care about nothing: but keep the surface easy, and have a good time. *Let us undermine one another. There is nothing to believe in, so let us undermine everything. But look out! No scenes, no spoiling the game. Stick to the rules of the game. Be sporting, and don't do anything that would make a commotion. Keep the game going smooth and jolly, and bear your bit like a sport. Never, by any chance, injure your fellow-man openly. But always injure him secretly. Make a fool of him, and undermine his nature. Break him up by undermining him, if you can. It's good sport.*

The evil! The mysterious potency of evil. She could see it all the time, in individuals, in society, in the press. There it was in socialism and bolshevism: the same evil. But bolshevism made a mess of the outside of life, so turn it down. Try fascism. Fascism would keep the surface of life intact, and carry on the undermining business all the better. All the better sport. Never draw blood. Keep the hæmorrhage internal, invisible.

And as soon as fascism makes a break—which it is bound to, because all evil works up to a break—then turn it down. With gusto, turn it down.

Mankind, like a horse, ridden by a stranger, smooth-faced, evil rider. Evil himself, smooth-faced and pseudo-handsome, riding mankind past the dead snake, to the last break.

Mankind no longer its own master. Ridden by this pseudo-handsome ghoul of outward loyalty, inward treachery, in a game of betrayal, betrayal, betrayal. The last of the gods of our era, Judas supreme!

People performing outward acts of loyalty, piety, self-sacrifice. But inwardly bent on undermining, betraying. Directing all their subtle evil will against any positive living thing. Masquerading as the ideal, in order to poison the real.

Creation destroys as it goes, throws down one tree for the rise of another. But ideal mankind would abolish death, multiply itself million upon million, rear up city upon city, save every parasite alive, until the accumulation of mere existence is swollen to a horror. But go on saving life, the ghastly salvation army of ideal mankind. At the same time secretly, viciously, potently undermine the natural creation, betray it with kiss after kiss, destroy it from the inside, till you have the swollen rottenness of our teeming existences.—But keep the game going. Nobody's going to make another bad break, such as Germany and Russia made.

Two bad breaks the secret evil has made: in Germany and in Russia. Watch it! Let evil keep a policeman's eye on evil! The surface of life must remain unruptured. Production must be heaped upon production. And the natural creation must be betrayed by many more kisses, yet. Judas is the last God, and, by heaven, the most potent.

But even Judas made a break: hanged himself, and his bowels gushed out. Not long after his triumph.

Man must destroy as he goes, as trees fall for trees to rise. The accumulation of life and things means rottenness. Life must destroy life, in the unfolding of creation. We save up life at the expense of the unfolding till all is full of rottenness. Then at last we make a break.

What's to be done? Generally speaking, nothing. The dead will have to bury their dead, while the earth stinks of corpses. The individual can but depart from the mass, and try to cleanse himself. Try to hold fast to the living thing, which destroys as it goes, but remains sweet. And in his soul fight, fight, fight to preserve that which is life in him from the ghastly kisses and poison-bites of the myriad evil ones. Retreat to the desert, and fight. But in his soul adhere to that which is life itself, creatively destroying as it goes: destroying the stiff old thing to let the new bud come through. The one passionate principle of creative being, which recognises the natural good, and has a sword for the swarms of evil. Fights, fights, fights to protect itself. But with itself, is strong and at peace.

Lou came to the farm, and got brandy, and asked the men to come out to carry in the injured.

It turned out that the kick in the face had knocked a couple of young Edwards's teeth out, and would disfigure him a little.

'To go through the war, and then get this!' he mumbled, with a vindictive glance at St Mawr.

And it turned out that Rico had two broken ribs and a crushed ankle. Poor Rico, he would limp for life.

'I want St Mawr *shot!*' was almost his first word when he was in bed at the farm and Lou was sitting beside him.

'What good would that do, dear?' she said.

'The brute is evil. I want him *shot!*'

Rico could make the last word sound like the spitting of a bullet.

'Do you want to shoot him yourself?'

'No. But I want to have him shot. I shall never be easy till I know he has a bullet through him. He's got a wicked character. I don't feel you are safe with him down there. I shall get one of the Manbys' gamekeepers to shoot him. You might tell Flora—or I'll tell her myself, when she comes.'

'Don't talk about it now, dear. You've got a temperature.'

Was it true St Mawr was evil? She would never forget him writhing and lunging on the ground, nor his awful face when he reared up. But then that noble look of his: surely he was not mean? Whereas all evil had an inner meanness, mean! Was he mean? Was he meanly treacherous? Did he know he could kill, and meanly wait his opportunity?

She was afraid. And if this were true, then he *should* be shot. Perhaps he ought to be shot.

This thought haunted her. Was there something mean and treacherous in St Mawr's spirit, the vulgar evil? If so, then have him shot. At moments, an anger would rise in her, as she thought of his frenzied rearing, and his mad, hideous writhing on the ground, and in the heat of her anger she would want to hurry down to her mother's house and have the creature shot at once. It would be a satisfaction, and a vindication of human rights. Because after all, Rico was so considerate of the brutal horse. But not a spark of consideration did the stallion have for Rico. No, it was the slavish malevolence of a domesticated creature that kept cropping up in St Mawr. The slave, taking his slavish vengeance, then dropping back into subservience.

All the slaves of this world, accumulating their preparations for slavish vengeance, and then, when they have taken it, ready to drop back into servility. Freedom! Most slaves can't be freed, no matter how you let them loose. Like domestic animals, they are, in the long run, more afraid of freedom than of masters: and freed by some generous master, they will at last crawl back to some mean boss, who will have no scruples about kicking them. Because, for them, far better kicks and servility than the hard, lonely responsibility of real freedom.

The wild animal is at every moment intensely self-disciplined, poised in the tension of self-defence, self-preservation and self-assertion. The moments of relaxation are rare and most carefully chosen. Even sleep is watchful, guarded, unrelaxing, the wild courage pitched one degree higher than the wild fear. Courage, the wild thing's courage to maintain itself alone and living in the midst of a diverse universe.

Did St Mawr have this courage?

And did Rico?

Ah, Rico! He was one of mankind's myriad conspirators, who conspire to live in absolute physical safety, whilst willing the minor disintegration of all positive living.

But St Mawr? Was it the natural wild thing in him which caused these disasters? Or was it the slave, asserting himself for vengeance?

If the latter, let him be shot. It would be a great satisfaction to see him dead.

But if the former—

When she could leave Rico with the nurse, she motored down to her mother for a couple of days. Rico lay in bed at the farm.

Everything seemed curiously changed. There was a new silence about the place, a new coolness. Summer had passed with several thunderstorms, and the blue, cool touch of autumn was about the house. Dahlias and perennial yellow sunflowers were out, the yellow of ending summer, the red coals of early autumn. First mauve tips of Michaelmas daisies were showing. Something suddenly carried her away to the great bare spaces of Texas, the blue sky, the flat, burnt earth, the miles of sunflowers. Another sky, another silence, towards the setting sun.

And suddenly she craved again for the more absolute silence of America. English stillness was so soft, like an inaudible murmur of voices, of presences. But the silence in the empty spaces of America was still unutterable, almost cruel.

St Mawr was in a small field by himself: she could not bear that he should be always in stable. Slowly she went through the gate towards him. And he stood there looking at her, the bright bay creature.

She could tell he was feeling somewhat subdued, after his late escapade. He was aware of the general human condemnation: the human damning. But something obstinate and uncanny in him made him not relent.

'Hello! St Mawr!' she said, as she drew near, and he stood watching her, his ears pricked, his big eyes glancing sideways at her.

But he moved away when she wanted to touch him.

'Don't trouble,' she said. 'I don't want to catch you or do anything to you.'
He stood still, listening to the sound of her voice, and giving quick, small glances at her. His underlip trembled. But he did not blink. His eyes remained wide and unrelenting. There was a curious malicious obstinacy in him which roused her anger.

'I don't want to touch you,' she said. 'I only want to look at you, and even you can't prevent that.'

She stood gazing hard at him, wanting to know, to settle the question of his meanness or his spirit. A thing with a brave spirit is not mean.

He was uneasy as she watched him. He pretended to hear something, the mares two fields away, and he lifted his head and neighed. She knew the powerful, splendid sound so well: like bells made of living membrane. And he looked so noble again, with his head tilted up, listening and his male eyes looking proudly over the distance, eagerly.

But it was all a bluff.

He knew, and became silent again. And as he stood there a few yards away from her, his head lifted and wary, his body full of power and tension, his face slightly averted from her, she felt a great animal sadness come from him. A strange animal atmosphere of sadness, that was vague and disseminated through the air, and made her feel as though she breathed grief. She breathed it into her breast, as if it were a great sigh down the ages, that passed into her breast. And she felt a great woe: the woe of human unworthiness. The race of men judged in the consciousness of the animals they have subdued, and there found unworthy, ignoble.

Ignoble men, unworthy of the animals they have subjugated, bred the woe in the spirit of their creatures. St Mawr, that bright horse, one of the kings of creation in the order below man, it had been a fulfilment for him to serve the brave, reckless, perhaps cruel men of the past, who had a flickering, rising flame of nobility in them. To serve that flame of mysterious further nobility. Nothing matters, but that strange flame, of inborn nobility that obliges men to be brave, and onward plunging. And the horse will bear him on.

But now where is the flame of dangerous, forward-pressing nobility in men? Dead, dead, guttering out in a stink of self-sacrifice whose feeble light is a light of exhaustion and *laissez-faire*.

And the horse, is he to go on carrying man forward into this?—this gutter?

No! Man wisely invents motor-cars and other machines, automobile and locomotive. The horse is superannuated for man.

But alas, man is even more superannuated for the horse.

Dimly in a woman's muse, Lou realised this, as she breathed the horse's sadness, his accumulated vague woe from the generations of latter-day ignobility. And a grief and a sympathy flooded her, for the horse. She realised now how his sadness recoiled into these frenzies of obstinacy and malevolence. Underneath it all was grief, an unconscious, vague, pervading animal grief, which perhaps only Lewis understood, because he felt the same. The grief of the generous creature which sees all ends turning to the morass of ignoble living.

She did not want to say any more to the horse: she did not want to look at him any more. The grief flooded her soul that made her want to be alone. She knew now what it all amounted to. She knew that the horse, born to serve nobly, had waited in vain for someone noble to serve. His spirit knew that nobility had gone out of men. And this left him high and dry, in a sort of despair.

As she walked away from him, towards the gate, slowly he began to walk after her.

Phœnix came striding through the gate towards her.

'You not afraid of that horse?' he asked sardonically, in his quiet, subtle voice.

'Not at the present moment,' she replied, even more quietly, looking direct at him. She was not in any mood to be jeered at.

And instantly the sardonic grimace left his face, followed by the sudden blankness, and the look of race misery in the keen eyes.

'Do you want me to be afraid?' she said, continuing to the gate.

'No, I don't want it,' he replied, dejected.

'Are you afraid of him yourself?' she said, glancing round. St Mawr had stopped, seeing Phœnix, and had turned away again.

'I'm not afraid of no horses,' said Phœnix.

Lou went on quietly. At the gate, she asked him:

'Don't you like St Mawr, Phœnix?'

'I like him. He's a very good horse.'

'Even after what he's done to Sir Henry?'

'That don't make no difference to him being a good horse.'

'But suppose he'd done it to you?'

'I don't care. I say it my own fault.'

'Don't you think he is wicked?'

'I don't think so. He don't kick anybody. He don't bite anybody. He don't pitch, he don't buck, he don't do nothing.'

'He rears,' said Lou.

'Well, what is rearing!' said the man, with a slow, contemptuous smile.

'A good deal, when a horse falls back on you.'

'That horse don't want to fall back on you, if you don't make him. If you know how to ride him. That horse wants his own way some time. If you don't let him, you got to fight him. Then look out!'

'Look out he doesn't kill you, you mean!'

'Look out you don't let him,' said Phœnix, with his slow, grim, sardonic smile.

Lou watched the smooth, golden face with its thin line of moustache and its sad eyes with the glint in them. Cruel–there was something cruel in him, right down in the abyss of him. But at the same time, there was an aloneness, and a grim little satisfaction in a fight, and the peculiar courage of an inherited despair. People who inherit despair may at last turn it into greater heroism. It was almost so with Phœnix. Three-quarters of his blood was probably Indian and the remaining quarter, that came through the Mexican father, had the Spanish-American despair to add to the Indian. It was almost complete enough to leave him free to be heroic.

'What are we going to do with him, though?' she asked.

'Why don't you and Mrs Witt go back to America–you never been West. You go West.'

'Where, to California?'

'No. To Arizona or New Mexico or Colorado or Wyoming, anywhere. Not to California.'

Phœnix looked at her keenly, and she saw the desire dark in him. He wanted to go back. But he was afraid to go back alone, empty-handed, as it were. He had suffered too much, and in that country his sufferings would overcome him, unless he had some other background. He had been too much in contact with the white world, and his own world was too dejected, in a sense, too hopeless for his own hopelessness. He needed an alien contact to give him relief.

But he wanted to go back. His necessity to go back was becoming too strong for him.

'What is it like in Arizona?' she asked. 'Isn't it all pale-coloured sand and alkali, and a few cactuses, and terribly hot and deathly?'

'No!' he cried. 'I don't take you there. I take you to the mountains—trees—' he lifted up his hand and looked at the sky—'big trees—pine! *Pino-real* and *pinovetes*, smell good. And then you come down, *piñon*, not very tall, and *cedro*, cedar, smell good in the fire. And then you see the desert, away below, go miles and miles, and where the canyon go, the crack where it look red! I know, I been there, working a cattle ranch.'

He looked at her with a haunted glow in his dark eyes. The poor fellow was suffering from nostalgia. And as he glowed at her in that queer, mystical way, she too seemed to see that country, with its dark, heavy mountains holding in their lap the great stretches of pale, creased, silent desert that still is virgin of idea, its word unspoken.

Phœnix was watching her closely and subtly. He wanted something of her. He wanted it intensely, heavily, and he watched her as if he could force her to give it him. He wanted her to take him back to America, because, rudderless, he was afraid to go back alone. He wanted her to take him back: avidly he wanted it. She was to be the means to his end.

Why shouldn't he go back by himself? Why should he crave for her to go too? Why should he want her there?

There was no answer, except that he did.

'Why, Phœnix,' she said. 'I might possibly go back to America. But you know, Sir Henry would never go there. He doesn't like America, though he's never been. But I'm sure he'd never go there to live.'

'Let him stay here,' said Phœnix abruptly, the sardonic look on his face as he watched her face. 'You come, and let him stay here.'

'Ah, that's a whole story!' she said, and moved away.

As she went, he looked after her, standing silent and arrested and watching as an Indian watches. It was not love. Personal love counts so little when the greater griefs, the greater hopes, the great despairs and the great resolutions come upon us.

She found Mrs Witt rather more silent, more firmly closed within herself, than usual. Her mouth was shut tight, her brows were arched rather more imperiously than ever, she was revolving some inward problem about which Lou was far too wise to inquire.

In the afternoon Dean Vyner and Mrs Vyner came to call on Lady Carrington.

'What bad luck this is, Lady Carrington!' said the Dean. 'Knocks Scotland on the head for you this year, I'm afraid. How did you leave your husband?'

'He seems to be doing as well as he could do!' said Lou.

'But how *very* unfortunate!' murmured the invalid Mrs Vyner. 'Such a handsome young man, in the bloom of youth! Does he suffer much pain?'

'Chiefly his foot,' said Lou.

'Oh, I *do* so hope they'll be able to restore the ankle. Oh, how dreadful, to be lamed at his age!'

'The doctor doesn't know. There *may* be a limp,' said Lou.

'That horse has certainly left his mark on two good-looking young fellows,' said the Dean. 'If you don't mind my saying so, Lady Carrington, I think he's a bad egg.'

'Who, St Mawr?' said Lou, in her American sing-song.

'Yes, Lady Carrington,' murmured Mrs Vyner, in her invalid's low tone. 'Don't you think he ought to be put away? He seems to me the incarnation of cruelty. His neigh. It goes through me like knives. Cruel! Cruel! Oh, I think he should be put away.'

'How put away?' murmured Lou, taking on an invalid's low tone herself.

'Shot, I suppose,' said the Dean.

'It is quite painless. He'll know nothing,' murmured Mrs Vyner hastily. 'And think of the harm he has done already! Horrible! Horrible!' she shuddered. 'Poor Sir Henry lame for life and Freddy Edwards disfigured. Besides all that has gone before. Ah, no, such a creature ought not to live!'

'To live, and have a groom to look after him and feed him,' said the Dean. 'It's a bit thick, while he's smashing up the very people that give him bread—or oats, since he's a horse. But I suppose you'll be wanting to get rid of him?'

'Rico does,' murmured Lou.

'Very naturally. So should I. A vicious horse is worse than a vicious man—except that you are free to put him six feet underground, and end his vice finally, by your own act.'

'Do you think St Mawr is vicious?' said Lou.

'Well, of course—if we're driven to definitions!—I *know* he's dangerous.'

'And do you think we ought to shoot everything that is dangerous?' asked Lou, her colour rising.

'But, Lady Carrington, have you consulted your husband? Surely his wish should be law, in a matter of this sort? And on such an occasion! For *you*, who are a woman, it is enough that the horse is cruel, cruel, evil! I felt it long before anything happened. That evil male cruelty! Ah!' and she clasped her hands convulsively.

'I suppose,' said Lou slowly, 'that St Mawr is really Rico's horse: I gave him to him, I suppose. But I don't believe I could let him shoot him, for all that.'

'Ah, Lady Carrington,' said the Dean breezily, 'you can shift the responsibility. The horse is a public menace, put it at that. We can get an order to have him done away with, at the public expense. And among ourselves we can find some suitable compensation for you, as a mark of sympathy. Which, believe me, is very sincere! One hates to have to destroy a fine-looking animal. But I would sacrifice a dozen rather than have our Rico limping.'

'Yes, indeed,' murmured Mrs Vyner.

'Will you excuse me one moment, while I see about tea,' said Lou, rising and leaving the room. Her colour was high, and there was a glint in her eyes. These people almost roused her to hatred. Oh, these awful, house-bred, house-inbred human beings, how repulsive they were!

She hurried to her mother's dressing-room. Mrs Witt was very carefully putting a touch of red on her lips.

'Mother, they want to shoot St Mawr,' she said.

'I know,' said Mrs Witt, as calmly as if Lou had said tea was ready.

'Well—' stammered Lou, rather put out. 'Don't you think it cheek?'

'It depends, I suppose, on the point of view,' said Mrs Witt dispassionately, looking closely at her lips. 'I don't think the English climate agrees with me. I need something to stand up against, no matter whether it's great heat or great cold. This climate, like the food and the people, is most always lukewarm or tepid, one or the other. And the tepid and the lukewarm are not really my line.' She spoke with a slow drawl.

'But they're in the drawing-room, mother, trying to force me to have St Mawr killed.'

'What about tea?' said Mrs Witt.

'I don't care,' said Lou.

Mrs Witt worked the bell-handle.

'I suppose, Louise,' she said, in her most beaming eighteenth-century manner, 'that these are your guests, so you will preside over the ceremony of pouring out.'

'No, mother, you do it. I can't smile to-day.'

'I can,' said Mrs Witt.

And she bowed her head slowly, with a faint, ceremoniously-effusive smile, as if handing a cup of tea.

Lou's face flickered to a smile.

'Then you pour out for them. You can stand them better than I can.'

'Yes,' said Mrs Witt. 'I saw Mrs Vyner's hat coming across the churchyard. It looks so like a crumpled cup and saucer, that I have been saying to myself ever since: "Dear Mrs Vyner, can't I fill your cup!"–and then pouring tea into that hat. And I hear the Dean responding: "My head is covered with cream, my cup runneth over."–That is the way they make *me* feel.'

They marched downstairs, and Mrs Witt poured tea with that devastating correctness which made Mrs Vyner, who was utterly impervious to sarcasm, pronounce her 'indecipherably vulgar'.

But the Dean was the old bull-dog, and he had set his teeth in a subject.

'I was talking to Lady Carrington about that stallion, Mrs Witt.'

'Did you say stallion' asked Mrs Witt, with perfect neutrality.

'Why, yes, I presume that's what he is.'

'I presume so,' said Mrs Witt colourlessly.

'I'm afraid Lady Carrington is a little sensitive on the wrong score,' said the Dean.

'I beg your pardon,' said Mrs Witt, leaning forward in her most colourless polite manner. 'You mean the stallion's score?'

'Yes,' said the Dean testily. 'The horse St Mawr.'

'The stallion St Mawr,' echoed Mrs Witt, with utmost mild vagueness. She completely ignored Mrs Vyner, who felt plunged like a specimen into methylated spirit. There was a moment's full-stop.

'Yes?' said Mrs Witt naïvely.

'You agree that we can't have any more of these accidents to your young men?' said the Dean rather hastily.

'I certainly do!' Mrs Witt spoke very slowly, and the Dean's lady began to look up. She might find a loop-hole through which to wriggle into the contest. 'You know, Dean, that my son-in-law calls me, for preference, *belle-mère!* It sounds so awfully English when he says it: I always see myself as an old grey mare with a bell round her neck, leading a bunch of horses.' She smiled a prim little smile, *very* conversationally. 'Well!' and she pulled herself up from the aside. 'Now as the bell-mare of the bunch of horses, I shall see to it that my son-in-law doesn't go too near that stallion again. That stallion won't stand mischief.'

She spoke so earnestly that the Dean looked at her with round, wide eyes, completely taken aback.

'We all know, Mrs Witt, that the author of the mischief is St Mawr himself,' he said, in a loud tone.

'Really! you think *that?*' Her voice went up in American surprise. 'Why, how *strange*–!' and she lingered over the last word.

'Strange, eh?–After what's just happened?' said the Dean, with a deadly little smile.

'Why, yes! Most strange! I saw with my own eyes my son-in-law pull that stallion over backwards, and hold him down with the reins as tight as he could hold them; pull St Mawr's head backwards on to the ground, till the groom had to crawl up and force the reins out of my son-in-law's hands. Don't you think that was mischievous on Sir Henry's part?'

The Dean was growing purple. He made an apoplectic movement with his hand. Mrs Vyner was turned to a seated pillar of salt, strangely dressed up.

'Mrs Witt, you are playing on words.'

'No, Dean Vyner, I am not. My son-in-law pulled that horse over backwards and pinned him down with the reins.'

'I am sorry for the horse,' said the Dean, with heavy sarcasm.

'I am *very*,' said Mrs Witt, 'sorry for that stallion: *very!*'

Here Mrs Vyner rose as if a chair-spring had suddenly propelled her to her feet. She was streaky pink in the face.

'Mrs Witt,' she panted, 'you misdirect your sympathies. That poor young man–in the beauty of youth.'

'Isn't he *beautiful*–' murmured Mrs Witt, extravagantly in sympathy. 'He's my daughter's husband!' And she looked at the petrified Lou.

'Certainly!' panted the Dean's wife. 'And you can defend that–that–'

'That stallion,' said Mrs Witt. 'But you see, Mrs Vyner,' she added, leaning forward female and confidential, 'if the old grey mare doesn't defend the stallion, who will? All the blooming young ladies will defend my beautiful son-in-law. You feel so *warmly* for him yourself! I'm an American woman, and I always have to stand up for the accused. And I stand up for that stallion. I say it is not right. He was pulled over backwards and then pinned down by my son-in-law–who may have meant to do it, or may not. And now people abuse him.–Just tell everybody, Mrs Vyner and Dean Vyner'–she looked round at the Dean–'that the *belle-mère's* sympathies are with the stallion.'

She looked from one to the other with a faint and gracious little bow, her black eyebrows arching in her eighteenth-century face like black rainbows, and her full, bold, grey eyes absolutely incomprehensible.

'Well, it's a peculiar message to have to hand round, Mrs Witt,' the Dean began to boom, when she interrupted him by laying her hand on his arm and leaning forward, looking up into his face like a clinging, pleading female:

'Oh, but *do* hand it, Dean, *do* hand it,' she pleaded, gazing intently into his face.

He backed uncomfortably from that gaze.

'Since you wish it,' he said, in a chest voice.

'I most certainly *do*–' she said, as if she were wishing the sweetest wish on earth. Then turning to Mrs Vyner:

'Good-bye, Mrs Vyner. We *do* appreciate your coming, my daughter and I.'

'I came out of kindness–' said Mrs Vyner.

'Oh, I know it, I know it,' said Mrs Witt. 'Thank you *so* much. Good-bye!

Good-bye, Dean! Who is taking the morning service on Sunday? I hope it is you, because I want to come.'

'It *is* me,' said the Dean. 'Good-bye! Well, good-bye, Lady Carrington. I shall be going over to see our young man to-morrow, and will gladly take you or anything you have to send.'

'Perhaps mother would like to go,' said Lou softly, plaintively.

'Well, we shall see,' said the Dean. 'Good-bye for the present!'

Mother and daughter stood at the window watching the two cross the churchyard. Dean and wife knew it, but daren't look round, and daren't admit the fact to one another.

Lou was grinning with a complete grin that gave her an odd, dryad or faun look, intensified.

'It was almost as good as pouring tea into her hat,' said Mrs Witt serenely. 'People like that tire me out. I shall take a glass of sherry.'

'So will I, mother.–It was even better than pouring tea in her hat.–You meant, didn't you, if you poured tea in her hat, to put cream and sugar in first?'

'I did,' said Mrs Witt.

But after the excitement of the encounter had passed away, Lou felt as if her life had passed away too. She went to bed, feeling she could stand no more.

In the morning she found her mother sitting at a window watching a funeral. It was raining heavily, so that some of the mourners even wore mackintosh coats. The funeral was in the poorer corner of the churchyard, where another new grave was covered with wreaths of sodden, shrivelling flowers. The yellowish coffin stood on wet earth in the rain: the curate held his hat, in a sort of permanent salute, above his head, like a little umbrella, as he hastened on with the service. The people seemed too wet to weep more wet.

It was a long coffin.

'Mother, do you really *like* watching?' asked Lou irritably, as Mrs Witt sat in complete absorption.

'I do, Louise, I really enjoy it.'

'Enjoy, mother!'–Lou was almost disgusted.

'I'll tell you why. I imagine I'm the one in the coffin–this is a girl of eighteen, who died of consumption–and those are my relatives, and I'm watching them put me away. And, you know, Louise, I've come to the conclusion that hardly anybody in the world really lives, and so hardly anybody really dies. They may well say: "Oh, Death, where is thy sting-a-ling-a-ling?" Even Death can't sting those that have never really lived.–I always used to want that–to die without death stinging me.–And I'm sure the girl in the coffin is saying to herself: "Fancy Aunt Emma putting on a drab slicker, and wearing it while they bury me. Doesn't show much respect. But then my mother's family always were common!" I feel there should be a solemn burial of a roll of newspapers containing the account of the death and funeral next week. It would be just as serious: the grave of all the world's remarks–'

'I don't want to think about it, mother. One ought to be able to laugh at it. I want to laugh at it.'

'Well, Louise, I think it's just as great a mistake to laugh at everything as to cry at everything. Laughter's not the one panacea, either. I should *really* like, before I do come to be buried in a box, to know where I am. That young girl in that coffin never was anywhere–any more than the newspaper remarks on her death and burial. And I begin to wonder if I've ever been anywhere. I seem to have been a daily sequence of newspaper remarks myself. I'm sure I never really conceived you and gave you birth. It all happened in newspaper notices. It's a newspaper fact that you are my child, and that's about all there is to it.'

Lou smiled as she listened.

'I always knew you were philosophic, mother. But I never dreamed it would come to elegies in a country churchyard, written to your motherhood.'

'Exactly, Louise! Here I sit and sing the elegy to my own motherhood. I never had any motherhood, except in newspaper fact. I never was a wife, except in newspaper notices. I never was a young girl, except in newspaper remarks. Bury everything I ever said or that was said about me, and you've buried *me*. But since Kind Words Can Never Die, I can't be buried, and death has no sting-a-ling-a-ling for *me*!—Now listen to me, Louise: I want death to be real to me—not as it was to that young girl. I *want* it to hurt me, Louise. If it hurts me enough, I shall know I was alive.'

She set her face and gazed under half-dropped lids at the funeral, stoic, fate-like, and yet, for the first time, with a certain pure wistfulness of a young virgin girl. This frightened Lou very much. She was so used to the matchless Amazon in her mother, that when she saw her sit there, still, wistful, virginal, tender as a girl who has never taken armour, wistful at the window that only looked on graves, a serious terror took hold of the young woman. The terror of *too late!*

Lou felt years, centuries older than her mother at that moment, with the tiresome responsibility of youth to protect and guide their elders.

'What can we do about it, mother?' she asked protectively.

'Do nothing, Louise. I'm not going to have anybody wisely steering my canoe, now I feel the rapids are near. I shall go with the river. Don't you pretend to do anything for me. I've done enough mischief myself, that way. I'm going down the stream at last.'

There was a pause.

'But in actuality, what?' asked Lou, a little ironically.

'I don't quite know. Wait a while.'

'Go back to America?'

'That is possible.'

'I may come too.'

'I've always waited for you to go back of your own will.'

Lou went away, wandering round the house. She was so unutterably tired of everything—weary of the house, the graveyard, weary of the thought of Rico. She would have to go back to him to-morrow, to nurse him. Poor old Rico, going on like an amiable machine from day to day. It wasn't his fault. But his life was a rattling nullity, and her life rattled in null correspondence. She had hardly strength enough to stop rattling and be still. Perhaps she had not strength enough.

She did not know. She felt so weak that unless something carried her away she would go on rattling her bit in the great machine of human life till she collapsed and her rattle rattled itself out, and there was a sort of barren silence where the sound of her had been.

She wandered out in the rain to the coach-house, where Lewis and Phœnix were sitting facing one another, one on a bin, the other on the inner doorstep.

'Well,' she said, smiling oddly. 'What's to be done?'

The two men stood up. Outside the rain fell steadily on the flagstones of the yard, past the leaves of trees. Lou sat down on the little iron step of the dog-cart.

'That's cold,' said Phœnix. 'You sit here.' And he threw a yellow horse-blanket on the box where he had been sitting.

'I don't want to take your seat,' she said.

'All right, you take it.'

He moved across and sat gingerly on the shaft of the dog-cart. Lou seated herself and loosened her soft tartan shawl. Her face was pink and fresh, and her dark hair curled almost merrily in the damp. But under her eyes were the finger-prints of deadly weariness.

She looked up at the two men, again smiling in her odd fashion.

'What are we going to do?' she asked.

They looked at her closely, seeking her meaning.

'What about?' said Phœnix, a faint smile reflecting on his face, merely because she smiled.

'Oh, everything,' she said, hugging her shawl again. 'You know what they want? They want to shoot St Mawr.'

The two men exchanged glances.

'Who want it?' said Phœnix.

'Why–all our *friends!*' She made a little *moue*. 'Dean Vyner does.'

Again the men exchanged glances. There was a pause. Then Phœnix said, looking aside:

'The boss is selling him.'

'Who?'

'Sir Henry.'–The half-breed always spoke the title with difficulty, and with a sort of sneer. 'He sell him to Miss Manby.'

'How do you know?'

'The man from Corrabach told me last night. Flora, she say it.'

Lou's eyes met the sardonic, empty-seeing eyes of Phœnix direct. There was too much sarcastic understanding. She looked aside.

'What else did he say?' she asked.

'I don't know,' said Phœnix evasively. 'He say they cut him–else shoot him. Think they cut him–and if he die, he die.'

Lou understood. He meant they would geld St Mawr–at his age.

She looked at Lewis. He sat with his head down, so she could not see his face.

'Do you think it is true?' she asked. 'Lewis? Do you think they would try to geld St Mawr–to make him a gelding?'

Lewis looked up at her. There was a faint deadly glimmer of contempt on his face.

'Very likely, Mam,' he said.

She was afraid of his cold, uncanny pale eyes, with their uneasy grey dawn of contempt. These two men, with their silent, deadly inner purpose, were not like other men. They seemed like two silent enemies of all the other men she knew. Enemies in the great white camp, disguised as servants, waiting the incalculable opportunity. What the opportunity might be, none knew.

'Sir Henry hasn't mentioned anything to me about selling St Mawr to Miss Manby,' she said.

The derisive flicker of a smile came on Phœnix's face.

'He sell him first, and tell you then,' he said, with his deadly impassive manner.

'But do you really think so?' she asked.

It was extraordinary how much corrosive contempt Phœnix could convey, saying nothing. She felt it almost as an insult. Yet it was a relief to her.

'You know, I can't believe it. I can't believe Sir Henry would want to have St

Mawr mutilated. I believe he'd rather shoot him.'
'You think so?' said Phœnix, with a faint grin.
Lou turned to Lewis.
'Lewis, will you tell me what you truly think?'
Lewis looked at her with a hard, straight, fearless British stare.
'That man Philips was in the "Moon and Stars" last night. He said Miss
Manby told him she was buying St Mawr, and she asked him if he thought it
would be safe to cut him and make a horse of him. He said it would be better,
take some of the nonsense out of him. He's no good for a sire, anyhow–'
   Lewis dropped his head again, and tapped a tattoo with the toe of his rather
small foot.
   'And what do you think?' said Lou. It occurred to her how sensible and
practical Miss Manby was, so much more so than the Dean.
   Lewis looked up at her with his pale eyes.
   'It won't have anything to do with me,' he said. 'I shan't go to Corrabach
Hall.'
   'What will you do, then?'
   Lewis did not answer. He looked at Phœnix.
   'Maybe him and me go to America,' said Phœnix, looking at the void.
   'Can he get in?' said Lou.
   'Yes, he can. I know how,' said Phœnix.
   'And the money?' she said.
   'We got money.'
   There was a silence, after which she asked of Lewis:
   'You'd leave St Mawr to his fate?'
   'I can't help his fate,' said Lewis. 'There's too many people in the world for
me to help anything.'
   'Poor St Mawr!'
   She went indoors again and up to her room: then higher, to the top rooms of
the tall Georgian house. From one window she could see the fields in the rain.
She could see St Mawr himself, alone as usual, standing with his head up,
looking across the fences. He was streaked dark with rain. Beautiful, with his
poised head and massive neck and his supple hindquarters. He was neighing to
Poppy. Clear on the wet wind came the sound of his bell-like, stallion's calling,
that Mrs Vyner called cruel. It was a strange noise, with a splendour that
belonged to another world age. The mean cruelty of Mrs Vyner's
humanitarianism, the barren cruelty of Flora Manby, the eunuch cruelty of
Rico. Our whole eunuch civilisation, nasty-minded as eunuchs are, with their
kind of sneaking, sterilising cruelty.
   Yet even she herself, seeing St Mawr's conceited march along the fence,
could not help addressing him:
   'Yes, my boy! If you knew what Miss Flora Manby was preparing for you!
She'll sharpen a knife that will settle you.'
   And Lou called her mother.
   The two American women stood high at the window, overlooking the wet,
close, hedged-and-fenced English landscape. Everything enclosed, enclosed,
to stifling. The very apples on the trees looked so shut in, it was impossible to
imagine any speck of 'Knowledge' lurking inside them. Good to eat, good to
cook, good even for show. But the wild sap of untameable and inexhaustible
knowledge–no! Bred out of them. Geldings, even the apples.
   Mrs Witt listened to Lou's half-humorous statements.

'You must admit, mother, Flora is a sensible girl,' she said.

'I admit it, Louise.'

'She goes straight to the root of the matter.'

'And eradicates the root. Wise girl! And what is your answer?'

'I don't know, mother. What would you say?'

'I know what *I* should say.'

'Tell me.'

'I should say: "Miss Manby, you may have my husband, but not my horse. My husband won't need emasculating and my horse I won't have you meddle with. I'll preserve one last male thing in the museum of this world, if I can."'

Lou listened, smiling faintly.

'That's what I will say,' she replied at length. 'The funny thing is, mother, they think all their men with their bare faces or their little quotation-mark moustaches *are* so tremendously male. That fox-hunting one!'

'I know it. Like little male motor-cars. Give him a little gas, and start him on the low gear, and away he goes: all his male gear rattling, like a cheap motor-car.'

'I'm afraid I dislike men altogether, mother.'

'You may, Louise. Think of Flora Manby, and how you love the fair sex.'

'After all, St Mawr is better. And I'm glad if he gives them a kick in the face.'

'Ah, Louise!' Mrs Witt suddenly clasped her hands with wicked passion. '*Ay, qué gozo!* as our Juan used to say, on your father's ranch in Texas.' She gazed in a sort of wicked ecstasy out of the window.

They heard Lou's maid softly calling Lady Carrington from below. Lou went to the stairs.

'What is it?'

'Lewis want to speak to you, my Lady.'

'Send him into the sitting-room.'

The two women went down.

'What is it, Lewis?' asked Lou.

'Am I to bring in St Mawr, in case they send for him from Corrabach?'

'No,' said Lou swiftly.

'Wait a minute,' put in Mrs Witt. 'What makes you think they will send for St Mawr from Corrabach, Lewis?' she asked, suave as a grey leopard cat.

'Miss Manby went up to Flints Farm with Dean Vyner this morning, and they've just come back. They stopped the car, and Miss Manby got out at the field gate to look at St Mawr. I'm thinking, if she made the bargain with Sir Henry, she'll be sending a man over this afternoon, and if I'd better brush St Mawr down a bit, in case.'

The man stood strangely still, and the words came like shadows of his real meaning. It was a challenge.

'I see,' said Mrs Witt slowly.

Lou's face darkened. She, too, saw.

'So that is her game,' she said. 'That is why they got me down here.'

'Never mind, Louise,' said Mrs Witt. Then to Lewis: 'Yes, please bring in St Mawr. You wish it, don't you, Louise?'

'Yes,' hesitated Lou. She saw by Mrs Witt's closed face that a counter-move was prepared.

'And Lewis,' said Mrs Witt, 'my daughter may wish you to ride St Mawr this afternoon—not to Corrabach Hall.'

'Very good, Mam.'

Mrs Witt sat silent for some time, after Lewis had gone, gathering inspiration from the wet, grisly grave-stones.

'Don't you think it's time we made a move, daughter?' she asked.

'Any move,' said Lou desperately.

'Very well then. My dearest friends, and my *only* friends, in this country, are in Oxfordshire. I will set off to *ride* to Merriton this afternoon, and Lewis will ride with me on St Mawr.'

'But you can't ride to Merriton in an afternoon,' said Lou.

'I know it. I shall ride across country. I shall *enjoy* it, Louise.–Yes.–I shall consider I am on my way back to America. I am most deadly tired of this country. From Merriton I shall make my arrangements to go to America, and take Lewis and Phœnix and St Mawr along with me. I think they want to go.–You will decide for yourself.'

'Yes, I'll come too,' said Lou casually.

'Very well. I'll start immediately after lunch, for I can't *breathe* in this place any longer. Where are Henry's automobile maps?'

Afternoon saw Mrs Witt, in a large waterproof cape, mounted on her horse, Lewis, in another cape, mounted on St Mawr, trotting through the rain, splashing in the puddles, moving slowly southwards. They took the open country, and would pass quite close to Flints Farm. But Mrs Witt did not care. With great difficulty she had managed to fasten a small waterproof roll behind her, containing her night things. She seemed to breathe the first breath of freedom.

And sure enough, an hour or so after Mrs Witt's departure arrived Flora Manby in a splashed-up motor-car, accompanied by her sister, and bringing a groom and a saddle.

'Do you know, Harry sold me St Mawr,' she said. 'I'm just wild to get that horse in hand.'

'How?' said Lou.

'Oh, I don't know. There are ways. Do you mind if Philips rides him over now to Corrabach?–Oh, I forgot, Harry sent you a note:

> Dearest Loulina: Have you been gone from here two days or two years? It seems the latter. You are terribly missed. Flora wanted so much to buy St Mawr, to save us further trouble, that I have sold him to her. She is giving me what we paid; rather, what you paid, so of course the money is yours. I am thankful we are rid of the animal, and that he falls into competent hands–I asked her please to remove him from your charge to-day. And I can't tell how much easier I am in my mind, to think of him gone. You are coming back to me to-morrow, aren't you? I shall think of nothing but you, till I see you. Arrivederci, darling dear! R.

'I'm so sorry,' said Lou. 'Mother went on horseback to see some friends, and Lewis went with her on St Mawr. He knows the road.'

'She'll be back this evening?' said Flora.

'I don't know. Mother is so uncertain. She may be away a day or two.'

'Well, here's the cheque for St Mawr.'

'No, I won't take it now–no, thank you–not till mother comes back with the goods.'

Flora was chagrined. The two women knew they hated one another. The visit was a brief one.

Mrs Witt rode on in the rain, which abated as the afternoon wore down, and the evening came without rain, and with a suffusion of pale yellow light. All the time she had trotted in silence, with Lewis just behind her. And she scarcely saw the heather-covered hills with the deep clefts between them, nor the oak woods, nor the lingering foxgloves, nor the earth at all. Inside herself she felt a profound repugnance for the English country: she preferred even the crudeness of Central Park in New York.

And she felt an almost savage desire to get away from Europe, from everything European. Now she was really *en route*, she cared not a straw for St Mawr or for Lewis or anything. Something just writhed inside her, all the time, against Europe. That closeness, that sense of cohesion, that sense of being fused into a lump with all the rest—no matter how much distance you kept—this drove her mad. In America the cohesion was a matter of choice and will. But in Europe it was organic, like the helpless particles of one sprawling body. And the great body in a state of incipient decay.

She was a woman of fifty-one: and she seemed hardly to have lived a day. She looked behind her—the thin trees and swamps of Louisiana, the sultry, sub-tropical excitement of decaying New Orleans, the vast bare dryness of Texas, with mobs of cattle in an illumined dust! The half-European thrills of New York! The false stability of Boston! A clever husband, who was a brilliant lawyer, but who was far more thrilled by his cattle ranch than by his law: and who drank heavily and died. The years of first widowhood in Boston, consoled by a self-satisfied sort of intellectual courtship from clever men.—For curiously enough, while she wanted it, she had always been able to compel men to pay court to her. All kinds of men.—Then a rather dashing time in New York—when she was in her early forties. Then the long *visual* philandering in Europe. She left off 'loving', save through the eye, when she came to Europe. And when she made her trips to America, she found it was finished there also, her 'loving'.

What was the matter? Examining herself, she had long ago decided that her nature was a destructive force. But then, she justified herself, she had only destroyed that which was destructible. If she could have found something indestructible, especially in men, though she would have fought against it, she would have been glad at last to be defeated by it.

That was the point. She really wanted to be defeated, in her own eyes. And nobody had ever defeated her. Men were never really her match. A woman of terrible strong health, she felt even that in her strong limbs there was far more electric power than in the limbs of any man she had met. That curious fluid electric force, that could make any man kiss her hand, if she so willed it. A queen, as far as she wished. And not having been very clever at school, she always had the greatest respect for the mental powers. Her own were not mental powers. Rather electric, as of some strange physical dynamo within her. So she had been ready to bow before Mind.

But alas! After a brief time, she had found Mind, at least the man who was supposed to have the mind, bowing before her. Her own peculiar dynamic force was stronger than the force of Mind. She could make Mind kiss her hand.

And not by any sensual tricks. She did not really care about sensualities, especially as a younger woman. Sex was a mere adjunct. She cared about the mysterious, intense, dynamic sympathy that could flow between her and some 'live' man—a man who was highly conscious, a real live wire. That she cared about.

But she had never rested until she had made the man she admired—and admiration was the roots of her attraction to any man—made him kiss her hand. In both cases, actual and metaphorical. Physical and metaphysical. Conquered his country.

She had always succeeded. And she believed that, if she cared, she always *would* succeed. In the world of living men. Because of the power that was in her, in her arms, in her strong, shapely, but terrible hands, in all the great dynamo of her body.

For this reason she had been so terribly contemptuous of Rico, and of Lou's infatuation. Ye gods! what was Rico in the scale of men!

Perhaps she despised the younger generation too easily. Because she did not see its sources of power, she concluded it was powerless. Whereas perhaps the power of accommodating oneself to any circumstance and committing oneself to no circumstance is the last triumph of mankind.

Her generation had had its day. She had had her day. The world of her men had sunk into a sort of insignificance. And with a great contempt she despised the world that had come into place instead: the world of Rico and Flora Manby, the world represented, to her, by the Prince of Wales.

In such a world there was nothing even to conquer. It gave everything and gave nothing to everybody and anybody all the time. *Dio benedetto!* as Rico would say. A great complicated tangle of nonentities ravelled in nothingness. So it seemed to her.

Great God! This was the generation she had helped to bring into the world.

She had had her day. And, as far as the mysterious battle of life went she had won all the way. Just as Cleopatra, in the mysterious business of a woman's life, won all the way.

Though that bald, tough Cæsar had drawn his iron from the fire without losing much of its temper. And he had gone his way. And Antony surely was splendid to die with.

In her life there had been no tough Cæsar to go his way in cold blood, away from her. Her men had gone from her like dogs on three legs, into the crowd. And certainly there was no gorgeous Antony to die for and with.

Almost she was tempted in her heart to cry: 'Conquer me, oh God, before I die!'—But then she had a terrible contempt for the God that was supposed to rule this universe. She felt she could make *Him* kiss her hand. Here she was a woman of fifty-one, past the change of life. And her great dread was to die an empty, barren death. Oh, if only Death might open dark wings of mystery and consolation. To die an easy, barren death. To pass out as she had passed in, without mystery or the rustling of darkness! That was her last, final, ashy dread.

'Old!' she said to herself. 'I am not *old*! I have lived many years, that is all. But I am as timeless as an hour-glass that turns morning and night, and spills the hours of sleep one way, the hours of consciousness the other way, without .itself being affected. Nothing in all my life has ever truly affected me.—I believe Cleopatra only tried the asp, as she tried her pearls in wine, to see if it would really, really have any effect on her. Nothing had ever really had any effect on her, neither Cæsar nor Antony nor any of them. Never once had she really been lost, lost to herself. Then try death, see if that trick would work. If she would lose herself to herself that way.—Ah, death—!'

But Mrs Witt mistrusted death too. She felt she might pass out as a bed of asters passes out in autumn, to mere nothingness.—And something in her longed to die, at least, *positively*: to be folded then at last into throbbing wings of mystery, like a hawk that goes to sleep. Not like a thing made into a parcel and put into the last rubbish-heap.

So she rode trotting across the hills, mile after mile, in silence. Avoiding the roads, avoiding everything, avoiding everybody, just trotting forwards, towards night.

And by nightfall they had travelled twenty-five miles. She had motored around this country, and knew the little towns and the inns. She knew where she would sleep.

The morning came beautiful and sunny. A woman so strong in health, why should she ride with the fact of death before her eyes? But she did.

Yet in sunny morning she must do something about it.

'Lewis!' she cried. 'Come here and tell me something, please! Tell me,' she said, 'do you believe in God?'

'In God!' he said, wondering. 'I never think about it.'

'But do you say your prayers?'

'No Mam!'

'Why don't you?'

He thought about it for some minutes.

'I don't like religion. My aunt and uncle were religious.'

'You don't like religion,' she repeated. 'And you don't believe in God.—Well, then—'

'Nay!' he hesitated. 'I never said I didn't believe in God.—Only I'm sure I'm not a Methodist. And I feel a fool in a proper church.—And I feel a fool saying my prayers.—And I feel a fool when ministers and parsons come getting at me.—I never think about God, if folks don't try to make me.' He had a small, sly smile, almost gay.

'And you don't like feeling a fool?' She smiled rather patronisingly.

'No, Mam.'

'Do I make you feel a fool?' she asked dryly.

He looked at her without answering.

'Why don't you answer?' she said, pressing.

'I think you'd like to make a fool of me sometimes,' he said.

'Now?' she pressed.

He looked at her with that slow, distant look.

'Maybe!' he said, rather unconcernedly.

Curiously, she couldn't touch him. He always seemed to be watching her from a distance, as if from another country. Even if she made a fool of him, something in him would all the time be far away from her, not implicated.

She caught herself up in the personal game and returned to her own isolated question. A vicious habit made her start the personal tricks. She didn't want to, really.

There was something about this little man—sometimes, to herself, she called him *Little Jack Horner, sat in a corner*—that irritated her and made her want to taunt him. His peculiar little inaccessibility, that was so tight and easy.

Then again, there was something, his way of looking at her as if he looked from out of another country, a country of which he was an inhabitant, and where she had never been: this touched her strangely. Perhaps behind this little man was the mystery. In spite of the fact that in actual life, in her world, he was only a groom, almost *chétif*, with his legs a little bit horsey and bowed; and of no education, saying 'Yes, Mam!' and 'No, Mam!' and accomplishing nothing, simply nothing at all on the face of the earth. Strictly a nonentity.

And yet, what made him perhaps the only real entity to her, his seeming to inhabit another world than hers. A world dark and still, where language never ruffled the growing leaves and seared their edges like a bad wind.

Was it an illusion, however? Sometimes she thought it was. Just bunkum, which she had faked up, in order to have something to mystify about.

But then, when she saw Phœnix and Lewis silently together, she knew there *was* another communion, silent, excluding her. And sometimes when Lewis was alone with St Mawr: and once when she saw him pick up a bird that had stunned itself against a wire: she had realised another world, silent, where each creature is alone in its own aura of silence, the mystery of power: as Lewis had power with St Mawr, and even with Phœnix.

The visible world and the invisible. Or rather, the audible and the inaudible. She had lived so long, and so completely, in the visible, audible world. She would not easily admit that other, inaudible. She always wanted to jeer as she approached the brink of it.

Even now she wanted to jeer at the little fellow, because of his holding himself inaccessible within the inaudible, silent world. And she knew he knew it.

'Did you never want to be rich, and be a gentleman, like Sir Henry?' she asked.

'I would many times have liked to be rich. But I never exactly wanted to be a gentleman,' he said.

'Why not?'

'I can't exactly say. I should be uncomfortable if I was like they are.'

'And are you comfortable now?'

'When I'm let alone.'

'And do they let you alone? Does the world let you alone?'

'No, they don't.'

'Well then–!'

'I keep to myself all I can.'

'And are you comfortable, as you call it, when you keep to yourself?'

'Yes, I am.'

'But when you keep to yourself, what do you keep to? What precious treasure have you to keep to?'

He looked and saw she was jeering.

'None,' he said. 'I've got nothing of that sort.'

She rode impatiently on ahead.

And the moment she had done so, she regretted it. She might put the little fellow, with contempt, out of her reckoning. But no, she would not do it.

She had put so much out of her reckoning: soon she would be left in an empty circle, with her empty self at the centre.

She reined in again.

'Lewis!' she said. 'I don't want you to take offence at anything I say.'

'No, Mam.'

'I don't want you to say just "No, Mam!" all the time!' she cried impulsively. 'Promise me.'

'Yes, Mam!'

'But really! Promise me you won't be offended at whatever I say.'

'Yes, Mam!'

She looked at him searchingly. To her surprise, she was almost in tears. A woman of her years! And with a servant!

But his face was blank and stony, with a stony, distant look of pride that made him inaccessible to her emotions. He met her eyes again: with that cold distant look, looking straight into her hot, confused, pained self. So cold and as if merely refuting her. He didn't believe her, nor trust her, nor like her even. She was an attacking enemy to him. Only he stayed really far away from her, looking down at her from a sort of distant hill where her weapons could not reach: not quite.

And at the same time, it hurt him in a dumb, living way, that she made these attacks on him. She could see the cloud of hurt in his eyes, no matter how distantly he looked at her.

They bought food in a village shop, and sat under a tree near a field where men were already cutting oats, in a warm valley. Lewis had stabled the horses for a couple of hours to feed and rest. But he came to join her under the tree, to eat.–He sat a little distance from her, with the bread and cheese in his small brown hands, eating silently, and watching the harvesters. She was cross with him, and therefore she was stingy, would give him nothing to eat but dry bread and cheese. Herself, she was not hungry.–So all the time he kept his face a little averted from her. As a matter of fact, he kept his whole being averted from her, away from her. He did not want to touch her, nor to be touched by her. He kept his spirit there, alert, on its guard, but out of contact. It was as if he had unconsciously accepted the battle, the old battle. He was her target, the old object of her deadly weapons. But he refused to shoot back. It was as if he caught all her missiles in full flight before they touched him, and silently threw them on the ground behind him. And in some essential part of himself he ignored her, staying in another world.

That other world! Mere male armour of artificial imperviousness! It angered her.

Yet she knew, by the way he watched the harvesters, and the grasshoppers popping into notice, that it was another world. And when a girl went by, carrying food to the field, it was at him she glanced. And he gave that quick, animal little smile that came from him unawares. Another world.

Yet also there was a sort of meanness about him: a *suffisance!* A keep-yourself-for-yourself, and don't give yourself away.

Well!–she rose impatiently.

It was hot in the afternoon, and she was rather tired. She went to the inn and slept, and did not start again till tea-time.

Then they had to ride rather late. The sun sank, among a smell of cornfields, clear and yellow-red behind motionless dark trees. Pale smoke rose from cottage chimneys. Not a cloud was in the sky, which held the floating light like a bowl inverted on purpose. A new moon sparkled and was gone. It was beginning of night.

Away in the distance, they saw a curious pinkish glare of fire, probably furnaces. And Mrs Witt thought she could detect the scent of furnace smoke, or factory smoke. But then she always said that of the English air: it was never quite free of the smell of smoke, coal smoke.

They were riding slowly on a path through fields, down a long slope. Away below was a puther of lights. All the darkness seemed full of half-spent crossing lights, a curious uneasiness. High in the sky a star seemed to be walking. It was an aeroplane with a light. Its buzz rattled above. Not a space, not a speck of this country that wasn't humanised, occupied by the human claim. Not even the sky.

They descended slowly through a dark wood, which they had entered through a gate. Lewis was all the time dismounting and opening gates, letting her pass, shutting the gate and mounting again.

So, in a while she came to the edge of the wood's darkness, and saw the open pale concave of the world beyond. The darkness was never dark. It shook with the concussion of many invisible lights, lights of towns, villages, mines, factories, furnaces, squatting in the valleys and behind all the hills.

Yet, as Rachel Witt drew rein at the gate emerging from the wood, a very big, soft star fell in heaven, cleaving the hubbub of this human night with a gleam from the greater world.

'See! a star falling!' said Lewis, as he opened the gate.

'I saw it,' said Mrs Witt, walking her horse past him.

There was a curious excitement of wonder, or magic, in the little man's voice. Even in this night something strange had stirred awake in him.

'You ask me about God,' he said to her, walking his horse alongside in the shadow of the wood's edge, the darkness of the old Pan, that kept our artificially-lit world at bay. 'I don't know about God. But when I see a star fall like that out of long-distance places in the sky: and the moon sinking saying Good-bye! Good-bye! Good-bye! and nobody listening: I think I hear something, though I wouldn't call it God.'

'What then?' said Rachel Witt.

'And you smell the smell of oak leaves now,' he said, 'now the air is cold. They smell to me more alive than people. The trees hold their bodies hard and still, but they watch and listen with their leaves. And I think they say to me: "Is that you passing there, Morgan Lewis? All right, you pass quickly, we shan't do anything to you. You are like a holly bush."'

'Yes,' said Rachel Witt dryly. 'Why?'

'All the time the trees grow and listen. And if you cut a tree down without asking pardon, trees will hurt you some time in your life, in the night-time.'

'I suppose,' said Rachel Witt, 'that's an old superstition.'

'They say that ash trees don't like people. When the other people were most in the country – I mean like what they call fairies, that have all gone now – they liked ash trees best. And you know the little green things with little small nuts in them, that come flying from ash trees – *pigeons*, we call them – they're the seeds – the other people used to catch them and eat them before they fell to the ground. And that made the people so they could hear trees living and feeling things. – But when all these people that there are now came to England, they liked the oak trees best, because their pigs ate the acorns. So now you can tell the ash trees are mad, they want to kill all these people. But the oak trees are many more than the ash trees.'

'And do you eat the ash tree seeds?' she asked.

'I always ate them when I was little. Then I wasn't frightened of ash trees, like most of the others. And I wasn't frightened of the moon. If you didn't go near the fire all day, and if you didn't eat any cooked food nor anything that had been in the sun, but only things like turnips or radishes or pig-nuts, and then went without any clothes on, in the full moon, then you could see the people in the moon, and go with them. They never have fire, and they never speak, and their bodies are clear almost like jelly. They die in a minute if there's a bit of fire near them. But they know more than we. Because unless fire touches them, they never die. They see people live and they see people perish, and they say, people are only like twigs on a tree, you break them off the tree, and kindle fire with them. You made a fire of them, and they are gone, the fire is gone, everything is gone. But the people of the moon don't die, and fire is nothing to them. They look at it from the distance of the sky, and see it burning things up, people all appearing and disappearing like twigs that come in spring and you cut them in autumn and make a fire of them and they are gone. And they say: What do people matter? If you want to matter, you must become a moon-boy. Then all your life, fire can't blind you and people can't hurt you. Because at full moon you can join the moon people, and go through the air and pass any cool places, pass through rocks and through the trunks of trees, and when you come to people lying warm in bed, you punish them.'

'How?'

'You sit on the pillow where they breathe, and you put a web across their mouth, so they can't breathe the fresh air that comes from the moon. So they go on breathing the same air again and again, and that makes them more and more stupefied. The sun gives out heat, but the moon gives out fresh air. That's what the moon people do: they wash the air clean with moonlight.'

He was talking with a strange, eager *naïveté* that amused Rachel Witt, and made her a little uncomfortable in her skin. Was he after all no more than a sort of imbecile?

'Who told you all this stuff?' she asked abruptly.

And, as abruptly he pulled himself up.

'We used to say it when we were children.'

'But you don't believe it? It *is* only childishness, after all.'

He paused a moment or two.

'No,' he said, in his ironical little day voice. 'I know I shan't make anything but a fool of myself, with that talk. But all sorts of things go through our heads, and some seem to linger, and some don't. But you asking me about God put it into my mind, I suppose. I don't know what sort of things I believe in: only I know it's not what the chapel folks believe in. We none of us believe in them when it comes to earning a living, or, with you people, when it comes to spending your fortune. Then we know that bread costs money, and even your sleep you have to pay for.–That's work. Or, with you people, it's just owning property and seeing you get your value for your money.–But a man's mind is always full of things. And some people's minds, like my aunt and uncle, are full of religion and hell for everybody except themselves. And some people's minds are all money, money, money, and how to get hold of something they haven't got hold of yet. And some people, like you, are always curious about what everybody else in the world is after. And some people are all for enjoying themselves and being thought much of, and some, like Lady Carrington, don't know what to do with themselves. Myself, I don't want to have in my mind the things other people have in their minds. I'm one that likes my own things best. And if, when I see a bright star fall, like to-night, I think to myself: "There's movement in the sky. The world is going to change again. They're throwing something to us from the distance, and we've got to have it, whether we want it or not. To-morrow there will be a difference for everybody, thrown out of the sky upon us, whether we want it or not: then that's how I want to think, so let me please myself."'

'You know what a shooting star actually is, I suppose?–and that there are always many in August, because we pass through a region of them?'

'Yes, Mam, I've been told. But stones don't come at us from the sky for nothing. Either it's like when a man tosses an apple to you out of his orchard, as you go by. Or it's like when somebody shies a stone at you to cut your head open. You'll never make me believe the sky is like an empty house with a slate falling from the roof. The world has its own life, the sky has a life of its own, and never is it like stones rolling down a rubbish-heap and falling into a pond. Many things twitch and twitter within the sky, and many things happen beyond us. My own way of thinking is my own way.'

'I never knew you talk so much.'

'No, Mam. It's your asking me that about God. Or else it's the night-time. I don't believe in God and being good and going to heaven. Neither do I worship idols, so I'm not a heathen as my aunt called me. Never from a boy did I want to believe the things they kept grinding in their guts at home, and at Sunday school, and at school. A man's mind has to be full of something, so I keep to what we used to think as lads. It's childish nonsense, I know it. But it suits me. Better than other people's stuff. Your man Phœnix is about the same, when he lets on. – Anyhow, it's my own stuff that we believed as lads, and I like it better than other people's stuff. – You asking about God made me let on. But I would never belong to any club, or trades union, and God's the same to my mind.'

With this he gave a little kick to his horse, and St Mawr went dancing excitedly along the highway they now entered, leaving Mrs Witt to trot after as rapidly as she could.

When she came to the hotel, to which she had telegraphed for rooms, Lewis disappeared, and she was left thinking hard.

It was not till they were twenty miles from Merriton, riding through a slow morning mist, and she had a rather far-away, wistful look on her face, unusual for her, that she turned to him in the saddle and said:

'Now don't be surprised, Lewis, at what I am going to say. I am going to ask you, now, supposing I wanted to marry you, what should you say?'

He looked at her quickly, and was at once on his guard.

'That you didn't mean it,' he replied hastily.

'Yes' – she hesitated, and her face looked wistful and tired. – 'Supposing I *did* mean it. Supposing I did *really*, from my heart, want to marry you and be a wife to you' – she looked away across the fields – 'then what should you say?'

Her voice sounded sad, a little broken.

'Why, Mam!' he replied, knitting his brow and shaking his head a little. 'I should say you didn't mean it, you know. Something would have come over you.'

'But supposing I *wanted* something to come over me?'

He shook his head.

'It would never do, Mam! Some people's flesh and blood is kneaded like bread: and that's me. And some are rolled like fine pastry, like Lady Carrington. And some are mixed with gunpowder. They're like a cartridge you put in a gun, Mam.'

She listened impatiently.

'Don't talk,' she said, 'about bread and cakes and pastry, it all means nothing. You used to answer short enough "Yes, Mam! No, Mam!" That will do now. Do you mean "Yes!" or "No!"?'

His eyes met hers. She was again hectoring.

'No, Mam!' he said, quite neutral.

'Why?'

As she waited for his answer, she saw the foundations of his loquacity dry up, his face go distant and mute again, as it always used to be, till these last two days, when it had had a funny touch of inconsequential merriness.

He looked steadily into her eyes, and his look was neutral, sombre, and hurt. He looked at her as if infinite seas, infinite spaces divided him and her. And his eyes seemed to put her away beyond some sort of fence. An anger congealed cold like lava, set impassive against her and all her sort.

'No, Mam. I couldn't give my body to any woman who didn't respect it.'

'But I do respect it, I do!'—she flushed hot like a girl.

'No, Mam. Not as *I* mean it,' he replied.

There was a touch of anger against her in his voice, and a distance of distaste.

'And how do *you* mean it?' she replied, the full sarcasm coming back into her tones. She could see that, as a woman to touch and fondle he saw her as repellent: only repellent.

'I have to be a servant to women now,' he said, 'even to earn my wage. I could never touch with my body a woman whose servant I was.'

'You're not my servant: my daughter pays your wages.—And all that is beside the point, between a man and a woman.'

'No woman who I touched with my body should ever speak to me as you speak to me, or think of me as you think of me,' he said.

'But!—' she stammered. 'I think of you—with love. And can you be so unkind as to notice the way I speak? You know it's only my way.'

'You, as a woman,' he said, 'you have no respect for a man.'

'Respect! Respect!' she cried. 'I'm likely to lose what respect I have left. I know I can *love* a man. But whether a man can love a woman—'

'No,' said Lewis. 'I never could, and I think I never shall. Because I don't want to. The thought of it makes me feel shame.'

'What do you mean?' she cried.

'Nothing in the world,' he said, 'would make me feel such shame as to have a woman shouting at me, or mocking at me, as I see women mocking and despising the men they marry. No woman shall touch my body and mock me or despise me. No woman.'

'But men must be mocked, or despised even, sometimes.'

'No. Not this man. Not by the woman I touch with my body.'

'Are you perfect?'

'I don't know. But if I touch a woman with my body, it must put a lock on her, to respect what I will never have despised: never!'

'What will you never have despised?'

'My body! And my touch upon the woman.'

'Why insist so on your body?'—And she looked at him with a touch of contemptuous mockery, raillery.

He looked her in the eyes steadily, and coldly, putting her away from him, and himself far away from her.

'Do you expect that any woman will stay your humble slave to-day?' she asked cuttingly.

But he only watched her coldly, distant, refusing any connection.

'Between men and women, it's a question of give and take. A man can't expect *always* to be humbly adored.'

He watched her still, cold, rather pale, putting her far from him. Then he turned his horse and set off rapidly along the road, leaving her to follow.

She walked her horse and let him go, thinking to herself:

'There's a little bantam cock. And a groom! Imagine it! Thinking he can dictate to a woman!'

She was in love with him. And he, in an odd way, was in love with her. She had known it by the odd, uncanny merriment in him, and his unexpected loquacity. But he would not have her come physically near him.

Unapproachable there as a cactus, guarding his 'body' from her contact. As if contact with her would be mortal insult and fatal injury to his marvellous 'body'.

What a little cock-sparrow!

Let him ride ahead. He would have to wait for her somewhere.

She found him at the entrance to the next village. His face was pallid and set. She could tell he felt he had been insulted, so he had congealed into stiff insentience.

'At the bottom of all men is the same,' she said to herself: 'an empty, male conceit of themselves.'

She, too, rode up with a face like a mask, and straight on to the hotel.

'Can you serve dinner to myself and my servant?' she asked at the inn: which, fortunately for her, accommodated motorists, otherwise they would have said 'No!'

'I think,' said Lewis as they came in sight of Merriton, 'I'd better give Lady Carrington a week's notice.'

A complete little stranger! And an impudent one.

'Exactly as you please,' she said.

She found several letters from her daughter at Marshal Place.

'Dear Mother: No sooner had you gone off than Flora appeared, not at all in the bud, but rather in full blow. She demanded her victim; Shylock demanding the pound of flesh: and wanted to hand over the shekels.

'Joyfully I refused them. She said "Harry" was much better, and invited him and me to stay at Corrabach Hall till he was quite well: it would be less strain on your household, while he was still in bed and helpless. So the plan is, that he shall be brought down on Friday, if he is really fit for the journey, and we drive straight to Corrabach. I am packing his bags and mine, clearing up our traces: his trunks to go to Corrabach, mine to stay here and make up their minds. – I am going to Flints Farm again to-morrow, dutifully, though I am no flower for the bedside. – I do so want to know if Rico has already called her Fiorita: or perhaps Florecita. It reminds me of old William's joke: "Now yuh tell me, little Missy: which is the best posey that grow?" And the hushed whisper in which he said the answer: "The Collyposy!" Oh dear, I am so tired of feeling spiteful, but how else is one to feel?

'You looked most prosaically romantic, setting off in a rubber cape, followed by Lewis. Hope the roads were not very slippery, and that you had a good time, à la Mademoiselle de Maupin. Do remember, dear, not to devour little Lewis before you have got half-way–'

'Dear Mother: I half expected word from you before I left, but nothing came. Forrester drove me up here just before lunch. Rico seems much better, almost himself, and a little more than that. He broached our staying at Corrabach very tactfully. I told him Flora had asked me, and it seemed a good plan. Then I told him about St Mawr. He was a little piqued, and there was a pause of very disapproving silence. Then he said: "Very well, darling. If you wish to keep the animal, do so by all means. I make a present of him again." Me: "That's so good of you, Rico. Because I know revenge is sweet." Rico: "Revenge, Loulina! I don't think I was selling him for vengeance! Merely to get rid of him to Flora, who can keep better hold over him." Me: "But you know, dear, she was going to geld him!" Rico: "I don't think anybody knew it. We only wondered if it were possible, to make him more amenable. Did she tell you?" Me: "No– Phœnix did. He had it from a groom." Rico: "Dear me! A concatenation of grooms! So your mother rode off with Lewis, and carried St Mawr out of danger! I understand! Let us hope worse won't befall." Me: "Whom?" Rico: "Never mind, dear! It's so lovely to see you. You are looking rested. I thought those Countess of Wilton roses the most marvellous things in the world, till you came, now they're quite in the background." He had some very lovely roses in a crystal bowl: the room smelled of roses." Me: "Where did they come from?" Rico: "Oh, Flora brought them!" Me: "Bowl and all?" Rico: "Bowl and all! Wasn't it dear of her?" Me: "Why, yes! But then she's the goddess of flowers, isn't she?" Poor darling, he was offended that I should twit him while he is ill, so I relented. He has had a couple of marvellous invalid's bed-jackets sent from London: one a pinkish yellow, with rose-arabesque facings: this one in fine cloth. But unfortunately he has already dropped soup on it. The other is a lovely silvery and blue and green, soft brocade. He had that one on to receive me, and I at once complimented him on it. He has got a new ring too: sent by Aspasia Weingartner, a rather lovely intaglio of Priapus under an apple bough, at least, so he says it is. He made a naughty face, and said: "The Priapus stage is rather advanced for poor me." I asked what the Priapus stage was, but he said: "Oh, nothing!" Then nurse said: "There's a big classical dictionary that Miss Manby brought up, if you wish to see it." So I have been studying the Classical Gods. The world always was a queer place. It's a very queer one when Rico is the god Priapus. He would go round the orchard painting life-like apples on the trees, and inviting nymphs to come and eat them. And the nymphs would pretend they were real: "Why, Sir Prippy, what stunningly naughty apples!" There's nothing so artificial as sinning nowadays. I suppose it once was real.

'I'm bored here: wish I had my horse.'

'Dear Mother: I'm so glad you are enjoying your ride. I'm sure it is like riding into history, like the Yankee at the Court of King Arthur, in those old by-lanes and Roman roads. They still fascinate me: at least, more before I get there than when I am actually there. I begin to feel real American and to resent the past. Why doesn't the past decently bury itself instead of waiting to be admired by the present?

'Phœnix brought Poppy. I am so fond of her: rode for five hours yesterday. I was glad to get away from this farm. The doctor came, and said Rico would be able to go down to Corrabach to-morrow. Flora came to hear the bulletin, and sailed back full of zest. Apparently Rico is going to do a portrait of her, sitting up in bed. What a mercy the bedclothes won't be mine when Priapus wields his palette from the pillow.

'Phœnix thinks you intend to go to America with St Mawr, and that I am coming too, leaving Rico this side. – I wonder. I feel so unreal, nowadays, as if I too were nothing more than a painting by Rico on a millboard. I feel almost too unreal even to make up my mind to anything. It is terrible when the life-flow dies out of one, and everything is like cardboard, and oneself is like cardboard. I'm sure it is worse than being dead. I realised it yesterday when Phœnix and I had a picnic lunch by a stream. You see, I must imitate you in all things. He found me some watercresses, and they tasted so damp and *alive*, I knew how deadened I was. Phœnix wants us to go and have a ranch in Arizona, and raise horses, with St Mawr, if willing, for Father Abraham. I wonder if it matters what one does: if it isn't all the same thing over again? Only Phœnix, his funny blank face, makes my heart melt and go sad. But I believe he'd be cruel too. I saw it in his face when he didn't know I was looking. Anything, though, rather than this deadness and this paint-Priapus business. *Au revoir*, mother dear! Keep on having a good time–'

'Dear Mother: I had your letter from Merriton: am so glad you arrived safe and sound in body and temper. There was such a funny letter from Lewis, too: I enclose it. What makes him take this extraordinary line? But I'm writing to tell him to take St Mawr to London, and wait for me there. I have telegraphed Mrs Squire to get the house ready for me. I shall go straight there.

'Things developed here, as they were bound to. I just couldn't bear it. No sooner was Rico put in the automobile than a self-conscious importance came over him, like when the wounded hero is carried into the middle of the stage. "Why so solemn, Rico dear?" I asked him, trying to laugh him out of it. "Not solemn, dear, only feeling a little transient." I don't think he knew himself what he meant. Flora was on the steps as the car drew up, dressed in severe white. She only needed an apron to become a nurse: or a veil to become a bride. Between the two, she had an unbearable air of a woman in seduced circumstances, as *The Times* said. She ordered two menservants about in subdued, you would have said hushed, but competent tones. And then I saw there was a touch of the priestess about her as well: Cassandra preparing for her violation: Iphigenia, with Rico for Orestes, on a stretcher: he looking like Adonis, fully prepared to be an unconscionable time in dying. They had given him a lovely room downstairs, with doors opening on to a little garden all of its own. I believe it was Flora's boudoir. I left nurse and the men to put him to bed. Flora was hovering anxiously in the passage outside. "Oh, what a marvellous room! Oh, how colourful, how beautiful!" came Rico's tones, the hero behind the scenes. I must say, it was like a harvest festival, with roses and gaillardias in the shadow, and cornflowers in the light, and a bowl of grapes, and nectarines among leaves. "I'm so anxious that he should be happy," Flora said to me in the passage. "You know him best. Is there anything else I could do for him?" Me: "Why, if you went to the piano and sang, I'm sure he'd love it. Couldn't you sing: Oh, my love is like a rred, rred rrose!"–You know how Rico imitates Scotch!

'Thank goodness I have a bedroom upstairs: nurse sleeps in a little ante-chamber to Rico's room. The Edwards are still here, the blond young man with some very futuristic plaster on his face. "Awfully good of you to come!" he said to me, looking at me out of one eye, and holding my hand fervently. How's that for cheek: "It's awfully good of Miss Manby to let me come," said I. He: "Ah, but Flora is always a sport, a topping good sport!"

'I don't know what's the matter, but it just all put me into a fiendish temper. I felt I couldn't sit there at luncheon with that bright, youthful company, and hear about their tennis and their polo and their hunting and have their flirtatiousness making me sick. So I asked for a tray in my room. Do as I might, I couldn't help being horrid.

'Oh, and Rico! He really is too awful. Lying there in bed with every ear open, like Adonis waiting to be persuaded not to die. Seizing a hushed moment to take Flora's hand and press it to his lips, murmuring: "How awfully good you are to me, dear Flora!" And Flora: "I'd be better if I knew how, Harry!" So cheerful with it all! No, it's too much. My sense of humour is leaving me: which means, I'm getting into too bad a temper to be able to ridicule it all. I suppose I feel in the minority. It's an awful thought, to think that most all the young people in the world are like this: so bright and cheerful, and *sporting*, and so brimming with libido. How awful!

'I said to Rico: "You're very comfortable here, aren't you?" He: "Comfortable! It's comparative heaven." Me: "Would you mind if I went away?" A deadly pause. He is deadly afraid of being left alone with Flora. He feels safe so long as I am about, and he can take refuge in his marriage ties. He: "Where do you want to go, dear?" Me: "To mother. To London. Mother is planning to go to America, and she wants me to go." Rico: "But you don't want to go t–he–e–re–e!" You know, mother, how Rico can put a venomous emphasis on a word, till it suggests pure poison. It nettled me. "I'm not sure," I said. Rico: "Oh, but you can't stand that awful America." Me: "I want to try again." Rico: "But Lou dear, it will be winter before you get there. And this is absolutely the wrong moment for me to go over there. I am only just making headway over here. When I am absolutely sure of a position in England, then we nip across the Atlantic and scoop in a few dollars, if you like. Just now, even when I am well, would be fatal. I've only just sketched in the outline of my success in London, and one ought to arrive in New York ready-made as a famous and important Artist." Me: "But mother and I didn't think of going to New York. We thought we'd sail straight to New Orleans–if we could: or to Havana. And then go west to Arizona." The poor boy looked at me in such distress. "But Loulina darling, do you mean you want to leave me in the lurch for the winter season? You can't mean it. We're just getting on so splendidly, really!"–I was surprised at the depth of feeling in his voice: how tremendously his career as an artist–a popular artist–matters to him. I can never believe it.–You know, mother, you and I feel alike about daubing paint on canvas: every possible daub that can be daubed has already been done, so people ought to leave off. Rico is so shrewd. I always think he's got his tongue in his cheek, and I'm always staggered once more to find that he takes it absolutely seriously. His career! The Modern British Society of Painters: perhaps even the Royal Academy! Those people we see in London, and those portraits Rico does! He may even be a second Laszlo, or a thirteenth Orpen, and die happy! Oh! mother! How can it really matter to anybody!

'But I was really rather upset when I realised how his heart was fixed on his career, and that I might be spoiling everything for him. So I went away to think about it. And then I realised how unpopular you are, and how unpopular I shall be myself, in a little while. A sort of hatred for people has come over me. I hate their ways and their bunk, and I feel like kicking them in the face, as St Mawr did that young man. Not that I should ever do it. And I don't think I should ever have made my final announcement to Rico, if he hadn't been such a beautiful pig in clover, here at Corrabach Hall. He has known the Manbys all his life; they and he are sections of one engine. He would be far happier with Flora: or I won't say happier, because there is something in him which rebels: but he would on the whole fit much better. I myself am at the end of my limit, and beyond it. I can't "mix" any more, and I refuse to. I feel like a bit of egg-shell in the mayonnaise: the only thing is to take it out, you can't beat it in. I *know* I shall cause a fiasco, even in Rico's career, if I stay. I shall go on being rude and hateful to people as I am at Corrabach, and Rico will lose all his nerve.

'So I have told him. I said this evening, when no one was about: "Rico dear, listen to me seriously. I can't stand these people. If you ask me to endure another week of them, I shall either become ill, or insult them, as mother does. And I don't want to do either." Rico: "But darling, isn't everybody perfect to you?" Me: "I tell you, I shall just make a break, like St Mawr, if I don't get out. I simply can't stand people."–The poor darling, his face goes so blank and anxious. He knows what I mean, because, except that they tickle his vanity all the time, he hates them as much as I do. But his vanity is the chief thing to him. He: "Lou darling, can't you wait till I get up, and we can go away to the Tyrol or somewhere for a spell?" Me: "Won't you come with me to America, to the South-West? I believe it's marvellous country."–I saw his face switch into hostility; quite vicious. He: "Are you so keen on spoiling everything for me? Is that what I married you for? Do you do it deliberately?" Me: "Everything is already spoilt for me. I tell you I can't stand people, your Floras and your Asparias, and your forthcoming young Englishmen. After all, I am an American, like mother, and I've got to go back." He: "Really! And am I to come along as part of the luggage? Labelled cabin!" Me: "You do as you wish, Rico." He: "I wish to God you did as you wished, Lou dear. I'm afraid you do as Mrs Witt wishes. I always heard that the holiest thing in the world was a mother." Me: "No, dear, it's just that I can't stand people." He (with a snarl): "And I suppose I'm lumped in as PEOPLE!" And when he'd said it, it was true. We neither of us said anything for a time. Then he said, calculating: "Very well, dear! You take a trip to the land of stars and stripes, and I'll stay here and go on with my work. And when you've seen enough of their stars and tasted enough of their stripes, you can come back and take your place again with me."–We left it at that.

'You and I are supposed to have important business connected with our estates in Texas–it sounds so well–so we are making a hurried trip to the States, as they call them. I shall leave for London early next week–'

Mrs Witt read this long letter with satisfaction. She herself had one strange craving: to get back to America. It was not that she idealised her native country: she was a tartar of restlessness there, quite as much as in Europe. It was not that she expected to arrive at any blessed abiding place. No, in America she would go on fuming and chafing the same. But at least she would be in America, in her own country. And that was what she wanted.

She picked up the sheet of poor paper that had been folded in Lou's letter. It was the letter from Lewis, quite nicely written. 'Lady Carrington, I write to tell you and Sir Henry that I think I had better quit your service, as it would be more comfortable all round. If you will write and tell me what you want me to do with St Mawr, I will do whatever you tell me. With kind regards to Lady Carrington and Sir Henry, I remain, Your obedient servant, Morgan Lewis.'

Mrs Witt put the letter aside, and sat looking out of the window. She felt, strangely, as if already her soul had gone away from her actual surroundings. She was there, in Oxfordshire, in the body, but her spirit had departed elsewhere. A listlessness was upon her. It was with an effort she roused herself, to write to her lawyer in London, to get her release from her English obligations. Then she wrote to the London hotel.

For the first time in her life she wished she had a maid to do little things for her. All her life she had had too much energy to endure anyone hanging round her, personally. Now she gave up. Her wrists seemed numb, as if the power in her were switched off.

When she went down they said Lewis had asked to speak to her. She had hardly seen him since they arrived at Merriton.

'I've had a letter from Lady Carrington, Mam. She says will I take St Mawr to London and wait for her there. But she says I am to come to you, Mam, for definite orders.'

'Very well, Lewis. I shall be going to London in a few days' time. You arrange for St Mawr to go up one day this week, and you will take him to the Mews. Come to me for anything you want. And don't talk of leaving my daughter. We want you to go with St Mawr to America, with us and Phœnix.'

'And your horse, Mam?'

'I shall leave him here at Merriton. I shall give him to Miss Atherton.'

'Very good, Mam!'

'Dear Daughter: I shall be in my old quarters in Mayfair next Saturday, calling the same day at your house to see if everything is ready for you. Lewis has fixed up with the railway: he goes to town to-morrow. The reason of his letter was that I had asked him if he would care to marry me, and he turned me down with emphasis. But I will tell you about it. You and I are the scribe and the Pharisee; I never could write a letter, and you could never leave off—'

'Dearest Mother: I smelt something rash, but I know it's no use saying: How *could* you? I only wonder, though, that you should think of marriage. You know, dear, I ache in every fibre to be left alone, from all that sort of thing. I feel all bruises, like one who has been assassinated. I do so understand why Jesus said: *"Noli me tangere."* Touch me not, I am not yet ascended unto the Father. Everything had hurt him so much, wearied him so beyond endurance, he felt he could not bear one little human touch on his body. I am like that. I can hardly bear even Elena to hand me a dress. As for a man—and marriage—ah, no! *Noli me tangere, homine!* I am not yet ascended unto the Father. Oh, leave me alone, leave me alone! That is all my cry to all the world.

'Curiously, I feel that Phœnix understands what I feel. He leaves me so understandingly alone, he almost gives me my sheath of aloneness: or at least, he protects me in my sheath. I am grateful for him.

'Whereas Rico feels my aloneness as a sort of shame to himself. He wants at least a blinding *pretence* of intimacy. Ah, intimacy! The thought of it fills me with aches, and the pretence of it exhausts me beyond myself.

'Yes, I long to go away to the West, to be away from the world like one dead and in another life, in a valley that life has not yet entered.

'Rico asked me: What are you doing with St Mawr? When I said we were taking him with us, he said: "Oh, the *Corpus delicti!*" Whether that means anything, I don't know. But he has grown sarcastic beyond my depth.

'I shall see you to-morrow—'

Lou arrived in town, at the dead end of August, with her maid and Phœnix. How wonderful it seemed to have London empty of all her set: her own little house to herself, with just the housekeeper and her own maid. The fact of being alone in those surroundings was so wonderful. It made the surroundings themselves seem all the more ghastly. Everything that had been actual to her was turning ghostly: even her little drawing-room was the ghost of a room, belonging to the dead people who had known it, or to all the dead generations that had brought such a room into being, evolved it out of their quaint domestic desires. And now, in herself, those desires were suddenly spent: gone out like a lamp that suddenly dies. And then she saw her pale, delicate room with its little green agate bowl and its two little porcelain birds and its soft, roundish chairs, turned into something ghostly, like a room set out in a museum. She felt like fastening little labels on the furniture: 'Lady Louise Carrington Lounge Chair, Last used August, 1923.' Not for the benefit of posterity: but to remove her own self into another world, another realm of existence.

'My house, my house, my house, how can I ever have taken so much pains about it!' she kept saying to herself. It was like one of her old hats, suddenly discovered neatly put away in an old hat-box. And what a horror: an old 'fashionable' hat.

Lewis came to see her, and he sat there in one of her delicate mauve chairs, with his feet on a delicate old carpet from Turkestan, and she just wondered. He wore his leather gaiters and khaki breeches as usual, and a faded blue shirt. But his beard and hair were trimmed, he was tidy. There was a certain fineness of contour about him, a certain subtle gleam, which made him seem, apart from his rough boots, not at all gross, or coarse, in that setting of rather silky, Oriental furnishings. Rather he made the Asiatic, sensuous exquisiteness of her old rugs and her old white Chinese figures seem a weariness. Beauty! What was beauty? she asked herself. The Oriental exquisiteness seemed to her all like dead flowers whose hour had come to be thrown away.

Lou could understand her mother's wanting, for a moment, to marry him. His detachedness and his acceptance of something in destiny which people cannot accept. Right in the middle of him he accepted something from destiny that gave him a quality of eternity. He did not care about persons, people, even events. In his own odd way he was an aristocrat, inaccessible in his aristocracy. But it was the aristocracy of the invisible powers, the greater influences, nothing to do with human society.

'You don't really want to leave St Mawr, do you?' Lou asked him. 'You don't really want to quit, as you said?'

He looked at her steadily from his pale grey eyes, without answering, not knowing what to say.

'Mother told me what she said to you.—But she doesn't mind, she says you are entirely within your rights. She has a real regard for you. But we mustn't let our regards run us into actions which are beyond our scope, must we? That makes everything unreal. But you will come with us to America with St Mawr, won't you? We depend on you.'

'I don't want to be uncomfortable,' he said.

'Don't be,' she smiled. 'I myself hate unreal situations—I feel I can't stand them any more. And most marriages are unreal situations. But apart from anything exaggerated, you like being with mother and me, don't you?'

'Yes, I do. I like Mrs Witt as well. But not—'

'I know. There won't be any more of that—'

'You see, Lady Carrington,' he said, with a little heat, 'I'm not by nature a marrying man. And I feel I was selling myself.'

'Quite!—Why do you think you are not a marrying man, though?'

'Me! I don't feel myself after I've been with women.' He spoke in a low tone, looking down at his hands. 'I feel messed up. I'm better to keep to myself.—Because—' and here he looked up with a flare in his eyes: 'women—they only want to make you give in to them, so that they feel almighty, and you feel small.'

'Don't you like feeling small?' Lou smiled. 'And don't you want to make them give in to you?'

'Not me,' he said. 'I don't want nothing. Nothing, I want.'

'Poor mother!' said Lou. 'She thinks if she feels moved by a man, it must result in marriage—or that kind of thing. Surely she makes a mistake. I think you and Phœnix and mother and I might live somewhere in a far-away wild place, and make a good life: so long as we didn't begin to mix up marriage, or love or that sort of thing into it. It seems to me men and women have really hurt one another so much nowadays that they had better stay apart till they have learned to be gentle with one another again. Not all this forced passion and destructive philandering. Men and women should stay apart till their hearts grow gentle towards one another again. Now, it's only each one fighting for his own–or her own–underneath the cover of tenderness.'

'*Dear!–darling!–Yes, my love!*' mocked Lewis, with a faint smile of amused contempt.

'Exactly. People always say *dearest!* when they hate each other most.'

Lewis nodded, looking at her with a sudden sombre gloom in his eyes. A queer bitterness showed on his mouth. But even then he was so still and remote.

The housekeeper came and announced The Honourable Laura Ridley. This was like a blow in the face to Lou. She rose hurriedly–and Lewis rose, moving to the door.

'Don't go, please, Lewis,' said Lou–and then Laura Ridley appeared in the doorway. She was a woman a few years older than Lou, but she looked younger. She might have been a shy girl of twenty-two, with her fresh complexion, her hesitant manner, her round, startled brown eyes, her bobbed hair.

'Hello!' said the newcomer. 'Imagine your being back! I saw you in Paddington.'

Those sharp eyes would see everything.

'I thought everyone was out of town,' said Lou. 'This is Mr Lewis.'

Laura gave him a little nod, then sat on the edge of her chair.

'No,' she said. 'I did go to Ireland to my people, but I came back. I prefer London when I can be more or less alone in it. I thought I'd just run in for a moment before you're gone again.–Scotland, isn't it?'

'No, mother and I are going to America.'

'America! Oh, I thought it was Scotland.'

'It was. But we have suddenly to go to America.'

'I see!–And what about Rico?'

'He is staying on in Shropshire. Didn't you hear of his accident?'

Lou told about it briefly.

'But how awful!' said Laura. 'But there! I knew it! I had a premonition when I saw that horse. We had a horse that killed a man. Then my father got rid of it. But ours was a mare, that one. Yours is a boy.'

'A full-grown man, I'm afraid.'

'Yes, of course, I remember.–But how awful! I suppose you won't ride in the Row. The awful people that ride there nowadays, anyhow! Oh, aren't they awful! Aren't people monstrous, really! My word, when I see the horses crossing Hyde Park Corner on a wet day and coming down smash to those slippery stones, giving their riders a fractured skull!–No joke!'

She inquired details of Rico.

'Oh, I suppose I shall see him when he gets back,' she said. 'But I'm sorry you are going. I shall miss you, I'm afraid. Though you won't be staying long in America. No one stays there longer than they can help.'

'I think the winter through, at least,' said Lou.

'Oh, all the winter! So long? I'm sorry to hear *that*. You're one of the few, very few people one can talk *really* simply with. Extraordinary, isn't it, how few really simple people there are! And they get fewer and fewer. I stayed a fortnight with my people, and a week of that I was in bed. It was really horrible. They really try to take the life out of me, *really!* Just because one won't be as they are, and play their game. I simply refused, and came away.'

'But you can't cut yourself off altogether,' said Lou.

'No, I suppose not. One has to see somebody. Luckily one has a few artists for friends. They're the only real people, anyhow—' She glanced round inquisitively at Lewis, and said with a slight, impertinent, elvish smile on her virgin face:

'Are you an artist?'

'No, Mam!' he said. 'I'm a groom.'

'Oh, I see!' She looked him up and down.

'Lewis is St Mawr's master,' said Lou.

'Oh, the horse! the terrible horse!' She paused a moment. Then again she turned to Lewis with that faint smile, slightly condescending, slightly impertinent, slightly flirtatious.

'Aren't you afraid of him?' she asked.

'No, Mam.'

'Aren't you, *really!*—And can you always master him?'

'Mostly. He knows me.'

'Yes! I suppose that's it.'—She looked him up and down again, then turned away to Lou.

'What have you been painting lately?' said Lou. Laura was not a bad painter.

'Oh, hardly anything. I haven't been able to get on at all. This is one of my bad intervals.'

Here Lewis rose and looked at Lou.

'All right,' she said. 'Come in after lunch, and we'll finish those arrangements.'

Laura gazed after the man, as he dived out of the room, as if her eyes were gimlets that could bore into his secret.

In the course of the conversation she said:

'What a curious little man that was!'

'Which?'

'The groom who was here just now. *Very* curious! Such peculiar eyes. I shouldn't wonder if he had psychic powers.'

'What sort of psychic powers?' said Lou.

'Could *see* things.—And hypnotic, too. He might have hypnotic powers.'

'What makes you think so?'

'He gives me that sort of feeling. Very curious! Probably he hypnotises the horse.—Are you leaving the horse here, by the way, in stable?'

'No, taking him to America.'

'Taking him to America! How extraordinary!'

'It's mother's idea. She thinks he might be valuable as a stock horse on a ranch. You know we still have interest in a ranch in Texas.'

'Oh, I see! Yes, probably he'd be very valuable to improve the breed of the horses over there.—My father has some very lovely hunters. Isn't it disgraceful, he would never let me ride!'

'Why?'

'Because we girls weren't important, in his opinion.—So you're taking the horse to America! With the little man?'

'Yes, St Mawr will hardly behave without him.'

'I see—I see—ee—ee! Just you and Mrs Witt and the little man. I'm sure you'll find he has psychic powers.'

'I'm afraid I'm not so good at finding things out,' said Lou.

'Aren't you? No, I suppose not. I am. I have a flair. I sort of *smell* things.—Then the horse is already here, is he? When do you think you'll sail?'

'Mother is finding a merchant boat that will go to Galveston, Texas, and take us along with the horse. She knows people who will find the right thing. But it takes time.'

'What a much nicer way to travel than on one of those great liners! Oh, how awful they are! So vulgar! Floating palaces they call them! My word, the people inside the palaces!–Yes, I should say that would be a much pleasanter way of travelling: on a cargo-boat.'

Laura wanted to go down to the Mews to see St Mawr. The two women went together.

St Mawr stood in his box, bright and tense as usual.

'Yes!' said Laura Ridley, with a slight hiss. 'Yes! Isn't he beautiful. Such very perfect legs!'–She eyed him round with those gimlet, sharp eyes of hers. 'Almost a pity to let him go out of England. We need some of his perfect *bone*, I feel.–But his eye. Hasn't he got a look in it, my word!'

'I can never see that he looks wicked,' said Lou.

'Can't you!'–Laura had a slight hiss in her speech, a sort of aristocratic decision in her enunciation, that got on Lou's nerves.–'He looks wicked to me!'

'He's not *mean*,' said Lou. 'He'd never do anything mean to you.'

'Oh, mean! I dare say not. No! I'll grant him that, he gives fair warning. His eye says *Beware!*–But isn't he a beauty, *isn't* he!' Lou could feel the peculiar reverence for St Mawr's breeding, his show qualities. Herself, all she cared about was the horse himself, his real nature. 'Isn't it extraordinary,' Laura continued, 'that you never get a *really* perfectly satisfactory animal! There's always something wrong. And in men too. Isn't it curious? there's always something–something wrong–or something missing. Why is it?'

'I don't know,' said Lou. She felt unable to cope with any more. And she was glad when Laura left her.

The days passed slowly, quietly, London almost empty of Lou's acquaintances. Mrs Witt was busy getting all sorts of papers and permits: such a fuss! The battle light was still in her eye. But about her nose was a dusky, pinched look that made Lou wonder.

Both women wanted to be gone: they felt they had already flown in spirit, and it was weary, having the body left behind.

At last all was ready: they only awaited the telegram to say when their cargo-boat would sail. Trunks stood there packed, like great stones locked for ever. The Westminster house seemed already a shell. Rico wrote and telegraphed tenderly, but there was a sense of relentless effort in it all, rather than of any tenderness. He had taken his position.

Then the telegram came, the boat was ready to sail.

'There, now!' said Mrs Witt, as if it had been a sentence of death.

'Why do you look like that, mother?'

'I feel I haven't an ounce of energy left in my body.'

'But how queer, for you, mother. Do you think you are ill?'

'No, Louise. I just feel that way: as if I hadn't an ounce of energy left in my body.'

'You'll feel yourself again, once you are away.'

'Maybe I shall.'

After all, it was only a matter of telephoning. The hotel and the railway porters and taxi-men would do the rest.

It was a grey, cloudy day, cold even. Mother and daughter sat in a cold first-class carriage and watched the little Hampshire country-side go past: little, old, unreal it seemed to them both, and passing away like a dream whose edges only are in consciousness. Autumn! Was this autumn? Were these trees, fields, villages? It seemed but the dim, dissolved edges of a dream, without inward substance.

At Southampton it was raining: and just a chaos, till they stepped on to a clean boat, and were received by a clean young captain, quite sympathetic, and quite a gentleman. Mrs Witt, however, hardly looked at him, but went down to her cabin and lay down in her bunk.

There, lying concealed, she felt the engines start, she knew the voyage had begun. But she lay still. She saw the clouds and the rain, and refused to be disturbed.

Lou had lunch with the young captain, and she felt she ought to be flirty. The young man was so polite and attentive. And she wished so much she were alone.

Afterwards, she sat on deck and saw the Isle of Wight pass shadowy, in a misty rain. She didn't know it was the Isle of Wight. To her, it was just the lowest bit of the British Isles. She saw it fading away: and with it, her life, going like a clot of shadow in a mist of nothingness. She had no feelings about it, none: neither about Rico, nor her London house, nor anything. All passing in a grey curtain of rainy drizzle, like a death, and she, with not a feeling left.

They entered the Channel, and felt the slow heave of the sea. And soon the clouds broke in a little wind. The sky began to clear. By mid-afternoon it was blue summer, on the blue, running waters of the Channel. And soon, the ship steering for Santander, there was the coast of France, the rocks twinkling like some magic world.

The magic world! And back of it, that post-war Paris, which Lou knew only too well, and which depressed her so thoroughly. Or that post-war Monte Carlo, the Riviera still more depressing even than Paris. No, no one must land, even on magic coasts. Else you found yourself in a railway station and a 'centre of civilisation' in five minutes.

Mrs Witt hated the sea, and stayed, as a rule, practically the whole time of the crossing in her bunk. There she was now, silent, shut up like a steel trap, as in her tomb. She did not even read. Just lay and stared at the passing sky. And the only thing to do was to leave her alone.

Lewis and Phœnix hung on the rail and watched everything. Or they went down to see St Mawr. Or they stood talking in the doorway of the wireless operator's cabin. Lou begged the captain to give them jobs to do.

The queer, transitory, unreal feeling, as the ship crossed the great, heavy Atlantic. It was rather bad weather. And Lou felt, as she had felt before, that this grey, wolf-like, cold-blooded ocean hated men and their ships and their smoky passage. Heavy grey waves, a low-sagging sky: rain: yellow, weird evenings with snatches of sun: so it went on. Till they got way south, into the westward-running stream. Then they began to get blue weather and blue water.

To go south! Always to go south, away from the Arctic horror as far as possible! That was Lou's instinct. To go out of the clutch of greyness and low skies, of sweeping rain, and of slow, blanketing snow. Never again to see the mud and rain and snow of a northern winter, nor to feel the idealistic, Christianised tension of the now irreligious North.

As they neared Havana, and the water sparkled at night with phosphorus, and the flying-fishes came like drops of bright water, sailing out of the massive-slippery waves, Mrs Witt emerged once more. She still had that shut-up, deathly look on her face. But she prowled round the deck, and manifested at least a little interest in affairs not her own. Here at sea she hardly remembered the existence of St Mawr or Lewis or Phœnix. She was not very deeply aware even of Lou's existence. – But, of course, it would all come back, once they were on land.

They sailed in hot sunshine out of a blue, blue sea, past the castle into the harbour of Havana. There was a lot of shipping: and this was already America. Mrs Witt had herself and Lou put ashore immediately. They took a motor-car and drove at once to the great boulevard that is the centre of Havana. Here they saw a long rank of motor-cars, all drawn up ready to take a couple of hundred American tourists for one more tour. There were the tourists, all with badges in their coats, lest they should get lost.

'They get so drunk by night,' said the driver in Spanish, 'that the policemen find them lying in the road – turn them over, see the badge – and, hup! – carry them to their hotel.' He grinned sardonically.

Lou and her mother lunched at the Hôtel d'Angleterre, and Mrs Witt watched transfixed while a couple of her countrymen, a stout successful man and his wife, lunched abroad. They had cocktails – then lobster – and a bottle of hock – then a bottle of champagne – then a half-bottle of port. – And Mrs Witt rose in haste as the liqueurs came. For that successful man and his wife had gone on imbibing with a sort of fixed and deliberate will, apparently tasting nothing, but saying to themselves: Now we're drinking Rhine wine! Now we're drinking 1912 champagne. Yah, Prohibition! Thou canst not put it over me. – Their complexions became more and more lurid. Mrs Witt fled, fearing a Havana *débâcle.* But she said nothing.

In the afternoon, they motored into the country to see the great brewery gardens, the new villa suburb, and through the lanes past the old, decaying plantations with palm trees. In one lane they met the fifty motor-cars with the two hundred tourists all with badges on their chests and self-satisfaction on their faces. Mrs Witt watched in grim silence.

'*Plus ça change, plus c'est la même chose,*' said Lou, with a wicked little smile. '*On n'est pas mieux ici,* mother.'

'I know it,' said Mrs Witt.

The hotels by the sea were all shut up: it was not yet the 'season'. Not till November. And then! – Why, then Havana would be an American city, in full leaf of green dollar bills. The green leaf of American prosperity shedding itself recklessly, from every roaming sprig of a tourist, over this city of sunshine and alcohol. Green leaves unfolded in Pittsburg and Chicago, showering in winter downfall in Havana.

Mother and daughter drank tea in a corner of the Hôtel d'Angleterre once more, and returned to the ferry.

The Gulf of Mexico was blue and rippling, with the phantom of islands on the south. Great porpoises rolled and leaped, running in front of the ship in the clear water, diving, travelling in perfect motion, straight, with the tip of the ship touching the tip of their tails, then rolling over, cork-screwing, and showing their bellies as they went. Marvellous! The marvellous beauty and fascination of natural wild things! The horror of man's unnatural life, his heaped-up civilisation!

The flying fishes burst out of the sea in clouds of silvery, transparent motion. Blue above and below, the Gulf seemed a silent, empty, timeless place where man did not really reach. And Lou was again fascinated by the glamour of the universe.

But bump! She and her mother were in a first-class hotel again, calling down the telephone for the bell-boy and iced water. And soon they were in a Pullman, off towards San Antonio.

It was America, it was Texas. They were at their ranch, on the great level of yellow autumn, with the vast sky above. And after all, from the hot, wide sky, and the hot, wide, red earth, there *did* come something new, something not used up. Lou *did* feel exhilarated.

The Texans were there, tall, blonde people, ingenuously cheerful, ingenuously, childishly intimate, as if the fact that you had never seen them before was as nothing compared to the fact that you'd all been living in one room together all your lives, so that nothing was hidden from either of you. The one room being the mere shanty of the world in which we all live. Strange, uninspired cheerfulness, filling, as it were, the blank of complete incomprehension.

And off they set in their motor-cars, chiefly high-legged Fords, rattling away down the red trails between yellow sunflowers or sere grass or dry cotton, away, away into great distances, cheerfully raising the dust of haste. It left Lou in a sort of blank amazement. But it left her amused, not depressed. The old screws of emotion and intimacy that had been screwed down so tightly upon her fell out of their holes here. The Texan intimacy weighed no more on her than a postage stamp, even if, for the moment, it stuck as close. And there was a certain underneath recklessness, even a stoicism in all the apparently childish people, which left one free. They might appear childish: but they stoically depended on themselves alone, in reality. Not as in England, where every man waited to pour the burden of himself upon you.

St Mawr arrived safely, a bit bewildered. The Texans eyed him closely, struck silent, as ever, by anything pure-bred and beautiful. He was somehow too beautiful, too perfected, in this great open country. The long-legged Texan horses, with their elaborate saddles, seemed somehow more natural.

Even St Mawr felt himself strange, as it were naked and singled out, in this rough place. Like a jewel among stones, a pearl before swine, maybe. But the swine were no fools. They knew a pearl from a grain of maize, and a grain of maize from a pearl. And they knew what they wanted. When it was pearls, it was pearls; though chiefly, it was maize. Which shows good sense. They could see St Mawr's points. Only he needn't draw the point too fine or it would just not pierce the tough skin of this country.

The ranch-man mounted him—just threw a soft skin over his back, jumped on, and away down the red trail, raising the dust among the tall, wild, yellow of sunflowers, in the hot, wild sun. Then back again in a fume, and the man slipped off.

'He's got the stuff in him, he sure has,' said the man.

And the horse seemed pleased with this rough handling. Lewis looked on in wonder, and a little envy.

Lou and her mother stayed a fortnight on the ranch. It was all so queer: so crude, so rough, so easy, so artificially civilised, and so meaningless. Lou could not get over the feeling that it all meant nothing. There were no roots of reality at all. No consciousness below the surface, no meaning in anything save the obvious, the blatantly obvious. It was like life enacted in a mirror. Visually, it was wildly vital. But there was nothing behind it. Or like a cinematograph: flat shapes, exactly like men, but without any substance of reality, rapidly rattling away with talk, emotions, activity, all in the flat, nothing behind it. No deeper consciousness at all. So it seemed to her.

One moved from dream to dream, from phantasm to phantasm.

But at least, this Texan life, if it had no bowels, no vitals, at least it could not prey on one's own vitals. It was this much better than Europe.

Lewis was silent, and rather piqued. St Mawr had already made advances to the boss's long-legged, arched-necked glossy-maned Texan mare. And the boss was pleased.

What a world!

Mrs Witt eyed it all shrewdly. But she failed to participate. Lou was a bit scared at the emptiness of it all, and the queer, phantasmal self-consciousness. Cowboys just as self-conscious as Rico, far more sentimental, inwardly vague and unreal. Cowboys that went after their cows in black Ford motor-cars: and who self-consciously saw Lady Carrington falling to them, as elegant young ladies from the East fall to the noble cowboy of the films, or in Zane Grey. It was all film-psychology.

And at the same time, these boys led a hard, hard life, often dangerous and gruesome. Nevertheless, inwardly they were self-conscious film heroes. The boss himself, a man over forty, long and lean and with a great deal of stringy energy, showed off before her in a strong silent manner, existing for the time being purely in his imagination of the sort of picture he made to her, the sort of impression he made on her.

So they all were, coloured up like a Zane Grey book-jacket, all of them living in the mirror. The kind of picture they made to somebody else.

And at the same time, with energy, courage, and a stoical grit getting their work done, and putting through what they had to put through.

It left Lou blank with wonder. And in the face of this strange, cheerful living in the mirror—a rather cheap mirror at that—England began to seem real to her again.

Then she had to remember herself back in England. And no, oh God, England was not real either, except poisonously.

What was real? What under heaven was real?

Her mother had gone dumb and, as it were, out of range. Phœnix was a bit assured and bouncy, back more or less in his own conditions. Lewis was a bit impressed by the emptiness of everything, the *lack* of concentration. And St Mawr followed at the heels of the boss's long-legged black Texan mare, almost slavishly.

What, in heaven's name, was one to make of it all?

Soon, she could not stand this sort of living in a film-setting, with the mechanical energy of 'making good', that is, making money, to keep the show going. The mystic duty to 'make good', meaning to make the ranch pay a laudable interest on the 'owners'' investment. Lou herself being one of the owners. And the interest that came to her, from her father's will, being the money she spent to buy St Mawr and to fit up that house in Westminster. Then also the mystic duty to 'feel good'. Everybody had to *feel good, fine!* 'How are you this morning, Mr Latham?'—'*Fine!* Eh! Don't you feel good out here, eh? Lady Carrington?'—'*Fine!*'—Lou pronounced it with the same ringing conviction. It was Coué all the time!

'Shall we stay here long, mother?' she asked.

'Not a day longer than you want to, Louise. I stay entirely for your sake.'

'Then let us go, mother.'

They left St Mawr and Lewis. But Phœnix wanted to come along. So they motored to San Antonio, got into the Pullman, and travelled as far as El Paso. Then they changed to go North. Santa Fé would be at least 'easy'. And Mrs Witt had acquaintances there.

They found the fiesta over in Santa Fé: Indians, Mexicans, artists had finished their great effort to amuse and attract the tourists. 'Welcome, Mr Tourist' said a great board on one side of the high-road. And on the other side, a little nearer to town: 'Thank You, Mr Tourist.'

'*Plus ça change–*' Lou began.

'*Ça ne change jamais*–except for the worse!' said Mrs Witt, like a pistol going off. And Lou held her peace, after she had sighed to herself, and said in her own mind: 'Welcome Also, Mrs and Miss Tourist!'

There was no getting a word out of Mrs Witt these days. Whereas Phœnix was becoming almost loquacious.

They stayed a while in Santa Fé, in the clean, comfortable, 'homely' hotel, where 'every room had its bath': a spotless white bath, with very hot water night and day. The tourists and commercial travellers sat in the big hall down below, everybody living in the mirror! And of course, they knew Lady Carrington down to her shoe-soles. And they all expected her to know them down to their shoe-soles. For the only object of the mirror is to reflect images.

For two days mother and daughter ate in the mayonnaise intimacy of the dining-room. Then Mrs Witt struck, and telephoned down every meal-time for her meal in her room. She got to staying in bed later and later, as on the ship. Lou became uneasy. This was worse than Europe.

Phœnix was still there, as a sort of half-friend, half-servant retainer. He was perfectly happy, roving round among the Mexicans and Indians, talking Spanish all day, and telling about England and his two mistresses, rolling the ball of his own importance.

'I'm afraid we've got Phœnix for life,' said Lou.

'Not unless we wish,' said Mrs Witt indifferently. And she picked up a novel which she didn't want to read, but which she was going to read.

'What shall we do next, mother?' Lou asked.

'As far as I am concerned, there is no next,' said Mrs Witt.

'Come, mother! Let's go back to Italy or somewhere, if it's as bad as that.'

'Never again, Louise, shall I cross that water. I have come home to die.'

'I don't see much home about it–the Gonsalez Hotel in Santa Fé.'

'Indeed not! But as good as anywhere else to die in.'

'Oh, mother, don't be silly! Shall we look for somewhere where we can be by ourselves?'

'I leave it to you, Louise. I have made my last decision.'

'What is that, mother?'

'Never, never to make another decision!'

'Not even to decide to die?'

'No, not even that.'

'Or *not* to die?'

'Not that either.'

Mrs Witt shut up like a trap. She refused to rise from her bed that day.

Lou went to consult Phœnix. The result was, the two set out to look at a little ranch that was for sale.

It was autumn, and the loveliest time in the south-west, where there is no spring, snow blowing into the hot lap of summer; and no real summer, hail falling in thick ice from the thunderstorms: and even no very definite winter, hot sun melting the snow and giving an impression of spring at any time. But autumn there is, when the winds of the desert are almost still, and the mountains fume no clouds. But morning comes cold and delicate, upon the wild sunflowers and the puffing, yellow-flowered greasewood. For the desert blooms in autumn. In spring it is grey ash all the time, and only the strong breath of the summer sun, and the heavy splashing of thunder rain succeeds at last, by September, in blowing it into soft puffy yellow fire.

It was such a delicate morning when Lou drove out with Phœnix towards the mountains, to look at this ranch that a Mexican wanted to sell. For the brief moment the high mountains had lost their snow: it would be back again in a fortnight: and stood dim and delicate with autumn haze. The desert stretched away pale, as pale as the sky, but silvery and sere, with hummock-mounds of shadow, and long wings of shadow, like the reflection of some great bird. The same eagle shadows came like rude paintings of the outstretched bird, upon the mountains, where the aspens were turning yellow. For the moment, the brief moment, the great desert-and-mountain landscape had lost its certain cruelty, and looked tender, dreamy. And many, many birds were flickering around.

Lou and Phœnix bumped and hesitated over a long trail: then wound down into a deep canyon: and then the car began to climb, climb, climb, in steep rushes, and in long, heart-breaking, uneven pulls. The road was bad, and driving was no joke. But it was the sort of road Phœnix was used to. He sat impassive and watchful, and kept on, till his engine boiled. He was *himself* in this country: impassive, detached, self-satisfied, and silently assertive. Guarding himself at every moment, but, on his guard, sure of himself. Seeing no difference at all between Lou or Mrs Witt and himself, except that they had money and he had none, while he had a native importance which they lacked. He depended on them for money, they on him for the power to live out here in the West. Intimately, he was as good as they. Money was their only advantage.

As Lou sat beside him in the front seat of the car, where it bumped less than behind, she felt this. She felt a peculiar, tough-necked arrogance in him, as if he were asserting himself to put something over her. He wanted her to allow him to make advances to her, to allow him to suggest that he should be her lover. And then, finally, she would marry him, and he would be on the same footing as she and her mother.

In return, he would look after her, and give her his support and countenance, as a man, and stand between her and the world. In this sense, he would be faithful to her, and loyal. But as far as other women went, Mexican women or Indian women: why, that was none of her business. His marrying her would be a pact between two aliens, on behalf of one another, and he would keep his part of it all right. But himself, as a private man and a predative alien-blooded male, this had nothing to do with her. It didn't enter into her scope and count. She was one of these nervous white women with lots of money. She was very nice, too. But as a squaw – as a real woman in a shawl whom a man went after for the pleasure of the night – why, she hardly counted. One of these white women who talk clever and know things like a man. She could hardly expect a half-savage male to acknowledge her as his female counterpart. – No! She had the bucks! And she had all the paraphernalia of the white man's civilisation, which a savage can play with and so escape his own hollow boredom. But his own real female counterpart? – Phœnix would just have shrugged his shoulders, and thought the question not worth answering. How could there be any answer in *her*, to the phallic male in him? Couldn't! Yet it would flatter his vanity and his self-esteem immensely, to possess her. That would be possessing the very clue to the white man's overwhelming world. And if she would let him possess her, he would be absolutely loyal to her, as far as affairs and appearances went. Only, the aboriginal phallic male in him simply couldn't recognise her as a woman at all. In this respect, she didn't exist. It needed the shawled Indian or Mexican women, with their squeaky, plaintive voices, their shuffling, watery humility, and the dark glances of their big, knowing eyes. When an Indian woman looked at him from under her black fringe, with dark, half-secretive suggestion in her big eyes: and when she stood before him hugged in her shawl, in such apparently complete quiescent humility: and when she spoke to him in her mousey squeak of a high, plaintive voice, as if it were difficult for her female bashfulness even to emit so much sound: and when she shuffled away with her legs wide apart, because of her wide-topped, white, high buckskin boots with tiny white feet, and her dark-knotted hair so full of hard, yet subtle lure: and when he remembered the almost watery softness of the Indian woman's dark, warm flesh: then he was a male, an old, secretive, rat-like male. But before Lou's straightforwardness and utter sexual incompetence, he just stood in contempt. And to him, even a French cocotte was utterly devoid of the right sort of sex. She couldn't really move him. She couldn't satisfy the furtiveness in him. He needed this plaintive, squeaky, dark-fringed Indian quality, something furtive and soft and rat-like, really to rouse him.

Nevertheless, he was ready to trade his sex, which, in his opinion, every white woman was secretly pining for, for the white woman's money and social privileges. In the day-time, all the thrill and excitement of the white man's motor-cars and moving pictures and ice-cream sodas, and so forth. In the night, the soft, watery-soft warmth of an Indian or half-Indian woman. This was Phœnix's idea of life for himself.

Meanwhile, if a white woman gave him the privileges of the white man's world, he would do his duty by her as far as all that went.

Lou, sitting very, very still beside him as he drove the car—he was not a very good driver, not quick and marvellous as some white men are, particularly some French chauffeurs she had known, but usually a little behindhand in his movements—she knew more or less all that he felt. More or less she divined as a woman does. Even from a certain rather assured stupidity of his shoulders, and a certain rather stupid assertiveness of his knees, she knew him.

But she did not judge him too harshly. Somewhere deep, deep in herself she knew she too was at fault. And this made her sometimes inclined to humble herself, as a woman, before the furtive assertiveness of this underground, 'knowing' savage. He was so different from Rico.

Yet, after all, *was* he? In his rootlessness, his drifting, his real meaninglessness, was he different from Rico? And his childish, spellbound absorption in the motor-car, or in the moving pictures, or in an ice-cream soda—was it very different from Rico? Anyhow, was it really any better? Pleasanter, perhaps, to a woman, because of the childishness of it.

The same with his opinion of himself as a sexual male! So childish, really, it was almost thrilling to a woman. But then, so stupid also, with that furtive lurking in holes and imagining it could not be detected. He imagined he kept himself dark, in his sexual rat-holes. He imagined he was not detected.

No, no, Lou was not such a fool as she looked, in his eyes, anyhow. She knew what she wanted. She wanted relief from the nervous tension and irritation of her life, she wanted to escape from the friction which is the whole stimulus in modern social life. She wanted to be still: only that, to be very, very still, and recover her own soul.

When Phœnix presumed she was looking for some secretly sexual male such as himself, he was ridiculously mistaken. Even the illusion of the beautiful St Mawr was gone. And Phœnix, roaming round like a sexual rat in promiscuous back yards!–*Merci, mon cher!* For that was all he was: a sexual rat in the great barn-yard of man's habitat, looking for female rats!

Merci, mon cher! You are had.

Nevertheless, in his very mistakenness, he was a relief to her. His mistake was amusing rather than impressive. And the fact that one half of his intelligence was a complete dark blank, that too was a relief.

Strictly, and perhaps in the best sense, he was a servant. His very unconsciousness and his very limitation served as a shelter, as one shelters within the limitations of four walls. The very decided limits to his intelligence were a shelter to her. They made her feel safe.

But that feeling of safety did not deceive her. It was the feeling one derived from having a *true* servant attached to one, a man whose psychic limitations left him incapable of anything but service, and whose strong flow of natural life, at the same time, made him need to serve.

And Lou, sitting there so very still and frail, yet self-contained, had not lived for nothing. She no longer wanted to fool herself. She had no desire at all to fool herself into thinking that a Phœnix might be a husband and a mate. No desire that way at all. His obtuseness was a servant's obtuseness. She was grateful to him for serving, and she paid him a wage. Moreover, she provided him with something to do, to occupy his life. In a sense, she gave him his life, and rescued him from his own boredom. It was a balance.

He did not know what she was thinking. There was a certain physical sympathy between them. His obtuseness made him think it was also a sexual sympathy.

'It's a nice trip, you and me,' he said suddenly, turning and looking her in the eyes with an excited look, and ending on a foolish little laugh.

She realised that she should have sat in the back seat.

'But it's a bad road,' she said. 'Hadn't you better stop and put the sides of the hood up? Your engine is boiling.'

He looked away with a quick switch of interest to the red thermometer in front of his machine.

'She's boiling,' he said, stopping, and getting out with a quick alacrity to go to look at the engine.

Lou got out also, and went to the back seat, shutting the door decisively.

'I think I'll ride at the back,' she said, 'it gets so frightfully hot in front when the engine heats up.–Do you think she needs some water? Have you got some in the canteen?'

'She's full,' he said, peering into the steaming valve.

'You can run a bit out, if you think there's any need. I wonder if its much farther!'

'*Quién sabe!*' said he, slightly impertinent.

She relapsed into her own stillness. She realised how careful, how very careful she must be of relaxing into sympathy, and reposing, as it were, on Phœnix. He would read it as a sexual appeal. Perhaps he couldn't help it. She had only herself to blame. He was obtuse, as a man and a savage. He had only one interpretation, sex, for any woman's approach to him.

And she knew, with the last clear knowledge of weary disillusion, that she did not want to be mixed up in Phœnix's sexual promiscuities. The very thought was an insult to her. The crude, clumsy servant-male: no, no, not that. He was a good fellow, a very good fellow, as far as he went. But he fell far short of physical intimacy.

'No, no,' she said to herself, 'I was wrong to ride in the front seat with him. I must sit alone, just alone. Because sex, mere sex, is repellent to me. I will never prostitute myself again. Unless something touches my very spirit, the very quick of me, I will stay alone, just alone. Alone, and give myself only to the unseen presences, serve only the other, unseen presences.'

She understood now the meaning of the Vestal Virgins, the Virgins of the holy fire in the old temples. They were symbolic of herself, of woman weary of the embrace of incompetent men, weary, weary, weary of all that, turning to the unseen gods, the unseen spirits, the hidden fire, and devoting herself to that, and that alone. Receiving thence her pacification and her fulfilment.

Not these little, incompetent, childish self-opinionated men! Not these to touch her. She watched Phœnix's rather stupid shoulders as he drove the car on between the piñon trees and cedars of the narrow mesa ridge, to the mountain foot. He was a good fellow. But let him run among women of his own sort. Something was beyond him. And this something must remain beyond him, never allow itself to come within his reach. Otherwise he would paw it and mess it up, and be as miserable as a child that has broken its father's watch.

No, no! She had loved an American, and lived with him for a fortnight. She had had a long, intimate friendship with an Italian. Perhaps it was love on his part. And she had yielded to him. Then her love and marriage to Rico.

And what of it all? Nothing. It was almost nothing. It was as if only the outside of herself, her top layers, were human. This inveigled her into intimacies. As soon as the intimacy penetrated, or attempted to penetrate, inside her, it was a disaster. Just a humiliation and a breaking down.

Within these outer layers of herself lay the successive inner sanctuaries of herself. And these were inviolable. She accepted it.

'I am not a marrying woman,' she said to herself. 'I'm not a lover nor a mistress nor a wife. It is no good. Love can't really come into me from the outside, and I can never, never mate with any man, since the mystic new man will never come to me. No, no, let me know myself and my role. I am one of the eternal Virgins, serving the eternal fire. My dealings with men have only broken my stillness and messed up my doorways. It has been my own fault. I ought to stay virgin, and still, very, very still, and serve the most perfect service. I want my temple and my loneliness and my Apollo mystery of the inner fire. And with men, only the delicate, subtler, more remote relations. No coming near. A coming near only breaks the delicate veils, and broken veils, like broken flowers, only lead to rottenness.'

She felt a great peace inside herself as she made this realisation. And a thankfulness. Because, after all, it seemed to her that the hidden fire was alive and burning in this sky, over the desert, in the mountains. She felt a certain latent holiness in the very atmosphere, a young, spring-fire of latent holiness, such as she had never felt in Europe or in the East. 'For me,' she said, as she looked away at the mountains in shadow and the pale, warm desert beneath, with wings of shadow upon it: 'For me, this place is sacred. It is blessed.'

But as she watched Phœnix: as she remembered the motor-cars and tourists, and the rather dreary Mexicans of Santa Fé, and the lurking, invidious Indians, with something of a rat-like secretiveness and defeatedness in their bearing, she realised that the latent fire of the vast landscape struggled under a great weight of dirt-like inertia. She had to mind the dirt, most carefully and vividly avoid it and keep it away from her, here in this place that at last seemed sacred to her.

The motor-car climbed up, past the tall pine trees, to the foot of the mountains, and came at last to a wire gate, where nothing was to be expected. Phœnix opened the gate, and they drove on, through more trees, into a clearing where dried-up bean plants were yellow.

'This man got no water for his beans,' said Phœnix. 'Not got much beans this year.'

They climbed slowly up the incline, through more pine trees, and out into another clearing, where a couple of horses were grazing. And there they saw the ranch itself, little low cabins with patched roofs, under a few pine trees, and facing the long twelve-acre clearing, or field, where the Michaelmas daises were purple mist, and spangled with clumps of yellow flowers.

'Not got no alfalfa here neither!' said Phœnix, as the car waded past the flowers. 'Must be a dry place up here. Got no water, sure they haven't.'

Yet it was the place Lou wanted. In an instant, her heart sprang to it. The instant the car stopped, and she saw the two cabins inside the rickety fence, the rather broken corral beyond, and behind all, tall, blue balsam pines, the round hills, the solid up-rise of the mountain flank: and getting down, she looked across the purple and gold of the clearing, downwards at the ring of pine trees standing so still, so crude and untameable, the motionless desert beyond the bristles of the pine crests, a thousand feet below: and beyond the desert, blue mountains, and far, far-off blue mountains in Arizona: 'This is the place,' she said to herself.

This little tumbledown ranch, only a homestead of a hundred and sixty acres, was, as it were, man's last effort towards the wild heart of the Rockies, at this point. Sixty years before, a restless schoolmaster had wandered out from the East, looking for gold among the mountains. He found a very little, then no more. But the mountains had got hold of him, he could not go back.

There was a little trickling spring of pure water, a thread of treasure perhaps better than gold. So the schoolmaster took up a homestead on the lot where this little spring arose. He struggled, and got himself his log cabin erected, his fence put up, sloping at the mountain-side through the pine trees and dropping into the hollows where the ghost-white mariposa lilies stood leafless and naked in flower, in spring, on tall, invisible stems. He made the long clearing for alfalfa.

And fell so into debt that he had to trade his homestead away, to clear his debt. Then he made a tiny living teaching the children of the few American prospectors who had squatted in the valleys, beside the Mexicans.

The trader who got the ranch tackled it with a will. He built another log cabin and a big corral, and brought water from the canyon two miles and more across the mountain slope, in a little runnel ditch, and more water, piped a mile or more down the little canyon immediately above the cabins. He got a flow of water for his houses: for being a true American, he felt he could not *really* say he had conquered his environment till he had got running water, taps, and wash-hand basins inside his house.

Taps, running water and wash-hand basins he accomplished. And, undaunted through the years, he prepared the basin for a fountain in the little fenced-in enclosure, and he built a little bath-house. After a number of years, he sent up the enamelled bath-tub to be put in the little log bath-house on the little wild ranch hung right against the savage Rockies, above the desert.

But here the mountains finished him. He was a trader down below, in the Mexican village. This little ranch was, as it were, his hobby, his ideal. He and his New England wife spent their summers there: and turned on the taps in the cabins and turned them off again, and felt really that civilisation had conquered.

All this plumbing from the savage ravines of the canyons–one of them nameless to this day–cost, however, money. In fact, the ranch cost a great deal of money. But it was all to be got back. The big clearing was to be irrigated for alfalfa, the little clearing for beans, and the third clearing, under the corral, for potatoes. All these things the trader could trade to the Mexicans, very advantageously.

And, moreover, since somebody had started a praise of the famous goats' cheese made by Mexican peasants in New Mexico, goats there should be.

Goats there were: five hundred of them, eventually. And they fed chiefly in the wild mountain hollows, the no-man's-land. The Mexicans call them fire-mouths, because everything they nibble dies. Not because of their flaming mouths, really, but because they nibble a live plant down, down to the quick, till it can put forth no more.

So, the energetic trader, in the course of five or six years, had got the ranch ready. The long three-roomed cabin was for him and his New England wife. In the two-roomed cabin lived the Mexican family who really had charge of the ranch. For the trader was mostly fixed to his store, seventeen miles away, down in the Mexican village.

The ranch lay over eight thousand feet up, the snows of winter came deep and the white goats, looking dirty yellow, swam in snow with their poor curved horns poking out like dead sticks. But the corral had a long, cosy, shut-in goat-shed all down one side, and into this crowded the five hundred, their acrid goat smell rising like hot acid over the snow. And the thin, pock-marked Mexican threw them alfalfa out of the log barn. Until the hot sun sank the snow again, and froze the surface, when patter-patter went the two thousand little goat-hoofs, over the silver-frozen snow, up at the mountain. Nibble, nibble, nibble, the fire-mouths, at every tender twig. And the goat-bell climbed, and the baa-ing came from among the dense and shaggy pine trees. And sometimes, in a soft drift under the trees, a goat, or several goats, went through, into the white depths, and some were lost thus, to reappear dead and frozen at the thaw.

By evening, they were driven down again, like a dirty yellowish-white stream carrying dark sticks on its yeasty surface, tripping and bleating over the frozen snow, past the bustling dark green pine trees, down to the trampled mess of the corral. And everywhere, everywhere over the snow, yellow stains and dark pills of goat-droppings melting into the surface crystal. On still, glittering nights, when the frost was hard, the smell of goats came up like some uncanny acid fire, and great stars sitting on the mountain's edge seemed to be watching like the eyes of a mountain lion, brought by the scent. Then the coyotes in the near canyon howled and sobbed, and ran like shadows over the snow. But the goat corral had been built tight.

In the course of years the goat-herd had grown from fifty to five hundred, and surely that was increase. The goat-milk cheeses sat drying on their little racks. In spring, there was a great flowing and skipping of kids. In summer and early autumn, there was a pest of flies, rising from all that goat smell and that cast-out whey of goats' milk, after the cheese-making. The rats came, and the pack-rats, swarming.

And after all, it was difficult to sell or trade the cheeses, and little profit to be made. And in dry summers, no water came down in the narrow ditch-channel, that straddled in wooden runnels over the deep clefts in the mountain-side. No water meant no alfalfa. In winter the goats scarcely drank at all. In summer they could be watered at the little spring. But the thirsty land was not so easy to accommodate.

Five hundred fine white Angora goats, with their massive handsome padres! They were beautiful enough. And the trader made all he could of them. Come summer, they were run down into the narrow tank filled with the fiery dipping fluid. Then their lovely white wool was clipped. It was beautiful, and valuable, but comparatively little of it.

And it all cost, cost, cost. And a man was always let down. At one time no water. At another a poison weed. Then a sickness. Always some mysterious malevolence fighting, fighting against the will of man. A strange invisible influence coming out of the livid rock fastnesses in the bowels of those uncreated Rocky Mountains, preying upon the will of man, and slowly wearing down his resistance, his onward-pushing spirit. The curious, subtle thing, like a mountain fever, got into the blood, so that the men at the ranch, and the animals with them, had bursts of queer, violent, half-frenzied energy, in which, however, they were wont to lose their wariness. And then, damage of some sort. The horses ripped and cut themselves, or they were struck by lightning, the men had great hurts or sickness. A curious disintegration working all the time, a sort of malevolent breath, like a stupefying, irritant gas coming out of the unfathomed mountains.

The pack-rats with their bushy tails and big ears came down out of the hills, and were jumping and bouncing about: symbols of the curious debasing malevolence that was in the spirit of the place. The Mexicans in charge, good honest men, worked all they could. But they were like most of the Mexicans in the south-west, as if they had been pithed, to use one of Kipling's words. As if the invidious malevolence of the country itself had slowly taken all the pith of manhood from them, leaving a hopeless sort of corpus of a man.

And the same happened to the white men, exposed to the open country. Slowly, they were pithed. The energy went out of them. And more than that, the interest. An inertia of indifference invading the soul, leaving the body healthy and active, but wasting the soul, the living interest, quite away.

It was the New England wife of the trader who put most energy into the ranch. She looked on it as her home. She had a little white fence put all round the two cabins: the bright brass water-taps she kept shining in the two kitchens: outside the kitchen door she had a little kitchen garden and nasturtiums, after a great fight with invading animals, that nibbled everything away. And she got so far as the preparation of the round concrete basin which was to be a little pool, under the few enclosed pine trees between the two cabins, a pool with a tiny fountain jet.

But this, with the bath-tub, was her limit, as the five hundred goats were her man's limit. Out of the mountains came two breaths of influence: the breath of the curious, frenzied energy, that took away one's intelligence as alcohol or any other stimulus does: and then the most strange indiviousness that ate away the soul. The woman loved her ranch, almost with passion. It was she who felt the stimulus more than the men. It seemed to enter her like a sort of sex passion, intensifying her ego, making her full of violence and of blind female energy. The energy and the blindness of it! A strange blind frenzy, like an intoxication while it lasted. And the sense of beauty that thrilled her New England woman's soul.

Her cabin faced the slow down-slope of the clearing, the alfalfa field: her long, low cabin, crouching under the great pine tree that threw up its trunk sheer in front of the house, in the yard. That pine tree was the guardian of the place. But a bristling, almost demonish guardian, from the far-off crude ages of the world. Its great pillar of pale, flakey-ribbed copper rose there in strange, callous indifference, and the grim permanence, which is in pine trees. A passionless, non-phallic column, rising in the shadows of the pre-sexual world, before the hot-blooded ithyphallic column ever erected itself. A cold, blossomless, resinous sap surging and oozing gum, from that pallid brownish bark. And the wind hissing in the needles, like a vast nest of serpents. And the pine cones falling plumb as the hail hit them. Then lying all over the yard, open in the sun like wooden roses, but hard, sexless, rigid with a blind will.

Past the column of that pine tree, the alfalfa field sloped gently down, to the circling guard of pine trees, from which silent, living barrier isolated pines rose to ragged heights at intervals, in blind assertiveness. Strange, those pine trees! In some lights all their needles glistened like polished steel, all subtly glittering with a whitish glitter among darkness, like real needles. Then again, at evening, the trunks would flare up orange red, and the tufts would be dark, alert tufts like a wolf's tail touching the air. Again, in the morning sunlight they would be soft and still, hardly noticeable. But all the same, present and watchful. Never sympathetic, always watchfully on their guard, and resistant, they hedged one in with the aroma and the power and the slight horror of the pre-sexual primeval world. The world where each creature was crudely limited to its own ego, crude and bristling and cold, and then crowding in packs like pine trees and wolves.

But beyond the pine trees, ah, there beyond, there was beauty for the spirit to soar in. The circle of pines, with the loose trees rising high and ragged at intervals, this was the barrier, the fence to the foreground. Beyond was only distance, the desert a thousand feet below, and beyond.

The desert swept its great fawn-coloured circle around, away beyond and below like a beach, with a long mountain-side of pure blue shadow closing in the near corner, and strange, bluish hummocks of mountains rising like wet rock from a vast strand, away in the middle distance, and beyond, in the farthest distance, pale blue crests of mountains looking over the horizon from the west, as if peering in from another world altogether.

Ah, that was beauty!—perhaps the most beautiful thing in the world. It was pure beauty, *absolute* beauty! There! That was it. To the little woman from New England, with her tense, fierce soul and her egoistic passion of service, this beauty was absolute, a *ne plus ultra*. From her doorway, from her porch, she could watch the vast, eagle-like wheeling of the daylight, that turned as the eagles which lived in the near rocks turned overhead in the blue, turning their luminous, dark-edged-patterned bellies and underwings upon the pure air, like winged orbs. So the daylight made the vast turn upon the desert, brushing the farthest out-watching mountains. And sometimes the vast strand of the desert would float with curious undulations and exhalations amid the blue fragility of mountains, whose upper edges were harder than the floating bases. And sometimes she would see the little brown adobe houses of the village Mexicans, twenty miles away, like little cube crystals of insect-houses dotting upon the desert, very distinct, with a cotton-wood tree or two rising near. And sometimes she would see the far-off rocks thirty miles away, where the canyon made a gateway between the mountains. Quite clear, like an open gateway out of the vast yard, she would see the cut-out bit of the canyon passage. And on the desert itself, curious, puckered folds of mesa-sides. And a blackish crack which in places revealed the otherwise invisible canyon of the Rio Grande. And beyond everything, the mountains like icebergs showing up from an outer sea. Then later, the sun would go down blazing above the shallow cauldron of simmering darkness, and the round mountains of Colorado would lump up into uncanny significance, northwards. That was always rather frightening. But morning came again, with the sun peeping over the mountain slopes and lighting the desert away in the distance long, long before it lighted on her yard. And then she would see another valley, like magic and very lovely, with green folds and long tufts of cotton-wood trees, and a few long-cubical adobe houses, lying floating in shallow light below, like a vision.

Ah! it was beauty, beauty absolute, at any hour of the day: whether the perfect clarity of morning or the mountains beyond the simmering desert at noon, or the purple lumping of northern mounds under a red sun at night. Or whether the dust whirled in tall columns, travelling across the desert far away, like pillars of cloud by day, tall, leaning pillars of dust hastening with ghostly haste: or whether, in the early part of the year, suddenly in the morning a whole sea of solid white would rise rolling below, a solid mist from melted snow, ghost-white under the mountain sun, the world below blotted out: or whether the black rain and cloud streaked down, far across the desert, and lightning stung down with sharp white stings on the horizon: or the cloud travelled and burst overhead, with rivers of fluid blue fire running out of heaven and exploding on earth, and hail coming down like a world of ice shattered above: or the hot sun rode in again: or snow fell in heavy silence: or the world was blinding white under a blue sky, and one must hurry under the pine trees for shelter against that vast, white, back-beating light which rushed up at one and made one almost unconscious, amid the snow.

It was always beauty, *always!* It was always great, and splendid, and, for some reason, natural. It was never grandiose or theatrical. Always, for some reason, perfect. And quite simple, in spite of it all.

So it was, when you watched the vast and living landscape. The landscape lived, and lived as the world of the gods, unsullied and unconcerned. The great circling landscape lived its own life, sumptuous and uncaring. Man did not exist for it.

And if it had been a question simply of living through the eyes, into the *distance*, then this would have been Paradise, and the little New England woman on her ranch would have found what she was always looking for, the earthly paradise of the spirit.

But even a woman cannot live only into the distance, the beyond. Willy-nilly she finds herself juxtaposed to the near things, the thing in itself. And willy-nilly she is caught up into the fight with the immediate object.

The New England woman had fought to make the nearness as perfect as the distance: for the distance was absolute beauty. She had been confident of success. She had felt quite assured, when the water came running out of her bright brass taps, the wild water of the hills caught, tricked into the narrow iron pipes, and led tamely to her kitchen, to jump out over her sink, into her wash-basin, at her service. 'There!' she said. 'I have tamed the waters of the mountain to my service.'

So she had, for the moment.

At the same time, the invisible attack was being made upon her. While she revelled in the beauty of the luminous world that wheeled around and below her, the grey, rat-like spirit of the inner mountains was attacking her from behind. She could not keep her attention. And, curiously, she could not keep even her speech. When she was saying something, suddenly the next word would be gone out of her, as if a pack-rat had carried it off. And she sat blank, stuttering, staring in the empty cupboard of her mind, like Mother Hubbard, and seeing the cupboard bare. And this irritated her husband intensely.

Her chickens, of which she was so proud, were carried away. Or they strayed. Or they fell sick. At first she could cope with their circumstances. But after a while, she couldn't. She couldn't care. A drug-like numbness possessed her spirit, and at the very middle of her, she couldn't care what happened to her chickens.

The same when a couple of horses were struck by lightning. It frightened her. The rivers of fluid fire that suddenly fell out of the sky and exploded on the earth near-by, as if the whole earth had burst like a bomb, frightened her from the very core of her, and made her know, secretly and with cynical certainty, *that there was no merciful God in the heavens.* A very tall, elegant pine tree just above her cabin took the lightning, and stood tall and elegant as before, but with a white seam spiralling from its crest, all down its tall trunk, to earth. The perfect scar, white and long as lightning itself. And every time she looked at it, she said to herself, in spite of herself: 'There is no Almighty loving God. The God there is shaggy as the pine trees, and horrible as the lightning.' Outwardly, she never confessed this. Openly, she thought of her dear New England Church as usual. But in the violent undercurrent of her woman's soul, after the storms, she would look at that living, seamed tree, and the voice would say in her, almost savagely: 'What nonsense about Jesus and a God of Love, in a place like this! This is more awful and more splendid. I like it better.' The very chipmunks, in their jerky helter-skelter, the blue jays wrangling in the pine tree in the dawn, the grey squirrel undulating to the tree-trunk, then pausing to chatter at her and scold her, with a shrewd fearlessness, as if she were the alien, the outsider, the creature that should not be permitted among the trees, all destroyed the illusion she cherished, of love, universal love. There was no love on this ranch. There was life, intense, bristling life, full of energy, but also, with an undertone of savage sordidness.

The black ants in her cupboard, the pack-rats bouncing on her ceiling like hippopotami in the night, the two sick goats: there was a peculiar undercurrent of squalor, flowing under the curious *tussle* of wild life. That was it. The wild life, even the life of the trees and flowers seemed one bristling, hair-raising tussle. The very flowers came up bristly, and many of them were fang-mouthed, like the dead-nettle: and none had any real scent. But they were very fascinating, too, in their very fierceness. In May, the curious columbines of the stream-beds, columbines scarlet outside and yellow in, like the red and yellow of a herald's uniform—farther from the dove nothing could be: then the beautiful rosy-blue of the great tufts of the flower they called bluebell, but which was really a flower of the snap-dragon family: these grew in powerful beauty in the little clearing of the pine trees, followed by the flower the settlers had mysteriously called herb honeysuckle: a tangle of long drops of pure fire-red, hanging from slim invisible stalks of smoke colour. The purest, most perfect vermilion scarlet, cleanest fire-colour, hanging in long drops like a shower of fire-rain that is just going to strike the earth. A little later, more in the open, there came another sheer fire-red flower, sparking, fierce red stars running up a bristly grey ladder, as if the earth's fire-centre had blown out some red sparks, white-speckled and deadly inside, puffing for a moment in the day air.

So it was! The alfalfa field was one raging, seething conflict of plants trying to get hold. One dry year, and the bristly wild things had got hold: the spiky, blue-leaved thistle-poppy with its moon-white flowers, the low clumps of blue nettle-flower, the later rush, after the sereneness of June and July, the rush of red sparks and Michaelmas daisies, and the tough, wild sunflowers, strangling and choking the dark, tender green of the clover-like alfalfa! A battle, a battle, with banners of bright scarlet and yellow.

When a really defenceless flower did issue, like the moth-still, ghost-centred mariposa lily, with its inner moth-dust of yellow, it came invisible. There was nothing to be seen but a hair of greyish grass near the oak scrub. Behold, this invisible long stalk was balancing a white, ghostly, three-petalled flower, naked out of nothingness. A mariposa lily!

Only the pink wild roses smelled sweet, like the old world. They were sweet-briar roses. And the dark blue harebells among the oak scrub, like the ice-dark bubbles of the mountain flowers in the Alps, the Alpenglocken.

The roses of the desert are the cactus flowers, crystal of translucent yellow or of rose-colour. But set among spines the devil himself must have conceived in a moment of sheer ecstasy.

Nay, it was a world before and after the God of Love. Even the very humming-birds hanging about the flowering squawberry bushes, when the snow had gone, in May, they were before and after the God of Love. And the blue jays were crested dark with challenge, and the yellow-and-dark woodpecker was fearless like a warrior in war-paint, as he struck the wood. While on the fence the hawks sat motionless, like dark fists clenched under heaven, ignoring man and his ways.

Summer, it was true, unfolded the tender cotton-wood leaves, and the tender aspen. But what a tangle and a ghostly aloofness in the aspen thickets high up on the mountains, the coldness that is in the eyes and the long cornelian talons of the bear.

Summer brought the little wild strawberries, with their savage aroma, and the late summer brought the rose-jewel raspberries in the valley cleft. But how lonely, how harsh-lonely and menacing it was, to be alone in that shadowy, steep cleft of a canyon just above the cabins, picking raspberries, while the thunder gathered thick and blue-purple at the mountain-tops. The many wild raspberries hanging rose-red in the thickets. But the stream bed below all silent, waterless. And the trees all bristling in silence, and waiting like warriors at an outpost. And the berries waiting for the sharp-eyed, cold, long-snouted bear to come rambling and shaking his heavy, sharp fur. The berries grew for the bears, and the little New England woman, with her uncanny sensitiveness to underlying influences, felt all the time she was stealing. Stealing the wild raspberries in the secret little canyon behind her home. And when she had made them into jam, she could almost taste the theft in her preserves.

She confessed nothing of this. She tried even to confess nothing of her dread.

But she was afraid. Especially she was conscious of the prowling, intense aerial electricity all the summer, after June. The air was thick with wandering currents of fierce electric fluid, waiting to discharge themselves. And almost every day there was the rage and battle of thunder. But the air was never cleared. There was no relief. However, the thunder raged, and spent itself, yet, afterwards, among the sunshine was the strange lurking and wandering of the electric currents, moving invisible, with strange menace, between the atoms of the air. She knew. Oh, she knew!

And her love for her ranch turned sometimes into a certain repulsion. The underlying rat-dirt, the everlasting bristling tussle of the wild life, with the tangle and the bones strewing. Bones of horses struck by lightning, bones of dead cattle, skulls of goats with little horns: bleached, unburied bones. Then the cruel electricity of the mountains. And then, most mysterious but worst of all, the animosity of the spirit of place: the crude, half-created spirit of place, like some serpent-bird for ever attacking man, in a hatred of man's onward struggle towards further creation.

The seething cauldron of lower life, seething on the very tissue of the higher life, seething the soul away, seething at the marrow. The vast and unrelenting will of the swarming lower life, working for ever against man's attempt at a higher life, a further created being.

At last, after many years, the little woman admitted to herself that she was glad to go down from the ranch, when November came with snows. She was glad to come to a more human home, her house in the village. And as winter passed by and spring came again, she knew she did not want to go up to the ranch again. It had broken something in her. It had hurt her terribly. It had maimed her for ever in her hope, her belief in paradise on earth. Now she hid from herself her own corpse, the corpse of her New England belief in a world ultimately all for love. The belief, and herself with it, was a corpse. The gods of those inner mountains were grim and invidious and relentless, huger than man, and lower than man. Yet man could never master them.

The little woman in her flower-garden away below, by the stream-irrigated village, hid away from the thought of it all. She would not go to the ranch any more.

The Mexicans stayed in charge, looking after the goats. But the place didn't pay. It didn't pay, not quite. It had paid. It might pay. But the effort, the effort! And as the marrow is eaten out of a man's bones and the soul out of his belly, contending with the strange rapacity of savage life, the lower stage of creation, he cannot make the effort any more.

Then also, the war came, making many men give up their enterprises at civilisation.

Every new stroke of civilisation has cost the lives of countless brave men, who have fallen defeated by the 'dragon', in their efforts to win the apples of the Hesperides, or the fleece of gold. Fallen in their efforts to overcome the old, half-sordid savagery of the lower stages of creation, and win to the next stage.

For all savagery is half sordid. And man is only himself when he is fighting on and on, to overcome the sordidness.

And every civilisation, when it loses its inward vision and its cleaner energy, falls into a new sort of sordidness, more vast and more stupendous than the old savage sort. An Augean stables of metallic filth.

And all the time, man has to rouse himself afresh to cleanse the new accumulations of refuse. To win from the crude, wild nature the victory and the power to make another start, and to cleanse behind him the century-deep desposits of layer upon layer of refuse: even of tin cans.

The ranch dwindled. The flock of goats declined. The water ceased to flow. And at length the trader gave it up.

He rented the place to a Mexican, who lived on the handful of beans he raised, and who was being slowly driven out by the vermin.

And now arrived Lou, new blood to the attack. She went back to Santa Fé, saw the trader and a lawyer, and bought the ranch for twelve hundred dollars. She was so pleased with herself.

She went upstairs to tell her mother.

'Mother, I've bought a ranch.'

'It is just as well, for I can't stand the noise of automobiles outside here another week.'

'It is quiet on my ranch, mother: the stillness simply speaks.'

'I had rather it held its tongue. I am simply drugged with all the bad novels I have read. I feel as if the sky was a big cracked bell and a million clappers were hammering human speech out of it.'

'Aren't you interested in my ranch, mother?'

'I hope I may be, by and by.'

Mrs Witt actually got up the next morning and accompanied her daughter in the hired motor-car, driven by Phœnix, to the ranch: which was called Las Chivas. She sat like a pillar of salt, her face looking what the Indians call a False Face, meaning a mask. She seemed to have crystallised into neutrality. She watched the desert with its tufts of yellow greasewood go lurching past: she saw the fallen apples on the ground in the orchards near the adobe cottages: she looked down into the deep arroyo, and at the stream they forded in the car, and at the mountains blocking up the sky ahead, all with indifference. High on the mountains was snow: lower, blue-grey livid rock: and below the livid rock the aspens were expiring their daffodil yellow, this year, and the oak scrub was dark and reddish, like gore. She saw it all with a sort of stony indifference.

'Don't you think it's lovely?' said Lou.

'I can *see* it is lovely,' replied her mother.

The Michaelmas daisies in the clearing as they drove up to the ranch were sharp-rayed with purple, like a coming night.

Mrs Witt eyed the two log cabins, one of which was dilapidated and practically abandoned. She looked at the rather rickety corral, whose long planks had silvered and warped in the fierce sun. On one of the roof-planks a pack-rat was sitting erect like an old Indian keeping watch on a pueblo roof. He showed his white belly, and folded his hands and lifted his big ears, for all the world like an old immobile Indian.

'Isn't it for all the world as if *he* were the real boss of the place, Louise?' she said cynically.

And turning to the Mexican, who was a rag of a man but a pleasant, courteous fellow, she asked him why he didn't shoot the rat.

'Not worth a shell!' said the Mexican, with a faint, hopeless smile.

Mrs Witt paced round and saw everything: it did not take long. She gazed in silence at the water of the spring, trickling out of an iron pipe into a barrel, under the cotton-wood tree in an arroyo.

'Well, Louise,' she said. 'I am glad you feel competent to cope with so much hopelessness and so many rats.'

'But, mother, you must admit it is beautiful.'

'Yes, I suppose it is. But to use one of your Henry's phrases, beauty is a cold egg, as far as I am concerned.'

'Rico never would have said that beauty was a cold egg to him.'

'No, he wouldn't. He sits on it like a broody old hen on a china imitation.—Are you going to bring him here?'

'*Bring* him!—No. But he can come if he likes,' stammered Lou.

'*Oh—h!* won't it be beau–ti–ful!' cried Mrs Witt, rolling her head and lifting her shoulders in savage imitation of her son-in-law.

'Perhaps he won't come, mother,' said Lou, hurt.

'He will most certainly come, Louise, to see what's doing: unless you tell him you don't want him.'

'Anyhow, I needn't think about it till spring,' said Lou, anxiously pushing the matter aside.

Mrs Witt climbed the steep slope above the cabins to the mouth of the little canyon. There she sat on a fallen tree and surveyed the world beyond: a world not of men. She could not fail to be roused.

'What is your idea in coming here, daughter?' she asked.

'I love it here, mother.'

'But what do you expect to achieve by it?'

'I was rather hoping, mother, to escape achievement. I'll tell you—and you mustn't get cross if it sounds silly. As far as people go, my heart is quite broken. And far as people go, I don't want any more. I can't stand any more. What heart I ever had for it—for life with people—is quite broken. I want to be alone, mother: with you here, and Phœnix perhaps to look after horses and drive a car. But I want to be by myself, really.'

'With Phœnix in the background! Are you sure he won't be coming into the foreground before long?'

'No, mother, no more of that. If I've got to say it, Phœnix is a servant: he's really placed, as far as I can see. Always the same, playing about in the old back yard. I can't take those men seriously. I can't fool round with them, or fool myself about them. I can't and I won't fool myself any more, mother, especially about men. They don't count. So why should you want them to pay me out?'

For the moment, this silenced Mrs Witt. Then she said:

'Why, *I* don't want it. Why should I! But after all, you've got to live. You've never *lived* yet: not in my opinion.'

'Neither, mother, in my opinion, have you,' said Lou dryly.

And this silenced Mrs Witt altogether. She had to be silent, or angrily on the defensive. And the latter she wouldn't be. She couldn't really, in honesty.

'What do you call life?' Lou continued. 'Wriggling half naked at a public show and going off in a taxi to sleep with some half-drunken fool who thinks he's a man because—Oh, mother, I don't even want to think of it. I know you have a lurking idea that *that is life*. Let it be so then. But leave me out. Men in that aspect simply nauseate me: so grovelling and ratty. Life in that aspect simply drains all my life away. I tell you, for all that sort of thing, I'm broken, absolutely broken: if I wasn't broken to start with.'

'Well, Louise,' said Mrs Witt after a pause, 'I'm convinced that ever since men and women were men and women, people who took things seriously, and had time for it, got their hearts broken. Haven't I had mine broken! It's as sure as having your virginity broken: and it amounts to about as much. It's a beginning rather than an end.'

'So it is, mother. It's the beginning of something else, and the end of something that's done with. I *know*, and there's no altering it, that I've got to live differently. It sounds silly, but I don't know how else to put it. I've got to live for something that matters, way, way down in me. And I think sex would matter, to my very soul, if it was really sacred. But cheap sex kills me.'

'You have had a fancy for rather cheap men, perhaps.'

'Perhaps I have. Perhaps I should always be a fool, where people are concerned. Now I want to leave off that kind of foolery. There's something else, mother, that I want to give myself to. I know it. I know it absolutely. Why should I let myself be shouted down any more?'

Mrs Witt sat staring at the distance, her face a cynical mask.

'What is the something bigger? And *pray*, what is it bigger than?' she asked, in that tone of honeyed suavity which was her deadliest poison. 'I want to learn. I am out to know. I'm terribly intrigued by it. Something bigger! Girls in my generation occasionally entered convents for *something bigger*. I always wondered if they found it. They seemed to me inclined in the imbecile direction, but perhaps that was because I was *something less–*'

There was a definite pause between the mother and daughter, a silence that was a pure breach. Then Lou said:

'You know quite well I'm not conventy, mother, whatever else I am–even a bit of an imbecile. But that kind of religion seems to me the other half of men. Instead of running after them you run away from them, and get the thrill that way. I don't hate men *because* they're men, as nuns do. I dislike them because they're not men enough: babies, and playboys, and poor things showing off all the time, even to themselves. I don't say I'm any better. I only wish, with all my soul, that some men *were* bigger and stronger and *deeper* than I am . . .'

'How do you know they're not?–' asked Mrs Witt.

'How *do* I know?–' said Lou mockingly.

And the pause that was a breach resumed itself. Mrs Witt was teasing with a little stick the bewildered black ants among the fir-needles.

'And no doubt you are right about men,' she said at length. 'But at your age, the only sensible thing is to try and keep up the illusion. After all, as you say, you may be no better.'

'I may be no better. But keeping up the illusion means fooling myself. And I won't do it. When I see a man who is even a bit attractive to me–even as much as Phœnix–I say to myself: "Would you care for him afterwards? Does he really mean anything to you, except just a sensation?"–And I know he doesn't. No, mother, of this I am convinced: either my taking a man shall have a meaning and a mystery that penetrates my very soul, or I will keep to myself.–And what I *know* is, that the time has come for me to keep to myself. No more messing about.'

'Very well, daughter. You will probably spend your life keeping to yourself.'

'Do you think I mind! There's something else for me, mother. There's something else even that loves me and wants me. I can't tell you what it is. It's a spirit. And it's here, on this ranch. It's here, in this landscape. It's something more real to me than men are, and it soothes me, and it holds me up. I don't know what it is, definitely. It's something wild, that will hurt me sometimes and will wear me down sometimes. I know it. But it's something big, bigger than men, bigger than people, bigger than religion. It's something to do with wild America. And it's something to do with me. It's a mission, if you like. I am imbecile enough for that!–But it's my mission to keep myself for the spirit that is wild, and has waited so long here: even waited for such as me. Now I've come!

Now I'm here. Now I am where I want to be: with the spirit that wants me.—And that's how it is. And neither Rico nor Phœnix nor anybody else really matters to me. They are in the world's back-yard. And I am here, right deep in America, where there's a wild spirit wants me, a wild spirit more than men. And it doesn't want to save me either. It needs me. It craves for me. And to it, my sex is deep and sacred, deeper than I am, with a deep nature aware deep down of my sex. It saves me from cheapness, mother. And even you could never do that for me.'

Mrs Witt rose to her feet and stood looking far, far away at the turquoise ridge of mountains half sunk under the horizon.

'How much did you say you paid for Las Chivas?' she asked.

'Twelve hundred dollars,' said Lou, surprised.

'Then I call it cheap, considering all there is to it: even the name.'

D.H. LAWRENCE

THE FOX

The two girls were usually known by their surnames, Banford and March. They had taken the farm together, intending to work it all by themselves: that is, they were going to rear chickens, make a living by poultry, and add to this by keeping a cow, and raising one or two young beasts. Unfortunately, things did not turn out well.

Banford was a small, thin, delicate thing with spectacles. She, however, was the principal investor, for March had little or no money. Banford's father, who was a tradesman in Islington, gave his daughter the start, for her health's sake, and because he loved her, and because it did not look as if she would marry. March was more robust. She had learned carpentry and joinery at the evening classes in Islington. She would be the man about the place. They had, moreover, Banford's old grandfather living with them at the start. He had been a farmer. But unfortunately the old man died after he had been at Bailey Farm for a year. Then the two girls were left alone.

They were neither of them young: that is, they were near thirty. But they certainly were not old. They set out quite gallantly with their enterprise. They had numbers of chickens, black Leghorns and white Leghorns, Plymouths and Wyandottes; also some ducks; also two heifers in the fields. One heifer, unfortunately, refused absolutely to stay in the Bailey Farm closes. No matter how March made up the fences, the heifer was out, wild in the woods, or trespassing on the neighbouring pasture, and March and Banford were away, flying after her, with more haste than success. So this heifer they sold in despair. Then, just before the other beast was expecting her first calf, the old man died, and the girls, afraid of the coming event, sold her in a panic, and limited their attentions to fowls and ducks.

In spite of a little chagrin, it was a relief to have no more cattle on hand. Life was not made merely to be slaved away. Both girls agreed in this. The fowls were quite enough trouble. March had set up her carpenter's bench at the end of the open shed. Here she worked, making coops and doors and other appurtenances. The fowls were housed in the bigger building, which had served as barn and cow-shed in old days. They had a beautiful home, and should have been perfectly content. Indeed, they looked well enough. But the girls were disgusted at their tendency to strange illnesses, at their exacting way of life, and at their refusal, obstinate refusal to lay eggs.

March did most of the outdoor work. When she was out and about, in her puttees and breeches, her belted coat and her loose cap, she looked almost like some graceful, loose-balanced young man, for her shoulders were straight, and her movements easy and confident, even tinged with a little indifference or irony. But her face was not a man's face, ever. The wisps of her crisp dark hair blew about her as she stooped, her eyes were big and wide and dark, when she looked up again, strange, startled, shy and sardonic at once. Her mouth, too, was almost pinched as if in pain and irony. There was something odd and unexplained about her. She would stand balanced on one hip, looking at the fowls pattering about in the obnoxious fine mud of the sloping yard, and calling to her favourite white hen, which came in answer to her name. But there was an almost satirical flicker in March's big, dark eyes as she looked at her three-toed flock pottering about under her gaze, and the same slight dangerous satire in her voice as she spoke to the favoured Patty, who pecked at March's boot by way of friendly demonstration.

Fowls did not flourish at Bailey Farm, in spite of all that March did for them. When she provided hot food for them in the morning, according to rule, she noticed that it made them heavy and dozy for hours. She expected to see them lean against the pillars of the shed in their languid processes of digestion. And she knew quite well that they ought to be busily scratching and foraging about, if they were to come to any good. So she decided to give them their hot food at night, and let them sleep on it. Which she did. But it made no difference.

War conditions, again, were very unfavourable to poultry-keeping. Food was scarce and bad. And when the Daylight Saving Bill was passed, the fowls obstinately refused to go to bed as usual, about nine o'clock in the summer-time. That was late enough, indeed, for there was no peace till they were shut up and asleep. Now they cheerfully walked around, without so much as glancing at the barn, until ten o'clock or later. Both Banford and March disbelieved in living for work alone. They wanted to read or take a cycle-ride in the evening, or perhaps March wished to paint curvilinear swans on porcelain, with green background, or else make a marvellous fire-screen by processes of elaborate cabinet work. For she was a creature of odd whims and unsatisfied tendencies. But from all these things she was prevented by the stupid fowls.

One evil there was greater than any other. Bailey Farm was a little homestead, with ancient wooden barn and low-gabled farm-house, lying just one field removed from the edge of the wood. Since the war the fox was a demon. He carried off the hens under the very noses of March and Banford. Banford would start and stare through her big spectacles with all her eyes, as another squawk and flutter took place at her heels. Too late! Another white Leghorn gone. It was disheartening.

They did what they could to remedy it. When it became permitted to shoot foxes, they stood sentinel with their guns, the two of them, at the favoured hours. But it was no good. The fox was too quick for them. So another year passed, and another, and they were living on their losses, as Banford said. They let their farm-house one summer, and retired to live in a railway-carriage that was deposited as a sort of out-house in a corner of the field. This amused them, and helped their finances. None the less, things looked dark.

Although they were usually the best of friends, because Banford, though nervous and delicate, was a warm, generous soul, and March, though so odd and absent in herself, had a strange magnanimity, yet, in the long solitude, they were apt to become a little irritable with one another, tired of one another. March had four-fifths of the work to do, and though she did not mind, there seemed no relief, and it made her eyes flash curiously sometimes. Then Banford, feeling more nerve-worn than ever, would become despondent, and March would speak sharply to her. They seemed to be losing ground, somehow, losing hope as the months went by. There alone in the fields by the wood, with the wide country stretching hollow and dim to the round hills of the White Horse, in the far distance, they seemed to have to live too much off themselves. There was nothing to keep them up—and no hope.

The fox really exasperated them both. As soon as they had let the fowls out, in the early summer mornings, they had to take their guns and keep guard: and then again as soon as evening began to mellow, they must go once more. And he was so sly. He slid along in the deep grass; he was difficult as a serpent to see. And he seemed to circumvent the girls deliberately. Once or twice March had caught sight of the white tip of his brush, or the ruddy shadow of him in the deep grass, and she had let fire at him. But he made no account of this.

One evening March was standing with her back to the sunset, her gun under her arm, her hair pushed under her cap. She was half watching, half musing. It was her constant state. Her eyes were keen and observant, but her inner mind took no notice of what she saw. She was always lapsing into this odd, rapt state, her mouth rather screwed up. It was a question whether she was there, actually conscious present, or not.

The trees on the wood-edge were a darkish, brownish green in the full light—for it was the end of August. Beyond, the naked, copper-like shafts and limbs of the pine trees shone in the air. Nearer the rough grass, with its long, brownish stalks all agleam, was full of light. The fowls were round about—the ducks were still swimming on the pond under the pine trees. March looked at it all, saw it all, and did not see it. She heard Banford speaking to the fowls in the distance—and she did not hear. What was she thinking about? Heaven knows. Her consciousness was, as it were, held back.

She lowered her eyes, and suddenly saw the fox. He was looking up at her. His chin was pressed down, and his eyes were looking up. They met her eyes. And he knew her. She was spellbound—she knew he knew her. So he looked into her eyes, and her soul failed her. He knew her, he was not daunted.

She struggled, confusedly she came to herself, and saw him making off, with slow leaps over some fallen boughs, slow, impudent jumps. Then he glanced over his shoulder, and ran smoothly away. She saw his brush held smooth like a feather, she saw his white buttocks twinkle. And he was gone, softly, soft as the wind.

She put her gun to her shoulder, but even then pursed her mouth, knowing it was nonsense to pretend to fire. So she began to walk slowly after him, in the direction he had gone, slowly, pertinaciously. She expected to find him. In her heart she was determined to find him. What she would do when she saw him again she did not consider. But she was determined to find him. So she walked abstractedly about on the edge of the wood, with wide, vivid dark eyes, and a faint flush in her cheeks. She did not think. In strange mindlessness she walked hither and thither.

At last she became aware that Banford was calling her. She made an effort of attention, turned, and gave some sort of screaming call in answer. Then again she was striding off towards the homestead. The red sun was setting, the fowls were retiring towards their roost. She watched them, white creatures, black creatures, gathering to the barn. She watched them spellbound, without seeing them. But her automatic intelligence told her when it was time to shut the door.

She went indoors to supper, which Banford had set on the table. Banford chatted easily. March seemed to listen, in her distant, manly way. She answered a brief word now and then. But all the time she was as if spellbound. And as soon as supper was over, she rose again to go out, without saying why.

She took her gun again and went to look for the fox. For he had lifted his eyes upon her, and his knowing look seemed to have entered her brain. She did not so much think of him: she was possessed by him. She saw his dark, shrewd, unabashed eye looking into her, knowing her. She felt him invisibly master her spirit. She knew the way he lowered his chin as he looked up, she knew his muzzle, the golden brown, and the greyish white. And again she saw him glance over his shoulder at her, half inviting, half contemptuous and cunning. So she went, with her great startled eyes glowing, her gun under her arm, along the wood edge. Meanwhile the night fell, and a great moon rose above the pine trees. And again Banford was calling.

So she went indoors. She was silent and busy. She examined her gun, and cleaned it, musing abstractedly by the lamp-light. Then she went out again, under the great moon, to see if everything was right. When she saw the dark crests of the pine trees against the blood-red sky, again her heart beat to the fox, the fox. She wanted to follow him, with her gun.

It was some days before she mentioned the affair to Banford. Then suddenly one evening she said:

'The fox was right at my feet on Saturday night.'

'Where?' said Banford, her eyes opening behind her spectacles.

'When I stood just above the pond.'

'Did you fire?' cried Banford.

'No, I didn't.'

'Why not?'

'Why, I was too much surprised, I suppose.'

It was the same old, slow, laconic way of speech March always had. Banford stared at her friend for a few moments.

'You saw him?' she cried.

'Oh yes! He was looking up at me, cool as anything.'

'I tell you,' cried Banford–'the cheek! They're not afraid of us, Nellie.'

'Oh no,' said March.

'Pity you didn't get a shot at him,' said Banford.

'Isn't it a pity! I've been looking for him ever since. But I don't suppose he'll come so near again.'

'I don't suppose he will,' said Banford.

And she proceeded to forget about it, except that she was more indignant than ever at the impudence of the beggar. March also was not conscious that she thought of the fox. But whenever she fell into her half-musing, when she was half rapt and half intelligently aware of what passed under her vision, then it was the fox which somehow dominated her unconsciousness, possessed the blank half of her musing. And so it was for weeks, and months. No matter whether she had been climbing the trees for the apples, or beating down the last of the damsons, or whether she had been digging out the ditch from the duck-pond, or clearing out the barn, when she had finished, or when she straightened herself, and pushed the wisps of hair away again from her forehead, and pursed up her mouth again in an odd, screwed fashion, much too old for her years, there was sure to come over her mind the old spell of the fox, as it came when he was looking at her. It was as if she could smell him at these times. And it always recurred, at unexpected moments, just as she was going to sleep at night, or just as she was pouring the water into the tea-pot to make tea–it was the fox, it came over her like a spell.

So the months passed. She still looked for him unconsciously when she went towards the wood. He had become a settled effect in her spirit, a state permanently established, not continuous, but always recurring. She did·not know what she felt or thought: only the state came over her, as when he looked at her.

The months passed, the dark evenings came, heavy, dark November, when March went about in high boots, ankle deep in mud, when the night began to fall at four o'clock, and the day never properly dawned. Both girls dreaded these times. They dreaded the almost continuous darkness that enveloped them on their desolate little farm near the wood. Banford was physically afraid. She was afraid of tramps, afraid lest someone should come prowling around. March was not so much afraid as uncomfortable, and disturbed. She felt discomfort and gloom in all her physique.

Usually the two girls had tea in the sitting-room. March lighted a fire at dusk, and put on the wood she had chopped and sawed during the day. Then the long evening was in front, dark, sodden, black outside, lonely and rather oppressive inside, a little dismal. March was content not to talk, but Banford could not keep still. Merely listening to the wind in the pines outside, or the drip of water, was too much for her.

One evening the girls had washed up the tea-cups in the kitchen, and March had put on her house-shoes, and taken up a roll of crochet-work, which she worked at slowly from time to time. So she lapsed into silence. Banford stared at the red fire, which, being of wood, needed constant attention. She was afraid to begin to read too early, because her eyes would not bear any strain. So she sat staring at the fire, listening to the distant sounds, sound of cattle lowing, of a dull, heavy moist wind, of the rattle of the evening train on the little railway not far off. She was almost fascinated by the red glow of the fire.

Suddenly both girls started, and lifted their heads. They heard a footstep–distinctly a footstep. Banford recoiled in fear. March stood listening. Then rapidly she approached the door that led into the kitchen. At the same time they heard the footsteps approach the back door. They waited a second. The back door opened softly. Banford gave a loud cry. A man's voice said softly:

'Hello!'

March recoiled, and took a gun from a corner.

'What do you want?' she cried, in a sharp voice.

Again the soft, softly-vibrating man's voice said:

'Hello! What's wrong?'

'I shall shoot!' cried March. 'What do you want?'

'Why, what's wrong? What's wrong?' came the soft, wondering, rather scared voice: and a young soldier, with his heavy kit on his back, advanced into the dim light.

'Why,' he said, 'who lives here then?'

'We live here,' said March. 'What do you want?'

'Oh!' came the long, melodious, wonder-note from the young soldier. 'Doesn't William Grenfel live here then?'

'No–you know he doesn't.'

'Do I? Do I? I don't, you see. He *did* live here, because he was my grandfather, and I lived here myself five years ago. What's become of him then?'

The young man–or youth, for he would not be more than twenty–now advanced and stood in the inner doorway. March, already under the influence of his strange, soft, modulated voice, stared at him spellbound. He had a ruddy, roundish face, with fairish hair, rather long, flattened to his forehead with sweat. His eyes were blue, and very bright and sharp. On his cheeks, on the fresh ruddy skin were fine, fair hairs, like a down, but sharper. It gave him a slightly glistening look. Having his heavy sack on his shoulders, he stooped, thrusting his head forward. His hat was loose in one hand. He stared brightly, very keenly from girl to girl, particularly at March, who stood pale, with great dilated eyes, in her belted coat and puttees, her hair knotted in a big crisp knot behind. She still had the gun in her hand. Behind her, Banford, clinging to the sofa-arm, was shrinking away, with half-averted head.

'I thought my grandfather still lived here? I wonder if he's dead.'

'We've been here for three years,' said Banford, who was beginning to recover her wits, seeing something boyish in the round head with its rather long, sweaty hair.

'Three years! You don't say so! And you don't know who was here before you?'

'I know it was an old man, who lived by himself.'

'Ay! Yes, that's him! And what became of him then?'

'He died. I know he died.'

'Ay! He's dead then!'

The youth stared at them without changing colour or expression. If he had any expression, besides a slight baffled look of wonder, it was one of sharp curiosity concerning the two girls; sharp, impersonal curiosity, the curiosity of that round young head.

But to March he was the fox. Whether it was the thrusting forward of his head, or the glisten of fine whitish hairs on the ruddy cheek-bones, or the bright, keen eyes, that can never be said: but the boy was to her the fox, and she could not see him otherwise.

'How is it you didn't know if your grandfather was alive or dead?' asked Banford, recovering her natural sharpness.

'Ay, that's it,' replied the softly-breathing youth. 'You see, I joined up in Canada, and I hadn't heard for three or four years. I ran away to Canada.'

'And now have you just come from France?'

'Well–from Salonika really.'

There was a pause, nobody knowing quite what to say.

'So you've nowhere to go now?' said Banford rather lamely.

'Oh, I know some people in the village. Anyhow, I can go to the "Swan".'

'You came on the train, I suppose. Would you like to sit down a bit?'

'Well–I don't mind.'

He gave an odd little groan as he swung off his kit. Banford looked at March.

'Put the gun down,' she said. 'We'll make a cup of tea.'

'Ay,' said the youth. 'We've seen enough of rifles.'

He sat down rather tired on the sofa, leaning forward.

March recovered her presence of mind, and went into the kitchen. There she heard the soft young voice musing:

'Well, to think I should come back and find it like this!' He did not seem sad, not at all–only rather interestedly surprised.

'And what a difference in the place, eh?' he continued, looking round the room.

'You see a difference, do you?' said Banford.

'Yes–don't I!'

His eyes were unnaturally clear and bright, though it was the brightness of abundant health.

March was busy in the kitchen preparing another meal. It was about seven o'clock. All the time, while she was active, she was attending to the youth in the sitting-room, not so much listening to what he said as feeling the soft run of his voice. She primmed up her mouth tighter and tighter, puckering it as if it were sewed, in her effort to keep her will uppermost. Yet her large eyes dilated and glowed in spite of her; she lost herself. Rapidly and carelessly she prepared the meal, cutting large chunks of bread and margarine—for there was no butter. She racked her brain to think of something else to put on the tray—she had only bread, margarine, and jam, and the larder was bare. Unable to conjure anything up, she went into the sitting-room with her tray.

She did not want to be noticed. Above all, she did not want him to look at her. But when she came in, and was busy setting the table just behind him, he pulled himself up from his sprawling, and turned and looked over his shoulder. She became pale and wan.

The youth watched her as she bent over the table, looked at her slim, well-shapen legs, at the belted coat dropping around her thighs, at the knot of dark hair, and his curiosity, vivid and widely alert, was again arrested by her.

The lamp was shaded with a dark-green shade, so that the light was thrown downwards and the upper half of the room was dim. His face moved bright under the light, but March loomed shadowy in the distance.

She turned round, but kept her eyes sideways, dropping and lifting her dark lashes. Her mouth unpuckered as she said to Banford:

'Will you pour out?'

Then she went into the kitchen again.

'Have your tea where you are, will you?' said Banford to the youth—'unless you'd rather come to the table.'

'Well,' said he, 'I'm nice and comfortable here, aren't I? I will have it here, if you don't mind.'

'There's nothing but bread and jam,' she said. And she put his plate on a stool by him. She was very happy now, waiting on him. For she loved company. And now she was no more afraid of him than if he were her own younger brother. He was such a boy.

'Nellie,' she called. 'I've poured you a cup out.'

March appeared in the doorway, took her cup, and sat down in a corner, as far from the light as possible. She was very sensitive in her knees. Having no skirts to cover them, and being forced to sit with them boldly exposed, she suffered. She shrank and shrank, trying not to be seen. And the youth, sprawling low on the couch, glanced up at her, with long, steady, penetrating looks, till she was almost ready to disappear. Yet she held her cup balanced, she drank her tea, screwed up her mouth and held her head averted. Her desire to be invisible was so strong that it quite baffled the youth. He felt he could not see her distinctly. She seemed like a shadow within the shadow. And ever his eyes came back to her, searching, unremitting, with unconscious fixed attention.

Meanwhile he was talking softly and smoothly to Banford, who loved nothing so much as gossip, and who was full of perky interest, like a bird. Also he ate largely and quickly and voraciously, so that March had to cut more chunks of bread and margarine, for the roughness of which Banford apologised.

'Oh, well,' said March, suddenly speaking, 'if there's no butter to put on it, it's no good trying to make dainty pieces.'

Again the youth watched her, and he laughed, with a sudden, quick laugh, showing his teeth and wrinkling his nose.

'It isn't, is it,' he answered in his soft, near voice.

It appeared he was Cornish by birth and upbringing. When he was twelve years old he had come to Bailey Farm with his grandfather, with whom he had never agreed very well. So he had run away to Canada, and worked far away in the West. Now he was here—and that was the end of it.

He was very curious about the girls, to find out exactly what they were doing. His questions were those of a farm youth; acute, practical, a little mocking. He was very much amused by their attitude to their losses: for they were amusing on the score of heifers and fowls.

'Oh, well,' broke in March, 'we don't believe in living for nothing but work.'

'Don't you?' he answered. And again the quick young laugh came over his face. He kept his eyes steadily on the obscure woman in the corner.

'But what will you do when you've used up all your capital?' he said.

'Oh, I don't know,' answered March laconically. 'Hire ourselves out for land-workers, I suppose.'

'Yes, but there won't be any demand for women landworkers now the war's over,' said the youth.

'Oh, we'll see. We shall hold on a bit longer yet,' said March, with a plangent, half-sad, half-ironical indifference.

'There wants a man about the place,' said the youth softly.

Banford burst out laughing.

'Take care what you say,' she interrupted. 'We consider ourselves quite efficient.'

'Oh,' came March's slow plangent voice, 'it isn't a case of efficiency, I'm afraid. If you're going to do farming you must be at it from morning till night, and you might as well be a beast yourself.'

'Yes, that's it,' said the youth. 'You aren't willing to put yourselves into it.'

'We aren't,' said March, 'and we know it.'

'We want some of our time for ourselves,' said Banford.

The youth threw himself back on the sofa, his face tight with laughter, and laughed silently but thoroughly. The calm scorn of the girls tickled him tremendously.

'Yes,' he said, 'but why did you begin then?'

'Oh,' said March, 'we had a better opinion of the nature of fowls then than we have now.'

'Of Nature altogether, I'm afraid,' said Banford. 'Don't talk to me about Nature.'

Again the face of the youth tightened with delighted laughter.

'You haven't a very high opinion of fowls and cattle, haven't you?' he said.

'Oh no—quite a low one,' said March.

He laughed out.

'Neither fowls nor heifers,' said Banford, 'nor goats nor the weather.'

The youth broke into a sharp yap of laughter, delighted. The girls began to laugh too, March turning aside her face and wrinkling her mouth in amusement.

'Oh, well,' said Banford, 'we don't mind, do we, Nellie?'

'No,' said March, 'we don't mind.'

The youth was very pleased. He had eaten and drunk his fill. Banford began to question him. His name was Henry Grenfel—no, he was not called Harry, always Henry. He continued to answer with courteous simplicity, grave and charming. March, who was not included, cast long, slow glances at him from her recess, as he sat there on the sofa, his hands clasping his knees, his face under the lamp bright and alert, turned to Banford. She became almost peaceful at last. He was identified with the fox—and he was here in full presence. She need not go after him any more. There in the shadow of her corner she gave herself up to a warm, relaxed peace, almost like sleep, accepting the spell that was on her. But she wished to remain hidden. She was only fully at peace whilst he forgot her, talking to Banford. Hidden in the shadow of the corner, she need not any more be divided in herself, trying to keep up two planes of consciousness. She could at last lapse into the odour of the fox.

For the youth, sitting before the fire in his uniform, sent a faint but distinct odour into the room, indefinable, but something like a wild creature. March no longer tried to reserve herself from it. She was still and soft in her corner like a passive creature in its cave.

At last the talk dwindled. The youth relaxed his clasp of his knees, pulled himself together a little, and looked around. Again he became aware of the silent, half-invisible woman in the corner.

'Well,' he said unwillingly, 'I suppose I'd better be going, or they'll be in bed at the "Swan".'

'I'm afraid they're in bed, anyhow,' said Banford. 'They've all got this influenza.'

'Have they!' he exclaimed. And he pondered. 'Well,' he continued, 'I shall find a place somewhere.'

'I'd say you could stay here, only—' Banford began.

He turned and watched her, holding his head forward.

'What?' he asked.

'Oh, well,' she said, 'propriety, I suppose.' She was rather confused.

'It wouldn't be improper, would it?' he said, gently surprised.

'Not as far as we're concerned,' said Banford.

'And not as far as *I'm* concerned,' he said, with grave naiveté. 'After all, it's my own home, in a way.'

Banford smiled at this.

'It's what the village will have to say,' she said.

There was a moment's blank pause.

'What do you say, Nellie?' asked Banford.

'I don't mind,' said March, in her distinct tone. 'The village doesn't matter to me, anyhow.'

'No,' said the youth, quick and soft. 'Why should it? I mean, what should they say?'

'Oh, well,' came March's plangent, laconic voice, 'they'll easily find something to say. But it makes no difference what they say. We can look after ourselves.'

'Of course you can,' said the youth.

'Well then, stop if you like,' said Banford. 'The spare room is quite ready.'

His face shone with pleasure.

'If you're quite sure it isn't troubling you too much,' he said, with that soft courtesy which distinguished him.

'Oh, it's no trouble,' they both said.

He looked, smiling with delight, from one to another.

'It's awfully nice not to have to turn out again, isn't it?' he said gratefully.

'I suppose it is,' said Banford.

March disappeared to attend the room. Banford was as pleased and thoughtful as if she had her own young brother home from France. It gave her just the same kind of gratification to attend on him, to get out the bath for him, and everything. Her natural warmth and kindliness had now an outlet. And the youth luxuriated in her sisterly attention. But it puzzled him slightly to know that March was silently working for him too. She was so curiously silent and obliterated. It seemed to him he had not really seen her. He felt he should not know her if he met her in the road.

That night March dreamed vividly. She dreamed she heard a singing outside which she could not understand, a singing that roamed round the house, in the fields, and in the darkness. It moved her so that she felt she must weep. She went out, and suddenly she knew it was the fox singing. He was very yellow and bright, like corn. She went nearer to him, but he ran away and ceased singing. He seemed near, and she wanted to touch him. She stretched out her hand, but suddenly he bit her wrist, and at the same instant, as she drew back, the fox, turning round to bound away, whisked his brush across her face, and it seemed his brush was on fire, for it seared and burned her mouth with a great pain. She awoke with the pain of it, and lay trembling as if she were really seared.

In the morning, however, she only remembered it as a distant memory. She arose and was busy preparing the house and attending to the fowls. Banford flew into the village on her bicycle to try and buy food. She was a hospitable soul. But alas, in the year 1918 there was not much food to buy. The youth came downstairs in his shirt-sleeves. He was young and fresh, but he walked with his head thrust forward, so that his shoulders seemed raised and rounded, as if he had a slight curvature of the spine. It must have been only a manner of bearing himself, for he was young and vigorous. He washed himself and went outside, whilst the women were preparing breakfast.

He saw everything, and examined everything. His curiosity was quick and insatiable. He compared the state of things with that which he remembered before, and cast over in his mind the effect of the changes. He watched the fowls and the ducks, to see their condition; he noticed the flight of wood-pigeons overhead: they were very numerous; he saw the few apples high up, which March had not been able to reach; he remarked that they had borrowed a draw-pump, presumably to empty the big soft-water cistern which was on the north side of the house.

'It's a funny, dilapidated old place,' he said to the girls, as he sat at breakfast.

His eyes were wise and childish, with thinking about things. He did not say much, but ate largely. March kept her face averted. She, too, in the early morning could not be aware of him, though something about the glint of his khaki reminded her of the brilliance of her dream-fox.

During the day the girls went about their business. In the morning he attended to the guns, shot a rabbit and a wild duck that was flying high towards the wood. That was a great addition to the empty larder. The girls felt that already he had earned his keep. He said nothing about leaving, however. In the afternoon he went to the village. He came back at tea-time. He had the same alert, forward-reaching look on his roundish face. He hung his hat on a peg with a little swinging gesture. He was thinking about something.

'Well,' he said to the girls, as he sat at table. 'What am I going to do?'

'How do you mean—what are you going to do?' said Banford.

'Where am I going to find a place in the village to stay?' he said.

'I don't know,' said Banford. 'Where do you think of staying?'

'Well'—he hesitated—'at the "Swan" they've got this 'flu, and at the "Plough and Harrow" they've got the soldiers who are collecting the hay for the army: besides, in the private houses, there's ten men and a corporal altogether billeted in the village, they tell me. I'm not sure where I could get a bed.'

He left the matter to them. He was rather calm about it. March sat with her elbows on the table, her two hands supporting her chin, looking at him unconsciously. Suddenly he lifted his clouded blue eyes, and unthinking looked straight into March's eyes. He was startled as well as she. He, too, recoiled a little. March felt the same sly, taunting, knowing spark leap out of his eyes, as he turned his head aside, and fall into her soul, as it had fallen from the dark eyes of the fox. She pursed her mouth as if in pain, as if asleep too.

'Well, I don't know,' Banford was saying. She seemed reluctant, as if she were afraid of being imposed upon. She looked at March. But, with her weak, troubled sight, she only saw the usual semi-abstraction on her friend's face. 'Why don't you speak, Nellie?' she said.

But March was wide-eyed and silent, and the youth, as if fascinated, was watching her without moving his eyes.

'Go on—answer something,' said Banford. And March turned her head slightly aside, as if coming to consciousness, or trying to come to consciousness.

'What do you expect me to say?' she asked automatically.

'Say what you think,' said Banford.

'It's all the same to me,' said March.

And again there was silence. A pointed light seemed to be on the boy's eyes, penetrating like a needle.

'So it is to me,' said Banford. 'You can stop on here if you like.'

A smile like a cunning little flame came over his face, suddenly and involuntarily. He dropped his head quickly to hide it, and remained with his head dropped, his face hidden.

'You can stop on here if you like. You can please yourself, Henry,' Banford concluded.

Still he did not reply, but remained with his head dropped. Then he lifted his face. It was bright with a curious light, as if exultant, and his eyes were strangely clear as he watched March. She turned her face aside, her mouth suffering as if wounded, and her consciousness dim.

Banford became a little puzzled. She watched the steady, pellucid gaze of the youth's eyes as he looked at March, with the invisible smile gleaming on his face. She did not know how he was smiling, for no feature moved. It seemed only in the gleam, almost the glitter of the fine hairs on his cheeks. Then he looked with quite a changed look at Banford.

'I'm sure,' he said in his soft, courteous voice, 'you're awfully good. You're too good. You don't want to be bothered with me, I'm sure.'

'Cut a bit of bread, Nellie,' said Banford uneasily, adding: 'It's no bother, if you like to stay. It's like having my own brother here for a few days. He's a boy like you are.'

'That's awfully kind of you,' the lad repeated. 'I should like to stay ever so much, if you're sure I'm not a trouble to you.'

'No, of course you're no trouble. I tell you, it's a pleasure to have somebody in the house besides ourselves,' said warm-hearted Banford.

'But Miss March?' he said in his soft voice, looking at her.

'Oh, it's quite all right as far as I'm concerned,' said March vaguely.

His face beamed, and he almost rubbed his hands with pleasure.

'Well then,' he said, 'I should love it, if you'd let me pay my board and help with the work.'

'You've no need to talk about board,' said Banford.

One or two days went by, and the youth stayed on at the farm. Banford was quite charmed by him. He was so soft and courteous in speech, not wanting to say much himself, preferring to hear what she had to say, and to laugh in his quick, half-mocking way. He helped readily with the work–but not too much. He loved to be out alone with the gun in his hands, to watch, to see. For his sharp-eyed, impersonal curiosity was insatiable, and he was most free when he was quite alone, half-hidden, watching.

Particularly he watched March. She was a strange character to him. Her figure, like a graceful young man's, piqued him. Her dark eyes made something rise in his soul, with a curious elate excitement, when he looked into them, an excitement he was afraid to let be seen, it was so keen and secret. And then her odd, shrewd speech made him laugh outright. He felt he must go further, he was inevitably impelled. But he put away the thought of her and went off towards the wood's edge with the gun.

The dusk was falling as he came home, and with the dusk, a fine, late November rain. He saw the fire-light leaping in the window of the sitting-room, a leaping light in the little cluster of the dark buildings. And he thought to himself it would be a good thing to have this place for his own. And then the thought entered him shrewdly: Why not marry March? He stood still in the middle of the field for some moments, the dead rabbit hanging still in his hand, arrested by this thought. His mind waited in amazement–it seemed to calculate–and then he smiled curiously to himself in acquiescence. Why not? Why not indeed? It was a good idea. What if it was rather ridiculous? What did it matter? What if she was older than he? It didn't matter. When he thought of her dark, startled, vulnerable eyes he smiled subtly to himself. He was older than she, really. He was master of her.

He scarcely admitted his intention even to himself. He kept it as a secret even from himself. It was all too uncertain as yet. He would have to see how things went. Yes, he would have to see how things went. If he wasn't careful, she would just simply mock at the idea. He knew, sly and subtle as he was, that if he went to her plainly and said: 'Miss March, I love you and want you to marry me,' her inevitable answer would be: 'Get out. I don't want any of that tomfoolery.' This was her attitude to men and their 'tomfoolery'. If he was not careful, she would turn round on him with her savage, sardonic ridicule, and dismiss him from the farm and from her own mind for ever. He would have to go gently. He would have to catch her as you catch a deer or a woodcock when you go out shooting. It's no good walking out into the forest and saying to the deer: 'Please fall to my gun.' No, it is a slow, subtle battle. When you really go out to get a deer, you gather yourself together, you coil yourself inside yourself, and you advance secretly, before dawn, into the mountains. It is not so much what you do, when you go out hunting, as how you feel. You have to be subtle and cunning and absolutely fatally ready. It becomes like a fate. Your own fate overtakes and determines the fate of the deer you are hunting. First of all, even before you come in sight of your quarry, there is a strange battle, like mesmerism. Your own soul, as a hunter, has gone out to fasten on the soul of the deer, even before you see any deer. And the soul of the deer fights to escape. Even before the deer has any wind of you, it is so. It is a subtle, profound battle of wills which takes place in the invisible. And it is a battle never finished till your bullet goes home. When you are *really* worked up to the true pitch, and you come at last into range, you don't then aim as you do when you are firing at a bottle. It is your own *will* which carries the bullet into the heart of your quarry. The bullet's flight home is a sheer projection of your own fate into the fate of the deer. It happens like a supreme wish, a supreme act of volition, not as a dodge of cleverness.

He was a huntsman in spirit, not a farmer, and not a soldier stuck in a regiment. And it was as a young hunter that he wanted to bring down March as his quarry, to make her his wife. So he gathered himself subtly together, seemed to withdraw into a kind of invisibility. He was not quite sure how he would go on. And March was suspicious as a hare. So he remained in appearance just the nice, odd, stranger-youth, staying for a fortnight on the place.

He had been sawing logs for the fire in the afternoon. Darkness came very early. It was still a cold, raw mist. It was getting almost too dark to see. A pile of short sawed logs lay beside the trestle. March came to carry them indoors, or into the shed, as he was busy sawing the last log. He was working in his shirt-sleeves, and did not notice her approach; she came unwillingly, as if shy. He saw her stooping to the brightended logs, and he stopped sawing. A fire like lightning flew down his legs in the nerves.

'March?' he said in his quiet, young voice.

She looked up from the logs she was piling.

'Yes!' she said.

He looked down on her in the dusk. He could see her not too distinctly.

'I wanted to ask you something,' he said.

'Did you? What was it?' she said. Already the fright was in her voice. But she was too much mistress of herself.

'Why'–his voice seemed to draw out soft and subtle, it penetrated her nerves–'why, what do you think it is?'

She stood up, placed her hands on her hips, and stood looking at him transfixed, without answering. Again he burned with a sudden power.

'Well,' he said, and his voice was so soft it seemed rather like a subtle touch, like the merest touch of a cat's paw, a feeling rather than a sound. 'Well–I wanted to ask you to marry me.'

March felt rather than heard him. She was trying in vain to turn aside her face. A great relaxation seemed to have come over her. She stood silent, her head slightly on one side. He seemed to be bending towards her, invisibly smiling. It seemed to her fine sparks came out of him.

Then very suddenly she said:

'Don't try any of your tomfoolery on me.'

A quiver went over his nerves. He had missed. He waited a moment to collect himself again. Then he said, putting all the strange softness into his voice, as if he were imperceptibly stroking her:

'Why, it's not tomfoolery. It's not tomfoolery. I mean it. I mean it. What makes you disbelieve me?'

He sounded hurt. And his voice had such a curious power over her; making her feel loose and relaxed. She struggled somewhere for her own power. She felt for a moment that she was lost–lost–lost. The word seemed to rock in her as if she were dying. Suddenly again she spoke.

'You don't know what you are talking about,' she said, in a brief and transient stroke of scorn. 'What nonsense! I'm old enough to be your mother.'

'Yes, I do know what I'm talking about. Yes, I do,' he persisted softly, as if he were producing his voice in her blood. 'I know quite well what I'm talking about. You're not old enough to be my mother. That isn't true. And what does it matter even if it was. You can marry me whatever age we are. What is age to me? And what is age to you! Age is nothing.'

A swoon went over her as he concluded. He spoke rapidly–in the rapid Cornish fashion–and his voice seemed to sound in her somewhere where she was helpless against it. 'Age is nothing!' The soft, heavy insistence of it made her sway dimly out there in the darkness. She could not answer.

A great exultance leaped like fire over his limbs. He felt he had won.

'I want to marry you, you see. Why shouldn't I?' he proceeded, soft and rapid. He waited for her to answer. In the dusk he saw her almost phosphorescent. Her eyelids were dropped, her face half-averted and unconscious. She seemed to be in his power. But he waited, watchful. He dared not yet touch her.

'Say then,' he said, 'say then you'll marry me. Say–say!' He was softly insistent.

'What?' she asked, faint, from a distance, like one in pain. His voice was now unthinkably near and soft. He drew very near to her.

'Say yes.'

'Oh, I can't,' she wailed helplessly, half-articulate, as if semi-conscious, and as if in pain, like one who dies. 'How can I?'

'You can,' he said softly, laying his hand gently on her shoulder as she stood with her head averted and dropped, dazed. 'You can. Yes, you can. What makes you say you can't? You can. You can.' And with awful softness he bent forward and just touched her neck with his mouth and his chin.

'Don't!' she cried, with a faint mad cry like hysteria, starting away and facing round on him. 'What do you mean?' But she had no breath to speak with. It was as if she was killed.

'I mean what I say,' he persisted softly and cruelly. 'I want you to marry me. I want you to marry me. You know that, now, don't you? You know that, now? Don't you? Don't you?'

'What?' she said.

'Know,' he replied.

'Yes,' she said. 'I know you say so.'

'And you know I mean it, don't you?'

'I know you say so.'

'You believe me?' he said.

She was silent for some time. Then she pursed her lips.

'I don't know what I believe,' she said.

'Are you out there?' came Banford's voice, calling from the house.

'Yes, we're bringing in the logs,' he answered.

'I thought you'd gone lost,' said Banford disconsolately. 'Hurry up, do, and come and let's have tea. The kettle's boiling.'

He stooped at once to take an armful of little logs and carry them into the kitchen, where they were piled in a corner. March also helped, filling her arms and carrying the logs on her breast as if they were some heavy child. The night had fallen cold.

When the logs were all in, the two cleaned their boots noisily on the scraper outside, then rubbed them on the mat. March shut the door and took off her old felt hat–her farm-girl hat. Her thick, crisp, black hair was loose, her face was pale and strained. She pushed back her hair vaguely and washed her hands. Banford came hurrying into the dimly-lighted kitchen, to take from the oven the scones she was keeping hot.

'Whatever have you been doing all this time?' she asked fretfully. 'I thought you were never coming in. And it's ages since you stopped sawing. What were you doing out there?'

'Well,' said Henry, 'we had to stop that hole in the barn to keep the rats out.'

'Why, I could see you standing there in the shed I could see your shirt-sleeves,' challenged Banford.

'Yes, I was just putting the saw away.'

They went in to tea. March was quite mute. Her face was pale and strained and vague. The youth, who always had the same ruddy, self-contained look on his face, as though he were keeping himself to himself, had come to tea in his shirt-sleeves as if he were at home. He bent over his plate as he ate his food.

'Aren't you cold?' said Banford spitefully. 'In your shirt-sleeves.'

He looked up at her, with his chin near his plate, and his eyes very clear, pellucid, and unwavering as he watched her.

'No, I'm not cold,' he said with his usual soft courtesy. 'It's much warmer in here than it is outside, you see.'

'I hope it is,' said Banford, feeling nettled by him. He had a strange, suave assurance and a wide-eyed bright look that got on her nerves this evening.

'But perhaps,' he said softly and courteously, 'you don't like me coming to tea without my coat. I forgot that.'

'Oh, I don't mind,' said Banford: although she *did*.

'I'll go and get it, shall I?' he said.

March's dark eyes turned slowly down to him.

'No, don't you bother,' she said in her queer, twanging tone. 'If you feel all right as you are, stop as you are.' She spoke with a crude authority.

'Yes,' said he, 'I *feel* all right, if I'm not rude.'

'It's usually considered rude,' said Banford. 'But we don't mind.'

'Go along, "considered rude",' ejaculated March. 'Who considers it rude?'

'Why, you do, Nellie, in anybody else,' said Banford, bridling a little behind her spectacles, and feeling her food stick in her throat.

But March had again gone vague and unheeding, chewing her food as if she did not know she was eating at all. And the youth looked from one to another, with bright, watching eyes.

Banford was offended. For all his suave courtesy and soft voice, the youth seemed to her impudent. She did not like to look at him. She did not like to meet his clear, watchful eyes, she did not like to see the strange glow in his face, his cheeks with their delicate fine hair, and his ruddy skin that was quite dull and yet which seemed to burn with a curious heat of life. It made her feel a little ill to look at him: the quality of his physical presence was too penetrating, too hot.

After tea the evening was very quiet. The youth rarely went into the village. As a rule, he read: he was a great reader, in his own hours. That is, when he did begin, he read absorbedly. But he was not very eager to begin. Often he walked about the fields and along the hedges alone in the dark at night, prowling with a queer instinct for the night, and listening to the wild sounds.

To-night, however, he took a Captain Mayne Reid book from Banford's shelf and sat down with knees wide apart and immersed himself in his story. His brownish fair hair was long, and lay on his head like a thick cap, combed sideways. He was still in his shirt-sleeves, and bending forward under the lamp-light, with his knees stuck wide apart and the book in his hand and his whole figure absorbed in the rather strenuous business of reading, he gave Banford's sitting-room the look of a lumber-camp. She resented this. For on her sitting-room floor she had a red Turkey rug and dark stain round, the fire-place had fashionable green tiles, the piano stood open with the latest dance music: she played quite well: and on the walls were March's hand-painted swans and water-lilies. Moreover, with the logs nicely, tremulously burning in the grate, the thick curtains drawn, the doors all shut, and the pine trees hissing and shuddering in the wind outside, it was cosy, it was refined and nice. She resented the big, raw, long-legged youth sticking his khaki knees out and sitting there with his soldier's shirt-cuffs buttoned on his thick red wrists. From time to time he turned a page, and from time to time he gave a sharp look at the fire, settling the logs. Then he immersed himself again in the intense and isolated business of reading.

March, on the far side of the table, was spasmodically crochetting. Her mouth was pursed in an odd way, as when she had dreamed the fox's brush burned it, her beautiful, crisp black hair strayed in wisps. But her whole figure was absorbed in its bearing, as if she herself was miles away. In a sort of semi-dream she seemed to be hearing the fox singing round the house in the wind, singing wildly and sweetly and like a madness. With red but well-shaped hands she slowly crochetted the white cotton, very slowly, awkwardly.

Banford was also trying to read, sitting in her low chair. But between those two she felt fidgetty. She kept moving and looking round and listening to the wind, and glancing secretly from one to the other of her companions. March, seated on a straight chair, with her knees in their close breeches crossed, and slowly, laboriously crochetting, was also a trial.

'Oh dear!' said Banford. 'My eyes are bad to-night.' And she pressed her fingers on her eyes.

The youth looked up at her with his clear, bright look, but did not speak.

'Are they, Jill?' said March absently.

Then the youth began to read again, and Banford perforce returned to her book. But she could not keep still. After a while she looked up at March, and a queer, almost malignant little smile was on her thin face.

'A penny for them, Nell,' she said suddenly.

March looked round with big, startled black eyes, and went pale as if with terror. She had been listening to the fox singing so tenderly, so tenderly, as he wandered round the house.

'What?' she said vaguely.

'A penny for them,' said Banford sarcastically. 'Or twopence, if they're as deep as all that.'

The youth was watching with bright, clear eyes from beneath the lamp.

'Why,' came March's vague voice, 'what do you want to waste your money for?'

'I thought it would be well spent,' said Banford.

'I wasn't thinking of anything except the way the wind was blowing,' said March.

'Oh dear,' replied Banford, 'I could have had as original thought as that myself. I'm afraid I *have* wasted my money this time.'

'Well, you needn't pay,' said March.

The youth suddenly laughed. Both women looked at him: March rather surprised-looking, as if she had hardly known he was there.

'Why, do you ever pay up on these occasions?' he asked.

'Oh yes,' said Banford. 'We always do. I've sometimes had to pass a shilling a week to Nellie, in the winter-time. It costs much less in summer.'

'What, paying for each other's thoughts?' he laughed.

'Yes, when we've absolutely come to the end of everything else.'

He laughed quickly, wrinkling his nose sharply like a puppy and laughing with quick pleasure, his eyes shining.

'It's the first time I ever heard of that,' he said.

'I guess you'd hear of it often enough if you stayed a winter on Bailey Farm,' said Banford lamentably.

'Do you get so tired, then?' he asked.

'So bored,' said Banford.

'Oh!' he said gravely. 'But why should you be bored?'

'Who wouldn't be bored?' said Banford.

'I'm sorry to hear that,' he said gravely.

'You must be, if you were hoping to have a lively time here,' said Banford.

He looked at her long and gravely.

'Well,' he said, with his odd, young seriousness, 'it's quite lively enough for me.'

'I'm glad to hear it,' said Banford.

And she returned to her book. In her thin, frail hair were already many threads of grey, though she was not yet thirty. The boy did not look down, but turned his eyes to March, who was sitting with pursed mouth laboriously crochetting, her eyes wide and absent. She had a warm, pale, fine skin and a delicate nose. Her pursed mouth looked shrewish. But the shrewish look was contradicted by the curious lifted arch of her dark brows, and the wideness of her eyes; a look of startled wonder and vagueness. She was listening again for the fox, who seemed to have wandered farther off into the night.

From under the edge of the lamp-light the boy sat with his face looking up, watching her silently, his eyes round and very clear and intent. Banford, biting her fingers irritably, was glancing at him under her hair. He sat there perfectly still, his ruddy face tilted up from the low level under the light, on the edge of the dimness, and watching with perfect abstract intentness. March suddenly lifted her great, dark eyes from her crochetting and saw him. She started, giving a little exclamation.

'There he is!' she cried involuntarily, as if terribly startled.

Banford looked around in amazement, sitting up straight.

'Whatever has got you, Nellie?' she cried.

But March, her face flushed a delicate rose colour, was looking away to the door.

'Nothing! Nothing!' she said crossly. 'Can't one speak?'

'Yes, if you speak sensibly,' said Banford. 'Whatever did you mean?'

'I don't know what I meant,' cried March testily.

'Oh, Nellie, I hope you aren't going jumpy and nervy. I feel I can't stand another *thing*! Whoever did you mean? Did you mean Henry?' cried poor, frightened Banford.

'Yes. I suppose so,' said March laconically. She would never confess to the fox.

'Oh dear, my nerves are all gone for to-night,' wailed Banford.

At nine o'clock March brought in a tray with bread and cheese and tea—Henry had confessed that he liked a cup of tea. Banford drank a glass of milk and ate a little bread. And soon she said:

'I'm going to bed, Nellie. I'm all nerves to-night. Are you coming?'

'Yes, I'm coming the minute I've taken the tray away,' said March.

'Don't be long then,' said Banford fretfully. 'Good-night, Henry. You'll see the fire is safe, if you come up last, won't you?'

'Yes, Miss Banford, I'll see it's safe,' he replied in his reassuring way.

March was lighting the candle to go to the kitchen. Banford took her candle and went upstairs. When March came back to the fire, she said to him:

'I suppose we can trust you to put out the fire and everything?' She stood there with her hand on her hip, and one knee loose, her head averted shyly, as if she could not look at him. He had his face lifted, watching her.

'Come and sit down a minute,' he said softly.

'No, I'll be going. Jill will be waiting, and she'll get upset, if I don't come.'

'What made you jump like that this evening?' he asked.

'When did I jump?' she retorted, looking at him.

'Why, just now you did,' he said. 'When you cried out.'

'Oh!' she said. 'Then!—Why, I thought you were the fox!' And her face screwed into a queer smile, half-ironic.

'The fox! Why the fox?' he asked softly.

'Why, one evening last summer when I was out with the gun I saw the fox in the grass nearly at my feet, looking straight up at me. I don't know—I suppose he made an impression on me.' She turned aside her head again and let one foot stray loose, self-consciously.

'And did you shoot him?' asked the boy.

'No, he gave me such a start, staring straight at me as he did, and then stopping to look back at me over his shoulder with a laugh on his face.'

'A laugh on his face!' repeated Henry, also laughing. 'He frightened you, did he?'

'No, he didn't frighten me. He made an impression on me, that's all.'

'And you thought I was the fox, did you?' he laughed, with the same queer, quick little laugh, like a puppy wrinkling his nose.

'Yes, I did, for the moment,' she said. 'Perhaps he'd been in my mind without my knowing.'

'Perhaps you think I've come to steal your chickens or something,' he said, with the same young laugh.

But she only looked at him with a wide, dark, vacant eye.

'It's the first time,' he said, 'that I've ever been taken for a fox. Won't you sit down for a minute?' His voice was very soft and cajoling.

'No,' she said. 'Jill will be waiting.' But still she did not go, but stood with one foot loose and her face turned aside, just outside the circle of light.

'But won't you answer my question?' he said, lowering his voice still more.

'I don't know what question you mean.'

'Yes, you do. Of course you do. I mean the question of you marrying me.'

'No, I shan't answer that question,' she said flatly.

'Won't you?' The queer, young laugh came on his nose again. 'Is it because I'm like the fox? Is that why?' And still he laughed.

She turned and looked at him with a long, slow look.

'I wouldn't let that put you against me,' he said. 'Let me turn the lamp low, and come and sit down a minute.'

He put his red hand under the glow of the lamp and suddenly made the light very dim. March stood there in the dimness quite shadowy, but unmoving. He rose silently to his feet, on his long legs. And now his voice was extraordinarily soft and suggestive, hardly audible.

'You'll stay a moment,' he said. 'Just a moment.' And he put his hand on her shoulder. She turned her face from him. 'I'm sure you don't really think I'm like the fox,' he said, with the same softness and with a suggestion of laughter in his tone, a subtle mockery. 'Do you now?' And he drew her gently towards him and kissed her neck, softly. She winced and trembled and hung away. But his strong, young arm held her, and he kissed her softly again, still on the neck, for her face was averted.

'Won't you answer my question? Won't you now?' came his soft, lingering voice. He was trying to draw her near to kiss her face. And he kissed her cheek softly, near the ear.

At that moment Banford's voice was heard calling fretfully, crossly from upstairs.

'There's Jill!' cried March, starting and drawing erect.

And as she did so, quick as lightning he kissed her on the mouth, with a quick, brushing kiss. It seemed to burn through her every fibre. She gave a queer little cry.

'You will, won't you? You will?' he insisted softly.

'Nellie! *Nellie!* Whatever are you so long for?' came Banford's faint cry from the outer darkness.

But he held her fast, and was murmuring with that intolerable softness and insistency:

'You will, won't you? Say yes! Say yes!'

March, who felt as if the fire had gone through her and scathed her, and as if she could do no more, murmured:

'Yes! Yes! Anything you like! Anything you like! Only let me go! Only let me go! Jill's calling.'

'You know you've promised,' he said insidiously.

'Yes! Yes! I do!' Her voice suddenly rose into a shrill cry. 'All right, Jill, I'm coming.'

Startled, he let her go, and she went straight upstairs.

In the morning at breakfast, after he had looked round the place and attended to the stock and thought to himself that one could live easily enough here, he said to Banford:

'Do you know what, Miss Banford?'

'Well, what?' said the good-natured, nervy Banford.

He looked at March, who was spreading jam on her bread.

'Shall I tell?' he said to her.

She looked up at him, and a deep pink colour flushed over her face.

'Yes, if you mean Jill,' she said. 'I hope you won't go talking all over the village, that's all.' And she swallowed her dry bread with difficulty.

'Whatever's coming?' said Banford, looking up with wide, tired, slightly reddened eyes. She was a thin, frail little thing, and her hair, which was delicate and thin, was bobbed, so it hung softly by her worn face in its faded brown and grey.

'Why, what do you think?' he said, smiling like one who has a secret.

'How do I know!' said Banford.

'Can't you guess?' he said, making bright eyes and smiling, pleased with himself.

'I'm sure I can't. What's more, I'm not going to try.'

'Nellie and I are going to be married.'

Banford put down her knife out of her thin, delicate fingers, as if she would never take it up to eat any more. She stared with blank, reddened eyes.

'You what?' she exclaimed.

'We're going to get married: Aren't we, Nellie?' and he turned to March.

'You say so, anyway,' said March, laconically. But again she flushed with an agonised flush. She, too, could swallow no more.

Banford looked at her like a bird that has been shot: a poor, little sick bird. She gazed at her with all her wounded soul in her face, at the deep-flushed March.

'Never!' she exclaimed, helpless.

'It's quite right,' said the bright and gloating youth.

Banford turned aside her face, as if the sight of the food on the table made her sick. She sat like this for some moments, as if she were sick. Then, with one hand on the edge of the table, she rose to her feet.

'I'll *never* believe it, Nellie,' she cried. 'It's absolutely impossible!'

Her plaintive, fretful voice had a thread of hot anger and despair.

'Why? Why shouldn't you believe it?' asked the youth, with all his soft, velvety impertinence in his voice.

Banford looked at him from her wide, vague eyes, as if he were some creature in a museum.

'Oh,' she said languidly, 'because she can never be such a fool. She can't lose her self-respect to such an extent.' Her voice was cold and plaintive, drifting.

'In what way will she lose her self-respect?' asked the boy.

Banford looked at him with vague fixity from behind her spectacles.

'If she hasn't lost it already,' she said.

He became very red, vermilion, under the slow, vague stare from behind the spectacles.

'I don't see it at all,' he said.

'Probably you don't. I shouldn't expect you would,' said Banford, with that straying mild tone of remoteness which made her words even more insulting.

He sat stiff in his chair, staring with hot, blue eyes from his scarlet face. An ugly look had come on his brow.

'My word, she doesn't know what she's letting herself in for,' said Banford, in her plaintive, drifting, insulting voice.

'What has it got to do with you, anyway?' said the youth, in a temper.

'More than it has to do with you, probably,' she replied, plaintive and venomous.

'Oh, has it! I don't see that at all,' he jerked out.

'No, you wouldn't,' she answered, drifting.

'Anyhow,' said March, pushing back her hair and rising uncouthly. 'It's no good arguing about it.' And she seized the bread and the tea-pot and strode away to the kitchen.

Banford let her fingers stray across her brow and along her hair, like one bemused. Then she turned and went away upstairs.

Henry sat stiff and sulky in his chair, with his face and his eyes on fire. March came and went, clearing the table. But Henry sat on, stiff with temper. He took no notice of her. She had regained her composure and her soft, even, creamy complexion. But her mouth was pursed up. She glanced at him each time as she came to take things from the table, glanced from her large, curious eyes, more in curiosity than anything. Such a long, red-faced, sulky boy! That was all he was. He seemed as remote from her as if his red face were a red chimney-pot on a cottage across the fields, and she looked at him just as objectively, as remotely.

At length he got up and stalked out into the fields with the gun. He came in only at dinner-time, with the devil still in his face, but his manners quite polite. Nobody said anything particular; they sat each one at the sharp corner of a triangle, in obstinate remoteness. In the afternoon he went out again at once with the gun. He came in at nightfall with a rabbit and a pigeon. He stayed in all the evening, but hardly opened his mouth. He was in the devil of a temper, feeling he had been insulted.

Banford's eyes were red, she had evidently been crying. But her manner was more remote and supercilious than ever; the way she turned her head if he spoke at all, as if he were some tramp or inferior intruder of that sort, made his blue eyes go almost black with rage. His face looked sulkier. But he never forgot his polite intonation, if he opened his mouth to speak.

March seemed to flourish in this atmosphere. She seemed to sit between the two antagonists with a little wicked smile on her face, enjoying herself. There was even a sort of complacency in the way she laboriously crochetted this evening.

When he was in bed, the youth could hear the two women talking and arguing in their room. He sat up in bed and strained his ears to hear what they said. But he could hear nothing, it was too far off. Yet he could hear the soft, plaintive drip of Banford's voice, and March's deeper note.

The night was quiet, frosty. Big stars were snapping outside, beyond the ridge-tops of the pine trees. He listened and listened. In the distance he heard a fox yelping: and the dogs from the farms barking in answer. But it was not that he wanted to hear. It was what the two women were saying.

He got stealthily out of bed and stood by his door. He could hear no more than before. Very, very carefully he began to lift the door latch. After quite a time he had his door open. Then he stepped stealthily out into the passage. The old oak planks were cold under his feet, and they creaked preposterously. He crept very, very gently up the one step, and along by the wall, till he stood outside their door. And there he held his breath and listened. Banford's voice:

'No, I simply couldn't stand it. I should be dead in a month. Which is just what he would be aiming at, of course. That would just be his game, to see me in the churchyard. No, Nellie, if you were to do such a thing as to marry him, you could never stop here. I couldn't, I couldn't live in the same house with him. Oh!–h! I feel quite sick with the smell of his clothes. And his red face simply turns me over. I can't eat my food when he's at the table. What a fool I was ever to let him stop. One ought *never* to try to do a kind action. It always flies back in your face like a boomerang.'

'Well, he's only got two more days,' said March.

'Yes, thank heaven. And when he's gone he'll never come in this house again. I feel so bad while he's here. And I know, I know he's only counting what he can get out of you. I *know* that's all it is. He's just a good-for-nothing, who doesn't want to work, and who thinks he'll live on us. But he won't live on me. If you're such a fool, then it's your own look-out. Mrs Burgess knew him all the time he was here. And the old man could never get him to do any steady work. He was off with the gun on every occasion, just as he is now. Nothing but the gun! Oh, I do hate it. You don't know what you're doing, Nellie, you don't. If you marry him he'll just make a fool of you. He'll go off and leave you stranded. I know he will, if he can't get Bailey Farm out of us–and he's not going to, while

I live. While I live he's never going to set foot here. I know what it would be. He'd soon think he was master of both of us, as he thinks he's master of you already.'

'But he isn't,' said Nellie.

'He thinks he is, anyway. And that's what he wants: to come and be master here. Yes, imagine it! That's what we've got the place together for, is it, to be bossed and bullied by a hateful, red-faced boy, a beastly labourer. Oh, we *did* make a mistake when we let him stop. We ought never to have lowered ourselves. And I've had such a fight with all the people here, not to be pulled down to their level. No, he's not coming here. And then you see—if he can't have the place, he'll run off to Canada or somewhere again, as if he'd never known you. And here you'll be, absolutely ruined and made a fool of. I know I shall never have any peace of mind again.'

'We'll tell him he can't come here. We'll tell him that,' said March.

'Oh, don't you bother; I'm going to tell him that, and other things as well, before he goes. He's not going to have all his own way while I've got the strength left to speak. Oh, Nellie, he'll despise you, he'll despise you, like the awful little beast he is, if you give way to him. I'd no more trust him than I'd trust a cat not to steal. He's deep, he's deep, and he's bossy, and he's selfish through and through, as cold as ice. All he wants is to make use of you. And when you're no more use to him, then I pity you.'

'I don't think he's as bad as all that,' said March.

'No, because he's been playing up to you. But you'll find out, if you see much of him. Oh, Nellie, I can't bear to think of it.'

'Well, it won't hurt you, Jill, darling.'

'Won't it! Won't it! I shall never know a moment's peace again while I live, nor a moment's happiness. No, Nellie—' and Banford began to weep bitterly.

The boy outside could hear the stifled sound of the woman's sobbing, and could hear March's soft, deep, tender voice comforting, with wonderful gentleness and tenderness, the weeping woman.

His eyes were so round and wide that he seemed to see the whole night, and his ears were almost jumping off his head. He was frozen stiff. He crept back to bed, but felt as if the top of his head were coming off. He could not sleep. He could not keep still. He rose, quietly dressed himself, and crept out on to the landing once more. The women were silent. He went softly downstairs and out to the kitchen.

Then he put on his boots and his overcoat and took the gun. He did not think to go away from the farm. No, he only took the gun. As softly as possible he unfastened the door and went out into the frosty December night. The air was still, the stars bright, the pine trees seemed to bristle audibly in the sky. He went stealthily away down a fenceside, looking for something to shoot. At the same time he remembered that he ought not to shoot and frighten the women.

So he prowled round the edge of the gorse cover, and through the grove of tall old hollies, to the woodside. There he skirted the fence, peering through the darkness with dilated eyes that seemed to be able to grow black and full of sight in the dark, like a cat's. An owl was slowly and mournfully whooing round a great oak tree. He stepped stealthily with his gun, listening, listening, watching.

As he stood under the oaks of the wood-edge he heard the dogs from the neighbouring cottage up the hill yelling suddenly and startlingly, and the wakened dogs from the farms around barking answer. And suddenly it seemed to him England was little and tight, he felt the landscape was constricted even in the dark, and that there were too many dogs in the night, making a noise like a fence of sound, like the network of English hedges netting the view. He felt the fox didn't have a chance. For it must be the fox that had started all this hullabaloo.

Why not watch for him, anyhow! He would, no doubt, be coming sniffing round. The lad walked downhill to where the farmstead with its few pine trees crouched blackly. In the angle of the long shed, in the black dark, he crouched down. He knew the fox would be coming. It seemed to him it would be the last of the foxes in this loudly-barking, thick-voiced England, tight with innumerable little houses.

He sat a long time with his eyes fixed unchanging upon the open gateway, where a little light seemed to fall from the stars or from the horizon, who knows. He was sitting on a log in a dark corner with the gun across his knees. The pine trees snapped. Once a chicken fell off its perch in the barn with a loud crawk and cackle and commotion that startled him, and he stood up, watching with all his eyes, thinking it might be a rat. But he *felt* it was nothing. So he sat down again with the gun on his knees and his hands tucked in to keep them warm, and his eyes fixed unblinking on the pale reach of the open gateway. He felt he could smell the hot, sickly, rich smell of live chickens on the cold air.

And then—a shadow. A sliding shadow in the gateway. He gathered all his vision into a concentrated spark, and saw the shadow of the fox, the fox creeping on his belly through the gate. There he went, on his belly like a snake. The boy smiled to himself and brought the gun to his shoulder. He knew quite well what would happen. He knew the fox would go to where the fowl door was boarded up and sniff there. He knew he would lie there for a minute, sniffing the fowls within. And then he would start again prowling under the edge of the old barn, waiting to get in.

The fowl door was at the top of a slight incline. Soft, soft as a shadow the fox slid up this incline, and crouched with his nose to the boards. And at the same moment there was the awful crash of a gun reverberating between the old buildings, as if all the night had gone smash. But the boy watched keenly. He saw even the white belly of the fox as the beast beat his paws in death. So he went forward.

There was a commotion everywhere. The fowls were scuffling and crawking, the ducks were quark-quarking, the pony had stamped wildly to his feet. But the fox was on his side, struggling in his last tremors. The boy bent over him and smelt his foxy smell.

There was a sound of a window opening upstairs, then March's voice calling: 'Who is it?'

'It's me,' said Henry; 'I've shot the fox.'

'Oh, goodness! You nearly frightened us to death.'

'Did I? I'm awfully sorry.'

'Whatever made you get up?'

'I heard him about.'

'And have you shot him?'

'Yes, he's here,' and the boy stood in the yard holding up the warm, dead brute. 'You can't see, can you? Wait a minute.' And he took his flash-light from his pocket and flashed it on to the dead animal. He was holding it by the brush. March saw, in the middle of the darkness, just the reddish fleece and the white belly and the white underneath of the pointed chin, and the queer, dangling paws. She did not know what to say.

'He's a beauty,' he said. 'He will make you a lovely fur.'

'You don't catch me wearing a fox fur,' she replied.

'Oh!' he said. And he switched off the light.

'Well, I should think you'll come in and go to bed again now,' she said.

'Probably I shall. What time is it?'

'What time is it, Jill?' called March's voice. It was a quarter to one.

That night March had another dream. She dreamed that Banford was dead, and that she, March, was sobbing her heart out. Then she had to put Banford into her coffin. And the coffin was the rough wood-box in which the bits of chopped wood were kept in the kitchen, by the fire. This was the coffin, and there was no other, and March was in agony and dazed bewilderment, looking for something to line the box with, something to make it soft with, something to cover up the poor, dead darling. Because she couldn't lay her in there just in her white, thin night-dress, in the horrible wood-box. So she hunted and hunted, and picked up thing after thing, and threw it aside in the agony of dream-frustration. And in her dream-despair all she could find that would do was a fox-skin. She knew that it wasn't right, that this was not what she should have. But it was all she could find. And so she folded the brush of the fox, and laid her darling Jill's head on this, and she brought round the skin of the fox and laid it on the top of the body, so that it seemed to make a whole ruddy, fiery coverlet, and she cried and cried, and woke to find the tears streaming down her face.

The first thing that both she and Banford did in the morning was to go out to see the fox. Henry had hung it up by the heels in the shed, with its poor brush falling backwards. It was a lovely dog-fox in its prime, with a handsome, thick, winter coat: a lovely golden-red colour, with grey as it passed to the belly, and belly all white, and a great full brush with a delicate black and grey and pure white tip.

'Poor brute!' said Banford. 'If it wasn't such a thieving wretch, you'd feel sorry for it.'

March said nothing, but stood with her foot trailing aside, one hip out; her face was pale and her eyes big and black, watching the dead animal that was suspended upside down. White and soft as snow his belly: white and soft as snow. She passed her hand softly down it. And his wonderful black-glinted brush was full and frictional, wonderful. She passed her hand down this also, and quivered. Time after time she took the full fur of that thick tail between her fingers, and passed her hand slowly downwards. Wonderful, sharp, thick, splendour of a tail. And he was dead! She pursed her lips, and her eyes went black and vacant. Then she took the head in her hand.

Henry was sauntering up, so Banford walked rather pointedly away. March stood there bemused, with the head of the fox in her hand. She was wondering, wondering, wondering over his long, fine muzzle. For some reason it reminded her of a spoon or a spatula. She felt she could not understand it. The beast was a strange beast to her, incomprehensible, out of her range. Wonderful silver whiskers he had, like ice-threads. And pricked ears with hair inside. But that long, long, slender spoon of a nose!—and the marvellous white teeth beneath! It was to thrust forward and bite with, deep, deep, deep into the living prey, to bite and bite the blood.

'He's a beauty, isn't he?' said Henry, standing by.

'Oh yes, he's a fine big fox. I wonder how many chickens he's responsible for,' she replied.

'A good many. Do you think he's the same one you saw in the summer?'

'I should think very likely he is,' she replied.

He watched her, but he could make nothing of her. Partly she was so shy and virgin, and partly she was so grim, matter-of-fact, shrewish. What she said seemed to him so different from the look of her big, queer, dark eyes.

'Are you going to skin him?' she asked.

'Yes, when I've had breakfast, and got a board to peg him on.'

'My word, what a strong smell he's got! Pooo! It'll take some washing off one's hands. I don't know why I was so silly as to handle him.' And she looked at her right hand, that had passed down his belly and along his tail, and had even got a tiny streak of blood from one dark place in his fur.

'Have you seen the chickens when they smell him, how frightened they are?' he said.

'Yes, aren't they!'

'You must mind you don't get some of his fleas.'

'Oh, fleas!' she replied, nonchalant.

Later in the day she saw the fox's skin nailed flat on a board, as if crucified. It gave her an uneasy feeling.

The boy was angry. He went about with his mouth shut, as if he had swallowed part of his chin. But in behaviour he was polite and affable. He did not say anything about his intention. And he left March alone.

That evening they sat in the dining-room. Banford wouldn't have him in her sitting-room any more. There was a very big log on the fire. And everybody was busy. Banford had letters to write, March was sewing a dress, and he was mending some little contrivance.

Banford stopped her letter-writing from time to time to look round and rest her eyes. The boy had his head down, his face hidden over his job.

'Let's see,' said Banford. 'What train do you go by, Henry?'

He looked up straight at her.

'The morning train. In the morning,' he said.

'What, the eight-ten or the eleven-twenty?'

'The eleven-twenty, I suppose,' he said.

'That is the day after to-morrow?' said Banford.

'Yes, the day after to-morrow.'

'Mm!' murmured Banford, and she returned to her writing. But as she was licking her envelope, she asked:

'And what plans have you made for the future, if I may ask?'

'Plans?' he said, his face very bright and angry.

'I mean about you and Nellie, if you are going on with this business. When do you expect the wedding to come off?' She spoke in a jeering tone.

'Oh, the wedding!' he replied. 'I don't know.'

'Don't you know anything?' said Banford. 'Are you going to clear out on Friday and leave things no more settled than they are?'

'Well, why shouldn't I? We can always write letters.'

'Yes, of course you can. But I wanted to know because of this place. If Nellie is going to get married all of a sudden, I shall have to be looking round for a new partner.'

'Couldn't she stay on here if she were married?' he said. He knew quite well what was coming.

'Oh,' said Banford, 'this is no place for a married couple. There's not enough work to keep a man going, for one thing. And there's no money to be made. It's quite useless your thinking of staying on here if you marry. Absolutely!'

'Yes, but I wasn't thinking of staying on here,' he said.

'Well, that's what I want to know. And what about Nellie, then? How long is *she* going to be here with me, in that case?'

The two antagonists looked at one another.

'That I can't say,' he answered.

'Oh, go along,' she cried petulantly. 'You must have some idea what you are going to do, if you ask a woman to marry you. Unless it's all a hoax.'

'Why should it be a hoax? I am going back to Canada.'

'And taking her with you?'

'Yes, certainly.'

'You hear that, Nellie?' said Banford.

March, who had had her head bent over her sewing, now looked up with a sharp, pink blush on her face, and a queer, sardonic laugh in her eyes and on her twisted mouth.

'That's the first time I've heard that I was going to Canada,' she said.

'Well, you have to hear it for the first time, haven't you?' said the boy.

'Yes, I suppose I have,' she said nonchalantly. And she went back to her sewing.

'You're quite ready, are you, to go to Canada? Are you, Nellie?' asked Banford.

March looked up again. She let her shoulders go slack, and let her hand that held the needle lie loose in her lap.

'It depends on *how* I'm going,' she said. 'I don't think I want to go jammed up in the steerage, as a soldier's wife. I'm afraid I'm not used to that way.'

The boy watched her with bright eyes.

'Would you rather stay over here while I go first?' he asked.

'I would, if that's the only alternative,' she replied.

'That's much the wisest. Don't make it any fixed engagement,' said Banford. 'Leave yourself free to go or not after he's got back and found you a place, Nellie. Anything else is madness, madness.'

'Don't you think,' said the youth, 'we ought to get married before I go—and then go together, or separate, according to how it happens?'

'I think it's a terrible idea,' cried Banford.

But the boy was watching March.

'What do you think?' he asked her.

She let her eyes stray vaguely into space.

'Well, I don't know,' she said. 'I shall have to think about it.'

'Why?' he asked pertinently.

'Why?' She repeated his question in a mocking way and looked at him laughing, though her face was pink again. 'I should think there's plenty of reasons why.'

He watched her in silence. She seemed to have escaped him. She had got into league with Banford against him. There was again the queer, sardonic look about her; she would mock stoically at everything he said or which life offered.

'Of course,' he said, 'I don't want to press you to do anything you don't wish to do.'

'I should think not, indeed,' cried Banford indignantly.

At bed-time Banford said plaintively to March:

'You take my hot bottle up for me, Nellie, will you?'

'Yes, I'll do it,' said March, with the kind of willing unwillingness she so often showed towards her beloved but uncertain Jill.

The two women went upstairs. After a time March called from the top of the stairs: 'Good-night, Henry. I shan't be coming down. You'll see to the lamp and the fire, won't you?'

The next day Henry went about with the cloud on his brow and his young cub's face shut up tight. He was cogitating all the time. He had wanted March to marry him and go back to Canada with him. And he had been sure she would do it. Why he wanted her he didn't know. But he did want her. He had set his mind on her. And he was convulsed with a youth's fury at being thwarted. To be thwarted, to be thwarted! It made him so furious inside that he did not know what to do with himself. But he kept himself in hand. Because even now things might turn out differently. She might come over to him. Of course she might. It was her business to do so.

Things drew to a tension again towards evening. He and Banford had avoided each other all day. In fact, Banford went in to the little town by the 11.20 train. It was market day. She arrived back on the 4.25. Just as the night was falling Henry saw her little figure in a dark-blue coat and a dark-blue tam-o'-shanter hat crossing the first meadow from the station. He stood under one of the wild pear trees, with the old dead leaves round his feet. And he watched the little blue figure advancing persistently over the rough winter-ragged meadow. She had her arms full of parcels, and advanced slowly, frail thing she was, but with that devilish little certainty which he so detested in her. He stood invisible under the pear tree, watching her every step. And if looks could have affected her, she would have felt a log of iron on each of her ankles as she made her way forward. 'You're a nasty little thing, you are,' he was saying softly, across the distance. 'You're a nasty little thing. I hope you'll be paid back for all the harm you've done me for nothing. I hope you will—you nasty little thing. I hope you'll have to pay for it. You will, if wishes are anything. You nasty little creature that you are.'

She was toiling slowly up the slope. But if she had been slipping back at every step towards the Bottomless Pit, he would not have gone to help her with her parcels. Aha, there went March, striding with her long, land stride in her breeches and her short tunic! Striding downhill at a great pace, and even running a few steps now and then, in her great solicitude and desire to come to the rescue of the little Banford. The boy watched her with rage in his heart. See her leap a ditch, and run, run as if a house was on fire, just to get to that creeping, dark little object down there! So, the Banford just stood still and waited. And March strode up and took *all* the parcels except a bunch of yellow chrysanthemums. These the Banford still carried—yellow chrysanthemums!

'Yes, you look well, don't you?' he said softly into the dusk air. 'You look well, pottering up there with a bunch of flowers, you do. I'd make you eat them for your tea if you hug them so tight. And I'd give them you for breakfast again, I would. I'd give you flowers. Nothing but flowers.'

He watched the progress of the two women. He could hear their voices: March always outspoken and rather scolding in her tenderness, Banford murmuring rather vaguely. They were evidently good friends. He could not hear what they said till they came to the fence of the home meadow, which they must climb. Then he saw March manfully climbing over the bars with all her packages in her arms, and on the still air he heard Banford's fretful:

'Why don't you let me help you with the parcels?' She had a queer, plaintive hitch in her voice. Then came March's robust and reckless:

'Oh, I can manage. Don't you bother about me. You've all you can do to get yourself over.'

'Yes, that's all very well,' said Banford fretfully. 'You say, *Don't you bother about me*, and then all the while you feel injured because nobody thinks of you.'

'When do I feel injured?' said March.

'Always. You always feel injured. Now you're feeling injured because I won't have that boy to come and live on the farm.'

'I'm not feeling injured at all,' said March.

'I know you are. When he's gone you'll sulk over it. I know you will.'

'Shall I?' said March. 'We'll see.'

'Yes, we *shall* see, unfortunately. I can't think how you can make yourself so cheap. I can't *imagine* how you can lower yourself like it.'

'I haven't lowered myself,' said March.

'I don't know what you call it, then. Letting a boy like that come so cheeky and impudent and make a mug of you. I don't know what you think of yourself. How much respect do you think he's going to have for you afterwards? My word, I wouldn't be in your shoes, if you married him.'

'Of course you wouldn't. My boots are a good bit too big for you, and not half dainty enough,' said March, with rather a misfire sarcasm.

'I thought you had too much pride, really I did. A woman's got to hold herself high, especially with a youth like that. Why, he's impudent. Even the way he forced himself on us at the start.'

'We asked him to stay,' said March.

'Not till he'd almost forced us to. And then he's so cocky and self-assured. My word, he puts my back up. I simply can't imagine how you can let him treat you so cheaply.'

'I don't let him treat me cheaply,' said March. 'Don't you worry yourself, nobody's going to treat me cheaply. And even you aren't, either.' She had a tender defiance and a certain fire in her voice.

'Yes, it's sure to come back to me,' said Banford bitterly. 'That's always the end of it. I believe you only do it to spite me.'

They went now in silence up the steep, grassy slope and over the brow, through the gorse bushes. On the other side of the hedge the boy followed in the dusk, at some little distance. Now and then, through the huge ancient hedge of hawthorn, risen into trees, he saw the two dark figures creeping up the hill. As he came to the top of the slope he saw the homestead dark in the twilight, with a huge old pear tree leaning from the near gable, and a little yellow light twinkling in the small side windows of the kitchen. He heard the clink of the latch and saw the kitchen door open into light as the two women went indoors. So they were at home.

And so!–this was what they thought of him. It was rather in his nature to be a listener, so he was not at all surprised whatever he heard. The things people said about him always missed him personally. He was only rather surprised at the women's way with one another. And he disliked the Banford with an acid dislike. And he felt drawn to the March again. He felt again irresistibly drawn to her. He felt there was a secret bond, a secret thread between him and her, something very exclusive, which shut out everybody else and made him and her possess each other in secret.

He hoped again that she would have him. He hoped with his blood suddenly firing up that she would agree to marry him quite quickly: at Christmas, very likely. Christmas was not far off. He wanted, whatever else happened, to snatch her into a hasty marriage and a consummation with him. Then for the future, they could arrange later. But he hoped it would happen as he wanted it. He hoped that to-night she would stay a little while with him, after Banford had gone upstairs. He hoped he could touch her soft, creamy cheek, her strange, frightened face. He hoped he could look into her dilated, frightened dark eyes, quite near. He hoped he might even put his hand on her bosom and feel her soft breasts under her tunic. His heart beat deep and powerful as he thought of that. He wanted very much to do so. He wanted to make sure of her soft woman's breasts under her tunic. She always kept the brown linen coat buttoned so close up to her throat. It seemed to him like some perilous secret, that her soft woman's breasts must be buttoned up in that uniform. It seemed to him, moreover, that they were so much softer, tenderer, more lovely and lovable, shut up in that tunic, than were the Banford's breasts, under her soft blouses and chiffon dresses. The Banford would have little iron breasts, he said to himself. For all her frailty and fretfulness and delicacy, she would have tiny iron breasts. But March, under her crude, fast, workman's tunic, would have soft, white breasts, white and unseen. So he told himself, and his blood burned.

When he went into tea, he had a surprise. He appeared at the inner door, his face very ruddy and vivid and his blue eyes shining, dropping his head forward as he came in, in his usual way, and hesitating in the doorway to watch the inside of the room, keenly and cautiously, before he entered. He was wearing a long-sleeved waistcoat. His face seemed extraordinarily like a piece of the out-of-doors come indoors: as holly-berries do. In his second of pause in the doorway he took in the two women sitting at table, at opposite ends, saw them sharply. And to his amazement March was dressed in a dress of dull, green silk crape. His mouth came open in surprise. If she had suddenly grown a moustache he could not have been more surprised.

'Why,' he said, 'do you wear a dress, then?'

She looked up, flushing a deep rose colour, and twisting her mouth with a smile, said:

'Of course I do. What else do you expect me to wear but a dress?'

'A land girl's uniform, of course,' said he.

'Oh,' she cried, nonchalant, 'that's only for this dirty, mucky work about here.'

'Isn't it your proper dress, then?' he said.

'No, not indoors it isn't,' she said. But she was blushing all the time as she poured out his tea. He sat down in his chair at table, unable to take his eyes off her. Her dress was a perfectly simple slip of bluey-green crape, with a line of gold stitching round the top and round the sleeves, which came to the elbow. It was cut just plain and round at the top, and showed her white, soft throat. Her arms he knew, strong and firm muscled, for he had often seen her with her sleeves rolled up. But he looked her up and down, up and down.

Banford, at the other end of the table, said not a word, but piggled with the sardine on her plate. He had forgotten her existence. He just simply stared at March while he ate his bread and margarine in huge mouthfuls, forgetting even his tea.

'Well, I never knew anything make such a difference!' he murmured, across his mouthfuls.

'Oh, goodness!' cried March, blushing still more. 'I might be a pink monkey!'

And she rose quickly to her feet and took the tea-pot to the fire, to the kettle.

And as she crouched on the hearth with her green slip about her, the boy stared more wide-eyed than ever. Through the crape her woman's form seemed soft and womanly. And when she stood up and walked he saw her legs move soft within her modernly short skirt. She had on black silk stockings, and small patent shoes with little gold buckles.

No, she was another being. She was something quite different. Seeing her always in the hard-cloth breeches, wide on the hips, buttoned on the knee, strong as armour, and in the brown puttees and thick boots, it had never occurred to him that she had a woman's legs and feet. Now it came upon him. She had a woman's soft, skirted legs, and she was accessible. He blushed to the roots of his hair, shoved his nose in his tea-cup and drank his tea with a little noise that made Banford simply squirm: and strangely, suddenly he felt a man, no longer a youth. He felt a man, with all a man's grave weight of responsibility. A curious quietness and gravity came over his soul. He felt a man, quiet, with a little of the heaviness of male destiny upon him.

She was soft and accessible in her dress. The thought went home in him like an everlasting responsibility.

'Oh, for goodness' sake, say something, somebody,' cried Banford fretfully. 'It might be a funeral.' The boy looked at her, and she could not bear his face.

'A funeral!' said March, with a twisted smile. 'Why, that breaks my dream.'

Suddenly she had thought of Banford in the wood-box for a coffin.

'What, have you been dreaming of a wedding?' said Banford sarcastically.

'Must have been,' said March.

'Whose wedding?' asked the boy.

'I can't remember,' said March.

She was shy and rather awkward that evening, in spite of the fact that, wearing a dress, her bearing was much more subdued than in her uniform. She felt unpeeled and rather exposed. She felt almost improper.

They talked desultorily about Henry's departure next morning, and made the trivial arrangement. But of the matter on their minds, none of them spoke. They were rather quiet and friendly this evening; Banford had practically nothing to say. But inside herself she seemed still, perhaps kindly.

At nine o'clock March brought in the tray with the everlasting tea and a little cold meat which Banford had managed to procure. It was the last supper, so Banford did not want to be disagreeable. She felt a bit sorry for the boy, and felt she must be as nice as she could.

He wanted her to go to bed. She was usually the first. But she sat on in her chair under the lamp, glancing at her book now and then, and staring into the fire. A deep silence had come into the room. It was broken by March asking, in a rather small tone:

'What time is it, Jill?'

'Five past ten,' said Banford, looking at her wrist.

And then not a sound. The boy had looked up from the book he was holding between his knees. His rather wide, cat-shaped face had its obstinate look, his eyes were watchful.

'What about bed?' said March at last.

'I'm ready when you are,' said Banford.

'Oh, very well,' said March. 'I'll fill your bottle.'

She was as good as her word. When the hot-water bottle was ready, she lit a candle and went upstairs with it. Banford remained in her chair, listening acutely. March came downstairs again.

'There you are, then,' she said. 'Are you going up?'

'Yes, in a minute,' said Banford. But the minute passed, and she sat on in her chair under the lamp.

Henry, whose eyes were shining like a cat's as he watched from under his brows, and whose face seemed wider, more chubbed and cat-like with unalterable obstinacy, now rose to his feet to try his throw.

'I think I'll go and look if I can see the she-fox,' he said. 'She may be creeping round. Won't you come as well for a minute, Nellie, and see if we see anything?'

'Me!' cried March, looking up with her startled, wondering face.

'Yes. Come on,' he said. It was wonderful how soft and warm and coaxing his voice could be, how near. The very sound of it made Banford's blood boil. 'Come on for a minute,' he said, looking down into her uplifted, unsure face.

And she rose to her feet as if drawn up by his young, ruddy face that was looking down on her.

'I should think you're never going out at this time of night, Nellie!' cried Banford.

'Yes, just for a minute,' said the boy, looking round on her, and speaking with an odd, sharp yelp in his voice.

March looked from one to the other, as if confused, vague. Banford rose to her feet for battle.

'Why, it's ridiculous. It's bitter cold. You'll catch your death in that thin frock. And in those slippers. You're not going to do any such thing.'

There was a moment's pause. Banford turtled up like a little fighting cock, facing March and the boy.

'Oh, I don't think you need worry yourself,' he replied. 'A moment under the stars won't do anybody any damage. I'll get the rug off the sofa in the dining-room. You're coming, Nellie.'

His voice had so much anger and contempt and fury in it as he spoke to Banford: and so much tenderness and proud authority as he spoke to March, that the latter answered:

'Yes, I'm coming.'

And she turned with him to the door.

Banford, standing there in the middle of the room, suddenly burst into a long wail and a spasm of sobs. She covered her face with her poor, thin hands, and her thin shoulders shook in an agony of weeping. March looked back from the door.

'Jill!' she cried in a frantic tone, like someone just coming awake. And she seemed to start towards her darling.

But the boy had March's arm in his grip, and she could not move. She did not know why she could not move. It was as in a dream when the heart strains and the body cannot stir.

'Never mind,' said the boy softly. 'Let her cry. Let her cry. She will have to cry sooner or later. And the tears will relieve her feelings. They will do her good.'

So he drew March slowly through the doorway. But her last look was back to the poor little figure which stood in the middle of the room with covered face and thin shoulders shaken with bitter weeping.

In the dining-room he picked up the rug and said:

'Wrap yourself up in this.'

She obeyed—and they reached the kitchen door, he holding her soft and firm by the arm, though she did not know it. When she saw the night outside she started back.

'I must go back to Jill,' she said. 'I *must*! Oh yes, I must.'

Her tone sounded final. The boy let go of her and she turned indoors. But he seized her again and arrested her.

'Wait a minute,' he said. 'Wait a minute. Even if you go, you're not going yet.'

'Leave go! Leave go!' she cried. 'My place is at Jill's side. Poor little thing, she's sobbing her heart out.'

'Yes,' said the boy bitterly. 'And your heart too, and mine as well.'

'Your heart?' said March. He still gripped her and detained her.

'Isn't it as good as her heart?' he said. 'Or do you think it's not?'

'Your heart?' she said again, incredulous.

'Yes, mine! Mine! Do you think I haven't *got* a heart?' And with his hot grasp he took her hand and pressed it under his left breast. 'There's my heart,' he said, 'if you don't believe in it.'

It was wonder which made her attend. And then she felt the deep, heavy, powerful stroke of his heart, terrible, like something from beyond. It was like something from beyond, something awful from outside, signalling to her. And the signal paralysed her. It beat upon her very soul, and made her helpless. She forgot Jill. She could not think of Jill any more. She could not think of her. That terrible signalling from outside!

The boy put his arm round her waist.

'Come with me,' he said gently. 'Come and let us say what we've got to say.'

And he drew her outside, closed the door. And she went with him darkly down the garden path. That he should have a beating heart! And that he should have his arm round her, outside the blanket! She was too confused to think who he was or what he was.

He took her to a dark corner of the shed, where there was a tool-box with a lid, long and low.

'We'll sit here a minute,' he said.

And obediently she sat down by his side.

'Give me your hand,' he said.

She gave him both her hands, and he held them between his own. He was young, and it made him tremble.

'You'll marry me. You'll marry me before I go back, won't you?' he pleaded.

'Why, aren't we both a pair of fools?' she said.

He had put her in the corner, so that she should not look out and see the lighted window of the house across the dark garden. He tried to keep her all there inside the shed with him.

'In what way a pair of fools?' he said. 'If you go back to Canada with me, I've got a job and a good wage waiting for me, and it's a nice place, near the mountains. Why shouldn't you marry me? Why shouldn't we marry? I should like to have you there with me. I should like to feel I'd got somebody there, at the back of me, all my life.'

'You'd easily find somebody else who'd suit you better,' she said.

'Yes, I might easily find another girl. I know I could. But not one I really wanted. I've never met one I really wanted for good. You see, I'm thinking of all my life. If I marry, I want to feel it's for all my life. Other girls: well, they're just girls, nice enough to go a walk with now and then. Nice enough for a bit of play. But when I think of my life, then I should be very sorry to have to marry one of them, I should indeed.'

'You mean they wouldn't make you a good wife.'

'Yes, I mean that. But I don't mean they wouldn't do their duty by me. I mean—I don't know what I mean. Only when I think of my life, and of you, then the two things go together.'

'And what if they didn't?' she said, with her odd, sardonic touch.

'Well, I think they would.'

They sat for some time silent. He held her hands in his, but he did not make love to her. Since he had realised that she was a woman, and vulnerable, accessible, a certain heaviness had possessed his soul. He did not want to make love to her. He shrank from any such performance, almost with fear. She was a woman, and vulnerable, accessible to him finally, and he held back from that which was ahead, almost with dread. It was a kind of darkness he knew he would enter finally, but of which he did not want as yet even to think. She was the woman, and he was responsible for the strange vulnerability he had suddenly realised in her.

'No,' she said at last, 'I'm a fool. I know I'm a fool.'

'What for?' he asked.

'To go on with this business.'

'Do you mean me?' he asked.

'No, I mean myself. I'm making a fool of myself, and a big one.'

'Why, because you don't want to marry me, really?'

'Oh, I don't know whether I'm against it, as a matter of fact. That's just it. I don't know.'

He looked at her in the darkness, puzzled. He did not in the least know what she meant.

'And don't you know whether you like to sit here with me this minute or not?' he asked.

'No, I don't really. I don't know whether I wish I was somewhere else, or whether I like being here. I don't know, really.'

'Do you wish you were with Miss Banford? Do you wish you'd gone to bed with her?' he asked, as a challenge.

She waited a long time before she answered.

'No,' she said at last. 'I don't wish that.'

'And do you think you would spend all your life with her—when your hair goes white, and you are old?' he said.

'No,' she said, without much hesitation. 'I don't see Jill and me two old women together.'

'And don't you think, when I'm an old man and you're an old woman, we might be together still, as we are now?' he said.

'Well, not as we are now,' she replied. 'But I could imagine—no, I can't. I can't imagine you an old man. Besides, it's dreadful!'

'What, to be an old man?'

'Yes, of course.'

'Not when the time comes,' he said. 'But it hasn't come. Only it will. And when it does, I should like to think you'd be there as well.'

'Sort of old age pensions,' she said dryly.

Her kind of witless humour always startled him. He never knew what she meant. Probably she didn't quite know herself.

'No,' he said, hurt.

'I don't know why you harp on old age,' she said. 'I'm not ninety.'

'Did anybody ever say you were?' he asked, offended.

They were silent for some time, pulling different ways in the silence.

'I don't want you to make fun of me,' he said.

'Don't you?' she replied, enigmatic.

'No, because just this minute I'm serious. And when I'm serious, I believe in not making fun of it.'

'You mean nobody else must make fun of you,' she replied.

'Yes, I mean that. And I mean I don't believe in making fun of it myself. When it comes over me so that I'm serious, then–there it is, I don't want it to be laughed at.'

She was silent for some time. Then she said, in a vague, almost pained voice: 'No, I'm not laughing at you.'

A hot wave rose in his heart.

'You believe me, do you?' he asked.

'Yes, I believe you,' she replied, with a twang of her old, tired nonchalance, as if she gave in because she was tired. But he didn't care. His heart was hot and clamorous.

'So you agree to marry me before I go?–perhaps at Christmas?'

'Yes, I agree.'

'There!' he exclaimed. 'That's settled it.'

And he sat silent, unconscious, with all the blood burning in all his veins, like fire in all the branches and twigs of him. He only pressed her two hands to his chest, without knowing. When the curious passion began to die down, he seemed to come awake to the world.

'We'll go in, shall we?' he said: as if he realised it was cold.

She rose without answering.

'Kiss me before we go, now you've said it,' he said.

And he kissed her gently on the mouth, with a young, frightened kiss. It made her feel so young, too, and frightened, and wondering: and tired, tired, as if she were going to sleep.

They went indoors. And in the sitting-room, there, crouched by the fire like a queer little witch, was Banford. She looked round with reddened eyes as they entered, but did not rise. He thought she looked frightening, unnatural, crouching there and looking round at them. Evil he thought her look was, and he crossed his fingers.

Banford saw the ruddy, elate face on the youth: he seemed strangely tall and bright and looming. And March had a delicate look on her face; she wanted to hide her face, to screen it, to let it not be seen.

'You've come at last,' said Banford uglily.

'Yes, we've come,' said he.

'You've been long enough for anything,' she said.

'Yes, we have. We've settled it. We shall marry as soon as possible,' he replied.

'Oh, you've settled it, have you! Well, I hope you won't live to repent it,' said Banford.

'I hope so too,' he replied.

'Are you going to bed *now*, Nellie?' said Banford.

'Yes, I'm going now.'

'Then for goodness' sake come along.'

March looked at the boy. He was glancing with his very bright eyes at her and at Banford. March looked at him wistfully. She wished she could stay with him. She wished she had married him already, and it was all over. For oh, she felt suddenly so safe with him. She felt so strangely safe and peaceful in his presence. If only she could sleep in his shelter, and not with Jill. She felt afraid of Jill. In her dim, tender state, it was agony to have to go with Jill and sleep with her. She wanted the boy to save her. She looked again at him.

And he, watching with bright eyes, divined something of what she felt. It puzzled and distressed him that she must go with Jill.

'I shan't forget what you've promised,' he said, looking clear into her eyes, right into her eyes, so that he seemed to occupy all herself with his queer, bright look.

She smiled to him faintly, gently. She felt safe again – safe with him.

But in spite of all the boy's precautions, he had a setback. The morning he was leaving the farm he got March to accompany him to the market-town, about six miles away, where they went to the registrar and had their names stuck up as two people who were going to marry. He was to come at Christmas, and the wedding was to take place then. He hoped in the spring to be able to take March back to Canada with him, now the war was really over. Though he was so young, he had saved some money.

'You never have to be without *some* money at the back of you, if you can help it,' he said.

So she saw him off in the train that was going West: his camp was on Salisbury Plain. And with big, dark eyes she watched him go, and it seemed as if everything real in life was retreating as the train retreated with his queer, chubby, ruddy face, that seemed so broad across the cheeks, and which never seemed to change its expression, save when a cloud of sulky anger hung on the brow, or the bright eyes fixed themselves in their stare. This was what happened now. He leaned there out of the carriage window as the train drew off, saying goodbye and staring back at her, but his face quite unchanged. There was no emotion on his face. Only his eyes tightened and became fixed and intent in their watching like a cat's when suddenly she sees something and stares. So the boy's eyes stared fixedly as the train drew away, and she was left feeling intensely forlorn. Failing his physical presence, she seemed to have nothing of him. And she had nothing of anything. Only his face was fixed in her mind: the full, ruddy, unchanging cheeks, and the straight snout of a nose and the two eyes staring above. All she could remember was how he suddenly wrinkled his nose when he laughed, as a puppy does when he is playfully growling. But him, himself, and what he was – she knew nothing, she had nothing of him when he left her.

On the ninth day after he had left her he received this letter.

Dear Henry,

I have been over it all again in my mind, this business of me and you, and it seems to me impossible. When you aren't there I see what a fool I am. When you are there you seem to blind me to things as they actually are. You make me see things all unreal, and I don't know what. Then when I am alone again with Jill I seem to come to my own senses and realise what a fool I am making of myself, and how I am treating you unfairly. Because it must be unfair to you for me to go on with this affair when I can't feel in my heart that I really love you. I know people talk a lot of stuff and nonsense about love, and I don't want to do that. I want to keep to plain facts and act in a sensible way. And that seems to be what I'm not doing. I don't see on what grounds I am going to marry you. I know I am not head over heels in love with you, as I have fancied myself to be with fellows when I was a young fool of a girl. You are an absolute stranger to me, and it seems to me you will always be one. So on what grounds am I going to marry you? When I think of Jill, she is ten times more real to me. I know her and I'm awfully fond of her, and I hate myself for a beast if I ever hurt her little finger. We have a life together. And even if it can't last for ever, it is a life while it does last. And it might last as long as either of us lives. Who knows how long we've got to live? She is a

The Fox

delicate little thing, perhaps nobody but me knows how delicate. And as for me, I feel I might fall down the well any day. What I don't seem to see at all is you. When I think of what I've been and what I've done with you, I'm afraid I am a few screws loose. I should be sorry to think that softening of the brain is setting in so soon, but that is what it seems like. You are such an absolute stranger, and so different from what I'm used to, and we don't seem to have a thing in common. As for love, the very word seems impossible. I know what love means even in Jill's case, and I know that in this affair with you it's an absolute impossibility. And then going to Canada. I'm sure I must have been clean off my chump when I promised such a thing. It makes me feel fairly frightened of myself. I feel I might do something really silly that I wasn't responsible for–and end my days in a lunatic asylum. You may think that's all I'm fit for after the way I've gone on, but it isn't a very nice thought for me. Thank goodness Jill is here, and her being here makes me feel sane again, else I don't know what I might do; I might have an accident with the gun one evening. I love Jill, and she makes me feel safe and sane, with her loving anger against me for being such a fool. Well, what I want to say is, won't you let us cry the whole thing off? I can't marry you, and really, I won't do such a thing if it seems to me wrong. It is all a great mistake. I've made a complete fool of myself, and all I can do is to apologise to you and ask you please to forget it, and please to take no further notice of me. Your fox-skin is nearly ready, and seems all right. I will post it to you if you will let me know if this address is still right, and if you will accept my apology for the awful and lunatic way I have behaved with you, and then let the matter rest.

Jill sends her kindest regards. Her mother and father are staying with us over Christmas.

Yours very sincerely,

ELLEN MARCH.

The boy read this letter in camp as he was cleaning his kit. He set his teeth, and for a moment went almost pale, yellow round the eyes with fury. He said nothing and saw nothing and felt nothing but a livid rage that was quite unreasoning. Balked! Balked again! Balked! He wanted the woman, he had fixed like doom upon having her. He felt that was his doom, his destiny, and his reward, to have this woman. She was his heaven and hell on earth, and he would have none elsewhere. Sightless with rage and thwarted madness he got through the morning. Save that in his mind he was lurking and scheming towards an issue, he would have committed some insane act. Deep in himself he felt like roaring and howling and gnashing his teeth and breaking things. But he was too intelligent. He knew society was on top of him, and he must scheme. So with his teeth bitten together, and his nose curiously slightly lifted, like some creature that is vicious, and his eyes fixed and staring, he went through the morning's affairs drunk with anger and suppression. In his mind was one thing–Banford. He took no heed of all March's outpouring: none. One thorn rankled, stuck in his mind. Banford. In his mind, in his soul, in his whole being, one thorn rankling to insanity. And he would have to get it out. He would have to get the thorn of Banford out of his life, if he died for it.

With this one fixed idea in his mind, he went to ask for twenty-four hours' leave of absence. He knew it was not due to him. His consciousness was supernaturally keen. He knew where he must go–he must go to the captain. But how could he get at the captain? In that great camp of wooden huts and tents he had no idea where his captain was.

But he went to the officers' canteen. There was his captain standing talking with three other officers. Henry stood in the doorway at attention.

'May I speak to Captain Berryman?' The captain was Cornish like himself.

'What do you want?' called the captain.

'May I speak to you, Captain?'

'What do you want?' replied the captain, not stirring from among his group of fellow officers.

Henry watched his superior for a minute without speaking.

'You won't refuse me, sir, will you?' he asked gravely.

'It depends what it is.'

'Can I have twenty-four hours' leave?'

'No, you've no business to ask.'

'I know I haven't. But I must ask you.'

'You've had your answer.'

'Don't send me away, Captain.'

There was something strange about the boy as he stood there so everlasting in the doorway. The Cornish captain felt the strangeness at once, and eyed him shrewdly.

'Why, what's afoot?' he said, curious.

'I'm in trouble about something. I must go to Blewbury,' said the boy.

'Blewbury, eh? After the girls?'

'Yes, it is a woman, Captain.' And the boy, as he stood there with his head reaching forward a little, went suddenly terribly pale, or yellow, and his lips seemed to give off pain. The captain saw and paled a little also. He turned aside.

'Go on, then,' he said. 'But for God's sake don't cause any trouble of any sort.'

'I won't, Captain, thank you.'

He was gone. The captain, upset, took a gin and bitters. Henry managed to hire a bicycle. It was twelve o'clock when he left the camp. He had sixty miles of wet and muddy crossroads to ride. But he was in the saddle and down the road without a thought of food.

At the farm, March was busy with a work she had had some time in hand. A bunch of Scotch fir trees stood at the end of the open shed, on a little bank where ran the fence between two of the gorse-shaggy meadows. The farthest of these trees was dead—it had died in the summer, and stood with all its needles brown and sere in the air. It was not a very big tree. And it was absolutely dead. So March determined to have it, although they were not allowed to cut any of the timber. But it would make such splendid firing, in these days of scarce fuel.

She had been giving a few stealthy chops at the trunk for a week or more, every now and then hacking away for five minutes, low down, near the ground, so no one should notice. She had not tried the saw, it was such hard work, alone. Now the tree stood with a great yawning gap in his base, perched, as it were, on one sinew, and ready to fall. But he did not fall.

It was late in the damp December afternoon, with cold mists creeping out of the woods and up the hollows, and darkness waiting to sink in from above. There was a bit of yellowness where the sun was fading away beyond the low woods of the distance. March took her axe and went to the tree. The small thud-thud of her blows resounded rather ineffectual about the wintry homestead. Banford came out wearing her thick coat, but with no hat on her head, so that her thin, bobbed hair blew on the uneasy wind that sounded in the pines and in the wood.

'What I'm afraid of,' said Banford, 'is that it will fall on the shed and we sh'll have another job repairing that.'

'Oh, I don't think so,' said March, straightening herself and wiping her arm over her hot brow. She was flushed red, her eyes were very wide open and queer, her upper lip lifted away from her two white, front teeth with a curious, almost rabbit look.

A little stout man in a black overcoat and a bowler hat came pottering across the yard. He had a pink face and a white beard and smallish, pale-blue eyes. He was not very old, but nervy, and he walked with little short steps.

'What do you think, father?' said Banford. 'Don't you think it might hit the shed in falling?'

'Shed, no!' said the old man. 'Can't hit the shed. Might as well say the fence.'

'The fence doesn't matter,' said March, in her high voice.

'Wrong as usual, am I!' said Banford, wiping her straying hair from her eyes.

The tree stood as it were on one spelch of itself, leaning, and creaking in the wind. It grew on the bank of a little dry ditch between the two meadows. On the top of the bank straggled one fence, running to the bushes up-hill. Several trees clustered there in the corner of the field near the shed and near the gate which led into the yard. Towards this gate, horizontal across the weary meadows, came the grassy, rutted approach from the high road. There trailed another rickety fence, long split poles joining the short, thick, wide-apart uprights. The three people stood at the back of the tree, in the corner of the shed meadow, just above the yard gate. The house, with its two gables and its porch, stood tidy in a little grassed garden across the yard. A little, stout, rosy-faced woman in a little red woollen shoulder shawl had come and taken her stand in the porch.

'Isn't it down yet,' she cried, in a high little voice.

'Just thinking about it,' called her husband. His tone towards the two girls was always rather mocking and satirical. March did not want to go on with her hitting while he was there. As for him, he wouldn't lift a stick from the ground if he could help it, complaining, like his daughter, of rheumatics in his shoulder. So the three stood there a moment silent in the cold afternoon, in the bottom corner near the yard.

They heard the far-off taps of a gate, and craned to look. Away across, on the green horizontal approach, a figure was just swinging on to a bicycle again, and lurching up and down over the grass, approaching.

'Why, it's one of our boys—it's Jack,' said the old man.

'Can't be,' said Banford.

March craned her head to look. She alone recognised the khaki figure. She flushed, but said nothing.

'No, it isn't Jack, I don't think,' said the old man, staring with little round blue eyes under his white lashes.

In another moment the bicycle lurched into sight, and the rider dropped off at the gate. It was Henry, his face wet and red and spotted with mud. He was altogether a muddy sight.

'Oh!' cried Banford, as if afraid. 'Why, it's Henry!'

'What!' muttered the old man. He had a thick, rapid, muttering way of speaking, and was slightly deaf. 'What? What? Who is it? Who is it, do you say? That young fellow? That young fellow of Nellie's? Oh! Oh!' And the satiric smile came on his pink face and white eyelashes.

Henry, pushing the wet hair off his steaming brow, had caught sight of them and heard what the old man said. His hot, young face seemed to flame in the cold light.

'Oh, are you all there!' he said, giving his sudden, puppy's little laugh. He was so hot and dazed with cycling he hardly knew where he was. He leaned the bicycle against the fence and climbed over into the corner on to the bank, without going into the yard.

'Well, I must say, we weren't expecting *you*,' said Banford laconically.

'No, I suppose not,' said he, looking at March.

She stood aside, slack, with one knee drooped and the axe resting its head loosely on the ground. Her eyes were wide and vacant, and her upper lip lifted from her teeth in that helpless, fascinated rabbit look. The moment she saw his glowing, red face it was all over with her. She was as helpless as if she had been bound. The moment she saw the way his head seemed to reach forward.

'Well, who is it? Who is it, anyway?' asked the smiling, satiric old man in his muttering voice.

'Why, Mr Grenfel, whom you've heard us tell about, father,' said Banford coldly.

'Heard you tell about, I should think so. Heard of nothing else practically,' muttered the elderly man, with his queer little jeering smile on his face. 'How do you do,' he added, suddenly reaching out his hand to Henry.

The boy shook hands just as startled. Then the two men fell apart.

'Cycled over from Salisbury Plain, have you?' asked the old man.

'Yes.'

'Hm! Longish ride. How long d'it take you, eh? Some time, eh? Several hours, I suppose.'

'About four.'

'Eh? Four! Yes, I should have thought so. When are you going back, then?'

'I've got till to-morrow evening.'

'Till to-morrow evening, eh? Yes. Hm! Girls weren't expecting you, were they?'

And the old man turned his pale-blue, round little eyes under their white lashes mockingly towards the girls. Henry also looked round. He had become a little awkward. He looked at March, who was still staring away into the distance as if to see where the cattle were. Her hand was on the pommel of the axe, whose head rested loosely on the ground.

'What were you doing there?' he asked in his soft, courteous voice. 'Cutting a tree down?'

March seemed not to hear, as if in a trance.

'Yes,' said Banford. 'We've been at it for over a week.'

'Oh! And have you done it all by yourselves then?'

'Nellie's done it all, I've done nothing,' said Banford.

'Really! You must have worked quite hard,' he said, addressing himself in a curious gentle tone direct to March. She did not answer, but remained half averted staring away towards the woods above as if in a trance.

'*Nellie!*' cried Banford sharply. 'Can't you answer?'

'What—me?' cried March, starting round and looking from one to the other. 'Did anyone speak to me?'

'Dreaming!' muttered the old man, turning aside to smile. 'Must be in love, eh, dreaming in the day-time!'

'Did you say anything to me?' said March, looking at the boy as from a strange distance, her eyes wide and doubtful, her face delicately flushed.

'I said you must have worked hard at the tree,' he replied courteously.

'Oh, that! Bit by bit. I thought it would have come down by now.'

'I'm thankful it hasn't come down in the night, to frighten us to death,' said Banford.

'Let me just finish it for you, shall I?' said the boy.

March slanted the axe-shaft in his direction.

'Would you like to?' she said.

'Yes, if you wish it,' he said.

'Oh, I'm thankful when the thing's down, that's all,' she replied, nonchalant.

'Which way is it going to fall?' said Banford. 'Will it hit the shed?'

'No, it won't hit the shed,' he said. 'I should think it will fall there–quite clear. Though it might give a twist and catch the fence.'

'Catch the fence!' cried the old man. 'What, catch the fence! When it's leaning at that angle? Why, it's farther off than the shed. It won't catch the fence.'

'No,' said Henry, 'I don't suppose it will. It has plenty of room to fall quite clear, and I suppose it will fall clear.'

'Won't tumble backwards on top of *us*, will it?' asked the old man, sarcastic.

'No, it won't do that,' said Henry, taking off his short overcoat and his tunic. 'Ducks! Ducks! Go back!'

A line of four brown-speckled ducks led by a brown-and-green drake were stemming away downhill from the upper meadow, coming like boats running on a ruffled sea, cockling their way top speed downwards towards the fence and towards the little group of people, and cackling as excitedly as if they brought news of the Spanish Armada.

'Silly things! Silly things!' cried Banford, going forward to turn them off. But they came eagerly towards her, opening their yellow-green beaks and quacking as if they were so excited to say something.

'There's no food. There's nothing here. You must wait a bit,' said Banford to them. 'Go away. Go away. Go round to the yard.'

They didn't go, so she climbed the fence to swerve them round under the gate and into the yard. So off they waggled in an excited string once more, wagging their rumps like the stems of little gondolas, ducking under the bar of the gate. Banford stood on the top of the bank, just over the fence, looking down on the other three.

Henry looked up at her, and met her queer, round-pupilled, weak eyes staring behind her spectacles. He was perfectly still. He looked away, up at the weak, leaning tree. And as he looked into the sky, like a huntsman who is watching a flying bird, he thought to himself: 'If the tree falls in just such a way, and spins just so much as it falls, then the branch there will strike her exactly as she stands on top of that bank.'

He looked at her again. She was wiping the hair from her brow again, with that perpetual gesture. In his heart he had decided her death. A terrible still force seemed in him, and a power that was just his. If he turned even a hair's breadth in the wrong direction, he would lose the power.

'Mind yourself, Miss Banford,' he said. And his heart held perfectly still, in the terrible pure will that she should not move.

'Who, me, mind myself?' she cried, her father's jeering tone in her voice. 'Why, do you think you might hit me with the axe?'

'No, it's just possible the tree might, though,' he answered soberly. But the tone of his voice seemed to her to imply that he was only being falsely solicitous, and trying to make her move because it was his will to move her.

'Absolutely impossible,' she said.

He heard her. But he held himself icy still, lest he should lose his power.

'No, it's just possible. You'd better come down this way.'

'Oh, all right. Let us see some crack Canadian tree-felling,' she retorted.

'Ready, then,' he said, taking the axe, looking round to see he was clear.

There was a moment of pure, motionless suspense, when the world seemed to stand still. Then suddenly his form seemed to flash up enormously tall and fearful, he gave two swift, flashing blows, in immediate succession, the tree was severed, turning slowly, spinning strangely in the air and coming down like a sudden darkness on the earth. No one saw what was happening except himself. No one heard the strange little cry which the Banford gave as the dark end of the bough swooped down, down on her. No one saw her crouch a little and receive the blow on the back of the neck. No one saw her flung outwards and laid, a little twitching heap, at the foot of the fence. No one except the boy. And he watched with intense bright eyes, as he would watch a wild goose he had shot. Was it winged or dead? Dead!

Immediately he gave a loud cry. Immediately March gave a wild shriek that went far, far down the afternoon. And the father started a strange bellowing sound.

The boy leapt the fence and ran to the fringe. The back of the neck and head was a mass of blood, of horror. He turned it over. The body was quivering with little convulsions. But she was dead really. He knew it, that it was so. He knew it in his soul and his blood. The inner necessity of his life was fulfilling itself, it was he who was to live. The thorn was drawn out of his bowels. So he put her down gently. She was dead.

He stood up. March was standing there petrified and absolutely motionless. Her face was dead white, her eyes big black pools. The old man was scrambling horribly over the fence.

'I'm afraid it's killed her,' said the boy.

The old man was making curious, blubbering noises as he huddled over the fence. 'What!' cried March, starting electric.

'Yes, I'm afraid,' repeated the boy.

March was coming forward. The boy was over the fence before she reached it.

'What do you say, killed her?' she asked in a sharp voice.

'I'm afraid so,' he answered softly.

She went still whiter, fearful. The two stood facing one another. Her black eyes gazed on him with the last look of resistance. And then in a last agonised failure she began to grizzle, to cry in a shivery little fashion of a child that doesn't want to cry, but which is beaten from within, and gives that little first shudder of sobbing which is not yet weeping, dry and fearful.

He had won. She stood there absolutely helpless, shuddering her dry sobs and her mouth trembling rapidly. And then, as in a child, with a little crash came the tears and the blind agony of sightless weeping. She sank down on the grass, and sat there with her hands on her breast and her face lifted in sightless, convulsed weeping. He stood above her, looking down on her, mute, pale, and everlasting seeming. He never moved, but looked down on her. And among all the torture of the scene, the torture of his own heart and bowels, he was glad, he had won.

After a long time he stooped to her and took her hands.

'Don't cry,' he said softly. 'Don't cry.'

She looked up at him with tears running from her eyes, a senseless look of helplessness and submission. So she gazed on him as if sightless, yet looking up to him. She would never leave him again. He had won her. And he knew it and was glad, because he wanted her for his life. His life must have her. And now he had won her. It was what his life must have.

But if he had won her, he had not yet got her. They were married at Christmas as he had planned, and he got again ten days' leave. They went to Cornwall, to his own village, on the sea. He realised that it was awful for her to be at the farm any more.

But though she belonged to him, though she lived in his shadow, as if she could not be away from him, she was not happy. She did not want to leave him: and yet she did not feel free with him. Everything round her seemed to watch her, seemed to press on her. He had won her, he had her with him, she was his wife. And she–she belonged to him, she knew it. But she was not glad. And he was still foiled. He realised that though he was married to her and possessed her in every possible way, apparently, and though she *wanted* him to possess her, she wanted it, she wanted nothing else, now, still he did not quite succeed.

Something was missing. Instead of her soul swaying with new life, it seemed to droop, to bleed, as if it were wounded. She would sit for a long time with her hand in his, looking away at the sea. And in her dark, vacant eyes was a sort of wound, and her face looked a little peaked. If he spoke to her, she would turn to him with a faint new smile, the strange, quivering little smile of a woman who has died in the old way of love, and can't quite rise to the new way. She still felt she ought to *do* something, to strain herself in some direction. And there was nothing to do, and no direction in which to strain herself. And she could not quite accept the submergence which his new love put upon her. If she was in love, she ought to *exert* herself, in some way, loving. She felt the weary need of our day to *exert* herself in love. But she knew that in fact she must no more exert herself in love. He would not have the love which exerted itself towards him. It made his brow go black. No, he wouldn't let her exert her love towards him. No, she had to be passive, to acquiesce, and to be submerged under the surface of love. She had to be like the seaweeds she saw as she peered down from the boat, swaying forever delicately under water, with all their delicate fibrils put tenderly out upon the flood, sensitive, utterly sensitive and receptive within the shadowy sea, and never, never rising and looking forth above water while they lived. Never. Never looking forth from the water until they died, only then washing, corpses, upon the surface. But while they lived, always submerged, always beneath the wave. Beneath the wave they might have powerful roots, stronger than iron; they might be tenacious and dangerous in their soft waving within the flood. Beneath the water they might be stronger, more indestructible than resistant oak trees are on land. But it was always under-water, always under-water. And she, being a woman, must be like that.

And she had been so used to the very opposite. She had had to take all the thought for love and for life, and all the responsibility. Day after day she had been responsible for the coming day, for the coming year: for her dear Jill's health and happiness and well-being. Verily, in her own small way, she had felt herself responsible for the well-being of the world. And this had been her great stimulant, this grand feeling that, in her own small sphere, she was responsible for the well-being of the world.

And she had failed. She knew that, even in her small way, she had failed. She had failed to satisfy her own feeling of responsibility. It was so difficult. It seemed so grand and easy at first. And the more you tried, the more difficult it became. It had seemed so easy to make one beloved creature happy. And the more you tried, the worse the failure. It was terrible. She had been all her life reaching, reaching, and what she reached for seemed so near, until she had stretched to her utmost limit. And then it was always beyond her.

Always beyond her, vaguely, unrealisably beyond her, and she was left with nothingness at last. The life she reached for, the happiness she reached for, the well-being she reached for all slipped back, became unreal, the farther she stretched her hand. She wanted some goal, some finality–and there was none.

Always this ghastly reaching, reaching, striving for something that might be just beyond. Even to make Jill happy. She was glad Jill was dead. For she had realised that she could never make her happy. Jill would always be fretting herself thinner and thinner, weaker and weaker. Her pains grew worse instead of less. It would be so for ever. She was glad she was dead.

And if Jill had married a man it would have been just the same. The woman striving, striving to make the man happy, striving within her own limits for the well-being of her world. And always achieving failure. Little, foolish successes in money or in ambition. But at the very point where she most wanted success, in the anguished effort to make some one beloved human being happy and perfect, there the failure was almost catastrophic. You wanted to make your beloved happy, and his happiness seemed always achievable. If only you did just this, that and the other. And you did this, that, and the other, in all good faith, and every time the failure became a little more ghastly. You could love yourself to ribbons and strive and strain yourself to the bone, and things would go from bad to worse, bad to worse, as far as happiness went. The awful mistake of happiness.

Poor March, in her good-will and her responsibility, she had strained herself till it seemed to her that the whole of life and everything was only a horrible abyss of nothingness. The more you reached after the fatal flower of happiness, which trembles so blue and lovely in a crevice just beyond your grasp, the more fearfully you become aware of the ghastly and awful gulf of the precipice below you, into which you will inevitably plunge, as into the bottomless pit, if you reach any farther. You pluck flower after flower—it is never *the* flower. The flower itself—its calyx is a horrible gulf, it is the bottomless pit.

That is the whole history of the search for happiness, whether it be your own or somebody else's that you want to win. It ends, and it always ends, in the ghastly sense of the bottomless nothingness into which you will inevitably fall if you strain any farther.

And women?—what goal can any woman conceive, except happiness? Just happiness for herself and the whole world. That, and nothing else. And so, she assumes the responsibility and set off towards her goal. She can see it there, at the foot of the rainbow. Or she can see it a little way beyond, in the blue distance. Not far, not far.

But the end of the rainbow is a bottomless gulf down which you can fall forever without arriving, and the blue distance is a void pit which can swallow you and all your efforts into its emptiness, and still be no emptier. You and all your efforts. So, the illusion of attainable happiness!

Poor March, she had set off so wonderfully towards the blue goal. And the farther and farther she had gone, the more fearful had become the realisation of emptiness. An agony, an insanity at last.

She was glad it was over. She was glad to sit on the shore and look westwards over the sea, and know the great strain had ended. She would never strain for love and happiness any more. And Jill was safely dead. Poor Jill, poor Jill. It must be sweet to be dead.

For her own part, death was not her destiny. She would have to leave her destiny to the boy. But then, the boy. He wanted more than that. He wanted her to give herself without defences, to sink and become submerged in him. And she—she wanted to sit still, like a woman on the last milestone, and watch. She wanted to see, to know, to understand. She wanted to be alone: with him at her side.

And he! He did not want her to watch any more, to see any more, to understand any more. He wanted to veil her woman's spirit, as Orientals veil the woman's face. He wanted her to commit herself to him, and to put her independent spirit to sleep. He wanted to take away from her all her effort, all that seemed her very *raison d'être*. He wanted to make her submit, yield, blindly pass away out of all her strenuous consciousness. He wanted to take away her consciousness, and make her just his woman. Just his woman.

And she was so tired, so tired, like a child that wants to go to sleep, but which fights against sleep as if sleep were death. She seemed to stretch her eyes wider in the obstinate effort and tension of keeping awake. She *would* keep awake. She *would* know. She *would* consider and judge and decide. She *would* have the reins of her own life between her own hands. She *would* be an independent woman to the last. But she was so tired, so tired of everything. And sleep seemed near. And there was such rest in the boy.

Yet there, sitting in a niche of the high, wild cliffs of West Cornwall, looking over the westward sea, she stretched her eyes wider and wider. Away to the West, Canada, America. She *would* know and she *would* see what was ahead. And the boy, sitting beside her, staring down at the gulls, had a cloud between his brows and the strain of discontent in his eyes. He wanted her asleep, at peace in him. He wanted her at peace, asleep in him. And *there* she was, dying with the strain of her own wakefulness. Yet she would not sleep: no, never. Sometimes he thought bitterly that he ought to have left her. He ought never to have killed Banford. He should have left Banford and March to kill one another.

But that was only impatience: and he knew it. He was waiting, waiting to go West. He was aching almost in torment to leave England, to go West, to take March away. To leave this shore! He believed that as they crossed the seas, as they left this England which he so hated, because in some way it seemed to have stung him with poison, she would go to sleep. She would close her eyes at last and give in to him.

And then he would have her, and he would have his own life at last. He chafed, feeling he hadn't got his own life. He would never have it till she yielded and slept in him. Then he would have all his own life as a young man and a male, and she would have all her own life as a woman and a female. There would be no more of this awful straining. She would not be a man any more, an independent woman with a man's responsibility. Nay, even the responsibility for her own soul she would have to commit to him. He knew it was so, and obstinately held out against her, waiting for the surrender.

'You'll feel better when once we get over the seas to Canada over there,' he said to her as they sat among the rocks on the cliff.

She looked away to the sea's horizon, as if it were not real. Then she looked round at him, with the strained, strange look of a child that is struggling against sleep.

'Shall I?' she said.

'Yes,' he answered quietly.

And her eyelids dropped with the slow motion, sleep weighing them unconscious. But she pulled them open again to say:

'Yes, I may. I can't tell. I can't tell what it will be like over there.'

'If only we could go soon!' he said, with pain in his voice.

D.H. LAWRENCE

THE WHITE PEACOCK

PART I

I

THE PEOPLE OF NETHERMERE

I stood watching the shadowy fish slide through the gloom of the millpond. They were grey, descendants of the silvery things that had darted away from the monks, in the young days when the valley was lusty. The whole place was gathered in the musing of old age. The thick-piled trees on the far shore were too dark and sober to dally with the sun; the weeds stood crowded and motionless. Not even a little wind flickered the willows of the islets. The water lay softly, intensely still. Only the thin stream falling through the millrace murmured to itself of the tumult of life which had once quickened the valley.

I was almost startled into the water from my perch on the alder roots by a voice saying:

'Well, what is there to look at?' My friend was a young farmer, stoutly built, brown-eyed, with a naturally fair skin burned dark and freckled in patches. He laughed, seeing me start, and looked down at me with lazy curiosity.

'I was thinking the place seemed old, brooding over its past.'

He looked at me with a lazy indulgent smile, and lay down on his back on the bank, saying:

'It's all right for a doss—here.'

'Your life is nothing else but a doss. I shall laugh when somebody jerks you awake,' I replied.

He smiled comfortably and put his hands over his eyes because of the light.

'Why shall you laugh?' he drawled.

'Because you'll be amusing,' said I.

We were silent for a long time, when he rolled over and began to poke with his finger in the bank.

'I thought,' he said in his leisurely fashion, 'there was some cause for all this buzzing.'

I looked, and saw that he had poked out an old, papery nest of those pretty field bees which seem to have dipped their tails into bright amber dust. Some agitated insects ran round the cluster of eggs, most of which were empty now, the crowns gone; a few young bees staggered about in uncertain flight before they could gather power to wing away in a strong course. He watched the little ones that ran in and out among the shadows of the grass, hither and thither in consternation.

'Come here—come here!' he said, imprisoning one poor little bee under a grass stalk, while with another stalk he loosened the folded blue wings.

'Don't tease the little beggar,' I said.

'It doesn't hurt him – I wanted to see if it was because he couldn't spread his wings that he couldn't fly. There he goes – no, he doesn't. Let's try another.'

'Leave them alone,' said I. 'Let them run in the sun. They're only just out of the shells. Don't torment them into flight.'

He persisted, however, and broke the wing of the next.

'Oh, dear – pity!' said he, and he crushed the little thing between his fingers. Then he examined the eggs, and pulled out some silk from round the dead larva, and investigated it all in a desultory manner, asking of me all I knew about the insects. When he had finished he flung the clustered eggs into the water and rose, pulling out his watch from the depth of his breeches' pocket.

'I thought it was about dinner-time,' said he, smiling at me. 'I always know when it's about twelve. Are you coming in?'

'I'm coming down at any rate,' said I as we passed along the pond bank, and over the plank bridge that crossed the brow of the falling sluice. The bankside where the grey orchard twisted its trees, was a steep declivity, long and sharp, dropping down to the garden.

The stones of the large house were burdened with ivy and honeysuckle, and the great lilac bush that had once guarded the porch now almost blocked the doorway. We passed out of the front garden into the farmyard, and walked along the brick path to the back door.

'Shut the gate, will you?' he said to me over his shoulder, as he passed on first.

We went through the large scullery into the kitchen. The servant-girl was just hurriedly snatching the table-cloth out of the table drawer, and his mother, a quaint little woman with big, brown eyes, was hovering round the wide fireplace with a fork.

'Dinner not ready?' said he with a shade of resentment.

'No, George,' replied his mother apologetically, 'it isn't. The fire wouldn't burn a bit. You shall have it in a few minutes, though.'

He dropped on the sofa and began to read a novel. I wanted to go, but his mother insisted on my staying.

'Don't go,' she pleaded. 'Emily will be so glad if you stay – and father will, I'm sure. Sit down, now.'

I sat down on a rush chair by the long window that looked out into the yard. As he was reading, and as it took all his mother's powers to watch the potatoes boil and the meat roast, I was left to my thoughts. George, indifferent to all claims, continued to read. It was very annoying to watch him pulling his brown moustache, and reading indolently while the dog rubbed against his leggings and against the knee of his old riding-breeches. He would not even be at the trouble to play with Trip's ears, he was so content with his novel and his moustache. Round and round twirled his thick fingers, and the muscles of his bare arm moved slightly under the red-brown skin. The little square window above him filtered a green light from the foliage of the great horse-chestnut outside and the glimmer fell on his dark hair, and trembled across the plates which Annie was reaching down from the rack, and across the face of the tall clock. The kitchen was very big; the table looked lonely, and the chairs mourned darkly for the lost companionship of the sofa; the chimney was a black cavern away at the back, and the inglenook seats shut in another little compartment ruddy with firelight, where the mother hovered. It was rather a desolate kitchen, such a bare expanse of uneven grey flagstones, such far-away dark corners and sober furniture. The only gay things were the chintz coverings of the sofa and the arm-chair cushions, bright red in the bare sombre room; some might smile at the old clock, adorned as it was with remarkable and vivid poultry; in me it only provoked wonder and contemplation.

In a little while we heard the scraping of heavy boots outside, and the father entered. He was a big burly farmer, with his half-bald head sprinkled with crisp little curls.

'Hullo, Cyril,' he said cheerfully. 'You've not forsaken us then,' and turning to his son:

'Have you many more rows in the coppice close?'

'Finished!' replied George, continuing to read.

'That's all right—you've got on with 'em. The rabbits has bitten them turnips down, Mother.'

'I expect so,' replied his wife, whose soul was in the saucepans. At last she deemed the potatoes cooked and went out with the steaming pan.

The dinner was set on the table and the father began to carve. George looked over his book to survey the fare, then read until his plate was handed him. The maid sat at her little table near the window, and we began the meal. There came the treading of four feet along the brick path, and a little girl entered, followed by her grown-up sister. The child's long brown hair was tossed wildly back beneath her sailor hat. She flung aside this article of her attire and sat down to dinner, talking endlessly to her mother. The elder sister, a girl of about twenty-one, gave me a smile and a bright look from her brown eyes, and went to wash her hands. Then she came and sat down, and looked disconsolately at the underdone beef on her plate.

'I do hate this raw meat,' she said.

'Good for you,' replied her brother, who was eating industriously. 'Give you some muscle to wallop the nippers.'

She pushed it aside, and began to eat the vegetables. Her brother re-charged his plate and continued to eat.

'Well, our George, I do think you might pass a body that gravy,' said Mollie, the younger sister, in injured tones.

'Certainly,' he replied. 'Won't you have the joint as well?'

'No!' retorted the young lady of twelve, 'I don't expect you've done with it yet.'

'Clever!' he exclaimed across a mouthful.

'Do you think so?' said the elder sister, Emily, sarcastically.

'Yes,' he replied complacently, 'you've made her as sharp as yourself, I see, since you've had her in Standard Six. I'll try a potato, Mother, if you can find one that's done.'

'Well, George, they seem mixed, I'm sure that was done that I tried. There—they are mixed—look at this one, it's soft enough. I'm sure they were boiling long enough.'

'Don't explain and apologise to him,' said Emily irritably.

'Perhaps the kids were too much for her this morning,' he said calmly, to nobody in particular.

'No,' chimed in Mollie, 'she knocked a lad across his nose and made it bleed.'

'Little wretch,' said Emily, swallowing with difficulty. 'I'm glad I did! Some of my lads belong to—to—'

'To the devil,' suggested George, but she would not accept it from him.

Her father sat laughing; her mother, with distress in her eyes, looked at her daughter, who hung her head and made patterns on the table-cloth with her finger.

'Are they worse than the last lot?' asked the mother, softly, fearfully.

'No–nothing extra,' was the curt answer.

'She merely felt like bashing 'em,' said George, calling, as he looked at the sugar-bowl and at his pudding:

'Fetch some more sugar, Annie.'

The maid rose from her little table in the corner, and the mother also hurried to the cupboard. Emily trifled with her dinner and said bitterly to him:

'I only wish you had a taste of teaching, it would cure your self-satisfaction.'

'Pf!' he replied contemptuously, 'I could easily bleed the noses of a handful of kids.'

'You wouldn't sit there bleating like a fatted calf,' she continued.

This speech so tickled Mollie that she went off into a burst of laughter, much to the terror of her mother, who stood up in trembling apprehension lest she should choke.

'You made a joke, Emily,' he said, looking at his younger sister's contortions.

Emily was too impatient to speak to him further, and left the table. Soon the two men went back to the fallow to the turnips, and I walked along the path with the girls as they were going to school.

'He irritates me in everything he does and says,' burst out Emily with much heat.

'He's a pig sometimes,' said I.

'He is!' she insisted. 'He irritates me past bearing, with his grand know-all way, and his heavy smartness–I can't bear it. And the way Mother humbles herself to him–!'

'It makes you wild,' said I.

'Wild!' she echoed, her voice vibrating with nervous passion. We walked on in silence, till she asked:

'Have you brought me those verses of yours?'

'No–I'm so sorry–I've forgotten them again. As a matter of fact, I've sent them away.'

'But you promised me.'

'You know what my promises are. I'm as irresponsible as a puff of wind.'

She frowned with impatience and her disappointment was greater than necessary. When I left her at the corner of the lane I felt a string of her deep reproach in my mind. I always felt the reproach when she had gone.

I ran over the little bright brook that came from the weedy, bottom pond. The stepping-stones were white in the sun, and the water slid sleepily among them. One or two butterflies, indistinguishable against the blue sky, trifled from flower to flower and led me up the hill, across the field where the hot sunshine stood as in a bowl, and I was entering the caverns of the wood, where the oaks bowed over and saved us a grateful shade. Within, everything was so still and cool that my steps hung heavily along the path. The bracken held out arms to me, and the bosom of the wood was full of sweetness, but I journeyed on, spurred by the attacks of an army of flies which kept up a guerrilla warfare round my head till I had passed the black rhododendron bushes in the garden, where they left me, scenting no doubt Rebecca's pots of vinegar and sugar.

The low red house, with its roof discoloured and sunken, dozed in sunlight, and slept profoundly in the shade thrown by the massive maples encroaching from the wood.

There was no one in the dining-room, but I could hear the whirr of a sewing-machine coming from the little study, a sound as of some great, vindictive insect buzzing about, now louder, now softer, now settling. Then came a jingling of four or five keys at the bottom of the keyboard of the drawing-room piano, continuing till the whole range had been covered in little leaps, as if some very fat frog had jumped from end to end.

'That must be mother dusting the drawing-room,' I thought. The unaccustomed sound of the old piano startled me. The vocal chords behind the green-silk bosom—you only discovered it was not a bronze-silk bosom by poking a fold aside—had become as thin and tuneless as a dried old woman's. Age had yellowed the teeth of my mother's little piano, and shrunken its spindle legs. Poor old thing, it could but screech in answer to Lettie's fingers flying across it in scorn, so the prim, brown lips were always closed save to admit the duster.

Now, however, the little old-maidish piano began to sing a tinkling Victorian melody, and I fancied it must be some demure little woman, with curls like bunches of hops on either side of her face, who was touching it. The coy little tune teased me with old sensations, but my memory would give me no assistance. As I stood trying to fix my vague feelings, Rebecca came in to remove the cloth from the table.

'Who is playing, Beck?' I asked.

'Your mother, Cyril.'

'But she never plays. I thought she couldn't.'

'Ah,' replied Rebecca, 'you forget when you was a little thing sitting playing against her frock with the prayer-book, and she singing to you. *You* can't remember her when her curls was long like a piece of brown silk. *You* can't remember her when she used to play and sing, before Lettie came and your father was—'

Rebecca turned and left the room. I went and peeped in the drawing-room. Mother sat before the little brown piano, with her plump, rather stiff fingers moving across the keys, a faint smile on her lips. At that moment Lettie came flying past me, and flung her arms round mother's neck, kissing her and saying:

'Oh, my Dear, fancy my Dear playing the piano! Oh, Little Woman, we never knew you could!'

'Nor can I,' replied Mother laughing, disengaging herself. 'I only wondered if I could just strum out this old tune; I learned it when I was quite a girl, on this piano. It was a cracked one then; the only one I had.'

'But play again, dearie, do play again. It was like the clinking of lustre glasses, and you look so quaint at the piano. Do play, my dear!' pleaded Lettie.

'Nay,' said my mother, 'the touch of the old keys on my fingers is making me sentimental—you wouldn't like to see me reduced to the tears of old age?'

'Old age!' scolded Lettie, kissing her again. 'You are young enough to play little romances. Tell us about it, Mother.'

'About what, child?'

'When you used to play.'

'Before my fingers were stiff with fifty-odd years? Where have you been, Cyril, that you weren't in to dinner?'

'Only down to Strelley Mill,' said I.

'Of course,' said Mother coldly.

'Why "of course"?' I asked.

'And you came away as soon as Em went to school?' said Lettie.

'I did,' said I.

They were cross with me, these two women. After I had swallowed my little resentment I said:

'They would have me stay to dinner.'

My mother vouchsafed no reply.

'And has the great George found a girl yet?' asked Lettie.

'No,' I replied, 'he never will at this rate. Nobody will ever be good enough for him.'

'I'm sure I don't know what you can find in any of them to take you there so much,' said my mother.

'Don't be so mean, Mater,' I answered, nettled. 'You know I like them.'

'I know you like *her*,' said my mother sarcastically. 'As for him—he's an unlicked cub. What can you expect when his mother has spoiled him as she has. But I wonder you are so interested in licking him.' My mother sniffed contemptuously.

'He is rather good-looking,' said Lettie with a smile.

'*You* could make a man of him, I am sure,' I said, bowing satirically to her.

'*I* am not interested,' she replied, also satirical.

Then she tossed her head, and all the fine hairs that were free from bonds made a mist of yellow light in the sun.

'What frock shall I wear, Mater?' she asked.

'Nay, don't ask me,' replied her mother.

'I think I'll wear the heliotrope—though this sun will fade it,' she said pensively. She was tall, nearly six feet in height, but slenderly formed. Her hair was yellow, tending towards a dun brown. She had beautiful eyes and brows, but not a nice nose. Her hands were very beautiful.

'Where are you going?' I asked.

She did not answer me.

'To Tempest's!' I said. She did not reply.

'Well, I don't know what you can see in *him*,' I continued.

'Indeed!' said she. 'He's as good as most folk—' then we both began to laugh.

'Not,' she continued blushing, 'that I think anything about him. I'm merely going for a game of tennis. Are you coming?'

'What shall you say if I agree?' I asked.

'Oh!' she tossed her head. 'We shall all be very pleased I'm sure.'

'Ooray!' said I with fine irony.

She laughed at me, blushed, and ran upstairs.

Half an hour afterwards she popped her head in the study to bid me good-bye, wishing to see if I appreciated her. She was so charming in her fresh linen frock and flowered hat, that I could not but be proud of her. She expected me to follow her to the window, for from between the great purple rhododendrons she waved me a lace mitten, then glinted on like a flower moving brightly through the green hazels. Her path lay through the wood in the opposite direction from Strelley Mill, down the red drive across the tree-scattered space to the high-road. This road ran along the end of our lakelet, Nethermere, for about a quarter of a mile. Nethermere is the lowest in a chain of three ponds. The other two are the upper and lower millponds at Strelley; this is the largest and most charming piece of water, a mile long and about a quarter of a mile in width. Our wood runs down to the water's edge. On the opposite side, on a hill beyond the farthest corner of the lake, stands Highclose. It looks across the water at us in Woodside with one eye as it were, while our cottage casts a side-long glance back again at the proud house, and peeps coyly through the trees.

I could see Lettie like a distant sail stealing along the water's edge, her parasol flowing above. She turned through the wicket under the pine clump, climbed the steep field, and was enfolded again in the trees beside Highclose.

Leslie was sprawled on a camp-chair, under a copper beech on the lawn, his cigar glowing. He watched the ash grow strange and grey in the warm daylight, and he felt sorry for poor Nell Wycherley, whom he had driven that morning to the station, for would she not be frightfully cut up as the train whirled her farther and farther away? These girls are so daft with a fellow! But she was a nice little thing—he'd get Marie to write to her.

At this point he caught sight of a parasol fluttering along the drive, and immediately he fell in a deep sleep, with just a tiny slit in his slumber to allow him to see Lettie approach. She, finding her watchman ungallantly asleep, and his cigar, instead of his lamp, untrimmed, broke off a twig of syringa whose ivory buds had not yet burst with luscious scent. I know not how the end of his nose tickled in anticipation before she tickled him in reality, but he kept bravely still until the petals swept him. Then, starting from his sleep, he exclaimed:

'Lettie! I was dreaming of kisses!'

'On the bridge of your nose?' laughed she—'But whose were the kisses?'

'Who produced the sensation?' he smiled.

'Since I only tapped your nose you should dream of—'

'Go on!' said he, expectantly.

'Of Doctor Slop,' she replied, smiling to herself as she closed her parasol.

'I do not know the gentleman,' he said, afraid that she was laughing at him.

'No—your nose is quite classic,' she answered, giving him one of those brief intimate glances with which women flatter men so cleverly. He radiated with pleasure.

2

DANGLING THE APPLE

The long-drawn booming of the wind in the wood, and the sobbing and moaning in the maples and oaks near the house, had made Lettie restless. She did not want to go anywhere, she did not want to do anything, so she insisted on my just going out with her as far as the edge of the water. We crossed the tangle of fern and bracken, bramble and wild-raspberry canes that spread in the open space before the house, and we went down the grassy slope to the edge of Nethermere. The wind whipped up noisy little wavelets, and the cluck and clatter of these among the pebbles, the swish of the rushes and the freshening of the breeze against our faces, roused us.

The tall meadow-sweet was in bud along the tiny beach and we walked knee-deep among it, watching the foamy race of the ripples and the whitening of the willows on the far shore. At the place where Nethermere narrows to the upper end, and receives the brook from Strelley, the wood sweeps down and stands with its feet washed round with waters. We broke our way along the shore, crushing the sharp-scented wild mint, whose odour checks the breath, and examining here and there among the marshy places ragged nests of water-fowl, now deserted. Some slim young lapwings started at our approach, and sped lightly from us, their necks outstretched in straining fear of that which could not hurt them. One, two, fled cheeping into cover of the wood; almost instantly they coursed back again to where we stood, to dart off from us at an angle, in an ecstasy of bewilderment and terror.

'What has frightened the crazy little things?' asked Lettie.

'I don't know. They've cheek enough sometimes; then they go whining, skelping off from a fancy as if they had a snake under their wings.'

Lettie, however, paid small attention to my eloquence. She pushed aside an elder bush, which graciously showered down upon her myriad crumbs from its flowers like slices of bread, and bathed her in a medicinal scent. I followed her, taking my dose, and was startled to hear her sudden, 'Oh, Cyril!'

On the bank before us lay a black cat, both hind paws torn and bloody in a trap. It had no doubt been bounding forward after its prey when it was caught. It was gaunt and wild; no wonder it frightened the poor lapwings into cheeping hysteria. It glared at us fiercely, growling low.

'How cruel—oh, how cruel!' cried Lettie, shuddering.

I wrapped my cap and Lettie's scarf over my hands and bent to open the trap. The cat struck with her teeth, tearing the cloth convulsively. When it was free, it sprang away with one bound, and fell panting, watching us.

I wrapped the creature in my jacket, and picked her up, murmuring:

'Poor Mrs Nickie Ben—we always prophesied it of you.'

'What will you do with it?' asked Lettie.

'It is one of the Strelley Mill cats,' said I, 'and so I'll take her home.'

The poor animal moved and murmured and I carried her, but we brought her home. They stared, on seeing me enter the kitchen coatless, carrying a strange bundle, while Lettie followed me.

'I have brought poor Mrs Nickie Ben,' said I, unfolding my burden.

'Oh, what a shame!' cried Emily, putting out her hand to touch the cat, but drawing quickly back, like the peewits.

'This is how they all go,' said the mother.

'I wish keepers had to sit two or three days with their bare ankles in a trap,' said Mollie in vindictive tones.

We laid the poor brute on the rug, and gave it warm milk. It drank very little, being too feeble. Mollie, full of anger, fetched Mr Nickie Ben, another fine black cat, to survey his crippled mate. Mr Nickie Ben looked, shrugged his sleek shoulders, and walked away with high steps. There was a general feminine outcry on masculine callousness.

George came in for hot water. He exclaimed in surprise on seeing us, and his eyes became animated.

'Look at Mrs Nickie Ben,' cried Mollie. He dropped on his knees on the rug and lifted the wounded paws.

'Broken,' said he.

'How awful!' said Emily, shuddering violently, and leaving the room.

'Both?' I asked.

'Only one—look!'

'You are hurting her!' cried Lettie.

'It's no good,' said he.

Mollie and the mother hurried out of the kitchen into the parlour.

'What are you going to do?' asked Lettie.

'Put her out of her misery,' he replied, taking up the poor cat. We followed him into the barn.

'The quickest way,' said he, 'is to swing her round and knock her head against the wall.'

'You make me sick,' exclaimed Lettie.

'I'll drown her then,' he said with a smile. We watched him morbidly, as he took a length of twine and fastened a noose round the animal's neck, and near it an iron goose; he kept a long piece of cord attached to the goose.

'You're not coming, are you?' said he. Lettie looked at him; she had grown rather white.

'It'll make you sick,' he said. She did not answer, but followed him across the yard to the garden. On the bank of the lower millpond he turned again to us and said:

'Now for it!–you are chief mourners.' As neither of us replied, he smiled, and dropped the poor writhing cat into the water, saying, 'Good-bye, Mrs Nickie Ben.'

We waited on the bank some time. He eyed us curiously.

'Cyril,' said Lettie quietly, 'isn't it cruel?–isn't it awful?'

I had nothing to say.

'Do you mean me?' asked George.

'Not you in particular–everything! If we move the blood rises in our heel-prints.'

He looked at her seriously, with dark eyes.

'I had to drown her out of mercy,' said he, fastening the cord he held to an ash-pole. Then he went to get a spade, and with it, he dug a grave in the old black earth.

'If,' said he, 'the poor old cat had made a prettier corpse, you'd have thrown violets on her.'

He had struck the spade into the ground, and hauled up the iron goose.

'Well,' he said, surveying the hideous object, 'haven't her good looks gone! She was a fine cat.'

'Bury it and have done,' Lettie replied.

He did so asking: 'Shall you have bad dreams after it?'

'Dreams do not trouble me,' she answered, turning away.

We went indoors, into the parlour, where Emily sat by a window, biting her finger. The room was long and not very high; there was a great rough beam across the ceiling. On the mantelpiece, and in the fireplace, and over the piano were wild flowers and fresh leaves plentifully scattered; the room was cool with the scent of the woods.

'Has he done it?' asked Emily–'and did you watch him? If I had seen it I should have hated the sight of him, and I'd rather have touched a maggot than him.'

'I shouldn't be particularly pleased if he touched me,' said Lettie.

'There is something so loathsome about callousness and brutality,' said Emily. 'He fills me with disgust.'

'Does he?' said Lettie, smiling coldly. She went across to the old piano. 'He's only healthy. He's never been sick, not anyway, yet.' She sat down and played at random, letting the numbed notes fall like dead leaves from the haughty, ancient piano.

Emily and I talked on by the window, about books and people. She was intensely serious, and generally succeeded in reducing me to the same state.

After a while, when the milking and feeding were finished, George came in. Lettie was still playing the piano. He asked her why she didn't play something with a tune in it, and this caused her to turn round in her chair to give him a withering answer. His appearance, however, scattered her words like startled birds. He had come straight from washing in the scullery, to the parlour, and he stood behind Lettie's chair, unconcernedly wiping the moisture from his arms. His sleeves were rolled up to the shoulder, and his shirt was opened wide at the breast. Lettie was somewhat taken aback by the sight of him standing with legs apart, dressed in dirty leggings and boots, and breeches torn at the knee, naked at the breast and arms.

'Why don't you play something with a tune in it?' he repeated, rubbing the towel over his shoulders beneath the shirt.

'A tune!' she echoed, watching the swelling of his arms as he moved them, and the rise and fall of his breast, wonderfully solid and white. Then having curiously examined the sudden meeting of the sunhot skin with the white flesh in his throat, her eyes met his, and she turned again to the piano, while the colour grew in her ears, mercifully sheltered by a profusion of bright curls.

'What shall I play?' she asked, fingering the keys somewhat confusedly.

He dragged out a book of songs from a little heap of music, and set it before her.

'Which do you want to sing?' she asked, thrilling a little as she felt his arms so near her.

'Anything you like.'

'A love song?' she said.

'If you like—yes, a love song—' he laughed with clumsy insinuation that made the girl writhe.

She did not answer, but began to play Sullivan's 'Tit Willow'. He had a passable bass voice, not of any great depth, and he sang with gusto. Then she gave him 'Drink to me only with thine eyes'. At the end she turned and asked him if he liked the words. He replied that he thought them rather daft. But he looked at her with glowing brown eyes, as if in hesitating challenge.

'That's because you have no wine in your eyes to pledge with,' she replied, answering his challenge with a blue blaze of her eyes. Then her eyelashes drooped on to her cheek. He laughed with a faint ring of consciousness, and asked her how could she know.

'Because,' she said slowly, looking up at him with pretended scorn, 'because there's no change in your eyes when I look at you. I always think people who are worth much talk with their eyes. That's why you are forced to respect many quite uneducated people. Their eyes are so eloquent, and full of knowledge.' She had continued to look at him as she spoke—watching his faint appreciation of her upturned face, and her hair, where the light was always tangled, watching his brief self-examination to see if he could feel any truth in her words, watching till he broke into a little laugh which was rather more awkward and less satisfied than usual. Then she turned away, smiling also.

'There's nothing in this book nice to sing,' she said, turning over the leaves discontentedly. I found her a volume, and she sang 'Should he upbraid'. She had a fine soprano voice, and the song delighted him. He moved nearer to her, and when at the finish she looked round with a flashing, mischievous air, she found him pledging her with wonderful eyes.

'You like that,' said she with the air of superior knowledge, as if, dear me, all one had to do was to turn over to the right page of the vast volume of one's soul to suit these people.

'I do,' he answered emphatically, thus acknowledging her triumph.

'I'd rather "dance and sing" round "wrinkled care" than carefully shut the door on him, while I slept in the chimney-seat—wouldn't you?' she asked.

He laughed, and began to consider what she meant before he replied.

'As you do,' she added.

'What?' he asked.

'Keep half your senses asleep—half alive.'

'Do I?' he asked.

'Of course you do;—"bosbovis; an ox." You are like a stalled ox, food and comfort, no more. Don't you love comfort?' she smiled.

'Don't you?' he replied, smiling shamefaced.

'Of course. Come and turn over for me while I play this piece. Well, I'll nod when you must turn—bring a chair.'

She began to play a romance of Schubert's. He leaned nearer to her to take hold of the leaf of music; she felt her loose hair touch his face, and turned to him a quick, laughing glance, while she played. At the end of the page she nodded, but he was oblivious; 'Yes!' she said, suddenly impatient, and he tried to get the leaf over; she quickly pushed his hand aside, turned the page herself and continued playing.

'Sorry!' said he, blushing actually.

'Don't bother,' she said, continuing to play without observing him. When she had finished:

'There!' she said, 'now tell me how you felt while I was playing.'

'Oh—a fool!'—he replied, covered with confusion.

'I'm glad to hear it,' she said—'but I didn't mean that. I meant how did the music make you feel?'

'I don't know—whether—it made me feel anything,' he replied deliberately, pondering over his answer, as usual.

'I tell you,' she declared, 'you're either asleep or stupid. Did you really see nothing in the music? But what did you think about?'

He laughed—and thought awhile—and laughed again.

'Why!' he admitted, laughing, and trying to tell the exact truth, 'I thought how pretty your hands are—and what they are like to touch—and I thought it was a new experience to feel somebody's hair tickling my cheek.' When he had finished his deliberate account she gave his hand a little knock, and left him saying:

'You are worse and worse.'

She came across the room to the couch where I was sitting talking to Emily, and put her arm around my neck.

'Isn't it time to go home, Pat?' she asked.

'Half-past eight—quite early,' said I.

'But I believe—I think I ought to be home now,' she said.

'Don't go,' said he.

'Why?' I asked.

'Stay to supper,' urged Emily.

'But I believe—' she hesitated.

'She has another fish to fry,' I said.

'I am not sure—' she hesitated again. Then she flashed into sudden wrath, exclaiming, 'Don't be so mean and nasty, Cyril!'

'Were you going somewhere?' asked George humbly.

'Why—no!' she said, blushing.

'Then stay to supper—will you?' he begged. She laughed, and yielded. We went into the kitchen. Mr Saxton was sitting reading. Trip, the big bull terrier, lay at his feet pretending to sleep; Mr Nickie Ben reposed calmly on the sofa; Mrs Saxton and Mollie were just going to bed. We bade them good night, and sat down. Annie, the servant, had gone home, so Emily prepared the supper.

'Nobody can touch that piano like you,' said Mr Saxton to Lettie, beaming upon her with admiration and deference. He was proud of the stately, mumbling old thing, and used to say that it was full of music for those that liked to ask for it. Lettie laughed, and said that so few folks ever tried it, that her honour was not great.

'What do you think of our George's singing?' asked the father proudly, but with a deprecating laugh at the end.

'I tell him, when he's in love he'll sing quite well,' she said.

'When he's in love!' echoed the father, laughing aloud, very pleased.

'Yes,' she said, 'when he finds out something he wants and can't have.'

George thought about it, and he laughed also.

Emily, who was laying the table, said, 'There is hardly any water in the pippin, George.'

'Oh, dash!' he exclaimed, 'I've taken my boots off.'

'It's not a very big job to put them on again,' said his sister.

'Why couldn't Annie fetch it—what's she here for?' he said angrily.

Emily looked at us, tossed her head, and turned her back on him.

'I'll go, I'll go, after supper,' said the father in a comforting tone.

'After supper!' laughed Emily.

George got up and shuffled out. He had to go into the spinney near the house to a well, and being warm disliked turning out.

We had just sat down to supper when Trip rushed barking to the door. 'Be quiet,' ordered the father, thinking of those in bed, and he followed the dog.

It was Leslie. He wanted Lettie to go home with him at once. This she refused to do, so he came indoors, and was persuaded to sit down at table. He swallowed a morsel of bread and cheese, and a cup of coffee, talking to Lettie of a garden party which was going to be arranged at Highclose for the following week.

'What is it for then?' interrupted Mr Saxton.

'For?' echoed Leslie.

'Is it for the missionaries, or the unemployed, or something?' explained Mr Saxton.

'It's a garden-party, not a bazaar,' said Leslie.

'Oh—a private affair. I thought it would be some church matter of your mother's. She's very big at the church, isn't she?'

'She is interested in the church—yes!' said Leslie, then proceeding to explain to Lettie that he was arranging a tennis tournament in which she was to take part. At this point he became aware that he was monopolising the conversation, and turned to George, just as the latter was taking a piece of cheese from his knife with his teeth, asking:

'Do you play tennis, Mr Saxton?—I know Miss Saxton does not.'

'No,' said George, working the piece of cheese into his cheek. 'I never learned any ladies' accomplishments.'

Leslie turned to Emily, who had nervously been pushing two plates over a stain in the cloth, and who was very startled when she found herself addressed.

'My mother would be so glad if you would come to the party, Miss Saxton.'

'I cannot. I shall be at school. Thanks very much.'

'Ah–it's very good of you,' said the father, beaming. But George smiled contemptuously.

When supper was over Leslie looked at Lettie to inform her that he was ready to go. She, however, refused to see his look, but talked brightly to Mr Saxton, who was delighted. George, flattered, joined in the talk with gusto. Then Leslie's angry silence began to tell on us all. After a dull lapse, George lifted his head and said to his father:

'Oh, I shouldn't be surprised if that little red heifer calved tonight.'

Lettie's eyes flashed with a sparkle of amusement at this thrust.

'No,' assented the father, 'I thought so myself.'

After a moment's silence, George continued deliberately, 'I felt her gristles–'

'George!' said Emily sharply.

'We will go,' said Leslie.

George looked up sideways at Lettie and his black eyes were full of sardonic mischief.

'Lend me a shawl, will you, Emily?' said Lettie. 'I brought nothing, and I think the wind is cold.'

Emily, however, regretted that she had no shawl, and so Lettie must needs wear a black coat over her summer dress. It fitted so absurdly that we all laughed, but Leslie was very angry that she should appear ludicrous before them. He showed her all the polite attentions possible, fastened the neck of her coat with his pearl scarf-pin, refusing the pin Emily discovered, after some search. Then we sallied forth.

When we were outside, he offered Lettie his arm with an air of injured dignity. She refused it and he began to remonstrate.

'I consider you ought to have been home as you promised.'

'Pardon me,' she replied, 'but I did not promise.'

'But you knew I was coming,' said he.

'Well–you found me,' she retorted.

'Yes,' he assented. 'I did find you; flirting with a common fellow,' he sneered.

'Well,' she returned. 'He did–it is true–call a heifer, a heifer.'

'And I should think you liked it,' he said.

'I didn't mind,' she said, with galling negligence.

'I thought your taste was more refined,' he replied sarcastically. 'But I suppose you thought it romantic.'

'Very! Ruddy, dark, and really thrilling eyes,' said she.

'I hate to hear a girl talk rot,' said Leslie. He himself had crisp hair of the 'ginger' class.

'But I mean it,' she insisted, aggravating his anger.

Leslie was angry. 'I'm glad he amuses you!'

'Of course, I'm not hard to please,' she said pointedly. He was stung to the quick.

'Then there's some comfort in knowing I don't please you,' he said coldly.

'Oh! but you do! You amuse me also,' she said.

After that he would not speak, preferring, I suppose, *not* to amuse her.

Lettie took my arm, and with her disengaged hand held her skirts above the wet grass. When he had left us at the end of the riding in the wood, Lettie said:

'What an infant he is!'

'A bit of an ass,' I admitted.

'But really!' she said, 'he's more agreeable on the whole than–than my Taurus.'

'Your bull!' I repeated, laughing.

3

A VENDOR OF VISIONS

The Sunday following Lettie's visit to the mill, Leslie came up in the morning, admirably dressed, and perfected by a grand air. I showed him into the dark drawing-room, and left him. Ordinarily he would have wandered to the stairs, and sat there calling to Lettie; today he was silent. I carried the news of his arrival to my sister, who was pinning on her brooch.

'And how is the dear boy?' she asked.

'I have not inquired,' said I.

She laughed, and loitered about till it was time to set off for church before she came downstairs. Then she also assumed the grand air and bowed to him with a beautiful bow. He was somewhat taken aback and had nothing to say. She rustled across the room to the window, where the white geraniums grew magnificently. 'I must adorn myself,' she said.

It was Leslie's custom to bring her flowers. As he had not done so this day, she was piqued. He hated the scent and chalky whiteness of the geraniums. So she smiled at him as she pinned them into the bosom of her dress, saying:

'They are very fine, are they not?'

He muttered that they were. Mother came downstairs, greeted him warmly, and asked him if he would take her to church.

'If you will allow me,' said he.

'You are modest today,' laughed Mother.

'Today!' he repeated.

'I hate modesty in a young man,' said Mother–'Come, we shall be late.' Lettie wore the geraniums all day–till evening. She brought Alice Gall home to tea, and bade me bring up 'Mon Taureau', when his farm work was over.

The day had been hot and close. The sun was reddening in the west as we leaped across the lesser brook. The evening scents began to awake, and wander unseen through the still air. An occasional yellow sunbeam would slant through the thick roof of leaves and cling passionately to the orange clusters of mountain-ash berries. The trees were silent, drawing together to sleep. Only a few pink orchids stood palely by the path, looking wistfully out at the ranks of red-purple bugle, whose last flowers, glowing from the top of the bronze column, yearned darkly for the sun.

We sauntered on in silence, not breaking the first hush of the woodlands. As we drew near home we heard a murmur from among the trees, from the lovers' seat, where a great tree had fallen and remained mossed and covered with fragile growth. There a crooked bough made a beautiful seat for two.

'Fancy being in love and making a row in such a twilight,' said I as we continued our way. But when we came opposite the fallen tree, we saw no lovers there, but a man sleeping, and muttering through his sleep. The cap had fallen from his grizzled hair, and his head leaned back against a profusion of the little wild geraniums that decorated the dead bough so delicately. The man's clothing was good, but slovenly and neglected. His face was pale and worn with sickness and dissipation. As he slept, his grey beard wagged, and his loose unlovely mouth moved in indistinct speech. He was acting over again some part of his life, and his features twitched during the unnatural sleep. He would give a little groan, gruesome to hear, and then talk to some woman. His features twitched as if with pain, and he moaned slightly.

The lips opened in a grimace, showing the yellow teeth behind the beard. Then he began again talking in his throat, thickly, so that we could only tell part of what he said. It was very unpleasant. I wondered how we should end it. Suddenly through the gloom of the twilight-haunted woods came the scream of a rabbit caught by a weasel. The man awoke with a sharp 'Ah!'–he looked round in consternation, then sinking down again wearily, said, 'I was dreaming again.'

'You don't seem to have nice dreams,' said George.

The man winced then, looking at us, said, almost sneering:

'And who are you?'

We did not answer, but waited for him to move. He sat still, looking at us.

'So!' he said at last, wearily, 'I do dream. I do, I do.' He sighed heavily. Then he added, sarcastically, 'Were you interested?'

'No,' said I. 'But you are out of your way surely. Which road did you want?'

'You want me to clear out,' he said.

'Well,' I said, laughing in deprecation, 'I don't mind your dreaming. But this is not the way to anywhere.'

'Where may you be going then?' he asked.

'I? Home,' I replied with dignity.

'You are a Beardsall?' he queried, eyeing me with bloodshot eyes.

'I am!' I replied with more dignity, wondering who the fellow could be.

He sat a few moments looking at me. It was getting dark in the wood. Then he took up an ebony stick with a gold head, and rose. The stick seemed to catch at my imagination. I watched it curiously as we walked with the old man along the path to the gate. We went with him into the open road. When we reached the clear sky where the light from the west fell full on our faces, he turned again and looked at us closely. His mouth opened sharply, as if he would speak, but he stopped himself, and only said, 'Good-bye–Good-bye.'

'Shall you be all right?' I asked, seeing him totter.

'Yes–all right–good-bye, lad.'

He walked away feebly into the darkness. We saw the lights of a vehicle on the high-road: after a while we heard the bang of a door, and a cab rattled away.

'Well–whoever's he?' said George, laughing.

'Do you know,' said I, 'it's made me feel a bit rotten.'

'Ay?' he laughed, turning up the end of the exclamation with indulgent surprise.

We went back home, deciding to say nothing to the women. They were sitting in the window seat watching for us, Mother and Alice and Lettie.

'You *have* been a long time!' said Lettie. 'We've watched the sun go down–it set splendidly–look–the rim of the hill is smouldering yet. What have you been doing?'

'Waiting till your Taurus finished work.'

'Now be quiet,' she said hastily, and–turning to him–'You have come to sing hymns?'

'Anything you like,' he replied.

'How nice of you, George!' exclaimed Alice, ironically. She was a short, plump girl, pale, with daring, rebellious eyes. Her mother was a Wyld, a family famous either for shocking lawlessness, or for extreme uprightness. Alice, with an admirable father, and a mother who loved her husband passionately, was wild and lawless on the surface, but at heart very upright and amenable. My mother and she were fast friends, and Lettie had a good deal of sympathy with her. But Lettie generally deplored Alice's outrageous behaviour, though she relished it–if 'superior' friends were not present. Most men enjoyed Alice in company, but they fought shy of being alone with her.

'Would you say the same to me?' she asked.

'It depends what you'd answer,' he said, laughingly.

'Oh, you're so bloomin' cautious. I'd rather have a tack in my shoe than a cautious man, wouldn't you, Lettie?'

'Well–it depends how far I had to walk,' was Lettie's reply–'but if I hadn't to limp too far–'

Alice turned away from Lettie, whom she often found rather irritating.

'You do look glum, Sybil,' she said to me, 'did somebody want to kiss you?'

I laughed–on the wrong side, understanding her malicious feminine reference–and answered:

'If they had, I should have looked happy.'

'Dear boy, smile now then'–and she tipped me under the chin. I drew away.

'Oh, Gum–we are solemn! What's the matter with you? Georgie–say something–else I's'll begin to feel nervous.'

'What shall I say?' he asked, shifting his feet and resting his elbows on his knees. 'Oh, Lor!' she cried in great impatience. He did not help her, but sat clasping his hands, smiling on one side of his face. He was nervous. He looked at the pictures, the ornaments, and everything in the room; Lettie got up to settle some flowers on the mantelpiece, and he scrutinised her closely. She was dressed in some blue foulard stuff, with lace at the throat, and lace cuffs to the elbow. She was tall and supple; her hair had a curling fluffiness very charming. He was no taller than she, and looked shorter, being strongly built. He too had a grace of his own, but not as he sat stiffly on a horse-hair chair. She was elegant in her movements.

After a little while Mother called us in to supper.

'Come,' said Lettie to him, 'take me in to supper.'

He rose, feeling very awkward.

'Give me your arm,' said she to tease him. He did so, and flushed under his tan, afraid of her round arm half hidden by lace, which lay along his sleeve.

When we were seated she flourished her spoon and asked him what he would have. He hesitated, looked at the strange dishes, and said he would have some cheese. They insisted on his eating new, complicated meats.

'I'm sure you like tantafflins, don't you, Georgie?' said Alice, in her mocking fashion. He was *not* sure. He could not analyse the flavours, he felt confused and bewildered even through his sense of taste! Alice begged him to have salad.

'No, thanks,' said he. 'I don't like it.'

'Oh, George!' she said. 'How *can* you say so when I'm *offering* it you.'

'Well–I've only had it once,' said he, 'and that was when I was working with Flint, and he gave us fat bacon and bits of lettuce soaked in vinegar–''Ave a bit more salit,'' he kept saying, but I'd had enough.'

'But all our lettuce,' said Alice with a wink, 'is as sweet as a nut, no vinegar about our lettuce.' George laughed in much confusion at her pun on my sister's name.

'I believe you,' he said, with pompous gallantry.

'Think of that!' cried Alice. 'Our Georgie believes me. Oh, I am so, so pleased!'

He smiled painfully. His hand was resting on the table, the thumb tucked tight under the fingers, his knuckles white as he nervously gripped his thumb. At last supper was finished, and he picked up his serviette from the floor and began to fold it. Lettie also seemed ill at ease. She had teased him till the sense of his awkwardness had become uncomfortable. Now she felt sorry, and a trifle repentant, so she went to the piano, as she always did to dispel her moods. When she was angry she played tender fragments of Tchaikovsky, when she was miserable, Mozart. Now she played Handel in a manner that suggested the plains of heaven in the long notes, and in the little trills as if she were waltzing up the ladder of Jacob's dream like the damsels in Blake's pictures. I often told her she flattered herself scandalously through the piano; but generally she pretended not to understand me, and occasionally she surprised me by a sudden rush of tears to her eyes. For George's sake, she played Gounod's 'Ave Maria', knowing that the sentiment of the chant would appeal to him, and make him sad, forgetful of the petty evils of this life. I smiled as I watched the cheap spell working. When she had finished, her fingers lay motionless for a minute on the keys, then she spun round, and looked him straight in the eyes, giving promise of a smile. But she glanced down at her knee.

'You are tired of music,' she said.

'No,' he replied, shaking his head.

'Like it better than salad?' she asked with a flash of raillery.

He looked up at her with a sudden smile, but did not reply. He was not handsome; his features were too often in a heavy repose; but when he looked up and smiled unexpectedly, he flooded her with an access of tenderness.

'Then you'll have a little more,' said she, and she turned again to the piano. She played soft, wistful morsels, then suddenly broke off in the midst of one sentimental plaint, and left the piano, dropping into a low chair by the fire. There she sat and looked at him. He was conscious that her eyes were fixed on him, but he dared not look back at her, so he pulled his moustache.

'You are only a boy, after all,' she said to him quietly. Then he turned and asked her why.

'It is a boy that you are,' she repeated, leaning back in her chair, and smiling lazily at him.

'I never thought so,' he replied seriously.

'Really?' she said, chuckling.

'No,' said he, trying to recall his previous impressions.

She laughed heartily, saying:

'You're growing up.'

'How?' he asked.

'Growing up,' she repeated, still laughing.

'But I'm sure I was never boyish,' said he.

'I'm teaching you,' said she, 'and when you're boyish you'll be a very decent man. A mere man daren't be a boy for fear of tumbling off his manly dignity, and then he'd be a fool, poor thing.'

He laughed, and sat still to think about it, as was his way.
'Do you like pictures?' she asked suddenly, being tired of looking at him.
'Better than anything,' he replied.
'Except dinner, and a warm hearth and a lazy evening,' she said.
He looked at her suddenly, hardening at her insult, and biting his lips at the taste of this humiliation. She repented, and smiled her plaintive regret to him.
'I'll show you some,' she said, rising and going out of the room. He felt he was nearer her. She returned, carrying a pile of great books.
'Jove–you're pretty strong!' said he.
'You are charming in your compliment,' she said.
He glanced at her to see if she were mocking.
'That's the highest you could say of me, isn't it?' she insisted.
'Is it?' he asked, unwilling to compromise himself.
'For sure,' she answered–and then, laying the books on the table, 'I know how a man will compliment me by the way he looks at me'–she kneeled before the fire. 'Some look at my hair, some watch the rise and fall of my breathing, some look at my neck, and a few–not you among them–look me in the eyes for my thoughts. To you, I'm a fine specimen, strong! Pretty strong! You primitive man!'
He sat twisting his fingers; she was very contrary.
'Bring your chair up,' she said, sitting down at the table and opening a book. She talked to him of each picture, insisting on hearing his opinion. Sometimes he disagreed with her and would not be persuaded. At such times she was piqued.
'If,' said she, 'an ancient Briton in his skins came and contradicted me as you do, wouldn't you tell him not to make an ass of himself?'
'I don't know,' said he.
'Then you ought to,' she replied. 'You know nothing.'
'How is it you ask me then?' he said.
She began to laugh.
'Why–that's a pertinent question. I think you might be rather nice, you know.'
'Thank you,' he said, smiling ironically.
'Oh!' she said. 'I know, you think you're perfect, but you're not, you're very annoying.'
'Yes,' exclaimed Alice, who had entered the room again, dressed ready to depart. 'He's so blooming slow! Great whizz! Who wants fellows to carry cold dinners? Shouldn't you like to shake him, Lettie?'
'I don't feel concerned enough,' replied the other calmly.
'Did you ever carry a boiled pudding, Georgie?' asked Alice with innocent interest, pinching me slyly.
'Me!–why?–what makes you ask?' he replied, quite at a loss.
'Oh, I only wondered if your people needed any indigestion mixture–Pa mixes it–$1/1\frac{1}{2}$ a bottle.'
'I don't see–' he began.
'Ta–ta, old boy, I'll give you time to think about it. Good night, Lettie. Absence makes the heart grow fonder–Georgie–of someone else. Farewell. Come along, Sybil love, the moon is shining–Good night all, good night!'
I escorted her home, while they continued to look at the pictures. He was a romanticist. He liked Copley, Fielding, Cattermole and Birket Foster; he could see nothing whatsoever in Girtin or David Cox. They fell out decidedly over George Clausen.

'But,' said Lettie, 'he is a real realist, he makes common things beautiful, he sees the mystery and magnificence that envelops us even when we work menially. I *do* know and I *can* speak. If I hoed in the fields beside you–' This was a very new idea for him, almost a shock to his imagination, and she talked unheeded. The picture under discussion was a water-colour–'Hoeing' by Clausen.

'You'd be just that colour in the sunset,' she said, thus bringing him back to the subject, 'and if you looked at the ground you'd find there was a sense of warm gold fire in it, and once you'd perceived the colour, it would strengthen till you'd see nothing else. You are blind; you are only half-born; you are gross with good living and heavy sleeping. You are a piano which will only play a dozen common notes. Sunset is nothing to you–it merely happens anywhere. Oh, but you make me feel as if I'd like to make you suffer. If you'd ever been sick; if you'd ever been born into a home where there was something oppressed you, and you couldn't understand; if ever you'd believed, or even doubted, you might have been a man by now. You never grow up, like bulbs which spend all summer getting fat and fleshy, but never wakening the germ of a flower. As for me, the flower is born in me, but it wants bringing forth. Things don't flower if they're overfed. You have to suffer before you blossom in this life. When death is just touching a plant, it forces it into a passion of flowering. You wonder how I have touched death. You don't know. There's always a sense of death in this home. I believe my mother hated my father before I was born. That was death in her veins for me before I was born. It makes a difference–'

As he sat listening, his eyes grew wide and his lips were parted, like a child who feels the tale but does not understand the words. She, looking away from herself at last, saw him, began to laugh gently, and patted his hand, saying:

'Oh! my dear heart, are you bewildered? How amiable of you to listen to me–there isn't any meaning in it all–there isn't really!'

'But,' said he, 'why do you say it?'

'Oh, the question!' she laughed. 'Let us go back to our muttons, we're gazing at each other like two dazed images.'

They turned on, chatting casually, till George suddenly exclaimed, 'There!' It was Maurice Griffinhagen's 'Idyll'.

'What of it?' she asked, gradually flushing. She remembered her own enthusiasm over the picture.

'Wouldn't it be fine?' he exlaimed, looking at her with glowing eyes, his teeth showing white in a smile that was not amusement.

'What?' she asked, dropping her head in confusion.

'That–a girl like that–half afraid–and passion!' He lit up curiously.

'She may well be half afraid, when the barbarian comes out in his glory, skins and all.'

'But don't you like it?' he asked.

She shrugged her shoulders, saying, 'Make love to the next girl you meet, and by the time the poppies redden the field, she'll hang in your arms. She'll have need to be more than half afraid, won't she?'

She played with the leaves of the book, and did not look at him.

'But,' he faltered, his eyes glowing, 'it would be–rather–'

'Don't, sweet lad, don't!' she cried, laughing.

'But I shouldn't–' he insisted. 'I don't know whether I should like any girl I know to–'

'Precious Sir Galahad,' she said in a mock caressing voice, and stroking his cheek with her finger, 'you ought to have been a monk–a martyr, a Carthusian.'

He laughed, taking no notice. He was breathlessly quivering under the new sensation of heavy, unappeased fire in his breast, and in the muscles of his arms. He glanced at her bosom and shivered.

'Are you studying just how to play the part?' she asked.

'No–but–' he tried to look at her, but failed. He shrank, laughing, and dropped his head.

'What?' she asked with vibrant curiosity.

Having become a few degrees calmer, he looked up at her now, his eyes wide and vivid with a declaration that made her shrink back as if flame had leaped towards her face. She bent down her head and picked at her dress.

'Didn't you know the picture before?' she said, in a low, toneless voice.

He shut his eyes and shrank with shame.

'No, I've never seen it before,' he said.

'I'm surprised,' she said. 'It is a very common one.'

'Is it?' he answered, and this make-belief conversation fell. She looked up, and found his eyes. They gazed at each other for a moment before they hid their faces again. It was a torture to each of them to look thus nakedly at the other, a dazzled, shrinking pain that they forced themselves to undergo for a moment, that they might the moment after tremble with a fierce sensation that filled their veins with fluid, fiery electricity. She sought, almost in panic, for something to say.

'I believe it's in Liverpool, the picture,' she contrived to say.

He dared not kill this conversation, he was too self-conscious. He forced himself to reply, 'I didn't know there was a gallery in Liverpool.'

'Oh yes, a very good one,' she said.

Their eyes met in the briefest flash of a glance, then both turned their faces aside. Thus averted, one from the other, they made talk. At last she rose, gathered the books together, and carried them off. At the door she turned. She must steal another keen moment: 'Are you admiring my strength?' she asked. Her pose was fine. With her head thrown back, the roundness of her throat ran finely down to the bosom, which swelled above the pile of books held by her straight arms. He looked at her. Their lips smiled curiously. She put back her throat as if she were drinking. They felt the blood beating madly in their necks. Then, suddenly breaking into a slight trembling, she turned round and left the room.

While she was out, he sat twisting his moustache. She came back along the hall talking madly to herself in French. Having been much impressed by Sarah Bernhardt's 'Dame aux Camélias' and 'Adrienne Lecouvreur', Lettie had caught something of the weird tone of this great actress, and her raillery and mockery came out in little wild waves. She laughed at him, and at herself, and at men in general, and at love in particular. Whatever he said to her, she answered in the same mad clatter of French, speaking high and harshly. The sound was strange and uncomfortable. There was a painful perplexity in his brow, such as I often perceived afterwards, a sense of something hurting, something he could not understand.

'Well, well, well, well!' she exclaimed at last. 'We must be mad sometimes, or we should be getting aged, *hein?*'

'I wish I could understand,' he said plaintively.

'Poor dear!' she laughed. 'How sober he is! And will you really go? They will think we've given you no supper, you look so sad.'

'I have supped–full–' he began, his eyes dancing with a smile as he ventured upon a quotation. He was very much excited.

'Of horrors!' she cried, completing it. 'Now that is worse than anything I have given you.'

'Is it?' he replied, and they smiled at each other.

'Far worse,' she answered. They waited in suspense for some moments. He looked at her.

'Good-bye,' she said, holding out her hand. Her voice was full of insurgent tenderness. He looked at her again, his eyes flickering. Then he took her hand. She pressed his fingers, holding them a little while. Then ashamed of her display of feeling, she looked down. He had a deep cut across his thumb.

'What a gash!' she exclaimed, shivering, and clinging a little tighter to his fingers before she released them. He gave a little laugh.

'Does it hurt you?' she asked very gently.

He laughed again–'No!' he said softly, as if his thumb were not worthy of consideration.

They smiled again at each other, and, with a blind movement, he broke the spell and was gone.

4

THE FATHER

Autumn set in, and the red dahlias which kept the warm light alive in their bosoms so late into the evening died in the night, and the morning had nothing but brown balls of rottenness to show.

They called me as I passed the post office door in Eberwich one evening, and they gave me a letter for my mother. The distorted, sprawling handwriting perplexed me with a dim uneasiness; I put the letter away, and forgot it. I remembered it later in the evening, when I wished to recall something to interest my mother. She looked at the handwriting, and began hastily and nervously to tear open the envelope; she held it away from her in the light of the lamp, and with eyes drawn half closed, tried to scan it. So I found her spectacles, but she did not speak her thanks, and her hand trembled. She read the short letter quickly; then she sat down, and read it again, and continued to look at it.

'What is it, Mother?' I asked.

She did not answer, but continued staring at the letter. I went up to her, and put my hand on her shoulder, feeling very uncomfortable. She took no notice of me, beginning to murmur, 'Poor Frank–Poor Frank.' That was my father's name.

'But what is it, Mother?–tell me what's the matter!'

She turned and looked at me as if I were a stranger; she got up, and began to walk about the room; then she left the room, and I heard her go out of the house.

The letter had fallen on to the floor. I picked it up. The handwriting was very broken. The address gave a village some few miles away; the date was three days before.

My Dear Lettice:

You will want to know I am gone. I can hardly last a day or two–my kidneys are nearly gone. I came over one day. I didn't see you, but I saw the girl by the window, and I had a few words with the lad. He never knew, and he felt nothing. I think the girl might have done. If you knew how awfully lonely I am, Lettice–how awfully I have been, you might feel sorry.

I have saved what I could, to pay you back. I have had the worst of it, Lettice, and I'm glad the end has come. I have had the worst of it.

> Good-bye–for ever–your husband,
> FRANK BEARDSALL.

I was numbed by this letter of my father's. With almost agonised effort I strove to recall him, but I knew that my image of a tall, handsome, dark man with pale grey eyes was made up from my mother's few words, and from a portrait I had once seen.

The marriage had been unhappy. My father was of frivolous, rather vulgar character, but plausible, having a good deal of charm. He was a liar, without notion of honesty, and he had deceived my mother thoroughly. One after another she discovered his mean dishonesties and deceits, and her soul revolted from him, and because the illusion of him had broken into a thousand vulgar fragments, she turned away with the scorn of a woman who finds her romance has been a trumpery tale. When he left her for other pleasures–Lettie being a baby of three years, while I was five–she rejoiced bitterly. She had heard of him indirectly–and of him nothing good, although he prospered–but he had never come to see her or written to her in all the eighteen years.

In a while my mother came in. She sat down, pleating up the hem of her black apron, and smoothing it out again.

'You know,' she said, 'he had a right to the children, and I've kept them all the time.'

'He could have come,' said I.

'I set them against him, I have kept them from him, and he wanted them. I ought to be by him now–I ought to have taken you to him long ago.'

'But how could you, when you knew nothing of him?'

'He would have come–he wanted to come–I have felt it for years. But I kept him away. I know I have kept him away. I have felt it, and he has. Poor Frank–he'll see his mistakes now. He would not have been as cruel as I have been–'

'Nay, Mother, it is only the shock that makes you say so.'

'This makes me know. I have felt in myself a long time that he was suffering; I have had the feeling of him in me. I knew, yes, I did know he wanted me, and you, I felt it. I have had the feeling of him upon me this last three months especially . . . I have been cruel to him.'

'Well–we'll go to him now, shall we?' I said.

'Tomorrow–tomorrow,' she replied, noticing me really for the first time. 'I go in the morning.'

'And I'll go with you.'

'Yes–in the morning. Lettie has her party to Chatsworth–don't tell her–we won't tell her.'

'No,' said I.

Shortly after, my mother went upstairs. Lettie came in rather late from Highclose; Leslie did not come in. In the morning they were going with a motor party into Matloch and Chatsworth, and she was excited, and did not observe anything.

After all, Mother and I could not set out until the warm tempered afternoon. The air was full of a soft yellowness when we stepped down from the train at Cossethay. My mother insisted on walking the long two miles to the village. We went slowly along the road, lingering over the little red flowers in the high hedge-bottom up the hillside. We were reluctant to come to our destination. As we came in sight of the little grey tower of the church, we heard the sound of braying, brassy music. Before us, filling a little croft, the Wakes was in full swing.

Some wooden horses careered gaily round, and the swing-boats leaped into the mild blue sky. We sat upon the stile, my mother and I, and watched. There were booths, and coconut shies and roundabouts scattered in the small field. Groups of children moved quietly from attraction to attraction. A deeply tanned man came across the field swinging two dripping buckets of water. Women looked from the doors of their brilliant caravans, and lean dogs rose lazily and settled down again under the steps. The fair moved slowly, for all its noise. A stout lady, with a husky masculine voice, invited the excited children into her peep-show. A swarthy man stood with his thin legs astride on the platform of the roundabouts, and sloping backwards, his mouth distended with a row of fingers, he whistled astonishingly to the coarse row of the organ, and his whistling sounded clear, like the flight of a wild goose high over the chimney tops, as he was carried round and round. A little fat man with an ugly swelling on his chest stood screaming from a filthy booth to a crowd of urchins, bidding them challenge a big, stolid young man who stood with folded arms, his fists pushing out his biceps. On being asked if he would undertake any of these prospective challenges, this young man nodded, not having yet attained a talking stage:–yes he would take two at a time, screamed the little fat man with the big excrescence on his chest, pointing at the cowering lads and girls. Farther off, Punch's quaint voice could be heard when the coconut man ceased grinding out screeches from his rattle. The coconut man was wroth, for these youngsters would not risk a penny shy, and the rattle yelled like a fiend. A little girl came along to look at us, daintily licking an ice-cream sandwich. We were uninteresting, however, so she passed on to stare at the caravans.

We had almost gathered courage to cross the wakes, when the cracked bell of the church sent its note falling over the babble.

'One–two–three'–had it really sounded three! Then it rang on a lower bell–'One–two–three.' A passing bell for a man! I looked at my mother–she turned away from me.

The organ flared on–the husky woman came forward to make another appeal. Then there was a lull. The man with the lump on his chest had gone inside the rag to spar with the solid fellow. The coconut man had gone to the 'Three Tunns' in fury, and a brazen girl of seventeen or so was in charge of the nuts. The horses careered round, carrying two frightened boys.

Suddenly the quick, throbbing note of the low bell struck again through the din. I listened–but could not keep count. One, two, three, four–for the third time that great lad had determined to go on the horses, and they had started while his foot was on the step, and he had been foiled–eight, nine, ten–no wonder that whistling man had such a big Adam's apple–I wondered if it hurt his neck when he talked, being so pointed–nineteen, twenty–the girl was licking more ice-cream, with precious, tiny licks–twenty-five, twenty-six–I wondered if I did count to twenty-six mechanically. At this point I gave it up, and watched for Lord Tennyson's bald head to come spinning round on the painted rim of the roundabouts, followed by a red-faced Lord Roberts, and a villainous-looking Disraeli.

'Fifty-one–' said my mother. 'Come–come along.'

We hurried through the fair, towards the church; towards a garden where the last red sentinels looked out from the top of the hollyhock spires. The garden was a tousled mass of faded pink chrysanthemums, and weak-eyed Michaelmas daisies, and spectre stalks of hollyhocks. It belonged to a low, dark house, which crouched behind a screen of yews. We walked along to the front. The blinds were down, and in one room we could see the stale light of candles burning.

'Is this Yew Cottage?' asked my mother of a curious lad.

'It's Mrs May's,' replied the boy.

'Does she live alone?' I asked.

'She 'ad French Carlin—but he's dead—an' she's letten th' candles ter keep th' owd lad off'n 'im.'

We went to the house and knocked.

'An' ye come about him?' hoarsely whispered a bent old woman, looking up with very blue eyes, nodding her old head with its velvet net significantly towards the inner room.

'Yes—' said my mother, 'we had a letter.'

'Ay, poor fellow—he's gone, missis,' and the old lady shook her head. Then she looked at us curiously, leaned forward, and, putting her withered old hand on my mother's arm, her hand with its dark blue veins, she whispered in confidence, 'And the candles 'as gone out twice. 'E wor a funny feller, very funny!'

'I must come in and settle things—I am his nearest relative,' said my mother, trembling.

'Yes—I must 'a dozed, for when I looked up, it wor black darkness. Missis, I dursn't sit up wi' 'im no more, an' many a one I've laid out. Eh, but his sufferin's, Missis—poor feller—eh, Missis!'—she lifted her ancient hands, and looked up at my mother, with her eyes so intensely blue.

'Do you know where he kept his papers?' asked my mother.

'Yis, I axed Father Burns about it; he said we mun pray for 'im. I bought him candles out o' my own pocket. He wor a rum feller, he wor!' and again she shook her grey head mournfully. My mother took a step forward.

'Did ye want to see 'im?' asked the old woman with half-timid questioning.

'Yes,' replied my mother, with a vigorous nod. She perceived now that the old lady was deaf.

We followed the woman into the kitchen, a long, low room, dark, with drawn blinds.

'Sit ye down,' said the old lady in the same low tone, as if she were speaking to herself:

'Ye are his sister, 'appen?'

My mother shook her head.

'Oh—his brother's wife!' persisted the old lady.

We shook our heads.

'Only a cousin?' she guessed, and looked at us appealingly. I nodded assent.

'Sit ye there a minute,' she said, and trotted off. She banged the door, and jarred a chair as she went. When she returned, she set down a bottle and two glasses with a thump on the table in front of us. Her thin, skinny wrist seemed hardly capable of carrying the bottle.

'It's one as he'd only just begun of—'ave a drop to keep ye up—do now, poor thing,' she said, pushing the bottle to my mother and hurrying off, returning with the sugar and the kettle. We refused.

''E won't want it no more, poor feller–an' it's good, Missis, he allers drank it good. Ay–an' 'e 'adn't a drop the last three days, poor man, poor feller, not a drop. Come now, it'll stay ye, come now.' We refused.

''T's in there,' she whispered, pointing to a closed door in a dark corner of the gloomy kitchen. I stumbled up a little step, and went plunging against a rickety table on which was a candle in a tall brass candlestick. Over went the candle, and it rolled on the floor, and the brass holder fell with much clanging.

'Eh!–Eh! Dear–Lord, Dear–Heart. Dear–Heart!' wailed the old woman. She hastened trembling round to the other side of the bed, and relit the extinguished candle at the taper which was still burning. As she returned, the light glowed on her old, wrinkled face, and on the burnished knobs of the dark mahogany bedstead, while a stream of wax dripped down on to the floor. By the glimmering light of the two tapers we could see the outlined form under the counterpane. She turned back the hem and began to make painful wailing sounds. My heart was beating heavily, and I felt choked. I did not want to look–but I must. It was the man I had seen in the woods–with the puffiness gone from his face. I felt the great wild pity, and a sense of terror, and a sense of horror, and a sense of awful littleness and loneliness among a great empty space. I felt beyond myself as if I were a mere fleck drifting unconsciously through the dark. Then I felt my mother's arm round my shoulders, and she cried pitifully, 'Oh, my son, my son!'

I shivered, and came back to myself. There were no tears in my mother's face, only a great pleading. 'Never mind, Mother–never mind,' I said incoherently.

She rose and covered the face again, and went round to the old lady, and held her still, and stayed her little wailings. The woman wiped from her cheeks the few tears of old age, and pushed her grey hair smooth under the velvet network.

'Where are all his things?' asked mother.

'Eh?' said the old lady, lifting up her ear.

'Are all his things here?' repeated mother in a louder tone.

'Here?'–the woman waved her hand round the room. It contained the great mahogany bedstead naked of hangings, a desk, and an oak chest, and two or three mahogany chairs. 'I couldn't get him upstairs; he's only been here about a three week.'

'Where's the key to the desk?' said my mother loudly in the woman's ear.

'Yes,' she replied–'it's his desk.' She looked at us, perplexed and doubtful, fearing she had misunderstood us. This was dreadful.

'Key!' I shouted. 'Where is the key?'

Her old face was full of trouble as she shook her head. I took it that she did not know.

'Where are his clothes? *Clothes*,' I repeated, pointing to my coat. She understood, and muttered, 'I'll fetch 'em ye.'

We should have followed her as she hurried upstairs through a door near the head of the bed, had we not heard a heavy footstep in the kitchen, and a voice saying, 'Is the old lady going to drink with the Devil? Hullo, Mrs May, come and drink with me!' We heard the tinkle of the liquor poured into a glass, and almost immediately the light tap of the empty tumbler on the table.

'I'll see what the old girl's up to,' he said, and the heavy tread came towards us. Like me, he stumbled at the little step, but escaped collision with the table.

'Damn that fool's step,' he said heartily. It was the doctor–for he kept his hat on his head, and did not hesitate to stroll about the house. He was a big, burly, red-faced man.

'I beg your pardon,' he said, observing my mother. My mother bowed.

'Mrs Beardsall?' he asked, taking off his hat.

My mother bowed.

'I posted a letter to you. You are a relative of his–of poor old Carlin's?'–he nodded sideways towards the bed.

'The nearest,' said my mother.

'Poor fellow–he was a bit stranded. Comes of being a bachelor, Ma'am.'

'I was very much surprised to hear from him,' said my mother.

'Yes, I guess he's not been much of a one for writing to his friends. He's had a bad time lately. You have to pay some time or other. We bring them on ourselves–silly devils as we are.–I beg your pardon.'

There was a moment of silence, during which the doctor sighed, and then began to whistle softly.

'Well–we might be more comfortable if we had the blind up,' he said, letting daylight in among the glimmer of the tapers as he spoke.

'At any rate,' he said, 'you won't have any trouble settling up–no debts or anything of that. I believe there's a bit to leave–so it's not so bad. Poor devil–he was very down at the last; but we have to pay at one end or the other. What on earth is the old girl after?' he asked, looking up at the raftered ceiling, which was rumbling and thundering with the old lady's violent rummaging.

'We wanted the key of his desk,' said my mother.

'Oh–I can find you that–and the will. He told me where they were, and to give them you when you came. He seemed to think a lot of you. Perhaps he might ha' done better for himself–'

Here we heard the heavy tread of the old lady coming downstairs. The doctor went to the foot of the stairs.

'Hello, now–be careful!' he bawled. The poor old woman did as he expected, and trod on the braces of the trousers she was trailing, and came crashing into his arms. He set her tenderly down, saying, 'Not hurt, are you?–no!' and he smiled at her and shook his head.

'Eh, Doctor–Eh, Doctor–bless ye, I'm thankful ye've come. Ye'll see to 'em now, will ye?'

'Yes–' he nodded in his bluff, winning way, and hurrying into the kitchen, he mixed her a glass of whisky, and brought one for himself, saying to her, 'There you are–'twas a nasty shaking for you.'

The poor old woman sat in a chair by the open door of the staircase, the pile of clothing tumbled about her feet. She looked round pitifully at us, and at the daylight struggling among the candle-light, making a ghostly gleam on the bed where the rigid figure lay unmoved; her hand trembled so that she could scarcely hold her glass.

The doctor gave us the keys, and we rifled the desk and the drawers, sorting out all the papers. The doctor sat sipping and talking to us all the time.

'Yes,' he said, 'he's only been here about two years. Felt himself beginning to break up then, I think. He'd been a long time abroad; they always called him Frenchy.' The doctor sipped and reflected, and sipped again, 'Ay–he'd run the rig in his day–used to dream dreadfully. Good thing the old woman was so deaf. Awful, when a man gives himself away in his sleep; played the deuce with him, knowing it.' Sip, sip, sip–and more reflections–and another glass to be mixed.

'But he was a jolly decent fellow–generous, open-handed. The folks didn't like him, because they couldn't get to the bottom of him; they always hate a thing they can't fathom. He was close, there's no mistake–save when he was asleep sometimes.' The doctor looked at his glass and sighed.

'However–we shall miss him–shan't we, Mrs May?' he bawled suddenly, startling us, making us glance at the bed.

He lit his pipe and puffed voluminously in order to obscure the attraction of his glass. Meanwhile we examined the papers. There were very few letters–one or two addressed to Paris. There were many bills, and receipts, and notes–business, all business.

There was hardly a trace of sentiment among all the litter. My mother sorted out such papers as she considered valuable; the others, letters and missives which she glanced at cursorily and put aside, she took into the kitchen and burned. She seemed afraid to find out too much.

The doctor continued to colour his tobacco smoke with a few pensive words. 'Ay,' he said, 'there are two ways. You can burn your lamp with a big draught, and it'll flare away, till the oil's gone, then it'll stink and smoke itself out. Or you can keep it trim on the kitchen table, dirty your fingers occasionally trimming it up, and it'll last a long time, and sink out mildly.' Here he turned to his glass, and finding it empty, was awakened to reality.

'Anything I can do, Madam?' he asked.

'No, thank you.'

'Ay, I don't suppose there's much to settle. Nor many tears to shed–when a fellow spends his years an' his prime on the Lord knows who, you can't expect those that remember him young to feel his loss too keenly. He'd had his fling in his day, though, ma'am. Ay–must ha' had some rich times. No lasting satisfaction in it though–always wanting, craving. There's nothing like marrying–you've got your dish before you then, and you've got to eat it.' He lapsed again into reflection, from which he did not rouse till we had locked up the desk, burned the useless papers, put the others into my pocket and the black bag, and were standing ready to depart. Then the doctor looked up suddenly and said:

'But what about the funeral?'

Then he noticed the weariness of my mother's look, and he jumped up, and quickly seized his hat, saying:

'Come across to my wife and have a cup of tea. Buried in these dam holes a fellow gets such a boor. Do come–my little wife is lonely–come just to see her.'

My mother smiled and thanked him. We turned to go. My mother hesitated in her walk; on the threshold of the room she glanced round at the bed, but she went on.

Outside, in the fresh air of the fading afternoon, I could not believe it was true. It was not true, that sad, colourless face with grey beard, wavering in the yellow candle-light. It was a lie–that wooden bedstead, that deaf woman, they were fading phrases of the untruth. That yellow blaze of little sunflowers was true, and the shadow from the sun-dial on the warm old almshouses–that was real. The heavy afternoon sunlight came round us warm and reviving; we shivered, and the untruth went out of our veins, and we were no longer chilled.

The doctor's house stood sweetly among the beech trees, and at the iron fence in front of the little lawn a woman was talking to a beautiful Jersey cow that pushed its dark nose through the fence from the field beyond. She was a little, dark woman with vivid colouring; she rubbed the nose of the delicate animal, peeped right into the dark eyes, and talked in a lovable Scottish speech; talked as a mother talks softly to her child.

When she turned round in surprise to greet us there was still the softness of a rich affection in her eyes. She gave us tea, and scones, and apple jelly, and all the time we listened with delight to her voice, which was musical as bees humming in the lime trees. Though she said nothing significant, we listened to her attentively.

Her husband was merry and kind. She glanced at him with quick glances of apprehension, and her eyes avoided him. He, in his merry, frank way, chaffed her, and praised her extravagantly, and teased her again. Then he became a trifle uneasy. I think she was afraid he had been drinking; I think she was shaken with horror when she found him tipsy, and bewildered and terrified when she saw him drunk. They had no children. I noticed he ceased to joke when she became a little constrained. He glanced at her often, and looked somewhat pitiful when she avoided his looks, and he grew uneasy, and I could see he wanted to go away.

'I had better go with you to see the vicar, then,' he said to me, and we left the room, whose windows looked south, over the meadows, the room where dainty little water-colours, and beautiful bits of embroidery, and empty flower-vases, and two dirty novels from the town library, and the closed piano, and the odd cups, and the chipped spout of the teapot causing stains on the cloth—all told one story.

We went to the joiner's and ordered the coffin, and the doctor had a glass of whisky on it; the graveyard fees were paid, and the doctor sealed the engagement with a drop of brandy; the vicar's port completed the doctor's joviality, and we went home.

This time the disquiet in the little woman's dark eyes could not dispel the doctor's merriment. He rattled away, and she nervously twisted her wedding-ring. He insisted on driving us to the station, in spite of our alarm.

'But you will be quite safe with him,' said his wife, in her caressing Highland speech. When she shook hands at parting I noticed the hardness of the little palm;—and I have always hated an old, black alpaca dress.

It is such a long way home from the station at Eberwich. We rode part way in the bus; then we walked. It is a very long way for my mother, when her steps are heavy with trouble.

Rebecca was out by the rhododendrons looking for us. She hurried to us all solicitous, and asked Mother if she had had tea.

'But you'll do with another cup,' she said, and ran back into the house.

She came into the dining-room to take my mother's bonnet and coat. She wanted us to talk; she was distressed on my mother's behalf; she noticed the blackness that lay under her eyes, and she fidgeted about, unwilling to ask anything, yet uneasy and anxious to know.

'Lettie has been home?' she said.

'And gone back again?' asked Mother.

'She only came to change her dress. She put the green poplin on. She wondered where you'd gone.'

'What did you tell her?'

'I said you'd just gone out a bit. She said she was glad. She was as lively as a squirrel.'

Rebecca looked wistfully at my mother. At length the latter said:

'He's dead, Rebecca. I have seen him.'

'Now thank God for that—no more need to worry over him.'

'Well!—He died all alone, Rebecca—all alone.'

'He died as you've lived,' said Becky with some asperity.

'But I've had the children, I've had the children—we won't tell Lettie, Rebecca.'

'No 'm.' Rebecca left the room.

'You and Lettie will have the money,' said mother to me. There was a sum of four thousand pounds or so. It was left to my mother; or, in default to Lettie and me.'

'Well, Mother—if it's ours, it's yours.'

There was silence for some minutes, then she said, 'You might have had a father—'

'We're thankful we hadn't, Mother. You spared us that.'

'But how can you tell?' said my mother.

'I can,' I replied. 'And I am thankful to you.'

'If ever you feel scorn for one who is near you rising in your throat, try and be generous, my lad.'

'Well—' said I.

'Yes,' she replied, 'we'll say no more. Sometime you must tell Lettie—you tell her.'

I did tell her, a week or so afterwards.

'Who knows?' she asked, her face hardening.

'Mother, Becky, and ourselves.'

'Nobody else?'

'No.'

'Then it's a good thing he is out of the way if he was such a nuisance to Mother. Where is she?'

'Upstairs.'

Lettie ran to her.

5

THE SCENT OF BLOOD

The death of the man who was our father changed our lives. It was not that we suffered a great grief; the chief trouble was the unanswered crying of failure. But we were changed in our feelings and in our relations; there was a new consciousness, a new carefulness.

We had lived between the woods and the water all our lives, Lettie and I, and she had sought the bright notes in everything. She seemed to hear the water laughing, and the leaves tittering and giggling like young girls; the aspen fluttered like the draperies of a flirt, and the sound of the wood-pigeons was almost foolish in its sentimentality.

Lately, however, she had noticed again the cruel, pitiful crying of a hedgehog caught in a gin, and she had noticed the traps for the fierce little murderers, traps walled in with a small fence of fir, and baited with the guts of a killed rabbit.

On an afternoon a short time after our visit to Cossethay, Lettie sat in the window seat. The sun clung to her hair, and kissed her with passionate splashes

of colour brought from the vermilion, dying creeper outside. The sun loved
Lettie, and was loath to leave her. She looked out over Nethermere to
Highclose, vague in the September mist. Had it not been for the scarlet light on
her face, I should have thought her look was sad and serious. She nestled up to
the window, and leaned her head against the wooden shaft. Gradually she
drooped into sleep. Then she became wonderfully childish again—it was the
girl of seventeen sleeping there, with her full pouting lips slightly apart, and the
breath coming lightly. I felt the old feeling of responsibility; I must protect her,
and take care of her.

There was a crunch of the gravel. It was Leslie coming. He lifted his hat to
her, thinking she was looking. He had that fine, lithe physique, suggestive of
much animal vigour; his person was exceedingly attractive; one watched him
move about, and felt pleasure. His face was less pleasing than his person. He
was not handsome; his eyebrows were too light, his nose was large and ugly,
and his forehead, though high and fair, was without dignity. But he had a frank,
good-natured expression, and a fine, wholesome laugh.

He wondered why she did not move. As he came nearer he saw. Then he
winked at me and came in. He tiptoed across the room to look at her. The sweet
carelessness of her attitude, the appealing, half-pitiful girlishness of her face
touched his responsive heart, and he leaned forward and kissed her cheek
where already was a crimson stain of sunshine.

She roused half out of her sleep with a little, petulant 'Oh!' as an awkward
child. He sat down behind her, and gently drew her head against him, looking
down at her with a tender, soothing smile. I thought she was going to fall asleep
thus. But her eyelids quivered, and her eyes beneath them flickered into
consciousness.

'Leslie!—oh!—Let me go!' she exclaimed, pushing him away. He loosed her,
and rose, looking at her reproachfully. She shook her dress, and went quickly to
the mirror to arrange her hair.

'You are mean!' she exclaimed, looking very flushed, vexed, and dishevelled.

He laughed indulgently, saying, 'You shouldn't go to sleep then and look so
pretty. Who could help?'

'It is not nice!' she said, frowning with irritation.

'We are not "nice"—are we? I thought we were proud of our uncon-
ventionality. Why shouldn't I kiss you?'

'Because it is a question of me, not of you alone.'

'Dear me, you *are* in a way!'

'Mother is coming.'

'Is she? You had better tell her.'

Mother was very fond of Leslie.

'Well, sir,' she said, 'why are you frowning?'

He broke into a laugh.

'Lettie is scolding me for kissing her when she was playing "Sleeping
Beauty".'

'The conceit of the boy, to play Prince!' said my mother.

'Oh, but it appears I was sadly out of character,' he said ruefully.

Lettie laughed and forgave him.

'Well,' he said, looking at her and smiling, 'I came to ask you to go out.'

'It is a lovely afternoon,' said Mother.

She glanced at him, and said:

'I feel dreadfully lazy.'

'Never mind!' he replied, 'you'll wake up. Go and put your hat on.'
He sounded impatient. She looked at him.
He seemed to be smiling peculiarly.
She lowered her eyes and went out of the room.
'She'll come all right,' he said to himself, and to me. 'She likes to play you on a string.'
She must have heard him. When she came in again, drawing on her gloves, she said quietly:
'You come as well, Pat.'
He swung round and stared at her in angry amazement.
'I had rather stay and finish this sketch,' I said, feeling uncomfortable.
'No, but do come, there's a dear.' She took the brush from my hand, and drew me from my chair. The blood flushed into his cheeks. He went quietly into the hall and brought my cap.
'All right!' he said angrily. 'Women like to fancy themselves Napoleons.'
'They do, dear Iron Duke, they do,' she mocked.
'Yet, there's a Waterloo in all their histories,' he said, since she had supplied him with the idea.
'Say Peterloo, my general, say Peterloo.'
'Ay, Peterloo,' he replied, with a splendid curl of the lip–'Easy conquests!'
'"He came, he saw, he conquered",' Lettie recited.
'Are you coming?' he said, getting more angry.
'When you bid me,' she replied, taking my arm.
We went through the wood, and through the dishevelled border-land to the high road, through the border-land that should have been park-like, but which was shaggy with loose grass and yellow mole-hills, ragged with gorse and bramble and briar, with wandering old thorn trees, and a queer clump of Scotch firs.
On the highway the leaves were falling, and they chattered under our steps. The water was mild and blue, and the corn stood drowsily in 'stook'.
We climbed the hill behind Highclose, and walked on along the upland, looking across towards the hills of arid Derbyshire, and seeing them not, because it was autumn. We came in sight of the head-stocks of the pit at Selsby, and of the ugly village standing blank and naked on the brow of the hill.
Lettie was in very high spirits. She laughed and joked continually. She picked bunches of hips and stuck them in her dress. Having got a thorn in her finger from a spray of blackberries, she went to Leslie to have it squeezed out. We were all quite gay as we turned off the high road and went along the bridle path, with the woods on our right, the high Strelley hills shutting in our small valley in front, and the fields and the common to the left. About half-way down the lane we heard the slurr of the scythe-stone on the scythe. Lettie went to the hedge to see. It was George mowing the oats on the steep hillside where the machine could not go. His father was tying up the corn into sheaves.
Straightening his back, Mr Saxton saw us, and called to us to come and help. We pushed through a gap in the hedge and went up to him.
'Now then,' said the father to me, 'take that coat off,' and to Lettie, 'Have you brought us a drink? No;–come, that sounds bad! Going a walk I guess. You see what it is to get fat,' and he pulled a wry face as he bent over to tie the corn. He was a man beautifully ruddy and burly, in the prime of life.
'Show me, I'll do some,' said Lettie.
'Nay,' he answered gently, 'it would scratch your wrists and break your

stays. Hark at my hands'–he rubbed them together–'like sandpaper!'

George had his back to us, and had not noticed us. He continued to mow. Leslie watched him.

'That's a fine movement!' he exclaimed.

'Yes,' replied the father, rising very red in the face from the tying, 'and our George enjoys a bit o' mowing. It puts you in fine condition when you get over the first stiffness.'

We moved across to the standing corn. The sun being mild, George had thrown off his hat, and his black hair was moist and twisted into confused half-curls. Firmly planted, he swung with a beautiful rhythm from the waist. On the hip of his belted breeches hung the scythe-stone; his shirt, faded almost white, was torn juśt above the belt, and showed the muscles of his back playing like lights upon the white sand of a brook. There was something exceedingly attractive in the rhythmic body.

I spoke to him, and he turned round. He looked straight at Lettie with a flashing, betraying smile. He was remarkably handsome. He tried to say some words of greeting, then he bent down and gathered an armful of corn, and deliberately bound it up.

Like him, Lettie had found nothing to say. Leslie, however, remarked:

'I should think mowing is a nice exercise.'

'It is,' he replied, and continued, as Leslie picked up the scythe, 'but it will make you sweat, and your hands will be sore.'

Leslie tossed his head a little, threw off his coat, and said briefly:

'How do you do it?' Without waiting for a reply he proceeded. George said nothing, but turned to Lettie.

'You are picturesque,' she said, a trifle awkwardly, 'quite fit for an Idyll.'

'And you?' he said.

She shrugged her shoulders, laughed, and turned to pick up a scarlet pimpernel.

'How do you bind the corn?' she asked.

He took some long straws, cleaned them, and showed her the way to hold them. Instead of attending, she looked at his hands, big, hard, inflamed by the snaith of the scythe.

'I don't think I could do it,' she said.

'No,' he replied quietly, and watched Leslie mowing. The latter who was wonderfully ready at everything, was doing fairly well, but he had not the invincible sweep of the other, nor did he make his same crisp crunching music.

'I bet he'll sweat,' said George.

'Don't you?' she replied.

'A bit–but I'm not dressed up.'

'Do you know,' she said suddenly, 'your arms tempt me to touch them. They are such a fine brown colour, and they look so hard.'

He held out one arm to her. She hesitated, then she swiftly put her finger-tips on the smooth brown muscle, and drew them along. Quickly she hid her hand into the folds of her skirt, blushing.

He laughed a low, quiet laugh, at once pleasant and startling to hear.

'I wish I could work here,' she said, looking away at the standing corn, and the dim blue woods. He followed her look, and laughed quietly, with indulgent resignation.

'I do!' she said emphatically.

'You feel so fine,' he said, pushing his hand through his open shirt-front, and gently rubbing the muscles of his side. 'It's a pleasure to work or to stand still. It's a pleasure to yourself–your own physique.'

She looked at him, full at his physical beauty, as if he were some great firm bud of life.

Leslie came up, wiping his brow.

'Jove,' said he, 'I do perspire.'

George picked up his coat and helped him into it, saying:

'You may take a chill.'

'It's a jolly nice form of exercise,' said he.

George, who had been feeling one finger-tip, now took out his pen-knife and proceeded to dig a thorn from his hand.

'What a hide you must have,' said Leslie.

Lettie said nothing, but she recoiled slightly.

The father, glad of an excuse to straighten his back and to chat, came to us.

'You'd soon had enough,' he said, laughing to Leslie.

George startled us with a sudden, 'Holloa'. We turned, and saw a rabbit, which had burst from the corn, go coursing through the hedge, dodging and bounding the sheaves. The standing corn was a patch along the hill-side some fifty paces in length, and ten or so in width.

'I didn't think there'd have been any in,' said the father, picking up a short rake, and going to the low wall of the corn. We all followed.

'Watch!' said the father, 'if you see the heads of the corn shake!'

We prowled round the patch of corn.

'Hold! Look out!' shouted the father excitedly, and immediately after a rabbit broke from the cover.

'Ay–Ay–Ay,' was the shout, 'turn him–turn him!' We set off full pelt. The bewildered little brute, scared by Leslie's wild running and crying, turned from its course, and dodged across the hill, threading its terrified course through the maze of lying sheaves, spurting on in a painful zigzag, now bounding over an untied bundle of corn, now swerving from the sound of a shout. The little wretch was hard pressed; George rushed upon it. It darted into some fallen corn, but he had seen it, and had fallen on it. In an instant he was up again, and the little creature was dangling from his hand.

We returned, panting, sweating, our eyes flashing, to the edge of the standing corn. I heard Lettie calling, and turning round saw Emily and the two children entering the field as they passed from school.

'There's another!' shouted Leslie.

I saw the oat-tops quiver. 'Here! Here!' I yelled. The animal leaped out, and made for the hedge. George and Leslie, who were on that side, dashed off, turned him, and he coursed back our way. I headed him off to the father who swept in pursuit for a short distance, but who was too heavy for the work. The little beast made towards the gate, but this time Mollie, with her hat in her hand and her hair flying, whirled upon him, and she and the little fragile làd sent him back again. The rabbit was getting tired. It dodged the sheaves badly, running towards the top hedge. I went after it. If I could have let myself fall on it I could have caught it, but this was impossible to me, and I merely prevented its dashing through the hole into safety. It raced along the hedge bottom. George tore after it. As he was upon it, it darted into the hedge. He fell flat, and shot his hand into the gap. But it had escaped. He lay there, panting in great sobs, and looking at me with eyes in which excitement and exhaustion struggled like flickering light and darkness. When he could speak, he said, 'Why didn't you fall on top of it?'

'I couldn't,' said I.

We returned again. The two children were peering into the thick corn also. We thought there was nothing more. George began to mow. As I walked round I caught sight of a rabbit skulking near the bottom corner of the patch. Its ears lay pressed against its back; I could see the palpitation of the heart under the brown fur, and I could see the shining dark eyes looking at me. I felt no pity for it, but still I could not actually hurt it. I beckoned to the father. He ran up, and aimed a blow with the rake. There was a sharp little cry which sent a hot pain through me as if I had been cut. But the rabbit ran out, and instantly I forgot the cry, and gave pursuit, fairly feeling my fingers stiffen to choke it. It was all lame. Leslie was upon it in a moment, and he almost pulled its head off in his excitement to kill it.

I looked up. The girls were at the gate, just turning away.

'There are no more,' said the father.

At that instant Mollie shouted.

'There's one down this hole.'

The hole was too small for George to get his hand in, so we dug it out with the rake-handle. The stick went savagely down the hole, and there came a squeak.

'Mice!' said George, and as he said it the mother slid out. Somebody knocked her on the back, and the hole was opened out. Little mice seemed to swarm everywhere. It was like killing insects. We counted nine little ones lying dead.

'Poor brute,' said George, looking at the mother. 'What a job she must have had rearing that lot!' He picked her up, handled her curiously and with pity. Then he said, 'Well, I may as well finish this tonight!'

His father took another scythe from off the hedge, and together they soon laid the proud, quivering heads low. Leslie and I tied up as they mowed, and soon all was finished.

The beautiful day was flushing to die. Over in the west the mist was gathering bluer. The intense stillness was broken by the rhythmic hum of the engines at the distant coal-mine, as they drew up the last bantles of men. As we walked across the fields the tubes of stubble tinkled like dulcimers. The scent of the corn began to rise gently. The last cry of the pheasants came from the wood, and the little clouds of birds were gone.

I carried a scythe, and we walked, pleasantly weary, down the hill towards the farm. The children had gone home with the rabbits.

When we reached the mill, we found the girls just rising from the table. Emily began to carry away the used pots, and to set clean ones for us. She merely glanced at us and said her formal greeting. Lettie picked up a book that lay in the ingle seat, and went to the window. George dropped into a chair. He had flung off his coat, and had pushed back his hair. He rested his great brown arms on the table and was silent for a moment.

'Running like that,' he said to me, passing his hand over his eyes, 'makes you more tired than a whole day's work. I don't think I shall do it again.'

'The sport's exciting while it lasts,' said Leslie.

'It does you more harm than the rabbits do us good,' said Mrs Saxton.

'Oh, I don't know, Mother,' drawled her son, 'it's a couple of shillings.'

'And a couple of days off your life.'

'What be that!' he replied, taking a piece of bread and butter, and biting a large piece from it.

'Pour us a drop of tea,' he said to Emily.

'I don't know that I shall wait on such brutes,' she replied, relenting, and flourishing the teapot.

'Oh,' said he, taking another piece of bread and butter, 'I'm not all alone in my savageness this time.'

'Men are all brutes,' said Lettie hotly, without looking up from her book.

'You can tame us,' said Leslie, in mighty good humour.

She did not reply. George began, in that deliberate voice that so annoyed Emily:

'It does make you mad, though, to touch the fur, and not be able to grab him'–he laughed quietly.

Emily moved off in disgust. Lettie opened her mouth sharply to speak, but remained silent.

'I don't know,' said Leslie. 'When it comes to killing it goes against the stomach.'

'If you can run,' said George, 'you should be able to run to death. When your blood's up, you don't hang half-way.'

'I think a man is horrible,' said Lettie, 'who can tear the head off a little mite of a thing like a rabbit, after running it in torture over a field.'

'When he is nothing but a barbarian to begin with–' said Emily.

'If you began to run yourself–you'd be the same,' said George.

'Why, women are cruel enough,' said Leslie, with a glance at Lettie. 'Yes,' he continued, 'they're cruel enough in their way'–another look, and a comical little smile.

'Well,' said George, 'what's the good finicking! If you feel like doing a thing–you'd better do it.'

'Unless you haven't courage,' said Emily, bitingly.

He looked up at her with dark eyes, suddenly full of anger.

'But,' said Lettie–she could not hold herself from asking, 'Don't you think it's brutal, now–now that you *do* think–isn't it degrading and mean to run the poor little things down?'

'Perhaps it is,' he replied, 'but it wasn't an hour ago.'

'You have no feeling,' she said bitterly.

He laughed deprecatingly, but said nothing.

We finished tea in silence, Lettie reading, Emily moving about the house. George got up and went out at the end. A moment or two after we heard him across the yard with the milk-buckets, singing 'The Ash Grove'.

'He doesn't care a scrap for anything,' said Emily with accumulated bitterness. Lettie looked out of the window across the yard, thinking. She looked very glum.

After a while we went out also, before the light faded altogether from the pond. Emily took us into the lower garden to get some ripe plums. The old garden was very low. The soil was black. The cornbind and goosegrass were clutching at the ancient gooseberry bushes, which sprawled by the paths. The garden was not very productive, save of weeds, and, perhaps, tremendous lank artichokes or swollen marrows. But at the bottom, where the end of the farm buildings rose high and grey, there was a plum tree which had been crucified to the wall, and which had broken away and leaned forward from bondage. Now under the boughs were hidden great mist-bloomed, crimson treasures, splendid globes. I shook the old, ragged trunk, green, with even the fresh gum dulled over, and the treasures fell heavily, thudding down among the immense rhubarb leaves below. The girls laughed, and we divided the spoil, and turned back to the yard. We went down to the edge of the garden, which skirted the bottom pond, a pool chained in a heavy growth of weeds. It was moving with rats, the father had said. The rushes were thick below us; opposite, the great bank fronted us, with orchard trees climbing it like a hillside. The lower pond received the overflow from the upper by a tunnel from the deep black sluice.

Two rats ran into the black culvert at our approach. We sat on some piled, mossy stones to watch. The rats came out again, ran a little way, stopped, ran again, listened, were reassured, and slid about freely, dragging their long naked tails. Soon six or seven grey beasts were playing round the mouth of the culvert, in the gloom. They sat and wiped their sharp faces, stroking their whiskers. Then one would give a little rush and a little squirm of excitement and would jump vertically into the air, alighting on four feet, running, sliding into the black shadow. One dropped with an ugly plop into the water, and swam towards us, the hoary imp, his sharp snout and his wicked little eyes moving at us. Lettie shuddered. I threw a stone into the dead pool, and frightened them all. But we had frightened ourselves more, so we hurried away, and stamped our feet in relief on the free pavement of the yard.

Leslie was looking for us. He had been inspecting the yard and the stock under Mr Saxton's supervision.

'Were you running away from me?' he asked.

'No,' she replied. 'I have been to fetch you a plum. Look!' And she showed him two in a leaf.

'They are too pretty to eat!' said he.

'You have not tasted yet,' she laughed.

'Come,' he said, offering her his arm. 'Let us go up to the water.' She took his arm.

It was a splendid evening, with the light all thick and yellow lying on the smooth pond. Lettie made him lift her on to a leaning bough of willow. He sat with his head resting against her skirts. Emily and I moved on. We heard him murmur something, and her voice reply, gently, caressingly:

'No—let us be still—it is all so still—I love it best of all now.'

Emily and I talked, sitting at the base of the alders, a little way on. After an excitement, and in the evening, especially in autumn, one is inclined to be sad and sentimental. We had forgotten that the darkness was weaving. I heard in the little distance Leslie's voice begin to murmur like a flying beetle that comes not too near. Then, away down in the yard, George began singing the old song, 'I sowed the seeds of love'.

This interrupted the flight of Leslie's voice, and as the singing came nearer, the hum of low words ceased. We went forward to meet George. Leslie sat up, clasping his knees, and did not speak. George came nearer, saying:

'The moon is going to rise.'

'Let me get down,' said Lettie, lifting her hands to him to help her. He, mistaking her wish, put his hands under her arms, and set her gently down, as one would a child. Leslie got up quickly, and seemed to hold himself separate, resenting the intrusion.

'I thought you were all four together,' said George quietly. Lettie turned quickly at the apology:

'So we were. So we are—five now. Is it there the moon will rise?'

'Yes—I like to see it come over the wood. It lifts slowly up to stare at you. I always think it wants to know something, and I always think I have something to answer, only I don't know what it is,' said Emily.

Where the sky was pale in the east over the rim of wood came the forehead of the yellow moon. We stood and watched in silence. Then, as the great disc, nearly full, lifted and looked straight upon us, we were washed off our feet in a vague sea of moonlight. We stood with the light like water on our faces. Lettie was glad, a little bit exalted; Emily was passionately troubled; her lips were parted, almost beseeching; Leslie was frowning, oblivious, and George was thinking, and the terrible, immense moonbeams braided through his feeling. At length Leslie said softly, mistakenly:

'Come along, dear'–and he took her arm.

She let him lead her along the bank of the pond, and across the plank over the sluice.

'Do you know,' she said, as we were carefully descending the steep bank of the orchard, 'I feel as if I wanted to laugh, or dance–something rather outrageous.'

'Surely not like that *now*,' Leslie replied in a low voice, feeling really hurt.

'I do though! I will race you to the bottom.'

'No, no, dear!' He held her back. When he came to the wicket leading on to the front lawns, he said something to her softly, as he held the gate.

I think he wanted to utter his half-finished proposal, and so bind her.

She broke free, and, observing the long lawn which lay in grey shadow between the eastern and western glows, she cried:

'Polka!–a polka–one can dance a polka when the grass is smooth and short–even if there are some fallen leaves. Yes, yes–how jolly!'

She held out her hands to Leslie, but it was too great a shock to his mood. So she called to me, and there was a shade of anxiety in her voice, lest after all she should be caught in the toils of the night's sentiment.

'Pat–you'll dance with me–Leslie hates a polka.' I danced with her. I do not know the time when I could not polka–it seems innate in one's feet, to dance that dance. We went flying round, hissing through the dead leaves. The night, the low-hung yellow moon, the pallor of the west, the blue cloud of evening overhead went round and through the fantastic branches of the old laburnum, spinning a little madness. You cannot tire Lettie; her feet are wings that beat the air. When at last I stayed her she laughed as fresh as ever, as she bound her hair.

'There!' she said to Leslie, in tones of extreme satisfaction. 'That was lovely. Do you come and dance now.'

'Not a polka,' said he, sadly, feeling the poetry in his heart insulted by the jigging measure.

'But one cannot dance anything else on wet grass, and through shuffling dead leaves. You, George?'

'Emily says I jump,' he replied.

'Come on–come on'–and in a moment they were bounding across the grass. After a few steps she fell in with him, and they spun round the grass. It was true, he leaped, sprang with large strides, carrying her with him. It was a tremendous, irresistible dancing. Emily and I must join, making an inner ring. Now and again there was a sense of something white flying near, and wild rustle of draperies, and a swish of disturbed leaves as they whirled past us. Long after we were tired they danced on.

At the end, he looked big, erect, nerved with triumph, and she was exhilarated like a Bacchante.

'Have you finished?' Leslie asked.

She knew she was safe from his question that day.

'Yes,' she panted. 'You should have danced. Give me my hat, please. Do I look very disgraceful?'

He took her hat and gave it to her.

'Disgraceful?' he repeated.

'Oh, you *are* solemn tonight! What is it?'

'Yes, what is it?' he repeated ironically.

'It must be the moon. Now, is my hat straight? Tell me now—you're not looking. Then put it level. Now then! Why, your hands are quite cold, and mine so hot! I feel so impish,' and she laughed.

'There—now I'm ready. Do you notice those little chrysanthemums trying to smell sadly; when the old moon is laughing and winking through those boughs. What business have they with their sadness!' She took a handful of petals and flung them into the air: 'There—if they sigh they ask for sorrow—I like things to wink and look wild.'

6

THE EDUCATION OF GEORGE

As I have said, Strelley Mill lies at the north end of the long Nethermere valley. On the northern slopes lay its pasture and arable lands. The shaggy common, now closed, and the cultivated land was bounded on the east by the sharp dip of the brook course, a thread of woodland broadening into a spinney and ending at the upper pond; beyond this, on the east, rose the sharp, wild, grassy hillside, scattered with old trees, ruinous with the gaunt, ragged bones of old hedge-rows, grown into thorn trees. Along the rim of the hills, beginning in the north-west, were dark woodlands, which swept round east and south till they raced down in riot to the very edge of southern Nethermere, surrounding our house. From the eastern hillcrest, looking straight across, you could see the spire of Selsby church, and a few roofs, and the head-stocks of the pit.

So on three sides the farm was skirted by woods, the dens of rabbits, and the common held another warren.

Now the squire of the estate, head of an ancient, once even famous, but now decayed house, loved his rabbits. Unlike the family fortunes, the family tree flourished amazingly; Sherwood could show nothing comparable. Its ramifications were stupendous; it was more like a banyan than a British oak. How was the good squire to nourish himself and his lady, his name, his tradition, and his thirteen lusty branches on his meagre estates? An evil fortune discovered to him that he could sell each of his rabbits, those bits of furry vermin, for a shilling or thereabout in Nottingham; since which time the noble family subsisted by rabbits.

Farms were gnawed away; corn and sweet grass departed from the face of the hills; cattle grew lean, unable to eat the defiled herbage. Then the farm became the home of a keeper, and the country was silent, with no sound of cattle, no clink of horses, no barking of lusty dogs.

But the squire loved his rabbits. He defended them against the snares of the despairing farmer, protected them with gun and notices to quit. How he glowed with thankfulness as he saw the dishevelled hillside heave when the gnawing hosts moved on!

'Are they not quails and manna?' said he to his sporting guest, early one Monday morning, as the high meadow broke into life at the sound of his gun. 'Quails and manna–in this wilderness?'

'They are, by Jove!' assented the sporting guest as he took another gun, while the saturnine keeper smiled grimly.

Meanwhile, Strelley Mill began to suffer under this gangrene. It was the outpost in the wilderness. It was an understood thing that none of the squire's tenants had a gun.

'Well,' said the squire to Mr Saxton, 'you have the land for next to nothing–next to nothing–at a rent really absurd. Surely the little that the rabbits eat–'

'It's not a little–come and look for yourself,' replied the farmer. The squire made a gesture of impatience.

'What *do* you want?' he inquired.

'Will you wire me off?' was the repeated request.

'Wire is–what does Halkett say–so much per yard–and it would come to–what did Halkett tell me now?–but a large sum. No, I can't do it.'

'Well, I can't live like this.'

'Have another glass of whisky? Yes, yes, I want another glass myself, and I can't drink alone–so if I am to enjoy my glass–That's it! Now surely you exaggerate a little. It's not so bad.'

'I can't go on like it, I'm sure.'

'Well, we'll see about compensation–we'll see. I'll have a talk with Halkett, and I'll come down and have a look at you. We all find a pinch somewhere–it's nothing but humanity's heritage.'

I was born in September, and love it best of all the months. There is no heat, no hurry, no thirst and weariness in corn harvest as there is in the hay. If the season is late, as is usual with us, then mid-September sees the corn still standing in stook. The mornings come slowly. The earth is like a woman married and fading; she does not leap up with a laugh for the first fresh kiss of dawn, but slowly, quietly, unexpectedly lies watching the waking of each new day. The blue mist, like memory in the eyes of a neglected wife, never goes from the wooded hill, and only at noon creeps from the near hedges. There is no bird to put a song in the throat of morning; only the crow's voice speaks during the day. Perhaps there is the regular breathing hush of the scythe–even the fretful jar of the mowing-machine. But next day, in the morning, all is still again. The lying corn is wet, and when you have bound it, and lift the heavy sheaf to make the stook, the tresses of oats wreathe round each other and drop mournfully.

As I worked with my friend through the still mornings we talked endlessly. I would give him the gist of what I knew of chemistry, and botany, and psychology. Day after day I told him what the professors had told me; of life, of sex and its origins; of Schopenhauer and William James. We had been friends for years, and he was accustomed to my talk. But this autumn fruited the first crop of intimacy between us. I talked a great deal of poetry to him, and of rudimentary metaphysics. He was very good stuff. He had hardly a single dogma, save that of pleasing himself. Religion was nothing to him. So he heard all I had to say with an open mind, and understood the drift of things very rapidly, and quickly made these ideas part of himself.

We tramped down to dinner with only the clinging warmth of the sunshine for a coat. In this still, enfolding weather a quiet companionship is very grateful. Autumn creeps through everything. The little damsons in the pudding taste of September, and are fragrant with memory. The voices of those at table are softer and more reminiscent than at haytime.

Afternoon is all warm and golden. Oat sheaves are lighter; they whisper to each other as they freely embrace. The long, stout stubble tinkles as the foot brushes over it; the scent of the straw is sweet. When the poor, bleached sheaves are lifted out of the hedge, a spray of nodding wild raspberries is disclosed, with belated berries ready to drop; among the damp grass lush blackberries may be discovered. Then one notices that the last bell hangs from the ragged spire of foxglove. The talk is of people, an odd book; of one's hopes—and the future; of Canada, where work is strenuous, but not life; where the plains are wide, and one is not lapped in a soft valley, like an apple that falls in a secluded orchard. The mist steals over the face of the warm afternoon. The tying-up is all finished, and it only remains to rear up the fallen bundles into shocks. The sun sinks into a golden glow in the west. The gold turns to red, the red darkens, like a fire burning low, the sun disappears behind the bank of milky mist, purple like the pale bloom on blue plums, and we put on our coats and go home.

In the evening, when the milking was finished, and all the things fed, then we went out to look at the snares. We wandered on across the stream and up the wild hillside. Our feet rattled through black patches of devil's-bit scabius; we skirted a swim of thistle-down, which glistened when the moon touched it. We stumbled on through wet, coarse grass, over soft mole-hills and black rabbit-holes. The hills and woods cast shadows; the pools of mist in the valleys gathered the moonbeams in cold, shivery light.

We came to an old farm that stood on the level brow of the hill. The woods swept away from it, leaving a great clearing of what was once cultivated land. The handsome chimneys of the house, silhouetted against a light sky, drew my admiration. I noticed that there was no light or glow in any window, though the house had only the width of one room, and though the night was only at eight o'clock. We looked at the long, impressive front. Several of the windows had been bricked in, giving a pitiful impression of blindness; the places where the plaster had fallen off the walls showed blacker in the shadow. We pushed open the gate, and as we walked down the path, weeds and dead plants brushed our ankles. We looked in at a window. The room was lighted also by a window from the other side, through which the moonlight streamed on to the flagged floor, dirty, littered with paper, and wisps of straw. The hearth lay in the light, with all its distress of grey ashes, and piled cinders of burnt paper, and a child's headless doll, charred and pitiful. On the border-line of shadow lay a round fur cap—a game-keeper's cap. I blamed the moonlight for entering the desolate room; the darkness alone was decent and reticent. I hated the little roses on the illuminated piece of wallpaper, I hated that fireside.

With farmer's instinct George turned to the outhouse. The cow-yard startled me. It was a forest of the tallest nettles I have ever seen—nettles far taller than six feet. The air was soddened with the dank scent of nettles. As I followed George along the obscure brick path, I felt my flesh creep. But the buildings, when we entered them, were in splendid condition; they had been restored within a small number of years; they were well-timbered, neat, and cosy. Here and there we saw feathers, bits of animal wreckage, even the remnants of a cat, which we hastily examined by the light of a match. As we entered the stable there was an ugly noise, and three great rats half rushed at us and threatened us with their vicious teeth. I shuddered, and hurried back, stumbling over a bucket, rotten with rust, and so filled with weeds that I thought it part of the jungle. There was a silence made horrible by the faint noises that rats and flying bats give out. The place was bare of any vestige of corn or straw or hay, only choked with a growth of abnormal weeds. When I found myself free in the orchard I could not stop shivering. There were no apples to be seen overhead between us and the clear sky. Either the birds had caused them to fall, when the rabbits had devoured them, or someone had gathered the crop.

'This,' said George bitterly, 'is what the mill will come to.'

'After your time,' I said.

'My time—my time. I shall never have a time. And I shouldn't be surprised if Father's time isn't short—with rabbits and one thing and another. As it is, we depend on the milkround, and on the carting which I do for the council. You can't call it farming. We're a miserable mixture of farmer, milkman, greengrocer, and carting contractor. It's a shabby business.'

'You have to live,' I retorted.

'Yes—but it's rotten. And Father won't move—and he won't change his methods.'

'Well—what about you?'

'Me! What should I change for?—I'm comfortable at home. As for my future, it can look after itself, so long as nobody depends on me.'

'*Laissez-faire*,' said I, smiling.

'This is no *laissez-faire*,' he replied, glancing round. 'This is pulling the nipple out of your lips, and letting the milk run away sour. Look there!'

Through the thin wall of moonlit mist that slid over the hillside we could see an army of rabbits bunched up, or hopping a few paces forward, feeding.

We set off at a swinging pace down the hill, scattering the hosts. As we approached the fence that bounded the Mill fields, he exclaimed, 'Hullo!' and hurried forward. I followed him, and observed the dark figure of a man rise from the hedge. It was a game-keeper. He pretended to be examining his gun. As we came up he greeted us with a calm 'Good evenin'!'

George replied by investigating the little gap in the hedge.

'I'll trouble you for that snare,' he said.

'Will yer?' answered Annable, a broad, burly, black-faced fellow. 'And *I* should like ter know what you're doin' on th' wrong side th' 'edge?'

'You can see what we're doing—hand over my snare—*and* the rabbit,' said George angrily.

'What rabbit?' said Annable, turning sarcastically to me.

'You know well enough—an' you can hand it over—or—' George replied.

'Or what? Spit it out! The sound won't kill me—' the man grinned with contempt.

'Hand over here!' said George, stepping up to the man in a rage.

'Now don't!' said the keeper, standing stock-still, and looking unmovedly at the proximity of George:

'You'd better get off home—both you an' 'im. You'll get neither snare nor rabbit—see!'

'We *will* see!' said George, and he made a sudden move to get hold of the man's coat. Instantly he went staggering back with a heavy blow under the left ear.

'Damn brute!' I ejaculated, bruising my knuckles against the fellow's jaw. Then I too found myself sitting dazedly on the grass, watching the great skirts of his velveteens flinging round him as if he had been a demon, as he strode away. I got up, pressing my chest where I had been struck. George was lying in the hedge-bottom. I turned him over, and rubbed his temples, and shook the drenched grass on his face. He opened his eyes and looked at me, dazed. Then he drew his breath quickly, and put his hand to his head.

'He–he nearly stunned me,' he said.

'The devil!' I answered.

'I wasn't ready.'

'No.'

'Did he knock me down?'

'Ay–me too.'

He was silent for some time, sitting limply. Then he pressed his hand against the back of his head, saying, 'My head does sing!!' He tried to get up, but failed. 'Good God–being knocked into this state by a damned keeper!'

'Come on,' I said, 'let's see if we can't get indoors.'

'No!' he said quickly, 'we needn't tell them–don't let them know.'

I sat thinking of the pain in my own chest, and wishing I could remember hearing Annable's jaw smash, and wishing that my knuckles were more bruised than they were–though that was bad enough. I got up, and helped George to rise. He swayed, almost pulling me over. But in a while he could walk unevenly.

'Am I,' he said, 'covered with clay and stuff?'

'Not much,' I replied, troubled by the shame and confusion with which he spoke.

'Get it off,' he said, standing still to be cleaned.

I did my best. Then we walked about the fields for a time, gloomy, silent, and sore.

Suddenly, as we went by the pond-side, we were startled by great, swishing black shadows that swept just above our heads. The swans were flying up for shelter, now that a cold wind had begun to fret Nethermere. They swung down on to the glassy millpond, shaking the moonlight in flecks across the deep shadows; the night rang with the clacking of their wings on the water; the stillness and calm were broken; the moonlight was furrowed and scattered, and broken. The swans, as they sailed into shadow, were dim, haunting spectres; the wind found us shivering.

'Don't–you won't say anything?' he asked as I was leaving him.

'No.'

'Nothing at all–not to anybody?'

'No.'

'Good night.'

About the end of September, our countryside was alarmed by the harrying of sheep by strange dogs. One morning, the squire, going the round of his fields as was his custom, to his grief and horror found two of his sheep torn and dead in the hedge-bottom, and the rest huddled in a corner swaying about in terror, smeared with blood. The squire did not recover his spirits for days.

There was a report of two grey wolvish dogs. The squire's keeper had heard yelping in the fields of Dr Collins of the Abbey, about dawn. Three sheep lay soaked in blood when the labourer went to tend the flocks. Then the farmers took alarm. Lord, of the White House farm, intended to put his sheep in pen, with his dogs in charge. It was Saturday, however, and the lads ran off to the little travelling theatre that had halted at Westwold. While they sat open-mouthed in the theatre, gloriously nicknamed the 'Blood-Tub', watching heroes die with much writhing and heaving, and struggling up to say a word, and collapsing without having said it, six of their silly sheep were slaughtered in the field. At every house it was inquired of the dog; nowhere had one been loose.

Mr Saxton had some thirty sheep on the Common. George determined that the easiest thing was for him to sleep out with them. He built a shelter of hurdles interlaced with brushwood, and in the sunny afternoon we collected piles of bracken, browning to the ruddy winter-brown now. He slept there for a week, but that week aged his mother like a year. She was out in the cold morning twilight watching, with her apron over her head, for his approach. She did not rest with the thought of him out on the Common.

Therefore, on Saturday night he brought down his rugs, and took up Gyp to watch in his stead. For some time we sat looking at the stars over the dark hills. Now and then a sheep coughed, or a rabbit rustled beneath the brambles, and Gyp whined. The mist crept over the gorse-bushes, and the webs on the brambles were white – the devil throws his net over the blackberries as soon as September's back is turned, they say.

'I saw two fellows go by with bags and nets,' said George, as we sat looking out of his little shelter.

'Poachers,' said I. 'Did you speak to them?'

'No – they didn't see me. I was dropping asleep when a rabbit rushed under the blanket, all of a shiver, and a whippet dog after it. I gave the whippet a punch in the neck, and he yelped off. The rabbit stopped with me quite a long time – then it went.'

'How did you feel?'

'I didn't care. I don't care much what happens just now. Father could get along without me, and Mother has the children. I think I shall emigrate.'

'Why didn't you before?'

'Oh, I don't know. There are a lot of little comforts and interests at home that one would miss. Besides, you feel somebody in your own countryside, and you're nothing in a foreign part, I expect.'

'But you're going?'

'What is there to stop here for? The valley is all running wild and unprofitable. You've no freedom for thinking of what the other folks think of you, and everything round you keeps the same, and so you can't change yourself – because everything you look at brings up the same old feeling, and stops you from feeling fresh things. And what is there that's worth anything? – What's worth having in my life?'

'I thought,' said I, 'your comfort was worth having.'

He sat still and did not answer.

'What's shaken you out of your nest?' I asked.

'I don't know. I've not felt the same since that row with Annable. And Lettie said to me, "Here, you can't live as you like – in any way or circumstance. You're like a bit out of those coloured marble mosaics in the hall, you have to fit in your own set, fit into your own pattern, because you're put there from the first. But you don't want to be like a fixed bit of a mosaic – you want to fuse into life, and melt and mix with the rest of folk, to have some things burned out of you—" She was downright serious.'

'Well, you need not believe her. When did you see her?'

'She came down on Wednesday, when I was getting the apples in the morning. She climbed a tree with me, and there was a wind, that was why I was getting all the apples, and it rocked us, me right up at the top, she sitting half-way down holding the basket. I asked her didn't she think that free kind of life was the best, and that was how she answered me.'

'You should have contradicted her.'

'It seemed true. I never thought of it being wrong, in fact.'

'Come—that sounds bad.'

'No—I thought she looked down on us—on our way of life. I thought she meant I was like a toad in a hole.'

'You should have shown her different.'

'How could I when I could see no different?'

'It strikes me you're in love.'

He laughed at the idea, saying, 'No, but it is rotten to find that there isn't a single thing you have to be proud of.'

'This is a new tune for you.'

He pulled the grass moodily.

'And when do you think of going?'

'Oh—I don't know—I've said nothing to Mother. Not yet—at any rate, not till spring.'

'Not till something has happened,' said I.

'What?' he asked.

'Something decisive.'

'I don't know what can happen—unless the squire turns us out.'

'No?' I said.

He did not speak.

'You should make things happen,' said I.

'Don't make me feel a worse fool, Cyril,' he replied despairingly.

Gyp whined and jumped, tugging her chain to follow us. The grey blurs among the blackness of the bushes were resting sheep. A chill, dim mist crept along the ground.

'But, for all that, Cyril,' he said, 'to have her laugh at you across the table; to hear her sing as she moved about, before you are washed at night, when the fire's warm, and you're tired; to have her sit by you on the hearth-seat, close and soft . . .'

'In Spain,' I said. 'In Spain.'

He took no notice, but turned suddenly, laughing.

'Do you know, when I was stooking up, lifting the sheaves, it felt like having your arm round a girl. It was quite a sudden sensation.'

'You'd better take care,' said I, 'you'll mesh yourself in the silk of dreams, and then—'

He laughed, not having heard my words.

'The time seems to go like lightning—thinking,' he confessed—'I seem to sweep the mornings up in a handful.'

'Oh Lord!' said I. 'Why don't you scheme for getting what you want, instead of dreaming fulfilments?'

'Well,' he replied. 'If it was a fine dream, wouldn't you want to go on dreaming?' And with that he finished, and I went home.

I sat at my window looking out, trying to get things straight. Mist rose, and wreathed round Nethermere, like ghosts meeting and embracing sadly. I thought of the time when my friend should not follow the harrow on our own snug valley side, and when Lettie's room next mine should be closed to hide its emptiness, not its joy. My heart clung passionately to the hollow which held us all; how could I bear that it should be desolate! I wondered what Lettie would do.

In the morning I was up early, when daybreak came with a shiver through the woods. I went out, while the moon still shone sickly in the west. The world shrank from the morning. It was then that the last of the summer things died. The wood was dark—and smelt damp and heavy with autumn. On the paths the leaves lay clogged.

As I came near the farm I heard the yelling of dogs. Running, I reached the Common, and saw the sheep huddled and scattered in groups; something leaped round them. George burst into sight pursuing. Directly, there was the bang, bang of a gun. I picked up a heavy piece of sandstone and ran forward. Three sheep scattered wildly before me. In the dim light I saw their grey shadows move among the gorse-bushes. Then a dog leaped, and I flung my stone with all my might. I hit. There came a high-pitched howling yelp of pain; I saw the brute make off, and went after him, dodging the prickly bushes, leaping the trailing brambles. The gunshots rang out again, and I heard the men shouting with excitement. My dog was out of sight, but I followed still, slanting down the hill. In a field ahead I saw someone running. Leaping the low hedge, I pursued, and overtook Emily, who was hurrying as fast as she could through the wet grass. There was another gunshot and great shouting. Emily glanced round, saw me, and started.

'It's gone to the quarries,' she panted. We walked on, without saying a word. Skirting the spinney, we followed the brook course, and came at last to the quarry fence. The old excavations were filled now with trees. The steep walls, twenty feet deep in places, were packed with loose stones, and trailed with hanging brambles. We climbed down the steep bank of the brook, and entered the quarries by the bed of the stream. Under the groves of ash and oak a pale primrose still lingered, glimmering wanly beside the hidden water. Emily found a smear of blood on a beautiful trail of yellow convolvulus. We followed the tracks on to the open, where the brook flowed on the hard rock bed, and the stony floor of the quarry was only a tangle of gorse and bramble and honeysuckle.

'Take a good stone,' said I, and we pressed on, where the grove in the great excavation darkened again, and the brook slid secretly under the arms of the bushes and the hair of the long grass. We beat the cover almost to the road. I thought the brute had escaped, and I pulled a bunch of mountain-ash berries, and stood tapping them against my knee. I was startled by a snarl and a little scream. Running forward, I came upon one of the old, horse-shoe lime-kilns that stood at the head of the quarry. There, in the mouth of one of the kilns, Emily was kneeling on the dog, her hands buried in the hair of its throat, pushing back its head. The little jerks of the brute's body were the spasms of death; already the eyes were turning inward, and the upper lip was drawn from the teeth by pain.

'Good Lord, Emily! But he is dead!' I exclaimed.

'Has he hurt you?' I drew her away. She shuddered violently, and seemed to feel a horror of herself.

'No—no,' she said, looking at herself, with blood all on her skirt, where she had knelt on the wound which I had given the dog, and pressed the broken rib into the chest. There was a trickle of blood on her arm.

'Did he bite you?' I asked, anxious.

'No—oh no—I just peeped in, and he jumped. But he had no strength, and I hit him back with my stone, and I lost my balance, and fell on him.'

'Let me wash your arm.'

'Oh!' she exclaimed, 'isn't it horrible! Oh, I think it is so awful.'

'What?' said I, busy bathing her arm in the cold water of the brook.

'This—this whole brutal affair.'

'It ought to be cauterised,' said I, looking at a score on her arm from the dog's tooth.

'That scratch—that's nothing! Can you get that off my skirt—I feel hateful to myself.'

I washed her skirt with my handkerchief as well as I could, saying:

'Let me just sear it for you; we can go to the Kennels. Do—you ought—I don't feel safe otherwise.'

'Really,' she said, glancing up at me, a smile coming into her fine dark eyes.

'Yes—come along.'

'Ha, ha!' she laughed. 'You look so serious.'

I took her arm and drew her away. She linked her arm in mine and leaned on me.

'It is just like Lorna Doone,' she said as if she enjoyed it.

'But you will let me do it,' said I, referring to the cauterising.

'You make me; but I shall feel—ugh, I daren't think of it. Get me some of those berries.'

I plucked a few bunches of guelder-rose fruits, transparent, ruby berries. She stroked them softly against her lips and cheek, caressing them. Then she murmured to herself:

'I have always wanted to put red berries in my hair.'

The shawl she had been wearing was thrown across her shoulders, and her head was bare, and her black hair, soft and short and ecstatic, tumbled wildly into loose light curls. She thrust the stalks of the berries under her combs. Her hair was not heavy or long enough to have held them. Then, with the ruby bunches glowing through the black mist of curls, she looked up at me, brightly, with wide eyes. I looked at her, and felt the smile winning into her eyes. Then I turned and dragged a trail of golden-leaved convolvulus from the hedge, and I twisted it into a coronet for her.

'There!' said I, 'you're crowned.'

She put back her head, and the low laughter shook in her throat.

'What!' she asked, putting all the courage and recklessness she had into the question, and in her soul trembling.

'Not Chloë, not Bacchante. You have always got your soul in your eyes, such an earnest, troublesome soul.'

The laughter faded at once, and her great seriousness looked out again at me, pleading.

'You are like Burne-Jones's damsels. Troublesome shadows are always crowding across your eyes, and you cherish them. You think the flesh of the apple is nothing, nothing. You only care for the eternal pips. Why don't you snatch your apple and eat it, and throw the core away?'

She looked at me sadly, not understanding, but believing that I in my wisdom spoke truth, as she always believed when I lost her in a maze of words. She stooped down, and the chaplet fell from her hair, and only one bunch of berries remained. The ground around us was strewn with the four-lipped burrs of beechnuts, and the quaint little nut-pyramids were scattered among the ruddy fallen leaves. Emily gathered a few nuts.

'I love beechnuts,' she said, 'but they make me long for my childhood again till I could almost cry out. To go out for beechnuts before breakfast; to thread them for necklaces before supper–to be the envy of the others at school next day! There was as much pleasure in a beech necklace then as there is in the whole autumn now–and no sadness. There are no more unmixed joys after you have grown up.' She kept her face to the ground as she spoke, and she continued to gather the fruits.

'Do you find any with nuts in?' I asked.

'Not many–here–here are two, three. You have them. No–I don't care about them.'

I stripped one of its horny brown coat and gave it to her. She opened her mouth slightly to take it, looking up into my eyes. Some people, instead of bringing with them clouds of glory, trail clouds of sorrow; they are born with 'the gift of Sorrow'; 'Sorrows,' they proclaim, 'alone are real. The veiled grey angels of sorrow work out slowly the beautiful shapes. Sorrow is beauty, and the supreme blessedness.' You read it in their eyes, and in the tones of their voices. Emily had the gift of sorrow. It fascinated me, but it drove me to rebellion.

We followed the soft, smooth-bitten turf road under the old beeches. The hillside fell away, dishevelled with thistles and coarse grass. Soon we were in sight of the Kennels, the red old Kennels which had been the scene of so much animation in the time of Lord Byron. They were empty now, overgrown with weeds. The barred windows of the cottages were grey with dust; there was no need now to protect the windows from cattle, dog or man. One of the three houses was inhabited. Clear water trickled through a wooden runnel into a great stone trough outside near the door.

'Come here,' said I to Emily. 'Let me fasten the back of your dress.'

'Is it undone?' she asked, looking quickly over her shoulder, and blushing.

As I was engaged in my task, a girl came out of the cottage with a black kettle and a tea-cup. She was so surprised to see me thus occupied that she forgot her own duty, and stood open-mouthed.

'S'r Ann! S'r Ann,' called a voice from inside. 'Are ter goin' ter come in an' shut that door?'

Sarah Ann hastily poured a few cupfuls of water into the kettle, then she put down both utensils and stood holding her bare arms to warm them. Her chief garment consisted of a skirt with grey bodice and red flannel skirt, very much torn. Her black hair hung in wild tails on to her shoulders.

'We must go in here,' said I, approaching the girl. She, however, hastily seized the kettle and ran indoors with an 'Oh, Mother–!'

A woman came to the door. One breast was bare, and hung over her blouse, which, like a dressing-jacket, fell loose over her skirt. Her fading, red-brown hair was all frowsy from the bed. In the folds of her skirt clung a swarthy urchin with a shockingly short shirt. He stared at us with big black eyes, the only portion of his face undecorated with egg and jam. The woman's blue eyes questioned us languidly. I told her our errand.

'Come in—come in,' she said, 'but dunna look at th' 'ouse. Th' childers not been long up. Go in, Billy, wi' nowt on!'

We entered, taking the forgotten kettle lid. The kitchen was large, but scantily furnished save, indeed, for children. The eldest, a girl of twelve or so, was standing toasting a piece of bacon with one hand, and holding back her night-dress in the other. As the toast hand got scorched, she transferred the bacon to the other, gave the hot fingers a lick to cool them, and then held back her night-dress again. Her auburn hair hung in heavy coils down her gown. A boy sat on the steel fender, catching the dropping fat on a piece of bread. 'One, two, three, four, five, six drops,' and he quickly bit off the tasty corner, and resumed the task with the other hand. When we entered he tried to draw his shirt over his knees, which caused the fat to fall wasted. A fat baby, evidently laid down from the breast, lay kicking on the squab, purple in the face, while another lad was pushing bread and butter into its mouth. The mother swept to the sofa, poked out the bread and butter, pushed her finger into the baby's throat, lifted the child up, punched its back, and was highly relieved when it began to yell. Then she administered a few sound spanks to the naked buttocks of the crammer. He began to howl, but stopped suddenly on seeing us laughing. On the sack-cloth which served as hearth-rug sat a beautiful child washing the face of a wooden doll with tea, and wiping it on her nightgown. At the table, an infant in a high chair sat sucking a piece of bacon, till the grease ran down his swarthy arms, oozing through his fingers. An old lad stood in the big armchair, whose back was hung with a calf-skin, and was industriously pouring the dregs of the tea-cups into a basin of milk. The mother whisked away the milk, and made a rush for the urchin, the baby hanging over her arm the while.

'I could half kill thee,' she said, but he had slid under the table—and sat serenely unconcerned.

'Could you'—I asked when the mother had put her bonny baby again to her breast—'could you lend me a knitting-needle?'

'Our S'r Ann, wheer's thy knittin'-needles?' asked the woman, wincing at the same time, and putting her hand to the mouth of the sucking child. Catching my eye, she said:

'You wouldn't credit how he bites. 'E's nobbut two teeth, but they like six needles.' She drew her brows together and pursed her lips, saying to the child, 'Naughty lad, naughty lad! Tha' shanna hae it, no, not if ter bites thy mother like that.'

The family interest was now divided between us and the private concerns in process when we entered—save, however, that the bacon-sucker had sucked on stolidly, immovable, all the time.

'Our Sam, wheer's my knittin', tha's 'ad it?' cried S'r Ann after a little search.

''A 'e na,' replied Sam from under the table.

'Yes, tha' 'as,' said the mother, giving a blind prod under the table with her foot.

''A 'e na then!' persisted Sam.

The mother suggested various possible places of discovery, and at last the knitting was found at the back of the table drawer, among forks and old wooden skewers.

'I 'an ter tell yer wheer ivrythink is,' said the mother in mild reproach. S'r Ann, however, gave no heed to her parent. Her heart was torn for her knitting, the fruit of her labours; it was a red woollen cuff for the winter; a corkscrew was bored through the web, and the ball of red wool was bristling with skewers.

'It's a' thee, our Sam,' she wailed. 'I know it's a' thee an' thy A. B. C.'
Samuel, under the table, croaked out in a voice of fierce monotony:

> 'P. is for Porkypine, whose bristles so strong
> Kill the bold lion by pricking 'is tongue.'

The mother began to shake with quiet laughter.

'His father learnt him that—made it all up,' she whispered proudly to us—and to him.

'Tell us what "B" is, Sam.'

'Shonna,' grunted Sam.

'Go on, there's a duckie; an' I'll ma' 'e a treacle-puddin'.'

'Today?' asked S'r Ann eagerly.

'Go on, Sam, my duck,' persisted the mother.

'Tha' 'as na got no treacle,' said Sam conclusively.

The needle was in the fire; the children stood about watching.

'Will you do it yourself?' I asked Emily.

'I!' she exclaimed, with wide eyes of astonishment, and she shook her head emphatically.

'Then I must.' I took out the needle, holding it in my handkerchief. I took her hand and examined the wound. But when she saw the hot glow of the needle, she snatched away her hand, and looked into my eyes, laughing in a half-hysterical fear and shame. I was very serious, very insistent. She yielded me her hand again, biting her lips in imagination of the pain, and looking at me. While my eyes were looking into hers she had courage; when I was forced to pay attention to my cauterising, she glanced down, and with a sharp 'Ah!' ending in a little laugh, she put her hands behind her, and looked again up at me with wide brown eyes, all quivering with apprehension, and a little shame, and a laughter that held much pleading.

One of the children began to cry.

'It is no good,' said I, throwing the fast cooling needle on to the hearth.

I gave the girls all the pennies I had—then I offered Sam, who had crept out of the shelter of the table, a sixpence.

'Shonna a'e that,' he said, turning from the small coin.

'Well—I have no more pennies, so nothing will be your share.'

I gave the other boy a rickety knife I had in my pocket. Sam looked fiercely at me. Eager for revenge, he picked up the 'porkypine quill' by the hot end. He dropped it with a shout of rage, and, seizing a cup off the table, flung it at the fortunate Jack. It smashed against the fireplace. The mother grabbed at Sam, but he was gone. A girl, a little girl, wailed, 'Oh, that's my rosey mug—my rosey mug.' We fled from the scene of confusion. Emily had already noticed it. Her thoughts were of herself, and of me.

'I am an awful coward,' said she humbly.

'But I can't help it—' She looked beseechingly.

'Never mind,' said I.

'All my flesh seems to jump from it. You don't know how I feel.'

'Well—never mind.'

'I couldn't help it, not for my life.'

'I wonder,' said I, 'if anything could possibly disturb that young bacon-sucker? He didn't even look round at the smash.'

'No,' said she, biting the tip of her finger moodily.

Further conversation was interrupted by howls from the rear. Looking round we saw Sam careering after us over the close-bitten turf, howling scorn and derision at us. 'Rabbit-tail, rabbit-tail,' he cried, his bare little legs twinkling, and his little shirt fluttering in the cold morning air. Fortunately, at last he trod on a thistle or a thorn, for when we looked round again to see why he was silent, he was capering on one leg, holding his wounded foot in his hands.

7

LETTIE PULLS DOWN THE SMALL GOLD GRAPES

During the falling of the leaves Lettie was very wilful. She uttered many banalities concerning men, and love, and marriage; she taunted Leslie and thwarted his wishes. At last he stayed away from her. She had been several times down to the mill, but because she fancied they were very familiar, receiving her on to their rough plane like one of themselves, she stayed away. Since the death of our father she had been restless; since inheriting her little fortune she had become proud, scornful, difficult to please. Difficult to please in every circumstance; she, who had always been so rippling in thoughtless life, sat down in the window-sill to think, and her strong teeth bit at her handkerchief till it was torn in holes. She would say nothing to me; she read all things that dealt with modern women.

One afternoon Lettie walked over to Eberwich. Leslie had not been to see us for a fortnight. It was a grey, dree afternoon. The wind drifted a clammy fog across the hills, and the roads were black and deep with mud. The trees in the wood slouched sulkily. It was a day to be shut out and ignored if possible. I heaped up the fire, and went to draw the curtains and make perfect the room. Then I saw Lettie coming along the path quickly, very erect. When she came in her colour was high.

'Tea not laid?' she said briefly.

'Rebecca has just brought in the lamp,' said I.

Lettie took off her coat and furs, and flung them on the couch. She went to the mirror, lifted her hair, all curled by the fog, and stared haughtily at herself. Then she swung round, looked at the bare table, and rang the bell.

It was so rare a thing for us to ring the bell from the dining-room, that Rebecca went first to the outer door. Then she came in the room saying:

'Did you ring?'

'I thought tea would have been ready,' said Lettie coldly. Rebecca looked at me, and at her, and replied:

'It is but half-past four. I can bring it in.'

Mother came down hearing the clink of the tea-cups.

'Well,' she said to Lettie, who was unlacing her boots, 'and did you find it a pleasant walk?'

'Except for the mud,' was the reply.

'Ah, I guess you wished you had stayed at home. What a state for your boots!—and your skirts too, I know. Here, let me take them into the kitchen.'

'Let Rebecca take them,' said Lettie—but Mother was out of the room.

When Mother had poured out the tea, we sat silently at table. It was on the tip of our tongues to ask Lettie what ailed her, but we were experienced and we refrained. After a while she said:

'Do you know, I met Leslie Tempest.'

'Oh,' said Mother tentatively. 'Did he come along with you?'

'He did not look at me.'

'Oh!' exclaimed Mother, and it was speaking volumes; then, after a moment, she resumed:

'Perhaps he did not see you.'

'Or was it a stony Britisher?' I asked.

'He saw me,' declared Lettie, 'or he wouldn't have made such a babyish show of being delighted with Margaret Raymond.'

'It may have been no show–he still may not have seen you.'

'I felt at once that he had; I could see his animation was extravagant. He need not have troubled himself. I was not going to run after him.'

'You seem very cross,' said I.

'Indeed I am not. But he knew I had to walk all this way home, and he could take up Margaret, who has only half the distance.'

'Was he driving?'

'In the dog-cart.' She cut her toast into strips viciously. We waited patiently. 'It was mean of him, wasn't it, Mother?'

'Well, my girl, you have treated him badly.'

'What a baby! What a mean, manly baby! Men are great infants.'

'And girls,' said Mother, 'do not know what they want.'

'A grown-up quality,' I added.

'Nevertheless,' said Lettie, 'he is a mean fop, and I detest him.'

She rose and sorted out some stitchery. Lettie never stitched unless she was in a bad humour. Mother smiled at me, sighed, and proceeded to Mr Gladstone for comfort; her breviary and missal were Morley's Life of Gladstone.

I had to take a letter to Highclose to Mrs Tempest–from my mother, concerning a bazaar in process at the church. 'I will bring Leslie back with me,' said I to myself.

The night was black and hateful. The lamps by the road from Eberwich ended at Nethermere; their yellow blur on the water made the cold, wet inferno of the night more ugly.

Leslie and Marie were both in the library–half a library, half a business office; used also as a lounge room, being cosy Leslie lay in a great arm-chair by the fire, immune among clouds of blue smoke. Marie was perched on the steps, a great volume on her knee. Leslie got up in his cloud, shook hands, greeted me curtly, and vanished again. Marie smiled me a quaint, vexed smile, saying:

'Oh, Cyril, I'm so glad you've come. I'm so worried, and Leslie says he's not a pastry-cook, though I'm sure I don't want him to be one, only he need not be a bear.'

'What's the matter?'

She frowned, gave the big volume a little smack and said:

'Why, I do so much want to make some of those Spanish tartlets of your mother's that are so delicious, and of course Mabel knows nothing of them, and they're not in my cookery book, and I've looked through page upon page of the encyclopædia, right through "Spain", and there's nothing yet, and there are fifty pages more, and Leslie won't help me, though I've got a headache, because he's frabous about something.' She looked at me in comical despair.

'Do you want them for the bazaar?'

'Yes–for tomorrow. Cook has done the rest, but I had fairly set my heart on these. Don't you think they are lovely?'

'Exquisitely lovely. Suppose I go and ask Mother.'

'If you would. But no, oh no, you can't make all that journey this terrible night. We are simply besieged by mud. The men are both out—William has gone to meet Father—and Mother has sent George to carry some things to the vicarage. I can't ask one of the girls on a night like this. I shall have to let it go—and the cranberry tarts too—it cannot be helped. I am so miserable.'

'Ask Leslie,' said I.

'He is too cross,' she replied, looking at him.

He did not deign a remark.

'Will you, Leslie?'

'What?'

'Go across to Woodside for me?'

'What for?'

'A recipe. Do, there's a dear boy.'

'Where are the men?'

'They are both engaged—they are out.'

'Send a girl, then.'

'At night like this? Who would go?'

'Cissy.'

'I shall not ask her. Isn't he mean, Cyril? Men are mean.'

'I will come back,' said I. 'There is nothing at home to do. Mother is reading, and Lettie is stitching. The weather disagrees with her, as it does with Leslie.'

'But it is not fair—' she said, looking at me softly. Then she put away the great book and climbed down.

'Won't you go, Leslie?' she said, laying her hand on his shoulder.

'Women!' he said, rising as if reluctantly. 'There's no end to their wants and their caprices.'

'I thought he would go,' said she warmly. She ran to fetch his overcoat. He put one arm slowly in the sleeve, and then the other, but he would not lift the coat on to his shoulders.

'Well!' she said, struggling on tiptoe, 'you are a great creature. Can't you get it on, naughty child?'

'Give her a chair to stand on,' he said.

She shook the collar of the coat sharply, but he stood like a sheep, impassive.

'Leslie, you are too bad. I can't get it on, you stupid boy.'

I took the coat and jerked it on.

'There,' she said, giving him his cap. 'Now don't be long.'

'What a damned dirty night!' said he, when we were out.

'It is,' said I.

'The town, anywhere's better than this hell of a country.'

'Ha! How did you enjoy yourself?'

He began a long history of three days in the metropolis. I listened, and heard little. I heard more plainly the cry of some night birds over Nethermere, and the peevish, wailing, yarling cry of some beast in the wood. I was thankful to slam the door behind me, to stand in the light of the hall.

'Leslie!' exclaimed Mother, 'I am glad to see you.'

'Thank you,' he said, turning to Lettie, who sat with her lap full of work, her head busily bent.

'You see I can't get up,' she said, giving him her hand, adorned as it was by the thimble. 'How nice of you to come! We did not know you were back.'

'But . . . !' he exclaimed, then he stopped.

'I suppose you enjoyed yourself,' she went on calmly.

'Immensely, thanks.'

Snap, snap, snap went her needle through the new stuff. Then, without looking up, she said:

'Yes, no doubt. You have the air of a man who has been enjoying himself.'

'How do you mean?'

'A kind of guilty—or shall I say embarrassed—look. Don't you notice it, Mother?'

'I do!' said my mother.

'I suppose it means we may not ask him questions,' Lettie concluded, always very busily sewing.

He laughed. She had broken her cotton, and was trying to thread the needle again.

'What have you been doing this miserable weather?' he enquired awkwardly.

'Oh, we have sat at home desolate. "Ever of thee I'm fo-o-ondly dreēaming"—and so on. Haven't we, Mother?'

'Well,' said Mother, 'I don't know. We imagined him all sorts of lions up there.'

'What a shame we may not ask him to roar his old roars over for us,' said Lettie.

'What are they like?' he asked.

'How should I know? Like a sucking dove, to judge from your present voice. "A monstrous little voice."'

He laughed uncomfortably.

She went on sewing, suddenly beginning to sing to herself:

'Pussy cat, Pussy cat, where have you been?
I've been up to London to see the fine queen:
Pussy cat, Pussy cat, what did you there—
I frightened a little mouse under a stair.'

'I suppose,' she added, 'that may be so. Poor mouse!—but I guess she's none the worse. You did not see the queen, though?'

'She was not in London,' he replied sarcastically.

'You don't—' she said, taking two pins from between her teeth. 'I suppose you don't mean by that, she was in Eberwich—your queen?'

'I don't know where she was,' he answered angrily.

'Oh!' she said, very sweetly, 'I thought perhaps you had met her in Eberwich. When did you come back?'

'Last night,' he replied.

'Oh—why didn't you come and see us before?'

'I've been at the offices all day.'

'I've been up to Eberwich,' she said innocently.

'Have you?'

'Yes. And I feel so cross because of it. I thought I might see you. I felt as if you were at home.'

She stitched a little, and glanced up secretly to watch his face redden, then she continued innocently, 'Yes—I felt you had come back. It is funny how one has a feeling occasionally that someone is near; when it is someone one has a sympathy with.' She continued to stitch, then she took a pin from her bosom, and fixed her work, all without the least suspicion of guile.

'I thought I might meet you when I was out—' another pause, another fixing, a pin to be taken from her lips—'but I didn't.'

'I was at the office till rather late,' he said quickly.

She stitched away calmly, provokingly.

She took the pin from her mouth again, fixed down a fold of stuff, and said softly:

'You little liar.'

Mother had gone out of the room for her recipe book.

He sat on his chair dumb with mortification. She stitched swiftly and unerringly. There was silence for some moments. Then he spoke:

'I did not know you wanted me for the pleasure of plucking this crow,' he said.

'I wanted you!' she exclaimed, looking up for the first time. 'Who said I wanted you?'

'No one. If you didn't want me I may as well go.'

The sound of stitching alone broke the silence for some moments, then she said deliberately:

'What made you think I wanted you?'

'I don't care a damn whether you wanted me or whether you didn't.'

'It seems to upset you! And don't use bad language. It is the privilege of those near and dear to one.'

'That's why you begin it, I suppose.'

'I cannot remember—' she said loftily.

He laughed sarcastically.

'Well—if you're so beastly cut up about it—' He put this tentatively, expecting the soft answer. But she refused to speak, and went on stitching. He fidgeted about, twisted his cap uncomfortably, and sighed. At last he said:

'Well—you—have we done then?'

She had the vast superiority, in that she was engaged in ostentatious work. She could fix the cloth, regard it quizzicaly, rearrange it, settle down and begin to sew before she replied. This humbled him. At last she said:

'I thought so this afternoon.'

'But, good God, Lettie, can't you drop it?'

'And then?'—the question startled him.

'Why!—forget it,' he replied.

'Well?'—she spoke softly, gently. He answered to the call like an eager hound. He crossed quickly to her side as she sat sewing, and said, in a low voice:

'You do care something for me, don't you, Lettie?'

'Well'—it was modulated kindly, a sort of promise of assent.

'You have treated me rottenly, you know, haven't you? You know I—well, I care a good bit.'

'It is a queer way of showing it.' Her voice was now a gentle reproof, the sweetest of surrenders and forgiveness. He leaned forward, took her face in his hands, and kissed her, murmuring:

'You are a little tease.'

She laid her sewing in her lap, and looked up.

The next day, Sunday, broke wet and dreary. Breakfast was late, and about ten o'clock we stood at the window looking upon the impossibility of our going to church.

There was a driving drizzle of rain, like a dirty curtain before the landscape. The nasturtium leaves by the garden walk had gone rotten in a frost, and the gay green discs had given place to the first black flags of winter, hung on flaccid stalks, pinched at the neck. The grass plot was strewn with fallen leaves, wet and brilliant: scarlet splashes of Virginia creeper, golden drift from the limes, ruddy brown shawls under the beeches, and away back in the corner, the black mat of maple leaves, heavy soddened; they ought to have been a vivid lemon colour. Occasionally one of these great black leaves would loose its hold, and zigzag down, staggering in the dance of death.

'There now!' said Lettie suddenly.

I looked up in time to see a crow close his wings and clutch the topmost bough of an old grey holly tree on the edge of the clearing. He flapped again, recovered his balance, and folded himself up in black resignation to the detestable weather.

'Why has the old wretch settled just over our noses,' said Lettie petulantly. 'Just to blot the promise of a sorrow.'

'Yours or mine?' I asked.

'He is looking at me, I declare.'

'You can see the wicked pupil of his eye at this distance,' I insinuated.

'Well,' she replied, determined to take this omen unto herself, 'I saw him first.'

> '"One for sorrow, two for joy,
> Three for a letter, four for a boy,
> Five for silver, six for gold,
> And seven for a secret never told."

– You may bet he's only a messenger in advance. There'll be three more shortly, and you'll have your four,' said I, comforting.

'Do you know,' she said, 'it is very funny, but whenever I've particularly noticed one crow, I've had some sorrow or other.'

'And when you notice four?' I asked.

'You should have heard old Mrs Wagstaffe,' was her reply. 'She declares an old crow croaked in their apple tree every day for a week before Jerry got drowned.'

'Great sorrow for her,' I remarked.

'Oh, but she wept abundantly. I felt like weeping too, but somehow I laughed. She hoped he had gone to heaven—but—I'm sick of that word "but"—it is always tangling one's thoughts.'

'But, Jerry!' I insisted.

'Oh, she lifted up her forehead, and the tears dripped off her nose. He must have been an old nuisance, Syb. I can't understand why women marry such men. I felt downright glad to think of the drunken old wretch toppling into the canal out of the way.'

She pulled the thick curtain across the window, and nestled down in it, resting her cheek against the edge, protecting herself from the cold window-pane. The wet, grey wind shook the half-naked trees, whose leaves dripped and shone sullenly. Even the trunks were blackened, trickling with the rain which drove persistently.

Whirled down the sky like black maple leaves caught up aloft, came two more crows. They swept down and clung hold of the trees in front of the house, staying near the old forerunner. Lettie watched them, half amused, half melancholy. One bird was carried past. He swerved round and began to battle up the wind, rising higher, and rowing laboriously against the driving wet current.

'Here comes your fourth,' said I.

She did not answer, but continued to watch. The bird wrestled heroically, but the wind pushed him aside, tilted him, caught under his broad wings and bore him down. He swept in level flight down the stream, outspread and still, as if fixed in despair. I grieved for him. Sadly two of his fellows rose and were carried away after him, like souls hunting for a body to inhabit, and despairing. Only the first ghoul was left on the withered, silver-grey skeleton of the holly.

'He won't even say "Nevermore",' I remarked.

'He has more sense,' replied Lettie. She looked a trifle lugubrious. Then she continued: 'Better say "Nevermore" than "Evermore".'

'Why?' I asked.

'Oh, I don't know. Fancy this "Evermore".'

She had been sure in her own soul that Leslie would come—now she began to doubt:—things were very perplexing.

The bell in the kitchen jangled, she jumped up. I went and opened the door. He came in. She gave him one bright look of satisfaction. He saw it, and understood.

'Helen has got some people over—I have been awfully rude to leave them now,' he said quietly.

'What a dreadful day!' said Mother.

'Oh, fearful! Your face *is* red, Lettie! What have you been doing?'

'Looking into the fire.'

'What did you see?'

'The pictures wouldn't come plain—nothing.'

He laughed. We were silent for some time.

'You were expecting me?' he murmured.

'Yes—I knew you'd come.'

They were left alone. He came up to her and put his arms round her, as she stood with her elbow on the mantelpiece.

'You do want me,' he pleaded softly.

'Yes,' she murmured.

He held her in his arms and kissed her repeatedly, again and again, till she was out of breath, and put up her hand, and gently pushed her face away.

'You are a cold little lover—you are a shy bird,' he said, laughing into her eyes. He saw her tears rise, swimming on her lids, but not falling.

'Why, my love, my darling—why!'—he put his face to hers and took the tear on his cheek:

'I know you love me,' he said, gently, all tenderness.

'Do you know,' he murmured. 'I can positively feel the tears rising up from my heart and throat. They are quite painful gathering, my love. There—you can do anything with me.'

They were silent for some time. After a while, a rather long while, she came upstairs and found Mother—and at the end of some minutes I heard my mother go to him.

I sat by my window and watched the low clouds reel and stagger past. It seemed as if everything were being swept along—I myself seemed to have lost my substance, to have become detached from concrete things and the firm trodden pavement of everyday life. Onward, always onward, not knowing where, nor why, the wind, the clouds, the rain and the birds and the leaves, everything whirling along—why?

All this time the old crow sat motionless, though the clouds tumbled, and were rent and piled, though the trees bent, and the window-pane shivered with running water. Then I found it had ceased to rain; that there was a sickly yellow sunlight, brightening on some great elm leaves near at hand till they looked like ripe lemons hanging. The crow looked at me – I was certain he looked at me.

'What do you think of it all?' I asked him.

He eyed me with contempt: great featherless, half-winged bird as I was, incomprehensible, contemptible, but awful. I believe he hated me.

'But,' said I, 'if a raven could answer, why won't you?'

He looked wearily away. Nevertheless my gaze disquieted him. He turned uneasily; he rose, waved his wings as if for flight, poised, then settled defiantly down again.

'You are no good,' said I, 'you won't help even with a word.'

He sat stolidly unconcerned. Then I heard the lapwings in the meadow crying, crying. They seemed to seek the storm, yet to rail at it. They wheeled in the wind, yet never ceased to complain of it. They enjoyed the struggle, and lamented it in wild lament, through which came a sound of exultation. All the lapwings cried, cried the same tale, 'Bitter, bitter, the struggle – for nothing, nothing, nothing' – and all the time they swung about on their broad wings, revelling.

'There,' said I to the crow, 'they try it, and find it bitter, but they wouldn't like to miss it, to sit still like you, you old corpse.'

He could not endure this. He rose in defiance, flapped his wings, and launched off, uttering one 'Caw' of sinister foreboding. He was soon whirled away.

I discovered that I was very cold, so I went downstairs.

Twisting a curl round his finger, one of those loose curls that always dance free from the captured hair, Leslie said:

'Look how fond your hair is of me; look how it twines round my finger. Do you know, your hair – the light in it is like – oh – buttercups in the sun.'

'It is like me – it won't be kept in bounds,' she replied.

'Shame if it were – like this, it brushes my face – so – and sets me tingling like music.'

'Behave! Now be still, and I'll tell you what sort of music you make.'

'Oh – well – tell me.'

'Like the calling of throstles and blackies, in the evening, frightening the pale little wood-anemones, till they run panting and swaying right up to our wall. Like the ringing of bluebells when the bees are at them; like Hippomenes, out-of-breath, laughing because he'd won.'

He kissed her with rapturous admiration.

'Marriage music, sir,' she added.

'What golden apples did I throw?' he asked lightly.

'What!' she exclaimed, half mocking.

'This Atalanta,' he replied, looking lovingly upon her, 'this Atalanta – I believe she just lagged at last on purpose.'

'You have it,' she cried, laughing, submitting to his caresses. 'It was you – the apples of your firm heels – the apples of your eyes – the apples Eve bit – that won me – *hein!*'

'That was it – you are clever, you are rare. And I've won, won the ripe apples of your cheeks, and your breasts, and your very fists – they can't stop me – and – and – all your roundness and warmness and softness – I've won you, Lettie.'

She nodded wickedly, saying:

'All those—those—yes.'
'All—she admits it—everything!'
'Oh!—but let me breathe. Did you claim everything?'
'Yes, and you gave it me.'
'Not yet. Everything though?'
'Every atom.'
'But—now you look—'
'Did I look aside?'
'With the inward eye. Suppose now we were two angels—'
'Oh, dear—a sloppy angel!'
'Well—don't interrupt now—suppose I were one—like the "Blessed Damosel".'
'With a warm bosom—!'
'Don't be foolish, now—I a "Blessed Damosel" and you kicking the brown beech leaves below thinking—'
'What *are* you driving at?'
'Would you be thinking—thoughts like prayers?'
'What on earth do you ask that for? Oh—I think I'd be cursing—eh?'
'No—saying fragrant prayers—that your thin soul might mount up—'
'Hang thin souls, Lettie! I'm not one of your souly sort. I can't stand Pre-Raphaelites. You—You're not a Burne-Jonesess—you're an Albert Moore. I think there's more in the warm touch of a soft body than in a prayer. I'll pray with kisses.'
'And when you can't?'
'I'll wait till prayer-time again. By Jove, I'd rather feel my arms full of you; I'd rather touch that red mouth—you grudger!—than sing hymns with you in any heaven.'
'I'm afraid you'll never sing hymns with me in heaven.'
'Well—I have you here—yes, I have you now.'
'Our life is but a fading dawn?'
'Liar!—Well, you called me! Besides, I don't care; "Carpe diem", my rose-bud, my fawn. There's a nice Carmen about a fawn. "Time to leave its mother, and venture into a warm embrace." Poor old Horace—I've forgotten him.'
'Then poor old Horace.'
'Ha! Ha!—Well, I shan't forget *you*. What's that queer look in your eyes?'
'What is it?'
'Nay—you tell me. You are such a tease, there's no getting to the bottom of you.'
'You can fathom the depth of a kiss—'
'I will—I will—'
After a while he asked:
'When shall we be properly engaged, Lettie?'
'Oh, wait till Christmas—till I am twenty-one.'
'Nearly three months! Why on earth—!'
'It will make no difference. I shall be able to choose thee of my own free choice then.'
'But three months!'
'I shall consider thee engaged—it doesn't matter about other people.'
'I thought we should be married in three months.'
'Ah—married in haste—But what will your mother say?'
'Say! Oh, she'll say it's the first wise thing I've done. You'll make a fine wife,

Lettie, able to entertain, and all that.'

'You will flutter brilliantly.'

'We will.'

'No—you'll be the moth—I'll paint your wings—gaudy feather-dust. Then when you lose your coloured dust, when you fly too near the light, or when you play dodge with a butterfly-net—away goes my part—you can't fly—I—alas, poor me! What becomes of the feather-dust when the moth brushes his wings against a butterfly-net?'

'What are you making so many words about? You don't know now, do you?'

'No—that I don't.'

'Then just be comfortable. Let me look at myself in your eyes.'

'Narcissus, Narcissus!—Do you see yourself well? Does the image flatter you?—Or is it a troubled stream, distorting your fair lineaments?'

'I can't see anything—only feel you looking—you are laughing at me.—What have you behind there—what joke?'

'I—I'm thinking you're just like Narcissus—a sweet, beautiful youth.'

'Be serious—do.'

'It would be dangerous. You'd die of it, and I—I should—'

'What!'

'Be just like I am now—serious.'

He looked proudly, thinking she referred to the earnestness of her love.

In the wood the wind rumbled and roared hoarsely overhead, but not a breath stirred among the saddened bracken. An occasional raindrop was shaken out of the trees; I slipped on the wet paths. Black bars striped the grey tree-trunks, where water had trickled down; the bracken was overthrown, its yellow ranks broken. I slid down the steep path to the gate, out of the wood.

Armies of cloud marched in rank across the sky, heavily laden, almost brushing the gorse on the common. The wind was cold and disheartening. The ground sobbed at every step. The brook was full, swirling along, hurrying, talking to itself, in absorbed intent tones. The clouds darkened; I felt the rain. Careless of the mud, I ran, and burst into the farm kitchen.

The children were painting, and they immediately claimed my help.

'Emily—and George—are in the front room,' said the mother quietly, for it was Sunday afternoon. I satisfied the little ones; I said a few words to the mother, and sat down to take off my clogs.

In the parlour, the father, big and comfortable, was sleeping in an arm-chair. Emily was writing at the table—she hurriedly hid her papers when I entered. George was sitting by the fire, reading. He looked up as I entered, and I loved him when he looked up at me, and as he lingered on his quiet 'Hullo!' His eyes were beautifully eloquent—as eloquent as a kiss.

We talked in subdued murmurs, because the father was asleep, opulently asleep, his tanned face as still as a brown pear against the wall. The clock itself went slowly, with languid throbs. We gathered round the fire, and talked quietly, about nothing—blissful merely in the sound of our voices, a murmured, soothing sound—a grateful, dispassionate love trio.

At last George rose, put down his book—looked at his father—and went out.

In the barn there was a sound of the pulper crunching the turnips. The crisp strips of turnip sprinkled quietly down on to a heap of gold which grew beneath the pulper. The smell of pulped turnips, keen and sweet, brings back to me the feeling of many winter nights, when frozen hoof-prints crunch in the yard, and

Orion is in the south; when a friendship was at its mystical best.

'Pulping on Sunday!' I exclaimed.

'Father didn't do it yesterday; it's his work; and I didn't notice it. You know—Father often forgets—he doesn't like to have to work in the afternoon—now.'

The cattle stirred in their stalls; the chains rattled round the posts; a cow coughed noisily. When George had finished pulping, and it was quiet enough for talk, just as he was spreading the first layers of chop and turnip and meal—in ran Emily—with her hair in silken, twining confusion, her eyes glowing—to bid us go in to tea before the milking was begun. It was the custom to milk before tea on Sunday—but George abandoned it without demur—his father willed it so, and his father was master, not to be questioned on farm matters, however one disagreed.

The last day in October had been dreary enough; the night could not come too early. We had tea by lamplight, merrily, with the father radiating comfort as the lamp shone yellow light. Sunday tea was imperfect without a visitor; with me, they always declared, it was perfect. I loved to hear them say so. I smiled, rejoicing quietly into my teacup when the father said:

'It seems proper to have Cyril here at Sunday tea, it seems natural.'

He was most loath to break the delightful bond of the lamplit tea-table; he looked up with a half-appealing glance when George at last pushed back his chair and said he supposed he'd better make a start.

'Ay,' said the father in a mild, conciliatory tone, 'I'll be out in a minute.'

The lamp hung against the barn wall, softly illuminating the lower part of the building, where bits of hay and white dust lay in the hollows between the bricks, where the curled chips of turnip scattered orange gleams over the earthen floor; the lofty roof, with its swallows' nests under the tiles, was deep in shadow, and the corners were full of darkness, hiding, half hiding, the hay, the chopper, the bins. The light shone along the passages before the stalls, glistening on the moist noses of the cattle, and on the whitewash of the walls.

George was very cheerful; but I wanted to tell him my message. When he had finished the feeding, and had at last sat down to milk, I said:

'I told you Leslie Tempest was at our house when I came away.'

He sat with the bucket between his knees, his hands at the cow's udder, about to begin to milk. He looked up a question at me.

'They are practically engaged now,' I said.

He did not turn his eyes away, but he ceased to look at me. As one who is listening for a far-off noise, he sat with his eyes fixed. Then he bent his head, and leaned it against the side of the cow, as if he would begin to milk. But he did not. The cow looked round and stirred uneasily. He began to draw the milk, and then to milk mechanically. I watched the movement of his hands, listening to the rhythmic clang of the jets of milk on the bucket, as a relief. After a while the movement of his hands became slower, thoughtful—then stopped.

'She has really said yes?'

I nodded.

'And what does your mother say?'

'She is pleased.'

He began to milk again. The cow stirred uneasily, shifting her legs. He looked at her angrily, and went on milking. Then, quite upset, she shifted again, and swung her tail in his face.

'Stand still!' he shouted, striking her on the haunch. She seemed to cower like a beaten woman. He swore at her, and continued to milk. She did not yield much that night; she was very restive; he took the stool from beneath him and gave her a good blow; I heard the stool knock on her prominent hipbone. After that she stood still, but her milk soon ceased to flow.

When he stood up, he paused before he went to the next beast, and I thought he was going to talk. But just then the father came along with his bucket. He looked in the shed, and, laughing in his mature, pleasant way, said:

'So you're an onlooker today, Cyril–I thought you'd have milked a cow or two for me by now.'

'Nay,' said I, 'Sunday is a day of rest–and milking makes your hands ache.'

'You only want a bit more practice,' he said, joking in his ripe fashion. 'Why, George, is that all you've got from Julia?'

'It is.'

'H'm–she's soon going dry. Julia, old lady, don't go and turn skinny.'

When he had gone, and the shed was still, the air seemed colder. I heard his good-humoured 'Stand over, old lass,' from the other shed, and the drum-beats of the first jets of milk on the pail.

'He has a comfortable time,' said George, looking savage. I laughed. He still waited.

'You really expected Lettie to have *him*,' I said.

'I suppose so,' he replied, 'then she'd made up her mind to it. It didn't matter–what she wanted–at the bottom.'

'You?' said I.

'If it hadn't been that he was a prize–with a ticket–she'd have had–'

'You!' said I.

'She was afraid–look how she turned and kept away–'

'From you?' said I.

'I should like to squeeze her till she screamed.'

'You should have gripped her before, and kept her,' said I.

'She–she's like a woman, like a cat–running to comforts–she strikes a bargain. Women are all tradesmen.'

'Don't generalise, it's no good.'

'She's like a prostitute–'

'It's banal! I believe she loves him.'

He started, and looked at me queerly. He looked quite childish in his doubt and perplexity.

'She what–?'

'Loves him–honestly.'

'She'd 'a loved me better,' he muttered, and turned to his milking. I left him and went to talk to his father. When the latter's four beasts were finished, George's light still shone in the other shed.

I went and found him at the fifth, the last cow. When at length he had finished he put down his pail, and going over to poor Julia, stood scratching her back, and her poll, and her nose, looking into her big, startled eye and murmuring. She was afraid; she jerked her head, giving him a good blow on the cheek with her horn.

'You can't understand them,' he said sadly, rubbing his face, and looking at me with his dark, serious eyes.

'I never knew I couldn't understand them. I never thought about it–till–But you know, Cyril, she led me on.'

I laughed at his rueful appearance.

8

THE RIOT OF CHRISTMAS

For some weeks, during the latter part of November and the beginning of December, I was kept indoors by a cold. At last came a frost which cleared the air and dried the mud. On the second Saturday before Christmas the world was transformed; tall, silver and pearl-grey trees rose pale against a dim blue sky, like trees in some rare, pale Paradise; the whole woodland was as if petrified in marble and silver and snow; the holly-leaves and long leaves of the rhododendron were rimmed and spangled with delicate tracery.

When the night came clear and bright, with a moon among the hoar-frost, I rebelled against confinement, and the house. No longer the mists and dank weather made the home dear; tonight even the glare of the distant little iron-works was not visible, for the low clouds were gone, and pale stars blinked from beyond the moon.

Lettie was staying with me; Leslie was in London again. She tried to remonstrate in a sisterly fashion when I said I would go out.

'Only down to the Mill,' said I. Then she hesitated a while–said she would come too. I suppose I looked at her curiously, for she said:

'Oh–if you would rather go alone–!'

'Come–come–yes, come!' said I, smiling to myself.

Lettie was in her old animated mood. She ran, leaping over rough places, laughing, talking to herself in French. We came to the Mill. Gyp did not bark. I opened the outer door and we crept softly into the great dark scullery, peeping into the kitchen through the crack of the door.

The mother sat by the hearth, where was a big bath half full of soapy water, and at her feet, warming his bare legs at the fire, was David, who had just been bathed. The mother was gently rubbing his fine fair hair into a cloud. Mollie was combing out her brown curls, sitting by her father, who, in the fire-seat, was reading aloud in a hearty voice, with quaint precision. At the table sat Emily and George: she was quickly picking over a pile of little yellow raisins, and he, slowly, with his head sunk, was stoning the large raisins. David kept reaching forward to play with the sleepy cat–interrupting his mother's rubbing. There was no sound but the voice of the father, full of zest; I am afraid they were not all listening carefully. I clicked the latch and entered.

'Lettie!' exclaimed George.

'Cyril!' cried Emily.

'Cyril, 'ooray!' shouted David.

'Hullo, Cyril!' said Mollie.

Six large brown eyes, round with surprise, welcomed me. They overwhelmed me with questions, and made much of us. At length they were settled and quiet again.

'Yes, I am a stranger,' said Lettie, who had taken off her hat and furs and coat. 'But you do not expect me often, do you? I may come at times, eh?'

'We are only too glad,' replied the mother. 'Nothing all day long but the sound of the sluice–and mists, and rotten leaves. I am thankful to hear a fresh voice.'

'Is Cyril really better, Lettie?' asked Emily softly.

'He's a spoiled boy–I believe he keeps a little bit ill so that we can cade him. Let me help you–let me peel the apples–yes, yes–I will.'

She went to the table, and occupied one side with her apple-peeling. George had not spoken to her. So she said:

'I won't help you, George, because I don't like to feel my fingers so sticky, and because I love to see you so domesticated.'

'You'll enjoy the sight a long time, then, for these things are numberless.'

'You should eat one now and then–I always do.'

'If I ate one I should eat the lot.'

'Then you may give me your one.'

He passed her a handful without speaking.

'That is too many, your mother is looking. Let me just finish this apple. There, I've not broken the peel!'

She stood up, holding up a long curling strip of peel.

'How many times must I swing it, Mrs Saxton?'

'Three times–but it's not All Hallows' Eve.'

'Never mind! Look!–' She carefully swung the long band of green peel over her head three times, letting it fall the third. The cat pounced on it, but Mollie swept him off again.

'What is it?' cried Lettie, blushing.

'G,' said the father, winking and laughing–the mother looked daggers at him.

'It isn't nothink,' said David naïvely, forgetting his confusion at being in the presence of a lady in his shirt. Mollie remarked in her cool way:

'It might be a "hess"–if you couldn't write.'

'Or an "L",' I added. Lettie looked over at me imperiously, and I was angry.

'What do you say, Emily?' she asked.

'Nay,' said Emily. 'It's only you can see the right letter.'

'Tell us what's the right letter,' said George to her.

'I!' exclaimed Lettie. 'Who can look into the seeds of Time?'

'Those who have set 'em and watched 'em sprout,' said I.

She flung the peel into the fire, laughing a short laugh, and went on with her work.

Mrs Saxton leaned over to her daughter and said softly, so that he should not hear, that George was pulling the flesh out of the raisins.

'George!' said Emily sharply, 'you're leaving nothing but the husks.'

He too was angry.

'"And he would fain fill his belly with the husks that the swine did eat,"' he said quietly, taking a handful of the fruit he had picked and putting some in his mouth. Emily snatched away the basin.

'It is too bad!' she said.

'Here,' said Lettie, handing him an apple she had peeled. 'You may have an apple, greedy boy.'

He took it and looked at it. Then a malicious smile twinkled round his eyes–as he said:

'If you give me the apple, to whom will you give the peel?'

'The swine,' she said, as if she only understood his first reference to the

Prodigal Son. He put the apple on the table.

'Don't you want it?' she said.

'Mother,' he said comically, as if jesting. 'She is offering me the apple like Eve.'

Like a flash, she snatched the apple from him, hid it in her skirts a moment, looking at him with dilated eyes, and then she flung it at the fire. She missed, and the father leaned forward and picked it off the hob, saying:

'The pigs may as well have it. You were slow, George—when a lady offers you a thing you don't have to make mouths.'

'*À ce qu'il paraît*,' she cried, laughing now at her ease, boisterously.

'Is she making love, Emily?' asked the father, laughing suggestively.

'She says it too fast for me,' said Emily.

George was leaning back in his chair, his hands in his breeches pockets.

'We shall have to finish his raisins after all, Emily,' said Lettie brightly. 'Look what a lazy animal he is.'

'He likes his comfort,' said Emily, with irony.

'The picture of content—solid, healthy, easy-moving content—' continued Lettie. As he sat thus, with his head thrown back against the end of the ingle-seat, coatless, his red neck seen in repose, he did indeed look remarkably comfortable.

'I shall never fret my fat away,' he said stolidly.

'No—you and I—we are not like Cyril. We do not burn our bodies in our heads—or our hearts, do we?'

'We have it in common,' said he, looking at her indifferently beneath his lashes, as his head was tilted back.

Lettie went on with the paring and coring of her apples—then she took the raisins. Meanwhile, Emily was making the house ring as she chopped the suet in a wooden bowl. The children were ready for bed. They kissed us all 'Good night'—save George. At last they were gone, accompanied by their mother. Emily put down her chopper, and sighed that her arm was aching, so I relieved her. The chopping went on for a long time, while the father read, Lettie worked, and George sat tilted back looking on. When at length the mincemeat was finished we were all out of work. Lettie helped to clear away—sat down—talked a little with effort—jumped up and said:

'Oh, I'm too excited to sit still—it's so near Christmas—let us play at something.'

'A dance?' said Emily.

'A dance—a dance!'

He suddenly sat straight and got up.

'Come on!' he said.

He kicked off his slippers, regardless of the holes in his stockinged feet, and put away the chairs. He held out his arm to her—she came with a laugh, and away they went, dancing over the great flagged kitchen at an incredible speed. her light flying steps followed his leaps; you could hear the quick light tap of her toes more plainly than the thud of his stockinged feet. Emily and I joined in. Emily's movements are naturally slow, but we danced at great speed. I was hot and perspiring, and she was panting, when I put her in a chair. But they whirled on in the dance, on and on till I was giddy, till the father, laughing, cried that they should stop. But George continued the dance; her hair was shaken loose, and fell in a great coil down her back; her feet began to drag; you could hear a light slur on the floor; she was panting—I could see her lips murmur to him, begging him to stop; he was laughing with open mouth, holding her tight; at last her feet trailed; he lifted her, clasping her tightly, and danced twice round the room with her thus. Then he fell with a crash on the sofa, pulling her beside him. His eyes glowed like coals; he was panting in sobs, and his hair was wet and glistening. She lay back on the sofa, with his arm still around her, not moving; she was quite overcome. Her hair was wild about her face. Emily was anxious; the father said, with a shade of inquietude:

'You've overdone it—it is very foolish.'

When at last she recovered her breath and her life, she got up, and laughing in a queer way, began to put up her hair. She went into the scullery where were the brush and combs, and Emily followed with a candle. When she returned, ordered once more, with a little pallor succeeding the flush, and with a great black stain of sweat on her leathern belt where his hand had held her, he looked up at her from his position on the sofa, with a peculiar glance of triumph, smiling.

'You great brute,' she said, but her voice was not as harsh as her words. He gave a deep sigh, sat up, and laughed quietly.

'Another?' he said.

'Will you dance with *me*?'

'At your pleasure.'

'Come then—a minuet.'

'Don't know it.'

'Nevertheless, you must dance it. Come along.'

He reared up, and walked to her side. She put him through the steps, even dragging him round the waltz. It was very ridiculous. When it was finished she bowed him to his seat, and, wiping her hands on her handkerchief, because his shirt where her hand had rested on his shoulders was moist, she thanked him.

'I hope you enjoyed it,' he said.

'Ever so much,' she replied.

'You made me look a fool—so no doubt you did.'

'Do you think you could look a fool? Why, you are ironical! *Ça marche!* In other words, you have come on. But it is a sweet dance.'

He looked at her, lowered his eyelids, and said nothing.

'Ah, well,' she laughed, 'some are bred for the minuet, and some for—'

'—Less tomfoolery,' he answered.

'Ah—you call it tomfoolery because you cannot do it. Myself, I like it—so—'

'And I can't do it?'

'Could you? Did you? You are not built that way.'

'Sort of Clarence MacFadden,' he said, lighting a pipe as if the conversation did not interest him.

'Yes—what ages since we sang that!'

> 'Clarence MacFadden he wanted to dance
> But his feet were not gaited that way . . .'

'I remember we sang it after one corn harvest—we had a fine time. I never thought of you before as Clarence. It is very funny. By the way—will you come to our party at Christmas?'

'When? Who's coming?'

'The twenty-sixth—Oh!—only the old people—Alice—Tom Smith—Fanny—those from Highclose.'

'And what will you do?'

'Sing–charades–dance a little–anything you like.'

'Polka?'

'And minuets–and valetas. Come and dance a valeta, Cyril.'

She made me take her through a valeta, a minuet, a mazurka, and she danced elegantly, but with a little of Carmen's ostentation–her dash and devilry. When we had finished, the father said:

'Very pretty–very pretty, indeed! They do look nice, don't they, George? I wish I was young.'

'As I am–' said George, laughing bitterly.

'Show me how to do them–some time, Cyril,' said Emily, in her pleading way, which displeased Lettie so much.

'Why don't you ask me?' said the latter quickly.

'Well–but you are not often here.'

'I am here now. Come–' and she waved Emily imperiously to the attempt.

Lettie, as I have said, is tall, approaching six feet; she is lissome, but firmly moulded, by nature graceful; in her poise and harmonious movement are revealed the subtle sympathies of her artist's soul. The other is shorter, much heavier. In her every motion you can see the extravagance of her emotional nature. She quivers with feeling; emotion conquers and carries havoc through her, for she had not a strong intellect, nor a heart of light humour; her nature is brooding and defenceless; she knows herself powerless in the tumult of her feelings, and adds to her misfortunes a profound mistrust of herself.

As they danced together, Lettie and Emily, they showed in striking contrast. My sister's ease and beautiful poetic movement were exquisite; the other could not control her movements, but repeated the same error again and again. She gripped Lettie's hand fiercely, and glanced up with eyes full of humiliation and terror of her continued failure, and passionate, trembling, hopeless desire to succeed. To show her, to explain, made matters worse. As soon as she trembled on the brink of an action, the terror of not being able to perform it properly blinded her, and she was conscious of nothing but that she must do something–in a turmoil. At last Lettie ceased to talk, and merely swung her through the dances haphazard. This way succeeded better. So long as Emily need not think about her actions, she had a large, free grace; and the swing and rhythm and time were imparted through her senses rather than through her intelligence.

It was time for supper. The mother came down for a while, and we talked quietly, at random. Lettie did not utter a word about her engagement, not a suggestion. She made it seem as if things were just as before, although I am sure she had discovered that I had told George. She intended that we should play as if ignorant of her bond.

After supper, when we were ready to go home, Lettie said to him:

'By the way–you must send us some mistletoe for the party–with plenty of berries, you know. Are there many berries on your mistletoe this year?'

'I do not know–I have never looked. We will go and see–if you like,' George answered.

'But will you come out into the cold?'

He pulled on his boots, and his coat, and twisted a scarf round his neck. The young moon had gone. It was very dark–the liquid stars wavered. The great night filled us with awe. Lettie caught hold of my arm, and held it tightly. He passed on in front to open the gates. We went down into the front garden, over the turf bridge where the sluice rushed coldly under, on to the broad slope of the bank. We could just distinguish the gnarled old apple trees leaning about us. We bent our heads to avoid the boughs, and followed George. He hesitated a moment, saying:

'Let me see—I think they are there—the two trees with mistletoe on.'

We again followed silently.

'Yes,' he said. 'Here they are!'

We went close and peered into the old trees. We could just see the dark bush of the mistletoe between the boughs of the tree. Lettie began to laugh.

'Have we come to count the berries?' she said. 'I can't even see the mistletoe.'

She leaned forward and upwards to pierce the darkness; he, also straining to look, felt her breath on his cheek, and turning, saw the pallor of her face close to his, and felt the dark glow of her eyes. He caught her in his arms, and held her mouth in a kiss. Then, when he released her, he turned away, saying something incoherent about going to fetch the lantern to look. She remained with her back towards me, and pretended to be feeling among the mistletoe for the berries. Soon I saw the swing of the hurricane lamp below.

'He is bringing the lantern,' said I.

When he came up, he said, and his voice was strange and subdued:

'Now we can see what it's like.'

He went near, and held up the lamp, so that it illuminated both their faces, and the fantastic boughs of the trees, and the weird bush of mistletoe sparsely pearled with berries. Instead of looking at the berries they looked into each other's eyes; his lids flickered, and he flushed, in the yellow light of the lamp looking warm and handsome; he looked upwards in confusion and said, 'There are plenty of berries.'

As a matter of fact, there were very few.

She too looked up, and murmured her assent. The light seemed to hold them as in a globe, in another world, apart from the night in which I stood. He put up his hand and broke off a sprig of mistletoe, with berries, and offered it to her. They looked into each other's eyes again. She put the mistletoe among her furs, looking down at her bosom. They remained still, in the centre of light with the lamp uplifted; the red and black scarf wrapped loosely round his neck gave him a luxurious, generous look. He lowered the lamp and said, affecting to speak naturally:

'Yes—there is plenty this year.'

'You will give me some,' she replied, turning away and finally breaking the spell.

'When shall I cut it?'—He strode beside her, swinging the lamp, as we went down the bank to go home. He came as far as the brooks without saying another word. Then he bade us good night. When he had lighted her over the stepping-stones, she did not take my arm as we walked home.

During the next two weeks we were busy preparing for Christmas, ranging the woods for the reddest holly, and pulling the gleaming ivy-bunches from the trees. From the farms around came the cruel yelling of pigs, and in the evening, later, was a scent of pork-pies. Far off on the high-way could be heard the sharp trot of ponies hastening with Christmas goods.

There the carts of the hucksters dashed by to the expectant villagers, triumphant with great bunches of light foreign mistletoe, gay with oranges peeping through the boxes, and scarlet intrusion of apples, and wild confusion of cold, dead poultry. The hucksters waved their whips triumphantly, the little ponies rattled bravely under the sycamores, towards Christmas.

In the late afternoon of the 24th, when dust was rising under the hazel brake, I was walking with Lettie. All among the mesh of twigs overhead was tangled a dark red sky. The boles of the trees grew denser–almost blue.

Tramping down the riding we met two boys, fifteen or sixteen years old. Their clothes were largely patched with tough cotton moleskin; scarves were knotted round their throats, and in their pockets rolled tin bottles full of tea, and the white knobs of their knotted snap-bags.

'Why!' said Lettie. 'Are you going to work on Christmas eve?'

'It looks like it, don't it?' said the elder.

'And what time will you be coming back?'

'About 'alf-past töw.'

'Christmas morning'

'You'll be able to look out for the herald Angels and the Star,' said I.

'They'd think we was two dirty little 'uns,' said the younger lad, laughing.

'They'll 'appen 'a done before we get up ter th' top,' added the elder boy, 'an' they'll none venture down th' shaft.'

'If they did,' put in the other, 'you'd ha'e ter bath 'em after. I'd gi'e 'em a bit o' my pasty.'

'Come on,' said the elder sulkily.

They tramped off, slurring their heavy boots.

'Merry Christmas!' I called after them.

'In th' mornin',' replied the elder.

'Same to you,' said the younger, and he began to sing with a tinge of bravado.

> 'In the fields with their flocks abiding.
> They lay on the dewy ground–'

'Fancy,' said Lettie, 'those boys are working for me!'

We were all going to the party at Highclose. I happened to go into the kitchen about half-past seven. The lamp was turned low, and Rebecca sat in the shadows. On the table, in the light of the lamp, I saw a glass vase with five or six very beautiful Christmas roses.

'Hullo, Becka, who's sent you these?' said I.

'They're not sent,' replied Rebecca from the depth of the shadow, with suspicion of tears in her voice.

'Why! I never saw them in the garden.'

'Perhaps not. But I've watched them these three weeks, and kept them under glass.'

'For Christmas? They are beauties. I thought someone must have sent them to you.'

'It's little as 'as ever been sent me,' replied Rebecca, 'an' less as will be.'

'Why–what's the matter?'

'Nothing. Who'm I, to have anything the matter! Nobody–nor ever was, nor ever will be. And I'm getting old as well.'

'Something's upset you, Becky.'

'What does it matter if it has? What are my feelings? A bunch o' fal-de-rol flowers as a gardener clips off wi' never a thought is preferred before mine as I've fettled after this three-week. I can sit at home to keep my flowers company–nobody wants 'em.'

I remembered that Lettie was wearing hot-house flowers; she was excited and full of the idea of the party at Highclose; I could imagine her quick 'Oh no, thank you, Rebecca. I have had a spray sent to me–'

'Never mind, Becky,' said I, 'she is excited tonight.'

'An' I'm easy forgotten.'

'So are we all, Becky–*tant mieux*.'

At Highclose Lettie made a stir. Among the little belles of the countryside, she was decidedly the most distinguished. She was brilliant, moving as if in a drama. Leslie was enraptured, ostentatious in his admiration, proud of being so well infatuated. They looked into each other's eyes when they met, both triumphant, excited, blazing arch looks at one another. Lettie was enjoying her public demonstration immensely; it exhilarated her into quite a vivid love for him. He was magnificent in response. Meanwhile, the honoured lady of the house, pompous and ample, sat aside with my mother conferring her patronage on the latter amiable little woman, who smiled sardonically and watched Lettie. It was a splendid party; it was brilliant, it was dazzling.

I danced with several ladies, and honourably kissed each under the mistletoe–except that two of them kissed me first, it was all done in a most correct manner.

'You wolf,' said Miss Wookey archly. 'I believe you are a wolf–a veritable *rôdeur des femmes*–and you look such a lamb too–such a dear.'

'Even my bleat reminds you of Mary's pet.'

'But you are not my pet–at least–it is well that my Golaud doesn't hear you–'

'If he is so very big–' said I.

'He is really; he's beefy. I've engaged myself to him, somehow or other. One never knows how one does those things, do they?'

'I couldn't speak from experience,' said I.

'Cruel man! I suppose I felt Christmasy, and I'd just been reading Maeterlinck–and he really is big.'

'Who?' I asked.

'Oh–He, of course. My Golaud. I can't help admiring men who are a bit avoirdupoisy. It is unfortunate they can't dance.'

'Perhaps fortunate,' said I.

'I can see you hate him. Pity I didn't think to ask him if he danced–before–'

'Would it have influenced you very much?'

'Well–of course–one can be free to dance all the more with the really nice men whom one never marries.'

'Why not?'

'Oh–you can only marry one–'

'Of course.'

'There he is–he's coming for me! Oh, Frank, you leave me to the tender mercies of the world at large. I thought you'd forgotten me, dear.'

'I thought the same,' replied her Golaud, a great fat fellow with a childish bare face. He smiled awesomely, and one never knew what he meant to say.

We drove home in the early Christmas morning. Lettie, warmly wrapped in her cloak, had had a little stroll with her lover in the shrubbery. She was still brilliant, flashing in her movements. He, as he bade her good-bye, was almost beautiful in his grace and his low musical tone. I nearly loved him myself. She was very fond towards him. As we came to the gate where the private road branched from the highroad, we heard John say 'Thank you'–and looking out, saw our two boys returning from the pit. They were very grotesque in the dark nights as the lamplight fell on them, showing them grimy, flecked with bits of snow. They shouted merrily, their good wishes. Lettie leaned out and waved to them, and they cried ''ooray!' Christmas came in with their acclamations.

9

LETTIE COMES OF AGE

Lettie was twenty-one on the day after Christmas. She woke me in the morning with cries of dismay. There was a great fall of snow, multiplying the cold morning light, startling the slow-footed twilight. The lake was black like the open eyes of a corpse; the woods were black like the beard on the face of a corpse. A rabbit bobbed out, and floundered in much consternation; little birds settled into the depth, and rose in a dusty whirr, much terrified at the universal treachery of the earth. The snow was eighteen inches deep, and drifted in places.

'They will never come!' lamented Lettie, for it was the day of her party.

'At any rate–Leslie will,' said I.

'One!' she exclaimed.

'That one is all, isn't it?' said I. 'And for sure George will come, though I've not seen him this fortnight. He's not been in one night, they say, for a fortnight.'

'Why not?'

'I cannot say.'

Lettie went away to ask Rebecca for the fiftieth time if she thought they would come. At any rate, ten o'clock when Leslie arrived, ruddy, with shining eyes, laughing like a boy. There was much stamping in the porch, and knocking of leggings with his stick, and crying of Lettie from the kitchen to know who had come, and loud, cheery answers from the porch bidding her come and see. She came, and greeted him with effusion.

'Ha, my little woman!' he said, kissing her. 'I declare you are a woman. Look at yourself in the glass now–' She did so–'What do you see?' he asked, laughing.

'You–mighty gay, looking at me.'

'Ah, but look at yourself. There! I declare you're more afraid of your own eyes than of mine, aren't you?'

'I am,' she said, and he kissed her with rapture.

'It's your birthday,' he said.

'I know,' she replied.

'So do I. You promised me something.'

'What?' she asked.

'Here–see if you like it'–he gave her a little case. She opened it, and instinctively slipped the ring on her finger. He made a movement of pleasure. She looked up, laughing breathlessly at him.

'Now!' said he, in times of finality.

'Ah!' she exclaimed in a strange, thrilled voice.

He caught her in his arms.

After a while, when they could talk rationally again, she said:

'Do you think they will come to my party?'

'I hope not–By Heaven!'

'But–oh yes! We have made all preparations.'

'What does that matter! Ten thousand folks here today–!'

'Not ten thousand–only five or six. I shall be wild if they can't come.'

'You want them?'

'We have asked them–and everything is ready–and I do want us to have a party one day.'

'But today–damn it all, Lettie!'

'But I did want my party today. Don't you think they'll come?'

'They won't if they've any sense!'

'You might help me–' she pouted.

'Well, I'll be–! and you've set your mind on having a houseful of people today?'

'You know how we look forward to it–my party. At any rate–I know Tom Smith will come–and I'm almost sure Emily Saxton will.'

He bit his moustache angrily, and said at last:

'Then I suppose I'd better send John round for the lot.'

'It wouldn't be much trouble, would it?'

'No *trouble* at all.'

'Do you know,' she said, twisting the ring on her finger, 'it makes me feel as if I tied something round my finger to remember by. It somehow remains in my consciousness all the time.'

'At any rate,' said he, 'I have got you.'

After dinner, when we were alone, Lettie sat at the table, nervously fingering her ring.

'It is pretty, Mother, isn't it?' she said a trifle pathetically.

'Yes, very pretty. I have always liked Leslie,' replied my mother.

'But it feels so heavy–it fidgets me. I should like to take it off.'

'You are like me, I never could wear rings. I hated my wedding ring for months.'

'Did you, Mother?'

'I longed to take it off and put it away. But after a while I got used to it.'

'I'm glad this isn't a wedding ring.'

'Leslie says it is as good,' said I.

'Ah well, yes! But still it is different–' She put the jewels round under her finger, and looked at the plain gold band–then she twisted it back quickly, saying:

'I'm glad it's not–not yet. I begin to feel a woman, little Mother–I feel grown up today.'

My mother got up suddenly and went and kissed Lettie fervently.

'Let me kiss my girl good-bye,' she said, and her voice was muffled with tears. Lettie clung to my mother, and sobbed a few quiet sobs, hidden in her bosom. Then she lifted her face, which was wet with tears, and kissed my mother, murmuring:

'No, Mother–no–o–!'

About three o'clock the carriage came with Leslie and Marie. Both Lettie and I were upstairs, and I heard Marie come tripping up to my sister.

'Oh, Lettie, he is in such a state of excitement, you never knew. He took me with him to buy it–let me see it on. I think it's awfully lovely. Here, let me help you to do your hair–all in those little rolls–it will look charming. You've really got beautiful hair—there's so much life in it—it's a pity to twist it into a coil as you do. I wish my hair were a bit longer—though really, it's all the better for this fashion—don't you like it?—it's "so chic"—I think these little puffs are just fascinating—it is rather long for them—but it will look ravishing. Really, my eyes, and eyebrows, and eyelashes are my best features, don't you think?'

Marie, the delightful, charming little creature, twittered on. I went downstairs.

Leslie started when I entered the room, but seeing only me, he leaned forward again, resting his arms on his knees, looking in the fire.

'What the Dickens is she doing?' he asked.

'Dressing.'

'Then we may keep on waiting. Isn't it a deuced nuisance, these people coming?'

'Well, we generally have a good time.'

'Oh—it's all very well—we're not in the same boat, you and me.'

'Fact,' said I, laughing.

'By Jove, Cyril, you don't know what it is to be in love. I never thought—I couldn't ha' believed I should be like it. And the time when it isn't at the top of your blood, it's at the bottom:—"the Girl, the Girl".'

He stared into the fire.

'It seems pressing you, pressing you on. Never leaves you alone a moment.'

Again he lapsed into reflection.

'Then, all at once, you remember how she kissed you, and all your blood jumps afire.'

He mused again for a while—or rather, he seemed fiercely to con over his sensations.

'You know,' he said, 'I don't think she feels for me as I do for her.'

'Would you want her to?' said I.

'I don't know. Perhaps not—but—still I don't think she feels—'

At this he lighted a cigarette to soothe his excited feelings, and there was silence for some time. Then the girls came down. We could hear their light chatter. Lettie entered the room. He jumped up and surveyed her. She was dressed in soft, creamy, silken stuff; her neck was quite bare; her hair was, as Marie promised, fascinating; she was laughing nervously. She grew warm, like a blossom in the sunshine, in the glow of his admiration. He went forward and kissed her.

'You are splendid!' he said.

She only laughed for answer. He drew her away to the great arm-chair, and made her sit in it beside him. She was indulgent and he radiant. He took her hand and looked at it, and at his ring which she wore.

'It looks all right!' he murmured.

'Anything would,' she replied.

'What do you mean—sapphires and diamonds—for I don't know?'

'Nor do I. Blue for hope, because Speranza in "Fairy Queen" had a blue gown—and diamonds for—the crystalline clearness of my nature.'

'Its glitter and hardness, you mean.—You are a hard little mistress. But why hope?'

'Why?—No reason whatever, like most things. No, that's not right. Hope! Oh—blindfolded—hugging a silly harp with no strings. I wonder why she didn't drop her harp framework over the edge of the globe, and take the handkerchief off her eyes, and have a look round! But of course she was a woman—and a man's woman. Do you know I believe most women can sneak a look down their noses from underneath the handkerchief of hope they've tied over their eyes. They could take the whole muffler off–but they don't do it, the dears.'

'I don't believe you know what you're talking about, and I'm sure I don't. Sapphires reminded me of your eyes–and–isn't it "Blue that kept the faith"? I remember something about it.'

'Here,' said she, pulling off the ring, 'you ought to wear it yourself, Faithful One, to keep me in constant mind.'

'Keep it on, keep it on. It holds you faster than that fair damsel tied to a tree in Millais's picture–I believe it's Millais.'

She sat shaking with laughter.

'What a comparison! Who'll be the brave knight to rescue me– discreetly–from behind?'

'Ah,' he answered, 'it doesn't matter. You don't want rescuing, do you?'

'Not yet,' she replied, teasing him.

They continued to talk half nonsense, making themselves eloquent by quick looks and gestures, and communion of warm closeness. The ironical tones went out of Lettie's voice, and they made love.

Marie drew me away into the dining-room, to leave them alone.

Marie is a charming little maid, whose appearance is neatness, whose face is confident little goodness. Her hair is dark, and lies low upon her neck in wavy coils. She does not affect the fashion in coiffure, and generally is a little behind the fashion in dress. Indeed she is a half-opened bud of a matron, conservative, full of proprieties, and of gentle indulgence. She now smiled at me with a warm delight in the romance upon which she had just shed her grace, but her demureness allowed nothing to be said. She glanced round the room, and out of the window, and observed:

'I always love Woodside, it is restful–there is something about it–oh– assuring–really–it comforts me–I've been reading Maxim Gorky.'

'You shouldn't,' said I.

'Dadda reads them–but I don't like them–I shall read no more. I like Woodside–it makes you feel–really at home–it soothes one like the old wood does. It seems right–life is proper here–not ulcery–'

'Just healthy living flesh,' said I.

'No, I don't mean that, because one feels–oh, as if the world were old and good, not old and bad.'

'Young, and undisciplined, and mad,' said I.

'No–but here, you, and Lettie, and Leslie, and me–it is so nice for us, and it seems so natural and good. Woodside is so old, and so sweet and serene–it does reassure one.'

'Yes,' said I, 'we just live, nothing abnormal, nothing cruel and extravagant –just natural–like doves in a dovecote.'

'Oh!–doves!–they are so–so mushy.'

'They are dear little birds, doves. You look like one yourself, with the black band round your neck. You a turtle-dove, and Lettie a wood-pigeon.'

'Lettie is splendid, isn't she? What a swing she has–what a mastery! I wish I had her strength–she just marches straight through in the right way–I think she's fine.'

I laughed to see her so enthusiastic in her admiration of my sister. Marie is such a gentle, serious little soul. She went to the window. I kissed her, and pulled two berries off the mistletoe. I made her a nest in the heavy curtains, and she sat there looking out on the snow.

'It is lovely,' she said reflectively. 'People must be ill when they write like Maxim Gorky.'

'They live in town,' said I.

'Yes–but then look at Hardy–life seems so terrible–it isn't, is it?'

'If you don't feel it, it isn't–if you don't see it. I don't see if for myself.'

'It's lovely enough for heaven.'

'Eskimo's heaven perhaps. And we're the angels, eh? And I'm an archangel.'

'No, you're a vain, frivolous man. Is that–? What is that moving through the trees?'

'Somebody coming,' said I.

It was a big, burly fellow moving curiously through the bushes.

'Doesn't he walk funnily?' exclaimed Marie. He did. When he came near enough we saw he was straddled upon Indian snow-shoes. Marie peeped, and laughed, and peeped, and hid again in the curtains laughing. He was very red, and looked very hot, as he hauled the great meshes, shuffling over the snow; his body rolled most comically. I went to the door and admitted him, while Marie stood stroking her face with her hands to smooth away the traces of her laughter.

He grasped my hand in a very large and heavy glove, with which he then wiped his perspiring brow.

'Well, Beardsall, old man,' he said, 'and how's things? God, I'm not 'alf hot! Fine idea though–' He showed me his snow-shoes.

'Ripping! ain't they? I've come like an Indian brave–' He rolled his 'r's', and lengthened out his 'ah's' tremendously–'brra-ave'.

'Couldn't resist it though,' he continued.

'Remember your party last year–Girls turned up? On the war-path, eh?' He pursed up his childish lips and rubbed his fat chin.

Having removed his coat, and the white wrap which protected his collar, not to mention the snowflakes, which Rebecca took almost as an insult to herself–he seated his fat, hot body on a chair, and proceeded to take off his gaiters and his boots. Then he donned his dancing-pumps, and I led him upstairs.

'Lord, I skimmed here like a swallow!' he continued–and I looked at his corpulence.

'Never met a soul, though they've had a snow-plough down the road. I saw the marks of a cart up the drive, so I guessed the Tempests were here. So Lettie's put her nose in Tempest's nosebag–leaves nobody a chance, that–some women have rum taste–only they're like ravens, they go for the gilding–don't blame 'em–only it leaves nobody a chance. Madie Howitt's coming, I suppose?'

I ventured something about the snow.

'She'll come,' he said, 'if it's up to the neck. Her mother saw me go past.'

He proceeded with his toilet. I told him that Leslie had sent the carriage for Alice and Madie. He slapped his fat legs, and exclaimed.

'Miss Gall–I smell sulphur! Beardsall, old boy, there's fun in the wind. Madie, and the coy little Tempest, and–' he hissed a line of a music-hall song through his teeth.

During all this he had straightened his cream and lavender waistcoat.

'Little pink of a girl worked it for me–a real juicy little peach–chipped somehow or other'–he had arranged his white bow–he had drawn forth two rings, one a great signet, the other gorgeous with diamonds, and had adjusted them on his fat white fingers; he had run his fingers delicately through his hair, which rippled backwards a trifle tawdrily–being fine and somewhat sapless; he had produced a box, containing a cream carnation with suitable greenery; he had flicked himself with a silk handkerchief, and had dusted his patent-leather shoes; lastly, he had pursued up his lips and surveyed himself with great satisfaction in the mirror. Then he was ready to be presented.

'Couldn't forget today, Lettie. Wouldn't have let old Pluto and all the bunch of 'em keep me away. I skimmed here like a "Brra-ave" on my snow-shoes, like Hiawatha coming to Minnehaha.'

'Ah–that was famine,' said Marie softly.

'And this is a feast, a gorgeous feast, Miss Tempest,' he said, bowing to Marie, who laughed.

'You have brought some music?' asked mother.

'Wish I was Orpheus,' he said, uttering his words with exaggerated enunciation, a trick he had caught from his singing, I suppose.

'I see you're in full feather, Tempest. Is she kind as she is fair?'

'Who?'

Will pursed up his smooth sensuous face that looked as if it had never needed shaving. Lettie went out with Marie, hearing the bell ring.

'She's an houri!' exclaimed William. 'Gad, I'm almost done for! She's a lotus-blossom!–But is that your ring she's wearing, Tempest?'

'Keep off,' said Leslie.

'And don't be a fool,' said I.

'Oh, O-O-Oh!' drawled Will, 'so we must look the other way! "*Le bel homme sans merci*"*!*'

He sighed profoundly, and ran his fingers through his hair, keeping one eye on himself in the mirror as he did so. Then he adjusted his rings and went to the piano. At first he only splashed about brilliantly. Then he sorted the music, and took a volume of Tchaikovsky's songs. He began the long opening of one song, was unsatisfied, and found another, a serenade of Don Juan. Then at last he began to sing.

His voice is a beautiful tenor, softer, more mellow, less strong and brassy than Leslie's. Now it was raised that it might be heard upstairs. As the melting gush poured forth, the door opened. William softened his tones, and sang "dolce", but he did not glance round.

'Rapture!–Choir of Angels,' exclaimed Alice, clasping her hands and gazing up at the lintel of the door like a sainted virgin.

'Persephone–Europa–' murmured Madie, at her side, getting tangled in her mythology.

Alice pressed her clasped hands against her bosom in ecstasy as the notes rose higher.

'Hold me, Madie, or I shall rush to extinction in the arms of this siren.' She clung to Madie. The song finished, and Will turned round.

'Take it calmly, Miss Gall,' he said. 'I hope you're not hit too badly.'

'Oh–how can you say "take it calmly"–how can the savage beast be calm!'

'I'm sorry for you,' said Will.

'You are the cause of my trouble, dear boy,' replied Alice.

'I never thought you'd come,' said Madie.

'Skimmed here like an Indian "brra-ave",' said Will. 'Like Hiawatha towards Minnehaha. I knew you were coming.'

'You know,' simpered Madie, 'it gave me quite a flutter when I heard the piano. It is a year since I saw you. How did you get here?'

'I came on snow-shoes,' said he. 'Real Indian–came from Canada–they're just ripping.'

'Oh–Aw-w *do* go and put them on and show us–*do!*–*do* perform for us, Billy dear!' cried Alice.

'Out in the cold and driving sleet–no fear,' said he, and he turned to talk to Madie. Alice sat chatting with Mother. Soon Tom Smith came, and took a seat next to Marie; and sat quietly looking over his spectacles with his sharp brown eyes, full of scorn for William, full of misgiving for Leslie and Lettie.

Shortly after, George and Emily came in. They were rather nervous. When they had changed their clogs, and Emily had taken off her brown-paper leggings, and he his leather ones, they were not anxious to go into the drawing-room. I was surprised–and so was Emily–to see that he had put on dancing shoes.

Emily, ruddy from the cold air, was wearing a wine-coloured dress, which suited her luxurious beauty. George's clothes were well made–it was a point on which he was particular, being somewhat self-conscious. He wore a jacket and a dark bow. The other men were in evening dress.

We took them into the drawing-room, where the lamp was not lighted, and the glow of the fire was becoming evident in the dusk. We had taken up the carpet–the floor was all polished–and some of the furniture was taken away–so that the room looked large and ample.

There was general hand-shaking, and the newcomers were seated near the fire. First Mother talked to them–then the candles were lighted at the piano, and Will played to us. He is an exquisite pianist, full of refinement and poetry. It is astonishing, and it is a fact. Mother went out to attend to the tea, and after a while, Lettie crossed over to Emily and George, and, drawing up a low chair, sat down to talk to them. Leslie stood in the window bay, looking out on the lawn where the snow grew bluer and bluer and the sky almost purple.

Lettie put her hands on Emily's lap, and said softly, 'Look–do you like it?'

'What! Engaged?' exclaimed Emily.

'I am of age, you see,' said Lettie.

'It is a beauty, isn't it? Let me try it on, will you? Yes, I've never had a ring. There, it won't go over my knuckle–no–I thought not. Aren't my hands red?–it's the cold–yes, it's too small for me. I do like it.'

George sat watching the play of the four hands in his sister's lap, two hands moving so white and fascinating in the twilight, the other two rather red, with rather large bones, looking so nervous, almost hysterical. The ring played between the four hands, giving an occasional flash from the twilight or candlelight.

'You must congratulate me,' she said, in a very low voice, and two of us knew she spoke to him.

'Ah, yes,' said Emily, 'I do.'

'And you?' she said, turning to him, who was silent.

'What do you want me to say?' he asked.

'Say what you like.'

'Some time, when I've thought about it.'

'Cold dinners!' laughed Lettie, awaking Alice's old sarcasm at his slowness.

'What?' he exclaimed, looking up suddenly at her taunt. She knew she was playing false; she put the ring on her finger and went across the room to Leslie, laying her arm over his shoulder, and leaning her head against him, murmuring softly to him. He, poor fellow, was delighted with her, for she did not display her fondness often.

We went in to tea. The yellow shaded lamp shone softly over the table, where Christmas roses spread wide open among some dark-coloured leaves; where the china and silver and the coloured dishes shone delightfully. We were all very gay and bright; who could be otherwise, seated round a well-laid table, with young company, and the snow outside? George felt awkward when he noticed his hands over the table, but for the rest, we enjoyed ourselves exceedingly.

The conversation veered inevitably to marriage.

'But what have you to say about it, Mr Smith?' asked little Marie.

'Nothing yet,' replied he in his peculiar grating voice. 'My marriage is in the unanalysed solution of the future—when I've done the analysis I'll tell you.'

'But what do you think about it—?'

'Do you remember, Lettie,' said Will Bancroft, 'that little red-haired girl who was in our year at college? She has just married old Craven out of Physic's department.'

'I wish her joy of it!' said Lettie; 'Wasn't she an old flame of yours?'

'Among the rest,' he replied, smiling. 'Don't you remember you were one of them; you had your day.'

'What a joke that was!' exclaimed Lettie. 'We used to go in the arboretum at dinner-time. You lasted half one autumn. Do you remember when we gave a concert, you and I, and Frank Wishaw, in the small lecture theatre?'

'When the Prinny was such an old buck, flattering you,' continued Will. 'And that night Wishaw took you to the station—sent old Gettim for a cab and saw you in, large as life—never was such a thing before. Old Wishaw won you with that cab, didn't he?'

'Oh, how I swelled!' cried Lettie. 'There were you all at the top of the steps gazing with admiration! But Frank Wishaw was not a nice fellow, though he played the violin beautifully. I never liked his eyes—'

'No,' added Will. 'He didn't last long, did he?—though long enough to oust me. We had a giddy ripping time in Coll., didn't we?'

'It was not bad,' said Lettie. 'Rather foolish. I'm afraid I wasted my three years.'

'I think,' said Leslie, smiling, 'you improved the shining hours to great purpose.'

It pleased him to think what a flirt she had been, since the flirting had been harmless, and only added to the glory of his final conquest. George felt very much left out during these reminiscences.

When we had finished tea, we adjourned to the drawing-room. It was in darkness, save for the fire-light. The mistletoe had been discovered, and was being appreciated.

'George, Sybil, Sybil, Georgie, come and kiss me,' cried Alice.

Will went forward to do her the honour. She ran to me, saying, 'Get away, you fat fool—keep on your own preserves. Now, Georgie dear, come and kiss me, 'cause you haven't got nobody else but me, no y' 'aven't. Do you want to run away, like Georgy-Porgy apple-pie? Shan't cry, sure I shan't, if you are ugly.'

She took him and kissed him on either cheek, saying softly, 'You shan't be so serious, old boy–buck up, there's a good fellow.'

We lighted the lamp, and charades were proposed, Leslie and Lettie, Will and Madie and Alice went out to play. The first scene was an elopement to Gretna Green–with Alice a maidservant, a part that she played wonderfully well as a caricature. It was very noisy, and extremely funny. Leslie was in high spirits. It was remarkable to observe that, as he became more animated, more abundantly energetic, Lettie became quieter. The second scene, which they were playing as excited melodrama, she turned into small tragedy with her bitterness. They went out, and Lettie blew us kisses from the doorway.

'Doesn't she act well?' exclaimed Marie, speaking to Tom.

'Quite realistic,' said he.

'She could always play a part well,' said Mother.

'I should think,' said Emily, 'she could take a role in life and play up to it.'

'I believe she could,' Mother answered. 'There would only be intervals when she would see herself in a mirror acting.'

'And what then?' said Marie.

'She would feel desperate, and wait till the fit passed off,' replied my mother, smiling significantly.

The players came in again. Lettie kept her part subordinate. Leslie played with brilliance; it was rather startling how he excelled. The applause was loud–but we could not guess the word. Then they laughed, and told us. We clamoured for more.

'Do go, dear,' said Lettie to Leslie, 'and I will be helping to arrange the room for the dances. I want to watch you–I am rather tired–it is so exciting–Emily will take my place.'

They went. Marie and Tom, and Mother and I played bridge in one corner. Lettie said she wanted to show George some new pictures, and they bent over a portfolio for some time. Then she bade him help her to clear the room for the dances.

'Well, you have had time to think,' she said to him.

'A short time,' he replied. 'What shall I say?'

'Tell me what you've been thinking.'

'Well–about you–' he answered, smiling foolishly.

'What about me?' she asked, venturesome.

'About you, how you were at college,' he replied.

'Oh! I had a good time. I had plenty of boys. I liked them all, till I found there was nothing in them; then they tired me.'

'Poor boys!' he said, laughing. 'Were they all alike?'

'All alike,' she replied, 'and they are still.'

'Pity,' he said, smiling. 'It's hard lines on you.'

'Why?' she said.

'It leaves you nobody to care for–' he replied.

'How very sarcastic you are. You make one reservation.'

'Do I?' he answered, smiling. 'But you fire sharp into the air, and then say we're all blank cartridges–except one, of course.'

'You?' she queried ironically–'Oh, you would for ever hang fire.'

' "Cold dinners!" ' he quoted in bitterness. 'But you knew I loved you. You knew well enough.'

'Past tense,' she replied, 'thanks–make it perfect next time.'

'It's you who hang fire–it's you who make me,' he said.

'"And so from the retort circumstantial to the retort direct",' she replied, smiling.

'You see—you put me off,' he insisted, growing excited. For reply, she held out her hand and showed him the ring. She smiled very quietly. He stared at her with darkening anger.

'Will you gather the rugs and stools together, and put them in that corner?' she said.

He turned away to do so, but he looked back again, and said, in low, passionate tones:

'You never counted me. I was a figure naught in the counting all along.'

'See—there is a chair that will be in the way,' she replied calmly; but she flushed, and bowed her head. She turned away, and he dragged an armful of rugs into a corner.

When the actors came in, Lettie was moving a vase of flowers. While they played, she sat looking on, smiling, clapping her hands. When it was finished Leslie came and whispered to her, whereon she kissed him unobserved, delighting and exhilarating him more than ever. Then they went out to prepare the next act.

George did not return to her till she called him to help her. Her colour was high in her cheeks.

'How do you know you did not count?' she said nervously, unable to resist the temptation to play this forbidden game.

He laughed, and for a moment could not find any reply.

'I do!' he said. 'You knew you could have me any day, so you didn't care.'

'Then we're behaving in quite the traditional fashion,' she answered with irony.

'But you know,' he said, 'you began it. You played with me, and showed me heaps of things—and those mornings—when I was binding corn, and when I was gathering the apples, and when I was finishing the straw-stack—you came then—I can never forget those mornings—things will never be the same—You have awakened my life—I imagine things that I couldn't have done.'

'Ah!—I am very sorry, I am so sorry.'

'Don't be!—don't say so. But what of me?'

'What?' she asked rather startled. He smiled again; he felt the situation, and was a trifle dramatic, though deadly in earnest.

'Well,' said he, 'you start me off—then leave me at a loose end. What am I going to do?'

'You are a man,' she replied.

He laughed. 'What does that mean?' he said contemptuously.

'You can go on—which way you like,' she answered.

'Oh well,' he said, 'we'll see.'

'Don't you think so?' she asked, rather anxious.

'I don't know—we'll see,' he replied.

They went out with some things. In the hall, she turned to him, with a break in her voice, saying, 'Oh, I am so sorry—I am so sorry.'

He said, very low and soft, 'Never mind—never mind.'

She heard the laughter of those preparing the charade. She drew away and went in the drawing-room, saying aloud:

'Now I think everything is ready—we can sit down now.'

After the actors had played the last charade, Leslie came and claimed her.

'Now, Madam—are you glad to have me back?'

'That I am,' she said. 'Don't leave me again, will you?'

'I won't,' he replied, drawing her beside him. 'I have left my handkerchief in the dining-room,' he continued; and they went out together.

Mother gave me permission for the men to smoke.

'You know,' said Marie to Tom, 'I am surprised that a scientist should smoke. Isn't it a waste of time?'

'Come and light me,' he said.

'Nay,' she replied, 'let science light you.'

'Science does–Ah, but science is nothing without a girl to set it going–Yes–Come on–now, don't burn my precious nose.'

'Poor George!' cried Alice. 'Does he want a ministering angel?'

He was half lying in a big arm-chair.

'I do,' he replied. 'Come on, be my box of soothing ointment. My matches are all loose.'

'I'll strike it on my heel, eh? Now, rouse up, or I shall have to sit on your knee to reach you.'

'Poor dear–he shall be luxurious,' and the dauntless girl perched on his knee. 'What if I singe your whiskers–would you send an Armada? Aw–aw–pretty!–You do look sweet–doesn't he suck prettily?'

'Do you envy me?' he asked, smiling whimsically.

'Ra–ther!'

'Shame to debar you,' he said, almost with tenderness.

'Smoke with me.'

He offered her the cigarette from his lips. She was surprised, and exceedingly excited by his tender tone. She took the cigarette.

'I'll make a heifer–like Mrs Daws,' she said.

'Don't call yourself a cow,' he said.

'Nasty thing–let me go,' she exclaimed.

'No–you fit me–don't go,' he replied, holding her.

'Then you must have growed. Oh–what great hands–let go. Lettie, come and pinch him.'

'What's the matter?' asked my sister.

'He won't let me go.'

'He'll be tired first,' Lettie answered.

Alice was released, but she did not move. She sat with wrinkled forehead trying his cigarette. She blew out little tiny whiffs of smoke, and thought about it; she sent a small puff down her nostrils, and rubbed her nose.

'It's not as nice as it looks,' she said.

He laughed at her with masculine indulgence.

'Pretty boy,' she said, stroking his chin.

'Am I?' he murmured languidly.

'Cheek!' she cried, and she boxed his ears. Then 'Oh, pore fing!' she said, and kissed him.

She turned round to wink at my mother and at Lettie. She found the latter sitting in the old position with Leslie, two in a chair. He was toying with her arm; holding it and stroking it.

'Isn't it lovely?' he said, kissing the forearm, 'so warm and yet so white. Io–it reminds one of Io.'

'Somebody else talking about heifers,' murmured Alice to George.

'Can you remember,' said Leslie, speaking low, 'that man in Merimée who wanted to bite his wife and taste her blood?'

'I do,' said Lettie. 'Have you a strain of wild beast too?'

'Perhaps,' he laughed. 'I wish these folks had gone. Your hair is all loose in your neck–it looks lovely like that, though–'

Alice, the mocker, had unbuttoned the cuff of the thick wrist that lay idly on her knee, and had pushed his sleeve a little way.

'Ah!' she said. 'What a pretty arm, brown as an over-baked loaf!'

He watched her smiling.

'Hard as a brick,' she added.

'Do you like it?' he drawled.

'No,' she said emphatically, in a tone that meant 'yes'. 'It makes me feel shivery.' He smiled again.

She superposed her tiny, pale, flower-like hands on his.

He lay back looking at them curiously.

'Do you feel as if your hands were full of silver?' she asked almost wistfully, mocking.

'Better than that,' he replied gently.

'And your heart full of gold?' she mocked.

'Of hell!' he replied briefly.

Alice looked at him searchingly.

'And am I like a blue-bottle buzzing in your window to keep you company?' she asked.

He laughed.

'Good-bye,' she said, slipping down and leaving him.

'Don't go,' he said–but too late.

The irruption of Alice into the quiet, sentimental party was like taking a bright light into a sleeping hen-roost. Everybody jumped up and wanted to do something. They cried out for a dance.

'Emily–play a waltz–you won't mind, will you, George? What! You don't dance, Tom? Oh, Marie!'

'I don't mind, Lettie,' protested Marie.

'Dance with me, Alice,' said George, smiling, 'and Cyril will take Miss Tempest.'

'Glory!–come on–do or die!' said Alice.

We began to dance. I saw Lettie watching, and I looked round. George was waltzing with Alice, dancing passably, laughing at her remarks. Lettie was not listening to what her lover was saying to her; she was watching the laughing pair. At the end she went to George.

'Why!' she said, 'you can–'

'Did you think I couldn't?' he said. 'You are pledged for a minuet and a valeta with me–you remember?'

'Yes.'

'You promise?'

'Yes. But–'

'I went to Nottingham and learned.'

'Why–because?–Very well, Leslie, a mazurka. Will you play it, Emily–Yes, it is quite easy. Tom, you look quite happy talking to the Mater.'

We danced the mazurka with the same partners. He did it better than I expected–without much awkwardness–but stiffly. However, he moved quietly through the dance, laughing and talking abstractedly all the time with Alice.

Then Lettie cried a change of partners, and they took their valeta. There was a little triumph in his smile.

'Do you congratulate me?' he said.

'I am surprised,' she answered.

'So am I. But I congratulate myself.'

'Do you? Well, so do I.'

'Thanks! You're beginning at last.'

'What?' she asked.

'To believe in me.'

'Don't begin to talk again,' she pleaded sadly, 'nothing vital.'

'Do you like dancing with me?' he asked.

'Now, be quiet—*that's* real,' she replied.

'By Heaven, Lettie, you make me laugh!'

'Do I?' she said—'What if you married Alice—soon.'

'I—Alice!—Lettie!! Besides, I've only a hundred pounds in the world, and no prospects whatever. That's why—well—I shan't marry anybody—unless it's somebody with money.'

'I've a couple of thousand or so of my own—'

'Have you? It would have done nicely,' he said, smiling.

'You are different tonight,' she said, leaning on him.

'Am I?' he replied—'It's because things are altered too. They're settled one way now—for the present at least.'

'Don't forget the two steps this time,' said she, smiling, and adding seriously, 'You see, I couldn't help it.'

'No, why not?'

'Things! I have been brought up to expect it—everybody expected it—and you're bound to do what people expect you to do—you can't help it. We can't help ourselves, we're all chess-men,' she said.

'Ay,' he agreed, but doubtfully.

'I wonder where it will end,' she said.

'Lettie!' he cried, and his hand closed in a grip on hers.

'Don't—don't say anything—it's no good now, it's too late. It's done; and what is done, is done. If you talk any more, I shall say I'm tired and stop the dance. Don't say another word.'

He did not—at least to her. Their dance came to an end. Then he took Marie, who talked winsomely to him. As he waltzed with Marie he regained his animated spirits. He was very lively the rest of the evening, quite astonishing and reckless. At supper he ate everything, and drank much wine.

'Have some more turkey, Mr Saxton.'

'Thanks—but give me some of that stuff in brown jelly, will you? It's new to me.'

'Have some of this trifle, Georgie?'

'I will—you are a jewel.'

'So will you be—a yellow topaz tomorrow!'

'Ah! tomorrow's tomorrow!'

After supper was over, Alice cried:

'Georgie, dear—have you finished?—don't die the death of a king—King John—I can't spare you, pet.'

'Are you so fond of me?'

'I am—Aw! I'd throw my best Sunday hat under a milkcart for you, I would!'

'No; throw yourself into the milk-cart—some Sunday, when I'm driving.'

'Yes–come and see us,' said Emily.

'How nice! Tomorrow you won't want me, Georgie dear, so I'll come. Don't you wish Pa would make Tono-Bungay? Wouldn't you marry me then?'

'I would,' said he.

When the cart came, and Alice, Madie, Tom and Will departed, Alice bade Lettie a long farewell–blew Georgie many kisses–promised to love him faithful and true–and was gone.

George and Emily lingered a short time.

Now the room seemed empty and quiet, and all the laughter seemed to have gone. The conversation dribbled away; there was an awkwardness.

'Well,' said George heavily, at last. 'Today is nearly gone–it will soon be tomorrow. I feel a bit drunk! We had a good time tonight.'

'I am glad,' said Lettie.

They put on their clogs and leggings, and wrapped themselves up, and stood in the hall.

'We must go,' said George, 'before the clock strikes–like Cinderella–look at my glass slippers–' he pointed to his clogs. 'Midnight, and rags, and fleeing. Very appropriate. I shall call myself Cinderella who wouldn't fit. I believe I'm a bit drunk–the world looks funny.'

We looked out at the haunting wanness of the hills beyond Nethermere.

'Good-bye, Lettie; good-bye.'

They were out in the snow, which peered pale and eerily from the depths of the black wood.

'Good-bye,' he called out of the darkness. Leslie slammed the door, and drew Lettie away into the drawing-room. The sound of his low, vibrating satisfaction reached us, as he murmured to her, and laughed now. Then he kicked the door of the room shut. Lettie began to laugh and mock and talk in a high strained voice. The sound of their laughter mingled was strange and incongruous. Then her voice died down.

Marie sat at the little piano–which was put in the dining-room–strumming and tinkling the false, quavering old notes. It was a depressing jingling in the deserted remains of the feast, but she felt sentimental, and enjoyed it.

This was a gap between today and tomorrow, a dreary gap, where one sat and looked at the dreary comedy of yesterdays, and the grey tragedies of dawning tomorrows, vacantly, missing the poignancy of an actual today.

The cart returned.

'Leslie, Leslie, John is here, come along!' called Marie.

There was no answer.

'Leslie–John is waiting in the snow.'

'All right.'

'But you must come at once.' She went to the door and spoke to him. Then he came out looking rather sheepish, and rather angry at the interruption. Lettie followed, tidying her hair. She did not laugh and look confused, as most girls do on similar occasions; she seemed very tired.

At last Leslie tore himself away, and after more returns for a farewell kiss, mounted the carriage, which stood in a pool of yellow light, blurred and splotched with shadows, and drove away, calling something about tomorrow.

PART II

I

STRANGE BLOSSOMS AND STRANGE NEW BUDDING

Winter lay a long time prostrate on the earth. The men in the mines of Tempest, Warrall and Co. came out on strike on a question of the rearranging of the working system down below. The distress was not awful, for the men were on the whole wise and well-conditioned, but there was a dejection over the face of the country-side, and some suffered keenly. Everywhere, along the lanes and in the streets, loitered gangs of men, unoccupied and spiritless. Week after week went on, and the agents of the Miners' Union held great meetings, and the ministers held prayer-meetings, but the strike continued. There was no rest. Always the crier's bell was ringing in the street; always the servants of the company were delivering handbills, stating the case clearly, and always the people talked and filled the months with bitter, and then hopeless, resenting. Schools gave breakfasts, chapels gave soup, well-to-do people gave teas—the children enjoyed it. But we, who knew the faces of the old men and the privations of the women, breathed a cold, disheartening atmosphere of sorrow and trouble.

Determined poaching was carried on in the squire's woods and warrens. Annable defended his game heroically. One man was at home with a leg supposed to be wounded by a fall on the slippery roads—but really, by a man-trap in the woods. Then Annable caught two men, and they were sentenced to two months' imprisonment.

On both the lodge gates of Highclose—on our side and on the far Eberwich side—were posted notices that trespassers on the drive or in the grounds would be liable to punishment. These posters were soon mudded over, and fresh ones fixed.

The men loitering on the road by Nethermere looked angrily at Lettie as she passed, in her black furs which Leslie had given her, and their remarks were pungent. She heard them, and they burned in her heart. From my mother she inherited democratic views, which she now proceeded to debate warmly with her lover.

Then she tried to talk to Leslie about the strike. He heard her with mild superiority, smiled, and said she did not know. Women jumped to conclusions at the first touch of feeling; men must look at a thing all round, then make a decision—nothing hasty and impetuous—careful, long-thought-out, correct decisions. Women could not be expected to understand these things, business was not for them; in fact, their mission was above business—etc., etc. Unfortunately Lettie was the wrong woman to treat thus.

'So!' said she, with a quiet, hopeless tone of finality.

'There now, you understand, don't you, Minnehaha, my Laughing Water.–So laugh again, darling, and don't worry about these things. We will not talk about them any more, eh?'

'No more.'

'No more–that's right–you are as wise as an angel. Come here–pooh, the wood is thick and lonely! Look, there is nobody in the world but us, and you are my heaven and earth!'

'And hell?'

'Ah–if you are so cold–how cold you are!–it gives me little shivers when you look so–and I am always hot–Lettie!'

'Well?'

'You are cruel! Kiss me–now–No, I don't want your cheek–kiss me yourself. Why don't you say something?'

'What for? What's the use of saying anything when there's nothing immediate to say?'

'You are offended!'

'It feels like snow today,' she answered.

At last, however, winter began to gather her limbs, to rise, and drift with saddened garments northward.

The strike was over. The men had compromised. It was a gentle way of telling them they were beaten. But the strike was over.

The birds fluttered and dashed; the catkins on the hazel loosened their winter rigidity, and swung soft tassels. All through the day sounded long, sweet whistlings from the bushes; then later, loud, laughing shouts of bird triumph on every hand.

I remember a day when the breast of the hills was heaving in a last quick waking sigh, and the blue eyes of the waters opened bright. Across the infinite skies of March great rounded masses of cloud had sailed stately all day, domed with white radiance, softened with faint, fleeting shadows as if companies of angels were gently sweeping past; adorned with resting, silken shadows likes those of a full white breast. All day the clouds had moved on to their vast destination, and I had clung to the earth yearning and impatient. I took a brush and tried to paint them, then I raged at myself. I wished that in all the wild valley where cloud shadows were travelling like pilgrims, something would call me forth from my rooted loneliness. Through all the grandeur of the white and blue day, the poised cloud masses swung their slow flight, and left me unnoticed.

At evening they were all gone, and the empty sky, like a blue bubble over us, swam on its pale bright rims.

Leslie came, and asked his betrothed to go out with him, under the darkening wonderful bubble. She bade me accompany her, and, to escape from myself, I went.

It was warm in the shelter of the wood and in the crouching hollows of the hills. But over the slanting shoulders of the hills the wind swept, whipping the redness into our faces.

'Get me some of those alder catkins, Leslie,' said Lettie, as we came down to the stream.

'Yes, those, where they hang over the brook. They are ruddy like new blood freshening under the skin. Look, tassels of crimson and gold!' She pointed to the dusty hazel catkins mingled with the alder on her bosom. Then she began to quote Christina Rossetti's 'A Birthday'.

'I'm glad you came to take me a walk,' she continued–'Doesn't Strelley Mill look pretty? Like a group of orange and scarlet fungi in a fairy picture. Do you know, I haven't been, no, not for quite a long time. Shall we call now?'

'The daylight will be gone if we do. It is half-past five–more! I saw him–the son–the other morning.'

'Where?'

'He was carting manure–I made haste by.'

'Did he speak to you–did you look at him?'

'No, he said nothing. I glanced at him–he's just the same, brick colour–stolid. Mind that stone–it rocks. I'm glad you've got strong boots on.'

'Seeing that I usually wear them–'

She stood poised a moment on a large stone, the fresh spring brook hastening towards her, deepening sidling round her.

'You won't call and see them, then?' she asked.

'No. I like to hear the brook tinkling, don't you?' he replied.

'Ah, yes–it's full of music.'

'Shall we go on?' he said, impatient but submissive.

'I'll catch up in a minute,' said I.

I went in and found Emily putting some bread into the oven.

'Come out for a walk,' said I.

'Now? Let me tell Mother–I was longing–'

She ran and put on her long grey coat and her red tam-o'-shanter. As we went down the yard, George called to me.

'I'll come back,' I shouted.

He came to the crew-yard gate to see us off. When we came out on to the path, we saw Lettie standing on the top bar of the stile, balancing with her hand on Leslie's head. She saw us, she saw George, and she waved to us. Leslie was looking up at her anxiously. She waved again, then we could hear her laughing, and telling him excitedly to stand still, and steady her while she turned. She turned round, and leaped with a great flutter, like a big bird launching, down from the top of the stile to the ground and into his arms. Then we climbed the steep hill-side–Sunny Bank, that had once shone yellow with wheat, and now waved black tattered ranks of thistles where the rabbits ran. We passed the little cottages in the hollow scooped out of the hill, and gained the highlands that look out over Leicestershire to Charnwood on the left, and away into the mountain knob of Derbyshire straight in front and towards the right.

The upper road is all grassy, fallen into long disuse. It used to lead from the Abbey to the Hall; but now it ends blindly on the hill-brow. Half-way along is the old White House farm, with its green mounting-steps mouldering outside. Ladies have mounted here and ridden towards the Vale of Belvoir–but now a labourer holds the farm.

We came to the quarries, and looked in at the lime-kilns.

'Let us go right into the woods out of the quarry,' said Leslie. 'I have not been since I was a little lad.'

'It is trespassing,' said Emily.

'We don't trespass,' he replied grandiloquently.

So we went along by the hurrying brook, which fell over little cascades in its haste, never looking once at the primroses that were glimmering all along its banks. We turned aside, and climbed the hill through the woods. Velvety green sprigs of dog-mercury were scattered on the red soil. We came to the top of a slope, where the wood thinned. As I talked to Emily I became dimly aware of a whiteness over the ground. She exclaimed with surprise, and I found that I was walking, in the first shades of twilight, over clumps of snowdrops. The hazels were thin, and only here and there an oak tree uprose. All the ground was white with snowdrops, like drops of manna scattered over the red earth, on the grey-green clusters of leaves. There was a deep little dell, sharp sloping like a cup, and white sprinkling of flowers all the way down, with white flowers showing pale among the first inpouring of shadow at the bottom. The earth was red and warm, pricked with the dark, succulent green of bluebell sheaths, and embroidered with grey-green clusters of spears, and many white flowerets. High above, above the light tracery of hazel, the weird oaks tangled in the sunset. Below, in the first shadows, drooped hosts of little white flowers, so silent and sad; it seemed like a holy communion of pure wild things, numberless, frail, and folded meekly in the evening light. Other flower companies are glad; stately barbaric hordes of bluebells, merry-headed cowslip groups, even light, tossing wood-anemones; but snowdrops are sad and mysterious. We have lost their meaning. They do not belong to us, who ravish them. The girls bent among them, touching them with their fingers, and symbolising the yearning which I felt. Folded in the twilight, these conquered flowerets are sad like forlorn little friends of dryads.

'What do they mean, do you think?' said Lettie in a low voice, as her white fingers touched the flowers, and her black furs fell on them.

'There are not so many this year,' said Leslie.

'They remind me of mistletoe, which is never ours, though we wear it,' said Emily to me.

'What do you think they say—what do they make you think, Cyril?' Lettie repeated.

'I don't know. Emily says they belong to some old wild lost religion. They were the symbol of tears, perhaps, to some strange-hearted Druid folk before us.'

'More than tears,' said Lettie. 'More than tears, they are so still. Something out of an old religion, that we have lost. They make me feel afraid.'

'What should you have to fear?' asked Leslie.

'If I knew I shouldn't fear,' she answered. 'Look at all the snowdrops'—they hung in dim, strange flecks among the dusky leaves—'look at them—closed up, retreating, powerless. They belong to some knowledge we have lost, that I have lost and that I need. I feel afraid. They seem like something in fate. Do you think, Cyril, we can lose things off the earth—like mastodons, and those old monstrosities—but things that matter—wisdom?'

'It is against my creed,' said I.

'I believe I have lost something,' said she.

'Come,' said Leslie, 'don't trouble with fancies. Come with me to the bottom of this cup, and see how strange it will be, with the sky marked with branches like a filigree lid.'

She rose and followed him down the steep side of the pit, crying, 'Ah, you are treading on the flowers.'

'No,' said he, 'I am being very careful.'

They sat down together on a fallen tree at the bottom. She leaned forward, her fingers wandering white among the shadowed grey spaces of leaves, plucking, as if it were a rite, flowers here and there. He could not see her face.

'Don't you care for me?' he asked softly.

'You?'–she sat up and looked at him, and laughed strangely. 'You do not seem real to me,' she replied, in a strange voice.

For some time they sat thus, both bowed and silent. Birds 'skirred' off from the bushes, and Emily looked up with a great start as a quiet, sardonic voice said above us:

'A dove-cot, my eyes if it ain't! It struck me I 'eered a cooin', an' 'ere's th' birds. Come on, sweethearts, it's th' wrong place for billin' an' cooin', in th' middle o' these 'ere snowdrops. Let's 'ave yer names, come on.'

'Clear off, you fool!' answered Leslie from below, jumping up in anger.

We all four turned and looked at the keeper. He stood in the rim of light, darkly; fine, powerful form, menacing us. He did not move, but like some malicious Pan looked down on us and said:

'Very pretty–pretty! Two–and two makes four. 'Tis true, two and two makes four. Come on, come on out o' this 'ere bridal bed, an' let's 'ave a look at yer.'

'Can't you use your eyes, you fool,' replied Leslie, standing up and helping Lettie with her furs. 'At any rate you can see there are ladies here.'

'Very sorry, Sir! You can't tell a lady from a woman at this distance at dusk. Who may you be, Sir?'

'Clear out! Come along, Lettie, you can't stay here now.'

They climbed into the light.

'Oh, very sorry, Mr Tempest–when yer look down on a man he never looks the same. I thought it was some young fools come here dallyin'–'

'Damn you–shut up!' exclaimed Leslie–'I beg your pardon, Lettie. Will you have my arm?'

They looked very elegant, the pair of them. Lettie was wearing a long coat which fitted close; she had a small hat whose feathers flushed straight back with her hair.

The keeper looked at them. Then, smiling, he went down the dell with great strides, and returned, saying, 'Well, the lady might as well take her gloves.'

She took them from him, shrinking to Leslie. Then she started, and said:

'Let me fetch my flowers.'

She ran for the handful of snowdrops that lay among the roots of the trees. We all watched her.

'Sorry I made such a mistake–a lady!' said Annable. 'But I've nearly forgot the sight o' one–save the squire's daughters, who are never out o' nights.'

'I should think you never have seen many–unless–! Have you ever been a groom?'

'No groom but a bridegroom, Sir, and then I think I'd rather groom a horse than a lady, for I got well bit–if you will excuse me, Sir.'

'And you deserved it–no doubt.'

'I got it–an' I wish you better luck, Sir. One's more a man here in th' wood, though, than in my lady's parlour, it strikes me.'

'A lady's parlour!' laughed Leslie, indulgent in his amusement at the facetious keeper.

'Oh, yes! "Will you walk into my parlour–"'

'You're very smart for a keeper.'

'Oh yes, Sir–I was once a lady's man. But I'd rather watch th' rabbits an' th' birds; an' it's easier breeding brats in th' Kennels than in th' town.'

'They are yours, are they?' said I.

'You know' em, do you, Sir? Aren't they a lovely little litter?–aren't they a pretty bag o' ferrets?–natural as weasels–that's what I said they should be–bred up like a bunch o' young foxes, to run as they would.'

Emily had joined Lettie, and they kept aloof from the man they instinctively hated.

'They'll get nicely trapped, one of these days,' said I.

'They're natural–they can fend for themselves like wild beasts do,' he replied, grinning.

'You are not doing your duty, it strikes me,' put in Leslie sententiously.

'Duties of parents!–tell me, I've need of it. I've nine–that is eight, and one not far off. She breeds well, the ow'd lass–one every two years–nine in fourteen years–done well, hasn't she?'

'You've done pretty badly, I think.'

'I–why? it's natural! When a man's more than nature he's a devil. Be a good animal, says I, whether it's man or woman. You, Sir, a good natural male animal; the lady there–a female un–that's proper as long as yer enjoy it.'

'And what then?'

'Do as th' animals do. I watch my brats–I let 'em grow. They're beauties, they are–sound as a young ash pole, every one. They shan't learn to dirty themselves wi' smirking deviltry–not if I can help it. They can be like birds, or weasels, or vipers, or squirrels, so long as they ain't human rot, that's what I say.'

'It's one way of looking at things,' said Leslie.

'Ay. Look at the women looking at us. I'm something between a bull and a couple of worms stuck together, I am. See that spink!' he raised his voice for the girls to hear, 'Pretty, isn't he? What for?–And what for do you wear a fancy vest and twist your moustache, Sir! What for, at the bottom! Ha–tell a woman not to come in a wood till she can look at natural things–she might see something.–Good night, Sir.'

He marched off into the darkness.

'Coarse fellow, that,' said Leslie when he had rejoined Lettie, 'but he's a character.'

'He makes you shudder,' she replied. 'But yet you are interested in him. I believe he has a history.'

'He seems to lack something,' said Emily.

'I thought him rather a fine fellow,' said I.

'Splendidly built fellow, but callous–no soul,' remarked Leslie, dismissing the question.

'No,' assented Emily. 'No soul–and among the snowdrops.'

Lettie was thoughtful, and I smiled.

It was a beautiful evening, still, with red, shaken clouds in the west. The moon in heaven was turning wistfully back to the east. Dark purple woods lay around us, painting out the distance. The near, wild, ruined land looked sad and strange under the pale afterglow. The turf path was fine and springy.

'Let us run!' said Lettie, and joining hands we raced wildly along, with a flutter and breathless laughter, till we were happy and forgetful. When we stopped we exclaimed at once, 'Hark!'

'A child!' said Lettie.

'At the Kennels,' said I.

We hurried forward. From the house came the mad yelling and yelping of children, and the wild hysterical shouting of a woman.

'Tha' little devil–tha' little devil–tha' shanna–that tha' shanna!' and this was accompanied by the hollow sound of blows, and a pandemonium of howling. We rushed in, and found the woman in a tousled frenzy belabouring a youngster with an enamelled pan. The lad was rolled up like a young hedgehog–the woman held him by the foot, and like a flail came the hollow utensil thudding on his shoulders and back. He lay in the firelight and howled, while scattered in various groups, with the leaping firelight twinkling over their tears and their open mouths, were the other children, crying too. The mother was in a state of hysteria; her hair streamed over her face, and her eyes were fixed in a stare of overwrought irritation. Up and down went her long arm like a windmill sail. I ran and held it. When she could hit no more, the woman dropped the pan from her nerveless hand, and staggered, trembling, to the squab. She looked desperately weary and foredone–she clasped and unclasped her hands continually. Emily hushed the children, while Lettie hushed the mother, holding her hard, cracked hands as she swayed to and fro. Gradually the mother became still, and sat staring in front of her; then aimlessly she began to finger the jewels on Lettie's finger.

Emily was bathing the cheek of a little girl, who lifted up her voice and wept loudly when she saw the speck of blood on the cloth. But presently she became quiet too, and Emily could empty the water from the late instrument of castigation, and at last light the lamp.

I found Sam under the table in a little heap. I put out my hand for him, and he wriggled away, like a lizard, into the passage. After a while I saw him in a corner, lying whimpering with little savage cries of pain. I cut off his retreat and captured him, bearing him struggling into the kitchen. Then, weary with pain, he became passive.

We undressed him, and found his beautiful white body all discoloured with bruises. The mother began to sob again, with a chorus of babies. The girls tried to soothe the weeping, while I rubbed butter into the silent, wincing boy. Then his mother caught him in her arms, and kissed him passionately, and cried with abandon. The boy let himself be kissed–then he too began to sob, till his little body was all shaken. They folded themselves together, the poor dishevelled mother and the half-naked boy, and wept themselves still. Then she took him to bed, and the girls helped the other little ones into their nightgowns, and soon the house was still.

'I canna manage 'em, I canna,' said the mother mournfully. 'They growin' beyont me–I dunna know what to do wi' 'em. An' niver a 'and does 'e lift ter 'elp me–no–'e cares not a thing for me–not a thing–nowt but makes a mock an' a sludge o' me.'

'Ah, baby!' said Lettie, setting the bonny boy on his feet, and holding up his trailing nightgown behind him, 'do you want to walk to your mother–go then–Ah!'

The child, a handsome little fellow of some sixteen months, toddled across to his mother, waving his hands as he went, and laughing, while his large hazel eyes glowed with pleasure. His mother caught him, pushed the silken brown hair back from his forehead, and laid his cheek against hers.

'Ah!' she said, 'tha's got a funny Dad, tha' has, not like another man, no, my duckie. 'E's got no 'art ter care for nobody, 'e 'asna, ma pigeon–no–lives like a stranger to his own flesh an' blood.'

The girl with the wounded cheek had found comfort in Leslie. She was seated on his knee, looking at him with solemn blue eyes, her solemnity increased by the quaint round head, whose black hair was cut short.

''S my chalk, yes it is, 'n our Sam says as it's 'issen, an' 'e ta'es it and marks it all gone, so I wouldna gie 't' 'im,'—she cluched in her fat little hand a piece of red chalk. 'My Dad gen it me, ter mark my dolly's face red, what's on'y wood—I'll show yer.'

She wriggled down, and holding up her trailing gown with one hand, trotted to a corner piled with a child's rubbish, and hauled out a hideous carven caricature of a woman, and brought it to Leslie. The face of the object was streaked with red.

''Ere sh' is, my dolly, what my Dad make me—'er name's Lady Mima.'

'Is it?' said Lettie, 'and are these her cheeks? She's not pretty, is she?'

'Um—sh' is. My Dad says sh' is—like a lady.'

'And he gave you her rouge, did he?'

'Rouge!' she nodded.

'And you wouldn't let Sam have it?'

'No—an' mi movver says, "Dun gie 't 'im"—'n 'e bite me.'

'What will your father say?'

'Me Dad?'

''E'd nobbut laugh,' put in the mother, 'an' say as a bite's bett'r'n a kiss.'

'Brute!' said Leslie feelingly.

'No, but 'e never laid a finger on' em—nor me neither. But 'e 's not like another man—niver tells yer nowt. He's more a stranger to me this day than 'e wor th' day I first set eyes on 'im.'

'Where was that?' asked Lettie.

'When I wor a lass at th' 'All—an' 'im a new man come—fair a gentleman, an' a, an' a! Ond even now can read an' talk like a gentleman—but 'e tells me nothing—Oh no—what am I in 'is eyes but a sludge bump?—'e 's above me, 'e is, an' above 'is own childer. God a-mercy, 'e 'll be in in a minute. Come on 'ere!'

She hustled the children to bed, swept the litter into a corner, and began to lay the table. The cloth was spotless, and she put him a silver spoon in the saucer.

We had only just got out of the house when he drew near. I saw his massive figure in the doorway, and the big, prolific woman moved subserviently about the room.

'Hullo, Proserpine—had visitors?'

'I never axed 'em—they come in 'earin' th' childer cryin'. I never encouraged 'em—'

We hurried away into the night.

'Ah, it's always the woman bears the burden,' said Lettie bitterly.

'If he'd helped her—wouldn't she have been a fine woman now—splendid? But she's dragged to bits. Men are brutes—and marriage just gives scope to them,' said Emily.

'Oh, you wouldn't take that as a fair sample of marriage,' replied Leslie. 'Think of you and me, Minnehaha.'

'Ay.'

'Oh—I meant to tell you—what do you think of Greymede old vicarage for us?'

'It's a lovely old place!' exclaimed Lettie, and we passed out of hearing.

We stumbled over the rough path. The moon was bright, and we stepped apprehensively on the shadows thrown from the trees, for they lay so black and substantial. Occasionally a moonbeam would trace out a suave white branch that the rabbits had gnawed quite bare in the hard winter. We came out of the woods into the full heavens. The northern sky was full of a gush of green light; in front, eclipsed Orion leaned over his bed, and the moon followed.

'When the northern lights are up,' said Emily, 'I feel so strange—half eerie—they do fill you with awe, don't they?'

'Yes,' said I, 'they make you wonder, and look, and expect something.'

'What do you expect?' she said softly, and looked up, and saw me smiling, and she looked down again, biting her lips.

When we came to the parting of the roads, Emily begged them just to step into the mill—just for a moment—and Lettie consented.

The kitchen window was uncurtained, and the blind, as usual, was not drawn. We peeped in through the cords of budding honeysuckle. George and Alice were sitting at the table playing chess; the mother was mending a coat, and the father, as usual, was reading. Alice was talking quietly, and George was bent on the game. His arms lay on the table.

We made a noise at the door, and entered. George rose heavily, shook hands, and sat down again.

'Hullo, Lettie Beardsall, you are a stranger,' said Alice. 'Are you *so* much engaged?'

'Ay—we don't see much of her nowadays,' added the father in his jovial way.

'And isn't she a toff, in her fine hat and furs and snowdrops. Look at her, George, you've never looked to see what a toff she is.'

He raised his eyes, and looked at her apparel and at her flowers, but not at her face:

'Ay, she is fine,' he said, and returned to the chess.

'We have been gathering snowdrops,' said Lettie, fingering the flowers in her bosom.

'They are pretty—give me some, will you?' said Alice, holding out her hand. Lettie gave her the flowers.

'Check!' said George deliberately.

'Get out!' replied his opponent, 'I've got some snowdrops—don't they suit me, an innocent little soul like me? Lettie won't wear them—she's not meek and mild and innocent like me. Do you want some?'

'If you like—what for?'

'To make you pretty, of course, and to show you an innocent little meekling.'

'You're in check,' he said.

'Where can you wear them?—there's only your shirt. Aw!—there'—she stuck a few flowers in his ruffled black hair—'Look, Lettie, isn't he sweet?'

Lettie laughed with a strained little laugh:

'He's like Bottom and the ass's head,' she said.

'Then I'm Titania—don't I make a lovely fairy queen, Bully Bottom?—and who's jealous Oberon?'

'He reminds me of that man in "Hedda Gabler"—crowned with vine leaves—oh yes, vine leaves,' said Emily.

'How's your mare's sprain, Mr Tempest?' George asked, taking no notice of the flowers in his hair.

'Oh—she'll soon be all right, thanks.'

'Ah—George told me about it,' put in the father, and he held Leslie in conversation.

'Am I in check, George?' said Alice, returning to the game. She knitted her brows and cogitated:

'Pooh!' she said, 'that's soon remedied!'–she moved her piece, and said triumphantly, 'Now, Sir!'

He surveyed the game, and, with deliberation moved. Alice pounced on him; with a leap of her knight she called, 'Check!'

'I didn't see it–you may have the game now,' he said.

'Beaten, my boy!–don't crow over a woman any more. Stalemate–with flowers in your hair!'

He put his hand to his head, and felt among his hair, and threw the flowers on the table.

'Would you believe it–!' said the mother, coming into the room from the dairy.

'What?' we all asked.

'Nickie Ben's been and eaten the sile-cloth. Yes! When I went to wash it, there sat Nickie Ben gulping, and wiping the froth off his whiskers.'

George laughed loudly and heartily. He laughed till he was tired. Lettie looked and wondered when he would be done.

'I imagined,' he gasped, 'how he'd feel with half a yard of muslin creeping down his throttle.'

This laughter was most incongruous. He went off into another burst. Alice laughed too–it was easy to infect her with laughter. Then the father began–and in walked Nickie Ben, stepping disconsolately–we all roared again, till the rafters shook. Only Lettie looked impatiently for the end. George swept his bare arms across the table, and the scattered little flowers fell broken to the ground.

'Oh–what a shame!' exclaimed Lettie.

'What?' said he, looking round. 'Your flowers? Do you feel sorry for them?–You're too tender-hearted; isn't she, Cyril?'

'Always was–for dumb animals, and things,' said I.

'Don't you wish you was a little dumb animal, Georgie?' said Alice.

He smiled, putting away the chess-men.

'Shall we go, dear?' said Lettie to Leslie.

'If you are ready,' he replied, rising with alacrity.

'I am tired,' she said plaintively.

He attended to her with little tender solicitations.

'Have we walked too far?' he asked.

'No, it's not that. No–it's the snowdrops, and the man, and the children–and everything. I feel just a bit exhausted.'

She kissed Alice, and Emily, and the mother.

'Good night, Alice,' she said. 'It's not altogether my fault we're strangers. You know–really–I'm just the same–really. Only you imagine, and then what can I do?'

She said farewell to George, and looked at him through a quiver of suppressed tears.

George was somewhat flushed with triumph over Lettie: She had gone home with tears shaken from her eyes unknown to her lover; at the farm George laughed with Alice.

We escorted Alice home to Eberwich–'Like a blooming little monkey dangling from two boughs,' as she put it, when we swung her along on our arms. We laughed and said many preposterous things. George wanted to kiss her at parting, but she tipped him under the chin and said, 'Sweet!' as one does to a canary. Then she laughed with her tongue between her teeth, and ran indoors.

'She is a little devil,' said he.

We took the long way home by Greymede, and passed the dark schools.

'Come on,' said he, 'let's go in the "Ram Inn"', and have a look at my cousin Meg.'

It was half-past ten when he marched me across the road and into the sanded passage of the little inn. The place had been an important farm in the days of George's grand-uncle, but since his decease it had declined, under the governance of the widow and a man-of-all-work. The old grand-aunt was propped and supported by a splendid granddaughter. The near kin of Meg were all in California, so she, a bonny delightful girl of twenty-four, stayed near her grandma.

As we tramped grittily down the passage, the red head of Bill poked out of the bar, and he said as he recognised George:

'Good ev'nin'–go forward–'er's non abed yit.'

We went forward, and unlatched the kitchen door. The great-aunt was seated in her little, round-backed arm-chair sipping her 'night-cap'.

'Well, George, my lad!' she cried, in her querulous voice. 'Tha' niver says it's thai, does ter? That's com'n for summat, for sure, else what brings thee ter see me?'

'No,' he said. 'Ah'n com ter see thee, nowt else. Wheer's Meg?'

'Ah!–Ha–Ha–Ah!–Me, did ter say?–come ter see me?–Ha–wheer's Meg!–an' who's this young gentleman?'

I was formally introduced, and shook the clammy corded hand of the old lady.

'Tha' looks delikit,' she observed, shaking her cap and its scarlet geraniums sadly: 'Cum now, sit thee down, an' dunna look so long o' th' leg.'

I sat down on the sofa, on the cushions covered with blue and red checks. The room was very hot, and I stared about uncomfortably. The old lady sat peering at nothing, in reverie. She was a hard-visaged, bosomless dame, clad in thick black cloth-like armour, and wearing an immense twisted gold brooch in the lace at her neck.

We heard heavy, quick footsteps above.

''Er's commin',' remarked the old lady, rousing from her apathy. The footsteps came downstairs–quickly, then cautiously round the bend. Meg appeared in the doorway. She started with surprise, saying:

'Well, I 'eered sumbody, but I never thought it was you.' More colour still flamed into her glossy cheeks, and she smiled in her fresh, frank way. I think I have never seen a woman who had more physical charm; there was a voluptuous fascination in her every outline and movement; one never listened to the words that came from her lips, one watched the ripe motion of those red fruits.

'Get 'em a drop o' whisky, Meg–you'll 'a'e a drop?'

I declined firmly, but did not escape.

'Nay,' declared the old dame. 'I s'll ha'e none o' thy no's. Should ter like it 'ot?–Say th' word, an' tha' 'as it.'

I did not say the word.

'Then gi'e 'im claret,' pronounced my hostess, 'though it's thin-bellied stuff ter go ter bed on'–and claret it was.

Meg went out again to see about closing. The grand-aunt sighed, and sighed again, for no perceptible reason but the whisky.

'It's well you've come ter see me now,' she moaned, 'for you'll none 'a'e a chance next time you come'n;—No—I'm all gone but my cap—' She shook that geraniumed erection, and I wondered what sardonic fate left it behind.

'An' I'm forced ter say it, I s'll be thankful to be gone,' she added, after a few sighs.

This weariness of the flesh was touching. The cruel truth is, however, that the old lady clung to life like a louse to a pig's back. Dying, she faintly, but emphatically declared herself, 'a bit better—a bit better. I s'll be up tomorrow.'

'I should a gone before now,' she continued, 'but for that blessed wench—I canna abear to think o' leavin' 'er—come drink up, my lad, drink up—nay, tha' 'rt nobbut young yet, tha' 'rt none topped up wi' a thimbleful.'

I took whisky in preference to the acrid stuff.

'Ay,' resumed the grand-aunt. 'I canna go in peace till 'er's settled—an' 'er's that tickle o' choosin'. Th' right sort 'asn't th' gumption ter ax' 'er.'

She sniffed, and turned scornfully to her glass. George grinned and looked conscious; as he swallowed a gulp of whisky it crackled in his throat. The sound annoyed the old lady.

'Tha' might be scar'd at summat,' she said. 'Tha' niver 'ad six drops o' spunk in thee.'

She turned again with a sniff to her glass. He frowned with irritation, half filled his glass with liquor, and drank again.

'I dare bet as tha' niver kissed a wench in thy life—not proper'—and she tossed the last drops of her toddy down her skinny throat.

Here Meg came along the passage.

'Come, Gran'ma,' she said. 'I'm sure it's time as you was in bed—come on.'

'Sit thee down an' drink a drop wi's—it's not ivry night as we 'a'e cumpny.'

'No, let me take you to bed—I'm sure you must be ready.'

'Sit thee down 'ere, I say, an' get thee a drop o' port. Come—no argy-bargyin'.'

Meg fetched more glasses and a decanter. I made a place for her between me and George. We all had port wine. Meg, naïve and unconscious, waited on us deliciously. Her cheeks gleamed like satin when she laughed, save when the dimples held the shadow. Her suave, tawny neck was bare and bewitching. She turned suddenly to George as he asked her a question, and they found their faces close together. He kissed her, and when she started back, jumped and kissed her neck with warmth.

'Là—là—dy—dà—là—dy—dà—dy—dà,' cried the old woman in delight, and she clutched her wineglass.

'Come on—chink!' she cried, 'all together—chink to him!'

We four chinked and drank. George poured wine in a tumbler, and drank it off. He was getting excited, and all the energy and passion that normally were bound down by his caution and self-instinct began to flame out.

'Here, Aunt!' said he, lifting his tumbler, 'here's to what you want—you know!'

'I knowed tha' wor as spunky as ony on'em,' she cried. 'Tha' nobbut wanted warmin' up. I'll see as you're all right. It's a bargain. Chink again, iverybody.'

'A bargain,' said he before he put his lips to the glass.

'What bargain's that?' said Meg.

The old lady laughed loudly and winked at George, who, with his lips wet with wine, got up and kissed Meg soundly, saying:

'There it is—that seals it.'

Meg wiped her face with her big pinafore, and seemed uncomfortable.

'Aren't you comin', Gran'ma?' she pleaded.

'Eh, tha' wants ter 'orry me off–what's thai say, George–a deep un, isna 'er?'

'Dunna go, Aunt, dunna be hustled off.'

'Tush–Pish,' snorted the old lady. 'Yah, tha' 'rt a slow un, an' no mistakes! Get a candle, Meg, I'm ready.'

Meg brought a brass bedroom candlestick. Bill brought in the money in a tin box, and delivered it into the hands of the old lady.

'Go thy ways to bed now, lad,' said she to the ugly, wizened serving-man. He sat in a corner and pulled off his boots.

'Come an' kiss me good night, George,' said the old woman–and as he did so she whispered in his ear, whereat he laughed loudly. She poured whisky into her glass and called to the serving-man to drink it. Then, pulling herself up heavily, she leaned on Meg and went upstairs. She had been a big woman, one could see, but now her shapeless, broken figure looked pitiful beside Meg's luxuriant form. We heard them slowly, laboriously climb the stairs. George sat pulling his moustache and half smiling; his eyes were alight with that peculiar childish look they had when he was experiencing new and doubtful sensations. Then he poured himself more whisky.

'I say, steady!' I admonished.

'What for!' he replied, indulging himself like a spoiled child and laughing.

Bill, who had sat for some time looking at the hole in his stocking, drained his glass, and with a sad 'Good night,' creaked off upstairs.

Presently Meg came down, and I rose and said we must be going.

'I'll just come an' lock the door after you,' said she, standing uneasily waiting.

George got up. He gripped the edge of the table to steady himself; then he got his balance, and, with his eyes on Meg, said:

''Ere!' he nodded his head to her. 'Come here, I want ter ax thee sumwhat.'

She looked at him, half smiling, half doubtful. He put his arm round her and looking down into her eyes, with his face very close to hers, said:

'Let's ha'e a kiss.'

Quite unresisting she yielded him her mouth, looking at him intently with her bright brown eyes. He kissed her, and pressed her closely to him.

'I'm going to marry thee,' he said.

'Go on!' she replied, softly, half glad, half doubtful.

'I am an' all,' he repeated, pressing her more tightly to him.

I went down the passage, and stood in the open doorway looking out into the night. It seemed a long time. Then I heard the thin voice of the old woman at the top of the stairs:

'Meg! Meg! Send 'im off now. Come on!'

In the silence that followed there was a murmur of voices, and then they came into the passage.

'Good night, my lad, good luck to thee!' cried the voice like a ghoul from upper regions.

He kissed his betrothed a rather hurried good night at the door.

'Good night,' she replied softly, watching him retreat. Then we heard her shoot the heavy bolts.

'You know,' he began, and he tried to clear his throat. His voice was husky and strangulated with excitement. He tried again:

'You know–she–she's a clinker.'

I did not reply, but he took no notice.

'Damn!' he ejaculated. 'What did I let her go for!'

We walked along in silence—his excitement abated somewhat.

'It's the way she swings her body—an' the curves as she stands. It's when you look at her—you feel—you know.'

I suppose I knew, but it was unnecessary to say so.

'You know—if ever I dream in the night—of women—you know—it's always Meg; she seems to look so soft, and to curve her body—'

Gradually his feet began to drag. When we came to the place where the colliery railway crossed the road, he stumbled, and pitched forward, only just recovering himself. I took hold of his arm.

'Good Lord, Cyril, am I drunk?' he said.

'Not quite,' said I.

'No,' he muttered, 'couldn't be.'

But his feet dragged again, and he began to stagger from side to side. I took hold of his arm. He murmured angrily—then, subsiding again, muttered, with slovenly articulation:

'I feel fit to drop with sleep.'

Along the dead, silent roadway, and through the uneven blackness of the wood, we lurched and stumbled. He was very heavy and difficult to direct. When at last we came to the brook we splashed straight through the water. I urged him to walk steadily and quietly across the yard. He did his best, and we made a fairly still entry into the farm. He dropped with all his weight on the sofa, and leaning down, began to unfasten his leggings. In the midst of his fumblings he fell asleep, and I was afraid he would pitch forward on to his head. I took off his leggings and his wet boots and his collar. Then, as I was pushing and shaking him awake to get off his coat, I heard a creaking on the stairs, and my heart sank, for I thought it was his mother. But it was Emily, in her long white nightgown. She looked at us with great dark eyes of terror, and whispered: 'What's the matter?'

I shook my head and looked at him. His head had dropped down on his chest again.

'Is he hurt?' she asked, her voice becoming audible, and dangerous. He lifted his head, and looked at her with heavy, angry eyes.

'George!' she said sharply, in bewilderment and fear. His eyes seemed to contract evilly.

'Is he drunk?' she whispered, shrinking away, and looking at me. 'Have you made him drunk—you?'

I nodded. I too was angry.

'Oh, if Mother gets up! I must get him to bed! Oh, how could you!'

This sibilant whispering irritated him, and me. I tugged at his coat. He snarled incoherently, and swore. She caught her breath. He looked at her sharply, and I was afraid he would wake himself into a rage.

'Go upstairs!' I whispered to her. She shook her head. I could see him taking heavy breaths, and the veins of his neck were swelling. I was furious at her disobedience.

'Go at once,' I said fiercely, and she went, still hesitating and looking back.

I had hauled off his coat and waistcoat, so I let him sink again into stupidity while I took off my boots. Then I got him to his feet, and, walking behind him impelled him slowly upstairs. I lit a candle in his bedroom. There was no sound from the other rooms. So I undressed him, and got him in bed at last, somehow. I covered him up and put over him the calf-skin rug, because the night was cold. Almost immediately he began to breathe heavily. I dragged him over to his side, and pillowed his head comfortably. He looked like a tired boy, asleep. I stood still, now I felt myself alone, and looked round. Up to the low roof rose the carven pillars of dark mahogany; there was a chair by the bed, and a little yellow chest of drawers by the windows; that was all the furniture, save the calf-skin rug on the floor. In the drawers I noticed a book. It was a copy of Omar Khayyam, that Lettie had given him in her Khayyam days, a little shilling book with coloured illustrations.

I blew out the candle, when I had looked at him again. As I crept on to the landing, Emily peeped from her room, whispering, 'Is he in bed?'

I nodded, and whispered good night. Then I went home, heavily.

After the evening at the farm, Lettie and Leslie drew closer together. They eddied unevenly down the little stream of courtship, jostling and drifting together and apart. He was unsatisfied and strove with every effort to bring her closer to him, submissive. Gradually she yielded, and submitted to him. She folded round her and him the snug curtain of the present, and they sat like children playing a game behind the hangings of an old bed. She shut out all distant outlooks, as an Arab unfolds his tent and conquers the mystery and space of the desert. So she lived gleefully in a little tent of present pleasures and fancies.

Occasionally, only occasionally, she would peep from her tent into the out space. Then she sat poring over books, and nothing would be able to draw her away; or she sat in her room looking out of the window for hours together. She pleaded headaches; Mother said liver; he, angry like a spoilt child denied his wish, declared it moodiness and perversity.

2

A SHADOW IN SPRING

With spring came trouble. The Saxtons declared they were being bitten off the estate by rabbits. Suddenly, in a fit of despair, the father bought a gun. Although he knew that the squire would not for one moment tolerate the shooting of that manna, the rabbits, yet he was out in the first cold morning twilight banging away. At first he but scared the brutes, and brought Annable on the scene; then, blooded by the use of the weapon, he played havoc among the furry beasts, bringing home some eight or nine couples.

George entirely approved of this measure; it rejoiced him even; yet he had never had the initiative to begin the life himself, or even to urge his father to it. He prophesied trouble, and possible loss of the farm. It disturbed him somewhat, to think they must look out for another place, but he postponed the thought of the evil day till the time should be upon him.

A vendetta was established between the Mill and the keeper, Annable. The latter cherished his rabbits:

'Call 'em vermin!' he said. 'I only know one sort of vermin—and that's the talkin' sort.' So he set himself to thwart and harass the rabbit-slayers.

It was about this time I cultivated the acquaintance of the keeper. All the world hated him—to the people in the villages he was like a devil of the woods.

Some miners had sworn vengeance on him for having caused their committal to gaol. But he had a great attraction for me; his magnificent physique, his great vigour and vitality, and his swarthy, gloomy face drew me.

He was a man of one idea: that all civilisation was the painted fungus of rottenness. He hated any sign of culture. I won his respect one afternoon when he found me trespassing in the woods because I was watching some maggots at work in a dead rabbit. That led us to a discussion of life. He was a thorough materialist—he scorned religion and all mysticism. He spent his days sleeping, making intricate traps for weasels and men, putting together a gun, or doing some amateur forestry, cutting down timber, splitting it in logs for use in the hall, and planting young trees. When he thought, he reflected on the decay of mankind—the decline of the human race into folly and weakness and rottenness. 'Be a good animal, true to your animal instinct,' was his motto. With all this, he was fundamentally very unhappy—and he made me also wretched. It was this power to communicate his unhappiness that made me somewhat dear to him, I think. He treated me as an affectionate father treats a delicate son; I noticed he liked to put his hand on my shoulder or my knee as we talked; yet withal, he asked me questions, and saved his thoughts to tell me, and believed in my knowledge like any acolyte.

I went up to the quarry woods one evening in early April, taking a look for Annable. I could not find him, however, in the wood. So I left the wildlands, and went along by the old red wall of the kitchen garden, along the main road as far as the mouldering church which stands high on a bank by the roadside, just where the trees tunnel the darkness, and the gloom of the highway startles the travellers at noon. Great trees growing on the banks suddenly fold over everything at this point in the swinging road, and in the obscurity rots the Hall church, black and melancholy above the shrinking head of the traveller.

The grassy path to the churchyard was still clogged with decayed leaves. The church is abandoned. As I drew near an owl floated softly out of the black tower. Grass overgrew the threshold. I pushed open the door, grinding back a heap of fallen plaster and rubbish and entered the place. In the twilight the pews were leaning in ghostly disorder, the prayer-books dragged from their ledges, scattered on the floor in the dust and rubble, torn by mice and birds. Birds scuffled in the darkness of the roof. I looked up. In the upward well of the tower I could see a bell hanging. I stooped and picked up a piece of plaster from the ragged confusion of feathers, and broken nests, and remnants of dead birds. Up into the vault overhead I tossed pieces of plaster until one hit the bell, and it 'tonged' out its faint remonstrance. There was a rustle of many birds like spirits. I sounded the bell again, and dark forms moved with cries of alarm overhead, and something fell heavily. I shivered in the dark, evil-smelling place, and hurried to get out of doors. I clutched my hands with relief and pleasure when I saw the sky above me quivering with the last crystal lights, and the lowest red of sunset behind the yew-boles. I drank the fresh air, that sparkled with the sound of the blackbirds and thrushes whistling their strong bright notes.

I strayed round to where the headstones, from their eminence, leaned to look on the Hall below, where great windows shone yellow light on the flagged courtyard, and the little fish-pool. A stone staircase descended from the graveyard to the court, between stone balustrades whose pock-marked grey columns still swelled gracefully and with dignity, encrusted with lichens. The staircase was filled with ivy and rambling roses—impassable. Ferns were unrolling round the big square halting-place, half-way down where the stairs turned.

A peacock, startled from the back premises of the Hall, came flapping up the terraces to the churchyard. Then a heavy footstep crossed the flags. It was the keeper. I whistled the whistle he knew, and he broke his way through the vicious rose-boughs up the stairs. The peacock flapped beyond me, on to the neck of an old bowed angel, rough and dark, an angel which had long ceased sorrowing for the lost Lucy, and had died also. The bird bent its voluptuous neck and peered about. Then it lifted up its head and yelled. The sound tore the dark sanctuary of twilight. The old grey grass seemed to stir, and I could fancy the smothered primroses and violets beneath it waking and gasping for fear.

The keeper looked at me and smiled. He nodded his head towards the peacock, saying:

'Hark at that damned thing!'

Again the bird lifted its crested head and gave a cry, at the same time turning awkwardly on its ugly legs, so that it showed us the full wealth of its tail glimmering like a stream of coloured stars over the sunken face of the angel.

'The proud fool!–look at it! Perched on an angel, too, as if it were a pedestal for vanity. That's the soul of a woman–or it's the devil.'

He was silent for a time, and we watched the great bird moving uneasily before us in the twilight.

'That's the very soul of a lady,' he said, 'the very, very soul. Damn the thing, to perch on that old angel. I should like to wring its neck.'

Again the bird screamed, and shifted awkwardly on its legs; it seemed to stretch its beak at us in derision. Annable picked up a piece of sod and flung it at the bird, saying:

'Get out, you screeching devil! God!' he laughed. 'There must be plenty of hearts twisting under here'–and he stamped on a grave–'when they hear that row.'

He kicked another sod from a grave and threw at the big bird. The peacock flapped away, over the tombs, down the terraces.

'Just look!' he said, 'the miserable brute has dirtied that angel. A woman to the end, I tell you, all vanity and screech and defilement.'

He sat down on a vault and lit his pipe. But before he had smoked two minutes, it was out again. I had not seen him in a state of perturbation before.

'The church,' said I, 'is rotten. I suppose they'll stand all over the country like this soon–with peacocks trailing the graveyards.'

'Ay,' he muttered, taking no notice of me.

'This stone is cold,' I said, rising.

He got up too, and stretched his arms as if he were tired. It was quite dark, save for the waxing moon which leaned over the east.

'It is a very fine night,' I said. 'Don't you notice a smell of violets?'

'Ay! The moon looks like a woman with child. I wonder what Time's got in her belly.'

'You?' I said. 'You don't expect anything exciting, do you?'

'Exciting!–No–about as exciting as this rotten old place–just rot off–Oh, my God!–I'm like a good house, built and finished, and left to tumble down again with nobody to live in it.'

'Why–what's up–really?'

He laughed bitterly, saying, 'Come and sit down.'

He led me off to a seat by the north door, between two pews, very black and silent. There we sat, he putting his gun carefully beside him. He remained perfectly still, thinking.

'Whot's up?' he said at last. 'Why–I'll tell you. I went to Cambridge–my father was a big cattle-dealer–he died bankrupt while I was in college, and I never took my degree. They persuaded me to be a parson, and a parson I was.

'I went a curate to a little place in Leicestershire–a bonnie place with not many people, and a fine old church, and a great rich parsonage, I hadn't over-much to do, and the rector–he was the son of an earl–was generous. He lent me a horse and would have me hunt like the rest. I always think of that place with a smell of honeysuckle while the grass is wet in the morning. It was fine, and I enjoyed myself, and did the parish work all right. I believe I was pretty good.

'A cousin of the rector's used to come in the hunting season–a Lady Crystabel, lady in her own right. The second year I was there she came in June. There wasn't much company, so she used to talk to me–I used to read then–and she used to pretend to be so childish and unknowing, and would get me telling her things, and talking to her, and I was hot on things. We must play tennis together, and ride together, and I must row her down the river. She said we were in the wilderness and could do as we liked. She made me wear flannels and soft clothes. She was very fine and frank and unconventional–ripping, I thought her. All the summer she stopped on. I should meet her in the garden early in the morning when I came from a swim in the river–it was cleared and deepened on purpose–and she'd blush and make me talk with her. I can remember I used to stand and dry myself on the bank full where she might see me–I was mad on her–and she was madder on me.

'We went to some caves in Derbyshire once, and she would wander from the rest, and loiter, and, for a game, we played a sort of hide and seek with the party. They thought we'd gone, and they went and locked the door. Then she pretended to be frightened and clung to me, and said what would they think, and hid her face in my coat. I took her and kissed her, and we made it up properly. I found out afterwards–she actually told me–she'd got the idea from a sloppy French novel–the *Romance of a Poor Young Man*. I was the Poor Young Man.

'We got married. She gave me a living she had in her parsonage, and we went to live at her Hall. She wouldn't let me out of her sight. Lord!–we were an infatuated couple–and she would choose to view me in an æsthetic light. I was Greek statues for her, bless you: Croton, Hercules, I don't know what! She had her own way too much–I let her do as she liked with me.

'Then gradually she got tired–it took her three years to be really glutted with me. I had a physique then–for that matter, I have now.'

He held out his arm to me, and bade me try his muscle. I was startled. The hard flesh almost filled his sleeve.

'Ah,' he continued, 'you don't know what it is to have the pride of a body like mine. But she wouldn't have children–no, she wouldn't–said she daren't. That was the root of the difference at first. But she cooled down, and if you don't know the pride of my body you'd never know my humiliation. I tried to remonstrate–and she looked simply astounded at my cheek. I never got over that amazement.

'She began to get souly. A poet got hold of her, and she began to affect Burne-Jones–or Waterhouse–it was Waterhouse–she was a lot like one of his women–Lady of Shalott, I believe. At any rate, she got souly, and I was her animal–*son animal–son bœuf*. I put up with that for above a year. Then I got some servants' clothes and went.

'I was seen in France–then in Australia–though I never left England. I was supposed to have died in the bush. She married a young fellow. Then I was proved to have died, and I read a little obituary notice on myself in a woman's paper she subscribed to. She wrote it herself–as a warning to other young ladies of position not to be seduced by plausible "Poor Young Men".

'Now she's dead. They've got the paper–her paper–in the kitchen down there, and it's full of photographs, even an old photo of me–"an unfortunate misalliance". I feel, somehow, as if I were at an end too. I thought I'd grown a solid, middle-aged man, and here I feel sore as I did at twenty-six, and I talk as I used to.

'One thing–I have got some children, and they're of a breed as you'd not meet anywhere. I was a good animal before everything, and I've got some children.'

He sat looking up where the big moon swam through the black branches of the yew.

'So she's dead–your poor peacock!' I murmured.

He got up, looking always at the sky, and stretched himself again. He was an impressive figure massed in blackness against the moonlight, with his arms outspread.

'I suppose,' he said, 'it wasn't all her fault.'

'A white peacock, we will say,' I suggested.

He laughed.

'Go home by the top road, will you!' he said. 'I believe there's something on in the bottom wood.'

'All right,' I answered, with a quiver of apprehension.

'Yes, she was fair enough,' he muttered.

'Ay,' said I, rising. I held out my hand from the shadow. I was startled myself by the white sympathy it seemed to express, extended towards him in the moonlight. He gripped it, and cleaved to me for a moment, then he was gone.

I went out of the churchyard feeling a sullen resentment against the tousled graves that lay inanimate across my way. The air was heavy to breathe, and fearful in the shadow of the great trees. I was glad when I came out on the bare white road, and could see the copper lights from the reflectors of a pony-cart's lamps, and could hear the amiable chat-chat of the hoofs trotting towards me. I was lonely when they had passed.

Over the hill, the big flushed face of the moon poised just above the tree-tops, very majestic, and far off–yet imminent. I turned with swift sudden friendliness to the net of elm-boughs spread over my head, dotted with soft clusters winsomely. I jumped up and pulled the cool soft tufts against my face for company; and as I passed, still I reached upward for the touch of this budded gentleness of the trees. The wood breathed fragrantly, with a subtle sympathy. The firs softened their touch to me, and the larches woke from the barren winter sleep, and put out velvet fingers to caress me as I passed. Only the clean, bare branches of the ash stood emblem of the discipline of life. I looked down on the blackness where trees filled the quarry and the valley bottoms, and it seemed that the world, my own home world, was strange again.

Some four or five days after Annable had talked to me in the churchyard, I went out to find him again. It was Sunday morning. The larch-wood was afloat with clear, lyric green, and some primroses scattered whitely on the edge under the fringing boughs. It was a clear morning, as when the latent life of the world begins to vibrate afresh in the air. The smoke from the cottage rose blue against the trees, and thick yellow against the sky. The fire, it seemed, was only just lighted, and the wood-smoke poured out.

Sam appeared outside the house, and looked round. Then he climbed the water-trough for a better survey. Evidently unsatisfied, paying slight attention to me, he jumped down and went running across the hill-side to the wood. 'He is going for his father,' I said to myself, and I left the path to follow him down hill across the waste meadow, crackling the blanched stems of last year's thistles as I went, and stumbling in rabbit-holes. He reached the wall that ran along the quarry's edge, and was over it in a twinkling.

When I came to the place, I was somewhat nonplussed, for sheer from the stone fence, the quarry-side dropped for some twenty or thirty feet, piled up with unmortared stones. I looked round—there was a plain dark thread down the hillside, which marked a path to this spot, and the wall was scored with the marks of heavy boots. Then I looked again down the quarry-side, and I saw—how could I have failed to see?—stones projecting to make an uneven staircase, such as is often seen in the Derbyshire fences. I saw this ladder was well used, so I trusted myself to it, and scrambled down, clinging to the face of the quarry wall. Once down, I felt pleased with myself for having discovered and used the unknown access, and I admired the care and ingenuity of the keeper, who had fitted and wedged the long stones into the uncertain pile.

It was warm in the quarry: there the sunshine seemed to thicken and sweeten; there the little mounds of overgrown waste were aglow with very early dog-violets; there the sparks were coming out on the bits of gorse, and among the stones the coltfoot plumes were already silvery. Here was spring sitting just awake, unloosening her glittering hair, and opening her purple eyes.

I went across the quarry, down to where the brook ran murmuring a tale to the primroses and the budding trees. I was startled from my wandering among the fresh things by a faint clatter of stones.

'What's that young rascal doing?' I said to myself, setting forth to see. I came towards the other side of the quarry: on this, the moister side, the bushes grew up against the wall, which was higher than on the other side, though piled the same with old dry stones. As I drew near I could hear the scrape and rattle of stones, and the vigorous grunting of Sam as he laboured among them. He was hidden by a great bush of sallow catkins, all yellow, and murmuring with bees, warm with spice. When he came in view I laughed to see him lugging and grunting among the great pile of stones that had fallen in a mass from the quarry-side; a pile of stones and earth and crushed vegetation. There was a great bare gap in the quarry wall. Somehow, the lad's labouring earnestness made me anxious, and I hurried up.

He heard me, and glancing round, his face red with exertion, eyes big with terror, he called, commanding me:

'Pull 'em off 'im—pull 'em off!'

Suddenly my heart beating in my throat nearly suffocated me. I saw the hand of the keeper lying among the stones. I set to tearing away the stones, and we worked for some time without a word. Then I seized the arm of the keeper and tried to drag him out. But I could not.

'Pull it off 'im!' whined the lad, working in a frenzy.

When we got him out I saw at once he was dead, and I sat down trembling with exertion. There was a great smashed wound on the side of the head. Sam put his face against his father's and snuffed round him like a dog, to feel the life in him. The child looked at me:

'He won't get up,' he said, and his little voice was hoarse with fear and anxiety.

I shook my head. Then the boy began to whimper. He tried to close the lips which were drawn with pain and death, leaving the teeth bare; then his fingers hovered round the eyes, which were wide open, glazed, and I could see he was trembling to touch them into life.

'He's not asleep,' he said, 'because his eyes is open—look!'

I could not bear the child's questioning terror. I took him up to carry him away, but he struggled and fought to be free.

'Ma'e 'im get up—ma'e 'im get up,' he cried in a frenzy, and I had to let the boy go.

He ran to the dead man, calling, 'Feyther! Feyther!' and pulling his shoulder; then he sat down, fascinated by the sight of the wound; he put out his finger to touch it, and shivered.

'Come away,' said I.

'Is it that?' he asked, pointing to the wound. I covered the face with a big silk handkerchief.

'Now,' said I, 'he'll go to sleep if you don't touch him—so sit still while I go and fetch somebody. Will *you* run to the Hall?'

He shook his head. I knew he would not. So I told him again not to touch his father, but to let him lie still till I came back. He watched me go, but did not move from his seat on the stones beside the dead man, though I know he was full of terror at being left alone.

I ran to the Hall—I dared not go to the Kennels. In a short time I was back with the squire and three men. As I led the way, I saw the child lifting a corner of the handkerchief to peep and see if the eyes were closed in sleep. Then he heard us, and started violently. When we removed the covering, and he saw the face unchanged in its horror, he looked at me with a look I have never forgotten.

'A bad business—an awful business!' repeated the squire. 'A bad business. I said to him from the first that the stones might come down when he was going up, and he said he had taken care to fix them. But you can't be sure, you can't be certain. And he'd be about half-way up—ay—and the whole wall would come down on him. An awful business, it is really; a terrible piece of work!'

They decided at the inquest that the death came by misadventure. But there were vague rumours in the village that this was revenge which had overtaken the keeper.

They decided to bury him in our churchyard at Greymede under the beeches; the widow would have it so, and nothing might be denied her in her state.

It was a magnificent morning in early spring when I watched among the trees to see the procession come down the hill-side. The upper air was woven with the music of the larks, and my whole world thrilled with the conception of summer. The young pale wind-flowers had arisen by the wood-gale, and under the hazels, when perchance the hot sun pushed his way, new little suns dawned, and blazed with real light. There was a certain thrill and quickening everywhere, as a woman must feel when she has conceived. A sallow tree in a favoured spot looked like a pale gold cloud of summer dawn; nearer it had poised a golden, fairy busby on every twig, and was voiced with a hum of bees, like any sacred golden bush, uttering its gladness in the thrilling murmur of bees, and in warm scent. Birds called and flashed on every hand; they made off exultant with streaming strands of grass, or wisps of fleece, plunging into the dark spaces of the wood, and out again into the blue.

A lad moved across the field from the farm below with a dog trotting behind him—a dog, no, a fussy, black-legged lamb trotting along on its toes, with its tail swinging behind. They were going to the mothers on the common, who moved like little grey clouds among the dark gorse.

I cannot help forgetting, and sharing the spink's triumph, when he flashes past with a fleece from a bramble bush. It will cover the bedded moss, it will weave among the soft red cow-hair, beautifully. It is a prize, it is an ecstasy to have captured it at the right moment, and the nest is nearly ready.

Ah, but the thrush is scornful, ringing out his voice from the hedge! He sets his breast against the mud, and models it warm for the turquoise eggs—blue, blue, bluest of eggs, which cluster so close and round against the breast, which round up beneath the breast, nestling content. You should see the bright ecstasy in the eyes of a nesting thrush, because of the rounded caress of the eggs against her breast!

What a hurry the jenny wren makes—hoping I shall not see her dart into the low bush. I have a delight in watching them against their shy little wills. But they have all risen with a rush of wings, and are gone, the birds. The air is brushed with agitation. There is no lark in the sky, not one; the heaven is clear of wings or twinkling dot—.

Till the heralds come—till the heralds wave like shadows in the bright air, crying, lamenting, fretting for ever. Rising and falling and circling round and round, the slow-waving peewits cry and complain, and lift their broad wings in sorrow. They stoop suddenly to the ground, the lapwings, then in another throb of anguish and protest, they swing up again, offering a glistening white breast to the sunlight, to deny it in black shadow, then a glisten of green, and all the time crying and crying in despair.

The pheasants are frightened into cover, they run and dart through the hedge. The cold cock must fly in his haste, spread himself on his streaming plumes, and sail into the wood's security.

There is a cry in answer to the peewits, echoing louder and stronger the lamentation of the lapwings, a wail which hushes the birds. The men come over the brow of the hill, slowly, with the old squire walking tall and straight in front; six bowed men bearing the coffin on their shoulders, treading heavily and cautiously, under the great weight of the glistening white coffin; six men following behind, ill at ease, waiting their turn for the burden. You can see the red handkerchiefs knotted round their throats, and their shirt-fronts blue and white between the open waistcoats. The coffin is of new unpolished wood, gleaming and glistening in the sunlight; the men who carry it remember all their lives after the smell of new, warm elm-wood.

Again a loud cry from the hill-top. The woman has followed thus far, the big, shapeless woman, and she cries with loud cries after the white coffin as it descends the hill, and the children that cling to her skirts weep aloud, and are not to be hushed by the other woman, who bends over them, but does not form one of the group. How the crying frightens the birds, and the rabbits; and the lambs away there run to their mothers. But the peewits are not frightened, they add their notes to the sorrow; they circle after the white, retreating coffin, they circle round the woman; it is they who for ever 'keen' the sorrows of this world. They are like priests in their robes, more black than white, more grief than hope, driving endlessly round and round, turning, lifting, falling and crying always in mournful desolation, repeating their last syllables like the broken accents of despair.

The bearers have at last sunk between the high banks, and turned out of sight. The big woman cannot see them, and yet she stands to look. She must go home, there is nothing left.

They have rested the coffin on the gate-posts, and the bearers are wiping the sweat from their faces. They put their hands to their shoulders on the place where the weight has pressed.

The other six are placing the pads on their shoulders, when a girl comes up with a jug and a blue pot. The squire drinks first, and fills for the rest. Meanwhile the girl stands back under the hedge, away from the coffin which smells of new elm-wood. In imagination she pictures the man shut up there in close darkness, while the sunlight flows all outside, and she catches her breast with terror. She must turn and rustle among the leaves of the violets for the flowers she does not see. Then, trembling, she comes to herself, and plucks a few flowers and breathes them hungrily into her soul, for comfort. The men put down the pots beside her, with thanks, and the squire gives the word. The bearers lift up the burden again, and the elm-boughs rattle along the hollow white wood, and the pitiful red clusters of elm-flowers sweep along it as if they whispered in sympathy—'We are so sorry, so sorry—'; always the compassionate buds in their fulness of life bend down to comfort the dark man shut up there. 'Perhaps,' the girl thinks, 'he hears them, and goes softly to sleep.' She shakes the tears out of her eyes on to the ground, and, taking up her pots, goes slowly down, over the brooks.

In a while, I too got up and went down to the mill, which lay red and peaceful, with the blue smoke rising as winsomely and carelessly as ever. On the other side of the valley I could see a pair of horses nod slowly across the fallow. A man's voice called to him now and again with a resonance that filled me with longing to follow my horses over the fallow, in the still, lonely valley, full of sunshine and eternal forgetfulness. The day had already forgotten. The water was blue and white and dark-burnished with shadows; two swans sailed across the reflected trees with perfect blithe grace. The gloom that had passed across was gone. I watched the swan with his ruffled wings swell onwards; I watched his slim consort go peeping into corners and under bushes; I saw him steer clear of the bushes, to keep full in view, turning his head to me imperiously, till I longed to pelt him with the empty husks of last year's flowers, knap-weed and scabious. I was too indolent, and I turned instead to the orchard.

There the daffodils were lifting their heads and throwing back their yellow curls. At the foot of each sloping, grey old tree stood a family of flowers, some bursten with golden fulness, some lifting their heads slightly, to show a modest, sweet countenance, others still hiding their faces, leaning forward pensively from the jaunty grey-green spears; I wished I had their language, to talk to them distinctly.

Overhead, the trees, with lifted fingers shook out their hair to the sun, decking themselves with buds as white and cool as a water-nymph's breasts.

I began to be very glad. The colts-foot discs glowed and laughed in a merry company down the path; I stroked the velvet faces, and laughed also, and I smelled the scent of blackcurrant leaves, which is full of childish memories.

The house was quiet and complacent; it was peopled with ghosts again; but the ghosts had only come to enjoy the warm place once more, carrying sunshine in their arms and scattering it through the dusk of gloomy rooms.

3

THE IRONY OF INSPIRED MOMENTS

It happened, the next day after the funeral, I came upon reproductions of Aubrey Beardsley's *Atalanta*, and of the tailpiece to *Salome*, and others. I sat and looked and my soul leaped out upon the new thing. I was bewildered, wondering, grudging, fascinated. I looked a long time, but my mind, or my soul, would come to no state of coherence. I was fascinated and overcome, but yet full of stubbornness and resistance.

Lettie was out, so, although it was dinner-time, even because it was dinner-time, I took the book and went down to the mill.

The dinner was over; there was the fragrance of cooked rhubarb in the room. I went straight to Emily, who was leaning back in her chair, and put the *Salome* before her.

'Look,' said I, 'look here!'

She looked; she was short-sighted, and peered close. I was impatient for her to speak. She turned slowly at last and looked at me, shrinking, with questioning.

'Well?' I said.

'Isn't it–fearful!' she replied softly.

'No!–why is it?'

'It makes you feel–Why have you brought it?'

'I wanted you to see it.'

Already I felt relieved, seeing that she too was caught in the spell.

George came and bent over my shoulder. I could feel the heavy warmth of him.

'Good Lord!' he drawled, half amused. The children came crowding to see, and Emily closed the book.

'I shall be late–Hurry up, Dave!' and she went to wash her hands before going to school.

'Give it me, will you?' George asked, putting out his hand for the book. I gave it him, and he sat down to look at the drawings. When Mollie crept near to look, he angrily shouted to her to get away. She pulled a mouth, and got her hat over her wild brown curls. Emily came in ready for school.

'I'm going–good-bye,' she said, and she waited hesitatingly. I moved to get my cap. He looked up with a new expression in his eyes, and said:

'Are you going?–wait a bit–I'm coming.'

I waited.

'Oh, very well–good-bye,' said Emily bitterly, and she departed.

When he had looked long enough he got up and we went out. He kept his finger between the pages of the book as he carried it. We went towards the fallow land without speaking. There he sat down on a bank, leaning his back against a holly tree, and saying, very calmly:

'There's no need to be in any hurry now–' whereupon he proceeded to study the illustrations.

'You know,' he said at last, 'I do want her.'

I started at the irrelevance of this remark, and said, 'Who?'

'Lettie. We've got notice, did you know?'

I started to my feet this time with amazement.

'Notice to leave?–What for?'

'Rabbits I expect. I wish she'd have me, Cyril.'

'To leave Strelley Mill!' I repeated.

'That's it–and I'm rather glad. But do you think she might have me, Cyril?'

'What a shame! Where will you go? And you lie there joking–!'

'I don't. Never mind about the damned notice. I want her more than anything.–And the more I look at these naked lines, the more I want her. It's a sort of fine sharp feeling, like these curved lines. I don't know what I'm saying–but do you think she'd have me? Has she seen these pictures?'

'No.'

'If she did perhaps she'd want me–I mean she'd feel it clear and sharp coming through her.'

'I'll show her and see.'

'I'd been sort of thinking about it–since Father had that notice. It seemed as if the ground was pulled from under our feet. I never felt so lost. Then I began to think of her, if she'd have me–but not clear, till you showed me those pictures. I must have her if I can–and I must have something. It's rather ghostish to have the road suddenly smudged out, and all the world anywhere, nowhere for you to go. I must get something sure soon, or else I feel as if I should fall from somewhere and hurt myself. I'll ask her.'

I looked at him as he lay there under the holly tree, his face all dreamy and boyish, very unusual.

'You'll ask Lettie?' said I. 'When–how?'

'I must ask her quick, while I feel as if everything had gone, and I was ghostish. I think I must sound rather a lunatic.'

He looked at me, and his eyelids hung heavy over his eyes as if he had been drinking, or as if he were tired.

'Is she at home?' he said.

'No, she's gone to Nottingham. She'll be home before dark.'

'I'll see her then. Can you smell violets?'

I replied that I could not. He was sure that he could, and he seemed uneasy till he had justified the sensation. So he arose, very leisurely, and went along the bank, looking closely for the flowers.

'I knew I could. White ones!'

He sat down and picked three flowers, and held them to his nostrils, and inhaled their fragrance. Then he put them to his mouth, and I saw his strong white teeth crush them. He chewed them for a while without speaking; then he spat them out and gathered more.

'They remind me of her too,' he said, and he twisted a piece of honeysuckle stem round the bunch and handed it to me.

'A white violet, is she?' I smiled.

'Give them to her, and tell her to come and meet me just when it's getting dark in the wood.'

'But if she won't?'

'She will.'

'If she's not at home?'

'Come and tell me.'

He lay down again with his head among the green violet leaves, saying: 'I ought to work, because it all counts in the valuation. But I don't care.' He lay looking at me for some time. Then he said:

'I don't suppose I shall have above twenty pounds left when we've sold up–but she's got plenty of money to start with–if she has me–in Canada. I could get well off–and she could have–what she wanted–I'm sure she'd have what she wanted.'

He took it all calmly as if it were realised. I was somewhat amused.

'What frock will she have on when she comes to meet me?' he asked.

'I don't know. The same as she's gone to Nottingham in, I suppose–a sort of gold-brown costume with a rather tight-fitting coat. Why?'

'I was thinking how she'd look.'

'What chickens are you counting now?' I asked.

'But what do you think I look best in?' he replied.

'You? Just as you are–no, put that old smooth cloth coat on–that's all.' I smiled as I told him, but he was very serious.

'Shan't I put my new clothes on?'

'No–you want to leave your neck showing.'

He put his hand to his throat, and said naïvely:

'Do I?'–and it amused him.

Then he lay looking dreamily up into the tree. I left him, and went wandering round the fields finding flowers and bird's nests.

When I came back, it was nearly four o'clock. He stood up and stretched himself. He pulled out his watch.

'Good Lord,' he drawled, 'I've lain there thinking all afternoon. I didn't know I could do such a thing. Where have you been? It's with being all upset, you see. You left the violets–here, take them, will you; and tell her; I'll come when it's getting dark. I feel like somebody else–or else really like myself. I hope I shan't wake up to the other things–you know, like I am always–before them.'

'Why not?'

'Oh, I don't know–only I feel as if I could talk straight off without arranging–like birds, without knowing what note is coming next.'

When I was going he said:

'Here, leave me that book–it'll keep me like this–I mean I'm not the same as I was yesterday, and that book'll keep me like it. Perhaps it's a bilious bout–I do sometimes have one, if something very extraordinary happens. When it's getting dark then!'

Lettie had not arrived when I went home. I put the violets in a little vase on the table. I remembered he had wanted her to see the drawings–it was perhaps as well he had kept them.

She came about six o'clock–in the motor-car with Marie. But the latter did not descend. I went out to assist with the parcels. Lettie had already begun to buy things; the wedding was fixed for July.

The room was soon over-covered with stuffs: table linen, underclothing, pieces of silken stuff and lace stuff, patterns for carpets and curtains, a whole gleaming, glowing array. Lettie was very delighted. She could hardly wait to take off her hat, but went round cutting the string of her parcels, opening them, talking all the time to my mother.

'Look, Little Woman. I've got a ready-made underskirt–isn't it lovely. Listen!' and she ruffled it through her hands. 'Shan't I sound splendid! Frou-Frou! But it is a charming shade, isn't it, and not a bit bulky or clumsy anywhere?' She put the band of the skirt against her waist, and put forward her foot, and looked down, saying, 'It's just the right length, isn't it. Little Woman?–and they said I was tall–it was a wonder. Don't you wish it were yours, Little?–oh, you won't confess it. Yes, you like to be as fine as anybody–that's why I bought you this piece of silk–isn't it sweet, though?–you needn't say there's too much lavender in it, there is not. Now!' She pleated it up and held it against my mother's chin. 'It suits you beautifully–doesn't it? Don't you like it, Sweet? You don't seem to like it a bit, and I'm sure it suits you–makes you look ever so young. I wish you wouldn't be so old-fashioned in your notions. You do like it, don't you?'

'Of course I do–I was only thinking what an extravagant mortal you are when you begin to buy. You know you mustn't keep on always–'

'Now–now, Sweet, don't be naughty and preachery. It's such a treat to go buying. You will come with me next time, won't you? Oh, I have enjoyed it–but I wished you were there–Marie takes anything, she's so easy to suit–I like to have a good buy–Oh, it was splendid!–and there's lots more yet. Oh, did you see this cushion-cover–these are the colours I want for that room–gold and amber–'

This was a bad opening. I watched the shadows darken farther and farther along the brightness, hushing the glitter of the water. I watched the golden ripeness come upon the west, and thought the rencontre was never to take place. At last, however, Lettie flung herself down with a sigh, saying she was tired.

'Come into the dining-room and have a cup of tea,' said Mother. 'I told Rebecca to mash when you came in.'

'All right. Leslie's coming up later on, I believe–about half-past eight, he said. Should I show him what I've bought?'

'There's nothing there for a man to see.'

'I shall have to change my dress, and I'm sure I don't want the fag. Rebecca, just go and look at the things I've bought–in the other room–and, Becky, fold them up for me, will you, and put them on my bed?'

As soon as she'd gone out, Lettie said:

'She'll enjoy doing it, won't she, Mother, they're so nice! Do you think I need dress, Mother?'

'Please yourself–do as you wish.'

'I suppose I shall have to; he doesn't like blouses and skirts of an evening, he says; he hates the belt. I'll wear that old cream cashmere; it looks nice now I've put that new lace on it. Don't those violets smell nice?–who got them?'

'Cyril brought them in.'

'George sent them you,' said I.

'Well, I'll just run up and take my dress off. Why are we troubled with men!'

'It's a trouble you like well enough,' said Mother.

'Oh, do I? such a bother!' and she ran upstairs.

The sun was red behind Highclose. I kneeled in the window seat and smiled at Fate and at people who imagine that strange states are near to the inner realities. The sun went straight down behind the cedar trees, deliberately, and, it seemed as I watched, swiftly lowered itself behind the trees, behind the rim of the hill.

'I must go,' I said to myself, 'and tell him she will not come.'

Yet I fidgeted about the room, loth to depart. Lettie came down, dressed in white – or cream – cut low round the neck. She looked very delightful and fresh again, with a sparkle of the afternoon's excitement still.

'I'll put some of these violets on me,' she said, glancing at herself in the mirror, and then taking the flowers from their water, she dried them, and fastened them among her lace.

'Don't Lettie and I look nice tonight?' she said, smiling, glancing from me to her reflection which was like a light in the dusky room.

'That reminds me,' I said, 'George Saxton wanted to see you this evening.'

'Whatever for?'

'I don't know. They've got notice to leave their farm, and I think he feels a bit sentimental.'

'Oh, well – is he coming here?'

'He said would you go just a little way in the wood to meet him.'

'Did he! Oh, indeed! Well, of course I can't.'

'Of course not – if you won't. They're his violets you're wearing, by the way.'

'Are they – let them stay, it makes no difference. But whatever did he want to see me for?'

'I couldn't say, I assure you.'

She glanced at herself in the mirror, and then at the clock.

'Let's see,' she remarked, 'it's only a quarter to eight. Three-quarters of an hour – ! But what can he want me for? – I never knew anything like it.'

'Startling, isn't it!' I observed satirically.

'Yes.' She glanced at herself in the mirror.

'I can't go out like this.'

'All right, you can't then.'

'Besides – it's nearly dark, it will be too dark to see in the wood, won't it?'

'It will directly.'

'Well, I'll just go to the end of the garden, for one moment – run and fetch that silk shawl out of my wardrobe – be quick, while it's light.'

I ran and brought the wrap. She arranged it carefully over her head.

We went out, down the garden path. Lettie held her skirts carefully gathered from the ground. A nightingale began to sing in the twilight; we stepped along in silence as far as the rhododendron bushes, now in rosy bud.

'I cannot go into the wood,' she said.

'Come to the top of the riding' – and we went round the dark bushes.

George was waiting. I saw at once he was half distrustful of himself now. Lettie dropped her skirts and trailed towards him. He stood awkwardly awaiting her, conscious of the clownishness of his appearance. She held out her hand with something of a grand air.

'See,' she said, 'I have come.'

'Yes – I thought you wouldn't – perhaps' – he looked at her, and suddenly gained courage.

'You have been putting white on – you, you do look nice – though not like – '

'What? – Who else?'

'Nobody else – only I – well, I'd – I'd thought about it different – like some pictures.'

She smiled with a gentle radiance, and asked indulgently, 'And how was I different?'

'Not all that soft stuff – plainer.'

'But don't I look very nice with all this soft stuff, as you call it?'—and she shook the silk away from her smiles.

'Oh, yes—better than those naked lines.'

'You are quaint tonight—what did you want me for—to say good-bye?'

'Good-bye?'

'Yes—you're going away, Cyril tells me. I'm very sorry—fancy horrid strangers at the Mill! But then I shall be gone away soon, too. We are all going, you see, now we've grown up'—she kept hold of my arm.

'Yes.'

'And where will you go—Canada? You'll settle there and be quite a patriarch, won't you?'

'I don't know.'

'You are not really sorry to go, are you?'

'No, I'm glad.'

'Glad to go away from us all.'

'I suppose so—since I must.'

'Ah, Fate—Fate! It separates you whether you want it or not.'

'What?'

'Why, you see, you have to leave. I mustn't stay out here—it is growing chilly. How soon are you going?'

'I don't know.'

'Not soon then?'

'I don't know.'

'Then I may see you again?'

'I don't know.'

'Oh yes, I shall. Well, I must go. Shall I say good-bye now?—that was what you wanted, was it not?'

'To say good-bye?'

'Yes.'

'No—it wasn't—I wanted, I wanted to ask you—'

'What?' she cried.

'You don't know, Lettie, now the old life's gone, everything—how I want you—to set out with—it's like beginning life, and I want you.'

'But what could I do—I could only hinder—what help should I be?'

'I should feel as if my mind was made up—as if I could do something clearly. Now it's all hazy—not knowing what to do next.'

'And if—if you had—what then?'

'If I had you I could go straight on.'

'Where?'

'Oh—I should take a farm in Canada—'

'Well, wouldn't it be better to get it first and make sure—?'

'I have no money.'

'Oh!—so you wanted me—?'

'I only wanted you, I only wanted you. I would have given you—'

'What?'

'You'd have me—you'd have all me, and everything you wanted.'

'That I paid for—a good bargain! No, oh no, George, I beg your pardon. This is one of my flippant nights. I don't mean it like that. But you know it's impossible—look how I'm fixed—it *is* impossible, isn't it now?'

'I suppose it is.'

'You know it is.—Look at me now, and say if it's not impossible—a farmer's wife—with you in Canada.'

'Yes—I didn't expect you like that. Yes, I see it is impossible. But I'd thought about it, and felt as if I must have you. Should have you . . . Yes, it doesn't do to go on dreaming. I think it's the first time, and it'll be the last. Yes, it is impossible. Now I have made up my mind.'

'And what will you do?'

'I shall not go to Canada.'

'Oh, you must not—you must not do anything rash.'

'No—I shall get married.'

'You will? Oh, I am glad. I thought—you—you were too fond—. But you're not—of yourself, I meant. I am so glad. Yes—do marry!'

'Well, I shall—since you are—'

'Yes,' said Lettie. 'It is best. But I thought that you—' she smiled at him in sad reproach.

'Did you think so?' he replied, smiling gravely.

'Yes,' she whispered. They stood looking at one another.

He made an impulsive movement towards her. She, however, drew back slightly, checking him.

'Well—I shall see you again some time—so good-bye,' he said, putting out his hand.

We heard a foot crunching on the gravel. Leslie halted at the top of the riding. Lettie, hearing him, relaxed into a kind of feline graciousness, and said to George:

'I am so sorry you are going to leave—it breaks the old life up. You said I would see you again—' She left her hand in his a moment or two.

'Yes,' George replied. 'Good night'—and he turned away. She stood for a moment in the same drooping, graceful attitude watching him, then she turned round slowly. She seemed hardly to notice Leslie.

'Who was that you were talking to?' he asked.

'He has gone now,' she replied irrelevantly, as if even then she seemed hardly to realise it.

'It appears to upset you—his going—who is it?'

'He!—Oh—why, it's George Saxton.'

'Oh, him!'

'Yes.'

'What did he want?'

'Eh? What did he want? Oh, nothing.'

'A mere trysting—in the interim, eh!' he said this laughing, generously passing off his annoyance in a jest.

'I feel so sorry,' she said.

'What for?'

'Oh—don't let us talk about him—talk about something else. I can't bear to talk about—him.'

'All right,' he replied—and after an awkward little pause, 'What sort of a time had you in Nottingham?'

'Oh, a fine time.'

'You'll enjoy yourself in the shops between now and—July. Some time I'll go with you and see them.'

'Very well.'

'That sounds as if you don't want me to go. Am I already in the way on a shopping expedition, like an old husband?'

'I should think you would be.'

'That's nice of you! Why?'

'Oh, I don't know.'

'Yes you do.'

'Oh, I suppose you'd hang about.'

'I'm much too well brought up.'

'Rebecca has lighted the hall lamp.'

'Yes, it's grown quite dark. I was here early. You never gave me a good word for it.'

'I didn't notice. There's a light in the dining-room, we'll go there.'

They went into the dining-room. She stood by the piano and carefully took off the wrap. Then she wandered listlessly about the room for a minute.

'Aren't you coming to sit down?' he said, pointing to the seat on the couch beside him.

'Not just now,' she said, trailing aimlessly to the piano. She sat down and began to play at random, from memory. Then she did that most irritating thing–played accompaniments to songs, with snatches of the air where the voice should have predominated.

'I say Lettie . . .' he interrupted after a time.

'Yes,' she replied, continuing to play.

'It's not very interesting. . . .'

'No?'–she continued to play.

'Nor very amusing. . . .'

She did not answer. He bore it for a little time longer, then he said:

'How much longer is it going to last, Lettie?'

'What?'

'That sort of business. . . .'

'The piano?–I'll stop playing if you don't like it.'

She did not, however, cease.

'Yes–and all this dry business.'

'I don't understand.'

'Don't you?–you make *me*.'

There she went on, tinkling away at 'If I built a world for you, dear'.

'I say, stop it, do!' he cried.

She tinkled to the end of the verse, and very slowly closed the piano.

'Come on–come and sit down,' he said.

'No, I don't want to–I'd rather have gone on playing.'

'Go on with your damned playing then, and I'll go where there's more interest.'

'You ought to like it.'

He did not answer, so she turned slowly round on the stool, opened the piano, and laid her fingers on the keys. At the sound of the chord he started up, saying: 'Then I'm going.'

'It's very early–why?' she said, through the calm jingle of 'Meine Ruh is hin–'

He stood biting his lips. Then he made one more appeal.

'Lettie!'

'Yes?'

'Aren't you going to leave off–and be–amiable?'

'Amiable?'

'You are a jolly torment. What's upset you now?'

'Nay, it's not I who am upset.'

'I'm glad to hear it–what do you call yourself?'

'I?–nothing.'

'Oh, well, I'm going then.'

'Must you?–so early tonight?'

He did not go, and she played more and more softly, languidly, aimlessly. Once she lifted her head to speak, but did not say anything.

'Look here!' he ejaculated all at once, so that she started, and jarred the piano, 'What do you mean by it?'

She jingled leisurely a few seconds before answering, then she replied: 'What a worry you are!'

'I suppose you want me out of the way while you sentimentalise over that milkman. You needn't bother. You can do it while I'm here. Or I'll go and leave you in peace. I'll go and call him back for you, if you like–if that's what you want–'

She turned on the piano stool slowly and looked at him, smiling faintly. 'It is very good of you!' she said.

He clenched his fists and grinned with rage.

'You tantalising little–' he began, lifting his fists expressively. She smiled. Then he swung round, knocked several hats flying off the stand in the hall, slammed the door, and was gone.

Lettie continued to play for some time, after which she went up to her own room.

Leslie did not return to us the next day, nor the day after. The first day Marie came and told us he had gone away to Yorkshire to see about the new mines that were being sunk there, and was likely to be absent for a week or so. These business visits to the north were rather frequent. The firm, of which Mr Tempest was director and chief shareholder, were opening important new mines in the other county, as the seams at home were becoming exhausted or unprofitable. It was proposed that Leslie should live in Yorkshire when he was married, to superintend the new workings. He at first rejected the idea, but he seemed later to approve of it more.

During the time he was away Lettie was moody and cross-tempered. She did not mention George nor the mill; indeed, she preserved her best, most haughty and ladylike manner.

On the evening of the fourth day of Leslie's absence we were out in the garden. The trees were 'uttering joyous leaves'. My mother was in the midst of her garden, lifting the dusky faces of the auriculas to look at the velvet lips, or tenderly taking a young weed from the black soil. The thrushes were calling and clamouring all round. The japonica flamed on the wall as the light grew thicker; the tassels of white cherry-blossom swung gently in the breeze.

'What shall I do, Mother?' said Lettie, as she wandered across the grass to pick at the japonica flowers. 'What shall I do? There's nothing to do.'

'Well, my girl–what do you want to do? You have been moping about all day–go and see somebody.'

'It's such a long way to Eberwich.'

'Is it? Then go somewhere nearer.'

Lettie fretted about with restless, petulant indecision.

'I don't know what to do,' she said, 'And I feel as if I might just as well never have lived at all as waste days like this. I wish we weren't buried in this dead little hole–I wish we were near the town–it's hateful having to depend on about two or three folk for your–your–your pleasure in life.'

'I can't help it, my dear–you must do something for yourself.'

'And what can I do?–I can do nothing.'

'Then I'd go to bed.'

'That I won't–with the dead weight of a wasted day on me. I feel as if I'd do something desperate.'

'Very well, then,' said Mother, 'do it, and have done.'

'Oh, it's no good talking to you–I don't want–' She turned away, went to the laurestinus, and began pulling off it the long red berries. I expected she would fret the evening wastefully away. I noticed all at once that she stood still. It was the noise of a motor-car running rapidly down the hill towards Nethermere–a light, quick-clicking sound. I listened also. I could feel the swinging drop of the car as it came down the leaps of the hill. We could see the dust trail up among the trees. Lettie raised her head and listened expectantly. The car rushed along the edge of Nethermere–then there was the jar of brakes, as the machine slowed down and stopped. In a moment with a quick flutter of sound, it was passing the lodge gates and whirling up the drive, through the wood, to us. Lettie stood with flushed cheeks and brightened eyes. She went towards the bushes that shut off the lawn from the gravelled space in front of the house, watching. A car came racing through the trees. It was the small car Leslie used on the firm's business–now it was white with dust. Leslie suddenly put on the brakes, and tore to a standstill in front of the house. He stepped to the ground. There he staggered a little, being giddy and cramped with the long drive. His motor-jacket and cap were thick with dust.

Lettie called to him, 'Leslie!'–and flew down to him. He took her into his arms, and clouds of dust rose round her. He kissed her, and they stood perfectly still for a moment. She looked up into his face–then she disengaged her arms to take off his disfiguring motor-spectacles. After she had looked at him a moment, tenderly, she kissed him again. He loosened his hold of her, and she said, in a voice full of tenderness:

'You are trembling, dear.'

'It's the ride. I've never stopped.'

Without further words she took him into the house.

'How pale you are–see, lie on the couch–never mind the dust. All right, I'll find you a coat of Cyril's. Oh, Mother, he's come all those miles in the car without stopping–make him lie down.'

She ran and brought him a jacket, and put the cushions round, and made him lie on the couch. Then she took off his boots and put slippers on his feet. He lay watching her all the time; he was white with fatigue and excitement.

'I wonder if I shall be had up for scorching–I can feel the road coming at me yet,' he said.

'Why were you so headlong?'

'I felt as if I should go wild if I didn't come–if I didn't rush. I didn't know how you might have taken me, Lettie–when I said–what I did.'

She smiled gently at him, and he lay resting, recovering, looking at her.

'It's a wonder I haven't done something desperate–I've been half mad since I said–Oh, Lettie, I was a damned fool and a wretch–I could have torn myself in two. I've done nothing but curse and rage at myself ever since. I feel as if I'd just come up out of hell. You don't know how thankful I am, Lettie, that you've not–oh–turned against me for what I said.'

She went to him and sat down by him, smoothing his hair from his forehead, kissing him, her attitude tender, suggesting tears, her movements impulsive, as if with a self-reproach she would not acknowledge, but which she must silence with lavish tenderness. He drew her to him, and they remained quiet for some time, till it grew dark.

The noise of my mother stirring in the next room disturbed them. Lettie rose, and he also got up from the couch.

'I suppose,' he said, 'I shall have to go home and get bathed and dressed—though,' he added in tones which made it clear he did not want to go, 'I shall have to get back in the morning—I don't know what they'll say.'

'At any rate,' she said, 'You could wash here—'

'But I must get out of these clothes—and I want a bath.'

'You could—you might have some of Cyril's clothes—and the water's hot I know. At all events, you can stay to supper—'

'If I'm going I shall have to go soon—or they'd not like it, if I go in late;—they have no idea I've come;—they don't expect me till next Monday or Tuesday—'

'Perhaps you could stay here—and they needn't know.'

They looked at each other with wide, smiling eyes—like children on the brink of a stolen pleasure.

'Oh, but what would your mother think!—no, I'll go.'

'She won't mind a bit.'

'Oh, but—'

'I'll ask her.'

He wanted to stay far more than she wished it, so it was she who put down his opposition and triumphed.

My mother lifted her eyebrows, and said very quietly:

'He'd better go home—and be straight.'

'But look how he'd feel—he'd have to tell them . . . and how would he feel! It's really my fault, in the end. Don't be piggling and mean and Grundyish, Matouchka.'

'It is neither meanness nor Grundyishness—'

'Oh, Ydgrun, Ydgrun—!' exclaimed Lettie, ironically.

'He may certainly stay if he likes,' said Mother, slightly nettled at Lettie's gibe.

'All right, Mutterchen—and be a sweetling, do!'

Lettie went out a little impatient at my mother's unwillingness, but Leslie stayed, nevertheless.

In a few moments Lettie was up in the spare bedroom, arranging and adorning, and Rebecca was running with hot-water bottles, and hurrying down with clean bedclothes. Lettie hastily appropriated my best brushes—which she had given me—and took the suit of pyjamas of the thinnest, finest flannel and discovered a new tooth-brush—and made selections from my shirts and handkerchiefs and underclothing—and directed me which suit to lend him. Altogether I was astonished, and perhaps a trifle annoyed, at her extraordinary thoughtfulness and solicitude.

He came down to supper, bathed, brushed, and radiant. He ate heartily and seemed to emanate a warmth of physical comfort and pleasure. The colour was flushed again into his face, and he carried his body with the old independent, assertive air. I have never known the time when he looked handsomer, when he was more attractive. There was a certain warmth about him, a certain glow that enhanced his words, his laughter, his movements; he was the predominant person, and we felt a pleasure in his mere proximity. My mother, however, could not quite get rid of her stiffness, and soon after supper she rose, saying she would finish her letter in the next room, bidding him good-night, as she would probably not see him again. The cloud of this little coolness was the thinnest and most transitory. He talked and laughed more gaily than ever, and was ostentatious in his movements, throwing back his head, taking little attitudes which displayed the broad firmness of his breast, the grace of his well-trained physique. I left them at the piano; he was sitting pretending to play, and looking up all the while at her, who stood with her hand on his shoulder.

In the morning he was up early, by six o'clock downstairs and attending to the car. When I got down I found him very busy, and very quiet.

'I know I'm a beastly nuisance,' he said, 'but I must get off early.'

Rebecca came and prepared breakfast, which we two ate alone. He was remarkably dull and wordless.

'It's a wonder Lettie hasn't got up to have breakfast with you—she's such a one for raving about the perfection of the early morning—its purity and promises and so forth,' I said.

He broke his bread nervously, and drank some coffee as if he were agitated, making noises in his throat as he swallowed.

'It's too early for her, I should think,' he replied, wiping his moustache hurriedly. Yet he seemed to listen for her. Lettie's bedroom was over the study, where Rebecca had laid breakfast, and he listened now and again, holding his knife and fork suspended in their action. Then he went on with his meal again.

When he was laying down his serviette, the door opened. He pulled himself together, and turned round sharply. It was Mother. When she spoke to him, his face twitched with a little frown, half of relief, half of disappointment.

'I must be going now,' he said—'thank you very much—Mother.'

'You are a harum-scarum boy. I wonder why Lettie doesn't come down. I know she is up.'

'Yes,' he replied. 'Yes. I've heard her. Perhaps she is dressing. I must get off.'

'I'll call her.'

'No—don't bother her—she'd come if she wanted—'

But Mother had called from the foot of the stairs.

'Lettie, Lettie—he's going.'

'All right,' said Lettie, and in another minute she came downstairs. She was dressed in dark, severe stuff, and she was somewhat pale. She did not look at any of us, but turned her eyes aside.

'Good-bye,' she said to him, offering him her cheek. He kissed her, murmuring, 'Good-bye—my love.'

He stood in the doorway a moment, looking at her with beseeching eyes. She kept her face half averted, and would not look at him, but stood pale and cold, biting her underlip. He turned sharply away with a motion of keen disappointment, set the engine of the car into action, mounted, and drove quickly away.

Lettie stood pale and inscrutable for some moments. Then she went in to breakfast and sat toying with her food, keeping her head bent down, her face hidden.

In less than an hour he was back again, saying he had left something behind. He ran upstairs, and then, hesitating, went into the room where Lettie was still sitting at table.

'I had to come back,' he said.

She lifted her face towards him, but kept her eyes averted, looking out of the window. She was flushed.

'What had you forgotten?' she asked.

'I'd left my cigarette-case,' he replied.

There was an awkward silence.

'But I shall have to be getting off,' he added.

'Yes, I suppose you will,' she replied.

After another pause, he asked:

'Won't you just walk down the path with me?'

She rose without answering. He took a shawl and put it round her carefully. She merely allowed him. They walked in silence down the garden.

'You—are you—are you angry with me?' he faltered.

Tears suddenly came to her eyes.

'What did you come back for?' she said, averting her face from him. He looked at her.

'I knew you were angry—and—' he hesitated.

'Why didn't you go away?' she said impulsively. He hung his head and was silent.

'I don't see why—why it should make trouble between us, Lettie,' he faltered. She made a swift gesture of repulsion, whereupon, catching sight of her hand, she hid it swiftly against her skirt again.

'You make my hands—my very hands disclaim me,' she struggled to say.

He looked at her clenched fist pressed against the folds of her dress.

'But—,' he began, much troubled.

'I tell you, I can't bear the sight of my own hands,' she said in low, passionate tones.

'But surely, Lettie, there's no need—if you love me—'

She seemed to wince. He waited, puzzled and miserable.

'And we're going to be married, aren't we?' he resumed, looking pleadingly at her.

She stirred, and exclaimed:

'Oh, why don't you go away? What did you come back for?'

'You'll kiss me before I go?' he asked.

She stood with averted face, and did not reply. His forehead was twitching in a puzzled frown.

'Lettie!' he said.

She did not move or answer, but remained with her face turned full away, so that he could see only the contour of her cheek. After waiting awhile, he flushed, turned swiftly and set his machine rattling. In a moment he was racing between the trees.

4

KISS WHEN SHE'S RIPE FOR TEARS

It was the Sunday after Lettie's visit. We had had a wretched week, with everybody mute and unhappy.

Though spring had come, none of us saw it. Afterwards it occurred to me that I had seen all the ranks of poplars suddenly bursten into a dark crimson glow, with a flutter of blood-red where the sun came through the leaves; that I had found high cradles where the swan's eggs lay by the water-side; that I had seen the daffodils leaning from the moss-grown wooden walls of the boathouse, and all, moss, daffodils, water, scattered with the pink scarves from the elm buds; that I had broken the half-spread fans of the sycamore, and had watched the white cloud of sloe-blossom go silver grey against the evening sky: but I had not perceived it, and I had not any vivid spring pictures left from the neglected week.

It was Sunday evening, just after tea, when Lettie suddenly said to me:

'Come with me down to Strelley Mill.'

I was astonished, but I obeyed unquestioningly.

On the threshold we heard a chattering of girls, and immediately Alice's voice greeted us:

'Hello, Sybil, love! Hello, Lettie! Come on, here's a gathering of the goddesses. Come on, you just make us right. You're Juno, and here's Meg, she's Venus, and I'm–here, somebody, who am I, tell us quick–did you say Minerva, Sybil dear? Well, you ought, then! Now, Paris, hurry up. He's putting his Sunday clothes on to take us a walk–Laws, what a time it takes him! Get your blushes ready, Meg–now, Lettie, look haughty, and I'll look wise. I wonder if he wants me to go and tie his tie. Oh, Glory–where on earth did you get that antimacassar?'

'In Nottingham–don't you like it?' said George, referring to his tie. 'Hello, Lettie–have you come?'

'Yes, it's a gathering of the goddesses. Have you that apple? If so, hand it over,' said Alice.

'What apple?'

'Oh, Lum, his education! Paris's apple–Can't you see we've come to be chosen?'

'Oh, well–I haven't got any apple–I've eaten mine.'

'Isn't he flat–he's like boiling magnesia that's done boiling for a week. Are you going to take us all to church then?'

'If you like.'

'Come on, then. Where's the Abode of Love? Look at Lettie looking shocked. Awfully sorry, old girl–thought love agreed with you.

'Did you say *love?*' inquired George.

'Yes, I did; didn't I, Meg? And you say "Love" as well, don't you?'

'I don't know what it is,' laughed Meg, who was very red and rather bewildered.

'"Amor est titillatio"–"Love is a tickling"–there–that's it, isn't it, Sybil?'

'How should I know.'

'Of *course* not, old fellow. Leave it to the girls. See how knowing Lettie looks–and, laws, Lettie, you are solemn.'

'It's love,' suggested George, over his new neck-tie.

'I'll bet it is "degustasse sat est"–ain't it, Lettie? "One lick's enough"–"and damned be he that first cries: Hold, enough!"–Which one do you like? But *are* you going to take us to church, Georgie, darling–one by one, or all at once?'

'What do you want me to do, Meg?' he asked.

'Oh, I don't mind.'

'And do you mind, Lettie?'

'I'm not going to church.'

'Let's go a walk somewhere–and let us start now,' said Emily somewhat testily. She did not like this nonsense.

'There you are, Syb—you've got your orders—don't leave me behind,' wailed Alice.

Emily frowned and bit her finger.

'Come on, Georgie. You look like the finger of a pair of scales—between two weights. Which'll draw?'

'The heavier,' he replied, smiling, and looking neither at Meg or Lettie.

'Then it's Meg,' cried Alice. 'Oh, I wish I was fleshy—I've no chance with Syb against Pem.'

Emily flashed looks of rage; Meg blushed and felt ashamed; Lettie began to recover from her first outraged indignation, and smiled.

Thus we went a walk, in two trios.

Unfortunately, as the evening was so fine, the roads were full of strollers: groups of three or four men dressed in pale trousers and shiny black cloth coats, following their suspicious little dogs: gangs of youths slouching along, occupied with nothing, often silent, talking now and then in raucous tones on some subjects of brief interest: then the gallant husbands, in their tail coats very husbandly, pushing a jingling perambulator, admonished by a much-dressed spouse round whom the small members of the family gyrated: occasionally, two lovers walking with a space between them, disowning each other; occasionally, a smartly dressed mother with two little girls in white silk frocks and much expanse of yellow hair, stepping mincingly, and, near by, a father awkwardly controlling his Sunday suit.

To endure all this it was necessary to chatter unconcernedly. George had to keep up the conversation behind, and he seemed to do it with ease, discoursing on the lambs, discussing the breed—when Meg exclaimed:

'Oh, aren't they black! They might ha' crept down th' chimney. I never saw any like them before.' He described how he had reared two on the bottle, exciting Meg's keen admiration by his mothering of the lambs. Then he went on to the peewits, harping on the same string: how they would cry and pretend to be wounded—'Just fancy, though!'—and how he had moved the eggs of one pair while he was ploughing, and the mother had followed them, and had even sat watching as he drew near again with the plough, watching him come and go—'Well, she knew you—but they *do* know those who are kind to them—'

'Yes,' he agreed, 'her little bright eyes seem to speak as you go by.'

'Oh, I do think they're nice little things—don't you, Lettie?' cried Meg in access of tenderness.

Lettie did—with brevity.

We walked over the hills and down into Greymede. Meg thought she ought to go home to her grandmother, and George bade her go, saying he would call and see her in an hour or so.

The dear girl was disappointed, but she went unmurmuring. We left Alice with a friend, and hurried home through Selsby to escape the after-church parade.

As you walk home past Selsby, the pit stands up against the west, with beautiful tapering chimneys marked in black against the swim of sunset, and the head-stocks etched with tall significance on the brightness. Then the houses are squat in rows of shadow at the foot of these high monuments.

'Do you know, Cyril,' said Emily, 'I *have* meant to go and see Mrs Annable—the keeper's wife—she's moved into Bonsart's Row, and the children come to school–Oh, it's awful!–they've never been to school, and they are unspeakable.'

'What's she gone there for?' I asked.

'I suppose the squire wanted the Kennels–and she chose it herself. But the way they live–it's fearful to think of!'

'And why haven't you been?'

'I don't know–I've meant to–but–' Emily stumbled.

'You didn't want, and you daren't?'

'Perhaps not–would you?'

'Pah–let's go now!–There, you hang back.'

'No, I don't,' she replied sharply.

'Come on then, we'll go through the twitchel. Let me tell Lettie.'

Lettie at once declared, 'No!'–with some asperity.

'All right,' said George. 'I'll take you home.'

But this suited Lettie still less.

'I don't know what you want to go for, Cyril,' she said, 'and Sunday night, and, everybody everywhere. I want to go home.'

'Well–you go then–Emily will come with you.'

'Ha,' cried the latter, 'you think I won't go to see her.'

I shrugged my shoulders, and George pulled his moustache.

'Well, I don't care,' declared Lettie, and we marched down the twitchel, Indian file.

We came near to the ugly rows of houses that back up against the pit-hill. Everywhere is black and sooty; the houses are back to back, having only one entrance, which is from a square garden where black-speckled weeds grow sulkily, and which looks on to a row of evil little ash-pit huts. The road everywhere is trodden over with a crust of soot and coal-dust and cinders.

Between the rows, however, was a crowd of women and children, bare hands, bare arms, white aprons, and black Sunday frocks bristling with gimp. One or two men squatted on their heels with their backs against a wall, laughing. The women were waving their arms and screaming up at the roof of the end house.

Emily and Lettie drew back.

'Look there–it's that little beggar, Sam!' said George.

There, sure enough, perched on the ridge of the roof against the end chimney, was the young imp, coatless, his shirtsleeves torn away from the cuffs. I knew his bright, reddish young head in a moment. He got up, his bare toes clinging to the tiles, and spread out his fingers fanwise from his nose, shouting something, which immediately caused the crowd to toss with indignation, and the women to shriek again. Sam sat down suddenly, having almost lost his balance.

The village constable hurried up, his thin neck stretching out of his tunic, and demanded the cause of the hubbub.

Immediately a woman, with bright brown squinting eyes and a birthmark on her cheek, rushed forward and seized the policeman by the sleeve.

'Ta'e 'im up, ta'e 'im up, an' birch 'im till 'is bloody back's raw,' she screamed.

The thin policeman shook her off, and wanted to know what was the matter.

'I'll smosh 'im like a rotten tater,' cried the woman, 'if I can lay 'ands on 'im. 'E's not fit ter live nowhere where there's decent folks–the thievin', brazen little devil–' thus she went on.

'But what's up!' interrupted the thin constable, 'What's up wi' 'im?'

'Up–it's 'im as 'is up, an' let 'im wait till I get 'im down. A crafty little–'

Sam, seeing her look at him, distorted his honest features, and overheated her wrath, till Lettie and Emily trembled with dismay.

The mother's head appeared at the bedroom window. She slid the sash back, and craned out, vainly trying to look over the gutter below the slates. She was even more dishevelled than usual, and the tears had dried on her pale face. She stretched farther out, clinging to the window-frame and to the gutter overhead, till I was afraid she would come down with a crash.

The men, squatting on their heels against the wall of the ash-pit laughed, saying:

'Nab 'im, Poll–can ter see 'im–clawk 'im!' and then the pitiful voice of the woman was heard crying, 'Come thy ways down, my duckie, come on–on'y come ter thy mother–they shanna touch thee. Du thy mother's biddin' now–Sam–Sam–Sam!' her voice rose higher and higher.

'Sammy, Sammy, go to thy mammy,' jeered the wits below.

'Shonna ter come, shonna ter come to thy mother, my duckie–come on, come thy ways down.'

Sam looked at the crowd, and at the eaves from under which rose his mother's voice. He was going to cry. A big gaunt woman, with the family steel comb stuck in her back hair, shouted, 'Tha' mun well bend thy face, tha' needs ter scraight,' and, aided by the woman with the birthmark and the squint, she reviled him. The little scoundrel, in a burst of defiance, picked a piece of mortar from between the slates, and in a second it flew into fragments against the family steel comb. The wearer thereof declared her head was laid open and there was general confusion. The policeman–I don't know how thin he must have been when he was taken out of his uniform–lost his head, and he too began brandishing his fists, spitting from under his sweep's-brush moustache as he commanded in tones of authority:

'Now then, no more on it–let's 'a'e thee down here, an' no more messin' about!'

The boy tried to creep over the ridge of the roof and escape down the other side. Immediately the brats rushed round yelling to the other side of the row, and pieces of red-burnt gravel began to fly over the roof. Sam crouched against the chimney.

'Got 'im!' yelled one little devil. 'Got 'im! Hi–go again!'

A shower of stones came down, scattering the women and the policeman. The mother rushed from the house and made a wild onslaught on the throwers. She caught one and flung him down. Immediately the rest turned and aimed their missiles at her. Then George and the policeman and I dashed after the young wretches, and the women ran to see what happened to their offspring. We caught two lads of fourteen or so, and made the policeman haul them after us. The rest fled.

When we returned to the field of battle, Sam had gone too.

'If 'e 'asna slived off!' cried the woman with a squint. 'But I'll see him locked up for this.'

At this moment a band of missioners from one of the chapels or churches arrived at the end of the row, and the little harmonium began to bray, and the place vibrated with the sound of a woman's powerful voice, propped round by several others, singing:

'At even 'ere the sun was set–'

Everybody hurried towards the new noise, save the policeman with his captives, the woman with the squint, and the woman with the family comb. I told the limb of the law he'd better get rid of the two boys and find out what mischief the others were after.

Then I enquired of the woman with the squint what was the matter.

'Thirty-seven young 'uns 'an we 'ad from that doe, an' there's no knowin' 'ow many more, if they 'adn't a-gone an' ate-n 'er,' she replied, lapsing, now her fury was spent, into sullen resentment.

'An' niver a word should we a' known,' added the family-comb-bearer, 'but for that blessed cat of ourn, as scrat it up.'

'Indeed,' said I, 'the rabbit?'

'No, there were nöwt left but th' skin—they'd seen ter that, a thieving, dirt-eatin' lot.'

'When was that?' said I.

'This mortal night—an' there was th' head an' th' back in th' dirty stewpot—I can show you this instant—I've got 'em in our pantry for a proof, 'aven't I, Martha?'

'A fat lot o' good it is—but I'll rip th' neck out of 'im, if ever I lay 'ands on 'im.'

At last I made out that Samuel had stolen a large, lop-eared doe out of a bunch in the coal-house of the squint-eyed lady, had skinned it, buried the skin, and offered his booty to his mother as a wild rabbit, trapped. The doe had been the chief item of the Annables' Sunday dinner—albeit a portion was unluckily saved till Monday, providing undeniable proof of the theft. The owner of the rabbit had supposed the creature to have escaped. This peaceful supposition had been destroyed by the comb-bearer's seeing her cat, scratching in the Annable garden, unearth the white and brown doe-skin, after which the trouble had begun.

The squint-eyed woman was not so hard to manage. I talked to her as if she were some male friend of mine, only appealing to her womanliness with all the soft sadness I could press into the tones of my voice. In the end she was mollified, and even tender and motherly in her feelings towards the unfortunate family. I left on her dresser the half-crown I shrank from offering her, and, having reduced the comb-wearer also, I marched off, carrying the stewpot and the fragments of the ill-fated doe to the cottage of the widow, where George and the girls awaited me.

The house was in a woeful state. In the rocking-chair, beside the high guard that surrounded the hearth, sat the mother, rocking, looking sadly shaken now her excitement was over. Lettie was nursing the little baby, and Emily the next child. George was smoking his pipe and trying to look natural. The little kitchen was crowded—there was no room—there was not even a place on the table for the stew-jar, so I gathered together cups and mugs containing tea sops, and set down the vessel of ignominy on the much-slopped tea-cloth. The four little children were striped and patched with tears—at my entrance one under the table recommenced to weep, so I gave him my pencil which pushed in and out, but which pushes in and out no more.

The sight of the stewpot affected the mother afresh. She wept again, crying:

'An' I niver thought as 'ow it were aught but a snared 'un; as if I should set 'im on ter thieve their old doe; an' tough it was an' all; an' 'im a thief, an' me called all the names they could lay their tongues to; an' then in my bit of a pantry, takin' the very pots out; that stewpot as I brought all the way from Nottingham, an' I've 'ad it afore our Minnie wor born—'

The baby, the little baby, then began to cry. The mother got up suddenly, and took it.

'Oh, come then, come then, my pet. Why, why cos they shanna, no they shanna. Yes, he's his mother's least little lad, he is, a little 'un. Hush then, there, there–what's a matter, my little?'

She hushed the baby, and herself. At length she asked:

''As th' p'liceman gone as well?'

'Yes–it's all right,' I said.

She sighed deeply, and her look of weariness was painful to see.

'How old is your eldest?' I asked.

'Fanny–she's fourteen. She's out service at Websters. Then Jim, as is thirteen next month–let's see, yes, it is next month–he's gone to Flints–farming. They can't do much–an' I shan't let 'em go into th' pit, if I can help it. My husband always used to say they should never go in th' pit.'

'They can't do much for you.'

'They dun what they can. But it's a hard job, it is, ter keep 'em all goin'. Wi' weshin', an' th' parish pay, an' five shillin' from th' squire–it's 'ard. It was diff'rent when my husband was alive. It ought ter 'a been me as should 'a died–I don't seem as if I can manage 'em–they get beyond me. I wish I was dead this minnit, an' 'im 'ere. I can't understand it: 'im as wor so capable, to be took, an' me left. 'E wor a man in a thousand, 'e wor–full o' management like a gentleman. I wisht it was me as 'ad a been took. 'An 'e's restless, 'cos 'e knows I find it 'ard. I stood at th' door last night, when they was all asleep, looking out over th' pit pond–an' I saw a light, an' I knowed it was 'im–cos it wor our weddin' day yesterday–by the day an' th' date. An' I said to 'im, "Frank, is it thee, Frank? I'm all right, I'm gettin' on all right"–an' then 'e went; seemed to go ower the whimsey an' back towards th' wood. I know it wor 'im, an' 'e couldna rest, thinkin' I couldna manage–'

After a while we left, promising to go again, and to see after the safety of Sam.

It was quite dark, and the lamps were lighted in the houses. We could hear the throb of the fan-house engines, and the soft whirr of the fan.

'Isn't it cruel?' said Emily plaintively.

'Wasn't the man a wretch to marry the woman like that,' added Lettie with decision.

'Speak of Lady Chrystabel,' said I, and then there was silence. 'I suppose he did not know what he was doing, any more than the rest of us.'

'I thought you were going to your aunt's–to the Ram Inn,' said Lettie to George when they came to the cross-roads.

'Not now–it's too late,' he answered quietly. 'You will come round our way, won't you?'

'Yes,' she said.

We were eating bread and milk at the farm, and the father was talking with vague sadness and reminiscence, lingering over the thought of their departure from the old house. He was a pure romanticist, forever seeking the colour of the past in the present's monotony. He seemed settling down to an easy contented middle age, when the unrest on the farm and development of his children quickened him with fresh activity. He read books on the land question and modern novels. In the end he became an advanced radical, almost a socialist. Occasionally his letters appeared in the newspapers. He had taken a new hold on life.

Over supper he became enthusiastic about Canada, and to watch him, his ruddy face lighted up, his burly form straight and nerved with excitement, was to admire him; to hear him, his words of thoughtful common sense all warm with a young man's hopes, was to love him. At forty-five he was more spontaneous and enthusiastic than George, and far more happy and hopeful.

Emily would not agree to go away with them—what should she do in Canada, she said—and she did not want the little ones 'to be drudges on a farm—in the end to be nothing but cattle'.

'Nay,' said her father gently, 'Mollie shall learn the dairying, and David will just be right to take to the place when I give up. It'll perhaps be a bit rough and hard at first, but when we've got over it we shall think it was one of the best times—like you do.'

'And you, George?' asked Lettie.

'I'm not going. What should I go for? There's nothing at the end of it only a long life. It's like a day here in June—a long work day, pleasant enough, and when it's done you sleep well—but it's work and sleep and comfort—half a life. It's not enough. What's the odds?—I might as well be Flower, the mare.'

His father looked at him gravely and thoughtfully.

'Now it seems to me so different,' he said sadly, 'it seems to me you can live your own life, and be independent, and think as you like without being choked with harassments. I feel as if I could keep on—like that—'

'I'm going to get more out of my life, I hope,' laughed George. 'No. Do you know?' and here he turned straight to Lettie. 'Do you know, I'm going to get pretty rich, so that I can do what I want for a bit. I want to see what it's like, to taste all sides—to taste the towns. I want to know what I've got in me. I'll get rich—or at least I'll have a good try.'

'And pray how will you manage it?' asked Emily.

'I'll begin by marrying—and then you'll see.'

Emily laughed with scorn—'Let us see you begin.'

'Ah, you're not wise!' said the father sadly—then, laughing, he said to Lettie in coaxing, confidential tones, 'But he'll come out there to me in a year or two—you see if he doesn't.'

'I wish I could come now,' said I.

'If you would,' said George, 'I'd go with you. But not by myself, to become a fat stupid fool, like my own cattle.'

While he was speaking Gyp burst into a rage of barking. The father got up to see what it was, and George followed. Trip, the great bull-terrier, rushed out of the house shaking the buildings with his roars. We saw the white dog flash down the yard, we heard a rattle from the hen-house ladder, and in a moment a scream from the orchard side.

We rushed forward, and there on the sharp bank-side lay a little figure, face down, and Trip standing over it, looking rather puzzled.

I picked up the child—it was Sam. He struggled as soon as he felt my hands, but I bore him off to the house. He wriggled like a wild hare, and kicked, but at last he was still. I set him on the hearth-rug to examine him. He was a quaint little figure, dressed in a man's trousers that had been botched small for him, and a coat hanging in rags.

'Did he get hold of you?' asked the father. 'Where was it he got hold of you?'

But the child stood unanswering, his little pale lips pinched together, his eyes staring out at nothing. Emily went on her knees before him, and put her face close to his, saying, with a voice that made one shrink from its unbridled emotion of caress:

'Did he hurt you, eh?—tell us where he hurt you.' She would have put her arms around him, but he shrank away.

'Look here,' said Lettie, 'it's here—and it's bleeding. Go and get some water, Emily, and some rags. Come on, Sam, let me look and I'll put some rags round it. Come along.'

She took the child and stripped him of his grotesque garments. Trip had given him a sharp grab on the thigh before he had realised that he was dealing with a little boy. It was not much, however, and Lettie soon had it bathed, and anointed with elder-flower ointment. On the boy's body were several scars and bruises—evidently he had rough times. Lettie tended to him and dressed him again. He endured these attentions like a trapped wild rabbit—never looking at us, never opening his lips—only shrinking slightly. When Lettie had put on him his torn little shirt, and had gathered the great breeches about him, Emily went to him to coax him and make him at home. She kissed him, and talked to him with her full vibration of emotional caress. It seemed almost to suffocate him. Then she tried to feed him with bread and milk from a spoon, but he would not open his mouth, and he turned his head away.

'Leave him alone—take no notice of him,' said Lettie, lifting him into the chimney seat, with the basin of bread and milk beside him. Emily fetched the two kittens out of their basket and put them too beside him.

'I wonder how many eggs he'd got,' said the father, laughing softly.

'Hush!' said Lettie. 'When do you think you will go to Canada, Mr Saxton?'

'Next spring—it's no good going before.'

'And then you'll marry?' asked Lettie of George.

'Before then—oh, before then,' he said.

'Why—how is it you are suddenly in such a hurry?—When will it be?'

'When are you marrying?' he asked in reply.

'I don't know,' she said, coming to a full stop.

'Then I don't know,' he said, taking a large wedge of cheese and biting a piece from it.

'It was fixed for June,' she said, recovering herself at his suggestion of hope.

'July!' said Emily.

'Father!' said he, holding the piece of cheese up before him as he spoke—he was evidently nervous: 'Would you advise me to marry Meg?'

His father started, and said:

'Why, was you thinking of doing?'

'Yes—all things considered.'

'Well—if she suits you—'

'We're cousins—'

'If you want her, I suppose you won't let that hinder you. She'll have a nice bit of money, and if you like her—'

'I like her all right—I shan't go out to Canada with her though. I shall stay at the Ram—for the sake of the life.'

'It's a poor life, that!' said the father, ruminating.

George laughed. 'A bit mucky!' he said—'But it'll do. It would need Cyril or Lettie to keep me alive in Canada.'

It was a bold stroke—everybody was embarrassed.

'Well,' said the father, 'I suppose we can't have everything we want–we generally have to put up with the next best thing–don't we, Lettie?'–he laughed. Lettie flushed furiously.

'I don't know,' she said. 'You can generally get what you want if you want it badly enough. Of course–if you *don't mind–*'

She rose and went across to Sam.

He was playing with the kittens. One was patting and cuffing his bare toe, which had poked through his stocking. He pushed and teased the little scamp with his toe till it rushed at him, clinging, tickling, biting till he gave little bubbles of laughter, quite forgetful of us. Then the kitten was tired, and ran off. Lettie shook her skirts, and directly the two playful mites rushed upon it, darting round her, rolling head over heels, and swinging from the soft cloth. Suddenly becoming aware that they felt tired, the young things trotted away and cuddled together by the fender, where in an instant they were asleep. Almost as suddenly, Sam sank into drowsiness.

'He'd better go to bed,' said the father.

'Put him in my bed,' said George. 'David would wonder what had happened.'

'Will you go to bed, Sam?' asked Emily, holding out her arms to him, and immediately startling him by the terrible gentleness of her persuasion. He retreated behind Lettie.

'Come along,' said the latter, and she quickly took him and undressed him. Then she picked him up, and his bare legs hung down in front of her. His head drooped drowsily on to her shoulder, against her neck.

She put down her face to touch the loose riot of his ruddy hair. She stood so, quiet, still and wistful, for a few moments; perhaps she was vaguely aware that the attitude was beautiful for her, and irresistibly appealing to George, who loved, above all in her, her delicate dignity of tenderness. Emily waited with the lighted candle for her some moments.

When she came down there was a softness about her.

'Now,' said I to myself, 'if George asks her again he is wise.'

'He is asleep,' she said quietly.

'I'm thinking we might as well let him stop while we're here, should we, George?' said the father.

'Eh?'

'We'll keep him here while we *are* here–'

'Oh–the lad! I should. Yes–he'd be better here than up yonder.'

'Ah, yes–ever so much. It is good of you,' said Lettie.

'Oh, he'll make no difference,' said the father.

'Not a bit,' added George.

'What about his mother?' asked Lettie.

'I'll call and tell her in the morning,' said George.

'Yes,' she said, 'call and tell her.'

Then she put on her things to go. He also put on his cap.

'Are you coming a little way, Emily?' I asked.

She ran, laughing, with bright eyes as we went out into the darkness.

We waited for them at the wood gate. We all lingered, not knowing what to say. Lettie said finally:

'Well–it's no good–the grass is wet–Good night–Good night, Emily.'

'Good night,' he said, with regret and hesitation, and a trifle of impatience in his voice and his manner. He lingered still a few moments; she hesitated–then she struck off sharply.

'He has not asked her, the idiot!' I said to myself.

'Really,' she said bitterly, when we were going up the garden path, 'you think rather quiet folks have a lot in them, but it's only stupidity–they are mostly fools.'

5

AN ARROW FROM THE IMPATIENT GOD

On an afternoon three or four days after the recovery of Sam, matters became complicated. George, as usual, discovered that he had been dawdling in the portals of his desires, when the doors came to with a bang. Then he hastened to knock.

'Tell her,' he said, 'I will come up tomorrow after milking–tell her I'm coming to see her.'

On the evening of that morrow, the first person to put in an appearance was a garrulous spinster who had called ostensibly to enquire into the absence of the family from church: 'I said to Elizabeth, "Now what a *thing* if anything happens to them just now, and the wedding is put off." I felt I *must* come and make myself sure–that nothing had happened. We all feel *so* interested in Lettie just now. I'm sure everybody is talking of her, she seems in the air.–I really think we shall have thunder: I *hope* we shan't.–Yes, we are all so glad that Mr Tempest is content with a wife from at home–the others, his father and Mr Robert and the rest–they were none of them to be suited at home, though to be sure the wives they brought were nothing–indeed they were not–as many a one said–Mrs Robert was a paltry choice–neither in looks or manner had she anything to boast of–if her family was older than mine. Family wasn't much to make up for what she lacked in other things, that I could easily have supplied her with; and, oh, dear, what an object she is now, with her wisp of hair and her spectacles She for one hasn't kept much of her youth. But when *is* the exact date, dear?–Some say this and some that, but as I always say, I never trust a "they say". It is so nice that you have that cousin a canon to come down for the service, Mrs Beardsall, and Sir Walter Houghton for the groom's man! What?–You don't think so–oh, but I know, dear, I know; you do like to treasure up these secrets, don't you; you are greedy for all the good things just now.'

She shook her head at Lettie, and the jet ornaments on her bonnet twittered like a thousand wagging little tongues. Then she sighed, and was about to recommence her song, when she happened to turn her head and to espy a telegraph-boy coming up the path.

'Oh, I hope nothing is wrong, dear–I hope nothing is wrong! I always feel so terrified of a telegram. You'd better not open it yourself, dear–don't now–let your brother go.'

Lettie, who had turned pale, hurried to the door. The sky was very dark–there was a mutter of thunder.

'It's all right,' said Lettie, trembling, 'it's only to say he's coming tonight.'

'I'm very thankful, very thankful,' cried the spinster. 'It might have been so much worse. I'm sure I never open a telegram without feeling as if I was opening a death-blow. I'm so glad, dear; it must have upset you. What news to take back to the village, supposing something had happened!' she sighed again, and the jet drops twinkled ominously in the thunder light, as if declaring they would make something of it yet.

It was six o'clock. The air relaxed a little, and the thunder was silent. George would be coming about seven; and the spinster showed no signs of departure; and Leslie might arrive at any moment. Lettie fretted and fidgeted, and the old woman gabbled on. I looked out of the window at the water and the sky.

The day had been uncertain. In the morning it was warm, and the sunshine had played and raced among the cloud-shadows on the hills. Later, great cloud masses had stalked up from the north-west and crowded thick across the sky; in this little night, sleet and wind, and rain whirled furiously. Then the sky had laughed at us again. In the sunshine came the spinster. But as she talked, over the hill-top rose the wide forehead of the cloud, rearing slowly, ominously higher. A first messenger of storm passed darkly over the sky, leaving the way clear again.

'I will go round to Highclose,' said Lettie. 'I am sure it will be stormy again. Are you coming down the road, Miss Slaighter, or do you mind if I leave you?'

'I will go, dear, if you think there is going to be another storm – I dread it so. Perhaps I had better wait – '

'Oh, it will not come over for an hour, I am sure. We read the weather well out here, don't we, Cyril? You'll come with me, won't you?'

We three set off, the gossip leaning on her toes, tripping between us. She was much gratified by Lettie's information concerning the proposals for the new home. We left her in a glow of congratulatory smiles on the highway. But the clouds had upreared, and stretched in two great arms, reaching overhead. The little spinster hurried along, but the black hands of the clouds kept pace and clutched her. A sudden gust of wind shuddered in the trees, and rushed upon her cloak, blowing its bugles.

An icy raindrop smote into her cheek. She hurried on, praying fervently for her bonnet's sake that she might reach Widow Harriman's cottage before the burst came. But the thunder crashed in her ear, and a host of hailstones flew at her. In despair and anguish she fled from under the ash trees; she reached the widow's garden gate, when out leapt the lightning full at her. 'Put me in the stair-hole!' she cried. 'Where is the stair-hole?'

Glancing wildly round, she saw a ghost. It was the reflection of the sainted spinster, Hilda Slaighter, in the widow's mirror; a reflection with a bonnet fallen backwards, and to it attached a thick rope of grey-brown hair. The author of the ghost instinctively twisted to look at the back of her head. She saw some ends of grey hair, and fled into the open stair-hole as into a grave.

We had gone back home till the storm was over, and then, restless, afraid of the arrival of George, we set out again into the wet evening. It was fine and chilly, and already a mist was rising from Nethermere, veiling the farther shore, where the trees rose loftily, suggesting groves beyond the Nile. The birds were singing riotously. The fresh green hedge glistened vividly and glowed again with intense green. Looking at the water, I perceived a delicate flush from the west hiding along it. The mist licked and wreathed up the shores; from the hidden white distance came the mournful cry of water-fowl. We went slowly along behind a heavy cart, which clanked and rattled under the dripping trees, with the hoofs of the horse moving with broad thuds in front. We passed over black patches where the ash flowers were beaten down, and under great massed clouds of green sycamore. At the sudden curve of the road, near the foot of the hill, I stopped to break off a spray of larch, where the soft cones were heavy as raspberries, and gay like flowers with petals. The shaken bough spattered a heavy shower on my face, of drops so cold that they seemed to sink into my blood and chill it.

'Hark!' said Lettie, as I was drying my face. There was the quick patter of a motor-car coming downhill. The heavy cart was drawn across the road to rest, and the driver hurried to turn the horse back. It moved with painful slowness, and we stood in the road in suspense. Suddenly, before we knew it, the car was dropping down on us, coming at us in a curve, having rounded the horse and cart. Lettie stood faced with terror. Leslie saw her, and swung round the wheels on the sharp, curving hill-side; looking only to see that he should miss her. The car slid sideways; the mud crackled under the wheels, and the machine went crashing into Nethermere. It caught the edge of the old stone wall with a smash. Then for a few moments I think I was blind. When I saw again, Leslie was lying across the broken hedge, his head hanging down the bank, his face covered with blood; the car rested strangely on the brink of the water, crumpled as if it had sunk down to rest.

Lettie, with hands shuddering, was wiping the blood from his eyes with a piece of her underskirt. In a moment she said:

'He is not dead—let us take him home—let us take him quickly.'

I ran and took the wicket-gate off its hinges and laid him on that. His legs trailed down, but we carried him thus, she at the feet, I at the head. She made me stop and put him down. I thought the weight was too much for her, but it was not that.

'I can't bear to see his hand hanging, knocking against the bushes and things.'

It was not many yards to the house. A maidservant saw us, came running out, and went running back, like the frightened lapwing from the wounded cat.

We waited until the doctor came. There was a deep graze down the side of the head—serious, but not dangerous; there was a cut across the cheek-bone that would leave a scar; and the collar-bone was broken. I stayed until he had recovered consciousness. 'Lettie.' He wanted Lettie, so she had to remain at Highclose all night. I went home to tell my mother.

When I went to bed I looked across at the lighted windows of Highclose, and the lights trailed mistily towards me across the water. The cedar stood dark guard against the house; bright the windows were, like the stars, covering their torment in brightness. The sky was glittering with sharp lights—they are too far off to take trouble for us, so little, little almost to nothingness. All the great hollow vastness roars overhead, and the stars are only sparks that whirl and spin in the restless space. The earth must listen to us; she covers her face with a thin veil of mist, and is sad; she soaks up our blood tenderly, in the darkness, grieving, and in the light she soothes and reassures us. Here on our earth is sympathy and hope, the heavens have nothing but distances.

A corncrake talked to me across the valley, talked and talked endlessly, asking and answering in hoarse tones from the sleeping, mist-hidden meadows. The monotonous voice, that on past summer evenings had had pleasant notes of romance, now was intolerable to me. Its inflexible harshness and cacophony seemed like the voice of fate speaking out its tuneless perseverance in the night.

In the morning Lettie came home wan, sad-eyed, and self-reproachful. After a short time they came for her, as he wanted her again.

When in the evening I went to see George, he too was very despondent.

'It's no good now,' said I. 'You should have insisted and made your own destiny.'

'Yes–perhaps so,' he drawled in his best reflective manner.

'I would have had her–she'd have been glad if you'd done as you wanted with her. She won't leave him till he's strong, and he'll marry her before then. You should have had the courage to risk yourself–you're always too careful of yourself and your own poor feelings–you never could brace yourself up to a shower-bath of contempt and hard usage, so you've saved your feelings and lost–not much, I suppose–you couldn't.'

'But–' he began, not looking up; and I laughed at him.

'Go on,' I said.

'Well–she was engaged to him–'

'Pah–you thought you were too good to be rejected.'

He was very pale, and when he was pale, the tan on his skin looked sickly. He regarded me with his dark eyes, which were now full of misery and a child's big despair.

'And nothing else,' I completed, with which the little, exhausted gunboat of my anger wrecked and sank utterly. Yet no thoughts would spread sail on the sea of my pity: I was like water that heaves with yearning, and is still.

Leslie was very ill for some time. He had a slight brain fever, and was delirious, insisting that Lettie was leaving him. She stayed most of her days at Highclose.

One day in June he lay resting on a deck-chair in the shade of the cedar, and she was sitting by him. It was a yellow, sultry day, when all the atmosphere seemed inert, and all things were languid.

'Don't you think, dear,' she said, 'it would be better for us not to marry?'

He lifted his head nervously from the cushions; his face was emblazoned with a livid red bar on a field of white, and he looked worn, wistful.

'Do you mean not yet?' he asked.

'Yes–and, perhaps–perhaps never.'

'Ha,' he laughed, sinking down again. 'I must be getting like myself again, if you begin to tease me.'

'But,' she said, struggling valiantly, 'I'm not sure I ought to marry you.'

He laughed again, though a little apprehensively.

'Are you afraid I shall always be weak in my noddle?' he asked. 'But you wait a month.'

'No, that doesn't bother me–'

'Oh, doesn't it!'

'Silly boy–no, it's myself.'

'I'm sure I've made no complaint about you.'

'Not likely–but I wish you'd let me go.'

'I'm a strong man to hold you, aren't I? Look at my muscular paw!'–he held out his hands, frail and white with sickness.

'You know you hold me–and I want you to let me go. I don't want to–'

'To what?'

'To get married at all–let me be, let me go.'

'What for?'

'Oh–for my sake.'

'You mean you don't love me?'

'Love–love–I don't know anything about it. But I can't–we can't be–don't you see–oh, what do they say–flesh of one flesh.'

'Why?' he whispered, like a child that is told some tale of mystery.

She looked at him, as he lay propped upon his elbow, turning towards her his white face of fear and perplexity, like a child that cannot understand, and is afraid, and wants to cry. Then slowly tears gathered full in her eyes, and she wept from pity and despair.

This excited him terribly. He got up from his chair, and the cushions fell on to the grass.

'What's the matter, what's the matter!–Oh, Lettie,–is it me?–don't you want me now?–is that it?–tell me, tell me now, tell me,'–he grasped her wrists, and tried to pull her hands from her face. The tears were running down his cheeks. She felt him trembling, and the sound of his voice alarmed her from herself. She hastily smeared the tears from her eyes, got up, and put her arms round him. He hid his head on her shoulder and sobbed, while she bent over him, and so they cried out their cries, till they were ashamed, looking round to see if anyone were near. Then she hurried about, picking up the cushions, making him lie down, and arranging him comfortably, so that she might be busy. He was querulous, like a sick, indulged child. He would have her arm under his shoulders, and her face near his.

'Well,' he said, smiling faintly again after a time. 'You are naughty to give us such rough times–is it for the pleasure of making up, bad little Schnucke–aren't you?'

She kept close to him, and he did not see the wince and quiver of her lips.

'I wish I was strong again–couldn't we go boating–or ride on horseback–and you'd have to behave then. Do you think I shall be strong in a month? Stronger than you?'

'I hope so,' she said.

'Why, I don't believe you do, I believe you like me like this–so that you can lay me down and smooth me–don't you, quiet girl?'

'When you're good.'

'Ah, well, in a month I shall be strong, and we'll be married and go to Switzerland–do you hear, Schnucke–you won't be able to be naughty any more then. Oh–do you want to go away from me again?'

'No–only my arm is dead,' she drew it from beneath him, standing up, swinging it, smiling because it hurt her.

'Oh, my darling–what a shame! Oh, I am a brute, a kiddish brute. I wish I was strong again, Lettie, and didn't do these things.'

'You boy–it's nothing.' She smiled at him again.

6

THE COURTING

During Leslie's illness I strolled down to the mill one Saturday evening. I met George tramping across the yard with a couple of buckets of swill, and eleven young pigs rushing squealing about his legs, shrieking in an agony of suspense. He poured the stuff into a trough with luscious gurgle, and instantly ten noses were dipped in, and ten little mouths began to slobber. Though there was plenty of room for ten, yet they shouldered and shoved and struggled to capture a larger space, and many little trotters dabbled and spilled the stuff, and the ten sucking, clapping snouts twitched fiercely, and twenty little eyes glared askance, like so many points of wrath. They gave uneasy, gasping grunts in their haste. The unhappy eleventh rushed from point to point trying to push in his snout, but for his pains he got rough squeezing, and sharp grabs on the ears. Then he lifted up his face and screamed screams of grief and wrath unto the evening sky.

But the ten little gluttons only twitched their ears to make sure there was no danger in the noise, and they sucked harder, with much spilling and slobbing. George laughed like a sardonic Jove, but at last he gave ear, and kicked the ten gluttons from the trough, and allowed the residue to the eleventh. This one, poor wretch, almost wept with relief as he sucked and swallowed in sobs, casting his little eyes apprehensively upwards, though he did not lift his nose from the trough, as he heard the vindictive shrieks of ten little fiends kept at bay by George. The solitary feeder, shivering with apprehension, rubbed the wood bare with his snout, then, turning up to heaven his eyes of gratitude, he reluctantly left the trough. I expected to see the ten fall upon him and devour him, but they did not; they rushed upon the empty trough, and rubbed the wood still drier, shrieking with misery.

'How like life,' I laughed.

'Fine litter,' said George; 'there were fourteen, only that damned she-devil, Circe, went and ate three of 'em before we got at her.'

The great ugly sow came leering up as he spoke.

'Why don't you fatten her up, and devour her, the old gargoyle? She's an offence to the universe.'

'Nay–she's a fine sow.'

I snorted, and he laughed, and the old sow grunted with contempt, and her little eyes twisted towards us with a demoniac leer as she rolled past.

'What are you going to do tonight!' I asked. 'Going out?'

'I'm going courting,' he replied, grinning.

'Oh!–wish *I* were!'

'You can come if you like–and tell me where I make mistakes, since you're an expert on such matters.'

'Don't you get on very well then?' I asked.

'Oh, all right–it's easy enough when you don't care a damn. Besides, you can always have a Johnny Walker. That's the best of courting at the Ram Inn. I'll go and get ready.'

In the kitchen Emily sat grinding out some stitching from a big old hand machine that stood on the table before her: she was making shirts for Sam, I presumed. That little fellow, who was installed at the farm, was seated by her side firing off words from a reading book. The machine rumbled and rattled on, like a whole factory at work, for an inch or two, during which time Sam shouted in shrill explosions like irregular pistol shots: 'Do–not–pot–' 'Put!' cried Emily from the machine; 'put–' shrilled the child, 'the soot–on–my–boot–,' there the machine broke down, and, frightened by the sound of his own voice, the boy stopped in bewilderment and looked round.

'Go on!' said Emily, as she poked in the teeth of the old machine with the scissors, then pulled and prodded again. He began, '–boot–but–you–' here he died off again, made nervous by the sound of his voice in the stillness. Emily sucked a piece of cotton and pushed it through the needle.

'Now go on,' she said, '–"but you may".'

'But–you–may–shoot':–he shouted away, reassured by the rumble of the machine: 'Shoot–the–fox. I–I–It–is–at–the–rot–'

'Root,' shrieked Emily, as she guided the stuff through the doddering jaws of the machine.

'Root,' echoed the boy, and he went off with these crackers: 'Root–of–the–tree.'

'Next one!' cried Emily.

'Put–the–ol–' began the boy.

'What?' cried Emily.

'Ole–on–'

'Wait a bit!' cried Emily, and then the machine broke down.

'Hang!' she ejaculated.

'Hang!' shouted the child.

She laughed, and leaned over to him:

'"Put the oil in the pan to boil, while I toil in the soil"–Oh, Cyril, I never knew you were there! Go along now, Sam: David 'll be at the back somewhere.'

'He's in the bottom garden,' said I, and the child ran out.

Directly George came in from the scullery, drying himself. He stood on the hearth-rug as he rubbed himself, and surveyed his reflection in the mirror above the high mantelpiece; he looked at himself and smiled. I wondered that he found such satisfaction in his image, seeing that there was a gap in his chin, and an uncertain moth-eaten appearance in one cheek. Mrs Saxton still held this mirror an object of dignity; it was fairly large, and had a well-carven frame; but it left gaps and spots and scratches in one's countenance, and even where it was brightest, it gave one's reflection a far-away dim aspect. Notwithstanding, George smiled at himself as he combed his hair, and twisted his moustache.

'You seem to make a good impression on yourself,' said I.

'I was thinking I looked all right–sort of face to go courting with,' he replied, laughing: 'You just arrange a patch of black to come and hide your faults–and you're all right.'

'I always used to think,' said Emily, 'that the black spots had swallowed so many faces they were full up, and couldn't take any more–and the rest was misty because there were so many faces lapped one over the other–reflected.'

'You do see yourself a bit ghostish–' said he, 'on a background of your ancestors. I always think when you stop in an old place like this you sort of keep company with your ancestors too much; I sometimes feel like a bit of the old building walking about; the old feelings of the old folks stick to you like the lichens on the walls; you sort of get hoary.'

'That's it–it's true,' asserted the father, 'people whose families have shifted about much don't know how it feels. That's why I'm going to Canada.'

'And I'm going in a pub,' said George, 'where it's quite different–plenty of life.'

'Life!' echoed Emily with contempt.

'That's the word, my wench,' replied her brother, lapsing into the dialect. 'That's what I'm after. We know such a lot, an' we know nöwt.'

'You do–' said the father, turning to me, 'you stay in one place, generation after generation, and you seem to get proud, an' look on things outside as foolishness. There's many a thing as any common man knows, as we haven't a glimpse of. We keep on thinking and feeling the same, year after year, till we've only got one side; an' I suppose they've done it before us.'

'It's "Good night an' God bless you," to th' owd place, granfeythers an' grammothers,' laughed George as he ran upstairs—'an' off we go on the gallivant,' he shouted from the landing.

His father shook his head, saying:

'I can't make out how it is, he's so different. I suppose it's being in love—'

We went into the barn to get the bicycles to cycle over to Greymede. George struck a match to look for his pump, and he noticed a great spider scuttle off into the corner of the wall, and sit peeping out at him like a hoary little ghoul.

'How are you, old chap?' said George, nodding to him—'Thought he looked like an old grandfather of mine,' he said to me, laughing, as he pumped up the tyres of the old bicycle for me.

It was Saturday night, so the bar parlour of the Ram Inn was fairly full.

'Hello, George—come co'tin'?' was the cry, followed by a nod and a 'Good evenin',' to me, who was a stranger in the parlour.

'It's raïght for thaïgh,' said a fat young fellow with an unwilling white moustache, '—tha can co'te as much as ter likes ter 'a'e, as well as th' lass, an' it cost thee nöwt—' at which the room laughed, taking pipes from mouths to do so. George sat down, looking round.

''Owd on a bit,' said a black-whiskered man, 'tha mun 'a 'e patience when tu 't co'tin' a lass. Ow's putting' th' öwd lady ter bed—'ark thee—can t' 'ear—that wor th' bed latts goin' bang. Ow'll be dern in a minnit now, gie 'er time ter tuck th' öwd lady up. Can' ter 'ear 'er say 'er prayers.'

'Strike!' cried the fat young man, exploding:

'Fancy th' öwd lady sayin' 'er prayers!—it 'ud be enough ter ma'e 'er false teeth drop out.'

The room laughed.

They began to tell tales about the old landlady. She had practised bone-setting, in which she was very skilful. People come to her from long distances that she might divine their trouble and make right their limbs. She would accept no fee.

Once she had gone up to Dr Fullwood to give him a piece of her mind, inasmuch as he had let a child go for three weeks with a broken collar-bone, whilst treating him for dislocation. The doctor had tried the high hand with her, since when, wherever he went, the miners placed their hands on their shoulders, and groaned: 'Oh my collar-bone!'

Here Meg came in. She gave a bright, quick, bird-like look at George, and flushed a brighter red.

'I thought you wasn't cummin',' she said.

'Dunna thee bother—'e'd none stop away,' said the black-whiskered man.

She brought us glasses of whisky, and moved about supplying the men, who chaffed with her honestly and good-naturedly. Then she went out, but we remained in our corner. The men talked on the most peculiar subjects: there was a bitter discussion as to whether London is or is not a seaport—the matter was thrashed out with heat; then an embryo artist set the room ablaze by declaring there were only three colours, red, yellow, and blue, and the rest were not colours, they were mixtures: this amounted almost to atheism and one man asked the artist to dare to declare that his brown breeches were not a colour, which the artist did, and almost had to fight for it; next they came to strength, and George won a bet of five shillings, by lifting a piano; then they settled down, and talked sex, sotto voce, one man giving startling accounts of Japanese and Chinese prostitutes in Liverpool. After this the talk split up: a farmer began to counsel George how to manage the farm attached to the inn, another bargained with him about horses, and argued about cattle, a tailor advised him thickly to speculate, and unfolded a fine secret by which a man might make money, if he had the go to do it—so on, till eleven o'clock. Then Bill came and called 'time!' and the place was empty, and the room shivered as a little fresh air came in between the foul tobacco smoke, and the smell of drink, and foul breath.

We were both affected by the whisky we had drunk. I was ashamed to find that when I put out my hand to take my glass, or to strike a match, I missed my mark, and fumbled; my hands seemed hardly to belong to me, and my feet were not much more sure. Yet I was acutely conscious of every change in myself and in him; it seemed as if I could make my body drunk, but could never intoxicate my mind, which roused itself and kept the sharpest guard. George was frankly half drunk: his eyelids sloped over his eyes and his speech was thick; when he put out his hand he knocked over his glass, and the stuff was spilled all over the table; he only laughed. I, too, felt a great prompting to giggle on every occasion, and I marvelled at myself.

Meg came into the room when all the men had gone.

'Come on, my duck,' he said, waving his arm with the generous flourish of a tipsy man. 'Come an' sit 'ere.'

'Shan't you come in th' kitchen?' she asked, looking round on the tables where pots and glasses stood in little pools of liquor, and where spent match and tobacco-ash littered the white wood.

'No—what for?—come an' sit 'ere!'—he was reluctant to get on his feet; I knew it and laughed inwardly; I also laughed to hear his thick speech, and his words which seemed to slur against his cheeks.

She went and sat by him, having moved the little table with its spilled liquor.

'They've been tellin' me how to get rich,' he said, nodding his head and laughing, showing his teeth, 'An' I'm goin' ter show 'em. You see, Meg, you see—I'm goin' ter show 'em I can be as good as them, you see.'

'Why,' said she, indulgent, 'what are you going to do?'

'You wait a bit an' see—they don't know yet what I can do—they don't know—*you* don't know—none of you know.'

'An' what shall you do when we're rich, George?'

'Do?—I shall do what I like. I can make as good a show as anybody else, can't I?'—he put his face very near to hers, and nodded at her, but she did not turn away. 'Yes—I'll see what it's like to have my fling. We've been too cautious, our family has—an' I have; we're frightened of ourselves, to do anything. I'm goin' to do what I like, my duck, now—I don't care—I don't care—that!'—he brought his hand down heavily on the table nearest him, and broke a glass. Bill looked in to see what was happening.

'But you won't do anything that's not right, George!'

'No—I don't want to hurt nobody—but I don't care—that!'

'You're too good-hearted to do anybody any harm.'

'I believe I am. You know me a bit, you do, Meg—you don't think I'm a fool now, do you?'

'I'm sure I don't—who does?'

'No—you don't—I know you don't. Gi'e me a kiss—thou'rt a little beauty, thou art—like a ripe plum! I could set my teeth in thee, thou'rt that nice—full o' red juice'–he playfully pretended to bite her. She laughed, and gently pushed him away.

'Tha likest me, doesna ta?' he asked softly.

'What do you want to know for?' she replied, with a tender archness.

'But tha does–say now, tha does.'

'I should a' thought you'd a' known, without telling.'

'Nay, but I want to hear thee.'

'Go on,' she said, and she kissed him.

'But what should you do if I went to Canada and left you?'

'Ah–you wouldn't do that.'

'But I might–and what then?'

'Oh, I don't know what I should do. But you wouldn't do it, I know you wouldn't–you couldn't.' He quickly put his arms round her and kissed her, moved by the trembling surety of her tone:

'No, I wouldna–I'd niver leave thee–tha'd be as miserable as sin, shouldna ta, my duck?'

'Yes,' she murmured.

'Ah,' he said, 'tha'rt a warm little thing–tha loves me, eh?'

'Yes,' she murmured, and he pressed her to him, and kissed her, and held her close.

'We'll be married soon, my bird–are ter glad?–in a bit–tha'rt glad, aren't ta?'

She looked up at him as if he were noble. Her love for him was so generous that it beautified him.

He had to walk his bicycle home, being unable to ride; his shins, I know, were a good deal barked by the pedals.

7

THE FASCINATION OF THE FORBIDDEN APPLE

On the first Sunday in June, when Lettie knew she would keep her engagement with Leslie, and when she was having a day at home from Highclose, she got ready to go down to the mill. We were in mourning for an aunt, so she wore a dress of fine black voile, and a black hat with long feathers. Then, when I looked at her fair hands, and her arms closely covered in the long black cuffs of her sleeves, I felt keenly my old brother-love shielding, indulgent.

It was a windy, sunny day. In shelter the heat was passionate, but in the open the wind scattered its fire. Every now and then a white cloud broad based, blue shadowed, travelled slowly along the sky-road after the forerunner small in the distance, and trailing over us a chill shade, a gloom which we watched creep on over the water, over the wood and the hill. These royal, rounded clouds had sailed all day along the same route, from the harbour of the south to the wastes in the northern sky, following the swift wild geese. The brook hurried along singing, only here and there lingering to whisper to the secret bushes, then setting off afresh with a new snatch of song.

The fowls pecked staidly in the farmyard, with Sabbath decorum. Occasionally a lost, sportive wind-puff would wander across the yard and ruffle them, and they resented it. The pigs were asleep in the sun, giving faint grunts now and then from sheer luxury. I saw a squirrel go darting down the mossy garden wall, up into the laburnum tree, where he lay flat along the bough, and listened. Suddenly away he went, chuckling to himself. Gyp all at once set off barking, but I soothed her down; it was the unusual sight of Lettie's dark dress that startled her, I suppose.

We went quietly into the kitchen. Mrs Saxton was just putting a chicken, wrapped in a piece of flannel, on the warm hob to coax it into life; it looked very feeble. George was asleep, with his head in his arms on the table; the father was asleep on the sofa, very comfortable and admirable; I heard Emily fleeing upstairs, presumably to dress.

'He stays out so late—up at the Ram Inn,' whispered the mother in a high whisper, looking at George, 'and then he's up at five—he doesn't get his proper rest,' she turned to the chicks, and continued in her whisper—'the mother left them just before they hatched out, so we've been bringing them on here. This one's a bit weak—I thought I'd hot him up a bit,' she laughed with a quaint little frown of deprecation. Eight or nine yellow, fluffy little mites were cheeping and scuffling in the fender. Lettie bent over them to touch them; they were tame, and ran among her fingers.

Suddenly George's mother gave a loud cry, and rushed to the fire. There was a smell of singed down. The chicken had toddled into the fire, and gasped its faint gasp among the red-hot cokes. The father jumped from the sofa; George sat up with wide eyes; Lettie gave a little cry and a shudder; Trip rushed round and began to bark. There was a smell of cooked meat.

'There goes number one!' said the mother, with her queer little laugh. It made me laugh too.

'What's a matter—what's a matter?' asked the father excitedly.

'It's a chicken been and walked into the fire—I put it on the hob to warm,' explained his wife.

'Goodness—I couldn't think what was up!' he said, and dropped his head to trace gradually the border between sleeping and waking.

George sat and smiled at us faintly, he was too dazed to speak. His chest still leaned against the table, and his arms were spread out thereon, but he lifted his face, and looked at Lettie with his dazed, dark eyes, and smiled faintly at her. His hair was all ruffled, and his shirt collar unbuttoned. Then he got up slowly, pushing his chair back with a loud noise, and stretched himself, pressing his arms upwards with a long, heavy stretch.

'Oh—h—h!' he said, bending his arms and then letting them drop to his sides. 'I never thought you'd come today.'

'I wanted to come and see you—I shan't have many more chances,' said Lettie, turning from him and yet looking at him again.

'No, I suppose not,' he said, subsiding into quiet. Then there was silence for some time. The mother began to enquire after Leslie, and kept the conversation up till Emily came down, blushing and smiling and glad.

'Are you coming out?' said she, 'there are two or three robins' nests, and a spinkie's—'

'I think I'll leave my hat,' said Lettie, unpinning it as she spoke, and shaking her hair when she was free. Mrs Saxton insisted on her taking a long white silk scarf; Emily also wrapped her hair in a gauze scarf, and looked beautiful.

George came out with us, coatless, hatless, his waistcoat all unbuttoned, as he was. We crossed the orchard, over the old bridge, and went to where the slopes ran down to the lower pond, a bank all covered with nettles, and scattered with a hazel bush or two. Among the nettles old pans were rusting, and old coarse pottery cropped up.

We came upon a kettle heavily coated with lime. Emily bent down and looked, and then we peeped in. There were the robin birds with their yellow beaks stretched so wide apart I feared they would never close them again. Among the naked little mites, that begged from us so blindly and confidently, were huddled three eggs.

'They are like Irish children peeping out of a cottage,' said Emily, with the family fondness for romantic similes.

We went on to where a tin lay with the lid pressed back, and inside it, snug and neat, was another nest, with six eggs, cheek to cheek.

'How warm they are,' said Lettie, touching them, 'you can fairly feel the mother's breast.'

He tried to put his hand into the tin, but the space was too small, and they looked into each other's eyes and smiled. 'You'd think the father's breast had marked them with red,' said Emily.

As we went up the orchard side we saw three wide displays of coloured pieces of pots arranged at the foot of three trees.

'Look,' said Emily, 'those are the children's houses. You don't know how our Mollie gets all Sam's pretty bits – she is a cajoling hussy!'

The two looked at each other again, smiling. Up on the pondside, in the full glitter of light, we looked round where the blades of clustering corn were softly healing the red bosom of the hill. The larks were overhead among the sunbeams. We straggled away across the grass. The field was all afroth with cowslips, a yellow, glittering, shaking froth on the still green of the grass. We trailed our shadows across the fields, extinguishing the sunshine on the flowers as we went. The air was tingling with the scent of blossoms.

'Look at the cowslips, all shaking with laughter,' said Emily, and she tossed back her head, and her dark eyes sparkled among the flow of gauze. Lettie was on in front, flitting darkly across the field, bending over the flowers, stooping to the earth like a sable Persephone come into freedom. George had left her at a little distance, hunting for something in the grass. He stopped, and remained standing in one place.

Gradually, as if unconsciously, she drew near to him, and when she lifted her head, after stooping to pick some chimney-sweeps, little grass flowers, she laughed with a slight surprise to see him so near.

'Ah!' she said. 'I thought I was all alone in the world – such a splendid world – it was so nice.'

'Like Eve in a meadow in Eden – and Adam's shadow somewhere on the grass,' said I.

'No – no Adam,' she asserted, frowning slightly, and laughing.

'Who ever would wants streets of gold,' Emily was saying to me, 'when you can have a field of cowslips! Look at that hedgebottom that gets the south sun – one stream and glitter of buttercups.'

'Those Jews always had an eye to the filthy lucre – they even made heaven out of it,' laughed Lettie, and, turning to him, she said. 'Don't you wish we were wild – hark, like wood-pigeons – or larks – or, look, like peewits? Shouldn't you love flying and wheeling and sparkling and – courting in the wind?' She lifted her eyelids, and vibrated the question. He flushed, bending over the ground.

'Look,' he said, 'here's a larkie's.'

Once a horse had left a hoof-print in the soft meadow; now the larks had rounded, softened the cup, and had laid there three dark-brown eggs. Lettie sat down and leaned over the nest; he leaned above her. The wind running over the flower-heads, peeped in at the little brown buds, and bounded off again gladly. The big clouds sent messages to them down the shadows, and ran in raindrops to touch them.

'I wish,' she said, 'I wish we were free like that. If we could put everything safely in a little place in the earth–couldn't we have a good time as well as the larks?'

'I don't see,' said he, 'why we can't.'

'Oh–but *I* can't–you know we can't'–and she looked at him fiercely.

'Why can't you?' he asked.

'You know we can't–you know as well as I do,' she replied, and her whole soul challenged him. 'We have to consider things,' she added. He dropped his head. He was afraid to make the struggle, to rouse himself to decide the question for her. She turned away, and went kicking through the flowers. He picked up the blossoms she had left by the nest–they were still warm from her hands–and followed her. She walked on towards the end of the field, the long strands of her white scarf running before her. Then she leaned back to the wind, while he caught her up.

'Don't you want your flowers?' he asked humbly.

'No, thanks–they'd be dead before I got home–throw them away, you look absurd with a posy.'

He did as he was bidden. They came near the hedge. A crab-apple tree blossomed up among the blue.

'You may get me a bit of that blossom,' said she, and suddenly added, 'No, I can reach it myself,' whereupon she stretched upward and pulled several sprigs of the pink and white, and put it in her dress.

'Isn't it pretty?' she said, and she began to laugh ironically, pointing to the flowers–'pretty, pink-cheeked petals, and stamens like yellow hair, and buds like lips promising something nice'–she stopped and looked at him, flickering with a smile. Then she pointed to the ovary beneath the flower, and said, 'Result: Crab-apples!'

She continued to look at him, and to smile. He said nothing. So they went on to where they could climb the fence into the spinney. She climbed to the top rail, holding by an oak bough. Then she let him lift her down bodily.

'Ah!' she said, 'you like to show me how strong you are–a veritable Samson!'–she mocked, although she had invited him with her eyes to take her in his arms.

We were entering the spinney of black poplar. In the hedge was an elm tree, with myriads of dark dots pointed against the bright sky, myriads of clusters of flaky green fruit.

'Look at that elm,' she said, 'you'd think it was in full leaf, wouldn't you? Do you know why it's so prolific?'

'No,' he said, with a curious questioning drawl of the monosyllable.

'It's casting its bread upon the winds–no, it is dying, so it puts out all its strength and loads its boughs with the last fruit. It'll be dead next year. If you're here then, come and see. Look at the ivy, the suave smooth ivy, with its fingers in the trees' throat. Trees know how to die, you see–we don't.'

With her whimsical moods she tormented him. She was at the bottom a seething confusion of emotion, and she wanted to make him likewise.

'If we were trees with ivy–instead of being fine humans with free active life–we should hug our thinning lives, shouldn't we?'

'I suppose we should.'

'You, for instance–fancy *your* sacrificing yourself–for the next generation– that reminds you of Schopenhauer, doesn't it?–for the next generation, or love, or anything!'

He did not answer her; she was too swift for him. They passed on under the poplars, which were hanging strings of green beads above them. There was a little open space, with tufts of bluebells. Lettie stooped over a wood-pigeon that lay on the ground on its breast, its wings half spread. She took it up–its eyes were bursten and bloody; she felt its breast, ruffling the dimming iris on its throat.

'It's been fighting,' he said.

'What for–a mate?' she asked, looking at him.

'I don't know,' he answered.

'Cold–he's quite cold, under the feathers! I think a wood-pigeon must enjoy being fought for–and being won; especially if the right one won. It would be a fine pleasure to see them fighting–don't you think?' she said, torturing him.

'The claws are spread–it fell dead off the perch,' he replied.

'Ah, poor thing–it was wounded–and sat and waited for death–when the other had won. Don't you think life is very cruel, George–and love the cruellest of all?'

He laughed bitterly under the pain of her soft, sad tones.

'Let me bury him–and have done with the beaten lover. But we'll make him a pretty grave.'

She scooped a hole in the dark soil, and snatching a handful of bluebells, threw them in on top of the dead bird. Then she smoothed the soil over all, and pressed her white hands on the black loam.

'There,' she said, knocking her hands one against the other to shake off the soil, 'He's done with. Come on.'

He followed her, speechless with his emotion.

The spinney opened out; the ferns were serenely uncoiling, the bluebells stood grouped with blue curls mingled. In the freer spaces forget-me-nots flowered in nebulæ, and dog-violets gave an undertone of dark purple, with primroses for planets in the night. There was a slight drift of woodruff, sweet new-mown hay, scenting the air under the boughs. On a wet bank was the design of golden saxifrage, glistening unholily as if varnished by its minister, the snail. George and Lettie crushed the veined belles of wood-sorrel and broke the silken mosses. What did it matter to them what they broke or crushed?

Over the fence of the spinney was the hill-side, scattered with old thorn trees. There the little grey lichens held up ruby balls to us unnoticed. What did it matter, when all the great red apples were being shaken from the Tree to be left to rot.

'If I were a man,' said Lettie, 'I would go out west and be free. I should love it.'

She took the scarf from her head and let it wave out on the wind; the colour was warm in her face with climbing, and her curls were freed by the wind, sparkling and rippling.

'Well–you're not a man,' he said, looking at her, and speaking with timid bitterness.

'No,' she laughed, 'if I were, I would shape things–oh, wouldn't I have my own way!'

'And don't you now?'

'Oh–I don't want it particularly–when I've got it. When I've had my way, I *do want* somebody to take it back from me.'

She put her head back and looked at him sideways, laughing through the glitter of her hair.

They came to the kennels. She sat down on the edge of the great stone water-trough, and put her hands in the water, moving them gently like submerged flowers through the clear pool.

'I love to see myself in the water,' she said, 'I don't mean *on* the water, Narcissus–but that's how I should like to be out west, to have a little lake of my own, and swim with my limbs quite free in the water.'

'Do you swim well?' he asked.

'Fairly.'

'I would race you–in your little lake.'

She laughed, took her hands out of the water, and watched the clear drops trickle off. Then she lifted her head suddenly, at some thought or other. She looked across the valley, and saw the red roofs of the Mill.

> *'Ilion, Ilion*
> *Fatalis incestusque judex*
> *Et mulier peregrina vertit.*
> *In pulverem–'*

'What's that?' he said.

'Nothing.'

'That's a private trough,' exclaimed a thin voice, high like a peewit's cry. We started in surprise to see a tall, black-bearded man looking at us and away from us nervously, fidgeting uneasily some ten yards off.

'Is it?' said Lettie, looking at her wet hands, which she proceeded to dry on a fragment of a handkerchief.

'You mustn't meddle with it,' said the man in the same reedy, oboe voice. Then he turned his head away, and his pale grey eyes roved the country-side–when he had courage, he turned his back to us, shading his eyes to continue his scrutiny. He walked hurriedly, a few steps, then craned his neck, peering into the valley, and hastened a dozen yards in another direction, again stretching and peering about. Then he went indoors.

'He is pretending to look for somebody,' said Lettie, 'but it's only because he's afraid we shall think he came out just to look at us'–and they laughed.

Suddenly a woman appeared at the gate; she had pale eyes like the mouse-voiced man.

'You'll get Bright's disease sitting on that there damp stone,' she said to Lettie, who at once rose apologetically.

'I ought to know,' continued the mouse-voiced woman, 'my own mother died of it.'

'Indeed,' murmured Lettie, 'I'm sorry.'

'Yes,' continued the woman, 'it behooves you to be careful. Do you come from Strelley Mill Farm?' she asked suddenly of George, surveying his shameful déshabille with bitter reproof.

He admitted the imputation.

'And you're going to leave, aren't you?'

Which also he admitted.

'Humph!–we s'll 'appen get some neighbours. It's a dog's life for loneliness.

I suppose you knew the last lot that was here.'

Another brief admission.

'A dirty lot–a dirty beagle she must have been. You should just ha' seen these grates.'

'Yes,' said Lettie. 'I have seen them.'

'Faugh–the state! But come in–come in, you'll see a difference.'

They entered, out of curiosity.

The kitchen was indeed different. It was clean and sparkling, warm with bright red chintzes on the sofa and on every chair cushion. Unfortunately the effect was spoiled by green and yellow antimacassars, and by a profusion of paper and woollen flowers. There were three cases of woollen flowers, and on the wall, four fans stitched over with ruffled green and yellow paper, adorned with yellow paper roses, carnations, arum lilies, and poppies; there were also wall pockets full of paper flowers; while the wood outside was loaded with blossom.

'Yes,' said Lettie, 'there is a difference.'

The woman swelled, and looked round. The black-bearded man peeped from behind the Christian Herald–those long blaring trumpets!–and shrank again. The woman darted at his pipe, which he had put on a piece of newspaper on the hob, and blew some imaginary ash from it. Then she caught sight of something–perhaps some dust–on the fireplace.

'There!' she cried, 'I knew it; I couldn't leave him one second! I haven't work enough burning wood, but he must be poke–poke–'

'I only pushed a piece in between the bars,' complained the mouse voice from behind the paper.

'Pushed a piece in!' she re-echoed, with awful scorn, seizing the poker and thrusting it over his paper. 'What do you call that, sitting there telling your stories before folks–'

They crept out and hurried away. Glancing round, Lettie saw the woman mopping the doorstep after them, and she laughed. He pulled his watch out of his breeches' pocket; it was half-past three.

'What are you looking at the time for?' she asked.

'Meg's coming to tea,' he replied.

She said no more, and they walked slowly on.

When they came on to the shoulder of the hill, and looked down on to the mill, and the millpond, she said:

'I will not come down with you–I will go home.'

'Not come down to tea!' he exclaimed, full of reproach and amazement. 'Why, what will they say?'

'No, I won't come down–let me say farewell–*jamque Vale!* Do you remember how Eurydice sank back into Hell?'

'But'–he stammered, 'you must come down to tea–how can I tell them? Why won't you come?'

She answered him in Latin, with two lines from Virgil. As she watched him, she pitied his helplessness, and gave him a last cut as she said, very softly and tenderly:

'It wouldn't be fair to Meg.'

He stood looking at her; his face was coloured only by the grey-brown tan; his eyes, the dark, self-mistrustful eyes of the family, were darker than ever, dilated with misery of helplessness; and she was infinitely pitiful. She wanted to cry in her yearning.

'Shall we go into the wood for a few minutes?' she said in a low, tremulous voice, as they turned aside.

The wood was high and warm. Along the ridings the forget-me-nots were knee deep, stretching, glimmering into the distance like the Milky Way through the night. They left the tall, flower-tangled paths to go in among the bluebells, breaking through the close-pressed flowers and ferns till they came to an oak which had fallen across the hazels, where they sat half screened. The hyacinths drooped magnificently with an over-weight of purple, or they stood pale and erect, like unripe ears of purple corn. Heavy bees swung down in a blunder of extravagance among the purple flowers. They were intoxicated even with the sight of so much blue. The sound of their hearty, wanton humming came clear upon the solemn boom of the wind overhead. The sight of their clinging, clambering riot gave satisfaction to the soul. A rosy campion flower caught the sun and shone out. An elm sent down a shower of flesh-tinted sheaths upon them.

'If there were fauns and hamadryads!' she said softly, turning to him to soothe his misery. She took his cap from his head, ruffled his hair, saying:

'If you were a faun, I would put guelder roses round your hair, and make you look Bacchanalian.' She left her hand lying on his knee, and looked up at the sky. Its blue looked pale and green in comparison with the purple tide ebbing about the wood. The clouds rose up like towers, and something had touched them into beauty, and poised them up among the winds. The clouds passed on, and the pool of sky was clear.

'Look,' she said, 'how we are netted down–boughs with knots of green buds. If we were free on the winds!–But I'm glad we're not.' She turned suddenly to him, and with the same movement, she gave him her hand, and he clasped it in both his. 'I'm glad we're netted down here; if we were free in the winds–Ah!' She laughed a peculiar little laugh, catching her breath.

'Look!' she said, 'it's a palace, with the ash-trunks smooth like a girl's arm, and the elm-columns, ribbed and bossed and fretted, with the great steel shafts of beech, all rising up to hold an embroidered care-cloth over us; and every thread of the care-cloth vibrates with music for us, and the little broidered birds sing; and the hazel-bushes fling green spray round us, and the honeysuckle leans down to pour our scent over us. Look at the harvest of bluebells–ripened for us! Listen to the bee, sounding among all the organ-play–if he sounded exultant for us!' She looked at him, with tears coming up into her eyes, and a little, winsome, wistful smile hovering round her mouth. He was very pale, and dared not look at her. She put her hand in his, leaning softly against him. He watched, as if fascinated, a young thrush with full pale breast who hopped near to look at them–glancing with quick, shining eyes.

'The clouds are going on again,' said Lettie.

'Look at that cloud face–see–gazing right up into the sky. The lips are opening–he is telling us something–now the form is slipping away–it's gone–come, we must go too.'

'No,' he cried, 'don't go–don't go away.'

Her tenderness made her calm. She replied in a voice perfect in restrained sadness and resignation.

'No, my dear, no. The threads of my life were untwined; they drifted about like floating threads of gossamer; and you didn't put out your hand to take them and twist them up into the chord with yours. Now another has caught them up, and the chord of my life is being twisted, and I cannot wrench it free and untwine it again–I can't. I am not strong enough. Besides, you have twisted another thread far and tight into your chord; could you get free?'

'Tell me what to do–yes, if you tell me.'

'I can't tell you–so let me go.'

'No, Lettie,' he pleaded, with terror and humility. 'No, Lettie; don't go. What should I do with my life? Nobody would love you like I do–and what should I do with my love for you?–hate it and fear it, because it's too much for me?'

She turned and kissed him gratefully. He then took her in a long, passionate embrace, mouth to mouth. In the end it had so wearied her that she could only wait in his arms till he was too tired to hold her. He was trembling already.

'Poor Meg!' she murmured to herself dully, her sensations having become vague.

He winced, and the pressure of his arms slackened. She loosened his hands and rose half dazed from her seat by him. She left him, while he sat dejected, raising no protest.

When I went out to look for them, when tea had already been waiting on the table half an hour or more, I found him leaning against the gatepost at the bottom of the hill. There was no blood in his face, and his tan showed livid; he was haggard as if he had been ill for some weeks.

'Whatever's the matter?' I said. 'Where's Lettie?'

'She's gone home,' he answered, and the sound of his own voice, and the meaning of his own words made him heave.

'Why?' I asked in alarm.

He looked at me as if to say, 'What are you talking about? I cannot listen!'

'Why?' I insisted.

'I don't know,' he replied.

'They are waiting tea for you,' I said.

He heard me, but took no notice.

'Come on,' I repeated, 'there's Meg and everybody waiting tea for you.'

'I don't want any,' he said.

I waited a minute or two. He was violently sick.

> '*Vae meum*
> *Fervens difficile bile tumet jecur,*'

I thought to myself.

When the sickness passed over, he stood up away from the post, trembling and lugubrious. His eyelids dropped heavily over his eyes, and he looked at me, and smiled a faint, sick smile.

'Come and lie down in the loft,' I said, 'and I'll tell them you've got a bilious bout.'

He obeyed me, not having energy to question; his strength had gone, and his splendid physique seemed shrunken; he walked weakly. I looked away from him, for in his feebleness he was already beginning to feel ludicrous.

We got into the barn unperceived, and I watched him climb the ladder to the loft. Then I went indoors to tell them.

I told them Lettie had promised to be at Highclose for tea, that George had a bilious attack, and was mooning about the barn till it was over; he had been badly sick. We ate tea without zest or enjoyment. Meg was wistful and ill at ease; the father talked to her and made much of her; the mother did not care for her much.

'I can't understand it,' said the mother, 'he so rarely has anything the matter with him—why, I've hardly known the day! Are you sure it's nothing serious, Cyril? It seems such a thing—and just when Meg happened to be down—just when Meg was coming—!'

About half-past six I had again to go and look for him, to satisfy the anxiety of his mother and his sweetheart. I went whistling to let him know I was coming. He lay on a pile of hay in a corner, asleep. He had put his cap under his head to stop the tickling of the hay, and he lay half curled up, sleeping soundly. He was still very pale, and there was on his face the repose and pathos that a sorrow always leaves. As he wore no coat, I was afraid he might be chilly, so I covered him up with a couple of sacks, and I left him. I would not have him disturbed—I helped the father about the cowsheds and with the pigs.

Meg had to go at half-past seven. She was so disappointed that I said: 'Come and have a look at him—I'll tell him you did.'

He had thrown off the sacks and spread out his limbs. As he lay on his back, flung out on the hay, he looked big again, and manly. His mouth had relaxed, and taken its old, easy lines. One felt for him now the warmth one feels for anyone who sleeps in an attitude of abandon. She leaned over him, and looked at him with a little rapture of love and tenderness; she longed to caress him. Then he stretched himself, and his eyes opened. Their sudden unclosing gave her a thrill. He smiled sleepily, and murmured, '''Allo, Meg!' Then I saw him awake. As he remembered, he turned with a great sighing yawn, hid his face again, and lay still.

'Come along, Meg,' I whispered, 'he'll be best asleep.'

'I'd better cover him up,' she said, taking the sack and laying it very gently over his shoulders. He kept perfectly still while I drew her away.

8

A POEM OF FRIENDSHIP

The magnificent promise of spring was broken before the May blossom was fully out. All through the beloved month the wind rushed in upon us from the north and north-east, bringing the rain fierce and heavy. The tender-budded trees shuddered and moaned; when the wind was dry, the young leaves flapped limp. The grass and corn grew lush, but the light of the dandelions was quite extinguished, and it seemed that only a long time back had we made merry before the broad glare of these flowers. The bluebells lingered and lingered; they fringed the fields for weeks like purple fringe of mourning. The pink campions came out only to hang heavy with rain; hawthorn buds remained tight and hard as pearls, shrinking into the brilliant green foliage; the forget-me-nots, the poor pleiades of the wood, were ragged weeds. Often at the end of the day the sky opened, and stately clouds hung over the horizon infinitely far away, glowing, through the yellow distance, with an amber lustre. They never came any nearer, always they remained far off, looking calmly and majestically over the shivering earth, then saddened, fearing their radiance might be dimmed, they drew away, and sank out of sight. Sometimes, towards sunset, a great shield stretched dark from the west to the zenith, tangling the light along its edges. As the canopy rose higher, it broke, dispersed, and the sky was primrose coloured, high and pale above the crystal moon. Then the cattle crouched among the gorse, distressed by the cold, while the long-billed snipe flickered round high overhead, round and round in great circles, seeming to carry a serpent from its throat, and crying a tragedy, more painful than the poignant lamentations and protests of the peewits. Following these evenings came mornings cold and grey.

Such a morning I went up to George, on the top fallow. His father was out with the milk—he was alone; as I came up the hill I could see him standing in the cart, scattering manure over the bare red fields; I could hear his voice calling now and then to the mare, and the creak and clank of the cart as it moved on. Starlings and smart wagtails were running briskly over the clods, and many little birds flashed, fluttered, hopped here and there. The lapwings wheeled and cried as ever between the low clouds and the earth, and some ran beautifully among the furrows, too graceful and glistening for the rough field.

I took a fork and scattered the manure along the hollows, and thus we worked, with a wide field between us, yet very near in the sense of intimacy. I watched him through the wheeling peewits, as the low clouds went stealthily overhead. Beneath us, the spires of the poplars in the spinney were warm gold, as if the blood shone through. Farther gleamed the grey water, and below it the red roofs. Nethermere was half hidden and far away. There was nothing in this grey, lonely world but the peewits swinging and crying, and George swinging silently at his work. The movement of active life held all my attention, and when I looked up, it was to see the motion of his limbs and his head, the rise and fall of his rhythmic body, and the rise and fall of the slow waving peewits. After a while, when the cart was empty, he took a fork and came towards me, working at my task.

It began to rain, so he brought a sack from the cart, and we crushed ourselves under the thick hedge. We sat close together and watched the rain fall like a grey striped curtain before us, hiding the valley; we watched it trickle in dark streams off the mare's back, as she stood dejectedly; we listened to the swish of the drops falling all about; we felt the chill of the rain, and drew ourselves together in silence. He smoked his pipe, and I lit a cigarette. The rain continued; all the little pebbles and the red earth glistened in the grey gloom. We sat together, speaking occasionally. It was at these times we formed the almost passionate attachment which later years slowly wore away.

When the rain was over, we filled our buckets with potatoes, and went along the wet furrows, sticking the spritted tubers in the cold ground. Being sandy, the field dried quickly. About twelve o'clock, when nearly all the potatoes were set, he left me, and fetching up Bob from the far hedge-side, harnessed the mare and him to the ridger, to cover the potatoes. The sharp light plough turned the soil in a fine furrow over the potatoes; hosts of little birds fluttered, settled, bounded off again after the plough. He called to the horses, and they came downhill, the white stars on the two brown noses nodding up and down, George striding firm and heavy behind. They came down upon me; at a call the horses turned, shifting awkwardly sideways; he flung himself against the plough, and leaning well in, brought it round with a sweep: a click, and they are off uphill again. There is a great rustle as the birds sweep round after him and follow up the new-turned furrow. Untackling the horses when the rows were all covered, we tramped behind them down the wet hill-side to dinner.

I kicked through the drenched grass, crushing the withered cowslips under my clogs, avoiding the purple orchids that were stunted with harsh upbringing, but magnificent in their powerful colouring, crushing the pallid lady smocks, the washed-out wild gillivers. I became conscious of something near my feet, something little and dark, moving indefinitely. I had found again the larkie's nest. I perceived the yellow beaks, the bulging eyelids of two tiny larks, and the blue lines of their wing quills. The indefinite movement was the swift rise and fall of the brown fledged backs, over which waved long strands of fine down. The two little specks of birds lay side by side, beak to beak, their tiny bodies rising and falling in quick unison. I gently put down my fingers to touch them; they were warm; gratifying to find them warm, in the midst of so much cold and wet. I became curiously absorbed in them, as an eddy of wind stirred the strands of down. When one fledgling moved uneasily, shifting his soft ball, I was quite excited; but he nestled down again, with his head close to his brother's. In my heart of hearts, I longed for someone to nestle against, someone who would come between me and the coldness and wetness of the surroundings. I envied the two little miracles exposed to any tread, yet so serene. It seemed as if I were always wandering, looking for something which they had found even before the light broke into their shell. I was cold; the lilacs in the Mill garden looked blue and perished. I ran with my heavy clogs, and my heart heavy with vague longing, down to the Mill, while the wind blanched the sycamores, and pushed the sullen pines rudely, for the pines were sulking because their million creamy sprites could not fly wet-winged. The horse-chestnuts bravely kept their white candles erect in the socket of every bough, though no sun came to light them. Drearily a cold swan swept up the water, trailing its black feet, clacking its great hollow wings, rocking the frightened water-hens, and insulting the staid black-necked geese. What did I want that I turned thus from one thing to another?

At the end of June the weather became fine again. Hay harvest was to begin as soon as it settled. There were only two fields to be mown this year, to provide just enough stuff to last until the spring. As my vacation had begun I decided I would help, and that we three, the father, George and I, would get in the hay without hired assistance.

I rose the first morning very early, before the sun was well up. The clear sound of challenging cocks could be heard along the valley. In the bottoms, over the water and over the lush wet grass, the night mist still stood white and substantial. As I passed along the edge of the meadow the cow-parsnip was as tall as I, frothing up to the top of the hedge, putting the faded hawthorn to a wan blush. Little, early birds—I had not heard the lark—fluttered in and out of the foamy meadow-sea, plunging under the surf of flowers washed high in one corner, swinging out again, dashing past the crimson sorrel cresset. Under the froth of flowers were the purple vetch-clumps, yellow milk vetches, and the scattered pink of the wood-betony, and the floating stars of marguerites. There was a weight of honeysuckle on the hedges, where pink roses were waking up for their broad-spread flight through the day.

Morning silvered the swaths of the far meadow, and swept in smooth, brilliant curves round the stones of the brook; morning ran in my veins; morning chased the silver, darting fish out of the depth, and I, who saw them, snapped my fingers at them, driving them back.

I heard Trip barking, so I ran towards the pond. The punt was at the island, where from behind the bushes I could hear George whistling. I called to him, and he came to the water's edge half dressed.

'Fetch a towel,' he called, 'and come on.'

I was back in a few moments, and there stood my Charon fluttering in the cool air. One good push sent us to the islet. I made haste to undress, for he was ready for the water, Trip dancing round, barking with excitement at his new appearance.

'He wonders what's happened to me,' he said, laughing, pushing the dog playfully away with his bare foot. Trip bounded back, and came leaping up, licking him with little caressing licks. He began to play with the dog, and directly they were rolling on the fine turf, the laughing, expostulating, naked man, and the excited dog, who thrust his great head on to the man's face, licking, and, when flung away, rushed forward again, snapping playfully at the naked arms and breasts. At last George lay back, laughing and panting, holding Trip by the two forefeet which were planted on his breast, while the dog, also panting, reached forward his head for a flickering lick at the throat pressed back on the grass, and the mouth thrown back out of reach. When the man had thus lain still for a few moments, and the dog was just laying his head against his master's neck to rest too, I called, and George jumped up, and plunged into the pond with me, Trip after us.

The water was icily cold, and for a moment deprived me of my senses. When I began to swim, soon the water was buoyant, and I was sensible of nothing but the vigorous poetry of action. I saw George swimming on his back laughing at me, and in an instant I had flung myself like an impulse after him. The laughing face vanished as he swung over and fled, and I pursued the dark head and the ruddy neck. Trip, the wretch, came paddling towards me, interrupting me; then all bewildered with excitement, he scudded to the bank. I chuckled to myself as I saw him run along, then plunge in and go plodding to George. I was gaining. He tried to drive off the dog, and I gained rapidly. As I came up to him and caught him, with my hand on his shoulder, there came a laughter from the bank. It was Emily.

I trod the water, and threw handfuls of spray at her. She laughed and blushed. Then Trip waded out to her and she fled swiftly from his shower-bath. George was floating just beside me, looking up and laughing.

We stood and looked at each other as we rubbed ourselves dry. He was well proportioned, and naturally of handsome physique, heavily limbed. He laughed at me, telling me I was like one of Aubrey Beardsley's long, lean, ugly fellows. I referred him to many classic examples of slenderness, declaring myself more exquisite than his grossness, which amused him.

But I had to give in, and bow to him, and he took on an indulgent, gentle manner. I laughed and submitted. For he knew how I admired the noble, white fruitfulness of his form. As I watched him, he stood in white relief against the mass of green. He polished his arm, holding it out straight and solid; he rubbed his hair into curls, while I watched the deep muscles of his shoulders, and the bands stand out in his neck as he held it firm; I remembered the story of Annable.

He saw I had forgotten to continue my rubbing, and laughing he took hold of me and began to rub me briskly, as if I were a child, or rather, a woman he loved and did not fear. I left myself quite limply in his hands, and, to get a better grip of me, he put his arm round me and pressed me against him, and the sweetness of the touch of our naked bodies one against the other was superb. It satisfied in some measure the vague, indecipherable yearning of my soul; and it was the same with him. When he had rubbed me all warm, he let me go, and we looked at each other with eyes of still laughter, and our love was perfect for a moment, more perfect than any love I have known since, either for man or woman.

We went together down to the fields, he to mow the island of grass he had left standing the previous evening, I to sharpen the machine knife, to mow out the hedge-bottoms with the scythe, and to rake the swarths from the way of the machine when the unmown grass was reduced to a triangle. The cool, moist fragrance of the morning, the intentional stillness of everything, of the tall bluish trees, of the wet, frank flowers, of the trustful moths folded and unfolded in the fallen swaths, was a perfect medium of sympathy. The horses moved with a still dignity, obeying his commands. When they were harnessed, and the machine oiled, still he was loth to mar the perfect morning, but stood looking down the valley.

'I shan't mow these fields any more,' he said, and the fallen, silvered swaths flickered back his regret, and the faint scent of the limes was wistful. So much of the field was cut, so much remained to cut; then it was ended. This year the elder flowers were widespread over the corner bushes, and the pink roses fluttered high above the hedge. There were the same flowers in the grass as we had known many years; we should not know them any more.

'But merely to have mown them is worth having lived for,' he said, looking at me.

We felt the warmth of the sun trickling through the morning's mist of coolness.

'You see that sycamore,' he said, 'that bushy one beyond the big willow? I remember when Father broke off the leading shoot because he wanted a fine straight stick, I can remember I felt sorry. It was running up so straight, with such a fine balance of leaves–you know how a young strong sycamore looks about nine feet high–it seemed a cruelty. When you are gone, and we are left from here, I shall feel like that, as if my leading shoot were broken off. You see, the tree is spoiled. Yet how it went on growing. I believe I shall grow faster. I can remember the bright red stalks of the leaves as he broke them off from the bough.'

He smiled at me, half proud of his speech. Then he swung into the seat of the machine, having attended to the horses' heads. He lifted the knife.

'Good-bye,' he said, smiling whimsically back at me. The machine started. The bed of the knife fell, and the grass shivered and dropped over. I watched the heads of the daisies and the splendid lines of the cocksfool grass quiver, shake against the crimson burnet, and drop over. The machine went singing down the field, leaving a track of smooth, velvet green in the way of the swath-board. The flowers in the wall of uncut grass waited unmoved, as the days wait for us. The sun caught in the up-licking scarlet sorrel flames, the butterflies woke, and I could hear the fine ring of his 'Whoa!' from the far corner. Then he turned, and I could see only the tossing ears of the horses, and the white of his shoulder as they moved along the wall of high grass on the hill slope. I sat down under the elm to file the sections of the knife. Always as he rode he watched the falling swath, only occasionally calling the horses into line. It was his voice which rang the morning awake. When we were at work we hardly noticed one another. Yet his mother had said:

'George is so glad when you're in the field–he doesn't care how long the day is.'

Later, when the morning was hot, and the honeysuckle had ceased to breathe, and all the other scents were moving in the air about us, when all the field was down, when I had seen the last trembling ecstasy of the harebells, trembling to fall; when the thick clump of purple vetch had sunk; when the green swaths were settling, and the silver swaths were glistening and glittering as the sun came along them, in the hot ripe morning we worked together turning the hay, tipping over the yesterday's swaths with our forks, and bringing yesterday's fresh, hidden flowers into the death of sunlight.

It was then that we talked of the past, and speculated on the future. As the day grew older and less wistful, we forgot everything, and worked on, singing, and sometimes I would recite him verses as we went, and sometimes I would tell him about books. Life was full of glamour for us both.

9

PASTORALS AND PEONIES

At dinner-time the father announced to us the exciting fact that Leslie had asked if a few of his guests might picnic that afternoon in the Strelley hayfields. The closes were so beautiful, with the brook under all its sheltering trees, running into the pond that was set with two green islets. Moreover, the squire's lady had written a book filling these meadows and the mill precincts with pot-pourri romance. The wedding guests at Highclose were anxious to picnic in so choice a spot.

The father, who delighted in a gay throng, beamed at us from over the table. George asked who were coming.

'Oh, not many—about half a dozen—mostly ladies down for the wedding.'

George at first swore warmly; then he began to appreciate the affair as a joke.

Mrs Saxton hoped they wouldn't want her to provide them pots, for she hadn't two cups that matched, nor had any of her spoons the least pretence to silver. The children were hugely excited, and wanted a holiday from school, which Emily at once vetoed firmly, thereby causing family dissension.

As we went round the field in the afternoon turning the hay, we were thinking apart, and did not talk. Every now and then—and at every corner—we stopped to look down towards the wood, to see if they were coming.

'Here they are!' George exclaimed suddenly, having spied the movement of white in the dark wood. We stood still and watched. Two girls, heliotrope and white, a man with two girls, pale green and white, and a man with a girl last.

'Can you tell who they are?' I asked.

'That's Marie Tempest, that first girl in white, and that's him and Lettie at the back, I don't know any more.'

He stood perfectly still until they had gone out of sight behind the banks down by the brooks, then he stuck his fork in the ground, saying:

'You can easily finish—if you like. I'll go and mow out that bottom corner.'

He glanced at me to see what I was thinking of him. I was thinking that he was afraid to meet her, and I was smiling to myself. Perhaps he felt ashamed, for he went silently away to the machine, where he belted his riding breeches tightly round his waist, and slung the scythe-strap on his hip. I heard the clanging slur of the scythe stone as he whetted the blade. Then he strode off to mow the far bottom corner, where the ground was marshy, and the machine might not go, to bring down the lush green grass and the tall meadow-sweet.

I went to the pond to meet the newcomers. I bowed to Louie Denys, a tall, graceful girl of the drooping type, elaborately gowned in heliotrope linen; I bowed to Agnes D'Arcy, an erect, intelligent girl with magnificent auburn hair–she wore no hat and carried a sunshade; I bowed to Hilda Seconde, a svelte, petite girl, exquisitely and delicately pretty; I bowed to Maria and to Lettie, and I shook hands with Leslie and with his friend, Freddy Cresswell. The latter was to be best man, a broad-shouldered, pale-faced fellow, with beautiful soft hair like red wheat, and laughing eyes, and a whimsical, drawling manner of speech, like a man who has suffered enough to bring him to manhood and maturity, but who in spite of all remains a boy, irresponsible, lovable–a trifle pathetic. As the day was very hot, both men were in flannels, and wore flannel collars, yet it was evident that they had dressed with scrupulous care. Instinctively I tried to pull my trousers into shape within my belt, and I felt the inferiority cast upon the father, big and fine as he was in his way, for his shoulders were rounded with work, and his trousers were much distorted.

'What can we do?' said Marie; 'you know we don't want to hinder, we want to help you. It was so good of you to let us come.'

The father laughed his fine indulgence, saying to them–they loved him for the mellow, laughing modulation of his voice:

'Come on, then–I see there's a bit of turning-over to do, as Cyril's left. Come and pick your forks.'

From among a sheaf of hay-forks he chose the lightest for them, and they began anywhere, just tipping at the swaths. He showed them carefully–Marie and the charming little Hilda–just how to do it, but they found the right way the hardest way, so they worked in their own fashion, and laughed heartily with him when he made playful jokes at them. He was a great lover of girls, and they blossomed from timidity under his hearty influence.

'Ain' it flippin' 'ot?' drawled Cresswell, who had just taken his M.A. degree in classics: 'This bloomin' stuff's dry enough–come an' flop on it.'

He gathered a cushion of hay, which Louie Denys carefully appropriated, arranging first her beautiful dress, that fitted close to her shape, without any belt or interruption, and then laying her arms, that were netted to the shoulder in open lace, gracefully at rest. Lettie, who was also in a close-fitting white dress which showed her shape down to the hips, sat where Leslie had prepared for her, and Miss D'Arcy reluctantly accepted my pile.

Cresswell twisted his clean-cut mouth in a little smile, saying:

'Lord, a giddy little pastoral–fit for old Theocritus, ain't it, Miss Denys?'

'Why do you talk to me about those classic people–I daren't even say their names. What would he say about us?'

He laughed, winking his blue eyes:

'He'd make old Daphnis there'–pointing to Leslie–'sing a match with me, Damoetas–contesting the merits of our various shepherdesses–begin Daphnis, sing up for Amaryllis, I mean Nais, damn 'em, they were for ever getting mixed up with their nymphs.'

'I say, Mr Cresswell, your language! Consider whom you're damning,' said Miss Denys, leaning over and tapping his head with her silk glove.

'You say any giddy thing in a pastoral,' he replied, taking the edge of her skirt, and lying back on it, looking up at her as she leaned over him. 'Strike up,

Daphnis, something about honey or white cheese—or else the early apples that'll be ripe in a week's time.'

'I'm sure the apples you showed me are ever so little and green,' interrupted Miss Denys; 'they will never be ripe in a week—ugh, sour!'

He smiled up at her in his whimsical way:

'Hear that, Tempest—"Ugh, sour!"—not much! Oh, love us, haven't you got a start yet?—isn't there aught to sing about, you blunt-faced kid?'

'I'll hear you first—I'm no judge of honey and cheese.'

'An' darn little apples—takes a woman to judge them; don't it, Miss Denys?'

'I don't know,' she said, stroking his soft hair from his forehead with her hand whereon rings were sparkling.

'"My love is not white, my hair is not yellow, like honey dropping through the sunlight—my love is brown, and sweet, and ready for the lips of love." Go on, Tempest—strike up, old cowherd. Who's that tuning his pipe?—oh, that fellow sharpening his scythe! It's enough to make your back ache to look at him working—go an' stop him, somebody.'

'Yes, let us go and fetch him,' said Miss D'Arcy. 'I'm sure he doesn't know what a happy pastoral state he's in—let us go and fetch him.'

'They don't like hindering at their work, Agnes—besides, where ignorance is bliss—' said Lettie, afraid lest she might bring him. The other hesitated, then with her eyes she invited me to go with her.

'Oh, dear,' she laughed, with a little *moue*, 'Freddy is such an ass, and Louie Denys is like a wasp at treacle. I wanted to laugh, yet I felt just a tiny bit cross. Don't you feel great when you go mowing like that? Father Timey sort of feeling? Shall we go and look! We'll say we want those foxgloves he'll be cutting down directly—and those bell flowers. I suppose you needn't go on with your labours—'

He did not know we were approaching till I called him, then he started slightly as he saw the tall, proud girl.

'Mr Saxton—Miss D'Arcy,' I said, and he shook hands with her. Immediately his manner became ironic, for he had seen his hand big and coarse and inflamed with the snaith clasping the lady's hand.

'We thought you looked so fine,' she said to him, 'and men are so embarrassing when they make love to somebody else—aren't they? Save us those foxgloves, will you—they are splendid—like savage soldiers drawn up against the hedge—don't cut them down—and those campanulas—bell-flowers, ah, yes! They are spinning idylls up there. I don't care for idylls, do you? Oh, you don't know what a classical pastoral person you are—but there, I don't suppose you suffer from idyllic love—' she laughed, '—one doesn't see the silly little god fluttering about in our hayfields, does one? Do you find much time to sport with Amaryllis in the shade?—I'm sure it's a shame they banish Phyllis from the fields—'

He laughed and went on with his work. She smiled a little, too, thinking she had made a great impression. She put out her hand with a dramatic gesture, and looked at me, when the scythe crunched through the meadow-sweet.

'Crunch! isn't it fine!' she exclaimed, 'a kind of inevitable fate—I think it's fine!'

We wandered about picking flowers and talking until tea-time. A manservant came with the tea-basket, and the girls spread the cloth under a great willow tree. Lettie took the little silver kettle, and went to fill it at the small spring which trickled into a stone trough all pretty with cranesbill and stellaria hanging over, while long blades of grass waved in the water. George, who had finished his work, and wanted to go home to tea, walked across to the spring where Lettie sat playing with the water, getting little cupfuls to put into the kettle, watching the quick skating of the water-beetles, and the large faint spots of their shadows darting on the silted mud at the bottom of the trough.

She glanced round on hearing him coming, and smiled nervously: they were mutually afraid of meeting each other again.

'It is about tea-time,' he said.

'Yes–it will be ready in a moment–this is not to make the tea with–it's only to keep a little supply of hot water.'

'Oh,' he said, 'I'll go on home–I'd rather.'

'No,' she replied, 'you can't because we are all having tea together: I had some fruits put up, because I know you don't trifle with tea–and your father's coming.'

'But,' he replied pettishly, 'I can't have my tea with all those folks–I don't want to–look at me!'

He held out his inflamed, barbaric hands.

She winced and said:

'It won't matter–you'll give the realistic touch.'

He laughed ironically.

'No–you must come,' she insisted.

'I'll have a drink then, if you'll let me,' he said, yielding.

She got up quickly, blushing, offering him the tiny, pretty cup.

'I'm awfully sorry,' she said.

'Never mind,' he muttered, and turning from the proffered cup he lay down flat, put his mouth to the water, and drank deeply. She stood and watched the motion of his drinking, and of his heavy breathing afterwards. He got up, wiping his mouth, not looking at her. Then he washed his hands in the water, and stirred up the mud. He put his hand to the bottom of the trough, bringing out a handful of silt, with the grey shrimps twisting in it. He flung the mud on the floor where the poor grey creatures writhed.

'It wants cleaning out,' he said.

'Yes,' she replied, shuddering. 'You won't be long,' she added, taking up the silver kettle.

In a few moments he got up and followed her reluctantly down. He was nervous and irritable.

The girls were seated on tufts of hay, with the men leaning in attendance on them, and the manservant waiting on all. George was placed between Lettie and Hilda. The former handed him his little egg-shell of tea, which, as he was not very thirsty, he put down on the ground beside him. Then she passed him the bread and butter, cut for five-o'clock tea, and fruits, grapes and peaches, and strawberries, in a beautifully-carved oak tray. She watched for a moment his thick, half-washed fingers fumbling over the fruits, then she turned her head away. All the gay tea-time, when the talk bubbled and frothed over all the cups, she avoided him with her eyes. Yet again and again, as someone said: 'I'm sorry, Mr Saxton–will you have some cake?'–or 'See, Mr Saxton–try this peach, I'm sure it will be mellow right to the stone,'–speaking very naturally, but making the distinction between him and the other men by their indulgence towards him, Lettie was forced to glance at him as he sat eating, answering in monosyllables, laughing with constraint and awkwardness, and her irritation flickered between her brows. Although she kept up the gay frivolity of the conversation, still the discord was felt by everybody, and we did not linger as we should have done over the cups. 'George,' they said afterwards, 'was a wet blanket on the party.' Lettie was intensely annoyed with him. His presence was unbearable to her. She wished him a thousand miles away. He sat listening to Cresswell's whimsical affectation of vulgarity which flickered with fantasy, and he laughed in a strained fashion.

He was the first to rise, saying he must get the cows up for milking.

'Oh, let us go–let us go. May we come and see the cows milked?' said Hilda, her delicate, exquisite features flushing, for she was very shy.

'No,' drawled Freddy, 'the stink o' live beef ain't salubrious. You be warned, and stop here.'

'I never could bear cows, except those lovely little Highland cattle, all woolly, in pictures,' said Louie Denys, smiling archly, with a little irony.

'No,' laughed Agnes D'Arcy, 'they–they're smelly,'–and she pursed up her mouth, and ended in a little trill of deprecatory laughter, as she often did. Hilda looked from one to the other, blushing.

'Come, Lettie,' said Leslie good-naturedly, 'I know you have a farmyard fondness–come on,' and they followed George down.

As they passed along the pond bank a swan and her tawny, fluffy brood sailed with them the length of the water, 'tipping on their little toes, the darlings–pitter-patter through the water, tiny little things,' as Marie said.

We heard George below calling 'Bully–Bully–Bully–Bully!' and then, a moment or two after, in the bottom garden: 'Come out, you little fool–are you coming out of it?' in manifestly angry tones.

'Has it run away?' laughed Hilda, delighted, and we hastened out of the lower garden to see.

There in the green shade, between the tall gooseberry bushes, the heavy crimson peonies stood gorgeously along the path. The full red globes, poised and leaning voluptuously, sank their crimson weight on to the seeding grass of the path, borne down by secret rain, and by their own splendour. The path was poured over with red rich silk of strewn petals. The great flowers swung their crimson grandly about the walk, like crowds of cardinals in pomp among the green bushes. We burst into the new world of delight. As Lettie stooped, taking between both hands the gorgeous silken fullness of one blossom that was sunk to the earth. George came down the path, with the brown bull-calf straddling behind him, its neck stuck out, sucking zealously at his middle finger.

The unconscious attitudes of the girls, all bent enraptured over the peonies, touched him with sudden pain. As he came up, with the calf stalking grudgingly behind, he said:

'There's a fine show of pyeenocks this year, isn't there?'

'What do you call them?' cried Hilda, turning to him her sweet, charming face full of interest.

'Pyeenocks,' he replied.

Lettie remained crouching with a red flower between her hands, glancing sideways unseen to look at the calf, which with its shiny nose uplifted was mumbling in its sticky gums the seductive finger. It sucked eagerly, but unprofitably, and it appeared to cast a troubled eye inwards to see if it were really receiving any satisfaction,–doubting, but not despairing. Marie, and Hilda, and Leslie laughed, while he, after looking at Lettie as she crouched, wistfully, as he thought, over the flower, led the little brute out of the garden, and sent it running into the yard with a smack on the haunch.

Then he returned, rubbing his sticky finger dry against his breeches. He stood near to Lettie, and she felt rather than saw the extraordinary pale cleanness of the one finger among the others. She rubbed her finger against her dress in painful sympathy.

'But aren't the flowers lovely!' exclaimed Marie again. 'I want to hug them.'

'Oh, yes!' assented Hilda.

'They are like a romance–D'Annunzio–a romance in passionate sadness,' said Lettie, in an ironical voice, speaking half out of conventional necessity of saying something, half out of desire to shield herself, and yet in a measure express herself.

'There is a tale about them,' I said.

The girls clamoured for the legend.

'Pray, do tell us,' pleaded Hilda, the irresistible.

'It was Emily told me–she says it's a legend, but I believe it's only a tale. She says the peonies were brought from the Hall long since by a fellow of this place–when it was a mill. He was brown and strong, and the daughter of the Hall, who was pale and fragile and young, loved him. When he went up to the Hall gardens to cut the yew hedges, she would hover round him in her white frock, and tell him tales of old days, in little snatches like a wren singing, till he thought she was a fairy who had bewitched him. He would stand and watch her, and one day, when she came near to him telling him a tale that set the tears swimming in her eyes, he took hold of her and kissed her and kept her. They used to tryst in the poplar spinney. She would come with her arms full of flowers, for she always kept to her fairy part. One morning she came early through the mists. He was out shooting. She wanted to take him unawares, like a fairy. Her arms were full of peonies. When she was moving beyond the trees he shot her, not knowing. She stumbled on, and sank down in their tryst place. He found her lying there among the red pyeenocks, white and fallen. He thought she was just lying talking to the red flowers, so he stood waiting. Then he went up, and bent over her, and found the flowers full of blood. It was he set the garden here with these pyeenocks.'

The eyes of the girls were round with pity of the tale and Hilda turned away to hide her tears.

'It is a beautiful ending,' said Lettie, in a low tone, looking at the floor.

'It's all a tale,' said Leslie, soothing the girls.

George waited till Lettie looked at him. She lifted her eyes to him at last. Then each turned aside, trembling.

Marie asked for some of the peonies.

'Give me just a few–and I can tell the others the story–it is so sad–I feel so sorry for him, it was so cruel for him–! And Lettie says it ends beautifully–!'

George cut the flowers with his great clasp-knife, and Marie took them, carefully, treating their romance with great tenderness. Then all went out of the garden and he turned to the cowshed.

'Good-bye for the present,' said Lettie, afraid to stay near him.

'Good-bye,' he laughed.

'Thank you *so* much for the flowers–and the story–it was splendid,' said Marie, '–but so sad!'

Then they went, and we did not see them again.

Later, when all had gone to bed at the mill, George and I sat together on opposite sides of the fire, smoking, saying little. He was casting up the total of discrepancies, and now and again he ejaculated one of his thoughts.

'And all day,' he said, 'Blench has been ploughing his wheat in, because it was that bitten off by the rabbits it was no manner of use, so he's ploughed it in: an' they say with idylls, eating peaches in our close.'

Then there was silence, while the clock throbbed heavily, and outside a wild bird called, and was still; softly the ashes rustled lower in the gate.

'She said it ended well—but what's the good of death—what's the good of that?' He turned his face to the ashes in the grate, and sat brooding.

Outside, among the trees, some wild animal set up a thin, wailing cry.

'Damn that row!' said I, stirring, looking also into the grey fire.

'It's some stoat or weasel, or something. It's been going on like that for nearly a week. I've shot in the trees ever so many times. There were two—one's gone.'

Continuously, through the heavy, chilling silence, came the miserable crying from the darkness among the trees.

'You know,' he said, 'she hated me this afternoon, and I hated her—'

It was midnight, full of sick thoughts.

'It is no good,' said I. 'Go to bed—it will be morning in a few hours.'

PART III

I

A NEW START IN LIFE

Lettie was wedded, as I had said, before Leslie lost all the wistful traces of his illness. They had been gone away to France five days before we recovered anything like the normal tone in the house. Then, though the routine was the same, everywhere was a sense of loss, and of change. The long voyage in the quiet home was over; we had crossed the bright sea of our youth, and already Lettie had landed and was travelling to a strange destination in a foreign land. It was time for us all to go, to leave the valley of Nethermere whose waters and whose woods were distilled in the essence of our veins. We were the children of the valley of Nethermere, a small nation with language and blood of our own, and to cast ourselves each one into separate exile was painful to us.

'I shall have to go now,' said George. 'It is my nature to linger an unconscionable time, yet I dread above all things this slow crumbling away from my foundations by which I free myself at last. I must wrench myself away now–'

It was the slack time between the hay and the corn harvest, and we sat together in the grey, still morning of August pulling the stack. My hands were sore with tugging the loose wisps from the lower part of the stack, so I waited for the touch of rain to send us indoors. It came at last, and we hurried into the barn. We climbed the ladder into the loft that was strewn with farming implements and with carpenters' tools. We sat together on the shavings that littered the bench before the high gable window, and looked out over the brooks and the woods and the ponds. The tree-tops were very near to us, and we felt ourselves the centre of the waters and the woods that spread down the rainy valley.

'In a few years,' I said, 'we shall be almost strangers.'

He looked at me with fond, dark eyes and smiled incredulously.

'It is as far,' said I, 'to the "Ram" as it is for me to London–farther.'

'Don't you want me to go there?' he asked, smiling quietly.

'It's all as one where you go, you will travel north, and I east, and Lettie south. Lettie has departed. In seven weeks I go.–And you?'

'I must be gone before you,' he said decisively.

'Do you know–' and he smiled timidly in confession, 'I feel alarmed at the idea of being left alone on a loose end. I must not be the last to leave–' he added almost appealingly.

'And you will go to Meg?' I asked.

He sat tearing the silken shavings into shreds, and telling me in clumsy fragments all he could of his feelings:

'You see, it's not so much what you call love. I don't know. You see, I built on Lettie'–he looked up at me shamefacedly, then continued tearing the shavings–'you must found your castles on something, and I founded mine on Lettie. You see, I'm like plenty of folks, I have nothing definite to shape my life to. I put brick upon brick, as they come, and if the whole topples down in the end, it does. But you see, you and Lettie have made me conscious, and now I'm at a dead loss. I have looked to marriage to set me busy on my house of life, something whole and complete, of which it will supply the design. I must marry or be in a lost lane. There are two people I could marry–and Lettie's gone. I love Meg just as well, as far as love goes. I'm not sure I don't feel better pleased at the idea of marrying her. You know I should always have been second to Lettie, and the best part of love is being made much of, being first and foremost in the whole world for somebody. And Meg's easy and lovely. I can have her without trembling, she's full of soothing and comfort. I can stroke her hair and pet her, and she looks up at me, full of trust and lovingness, and there is no flaw, all restfulness in one another–'

Three weeks later, as I lay in the August sunshine in a deck-chair on the lawn, I heard the sound of wheels along the gravel path. It was George calling for me to accompany him to his marriage. He pulled up the dog-cart near the door and came up the steps to me on the lawn. He was dressed as if for the cattle market, in jacket and breeches and gaiters.

'Well, are you ready?' he said, standing smiling down on me. His eyes were dark with excitement, and had that vulnerable look which was so peculiar to the Saxtons in their emotional moments.

'You are in good time,' said I, 'it is but half-past nine.'

'It wouldn't do to be late on a day like this,' he said gaily, 'see how the sun shines. Come, you don't look as brisk as a best man should. I thought you would have been on tenterhooks of excitement. Get up, get up! Look here, a bird has given me luck'–he showed me a white smear on his shoulder.

I drew myself up lazily.

'All right,' I said, 'but we must drink a whisky to establish it.'

He followed me out of the fragrant sunshine into the dark house. The rooms were very still and empty, but the cool silence responded at once to the gaiety of our sun-warm entrance. The sweetness of the summer morning hung invisible like glad ghosts of romance through the shadowy room. We seemed to feel the sunlight dancing golden in our veins as we filled again the pale liqueur.

'Joy to you–I envy you today.'

His teeth were white, and his eyes stirred like dark liquor as he smiled.

'Here is my wedding present!'

I stood the four large water-colours along the wall before him. They were drawings among the waters and the fields of the mill, grey rain and twilight, morning with the sun pouring gold into the mist, and the suspense of a midsummer noon upon the pond. All the glamour of our yesterdays came over him like an intoxicant, and he quivered with the wonderful beauty of life that was weaving him into the large magic of the years. He realised the splendour of the pageant of days which had him in train.

'It's been wonderful, Cyril, all the time,' he said, with surprised joy.

We drove away through the freshness of the wood, and among the flowing of the sunshine along the road. The cottages of Greymede filled the shadows with colour of roses, and the sunlight with odour of pinks and the blue of cornflowers and larkspur. We drove briskly up the long, sleeping hill, and bowled down the hollow past the farms where the hens were walking with the red gold cocks in the orchard, and the ducks like white cloudlets under the aspen trees revelled on the pond.

'I told her to be ready any time,' said George–'but she doesn't know it's today. I didn't want the public-house full of the business.'

The mare walked up the sharp little rise on top of which stood the Ram Inn. In the quiet, as the horse slowed to a standstill, we heard the crooning of a song in the garden. We sat still in the cart, and looked across the flagged yard to where the tall madonna lilies rose in clusters out of the alyssum. Beyond the border of flowers was Meg, bending over the gooseberry bushes. She saw us and came swinging down the path, with a bowl of gooseberries poised on her hip. She was dressed in a plain, fresh holland frock, with a white apron. Her black, heavy hair reflected the sunlight, and her ripe face was luxuriant with laughter.

'Well, I never!' she exclaimed, trying not to show that she guessed his errand. 'Fancy you here at this time o' morning!'

Her eyes, delightful black eyes like polished jet, untroubled and frank, looked at us as a robin might, with bright questioning. Her eyes were so different from the Saxtons': darker, but never still and full, never hesitating, dreading a wound, never dilating with hurt or with timid ecstasy.

'Are you ready then?' he asked, smiling down on her.

'What?' she asked in confusion.

'To come to the registrar with me–I've got the licence.'

'But I'm just going to make the pudding,' she cried, in full expostulation.

'Let them make it themselves–put your hat on.'

'But look at me! I've just been getting the gooseberries. Look!' She showed us the berries, and the scratches on her arms and hands.

'What a shame!' he said, bending down to stroke her hand and her arm. She drew back smiling, flushing with joy. I could smell the white lilies where I sat.

'But you don't mean it, do you?' she said, lifting to him her face that was round and glossy like a blackheart cherry. For answer, he unfolded the marriage licence. She read it, and turned aside her face in confusion, saying:

'Well, I've got to get ready. Shall you come an' tell Gran'ma?'

'Is there any need?' he answered reluctantly.

'Yes, you come an' tell 'er,' persuaded Meg.

He got down from the trap. I preferred to stay out of doors. Presently Meg ran out with a glass of beer for me.

'We shan't be many minutes,' she apologised. 'I've o'ny to slip another frock on.'

I heard George go heavily up the stairs and enter the room over the bar-parlour, where the grandmother lay bedridden.

'What, is it thaïgh, ma lad? What are thaïgh doin' 'ere this mornin'?' she asked.

'Well A'nt, how does ta feel by now?' he said.

'Eh, sadly, lad, sadly! It'll not be long afore they carry me downstairs head first–'

'Nay, dunna thee say so!–I'm just off to Nottingham–I want Meg ter come.'

'What for?' cried the old woman sharply.

'I wanted 'er to get married,' he replied.

'What! What does't say? An' what about th' licence, an' th' ring, an' ivrything?'

'I've seen to that all right,' he answered.

'Well, tha 'rt a nice'st 'un, I must say! What's want goin' in this pig-in-a-poke fashion for? This is a nice shabby trick to serve a body! What does ta mean by it?'

'You knowed as I wor goin' ter marry 'er directly, so I can't see as it matters o' th' day. I non wanted a' th' pub talkin'—'

'Tha 'rt mighty particklar, an' all, an' all! An' why shouldn't the pub talk? Tha 'rt non marryin' a nigger, as ta should be so frightened—I niver thought it on thee!—An' what's thy 'orry, all of a sudden?'

'No hurry as I know of.'

'No 'orry—!' replied the old lady, with withering sarcasm. 'Tha wor niver in a 'orry a' thy life! She's non commin' wi' thee this day, though.'

He laughed, also sarcastic. The old lady was angry. She poured on him her abuse, declaring she would not have Meg in the house again, nor leave her a penny, if she married him that day.

'Tha can please thysen,' answered George, also angry.

Meg came hurriedly into the room.

'Ta'e that 'at off—ta'e it off! Tha non goos wi' 'im this day, not if I know it! Does 'e think tha 'rt a cow, or a pig, to be fetched wheniver 'e thinks fit. Ta'e that 'at off, I say!'

The old woman was fierce and peremptory.

'But Gran'ma—!' began Meg.

The bed creaked as the old lady tried to rise.

'Ta'e that 'at off, afore I pull it off!' she cried.

'Oh, be still, Gran'ma—you'll be hurtin' yourself, you know you will—'

'Are you coming, Meg?' said George suddenly.

'She is not!' cried the old woman.

'Are you coming, Meg?' repeated George, in a passion.

Meg began to cry. I suppose she looked at him through her tears. The next thing I heard was a cry from the old woman, and the sound of staggering feet.

'Would ta drag 'er from me!—if tha goos, ma wench, tha enters this 'ouse no more, tha 'eers that! Tha does thysen, my lady! Dunna venture anigh me after this, my gel!'—the old woman called louder and louder. George appeared in the doorway, holding Meg by the arm. She was crying in a little distress. Her hat, with its large silk roses, was slanting over her eyes. She was dressed in white linen. They mounted the trap. I gave him the reins and scrambled up behind. The old woman heard us through the open window, and we listened to her calling as we drove away:

'Dunna let me clap eyes on thee again, tha ungrateful 'ussy, tha ungrateful 'ussy! Tha'll rue it, my wench, tha'll rue it, an' then dunna come ter me—'

We drove out of hearing. George sat with a shut mouth, scowling. Meg wept a while to herself woefully. We were swinging at a good pace under the beeches of the churchyard which stood above the level of the road. Meg, having settled her hat, bent her head to the wind, too much occupied with her attire to weep. We swung round the hollow by the bog end, and rattled a short distance up the steep hill to Watnall. Then the mare walked slowly. Meg, at leisure to collect herself, exclaimed plaintively:

'Oh, I've only got one glove!'

She looked at the odd silk glove that lay in her lap, then peered about among her skirts.

'I must 'a left it in th' bedroom' she said piteously.

The White Peacock 615

He laughed, and his anger suddenly vanished.

'What does it matter? You'll do without all right.'

At the sound of his voice, she recollected, and her tears and her weeping returned.

'Nay,' he said, 'don't fret about the old woman. She'll come round tomorrow–an' if she doesn't, it's her lookout. She's got Polly to attend to her.'

'But she'll be that miserable–!' wept Meg.

'It's her own fault. At any rate, don't let it make you miserable'–he glanced to see if anyone were in sight, then he put his arm round her waist and kissed her, saying softly, coaxingly, 'She'll be all right tomorrow. We'll go an' see her then, an' she'll be glad enough to have us. We'll give in to her then, poor old gran'ma. She can boss you about, an' me as well, tomorrow as much as she likes. She feels it hard, being tied to her bed. But today is ours, surely–isn't it? Today is ours, an' you're not sorry, are you?'

'But I've got no gloves, an' I'm sure my hair's a sight. I never thought she could 'a reached up like that.'

George laughed, tickled.

'No,' he said, 'she *was* in a temper. But we can get you some gloves directly we get to Nottingham.'

'I haven't a farthing of money,' she said.

'I've plenty!' he laughed. 'Oh, an' let's try this on.'

They were merry together as he tried on her wedding ring, and they talked softly, he gentle and coaxing, she rather plaintive. The mare took her own way, and Meg's hat was disarranged once more by the sweeping elm-boughs. The yellow corn was dipping and flowing in the fields, like a cloth of gold pegged down at the corners under which the wind was heaving. Sometimes we passed cottages where the scarlet lilies rose like bonfires, and the tall larkspur like bright blue leaping smoke. Sometimes we smelled the sunshine on the browning corn, sometimes the fragrance of the shadow of leaves. Occasionally it was the dizzy scent of new haystacks. Then we rocked and jolted over the rough cobblestones of Cinderhill, and bounded forward again at the foot of the enormous pit hill, smelling of sulphur, inflamed with slow red fires in the daylight, and crusted with ashes. We reached the top of the rise and saw the city before us, heaped high and dim upon the broad range of the hill. I looked for the square tower of my old school, and the sharp proud spire of St Andrew's. Over the city hung a dullness, a thin dirty canopy against the blue sky.

We turned and swung down the slope between the last sullied cornfields towards Basford, where the swollen gasometers stood like toadstools. As we neared the mouth of the street, Meg rose excitedly, pulling George's arm, crying:

'Oh, look, the poor little thing!'

On the causeway stood two small boys lifting their faces and weeping to the heedless heavens, while before them, upside down, lay a baby strapped to a shut-up baby-chair. The gimcrack carpet-seated thing had collapsed as the boys were dismounting the kerb-stone with it. It had fallen backwards, and they were unable to right it. There lay the infant strapped head downwards to its silly cart, in imminent danger of suffocation. Meg leaped out, and dragged the child from the wretched chair. The two boys, drenched with tears, howled on. Meg crouched on the road, the baby on her knee, its tiny feet dangling against her skirt. She soothed the pitiful tear-wet mite. She hugged it to her, and kissed it, and hugged it, and rocked it in an abandonment of pity. When at last the childish trio were silent, the boys shaken only by the last ebbing sobs, Meg calmed also from her frenzy of pity for the little thing. She murmured to it tenderly, and wiped its wet little cheeks with her handkerchief, soothing, kissing, fondling the bewildered mite, smoothing the wet strands of brown hair under the scrap of cotton bonnet, twitching the inevitable baby cape into order. It was a pretty baby, with wisps of brown-gold silken hair and large blue eyes.

'Is it a girl?' I asked one of the boys–'How old is she?'

'I don't know,' he answered awkwardly. 'We've 'ad 'er about a three week.'

'Why, isn't she your sister?'

'No–my mother keeps 'er'–they were very reluctant to tell us anything.

'Poor little lamb!' cried Meg, in another access of pity, clasping the baby to her bosom with one hand, holding its winsome slippered feet in the other. She remained thus, stung through with acute pity, crouching, folding herself over the mite. At last she raised her head, and said, in a voice difficult with emotion:

'But you love her–don't you?'

'Yes–she's–she's all right. But we 'ave to mind 'er,' replied the boy in great confusion.

'Surely,' said Meg, 'surely you don't begrudge that. Poor little thing–so little, she is–surely you don't grumble at minding her a bit–?'

The boys would not answer.

'Oh, poor little lamb, poor little lamb!' murmured Meg over the child, condemning with bitterness the boys and the whole world of men.

I taught one of the lads how to fold and unfold the wretched chair. Meg very reluctantly seated the unfortunate baby therein, gently fastening her with the strap.

'Wheer's 'er dummy?' asked one of the boys in muffled, self-conscious tones. The infant began to cry thinly. Meg crouched over it. The 'dummy' was found in the gutter and wiped on the boy's coat, then plugged into the baby's mouth. Meg released the tiny clasping hand from over her finger, and mounted the dog-cart, saying sternly to the boys:

'Mind you look after her well, poor little baby with no mother. God's watching to see what you do to her–so you be careful, mind.'

They stood very shamefaced. George clicked to the mare, and as we started threw coppers to the boys. While we drove away I watched the little group diminish down the road.

'It's such a shame,' she said, and the tears were in her voice, '–A sweet little thing like that–'

'Ay,' said George softly, 'there's all sorts of things in towns.'

Meg paid no attention to him, but sat woman-like, thinking of the forlorn baby, and condemning the hard world. He, full of tenderness and protectiveness towards her, having watched her with softening eyes, felt a little bit rebuffed that she ignored him, and sat alone in her fierce womanhood. So he busied himself with the reins, and the two sat each alone until Meg was roused by the bustle of the town. The mare sidled past the electric cars nervously, and jumped when a traction engine came upon us. Meg, rather frightened, clung to George again. She was very glad when we had passed the cemetery with its white population of tombstones, and drew up in a quiet street.

But when we had dismounted, and given the horse's head to a loafer, she became confused and bashful and timid to the last degree. He took her on his arm; he took the whole charge of her, and laughing, bore her away towards the steps of the office. She left herself entirely in his hands; she was all confusion, so he took the charge of her.

When, after a short time, they came out, she began to chatter with blushful animation. He was very quiet, and seemed to be taking his breath.

'Wasn't he a funny little man? Did I do it all proper?–I didn't know what I was doing. I'm sure they were laughing at me–do you think they were? Oh, just look at my frock–what a sight! What would they think–!' The baby had slightly soiled the front of her dress.

George drove up the long hill into the town. As we came down between the shops on Mansfield Road he recovered his spirits.

'Where are we going–where are you taking us?' asked Meg.

'We may as well make a day of it while we are here,' he answered, smiling and flicking the mare. They both felt that they were launched forth on an adventure. He put up at the Spread Eagle, and we walked towards the market-place for Meg's gloves. When he had bought her these and a large lace scarf to give her a more clothed appearance, he wanted dinner.

'We'll go,' he said, 'to an hotel.'

His eyes dilated as he said it, and she shrank away with delighted fear. Neither of them had ever been to an hotel. She was really afraid. She begged him to go to an eating-house, to a café. He was obdurate. His one idea was to do the thing that he was half afraid to do. His passion–and it was almost intoxication–was to dare to play with life. He was afraid of the town. He was afraid to venture into the foreign places of life, and all was foreign save the valley of Nethermere. So he crossed the borders flauntingly, and marched towards the heart of the unknown. We went to the Victoria Hotel–the most imposing he could think of–and we had luncheon according to the menu. They were like two children, very much afraid, yet delighting in the adventure. He dared not, however, give the orders. He dared not address anybody, waiters or otherwise. I did that for him, and he watched me, absorbing, learning, wondering that things were so easy and so delightful. I murmured them injunctions across the table and they blushed and laughed with each other nervously. It would be hard to say whether they enjoyed that luncheon. I think Meg did not–even though she was with him. But of George I am doubtful. He suffered exquisitely from self-consciousness and nervous embarrassment, but he felt also the intoxication of the adventure, he felt as a man who has lived in a small island when he first sets foot on a vast continent. This was the first step into a new life, and he mused delightedly upon it over his brandy. Yet he was nervous. He could not get over the feeling that he was trespassing.

'Where shall we go this afternoon?' he asked.

Several things were proposed, but Meg pleaded warmly for Colwick.

'Let's go on a steamer to Colwick Park. There'll be entertainments there this afternoon. It'll be lovely.'

In a few moments we were on the top of the car swinging down to the Trent Bridges. It was dinner-time, and crowds of people from shops and warehouses were hurrying in the sunshine along the pavements. Sun-blinds cast their shadows on the shop-fronts, and in the shade streamed the people dressed brightly for summer. As our car stood in the great space of the market-place we could smell the mingled scent of fruit, oranges, and small apricots, and pears piled in their vividly coloured sections on the stalls. Then away we sailed through the shadows of the dark streets and the open pools of sunshine. The castle on its high rock stood in the dazzling dry sunlight; the fountain stood shadowy in the green glimmer of the lime trees that surrounded the alms-houses.

There were many people at the Trent. We stood a while on the bridge to watch the bright river swirling in a silent dance to the sea, while the light pleasure-boats lay asleep along the banks. We went on board the little paddle-steamer and paid our 'sixpence return'. After much waiting we set off, with great excitement, for our mile-long voyage. Two banjos were tumming somewhere below, and the passengers hummed and sang to their tunes. A few boats dabbled on the water. Soon the river meadows with their high thorn hedges lay green on our right, while the scarp of red rock rose on our left, covered with the dark trees of summer.

We landed at Colwick Park. It was early, and few people were there. Dead glass fairy-lamps were slung about the trees. The grass in places was worn threadbare. We walked through the avenues and small glades of the park till we came to the boundary where the race-course stretched its level green, its winding white barriers running low into the distance. They sat in the shade for some time while I wandered about. Then many people began to arrive. It became noisy, even rowdy. We listened for some time to an open-air concert, given by the pierrots. It was rather vulgar, and very tiresome. It took me back to Cowes, to Yarmouth. There were the same foolish over-eyebrowed faces, the same perpetual jingle from an out-of-tune piano, the restless jigging to the songs, the same choruses, the same escapading. Meg was well pleased. The vulgarity passed by her. She laughed, and sang the choruses half audibly, daring, but not bold. She was immensely pleased. 'Oh, it's Ben's turn now. I like him, he's got such a wicked twinkle in his eye. Look at Joey trying to be funny!—He can't to save his life. Doesn't he look soft—!' She began to giggle in George's shoulder. He saw the funny side of things for the time and laughed with her.

During tea, which we took on the green veranda of the degraded hall, she was constantly breaking forth into some chorus, and he would light up as she looked at him and sing with her, *sotto voce*. He was not embarrassed at Colwick. There he had on his best careless, superior air. He moved about with a certain scornfulness, and ordered lobster for tea off-handedly. This also was a new walk of life. Here he was not hesitating or tremulously strung; he was patronising. Both Meg and he thoroughly enjoyed themselves.

When we got back into Nottingham she entreated him not to go to the hotel as he had proposed, and he readily yielded. Instead they went to the Castle. We stood on the high rock in the cool of the day, and watched the sun sloping over the great river-flats where the menial town spread out, and ended, while the river and the meadows continued into the distance. In the picture-galleries there was a fine collection of Arthur Melville's paintings. Meg thought them very ridiculous. I began to expound them, but she was manifestly bored, and he was half-hearted. Outside in the grounds was a military band playing. Meg longed to be there. The townspeople were dancing on the grass. She longed to join them, but she could not dance. So they sat a while looking on.

We were to go to the theatre in the evening. The Carl Rosa Company was giving 'Carmen' at the Royal. We went into the dress circle 'like giddy dukes', as I said to him, so that I could see his eyes dilate with adventure again as he laughed. In the theatre, among the people in evening dress, he became once more childish and timorous. He had always the air of one who does something forbidden, and is charmed, yet fearful, like a trespassing child. He had begun to trespass that day outside his own estates of Nethermere.

'Carmen' fascinated them both. The gaudy, careless Southern life amazed them. The bold free way in which Carmen played with life startled them with hints of freedom. They stared on the stage fascinated. Between the acts they held each other's hands, and looked full into each other's wide bright eyes, and laughing with excitement, talked about the opera. The theatre surged and roared dimly like a hoarse shell. Then the music rose like a storm, and swept and rattled at their feet. On the stage the strange storm of life clashed in music towards tragedy and futile death. The two were shaken with a tumult of wild feeling. When it was all over they rose bewildered, stunned, she with tears in her eyes, he with a strange wild beating of his heart.

They were both in a tumult of confused emotion. Their ears were full of the roaring passion of life, and their eyes were blinded by a spray of tears and that strange quivering laughter which burns with real pain. They hurried along the pavement to the Spread Eagle, Meg clinging to him, running, clasping her lace scarf over her white frock, like a scared white butterfly shaken through the night. We hardly spoke as the horse was being harnessed and the lamps lighted. In the little smoke-room he drank several whiskies, she sipping out of his glass, standing all the time ready to go. He pushed into his pocket great pieces of bread and cheese, to eat on the way home. He seemed now to be thinking with much acuteness. His few orders were given sharp and terse. He hired an extra light rug in which to wrap Meg, and then we were ready.

'Who drives?' said I.

He looked at me and smiled faintly.

'You,' he answered.

Meg, like an impatient white flame, stood waiting in the light of the lamps. He covered her, extinguished her in the dark rug.

2

PUFFS OF WIND IN THE SAIL

The year burst into glory to usher us forth out of the valley of Nethermere. The cherry trees had been gorgeous with heavy out-reaching boughs of red and gold. Immense vegetable marrows lay prostrate in the bottom garden, their great tentacles clutching the pond bank. Against the wall the globed crimson plums hung close together, and dropped occasionally with a satisfied plunge into the rhubarb leaves. The crop of oats was very heavy. The stalks of corn were like strong reeds of bamboo; the heads of grain swept heavily over like tresses weighted with drops of gold.

George spent his time between the Mill and the Ram. The grandmother had received them with much grumbling but with real gladness. Meg was re-installed, and George slept at the Ram. He was extraordinarily bright, almost gay. The fact was that his new life interested and pleased him keenly. He often talked to me about Meg, how quaint and naïve she was, how she amused him and delighted him. He rejoiced in having a place of his own, a home, and a beautiful wife who adored him. Then the public house was full of strangeness and interest. No hour was ever dull. If he wanted company he could go into the smoke-room, if he wanted quiet he could sit with Meg, and she was such a treat, so soft and warm, and so amusing. He was always laughing at her quaint crude notions, and at her queer little turns of speech. She talked to him with a little language, she sat on his knee and twisted his moustache, finding small, unreal fault with his features for the delight of dwelling upon them. He was, he said, incredibly happy. Really he could not believe it. Meg was, ah! she was a treat. Then he would laugh, thinking how indifferent he had been about taking her. A little shadow might cross his eyes, but he would laugh again, and tell me one of his wife's funny little notions. She was quite uneducated, and such fun, he said. I looked at him as he sounded this note. I remembered his crude superiority of early days, which had angered Emily so deeply. There was in him something of the prig. I did not like his amused indulgence of his wife.

At threshing day, when I worked for the last time at the Mill, I noticed the new tendency in him. The Saxtons had always kept up a certain proud reserve. In former years, the family had moved into the parlour on threshing day, and an extra woman had been hired to wait on the men who came with the machine. This time George suggested: 'Let us have dinner with the men in the kitchen, Cyril. They are a rum gang. It's rather good sport mixing with them. They've seen a bit of life, and I like to hear them, they're so blunt. They're good studies though.'

The farmer sat at the head of the table. The seven men trooped in, very sheepish, and took their places. They had not much to say at first. They were a mixed set, some rather small, young, and furtive looking, some unshapely and coarse, with unpleasant eyes, the eyelids slack. There was one man whom we called the Parrot, because he had a hooked nose, and put forward his head as he talked. He had been a very large man, but he was grey, and bending at the shoulders. His face was pale and fleshy, and his eyes seemed dull-sighted.

George patronised the men, and they did not object. He chaffed them, making a good deal of demonstration in giving them more beer. He invited them to pass up their plates, called the woman to bring more bread, and altogether played mine host of a feast of beggars. The Parrot ate very slowly.

'Come, Dad,' said George, 'you're not getting on. Not got many grinders–?'

'What I've got's in th' road. Is'll 'a'e ter get 'em out. I can manage wi' bare gums, like a baby again.'

'Second childhood, eh? Ah well, we must all come to it,' George laughed.

The old man lifted his head and looked at him, and said slowly:

'You'n got ter get ower th' first afore that.'

George laughed, unperturbed. Evidently he was well used to the thrusts of the public house.

'I suppose you soon got over yours,' he said.

The old man raised himself and his eyes flickered into life. He chewed slowly, then said:

'I'd married, an' paid for it; I'd broke a constable's jaw an' paid for it; I'd deserted from the army, an' paid for that: I'd had a bullet through my cheek in India atop of it all, by I was your age.'

'Oh!' said George, with condescending interest, 'you've seen a bit of life then?'

They drew the old man out, and he told them in his slow, laconic fashion, a few brutal stories. They laughed and chaffed him. George seemed to have a thirst for tales of brutal experience, the raw gin of life. He drank it all in with relish, enjoying the sensation. The dinner was over. It was time to go out again to work.

'And how old are you, Dad?' George asked. The Parrot looked at him again with his heavy, tired, ironic eyes, and answered:

'If you'll be any better for knowing–sixty-four.'

'It's a bit rough on you, isn't it?' continued the young man, 'going round with the threshing machine and sleeping outdoors at that time of life? I should 'a thought you'd 'a wanted a bit o' comfort–'

'How do you mean, "rough on me"?' the Parrot replied slowly.

'Oh, I think you know what I mean,' answered George easily.

'Don't know as I do,' said the slow old Parrot.

'Well, you haven't made exactly a good thing out of life, have you?'

'What d'you mean by a good thing? I've had my life, an' I'm satisfied wi' it. Is'll die with a full belly.'

'Oh, so you have saved a bit?'

'No,' said the old man deliberately, 'I've spent as I've gone on. An' I've had all I wish for. But I pity the angels, when the Lord sets me before them like a book to read. Heaven won't be heaven just then.'

'You're a philosopher in your way,' laughed George.

'And you,' replied the old man, 'toddling about your backyard, think yourself mighty wise. But your wisdom 'll go with your teeth. You'll learn in time to say nothing.'

The old man went out and began his work, carrying the sacks of corn from the machine to the chamber.

'There's a lot in the old Parrot,' said George, 'as he'll never tell.'

I laughed.

'He makes you feel, as well, as if you'd a lot to discover in life,' he continued, looking thoughtfully over the dusty strawstack at the chuffing machine.

After the harvest was ended the father began to deplete his farm. Most of the stock was transferred to the Ram. George was going to take over his father's milk business, and was going to farm enough of the land attaching to the Inn to support nine or ten cows. Until the spring, however, Mr Saxton retained his own milk round, and worked at improving the condition of the land ready for the valuation. George, with three cows, started a little milk supply in the neighbourhood of the Inn, prepared his land for the summer, and helped in the public-house.

Emily was the first to depart finally from the Mill. She went to a school in Nottingham, and shortly afterwards Mollie, her younger sister, went to her. In October I moved to London. Lettie and Leslie were settled in their home in Brentwood, Yorkshire. We all felt very keenly our exile from Nethermere. But as yet the bonds were not broken; only use could sever them. Christmas brought us all home again, hastening to greet each other. There was a slight change in everybody. Lettie was brighter, more imperious, and very gay; Emily was quiet, self-restrained, and looked happier; Leslie was jollier and at the same time more subdued and earnest; George looked very healthy and happy, and sounded well pleased with himself; my mother with her gaiety at our return brought tears to our eyes.

We dined one evening at Highclose with the Tempests. It was dull as usual, and we left before ten o'clock. Lettie had changed her shoes and put on a fine cloak of greenish blue. We walked over the frost-bound road. The ice on Nethermere gleamed mysteriously in the moonlight, and uttered strange, half-audible whoops and yelps. The moon was very high in the sky, small and brilliant like a vial full of the pure white liquid of light. There was no sound in the night save the haunting movement of the ice, and the clear twinkle of Lettie's laughter.

On the drive leading to the wood we saw someone approaching. The wild grass was grey on either side, the thorn trees stood with shaggy black beards sweeping down, the pine trees were erect like dark soldiers. The black shape of the man drew near, with a shadow running at its feet. I recognised George, obscured as he was in his cap and his upturned collar. Lettie was in front with her husband. As George was passing, she said, in bright clear tones:

'A Happy New Year to you.'

He stopped, swung round, and laughed.

'I thought you wouldn't have known me,' he said.

'What, is it you, George?' cried Lettie in great surprise–'Now, what a joke! How are you?'–she put out her white hand from her draperies. He took it, and answered, 'I am very well–and you–?' However meaningless the words were, the tone was curiously friendly, intimate, informal.

'As you see,' she replied, laughing, interested in his attitude–'but where are you going?'

'I am going home,' he answered, in a voice that meant 'have you forgotten that I too am married'?

'Oh, of course!' cried Lettie. 'You are now mine host of the Ram. You must tell me about it. May I ask him to come home with us for an hour, Mother?–It is New Year's Eve, you know.'

'You have asked him already,' laughed Mother.

'Will Mrs Saxton spare you for so long?' asked Lettie of George.

'Meg? Oh, she does not order my comings and goings.'

'Does she not?' laughed Lettie. 'She is very unwise. Train up a husband in the way he should go, and in after life–I never could quote a text from end to end. I am full of beginnings, but as for a finish–! Leslie, my shoe-lace is untied–shall I wait till I can put my foot on the fence?'

Leslie knelt down at her feet. She shook the hood back from her head, and her ornaments sparkled in the moonlight. Her face with its whiteness and its shadows was full of fascination, and in their dark recesses her eyes thrilled George with hidden magic. She smiled at him along her cheeks while her husband crouched before her. Then, as the three walked along towards the wood she flung her draperies into loose eloquence and there was a glimpse of her bosom white with the moon. She laughed and chattered, and shook her silken stuffs, sending out a perfume exquisite on the frosted air. When we reached the house Lettie dropped her draperies and rustled into the drawing-room. There the lamp was low-lit, shedding a yellow twilight from the window space. Lettie stood between the firelight and the dusky lamp-glow, tall and warm between the lights. As she turned laughing to the two men, she let her cloak slide over her white shoulder and fall with silk splendour of a peacock's gorgeous blue over the arm of the large settee. There she stood, with her white hand upon the peacock of her cloak, where it tumbled against her dull orange dress. She knew her own splendour, and she drew up her throat laughing and brilliant with triumph. Then she raised both her arms to her head and remained for a moment delicately touching her hair into order, still fronting the two men. Then with a final little laugh she moved slowly and turned up the lamp, dispelling some of the witchcraft from the room. She had developed strangely in six months. She seemed to have discovered the wonderful charm of her womanhood. As she leaned forward with her arm outstretched to the lamp, as she delicately adjusted the wicks with mysterious fingers, she seemed to be moving in some alluring figure of a dance, her hair like a nimbus clouding the light, her bosom lit with wonder. The soft outstretching of her hand was like the whispering of strange words into the blood, and as she fingered a book the heart watched silently for the meaning.

'Won't you take off my shoes, darling?' she said, sinking among the cushions of the settee. Leslie kneeled again before her, and she bent her head and watched him.

'My feet are a tiny bit cold,' she said plaintively, giving him her foot, that seemed like gold in the yellow silk stocking. He took it between his hands, stroking it.

'It is quite cold,' he said, and he held both her feet in his hands.

'Ah, you dear boy!' she cried with sudden gentleness, bending forward and touching his cheek.

'Is it great fun being mine host of "Ye Ramme Inne"!' she said playfully to George. There seemed a long distance between them now as she sat, with the man in evening dress crouching before her putting golden shoes on her feet.

'It is rather,' he replied, 'the men in the smoke-room say such rum things. My word, you hear some tales there.'

'Tell us, do!' she pleaded.

'Oh! I couldn't. I never could tell a tale, and even if I could–well–'

'But I do long to hear,' she said, 'what the men say in the smoke-room of "Ye Ramme Inne". Is it quite untellable?'

'Quite!' he laughed.

'What a pity! See what a cruel thing it is to be a woman, Leslie: we never know what men say in smoke-rooms, while you read in your novels everything a woman ever uttered. It is a shame! George, you are a wretch, you should tell me. I do envy you–'

'What do you envy me, exactly?' he asked, laughing always at her whimsical way.

'Your smoke-room. The way you see life–or the way you hear it, rather.'

'But I should have thought you saw life ten times more than me,' he replied.

'I! I only see manners–good manners and bad manners. You know "manners maketh a man". That's when a woman's there. But you wait a while, you'll see.'

'When shall I see?' asked George, flattered and interested.

'When you have made the fortune you talked about,' she replied.

He was uplifted by her remembering the things he had said.

'But when I have made it–when!'–he said sceptically–'even then–well, I shall only be, or have been, landlord of "Ye Ramme Inne".' He looked at her, waiting for her to lift up his hopes with her gay balloons.

'Oh, that doesn't matter! Leslie might be landlord of some "Ram Inn" when he's at home, for all anybody would know–mightn't you, hubby, dear?'

'Thanks!' replied Leslie, with good-humoured sarcasm.

'You can't tell a publican from a peer, if he's a rich publican,' she continued. 'Money maketh the man, you know.'

'Plus manners,' added George, laughing.

'Oh, they are always there–where I am. I give you ten years. At the end of that time you must invite us to your swell place–say the Hall at Eberwich–and we will come–"with all our numerous array".'

She sat among her cushions smiling upon him. She was half ironical, half sincere. He smiled back at her, his dark eyes full of trembling hope, and pleasure, and pride.

'How is Meg?' she asked. 'Is she as charming as ever–or have you spoiled her?'

'Oh, she is as charming as ever,' he replied. 'And we are tremendously fond of one another.'

'That is right!–I do think men are delightful,' she added, smiling.

'I am glad you think so,' he laughed.

They talked on brightly about a thousand things. She touched on Paris, and pictures, and new music, with her quick chatter, sounding to George wonderful in her culture and facility. And at last he said he must go.

'Not until you have eaten a biscuit and drunk good luck with me,' she cried, catching her dress about her like a dim flame and running out of the room. We all drank to the New Year in the cold champagne.

'To the *Vita Nuova!*' said Lettie, and we drank, smiling.

'Hark!' said George, 'the hooters.'

We stood still and listened. There was a faint booing noise far away outside. It was midnight. Lettie caught up a wrap and we went to the door. The wood, the ice, the grey dim hills lay frozen in the light of the moon. But outside the valley, far away in Derbyshire, away towards Nottingham, on every hand the distant hooters and buzzers of mines and ironworks crowed small on the borders of the night, like so many strange, low voices of cockerels bursting forth at different pitch, with different tone, warning us of the dawn of the New Year.

3

THE FIRST PAGES OF SEVERAL ROMANCES

I found a good deal of difference in Leslie since his marriage. He had lost his assertive self-confidence. He no longer pronounced emphatically and ultimately on every subject, nor did he seek to dominate, as he had always done, the company in which he found himself. I was surprised to see him so courteous and attentive to George. He moved unobtrusively about the room while Lettie was chattering, and in his demeanour there was a new reserve, a gentleness and grace. It was charming to see him offering the cigarettes to George, or, with beautiful tact, asking with his eyes only whether he should refill the glass of his guest, and afterward replacing it softly close to the other's hand.

To Lettie he was unfailingly attentive, courteous, and undemonstrative.

Towards the end of my holiday he had to go to London on business, and we agreed to take the journey together. We must leave Woodside soon after eight o'clock in the morning. Lettie and he had separate rooms. I thought she would not have risen to take breakfast with us, but at a quarter-past seven, just as Rebecca was bringing in the coffee, she came downstairs. She wore a blue morning-gown, and her hair was as beautifully dressed as usual.

'Why, my darling, you shouldn't have troubled to come down so early,' said Leslie, as he kissed her.

'Of course, I should come down,' she replied, lifting back the heavy curtains and looking out on the snow where the darkness was wilting into daylight. 'I should not let you go away into the cold without having seen you take a good breakfast. I think it is thawing. The snow on the rhododendrons looks sodden and drooping. Ah, well, we can keep out the dismal of the morning for another hour.' She glanced at the clock–'just an hour!' she added. He turned to her with a swift tenderness. She smiled to him, and sat down at the coffee-maker. We took our places at table.

'I think I shall come back tonight,' he said quietly, almost appealingly.

She watched the flow of the coffee before she answered. Then the brass urn swung back, and she lifted her face to hand him the cup.

'You will not do anything so foolish, Leslie,' she said calmly.

He took his cup, thanking her, and bent his face over the fragrant steam.

'I can easily catch the 7.15 from St Pancras,' he replied, without looking up.

'Have I sweetened to your liking Cyril?' she asked, and then, as she stirred her coffee she added, 'It is ridiculous, Leslie! You catch the 7.15 and very probably miss the connection at Nottingham. You can't have the motor-car there, because of the roads. Besides, it is absurd to come toiling home in the cold slushy night when you can just as well stay in London and be comfortable.'

'At any rate I should get the 10.30 down to Lawton Hill,' he urged.

'But there is no need,' she replied, 'there is not the faintest need for you to come home tonight. It is really absurd of you. Think of all the discomfort! Indeed I should not want to come trailing dismally home at midnight, I should not indeed. You would be simply wretched. Stay and have a jolly evening with Cyril.'

He kept his head bent over his plate and did not reply. His persistence irritated her slightly.

'That is what you can do!' she said. 'Go to the pantomime. Or wait–go to Maeterlinck's "Blue Bird". I am sure that is on somewhere. I wonder if Rebecca has destroyed yesterday's paper. Do you mind touching the bell, Cyril?' Rebecca came, and the paper was discovered. Lettie carefully read the notices, and planned for us with zest a delightful programme for the evening. Leslie listened to it all in silence.

When the time had come for our departure Lettie came with us into the hall to see that we were well wrapped up. Leslie had spoken very few words. She was conscious that he was deeply offended, but her manner was quite calm, and she petted us both brightly.

'Good-bye dear!' she said to him, when he came mutely to kiss her. 'You know it would have been miserable for you to sit all those hours in the train at night. You will have ever such a jolly time. I know you will. I shall look for you tomorrow. Good-bye, then, good-bye!'

He went down the steps and into the car without looking at her. She waited in the doorway as we moved round. In the black-grey morning she seemed to harbour the glittering blue sky and the sunshine of March in her dress and her luxuriant hair. He did not look at her till we were curving to the great, snow-cumbered rhododendrons, when, at the last moment he stood up in a sudden panic to wave to her. Almost as he saw her the bushes came between them and he dropped dejectedly into his seat.

'Good-bye!' we heard her call cheerfully and tenderly like a blackbird.

'Good-bye!' I answered, and: 'Good-bye Darling, good-bye!' he cried, suddenly starting up in a passion of forgiveness and tenderness.

The car went cautiously down the soddened white path, under the trees.

I suffered acutely the sickness of exile in Norwood. For weeks I wandered the streets of the suburb, haunted by the spirit of some part of Nethermere. As I went along the quiet roads where the lamps in yellow loneliness stood among the leafless trees of the night I would feel the feeling of the dark, wet bit of path between the wood meadow and the brooks. The spirit of that wild little slope to the Mill would come upon me, and there in the suburb of London I would walk wrapt in the sense of a small wet place in the valley of Nethermere. A strange voice within me rose and called for the hill path; again I could feel the wood waiting for me, calling and calling, and I crying for the wood, yet the space of many miles was between us. Since I left the valley of home I have not much feared any other loss. The hills of Nethermere had been my walls, and the sky of Nethermere my roof overhead. It seemed almost as if, at home, I might lift my hand to the ceiling of the valley, and touch my own beloved sky, whose familiar clouds came again and again to visit me, whose stars were constant to me, born when I was born, whose sun had been all my father to me. But now the skies were strange over my head, and Orion walked past me unnoticing, he who night after night had stood over the woods to spend with me a wonderful hour. When does day now lift up the confines of my dwelling place, when does the night throw open her vastness for me, and send me the stars for company? There is no night in a city. How can I lose myself in the magnificent forest of darkness when night is only a thin scattering of the trees of shadow with barrenness of lights between!

I could never lift my eyes save to the Crystal Palace, crouching, cowering wretchedly among the yellow-grey clouds, pricking up its two round towers like pillars of anxious misery. No landmark could have been more foreign to me, more depressing, than the great dilapidated palace which lay for ever prostrate above us, fretting because of its own degradation and ruin.

I watched the buds coming on the brown almond trees; I heard the blackbirds, and saw the restless starlings; in the streets were many heaps of violets, and men held forward to me snowdrops whose white mute lips were pushed upwards in a bunch: but these things had no meaning for me, and little interest.

Most eagerly I waited for my letters. Emily wrote to me very constantly:

'Don't you find it quite exhilarating, almost intoxicating, to be so free? I think it is quite wonderful. At home you cannot live your own life. You have to struggle to keep even a little apart for yourself. It is so hard to stand aloof from our mothers, and yet they are only hurt and insulted if you tell them what is in your heart. It is such a relief not to have to be anything to anybody, but just to please yourself. I am sure Mother and I have suffered a great deal from trying to keep up our old relations. Yet she would not let me go. When I come home in the evening and think that I needn't say anything to anybody, nor do anything for anybody, but just have the evening for myself, I am overjoyed.

'I have begun to write a story—'

Again, a little later, she wrote:

'As I go to school by Old Brayford village in the morning the birds are thrilling wonderfully and everything seems stirring. Very likely there will be a set-back, and after that spring will come in truth.

'When shall you come and see me? I cannot think of a spring without you. The railways are the only fine exciting things here—one is only a few yards away from school. All day long I am watching the great Midland trains go south. They are very lucky to be able to rush southward through the sunshine.

'The crows are very interesting. They flap past all the time we're out in the yard. The railways and the crows make the charm of my life in Brayford. The other day I saw no end of pairs of crows. Do you remember what they say at home?–"One for sorrow." Very often one solitary creature sits on the telegraph wires. I almost hate him when I look at him. I think my badge for life ought to be–one crow–'

Again, a little later:

'I have been home for the week-end. Isn't it nice to be made much of, to be an important cherished person for a little time? It is quite a new experience for me.

'The snowdrops are full out among the grass in the front garden–and such a lot. I imagined you must come in the sunshine of the Sunday afternoon to see them. It did not seem possible you should not. The winter aconites are out along the hedge. I knelt and kissed them. I have been so glad to go away, to breathe the free air of life, but I felt as if I could not come away from the aconites. I have sent you some–are they much withered?

'Now I am in my lodgings, I have the quite unusual feeling of being contented to stay here a little while–not long–not above a year, I am sure. But even to be contented for a little while is enough for me–'

In the beginning of March I had a letter from the father:

'You'll not see us again in the old place. We shall be gone in a fortnight. The things are most of them gone already. George has got Bob and Flower. I have sold three of the cows, Stafford, and Julia and Hannah. The place looks very empty. I don't like going past the cowsheds, and we miss hearing the horses stamp at night. But I shall not be sorry when we have really gone. I begin to feel as if we'd stagnated here. I begin to feel as if I was settling and getting narrow and dull. It will be a new lease of life to get away.

'But I'm wondering how we shall be over there. Mrs Saxton feels very nervous about going. But at the worst we can but come back. I feel as if I must go somewhere, it's stagnation and starvation for us here. I wish George would come with me. I never thought he would have taken to public-house keeping, but he seems to like it all right. He was down with Meg on Sunday. Mrs Saxton says he's getting a public-house tone. He is certainly much livelier, more full of talk than he was. Meg and he seem very comfortable, I'm glad to say. He's got a good milk round, and I've no doubt but what he'll do well. He is very cautious at the bottom; he'll never lose much if he never makes much.

'Sam and David are very great friends. I'm glad I've got the boy. We often talk of you. It would be very lonely if it wasn't for the excitement of selling things and so on. Mrs Saxton hopes you will stick by George. She worries a bit about him, thinking he may go wrong. I don't think he will ever go far. But I should be glad to know you were keeping friends. Mrs Saxton says she will write to you about it–'

George was a very poor correspondent. I soon ceased to expect a letter from him. I received one directly after the father's.

My Dear Cyril,

Forgive me for not having written you before, but you see, I cannot sit down and write to you any time. If I cannot do it just when I am in the mood, I cannot do it at all. And it so often happens that the mood comes upon me when I am in the fields at work, when it is impossible to write. Last night I sat by myself in the kitchen on purpose to write to you, and then I could not. All day, at Greymede, when I was drilling in the fallow at the back of the church, I had been thinking of you, and I could have written there if I had had materials, but I had not, and at night I could not.

I am sorry to say that in my last letter I did not thank you for the books. I have not read them both, but I have nearly finished Evelyn Innes. I get a bit tired of it towards the end. I do not do much reading now. There seems to be hardly any chance for me, either somebody is crying for me in the smoke-room, or there is some business, or else Meg won't let me. She doesn't like me to read at night, she says I ought to talk to her, so I have to.

It is half-past seven, and I am sitting ready dressed to go and talk to Harry Jackson about a young horse he wants to sell to me. He is in pretty low water, and it will make a pretty good horse. But I don't care much whether I have it or not. The mood seized me to write to you. Somehow at the bottom I feel miserable and heavy, yet there is no need. I am making pretty good money, and I've got all I want. But when I've been ploughing and getting the oats in those fields on the hillside at the back of Greymede church, I've felt as if I didn't care whether I got on or not. It's very funny. Last week I made over five pounds clear, one way and another, and yet now I'm as restless, and discontented as I can be, and I seem eager for something, but I don't know what it is. Sometimes I wonder where I am going. Yesterday I watched broken white masses of cloud sailing across the sky in a fresh strong wind. They all seemed to be going somewhere. I wondered where the wind was blowing them. I don't seem to have hold on anything, do I? Can you tell me what I want at the bottom of my heart? I wish you were here, then I think I should not feel like this. But generally I don't, generally I am quite jolly, and busy.

By jove, here's Harry Jackson come for me. I will finish this letter when I get back.

— I have got back, we have turned out, but I cannot finish. I cannot tell you all about it. I've had a little row with Meg. Oh, I've had a rotten time. But I cannot tell you about it tonight, it is late, and I am tired, and have a headache. Some other time perhaps—

GEORGE SAXTON.

The spring came bravely, even in south London, and the town was filled with magic. I never knew the sumptuous purple of evening till I saw the round arc-lamps fill with light, and roll like golden bubbles along the purple dusk of the high road. Everywhere at night the city is filled with the magic of lamps: over the river they pour in golden patches their floating luminous oil on the restless darkness; the bright lamps float in and out of the cavern of London Bridge Station like round shining bees in and out of a black hive; in the suburbs the street lamps glimmer with the brightness of lemons among the trees. I began to love the town.

In the mornings I loved to move in the aimless street's procession, watching the faces come near to me, with the sudden glance of dark eyes, watching the mouths of the women blossom with talk as they passed, watching the subtle movements of the shoulders of men beneath their coats, and the naked warmth of their necks that went glowing along the street. I loved the city intensely for its movement of men and women, the soft, fascinating flow of the limbs of men and women, and the sudden flash of eyes and lips as they pass. Among all the faces of the street my attention roved like a bee which clambers drunkenly among blue flowers. I became intoxicated with the strange nectar which I sipped out of the eyes of the passers-by.

I did not know how time was hastening by on still bright wings, till I saw the scarlet hawthorn flaunting over the road, and the lime buds lit up like wine drops in the sun, and the pink scarves of the lime buds pretty as louse-wort a-blossom in the gutters, and a silver-pink tangle of almond boughs against the blue sky. The lilacs came out, and in the pensive stillness of the suburb, at night, came the delicious tarry scent of lilac flowers, wakening a silent laughter of romance.

Across all this, strangely, came the bleak sounds of home. Alice wrote to me at the end of May:

'Cyril dear, prepare yourself. Meg has got twins—yesterday. I went up to see how she was this afternoon, not knowing anything, and there I found a pair of bubs in the nest, and old Ma Stainwright bossing the show. I nearly fainted. Sybil dear, I hardly knew whether to laugh or to cry when I saw those two rummy little round heads, like two larch cones cheek by cheek on a twig. One is a darkie, with lots of black hair, and the other is red, would you believe it, just lit up with thin red hair like a flicker of firelight. I gasped. I believe I did shed a few tears, though what for, I don't know.

'The old grandma is a perfect old wretch over it. She lies chuckling and passing audible remarks in the next room, as pleased as punch really, but so mad because Ma Stainwright wouldn't have them taken in to her. You should have heard her when we took them in at last. They are both boys. She did make a fuss, poor old woman. I think she's going a bit funny in the head. She seemed sometimes to think they were hers, and you should have heard her, the way she talked to them, it made me feel quite funny. She wanted them lying against her on the pillow, so that she could feel them with her face. I shed a few more tears, Sybil. I think I must be going dotty also. But she came round when we took them away, and began to chuckle to herself, and talk about the things she'd say to George when he came—awful shocking things, Sybil, made me blush dreadfully.

'Georgie didn't know about it then. He was down at Bingham, buying some horses, I believe. He seems to have got a craze for buying horses. He got in with Harry Jackson and Mayhew's sons—you know, they were horse dealers—at least their father was. You remember he died bankrupt about three years ago. There are Fred and Duncan left, and they pretend to keep on the old business. They are always up at the Ram, and Georgie is always driving about with them. I don't like it—they are a loose lot, rather common, and poor enough now.

'Well, I thought I'd wait and see Georgie. He came about half-past five. Meg had been fidgeting about him, wondering where he was, and how he was, and so on. Bless me if I'd worry and whittle about a man. The old grandma heard the cart, and before he could get down she shouted—you know her room is in the front—"Hi, George, ma lad, sharpen thy shins an' com' an' a'e a look at 'em—thee'r's two on 'em, two on 'em!" and she laughed something awful.

'"'Ello Granma, what art ter shoutin' about?" he said, and at the sound of his voice Meg turned to me so pitiful, and said:

'"He's been wi' them Mayhews."

'"Tha's gotten twins, a couple at a go, ma lad!" shouted the old woman, and you know how she gives squeal before she laughs! She made the horse shy, and he swore at it something awful. Then Bill took it, and Georgie came upstairs. I saw Meg seem to shrink when she heard him kick at the stairs as he came up, and she went white. When he got to the top he came in. He fairly reeked of whisky and horses. Bah, a man is hateful when he reeks of drink! He stood by the side of the bed grinning like a fool, and saying, quite thick:

'"You've bin in a bit of a 'urry, 'aven't you Meg. An' how are ter feeling' then?"

'"Oh, I'm a' right," said Meg.

'"Is it twins, straight?" he said; "Wheer is 'em?"

'Meg looked over at the cradle, and he went round the bed to it, holding to the bed-rail. He had never kissed her, nor anything. When he saw the twins, asleep with their fists shut tight as wax, he gave a laugh as if he was amused, and said:

'"Two right enough—an' one on 'em red! Which is the girl, Meg, the black 'un?"

'"They're both boys," said Meg, quite timidly.

'He turned round, and his eyes went little.

'"Blast 'em then!" he said. He stood there looking like a devil. Sybil dear, I did not know our George could look like that. I thought he could only look like a faithful dog or a wounded stag. But he looked fiendish. He stood watching the poor little twins, scowling at them, till at last the little red one began to whine a bit. Ma Stainwright came pushing her fat carcass in front of him and bent over the baby, saying:

'"Why, my pretty, what are they doin' to thee, what are they?—What are they doin' to thee?"

'Georgie scowled blacker than ever, and went out, lurching against the washstand and making the pots rattle till my heart jumped in my throat.

'"Well, if you don't call that scandylos—!" said old Ma Stainwright, and Meg began to cry. You don't know, Cyril! She sobbed fit to break her heart. I felt as if I could have killed him.

'That old gran'ma began talking to him, and he laughed at her. I do hate to hear a man laugh when he's half drunk. It makes my blood boil all of a sudden. That old grandmother backs him up in everything, she's a regular nuisance. Meg has cried to me before over the pair of them. The wicked, vulgar old thing that she is—'

I went home to Woodside early in September. Emily was staying at the Ram. It was strange that everything was so different. Nethermere even had changed. Nethermere was no longer a complete, wonderful little world that held us charmed inhabitants. It was a small, insignificant valley lost in the spaces of the earth. The tree that had drooped over the brook with such delightful, romantic grace was a ridiculous thing when I came home after a year of absence in the south. The old symbols were trite and foolish.

Emily and I went down one morning to Strelley Mill. The house was occupied by a labourer and his wife, strangers from the north. He was tall, very thin, and silent, strangely suggesting kinship with the rats of the place. She was small and very active, like some ragged domestic fowl run wild. Already Emily had visited her, so she invited us into the kitchen of the mill, and set forward the chairs for us. The large room had the barren air of a cell. There was a small table stranded towards the fireplace, and a few chairs by the walls; for the rest, desert spaces of flagged floor retreating into shadow. On the walls by the windows were five cages of canaries, and the small sharp movements of the birds made the room more strange in its desolation. When we began to talk the birds began to sing, till we were quite bewildered, for the little woman spoke Glasgow Scotch, and she had a hare lip. She rose and ran towards the cages, crying herself like some wild fowl, and flapping a duster at the warbling canaries.

'Stop it, stop it!' she cried, shaking her thin weird body at them. 'Silly little devils, fools, fools, fools!!' and she flapped the duster till the birds were subdued. Then she brought us delicious scones and apple jelly, urging us, almost nudging us with her thin elbows to make us eat.

'Don't you like 'em, don't you? Well, eat 'em, eat 'em then. Go on, Emily, go on, eat some more. Only don't tell Tom—don't tell Tom when 'e comes in'—she shook her head and laughed her shrilling, weird laughter.

As we were going she came out with us, and went running on in front. We could not help noting how ragged and unkempt was her short black skirt. But she hastened around us, hither and thither like an excited fowl, talking in her high-pitched, unintelligible manner. I could not believe the brooding mill was in her charge. I could not think this was the Strelley Mill of a year ago. She fluttered up the steep orchard bank in front of us. Happening to turn round and see Emily and me smiling at each other she began to laugh her strident, weird laughter, saying, with a leer:

'Emily, he's your sweetheart, your sweetheart, Emily! You never told me!' and she laughed aloud.

We blushed furiously. She came away from the edge of the sluice gully, nearer to us, crying:

'You've been here o' nights, haven't you, Emily—haven't you?' and she laughed again. Then she sat down suddenly, and pointing above our heads, shrieked:

'Ah, look there!'—we looked and saw the mistletoe. 'Look at her, look at her! How many kisses a night, Emily?—Ha! Ha! Kisses all the year! Kisses o' nights in a lonely place.'

She went on wildly for a short time, then she dropped her voice and talked in low, pathetic tones. She pressed on us scones and jelly and oat-cakes, and we left her.

When we were out on the road by the brook Emily looked at me with shamefaced, laughing eyes. I noticed a small movement of her lips, and in an instant I found myself kissing her, laughing with some of the little woman's wildness.

4

DOMESTIC LIFE AT THE RAM

George was very anxious to receive me at his home. The Ram had as yet only a six days' licence, so on Sunday afternoon I walked over to tea. It was very warm and still and sunny as I came through Greymede. A few sweethearts were sauntering under the horse-chestnut trees, or crossing the road to go into the fields that lay smoothly carpeted after the hay-harvest.

As I came round the flagged track to the kitchen door of the inn I heard the slur of a baking-tin and the bang of the oven door, and Meg saying crossly:

'No, don't you take him, Emily—naughty little thing! Let his father hold him!'

One of the babies was crying.

I entered, and found Meg all flushed and untidy, wearing a large white apron, just rising from the oven. Emily, in a cream dress, was taking a red-haired, crying baby from out of the cradle. George sat in the small arm-chair, smoking and looking cross.

'I can't shake hands,' said Meg, rather flurried. 'I am all floury. Sit down, will you—' and she hurried out of the room. Emily looked up from the complaining baby to me and smiled a woman's rare, intimate smile, which says: 'See, I am engaged thus for a moment, but I keep my heart for you all the time.'

George rose and offered me the round arm-chair. It was the highest honour he could do me. He asked me what I would drink. When I refused everything, he sat down heavily on the sofa, frowning, and angrily cudgelling his wits for something to say—in vain.

The room was large and comfortably furnished with rush-chairs, a glass-knobbed dresser, a cupboard with glass doors, perched on a shelf in the corner, and the usual large sofa whose cosy loose-bed and pillows were covered with red cotton stuff. There was a peculiar reminiscence of victuals and drink in the room; beer, and a touch of spirits, and bacon. Teenie, the sullen, black-browed servant girl came in carrying the other baby, and Meg called from the scullery to ask her if the child were asleep. Meg was evidently in a bustle and a flurry, a most uncomfortable state.

'No,' replied Teenie, 'he's not for sleep this day.'

'Mend the fire and see to the oven, and then put him his frock on,' replied Meg testily. Teenie set the black-haired baby in the second cradle. Immediately he began to cry, or rather to shout his remonstrance. George went across to him and picked up a white furry rabbit, which he held before the child.

'Here, look at bun-bun! Have your nice rabbit! Hark at it squeaking!'

The baby listened for a moment, then, deciding that this was only a put-off, began to cry again. George threw down the rabbit and took the baby, swearing inwardly. He dandled the child on his knee.

'What's up then?–What's up wi' thee? Have a ride then–dee-de-dee-de-dee!'

But the baby knew quite well what was the father's feeling towards him, and he continued to cry.

'Hurry up, Teenie!' said George as the maid rattled the coal on the fire. Emily was walking about hushing her charge, and smiling at me, so that I had a peculiar pleasure in gathering for myself the honey of endearment which she shed on the lips of the baby. George handed over his child to the maid, and said to me with patient sarcasm:

'Will you come in the garden?'

I rose and followed him across the sunny flagged yard, along the path between the bushes. He lit his pipe and sauntered along as a man on his own estate does, feeling as if he were untrammeled by laws or conventions.

'You know,' he said, 'she's a dam rotten manager.'

I laughed, and remarked how full of plums the trees were.

'Yes!' he replied heedlessly–'you know she ought to have sent the girl out with the kids this afternoon, and have got dressed directly. But no, she must sit gossiping with Emily all the time they were asleep, and then as soon as they wake up she begins to make cake–'

'I suppose she felt she'd enjoy a pleasant chat, all quiet,' I answered.

'But she knew quite well you were coming, and what it would be. But a woman's no dam foresight.'

'Nay, what does it matter!' said I.

'Sunday's the only day we can have a bit of peace, so she might keep 'em quiet then.'

'I suppose it was the only time, too, that she could have a quiet gossip,' I replied.

'But you don't know,' he said, 'there seems to be never a minute of freedom. Teenie sleeps in now, and lives with us in the kitchen–Oswald as well–so I never know what it is to have a moment private. There doesn't seem a single spot anywhere where I can sit quiet. It's the kids all day, and the kids all night, and the servants, and then all the men in the house–I sometimes feel as if I should like to get away. I shall leave the pub as soon as I can–only Meg doesn't want to.'

'But if you leave the public-house–what then?'

'I should like to get back on a farm. This is no sort of a place, really, for farming. I've always got some business on hand. There's a traveller to see, or

I've got to go to the brewers, or I've somebody to look at a horse, or something. Your life's all messed up. If I had a place of my own, and farmed it in peace—'

'You'd be as miserable as you could be,' I said.

'Perhaps so,' he assented, in his old reflective manner. 'Perhaps so! Anyhow, I needn't bother, for I feel as if I never shall go back—to the land.'

'Which means at the bottom of your heart you don't intend to,' I said, laughing.

'Perhaps so!' he again yielded. 'You see, I'm doing pretty well here—apart from the public-house: I always think that's Meg's. Come and look in the stable. I've got a shire mare and two nags: pretty good; I went down to Melton Mowbray with Tom Mayhew, to a chap they've had dealings with. Tom's all right, and he knows how to buy, but he is such a lazy, careless devil, too lazy to be bothered to sell—'

George was evidently interested. As we went round to the stables, Emily came out with the baby, which was dressed in a new silk frock. She advanced, smiling to me with dark eyes.

'See, now he is good! Doesn't he look pretty?'

She held the baby for me to look at. I glanced at it, but I was only conscious of the near warmth of her cheek, and of the scent of her hair.

'Who is he like?' I asked, looking up and finding myself full in her eyes. The question was quite irrelevant: her eyes spoke a whole clear message that made my heart throb; yet she answered.

'Who is he? Why, nobody, of course! But he *will* be like Father, don't you think?'

The question drew my eyes to hers again, and again we looked each other the strange intelligence that made her flush and me breathe in as I smiled.

'Ay! Blue eyes like your father's—not like yours—'

Again the wild messages in her looks.

'No!' she answered very softly. 'And I think he'll be jolly, like Father—they have neither of them our eyes, have they?'

'No,' I answered, overcome by a sudden hot flush of tenderness. 'No—not vulnerable. To have such soft, vulnerable eyes as you used makes one feel nervous and irascible. But you have clothed over the sensitiveness of yours, haven't you?—like naked life, naked defenceless protoplasm they were, is it not so?'

She laughed, and at the old painful memories she dilated in the old way, and I felt the old tremor at seeing her soul flung quivering on my pity.

'And were mine like that?' asked George, who had come up.

He must have perceived the bewilderment of my look as I tried to adjust myself to him. A slight shadow, a slight chagrin appeared on his face.

'Yes,' I answered, 'yes—but not so bad. You never gave yourself away so much—you were most cautious: but just as defenceless.'

'And am I altered?' he asked, with quiet irony, as if he knew I was not interested in him.

'Yes, more cautious. You keep in the shadow. But Emily has clothed herself, and can now walk among the crowd at her own gait.'

It was with an effort I refrained from putting my lips to kiss her at that moment as she looked at me with womanly dignity and tenderness. Then I remembered, and said:

'But you are taking me to the stable, George! Come and see the horses too, Emily.'

'I will. I admire them so much,' she replied, and thus we both indulged him. He talked to his horses and of them, laying his hand upon them, running over their limbs. The glossy, restless animals interested him more than anything. He broke into a little flush of enthusiasm over them. They were his new interest. They were quiet and yet responsive; he was their master and owner. This gave him real pleasure.

But the baby became displeased again. Emily looked at me for sympathy with him.

'He is a little wanderer,' she said, 'he likes to be always moving. Perhaps he objects to the ammonia of stables too,' she added, frowning and laughing slightly; 'It is not very agreeable, is it?'

'Not particularly,' I agreed, and as she moved off I went with her, leaving him in the stables. When Emily and I were alone we sauntered aimlessly back to the garden. She persisted in talking to the baby, and in talking to me about the baby, till I wished the child in Jericho. This made her laugh, and she continued to tantalise me. The hollyhock flowers of the second whorl were flushing to the top of the spires. The bees, covered with pale crumbs of pollen, were swaying a moment outside the wide gates of the florets, then they swung in with excited hum, and clung madly to the furry white capitals, and worked riotously round the waxy bases. Emily held out the baby to watch, talking all the time in low, fond tones. The child stretched towards the bright flowers. The sun glistened on his smooth hair as on bronze dust, and the wondering blue eyes of the baby followed the bees. Then he made small sounds, and suddenly waved his hands, like rumpled pink hollyhock buds.

'Look!' said Emily, 'look at the little bees! Ah, but you mustn't touch them, they bite. They're coming!' she cried, with sudden laughing apprehension, drawing the child away. He made noises of remonstrance. She put him near to the flowers again till he knocked the spire with his hand and two indignant bees came sailing out. Emily drew back quickly crying in alarm, then laughing with excited eyes at me, as if she had just escaped a peril in my presence. Thus she teased me by flinging me all kinds of bright gages of love while she kept me aloof because of the child. She laughed with pure pleasure at this state of affairs, and delighted the more when I frowned, till at last I swallowed my resentment and laughed too, playing with the hands of the baby, and watching his blue eyes change slowly like a softly sailing sky.

Presently Meg called us in to tea. She wore a dress of fine blue stuff with cream silk embroidery, and she looked handsome, for her hair was very hastily dressed.

'What, have you had that child all this time?' she exclaimed, on seeing Emily. 'Where is his father?'

'I don't know—we left him in the stable, didn't we, Cyril? But I like nursing him, Meg. I like it ever so much,' replied Emily.

'Oh yes, you may be sure George would get off it if he could. He's always in the stable. As I tell him, he fair stinks of horses. He's not that fond of the children, I can tell you. Come on, my pet—why, come to its mammy.'

She took the baby and kissed it passionately, and made extravagant love to it. A clean-shaven young man with thick bare arms went across the yard.

'Here, just look and tell George as tea is ready,' said Meg.

'Where is he?' asked Oswald, the sturdy youth who attended to the farm business.

'You know where to find him,' replied Meg, with that careless freedom which was so subtly derogatory to her husband.

George came hurrying from the out-building. 'What, is it tea already?' he said.

'It's a wonder you haven't been crying out for it this last hour,' said Meg.

'It's a marvel you've got dressed so quick,' he replied.

'Oh, is it?' she answered–'well, it's not with any of your help that I've done it, that is a fact. Where's Teenie?'

The maid, short, stiffly built, very dark and sullen-looking, came forward from the gate.

'Can you take Alfy as well, just while we have tea?' she asked. Teenie replied that she should think she could, whereupon she was given the ruddy-haired baby, as well as the dark one. She sat with them on a seat at the end of the yard. We proceeded to tea.

It was a very great spread. There were hot cakes, three or four kinds of cold cakes, tinned apricots, jellies, tinned lobster, and trifles in the way of jam, cream, and rum.

'I don't know what those cakes are like,' said Meg. 'I made them in such a fluster. Really, you have to do things as best you can when you've got children–especially when there's two. I never seem to have time to do my hair up even–look at it now.'

She put up her hands to her head, and I could not help noticing how grimy and rough were her nails.

The tea was going on pleasantly when one of the babies began to cry. Teenie bent over it crooning gruffly. I leaned back and looked out of the door to watch her. I thought of the girl in Tchekoff's story, who smothered her charge, and I hoped the grim Teenie would not be driven to such desperation. The other child joined in this chorus. Teenie rose from her seat and walked about the yard, gruffly trying to soothe the twins.

'It's a funny thing, but whenever anybody comes they're sure to be cross,' said Meg, beginning to simmer.

'They're no different from ordinary,' said George, 'it's only that you're forced to notice it then.'

'No, it is not!' cried Meg in a sudden passion:

'Is it now, Emily? Of course, *he* has to say something! Weren't they as good as gold this morning, Emily?–and yesterday!–Why, they never murmured, as good as gold they were. But he wants them to be as dumb as fishes: he'd like them shutting up in a box as soon as they make a bit of noise.'

'I was not saying anything about it,' he replied.

'Yes, you were,' she retorted. 'I don't know what you call it then–'

The babies outside continued to cry.

'Bring Alfy to me,' called Meg, yielding to the mother feeling.

'Oh no, damn it!' said George, 'let Oswald take him.'

'Yes,' replied Meg bitterly, 'let anybody take him so long as he's out of your sight. You never ought to have children, you didn't–'

George murmured something about 'today'.

'Come then!' said Meg, with a whole passion of tenderness, as she took the red-haired baby and held it to her bosom. 'Why, what is it then, what is it, my precious? Hush then, pet, hush then!'

The baby did not hush. Meg rose from her chair and stood rocking the baby in her arms, swaying from one foot to the other.

'He's got a bit of wind,' she said.

We tried to continue the meal, but everything was awkward and difficult.

'I wonder if he's hungry,' said Meg, 'let's try him.'

She turned away and gave him her breast. Then he was still, so she covered herself as much as she could, and sat down again to tea. We had finished, so we sat and waited while she ate. This disjointing of the meal, by reflex action, made Emily and me more accurate. We were exquisitely attentive, and polite to a nicety. Our very speech was clipped with precision, as we drifted to a discussion of Strauss and Dèbussy. This of course put a breach between us two and our hosts, but we could not help it; it was our only way of covering over the awkwardness of the occasion. George sat looking glum and listening to us. Meg was quite indifferent. She listened occasionally, but her position as mother made her impregnable. She sat eating calmly, looking down now and again at her baby, holding us in slight scorn, babblers that we were. She was secure in her high maternity; she was mistress and sole authority. George, as father, was first servant; as an indifferent father, she humiliated him and was hostile to his wishes. Emily and I were mere intruders, feeling ourselves such. After tea we went upstairs to wash our hands. The grandmother had had a second stroke of paralysis, and lay inert, almost stupefied. Her large bulk upon the bed was horrible to me, and her face, with the muscles all slack and awry, seemed like some cruel cartoon. She spoke a few thick words to me. George asked her if she felt all right, or should he rub her. She turned her old eyes slowly to him.

'My leg—my leg a bit,' she said in her strange guttural.

He took off his coat, and pushing his hand under the bed-clothes, sat rubbing the poor old woman's limb patiently, slowly, for some time. She watched him for a moment, then without her turning her eyes from him, he passed out of her vision and she lay staring at nothing, in his direction.

'There,' he said at last, 'is that any better then, Mother?'

'Ay, that's a bit better,' she said slowly.

'Should I gi'e thee a drink?' he asked, lingering, wishing to minister all he could to her before he went.

She looked at him, and he brought the cup. She swallowed a few drops with difficulty.

'Doesn't it make you miserable to have her always there?' I asked him, when we were in the next room. He sat down on the large white bed and laughed shortly.

'We're used to it—we never notice her, poor old gran'ma.'

'But she must have made a difference to you—she must make a big difference at the bottom, even if you don't know it,' I said.

'She'd got such a strong character,' he said, musing, '—she seemed to understand me. She was a real friend to me before she was so bad. Sometimes I happen to look at her—generally I never see her, you know how I mean—but sometimes I do—and then—it seems a bit rotten—'

He smiled at me peculiarly, '—it seems to take the shine off things,' he added, and then, smiling again with ugly irony—'She's our skeleton in the closet.' He indicated her large bulk.

The church bells began to ring. The grey church stood on a rise among the fields not far away, like a handsome old stag looking over towards the inn. The five bells began to play, and the sound came beating upon the window.

'I hate Sunday night,' he said restlessly.

'Because you've nothing to do?' I asked.

'I don't know,' he said. 'It seems like a gag, and you feel helpless. I don't

want to go to church, and hark at the bells, they make you feel uncomfortable.'
'What do you generally do?' I asked.

'Feel miserable–I've been down to Mayhew's these last two Sundays, and Meg's been pretty mad. She says it's the only night I could stop with her, or go out with her. But if I stop with her, what can I do?–and if we go out, it's only for half an hour. I hate Sunday night–it's a dead end.'

When we went downstairs, the table was cleared, and Meg was bathing the dark baby. Thus she was perfect. She handled the bonny, naked child with beauty of gentleness. She kneeled over him nobly. Her arms and her bosom and her throat had a nobility of roundness and softness. She drooped her head with the grace of a Madonna, and her movements were lovely, accurate and exquisite, like an old song perfectly sung. Her voice, playing and soothing round the curved limbs of the baby, was like water, soft as wine in the sun, running with delight.

We watched humbly, sharing the wonder from afar.

Emily was very envious of Meg's felicity. She begged to be allowed to bathe the second baby. Meg granted her bounteous permission:

'Yes, you can wash him if you like, but what about your frock?'

Emily, delighted, began to undress the baby whose hair was like crocus petals. Her fingers trembled with pleasure as she loosed the little tapes. I always remember the inarticulate delight with which she took the child in her hands, when at last his little shirt was removed, and felt his soft white limbs and body. A distinct, glowing atmosphere seemed suddenly to burst out around her and the child, leaving me outside. The moment before she had been very near to me, her eyes searching mine, her spirit clinging timidly about me. Now I was put away, quite alone, neglected, forgotten, outside the glow which surrounded the woman and the baby.

'Ha!–Ha-a-a!' she said with a deep-throated vowel, as she put her face against the child's small breasts, so round, almost like a girl's, silken and warm and wonderful. She kissed him, and touched him, and hovered over him, drinking in his baby sweetnesses, the sweetness of the laughing little mouth's wide, wet kisses, of the round, waving limbs, of the little shoulders so winsomely curving to the arms and the breasts, of the tiny soft neck hidden very warm beneath the chin, tasting deliciously with her lips and her cheeks all the exquisite softness, silkiness, warmth, and tender life of the baby's body.

A woman is so ready to disclaim the body of a man's love; she yields him her own soft beauty with so much gentle patience and regret; she clings to his neck, to his head and his cheeks, fondling them for the soul's meaning that is there, and shrinking from his passionate limbs and his body. It was with some perplexity, some anger and bitterness that I watched Emily moved almost to ecstasy by the baby's small, innocuous person.

'Meg never found any pleasure in me as she does in the kids,' said George bitterly, for himself.

The child, laughing and crowing, caught his hands in Emily's hair and pulled dark tresses down, while she cried out in remonstrance, and tried to loosen the small fists that were shut so fast. She took him from the water and rubbed him dry, with marvellous gentle little rubs, he kicking and expostulating. She brought his fine hair into one silken up-springing of ruddy gold like an aureole. She played with his tiny balls of toes, like wee pink mushrooms, till at last she dare detain him no longer, when she put on his flannel and his night-gown and gave him to Meg.

Before carrying him to bed Meg took him to feed him. His mouth was stretched round the nipple as he sucked, his face was pressed closer and closer to the breast, his fingers wandered over the fine white globe, blue-veined and heavy, trying to hold it. Meg looked down upon him with a consuming passion of tenderness, and Emily clasped her hands and leaned forward to him. Even thus they thought him exquisite.

When the twins were both asleep, I must tiptoe upstairs to see them. They lay cheek by cheek in the crib next the large white bed, breathing little, ruffling breaths, out of unison, so small and pathetic with their tiny shut fingers. I remembered the two larks.

From the next room came a heavy sound of the old woman's breathing. Meg went in to her. As in passing I caught sight of the large, prone figure in the bed, I thought of Guy de Maupassant's 'Toine', who acted as an incubator.

5

THE DOMINANT MOTIF OF SUFFERING

The old woman lay still another year, then she suddenly sank out of life. George ceased to write to me, but I learned his news elsewhere. He became more and more intimate with the Mayhews. After old Mayhew's bankruptcy, the two sons had remained on in the large dark house that stood off the Nottingham Road in Eberwich. This house had been bequeathed to the oldest daughter by the mother. Maud Mayhew, who was married and separated from her husband, kept house for her brothers. She was a tall, large woman with high cheek-bones and oily black hair looped over her ears. Tom Mayhew was also a handsome man, very dark and ruddy, with insolent bright eyes.

The Mayhews' house was called the 'Hollies'. It was a solid building, of old red brick, standing fifty yards back from the Eberwich highroad. Between it and the road was an unkempt lawn, surrounded by very high black holly trees. The house seemed to be imprisoned among the bristling hollies. Passing through the large gate, one came immediately upon the bare side of the house and upon the great range of stables. Old Mayhew had in his day stabled thirty or more horses there. Now grass was between the red bricks, and all the bleaching doors were shut, save perhaps two or three which were open for George's horses.

The 'Hollies' became a kind of club for the disconsolate, 'better-off' men of the district. The large dining-room was gloomily and sparsely furnished, the drawing-room was a desert, but the smaller morning-room was comfortable enough, with wicker arm-chairs, heavy curtains, and a large sideboard. In this room George and the Mayhews met with several men two or three times a week. There they discussed horses and made mock of the authority of women. George provided the whisky, and they all gambled timidly at cards. These bachelor parties were the source of great annoyance to the wives of the married men who attended them.

'He's quite unbearable when he's been at those Mayhews',' said Meg. 'I'm sure they do nothing but cry us down.'

Maud Mayhew kept apart from these meetings, watching over her two children. She had been very unhappily married, and now was reserved, silent. The women of Eberwich watched her as she went swiftly along the street in the morning with her basket, and they gloried a little in her overthrow, because she was too proud to accept consolation, yet they were sorry in their hearts for her, and she was never touched with calumny. George saw her frequently, but she treated him coldly as she treated the other men, so he was afraid of her.

He had more facilities now for his horse-dealing. When the grandmother died, in the October two years after the marriage of George, she left him seven hundred pounds. To Meg she left the Inn, and the two houses she had built in Newerton, together with brewery shares to the value of nearly a thousand pounds. George and Meg felt themselves to be people of property. The result, however, was only a little further coldness between them. He was very careful that she had all that was hers. She said to him once when they were quarrelling, that he needn't go feeding the Mayhews on the money that came out of her business. Thenceforward he kept strict accounts of all his affairs, and she must audit them, receiving her exact dues. This was a mortification to her woman's capricious soul of generosity and cruelty.

The Christmas after the grandmother's death another son was born to them. For the time George and Meg became very good friends again.

When in the following March I heard he was coming down to London with Tom Mayhew on business, I wrote and asked him to stay with me. Meg replied, saying she was so glad I had asked him: she did not want him going off with that fellow again; he had been such a lot better lately, and she was sure it was only those men at Mayhews' made him what he was.

He consented to stay with me. I wrote and told him Lettie and Leslie were in London, and that we should dine with them one evening. I met him at King's Cross and we all three drove west. Mayhew was a remarkably handsome, well-built man; he and George made a notable couple. They were both in breeches and gaiters, but George still looked like a yeoman, while Mayhew had all the braggadocio of the stable. We made an impossible trio. Mayhew laughed and jested broadly for a short time, then he grew restless and fidgety. He felt restrained and awkward in my presence. Later, he told George I was a damned parson. On the other hand, I was content to look at his rather vulgar beauty—his teeth were blackened with smoking—and to listen to his ineffectual talk, but I could find absolutely no response. George was go-between. To me he was cautious and rather deferential, to Mayhew he was careless, and his attitude was tinged with contempt.

When the son of the horse-dealer at last left us to go to some of his father's old cronies, we were glad. Very uncertain, very sensitive and wavering, our old intimacy burned again like the fragile burning of alcohol. Closed together in the same blue flames, we discovered and watched the pageant of life in the town revealed wonderfully to us. We laughed at the tyranny of old romance. We scorned the faded procession of old years, and made mock of the vast pilgrimage of by-gone romances travelling farther into the dim distance. Were we not in the midst of the bewildering pageant of modern life, with all its confusion of bannerets and colours, with its infinite inter-weaving of sounds, the screech of the modern toys of haste striking like keen spray, the heavy boom of busy mankind gathering its bread, earnestly, forming the bed of all other sounds; and between these two the swiftness of songs, the triumphant tilt of the joy of life, the hoarse oboes of privation, the shuddering drums of tragedy, and the eternal scraping of the two deep-toned strings of despair?

We watched the taxi-cabs coursing with their noses down to the street, we watched the rocking hansoms, and the lumbering stateliness of buses. In the silent green cavern of the park we stood and listened to the surging of the ocean of life. We watched a girl with streaming hair go galloping down the Row, a dark man, laughing and showing his white teeth, galloping more heavily at her elbow. We saw a squad of life-guards enter the gates of the park, erect and glittering with silver and white and red. They came near to us, and we thrilled a little as we watched the muscles of their white smooth thighs answering the movement of the horses, and their cheeks and their chins bending with proud manliness to the rhythm of the march. We watched the exquisite rhythm of the body of men moving in scarlet and silver farther down the leafless avenue, like a slightly wavering spark of red life blown along. At the Marble Arch Corner we listened to a little socialist who was flaring fiercely under a plane tree. The hot stream of his words flowed over the old wounds that the knowledge of the unending miseries of the poor had given me, and I winced. For him the world was all East End, and all the East End was as a pool from which the waters are drained off, leaving the water-things to wrestle in the wet mud under the sun, till the whole of the city seems a heaving, shuddering struggle of black-mudded objects deprived of the elements of life. I felt a great terror of the little man, lest he should make me see all mud, as I had seen before. Then I felt a breathless pity for him, that his eyes should be always filled with mud, and never brightened. George listened intently to the speaker, very much moved by him.

At night, after the theatre, we saw the outcasts sleep in a rank under the Waterloo Bridge, their heads to the wall, their feet lying out on the pavement: a long, black, ruffled heap at the foot of the wall. All the faces were covered but two, that of a peaked, pale little man, and that of a brutal woman. Over these two faces, floating like uneasy pale dreams on their obscurity, swept now and again the trailing light of the tram-cars. We picked our way past the line of abandoned feet, shrinking from the sight of the thin bare ankles of a young man, from the draggled edge of the skirts of a bunched-up woman, from the pitiable sight of the men who had wrapped their legs in newspaper for a little warmth, and lay like worthless parcels. It was raining. Some men stood at the edge of the causeway fixed in dreary misery, finding no room to sleep. Outside, on a seat in the blackness and the rain, a woman sat sleeping, while the water trickled and hung heavily at the ends of her loosened strands of hair. Her hands were pushed in the bosom of her jacket. She lurched forward in her sleep, started, and one of her hands fell out of her bosom. She sank again to sleep. George gripped my arm.

'Give her something,' he whispered in panic. I was afraid. Then suddenly getting a florin from my pocket, I stiffened my nerves and slid it into her palm. Her hand was soft, and warm, and curled in sleep. She started violently, looking up at me, then down at her hand. I turned my face aside, terrified lest she should look in my eyes, and full of shame and grief I ran down the embankment to him. We hurried along under the plane trees in silence. The shining cars were drawing tall in the distance over Westminster Bridge, a fainter, yellow light running with them on the water below. The wet streets were spilled with golden liquor of light, and on the deep blackness of the river were the restless yellow slashes of the lamps.

Lettie and Leslie were staying up at Hampstead with a friend of the Tempests, one of the largest shareholders in the firm of Tempest, Wharton & Co. The

Raphaels had a substantial house, and Lettie preferred to go to them rather than to an hotel, especially as she had brought with her her infant son, now ten months old, with his nurse. They invited George and me to dinner on the Friday evening. The party included Lettie's host and hostess, and also a Scottish poetess, and an Irish musician, composer of songs and pianoforte rhapsodies.

Lettie wore a black lace dress in mourning for one of Leslie's maternal aunts. This made her look older, otherwise there seemed to be no change in her. A subtle observer might have noticed a little hardness about her mouth, and disillusion hanging slightly on her eyes. She was, however, excited by the company in which she found herself, therefore she overflowed with clever speeches and rapid, brilliant observations. Certainly on such occasions she was admirable. The rest of the company formed, as it were, the orchestra which accompanied her.

George was exceedingly quiet. He spoke a few words now and then to Mrs Raphael, but on the whole he was altogether silent, listening.

'Really!' Lettie was saying, 'I don't see that one thing is worth doing any more than another. It's like dessert: you are equally indifferent whether you have grapes, or pears, or pineapple.'

'Have you already dined so far?' sang the Scottish poetess in her musical, plaintive manner.

'The only thing worth doing is producing,' said Lettie.

'Alas, that is what all the young folk are saying nowadays!' sighed the Irish musician.

'That is the only thing one finds any pleasure in–that is to say, any satisfaction,' continued Lettie, smiling, and turning to the two artists.

'Do you not think so?' she added.

'You do come to a point at last,' said the Scottish poetess, 'when your work is a real source of satisfaction.'

'Do you write poetry then?' asked George of Lettie.

'I! Oh, dear no! I have tried strenuously to make up a Limerick for a competition, but in vain. So you see, I am a failure there. Did you know I have a son, though?–A marvellous little fellow, is he not, Leslie?–He is my work. I am a wonderful mother, am I not, Leslie?'

'Too devoted,' he replied.

'There!' she exclaimed in triumph–'When I have to sign my name and occupation in a visitor's book, it will be, "–Mother". I hope my business will flourish,' she concluded, smiling.

There was a touch of ironical brutality in her now. She was, at the bottom, quite sincere. Having reached that point in a woman's career when most, perhaps all, of the things in life seem worthless and insipid, she had determined to put up with it, to ignore her own self, to empty her own potentialities into the vessel of another or others, and to live her life at second-hand. This peculiar abnegation of self is the resource of a woman for the escaping of the responsibilities of her own development. Like a nun, she puts over her living face a veil, as a sign that the woman no longer exists for herself: she is the servant of God, of some man, of her children, or maybe of some cause. As a servant, she is no longer responsible for her self, which would make her terrified and lonely. Service is light and easy. To be responsible for the good progress of one's life is terrifying. It is the most insufferable form of loneliness, and the heaviest of responsibilities. So Lettie indulged her husband, but did not yield her independence to him; rather it was she who took much of the responsibility of him into her hands, and therefore he was so devoted to her. She had, however, now determined to abandon the charge of herself to serve her children. When the children grew up, either they would unconsciously fling her away, back upon herself again in bitterness and loneliness, or they would tenderly cherish her, chafing at her love-bonds occasionally.

George looked and listened to all the flutter of conversation, and said nothing. It seemed to him like so much unreasonable rustling of pieces of paper, of leaves of books, and so on. Later in the evening Lettie sang, no longer Italian folk songs, but the fragmentary utterances of Dèbussy and Strauss. These also to George were quite meaningless, and rather wearisome. It made him impatient to see her wasting herself upon them.

'Do you like those songs?' she asked in the frank, careless manner she affected.

'Not much,' he replied, ungraciously.

'Don't you?' she exclaimed, adding with a smile, 'Those are the most wonderful things in the world, those little things'–she began to hum a Dèbussy idiom. He could not answer her on the point, so he sat with the arrow sticking in him, and did not speak.

She enquired of him concerning Meg and his children and the affairs of Eberwich, but the interest was flimsy, as she preserved a wide distance between them, although apparently she was so unaffected and friendly. We left before eleven.

When we were seated in the cab and rushing downhill, he said:

'You know, she makes me mad.'

He was frowning, looking out of the window away from me.

'Who, Lettie? Why, what riles you?' I asked.

He was some time in replying.

'Why, she's so affected.'

I sat in the small, close space and waited.

'Do you know–?' he laughed, keeping his face averted from me. 'She makes my blood boil. I could hate her.'

'Why?' I said gently.

'I don't know. I feel as if she'd insulted me. She does lie, doesn't she?'

'I didn't notice it,' I said, but I knew he meant her shirking, her shuffling of her life.

'And you think of those poor devils under the bridge–and then of her and them frittering away themselves and money in that idiocy–'

He spoke with passion.

'You are quoting Longfellow,' I said.

'What?' he asked, looking at me suddenly.

'"Life is real, life is earnest–"'

He flushed slightly at my good-natured gibe.

'I don't know what it is,' he replied. 'But it's a pretty rotten business, when you think of her fooling about wasting herself, and all the waste that goes on up there, and the poor devils rotting on the Embankment–and–'

'And you–and Mayhew–and me–' I continued.

He looked at me very intently to see if I was mocking. He laughed. I could see he was very much moved.

'Is the time quite out of joint?' I asked.

'Why!'–he laughed. 'No. But she makes me feel so angry–as if I should burst.—I don't know when I felt in such a rage. I wonder why. I'm sorry for him, poor devil. "Lettie and Leslie"—they seemed christened for one another, didn't they?'

'What if you'd had her?' I asked.

'We should have been like a cat and dog; I'd rather be with Meg a thousand times—now!' he added significantly. He sat watching the lamps and the people and the dark buildings slipping past us.

'Shall we go and have a drink?' I asked him, thinking we would call in Frascati's to see the come-and-go.

'I could do with a brandy,' he replied, looking at me slowly.

We sat in the restaurant listening to the jigging of the music, watching the changing flow of the people. I like to sit a long time by the hollyhocks watching the throng of varied bees which poise and hesitate outside the wild flowers, then swing in with a hum which sets everything aquiver. But still more fascinating it is to watch the come and go of people weaving and intermingling in the complex mesh of their intentions, with all the subtle grace and mystery of their moving, shapely bodies.

I sat still, looking out across the amphitheatre. George looked also, but he drank glass after glass of brandy.

'I like to watch the people,' said I.

'Ay—and doesn't it seem an aimless, idiotic business—look at them!' he replied in tones of contempt. I looked instead at him, in some surprise and resentment. His face was gloomy, stupid and unrelieved. The amount of brandy he had drunk had increased his ill humour.

'Shall we be going?' I said. I did not want him to get drunk in his present state of mind.

'Ay—in half a minute,' he finished the brandy, and rose. Although he had drunk a good deal, he was quite steady, only there was a disagreeable look always on his face, and his eyes seemed smaller and more glittering than I had seen them. We took a bus to Victoria. He sat swaying on his seat in the dim, clumsy vehicle, saying not a word. In the vast cavern of the station the theatre-goers were hastening, crossing the pale grey strand, small creatures scurrying hither and thither in the space beneath the lonely lamps. As the train crawled over the river we watched the far-flung hoop of diamond lights curving slowly round and striping with bright threads the black water. He sat looking with heavy eyes, seeming to shrink from the enormous unintelligible lettering of the poem of London.

The town was too large for him, he could not take in its immense, its stupendous poetry. What did come home to him was its flagrant discords. The unintelligibility of the vast city made him apprehensive, and the crudity of its big, coarse contrasts wounded him unutterably.

'What is the matter?' I asked him as we went along the silent pavement at Norwood.

'Nothing,' he replied. 'Nothing!' and I did not trouble him further.

We occupied a large, two-bedded room—that looked down the hill and over to the far woods of Kent. He was morose and untalkative. I brought up a soda-syphon and whisky, and we proceeded to undress. When he stood in his pyjamas he waited as if uncertain.

'Do you want a drink?' he asked.

I did not. He crossed to the table, and as I got into my bed I heard the brief fizzing of the syphon. He drank his glass at one draught, then switched off the light. In the sudden darkness I saw his pale shadow go across to the sofa in the window-space. The blinds were undrawn, and the stars looked in. He gazed out on the great bay of darkness wherein, far away and below, floated a few sparks of lamps like herring-boats at sea.

'Aren't you coming to bed?' I asked.

'I'm not sleepy–you go to sleep,' he answered, resenting having to speak at all.

'Then put on a dressing-gown–there's one in that corner–turn the light on.'

He did not answer, but fumbled for the garment in the darkness. When he had found it, he said:

'Do you mind if I smoke?'

I did not. He fumbled again in his pockets for cigarettes, always refusing to switch on the light. I watched his face bowed to the match as he lighted his cigarette. He was still handsome in the ruddy light, but his features were coarser. I felt very sorry for him, but I saw that I could get no nearer to him, to relieve him. For some time I lay in the darkness watching the end of his cigarette like a ruddy, malignant insect hovering near his lips, putting the timid stars immensely far away. He sat quite still, leaning on the sofa arm. Occasionally there was a little glow on his cheeks as the cigarette burned brighter, then again I could see nothing but the dull red bee.

I suppose I must have dropped asleep. Suddenly I started as something fell to the floor. I heard him cursing under his breath.

'What's the matter?' I asked.

'I've only knocked something down–cigarette-case or something,' he replied, apologetically.

'Aren't you coming to bed?' I asked.

'Yes, I'm coming,' he answered quite docile.

He seemed to wander about and knock against things as he came. He dropped heavily into bed.

'Are you sleepy now?' I asked.

'I dunno–I shall be directly,' he replied.

'What's up with you?' I asked.

'I dunno,' he answered. 'I'm like this sometimes, when there's nothing I want to do, and nowhere I want to go, and nobody I want to be near. Then you feel so rottenly lonely, Cyril. You feel awful, like a vacuum, with a pressure on you, a sort of pressure of darkness, and you yourself–just nothing, a vacuum–that's what it's like–a little vacuum that's not dark, all loose in the middle of a space of darkness, that's pressing on you.'

'Good gracious!' I exclaimed, rousing myself in bed. 'That sounds bad!'

He laughed slightly.

'It's all right,' he said, 'it's only the excitement of London, and that little man in the park, and that woman on the seat–I wonder where she is tonight, poor devil–and then Lettie. I seem thrown off my balance.–I think really, I ought to have made something of myself–'

'What?' I asked, as he hesitated.

'I don't know,' he replied slowly, '–a poet or something, like Burns–I don't know. I shall laugh at myself for thinking so, tomorrow. But I am born a generation too soon–I wasn't ripe enough when I came. I wanted something I hadn't got. I'm something short. I'm like corn in a wet harvest–full, but pappy, no good. I s'll rot. I came too soon; or I wanted something that would ha' made me grow fierce. That's why I wanted Lettie–I think. But am I talking damn rot? What am I saying? What are you making me talk for? What are you listening for?'

I rose and went across to him, saying:

'I don't want you to talk! If you sleep till morning things will look different.'

I sat on his bed and took his hand. He lay quite still.

'I'm only a kid after all, Cyril,' he said, a few moments later.

'We all are,' I answered, still holding his hand. Presently he fell asleep.

When I awoke the sunlight was laughing with the young morning in the room. The large blue sky shone against the window, and the birds were calling in the garden below, shouting to one another and making fun of life. I felt glad to have opened my eyes. I lay for a moment looking out on the morning as on a blue bright sea in which I was going to plunge.

Then my eyes wandered to the little table near the couch. I noticed the glitter of George's cigarette-case, and then, with a start, the whisky decanter. It was nearly empty. He must have drunk three-quarters of a pint of liquor while I was dozing. I could not believe it. I thought I must have been mistaken as to the quantity the bottle contained. I leaned out to see what it was that had startled me by its fall the night before. It was the large, heavy drinking glass which he had knocked down but not broken. I could see no stain on the carpet.

George was still asleep. He lay half uncovered, and was breathing quietly. His face looked inert like a mask. The pallid, uninspired clay of his features seemed to have sunk a little out of shape, so that he appeared rather haggard, rather ugly, with grooves of ineffectual misery along his cheeks. I wanted him to wake, so that his inert, flaccid features might be inspired with life again. I could not believe his charm and his beauty could have forsaken him so, and left his features dreary, sunken clay.

As I looked he woke. His eyes opened slowly. He looked at me and turned away, unable to meet my eyes. He pulled the bedclothes up over his shoulders, as though to cover himself from me, and he lay with his back to me, quite still, as if he were asleep, although I knew he was quite awake; he was suffering the humiliation of lying waiting for his life to crawl back and inhabit his body. As it was, his vitality was not yet sufficient to inform the muscles of his face and give him an expression, much less to answer by challenge.

6

PISGAH

When her eldest boy was three years old Lettie returned to live at Eberwich. Old Mr Tempest died suddenly, so Leslie came down to inhabit Highclose. He was a very much occupied man. Very often he was in Germany or in the South of England engaged on business. At home he was unfailingly attentive to his wife and his two children. He had cultivated a taste for public life. In spite of his pressure of business he had become a County Councillor, and one of the prominent members of the Conservative Association. He was very fond of answering or proposing toasts at some public dinner, of entertaining political men at Highclose, of taking the chair at political meetings, and finally, of speaking on this or that platform. His name was fairly often seen in the newspapers. As a mine-owner, he spoke as an authority on the employment of labour, on royalties, land-owning and so on.

At home he was quite tame. He treated his wife with respect, romped in the nursery, and domineered the servants royally. They liked him for it—her they did not like. He was noisy, but unobservant, she was quiet and exacting. He would swear and bluster furiously, but when he was round the corner they smiled. She gave her orders and passed very moderate censure, but they went away cursing to themselves. As Lettie was always a very good wife, Leslie adored her when he had the time, and when he had not, forgot her comfortably.

She was very contradictory. At times she would write to me in terms of passionate dissatisfaction: she had nothing at all in her life, it was a barren futility.

'I hope I shall have another child next spring,' she would write, 'there is only that to take away the misery of this torpor. I seem full of passion and energy, and it all fizzles out in day-to-day domestics—'

When I replied to her, urging her to take some work that she could throw her soul into, she would reply indifferently. Then later:

'You charge me with contradiction. Well, naturally. You see I wrote that screeching letter in a mood which won't come again for some time. Generally I am quite content to take the rain and the calm days just as they come, then something flings me out of myself—and I am a trifle demented:—very, very blue, as I tell Leslie.'

Like so many women, she seemed to live, for the most part contentedly, a small indoor existence with artificial light and padded upholstery. Only occasionally, hearing the winds of life outside, she clamoured to be out in the black, keen storm. She was driven to the door, she looked out and called into the tumult wildly, but feminine caution kept her from stepping over the threshold.

George was flourishing in his horse-dealing.

In the morning, processions of splendid shire horses, tied tail and head, would tramp grandly along the quiet lanes of Eberwich, led by George's man, or by Tom Mayhew, while in the fresh clean sunlight George would go riding by, two restless nags dancing beside him.

When I came home from France five years after our meeting in London I found him installed in the Hollies. He had rented the house from the Mayhews, and had moved there with his family, leaving Oswald in charge of the Ram. I called at the large house one afternoon, but George was out. His family surprised me. The twins were tall lads of six. There were two more boys, and Meg was nursing a beautiful baby girl about a year old. This child was evidently mistress of the household. Meg, who was growing stouter, indulged the little creature in every way.

'How is George?' I asked her.

'Oh, he's very well,' she replied. 'He's always got something on hand. He hardly seems to have a spare moment; what with his socialism, and one thing and another.'

It was true, the outcome of his visit to London had been a wild devotion to the cause of the down-trodden. I saw a picture of Watts's 'Mammon' on the walls of the morning-room, and the works of Blatchford, Masterman, and Chiozza Money on the side-table. The socialists of the district used to meet every other Thursday evening at the Hollies to discuss reform. Meg did not care for these earnest souls.

'They're not my sort,' she said, 'too jerky and bumptious. They think everybody's slow-witted but them. There's one thing about them, though, they don't drink, so that's a blessing.'

'Why!' I said, 'Have you had much trouble that way?'

She lowered her voice to a pitch which was sufficiently mysterious to attract the attention of the boys.

'I shouldn't say anything if it wasn't that you were like brothers,' she said. 'But he did begin to have dreadful drinking bouts. You know it was always spirits, and generally brandy–and that makes such work with them. You've no idea what he's like when he's evil-drunk. Sometimes he's all for talk, sometimes he's laughing at everything, and sometimes he's just snappy. And then–' here her tones grew ominous, '–he'll come home evil-drunk.'

At the memory she grew serious.

'You couldn't imagine what it's like, Cyril,' she said. 'It's like having Satan in the house with you, or a black tiger glowering at you. I'm sure nobody knows what I've suffered with him–'

The children stood with large awful eyes and paling lips, listening.

'But he's better now?' I said.

'Oh, yes–since Gertie came,'–she looked fondly at the baby in her arms–'He's a lot better now. You see he always wanted a girl, and he's very fond of her–isn't he, pet?–are you your Dadda's girlie?–and Mamma's too, aren't you?'

The baby turned with sudden coy shyness, and clung to her mother's neck. Meg kissed her fondly, then the child laid her cheek against her mother's. The mother's dark eyes, and the baby's large, hazel eyes looked at me serenely. The two were very calm, very complete and triumphant together. In their completeness was a security which made me feel alone and ineffectual. A woman who has her child in her arms is a tower of strength, a beautiful, unassailable tower of strength that may in its turn stand quietly dealing death.

I told Meg I would call again to see George. Two evenings later I asked Lettie to lend me a dog-cart to drive over to the Hollies. Leslie was away on one of his political jaunts, and she was restless. She proposed to go with me. She had called on Meg twice before in the new large home.

We started about six o'clock. The night was dark and muddy. Lettie wanted to call in Eberwich village, so she drove the long way round Selsby. The horse was walking through the gate of the Hollies at about seven o'clock. Meg was upstairs in the nursery, the maid told me, and George was in the dining-room getting baby to sleep.

'All right!' I said, 'we will go in to him. Don't bother to tell him.'

As we stood in the gloomy, square hall we heard the rumble of a rocking-chair, the stroke coming slow and heavy to the tune of 'Henry Martin', one of our Strelley Mill folk songs. Then, through the man's heavily-accented singing floated the long light crooning of the baby as she sang, in her quaint little fashion, a mischievous second to her father's lullaby. He waxed a little louder; and without knowing why, we found ourselves smiling with piquant amusement. The baby grew louder too, till there was a shrill ring of laughter and mockery in her music. He sang louder and louder, the baby shrilled higher and higher, the chair swung in long, heavy beats. Then suddenly he began to laugh. The rocking stopped, and he said, still with laughter and enjoyment in his tones:

'Now that is very wicked! Ah, naughty Girlie–go to boh, go to bohey!–at once.'

The baby chuckled her small, insolent mockery.

'Come, Mamma!' he said, 'come and take Girlie to bohey!'

The baby laughed again, but with an uncertain touch of appeal in her tone. We opened the door and entered. He looked up very much startled to see us. He was sitting in a tall rocking-chair by the fire, coatless, with white shirtsleeves. The baby, in her high-waisted, tight little night-gown, stood on his knee, her wide eyes fixed on us, wild wisps of her brown hair brushed across her forehead and glinting like puffs of bronze dust over her ears. Quickly she put her arms round his neck and tucked her face under his chin, her small feet poised on his thigh, the night-gown dropping upon them. He shook his head as the puff of soft brown hair tickled him. He smiled at us, saying:

'You see I'm busy!'

Then he turned again to the little brown head tucked under his chin, blew away the luminous cloud of hair, and rubbed his lips and his moustache on the small white neck, so warm and secret. The baby put up her shoulders, and shrank a little, bubbling in his neck with hidden laughter. She did not lift her face or loosen her arms.

'She thinks she is shy,' he said. 'Look up, young hussy, and see the lady and gentleman. She is a positive owl, she won't go to bed—will you, young brown-owl?'

He tickled her neck again with his moustache, and the child bubbled over with naughty, merry laughter.

The room was very warm, with a red bank of fire up the chimney mouth. It was half lighted from a heavy bronze chandelier, black and gloomy, in the middle of the room. There was the same sombre, sparse furniture that the Mayhews had had. George looked large and handsome, the glossy black silk of his waistcoat fitting close to his sides, the roundness of the shoulder muscle filling the white linen of his sleeves.

Suddenly the baby lifted her head and stared at us, thrusting into her mouth the dummy that was pinned to the breast of her night-gown. The faded pink sleeves of the night-gown were tight on her fat little wrists. She stood thus sucking her dummy, one arm round her father's neck, watching us with hazel solemn eyes. Then she pushed her fat little fist up among the bush of small curls, and began to twist her fingers about her ear that was white like a camellia flower.

'She is really sleepy,' said Lettie.

'Come then!' said he, folding her for sleep against his breast. 'Come and go to boh.'

But the young rascal immediately began to cry her remonstrance. She stiffened herself, freed herself, and stood again on his knee, watching us solemnly, vibrating the dummy in her mouth as she suddenly sucked at it, twisting her father's ear in her small fingers till he winced.

'Her nails *are* sharp,' he said, smiling.

He began asking and giving the small information that pass between friends who have not met for a long time. The baby laid her head on his shoulder, keeping her tired, owl-like eyes fixed darkly on us. Then gradually the lids fluttered and sank, and she dropped on to his arm.

'She is asleep,' whispered Lettie.

Immediately the dark eyes opened again. We looked significantly at one another, continuing our subdued talk. After a while the baby slept soundly.

Presently Meg came downstairs. She greeted us in breathless whispers of surprise, and then turned to her husband.

'Has she gone?' she whispered, bending over the sleeping child in astonishment. 'My, this is wonderful, isn't it!'

She took the sleeping drooping baby from his arms, putting her mouth close to its forehead, murmuring with soothing, inarticulate sounds.

We stayed talking for some time when Meg had put the baby to bed. George had a new tone of assurance and authority. In the first place he was an established man, living in a large house, having altogether three men working for him. In the second place he had ceased to value the conventional treasures of social position and ostentatious refinement. Very, very many things he condemned as flummery and sickly waste of time. The life of an ordinary well-to-do person he set down as adorned futility, almost idiocy. He spoke passionately of the monstrous denial of life to the many of the fortunate few. He talked at Lettie most flagrantly.

'Of course,' she said, 'I have read Mr Wells and Mr Shaw, and even Niel Lyon and a Dutchman – what is his name, Querido? But what can I do? I think the rich have as much misery as the poor, and of quite as deadly a sort. What can I do? It is a question of life and the development of the human race. Society and its regulations is not a sort of drill that endless Napoleons have forced on us: it is the only way we have yet found of living together.'

'Pah!' said he, 'that is rank cowardice. It is feeble and futile to the last degree.'

'We can't grow consumption-proof in a generation, nor can we grow poverty-proof.'

'We can begin to take active measures,' he replied contemptuously.

'We can all go into a sanatorium and live miserably and dejectedly warding off death,' she said, 'but life is full of goodliness for all that.'

'It is fuller of misery,' he said.

Nevertheless, she had shaken him. She still kept her astonishing power of influencing his opinions. All his passion, and heat, and rude speech, analysed out, was only his terror at her threatening of his life-interest.

She was rather piqued by his rough treatment of her, and by his contemptuous tone. Moreover, she could never quite let him be. She felt a driving force which impelled her against her will to interfere in his life. She invited him to dine with them at Highclose. He was now quite possible. He had, in the course of his business, been sufficiently in the company of gentlemen to be altogether '*comme il faut*' at a private dinner, and after dinner.

She wrote me concerning him occasionally:

'George Saxton was here to dinner yesterday. He and Leslie had frightful battles over the nationalisation of industries. George is rather more than a match for Leslie, which, in his secret heart, makes our friend gloriously proud. It is very amusing. I, of course, have to preserve the balance of power, and, of course, to bolster my husband's dignity. At a crucial dangerous moment, when George is just going to wave his bloody sword and Leslie lies bleeding with rage, I step in and prick the victor under the heart with some little satire or some esoteric question, I raise Leslie and say his blood is luminous for the truth, and *vous voilà*! Then I abate for the thousandth time Leslie's conservative crow, and I appeal once more to George – it is no use my arguing with him, he gets so angry – I make an abstruse appeal for all the wonderful, sad, and beautiful expressions on the countenance of life, expressions which he does not see or which he distorts by his oblique vision of socialism into grimaces—and there I am! I think I am something of a Machiavelli, but it is quite true, what I say—'

Again she wrote:

'We happened to be motoring from Derby on Sunday morning, and as we came to the top of the hill, we had to thread our way through quite a large crowd. I looked up, and whom should I see but our friend George, holding forth about the state endowment of mothers. I made Leslie stop while we listened. The market-place was quite full of people. George saw us, and became fiery. Leslie then grew excited, and although I clung to the skirts of his coat with all my strength, he jumped up and began to question. I must say it with shame and humility—he made an ass of himself. The men all round were jeering and muttering under their breath. I think Leslie is not very popular among them, he is such an advocate of machinery which will do the work of men. So they cheered our friend George when he thundered forth his replies and his demonstrations. He pointed his fingers at us, and flung his hand at us, and shouted till I quailed in my seat. I cannot understand why he should become so frenzied as soon as I am within range. George had a triumph that morning, but when I saw him a few days later he seemed very uneasy, rather self-mistrustful—'

Almost a year later I heard from her again on the same subject.

'I have had such a lark. Two or three times I have been to the Hollies: to socialist meetings. Leslie does not know. They are great fun. Of course, I am in sympathy with the socialists, but I cannot narrow my eyes till I see one thing only. Life is like a large, rather beautiful man who is young and full of vigour, but hairy, barbaric, with hands hard and dirty, the dirt ingrained. I know his hands are very ugly, I know his mouth is not firmly shapen, I know his limbs are hairy and brutal: but his eyes are deep and very beautiful. That is what I tell George.

'The people are so earnest, they make me sad. But then, they are so didactic, they hold forth so much, they are so cock-sure and so narrow-eyed, they make me laugh. George laughs too. I am sure we made such fun of a straight-haired goggle of a girl who had suffered in prison for the cause of women, that I am ashamed when I see my "Woman's League" badge. At the bottom, you know, Cyril, I don't care for anything very much, except myself. Things seem so frivolous. I am the only real thing, I and the children—'

Gradually George fell out of the socialist movement. It wearied him. It did not feed him altogether. He began by mocking his friends of the confraternity. Then he spoke in bitter dislike of Hudson, the wordy, humorous, shallow leader of the movement in Eberwich; it was Hudson with his wriggling and his clap-trap who disgusted George with the cause. Finally the meetings at the Hollies ceased, and my friend dropped all connection with his former associates.

He began to speculate in land. A hosiery factory moved to Eberwich, giving the place a new stimulus to growth. George happened to buy a piece of land at the end of the street of the village. When he got it, it was laid out in allotment gardens. These were becoming valueless owing to the encroachment of houses. He took it, divided it up, and offered it as sites for a new row of shops. He sold at a good profit.

Altogether he was becoming very well off. I heard from Meg that he was flourishing, that he did not drink 'anything to speak of,' but that he was always out, she hardly saw anything of him. If getting-on was to keep him so much away from home, she would be content with a little less fortune. He complained that she was narrow, and that she would not entertain any sympathy with any of his ideas.

'Nobody comes here to see me twice,' he said. 'Because Meg receives them in such an off-hand fashion. I asked Jim Curtiss and his wife from Everley Hall one evening. We were uncomfortable all the time. Meg had hardly a word for anybody – "Yes" and "No" and "Hm Hm!" – They'll never come again.'

Meg herself said:

'Oh, I can't stand stuck-up folks. They make me feel uncomfortable. As soon as they begin mincing their words I'm done for – I can no more talk than a lobster – '

Thus their natures contradicted each other. He tried hard to gain a footing in Eberwich. As it was he belonged to no class of society whatsoever. Meg visited and entertained the wives of small shop-keepers and publicans: this was her set.

George voted the women loud-mouthed, vulgar, and narrow – not without some cause. Meg, however, persisted. She visited when she thought fit, and entertained when he was out. He made acquaintance after acquaintance: Dr Francis; Mr Cartridge, the veterinary surgeon; Toby Heswall, the brewer's son; the Curtisses, farmers of good standing from Everley Hall. But it was no good. George was by nature a family man. He wanted to be private and secure in his own rooms, then he was at ease. As Meg never went out with him, and as every attempt to entertain at the Hollies filled him with shame and mortification, he began to give up trying to place himself, and remained suspended in social isolation at the Hollies.

The friendship between Lettie and himself had been kept up, in spite of all things. Leslie was sometimes jealous, but he dared not show it openly, for fear of his wife's scathing contempt. George went to Highclose perhaps once in a fortnight, perhaps not so often. Lettie never went to the Hollies, as Meg's attitude was too antagonistic.

Meg complained very bitterly of her husband. He often made a beast of himself drinking, he thought more of himself than he ought, home was not good enough for him, he was selfish to the back-bone, he cared neither for her nor the children, only for himself.

I happened to be at home for Lettie's thirty-first birthday. George was then thirty-five. Lettie had allowed her husband to forget her birthday. He was now very much immersed in politics, foreseeing a general election in the following year, and intending to contest the seat in Parliament. The division was an impregnable Liberal stronghold, but Leslie had hopes that he might capture the situation. Therefore he spent a great deal of time at the Conservative Club, and among the men of influence in the southern division. Lettie encouraged him in these affairs. It relieved her of him. It was thus that she let him forget her birthday, while, for some unknown reason, she let the intelligence slip to George. He was invited to dinner, as I was at home.

George came at seven o'clock. There was a strange feeling of festivity in the house, although there were no evident signs. Lettie had dressed with some magnificence in a blackish purple gauze over soft satin of lighter tone, nearly the colour of double violets. She wore vivid green azurite ornaments on the fairness of her bosom, and her bright hair was bound by a band of the same colour. It was rather startling. She was conscious of her effect, and was very excited. Immediately George saw her his eyes wakened with a dark glow. She stood up as he entered, her hand stretched straight out to him, her body very erect, her eyes bright and rousing, like two blue pennants.

'Thank you so much,' she said softly, giving his hand a last pressure before she let it go. He could not answer, so he sat down, bowing his head, then looking up at her in suspense. He smiled at her.

Presently the children came in. They looked very quaint, like acolytes, in their long straight dressing-gowns of quilted blue silk. The boy, particularly, looked as if he were going to light the candles in some childish church in paradise. He was very tall and slender and fair, with a round fine head, and serene features. Both children looked remarkable, almost transparently clean: it is impossible to consider anything more fresh and fair. The girl was a merry, curly-headed puss of six. She played with her mother's green jewels and prattled prettily, while the boy stood at his mother's side, a slender and silent acolyte in his pale blue gown. I was impressed by his patience and his purity. When the girl had bounded away into George's arms, the lad laid his hand timidly on Lettie's knee and looked with a little wonder at her dress.

'How pretty those green stones are, Mother!' he said.

'Yes,' replied Lettie brightly, lifting them and letting their strange pattern fall again on her bosom. 'I like them.'

'Are you going to sing, Mother?' he asked.

'Perhaps. But why?' said Lettie, smiling.

'Because you generally sing when Mr Saxton comes.'

He bent his head and stroked Lettie's dress shyly.

'Do I?' she said, laughing. 'Can you hear?'

'Just a little,' he replied. 'Quite small, as if it were nearly lost in the dark.'

He was hesitating, shy as boys are. Lettie laid her hand on his head and stroked his smooth fair hair.

'Sing a song for us before we go, Mother—' he asked, almost shamefully. She kissed him.

She played without a copy of the music. He stood at her side, while Lucy, the little mouse, sat on her mother's skirts, pressing Lettie's silk slippers in turn upon the pedals. The mother and the boy sang their song.

> 'Gaily the troubadour touched his guitar
> As he was hastening from the war.'

The boy had a pure treble, clear as the flight of swallows in the morning. The light shone on his lips. Under the piano the girl child sat laughing, pressing her mother's feet with all her strength, and laughing again. Lettie smiled as she sang.

At last they kissed us a gentle 'good night', and flitted out of the room. The girl popped her curly head round the door again. We saw the white cuff of the nurse's wrist as she held the youngster's arm.

'You'll come and kiss us when we're in bed, Mum?' asked the rogue. Her mother laughed and agreed.

Lucy was withdrawn for a moment; then we heard her, 'Just a tick, nurse, just half a tick!'

The curly head appeared round the door again.

'And *one* teenie sweetie,' she suggested, 'only *one*!'

'Go, you—!' Lettie clapped her hands in mock wrath. The child vanished, but immediately there appeared again round the door two blue laughing eyes and the snub tip of a nose.

'A nice one, Mum–not a jelly one!'

Lettie rose with a rustle to sweep upon her. The child vanished with a glitter of laughter. We heard her calling breathlessly on the stairs–'Wait a bit, Freddies–wait for me!'

George and Lettie smiled at each other when the children had gone. As the smile died from their faces they looked down sadly, and until dinner was announced they were very still and heavy with melancholy. After dinner Lettie debated pleasantly which bon-bon she should take for the children. When she came down again she smoked a cigarette with us over coffee. George did not like to see her smoking, yet he brightened a little when he sat down after giving her a light, pleased with the mark of recklessness in her.

'It is ten years today since my party at Woodside,' she said, reaching for the small Roman salt-cellar of green jade that she used as an ash-tray.

'My Lord–ten years!' he exclaimed bitterly. 'It seems a hundred.'

'It does and it doesn't,' she answered, smiling.

'If I look straight back, and think of my excitement, it seems only yesterday. If I look between then and now, at all the days that lie between, it is an age.'

'If I look at myself,' he said, 'I think I am another person altogether.'

'You have changed,' she agreed, looking at him sadly. 'There is a great change–but you are not another person. I often think–there is one of his old looks, he is just the same at the bottom!'

They embarked on a barge of gloomy recollections and drifted along the soiled canal of their past.

'The worst of it is,' he said, 'I have got a miserable carelessness, a contempt for things. You know I had such a faculty for reverence. I always believed in things.'

'I know you did,' she smiled. 'You were so humbly-minded–too humbly-minded, I always considered. You always thought things had a deep religious meaning, somewhere hidden, and you reverenced them. Is it different now?'

'You know me very well,' he laughed. 'What is there left for me to believe in, if not in myself?'

'You have to live for your wife and children,' she said with firmness.

'Meg has plenty to secure her and the children as long as they live,' he said, smiling. 'So I don't know that I'm essential.'

'But you are,' she replied. 'You are necessary as a father and a husband, if not as a provider.'

'I think,' said he, 'marriage is more of a duel than a duet. One party wins and takes the other captive, slave, servant–what you like. It is so, more or less.'

'Well?' said Lettie.

'Well!' he answered. 'Meg is not like you. She wants me, part of me, so she'd kill me rather than let me go loose.'

'Oh, no!' said Lettie, emphatically.

'You know nothing about it,' he said quietly. 'In the marital duel Meg is winning. The woman generally does; she has the children on her side. I can't give her any of the real part of me, the vital part that she wants–I can't, any more than you could give kisses to a stranger. And I feel that I'm losing–and don't care.'

'No,' she said, 'you are getting morbid.'

He put the cigarette between his lips, drew a deep breath, then slowly sent the smoke down his nostrils.

'No,' he said.

'Look here!' she said. 'Let me sing to you, shall I, and make you cheerful again?'

She sang from Wagner. It was the music of resignation and despair. She had not thought of it. All the time he listened he was thinking. The music stimulated his thoughts and illuminated the trend of his brooding. All the time he sat looking at her his eyes were dark with his thoughts. She finished the 'Star of Eve' from *Tannhäuser* and came over to him.

'Why are you so sad tonight, when it is my birthday?' she asked plaintively.

'Am I slow?' he replied. 'I am sorry.'

'What is the matter?' she said, sinking on to the small sofa near to him.

'Nothing!' he replied–'You are looking very beautiful.'

'There, I wanted you to say that! You ought to be quite gay, you know, when I am so smart tonight.'

'Nay,' he said, 'I know I ought. But the tomorrow seems to have fallen in love with me. I can't get out of its lean arms.'

'Why!' she said. 'Tomorrow's arms are not lean. They are white, like mine.' She lifted her arms and looked at them, smiling.

'How do you know?' he asked, pertinently.

'Oh, of course they are,' was her light answer.

He laughed, brief and sceptical.

'No!' he said. 'It came when the children kissed us.'

'What?' she asked.

'These lean arms of tomorrow's round me, and the white arms round you,' he replied, smiling whimsically. She reached out and clasped his hand.

'You foolish boy,' she said.

He laughed painfully, not able to look at her.

'You know,' he said, and his voice was low and difficult, 'I have needed you for a light. You will soon be the only light again.'

'Who is the other?' she asked.

'My little girl!' he answered. Then he continued, 'And you know, I couldn't endure complete darkness, I couldn't. It's the solitariness.'

'You mustn't talk like this,' she said. 'You know you mustn't.' She put her hand on his head and ran her fingers through the hair he had so ruffled.

'It is as thick as ever, your hair,' she said.

He did not answer, but kept his face bent out of sight. She rose from her seat and stood at the back of his low armchair. Taking an amber comb from her hair, she bent over him, and with the translucent comb and her white fingers she busied herself with his hair.

'I believe you *would* have a parting,' she said softly.

He laughed shortly at her playfulness. She continued combing, just touching, pressing the strands in place with the tips of her fingers.

'I was only a warmth to you,' he said, pursuing the same train of thought. 'So you could do without me. But you were like the light to me, and otherwise it was dark and aimless. Aimlessness is horrible.'

She had finally smoothed his hair, so she lifted her hands and put back her head.

'There!' she said. 'It looks fair fine, as Alice would say. Raven's wings are raggy in comparison.'

He did not pay any attention to her.

'Aren't you going to look at yourself?' she said, playfully reproachful. She put her finger-tips under his chin. He lifted his head and they looked at each other, she smiling, trying to make him play, he smiling with his lips, but not with eyes, dark with pain.

'We can't go on like this, Lettie, can we?' he said softly.

'Yes,' she answered him, 'Yes; why not?'

'It can't!' he said, 'it can't, I couldn't keep it up, Lettie.'

'But don't think about it,' she answered. 'Don't think of it.'

'Lettie,' he said. 'I have to set my teeth with loneliness.'

'Hush!' she said. 'No! There are the children. Don't say anything–do not be serious, will you?'

'No, there are the children,' he replied, smiling dimly.

'Yes! Hush now! Stand up and look what a fine parting I have made in your hair. Stand up, and see if my style becomes you.'

'It is no good, Lettie,' he said, 'we can't go on.'

'Oh, but come, come, come!' she exclaimed. 'We are not talking about going on; we are considering what a fine parting I have made down the middle, like two wings of a spread bird–' she looked down, smiling playfully on him, just closing her eyes slightly in petition.

He rose and took a deep breath, and set his shoulders.

'No,' he said, and at the sound of his voice, Lettie went pale and also stiffened herself.

'No!' he repeated. 'It is impossible. I felt as soon as Fred came into the room –it must be one way or another.'

'Very well then,' said Lettie, coldly. Her voice was 'muted' like a violin.

'Yes,' he replied, submissive. 'The children.' He looked at her, contracting his lips in a smile of misery.

'Are you sure it must be so final?' she asked, rebellious, even resentful. She was twisting the azurite jewels on her bosom, and pressing the blunt points into her flesh. He looked up from the fascination of her action when he heard the tone of her last question. He was angry.

'Quite sure!' he said at last, simply, ironically.

She bowed her head in assent. His face twitched sharply as he restrained himself from speaking again. Then he turned and quietly left the room. She did not watch him go, but stood as he had left her. When, after some time, she heard the grating of his dog-cart on the gravel, and then the sharp trot of hoofs down the frozen road, she dropped herself on the settee, and lay with her bosom against the cushions, looking fixedly at the wall.

7

THE SCARP SLOPE

Leslie won the Conservative victory in the general election which took place a year or so after my last visit to Highclose.

In the interim the Tempests had entertained a continuous stream of people. I heard occasionally from Lettie how she was busy, amused, or bored. She told me that George had thrown himself into the struggle on behalf of the candidate of the Labour Party; that she had not seen him, except in the streets, for a very long time.

When I went down to Eberwich in the March succeeding the election, I found several people staying with my sister. She had under her wing a young literary fellow who affected the 'Doady' style–Dora Copperfield's 'Doady'. He had bunches of half-curly hair, and a romantic black cravat; he played the impulsive part, but was really as calculating as any man on the stock-exchange. It delighted Lettie to 'mother' him. He was so shrewd as to be less than harmless. His fellow guests, a woman much experienced in music and an elderly man who was in the artistic world without being of it, were interesting for a time. Bubble after bubble of floating fancy and wit we blew with our breath in the evenings. I rose in the morning loathing the idea of more bubble-blowing.

I wandered around Nethermere, which had now forgotten me. The daffodils under the boat-house continued their golden laughter, and nodded to one another in gossip, as I watched them, never for a moment pausing to notice me. The yellow reflection of daffodils among the shadows of grey willow in the water trembled faintly as they told haunted tales in the gloom. I felt like a child left out of the group of my playmates. There was a wind running across Nethermere, and on the eager water blue and glistening grey shadows changed places swiftly. Along the shore the wild birds rose, flapping in expostulation as I passed, peewits mewing fiercely round my head, while two white swans lifted their glistening feathers till they looked like grand double water-lilies, laying back their orange beaks among the petals, and fronting me with haughty resentment, charging towards me insolently.

I wanted to be recognised by something. I said to myself that the dryads were looking out for me from the wood's edge. But as I advanced they shrank, and glancing wistfully, turned back like pale flowers falling in the shadow of the forest. I was a stranger, an intruder. Among the bushes a twitter of lively birds exclaimed upon me. Finches went leaping past in bright flashes, and a robin sat and asked rudely, 'Hello! Who are you?'

The bracken lay sere under the trees, broken and chavelled by the restless wild winds of the long winter.

The trees caught the wind in their tall netted twigs, and the young morning wind moaned at its captivity. As I trod the discarded oak-leaves and the bracken they uttered their last sharp gasps, pressed into oblivion. The wood was roofed with a wide young sobbing sound, and floored with a faint hiss like the intaking of the last breath. Between, was all the glad out-peeping of buds and anemone flowers and the rush of birds. I, wandering alone, felt them all, the anguish of the bracken fallen face down in defeat, the careless dash of the birds, the sobbing of the young wind arrested in its haste, the trembling, expanding delight of the buds. I alone among them could hear the whole succession of chords.

The brooks talked on just the same, just as gladly, just as boisterously as they had done when I had netted small, glittering fish in the rest-pools. At Strelley Mill a servant girl in a white cap, and white apron-bands, came running out of the house with purple prayer-books, which she gave to the elder of two finicking girls who sat disconsolately with their black-silked mother in the governess cart at the gate, ready to go to church. Near Woodside there was barbed-wire along the path, and at the end of every riding it was tarred on the tree-trunks, 'Private'.

I had done with the valley of Nethermere. The valley of Nethermere had cast me out many years before, while I had fondly believed it cherished me in memory.

I went along the road to Eberwich. The church bells were ringing boisterously, with the careless boisterousness of the brooks and the birds and the rollicking coltsfoots and celandines.

A few people were hastening blithely to service. Miners and other labouring men were passing in aimless gangs, walking nowhere in particular, so long as they reached a sufficiently distant public-house.

I reached the Hollies. It was much more spruce than it had been. The yard, however, and the stables had again a somewhat abandoned air. I asked the maid for George.

'Oh, master's not up yet,' she said, giving a little significant toss of her head, and smiling. I waited a moment.

'But he rung for a bottle of beer about ten minutes since, so I should think–' she emphasised the word with some ironical contempt, '–he won't be very long,' she added, in tones which conveyed that she was not by any means sure. I asked for Meg.

'Oh, Missis is gone to church–and the children–but Miss Saxton is in, she might–'

'Emily!' I exclaimed.

The maid smiled.

'She's in the drawing-room. She's engaged, but perhaps if I tell her–'

'Yes, do,' said I, sure that Emily would receive me.

I found my old sweetheart sitting in a low chair by the fire, a man standing on the hearth-rug pulling his moustache. Emily and I both felt a thrill of old delight at meeting.

'I can hardly believe it is really you,' she said, laughing me one of the old intimate looks. She had changed a great deal. She was very handsome, but she had now a new self-confidence, a fine, free indifference.

'Let me introduce you. Mr Renshaw, Cyril. Tom, you know who it is; you have heard me speak often enough of Cyril. I am going to marry Tom in three weeks' time,' she said, laughing.

'The devil you are!' I exclaimed involuntarily.

'If he will have me,' she added, quite as a playful after-thought.

Tom was a well-built fair man, smoothly, almost delicately tanned. There was something soldierly in his bearing, something self-conscious in the way he bent his head and pulled his moustache, something charming and fresh in the way he laughed at Emily's last preposterous speech.

'Why didn't you tell me?' I asked.

'Why didn't you ask me?' she retorted, arching her brows.

'Mr Renshaw,' I said. 'You have out-manœuvred me all unawares, quite indecently.'

'I am very sorry,' he said, giving one more twist to his moustache, then breaking into a loud, short laugh at his joke.

'Do you really feel cross?' said Emily to me, knitting her brows and smiling quaintly.

'I do!' I replied, with truthful emphasis.

She laughed, and laughed again, very much amused.

'It is such a joke,' she said. 'To think you should feel cross now, when it is–how long is it ago–?'

'I will not count up,' said I.

'Are you not sorry for me?' I asked of Tom Renshaw.

He looked at me with his young blue eyes, eyes so bright, so naïvely inquisitive, so winsomely meditative. He did not know quite what to say, or how to take it.

'Very!' he replied in another short burst of laughter, quickly twisting his moustache again and looking down at his feet.

He was twenty-nine years old; had been a soldier in China for five years, was now farming his father's farm at Papplewick, where Emily was schoolmistress. He had been at home eighteen months. His father was an old man of seventy who had had his right hand chopped to bits in the chopping machine. So they told me. I liked Tom for his handsome bearing and his fresh, winsome way. He was exceedingly manly: that is to say, he did not dream of questioning or analysing anything. All that came his way was ready labelled nice or nasty, good or bad. He did not imagine that anything could be other than just what it appeared to be—and with this appearance, he was quite content. He looked up to Emily as one wiser, nobler, nearer to God than himself.

'I am a thousand years older than he,' she said to me, laughing. 'Just as you are centuries older than I.'

'And you love him for his youth?' I asked.

'Yes,' she replied. 'For that and—he is wonderfully sagacious—and so gentle.'

'And I was never gentle, was I?' I said.

'No! As restless and as urgent as the wind,' she said, and I saw a last flicker of the old terror.

'Where is George?' I asked.

'In bed,' she replied briefly. 'He's recovering from one of his orgies. If I were Meg I would not live with him.'

'Is he so bad?' I asked.

'Bad!' she replied. 'He's disgusting, and I'm sure he's dangerous. I'd have him removed to an inebriates' home.'

'You'd have to persuade him to go,' said Tom, who had come into the room again. 'He does have dreadful bouts, though! He's killing himself, sure enough. I feel awfully sorry for the fellow.'

'It seems so contemptible to me,' said Emily, 'to become enslaved to one of your likings till it makes a beast of you. Look what a spectacle he is for his children, and what a disgusting disgrace for his wife.'

'Well, if he can't help it, he can't, poor chap,' said Tom. 'Though I do think a man should have more backbone.'

We heard heavy noises from the room above.

'He is getting up,' said Emily. 'I suppose I'd better see if he'll have any breakfast.' She waited, however. Presently the door opened, and there stood George with his hand on the knob, leaning, looking in.

'I thought I heard three voices,' he said, as if it freed him from a certain apprehension. He smiled. His waistcoat hung open over his woollen shirt, he wore no coat and was slipperless. His hair and his moustache were dishevelled, his face pale and stupid with sleep, his eyes small. He turned aside from our looks as from a bright light. His hand as I shook it was flaccid and chill.

'How do you come to be here, Cyril?' he said subduedly, faintly smiling.

'Will you have any breakfast?' Emily asked him coldly.

'I'll have a bit if there's any for me,' he replied.

'It has been waiting for you long enough,' she answered. He turned and went with a dull thud of his stockinged feet across to the dining-room. Emily rang for the maid, I followed George, leaving the betrothed together. I found my host moving about the dining-room, looking behind the chairs and in the corners.

'I wonder where the devil my slippers are!' he muttered explanatorily. Meanwhile he continued his search. I noticed he did not ring the bell to have them found for him. Presently he came to the fire, spreading his hands over it. As he was smashing the slowly burning coal the maid came in with the tray. He desisted, and put the poker carefully down. While the maid spread his meal on one corner of the table, he looked in the fire, paying her no heed. When she had finished:

'It's fried white-bait,' she said. 'Shall you have that?'

He lifted his head and looked at the plate.

'Ay,' he said. 'Have you brought the vinegar?'

Without answering, she took the cruet from the sideboard and set it on the table. As she was closing the door, she looked back to say:

'You'd better eat it now, while it's hot.'

He took no notice, but sat looking in the fire.

'And how are you going on?' he asked me.

'I? Oh, very well! And you–?'

'As you see,' he replied, turning his head on one side with a little gesture of irony.

'As I am very sorry to see,' I rejoined.

He sat forward with his elbows on his knees, tapping the back of his hand with one finger, in monotonous two-pulse like heart-beats.

'Aren't you going to have breakfast?' I urged. The clock at that moment began to ring a sonorous twelve. He looked up at it with subdued irritation.

'Ay, I suppose so,' he answered me, when the clock had finished striking. He rose heavily and went to the table. As he poured out a cup of tea he spilled it on the cloth, and stood looking at the stain. It was still some time before he began to eat. He poured vinegar freely over the hot fish, and ate with an indifference that made eating ugly, pausing now and again to wipe the tea off his moustache, or to pick a bit of fish from off his knee.

'You are not married, I suppose?' he said in one of his pauses.

'No,' I replied. 'I expect I shall have to be looking round.'

'You're wiser not,' he replied, quiet and bitter.

A moment or two later the maid came in with a letter.

'This came this morning,' she said, as she laid it on the table beside him. He looked at it, then he said:

'You didn't give me a knife for the marmalade.'

'Didn't I?' she replied. 'I thought you wouldn't want it. You don't as a rule.'

'And do you know where my slippers are?' he asked.

'They ought to be in their usual place.' She went and looked in the corner. 'I suppose Miss Gertie's put them somewhere. I'll get you another pair.'

As he waited for her he read the letter. He read it twice, then he put it back in the envelope, quietly, without any change of expression. But he ate no more breakfast, even after the maid had brought the knife and his slippers, and though he had had but a few mouthfuls.

At half-past twelve there was an imperious woman's voice in the house. Meg came to the door. As she entered the room, and saw me, she stood still. She sniffed, glanced at the table, and exclaimed, coming forward effusively:

'Well I never, Cyril! Who'd a thought of seeing you here this morning! How are you?'

She waited for the last of my words, then immediately she turned to George, and said:

'I must say you're in a nice state for Cyril to see you! Have you finished?–If you have, Kate can take that tray out. It smells quite sickly. Have you finished?'

He did not answer, but drained his cup of tea and pushed it away with the back of his hand. Meg rang the bell, and having taken off her gloves, began to put the things on the tray, tipping the fragments of fish and bones from the edge of his plate to the middle with short, disgusted jerks of the fork. Her attitude and expression were of resentment and disgust. The maid came in.

'Clear the table, Kate, and open the window. Have you opened the bedroom windows?'

'No'm–not yet'–she glanced at George as if to say he had only been down a few minutes.

'Then do it when you have taken the tray,' said Meg.

'You don't open this window,' said George churlishly. 'It's cold enough as it is.'

'You should put a coat on then if you're starved,' replied Meg contemptuously. 'It's warm enough for those that have got any life in their blood. You do not find it cold, do you, Cyril?'

'It is fresh this morning,' I replied.

'Of course it is, not cold at all. And I'm sure this room needs airing.'

The maid, however, folded the cloth and went out without approaching the windows.

Meg had grown stouter, and there was a certain immovable confidence in her. She was authoritative, amiable, calm. She wore a handsome dress of dark green, and a toque with opulent ostrich feathers. As she moved about the room she seemed to dominate everything, particularly her husband, who sat ruffled and dejected, his waistcoat hanging loose over his shirt.

A girl entered. She was proud and mincing in her deportment. Her face was handsome, but too haughty for a child. She wore a white coat, with ermine tippet, muff, and hat. Her long brown hair hung twining down her back.

'Has Dad only just had his breakfast?' she exclaimed in high censorious tones as she came in.

'He has!' replied Meg.

The girl looked at her father in calm, childish censure.

'And we have been to church, and come home to dinner,' she said, as she drew off her little white gloves. George watched her with ironical amusement.

'Hello!' said Meg, glancing at the opened letter which lay near his elbow. 'Who is that from?'

He glanced round, having forgotten it. He took the envelope, doubled it and pushed it in his waistcoat pocket.

'It's from William Housley,' he replied.

'Oh! And what has he to say?' she asked.

George turned his dark eyes at her.

'Nothing!' he said.

'Hm–Hm!' sneered Meg. 'Funny letter, about nothing!'

'I suppose,' said the child, with her insolent, high-pitched superiority, 'it's some money that he doesn't want us to know about.'

'That's about it!' said Meg, giving a small laugh at the child's perspicuity.

'So's he can keep it for himself, that's what it is,' continued the child, nodding her head in rebuke at him.

'I've no right to any money, have I?' asked the father sarcastically.

'No, you haven't,' the child nodded her head at him dictatorially, 'you haven't, because you only put it in the fire.'

'You've got it wrong,' he sneered. 'You mean it's like giving a child fire to play with.'

'Um!–and it is, isn't it, Mam?'–the small woman turned to her mother for corroboration. Meg had flushed at his sneer, when he quoted for the child its mother's dictum.

'And you're very naughty!' preached Gertie, turning her back disdainfully on her father.

'Is that what the parson's been telling you?' he asked, a grain of amusement still in his bitterness.

'No, it isn't!' retorted the youngster. 'If you want to know you should go and listen for yourself. Everybody that goes to church looks nice–' she glanced at her mother and at herself, pruning herself proudly, '–and God loves them,' she added. She assumed a sanctified expression, and continued after a little thought, 'Because they look nice and are meek.'

'What!' exclaimed Meg, laughing, glancing with secret pride at me.

'Because they're meek!' repeated Gertie, with a superior little smile of knowledge.

'You're off the mark this time,' said George.

'No, I'm not, am I, Mam? Isn't it right, Mam? "The meek shall inevit the erf"?'

Meg was too much amused to answer.

'The meek shall have herrings on earth,' mocked the father, also amused. His daughter looked dubiously at him. She smelled impropriety.

'It's not, Mam, is it?' she asked, turning to her mother. Meg laughed.

'The meek shall have herrings on earth,' repeated George with soft banter.

'No, it's not, Mam, is it?' cried the child in real distress.

'Tell your father he's always teaching you something wrong,' answered Meg. Then I said I must go. They pressed me to stay.

'Oh yes–do stop to dinner,' suddenly pleaded the child, smoothing her wild ravels of curls after having drawn off her hat. She asked me again and again, with much earnestness.

'But why?' I asked.

'So's you can talk to us this afternoon–an' so's Dad won't be so dis'greeable,' she replied plaintively, poking the black spots on her muff.

Meg moved nearer to her daughter with a little gesture of compassion.

'But,' said I, 'I promised a lady I would be back for lunch, so I must. You have some more visitors, you know.'

'Oh, well!' she complained. 'They go in another room, and Dad doesn't care about them.'

'But come!' said I.

'Well, he's just as dis'greeable when Auntie Emily's here–he is with her an' all.'

'You *are* having your character given away,' said Meg brutally, turning to him.

I bade him good-bye. He did me the honour of coming with me to the door. We could neither of us find a word to say, though we were both moved. When at last I held his hand and was looking at him as I said 'Good-bye', he looked back at me for the first time during our meeting. His eyes were heavy, and as he lifted them to me, seemed to recoil in an agony of shame.

8

A PROSPECT AMONG THE MARSHES OF LETHE

George steadily declined from this time. I went to see him two years later. He was not at home. Meg wept to me as she told me of him, how he let the business slip, how he drank, what a brute he was in drink, and how unbearable afterwards. He was ruining his constitution, he was ruining her life and the children's. I felt very sorry for her as she sat, large and ruddy, brimming over with bitter tears. She asked me if I did not think I might influence him. He was, she said, at the Ram. When he had an extra bad bout on he went up there, and stayed sometimes for a week at a time, with Oswald, coming back to the Hollies when he had recovered–'though,' said Meg, 'he's sick every morning and almost after every meal.'

All the time Meg was telling me this, sat curled up in a large chair their youngest boy, a pale, sensitive, rather spoiled lad of seven or eight years, with a petulant mouth and nervous dark eyes. He sat watching his mother as she told her tale, heaving his shoulders and settling himself in a new position when his feelings were nearly too much for him. He was full of wild, childish pity for his mother, and furious, childish hate of his father, the author of all their trouble. I called at the Ram and saw George. He was half drunk.

I went up to Highclose with a heavy heart. Lettie's last child had been born, much to the surprise of everybody, some few months before I came down. There was a space of seven years between her youngest girl and this baby. Lettie was much absorbed in motherhood.

When I went up to talk to her about George, I found her in the bedroom nursing the baby, who was very good and quiet on her knee. She listened to me sadly, but her attention was caught away by each movement made by the child. As I was telling her of the attitude of George's children towards their father and mother, she glanced from the baby to me, and exclaimed:

'See how he watches the light flash across your spectacles when you turn suddenly–Look!'

But I was weary of babies. My friends had all grown up and married and inflicted them on me. There were storms of babies. I longed for a place where they would be obsolete, and young, arrogant, impervious mothers might be a forgotten tradition. Lettie's heart would quicken in answer to only one pulse, the easy, light ticking of the baby's blood.

I remembered, one day as I sat in the train hastening to Charing Cross on my way from France, that that was George's birthday. I had the feeling of him upon me, heavily, and I could not rid myself of the depression. I put it down to travel fatigue, and tried to dismiss it. As I watched the evening sun glitter along the new corn-stubble in the fields we passed, trying to describe the effect to myself, I found myself asking, 'But–what's the matter? I've not had bad news, have I, to make my chest feel so weighted?'

I was surprised when I reached my lodging in New Malden to find no letters for me, save one fat budget from Alice. I knew her squat, saturnine handwriting on the envelope, and I thought I knew what contents to expect from the letter.

She had married an old acquaintance who had been her particular aversion. This young man had got himself into trouble, so that the condemnations of the righteous pursued him like clouds of gnats on a summer evening. Alice immediately rose to sting back his vulgar enemies, and having rendered him a service, felt she could only wipe out the score by marrying him. They were fairly comfortable. Occasionally, as she said, there were displays of small fireworks in the back yard. He worked in the offices of some iron foundries just over the Erewash in Derbyshire. Alice lived in a dirty little place in the valley a mile and a half from Eberwich, not far from his work. She had no children, and practically no friends; a few young matrons for acquaintances. As wife of a superior clerk, she had to preserve her dignity among the work-people. So all her little crackling fires were sodded down with the sods of British respectability. Occasionally she smouldered a fierce smoke that made one's eyes water. Occasionally, perhaps once a year, she wrote me a whole venomous budget, much to my amusement.

I was not in any haste to open this fat letter until, after supper, I turned to it as a resource from my depression.

'Oh dear, Cyril, I'm in a bubbling state, I want to yell, not write. Oh, Cyril, why didn't *you* marry me, or why didn't our Georgie Saxton, or somebody. I'm deadly sick. Percival Charles is enough to stop a clock. Oh, Cyril, he lives in an eternal Sunday suit, holy broadcloth and righteous three inches of cuffs! He goes to bed in it. Nay, he wallows in Bibles when he goes to bed. I can feel the brass covers of all his family Bibles sticking in my ribs as I lie by his side. I could weep with wrath, yet I put on my black hat and trot to chapel with him like a lamb.

'Oh, Cyril, nothing's happened. Nothing has happened to me all these years. I shall die of it. When I see Percival Charles at dinner, after having asked a blessing, I feel as if I should never touch a bit at his table again. In about an hour I shall hear him hurrying up the entry—prayers always make him hungry—and his first look will be on the table. But I'm not fair to him—he's really a good fellow—I only wish he wasn't.

'It's George Saxton who's put this Seidlitz powder in my marital cup of cocoa. Cyril, I must a tale unfold. It is fifteen years since our George married Meg. When I count up, and think of the future, it nearly makes me scream. But my tale, my tale!

'Can you remember his faithful-dog, wounded-stag, gentle-gazelle eyes? Cyril, you can see the whisky, or the brandy combusting in them. He's got d.t.'s, blue-devils—and I've seen him, and I'm swarming myself with little red devils after it. I went up to Eberwich on Wednesday afternoon for a pound of fry for Percival Charles's Thursday dinner. I walked by that little path which you know goes round the back of the Hollies—it's as near as any way for me. I thought I heard a row in the paddock at the back of the stables, so I said I might as well see the fun. I went to the gate, basket in one hand, ninepence in coppers in the other, a demure deacon's wife. I didn't take in the scene at first.

'There was our Georgie, in leggings and breeches as of yore, and a whip. He was flourishing, and striding, and yelling. "Go it, old boy," I said, "you'll want your stocking round your throat tonight." But, Cyril, I had spoken too soon. Oh, lum! There came raking up the croft that long, wire-springy racehorse of his, ears flat, and, clinging to its neck, the pale-faced lad, Wilfred. The kid was white as death, and squealing "Mam! Mam!" I thought it was a bit rotten of Georgie trying to teach the kid to jockey. The race-horse, Bonny-Boy–Boney Boy, I call him–came bouncing round like a spiral egg-whish. Then I saw our Georgie rush up screaming, nearly spitting the moustache off his face, and fetch the horse a cut with the whip. It went off like a flame along hot paraffin. The kid shrieked and clung. Georgie went rushing after him, running staggery, and swearing, fairly screaming–awful–"a lily-livered little swine!" The high lanky race-horse went larroping round as if it was going mad. I was dazed. Then Meg came rushing, and the other two lads, all screaming. She went for George, but he lifted his whip like the devil. She daren't go near him–she rushed at him, and stopped, rushed at him, and stopped, striking at him with her two fists. He waved his whip and kept her off, and the race-horse kept tearing along. Meg flew to stop it, he ran with his drunken totter-step, brandishing his whip. I flew as well. I hit him with my basket. The kid fell off, and Meg rushed to him. Some men came running. George stood fairly shuddering. You would never have known his face, Cyril. He was mad, demoniacal. I feel sometimes as if I should burst and shatter to bits like a sky-rocket when I think of it. I've got such a weal on my arm.

'I lost Percival Charles's ninepence and my nice white cloth out of the basket, and everything, besides having black looks on Thursday because it was mutton-chops, which he hates. Oh, Cyril, "I wish I was a cassowary, on the banks of the Timbuctoo." When I saw Meg sobbing over that lad–thank goodness he wasn't hurt!–I wished our Georgie was dead; I do now, also; I wish we only had to remember him. I haven't been to see them lately–can't stand Meg's ikeyness. I wonder how it all will end.

'There's P. C. bidding "Good night and God bless You" to Brother Jakes, and no supper ready–'

As soon as I could, after reading Alice's letter, I went down to Eberwich to see how things were. Memories of the old days came over me again till my heart hungered for its old people.

They told me at the Hollies that, after a bad attack of delirium tremens, George had been sent to Papplewick in the lonely country to stay with Emily. I borrowed a bicycle to ride the nine miles. The summer had been wet, and everything was late. At the end of September the foliage was heavy green, and the wheat stood dejectedly in stook. I rode through the still sweetness of an autumn morning. The mist was folded blue along the hedges; the elm trees loomed up along the dim walls of the morning, the horse-chestnut trees at hand flickered with a few yellow leaves like bright blossoms. As I rode through the tree tunnel by the church where, on his last night, the keeper had told me his story, I smelled the cold rotting of the leaves of the cloudy summer.

I passed silently through the lanes, where the chill grass was weighed down with grey-blue seed-pearls of dew in the shadow, where the wet woollen spider-cloths of autumn were spread as on a loom. Brown birds rustled in flocks like driven leaves before me. I heard the far-off hooting of the 'loose-all' at the pits, telling me it was half-past eleven, that the men and boys would be sitting in the narrow darkness of the mines eating their 'snap', while shadowy mice darted for the crumbs, and the boys laughed with red mouths rimmed with grime, as the bold little creatures peeped at them in the dim light of the lamps. The dogwood berries stood jauntily scarlet on the hedge-tops, the bunched scarlet and green berries of the convolvulus and bryony hung amid golden trails, the blackberries dropped ungathered. I rode slowly on, the plants dying around me, the berries leaning their heavy ruddy mouths, and languishing for the birds, the men imprisoned underground below me, the brown birds dashing in haste along the hedges.

Swineshed Farm, where the Renshaws lived, stood quite alone among its fields, hidden from the highway and from everything. The lane leading up to it was deep and unsunned. On my right, I caught glimpses through the hedge of the cornfields, where the shocks of wheat stood like small yellow-sailed ships in a widespread flotilla. The upper part of the field was cleared. I heard the clank of a wagon and the voices of men, and I saw the high load of sheaves go lurching, rocking up the incline to the stack-yard.

The lane debouched into a close-bitten field, and out of this empty land the farm rose up with its buildings like a huddle of old, painted vessels floating in still water. White fowls went stepping discreetly through the mild sunshine and the shadow. I leaned my bicycle against the grey, silken doors of the old coach-house. The place was breathing with silence. I hesitated to knock at the open door. Emily came. She was rich as always with her large beauty, and stately now with the stateliness of a strong woman six months gone with child.

She exclaimed with surprise, and I followed her into the kitchen, catching a glimpse of the glistening pans and the white wood baths as I passed through the scullery. The kitchen was a good-sized, low room that through long course of years had become absolutely a home. The great beams of the ceiling bowed easily, the chimney-seat had a bit of dark-green curtain, and under the high mantelpiece was another low shelf that the men could reach with their hands as they sat in the inglenook. There the pipes lay. Many generations of peaceful men and fruitful women had passed through the room, and not one but had added a new small comfort; a chair in the right place, a hook, a stool, a cushion, a certain pleasing cloth for the sofa covers, a shelf of books. The room, that looked so quiet and crude, was a home evolved through generations to fit the large bodies of the men who dwelled in it, and the placid fancy of the women. At last, it had an individuality. It was the home of the Renshaws, warm, lovable, serene. Emily was in perfect accord with its brownness, its shadows, its ease. I, as I sat on the sofa under the window, felt rejected by the kind room. I was distressed with a sense of ephemerality, of pale, erratic fragility.

Emily, in her full-blooded beauty, was at home. It is rare now to feel a kinship between a room and the one who inhabits it, a close bond of blood relation. Emily had at last found her place, and had escaped from the torture of strange, complex modern life. She was making a pie, and the flour was white on her brown arms. She pushed the tickling hair from her face with her arm, and looked at me with tranquil pleasure, as she worked the paste in the yellow bowl. I was quiet, subdued before her.

'You are very happy?' I said.

'Ah, very!' she replied. 'And you?—you are not, you look worn.'

'Yes,' I replied. 'I am happy enough. I am living my life.'

'Don't you find it wearisome?' she asked pityingly.

She made me tell her all my doings, and she marvelled, but all the time her eyes were dubious and pitiful.

'You have George here,' I said.

'Yes. He's in a poor state, but he's not as sick as he was.'

'What about the delirium tremens?'

'Oh, he was better of that—very nearly—before he came here. He sometimes fancies they're coming on again, and he's terrified. Isn't it awful! And he's brought it all on himself. Tom's very good to him.'

'There's nothing the matter with him–physically, is there?' I asked.

'I don't know,' she replied, as she went to the oven to turn a pie that was baking. She put her arm to her forehead and brushed aside her hair, leaving a mark of flour on her nose. For a moment or two she remained kneeling on the fender, looking into the fire and thinking. 'He was in a poor way when he came here, could eat nothing, sick every morning. I suppose it's his liver. They all end like that.' She continued to wipe the large black plums and put them in the dish.

'Hardening of the liver?' I asked. She nodded.

'And is he in bed?' I asked again.

'Yes,' she replied. 'It's as I say, if he'd get up and potter about a bit, he'd get over it. But he lies there skulking.'

'And what time will he get up?' I insisted.

'I don't know. He may crawl down somewhere towards tea-time. Do you want to see him? That's what you came for, isn't it?'

She smiled at me with a little sarcasm, and added. 'You always thought more of him than anybody, didn't you? Ah, well, come up and see him.'

I followed her up the back stairs, which led out of the kitchen, and which emerged straight in a bedroom. We crossed the hollow-sounding plaster-floor of this naked room and opened a door at the opposite side. George lay in bed watching us with apprehensive eyes.

'Here is Cyril come to see you,' said Emily, 'so I've brought him up, for I didn't know when you'd be downstairs.'

A small smile of relief came on his face, and he put out his hand from the bed. He lay with the disorderly clothes pulled up to his chin. His face was discoloured and rather bloated, his nose swollen.

'Don't you feel so well this morning?' asked Emily, softening with pity when she came into contact with his sickness.

'Oh, all right,' he replied, wishing only to get rid of us.

'You should try to get up a bit, it's a beautiful morning, warm and soft–' she said gently. He did not reply, and she went downstairs.

I looked round to the cold, whitewashed room, with its ceiling curving and sloping down the walls. It was sparsely furnished, and bare of even the slightest ornament. The only things of warm colour were the cow and horse skins on the floor. All the rest was white or grey or drab. On one side, the room sloped down so that the window was below my knees, and nearly touching the floor, on the other side was a larger window, breast high. Through it one could see the jumbled, ruddy roofs of the sheds and the skies. The tiles were shining with patches of vivid orange lichen. Beyond was the cornfield, and the men, small in the distance, lifting the sheaves on the cart.

'You will come back to farming again, won't you?' I asked him, turning to the bed. He smiled.

'I don't know,' he answered dully.

'Would you rather I went downstairs?' I asked.

'No, I'm glad to see you,' he replied, in the same uneasy fashion.

'I've only just come back from France,' I said.

'Ah!' he replied, indifferent.

'I am sorry you're ill,' I said.

He stared unmovedly at the opposite wall. I went to the window and looked out. After some time, I compelled myself to say, in a casual manner:

'Won't you get up and come out a bit?'

'I suppose I s'll have to,' he said, gathering himself slowly together for the effort. He pushed himself up in bed.

When he took off the jacket of his pyjamas to wash himself I turned away. His arms seemed thin, and he had bellied, and was bowed and unsightly. I remembered the morning we swam in the millpond. I remembered that he was now in the prime of his life. I looked at his bluish feeble hands as he laboriously washed himself. The soap once slipped from his fingers as he was picking it up, and fell, rattling the pot loudly. It startled us, and he seemed to grip the sides of the washstand to steady himself. Then he went on with his slow, painful toilet. As he combed his hair he looked at himself with dull eyes of shame.

The men were coming in from the scullery when we got downstairs. Dinner was smoking on the table. I shook hands with Tom Renshaw, and with the old man's hard, fierce left hand. Then I was introduced to Arthur Renshaw, a clean-faced, large, bashful lad of twenty. I nodded to the man, Jim, and to Jim's wife, Annie. We all sat down to table.

'Well, an' 'ow are ter feelin' by now, like?' asked the old man heartily of George. Receiving no answer, he continued, 'Tha should 'a gor up an' com' an' gen us a 'and wi' th' wheat, it 'ud 'a done thee good.'

'You will have a bit of this mutton, won't you?' Tom asked him, tapping the joint with the carving-knife. George shook his head.

'It's quite lean and tender,' he said gently.

'No, thanks,' said George.

'Gi'e 'im a bit, gi'e 'im a bit!' cried the old man. 'It'll do 'im good–it's what 'e wants, a bit o' strengthenin' nourishment.'

'It's no good if his stomach won't have it.' said Tom, in mild reproof, as if he were speaking of a child. Arthur filled George's glass with beer without speaking. The two young men were full of kind, gentle attention.

'Let im 'a'e a spoonful o' tonnup then,' persisted the old man. 'I canna eat while 'is plate stands there emp'y.'

So they put turnip and onion sauce on George's plate, and he took up his fork and tasted a few mouthfuls. The men ate largely, and with zest. The sight of their grand satisfaction, amounting almost to gusto, sickened him.

When at last the old man laid down the dessert-spoon which he used in place of a knife and fork, he looked again at George's plate, and said:

'Why tha 'asna aten a smite, not a smite! Tha non goos th' raight road to be better.'

George maintained a stupid silence.

'Don't bother him, Father,' said Emily.

'Tha art an öwd whittle, Feythey,' added Tom, smiling good-naturedly. He spoke to his father in dialect, but to Emily in good English. Whatever she said had Tom's immediate support. Before serving us with pie, Emily gave her brother junket and damsons, setting the plate and the spoon before him as if he were a child. For this act of grace Tom looked at her lovingly, and stroked her hand as she passed.

After dinner, George said, with a miserable struggle for an indifferent tone:

'Aren't you going to give Cyril a glass of whisky?'

He looked up furtively, in a conflict of shame and hope. A silence fell on the room.

'Ay!' said the old man softly. 'Let 'im 'ave a drop.'

'Yes!' added Tom, in submissive pleading.

All the men in the room shrank a little, awaiting the verdict of the woman.

'I don't know,' she said clearly, 'that Cyril wants a glass.'

'I don't mind,' I answered, feeling myself blush. I had not the courage to counteract her will directly. Not even the old man had that courage. We waited in suspense. After keeping us so for a few minutes, while we smouldered with mortification, she went into another room, and we heard her unlocking a door. She returned with a decanter containing rather less than half a pint of liquor. She put out five tumblers.

'Tha neda gi'e me none,' said the old man. 'Ah'm non a proud chap. Ah'm not.'

'Nor me neither,' said Arthur.

'You will, Tom?' she asked.

'Do you want me to?' he replied, smiling.

'I don't,' she answered sharply. 'I want nobody to have it, when you look at the results of it. But if Cyril is having a glass, you may as well have one with him.'

Tom was pleased with her. She gave her husband and me fairly stiff glasses.

'Steady, steady!' he said. 'Give that to George, and give me not so much. Two fingers, two of your fingers, you know.'

But she passed him the glass. When George had had his share, there remained but a drop in the decanter.

Emily watched the drunkard coldly as he took this remainder.

George and I talked for a time while the men smoked. He, from his glum stupidity, broke into a harsh, almost imbecile loquacity.

'Have you seen my family lately?' he asked, continuing. 'Yes! Not badly set up, are they, the children? But the little devils are soft, mard-soft, every one of 'em. It's their mother's bringin' up–she marded 'em till they were soft, an' would never let me have a say in it. I should 'a brought 'em up different, you know I should.'

Tom looked at Emily, and, remarking her angry contempt, suggested that she should go out with him to look at the stacks. I watched the tall, square-shouldered man leaning with deference and tenderness towards his wife as she walked calmly at his side. She was the mistress, quiet and self-assured, he her rejoiced husband and servant.

George was talking about himself. If I had not seen him, I should hardly have recognised the words as his. He was lamentably decayed. He talked stupidly, with vulgar contumely of others, and in weak praise of himself.

The old man rose, with a:

'Well, I suppose we mun ma'e another dag at it,' and the men left the house.

George continued his foolish, harsh monologue, making gestures of emphasis with his head and his hands. He continued when we were walking round the buildings into the fields, the same babble of bragging and abuse. I was wearied and disgusted. He looked, and he sounded, so worthless.

Across the empty cornfield the partridges were running. We walked through the September haze slowly, because he was feeble on his legs. As he became tired he ceased to talk. We leaned for some time on a gate, in the brief glow of the transient afternoon, and he was stupid again. He did not notice the brown haste of the partridges, he did not care to share with me the handful of ripe blackberries, and when I pulled the bryony ropes off the hedges, and held the great knots of red and green berries in my hand, he glanced at them without interest or appreciation.

'Poison-berries, aren't they?' he said dully.

Like a tree that is falling, going soft and pale and rotten, clammy with small fungi, he stood leaning against the gate, while the dim afternoon drifted with a flow of thick sweet sunshine past him, not touching him.

In the stackyard, the summer's splendid monuments of wheat and grass were reared in gold and grey. The wheat was littered brightly round the rising stack. The loaded wagon clanked slowly up the incline, drew near, and rode like a ship at anchor against the scotches, brushing the stack with a crisp, sharp sound. Tom climbed the ladder and stood a moment there against the sky, amid the brightness and fragrance of the gold corn, and waved his arm to his wife who was passing in the shadow of the building. Then Arthur began to lift the sheaves to the stack, and the two men worked in an exquisite, subtle rhythm, their white sleeves and their dark heads gleaming, moving against the mild sky and the corn. The silence was broken only by the occasional lurch of the body of the wagon, as the teamer stepped to the front, or again to the rear of the load. Occasionally I could catch the blue glitter of the prongs of the forks. Tom, now lifted high above the small wagon load, called to his brother some question about the stack. The sound of his voice was strong and mellow.

I turned to George, who was also watching, and said:

'You ought to be like that.'

We heard Tom calling, 'All right!' and saw him standing high up on the tallest corner of the stack, as on the prow of a ship.

George watched, and his face slowly gathered expression. He turned to me, his dark eyes alive with horror and despair.

'I shall soon—be out of everybody's way!' he said. His moment of fear and despair was cruel. I cursed myself for having roused him from his stupor.

'You will be better,' I said.

He watched again the handsome movement of the men at the stack.

'I couldn't team ten sheaves,' he said.

'You will in a month or two,' I urged.

He continued to watch, while Tom got on the ladder and came down the front of the stack.

'Nay, the sooner I clear out, the better,' he repeated to himself.

When we went in to tea, he was, as Tom said, 'downcast'. The men talked uneasily with abated voices. Emily attended to him with a little, palpitating solicitude. We were all uncomfortably impressed with the sense of our alienation from him. He sat apart and obscure among us, like a condemned man.

D.H. LAWRENCE

LOVE AMONG THE HAYSTACKS

I

The two large fields lay on a hillside facing south. Being newly cleared of hay, they were golden green, and they shone almost blindingly in the sunlight. Across the hill, half-way up, ran a high hedge, that flung its black shadow finely across the molten glow of the sward. The stack was being built just above the hedge. It was of great size, massive, but so silvery and delicately bright in tone that it seemed not to have weight. It rose dishevelled and radiant among the steady, golden-green glare of the field. A little farther back was another, finished stack.

The empty wagon was just passing through the gap in the hedge. From the far-off corner of the bottom field, where the sward was still striped grey with winrows, the loaded wagon launched forward to climb the hill to the stack. The white dots of the hay-makers showed distinctly among the hay.

The two brothers were having a moment's rest, waiting for the load to come up. They stood wiping their brows with their arms, sighing from the heat and the labour of placing the last load. The stack they rode was high, lifting them up above the hedge-tops, and very broad, a great slightly-hollowed vessel into which the sunlight poured, in which the hot, sweet scent of hay was suffocating. Small and inefficacious the brothers looked, half-submerged in the loose, great trough, lifted high up as if on an altar reared to the sun.

Maurice, the younger brother, was a handsome young fellow of twenty-one, careless and debonair, and full of vigour. His grey eyes, as he taunted his brother, were bright and baffled with a strong emotion. His swarthy face had the same peculiar smile, expectant and glad and nervous, of a young man roused for the first time in passion.

'Tha sees,' he said, as he leaned on the pommel of his fork, 'tha thowt as tha'd done me one, didna ter?' He smiled as he spoke, then fell again into his pleasant torment of musing.

'I thought nowt – tha knows so much,' retorted Geoffrey, with the touch of a sneer. His brother had the better of him. Geoffrey was a very heavy, hulking fellow, a year older than Maurice. His blue eyes were unsteady, they glanced away quickly; his mouth was morbidly sensitive. One felt him wince away, through the whole of his great body. His inflamed self-consciousness was a disease in him.

'Ah, but though, I know tha did,' mocked Maurice. 'Tha went slinkin' off' – Geoffrey winced convulsively – 'thinking as that wor the last night as any of us'ud ha'e ter stop here, an' so tha'd leave me to sleep out, though it wor thy turn–'

He smiled to himself, thinking of the result of Geoffrey's ruse.

'I didna go slinkin' off neither,' retorted Geoffrey, in his heavy, clumsy manner, wincing at the phrase. 'Didna my feyther send me to fetch some coal–'

'Oh yes, oh yes – we know all about it. But tha sees what tha missed, my lad.'

Maurice, chuckling, threw himself on his back in the bed of hay. There was absolutely nothing in his world, then, except the shallow ramparts of the stack, and the blazing sky. He clenched his fists tight, threw his arms across his face, and braced his muscles again. He was evidently very much moved, so acutely that it was hardly pleasant, though he still smiled. Geoffrey, standing behind him, could just see his red mouth, with the young moustache like black fur, curling back and showing the teeth in a smile. The elder brother leaned his chin on the pommel of his fork, looking out across the country.

Far away was the faint blue heap of Nottingham. Between, the country lay under a haze of heat, with here and there a flag of colliery smoke waving. But near at hand, at the foot of the hill, across the deep-hedged high road, was only the silence of the old church and the castle farm, among their trees. The large view only made Geoffrey more sick. He looked away, to the wagons crossing the field below him, the empty cart like a big insect moving down-hill, the load coming up, rocking like a ship, the brown head of the horse ducking, the brown knees lifted and planted strenuously. Geoffrey wished it would be quick.

'Tha didna think—'

Geoffrey started, coiled within himself, and looked down at the handsome lips moving in speech below the brown arms of his brother.

'Tha didna think 'er'd be thur wi' me—or tha wouldna ha' left me to it,' Maurice said, ending with a little laugh of excited memory. Geoffrey flushed with hate, and had an impulse to set his foot on that moving, taunting mouth, which was there below him. There was silence for a time, then, in a peculiar tone of delight, Maurice's voice came again, spelling out the words, as it were:

'Ich bin klein, mein Herz ist rein,
Ist niemand d'rin als Christ allein.'

Maurice chuckled, then, convulsed at a twinge of recollection, keen as pain, he twisted over, pressed himself into the hay.

'Can thee say thy prayers in German?' came his muffled voice.

'I non want,' growled Geoffrey.

Maurice chuckled. His face was quite hidden, and in the dark he was going over again his last night's experiences.

'What about kissing 'er under th' ear, Sonny,' he said, in a curious, uneasy tone. He writhed, still startled and inflamed by his first contact with love.

Geoffrey's heart swelled within him, and things went dark. He could not see the landscape.

'An' there's just a nice two-handful of her bosom,' came the low, provocative tones of Maurice, who seemed to be talking to himself.

The two brothers were both fiercely shy of women, and until this hay harvest, the whole feminine sex had been represented by their mother and in presence of any other women they were dumb louts. Moreover, brought up by a proud mother, a stranger in the country, they held the common girls as beneath them, because beneath their mother, who spoke pure English, and was very quiet. Loud-mouthed and broad-tongued the common girls were. So these two young men had grown up virgin but tormented.

Now again Maurice had the start of Geoffrey, and the elder brother was deeply mortified. There was a danger of his sinking into a morbid state, from sheer lack of living, lack of interest. The foreign governess at the Vicarage, whose garden lay beside the top field, had talked to the lads through the hedge, and had fascinated them. There was a great elder bush, with its broad creamy flowers crumbling on to the garden path, and into the field. Geoffrey never smelled elder-flower without starting and wincing, thinking of the strange foreign voice that had so startled him as he mowed out with the scythe in the hedge bottom. A baby had run through the gap, and the Fräulein, calling in German, had come brushing down the flowers in pursuit. She had started so on seeing a man standing there in the shade, that for a moment she could not move: and then she had blundered into the rake which was lying by his side. Geoffrey, forgetting she was a woman when he saw her pitch forward, had picked her up carefully, asking: 'Have you hurt you?'

Then she had broken into a laugh, and answered in German, showing him her arms, and knitting her brows. She was nettled rather badly.

'You want a dock leaf,' he said. She frowned in a puzzled fashion.

'A dock leaf?' she repeated. He had rubbed her arms with the green leaf.

And now, she had taken to Maurice. She had seemed to prefer himself at first. Now she had sat with Maurice in the moonlight, and had let him kiss her. Geoffrey sullenly suffered, making no fight.

Unconsciously, he was looking at the Vicarage garden. There she was, in a golden-brown dress. He took off his hat, and held up his right hand in greeting to her. She, a small, golden figure, waved her hand negligently from among the potato rows. He remained, arrested, in the same posture, his hat in his left hand, his right arm upraised, thinking. He could tell by the negligence of her greeting that she was waiting for Maurice. What did she think of himself? Why wouldn't she have him?

Hearing the voice of the wagoner leading the load, Maurice rose. Geoffrey still stood in the same way, but his face was sullen, and his upraised hand was slack with brooding. Maurice faced up-hill. His eyes lit up and he laughed. Geoffrey dropped his own arm, watching.

'Lad!' chuckled Maurice. 'I non knowed 'er wor there.' He waved his hand clumsily. In these matters Geoffrey did better. The elder brother watched the girl. She ran to the end of the path, behind the bushes, so that she was screened from the house. Then she waved her handkerchief wildly. Maurice did not notice the manoeuvre. There was the cry of a child. The girl's figure vanished, reappeared holding up a white childish bundle, and came down the path. There she put down her charge, sped up-hill to a great ash tree, climbed quickly to a large horizontal bar that formed the fence there, and, standing poised, blew kisses with both her hands, in a foreign fashion that excited the brothers. Maurice laughed aloud, as he waved his red handkerchief.

'Well, what's the danger?' shouted a mocking voice from below. Maurice collapsed, blushing furiously.

'Nowt!' he called.

There was a hearty laugh from below.

The load rode up, sheered with a hiss against the stack, then sank back again upon the scotches. The brothers ploughed across the mass of hay, taking the forks. Presently a big burly man, red and glistening, climbed to the top of the load. Then he turned round, scrutinised the hillside from under his shaggy brows. He caught sight of the girl under the ash tree.

'Oh, that's who it is,' he laughed. 'I thought it was some such bird, but I couldn't see her.'

The father laughed in a hearty, chaffing way, then began to teem the load. Geoffrey, on the stack above, received his great forkfuls, and swung them over to Maurice, who took them, placed them, building the stack. In the intense sunlight, the three worked in silence, knit together in a brief passion of work. The father stirred slowly for a moment, getting the hay from under his feet. Geoffrey waited, the blue tines of his fork glittering in expectation: the mass rose, his fork swung beneath it, there was a light clash of blades, then the hay was swept on to the stack, caught by Maurice, who placed it judiciously. One after another, the shoulders of the three men bowed and braced themselves. All wore light blue, bleached shirts, that stuck close to their backs. The father moved mechanically, his thick, rounded shoulders bending and lifting dully: he worked monotonously. Geoffrey flung away his strength. His massive shoulders swept and flung the hay extravagantly.

'Dost want to knock me ower?' asked Maurice angrily. He had to brace himself against the impact. The three men worked intensely, as if some will urged them. Maurice was light and swift at the work, but he had to use his judgment. Also, when he had to place the hay along the far ends, he had some distance to carry it. So he was too slow for Geoffrey. Ordinarily, the elder would have placed the hay as far as possible where his brother wanted it. Now, however, he pitched his forkfuls into the middle of the stack. Maurice strode swiftly and handsomely across the bed, but the work was too much for him. The other two men, clenched in their receive and deliver, kept up a high pitch of labour. Geoffrey still flung the hay at random. Maurice was perspiring heavily with heat and exertion, and was getting worried. Now and again, Geoffrey wiped his arm across his brow, mechanically, like an animal. Then he glanced with satisfaction at Maurice's moiled condition, and caught the next forkful.

'Wheer dost think thou'rt hollin' it, fool!' panted Maurice, as his brother flung a forkful out of reach.

'Wheer I've a mind,' answered Geoffrey.

Maurice toiled on, now very angry. He felt the sweat trickling down his body: drops fell into his long black lashes, blinding him, so that he had to stop and angrily dash his eyes clear. The veins stood out in his swarthy neck. He felt he would burst, or drop, if the work did not soon slacken off. He heard his father's fork dully scrape the cart bottom.

'There, the last,' the father panted. Geoffrey tossed the last light lot at random, took off his hat, and, steaming in the sunshine as he wiped himself, stood complacently watching Maurice struggle with clearing the bed.

'Don't you think you've got your bottom corner a bit far out?' came the father's voice from below. 'You'd better be drawing in now, hadn't you?'

'I thought you said next load,' Maurice called sulkily.

'Aye! All right. But isn't this bottom corner–?'

Maurice, impatient, took no notice.

Geoffrey strode over the stack, and stuck his fork in the offending corner. 'What–here?' he bawled in his great voice.

'Aye–isn't it a bit loose?' came the irritating voice.

Geoffrey pushed his fork in the jutting corner, and, leaning his weight on the handle, shoved. He thought it shook. He thrust again with all his power. The mass swayed.

'What art up to, tha fool!' cried Maurice, in a high voice.

'Mind who tha'rt callin' a fool,' said Geoffrey, and he prepared to push again. Maurice sprang across, and elbowed his brother aside. On the yielding, swaying bed of hay, Geoffrey lost his foothold and fell grovelling. Maurice tried the corner.

'It's solid enough,' he shouted angrily.

'Aye–all right,' came the conciliatory voice of the father; 'you do get a bit of rest now there's such a long way to cart it,' he added reflectively.

Geoffrey had got to his feet.

'Tha'll mind who tha'rt nudging, I can tell thee,' he threatened heavily; adding, as Maurice continued to work, 'an' tha non ca's him a fool again, dost hear?'

'Not till next time,' sneered Maurice.

As he worked silently round the stack, he neared where his brother stood like a sullen statue, leaning on his fork-handle, looking out over the countryside. Maurice's heart quickened in its beat. He worked forward, until a point of his fork caught in the leather of Geoffrey's boot, and the metal rang sharply.

'Are ter going ta shift thysen?' asked Maurice threateningly. There was no reply from the great block. Maurice lifted his upper lips like a dog. Then he put out his elbow and tried to push his brother into the stack, clear of his way.

'Who are ter shovin'?' came the deep, dangerous voice.

'Thaïgh,' replied Maurice, with a sneer, and straightway the two brothers set themselves against each other, like opposing bulls, Maurice trying his hardest to shift Geoffrey from his footing, Geoffrey leaning all his weight in resistance. Maurice, insecure in his footing, staggered a little, and Geoffrey's weight followed him. He went slithering over the edge of the stack.

Geoffrey turned white to the lips, and remained standing, listening. He heard the fall. Then a flush of darkness came over him, and he remained standing only because he was planted. He had not strength to move. He could hear no sound from below, was only faintly aware of a sharp shriek from a long way off. He listened again. Then he filled with sudden panic.

'Feyther!' he roared, in his tremendous voice: 'Feyther! Feyther!'

The valley re-echoed with the sound. Small cattle on the hillside looked up. Men's figures came running from the bottom field, and much nearer a woman's figure was racing across the upper field. Geoffrey waited in terrible suspense.

'Ah-h!' he heard the strange, wild voice of the girl cry out. 'Ah-h!'–and then some foreign wailing speech. Then: 'Ah-h! Are you dea-ed!'

He stood sullenly erect on the stack, not daring to go down, longing to hide in the hay, but too sullen to stoop out of sight. He heard his eldest brother come up, panting:

'Whatever's amiss!' and then the labourer, and then his father.

'Whatever have you been doing?' he heard his father ask, while yet he had not come round the corner of the stack. And then, in a low, bitter tone:

'Eh, he's done for! I'd no business to ha' put it all on that stack.'

There was a moment or two of silence, then the voice of Henry, the eldest brother, said crisply:

'He's not dead–he's coming round.'

Geoffrey heard, but was not glad. He had as lief Maurice were dead. At least that would be final: better than meeting his brother's charges, and of seeing his mother pass to the sick-room. If Maurice was killed, he himself would not explain, no, not a word, and they could hang him if they liked. If Maurice were only hurt, then everybody would know, and Geoffrey could never lift his face again. What added torture, to pass along, everybody knowing. He wanted something that he could stand back to, something definite, if it were only the knowledge that he had killed his brother. He *must* have something firm to back up to, or he would go mad. He was so lonely, he who above all needed the support of sympathy.

'No, he's commin' to; I tell you he is,' said the labourer.   ·

'He's not dea-ed, he's not dea-ed,' came the passionate, strange sing-song of the foreign girl. 'He's not dead–no-o.'

'He wants some brandy–look at the colour of his lips,' said the crisp, cold voice of Henry. 'Can you fetch some?'

'Wha-at? Fetch?' Fräulein did not understand.

'Brandy,' said Henry, very distinct.

'Brrandy!' she re-echoed.

'You go, Bill,' groaned the father.

'Aye, I'll go,' replied Bill, and he ran across the field..

Maurice was not dead, nor going to die. This Geoffrey now realised. He was glad after all that the extreme penalty was revoked. But he hated to think of himself going on. He would always shrink now. He had hoped and hoped for the time when he would be careless, bold as Maurice, when he would not wince and shrink. Now he would always be the same, coiling up in himself like a tortoise with no shell.

'Ah-h! He's getting better!' came the wild voice of the Fräulein, and she began to cry, a strange sound, that startled the men, made the animal bristle within them. Geoffrey shuddered as he heard, between her sobbing, the impatient moaning of his brother as the breath came back.

The labourer returned at a run, followed by the Vicar. After the brandy, Maurice made more moaning, hiccuping noise. Geoffrey listened in torture. He heard the Vicar asking for explanations. All the united, anxious voices replied in brief phrases.

'It was that other,' cried the Fräulein. 'He knocked him over–Ha!'

She was shrill and vindictive.

'I don't think so,' said the father to the Vicar, in a quite audible but private tone, speaking as if the Fräulein did not understand his English.

The Vicar addressed his children's governess in bad German. She replied in a torrent which he would not confess was too much for him. Maurice was making little moaning, sighing noises.

'Where's your pain, boy, eh?' the father asked pathetically.

'Leave him alone a bit,' came the cool voice of Henry. 'He's winded, if no more.'

'You'd better see that no bones are broken,' said the anxious Vicar.

'It wor a blessing as he should a dropped on that heap of hay just there,' said the labourer. 'If he'd happened to ha' catched hisself on this nog o' wood 'e wouldna ha' stood much chance.'

Geoffrey wondered when he would have courage to venture down. He had wild notions of pitching himself head foremost from the stack: if he could only extinguish himself, he would be safe. Quite frantically, he longed not to be. The idea of going through life thus coiled up within himself in morbid self-consciousness, always lonely, surly, and a misery, was enough to make him cry out. What would they all think when they knew he had knocked Maurice off that high stack?

They were talking to Maurice down below. The lad had recovered in great measure, and was able to answer faintly.

'Whatever was you doin'?' the father asked gently. 'Was you playing about with our Geoffrey?–Aye, and where is he?'

Geoffrey's heart stood still.

'I dunno,' said Henry, in a curious, ironic tone.

'Go an' have a look,' pleaded the father, infinitely relieved over one son, anxious now concerning the other. Geoffrey could not bear that his eldest brother should climb up and question him in his high-pitched drawl of curiosity. The culprit doggedly set his feet on the ladder. His nailed boots slipped a rung.

'Mind yourself,' shouted the over-wrought father.

Geoffrey stood like a criminal at the foot of the ladder, glancing furtively at the group. Maurice was lying, pale and slightly convulsed, upon a heap of hay. The Fräulein was kneeling beside his head. The Vicar had the lad's shirt full open down the breast, and was feeling for broken ribs. The father knelt on the other side, the labourer and Henry stood aside.

'I can't find anything broken,' said the Vicar, and he sounded slightly disappointed.

'There's nowt broken to find,' murmured Maurice, smiling.

The father started. 'Eh?' he said. 'Eh?' and he bent over the invalid.

'I say it's not hurt me,' repeated Maurice.

'What were you doing?' asked the cold, ironic voice of Henry. Geoffrey turned his head away: he had not yet raised his face.

'Nowt as I know on,' he muttered in a surly tone.

'Why!' cried Fräulein in a reproachful tone. 'I see him–knock him over!' She made a fierce gesture with her elbow. Henry curled his long moustache sardonically.

'Nay lass, niver,' smiled the wan Maurice. 'He was fur enough away from me when I slipped.'

'Oh, ah!' cried the Fräulein, not understanding.

'Yi,' smiled Maurice indulgently.

'I think you're mistaken,' said the father, rather pathetically, smiling at the girl as if she were 'wanting'.

'Oh no,' she cried. 'I *see* him.'

'Nay, lass,' smiled Maurice quietly.

She was a Pole, named Paula Jablonowsky: young, only twenty years old, swift and light as a wild cat, with a strange wild-cat way of grinning. Her hair was blonde and full of life, all crisped into many tendrils with vitality, shaking round her face. Her fine blue eyes were peculiarly lidded, and she seemed to look piercingly, then languorously, like a wild cat. She had somewhat Slavonic cheek-bones, and was very much freckled. It was evident that the Vicar, a pale, rather cold man, hated her.

Maurice lay pale and smiling in her lap, whilst she cleaved to him like a mate. One felt instinctively that they were mated. She was ready at any minute to fight with ferocity in his defence, now he was hurt. Her looks at Geoffrey were full of fierceness. She bowed over Maurice and caressed him with her foreign-sounding English.

'You say what you lai-ike,' she laughed, giving him lordship over her.

'Hadn't you better be going and looking what has become of Margery?' asked the Vicar in tones of reprimand.

'She is with her mother–I heared her. I will go in a whai-ile,' smiled the girl coolly.

'Do you feel as if you could stand?' asked the father, still anxiously.

'Aye, in a bit,' smiled Maurice.

'You want to get up?' caressed the girl, bowing over him, till her face was not far from his.

'I'm in no hurry,' he replied, smiling brilliantly.

This accident had given him quite a strange new ease, an authority. He felt extraordinarily glad. New power had come to him all at once.

'You in no hurry,' she repeated, gathering his meaning. She smiled tenderly: she was in his service.

'She leaves us in another month—Mrs Inwood could stand no more of her,' apologised the Vicar quietly to the father.

'Why, is she—'

'Like a wild thing—disobedient and insolent.'

'Ha!'

The father sounded abstract.

'No more foreign governesses for me.'

Maurice stirred, and looked up at the girl.

'You stand up?' she asked brightly. 'You well?'

He laughed again, showing his teeth winsomely. She lifted his head, sprang to her feet, her hands still holding his head, then she took him under the armpits and had him on his feet before anyone could help. He was much taller than she. He grasped her strong shoulders heavily, leaned against her, and, feeling her round, firm breast doubled up against his side, he smiled, catching his breath.

'You see, I'm all right,' he gasped. 'I was only winded.'

'You all raïght?' she cried, in great glee.

'Yes, I am.'

He walked a few steps after a moment.

'There's nowt ails me, father,' he laughed.

'Quite well, you?' she cried in a pleading tone. He laughed outright, looked down at her, touching her cheek with his fingers.

'That's it—if tha likes.'

'If I lai-ike!' she repeated, radiant.

'She's going at the end of three weeks,' said the Vicar consolingly to the farmer.

2

While they were talking, they heard the far-off hooting of a pit.

'There goes th' loose 'a,' said Henry coldly. 'We're *not* going to get that corner up to-day.'

The father looked round anxiously.

'Now, Maurice, are you sure you're all right?' he asked.

'Yes, I'm all right. Haven't I told you?'

'Then you sit down there, and in a bit you can be getting dinner out. Henry, you go on the stack. Wheer's Jim? Oh, he's minding the hosses. Bill, and you, Geoffrey, you can pick while Jim loads.'

Maurice sat down under the wych elm to recover. The Fräulein had fled back. He made up his mind to ask her to marry him. He had got fifty pounds of his own, and his mother would help him. For a long time he sat musing, thinking what he would do. Then, from the float he fetched a big basket covered with a cloth, and spread the dinner. There was an immense rabbit-pie, a dish of cold potatoes, much bread, a great piece of cheese, and a solid rice pudding.

These two fields were four miles from the home farm. But they had been in the hands of the Wookeys for several generations, therefore the father kept them on, and everyone looked forward to the hay harvest at Greasley: it was a kind of picnic. They brought dinner and tea in the milk-float, which the father drove over in the morning. The lads and the labourers cycled. Off and on, the harvest lasted a fortnight. As the high road from Alfreton to Nottingham ran at the foot of the fields, someone usually slept in the hay under the shed to guard the tools. The sons took it in turns. They did not care for it much, and were for that reason anxious to finish the harvest on this day. But work went slack and disjointed after Maurice's accident.

When the load was teemed, they gathered round the white cloth, which was spread under a tree between the hedge and the stack, and, sitting on the ground, ate their meal. Mrs Wookey sent always a clean cloth, and knives and forks and plates for everybody. Mr Wookey was always rather proud of this spread: everything was so proper.

'There now,' he said, sitting down jovially. 'Doesn't this look nice now–eh?'

They all sat round the white spread, in the shadow of the tree and the stack, and looked out up the fields as they ate. From their shady coolness, the gold sward seemed liquid, molten with heat. The horse with the empty wagon wandered a few yards, then stood feeding. Everything was still as a trance. Now and again, the horse between the shafts of the load that stood propped beside the stack, jingled his loose bit as he ate. The men ate and drank in silence, the father reading the newspaper, Maurice leaning back on a saddle, Henry reading the *Nation*, the others eating busily.

Presently 'Helloa! 'Er's 'ere again!' exclaimed Bill. All looked up. Paula was coming across the field carrying a plate.

'She's bringing something to tempt your appetite, Maurice,' said the eldest brother ironically. Maurice was midway through a large wedge of rabbit-pie and some cold potatoes.

'Aye, bless me if she's not,' laughed the father. 'Put that away, Maurice, it's a shame to disappoint her.'

Maurice looked round very shamefaced, not knowing what to do with his plate.

'Give it over here,' said Bill. 'I'll polish him off.'

'Bringing something for the invalid?' laughed the father to the Fräulein. 'He's looking up nicely.'

'I bring him some chicken, him!' She nodded her head at Maurice childishly. He flushed and smiled.

'Tha doesna mean ter bust 'im,' said Bill.

Everybody laughed aloud. The girl did not understand, so she laughed also. Maurice ate his portion very sheepishly.

The father pitied his son's shyness.

'Come here and sit by me,' he said. 'Eh, Fräulein! Is that what they call you?'

'I sit by you, father,' she said innocently.

Henry threw his head back and laughed long and noiselessly.

She settled near to the big, handsome man.

'My name,' she said, 'is Paula Jablonowsky.'

'Is what?' said the father, and the other men went into roars of laughter.

'Tell me again,' said the father. 'Your name—'

'Paula.'

'Paula? Oh—well, it's a rum sort of name, eh? His name—' he nodded at his son.

'Maurice—I know.' She pronounced it sweetly, then laughed into the father's eyes. Maurice blushed to the roots of his hair.

They questioned her concerning her history, and made out that she came from Hanover, that her father was a shopkeeper, and that she had run away from home because she did not like her father. She had gone to Paris.

'Oh,' said the father, now dubious. 'And what did you do there?'

'In school—in a young ladies' school.'

'Did you like it?'

'Oh no—no laïfe—no life!'

'What?'

'When we go out—two and two—all together—no more. Ah, no life, no life.'

'Well, that's a winder!' exclaimed the father. 'No life in Paris! And have you found much life in England?'

'No—ah no. I don't like it.' She made a grimace at the Vicarage.

'How long have you been in England?'

'Chreestmas—so.'

'And what will you do?'

'I will go to London, or to Paris. Ah, Paris!—Or get married!' She laughed into the father's eyes.

The father laughed heartily.

'Get married, eh? And who to?'

'I don't know. I am going away.'

'The country's too quiet for you?' asked the father.

'Too quiet—hm!' she nodded in assent.

'You wouldn't care for making butter and cheese?'

'Making butter—hm!' She turned to him with a glad, bright gesture. 'I like it.'

'Oh,' laughed the father. 'You would, would you?'

She nodded vehemently, with glowing eyes.

'She'd like anything in the shape of a change,' said Henry judicially.

'I think she would,' agreed the father. It did not occur to them that she fully understood what they said. She looked at them closely, then thought with bowed head.

'Hullo!' exclaimed Henry, the alert. A tramp was slouching towards them through the gap. He was a very seedy, slinking fellow, with a tang of horsey braggadocio about him. Small, thin, and ferrety, with a week's red beard bristling on his pointed chin, he came slouching forward.

'Have yer got a bit of a job goin'?' he asked

'A bit of a job,' repeated the father. 'Why, can't you see as we've a'most done?'

'Aye—but I noticed you was a hand short, an' I thowt as 'appen you'd gie me half a day.'

'What, are *you* any good in a hay close?' asked Henry, with a sneer.

The man stood slouching against the haystack. All the others were seated on the floor. He had an advantage.

'I could work aside any on yer,' he bragged.

'Tha looks it,' laughed Bill.

'And what's your regular trade?' asked the father.

'I'm a jockey by rights. But I did a bit o' dirty work for a boss o' mine, an' I was landed. *'E* got the benefit, *I* got kicked out. *'E* axed me–an' then 'e looked as if 'e'd never seed me.'

'Did he, though!' exclaimed the father sympathetically.

''E did that!' asserted the man.

'But we've got nothing for you,' said Henry coldly.

'What does the boss say?' asked the man, impudent.

'No, we've no work you can do,' said the father. 'You can have a bit o' something to eat, if you like.'

'I should be glad of it,' said the man.

He was given the chunk of rabbit-pie that remained. This he ate greedily. There was something debased, parasitic, about him, which disgusted Henry. The others regarded him as a curiosity.

'That was nice and tasty,' said the tramp, with gusto.

'Do you want a piece of bread 'n' cheese?' asked the father.

'It'll help to fill up,' was the reply.

The man ate this more slowly. The company was embarrassed by his presence, and could not talk. All the men lit their pipes, the meal over.

'So you dunna want any help?' said the tramp at last.

'No–we can manage what bit there is to do.'

'You don't happen to have a fill of bacca to spare, do you?'

The father gave him a good pinch.

'You're all right here,' he said, looking round. They resented this familiarity. However, he filled his clay pipe and smoked with the rest.

As they were sitting silent, another figure came through the gap in the hedge, and noiselessly approached. It was a woman. She was rather small and finely made. Her face was small, very ruddy, and comely, save for the look of bitterness and aloofness that it wore. Her hair was drawn tightly back under a sailor hat. She gave an impression of cleanness, of precision and directness.

'Have you got some work?' she asked of her man. She ignored the rest. He tucked his tail between his legs.

'No, they haven't got no work for me. They've just gave me a draw of bacca.' He was a mean crawl of a man.

'An' am I goin' to wait for you out there on the lane all day?'

'You needn't if you don't like. You could go on.'

'Well, are you coming?' she asked contemptuously. He rose to his feet in a rickety fashion.

'You needn't be in such a mighty hurry,' he said. 'If you'd wait a bit you might get summat.'

She glanced for the first time over the men. She was quite young, and would have been pretty, were she not so hard and callous-looking.

'Have you had your dinner?' asked the father.

She looked at him with a kind of anger and turned away. Her face was so childish in its contours, contrasting strangely with her expression.

'Are you coming?' she said to the man.

'He's had his tuck-in. Have a bit, if you want it,' coaxed the father.

'What have you had?' she flashed to the man.

'He's had all what was left o' th' rabbit-pie,' said Geoffrey, in an indignant, mocking tone, 'and a great hunk o' bread an' cheese.'

'Well, it was gave me,' said the man.

The young woman looked at Geoffrey, and he at her. There was a sort of kinship between them. Both were at odds with the world. Geoffrey smiled satirically. She was too grave, too deeply incensed even to smile.

'There's a cake here, though—you can have a bit o' that,' said Maurice blithely.

She eyed him with scorn.

Again she looked at Geoffrey. He seemed to understand her. She turned, and in silence departed. The man remained obstinately sucking at his pipe. Everybody looked at him with hostility.

'We'll be getting to work,' said Henry, rising, pulling off his coat. Paula got to her feet. She was a little bit confused by the presence of the tramp.

'I go,' she said, smiling brilliantly. Maurice rose and followed her sheepishly.

'A good grind, eh?' said the tramp, nodding after the Fräulein. The men only half understood him, but they hated him.

'Hadn't you better be getting off?' said Henry.

The man rose obediently. He was all slouching, parasitic insolence. Geoffrey loathed him, longed to exterminate him. He was exactly the worst foe of the hypersensitive: insolence without sensibility, preying on sensibility.

'Aren't you goin' to give me summat for her? It's nowt she's had all day, to my knowin'. She'll 'appen eat it if I take it 'er—though she gets more than I've any knowledge of'—this with a lewd wink of jealous spite. 'And then tries to keep a tight hand on me,' he sneered, taking the bread and cheese, and stuffing it in his pocket.

3

Geoffrey worked sullenly all the afternoon, and Maurice did the horse-raking. It was exceedingly hot. So the day wore on, the atmosphere thickened, and the sunlight grew blurred. Geoffrey was picking with Bill—helping to load the wagons from the winrows. He was sulky, though extraordinarily relieved: Maurice would not tell. Since the quarrel neither brother had spoken to the other. But their silence was entirely amicable, almost affectionate. They had both been deeply moved, so much so that their ordinary intercourse was interrupted: but underneath, each felt a strong regard for the other. Maurice was peculiarly happy, his feeling of affection swimming over everything. But Geoffrey was still sullenly hostile to the most part of the world. He felt isolated. The free and easy inter-communication between the other workers left him distinctly alone. And he was a man who could not bear to stand alone, he was too much afraid of the vast confusion of life surrounding him, in which he was helpless. Geoffrey mistrusted himself with everybody.

The work went on slowly. It was unbearably hot, and everyone was disheartened.

'We s'll have getting-on-for another day of it,' said the father at tea-time, as they sat under the tree.

'Quite a day,' said Henry.

'Somebody'll have to stop, then,' said Geoffrey. 'It 'ud better be me.'

'Nay, lad, I'll stop,' said Maurice, and he hid his head in confusion.

'Stop again to-night!' exclaimed the father. 'I'd rather you went home.'

'Nay, I'm stoppin',' protested Maurice.

'He wants to do his courting,' Henry enlightened them.

The father thought seriously about it.

'I don't know . . .' he mused, rather perturbed.

But Maurice stayed. Towards eight o'clock, after sundown, the men mounted their bicycles, the father put the horse in the float, and all departed. Maurice stood in the gap of the hedge and watched them go, the cart rolling and swinging down-hill, over the grass stubble, the cyclists dipping swiftly like shadows in front. All passed through the gate, there was a quick clatter of hoofs on the roadway under the lime trees, and they were gone. The young man was very much excited, almost afraid, at finding himself alone.

Darkness was rising from the valley. Already, up the steep hill the cart-lamps crept indecisively, and the cottage windows were lit. Everything looked strange to Maurice, as if he had not seen it before. Down the hedge a large lime tree teemed with scent that seemed almost like a voice speaking. It startled him. He caught a breath of the over-sweet fragrance, then stood still, listening expectantly.

Up-hill, a horse whinneyed. It was the young mare. The heavy horses went thundering across to the far hedge.

Maurice wondered what to do. He wandered round the deserted stacks restlessly. Heat came in wafts, in thick strands. The evening was a long time cooling. He thought he would go and wash himself. There was a trough of pure water in the hedge bottom. It was filled by a tiny spring that filtered over the brim of the trough down the lush hedge bottom of the lower field. All round the trough, in the upper field, the land was marshy, and there the meadow-sweet stood like clots of mist, very sickly-smelling in the twilight. The night did not darken, for the moon was in the sky, so that as the tawny colour drew off the heavens they remained pallid with a dimmed moon. The purple bell-flowers in the hedge went black, the ragged robin turned its pink to a faded white, the meadow-sweet gathered light as if it were phosphorescent, and it made the air ache with scent.

Maurice kneeled on the slab of stone bathing his hands and arms, then his face. The water was deliciously cool. He had still an hour before Paula would come: she was not due till nine. So he decided to take his bath at night instead of waiting till morning. Was he not sticky, and was not Paula coming to talk to him? He was delighted the thought had occurred to him. As he soused his head in the trough, he wondered what the little creatures that lived in the velvety silt at the bottom would think of the taste of soap. Laughing to himself, he squeezed his cloth into the water. He washed himself from head to foot, standing in the fresh, forsaken corner of the field, where no one could see him by daylight, so that now, in the veiled grey tinge of moonlight, he was no more noticeable than the crowded flowers. The night had on a new look: he never remembered to have seen the lustrous grey sheen of it before, nor to have noticed how vital the lights looked, like live folk inhabiting the silvery spaces. And the tall trees, wrapped obscurely in their mantles, would not have surprised him had they begun to move in converse. As he dried himself, he discovered little wanderings in the air, felt on his sides soft touches and caresses that were peculiarly delicious: sometimes they startled him, and he laughed as if he were not alone. The flowers, the meadow-sweet particularly, haunted him.

He reached to put his hand over their fleeciness. They touched his thighs. Laughing, he gathered them and dusted himself all over with their cream dust and fragrance. For a moment he hesitated in wonder at himself: but the subtle glow in the hoary and black night reassured him. Things never had looked so personal and full of beauty, he had never known the wonder in himself before.

At nine o'clock he was waiting under the elder bush, in a state of high trepidation, but feeling that he was worthy, having a sense of his own wonder. She was late. At a quarter-past nine she came, flitting swiftly, in her own eager way.

'No, she would *not* go to sleep,' said Paula, with a world of wrath in her tone. He laughed bashfully. They wandered out into the dim, hill-side field.

'I have sat–in that bedroom–for an hour, for hours,' she cried indignantly. She took a deep breath: 'Ah, breathe!' she smiled.

She was very intense, and full of energy.

'I want'–she was clumsy with the language–'I want–I should laike–to run–there!' She pointed across the field.

'Let's run, then,' he said curiously.

'Yes!'

And in an instant she was gone. He raced after her. For all he was so young and limber, he had difficulty in catching her. At first he could scarcely see her, though he could hear the rustle of her dress. She sped with astonishing fleetness. He overtook her, caught her by the arm, and they stood panting, facing one another with laughter.

'I could win,' she asserted blithely.

'Tha couldna,' he replied, with a peculiar, excited laugh. They walked on, rather breathless. In front of them suddenly appeared the dark shapes of the three feeding horses.

'We ride a horse?' she said.

'What, bareback?' he asked.

'You say?' She did not understand.

'With no saddle?'

'No saddle–yes–no saddle.'

'Coop, lass!' he said to the mare, and in a minute he had her by the forelock, and was leading her down to the stacks, where he put a halter on her. She was a big, strong mare. Maurice seated the Fräulein, clambered himself in front of the girl, using the wheel of the wagon as a mount, and together they trotted uphill, she holding lightly round his waist. From the crest of the hill they looked round.

The sky was darkening with an awning of cloud. On the left the hill rose black and wooded, made cosy by a few lights from cottages along the highway. The hill spread to the right, and tufts of trees shut round. But in front was a great vista of night, a sprinkle of cottage candles, a twinkling cluster of lights, like an elfish fair in full swing, at the colliery an encampment of light at a village, a red flare on the sky far off, above an iron-foundry, and in the farthest distance the dim breathing of town lights. As they watched the night stretch far out, her arms tightened round his waist, and he pressed his elbows to his side, pressing her arms closer still. The horse moved restlessly. They clung to each other.

'Tha daesna want to go right away?' he asked the girl behind him.

'I stay with you,' she answered softly, and he felt her crouching close against him. He laughed curiously. He was afraid to kiss her, though he was urged to do so. They remained still, on the restless horse, watching the small lights lead deep into the night, an infinite distance.

'I don't want to go,' he said, in a tone half pleading.

She did not answer. The horse stirred restlessly.

'Let him run,' cried Paula, 'fast!'

She broke the spell, startled him into a little fury. He kicked the mare, hit her, and away she plunged down-hill. The girl clung tightly to the young man. They were riding bareback down a rough, steep hill. Maurice clung hard with hands and knees. Paula held him fast round the waist, leaning her head on his shoulders, and thrilling with excitement.

'We shall be off, we shall be off,' he cried, laughing with excitement; but she only crouched behind and pressed tight to him. The mare tore across the field. Maurice expected every moment to be flung on to the grass. He gripped with all the strength of his knees. Paula tucked herself behind him, and often wrenched him almost from his hold. Man and girl were taut with effort.

At last the mare came to a standstill, blowing. Paula slid off, and in an instant Maurice was beside her. They were both highly excited. Before he knew what he was doing, he had her in his arms, fast, and was kissing her, and laughing. They did not move for some time. Then, in silence, they walked towards the stacks.

It had grown quite dark, the night was thick with cloud. He walked with his arm round Paula's waist, she with her arm round him. They were near the stacks when Maurice felt a spot of rain.

'It's going to rain,' he said.

'Rain!' she echoed, as if it were trivial.

'I s'll have to put the stack-cloth on,' he said gravely. She did not understand.

When they got to the stacks, he went round to the shed, to return staggering in the darkness under the burden of the immense and heavy cloth. It had not been used once during the hay harvest.

'What are you going to do?' asked Paula, coming close to him in the darkness.

'Cover the top of the stack with it,' he replied. 'Put it over the stack, to keep the rain out.'

'Ah!' she cried, 'up there!' He dropped his burden. 'Yes,' he answered.

Fumblingly he reared the long ladder up the side of the stack. He could not see the top.

'I hope it's solid,' he said softly.

A few smart drops of rain sounded drumming on the cloth. They seemed like another presence. It was very dark indeed between the great buildings of hay. She looked up the black wall and shrank to him.

'You carry it up there?' she asked.

'Yes,' he answered.

'I help you?' she said.

And she did. They opened the cloth. He clambered first up the steep ladder, bearing the upper part, she followed closely, carrying her full share. They mounted the shaky ladder in silence, stealthily.

4

As they climbed the stacks a light stopped at the gate on the high road. It was Geoffrey, come to help his brother with the cloth. Afraid of his own intrusion, he wheeled his bicycle silently towards the shed. This was a corrugated iron erection, on the opposite side of the hedge from the stacks. Geoffrey let his light go in front of him, but there was no sign from the lovers. He thought he saw a shadow slinking away. The light of the bicycle lamp sheered yellowly across the dark, catching a glint of raindrops, a mist of darkness, shadow of leaves and strokes of long grass. Geoffrey entered the shed—no one was there. He walked slowly and doggedly round to the stacks. He had passed the wagon, when he heard something sheering down upon him. Starting back under the wall of hay, he saw the long ladder slither across the side of the stack, and fall with a bruising ring.

'What wor that?' he heard Maurice, aloft, ask cautiously.

'Something fall,' came the curious, almost pleased voice of the Fräulein.

'It wor niver th' ladder,' said Maurice. He peered over the side of the stack. He lay down, looking.

'It is an' a'!' he exclaimed. 'We knocked it down with the cloth, dragging it over.'

'We fast up here?' she exclaimed with a thrill.

'We are that—without I shout and make 'em hear at the Vicarage.'

'Oh no,' she said quickly.

'I don't want to,' he replied, with a short laugh. There came a swift clatter of raindrops on the cloth. Geoffrey crouched under the wall of the other stack.

'Mind where you tread—here, let me straighten this end,' said Maurice, with a peculiar intimate tone—a command and an embrace. 'We s'll have to sit under it. At any rate, we shan't get wet.'

'Not get wet!' echoed the girl, pleased, but agitated.

Geoffrey heard the slide and rustle of the cloth over the top of the stack, heard Maurice telling her to 'Mind!'

'Mind!' she repeated. 'Mind! you say "Mind!"'

'Well, what if I do?' he laughed. 'I don't want you to fall over th' side, do I?' His tone was masterful, but he was not quite sure of himself.

There was silence a moment or two.

'Maurice!' she said plaintively.

'I'm here,' he answered tenderly, his voice shaky with excitement that was near to distress. 'There, I've done. Now should we—we'll sit under this corner.'

'Maurice!' she was rather pitiful.

'What? You'll be all right,' he remonstrated, tenderly indignant.

'I be all raïght,' she repeated, 'I be all raïght, Maurice?'

'Tha knows tha will—I canna ca' thee Powla. Should I ca' thee, Minnie?' It was the name of a dead sister.

'Minnie?' she exclaimed in surprise.

'Aye, should I?'

She answered in full-throated German. He laughed shakily.

'Come on—come on under. But do yer wish you was safe in th' Vicarage? Should I shout for somebody?' he asked.

'I don't wish, no!' She was vehement.

'Art sure?' he insisted, almost indignantly.

'Sure—I quite sure.' She laughed.

Geoffrey turned away at the last words. Then the rain beat heavily. The lonely brother slouched miserably to the hut, where the rain played a mad tattoo. He felt very miserable, and jealous of Maurice.

His bicycle lamp, downcast, shone a yellow light on the stark floor of the shed or hut with one wall open. It lit up the trodden earth, the shafts of tools lying piled under the beam, beside the dreary grey metal of the building. He took off the lamp, shone it round the hut. There were piles of harness, tools, a big sugar-box, a deep bed of hay—then the beams across the corrugated iron, all very dreary and stark. He shone the lamp into the night: nothing but the furtive glitter of raindrops through the mist of darkness, and black shapes hovering round.

Geoffrey blew out the light and flung himself on to the hay. He would put the ladder up for them in a while, when they would be wanting it. Meanwhile he sat and gloated over Maurice's felicity. He was imaginative, and now he had something concrete to work upon. Nothing in the whole of life stirred him so profoundly, and so utterly, as the thought of this woman. For Paula was strange, foreign, different from the ordinary girls: the rousing, feminine quality seemed in her concentrated, brighter, more fascinating than in anyone he had known, so that he felt most like a moth near a candle. He would have loved her wildly—but Maurice had got her. His thoughts beat the same course, round and round. What was it like when you kissed her, when she held you tight round the waist, how did she feel towards Maurice, did she love to touch him, was he fine and attractive to her; what did she think of himself—she merely disregarded him, as she would disregard a horse in a field; why would she do so, why couldn't he make her regard himself, instead of Maurice: he would never command a woman's regard like that, he always gave in to her too soon; if only some woman would come and take him for what he was worth, though he was such a stumbler and showed to such disadvantage, ah, what a grand thing it would be; how he would kiss her. Then round he went again in the same course, brooding almost like a madman. Meanwhile the rain drummed deep on the shed, then grew lighter and softer. There came the drip, drip of the drops falling outside.

Geoffrey's heart leaped up his chest, and he clenched himself, as a black shape crept round the post of the shed and, bowing, entered silently. The young man's heart beat so heavily in plunges, he could not get his breath to speak. It was shock, rather than fear. The form felt towards him. He sprang up, gripped it with his great hand's panting 'Now, then!'

There was no resistance, only a little whimper of despair.

'Let me go,' said a woman's voice.

'What are you after?' he asked, in deep, gruff tones.

'I thought 'e was 'ere,' she wept despairingly, with little, stubborn sobs.

'An' you've found what you didn't expect, have you?'

At the sound of his bullying she tried to get away from him.

'Let me go,' she said.

'Who did you expect to find here?' he asked, but more his natural self.

'I expected my husband—him as you saw at dinner. Let me go.'

'Why, is it you?' exclaimed Geoffrey. 'Has he left you?'

'Let me go,' said the woman sullenly, trying to draw away. He realised that her sleeve was very wet, her arm slender under his grasp. Suddenly he grew ashamed of himself: he had no doubt hurt her, gripping her so hard. He relaxed, but did not let her go.

'An' are you searching round after that snipe as was here at dinner?' he asked. She did not answer.

'Where did he leave you?'

'I left him—here. I've seen nothing of him since.'

'I s'd think it's good riddance,' he said. She did not answer. He gave a short laugh, saying:

'I should ha' thought you wouldn't ha' wanted to clap eyes on him again.'

'He's my husband—an' he's not go n' to run off if I can stop him.'

Geoffrey was silent, not knowing what to say.

'Have you got a jacket on?' he asked at last.

'What do you think? You've got hold of it.'

'You're wet through, aren't you?'

'I shouldn't be dry, comin' through that teemin' rain. But 'e's not here, so I'll go.'

'I mean,' he said humbly, 'are you wet through?'

She did not answer. He felt her shiver.

'Are you cold?' he asked, in surprise and concern.

She did not answer. He did not know what to say.

'Stop a minute,' he said, and he fumbled in his pocket for his matches. He struck a light, holding it in the hollow of his large, hard palm. He was a big man, and he looked anxious. Shedding the light on her, he saw she was rather pale, and very weary looking. Her old sailor hat was sodden and drooping with rain. She wore a fawn-coloured jacket of smooth cloth. This jacket was black-wet where the rain had beaten, her skirt hung sodden, and dripped on to her boots. The match went out.

'Why, you're wet through!' he said.

She did not answer.

'Shall you stop in here while it gives over?' he asked. She did not answer.

''Cause if you will, you'd better take your things off, an' have th' rug. There's a horse-rug in the box.'

He waited, but she would not answer. So he lit his bicycle lamp, and rummaged in the box, pulling out a large brown blanket, striped with scarlet and yellow. She stood stock still. He shone the light on her. She was very pale, and trembling fitfully.

'Are you that cold?' he asked in concern. 'Take your jacket off, and your hat, and put this right over you.'

Mechanically, she undid the enormous fawn-coloured buttons, and unpinned her hat. With her black hair drawn back from her low, honest brow, she looked little more than a girl, like a girl driven hard with womanhood by stress of life. She was small, and natty, with neat little features. But she shivered convulsively.

'Is something a-matter with you?' he asked.

'I've walked to Bulwell and back,' she quivered, 'looking for him—an' I've not touched a thing since this morning.' She did not weep—she was too dreary-hardened to cry. He looked at her in dismay, his mouth half open: 'Gormin' as Maurice would have said.

''Aven't you had nothing to eat?' he said.

Then he turned aside to the box. There, the bread remaining was kept, and the great piece of cheese, and such things as sugar and salt, with all table utensils: there was some butter.

She sat down drearily on the bed of hay. He cut her a piece of bread and butter, and a piece of cheese. This she took, but ate listlessly.

'I want a drink,' she said.

'We 'aven't got no beer,' he answered. 'My father doesn't have it.'

'I want water,' she said.

He took a can and plunged through the wet darkness, under the great black hedge, down to the trough. As he came back he saw her in the half-lit little cave sitting bunched together. The soaked grass wet his feet—he thought of her. When he gave her a cup of water, her hand touched his and he felt her fingers hot and glossy. She trembled so she spilled the water.

'Do you feel badly?' he asked.

'I can't keep myself still—but it's only with being tired and having nothing to eat.'

He scratched his head contemplatively, waited while she ate her piece of bread and butter. Then he offered her another piece.

'I don't want it just now,' she said.

'You'll have to eat summat,' he said.

'I couldn't eat any more just now.'

He put the piece down undecidedly on the box. Then there was another long pause. He stood up with bent head. The bicycle, like a restful animal, glittered behind him, turning towards the wall. The woman sat hunched on the hay, shivering.

'Can't you get warm?' he asked.

'I shall by an' by—don't you bother. I'm taking your seat—are you stopping here all night?'

'Yes.'

'I'll be goin' in a bit,' she said.

'Nay, I non want you to go. I'm thinkin' how you could get warm.'

'Don't you bother about me,' she remonstrated, almost irritably.

'I just want to see as the stacks is all right. You take your shoes an' stockin's an' all your wet things off: you can easy wrap yourself all over in that rug, there's not so much of you.'

'It's raining—I s'll be all right—I s'll be going in a minute.'

'I've got to see as the stacks is safe. Take your wet things off.'

'Are you coming back?' she asked.

'I mightn't, not till morning.'

'Well, I s'll be gone in ten minutes, then. I've no rights to be here, an' I s'll not let anybody be turned out for me.'

'You won't be turning me out.'

'Whether or no, I shan't stop.'

'Well, shall you if I come back?' he asked. She did not answer.

He went. In a few moments, she blew the light out. The rain was falling steadily, and the night was a black gulf. All was intensely still. Geoffrey listened everywhere: no sound save the rain. He stood between the stacks, but only heard the trickle of water, and the light swish of rain. Everything was lost in blackness. He imagined death was like that, many things dissolved in silence and darkness, blotted out, but existing. In the dense blackness he felt himself almost extinguished. He was afraid he might not find things the same. Almost frantically, he stumbled, feeling his way, till his hand touched the wet metal. He had been looking for a gleam of light.

'Did you blow the lamp out?' he asked, fearful lest the silence should answer him.

'Yes,' she answered humbly. He was glad to hear her voice. Groping into the pitch-dark shed, he knocked against the box, part of whose cover served as table. There was a clatter and fall.

'That's the lamp, an' the knife, an' the cup,' he said. He struck a match.

'Th' cup's not broke.' He put it into the box.

'But th' oil's spilled out o' th' lamp. It always was a rotten old thing.' He hastily blew out his match, which was burning his fingers. Then he struck another light.

'You don't want a lamp, you know you don't, and I s'll be going directly, so you come an' lie down an' get your night's rest. I'm not taking any of your place.'

He looked at her by the light of another match. She was a queer little bundle, all brown, with gaudy border folding in and out, and her little face peering at him. As the match went out she saw him beginning to smile.

'I can sit right at this end,' she said. 'You lie down.'

He came and sat on the hay, at some distance from her. After a spell of silence:

'Is he really your husband?' he asked.

'He is!' she answered grimly.

'Hm!' Then there was silence again.

After a while: 'Are you warm now?'

'Why do you bother yourself?'

'I don't bother myself—do you follow him because you like him?' He put it very timidly. He wanted to know.

'I don't—I wish he was dead,' this with bitter contempt. Then doggedly: 'But he's my husband.'

He gave a short laugh.

'By Gad!' he said.

Again, after a while: 'Have you been married long?'

'Four years.'

'Four years—why, how old are you?'

'Twenty-three.'

'Are you turned twenty-three?'

'Last May.'

'Then you're four month older than me.' He mused over it. They were only two voices in the pitch-black night. It was eerie silence again.

'And do you just tramp about?' he asked.

'He reckons he's looking for a job. But he doesn't like work in any shape or form. He was a stableman when I married him, at Greenhalgh's, the horse-dealers, at Chesterfield, where I was housemaid. He left that job when the baby was only two months, and I've been badgered about from pillar to post ever sin'. They say a rolling stone gathers no moss. . . .'

'An' where's the baby?'

'It died when it was ten months old.'

Now the silence was clinched between them. It was quite a long time before Geoffrey ventured to say sympathetically: 'You haven't much to look forward to.'

'I've wished many a score time when I've started shiverin' an' shakin' at nights, as I was taken bad for death. But we're not that handy at dying.'

He was silent. 'But whatever shall you do?' he faltered.

'I s'll find him, if I drop by th' road.'

'Why?' he asked, wondering, looking her way, though he saw nothing but solid darkness.

'Because I shall. He's not going to have it all his own road.'

'But why don't you leave him?'

'Because he's *not goin' to have it all his own road.*'

She sounded very determined, even vindictive. He sat in wonder, feeling uneasy, and vaguely miserable on her behalf. She sat extraordinarily still. She seemed like a voice only, a presence.

'Are you warm now?' he asked, half afraid.

'A bit warmer–but my feet!' She sounded pitiful.

'Let me warm them with my hands,' he asked her. 'I'm hot enough.'

'No, thank you,' she said coldly.

Then, in the darkness, she felt she had wounded him. He was writhing under her rebuff, for his offer had been pure kindness.

'They're 'appen dirty,' she said, half mocking.

'Well–mine is–an' I have a bath a'most every day,' he answered.

'I don't know when they'll get warm,' she moaned to herself.

'Well, then, put them in my hands.'

She heard him faintly rattling the match-box, and then a phosphorescent glare began to fume in his direction. Presently he was holding two smoking, blue-green blotches of light towards her feet. She was afraid. But her feet ached so, and the impulse drove her on, so she placed her soles lightly on the two blotches of smoke. His large hands clasped over her instep, warm and hard.

'They're like ice!' he said, in deep concern.

He warmed her feet as best he could, putting them close against him. Now and again convulsive tremors ran over her. She felt his warm breath on the balls of her toes, that were bunched up in his hands. Leaning forward, she touched his hair delicately with her fingers. He thrilled. She fell to gently stroking his hair, with timid, pleading finger-tips.

'Do they feel any better?' he asked, in a low voice, suddenly lifting his face to her. This sent her hand sliding softly over his face, and her finger-tips caught on his mouth. She drew quickly away. He put his hand out to find hers, in his other palm holding both her feet. His wandering hand met her face. He touched it curiously. It was wet. He put his big fingers cautiously on her eyes, into two little pools of tears.

'What's a matter?' he asked in a low, choked voice.

She leaned down to him and gripped him tightly round the neck, pressing him to her bosom in a little frenzy of pain. Her bitter disillusionment with life, her unalleviated shame and degradation during the last four years, had driven her into loneliness, and hardened her till a large part of her nature was caked and sterile. Now she softened again, and her spring might be beautiful. She had been in a fair way to make an ugly old woman.

She clasped the head of Geoffrey to her breast, which heaved and fell, and heaved again. He was bewildered, full of wonder. He allowed the woman to do as she would with him. Her tears fell on his hair, as she wept noiselessly; and he breathed deep as she did. At last she let go her clasp. He put his arms round her.

'Come and let me warm you,' he said, folding up on his knee and lapping her with his heavy arms against himself. She was small and *câline.* He held her very warm and close. Presently she stole her arms round him.

'You *are* big,' she whispered.

He gripped her hard, started, put his mouth down wanderingly, seeking her out. His lips met her temple. She slowly, deliberately turned her mouth to his, and with opened lips, met him in a kiss, his first love kiss.

5

It was breaking cold dawn when Geoffrey woke. The woman was still sleeping in his arms. Her face in sleep moved all his tenderness: the tight shutting of her mouth, as if in resolution to bear what was very hard to bear, contrasted so pitifully with the small mould of her features. Geoffrey pressed her to his bosom: having her, he felt he could bruise the lips of the scornful, and pass on erect, unabateable. With her to complete him, to form the core of him, he was firm and whole. Needing her so much, he loved her fervently.

Meanwhile the dawn came like death, one of those slow, livid mornings that seem to come in a cold sweat. Slowly, and painfully, the air began to whiten. Geoffrey saw it was not raining. As he was watching the ghastly transformation outside, he felt aware of something. He glanced down: she was open-eyed, watching him; she had golden-brown, calm eyes, that immediately smiled into his. He also smiled, bowed softly down and kissed her. They did not speak for some time. Then:

'What's thy name?' he asked curiously.

'Lydia,' she said.

'Lydia!' he repeated wonderingly. He felt rather shy.

'Mine's Geoffrey Wookey,' he said.

She merely smiled at him.

They were silent for a considerate time. By morning light, things look small. The huge trees of the evening were dwindled to hoary, small, uncertain things, trespassing in the sick pallor of the atmosphere. There was a dense mist, so that the light could scarcely breathe. Everything seemed to quiver with cold and sickliness.

'Have you often slept out?' he asked her.

'Not so very,' she answered.

'You won't go after *him?*' he asked.

'I s'll have to,' she replied, but she nestled in to Geoffrey. He felt a sudden panic.

'You mustn't,' he exclaimed, and she saw he was afraid for himself. She let it be, was silent.

'We couldn't get married?' he asked thoughtfully.

'No.'

He brooded deeply over this. At length:

'Would you go to Canada with me?'

'We'll see what you think in two months' time,' she replied quietly, without bitterness.

'I s'll think the same,' he protested, hurt.

She did not answer, only watched him steadily. She was there for him to do as he liked with; but she would not injure his fortunes; no, not to save his soul.

'Haven't you got no relations?' he asked.

'A married sister at Crick.'

'On a farm?'

'No—married a farm labourer—but she's very comfortable. I'll go there, if you want me to, just till I can get another place in service.'

He considered this.

'Could you get on a farm?' he asked wistfully.

'Greenhalgh's was a farm.'

He saw the future brighten: she would be a help to him. She agreed to go to her sister, and to get a place of service—until spring, he said, when they would sail for Canada. He waited for her assent.

'You will come with me, then?' he asked.

'When the time comes,' she said.

Her want of faith made him bow his head: she had reason for it.

'Shall you walk to Crick, or go from Langley Mill to Ambergate? But it's only ten mile to walk. So we can go together up Hunt's Hill—you'd have to go past our lane-end, then I could easy nip down an' fetch you some money,' he said humbly.

'I've got half a sovereign by me—it's more than I s'll want.'

'Let's see it,' he said.

After a while, fumbling under the blanket, she brought out the piece of money. He felt she was independent of him. Brooding rather bitterly, he told himself she'd forsake him. His anger gave him courage to ask:

'Shall you go in service in your maiden name?'

'No.'

He was bitterly wrathful with her—full of resentment.

'I bet I s'll niver see you again,' he said, with a short, hard laugh. She put her arms round him, pressed him to her bosom, while the tears rose to her eyes. He was reassured, but not satisfied.

'Shall you write to me to-night?'

'Yes, I will.'

'And can I write to you—who shall I write to?'

'Mrs Bredon.'

'"Bredon"!' he repeated bitterly.

He was exceedingly uneasy.

The dawn had grown quite wan. He saw the hedges drooping wet down the grey mist. Then he told her about Maurice.

'Oh, you *shouldn't!*' she said. 'You should ha' put the ladder up for them, you *should.*'

'Well—I don't care.'

'Go and do it now—and I'll go.'

'No, don't you. Stop an' see our Maurice; go on, stop an' see him—then I'll be able to tell him.'

She consented in silence. He had her promise she would not go before he returned. She adjusted her dress, found her way to the trough, where she performed her toilet.

Geoffrey wandered round to the upper field. The stacks looked wet in the mist, the hedge was drenched. Mist rose like steam from the grass, and the near hills were veiled almost to a shadow. In the valley, some peaks of black poplar showed fairly definite, jutting up. He shivered with chill.

There was no sound from the stacks, and he could see nothing. After all, he wondered, were they up there? But he reared the ladder to the place whence it had been swept, then went down the hedge to gather dry sticks. He was breaking off thin dead twigs under a holly tree when he heard, on the perfectly still air: 'Well, I'm dashed!'

He listened intently. Maurice was awake.

'Sithee here!' the lad's voice exclaimed. Then, after a while, the foreign sound of the girl:

'What–oh, thair!'

'Aye, th' ladder's there, right enough.'

'You said it had fall down.'

'Well, I heard it drop–an' I couldna feel it nor see it.'

'You said it had fall down–you lie, you liar.'

'Nay, as true as I'm here–'

'You tell me lies–make me stay here–you tell me lies–' She was passionately indignant.

'As true as I'm standing here–' he began.

'Lies!–lies!–lies!' she cried. 'I don't believe you, never. You *mean*, you *mean*, mean, mean!*'

'A' raïght, then!' He was now incensed, in his turn.

'You are bad, mean, mean, mean.'

'Are ter commin' down?' asked Maurice coldly.

'No–I will not come with you–mean, to tell me lies.'

'Are ter commin' down?'

'No, I don't want you.'

'A' raïght, then!'

Geoffrey, peering through the holly tree, saw Maurice negotiating the ladder. The top rung was below the brim of the stack, and rested on the cloth, so it was dangerous to approach. The Fräulein watched him from the end of the stack, where the cloth thrown back showed the light, dry hay. He slipped slightly, she screamed. When he had got on to the ladder, he pulled the cloth away, throwing it back, making it easy for her to descend.

'Now are ter commin'?' he asked.

'No!' She shook her head violently, in a pet.

Geoffrey felt slightly contemptuous of her. But Maurice waited.

'Are ter commin'?' he called again.

'No,' she flashed, like a wild cat.

'All right, then I'm going.'

He descended. At the bottom, he stood holding the ladder.

'Come on, while I hold it steady,' he said.

There was no reply. For some minutes he stood patiently with his foot on the bottom rung of the ladder. He was pale, rather washed-out in his appearance, and he drew himself together with cold.

'Are ter commin', or aren't ter?' he asked at length. Still there was no reply.

'Then stop up till tha'rt ready,' he muttered, and he went away. Round the other side of the stacks he met Geoffrey.

'What, are thaïgh here?' he exclaimed.

'Bin here a' naïght,' replied Geoffrey. 'I come to help thee wi' th' cloth, but I found it on, an' th' ladder down, so I thowt tha'd gone.'

'Did ter put th' ladder up?'

'I did a bit sin'.'

Maurice brooded over this, Geoffrey struggled with himself to get out his own news. At last he blurted:

'Tha knows that woman as wor here yis'day dinner–'er come back, an' stopped i' th' shed a' night, out o' th' rain.'

'Oh–ah!' said Maurice, his eye kindling, and a smile crossing his pallor.

'An' I s'll gi'e her some breakfast.'

'Oh–ah!' repeated Maurice.

'It's th' man as is good-for-nowt, not her,' protested Geoffrey. Maurice did not feel in a position to cast stones.

'Tha pleases thysen,' he said, 'what ter does.' He was very quiet, unlike himself. He seemed bothered and anxious, as Geoffrey had not seen him before.

'What's up wi' thee?' asked the elder brother, who in his own heart was glad, and relieved.

'Nowt,' was the reply.

They went together to the hut. The woman was folding the blanket. She was fresh from washing, and looked very pretty. Her hair, instead of being screwed tightly back, was coiled in a knot low down, partly covering her ears. Before she had deliberately made herself plain-looking: now she was neat and pretty, with a sweet, womanly gravity.

'Hello. I didn't think to find you here,' said Maurice, very awkwardly, smiling. She watched him gravely without reply. 'But it was better in shelter than outside last night,' he added.

'Yes,' she replied.

'Shall you get a few more sticks?' Geoffrey asked him. It was a new thing for Geoffrey to be leader. Maurice obeyed. He wandered forth into the damp, raw morning. He did not go to the stack, as he shrank from meeting Paula.

At the mouth of the hut, Geoffrey was making the fire. The woman got out coffee from the box: Geoffrey set the tin to boil. They were arranging breakfast when Paula appeared. She was hatless. Bits of hay stuck in her hair, and she was white-faced–altogether, she did not show to advantage.

'Ah–you!' she exclaimed, seeing Geoffrey.

'Hello!' he answered. 'You're out early.'

'Where's Maurice?'

'I dunno, he should be back directly.'

Paula was silent.

'When have you come?' she asked.

'I come last night, but I could see nobody about. I got up half an hour sin', an' put th' ladder up ready to take the stack-cloth up.'

Paula understood, and was silent. When Maurice returned with the faggots, she was crouched warming her hands. She looked up at him, but he kept his eyes averted from her. Geoffrey met the eyes of Lydia, and smiled. Maurice put his hands to the fire.

'You cold?' asked Paula tenderly.

'A bit,' he answered, quite friendly, but reserved. And all the while the four sat round the fire, drinking their smoked coffee, eating each a small piece of toasted bacon, Paula watched eagerly for the eyes of Maurice, and he avoided her. He was gentle, but would not give his eyes to her looks. And Geoffrey smiled constantly to Lydia, who watched gravely.

The German girl succeeded in getting safely into the Vicarage, her escapade unknown to anyone save the housemaid. Before a week was out, she was openly engaged to Maurice, and when her month's notice expired, she went to live at the farm.

Geoffrey and Lydia kept faith one with the other.

D. H. LAWRENCE

THE VIRGIN
AND THE GIPSY

I

When the vicar's wife went off with a young and penniless man the scandal knew no bounds. Her two little girls were only seven and nine years old respectively. And the vicar was such a good husband. True, his hair was grey. But his moustache was dark, he was handsome, and still full of furtive passion for his unrestrained and beautiful wife.

Why did she go? Why did she burst away with such an *èclat* of revulsion, like a touch of madness?

Nobody gave any answer. Only the pious said she was a bad woman. While some of the good women kept silent. They knew.

The two little girls never knew. Wounded, they decided that it was because their mother found them negligible.

The ill wind that blows nobody any good swept away the vicarage family on its blast. Then lo and behold! the vicar, who was somewhat distinguished as an essayist and a controversialist, and whose case had aroused sympathy among the bookish men, received the living of Papplewick. The Lord had tempered the wind of misfortune with a rectorate in the north country.

The rectory was a rather ugly stone house down by the River Papple, before you come into the village. Farther on, beyond where the road crosses the stream, were the big old stone cotton-mills, once driven by water. The road curved uphill, into the bleak stone streets of the village.

The vicarage family received decided modification, upon its transference into the rectory. The vicar, now the rector, fetched up his old mother and his sister, and a brother from the city. The two little girls had a very different milieu from the old house.

The rector was now forty-seven years old; he had displayed an intense and not very dignified grief after the flight of his wife. Sympathetic ladies had stayed him from suicide. His hair was almost white, and he had a wild-eyed, tragic look. You had only to look at him to know how dreadful it all was, and how he had been wronged.

Yet somewhere there was a false note. And some of the ladies, who had sympathised most profoundly with the vicar, secretly rather disliked the rector. There was a certain furtive self-righteousness about him, when all was said and done.

The little girls, of course, in the vague way of children, accepted the family verdict. Granny, who was over seventy and whose sight was failing, became the central figure in the house. Aunt Cissie, who was over forty, pale, pious, and gnawed by an inward worm, kept house. Uncle Fred, a stingy and grey-faced man of forty, who just lived dingily for himself, went into town every day. And the rector, of course, was the most important person, after Granny.

They called her the Mater. She was one of those physically vulgar, clever old bodies who had got her own way all her life by buttering the weaknesses of her men-folk. Very quickly she took her cue. The rector still 'loved' his delinquent wife, and would 'love her' till he died. Therefore hush! The rector's feeling was sacred. In his heart was enshrined the pure girl he had wedded and worshipped.

Out in the evil world, at the same time, there wandered a disreputable woman who had betrayed the rector and abandoned his little children. She was now yoked to a young and despicable man, who no doubt would bring her the degradation she deserved. Let this be clearly understood, and then hush! For in the pure loftiness of the rector's heart still bloomed the pure white snow-flower of his young bride. This white snow-flower did not wither. That other creature, who had gone off with that despicable young man, was none of his affair.

The Mater, who had been somewhat diminished and insignificant as a widow in a small house, now climbed into the chief arm-chair in the rectory, and planted her old bulk firmly again. She was not going to be dethroned. Astutely she gave a sigh of homage to the rector's fidelity to the pure white snow-flower, while she pretended to disapprove. In sly reverence for her son's great love, she spoke no word against that nettle which flourished in the evil world, and which had once been called Mrs Arthur Saywell. Now, thank heaven, having married again, she was no more Mrs Arthur Saywell. No woman bore the rector's name. The pure white snow-flower bloomed *in perpetuum*, without nomenclature. The family even thought of her as She-who-was-Cynthia.

All this was water on the Mater's mill. It secured her against Arthur's ever marrying again. She had him by his feeblest weakness, his skulking self-love. He had married an imperishable white snow-flower. Lucky man! He had been injured. Unhappy man! He had suffered. Ah, what a heart of love! And he had—forgiven! Yes, the white snow-flower was forgiven. He even had made provision in his will for her, when that other scoundrel—But hush! Don't even *think* too near to that horrid nettle in the rank outer world! She-who-was-Cynthia. Let the white snow-flower bloom inaccessible on the heights of the past. The present is another story.

The children were brought up in this atmosphere of cunning self-sanctification and of unmentionability. They, too, saw the snow-flower on inaccessible heights. They, too, knew that it was throned in lone splendour aloft their lives, never to be touched.

At the same time, out of the squalid world sometimes would come a rank, evil smell of selfishness and degraded lust, the smell of that awful nettle, She-who-was-Cynthia. This nettle actually contrived at intervals, to get a little note through to the girls, her children. And at this the silver-haired Mater shook inwardly with hate. For if She-who-was-Cynthia ever came back, there wouldn't be much left of the Mater. A secret gust of hate went from the old granny to the girls, children of that foul nettle of lust, that Cynthia who had had such an affectionate contempt for the Mater.

Mingled with all this was the children's perfectly distinct recollection of their real home, the vicarage in the south, and their glamorous but not very dependable mother, Cynthia. She had made a great glow, a flow of life, like a swift and dangerous sun in the home, forever coming and going. They always associated her presence with brightness, but also with danger; with glamour, but with fearful selfishness.

Now the glamour was gone, and the white snow-flower, like a porcelain wreath, froze on its grave. The danger of instability, the peculiarly *dangerous* sort of selfishness, like lions and tigers, was also gone. There was now a complete stability, in which one could perish safely.

But they were growing up. And as they grew, they became more definitely confused, more actively puzzled. The Mater, as she grew older, grew blinder. Somebody had to lead her about. She did not get up till towards midday. Yet blind or bed-ridden, she held the house.

Besides, she wasn't bed-ridden. Whenever the *men* were present, the Mater was in her throne. She was too cunning to court neglect. Especially as she had rivals.

Her great rival was the younger girl, Yvette. Yvette had some of the vague, careless blitheness of She-who-was-Cynthia. But this one was more docile. Granny perhaps had caught her in time. Perhaps!

The rector adored Yvette, and spoiled her with a doting fondness; as much as to say: am I not a soft-hearted, indulgent old boy! He liked to have this opinion of himself, and the Mater knew his weaknesses to a hair's-breadth. She knew them, and she traded on them by turning them into decorations for him, for his character. He wanted, in his own eyes, to have a fascinating character, as women want to have fascinating dresses. And the Mater cunningly put beauty-spots over his defects and deficiencies. Her mother-love gave her the clue to his weaknesses, and she hid them for him with decorations. Whereas She-who-was-Cynthia–! But don't mention *her* in this connection. In her eyes, the rector was almost hump-backed and an idiot.

The funny thing was, Granny secretly hated Lucille, the elder girl, more than the pampered Yvette. Lucille, the uneasy and irritable, was more conscious of being under Granny's power than was the spoilt and vague Yvette.

On the other hand, Aunt Cissie hated Yvette. She hated her very name. Aunt Cissie's life had been sacrificed to the Mater, and Aunt Cissie knew it, and the Mater knew she knew it. Yet as the years went on, it became a convention. The convention of Aunt Cissie's sacrifice was accepted by everybody, including the self-same Cissie. She prayed a good deal about it. Which also showed that she had her own private feelings somewhere, poor thing. She had ceased to be Cissie, she had lost her life and her sex. And now she was creeping towards fifty, strange green flares of rage would come up in her, and at such times she was insane.

But Granny held her in her power. And Aunt Cissie's one object in life was to look after the Mater.

Aunt Cissie's green flares of hellish hate would go up against all young things, sometimes. Poor thing, she prayed and tried to obtain forgiveness from heaven. But what had been done to her, *she* could not forgive, and the vitriol would spurt in her veins sometimes.

It was not as if the Mater were a warm, kindly soul. She wasn't. She only seemed it, cunningly. And the fact dawned gradually on the girls. Under her old-fashioned lace cap, under her silver hair, under the black silk of her stout, short, forward-bulging body, this old woman had a cunning heart, seeking forever her own female power. And through the weakness of the unfresh, stagnant men she had bred, she kept her power, as her years rolled on, from seventy to eighty, and from eighty on the new lap, towards ninety.

For in the family there was a whole tradition of 'loyalty'; loyalty to one another, and especially to the Mater. The Mater, of course, was the pivot of the family. The family was her own extended ego. Naturally she covered it with her power. And her sons and daughters, being weak and disintegrated, naturally were loyal. Outside the family, what was there for them but danger and insult and ignominy? Had not the rector experienced it in his marriage? So now, caution! Caution and loyalty, fronting the world! Let there bé as much hate and friction *inside* the family as you like. To the outer world, a stubborn fence of unison.

<hr>

2

<hr>

But it was not until the girls finally came home from school that they felt the full weight of Granny's dead old hand on their lives. Lucille was now nearly twenty-one, and Yvette nineteen. They had been to a good girls' school, and had had a finishing year in Lausanne, and were quite the usual thing, tall young creatures with fresh, sensitive faces and bobbed hair and young-manly, deuce-take-it manners.

'What's so awfully *boring* about Papplewick,' said Yvette, as they stood on the Channel boat watching the grey, grey cliffs of Dover draw near, 'is that there are no *men* about. Why doesn't Daddy have some good old sports for friends? As for Uncle Fred, he's the limit!'

'Oh, you never know what will turn up,' said Lucille, more philosophic.

'You jolly well know what to expect,' said Yvette. 'Choir on Sundays, and I hate mixed choirs. Boys' voices are *lovely* when there are no women. And Sunday School and Girls' Friendly, and socials, all the dear old souls that inquire after Granny! Not a decent young fellow for miles.'

'Oh, I don't know!' said Lucille. 'There's always the Framleys. And you know Gerry Somercotes *adores* you.'

'Oh, but I *hate* fellows who adore me!' cried Yvette, turning up her sensitive nose. 'They *bore* me. They hang on like lead.'

'Well, what *do* you want, if you can't stand being adored? *I* think it's perfectly all right to be adored. You know you'll never marry them, so why not let them go on adoring, if it amuses them.'

'Oh, but I *want* to get married,' cried Yvette.

'Well, in that case, let them go on adoring you till you find one that you can *possibly* marry.'

'I never should, that way. Nothing puts me off like an adoring fellow. They *bore* me so! They make me feel beastly.'

'Oh, so they do me, if they get pressing. But at a distance, I think they're rather nice.'

'I should like to fall *violently* in love.'

'Oh, very likely! I shouldn't! I should hate it. Probably so would you, if it actually happened. After all, we've got to settle down a bit before we know what we want.'

'But don't you *hate* going back to Papplewick?' cried Yvette, turning up her young, sensitive nose.

'No, not particularly. I suppose we shall be rather bored. I wish Daddy would get a car. I suppose we shall have to drag the old bikes out. Wouldn't you like to go to Tansy Moor?'

'Oh, *love* it! Though it's an awful *strain*, shoving an old push-bike up those hills.'

The ship was nearing the grey cliffs. It was summer, but a grey day. The two girls wore their coats with fur collars turned up, and little *chic* hats pulled down over their ears. Tall, slender, fresh-faced, naïve, yet confident, too confident, in their school-girlish arrogance, they were so terribly English. They seemed so free, and were, as a matter of fact, so tangled and tied up, inside themselves. They seemed so dashing and unconventional, and were really so conventional, so, as it were, shut up indoors inside themselves. They looked like bold, tall young sloops, just slipping from the harbour into the wide seas of life. And they were, as a matter of fact, two poor, young, rudderless lives, moving from one chain anchorage to another.

The rectory struck a chill into their hearts as they entered. It seemed ugly, and almost sordid, with the dank air of that middle-class, degenerate comfort which has ceased to be comfortable and has turned stuffy, unclean. The hard, stone house struck, the girls as being unclean, they could not have said why. The shabby furniture seemed somehow sordid, nothing was fresh. Even the food at meals had that awful, dreary sordidness which is so repulsive to a young thing coming from abroad. Roast beef and wet cabbage, cold mutton and mashed potatoes, sour pickles, inexcusable puddings.

Granny, who 'loved a bit of pork', also had special dishes, beef-tea and rusks, or a small savoury custard. The grey-faced Aunt Cissie ate nothing at all. She would sit at table and take a single lonely and naked boiled potato on to her plate. She never ate meat. So she sat in sordid durance, while the meal went on, and Granny quickly slobbered her portion–lucky if she spilled nothing on her protuberant stomach. The food was not appetising in itself: how could it be, when Aunt Cissie hated food herself, hated the fact of eating, and never could keep a maid-servant for three months? The girls ate with repulsion, Lucille bravely bearing up, Yvette's tender nose showing her disgust. Only the rector, white-haired, wiped his long grey moustache with his serviette, and cracked jokes. He, too, was getting heavy and inert, sitting in his study all day, never taking exercise. But he cracked sarcastic little jokes all the time, sitting there under the shelter of the Mater.

The country, with its steep hills and its deep, narrow valleys, was dark and gloomy, yet had a certain powerful strength of its own. Twenty miles away was the black industrialism of the north. Yet the village of Papplewick was comparatively lonely, almost lost, the life in it stony and dour. Everything was stone, with a hardness that was almost poetic, it was so unrelenting.

It was as the girls had known: they went back into the choir, they helped in the parish. But Yvette struck absolutely against Sunday School, the Band of Hope, the Girls' Friendlies–indeed against all those functions that were conducted by determined old maids and obstinate, stupid, elderly men. She avoided church duties as much as possible, and got away from the rectory whenever she could. The Framleys, a big, untidy, jolly family up at the Grange, were an enormous stand-by. And if anybody asked her out to a meal, even if a woman in one of the workmen's houses asked her to stay to tea, she accepted at once. In fact, she was rather thrilled. She liked talking to the working men, they had often such fine, hard heads. But of course they were in another world.

So the months went by. Gerry Somercotes was still an adorer. There were others, too, sons of farmers or mill-owners. Yvette really ought to have had a good time. She was always out to parties and dances, friends came for her in their motor-cars, and off she went to the city, to the afternoon dance in the chief hotel, or in the gorgeous new Palais de Danse, called the Pally.

Yet she always seemed like a creature mesmerised. She was never free to be quite jolly. Deep inside her worked an intolerable irritation, which she thought she *ought* not to feel, and which she hated feeling, thereby making it worse. She never understood at all whence it arose.

At home, she truly was irritable, and outrageously rude to Aunt Cissie. In fact, Yvette's awful temper became one of the family by-words.

Lucille, always more practical, got a job in the city as private secretary to a man who needed somebody with fluent French and shorthand. She went back and forth every day by the same train as Uncle Fred. But she never travelled with him, and wet or fine, bicycled to the station, while he went on foot.

The two girls were both determined that what they wanted was a really jolly social life. And they resented with fury that the rectory was, for their friends, impossible. There were only four rooms downstairs: the kitchen, where lived the two discontented maid-servants: the dark dining-room: the rector's study: and the big, 'homely', dreary living-room or drawing-room. In the dining-room there was a gas fire. Only in the living-room was a good hot fire kept going. Because, of course, here Granny reigned.

In this room the family was assembled. At evening, after dinner, Uncle Fred and the rector invariably played crossword puzzles with Granny.

'Now, Mater, are you ready? N blank blank blank blank W: a Siamese functionary.'

'Eh? Eh? M blank blank blank blank W?'

Granny was hard of hearing.

'No, Mater. Not M! N blank blank blank blank W: a Siamese functionary.'

'N blank blank blank blank W: a Chinese functionary.'

'SIAMESE.'

'Eh?'

'SIAMESE! SIAM!'

'A Siamese functionary! Now what can that be?' said the old lady profoundly, folding her hands on her round stomach. Her two sons proceeded to make suggestions, at which she said Ah! Ah! The rector was amazingly clever at crossword puzzles. But Fred had a certain technical vocabulary.

'This certainly is a hard nut to crack,' said the old lady, when they were all stuck.

Meanwhile Lucille sat in a corner with her hands over her ears, pretending to read, and Yvette irritably made drawings, or hummed loud and exasperating tunes, to add to the family concert. Aunt Cissie continually reached for a chocolate, and her jaws worked ceaselessly. She literally lived on chocolates. Sitting in the distance, she put another into her mouth, then looked again at the parish magazine. Then she lifted her head, and saw it was time to fetch Granny's cup of Horlicks.

While she was gone, in nervous exasperation Yvette would open the window. The room was never fresh, she imagined it smelt: smelt of Granny. And Granny, who was hard of hearing, heard like a weasel when she wasn't wanted to.

'Did you open the window, Yvette? I think you might remember there are older people than yourself in the room,' she said.

'It's stifling! It's unbearable! No wonder we've all of us always got colds.'

'I'm sure the room is large enough, and a good fire burning.' The old lady gave a little shudder. 'A draught to give us all our death.'

'Not a draught at all,' roared Yvette. 'A breath of fresh air.'

The old lady shuddered again, and said: 'Indeed!'

The rector, in silence, marched to the window and firmly closed it. He did not look at his daughter meanwhile. He hated thwarting her. But she must know what's what!

The crossword puzzles, invented by Satan himself, continued till Granny had had her Horlicks, and was to go to bed. Then came the ceremony of Good-night! Everybody stood up. The girls went to be kissed by the blind old woman, the rector gave his arm, and Aunt Cissie followed with a candle.

But this was already nine o'clock, although Granny was really getting old, and should have been in bed sooner. But when she was in bed, she could not sleep, till Aunt Cissie came.

'You see,' said Granny, 'I have *never* slept alone. For fifty-four years I never slept a night without the Pater's arm round me. And when he was gone I tried to sleep alone. But as sure as my eyes closed to sleep, my heart nearly jumped out of my body, and I lay in a palpitation. Oh, you may think what you will, but it was a fearful experience, after fifty-four years of perfect married life! I would have prayed to be taken first, but the Pater, well, no, I don't think he would have been able to bear up.'

So Aunt Cissie slept with Granny. And she hated it. She said *she* could never sleep. And she grew greyer and greyer, and the food in the house got worse, and Aunt Cissie had to have an operation.

But the Mater rose as ever, towards noon, and at the midday meal she presided from her arm-chair, with her stomach protruding; her reddish, pendulous face, that had a sort of horrible majesty, dropping soft under the wall of her high brow, and her blue eyes peering unseeing. Her white hair was getting scanty, it was altogether a little indecent. But the rector jovially cracked his jokes to her, and she pretended to disapprove. But she was perfectly complacent, sitting in her ancient obesity, and after meals, getting the wind from her stomach, pressing her bosom with her hand as she 'rifted' in gross physical complacency.

What the girls minded most was that, when they brought their young friends to the house, Granny always was there, like some awful idol of old flesh, consuming all the attention. There was only the one room for everybody. And there sat the old lady, with Aunt Cissie keeping an acrid guard over her. Everybody must be presented first to Granny: she was ready to be genial, she liked company. She had to know who everybody was, where they came from, every circumstance of their lives. And then, when she was *au fait*, she could get hold of the conversation.

Nothing could be more exasperating to the girls. 'Isn't old Mrs Saywell wonderful! She takes *such* an interest in life, at nearly ninety!'

'She does take an interest in people's affairs, if that's life,' said Yvette.

Then she would immediately feel guilty. After all, it *was* wonderful to be nearly ninety, and have such a clear mind! And Granny never *actually* did anybody any harm. It was more that she was in the way. And perhaps it was rather awful to hate somebody because they were old and in the way.

Yvette immediately repented, and was nice. Granny blossomed forth into reminiscences of when she was a girl in the little town in Buckinghamshire. She talked and talked away, and was *so* entertaining. She really *was* rather wonderful.

Then in the afternoon Lottie and Ella and Bob Framley came, with Leo
Wetherell.

'Oh, come in!'–and in they all trooped to the sitting-room, where Granny, in
her white cap, sat by the fire.

'Granny, this is Mr Wetherell.'

'Mr what-did-you-say? You must excuse me, I'm a little deaf!'

Granny gave her hand to the uncomfortable young man, and gazed silently at
him, sightlessly.

'You are not from our parish?' she asked him.

'Dinnington!' he shouted.

'We want to go a picnic to-morrow, to Bonsall Head, in Leo's car. We can all
squeeze in,' said Ella, in a low voice.

'Did you say Bonsall Head?' asked Granny.

'Yes!'

There was a blank silence.

'Did you say you were going in a car?'

'Yes! In Mr Wetherell's.'

'I hope he's a good driver. It's a very dangerous road.'

'He's a *very* good driver.'

'Not a very good driver?'

'Yes! He *is* a very good driver.'

'If you go to Bonsall Head, I think I must send a message to Lady Louth.'

Granny always dragged in this miserable Lady Louth when there was
company.

'Oh, we shan't go that way,' cried Yvette.

'Which way?' said Granny. 'You must go by Heanor.'

The whole party sat, as Bob expressed it, like stuffed ducks, fidgeting on
their chairs.

Aunt Cissie came in–and then the maid with the tea. There was the eternal
and everlasting piece of bought cake. Then appeared a plate of little fresh cakes.
Aunt Cissie had actually sent to the baker's.

'Tea, Mater!'

The old lady gripped the arms of her chair. Everybody rose and stood, while
she waded slowly across, on Aunt Cissie's arm, to her place at table.

During tea Lucille came in from town, from her job. She was simply worn
out, with black marks under her eyes. She gave a cry, seeing all the company.

As soon as the noise had subsided, and the awkwardness was resumed,
Granny said:

'You have never mentioned Mr Wetherell to me, have you, Lucille?'

'I don't remember,' said Lucille.

'You can't have done. The name is strange to me.'

Yvette absently grabbed another cake from the now almost empty plate.
Aunt Cissie, who was driven almost crazy by Yvette's vague and inconsiderate
ways, felt the green rage fuse in her heart. She picked up her own plate, on
which was the one cake she allowed herself, and said with vitriolic politeness,
offering it to Yvette:

'Won't you have mine?'

'Oh, thanks!' said Yvette, starting in her angry vagueness. And with an
appearance of the same insouciance, she helped herself to Aunt Cissie's cake
also, adding as an afterthought: 'If you're sure you don't want it.'

She now had two cakes on her plate. Lucille had gone white as a ghost, bending to her tea. Aunt Cissie sat with a green look of poisonous resignation. The awkwardness was an agony.

But Granny, bulkily enthroned and unaware, only said, in the centre of the cyclone:

'If you are motoring to Bonsall Head to-morrow, Lucille, I wish you would take a message from me to Lady Louth.'

'Oh!' said Lucille, giving a queer look across the table at the sightless old woman. Lady Louth was the King Charles's Head of the family, invariably produced by Granny for the benefit of visitors. 'Very well!'

'She was so very kind last week. She sent her chauffeur over with a Crossword Puzzle book for me.'

'But you thanked her then,' cried Yvette.

'I should like to send her a note.'

'We can post it,' cried Lucille.

'Oh no! I should like you to take it. When Lady Louth called last time . . .'

The young ones sat like a shoal of young fishes dumbly mouthing at the surface of the water, while Granny went on about Lady Louth. Aunt Cissie, the two girls knew, was still helpless, almost unconscious in a paroxysm of rage about the cake. Perhaps, poor thing, she was praying.

It was a mercy when the friends departed. But by that time the two girls were both haggard-eyed. And it was then that Yvette, looking round, suddenly saw the stony, implacable will-to-power in the old and motherly-seeming Granny. She sat there bulging backwards in her chair, impassive, her reddish, pendulous old face rather mottled, almost unconscious, but implacable, her face like a mask that hid something stony, relentless. It was the static inertia of her unsavoury power. Yet in a minute she would open her ancient mouth to find out every detail about Leo Wetherell. For the moment she was hibernating in her oldness, her agedness. But in a minute her mouth would open, her mind would flicker awake and with her insatiable greed for life, other people's life, she would start on her quest for every detail. She was like the old toad which Yvette had watched, fascinated, as it sat on the ledge of the beehive, immediately in front of the little entrance by which the bees emerged, and which, with a demonish lightning-like snap of its pursed jaws, caught every bee as it came out to launch into the air, swallowed them one after the other, as if it could consume the whole hiveful, into its aged, bulging, purse-like wrinkledness. It had been swallowing bees as they launched into the air of spring, year after year, year after year, for generations.

But the gardener, called by Yvette, was in a rage, and killed the creature with a stone.

''Appen tha *art* good for th' snails,' he said, as he came down with the stone. 'But tha 'rt none goin' ter emp'y th' bee-'ive into thy guts.'

3

The next day was dull and low, and the roads were awful, for it had been raining for weeks, yet the young ones set off on their trip, without taking Granny's message either. They just slipped out while she was making her slow trip upstairs after lunch. Not for anything would they have called at Lady Louth's house. That widow of a knighted doctor, a harmless person indeed, had become an obnoxity in their lives.

Six young rebels, they sat very perkily in the car as they swished through the mud. Yet they had a peaked look too. After all, they had nothing really to rebel against, any of them. They were left so very free in their movements. Their parents let them do almost entirely as they liked. There wasn't really a fetter to break, nor a prison bar to file through, nor a bolt to shatter. The keys of their lives were in their own hands. And there they dangled inert.

It is very much easier to shatter prison bars than to open undiscovered doors to life. As the younger generation finds out somewhat to its chagrin. True, there was Granny. But poor old Granny, you couldn't actually say to her: 'Lie down and die, you old woman!' She might be an old nuisance, but she never really *did* anything. It wasn't fair to hate her.

So the young people set off on their jaunt, trying to be very full of beans. They could really do as they liked. And so, of course, there was nothing to do but sit in the car and talk a lot of criticism of other people, and silly flirty gallantry that was really rather a bore. If there had only been a few 'strict orders' to be disobeyed! But nothing: beyond the refusal to carry the message to Lady Louth, of which the rector would approve because he didn't encourage King Charles's Head either.

They sang, rather scrappily, the latest would-be comic songs as they went through the grim villages. In the great park the deer were in groups near the road, roe deer and fallow, nestling in the gloom of the afternoon under the oaks by the road, as if for the stimulus of human company.

Yvette insisted on stopping and getting out to talk to them. The girls, in their Russian boots, tramped through the damp grass, while the deer watched them with big, unfrightened eyes. The hart trotted away mildly, holding back his head, because of the weight of the horns. But the doe, balancing her big ears, did not rise from under the tree, with her half-grown young ones, till the girls were almost in touch. Then she walked light-foot away, lifting her tail from her spotted flanks, while the young ones nimbly trotted.

'Aren't they awfully dainty and nice!' cried Yvette. 'You'd wonder they could lie so cosily in this horrid wet grass.'

'Well, I suppose they've got to lie down *some time*,' said Lucille. 'And it's *fairly* dry under the tree.' She looked at the crushed grass, where the deer had lain.

Yvette went and put her hand down to feel how it felt.

'Yes!' she said doubtfully, 'I believe it's a bit warm.'

The deer had bunched again a few yards away, and were standing motionless in the gloom of the afternoon. Away below the slopes of grass and trees, beyond the swift river with its balustraded bridge, sat the huge ducal house, one or two chimneys smoking bluely. Behind it rose purplish woods.

The girls, pushing their fur collars up to their ears, dangling one long arm, stood watching in silence, their wide Russian boots protecting them from the wet grass. The great house squatted square and creamy-grey below. The deer, in little groups, were scattered under the old trees close by. It all seemed so still, so unpretentious, and so sad.

'I wonder where the Duke is now,' said Ella.

'Not here, wherever he is,' said Lucille. 'I expect he's abroad where the sun shines.'

The motor-horn called from the road, and they heard Leo's voice:

'Come on, boys! If we're going to get to the Head and down to Amberdale for tea, we'd better move.'

They crowded into the car again, with chilled feet, and set off through the park past the silent spire of the church, out through the great gates and over the bridge, on into the wide, damp, stony village of Woodlinkin, where the river ran. And thence, for a long time, they stayed in the mud and dark and dampness of the valley, often with sheer rock above them; the water brawling on one hand, the steep rock or dark trees on the other.

Till, through the darkness of overhanging trees, they began to climb, and Leo changed the gear. Slowly the car toiled up through the whitey-grey mud, into the stony village of Bolehill, that hung on the slope, round the old cross, with its steps, that stood where the road branched, on past the cottages whence came a wonderful smell of hot tea-cakes, and beyond, still upwards, under dripping trees and past broken slopes of bracken, always climbing. Until the cleft became shallower, and the trees finished, and the slopes on either side were bare, gloomy grass, with low dry-stone walls. They were emerging on to the Head.

The party had been silent for some time. On either side the road was grass, then a low stone fence, and the swelling curve of the hill-summit, traced with the low, dry-stone walls. Above this, the low sky.

The car ran out, under the low, grey sky, on the naked tops.

'Shall we stay a moment?' called Leo.

'Oh yes!' cried the girls.

And they scrambled out once more, to look around. They knew the place quite well. But still, if one came to the Head, one got out to look.

The hills were like the knuckles of a hand, the dales were below, between the fingers, narrow, steep, and dark. In the deeps a train was steaming, slowly pulling north: a small thing of the underworld. The noise of the engine re-echoed curiously upwards. Then came the dull, familiar sound of blasting in a quarry.

Leo, always on the go, moved quickly.

'Shall we be going?' he said. 'Do we *want* to get down to Amberdale for tea? Or shall we try somewhere nearer?'

They all voted for Amberdale, for the 'Marquis of Grantham'.

'Well, which way shall we go back? Shall we go by Codnor and over Crosshill, or shall we go by Ashbourne?'

There was the usual dilemma. Then they finally decided on the Codnor top road. Off went the car gallantly.

They were on the top of the world, now, on the back of the fist. It was naked, too, as the back of your fist, high under heaven, and dull, heavy green. Only it was veined with a network of old stone walls, dividing the fields, and broken here and there with ruins of old lead-mines and works. A sparse stone farm bristled with six naked sharp trees. In the distance was a patch of smoky grey stone, a hamlet. In some fields grey, dark sheep fed silently, sombrely. But there was not a sound nor a movement. It was the roof of England, stony and arid as any roof. Beyond, below, were the shires.

'"And see the coloured counties,"' said Yvette to herself. Here, anyhow, they were not coloured. A stream of rooks trailed out from nowhere. They had been walking, pecking, on a naked field that had been manured. The car ran on between the grass and the stone walls of the upland lane, and the young people were silent, looking out over the far network of stone fences, under the sky, looking for the curves downward that indicated a drop to one of the underneath, hidden dales.

Ahead was a light cart, driven by a man, and trudging along at the side was a woman, sturdy and elderly, with a pack on her back. The man in the cart had caught her up, and now was keeping pace.

The road was narrow. Leo sounded the horn sharply. The man on the cart looked round, but the woman on foot only trudged steadily, rapidly forward, without turning her head.

Yvette's heart gave a jump. The man on the cart was a gipsy, one of the black, loose-bodied, handsome sort. He remained seated on his cart, turning round and gazing at the occupants of the motor-car from under the brim of his cap. And his pose was loose, his gaze insolent in its indifference. He had a thin black moustache under his thin, straight nose, and a big silk handkerchief of red and yellow tied round his neck. He spoke a word to the woman. She stood a second, solid, to turn round and look at the occupants of the car, which had now drawn quite close. Leo honked the horn again imperiously. The woman, who had a grey-and-white kerchief tied round her head, turned sharply, to keep pace with the cart, whose driver also had settled back, and was lifting the reins, moving his loose, light shoulders. But still he did not pull aside.

Leo made the horn scream as he put the brakes on, and the car slowed up near the back of the cart. The gipsy turned round at the din, laughing in his dark face under his dark-green cap, and said something which they did not hear, showing white teeth under the line of black moustache, and making a gesture with his dark, loose hand.

'Get out o' the way then!' yelled Leo.

For answer the man delicately pulled the horse to a standstill as it curved to the side of the road. It was a good roan horse and a good, natty, dark-green cart.

Leo, in a rage, had to jam on the brake and pull up too.

'Don't the pretty young ladies want to hear their fortunes?' said the gipsy on the cart, laughing except for his dark, watchful eyes, which went from face to face, and lingered on Yvette's young, tender face.

She met his dark eyes for a second, their level search, their insolence, their complete indifference to people like Bob and Leo, and something took fire in her breast. She thought: 'He is stronger than I am! He doesn't care!'

'Oh yes! Let's!' cried Lucille at once.

'Oh yes!' chorused the girls.

'I say! What about the time?' cried Leo.

'Oh, bother the old time! Somebody's always dragging in time by the forelock,' cried Lucille.

'Well, if you don't mind *when* we get back, *I* don't!' said Leo heroically.

The gipsy man had been sitting loosely on the side of his cart, watching the faces. He now jumped softly down from the shaft, his knees a bit stiff. He was apparently a man something over thirty, and a beau in his way. He wore a sort of shooting-jacket, double-breasted, coming only to the hips, of dark green-and-black frieze; rather tight black trousers, black boots, and a dark-green cap; with the big yellow-and-red bandanna handkerchief round his neck. His appearance was curiously elegant, and quite expensive in its gipsy style. He was handsome, too, pressing in his chin with the old, gipsy conceit, and now apparently not heeding the strangers any more, as he led his good roan horse off the road, preparing to back his cart.

The girls saw for the first time a deep recess in the side of the road, and two caravans smoking. Yvette got quickly down. They had suddenly come upon a disused quarry, cut into the slope of the road-side, and in this sudden lair, almost like a cave, were three caravans, dismantled for the winter. There was also, deep at the back, a shelter built of boughs, as a stable for the horse. The grey, crude rock rose high above the caravans, and curved round towards the road. The floor was heaped chips of stone, with grasses growing among. It was a hidden, snug winter camp.

The elderly woman with the pack had gone into one of the caravans, leaving the door open. Two children were peeping out, showing black heads. The gipsy man gave a little call as he backed his cart into the quarry, and an elderly man came out to help him untackle.

The gipsy himself went up the steps into the newest caravan, that had its door closed. Underneath, a tied-up dog ranged forth. It was a white hound spotted liver-coloured. It gave a low growl as Leo and Bob approached.

At the same moment, a dark-faced gipsy woman with a pink shawl or kerchief round her head and big gold ear-rings in her ears, came down the steps of the newest caravan, swinging her flounced, voluminous green skirt. She was handsome in a bold, dark, long-faced way, just a bit wolfish. She looked like one of the bold, loping Spanish gipsies.

'Good-morning, my ladies and gentlemen,' she said, eyeing the girls from her bold, predative eyes. She spoke with a certain foreign stiffness.

'Good-afternoon!' said the girls.

'Which beautiful little lady like to hear her fortune? Give me her little hand?'

She was a tall woman, with a frightening way of reaching forward her neck like a menace. Her eyes went from face to face, very active, heartlessly searching out what she wanted. Meanwhile the man, apparently her husband, appeared at the top of the caravan steps smoking a pipe, and with a small, black-haired child in his arms. He stood on his limber legs, casually looking down on the group, as if from a distance, his long, black lashes lifted from his full, conceited, impudent black eyes. There was something peculiarly transfusing in his stare. Yvette felt it, felt it in her knees. She pretended to be interested in the white-and-liver-coloured hound.

'How much do you want if we all have our fortunes told?' asked Lottie Framley, as the six fresh-faced young Christians hung back rather reluctantly from this pagan pariah woman.

'All of you? ladies and gentlemen, all?' said the woman shrewdly.

'I don't want mine told! You go ahead!' cried Leo.

'Neither do I,' said Bob. 'You four girls.'

'The four ladies? said the gipsy woman, eyeing them shrewdly, after having looked at the boys. And she fixed her price. 'Each one give me a sheeling, and a little bit more for luck? a little bit!' She smiled in a way that was more wolfish than cajoling, and the force of her will was felt, heavy as iron beneath the velvet of her words.

'All right,' said Leo. 'Make it a shilling a head. Don't spin it out too long.'

'Oh, *you!*' cried Lucille at him. 'We want to hear it *all.*'

The woman took two wooden stools from under a caravan and placed them near the wheel. Then she took the tall, dark Lottie Framley by the hand and bade her sit down.

'You don't care if everybody hear?' she said, looking up curiously into Lottie's face.

Lottie blushed dark with nervousness as the gipsy woman held her hand, and stroked her palm with hard, cruel-seeming fingers.

'Oh, I don't mind,' she said.

The gipsy woman peered into the palm tracing the lines of the hand with a hard, dark forefinger. But she seemed clean.

And slowly she told the fortune, while the others, standing listening, kept on crying out: 'Oh, that's Jim Baggaley! Oh, I don't believe it! Oh, that's not true! A fair woman who lives beneath a tree! Why, whoever's this?' until Leo stopped them with a manly warning:

'Oh, hold on, girls! You give everything away.'

Lottie retired blushing and confused, and it was Ella's turn. She was much more calm and shrewd, trying to read the oracular words. Lucille kept breaking out with: 'Oh, I say!' The gipsy man at the top of the steps stood imperturbable, without any expression at all. But his bold eyes kept staring at Yvette, she could feel them on her cheek, on her neck, and she dared not look up. But Framley would sometimes look up at him, and got a level stare back from the handsome face of the male gipsy, from the dark, conceited, proud eyes. It was a peculiar look, in the eyes that belonged to the tribe of the humble: the pride of the pariah, the half-sneering challenge of the outcast, who sneered at law-abiding men, and went his own way. All the time the gipsy man stood there, holding his child in his arms, looking on without being concerned.

Lucille was having her hand read–'You have been across the sea, and there you met a man–a brown-haired man–but he was too old–'

'Oh, I *say!*' cried Lucille, looking round at Yvette.

But Yvette was abstracted, agitated, hardly heeding: in one of her mesmerised states.

'You will marry in a few years–not now, but a few years–perhaps four–and you will not be rich, but you will have plenty–enough–and you will go away, a long journey.'

'With my husband, or without?' cried Lucille.

'With him–'

When it came to Yvette's turn, and the woman looked up boldly, cruelly, searching for a long time in her face, Yvette said nervously:

'I don't think I want mine told. No, I won't have mine told! No, I won't, really!'

'You are afraid of something?' said the gipsy woman cruelly.

'No, it's not that–' Yvette fidgeted.

'You have some secret? You are afraid I shall say it? Come, would you like to go in the caravan, where nobody hears?'

The woman was curiously insinuating; while Yvette was always wayward, perverse. The look of perversity was on her soft, frail young face now, giving her a queer hardness.

'Yes!' she said suddenly. 'Yes! I might do that!'

'Oh, I say!' cried the others. 'Be a sport!'

'I don't think you'd *better*!' cried Lucille.

'Yes!' said Yvette, with that hard little way of hers. 'I'll do that. I'll go in the caravan.'

The gipsy woman called something to the man on the steps. He went into the caravan for a moment or two, then reappeared, and came down the steps, setting the small child on its uncertain feet, and holding it by the hand. A dandy, in his polished black boots, tight black trousers and tight, dark-green jersey, he walked slowly across with the toddling child to where the elderly gipsy was giving the roan horse a feed of oats, in the bough shelter between pits of grey rock, with dry bracken upon the stone chip floor. He looked at Yvette as he passed, staring her full in the eyes, with his pariah's bold yet dishonest stare. Something hard inside her met his stare. But the surface of her body seemed to turn to water. Nevertheless, something hard in her registered the peculiar pure lines of his face, of his straight, pure nose, of his cheeks and temples. The curious dark, suave purity of all his body, outlined in the green jersey: a purity like a living sneer.

And as he loped slowly past her, on his flexible hips, it seemed to her still that he was stronger than she was. Of all the men she had ever seen, this one was the only one who was stronger than she was, in her own kind of strength, her own kind of understanding.

So, with curiosity, she followed the woman up the steps of the caravan, the skirts of her well-cut tan coat swinging and almost showing her knees, under the pale-green cloth dress. She had long, long-striding, fine legs, too slim rather than too thick, and she wore curiously-patterned pale-and-fawn stockings of fine wool, suggesting the legs of some delicate animal.

At the top of the steps she paused and turned, debonair, to the others, saying in her naïve, lordly way, so off-hand:

'I won't let her be long.'

Her grey fur collar was open, showing her soft throat and pale green dress, her little plaited tan-coloured hat came down to her ears, round her soft, fresh face. There was something soft and yet overbearing, unscrupulous, about her. She knew the gipsy man had turned to look at her. She was aware of the pure dark nape of his neck, the black hair groomed away. He watched as she entered his house.

What the gipsy told her, no one ever knew. It was a long time to wait, the others felt. Twilight was deepening on the gloom, and it was turning raw and cold. From the chimney on the second caravan came smoke and a smell of rich food. The horse was fed, a yellow blanket strapped round him, and two gipsy men talked together in the distance in low tones. There was a peculiar feeling of silence and secrecy in that lonely, hidden quarry.

At last the caravan door opened, and Yvette emerged, bending forward and stepping with long, witch-like slim legs down the steps. There was a stooping, witch-like silence about her as she emerged on the twilight.

'Did it seem long?' she said vaguely, not looking at anybody and keeping her own counsel hard within her soft, vague waywardness. 'I hope you weren't bored! Wouldn't tea be nice! Shall we go?'

'You get in!' said Bob. 'I'll pay.'

The gipsy woman's full, metallic skirts of jade-green alpaca came swinging down the steps. She rose to her height, a big, triumphant-looking woman with a dark wolf face. The pink cashmere kerchief stamped with red roses was slipping to one side over her black and crimped hair. She gazed at the young people in the twilight with bold arrogance.

Bob put two half-crowns in her hand.

'A little bit more for luck, for your young lady's luck,' she wheedled, like a wheedling wolf. 'Another bit of silver, to bring you luck.'

'You've got a shilling for luck, that's enough,' said Bob calmly and quietly, as they moved away to the car.

'A little bit of silver! Just a little bit, for your luck in love!'

Yvette, with the sudden long, startling gestures of her long limbs, swung round as she was entering the car, and with long arm outstretched, strode and put something into the gipsy's hand, then stepped, bending her height, into the car.

'Prosperity to the beautiful young lady, and the gipsy's blessing on her,' came the suggestive, half-sneering voice of the woman.

The engine *birred!* then *birred!* again more fiercely, and started. Leo switched on the lights, and immediately the quarry with the gipsies fell back into the blackness of night.

'Good-night!' called Yvette's voice, as the car started. But hers was the only voice that piped up, chirpy and impudent in its nonchalance. The headlights glared down the stone lane.

'Yvette, you've got to tell us what she said to you,' cried Lucille, in the teeth of Yvette's silent will *not* to be asked.

'Oh, nothing at *all* thrilling,' said Yvette, with false warmth. 'Just the usual old thing: a dark man who means good luck, and a fair one who means bad: and a death in the family, which if it means Granny, won't be so *very* awful: and I shall marry when I'm twenty-three, and have heaps of money and heaps of love, and two children. All sounds very nice, but it's a bit too much of a good thing, you know.'

'Oh, but why did you give her more money?'

'Oh, well, I wanted to! You *have* to be a bit lordly with people like that–'

4

There was a terrific rumpus down at the rectory, on account of Yvette and the Window Fund. After the war, Aunt Cissie had set her heart on a stained glass window in the church, as a memorial for the men of the parish who had fallen. But the bulk of the fallen had been Nonconformists, so the memorial took the form of an ugly little monument in front of the Wesleyan chapel.

This did not vanquish Aunt Cissie. She canvassed, she had bazaars, she made the girls get up amateur theatrical shows, for her precious window. Yvette, who quite liked the acting and showing-off part of it, took charge of the farce called

Mary in the Mirror, and gathered in the proceeds, which were to be paid to the Window Fund when accounts were settled. Each of the girls was supposed to have a money-box for the Fund.

Aunt Cissie, feeling that the united sums must now almost suffice, suddenly called in Yvette's box. It contained fifteen shillings. There was a moment of green horror.

'Where is all the rest?'

'Oh!' said Yvette casually. 'I just borrowed it. It wasn't so awfully much.'

'What about the three pounds thirteen for *Mary in the Mirror*?' asked Aunt Cissie, as if the jaws of Hell were yawning.

'Oh, quite! I just borrowed it. I can pay it back.'

Poor Aunt Cissie! The green tumour of hate burst inside her, and there was a ghastly, abnormal scene, which left Yvette shivering with fear and nervous loathing.

Even the rector was rather severe.

'If you needed money, why didn't you tell me?' he said coldly. 'Have you ever been refused anything in reason?'

'I – I thought it didn't matter,' stammered Yvette.

'And what have you done with the money?'

'I suppose I've spent it,' said Yvette, with wide, distraught eyes and a peaked face.

'Spent it, on what?'

'I can't remember everything: stockings and things, and I gave some of it away.'

Poor Yvette! Her lordly airs and ways were already hitting back at her, on the reflex. The rector was angry: his face had a snarling, doggish look, a sort of sneer. He was afraid his daughter was developing some of the rank, tainted qualities of She-who-was-Cynthia.

'You *would* do the large with somebody else's money, wouldn't you?' he said, with a cold, mongrel sort of sneer, which showed what an utter unbeliever he was at the heart. The inferiority of a heart which has no core of warm belief in it, no pride in life. He had utterly no belief in her.

Yvette went pale and very distant. Her pride, that frail, precious flame which everybody tried to quench, recoiled like a flame blown far away on a cold wind, as if blown out, and her face, white now and still like a snowdrop, the white snow-flower of his conceit, seemed to have no life in it, only this pure, strange abstraction.

'He has no belief in me!' she thought in her soul. 'I am really nothing to him. I am nothing, only a shameful thing. Everything is shameful, everything is shameful!'

A flame of passion or rage, while it might have overwhelmed or infuriated her, would not have degraded her as did her father's unbelief, his final attitude of a sneer against her.

He became a little afraid, in the silence of sterile thought. After all, he needed the *appearance* of love and belief and bright life, he would never dare to face the fat worm of his own unbelief, that stirred in his heart.

'What have you to say for yourself?' he asked.

She only looked at him from that senseless snowdrop face which haunted him with fear, and gave him a helpless sense of guilt. That other one, She-who-was-Cynthia, she had looked back at him with the same numb, white fear, the fear of his degrading unbelief, the worm which was his heart's core. He *knew* his heart's core was a fat, awful worm. His dread was lest anyone else should know. His anguish of hate was against anyone who knew and recoiled.

He saw Yvette recoiling, and immediately his manner changed to the worldly old good-humoured cynic which he affected.

'Ah well!' he said. 'You have to pay it back, my girl, that's all. I will advance you the money out of your allowance. But I shall charge you four per cent a month interest. Even the devil himself must pay a percentage on his debts. Another time, if you can't trust yourself, don't handle money which isn't your own. Dishonesty isn't pretty.'

Yvette remained crushed, and deflowered and humiliated. She crept about, trailing the rays of her pride. She had a revulsion even from herself. Oh, why had she ever touched the leprous money! Her whole flesh shrank as if it were defiled. Why was that? Why, why was that?

She admitted herself wrong in having spent the money. 'Of course I shouldn't have done it. They are quite right to be angry,' she said to herself.

But where did the horrible wincing of her flesh come from? Why did she feel she had caught some physical contagion?

'Where you're so *silly*, Yvette,' Lucille lectured her: poor Lucille was in great distress—'is that you give yourself away to them all. You might *know* they'd find out. I could have raised the money for you, and saved all this bother. It's perfectly awful! But you never will think beforehand where your actions are going to land you! Fancy Aunt Cissie saying all those things to you! How *awful!* Whatever would Mamma have said if she'd heard it?'

When things went very wrong, they thought of their mother, and despised their father and all the low brood of the Saywells. Their mother, of course, had belonged to a higher, if more dangerous and 'immortal', world. More selfish, decidedly. But with a showier gesture. More unscrupulous and more easily moved to contempt: but not so humiliating.

Yvette always considered that she got her fine, delicate flesh from her mother. The Saywells were all a bit leathery, and grubby somewhere inside. But then the Saywells never let you down. Whereas the fine She-who-was-Cynthia had let the rector down with a bang, and his little children along with him. Her little children? They could not quite forgive her.

Only dimly, after the row, Yvette began to realise the other sanctity of herself, the sanctity of her sensitive, clean flesh and blood, which the Saywells with their so-called morality succeeded in defiling. They always wanted to defile it. They were the life unbelievers. Whereas, perhaps She-who-was-Cynthia had only been a moral unbeliever.

Yvette went about dazed and peaked and confused. The rector paid in the money to Aunt Cissie, much to that lady's rage. The helpless tumour of her rage was still running. She would have liked to announce her niece's delinquency in the parish magazine. It was anguish to the destroyed woman that she could not publish the news to all the world. The selfishness! The selfishness! The selfishness!

Then the rector handed his daughter a little account with himself: her debt to him, interest thereon, the amount deducted from her small allowance. But to her credit he had placed a guinea, which was the fee he had to pay for complicity.

'As father of the culprit,' he said humorously, 'I am fined one guinea. And with that I wash the ashes out of my hair.'

He was always generous about money. But somehow he seemed to think that by being free about money he could absolutely call himself a generous man.

Whereas he used money, even generosity, as a hold over her.

But he let the affair drop entirely. He was by this time more amused than anything, to judge from appearances. He thought still he was safe.

Aunt Cissie, however, could not get over her convulsion. One night when Yvette had gone rather early, miserably, to bed, when Lucille was away at a party, and she was lying with soft, peaked limbs aching with a sort of numbness and defilement, the door softly opened, and there stood Aunt Cissie, pushing her grey-green face through the opening of the door. Yvette started up in terror.

'Liar! Thief! Selfish little beast!' hissed the maniacal face of Aunt Cissie. 'You little hypocrite! You liar! You selfish beast! You greedy little beast!'

There was such extraordinary impersonal hatred in that grey-green mask, and those frantic words, that Yvette opened her mouth to scream with hysterics. But Aunt Cissie shut the door as suddenly as she had opened it and disappeared. Yvette leaped from her bed and turned the key. Then she crept back, half demented with fear of the squalid abnormal, half numbed with paralysis of damaged pride. And amid it all, up came a bubble of distracted laughter. It *was* so filthily ridiculous!

Aunt Cissie's behaviour did not hurt the girl so very much. It was, after all, somewhat fantastic. Yet hurt she was: in her limbs, in her body, in her sex, hurt. Hurt, numbed, and half destroyed, with only her nerves vibrating and jangled. And still so young, she could not conceive what was happening.

Only she lay and wished she were a gipsy. To live in a camp, in a caravan, and never set foot in a house, not know the existence of a parish, never look at a church. Her heart was hard with repugnance against the rectory. She loathed these houses with their indoor sanitation and their bathrooms, and their extraordinary repulsiveness. She hated the rectory and everything it implied. The whole stagnant, sewerage sort of life, where sewerage is never mentioned, but where it seems to smell from the centre to every two-legged inmate, from Granny to the servants, was foul. If gipsies had no bathrooms, at least they had no sewerage. There was fresh air. In the rectory there was *never* fresh air. And in the souls of the people, the air was stale till it stank.

Hate kindled her heart, as she lay with numbed limbs. And she thought of the words of the gipsy woman: 'There is a dark man who never lived in a house. He loves you. The other people are treading on your heart. They will tread on your heart till you think it is dead. But the dark man will blow the one spark up into fire again, good fire. You will see what good fire.'

Even as the woman was saying it, Yvette felt there was some duplicity somewhere. But she didn't mind. She hated with the cold, acrid hatred of a child the rectory interior, the sort of putridity in the life. She liked that big, swarthy, wolf-like gipsy woman, with the big gold rings in her ears, the pink scarf over her wavy black hair, the tight bodice of brown velvet, the green, fan-like skirt. She liked her dusky, strong, relentless hands, that had pressed so firm, like wolf's paws, in Yvette's own soft palm. She liked her. She liked the danger and the covert fearlessness of her. She liked her covert, unyielding sex, that was immoral, but with a hard, defiant pride of its own. Nothing would ever get that woman under. She would despise the rectory and the rectory morality utterly! She would strangle Granny with one hand. And she would have the same contempt for Daddy and for Uncle Fred, as men, as she would have for fat old slobbery Rover, the Newfoundland dog. A great, sardonic female contempt, for such domesticated dogs, calling themselves men.

And the gipsy man himself! Yvette quivered suddenly, as if she had seen his big, bold eyes upon her, with the naked insinuation of desire in them. The absolutely naked insinuation of desire made her lie prone and powerless in the bed, as if a drug had cast her in a new, molten mould.

She never confessed to anybody that two of the ill-starred Window Fund pounds had gone to the gipsy woman. What if Daddy and Aunt Cissie knew *that*! Yvette stirred luxuriously in the bed. The thought of the gipsy had released the life of her limbs, and crystallised in her heart the hate of the rectory: so that now she felt potent, instead of impotent.

When, later, Yvette told Lucille about Aunt Cissie's dramatic interlude in the bedroom doorway, Lucille was indignant.

'Oh, hang it all!' cried she. 'She might let it drop now. I should think we've heard enough about it by now! Good heavens, you'd think Aunt Cissie was a perfect bird of paradise! Daddy's dropped it, and after all, it's his business if it's anybody's. Let Aunt Cissie shut up!'

It was the very fact that the rector had dropped it, and that he again treated the vague and inconsiderate Yvette as if she were some specially-licensed being, that kept Aunt Cissie's bile flowing. The fact that Yvette really was most of the time unaware of other people's feelings, and being unaware, couldn't care about them, nearly sent Aunt Cissie mad. Why should that young creature, with a delinquent mother, go through life as a privileged being, even unaware of other people's existence, though they were under her nose?

Lucille at this time was very irritable. She seemed as if she simply went a little unbalanced, when she entered the rectory. Poor Lucille, she was so thoughtful and responsible. She did all the extra troubling, thought about doctors, medicines, servants, and all that sort of thing. She slaved conscientiously at her job all day in town, working in a room with artificial light from ten till five. And she came home to have her nerves rubbed almost to frenzy by Granny's horrible and persistent inquisitiveness and parasitic agedness.

The affair of the Window Fund had apparently blown over, but there remained a stuffy tension in the atmosphere. The weather continued bad. Lucille stayed at home on the afternoon of her half holiday, and did herself no good by it. The rector was in his study, she and Yvette were making a dress for the latter young woman, Granny was resting on the couch.

The dress was of blue silk velours, French material, and was going to be very becoming. Lucille made Yvette try it on again: she was nervously uneasy about the hang under the arms.

'Oh, bother!' cried Yvette, stretching her long, tender, childish arms, that tended to go bluish with the cold. 'Don't be so frightfully *fussy*, Lucille! It's quite all right.'

'If that's all the thanks I get, slaving my half-day away making dresses for you, I might as well do something for myself!'

'Well, Lucille! You know I never *asked* you! You know you can't bear it unless you *do* supervise,' said Yvette, with that irritating blandness of hers, as she raised her naked elbows and peered over her shoulder into the long mirror.

'Oh yes! you never *asked* me!' cried Lucille. 'As if I didn't know what you meant, when you started sighing and flouncing about.'

'I?' said Yvette, with vague surprise. 'Why, when did I start sighing and flouncing about?'

'Of course, you know you did.'

'Did I? No, I didn't know! When was it?' Yvette could put a peculiar annoyance into her mild, straying questions.

'I shan't do another thing to this frock, if you don't stand still and *stop* it,' said Lucille, in her rather sonorous, burning voice.

'You know you are most awfully nagging and irritable, Lucille,' said Yvette, standing as if on hot bricks.

'Now, Yvette!' cried Lucille, her eyes suddenly flashing in her sister's face, with wild flashes. 'Stop it at once! Why should everybody put up with your abominable and overbearing temper?'

'Well, I don't know about *my* temper,' said Yvette, writhing slowly out of the half-made frock, and slipping into her dress again.

Then, with an obstinate little look on her face, she sat down again at the table, in the gloomy afternoon, and began to sew at the blue stuff. The room was littered with blue clippings, the scissors were lying on the floor, the work-basket was spilled in chaos all over the table, and a second mirror was perched perilously on the piano.

Granny, who had been in a semi-coma, called a doze, roused herself on the big, soft couch and put her cap straight.

'I don't get much peace for my nap,' she said, slowly feeling her thin white hair, to see that it was in order. She had heard vague noises.

Aunt Cissie came in, fumbling in a bag for a chocolate.

'I never saw such a mess!' she said. 'You'd better clear some of that litter away, Yvette.'

'All right,' said Yvette. 'I will in a minute.'

'Which means never!' sneered Aunt Cissie, suddenly darting and picking up the scissors.

There was silence for a few moments, and Lucille slowly pushed her hands in her hair, as she read a book.

'You'd better clear away, Yvette,' persisted Aunt Cissie.

'I will, before tea,' replied Yvette, rising once more and pulling the blue dress over her head, flourishing her long, naked arms through the sleeveless arm-holes. Then she went between the mirrors to look at herself once more.

As she did so, she sent the second mirror, that she had perched carelessly on the piano, sliding with a rattle to the floor. Luckily it did not break. But everybody started badly.

'She's smashed the mirror!' cried Aunt Cissie.

'Smashed a mirror! Which mirror! Who's smashed it?' came Granny's sharp voice.

'I haven't smashed anything,' came the calm voice of Yvette. 'It's quite all right.'

'You'd better not perch it up there again,' said Lucille.

Yvette, with a little impatient shrug at all the fuss, tried making the mirror stand in another place. She was not successful.

'If one had a fire in one's own room,' she said crossly, 'one needn't have a lot of people fussing when one wants to sew.'

'Which mirror are you moving about?' asked Granny.

'One of our own that came from the vicarage,' said Yvette rudely.

'Don't break it in *this* house, wherever it came from,' said Granny.

There was a sort of family dislike for the furniture that had belonged to She-who-was-Cynthia. It was most of it shoved into the kitchen and the servants' bedrooms.

'Oh, *I'm* not superstitious,' said Yvette, 'about mirrors or any of that sort of thing.'

'Perhaps you're not,' said Granny. 'People who never take the responsibility for their own actions usually don't see what happens.'

'After all,' said Yvette, 'I may say it's my own looking-glass, even if I did break it.'

'And I say,' said Granny, 'that there shall be no mirrors broken in *this* house, if we can help it; no matter who they belong to, or did belong to. Cissie, have I got my cap straight?'

Aunt Cissie went over and straightened the old lady. Yvette loudly and irritatingly trilled a tuneless tune.

'And now, Yvette, will you please clear away?' said Aunt Cissie.

'Oh, bother!' cried Yvette angrily. 'It's simply *awful* to live with a lot of people who are always nagging and fussing over trifles.'

'What people, may I ask?' said Aunt Cissie ominously.

Another row was imminent. Lucille looked up with a queer cast in her eyes. In the two girls, the blood of She-who-was-Cynthia was roused.

'Of course you may ask! You know quite well I mean the people in this beastly house,' said the outrageous Yvette.

'At least,' said Granny, 'we don't come of half-depraved stock.'

There was a second's electric pause. Then Lucille sprang from her low seat, with sparks flying from her.

'You shut up!' she shouted, in a blast full upon the mottled majesty of the old lady.

The old woman's breast began to heave with heaven knows what emotions. The pause this time, as after the thunderbolt, was icy.

Then Aunt Cissie, livid, sprang upon Lucille, pushing her like a fury.

'Go to your room!' she cried hoarsely. 'Go to your room!'

And she proceeded to push the white but fiery-eyed Lucille from the room. Lucille let herself be pushed, while Aunt Cissie vociferated:

'Stay in your room till you've apologised for this!—till you've apologised to the Mater for this!'

'I shan't apologise!' came the clear voice of Lucille, from the passage, while Aunt Cissie shoved her.

Aunt Cissie drove her more wildly upstairs.

Yvette stood tall and bemused in the sitting-room, with the air of offended dignity, at the same time bemused, which was so odd on her. She still was bare-armed, in the half-made blue dress. And even *she* was half aghast at Lucille's attack on the majesty of age. But also, she was coldly indignant against Granny's aspersion of the maternal blood in their veins.

'Of course I meant no offence,' said Granny.

'Didn't you?' said Yvette coolly.

'Of course not. I only said we're not depraved, just because we happen to be superstitious about breaking mirrors.'

Yvette could hardly believe her ears. Had she heard right? Was it possible! Or was Granny, at her age, just telling a barefaced lie?

Yvette knew that the old woman was telling a cool, barefaced lie. But already, so quickly, Granny believed her own statement.

The rector appeared, having left time for a lull.

'What's wrong?' he asked cautiously, genially.

'Oh, nothing!' drawled Yvette. 'Lucille told Granny to shut up when she was saying something. And Aunt Cissie drove her up to her room. *Tant de bruit pour une omelette!* Though Lucille *was* a bit over the mark, that time.'

The old lady couldn't catch what Yvette said.

'Lucille really will have to learn to control her nerves,' said the old woman. 'The mirror fell down, and it worried me. I said so to Yvette, and she said something about superstitions and the people in the beastly house. I told her the people in the house were not depraved, if they happened to mind when a mirror was broken. And at that Lucille flew at me and told me to shut up. It really is disgraceful how these children give way to their nerves. I know it's nothing but nerves.'

Aunt Cissie had come in during this speech. At first even she was dumb. Then it seemed to her, it was as Granny had said.

'I have forbidden her to come down until she comes to apologise to the Mater,' she said.

'I doubt if she'll apologise,' said the calm, queenly Yvette, holding her bare arms.

'And I don't want any apology,' said the old lady. 'It is merely nerves. I don't know what they'll come to, if they have nerves like that, at their age! She must take Vibrofat.—I am sure Arthur would like his tea, Cissie.'

Yvette swept her sewing together, to go upstairs. And again she trilled her tune, rather shrill and tuneless. She was trembling inwardly.

'More glad rags!' said her father to her genially.

'More glad rags!' she reiterated sagely, as she sauntered upstairs, with her day dress over her arm. She wanted to console Lucille, and ask her how the blue stuff hung now.

At the first landing she stood as she nearly always did, to gaze through the window that looked to the road and the bridge. Like the Lady of Shalott, she seemed always to imagine that someone would come along singing *Tirra-lirra!* or something equally intelligent, by the river.

5

It was nearly tea-time. The snowdrops were out by the short drive going to the gate from the side of the house, and the gardener was pottering at the round, damp flower-beds on the wet grass that sloped to the stream. Past the gate went the whitish, muddy road, crossing the stone bridge almost immediately, and winding in a curve up to the steep, clustering, stony, smoking northern village, that perched over the grim stone mills which Yvette could see ahead down the narrow valley, their tall chimneys long and erect.

The rectory was on one side the Papple, in the rather steep valley, the village was beyond and above, farther down, on the other side the swift stream. At the back of the rectory the hill went up steep, with a grove of dark, bare larches, through which the road disappeared. And immediately across stream from the rectory, facing the house, the river-bank rose steep and bushy, up to the sloping, dreary meadows, that sloped up again to dark hillsides of trees, with grey rock cropping out.

But from the end of the house, Yvette could only see the road curving round past the wall with its laurel hedge, down to the bridge, then up again round the shoulder to that first hard cluster of houses in Papplewick village, beyond the dry-stone walls of the steep fields.

She always expected *something* to come down the slant of the road from Papplewick, and she always lingered at the landing window. Often a cart came, or a motor-car, or a lorry with stone, or a labourer, or one of the servants. But never anybody who sang *Tirra-lirra!* by the river. The tirra-lirraing days seem to have gone by.

This day, however, round the corner on the white-grey road, between the grass and the low stone walls, a roan horse came stepping bravely and briskly downhill, driven by a man in a cap, perched on the front of his light cart. The man swayed loosely to the swing of the cart, as the horse stepped downhill, in the silent sombreness of the afternoon. At the back of the cart, long duster-brooms of reed and feather stuck out, nodding on their stalks of cane.

Yvette stood close to the window, and put the casement-cloth curtains behind her, clutching her bare upper arms with her hands.

At the foot of the slope the horse started into a brisk trot to the bridge. The cart rattled on the stone bridge, the brooms bobbed and flustered, the driver sat as if in a kind of dream, swinging along. It was like something seen in a sleep.

But as he crossed the end of the bridge, and was passing along the rectory wall, he looked up at the grim stone house that seemed to have backed away from the gate, under the hill. Yvette moved her hands quickly on her arms. And as quickly, from under the peak of his cap, he had seen her, his swarthy predative face was alert.

He pulled up suddenly at the white gate, still gazing upwards at the landing window; while Yvette, always clasping her cold and mottled arms, still gazed abstractedly down at him from the window.

His head gave a little, quick jerk of signal, and he led his horse well aside, on to the grass. Then, limber and alert, he turned back the tarpaulin of the cart, fetched out various articles, pulled forth two or three of the long brooms of reed or turkey-feathers, covered the cart, and turned towards the house, looking up at Yvette as he opened the white gate.

She nodded to him, and flew to the bathroom to put on her dress, hoping she had disguised her nod so that he wouldn't be sure she had nodded. Meanwhile she heard the hoarse, deep roaring of that old fool, Rover, punctuated by the yapping of that young idiot, Trixie.

She and the housemaid arrived at the same moment at the sitting-room door. 'Was it the man selling brooms?' said Yvette to the maid. 'All right!' and she opened the door. 'Aunt Cissie, there's a man selling brooms. Shall I go?'

'What sort of a man?' said Aunt Cissie, who was sitting at tea with the rector and the Mater: the girls having been excluded for once from the meal.

'A man with a cart,' said Yvette.

'A gipsy,' said the maid.

Of course Aunt Cissie rose at once. She had to look at him.

The gipsy stood at the back door, under the steep, dark bank where the larches grew. The long brooms flourished from one hand, and from the other hung various objects of shining copper and brass: a saucepan, a candlestick, plates of beaten copper. The man himself was neat and dapper, almost rakish, in his dark-green cap and double-breasted green check coat. But his manner was subdued, very quiet: and at the same time proud, with a touch of condescension and aloofness.

'Anything to-day, lady?' he said, looking at Aunt Cissie with dark, shrewd, searching eyes, but putting a very quiet tenderness into his voice.

Aunt Cissie saw how handsome he was, saw the flexible curve of his lips under the line of black moustache, and she was fluttered. The merest hint of roughness or aggression on the man's part would have made her shut the door contemptuously in his face. But he managed to insinuate such a subtle suggestion of submission into his male bearing, that she began to hesitate.

'The candlestick is lovely!' said Yvette. 'Did you make it?'

And she looked up at the man with her naïve, childlike eyes, that were as capable of double meaning as his own.

'Yes, lady!' He looked back into her eyes for a second, with that naked suggestion of desire which acted on her like a spell, and robbed her of her will. Her tender face seemed to go into a sleep.

'It's awfully nice!' she murmured vaguely.

Aunt Cissie began to bargain for the candlestick: which was a low, thick stem of copper, rising from a double bowl. With patient aloofness the man attended to her, without ever looking at Yvette, who leaned against the doorway and watched in a muse.

'How is your wife?' she asked him suddenly, when Aunt Cissie had gone indoors to show the candlestick to the rector, and ask him if he thought it was worth it.

The man looked fully at Yvette, and a scarcely discernible smile curled his lips. His eyes did not smile: the insinuation in them only hardened to a glare.

'She's all right. When are you coming that way again?' he murmured in a low, caressive, intimate voice.

'Oh, I don't know,' said Yvette vaguely.

'You come Fridays, when I'm there,' he said.

Yvette gazed over his shoulder as if she had not heard him. Aunt Cissie returned, with the candlestick and the money to pay for it. Yvette turned nonchalant away, trilling one of her broken tunes, abandoning the whole affair with a certain rudeness.

Nevertheless, hiding this time at the landing window, she stood to watch the man go. What she wanted to know was whether he really had any power over her. She did not intend him to see her this time.

She saw him go down to the gate, with his brooms and pans, and out to the cart. He carefully stowed away his pans and his brooms and fixed down the tarpaulin over the cart. Then with a slow, effortless spring of his flexible loins, he was on the cart again, and touching the horse with the reins. The roan horse was away at once, the cart-wheels grinding uphill, and soon the man was gone, without looking round. Gone like a dream which was only a dream, yet which she could not shake off.

'No, he hasn't any power over me!' she said to herself: rather disappointed really, because she wanted somebody, or something, to have power over her.

She went up to reason with the pale and overwrought Lucille, scolding her for getting into a state over nothing.

'What does it *matter*,' she expostulated, 'if you told Granny to shut up! Why, everybody ought to be told to shut up when they're being beastly. But she didn't mean it, you know. No, she didn't mean it. And she's quite sorry she said it. There's absolutely no reason to make a fuss. Come on, let's dress ourselves up and sail down to dinner like duchesses. Let's have our own back that way. Come on, Lucille!'

There was something strange and mazy, like having cobwebs over one's face, about Yvette's vague blitheness; her queer, misty side-stepping from an unpleasantness. It was cheering, too. But it was like walking in one of those autumn mists, when gossamer strands blow over your face. You don't quite know where you are.

She succeeded, however, in persuading Lucille, and the girls got out their best party frocks: Lucille in green and silver, Yvette in a pale lilac colour with turquoise chenille threading. A little rouge and powder, and their best slippers, and the gardens of paradise began to blossom. Yvette hummed and looked at herself, and put on her most *dégagé* airs of one of the young marchionesses. She had an odd way of slanting her eyebrows and pursing her lips, and to all appearances detaching herself from every earthly consideration, and floating through the cloud of her own pearl-coloured reserves. It was amusing, and not quite convincing.

'Of course I am beautiful, Lucille,' she said blandly. 'And you're perfectly lovely, now you look a bit reproachful. Of course you're the most aristocratic of the two of us, with your nose! And now your eyes look reproachful, that adds an appealing look, and you're perfect, perfectly lovely. But I'm more *winning*, in a way.–Don't you agree?' She turned with arch, complicated simplicity to Lucille.

She was truly simple in what she said. It was just what she thought. But it gave no hint of the very different *feeling* that also preoccupied her: the feeling that she had been looked upon, not from the outside, but from the inside, from her secret female self. She was dressing herself up and looking her most dazzling, just to counteract the effect that the gipsy had had on her, when he had looked at her, and seen none of her pretty face and her pretty ways, but just the dark, tremulous potent secret of her virginity.

The two girls started downstairs in state when the dinner-gong rang: but they waited till they heard the voices of the men. Then they sailed down and into the sitting-room, Yvette preening herself in her vague, debonair way, always a little bit absent; and Lucille shy, ready to burst into tears.

'My goodness gracious!' exclaimed Aunt Cissie, who was still wearing her dark-brown knitted sports coat. 'What an apparition! Wherever do you think you're going?'

'We're dining with the family,' said Yvette naïvely, 'and we've put on our best gewgaws in honour of the occasion.'

The rector laughed aloud, and Uncle Fred said:

'The family feels itself highly honoured.'

Both the elderly men were quite gallant, which was what Yvette wanted.

'Come and let me feel your dresses, do!' said Granny. 'Are they your best? It *is* a shame I can't see them.'

'To-night, Mater,' said Uncle Fred, 'we shall have to take the young ladies in to dinner, and live up to the honour. Will you go with Cissie?'

'I certainly will,' said Granny. 'Youth and beauty must come first.'

'Well, to-night, Mater!' said the rector, pleased.

And he offered his arm to Lucille, while Uncle Fred escorted Yvette.

But it was a draggled, dull meal, all the same. Lucille tried to be bright and sociable, and Yvette really was most amiable in her vague, cobwebby way. Dimly, at the back of her mind, she was thinking: Why are we all only like mortal pieces of furniture? Why is nothing *important?*

That was her constant refrain to herself: Why is nothing important? Whether she was in church, or at a party of young people, or dancing in the hotel in the city, the same little bubble of a question rose repeatedly on her consciousness: Why is nothing important?

There were plenty of young men to make love to her: even devotedly. But with impatience she had to shake them off. Why were they so unimportant?–so irritating!

She never even thought of the gipsy. He was a perfectly negligible incident. Yet the approach of Friday loomed strangely significant. 'What are we doing on Friday?' she said to Lucille. To which Lucille replied that they were doing nothing. And Yvette was vexed.

Friday came, and in spite of herself she thought all day of the quarry off the road up high Bonsall Head. She wanted to be there. That was all she was conscious of. She wanted to be there. She had not even a dawning idea of going there. Besides, it was raining again. But as she sewed the blue dress, finishing it for the party up at Lambley Close to-morrow, she just felt that her soul was up there, at the quarry, among the caravans, with the gipsies. Like one lost, or whose soul was stolen, she was not present in her body, the shell of her body. Her intrinsic body was away at the quarry, among the caravans.

The next day, at the party, she had no idea that she was being sweet to Leo. She had no idea that she was snatching him away from the tortured Ella Framley. Not until, when she was eating her pistachio ice, he said to her:

'Why don't you and me get engaged, Yvette? I'm absolutely sure it's the right thing for us both.'

Leo was a bit common, but good-natured and well off. Yvette quite liked him. But engaged! How perfectly silly! She felt like offering him a set of her silk underwear, to get engaged to.

'But I thought it was Ella!' she said, in wonder.

'Well! It might ha' been, but for you. It's your doings, you know! Ever since those gipsies told your fortune, I felt it was me or nobody, for you, and you or nobody, for me.'

'Really!' said Yvette, simply lost in amazement. 'Really!'

'Didn't you feel a bit the same?' he asked.

'Really!' Yvette kept on gasping softly, like a fish.

'You felt a bit the same, didn't you?' he said.

'What? About what?' she asked, coming to.

'About me, as I feel about you.'

'Why? What? Getting engaged, you mean? I? No! Why, how *could* I? I could never have dreamed of such an impossible thing.'

She spoke with her usual heedless candour, utterly unoccupied with his feelings.

'What was to prevent you?' he said, a bit nettled. 'I thought you did.'

'Did you *really now?*' she breathed in amazement, with that soft, virgin, heedless candour which made her her admirers and her enemies.

She was so completely amazed, there was nothing for him to do but twiddle his thumbs in annoyance.

The music began, and he looked at her.

'No! I won't dance any more,' she said, drawing herself up and gazing away rather loftily over the assembly, as if he did not exist. There was a touch of puzzled wonder on her brow, and her soft, dim, virgin face did indeed suggest the snowdrop of her father's pathetic imagery.

'But of course *you* will dance,' she said, turning to him with young condescension. 'Do ask somebody to have this with you.'

He rose, angry, and went down the room.

She remained soft and remote in her amazement. Expect Leo to propose to her! She might as well have expected old Rover the Newfoundland dog to propose to her. Get engaged, to any man on earth? No, good heavens, nothing more ridiculous could be imagined!

It was then, in a fleeting side-thought, that she realised that the gipsy existed. Instantly, she was indignant. Him, of all things! Him! Never!

'Now why?' she asked herself, again in hushed amazement. 'Why? It's *absolutely* impossible: absolutely! So why is it?'

This was a nut to crack. She looked at the young men dancing, elbows out, hips prominent, waists elegantly in. They gave her no clue to her problem. Yet she did particularly dislike the forced elegance of the waists and the prominent hips, over which the well-tailored coats hung with such effeminate discretion.

'There is something about me which they don't see and never would see,' she said angrily to herself. And at the same time, she was relieved that they didn't and couldn't. It made life so very much simpler.

And again, since she was one of the people who are conscious in visual images, she saw the dark-green jersey rolled on the black trousers of the gipsy, his fine, quick hips, alert as eyes. They were elegant. The elegance of these dancers seemed so stuffed, hips merely wadded with flesh. Leo the same, thinking himself such a fine dancer! and a fine figure of a fellow!

Then she saw the gipsy's face; the straight nose, the slender mobile lips, and the level, significant stare of the black eyes, which seemed to shoot her in some vital, undiscovered place, unerring.

She drew herself up angrily. How dared he look at her like that? So she gazed glaringly at the insipid beaux on the dancing-floor. And she despised him. Just as the raggle-taggle gipsy women despise men who are not gipsies, despise their dog-like walk down the streets, she found herself despising this crowd. Where among them was the subtle, lonely, insinuating challenge that could reach her?

She did not want to mate with a house-dog.

Her sensitive nose turned up, her soft brown hair fell like a soft sheath round her tender, flower-like face, as she sat musing. She seemed so virginal. At the same time, there was a touch of the tall young virgin *witch* about her, that made the house-dog men shy off. She might metamorphose into something uncanny before you knew where you were.

This made her lonely, in spite of all the courting. Perhaps the courting only made her lonelier.

Leo, who was a sort of mastiff among the house-dogs, returned after his dance, with fresh cheery-o! courage.

'You've had a little think about it, haven't you?' he said, sitting down beside her: a comfortable, well-nourished, determined sort of fellow. She did not know why it irritated her so unreasonably, when he hitched up his trousers at the knee, over his good-sized but not very distinguished legs, and lowered himself assuredly on to a chair.

'Have I?' she said vaguely. 'About what?'

'You know what about,' he said. 'Did you make up your mind?'

'Make up my mind about what?' she asked innocently.

In her upper consciousness, she truly had forgotten.

'Oh!' said Leo, settling his trousers again. 'About me and you getting engaged, you know.' He was almost as off-hand as she.

'Oh, that's *absolutely* impossible,' she said, with mild amiability, as if it were some stray question among the rest. 'Why, I never even thought of it again. Oh, don't talk about that sort of nonsense! That sort of thing is *absolutely* impossible,' she reiterated like a child.

'That sort of thing is, is it?' he said, with an odd smile at her calm, distant assertion. 'Well, what sort of thing *is* possible, then? You don't want to die an old maid, do you?'

'Oh, I don't mind,' she said absently.

'I do,' he said.

She turned round and looked at him in wonder.

'Why?' she said. 'Why should you mind if I was an old maid?'

'Every reason in the world,' he said, looking up at her with a bold, meaningful smile, that wanted to make its meaning blatant, if not patent.

But instead of penetrating into some deep, secret place, and shooting her there, Leo's bold and patent smile only hit her on the outside of the body, like a tennis ball, and caused the same kind of sudden irritated reaction.

'I think this sort of thing is awfully silly,' she said, with minx-like spite. 'Why, you're practically engaged to–to–' she pulled herself up in time– 'probably half a dozen other girls. I'm not flattered by what you've said. I should hate it if anybody knew!–Hate it!–I shan't breathe a word of it, and I hope you'll have the sense not to.–There's Ella!'

And keeping her face averted from him, she sailed away like a tall, soft flower, to join poor Ella Framley.

Leo flapped his white gloves.

'Catty little bitch!' he said to himself. But he was of the mastiff type, he rather liked the kitten to fly in his face. He began definitely to single her out.

6

The next week it poured again with rain. And this irritated Yvette with strange anger. She had intended it should be fine. Especially she insisted it should be fine towards the week-end. Why, she did not ask herself.

Thursday, the half-holiday, came with a hard frost, and sun. Leo arrived with his car, the usual bunch. Yvette disagreeably and unaccountably refused to go.

'No, thanks, I don't feel like it,' she said.

She rather enjoyed being Mary-Mary-quite contrary.

Then she went for a walk by herself, up the frozen hills, to the Black Rocks.

The next day also came sunny and frosty. It was February, but in the north country the ground did not thaw in the sun. Yvette announced that she was going for a ride on her bicycle, and taking her lunch as she might not be back till afternoon.

She set off, not hurrying. In spite of the frost, the sun had a touch of spring. In the park, the deer were standing in the distance, in the sunlight, to be warm.

One doe, white-spotted, walked slowly across the motionless landscape.

Cycling, Yvette found it difficult to keep her hands warm, even when bodily she was quite hot. Only when she had to walk up the long hill, to the top, and there was no wind.

The upland was very bare and clear, like another world. She had climbed on to another level. She cycled slowly, a little afraid of taking the wrong lane, in the vast maze of stone fences. As she passed along the lane she thought was the right one, she heard a faint tapping noise, with a slight metallic resonance.

The gipsy man was seated on the ground with his back to the cart shaft, hammering a copper bowl. He was in the sun, bare-headed, but wearing his green jersey. Three small children were moving quietly round, playing in the horse's shelter: the horse and cart were gone. An old woman, bent, with a kerchief round her head, was cooking over a fire of sticks. The only sound was the rapid, ringing tap-tap-tap of the small hammer on the dull copper.

The man looked up at once, as Yvette stepped from her bicycle, but he did not move, though he ceased hammering. A delicate, barely discernible smile of triumph was on his face. The old woman looked round, keenly, from under her dirty grey hair. The man spoke a half-audible word to her, and she turned again to her fire. He looked up at Yvette.

'How are you all getting on?' she asked politely.

'All right, eh! You sit down a minute?' He turned as he sat, and pulled a stool from under the caravan for Yvette. Then, as he wheeled her bicycle to the side of the quarry, he started hammering again, with that bird-like, rapid light stroke.

Yvette went to the fire to warm her hands.

'Is this the dinner cooking?' she asked childishly of the old gipsy, as she spread her long tender hands, mottled red with the cold, to the embers.

'Dinner, yes!' said the old woman. 'For him! And for the children.'

She pointed with the long fork at the three black-eyed staring children, who were staring at her from under their black fringes. But they were clean. Only the old woman was not clean. The quarry itself they had kept perfectly clean.

Yvette crouched in silence, warming her hands. The man rapidly hammered away with intervals of silence. The old hag slowly climbed the steps to the third, oldest caravan. The children began to play again, like little wild animals, quiet and busy.

'Are they your children?' asked Yvette, rising from the fire and turning to the man.

He looked her in the eyes and nodded.

'But where's your wife?'

'She's gone out with the basket. They've all gone out, cart and all, selling things. I don't go selling things, I make them, but I don't go selling them. Not often. I don't often.'

'You make all the copper and brass things?' she said.

He nodded, and again offered her the stool. She sat down.

'You said you'd be here on Fridays,' she said. 'So I came this way, as it was so fine.'

'Very fine day!' said the gipsy, looking at her cheek, that was still a bit blanched by the cold, and the soft hair over her reddened ear, and the long, still mottled hands on her knee.

'You get cold, riding a bicycle?' he asked.

'My hands!' she said, clasping them nervously.

'You didn't wear gloves?'

'I did, but they weren't much good.'

'Cold comes through,' he said.

'Yes!' she replied.

The old woman came slowly, grotesquely down the steps of the caravan, with some enamel plates.

'The dinner cooked, eh?' he called softly.

The old woman muttered something as she spread the plates near the fire. Two pots hung from a long, iron, horizontal bar over the embers of the fire. A little pan seethed on a small iron tripod. In the sunshine, heat and vapour wavered together.

He put down his tools and the pot and rose from the ground.

'You eat something along of us?' he asked Yvette, not looking at her.

'Oh, I brought my lunch,' said Yvette.

'You eat some stew?' he said. And again he called quietly, secretly to the old woman, who muttered in answer, as she slid the iron pot towards the end of the bar.

'Some beans, and some mutton in it,' he said.

'Oh, thanks awfully!' said Yvette. Then, suddenly taking courage, added: 'Well, yes, just a very little, if I may.'

She went across to untie her lunch from her bicycle, and he went up the steps to his own caravan. After a minute, he emerged, wiping his hands on a towel.

'You want to come up and wash your hands?' he said.

'No, I think not,' she said. 'They are clean.'

He threw away his wash-water and set off down the road with a high brass jug to fetch clean water from the spring that trickled into a small pool, taking a cup to dip it with.

When he returned, he set the jug and the cup by the fire, and fetched himself a short log to sit on. The children sat on the floor by the fire, in a cluster, eating beans and bits of meat with spoon or fingers. The man on the log ate in silence, absorbedly. The woman made coffee in the black pot on the tripod, hobbling upstairs for the cups. There was silence in the camp. Yvette sat on her stool, having taken off her hat and shaken her hair in the sun.

'How many children have you?' Yvette asked suddenly.

'Say five,' he replied slowly, as he looked up into her eyes.

And again the bird of her heart sank down and seemed to die. Vaguely, as in a dream, she received from him the cup of coffee. She was aware only of his silent figure, sitting like a shadow there on the log, with an enamel cup in his hand, drinking his coffee in silence. Her will had departed from her limbs, he had power over her: his shadow was on her.

And he, as he blew his hot coffee, was aware of one thing only, the mysterious fruit of her virginity, her perfect tenderness in the body.

At length he put down his coffee-cup by the fire, then looked round at her. Her hair fell across her face as she tried to sip from the hot cup. On her face was that tender look of sleep, which a nodding flower has when it is full out. Like a mysterious early flower, she was full out, like a snowdrop which spreads its three white wings in a flight into the waking sleep of its brief blossoming. The waking sleep of her full-opened virginity, entranced like a snowdrop in the sunshine, was upon her.

The gipsy, supremely aware of her, waited for her like the substance of shadow, as shadow waits and is there.

At length his voice said, without breaking the spell:

'You want to go in my caravan now and wash your hands?'

The childlike, sleep-waking eyes of her moment of perfect virginity looked into his, unseeing. She was only aware of the dark, strange effluence of him bathing her limbs, washing her at last purely will-less. She was aware of *him*, as a dark, complete power.

'I think I might,' she said.

He rose silently, then turned to speak, in a low command, to the old woman. And then again he looked at Yvette, and putting his power over her, so that she had no burden of herself, or of action.

'Come!' he said.

She followed simply, followed the silent, secret, over-powering motion of his body in front of her. It cost her nothing. She was gone in his will.

He was at the top of the steps, and she at the foot, when she became aware of an intruding sound. She stood still at the foot of the steps. A motor-car was coming. He stood at the top of the steps, looking round strangely. The old woman harshly called something, as with rapidly increasing sound a car rushed near. It was passing.

Then they heard the cry of a woman's voice and the brakes on the car. It had pulled up just beyond the quarry.

The gipsy came down the steps, having closed the door of the caravan.

'You want to put your hat on,' he said to her.

Obediently she went to the stool by the fire and took up her hat. He sat down by the cart-wheel, darkly, and took up his tools. The rapid tap-tap-tap of his hammer, rapid and angry now like the sound of a tiny machine-gun, broke out just as the voice of the woman was heard crying:

'May we warm our hands at the camp-fire?'

She advanced, dressed in a sleek but bulky coat of sable fur. A man followed, in a blue greatcoat; pulling off his fur gloves and pulling out a pipe.

'It looked so tempting,' said the woman in the coat of many dead little animals, smiling a broad, half-condescending, half-hesitant simper around the company.

No one said a word.

She advanced to the fire, shuddering a little inside her coat with the cold. They had been driving in an open car.

She was a very small woman, with a rather large nose: probably a Jewess. Tiny almost as a child, in that sable coat she looked much more bulky than she should, and her wide, rather resentful brown eyes of a spoilt Jewess gazed oddly out of her expensive get-up.

She crouched over the low fire, spreading her little hands, on which diamonds and emeralds glittered.

'Ugh!' she shuddered. 'Of course we ought not to have come in an open car! But my husband won't even let me say I'm cold!' She looked round at him with her large, childish, reproachful eyes, that had still the canny shrewdness of a bourgeois Jewess: a rich one, probably.

Apparently she was in love, in a Jewess's curious way, with the big, blond man. He looked back at her with his abstracted blue eyes, that seemed to have no lashes, and a small smile creased his smooth, curiously naked cheeks. The smile didn't mean anything at all.

He was a man one connects instantly with winter sports, ski-ing and skating. Athletic, unconnected with life, he slowly filled his pipe, pressing in the tobacco with long, powerful, reddened finger.

The Jewess looked at him to see if she got any response from him. Nothing at all, but that odd, blank smile. She turned again to the fire, tilting her eyebrows and looking at her small, white, spread hands.

He slipped off his heavily-lined coat and appeared in one of the handsome, sharp-patterned knitted jerseys, in yellow and grey and black, over well-cut trousers, rather wide. Yes, they were both expensive! And he had a magnificent figure, an athletic, prominent chest. Like an experienced camper, he began building the fire together quietly: like a soldier on campaign.

'D'you think they'd mind if we put some fir-cones on to make a blaze?' he asked of Yvette, with a silent glance at the hammering gipsy.

'Love it, I should think,' said Yvette in a daze, as the spell of the gipsy slowly left her, feeling stranded and blank.

The man went to the car, and returned with a little sack of cones, from which he drew a handful.

'Mind if we make a blaze?' he called to the gipsy.

'Eh?'

'Mind if we make a blaze with a few cones?'

'You go ahead!' said the gipsy.

The man began placing the cones lightly, carefully on the red embers. And soon, one by one, they caught fire, and burned like roses of flame, with a sweet scent.

'Ah, lovely! lovely!' cried the little Jewess, looking up at her man again. He looked down at her quite kindly, like the sun on ice. 'Don't you love fire? Oh, I love it!' the little Jewess cried to Yvette, across the hammering.

The hammering annoyed her. She looked round with a slight frown on her fine little brows, as if she would bid the man stop. Yvette looked round too. The gipsy was bent over his copper bowl, legs apart, head down, lithe arm lifted. Already he seemed so far from her.

The man who accompanied the little Jewess strolled over to the gipsy and stood in silence looking down on him, holding his pipe in his mouth. Now they were two men, like two strange male dogs, having to sniff one another.

'We're on our honeymoon,' said the little Jewess, with an arch, resentful look at Yvette. She spoke in a rather high, defiant voice, like some bird, a jay, or a rook, calling.

'Are you really?' said Yvette.

'Yes! Before we're married! Have you heard of Simon Fawcett?'–she named a wealthy and well-known engineer of the north country. 'Well, I'm Mrs Fawcett, and he's just divorcing me!' She looked at Yvette with curious defiance and wistfulness.

'Are you really!' said Yvette.

She understood now the look of resentment and defiance in the little Jewess's big, childlike brown eyes. She was an honest little thing, but perhaps her honesty was *too* rational. Perhaps it partly explained the notorious unscrupulousness of the well-known Simon Fawcett.

'Yes! As soon as we get the divorce, I'm going to marry Major Eastwood.'

Her cards were now all on the table. She was not going to deceive anybody.

Behind her, the two men were talking briefly. She glanced round, and fixed the gipsy with her big brown eyes.

He was looking up, as if shyly, at the big fellow in the sparkling jersey, who was standing pipe in mouth, man to man, looking down.

'With the horses back of Arras,' said the gipsy, in a low voice.

They were talking war. The gipsy had served with the artillery teams in the Major's own regiment.

'*Ein schöner Mensch!*' said the Jewess. 'A handsome man, eh?'

For her, too, the gipsy was one of the common men, the Tommies.

'Quite handsome!' said Yvette.

'You are cycling?' asked the Jewess in a tone of surprise.

'Yes! Down to Papplewick. My father is rector of Papplewick: Mr Saywell!'

'Oh!' said the Jewess. 'I know! A clever writer! Very clever! I have read him.'

The fir-cones were all consumed already, the fire was a tall pile now of crumbling, shattering fire-roses. The sky was clouding over for afternoon. Perhaps towards evening it would snow.

The Major came back and slung himself into his coat.

'I thought I remembered his face!' he said. 'One of our grooms, A1 man with horses.'

'Look!' cried the Jewess to Yvette. 'Why don't you let us motor you down to Normanton. We live in Scoresby. We can tie the bicycle on behind.'

'I think I will,' said Yvette.

'Come!' called the Jewess to the peeping children, as the blond man wheeled away the bicycle. 'Come! Come here!' and taking out her little purse, she held out a shilling.

'Come!' she cried. 'Come and take it!'

The gipsy had laid down his work and gone into his caravan. The old woman called hoarsely to the children from her enclosure. The two elder children came stealing forward. The Jewess gave them the two bits of silver, a shilling and a florin, which she had in her purse, and again the hoarse voice of the unseen old woman was heard.

The gipsy descended from his caravan and strolled to the fire. The Jewess searched his face with the peculiar bourgeois boldness of her race.

'You were in the war, in Major Eastwood's regiment?' she said.

'Yes, lady!'

'Imagine you both being here now! – It's going to snow.' She looked up at the sky.

'Later on,' said the man, looking at the sky.

He too had gone inaccessible. His race was very old, in its peculiar battle with established society, and had no conception of winning. Only now and then it could score.

But since the war, even the old sporting chance of scoring now and then was pretty well quenched. There was no question of yielding. The gipsy's eyes still had their bold look: but it was hardened and directed far away, the touch of insolent intimacy was gone. He had been through the war.

He looked at Yvette.

'You're going back in the motor-car?' he said.

'Yes!' she replied, with a rather mincing mannerism. 'The weather is so treacherous!'

'Treacherous weather!' he repeated, looking at the sky.

She could not tell in the least what his feelings were. In truth, she wasn't very much interested. She was rather fascinated, now, by the little Jewess, mother of two children, who was taking her wealth away from the well-known engineer and transferring it to the penniless, sporting young Major Eastwood, who must be five or six years younger than she. Rather intriguing!

The blond man returned.

'A cigarette, Charles!' cried the little Jewess plaintively.

He took out his case slowly, with his slow, athletic movement. Something sensitive in him made him slow, cautious, as if he had hurt himself against people. He gave a cigarette to his wife, then one to Yvette, then offered the case, quite simply, to the gipsy. The gipsy took one.

'Thank you, sir!'

And he went quietly to the fire, and stooping, lit it at the red embers. Both women watched him.

'Well, good-bye!' said the Jewess, with her old bourgeois freemasonry. 'Thank you for the warm fire.'

'Fire is everybody's,' said the gipsy.

The young child came toddling to him.

'Good-bye!' said Yvette. 'I hope it won't snow for you.'

'We don't mind a bit of snow,' said the gipsy.

'Don't you?' said Yvette. 'I should have thought you would!'

'No!' said the gipsy.

She flung her scarf royally over her shoulder and followed the fur coat of the Jewess, which seemed to walk on little legs of its own.

7

Yvette was rather thrilled by the Eastwoods, as she called them. The little Jewess had only to wait three months now for the final decree. She had boldly rented a small summer cottage by the moors up at Scoresby, not far from the hills. Now it was dead winter, and she and the Major lived in comparative isolation, without any maid-servant. He had already resigned his commission in the regular army, and called himself Mr Eastwood. In fact, they were already Mr and Mrs Eastwood to the common world.

The little Jewess was thirty-six, and her two children were both over twelve years of age. The husband had agreed that she should have the custody, as soon as she was married to Eastwood.

So there they were, this queer couple, the tiny, finely-formed little Jewess with her big, resentful, reproachful eyes, and her mop of carefully-barbered black, curly hair, an elegant little thing in her way; and the big, pale-eyed young man, powerful and wintry, the remnant, surely, of some old uncanny Danish stock: living together in a small modern house near the moors and the hills, and doing their own housework.

It was a funny household. The cottage was hired furnished, but the little Jewess had brought along her dearest pieces of furniture. She had an odd little taste for the rococo, strange curving cupboards inlaid with mother-of-pearl, tortoise-shell, ebony, heaven knows what; strange, tall, flamboyant chairs from Italy, with sea-green brocade: astonishing saints with wind-blown, richly-coloured carven garments and pink faces: shelves of weird old Saxe and Capo di Monte figurines: and finally, a strange assortment of astonishing pictures painted on the back of glass, done probably in the early years of the nineteenth century or in the late eighteenth.

In this crowded and extraordinary interior she received Yvette, when the latter made a stolen visit. A whole system of stoves had been installed into the cottage, every corner was warm, almost hot. And there was the tiny rococo figurine of the Jewess herself, in a perfect little frock and an apron, putting slices of ham on the dish, while the great snow-bird of a major, in a white sweater and grey trousers, cut bread, mixed mustard, prepared coffee, and did all the rest. He had even made the dish of jugged hare which followed the cold meats and caviare.

The silver and the china were really valuable, part of the bride's trousseau. The Major drank beer from a silver mug, the little Jewess and Yvette had champagne in lovely glasses, the Major brought in coffee. They talked away. The little Jewess had a burning indignation against her first husband. She was intensely moral, so moral, that she was a divorcée. The Major, too, strange wintry bird, so powerful, handsome, too, in his way, but pale round the eyes as if he had no eyelashes, like a bird, he, too, had a curious indignation against life, because of the false morality. That powerful, athletic chest hid a strange, snowy sort of anger. And his tenderness for the little Jewess was based on his sense of outraged justice, the abstract morality of the north blowing him, like a strange wind, into isolation.

As the afternoon drew on, they went to the kitchen, the Major pushed back his sleeves, showing his powerful athletic white arms, and carefully, deftly washed the dishes, while the women wiped. It was not for nothing his muscles were trained. Then he went round attending to the stoves of the small house, which only needed a moment or two of care each day. And after this he brought out the small, closed car and drove Yvette home, in the rain, depositing her at the back gate, a little wicket among the larches, through which the earthen steps sloped downwards to the house.

She was really amazed by this couple.

'Really, Lucille!' she said. 'I do meet the most extraordinary people!' And she gave a detailed description.

'I think they sound rather nice!' said Lucille. 'I like the Major doing the housework, and looking so frightfully Bond Streety with it all. I should think, *when they're married*, it would be rather fun knowing them.'

'Yes!' said Yvette vaguely. 'Yes! Yes, it would!'

The very strangeness of the connection between the tiny Jewess and that pale-eyed, athletic young officer made her think again of her gipsy, who had been utterly absent from her consciousness, but who now returned with sudden painful force.

'What is it, Lucille,' she asked, 'that brings people together? People like the Eastwoods, for instance? and Daddy and Mamma, so frightfully unsuitable?—and that gipsy woman who told my fortune, like a great horse, and the gipsy man, so fine and delicately cut? What is it?'

'I suppose it's sex, whatever that is,' said Lucille.

'Yes, what is it? It's not really anything *common*, like common sensuality, you know, Lucille. It really isn't.'

'No, I suppose not,' said Lucille. 'Anyhow, I suppose it needn't be.'

'Because you see, the *common* fellows, you know, who make a girl feel *low*: nobody cares much about them. Nobody feels any connection with them. Yet they're supposed to be the sexual sort.'

'I suppose,' said Lucille, 'there's the low sort of sex, and there's the other sort, that isn't low. It's frightfully complicated, really! I *loathe* common fellows. And I never feel anything *sexual*'—she laid a rather disgusted stress on the word—'for fellows who aren't common. Perhaps I haven't got any sex.'

'That's just it!' said Yvette. 'Perhaps neither of us has. Perhaps we haven't really *got* any sex, to connect us with men.'

'How horrible it sounds: *connect us with men!*' cried Lucille, with revulsion. 'Wouldn't you hate to be connected with men that way? Oh, I think it's an awful pity there has to *be* sex! It would be so much better if we could still be men and women, without that sort of thing.'

Yvette pondered. Far in the background was the image of the gipsy as he had looked round at her, when she had said: 'The weather is so treacherous.' She felt rather like Peter when the cock crew, as she denied him. Or rather, she did not deny the gipsy; she didn't care about his part in the show, anyhow. It was some hidden part of herself which she denied: that part which mysteriously and unconfessedly responded to him. And it was a strange, lustrous black cock which crew in mockery of her.

'Yes!' she said vaguely. 'Yes! Sex is an awful bore, you know, Lucille. When you haven't got it, you feel you *ought* to have it, somehow. And when you've got it—or *if* you have it'—she lifted her head and wrinkled her nose disdainfully—'you hate it.'

'Oh, I don't know!' cried Lucille. 'I think I should *like* to be awfully in love with a man.'

'You think so!' said Yvette, again wrinkling her nose. 'But if you were you wouldn't.'

'How do you know?' asked Lucille.

'Well, I don't really,' said Yvette. 'But I think so! Yes, I think so!'

'Oh, it's very likely!' said Lucille disgustedly. 'And, anyhow, one would be sure to get out of love again, and it would be merely disgusting.'

'Yes,' said Yvette. 'It's a problem.' She hummed a little tune.

'Oh, hang it all, it's not a problem for us two yet. We're neither of us really in love, and we probably never shall be, so the problem is settled that way.'

'I'm not so sure!' said Yvette sagely. 'I'm not so sure. I believe, one day, I shall fall *awfully* in love.'

'Probably you never will,' said Lucille brutally. 'That's what most old maids are thinking all the time.'

Yvette looked at her sister from pensive but apparently insouciant eyes.

'Is it?' she said. 'Do you really think so, Lucille? How perfectly awful for them, poor things! Why ever do they *care?*'

'Why do they?' said Lucille. 'Perhaps they don't, really.—Probably it's all because people say: "Poor old girl, she couldn't catch a man."'

'I suppose it is!' said Yvette. 'They get to mind the beastly things people always do say about old maids. What a shame!'

'Anyhow, we have a good time, and we do have lots of boys who make a fuss of us,' said Lucille.

'Yes!' said Yvette. 'Yes! But I couldn't possibly marry any of them.'

'Neither could I,' said Lucille. 'But why shouldn't we? Why should we bother about marrying, when we have a perfectly good time with the boys, who are awfully good sorts, and you must say, Yvette, awfully sporting and *decent* to us.'

'Oh, they are!' said Yvette absently.

'I think it's time to think of marrying somebody,' said Lucille, 'when you feel you're *not* having a good time any more. Then marry, and just settle down.'

'Quite!' said Yvette.

But now, under all her bland, soft amiability, she was annoyed with Lucille. Suddenly she wanted to turn her back on Lucille.

Besides, look at the shadows under poor Lucille's eyes, and the wistfulness in the beautiful eyes themselves. Oh, if some awfully nice, kind, protective sort of man would but marry her! And if the sporting Lucille would let him!

Yvette did not tell the rector or Granny about the Eastwoods. It would only have started a lot of talk, which she detested. The rector wouldn't have minded, for himself, privately. But he, too, knew the necessity of keeping as clear as possible from that poisonous, many-headed serpent, the tongue of the people.

'But I don't *want* you to come if your father doesn't know,' cried the little Jewess.

'I suppose I'll have to tell him,' said Yvette. 'I'm sure he doesn't mind, really. But if he knew, he'd have to, I suppose.'

The young officer looked at her with an odd amusement, bird-like and unemotional, in his keen eyes. He, too, was by way of falling in love with Yvette. It was her peculiar virgin tenderness, and her straying, absent-minded detachment from things, which attracted him.

She was aware of what was happening, and she rather preened herself. Eastwood piqued her fancy. Such a smart young officer, awfully good class, so calm and amazing with a motor-car, and quite a champion swimmer, it was intriguing to see him quietly, calmly washing dishes, smoking his pipe, doing his job so alert and skilful. Or, with the same interested care with which he made his investigation into the mysterious inside of an automobile, concocting jugged hare in the cottage kitchen. Then going out in the icy weather and cleaning his car till it looked like a live thing, like a cat when she has licked herself. Then coming in to talk so unassumingly and responsively, if briefly, with the little Jewess. And apparently, never bored. Sitting at the window with his pipe in bad weather, silent for hours, abstracted, musing, yet with his athletic body alert in its stillness.

Yvette did not flirt with him. But she *did* like him.

'But what about your future?' she asked him.

'What about it?' he said, taking his pipe from his mouth, the unemotional point of a smile in his bird's eyes.

'A career! Doesn't every man have to carve out a career?—like some huge goose with gravy?' She gazed with odd naïveté into his eyes.

'I'm perfectly all right to-day, and I shall be all right to-morrow,' he said, with a cold, decided look. 'Why shouldn't my future be continuous to-days and to-morrows?'

He looked at her with unmoved searching.

'Quite!' she said. 'I hate jobs, and all that side of life.' But she was thinking of the Jewess's money.

To which he did not answer. His anger was of the soft, snowy sort, which comfortably muffles the soul.

They had come to the point of talking philosophically together. The little Jewess looked a bit wan. She was curiously naïve, and not possessive in her attitude to the man. Nor was she at all catty with Yvette. Only rather wan and dumb.

Yvette, on a sudden impulse, thought she had better clear herself.

'I think life's *awfully* difficult,' she said.

'Life is!' cried the Jewess.

'What's so beastly, is that one is supposed to *fall in love* and get married!' said Yvette, curling up her nose.

'Don't you *want* to fall in love and get married?' cried the Jewess, with great glaring eyes of astounded reproach.

'No, not particularly!' said Yvette. 'Especially as one feels there's nothing else to do. It's an awful chicken-coop one has to run into.'

'But you don't know what love is?' cried the Jewess.

'No!' said Yvette. 'Do you?'

'I?' bawled the tiny Jewess. 'I? My goodness, don't I!' She looked with reflective gloom at Eastwood, who was smoking his pipe, the dimples of his disconnected amusement showing on his smooth, scrupulous face. He had a very fine, smooth skin, which yet did not suffer from the weather, so that his face looked naked as a baby's. But it was not a round face: it was characteristic enough, and took queer, ironical dimples, like a mask which is comic but frozen.

'Do you mean to say you don't know what love is?' insisted the Jewess.

'No!' said Yvette, with insouciant candour. 'I don't believe I do! Is it awful of me, at my age?'

'Is there never any man that makes you feel quite, quite different?' said the Jewess, with another big-eyed look at Eastwood. He smoked, utterly unimplicated.

'I don't think there is,' said Yvette. 'Unless–yes!–unless it is that gipsy'–she had put her hand pensively sideways.

'Which gipsy?' bawled the little Jewess.

'The one who was a Tommy and looked after horses in Major Eastwood's regiment in the war,' said Yvette coolly.

The little Jewess gazed at Yvette with great eyes of stupor.

'You're not in love with that *gipsy!*' she said.

'Well!' said Yvette. 'I don't know. He's the only one that makes me feel–different! He really is!'

'But how? How? Has he ever *said* anything to you?'

'No! No!'

'Then how? What has he done?'

'Oh, just looked at me!'

'How?'

'Well, you see, I don't know. But different! Yes, different! Different, quite different from the way any man ever looked at me.'

'But *how* did he look at you?' insisted the Jewess.

'Why–as if he really, but *really, desired* me,' said Yvette, her meditative face looking like the bud of a flower.

'What a vile fellow! What *right* had he to look at you like that?' cried the indignant Jewess.

'A cat may look at a king,' calmly interposed the Major, and now his face had the smiles of a cat's face.

'You think he oughtn't to?' asked Yvette, turning to him.

'Certainly not! A gipsy fellow, with half a dozen dirty women trailing after him! Certainly not!' cried the tiny Jewess.

'I wondered!' said Yvette. 'Because it *was* rather wonderful, really! And it was something quite different in my life.'

'I think,' said the Major, taking his pipe from his mouth, 'that desire is the most wonderful thing in life. Anybody who can really feel it is a king, and I envy nobody else!' He put back his pipe.

The Jewess looked at him stupefied.

'But, Charles!' she cried. 'Every common low man in Halifax feels nothing else!'

He again took his pipe from his mouth.

'That's merely appetite,' he said.

And he put back his pipe.

'You think the gipsy is the real thing?' Yvette asked him.

He lifted his shoulders.

'It's not for me to say,' he replied. 'If I were you, I should know, I shouldn't be asking other people.'

'Yes—but—' Yvette trailed out.

'Charles! You're wrong! How *could* it be a real thing! As if she could possibly marry him and go round in a caravan!'

'I didn't say marry him,' said Charles.

'Or a love affair! Why, it's monstrous! What would she think of herself!—That's not love! That's—that's prostitution!'

Charles smoked for some moments.

'That gipsy was the best man we had, with horses. Nearly died of pneumonia. I thought he *was* dead. He's a resurrected man to me. I'm a resurrected man myself, as far as that goes.' He looked at Yvette. 'I was buried for twenty hours under snow,' he said. 'And not much the worse for it, when they dug me out.'

There was a frozen pause in the conversation.

'Life's awful!' said Yvette.

'They dug me out by accident,' he said.

'Oh!—' Yvette trailed slowly. 'It might be destiny, you know.'

To which he did not answer.

8

The rector heard about Yvette's intimacy with the Eastwoods, and she was somewhat startled by the result. She had thought he wouldn't care. Verbally, in his would-be humorous fashion, he was so entirely unconventional, such a frightfully good sport. As he said himself, he was a conservative anarchist; which meant, he was like a great many more people, a mere unbeliever. The anarchy extended to his humorous talk, and his secret thinking. The conservatism, based on a mongrel fear of the anarchy, controlled every action. His thoughts, secretly, were something to be scared of. Therefore, in his life he was fanatically afraid of the unconventional.

When his conservatism and his abject sort of fear were uppermost, he always lifted his lip and bared his teeth a little, in a dog-like sneer.

'I hear your latest friends are the half-divorced Mrs Fawcett and the *maquereau* Eastwood,' he said to Yvette.

She didn't know what a *maquereau* was, but she felt the poison in the rector's fangs.

'I just know them,' she said. 'They're awfully nice, really. And they'll be married in about a month's time.'

The rector looked at her insouciant face with hatred. Somewhere inside him he was cowed, he had been born cowed. And those who are born cowed are natural slaves, and deep instinct makes them fear with poisonous fear those who might suddenly snap the slave's collar round their necks.

It was for this reason the rector had so abjectly curled up, still so abjectly curled up before She-who-was-Cynthia: because of his slave's fear of her contempt, the contempt of a born-free nature for a base-born nature.

Yvette too had a free-born quality. She, too, one day, would know him, and clap the slave's collar of her contempt round his neck.

But should she? He would fight to the death, this time, first. The slave in him was cornered this time, like a cornered rat, and with the courage of a cornered rat.

'I suppose they're your sort!' he sneered.

'Well, they are, really,' she said, with that blithe vagueness. 'I do like them awfully. They seem so solid, you know, so honest.'

'You've got a peculiar notion of honesty!' he sneered. 'A young sponge going off with a woman older than himself, so that he can live on her money! The woman leaving her home and her children! I don't know where you get your idea of honesty. Not from me, I hope – And you seem to be very well acquainted with them, considering you say you just know them. Where did you meet them?'

'When I was out bicycling. They came along in their car, and we happened to talk. She told me at once who she was, so that I shouldn't make a mistake. She *is* honest.'

Poor Yvette was struggling to bear up.

'And how often have you seen them since?'

'Oh, I've just been over twice.'

'Over where?'

'To their cottage in Scoresby.'

He looked at her in hate, as if he could kill her. And he backed away from her, against the window-curtains of his study, like a rat at bay. Somewhere in his mind he was thinking unspeakable depravities about his daughter, as he had thought them of She-who-was-Cynthia. He was powerless against the lowest insinuations of his own mind. And these depravities which he attributed to the still-uncowed but frightened girl in front of him, made him recoil, showing all his fangs in his handsome face.

'So you just know them, do you?' he said. 'Lying is in your blood, I see. I don't believe you get it from me.'

Yvette half averted her mute face, and thought of Granny's bare-faced prevarication. She did not answer.

'What takes you creeping round such couples?' he sneered. 'Aren't there enough decent people in the world for you to know? Anyone would think you were a stray dog, having to run round indecent couples, because the decent ones wouldn't have you. Have you got something worse than lying in your blood?'

'What have I got worse than lying in my blood?' she asked. A cold deadness was coming over her. Was she abnormal, one of the semi-criminal abnormals? It made her feel cold and dead.

In his eyes, she was just brazening out the depravity that underlay her virgin, tender, bird-like face. She-who-was-Cynthia had been like this: a snow-flower. And he had convulsions of sadistic horror, thinking what might be the *actual* depravity of She-who-was-Cynthia. Even his *own* love for her, which had been the lust-love of the born cowed, had been a depravity, in secret, to him. So what must an illegal love be?

'You know best yourself, what you have got,' he sneered. 'But it is something you had best curb, and quickly, if you don't intend to finish in a criminal-lunacy asylum.'

'Why?' she said, pale and muted, numbed with frozen fear. 'Why criminal lunacy? What have I done?'

'That is between you and your Maker,' he jeered. 'I shall never ask. But certain tendencies end in criminal lunacy, unless they are curbed in time.'

'Do you mean like knowing the Eastwoods?' asked Yvette, after a pause of numb fear.

'Do I mean like nosing round such people as Mrs Fawcett, a Jewess, and ex-Major Eastwood, a man who goes off with an older woman for the sake of her money? Why, yes, I do!'

'But you *can't* say that,' cried Yvette. 'He's an awfully simple, straightforward man.'

'He is apparently one of your sort.'

'Well.–In a way, I thought he was. I thought you'd like him, too,' she said simply, hardly knowing what she said.

The rector backed into the curtains, as if the girl menaced him with something fearful.

'Don't say any more,' he snarled, abject. 'Don't say any more. You've said too much to implicate you. I don't want to learn any more horrors.'

'But what horrors?' she persisted.

The very naïveté of her unscrupulous innocence repelled him, cowed him still more.

'Say no more!' he said in a low, hissing voice. 'But I will kill you before you shall go the way of your mother.'

She looked at him as he stood there backed against the velvet curtains of his study, his face yellow, his eyes distraught like a rat's with fear and rage and hate, and a numb, frozen loneliness came over her. For her, too, the meaning had gone out of everything.

It was hard to break the frozen, sterile silence that ensued. At last, however, she looked at him. And in spite of herself, beyond her own knowledge, the contempt for him was in her young, clear, baffled eyes. It fell like the slave's collar over his neck, finally.

'Do you mean I mustn't know the Eastwoods?' she said.

'You can know them if you wish,' he sneered. 'But you must not expect to associate with your Granny, and your Aunt Cissie, and Lucille, if you do. I cannot have *them* contaminated. Your Granny was a faithful wife and a faithful mother, if ever one existed. She has already had one shock of shame and abomination to endure. She shall never be exposed to another.'

Yvette heard it dimly, half hearing.

'I can send a note and say you disapprove,' she said dimly.

'You can follow your own course of action. But remember, you have to choose between clean people and reverence for your Granny's blameless old age, and people who are unclean in their minds and their bodies.'

Again there was a silence. Then she looked at him, and her face was more puzzled than anything. But somewhere at the back of her perplexity was that peculiar calm, virgin contempt of the free-born for the base-born. He, and all the Saywells, were base-born.

'All right,' she said. 'I'll write and say you disapprove.'

He did not answer. He was partly flattered, secretly triumphant, but abjectly.

'I have tried to keep this from your Granny and Aunt Cissie,' he said. 'It need not be public property, since you choose to make your friendship clandestine.'

There was a dreary silence.

'All right,' she said. 'I'll go and write.'

And she crept out of the room.

She addressed her little note to Mrs Eastwood. 'Dear Mrs Eastwood, Daddy doesn't approve of my coming to see you. So you will understand if we have to break it off. I'm awfully sorry—' That was all.

Yet she felt a dreary blank when she had posted her letter. She was now even afraid of her own thoughts. She wanted, now, to be held against the slender, fine-shaped breast of the gipsy. She wanted him to hold her in his arms, if only for once, for once, and comfort and confirm her. She wanted to be confirmed by him against her father, who had only a repulsive fear of her.

And at the same time she cringed and winced, so that she could hardly walk, for fear the thought was obscene, a criminal lunacy. It seemed to wound her heels as she walked, the fear. The fear, the great cold fear of the base-born, her father, everything human and swarming. Like a great bog humanity swamped her, and she sank in, weak at the knees, filled with repulsion and fear of every person she met.

She adjusted herself, however, quite rapidly to her new conception of people. She had to live. It is useless to quarrel with one's bread and butter. And to expect a great deal out of life is puerile. So, with the rapid adaptability of the post-war generation, she adjusted herself to the new facts. Her father was what he was. He would always play up to appearances. She would do the same. She, too, would play up to appearances.

So, underneath the blithe, gossamer-straying insouciance, a certain hardness formed, like rock crystallising in her heart. She lost her illusions in the collapse of her sympathies. Outwardly, she seemed the same. Inwardly she was hard and detached, and, unknown to herself, revengeful.

Outwardly she remained the same. It was part of her game. While circumstances remained as they were, she must remain, at least in appearance, true to what was expected of her.

But the revengefulness came out in her new vision of people. Under the rector's apparently gallant handsomeness, she saw the weak, feeble nullity. And she despised him. Yet still, in a way, she liked him too. Feelings are so complicated.

It was Granny whom she came to detest with all her soul. That obese old woman, sitting there in her blindness like some great red-blotched fungus, her neck swallowed between her heaped-up shoulders and her rolling, ancient chins, so that she was neckless as a double potato, her Yvette really hated, with that pure, sheer hatred which is almost a joy. Her hate was so clear, that while she was feeling strong, she enjoyed it.

The old woman sat with her big, reddened face pressed a little back, her lace cap perched on her thin white hair, her stub nose still assertive, and her old mouth shut like a trap. This motherly old soul, her mouth gave her away. It always had been one of the compressed sort. But in her great age, it had gone like a toad's, lipless, the jaw pressing up like the lower jaw of a trap. The look Yvette most hated was the look of that lower jaw pressing relentlessly up, with an ancient prognathous thrust, so that the snub nose in turn was forced to press upwards, and the whole face was pressed a little back, beneath the big, wall-like forehead. The will, the ancient, toad-like, obscene *will* in the old woman, was fearful, once you saw it: a toad-like self-will that was godless, and less than human! It belonged to the old, enduring race of toads, or tortoises. And it made one feel that Granny would never die. She would live on like these higher reptiles, in a state of semi-coma, for ever.

Yvette dared not even suggest to her father that Granny was not perfect. He would have threatened his daughter with the lunatic asylum. That was the threat he always seemed to have up his sleeve: the lunatic asylum. Exactly as if a distaste for Granny and for that horrible house of relatives was in itself a proof of lunacy, dangerous lunacy.

Yet in one of her moods of irritable depression, she did once fling out:

'How perfectly beastly this house is! Aunt Lucy comes, and Aunt Nell, and Aunt Alice, and they make a ring like a ring of crows, with Granny and Aunt Cissie, all lifting their skirts up and warming their legs at the fire, and shutting Lucille and me out. We're nothing but outsiders in this beastly house!'

Her father glanced at her curiously. But she managed to put a petulance into her speech and a mere cross rudeness into her look, so that he could laugh, as at a childish tantrum. Somewhere, though, he knew that she coldly, venomously meant what she said, and he was wary of her.

Her life seemed now nothing but an irritable friction against the unsavoury household of the Saywells, in which she was immersed. She loathed the rectory with a loathing that consumed her life, a loathing so strong that she could not really go away from the place. While it endured, she was spell-bound to it, in revulsion.

She forgot the Eastwoods again. After all, what was the revolt of the little Jewess, compared to Granny and the Saywell bunch! A husband was never more than a semi-casual thing! But a family!—an awful, smelly family that would never disperse, stuck half dead round the base of a fungoid old woman! How was one to cope with that?

She did not forget the gipsy entirely. But she had no time for him. She, who was bored almost to agony, and who had nothing at all to do, she had not time to think even, seriously, of anything. Time being, after all, only the current of the soul in its flow.

She saw the gipsy twice. Once he came to the house with things to sell. And she, watching him from the landing window, refused to go down. He saw her, too, as he was putting his things back into his cart. But he, too, gave no sign. Being of a race that exists only to be harrying the outskirts of our society, forever hostile and living only by spoil, he was too much master of himself, and too wary, to expose himself openly to the vast and gruesome clutch of our law. He had been through the war. He had been enslaved against his will, that time.

So now, he showed himself at the rectory, and slowly, quietly busied himself at his cart outside the white gate, with that air of silent and for ever-unyielding outsideness which gave him his lonely, predative grace. He knew she saw him. And she should see him unyielding, quietly hawking his copper vessels, on an old, old war-path against such as herself.

Such as herself? Perhaps he was mistaken. Her heart, in its stroke, now rang hard as his hammer upon his copper, beating against circumstances. But he struck stealthily on the outside, and she still more secretly on the inside of the establishment. She liked him. She liked the quiet, noiseless, clean-cut presence of him. She liked that mysterious endurance in him, which endures in opposition, without any idea of victory. And she liked that peculiar added relentlessness, the disillusion in hostility, which belongs to after the war. Yes, if she belonged to any side, and to any clan, it was to his. Almost she could have found it in her heart to go with him, and be a pariah gipsy woman.

But she was born inside the pale. And she liked comfort, and a certain prestige. Even as a mere rector's daughter, one did have a certain prestige. And she liked that. Also she liked to chip against the pillars of the temple from the inside. She wanted to be safe under the temple roof. Yet she enjoyed chipping fragments off the supporting pillars. Doubtless many fragments had been whittled away from the pillars of the Philistine before Samson pulled the temple down.

'I'm not sure one shouldn't have one's fling till one is twenty-six, and then give in, and marry!'

This was Lucille's philosophy, learned from older women. Yvette was twenty-one. It meant she had five more years in which to have this precious fling. And the fling meant, at the moment, the gipsy. The marriage, at the age of twenty-six, meant Leo or Gerry.

So, a woman could eat her cake and have her bread and butter.

Yvette, pitched in gruesome, deadlocked hostility to the Saywell household, was very old and very wise: with the agedness and the wisdom of the young, which always overleaps the agedness and the wisdom of the old or the elderly.

The second time she met the gipsy by accident. It was March, and sunny weather, after unheard-of rains. Celandines were yellow in the hedges, and primroses among the rocks. But still there came a smell of sulphur from far-away steel-works, out of the steel-blue sky.

And yet it was spring!

Yvette was cycling slowly along by Codnor Gate, past the lime quarries, when she saw the gipsy coming away from the door of a stone cottage. His cart stood there in the road. He was returning with his brooms and copper things to the cart.

She got down from her bicycle. As she saw him, she loved with curious tenderness the slim lines of his body in the green jersey, the turn of his silent face. She felt she knew him better than she knew anybody on earth, even Lucille, and belonged to him, in some way, for ever.

'Have you made anything new and nice?' she asked innocently, looking at his copper things.

'I don't think,' he said, glancing back at her.

The desire was still there, still curious and naked, in his eyes. But it was more remote, the boldness was diminished. There was a tiny glint, as if he might dislike her. But this dissolved again as he saw her looking among his bits of copper and brasswork. She searched them diligently.

There was a little oval brass plate, with a queer figure like a palm tree beaten upon it.

'I like that,' she said. 'How much is it?'

'What you like,' he said.

This made her nervous: he seemed off-hand, almost mocking.

'I'd rather you said,' she told him, looking up at him.

'You give me what you like,' he said.

'No!' she said suddenly. 'If you won't tell me I won't have it.'

'All right,' he said. 'Two shilling.'

She found half a crown, and he drew from his pocket a handful of silver, from which he gave her sixpence.

'The old gipsy dreamed something about you,' he said, looking at her with curious, searching eyes.

'Did she!' cried Yvette, at once interested. 'What was it?'

'She said: "Be braver in your heart, or you lose your game." She said it this way: "Be braver in your body, or your luck will leave you." And she said as well: "Listen for the voice of water."'

Yvette was very much impressed.

'And what does it mean?' she asked.

'I asked her,' he said. 'She says she don't know.'

'Tell me again what it was,' said Yvette.

'"Be braver in your body, or your luck will go." And: "Listen for the voice of water."'

He looked in silence at her soft, pondering face. Something almost like a perfume seemed to flow from her young bosom direct to him, in a grateful connection.

'I'm to be braver in my body, and I'm to listen for the voice of water! All right!' she said. 'I don't understand, but perhaps I shall.'

She looked at him with clear eyes. Man or woman is made up of many selves. With one self, she loved this gipsy man. With many selves, she ignored him or had a distaste for him.

'You're not coming up to the Head no more?' he asked.

Again she looked at him absently.

'Perhaps I will,' she said, 'some time. Some time.'

'Spring weather!' he said, smiling faintly and glancing round at the sun. 'We're going to break camp soon and go away.'

'When?' she said.

'Perhaps next week.'

'Where to?'

Again he made a move with his head.

'Perhaps up north,' he said.

She looked at him.

'All right!' she said. 'Perhaps I *will* come up before you go, and say good-bye to your wife and to the old woman who sent me the message.'

9

Yvette did not keep her promise. The few March days were lovely, and she let them slip. She had a curious reluctance, always, towards taking action, or making any real move of her own. She always wanted someone else to make a move for her, as if she did not want to play her own game of life.

She lived as usual, went out to her friends, to parties, and danced with the undiminished Leo. She wanted to go up and say good-bye to the gipsies. She wanted to. And nothing prevented her.

On the Friday afternoon especially she wanted to go. It was sunny, and the last yellow crocuses down the drive were in full blaze, wide open, the first bees rolling in them. The Papple rushed under the stone bridge, uncannily full, nearly filling the arches. There was the scent of a mezereon tree.

And she felt too lazy, too lazy, too lazy. She strayed in the garden by the river, half dreamy, expecting something. While the gleam of spring sun lasted, she would be out of doors. Indoors Granny, sitting back like some awful old prelate, in her bulk of black silk and her white lace cap, was warming her feet by the fire, and hearing everything that Aunt Nell had to say. Friday was Aunt Nell's day. She usually came for lunch, and left after an early tea. So the mother and the large, rather common daughter, who was a widow at the age of forty, sat gossiping by the fire, while Aunt Cissie prowled in and out. Friday was the rector's day for going to town: it was also the housemaid's half-day.

Yvette sat on a wooden seat in the garden, only a few feet above the bank of the swollen river, which rolled a strange, uncanny mass of water. The crocuses were passing in the ornamental beds, the grass was dark green where it was mown, the laurels looked a little brighter. Aunt Cissie appeared at the top of the porch steps, and called to ask if Yvette wanted that early cup of tea. Because of the river just below, Yvette could not hear what Aunt Cissie said, but she guessed, and shook her head. An early cup of tea, indoors, when the sun actually shone? No, thanks!

She was conscious of her gipsy, as she sat there musing in the sun. Her soul had the half painful, half easing knack of leaving her, and straying away to some place, to somebody that had caught her imagination. Some days she would be at the Framleys', even though she did not go near them. Some days she was all the time in spirit with the Eastwoods. And to-day it was the gipsies. She was up at their encampment in the quarry. She saw the man hammering his copper, lifting his head to look at the road; and the children playing in the horse-shelter: and the women, the gipsy's wife and the strong, elderly woman, coming home with their packs, along with the elderly man. For this afternoon, she felt intensely that *that* was home for her: the gipsy camp, the fire, the stool, the man with the hammer, the old crone.

It was part of her nature, to get these fits of yearning for some place she knew; to be in a certain place; with somebody who meant home to her. This afternoon it was the gipsy camp. And the man in the green jersey made it home to her. Just to be where he was, that was to be at home. The caravans, the brats, the other women: everything was natural to her, her home, as if she had been born there. She wondered if the gipsy was aware of her: if he could see her sitting on the stool by the fire; if he would lift his head and see her as she rose, looking at him slowly and significantly, turning towards the steps of his caravan. Did he know? Did he know?

Vaguely she looked up the steep of dark larch trees north of the house, where unseen the road climbed, going towards the Head. There was nothing, and her glance strayed down again. At the foot of the slope the river turned, thrown back harshly, ominously, against the low rocks across stream, then pouring past the garden to the bridge. It was unnaturally full, and whitey-muddy, and ponderous. 'Listen for the voice of water,' she said to herself. 'No need to listen for it, if the voice means the noise!'

And again she looked at the swollen river breaking angrily as it came round the bend. Above it the black-looking kitchen garden hung, and the hard-natured fruit trees. Everything was on the tilt, facing south and south-west, for the sun. Behind, above the house and the kitchen garden hung the steep little wood of withered-seeming larches. The gardener was working in the kitchen garden, high up there, by the edge of the larch-wood.

She heard a call. It was Aunt Cissie and Aunt Nell. They were on the drive, waving good-bye! Yvette waved back. Then Aunt Cissie, pitching her voice against the waters, called:

'I shan't be long. Don't forget Granny is alone!'

'All right!' screamed Yvette rather ineffectually.

And she sat on her bench and watched the two undignified, long-coated women walk slowly over the bridge and begin the curving climb on the opposite slope. Aunt Nell carrying a sort of suit-case in which she brought a few goods for Granny and took back vegetables or whatever the rectory garden or cupboard was yielding. Slowly the two figures diminished on the whitish, up-curving road, labouring slowly up towards Papplewick village. Aunt Cissie was going as far as the village for something.

The sun was yellowing to decline. What a pity! Oh, what a pity the sunny day was going, and she would have to turn indoors, to those hateful rooms, and Granny! Aunt Cissie would be back directly: it was past five. And all the others would be arriving from town, rather irritable and tired, soon after six.

As she looked uneasily round, she heard, across the running water, the sharp noise of a horse and cart rattling on the road hidden in the larch trees. The gardener was looking up too. Yvette turned away again, lingering, strolling by the full river a few paces, unwilling to go in; glancing up the road to see if Aunt Cissie were coming. If she saw her, she would go indoors.

She heard somebody shouting, and looked round. Down the path through the larch trees the gipsy was bounding. The gardener, away beyond, was also running. Simultaneously she became aware of a great roar, which before she could move, accumulated to a vast deafening snarl. The gipsy was gesticulating. She looked round behind her.

And to her horror and amazement, round the bend of the river she saw a shaggy, tawny wave-front of water advancing like a wall of lions. The roaring sound wiped out everything. She was powerless, too amazed and wonder-struck, she wanted to see it.

Before she could think twice, it was near, a roaring cliff of water. She almost fainted with horror. She heard the scream of the gipsy, and looked up to see him bounding upon her, his black eyes starting out of his head.

'Run!' he screamed, seizing her arm.

And in the instant the first wave was washing her feet from under her, swirling, in the insane noise, which suddenly for some reason, seemed like stillness, with a devouring flood over the garden. The horrible mowing of water!

The gipsy dragged her heavily, lurching, plunging, but still keeping foot-hold both of them, towards the house. She was barely conscious: as if the flood was in her soul.

There was one grass-banked terrace of the garden, near the path round the house. The gipsy clawed his way up this terrace to the dry level of the path, dragging her after him, and sprang with her past the windows to the porch steps. Before they got there, a new great surge of water came mowing, mowing trees down even, and mowed them down too.

Yvette felt herself gone in an agonising mill race of icy water, whirled, with only the fearful grip of the gipsy's hand on her wrist. They were both down and gone. She felt a dull but stunning bruise somewhere.

Then he pulled her up. He was up, streaming forth water, clinging to the stem of the great wisteria that grew against the wall, crushed against the wall by the water. Her head was above water, he held her arm till it seemed dislocated: but she could not get her footing. With a ghastly sickness like a dream, she struggled and struggled, and could not get her feet. Only his hand was locked on her wrist.

He dragged her nearer till her one hand caught his leg. He nearly went down again. But the wisteria held him, and he pulled her up to him. She clawed at him, horribly; and got to her feet, he hanging on like a man torn in two to the wisteria trunk.

The water was above her knees. The man and she looked into each other's ghastly, streaming faces.

'Get to the steps!' he screamed.

It was only just round the corner: four strides! She looked at him: she could not go. His eyes glared on her like a tiger's, and he pushed her from him. She clung to the wall, and the water seemed to abate a little. Round the corner she staggered, but staggering, reeled and was pitched up against the cornice of the balustrade of the porch steps, the man after her.

They got on to the steps, when another roar was heard amid the roar, and the wall of the house shook. Up heaved the water round their legs again, but the gipsy had opened the hall door. In they poured with the water, reeling to the stairs. And as they did so, they saw the short but strange bulk of Granny emerge in the hall, away down from the dining-room door. She had her hands lifted and clawing, as the first water swirled round her legs, and her coffin-like mouth was opened in a hoarse scream.

Yvette was blind to everything but the stairs. Blind, unconscious of everything save the steps rising beyond the water, she clambered up like a wet, shuddering cat, in a state of unconsciousness. It was not till she was on the landing, dripping and shuddering till she could not stand erect, clinging to the banisters, while the house shook and the water raved below, that she was aware of the sodden gipsy, in paroxysms of coughing at the head of the stairs, his cap gone, his black hair over his eyes, peering between his washed-down hair at the sickening heave of water below in the hall. Yvette fainting, looked, too, and saw Granny bob up, like a strange float, her face purple, her blind blue eyes bolting, spume hissing from her mouth. One old purple hand clawed at a banister-rail and held for a moment, showing the glint of a wedding ring.

The gipsy, who had coughed himself free and pushed back his hair, said to that awful float-like face below:

'Not good enough! Not good enough!'

With a low thud like thunder, the house was struck again, and shuddered, and a strange cracking, rattling, spitting noise began. Up heaved the water like a sea. The hand was gone, all sign of anything was gone, but upheaving water.

Yvette turned in blind unconscious frenzy, staggering like a wet cat to the upper staircase, and climbing swiftly. It was not till she was at the door of her room that she stopped, paralysed by the sound of a sickening, tearing crash, while the house swayed.

'The house is coming down!' yelled the green-white face of the gipsy in her face.

He glared into her crazed face.

'Where is the chimney? the back chimney?–which room? The chimney will stand–'

He glared with strange ferocity into her face, forcing her to understand. And she nodded with a strange, crazed poise, nodded quite serenely, saying:

'In here! In here! It's all right.'

They entered her room, which had a narrow fire-place. It was a back room with two windows, one on each side the great chimney-flue. The gipsy, coughing bitterly and trembling in every limb, went to the window to look out.

Below, between the house and the steep rise of the hill, was a wild mill-race of water rushing with refuse, including Rover's green dog-kennel. The gipsy coughed and coughed, and gazed down blankly. Tree after tree went down, mown by the water, which must have been ten feet deep.

Shuddering and pressing his sodden arms on his sodden breast, a look of resignation on his livid face, he turned to Yvette. A fearful tearing noise tore the house, then there was a deep, watery explosion. Something had gone down, some part of the house, the floor heaved and wavered beneath them. For some moments both were suspended, stupefied. Then he roused.

'Not good enough! Not good enough! This will stand. This here will stand. See! that chimney! like a tower. Yes! All right! All right! You take your clothes off and go to bed. You'll die of the cold.'

'It's all right! It's quite all right!' she said to him, sitting on a chair and looking up into his face with her white, insane little face, round which the hair was plastered.

'No!' he cried. 'No! Take your things off and I'll rub you with this towel. I rub myself. If the house falls then die warm. If it don't fall, then live, not die of pneumonia.'

Coughing, shuddering violently, he pulled up his jersey hem and wrestled with all his shuddering, cold-racked might, to get off his wet, tight jersey.

'Help me!' he cried, his face muffled.

She seized the edge of the jersey, obediently, and pulled with all her 'might. The garment came over his head, and he stood in his braces.

'Take your things off! Rub with this towel!' he commanded ferociously, the savageness of the war on him. And like a thing obsessed, he pushed himself out of his trousers and got out of his wet, clinging shirt, emerging slim and livid, shuddering in every fibre with cold and shock.

He seized a towel, and began quickly to rub his body, his teeth chattering like plates rattling together. Yvette dimly saw it was wise. She tried to get out of her dress. He pulled the horrible, wet, death-gripping thing off her, then, resuming his rubbing, went to the door, tiptoeing on the wet floor.

There he stood, naked, towel in hand, petrified. He looked west, towards where the upper landing window had been, and was looking into the sunset, over an insane sea of waters, bristling with up-torn trees and refuse. The end corner of the house where the porch had been, and the stairs, had gone. The wall had fallen, leaving the floors sticking out. The stairs had gone.

Motionless, he watched the water. A cold wind blew in upon him. He clenched his rattling teeth with a great effort of will, and turned into the room again, closing the door.

Yvette, naked, shuddering so much that she was sick, was trying to wipe herself dry.

'All right!' he cried. 'All right! The water don't rise no more! All right!'

With his towel he began to rub her, himself shaking all over, but holding her gripped by the shoulder, and slowly numbedly rubbing her tender body, even trying to rub up into some dryness the pitiful hair of her small head.

Suddenly he left off.

'Better lie in the bed,' he commanded, 'I want to rub myself.'

His teeth went snap-snap-snap-snap in great snaps, cutting off his words. Yvette crept shaking and semi-conscious into her bed. He, making strained efforts to hold himself still and rub himself warm, went again to the north window to look out.

The water had risen a little. The sun had gone down, and there was a reddish glow. He rubbed his hair into a black, wet tangle, then paused for breath, in a sudden access of shuddering, then looked out again, then rubbed again on his breast, and began to cough afresh, because of the water he had swallowed. His towel was red: he had hurt himself somewhere: but he felt nothing.

There was still the strange, huge noise of water, and the horrible bump of things bumping against the walls. The wind was rising with sundown, cold and hard. The house shook with explosive thuds, and weird, weird, frightening noises came up.

A terror creeping over his soul, he went again to the door. The wind, roaring with the waters, blew in as he opened it. Through the awesome gap in the house he saw the world, the waters, the chaos of horrible waters, the twilight, the perfect new moon high above the sunset, a faint thing, and clouds pushing dark into the sky, on the cold, blustery wind.

Clenching his teeth again, fear mingling with resignation, or fatalism, in his soul, he went into the room and closed the door, picking up her towel to see if it were drier than his own, and less blood-stained, again rubbing his head and going to the window.

He turned away, unable to control his spasms of shivering. Yvette had disappeared right under the bedclothes, and nothing of her was visible but a shivering mound under the white quilt. He laid his hand on this shivering mound, as if for company. It did not stop shivering.

'All right!' he said. 'All right! Water's going down!'

She suddenly uncovered her head and peered out at him from a white face. She peered into his greenish, curiously calm face, semi-conscious. His teeth were chattering, unheeded as he gazed down at her, his black eyes still full of the fire of life and a certain vagabond calm of fatalistic resignation.

'Warm me!' she moaned, with chattering teeth. 'Warm me! I shall die of shivering.'

A terrible convulsion went through her curled-up white body, enough indeed to rupture her and cause her to die.

The gipsy nodded, and took her in his arms, and held her in a clasp like a vice, to still his own shuddering. He himself was shuddering fearfully, and only semi-conscious. It was the shock.

The vice-like grip of his arms round her seemed to her the only stable point in her consciousness. It was a fearful relief to her heart, which was strained to bursting. And though his body, wrapped round her strange and lithe and powerful, like tentacles, rippled with shuddering as an electric current, still the rigid tension of the muscles that held her clenched steadied them both, and gradually the sickening violence of the shuddering, caused by shock, abated, in his body first, then in hers, and the warmth revived between them. And as it roused, their tortured semi-conscious minds became unconscious, they passed away into sleep.

10

The sun was shining in heaven before men were able to get across the Papple with ladders. The bridge was gone. But the flood had abated, and the house, that leaned forwards as if it were making a stiff bow to the stream, stood now in mud and wreckage, with a great heap of fallen masonry and debris at the south-west corner. Awful were the gaping mouths of rooms!

Inside, there was no sign of life. But across-stream the gardener had come to reconnoitre, and the cook appeared, thrilled with curiosity. She had escaped from the back door and up through the larches to the high-road, when she saw the gipsy bound past the house: thinking he was coming to murder somebody. At the little top gate she had found his cart standing. The gardener had led the horse away to the 'Red Lion' up at Darley, when night had fallen.

This the men from Papplewick learned when at last they got across the stream with ladders, and to the back of the house. They were nervous, fearing a collapse of the building, whose front was all undermined and whose back was choked up. They gazed with horror at the silent shelves of the rector's rows of books in his torn-open study; at the big brass bedstead of Granny's room, the bed so deep and comfortably made, but one brass leg of the bedstead perching tentatively over the torn void; at the wreckage of the maid's room upstairs. The housemaid and the cook wept. Then a man climbed in cautiously through a smashed kitchen window, into the jungle and morass of the ground floor. He found the body of the old woman: or at least he saw her foot, in its flat black slipper, muddily protruding from a mud-heap of debris. And he fled.

The gardener said he was sure that Miss Yvette was not in the house. He had seen her and the gipsy swept away. But the policeman insisted on a search, and the Framley boys rushing up at last, the ladders were roped together. Then the whole party set up a loud yell. But without result. No answer from within.

A ladder was up, Bob Framley climbed, smashed a window, and clambered into Aunt Cissie's room. The perfect homely familiarity of everything terrified him like ghosts. The house might go down any minute.

They had just got the ladder up to the top floor when men came running from Darley, saying the old gipsy had been to the 'Red Lion' for the horse and cart, leaving word that his son had seen Yvette at the top of the house. But by that time the policeman was smashing the window of Yvette's room.

Yvette, fast asleep, started from under the bedclothes with a scream as the glass flew. She clutched the sheets round her nakedness. The policeman uttered a startled yell, which he converted into a cry of: 'Miss Yvette! Miss Yvette!'

He turned round on the ladder and shouted to the faces below:

'Miss Yvette's in bed!—in bed!'

And he perched there on the ladder, an unmarried man, clutching the window in peril, not knowing what to do.

Yvette sat up in bed, her hair in a matted tangle, and stared with wild eyes, clutching up the sheets at her naked breast. She had been so very fast asleep, that she was still not there.

The policeman, terrified at the flabby ladder, climbed into the room, saying: 'Don't be frightened, miss! Don't you worry any more about it. You're safe now.'

And Yvette, so dazed, thought he meant the gipsy. Where was the gipsy? This was the first thing in her mind. Where was her gipsy of this world's-end night?

He was gone! He was gone! And a policeman was in the room! A policeman! She rubbed her hand over her dazed brow.

'If you'll get dressed, miss, we can get you down to safe ground. The house is likely to fall. I suppose there's nobody in the other rooms?'

He stepped gingerly into the passage and gazed in terror through the torn-out end of the house, and far off saw the rector coming down in a motor-car, on the sunlit hill.

Yvette, her face gone numb and disappointed, got up quickly, closing the bedclothes, and looked at herself a moment, then opened her drawers for clothing. She dressed herself, then looked in a mirror, and saw her matted hair with horror. Yet she did not care. The gipsy was gone, anyhow.

Her own clothes lay in a sodden heap. There was a great sodden place on the carpet where his had been, and two blood-stained filthy towels. Otherwise there was no sign of him.

She was tugging at her hair when the policeman tapped at her door. She called him to come in. He saw with relief that she was dressed and in her right senses.

'We'd better get out of the house as soon as possible, miss,' he reiterated. 'It might fall any minute.'

'Really!' said Yvette calmly. 'Is it as bad as that?'

There were great shouts. She had to go to the window. There, below, was the rector, his arms wide open, tears streaming down his face.

'I'm perfectly all right, daddy!' she said, with the calmness of her contradictory feelings. She would keep the gipsy a secret from him. At the same time, tears ran down her face.

'Don't you cry, miss, don't you cry! The rector's lost his mother, but he's thanking his stars to have his daughter. We all thought you were gone as well, we did that!'

'Is Granny drowned?' said Yvette.

'I'm afraid she is, poor lady!' said the policeman, with a grave face.

Yvette wept away into her hanky, which she had had to fetch from a drawer.

'Dare you go down that ladder, miss?' said the policeman.

Yvette looked at the sagging depth of it, and said promptly to herself: 'No! Not for anything!'—But then she remembered the gipsy's saying: 'Be braver in the body.'

'Have you been in all the other rooms?' she said, in her weeping, turning to the policeman.

'Yes, miss! But you was the only person in the house, you know, save the old lady. Cook got away in time, and Lizzie was up at her mother's. It was only you and the poor old lady we was fretting about. Do you think you dare go down that ladder?'

'Oh yes!' said Yvette, with indifference. The gipsy was gone, anyway.

And now the rector in torment watched his tall, slender daughter slowly stepping backwards down the sagging ladder, the policeman, peering heroically from the smashed window, holding the ladder's top end.

At the foot of the ladder Yvette appropriately fainted in her father's arms, and was borne away with him, in the car, by Bob, to the Framley home. There the poor Lucille, a ghost of ghosts, wept with relief till she had hysterics, and even Aunt Cissie cried out among her tears: 'Let the old be taken and the young spared! Oh, I *can't* cry for the Mater, now Yvette is spared!'

And she wept gallons.

The flood was caused by the sudden bursting of the great reservoir, up in Papple Highdale, five miles from the rectory. It was found out later that an ancient, perhaps even a Roman mine tunnel, unsuspected, undreamed of, beneath the reservoir dam, had collapsed, undermining the whole dam. That was why the Papple had been, for that last day, so uncannily full. And then the dam had burst.

The rector and the two girls stayed on at the Framley's till a new home could be found. Yvette did not attend Granny's funeral. She stayed in bed.

Telling her tale, she only told how the gipsy had got her inside the porch, and she had crawled to the stairs out of the water. It was known that he had escaped: the old gipsy had said so, when he fetched the horse and cart from the 'Red Lion'.

Yvette could tell little. She was vague, confused, she seemed hardly to remember anything. But that was just like her.

It was Bob Framley who said:

'You know, I think that gipsy deserves a medal.'

The whole family suddenly was struck.

'Oh, we *ought* to thank him!' cried Lucille.

The rector himself went with Bob in the car. But the quarry was deserted. The gipsies had lifted camp and gone, no one knew whither.

And Yvette, lying in bed, moaned in her heart: 'Oh, I love him! I love him! I love him!' The grief over him kept her prostrate. Yet practically she too was acquiescent in the fact of his disappearance. Her young soul knew the wisdom of it.

But after Granny's funeral, she received a little letter, dated from some unknown place.

'Dear Miss, I see in the paper you are all right after your ducking, as is the same with me. I hope I see you again one day, maybe at Tideswell cattle fair, or maybe we come that way again. I come that day to say good-bye! and I never said it, well, the water give no time, but I live in hopes. Your obdt. servant, Joe Boswell.'

And only then she realised that he had a name.

D.H. LAWRENCE

LADY CHATTERLEY'S
LOVER

I

Ours is essentially a tragic age, so we refuse to take it tragically. The cataclysm has happened, we are among the ruins, we start to build up new little habitats, to have new little hopes. It is rather hard work: there is now no smooth road into the future: but we go round, or scramble over the obstacles. We've got to live, no matter how many skies have fallen.

This was more or less Constance Chatterley's position. The war had brought the roof down over her head. And she had realized that one must live and learn.

She married Clifford Chatterley in 1917, when he was home for a month on leave. They had a month's honeymoon. Then he went back to Flanders: to be shipped over to England again six months later, more or less in bits. Constance, his wife, was then twenty-three years old, and he was twenty-nine.

His hold on life was marvellous. He didn't die, and the bits seemed to grow together again. For two years he remained in the doctor's hands. Then he was pronounced a cure, and could return to life again, with the lower half of his body, from the hips down, paralysed for ever.

This was in 1920. They returned, Clifford and Constance, to his home, Wragby Hall, the family 'seat'. His father had died, Clifford was now a baronet, Sir Clifford, and Constance was Lady Chatterley. They came to start housekeeping and married life in the rather forlorn home of the Chatterleys on a rather inadequate income. Clifford had a sister, but she had departed. Otherwise there were no near relatives. The elder brother was dead in the war. Crippled for ever, knowing he could never have any children, Clifford came home to the smoky Midlands to keep the Chatterley name alive while he could.

He was not really downcast. He could wheel himself about in a wheeled chair, and he had a bath-chair with a small motor attachment, so he could drive himself slowly round the garden and into the fine melancholy park, of which he was really so proud, though he pretended to be flippant about it.

Having suffered so much, the capacity for suffering had to some extent left him. He remained strange and bright and cheerful, almost, one might say, chirpy, with his ruddy, healthy-looking face, and his pale-blue, challenging bright eyes. His shoulders were broad and strong, his hands were very strong. He was expensively dressed, and wore handsome neckties from Bond Street. Yet still in his face one saw the watchful look, the slight vacancy of a cripple.

He had so very nearly lost his life, that what remained was wonderfully precious to him. It was obvious in the anxious brightness of his eyes, how proud he was, after the great shock, of being alive. But he had been so much hurt that something inside him had perished, some of his feelings had gone. There was a blank of insentience.

Constance, his wife, was a ruddy, country-looking girl with soft brown hair and sturdy body, and slow movements, full of unusual energy. She had big, wondering eyes, and a soft mild voice, and seemed just to have come from her native village. It was not so at all. Her father was the once well-known R.A., old Sir Malcolm Reid. Her mother had been one of the cultivated Fabians in the palmy, rather pre-Raphaelite days. Between artists and cultured socialists, Constance and her sister Hilda had had what might be called an aesthetically unconventional upbringing. They had been taken to Paris and Florence and Rome to breathe in art, and they had been taken also in the other direction, to the Hague and Berlin, to great Socialist conventions, where the speakers spoke in every civilized tongue, and no one was abashed.

The two girls, therefore, were from an early age not the least daunted by either art or ideal politics. It was their natural atmosphere. They were at once cosmopolitan and provincial, with the cosmopolitan provincialism of art that goes with pure social ideals.

They had been sent to Dresden at the age of fifteen, for music among other things. And they had had a good time there. They lived freely among the students, they argued with the men over philosophical, sociological and artistic matters, they were just as good as the men themselves: only better, since they were women. And they tramped off to the forests with sturdy youths bearing guitars, twang-twang! They sang the Wandervogel songs, and they were free. Free! That was the great word. Out in the open world, out in the forests of the morning, with lusty and splendid-throated young fellows, free to do as they liked, and–above all–to say what they liked. It was the talk that mattered supremely: the impassioned interchange of talk. Love was only a minor accompaniment.

Both Hilda and Constance had had their tentative love-affairs by the time they were eighteen. The young men with whom they talked so passionately and sang so lustily and camped under the trees in such freedom wanted, of course, the love connexion. The girls were doubtful, but then the thing was so much talked about, it was supposed to be so important. And the men were so humble and craving. Why couldn't a girl be queenly, and give the gift of herself?

So they had given the gift of themselves, each to the youth with whom she had the most subtle and intimate arguments. The arguments, the discussions were the great thing: the love-making and connexion were only a sort of primitive reversion and a bit of an anti-climax. One was less in love with the boy afterwards, and a little inclined to hate him, as if he had trespassed on one's privacy and inner freedom. For, of course, being a girl, one's whole dignity and meaning in life consisted in the achievement of an absolute, a perfect, a pure and noble freedom. What else did a girl's life mean? To shake off the old and sordid connexions and subjections.

And however one might sentimentalize it, this sex business was one of the most ancient, sordid connexions and subjections. Poets who glorified it were mostly men. Women had always known there was something better, something higher. And now they knew it more definitely than ever. The beautiful pure freedom of a woman was infinitely more wonderful than any sexual love. The only unfortunate thing was that men lagged so far behind women in the matter. They insisted on the sex thing like dogs.

And a woman had to yield. A man was like a child with his appetites. A woman had to yield him what he wanted, or like a child he would probably turn nasty and flounce away and spoil what was a very pleasant connexion. But a woman could yield to a man without yielding her inner, free self. That the poets and talkers about sex did not seem to have taken sufficiently into account. A woman could take a man without really giving herself away. Certainly she could take him without giving herself into his power. Rather she could use this sex thing to have power over him. For she only had to hold herself back in sexual intercourse, and let him finish and expend himself without herself coming to the crisis: and then she could prolong the connexion and achieve her orgasm and her crisis while he was merely her tool.

Both sisters had had their love experience by the time the war came, and they were hurried home. Neither was ever in love with a young man unless he and she were verbally very near: that is unless they were profoundly interested, TALKING to one another. The amazing, the profound, the unbelievable thrill there was in passionately talking to some really clever young man by the hour, resuming day after day for months ... this they had never realized till it happened! The paradisal promise: Thou shalt have men to talk to!–had never been uttered. It was fulfilled before they knew what a promise it was.

And if after the roused intimacy of these vivid and soul-enlightening discussions the sex thing became more or less inevitable, then let it. It marked the end of a chapter. It had a thrill of its own too: a queer vibrating thrill inside the body, a final spasm of self-assertion, like the last word, exciting, and very like the row of asterisks that can be put to show the end of a paragraph, and a break in the theme.

When the girls came home for the summer holidays of 1913, when Hilda was twenty and Connie eighteen, their father could see plainly that they had had the love experience.

L'amour avait passé par là, as somebody puts it. But he was a man of experience himself, and let life take its course. As for the mother, a nervous invalid in the last few months of her life, she only wanted her girls to be 'free', and to 'fulfil themselves'. She herself had never been able to be altogether herself: it had been denied her. Heaven knows why, for she was a woman who had her own income and her own way. She blamed her husband. But as a matter of fact, it was some old impression of authority on her own mind or soul that she could not get rid of. It had nothing to do with Sir Malcolm, who left his nervously hostile, high-spirited wife to rule her own roost, while he went his own way.

So the girls were 'free', and went back to Dresden, and their music, and the university and the young men. They loved their respective young men, and their respective young men loved them with all the passion of mental attraction. All the wonderful things the young men thought and expressed and wrote, they thought and expressed and wrote for the young women. Connie's young man was musical, Hilda's was technical. But they simply lived for their young women. In their minds and their mental excitements, that is. Somewhere else they were a little rebuffed, though they did not know it.

It was obvious in them too that love had gone through them: that is, the physical experience. It is curious what a subtle but unmistakable transmutation it makes, both in the body of men and women: the women more blooming, more subtly rounded, her young angularities softened, and her expression either anxious or triumphant: the man much quieter, more inward, the very shapes of his shoulders and his buttocks less assertive, more hesitant.

In the actual sex-thrill within the body, the sisters nearly succumbed to the strange male power. But quickly they recovered themselves, took the sex-thrill as a sensation, and remained free. Whereas the men, in gratitude to the woman for the sex experience, let their souls go out to her. And afterwards looked rather as if they had lost a shilling and found sixpence. Connie's man could be a bit sulky, and Hilda's a bit jeering. But that is how men are! Ungrateful and never satisfied. When you don't have them they hate you because you won't; and when you do have them they hate you again, for some other reason. Or for no reason at all, except that they are discontented children, and can't be satisfied whatever they get, let a woman do what she may.

However, came the war, Hilda and Connie were rushed home again after having been home already in May, to their mother's funeral. Before Christmas of 1914 both their German young men were dead: whereupon the sisters wept, and loved the young men passionately, but underneath forgot them. They didn't exist any more.

Both sisters lived in their father's, really their mother's, Kensington house, and mixed with the young Cambridge group, the group that stood for 'freedom' and flannel trousers, and flannel shirts open at the neck, and a well-bred sort of emotional anarchy, and a whispering, murmuring sort of voice, and an ultra-sensitive sort of manner. Hilda, however, suddenly married a man ten years older than herself, an elder member of the same Cambridge group, a man with a fair amount of money, and a comfortable family job in the government: he also wrote philosophical essays. She lived with him in a smallish house in Westminster, and moved in that good sort of society of people in the government who are not tip-toppers, but who are, or would be, the real intelligent power in the nation: people who know what they're talking about, or talk as if they did.

Connie did a mild form of war-work, and consorted with the flannel-trousers Cambridge intransigents, who gently mocked at everything, so far. Her 'friend' was a Clifford Chatterley, a young man of twenty-two, who had hurried home from Bonn, where he was studying the technicalities of coal-mining. He had previously spent two years at Cambridge. Now he had become a first lieutenant in a smart regiment, so he could mock at everything more becomingly in uniform.

Clifford Chatterley was more upper-class than Connie. Connie was well-to-do intelligentsia, but he was aristocracy. Not the big sort, but still *it*. His father was a baronet, and his mother had been a viscount's daughter.

But Clifford, while he was better bred than Connie, and more 'society', was in his own way more provincial and more timid. He was at his ease in the narrow 'great world', that is landed aristocracy society, but he was shy and nervous of all that other big world which consists of the vast hordes of the middle and lower classes, and foreigners. If the truth must be told, he was just a little bit frightened of middle- and lower-class humanity, and of foreigners not of his own class. He was, in some paralysing way, conscious of his own defencelessness, though he had all the defence of privilege. Which is curious, but a phenomenon of our day.

Therefore the peculiar soft assurance of a girl like Constance Reid fascinated him. She was so much more mistress of herself in that outer world of chaos than he was master of himself.

Nevertheless he too was a rebel: rebelling even against his class. Or perhaps rebel is too strong a word; far too strong. He was only caught in the general, popular recoil of the young against convention and against any sort of real authority. Fathers were ridiculous: his own obstinate one supremely so. And governments were ridiculous: our own wait-and-see sort especially so. And armies were ridiculous, and old buffers of generals altogether, the red-faced

Kitchener supremely. Even the war was ridiculous, though it did kill rather a lot of people.

In fact everything was a little ridiculous, or very ridiculous: certainly everything connected with authority, whether it were in the army or the government or the universities, was ridiculous to a degree. And so far as the governing class made any pretensions to govern, they were ridiculous too. Sir Geoffrey, Clifford's father, was intensely ridiculous, chopping down his trees, and weeding men out of his colliery to shove them into the war; and himself being so safe and patriotic; but, also, spending more money on his country than he'd got.

When Miss Chatterley—Emma—came down to London from the Midlands to do some nursing work, she was very witty in a quiet way about Sir Geoffrey and his determined patriotism. Herbert, the elder brother and heir, laughed outright, though it was his trees that were falling for trench props. But Clifford only smiled a little uneasily. Everything was ridiculous, quite true. But when it came too close and oneself became ridiculous too . . .? At least people of a different class, like Connie, were earnest about something. They believed in something.

They were rather earnest about the Tommies, and the threat of conscription, and the shortage of sugar and toffee for the children. In all these things, of course, the authorities were ridiculously at fault. But Clifford could not take it to heart. To him the authorities were ridiculous *ab ovo*, not because of toffee or Tommies.

And the authorities felt ridiculous, and behaved in a rather ridiculous fashion, and it was all a mad hatter's tea-party for a while. Till things developed over there, and Lloyd George came to save the situation over here. And this surpassed even ridicule, the flippant young laughed no more.

In 1916 Herbert Chatterley was killed, so Clifford became heir. He was terrified even of this. His importance as son of Sir Geoffrey, and child of Wragby, was so ingrained in him, he could never escape it. And yet he knew that this too, in the eyes of the vast seething world, was ridiculous. Now he was heir and responsible for Wragby. Was that not terrible? and also splendid and at the same time, perhaps, purely absurd?

Sir Geoffrey would have none of the absurdity. He was pale and tense, withdrawn into himself, and obstinately determined to save his country and his own position, let it be Lloyd George or who it might. So cut off he was, so divorced from the England that was really England, so utterly incapable, that he even thought well of Horatio Bottomley. Sir Geoffrey stood for England and Lloyd George as his forebears had stood for England and St George: and he never knew there was a difference. So Sir Geoffrey felled timber and stood for Lloyd George and England, England and Lloyd George.

And he wanted Clifford to marry and produce an heir. Clifford felt his father was a hopeless anachronism. But wherein was he himself any further ahead, except in a wincing sense of the ridiculousness of everything, and the paramount ridiculousness of his own position? For willy-nilly he took his baronetcy and Wragby with the last seriousness.

The gay excitement had gone out of the war . . . dead. Too much death and horror. A man needed support and comfort. A man needed to have an anchor in the safe world. A man needed a wife.

The Chatterleys, two brothers and a sister, had lived curiously isolated, shut in with one another at Wragby, in spite of all their connexions. A sense of isolation intensified the family tie, a sense of the weakness of their position, a sense of defencelessness, in spite of, or because of, the title and the land. They were cut off from those industrial Midlands in which they passed their lives. And they were cut off from their own class by the brooding, obstinate, shut-up nature of Sir Geoffrey, their father, whom they ridiculed, but whom they were so sensitive about.

The three had said they would all live together always. But now Herbert was dead, and Sir Geoffrey wanted Clifford to marry. Sir Geoffrey barely mentioned it: he spoke very little. But his silent, brooding insistence that it should be so was hard for Clifford to bear up against.

But Emma said No! She was ten years older than Clifford, and she felt his marrying would be a desertion and a betrayal of what the young ones of the family had stood for.

Clifford married Connie, nevertheless, and had his month's honeymoon with her. It was the terrible year 1917, and they were intimate as two people who stand together on a sinking ship. He had been virgin when he married: and the sex part did not mean much to him. They were so close, he and she, apart from that. And Connie exulted a little in this intimacy which was beyond sex, and beyond a man's 'satisfaction'. Clifford anyhow was not just keen on his 'satisfaction', as so many men seemed to be. No, the intimacy was deeper, more personal than that. And sex was merely an accident, or an adjunct, one of the curious obsolete, organic processes which persisted in its own clumsiness, but was not really necessary. Though Connie did want children: if only to fortify her against her sister-in-law Emma.

But early in 1918 Clifford was shipped home smashed, and there was no child. And Sir Geoffrey died of chagrin.

2

Connie and Clifford came home to Wragby in the autumn of 1920. Miss Chatterley, still disgusted at her brother's defection, had departed and was living in a little flat in London.

Wragby was a long low old house in brown stone, begun about the middle of the eighteenth century, and added on to, till it was a warren of a place without much distinction. It stood on an eminence in a rather fine old park of oak trees, but alas, one could see in the near distance the chimney of Tevershall pit, with its clouds of steam and smoke, and on the damp, hazy distance of the hill the raw straggle of Tevershall village, a village which began almost at the park gates, and trailed in utter hopeless ugliness for a long and gruesome mile: houses, rows of wretched, small, begrimed, brick houses, with black slate roofs for lids, sharp angles and wilful, blank dreariness.

Connie was accustomed to Kensington or the Scotch hills or the Sussex downs: that was her England. With the stoicism of the young she took in the utter, soulless ugliness of the coal-and-iron Midlands at a glance, and left it at what it was: unbelievable and not to be thought about. From the rather dismal rooms at Wragby she heard the rattle-rattle of the screens at the pit, the puff of the winding-engine, the clink-clink of shunting trucks, and the hoarse little whistle of the colliery locomotives. Tevershall pit-bank was burning, had been burning for years, and it would cost thousands to put it out. So it had to burn. And when the wind was that way, which was often, the house was full of the stench of this sulphurous combustion of the earth's excrement. But even on windless days the air always smelt of something under-earth: sulphur, iron, coal, or acid. And even on the Christmas roses the smuts settled persistently, incredible, like black manna from the skies of doom.

Well, there it was: fated like the rest of things! It was rather awful, but why kick? You couldn't kick it away. It just went on. Life, like all the rest! On the low dark ceiling of cloud at night red blotches burned and quavered, dappling and swelling and contracting, like burns that give pain. It was the furnaces. At first they fascinated Connie with a sort of horror; she felt she was living underground. Then she got used to them. And in the morning it rained.

Clifford professed to like Wragby better than London. This country had a grim will of its own, and the people had guts. Connie wondered what else they had: certainly neither eyes nor minds. The people were as haggard, shapeless, and dreary as the countryside, and as unfriendly. Only there was something in their deep-mouthed slurring of the dialect, and the thresh-thresh of their hob-nailed pit-boots as they trailed home in gangs on the asphalt from work, that was terrible and a bit mysterious.

There had been no welcome home for the young squire, no festivities, no deputation, not even a single flower. Only a dank ride in a motor-car up a dark, damp drive, burrowing through gloomy trees, out to the slope of the park where grey damp sheep were feeding, to the knoll where the house spread its dark brown façade, and the housekeeper and her husband were hovering, like unsure tenants on the face of the earth, ready to stammer a welcome.

There was no communication between Wragby Hall and Tevershall village, none. No caps were touched, no curtseys bobbed. The colliers merely stared; the tradesmen lifted their caps to Connie as to an acquaintance, and nodded awkwardly to Clifford; that was all. Gulf impassable, and a quiet sort of resentment on either side. At first Connie suffered from the steady drizzle of resentment that came from the village. Then she hardened herself to it, and it became a sort of tonic, something to live up to. It was not that she and Clifford were unpopular, they merely belonged to another species altogether from the colliers. Gulf impassable, breach indescribable, such as is perhaps non-existent south of the Trent. But in the Midlands and the industrial North gulf impassable, across which no communication could take place. You stick to your side, I'll stick to mine! A strange denial of the common pulse of humanity.

Yet the village sympathized with Clifford and Connie in the abstract. In the flesh it was—You leave me alone!—on either side.

The rector was a nice man of about sixty, full of his duty, and reduced, personally, almost to a nonentity by the silent—You leave me alone!—of the village. The miners' wives were nearly all Methodists. The miners were nothing. But even so much official uniform as the clergyman wore was enough to obscure entirely the fact that he was a man like any other man. No, he was Mester Ashby, a sort of automatic preaching and praying concern.

This stubborn, instinctive—We think ourselves as good as you, if you *are* Lady Chatterley!—puzzled and baffled Connie at first extremely. The curious, suspicious, false amiability with which the miners' wives met her overtures; the curiously offensive tinge of—Oh dear me! I *am* somebody now, with Lady

Chatterley talking to me! But she needn't think I'm not as good as her for all that!—which she always heard twanging in the women's half-fawning voices, was impossible. There was no getting past it. It was hopelessly and offensively Nonconformist.

Clifford left them alone, and she learnt to do the same: she just went by without looking at them , and they stared as if she were a walking wax figure. When he had to deal with them, Clifford was rather haughty and contemptuous; one could no longer afford to be friendly. In fact he was altogether rather supercilious and contemptuous of anyone not in his own class. He stood his ground, without any attempt at conciliation. And he was neither liked nor disliked by the people: he was just part of things, like the pit-bank and Wragby itself.

But Clifford was extremely shy and self-conscious now he was lamed. He hated seeing anyone except just the personal servants. For he had to sit in a wheeled chair or a sort of bath-chair. Nevertheless he was just as carefully dressed as ever by his expensive tailors, and he wore the careful Bond Street neckties just as before, and from the top he looked just as smart and impressive as ever. He had never been one of the modern ladylike young men: rather bucolic even, with his ruddy face and broad shoulders. But his very quiet, hesitating voice, and his eyes, at the same time bold and frightened, assured and uncertain, revealed his nature. His manner was often offensively supercilious, and then again modest and self effacing, almost tremulous.

Connie and he were attached to one another, in the aloof modern way. He was much too hurt in himself, the great shock of his maiming, to be easy and flippant. He was a hurt thing. And as such Connie stuck to him passionately.

But she could not help feeling how little connexion he really had with people. The miners were, in a sense, his own men; but he saw them as objects rather than men, parts of the pit rather than parts of life, crude raw phenomena rather than human beings along with him. He was in some way afraid of them, he could not bear to have them look at him now he was lame. And their queer, crude life seemed as unnatural as that of hedgehogs.

He was remotely interested; but like a man looking down a microscope, or up a telescope. He was not in touch. He was not in actual touch with anybody, save, traditionally, with Wragby, and, through the close bond of family defence, with Emma. Beyond this nothing really touched him. Connie felt that she herself didn't really, not really touch him; perhaps there was nothing to get at ultimately; just a negation of human contact.

Yet he was absolutely dependent on her, he needed her every moment. Big and strong as he was, he was helpless. He could wheel himself about in a wheeled chair, and he had a sort of bath-chair with a motor attachment, in which he could puff slowly round the park. But alone he was like a lost thing. He needed Connie to be there, to assure him he existed at all.

Still he was ambitious. He had taken to writing stories; curious, very personal stories about people he had known. Clever, rather spiteful, and yet, in some mysterious way, meaningless. The observation was extraordinary and peculiar. But there was no touch, no actual contact. It was as if the whole thing took place in a vacuum. And since the field of life is largely an artificially-lighted stage today, the stories were curiously true to modern life, to the modern psychology, that is.

Clifford was almost morbidly sensitive about these stories. He wanted everyone to think them good, of the best, *ne plus ultra.* They appeared in the most modern magazines, and were praised and blamed as usual. But to Clifford the blame was torture, like knives goading him. It was as if the whole of his being were in his stories.

Connie helped him as much as she could. At first she was thrilled. He talked everything over with her monotonously, insistently, persistently, and she had to respond with all her might. It was as if her whole soul and body and sex had to rouse up and pass into these stories of his. This thrilled her and absorbed her.

Of physical life they lived very little. She had to superintend the house. But the housekeeper had served Sir Geoffrey for many years, and the dried-up, elderly, superlatively correct female . . . you could hardly call her a parlourmaid, or even a woman . . . who waited at table, had been in the house for forty years. Even the very housemaids were no longer young. It was awful! What could you do with such a place, but leave it alone! All these endless rooms that nobody used, all the Midlands routine, the mechanical cleanliness and the mechanical order! Clifford had insisted on a new cook, an experienced woman who had served him in his rooms in London. For the rest the place seemed run by mechanical anarchy. Everything went on in pretty good order, strict cleanliness, and strict punctuality; even pretty strict honesty. And yet, to Connie, it was a methodical anarchy. No warmth of feeling united it organically. The house seemed as dreary as a disused street.

What could she do but leave it alone. . . .? So she left it alone. Miss Chatterley came sometimes, with her aristocratic thin face, and triumphed, finding nothing altered. She would never forgive Connie for ousting her from her union in consciousness with her brother. It was she, Emma, who should be bringing forth the stories, these books, with him; the Chatterley stories, something new in the world, that *they*, the Chatterleys, had put there. There was no other standard. There was no organic connexion with the thought and expression that had gone before. Only something new in the world: the Chatterley books, entirely personal.

Connie's father, when he paid a flying visit to Wragby, said in private to his daughter: As for Clifford's writing, it's smart, but there's nothing in it. It won't last! . . . Connie looked at the burly Scottish knight who had done himself well all his life, and her eyes, her big, still-wondering blue eyes became vague. Nothing in it! What did he mean by *nothing in it?* If the critics praised it, and Clifford's name was almost famous, and it even brought in money . . . what did her father mean by saying there was nothing in Clifford's writing? What else could there be?

For Connie had adopted the standard of the young: what there was in the moment was everything. And moments followed one another without necessarily belonging to one another.

It was in her second winter at Wragby her father said to her: 'I hope, Connie, you won't let circumstances force you into being a demi-vierge.'

'A demi-vierge!' replied Connie vaguely. 'Why? Why not?'

'Unless you like it, of course!' said her father hastily. To Clifford he said the same, when the two men were alone: 'I'm afraid it doesn't quite suit Connie to be a demi-vierge.'

'A half-virgin!' replied Clifford, translating the phrase to be sure of it.

He thought for a moment, then flushed very red. He was angry and offended.

'In what way doesn't it suit her?' he asked stiffly.

'She's getting thin . . . angular. It's not her style. She's not the pilchard sort of little slip of a girl, she's a bonny Scotch trout.'

'Without the spots, of course!' said Clifford.

He wanted to say something later to Connie about the demi-vierge business . . . the half-virgin state of her affairs. But he could not bring himself to do it. He was at once too intimate with her and not intimate enough. He was so very much at one with her, in his mind and hers, but bodily they were non-existent to one another, and neither could bear to drag in the *corpus delicti.* They were so intimate, and utterly out of touch.

Connie guessed, however, that her father had said something, and that something was in Clifford's mind. She knew that he didn't mind whether she were demi-vierge or demi-monde, so long as he didn't absolutely know, and wasn't made to see. What the eye doesn't see and the mind doesn't know, doesn't exist.

Connie and Clifford had now been nearly two years at Wragby, living their vague life of absorption in Clifford and his work. Their interests had never ceased to flow together over his work. They talked and wrestled in the throes of composition, and felt as if something were happening, really happening, really in the void.

And thus far it was a life: in the void. For the rest it was non-existence. Wragby was there, the servants . . . but spectral, not really existing. Connie went for walks in the park, and in the woods that joined the park, and enjoyed the solitude and the mystery, kicking the brown leaves of autumn, and picking the primroses of spring. But it was all a dream; or rather it was like the simulacrum of reality. The oak-leaves were to her like oak-leaves seen ruffling in a mirror, she herself was a figure somebody had read about, picking primroses that were only shadows or memories, or words. No substance to her or anything . . . no touch, no contact! Only this life with Clifford, this endless spinning of webs of yarn, of the minutiae of consciousness, these stories Sir Malcolm said there was nothing in, and they wouldn't last. Why should there be anything in them, why should they last? Sufficient unto the day is the evil thereof. Sufficient unto the moment is the *appearance* of reality.

Clifford had quite a number of friends, acquaintances really, and he invited them to Wragby. He invited all sorts of people, critics and writers, people who would help to praise his books. And they were flattered at being asked to Wragby, and they praised. Connie understood it all perfectly. But why not? This was one of the fleeting patterns in the mirror. What was wrong with it?

She was hostess to these people . . . mostly men. She was hostess also to Clifford's occasional aristocratic relations. Being a soft, ruddy, country-look-ing girl, inclined to freckles, with big blue eyes, and curling, brown hair, a soft voice, and rather strong, female loins she was considered a little old-fashioned and 'womanly'. She was not a 'little pilchard sort of fish', like a boy, with a boy's flat breast and little buttocks. She was too feminine to be quite smart.

So the men, especially those no longer young, were very nice to her indeed. But, knowing what torture poor Clifford would feel at the slightest sign of flirting on her part, she gave them no encouragement at all. She was quiet and vague, she had no contact with them and intended to have none. Clifford was extraordinarily proud of himself.

His relatives treated her quite kindly. She knew that the kindliness indicated a lack of fear, and that these people had no respect for you unless you could frighten them a little. But again she had no contact. She let them be kindly and disdainful, she let them feel they had no need to draw their steel in readiness. She had no real connexion with them.

Time went on. Whatever happened, nothing happened, because she was so beautifully out of contact. She and Clifford lived in their ideas and his books. She entertained . . . there were always people in the house. Time went on as the clock does, half past eight instead of half past seven.

3

Connie was aware, however, of a growing restlessness. Out of her disconnexion, a restlessness was taking possession of her like madness. It twitched her limbs when she didn't want to twitch them, it jerked her spine when she didn't want to jerk upright but preferred to rest comfortably. It thrilled inside her body, in her womb, somewhere, till she felt she must jump into water and swim to get away from it; a mad restlessness. It made her heart beat violently for no reason. And she was getting thinner.

It was just restlessness. She would rush off across the park, abandon Clifford, and lie prone in the bracken. To get away from the house . . . she must get away from the house and everybody. The wood was her one refuge, her sanctuary.

But it was not really a refuge, a sanctuary, because she had no connexion with it. It was only a place where she could get away from the rest. She never really touched the spirit of the wood itself . . . if it had any such nonsensical thing.

Vaguely she knew herself that she was going to pieces in some way. Vaguely she knew she was out of connexion: she had lost touch with the substantial and vital world. Only Clifford and his books, which did not exist . . . which had nothing in them! Void to void. Vaguely she knew. But it was like beating her head against a stone.

Her father warned her again: 'Why don't you get yourself a beau, Connie? Do you all the good in the world.'

That winter Michaelis came for a few days. He was a young Irishman who had already made a large fortune by his plays in America. He had been taken up quite enthusiastically for a time by smart society in London, for he wrote smart society plays. Then gradually smart society realized that it had been made ridiculous at the hands of a down-at-heel Dublin street-rat, and revulsion came. Michaelis was the last word in what was caddish and bounderish. He was discovered to be anti-English, and to the class that made this discovery this was worse than the dirtiest crime. He was cut dead, and his corpse thrown into the refuse-can.

Nevertheless Michaelis had his apartment in Mayfair, and walked down Bond Street the image of a gentleman, for you cannot get even the best tailors to cut their low-down customers, when the customers pay.

Clifford was inviting the young man of thirty at an inauspicious moment in that young man's career. Yet Clifford did not hesitate. Michaelis had the ear of a few million people, probably; and, being a hopeless outsider, he would no doubt be grateful to be asked down to Wragby at this juncture, when the rest of the smart world was cutting him. Being grateful, he would no doubt do Clifford 'good' over there in America. Kudos! A man gets a lot of kudos, whatever that may be, by being talked about in the right way, especially 'over there'. Clifford was a coming man; and it was remarkable what a sound publicity instinct he had. In the end Michaelis did him most nobly in a play, and Clifford was a sort of popular hero. Till the reaction, when he found he had been made ridiculous.

Connie wondered a little over Clifford's blind, imperious instinct to become known: known, that is, to the vast amorphous world he did not himself know, and of which he was uneasily afraid; known as a writer, as a first-class modern writer. Connie was aware from successful, old, hearty, bluffing Sir Malcolm, that artists did advertise themselves, and exert themselves to put their goods over. But her father used channels ready-made, used by all the other R.A.s who sold their pictures. Whereas Clifford discovered new channels of publicity, all kinds. He had all kinds of people at Wragby, without exactly lowering himself. But, determined to build himself a monument of a reputation quickly, he used any handy rubble in the making.

Michaelis arrived duly, in a very neat car, with a chauffeur and a manservant. He was absolutely Bond Street! But at sight of him something in Clifford's county soul recoiled. He wasn't exactly . . . not exactly . . . in fact, he wasn't at all, well, what his appearance intended to imply. To Clifford this was final and enough. Yet he was very polite to the man; to the amazing success in him. The bitch-goddess, as she is called, of Success, roamed, snarling and protective, round the half-humble, half-defiant Michael's heels, and intimidated Clifford completely: for he wanted to prostitute himself to the bitch-goddess. Success also, if only she would have him.

Michaelis obviously wasn't an Englishman, in spite of all the tailors, hatters, barbers, booters of the very best quarter of London. No, no, he obviously wasn't an Englishman: the wrong sort of flattish, pale face and bearing; and the wrong sort of grievance. He had a grudge and a grievance: that was obvious to any true-born English gentleman, who would scorn to let such a thing appear blatant in his own demeanour. Poor Michaelis had been much kicked, so that he had a slightly tail-between-the-legs look even now. He had pushed his way by sheer instinct and sheerer effrontery on to the stage and to the front of it, with his plays. He had caught the public. And he had thought the kicking days were over. Alas, they weren't . . . They never would be. For he, in a sense, asked to be kicked. He pined to be where he didn't belong . . . among the English upper classes. And how they enjoyed the various kicks they got at him! And how he hated them!

Nevertheless he travelled with his manservant and his very neat car, this Dublin mongrel.

There was something about him that Connie liked. He didn't put on airs to himself; he had no illusions about himself. He talked to Clifford sensibly, briefly, practically, about all the things Clifford wanted to know. He didn't expand or let himself go. He knew he had been asked down to Wragby to be made use of, and like an old, shrewd, almost indifferent business man, or big-business man, he let himself be asked questions, and he answered with as little waste of feeling as possible.

'Money!' he said. 'Money is a sort of instinct. It's a sort of property of nature in a man to make money. It's nothing you do. It's no trick you play. It's a sort of permanent accident of your own nature; once you start, you make money, and you go on; up to a point, I suppose.'

'But you've got to begin,' said Clifford.

'Oh, quite! You've got to get *in*. You can do nothing if you are kept outside.

You've got to beat your way in. Once you've done that, you can't help it.'

'But could you have made money except by plays?' asked Clifford.

'Oh, probably not! I may be a good writer or I may be a bad one, but a writer and a writer of plays is what I am, and I've got to be. There's no question of that.'

'And you think it's a writer of popular plays that you've got to be?' asked Connie.

'There, exactly!' he said, turning to her in a sudden flash. 'There's nothing in it! There's nothing in popularity. There's nothing in the public, if it comes to that. There's nothing really in my plays to *make* them popular, It's not that. They just are like the weather . . . the sort that will *have* to be . . . for the time being.'

He turned his slow, rather full eyes, that had been drowned in such fathomless disillusion, on Connie, and she trembled a little. He seemed so old . . . endlessly old, built up of layers of disillusion, going down in him generation after generation, like geological strata; and at the same time he was forlorn like a child. An outcast, in a certain sense; but with the desperate bravery of his rat-like existence.

'At least it's wonderful what you've done at your time of life,' said Clifford contemplatively.

'I'm thirty . . . yes, I'm thirty!' said Michaelis, sharply and suddenly, with a curious laugh; hollow, triumphant, and bitter.

'And are you alone?' asked Connie.

'How do you mean? Do I live alone? I've got my servant. He's a Greek, so he says, and quite incompetent. But I keep him. And I'm going to marry, Oh, yes, I must marry.'

'It sounds like going to have your tonsils cut,' laughed Connie. 'Will it be an effort?'

He looked at her admiringly. 'Well, Lady Chatterley, somehow it will! I find . . . excuse me . . . I find I can't marry an Englishwoman, not even an Irishwoman . . .'

'Try an American,' said Clifford.

'Oh, American!' He laughed a hollow laugh. 'No, I've asked my man if he will find me a Turk or something . . . something nearer to the Oriental.'

Connie really wondered at this queer, melancholy specimen of extraordinary success; it was said he had an income of fifty thousand dollars from America alone. Sometimes he was handsome: sometimes as he looked sideways, downwards, and the light fell on him, he had the silent, enduring beauty of a carved ivory Negro mask, with his rather full eyes, and the strong queerly-arched brows, the immobile, compressed mouth; that momentary but revealed immobility, an immobility, a timelessness which the Buddha aims at, and which Negroes express sometimes without ever aiming at it; something old, old, and acquiescent in the race! Aeons of acquiescence in race destiny, instead of our individual resistance. And then a swimming through, like rats in a dark river. Connie felt a sudden, strange leap of sympathy for him, a leap mingled with compassion, and tinged with repulsion, amounting almost to love. The outsider! The outsider! And they called him a bounder! How much more bounderish and assertive Clifford looked! How much stupider!

Michaelis knew at once he had made an impression on her. He turned his full, hazel, slightly prominent eyes on her in a look of pure detachment. He was estimating her, and the extent of the impression he had made. With the English nothing could save him from being the eternal outsider, not even love. Yet women sometimes fell for him . . . Englishwomen too.

He knew just where he was with Clifford. They were two alien dogs which would have liked to snarl at one another, but which smiled instead, perforce. But with the woman he was not quite so sure.

Breakfast was served in the bedrooms; Clifford never appeared before lunch, and the dining-room was a little dreary. After coffee Michaelis, restless and ill-sitting soul, wondered what he should do. It was a fine November day . . . fine for Wragby. He looked over the melancholy park. My God! What a place!

He sent a servant to ask, could he be of any service to Lady Chatterley: he thought of driving into Sheffield. The answer came, would he care to go up to Lady Chatterley's sitting-room.

Connie had a sitting-room on the third floor, the top floor of the central portion of the house. Clifford's rooms were on the ground floor, of course. Michaelis was flattered by being asked up to Lady Chatterley's own parlour. He followed blindly after the servant . . . he never noticed things, or had contact with his surroundings. In her room he did glance vaguely round at the fine German reproductions of Renoir and Cézanne.

'It's very pleasant up here,' he said, with his queer smile, as if it hurt him to smile, showing his teeth. 'You are wise to get up to the top.'

'Yes, I think so,' she said.

Her room was the only gay, modern one in the house, the only spot in Wragby where her personality was at all revealed. Clifford had never seen it, and she asked very few people up.

Now she and Michaelis sat on opposite sides of the fire and talked. She asked him about himself, his mother and father, his brothers . . . other people were always something of a wonder to her, and when her sympathy was awakened she was quite devoid of class feeling. Michaelis talked frankly about himself, quite frankly, with affection, simply revealing his bitter, indifferent, stray-dog's soul, then showing a gleam of revengeful pride in his success.

'But why are you such a lonely bird?' Connie asked him; and again he looked at her, with his full, searching, hazel look.

'Some birds *are* that way,' he replied. Then, with a touch of familiar irony: 'but, look here, what about yourself? Aren't you by way of being a lonely bird yourself?' Connie, a little startled, thought about it for a few moments, and then she said: 'Only in a way! Not altogether, like you!'

'Am I altogether a lonely bird?' he asked, with his queer grin of a smile, as if he had toothache; it was so wry, and his eyes were so perfectly unchangingly melancholy, or stoical, or disillusioned, or afraid.

'Why?' she said, a little breathless, as she looked at him. 'You are, aren't you?'

She felt a terrible appeal coming to her from him, that made her almost lose her balance.

'Oh, you're quite right!' he said, turning his head away, and looking sideways, downwards, with that strange immobility of an old race that is hardly here in our present day. It was that that really made Connie lose her power to see him detached from herself.

He looked up at her with the full glance that saw everything, registered everything. At the same time, the infant crying in the night was crying out of his breast to her, in a way that affected her very womb.

'It's awfully nice of you to think of me,' he said laconically.

'Why shouldn't I think of you?' she exclaimed, with hardly breath to utter it.

He gave the wry, quick hiss of a laugh.

'Oh, in that way! . . . May I hold your hand for a minute?' he asked suddenly, fixing his eyes on her with almost hypnotic power, and sending out an appeal that affected her direct in the womb.

She stared at him, dazed and transfixed, and he went over and kneeled beside her, and took her two feet close in his two hands, and buried his face in her lap, remaining motionless. She was perfectly dim and dazed, looking down in a sort of amazement at the rather tender nape of his neck, feeling his face pressing her thighs. In all her burning dismay, she could not help putting her hand, with tenderness and compassion, on the defenceless nape of his neck, and he trembled, with a deep shudder.

Then he looked up at her with that awful appeal in his full, glowing eyes. She was utterly incapable of resisting it. From her breast flowed the answering, immense yearning over him; she must give him anything, anything.

He was a curious and very gentle lover, very gentle with the woman, trembling uncontrollably, and yet at the same time detached, aware, aware of every sound outside.

To her it meant nothing except that she gave herself to him. And at length he ceased to quiver any more, and lay quite still, quite still. Then, with dim, compassionate fingers, she stroked his head, that lay on her breast.

When he rose, he kissed both her hands, then both her feet, in their suède slippers, and in silence went away to the end of the room where he stood with his back to her. There was silence for some minutes. Then he turned and came to her again as she sat in her old place by the fire.

'And now, I suppose you'll hate me!' he said in a quiet, inevitable way. She looked up at him quickly.

'Why should I?' she asked.

'They mostly do,' he said; then he caught himself up. 'I mean . . . a woman is supposed to.'

'This is the last moment when I ought to hate you,' she said resentfully.

'I know! I know! It should be so! You're *frightfully* good to me . . .' he cried miserably.

She wondered why he should be so miserable. 'Won't you sit down again?' she said. He glanced at the door.

'Sir Clifford!' he said, 'won't he . . . won't he be . . . ?' She paused a moment to consider. 'Perhaps!' she said. And she looked up at him 'I don't want Clifford to know . . . not even to suspect. It would hurt him so much. But I don't think it's wrong, do you?'

'Wrong! Good God, no! You're only too infinitely good to me . . . I can hardly bear it.'

He turned aside, and she saw that in another moment he would be sobbing.

'But we needn't let Clifford know, need we?' she pleaded. 'It *would* hurt him so. And if he never knows, never suspects, it hurts nobody.'

'Me! he said, almost fiercely; 'he'll know nothing from me! You see if he does. Me give myself away! Ha! Ha!' he laughed hollowly, cynically, at such an idea. She watched him in wonder. He said to her: 'May I kiss your hand and go? I'll run into Sheffield I think, and lunch there, if I may, and be back to tea. May I do anything for you? May I be sure you don't hate me?–and that you won't?'–he ended with a desperate note of cynicism.

'No, I don't hate you,' she said. 'I think you're nice.'

'Ah!' he said to her fiercely, 'I'd rather you said that to me than you said you love me! It means such a lot more . . . Till afternoon then. I've plenty to think about till then.' He kissed her hands humbly and was gone.

'I don't think I can stand that young man,' said Clifford at lunch.

'Why?' asked Connie.

'He's such a bounder underneath his veneer . . . just waiting to bounce us.'

'I think people have been so unkind to him,' said Connie.

'Do you wonder? And do you think he employs his shining hours doing deeds of kindness?'

'I think he has a certain sort of generosity.'

'Towards whom?'

'I don't quite know.'

'Naturally you don't. I'm afraid you mistake unscrupulousness for generosity.'

Connie paused. Did she? It was just possible. Yet the unscrupulousness of Michaelis had a certain fascination for her. He went whole lengths where Clifford only crept a few timid paces. In his way he had conquered the world, which was what Clifford wanted to do. Ways and means. . .? Were those of Michaelis more despicable than those of Clifford? Was the way the poor outsider had shoved and bounced himself forward in person, and by the back doors, any worse than Clifford's way of advertising himself into prominence? The bitch-goddess, Success, was trailed by thousands of gasping dogs with lolling tongues. The one that got her first was the real dog among dogs, if you go by success! So Michaelis could keep his tail up.

The queer thing was, he didn't. He came back towards tea-time with a large handful of violets and lilies, and the same hang-dog expression. Connie wondered sometimes if it were a sort of mask to disarm opposition, because it was almost too fixed. Was he really such a sad dog?

His sad-dog sort of extinguished self persisted all the evening, though through it Clifford felt the inner effrontery. Connie didn't feel it, perhaps because it was not directed against women; only against men, and their presumptions and assumptions. That indestructible, inward effrontery in the meagre fellow was what made men so down on Michaelis. His very presence was an affront to a man of society, cloak it as he might in an assumed good manner.

Connie was in love with him, but she managed to sit with her embroidery and let the men talk, and not give herself away. As for Michaelis, he was perfect; exactly the same melancholic, attentive, aloof young fellow of the previous evening, millions of degrees remote from his hosts, but laconically playing up to them to the required amount, and never coming forth to them for a moment. Connie felt he must have forgotten the morning. He had not forgotten. But he knew where he was . . . in the same old place outside, where the born outsiders are. He didn't take the love-making altogether personally. He knew it would not change him from an ownerless dog, whom everybody begrudges its golden collar, into a comfortable society dog.

The final fact being that at the very bottom of his soul he *was* an outsider, and anti-social, and he accepted the fact inwardly, no matter how Bond-Streety he was on the outside. His isolation was a necessity to him; just as the appearance of conformity and mixing-in with the smart people was also a necessity.

But occasional love, as a comfort and soothing, was also a good thing, and he was not ungrateful. On the contrary, he was burningly, poignantly grateful for a piece of natural, spontaneous kindness: almost to tears. Beneath his pale,

immobile, disillusioned face, his child's soul was sobbing with gratitu⌐
woman, and burning to come to her again; just as his outcast soul was know⌐
he would keep really clear of her.

He found an opportunity to say to her, as they were lighting the candles in the hall:

'May I come?'

'I'll come to you,' she said.

'Oh, good!'

He waited for her a long time . . . but she came.

He was the trembling excited sort of lover, whose crisis soon came, and was finished. There was something curiously child-like and defenceless about his naked body: as children are naked. His defences were all in his wits and cunning, his very instincts of cunning, and when these were in abeyance he seemed doubly naked and like a child, of unfinished, tender flesh, and somehow struggling helplessly.

He roused in the woman a wild sort of compassion and yearning, and a wild, craving physical desire. The physical desire he did not satisfy in her; he was always come and finished so quickly, then shrinking down on her breast, and recovering somewhat his effrontery while she lay dazed, disappointed, lost.

But then she soon learnt to hold him, to keep him there inside her when his crisis was over. And there he was generous and curiously potent; he stayed firm inside her, giving to her, while she was active . . . wildly, passionately active, coming to her own crisis. And as he felt the frenzy of her achieving her own orgasmic satisfaction from his hard, erect passivity, he had a curious sense of pride and satisfaction.

'Ah, how good!' she whispered tremulously, and she became quite still, clinging to him. And he lay there in his own isolation, but somehow proud.

He stayed that time only the three days, and to Clifford was exactly the same as on the first evening; to Connie also. There was no breaking down his external man.

He wrote to Connie with the same plaintive melancholy note as ever, sometimes witty, and touched with a queer, sexless affection. A kind of hopeless affection he seemed to feel for her, and the essential remoteness remained the same. He was hopeless at the very core of him, and he wanted to be hopeless. He rather hated hope. '*Une immense espérance a traversé la terre*', he read somewhere, and his comment was: '–and it's darned-well drowned everything worth having.'

Connie never really understood him, but, in her way, she loved him. And all the time she felt the reflection of his hopelessness in her. She couldn't quite, quite love in hopelessness. And he, being hopeless, couldn't ever quite love at all.

So they went on for quite a time, writing, and meeting occasionally in London. She still wanted the physical, sexual thrill she could get with him by her own activity, his little orgasm being over. And he still wanted to give it her. Which was enough to keep them connected.

And enough to give her a subtle sort of self-assurance, something blind and a little arrogant. It was an almost mechanical confidence in her own powers, and went with a great cheerfulness.

She was terrifically cheerful at Wragby. And she used all her aroused cheerfulness and satisfaction to stimulate Clifford, so that he wrote his best at this time, and was almost happy in his strange blind way. He really reaped the fruits of the sensual satisfaction she got out of Michaelis's male passivity erect inside her. But of course he never knew it, and if he had, he wouldn't have said thank you!

Yet when those days of her grand joyful cheerfulness and stimulus were gone, quite gone, and she was depressed and irritable, how Clifford longed for them again! Perhaps if he'd known he might even have wished to get her and Michaelis together again.

4

Connie always had a foreboding of the hopelessness of her affair with Mick, as people called him. Yet other men seemed to mean nothing to her. She was attached to Clifford. He wanted a good deal of her life and she gave it to him. But she wanted a good deal from the life of a man, and this Clifford did not give her; could not. There were occasional spasms of Michaelis. But, as she knew by foreboding, that would come to an end. Mick *couldn't* keep anything up. It was part of his very being that he must break off any connexion, and be loose, isolated, absolutely lone dog again. It was his major necessity, even though he always said: She turned me down!

The world is supposed to be full of possibilities, but they narrow down to pretty few in most personal experience. There's lots of good fish in the sea . . . maybe . . . but the vast masses seemed to be mackerel or herring, and if you're not mackerel or herring yourself, you are likely to find very few good fish in the sea.

Clifford was making strides into fame, and even money. People came to see him. Connie nearly always had somebody at Wragby. But if they weren't mackerel they were herring, with an occasional cat-fish, or conger-eel.

There were a few regular men, constants; men who had been at Cambridge with Clifford. There was Tommy Dukes, who had remained in the army, and was a Brigadier-General. 'The army leaves me time to think, and saves me from having to face the battle of life,' he said.

There was Charles May, an Irishman, who wrote scientifically about stars. There was Hammond, another writer. All were about the same age as Clifford; the young intellectuals of the day. They all believed in the life of the mind. What you did apart from that was your private affair, and didn't much matter. No one thinks of inquiring of another person at what hour he retires to the privy. It isn't interesting to anyone but the person concerned.

And so with most of the matters of ordinary life . . . how you make your money, or whether you love your wife, or if you have 'affairs'. All these matters concern only the person concerned, and, like going to the privy, have no interest for anyone else.

'The whole point about the sexual problem,' said Hammond, who was a tall thin fellow with a wife and two children, but much more closely connected with a typewriter, 'is that there is no point to it. Strictly there is no problem. We don't want to follow a man into the W.C., so why should we want to follow him into bed with a woman? And therein lies the problem. If we took no more notice of the one thing than the other, there'd be no problem. It's all utterly senseless and pointless; a matter of misplaced curiosity.'

'Quite, Hammond, quite! But if someone starts making love to Julia, you begin to simmer; and if he goes on, you are soon at boiling point.' . . . Julia was Hammond's wife.

'Why, exactly! So I should be if he began to urinate in a corner of my drawing-room. There's a place for all these things.'

'You mean you wouldn't mind if he made love to Julia in some discreet alcove?'

Charlie May was slightly satirical, for he had flirted a very little with Julia, and Hammond had cut up very roughly.

'Of course I should mind. Sex is a private thing between me and Julia; and of course I should mind anyone else trying to mix in.'

'As a matter of fact,' said the lean and freckled Tommy Dukes, who looked much more Irish than May, who was pale and rather fat: 'As a matter of fact, Hammond, you have a strong property instinct, and a strong will to self-assertion, and you want success. Since I've been in the army definitely, I've got out of the way of the world, and now I see how inordinately strong the craving for self-assertion and success is in men. It is enormously over-developed. All our individuality has run that way. And of course men like you think you'll get through better with a woman's backing. That's why you're so jealous. That's what sex is to you . . . a vital little dynamo between you and Julia, to bring success. If you began to be unsuccessful you'd begin to flirt, like Charlie, who isn't successful. Married people like you and Julia have labels on you, like travellers' trunks. Julia is labelled *Mrs Arnold B. Hammond* . . . just like a trunk on the railway that belongs to somebody. And you are labelled *Arnold B. Hammond, c/o Mrs Arnold B. Hammond.* Oh, you're quite right, you're quite right! The life of the mind needs a comfortable house and decent cooking. You're quite right. It even needs posterity. But it all hinges on the instinct for success. That is the pivot on which all things turn.'

Hammond looked rather piqued. He was rather proud of the integrity of his mind, and of his *not* being a time-server. None the less, he did want success.

'It's quite true, you can't live without cash,' said May. 'You've got to have a certain amount of it to be able to live and get along . . . even to be free to *think* you must have a certain amount of money, or your stomach stops you. But it seems to me you might leave the labels off sex. We're free to talk to anybody; so why shouldn't we be free to make love to any woman who inclines us that way?'

'There speaks the lascivious Celt,' said Clifford.

'Lascivious! well, why not–? I can't see I do a woman any more harm by sleeping with her than by dancing with her . . . or even talking to her about the weather. It's just an interchange of sensations instead of ideas, so why not?'

'Be as promiscuous as the rabbits!' said Hammond.

'Why not? What's wrong with rabbits? Are they any worse than a neurotic, revolutionary humanity, full of nervous hate?'

'But we're not rabbits, even so,' said Hammond.

'Precisely! I have my mind: I have certain calculations to make in certain astronomical matters that concern me almost more than life or death. Sometimes indigestion interferes with me. Hunger would interfere with me disastrously. In the same way starved sex interferes with me. What then?'

'I should have thought sexual indigestion from surfeit would have interfered with you more seriously,' said Hammond satirically.

'Not it! I don't over-eat myself, and I don't over-fuck myself. One has a choice about eating too much. But you would absolutely starve me.'

'Not at all! You can marry.'

'How do you know I can? It may not suit the process of my mind. Marriage might . . . and would . . . stultify my mental processes. I'm not properly pivoted that way . . . and so must I be chained in a kennel like a monk? All rot and funk, my boy. I must live and do my calculations. I need women sometimes. I refuse to make a mountain of it, and I refuse anybody's moral condemnation or prohibition. I'd be ashamed to see a woman walking around with my name-label on her, address and railway station, like a wardrobe trunk.'

These two men had not forgiven each other about the Julia flirtation.

'It's an amusing idea, Charlie,' said Dukes, 'that sex is just another form of talk, where you act the words instead of saying them. I suppose it's quite true. I suppose we might exchange as many sensations and emotions with women as we do ideas about the weather, and so on. Sex might be a sort of normal physical conversation between a man and a woman. You don't talk to a woman unless you have ideas in common: that is you don't talk with any interest. And in the same way, unless you had some emotion or sympathy in common with a woman you wouldn't sleep with her. But if you had . . .'

'If you *have* the proper sort of emotion or sympathy with a woman, you *ought* to sleep with her,' said May. 'It's the only decent thing, to go to bed with her. Just as, when you are interested talking to someone, the only decent thing is to have the talk out. You don't prudishly put your tongue between your teeth and bite it. You just say out your say. And the same the other way.'

'No,' said Hammond. 'It's wrong. You, for example, May, you squander half your force with women. You'll never really do what you should do, with a fine mind such as yours. Too much of it goes the other way.'

'Maybe it does . . . and too little of you goes that way, Hammond, my boy, married or not. You can keep the purity and integrity of your mind, but it's going damned dry. Your pure mind is going as dry as fiddlesticks, from what I see of it. You're simply talking it down.'

Tommy Dukes burst into a laugh.

'Go it, you two minds!' he said. 'Look at me . . . I don't do any high and pure mental work, nothing but jot down a few ideas. And yet I neither marry nor run after women. I think Charlie's quite right; if he wants to run after the women, he's quite free not to run too often. But I wouldn't prohibit him from running. As for Hammond, he's got a property instinct, so naturally the straight road and the narrow gate are right for him. You'll see he'll be an English Man of Letters before he's done, A.B.C. from top to toe. Then there's me. I'm nothing. Just a squib. And what about you, Clifford? Do you think sex is a dynamo to help a man on to success in the world?'

Clifford rarely talked much at these times. He never held forth; his ideas were really not vital enough for it, he was too confused and emotional. Now he blushed and looked uncomfortable.

'Well!' he said, 'being myself *hors de combat*, I don't see I've anything to say on the matter.'

'Not at all,' said Dukes; 'the top of you's by no means *hors de combat*. You've got the life of the mind sound and intact. So let us hear your ideas.'

'Well,' stammered Clifford, 'even then I don't suppose I have much idea . . . I suppose marry-and-have-done-with-it would pretty well stand for what I think. Though of course between a man and woman who care for one another, it is a great thing.'

'What sort of a great thing?' said Tommy.

'Oh . . . it perfects the intimacy,' said Clifford, uneasy as a woman in such talk.

'Well, Charlie and I believe that sex is a sort of communication like speech. Let any woman start a sex conversation with me, and it's natural for me to go to bed with her to finish it, all in due season. Unfortunately no woman makes any particular start with me, so I go to bed by myself; and am none the worse for it . . . I hope so, anyway, for how should I know? Anyhow I've no starry calculations to be interfered with, and no immortal works to write. I'm merely a fellow skulking in the army . . .'

Silence fell. The four men smoked. And Connie sat there and put another stitch in her sewing . . . Yes, she sat there! She had to sit mum. She had to be quiet as a mouse, not to interfere with the immensely important speculations of these highly-mental gentlemen. But she had to be there. They didn't get on so well without her; their ideas didn't flow so freely. Clifford was much more hedgy and nervous, he got cold feet much quicker in Connie's absence, and the talk didn't run. Tommy Dukes came off best; he was a little inspired by her presence. Hammond she didn't really like; he seemed so selfish in a mental way. And Charles May, though she liked something about him, seemed a little distasteful and messy, in spite of his stars.

How many evenings had Connie sat and listened to the manifestations of these four men! these, and one or two others. That they never seemed to get anywhere didn't trouble her deeply. She liked to hear what they had to say, especially when Tommy was there. It was fun. Instead of men kissing you, and touching you with their bodies, they revealed their minds to you. It was great fun! But what cold minds!

And also it was a little irritating. She had more respect for Michaelis, on whose name they all poured such withering contempt, as a little mongrel arriviste, and uneducated bounder of the worst sort. Mongrel and bounder or not, he jumped to his own conclusions. He didn't merely walk round them with millions of words, in the parade of the life of the mind.

Connie quite liked the life of the mind, and got a great thrill out of it. But she did think it overdid itself a little. She loved being there, amidst the tobacco smoke of those famous evenings of the cronies, as she called them privately to herself. She was infinitely amused, and proud too, that even their talking they could not do, without her silent presence. She had an immense respect for thought . . . and these men, at least, tried to think honestly. But somehow there was a cat, and it wouldn't jump. They all alike talked at something, though what it was for the life of her she couldn't say. It was something that Mick didn't clear, either.

But then Mick wasn't trying to do anything, but just get through his life, and put as much across other people as they tried to put across him. He was really anti-social, which was what Clifford and his cronies had against him. Clifford and his cronies were not anti-social; they were more or less bent on saving mankind, or on instructing it, to say the least.

There was a gorgeous talk on Sunday evening, when the conversation drifted again to love.

'Blest be the tie that binds
Our hearts in kindred something-or-other'–

said Tommy Dukes. 'I'd like to know what the tie is . . . The tie that binds *us* just now is mental friction on one another. And, apart from that, there's damned little tie between us. We bust apart, and say spiteful things about one another, like all the other damned intellectuals in the world. Damned everybodies, as far as that goes, for they all do it. Else we bust apart, and cover up the spiteful things we feel against one another by saying false sugaries. It's a curious thing that the mental life seems to flourish with its roots in spite, ineffable and fathomless spite. Always has been so! Look at Socrates, in Plato, and his bunch round him! The sheer spite of it all, just sheer joy in pulling somebody else to bits . . . Protagoras, or whoever it was! And Alcibiades, and all the other little disciple dogs joining in the fray! I must say it makes one prefer Buddha, quietly sitting under a bo-tree, or Jesus, telling his disciples little Sunday stories, peacefully, and without any mental fireworks. No, there's something wrong with the mental life, radically. It's rooted in spite and envy, envy and spite. Ye shall know the tree by its fruit.'

'I don't think we're altogether so spiteful,' protested Clifford.

'My dear Clifford, think of the way we talk each other over, all of us. I'm rather worse than anybody else, myself. Because I infinitely prefer the spontaneous spite to the concocted sugaries; now they *are* poison; when I begin saying what a fine fellow Clifford is, etc., etc., then poor Clifford is to be pitied. For God's sake, all of you, say spiteful things about me, then I shall know I mean something to you. Don't say sugaries, or I'm done.'

'Oh, but I do think we honestly like one another,' said Hammond.

'I tell you we must . . . we say such spiteful things to one another, about one another, behind our backs! I'm the worst.'

'And I do think you confuse the mental life with the critical activity. I agree with you, Socrates gave the critical activity a grand start, but he did more than that,' said Charlie May, rather magisterially. The cronies had such a curious pomposity under their assumed modesty. It was all so *ex cathedra*, and it all pretended to be so humble.

Dukes refused to be drawn about Socrates.

'That's quite true, criticism and knowledge are not the same thing,' said Hammond.

'They aren't, of course,' chimed in Berry, a brown, shy young man, who had called to see Dukes, and was staying the night.

They all looked at him as if the ass had spoken.

'I wasn't talking about knowledge . . . I was talking about the mental life,' laughed Dukes. 'Real knowledge comes out of the whole corpus of the consciousness; out of your belly and your penis as much as out of your brain and mind. The mind can only analyse and rationalize. Set the mind and the reason to cock it over the rest, and all they can do is to criticize, and make a deadness. I say *all* they can do. It is vastly important. My God, the world needs criticizing today . . . criticizing to death. Therefore let's live the mental life, and glory in our spite, and strip the rotten old show. But, mind you, it's like this: while you *live* your life, you are in some way an organic whole with all life. But once you start the mental life you pluck the apple. You've severed the connexion between the apple and the tree: the organic connexion. And if you've got nothing in your life *but* the mental life, then you yourself are a plucked apple . . . you've fallen off the tree. And then it is a logical necessity to be spiteful, just as it's a natural necessity for a plucked apple to go bad.'

Clifford made big eyes: it was all stuff to him. Connie secretly laughed to herself.

'Well then we're all plucked apples,' said Hammond, rather acidly and petulantly.

'So let's make cider of ourselves,' said Charlie.

'But what do you think of Bolshevism?' put in the brown Berry, as if everything had led up to it.

'Bravo!' roared Charlie. 'What do you think of Bolshevism?'

'Come on! Let's make hay of Bolshevism!' said Dukes.

'I'm afraid Bolshevism is a large question,' said Hammond, shaking his head seriously.

'Bolshevism, it seems to me,' said Charlie, 'is just a superlative hatred of the thing they call the bourgeois; and what the bourgeois is, isn't quite defined. It is Capitalism, among other things. Feelings and emotions are also so decidedly bourgeois that you have to invent a man without them.

'Then the individual, especially the *personal* man, is bourgeois: so he must be suppressed. You must submerge yourselves in the greater thing, the Soviet-social thing. Even an organism is bourgeois: so the ideal must be mechanical. The only thing that is a unit, non-organic, composed of many different, yet equally essential parts, is the machine. Each man a machine-part, and the driving power of the machine, hate . . . hate of the bourgeois. That, to me, is Bolshevism.'

'Absolutely!' said Tommy. 'But also, it seems to me a perfect description of the whole of the industrial ideal. It's the factory-owner's ideal in a nut-shell; except that he would deny that the driving power was hate. Hate it is, all the same: hate of life itself. Just look at these Midlands, if it isn't plainly written up . . . but it's all part of the life of the mind, it's a logical development.'

'I deny that Bolshevism is logical, it rejects the major part of the premises,' said Hammond.

'My dear man, it allows the material premiss; so does the pure mind . . . exclusively.'

'At least Bolshevism has got down to rock bottom,' said Charlie.

'Rock bottom! The bottom that has no bottom! The Bolshevists will have the finest army in the world in a very short time, with the finest mechanical equipment.'

'But this thing can't go on . . . this hate business. There must be a reaction . . .' said Hammond.

'Well, we've been waiting for years . . . we wait longer. Hate's a growing thing like anything else. It's the inevitable outcome of forcing ideas on to life, of forcing one's deepest instincts; our deepest feelings we force according to certain ideas. We drive ourselves with a formula, like a machine. The logical mind pretends to rule the roost, and the roost turns into pure hate. We're all Bolshevists, only we are hypocrites. The Russians are Bolshevists without hypocrisy.'

'But there are many other ways,' said Hammond, 'than the Soviet way. The Bolshevists aren't really intelligent.'

'Of course not. But sometimes it's intelligent to be half-witted: if you want to make your end. Personally, I consider Bolshevism half-witted; but so do I consider our social life in the west half-witted. So I even consider our far-famed mental life half-witted. We're all as cold as cretins, we're all as passionless as idiots. We're all of us Bolshevists, only we give it another name. We think we're gods . . . men like gods! It's just the same as Bolshevism. One has to be human, and have a heart and a penis if one is going to escape being either a god or a Bolshevist . . . for they are the same thing; they're both too good to be true.'

Out of the disapproving silence came Berry's anxious question:
'You do believe in love then, Tommy, don't you?'
'You lovely lad!' said Tommy. 'No, my cherub, nine times out of ten, no!
Love's another of those half-witted performances today. Fellows with swaying
waists fucking little jazz girls with small boy buttocks, like two collar studs! Do
you mean that sort of love? Or the joint-property, make-a-success-of-it, My-
husband-my-wife sort of love? No, my fine fellow, I don't believe in it at all!'
'But you do believe in something?'
'Me? Oh, intellectually I believe in having a good heart, a chirpy penis, a
lively intelligence, and the courage to say "shit!" in front of a lady.'
'Well, you've got them all,' said Berry.
Tommy Dukes roared with laughter. 'You angel boy! If only I had! If only I
had! No; my heart's as numb as a potato, my penis droops and never lifts its
head up, I dare rather cut him clean off than say "shit!" in front of my mother
or my aunt . . . they are real ladies, mind you; and I'm not really intelligent, I'm
only a "mental-lifer". It would be wonderful to be intelligent: then one would
be alive in all the parts mentioned and unmentionable. The penis rouses his
head and says: How do you do?–to any really intelligent person. Renoir said he
painted his pictures with his penis . . . he did too, lovely pictures! I wish I did
something with mine. God! when one can only talk! Another torture added to
Hades! And Socrates started it.'
'There are nice women in the world,' said Connie, lifting her head up and
speaking at last.
The men resented it . . . she should have pretended to hear nothing. They
hated her admitting she had attended so closely to such talk.

> '*My God!*   "If they be not nice to me
> What care I how nice they be?"

'No, it's hopeless! I just simply can't vibrate in unison with a woman.
There's no woman I can really want when I'm faced with her, and I'm
not going to start forcing myself to it . . . My God, no! I'll remain as I am, and
lead the mental life. It's the only honest thing I can do. I can be quite happy
talking to women; but it's all pure, hopelessly pure. Hopelessly pure! What do
you say, Hildebrand, my chicken?'
'It's much less complicated if one stays pure,' said Berry.
'Yes, life is all to simple!'

5

On a frosty morning with a little February sun, Clifford and Connie went for a
walk across the park to the wood. That is, Clifford chuffed in his motor-chair,
and Connie walked beside him.
The hard air was still sulphurous, but they were both used to it. Round the
near horizon went the haze, opalescent with frost and smoke, and on the top lay
the small blue sky; so that it was like being inside an enclosure, always inside.
Life always a dream or a frenzy, inside an enclosure.

The sheep coughed in the rough, sere grass of the park, where frost lay bluish in the sockets of the tufts. Across the park ran a path to the wood-gate, a fine ribbon of pink. Clifford had had it newly gravelled with sifted gravel from the pit-bank. When the rock and refuse of the underworld had burned and given off its sulphur, it turned bright pink, shrimp-coloured on dry days, darker, crab-coloured on wet. Now it was pale shrimp-colour, with a bluish-white hoar of frost. It always pleased Connie, this underfoot of sifted, bright pink. It's an ill wind that brings nobody good.

Clifford steered cautiously down the slope of the knoll from the hall, and Connie kept her hand on the chair. In front lay the wood, the hazel thicket nearest, the purplish density of oaks beyond. From the wood's edge rabbits bobbed and nibbled. Rooks suddenly rose in a black train, and went trailing off over the little sky.

Connie opened the wood-gate, and Clifford puffed slowly through into the broad rising that ran up an incline between the clean-whipped thickets of the hazel. The wood was a remnant of the great forest where Robin Hood hunted, and this riding was an old, old thoroughfare coming across country. But now, of course, it was only a riding through the private wood. The road from Mansfield swerved round to the north.

In the wood everything was motionless, the old leaves on the ground keeping the frost on their underside. A jay called harshly, many little birds fluttered. But there was no game; no pheasants. They had been killed off during the war, and the wood had been left unprotected, till now Clifford had got his game-keeper again.

Clifford loved the wood; he loved the old oak-trees. He felt they were his own through generations. He wanted to protect them. He wanted this place inviolate, shut off from the world.

The chair chuffed slowly up the incline, rocking and jolting on the frozen clods. And suddenly, on the left, came a clearing where there was nothing but a ravel of dead bracken, a thin and spindly sapling leaning here and there, big sawn stumps, showing their tops and their grasping roots, lifeless. And patches of blackness where the woodmen had burned the brushwood and rubbish.

This was one of the places that Sir Geoffrey had cut during the war for trench timber. The whole knoll, which rose softly on the right of the riding, was denuded and strangely forlorn. On the crown of the knoll where the oaks had stood, now was bareness; and from there you could look out over the trees to the colliery railway, and the new works at Stacks Gate. Connie had stood and looked, it was a breach in the pure seclusion of the wood. It let in the world. But she didn't tell Clifford.

This denuded place always made Clifford curiously angry. He had been through the war, had seen what it meant. But he didn't get really angry till he saw this bare hill. He was having it replanted. But it made him hate Sir Geoffrey.

Clifford sat with a fixed face as the chair slowly mounted. When they came to the top of the rise he stopped; he would not risk the long and very jolty down-slope. He sat looking at the greenish sweep of the riding downwards, a clear way through the bracken and oaks. It swerved at the bottom of the hill and disappeared; but it had such a lovely easy curve, of knights riding and ladies on palfreys.

'I consider this is really the heart of England,' said Clifford to Connie, as she sat there in the dim February sunshine.

'Do you?' she said, seating herself, in her blue knitted dress, on a stump by the path.

'I do! this is the old England, the heart of it; and I intend to keep it intact.'

'Oh yes!' said Connie. But, as she said it she heard the eleven-o'clock hooters at Stacks Gate colliery. Clifford was too used to the sound to notice.

'I want this wood perfect . . . untouched. I want nobody to trespass in it,' said Clifford.

There was a certain pathos. The wood still had some of the mystery of wild, old England; but Sir Geoffrey's cuttings during the war had given it a blow. How still the trees were, with their crinkly, innumerable twigs against the sky, and their grey, obstinate trunks rising from the brown bracken! How safely the birds flitted among them! And once there had been deer, and archers, and monks padding along on asses. The place remembered, still remembered.

Clifford sat in the pale sun, with the light on his smooth, rather blond hair, his reddish full face inscrutable.

'I mind more, not having a son, when I come here, than any other time,' he said.

'But the wood is older than your family,' said Connie gently.

'Quite!' said Clifford. 'But we've preserved it. Except for us it would go . . . it would be gone already, like the rest of the forest. One must preserve some of the old England!'

'Must one?' said Connie. 'If it has to be preserved, and preserved against the new England? It's sad, I know.'

'If some of the old England isn't preserved, there'll be no England at all,' said Clifford. 'And we who have this kind of property, and the feeling for it, *must* preserve it.'

There was a sad pause.

'Yes, for a little while,' said Connie.

'For a little while! It's all we can do. We can only do our bit. I feel every man of my family has done his bit here, since we've had the place. One may go against convention, but one must keep up tradition.' Again there was a pause.

'What tradition?' asked Connie.

'The tradition of England! of this!'

'Yes,' she said slowly.

'That's why having a son helps; one is only a link in a chain,' he said.

Connie was not keen on chains, but she said nothing. She was thinking of the curious impersonality of his desire for a son.

'I'm sorry we can't have a son,' she said.

He looked at her steadily, with his full, pale-blue eyes.

'It would almost be a good thing if you had a child by another man,' he said. 'If we brought it up at Wragby, it would belong to us and to the place. I don't believe very intensely in fatherhood. If we had the child to rear, it would be our own, and it would carry on. Don't you think it's worth considering?'

Connie looked up at him at last. The child, her child, was just an 'it' to him. It . . . it . . . it!

'But what about the other man?' she asked.

'Does it matter very much? Do these things really affect us very deeply? . . . You had that lover in Germany . . . what is it now? Nothing almost. It seems to me that it isn't these little acts and little connexions we make in our lives that matter so very much. They pass away, and where are they? Where . . . Where are the snows of yesteryear? . . . It's what endures through one's life that matters; my own life matters to me, in its long continuance and development. But what do the occasional connexions matter? And the occasional sexual connexions especially! If people don't exaggerate them ridiculously, they pass like the mating of birds. And so they should. What does it matter? It's the life-long companionship that matters. It's the living together from day to day, not the sleeping together once or twice. You and I are married, no matter what happens to us. We have the habit of each other. And habit, to my thinking, is more vital than any occasional excitement. The long, slow, enduring thing . . . that's what we live by . . . not the occasional spasm of any sort. Little by little, living together, two people fall into a sort of unison, they vibrate so intricately to one another. That's the real secret of marriage, not sex; at least not the simple function of sex. You and I are interwoven in a marriage. If we stick to that we ought to be able to arrange this sex thing, as we arrange going to the dentist; since fate has given us a checkmate physically there.'

Connie sat and listened in a sort of wonder, and a sort of fear. She did not know if he was right or not. There was Michaelis, whom she loved; so she said to herself. But her love was somehow only an excursion from her marriage with Clifford; the long, slow habit of intimacy, formed through years of suffering and patience. Perhaps the human soul needs excursions, and must not be denied them. But the point of an excursion is that you come home again.

'And wouldn't you mind *what* man's child I had?' she asked.

'Why, Connie, I should trust your natural instinct of decency and selection. You just wouldn't let the wrong sort of fellow touch you.'

She thought of Michaelis! He was absolutely Clifford's idea of the wrong sort of fellow.

'But men and women may have different feelings about the wrong sort of fellow,' she said.

'No,' he replied. 'You care for me. I don't believe you would ever care for a man who was purely antipathetic to me. Your rhythm wouldn't let you.'

She was silent. Logic might be unanswerable because it was so absolutely wrong.

'And should you expect me to tell you?' she asked, glancing up at him almost furtively.

'Not at all, I'd better not know . . . But you do agree with me, don't you, that the casual sex thing is nothing, compared to the long life lived together? Don't you think one can just subordinate the sex thing to the necessities of a long life? Just use it, since that's what we're driven to? After all, *do* these temporary excitements matter? Isn't the whole problem of life the slow building up of an integral personality, through the years? living an integrated life? There's no point in a disintegrated life. If lack of sex is going to disintegrate you, then go out and have a love-affair. If lack of a child is going to disintegrate you, then have a child if you possibly can. But only do these things so that you have an integrated life, that makes a long harmonious thing. And you and I can do that together . . . don't you think? . . . if we adapt ourselves to the necessities, and at the same time weave the adaptation together into a piece with our steadily-lived life. Don't you agree?'

Connie was a little overwhelmed by his words. She knew he was right theoretically. But when she actually touched her steadily-lived life with him she . . . hesitated. Was it actually her destiny to go on weaving herself into his life all the rest of her life? Nothing else?

Was it just that? She was to be content to weave a steady life with him, all one fabric, but perhaps brocaded with the occasional flower of an adventure. But how could she know what she would feel next year? How could one ever know? How could one say Yes? for years and years? The little yes, gone on a breath! Why should one be pinned down by that butterfly word? Of course it had to flutter away and be gone, to be followed by other yes's and no's! Like the straying of butterflies.

'I think you're right, Clifford. And as far as I can see I agree with you. Only life may turn quite a new face on it all.'

'But until life turns a new face on it all, you do agree?'

'Oh yes! I think I do, really.'

She was watching a brown spaniel that had run out of a side-path, and was looking towards them with lifted nose, making a soft, fluffy bark. A man with a gun strode swiftly, softly out after the dog, facing their way as if about to attack them; then stopped instead, saluted, and was turning downhill. It was only the new game-keeper, but he had frightened Connie, he seemed to emerge with such a swift menace. That was how she had seen him, like the sudden rush of a threat out of nowhere.

He was a man in dark green velveteens and gaiters . . . the old style, with a red face and red moustache and distant eyes. He was going quickly downhill.

'Mellors!' called Clifford.

The man faced lightly round, and saluted with a quick little gesture, a soldier!

'Will you turn the chair round and get it started? That makes it easier,' said Clifford.

The man at once slung his gun over his shoulder, and came forward with the same curious swift, yet soft movements, as if keeping invisible. He was moderately tall and lean, and was silent. He did not look at Connie at all, only at the chair.

'Connie, this is the new game-keeper, Mellors. You haven't spoken to her ladyship yet, Mellors?'

'No, Sir!' came the ready, neutral words.

The man lifted his hat as he stood, showing his thick, almost fair hair. He stared straight into Connie's eyes, with a perfect, fearless, impersonal look, as if he wanted to see what she was like. He made her feel shy. She bent her head to him shyly, and he changed his hat to his left hand and made her a slight bow, like a gentleman; but he said nothing at all. He remained for a moment still, with his hat in his hand.

'But you've been here some time, haven't you?' Connie said to him.

'Eight months, Madam . . . your Ladyship!' he corrected himself calmly.

'And do you like it?'

She looked him in the eyes. His eyes narrowed a little, with irony, perhaps with impudence.

'Why, yes, thank you, your Ladyship! I was reared here. . . .' He gave another slight bow, turned, put his hat on, and strode to take hold of the chair. His voice on the last words had fallen into the heavy broad drag of the dialect . . . perhaps also in mockery, because there had been no trace of dialect before. He might almost be a gentleman. Anyhow, he was a curious, quick, separate fellow, alone, but sure of himself.

Clifford started the little engine, the man carefully turned the chair, and set it nose-forwards to the incline that curved gently to the dark hazel thicket.

'Is that all then, Sir Clifford?' asked the man.

'No, you'd better come along in case she sticks. The engine isn't really strong enough for the uphill work.' The man glanced round for his dog . . . a thoughtful glance. The spaniel looked at him and faintly moved its tail. A little smile, mocking or teasing her, yet gentle, came into his eyes for a moment, then faded away, and his face was expressionless. They went fairly quickly down the slope, the man with his hand on the rail of the chair, steadying it. He looked like a free soldier rather than a servant. And something about him reminded Connie of Tommy Dukes.

When they came to the hazel grove, Connie suddenly ran forward, and opened the gate into the park. As she stood holding it, the two men looked at her in passing. Clifford critically, the other man with a curious, cool wonder; impersonally wanting to see what she looked like. And she saw in his blue, impersonal eyes a look of suffering and detachment, yet a certain warmth. But why was he so aloof, apart?

Clifford stopped the chair, once through the gate, and the man came quickly, courteously, to close it.

'Why did you run to open?' asked Clifford in his quiet, calm voice, that showed he was displeased. 'Mellors would have done it.'

'I thought you would go straight ahead,' said Connie.

'And leave you to run after us?' said Clifford.

'Oh, well, I like to run sometimes!'

Mellors took the chair again, looking perfectly unheeding, yet Connie felt he noted everything. As he pushed the chair up the steepish rise of the knoll in the park, he breathed rather quickly, through parted lips. He was rather frail really. Curiously full of vitality, but a little frail and quenched. Her woman's instinct sensed it.

Connie fell back, let the chair go on. The day had greyed over; the small blue sky that had poised low on its circular rims of haze was closed in again, the lid was down, there was a raw coldness. It was going to snow. All grey, all grey! the world looked worn out.

The chair waited at the top of the pink path. Clifford looked round for Connie.

'Not tired, are you?' he asked.

'Oh, no!' she said.

But she was. A strange, weary yearning, a dissatisfaction had started in her. Clifford did not notice: those were not things he was aware of. But the stranger knew. To Connie, everything in her world and life seemed worn out, and her dissatisfaction was older than the hills.

They came to the house, and around to the back, where there were no steps. Clifford managed to swing himself over on to the low, wheeled house-chair; he was very strong and agile with his arms. Then Connie lifted the burden of his dead legs after him.

The keeper, waiting at attention to be dismissed, watched everything narrowly, missing nothing. He went pale, with a sort of fear, when he saw Connie lifting the inert legs of the man in her arms, into the other chair, Clifford pivoting round as she did so. He was frightened.

'Thanks, then, for the help, Mellors,' said Clifford casually, as he began to wheel down the passage to the servants' quarters.

'Nothing else, Sir?' came the neutral voice, like one in a dream.

'Nothing, good morning!'

'Good morning, Sir.'

'Good morning! it was kind of you to push the chair up that hill . . . I hope it wasn't heavy for you,' said Connie, looking back at the keeper outside the door. His eyes came to hers in an instant, as if wakened up. He was aware of her. 'Oh no, not heavy!' he said quickly. Then his voice dropped again into the broad sound of the vernacular: 'Good mornin' to your Ladyship!'

'Who is your game-keeper?' Connie asked at lunch.

'Mellors! You saw him,' said Clifford.

'Yes, but where did he come from?'

'Nowhere! He was a Tevershall boy . . . son of a collier, I believe.'

'And was he a collier himself?'

'Blacksmith on the pit-bank, I believe: overhead smith. But he was keeper here for two years before the war . . . before he joined up. My father always had a good opinion of him, so when he came back, and went to the pit for a blacksmith's job, I just took him back here as keeper. I was really very glad to get him . . . it's almost impossible to find a good man round here for a game-keeper . . . and it needs a man who knows the people.'

'And isn't he married?'

'He was. But his wife went off with . . . with various men . . . but finally with a collier at Stacks Gate, and I believe she's living there still.'

'So this man is alone?'

'More or less! He has a mother in the village . . . and a child, I believe.'

Clifford looked at Connie, with his pale, slightly prominent blue eyes, in which a certain vagueness was coming. He seemed alert in the foreground, but the background was like the Midlands atmosphere, haze, smoky mist. And the haze seemed to be creeping forward. So when he stared at Connie in his peculiar way, giving her his peculiar, precise information, she felt all the background of his mind filling up with mist, with nothingness. And it frightened her. It made him seem impersonal, almost to idiocy.

And dimly she realized one of the great laws of the human soul: that when the emotional soul receives a wounding shock, which does not kill the body, the soul seems to recover as the body recovers. But this is only appearance. It is really only the mechanism of the reassumed habit. Slowly, slowly the wound to the soul begins to make itself felt, like a bruise, which only slowly deepens its terrible ache, till it fills all the psyche. And when we think we have recovered and forgotten, it is then that the terrible after-effects have to be encountered at their worst.

So it was with Clifford. Once he was 'well', once he was back at Wragby, and writing his stories, and feeling sure of life, in spite of all, he seemed to forget, and to have recovered all his equanimity. But now, as the years went by, slowly, slowly, Connie felt the bruise of fear and horror coming up, and spreading in him. For a time it had been so deep as to be numb, as it were non-existent. Now slowly it began to assert itself in a spread of fear, almost paralysis. Mentally he still was alert. But the paralysis, the bruise of the too-great shock, was gradually spreading in his affective self.

And as it spread in him, Connie felt it spread in her. An inward dread, an emptiness, an indifference to everything gradually spread in her soul. When Clifford was roused, he could still talk brilliantly and, as it were, command the future: as when, in the wood, he talked about her having a child, and giving an heir to Wragby. But the day after, all the brilliant words seemed like dead leaves, crumpling up and turning to powder, meaning really nothing, blown away on any gust of wind. They were not the leafy words of an effective life, young with energy and belonging to the tree. They were the hosts of fallen leaves of a life that is ineffectual.

So it seemed to her everywhere. The colliers at Tevershall were talking again of a strike, and it seemed to Connie there again it was not a manifestation of energy, it was the bruise of the war that had been in abeyance, slowly rising to the surface and creating the great ache of unrest, and stupor of discontent. The bruise went deep, deep, deep . . . the bruise of the false inhuman war. It would take many years for the living blood of the generations to dissolve the vast black clot of bruised blood, deep inside their souls and bodies. And it would need a new hope.

Poor Connie! As the years drew on it was the fear of nothingness in her life that affected her. Clifford's mental life and hers gradually began to feel like nothingness. Their marriage, their integrated life based on a habit of intimacy, that he talked about: there were days when it all became utterly blank and nothing. It was words, just so many words. The only reality was nothingness, and over it a hypocrisy of words.

There was Clifford's success: the bitch-goddess! It was true he was almost famous, and his books brought him in a thousand pounds. His photograph appeared everywhere. There was a bust of him in one of the galleries, and a portrait of him in two galleries. He seemed the most modern of modern voices. With his uncanny lame instinct for publicity, he had become in four or five years one of the best known of the young 'intellectuals'. Where the intellect came in, Connie did not quite see. Clifford was really clever at that slightly humorous analysis of people and motives which leaves everything in bits at the end. But it was rather like puppies tearing the sofa cushions to bits; except that it was not young and playful, but curiously old, and rather obstinately conceited. It was weird and it was nothing. This was the feeling that echoed and re-echoed at the bottom of Connie's soul: it was all nothing, a wonderful display of nothingness. At the same time a display. A display! a display! a display!

Michaelis had seized upon Clifford as the central figure for a play; already he had sketched in the plot, and written the first act. For Michaelis was even better than Clifford at making a display of nothingness. It was the last bit of passion left in these men: the passion for making a display. Sexually they were passionless, even dead. And now it was not money that Michaelis was after. Clifford had never been primarily out for money, though he made it where he could, for money is the seal and stamp of success. And success was what they wanted. They wanted, both of them, to make a real display . . . a man's own very display of himself, that should capture for a time the vast populace.

It was strange . . . the prostitution to the bitch-goddess. To Connie, since she was really outside of it, and since she had grown numb to the thrill of it, it was again nothingness. Even the prostitution to the bitch-goddess was nothingness, though the men prostituted themselves innumerable times. Nothingness even that.

Michaelis wrote to Clifford about the play. Of course she knew about it long ago. And Clifford was again thrilled. He was going to be displayed again this time, somebody was going to display him, and to advantage. He invited Michaelis down to Wragby with Act I.

Michaelis came: in summer, in a pale-coloured suit and white suède gloves, with mauve orchids for Connie, very lovely, and Act I was a great success. Even Connie was thrilled . . . thrilled to what bit of marrow she had left. And

Michaelis, thrilled by his power to thrill, was really wonderful . . . and quite beautiful, in Connie's eyes. She saw in him that ancient motionless of a race that can't be disillusioned any more, an extreme, perhaps, of impurity that is pure. On the far side of his supreme prostitution to the bitch-goddess he seemed pure, pure as an African ivory mask that dreams impurity into purity, in its ivory curves and planes.

His moment of sheer thrill with the two Chatterleys, when he simply carried Connie and Clifford away, was one of the supreme moments of Michaelis's life. He had succeeded; he had carried them away. Even Clifford was temporarily in love with him . . . if that is the way one can put it.

So next morning Mick was more uneasy than ever: restless, devoured, with his hands restless in his trousers pockets. Connie had not visited him in the night . . . and he had not known where to find her. Coquetry! . . . at his moment of triumph.

He went up to her sitting-room in the morning. She knew he would come. And his restlessness was evident. He asked her about his play . . . did she think it good? He *had* to hear it praised: that affected him with the last thin thrill of passion beyond any sexual orgasm. And she praised it rapturously. Yet all the while, at the bottom of her soul, she knew it was nothing.

'Look here!' he said suddenly at last. 'Why don't you and I make a clean thing of it? Why don't we marry?'

'But I am married,' she said, amazed, and yet feeling nothing.

'Oh that! . . . he'll divorce you all right . . . Why don't you and I marry? I want to marry. I know it would be the best thing for me . . . marry and lead a regular life. I lead the deuce of a life, simply tearing myself to pieces. Look here, you and I, we're made for one another . . . hand and glove. Why don't we marry? Do you see any reason why we shouldn't?'

Connie looked at him amazed: and yet she felt nothing. These men, they were all alike, they left everything out. They just went off from the top of their heads as if they were squibs, and expected you to be carried heavenwards along with their own thin sticks.

'But I am married already,' she said. 'I can't leave Clifford, you know.'

'Why not? but why not?' he cried. 'He'll hardly know you've gone, after six months. He doesn't know that anybody exists, except himself. Why the man has no use for you at all, as far as I can see; he's entirely wrapped up in himself.'

Connie felt there was truth in this. But she also felt that Mick was hardly making a display of selflessness.

'Aren't all men wrapped up in themselves?' she asked.

'Oh, more or less, I allow. A man's got to be, to get through. But that's not the point. The point is, what sort of a time can a man give a woman? Can he give her a damn good time, or can't he? If he can't he's no right to the woman . . .' He paused and gazed at her with his full, hazel eyes, almost hypnotic. 'Now I consider,' he added, 'I can give a woman the darndest good time she can ask for. I think I can guarantee myself.'

'And what sort of a good time?' asked Connie, gazing on him still with a sort of amazement, that looked like thrill; and underneath feeling nothing at all.

'Every sort of a good time, damn it, every sort! Dress, jewels up to a point, any nightclub you like, know anybody you want to know, live the pace . . . travel and be somebody wherever you go . . . Darn it, every sort of good time.'

He spoke it almost in a brilliancy of triumph, and Connie looked at him as if dazzled, and really feeling nothing at all. Hardly even the surface of her mind was tickled at the glowing prospects he offered her. Hardly even her most outside self responded, that at any other time would have been thrilled. She just got no feeling from it, she couldn't 'go off'. She just sat and stared and looked dazzled, and felt nothing, only somewhere she smelt the extraordinarily unpleasant smell of the bitch-goddess.

Mick sat on tenterhooks, leaning forward in his chair, glaring at her almost hysterically: and whether he was more anxious out of vanity for her to say Yes! or whether he was more panic-stricken for fear she *should* say Yes!–who can tell?

'I should have to think about it,' she said. 'I couldn't say now. It may seem to you Clifford doesn't count, but he does. When you think how disabled he is . . .'

'Oh damn it all! If a fellow's going to trade on his disabilities, I might begin to say how lonely I am, and always have been, and all the rest of my-eye-Betty-Martin sob-stuff! Damn it all, if a fellow's got nothing but disabilities to recommend him . . .'

He turned aside, working his hands furiously in his trousers pockets. That evening he said to her:

'You're coming round to my room tonight, aren't you? I don't darn know where your room is.'

'All right!' she said.

He was a more excited lover that night, with his strange, small boy's frail nakedness. Connie found it impossible to come to her crisis before he had really finished his. And he roused a certain craving passion in her, with his little boy's nakedness and softness; she had to go on after he had finished, in the wild tumult and heaving of her loins, while he heroically kept himself up, and present in her, with all his will and self-offering, till she brought about her own crisis, with weird little cries.

When at last he drew away from her, he said, in a bitter, almost sneering little voice:

'You couldn't go off at the same time as a man, could you? You'd have to bring yourself off! You'd have to run the show!'

This little speech, at the moment, was one of the shocks of her life. Because that passive sort of giving himself was so obviously his only real mode of intercourse.

'What do you mean?' she said.

'You know what I mean. You keep on for hours after I've gone off . . . and I have to hang on with my teeth till you bring yourself off by your own exertions.'

She was stunned by this unexpected piece of brutality, at the moment when she was glowing with a sort of pleasure beyond words, and a sort of love for him. Because, after all, like so many modern men, he was finished almost before he had begun. And that forced a woman to be active.

'But you want me to go on, to get my own satisfaction?' she said.

He laughed grimly: 'I want it!' he said. 'That's good! I want to hang on with my teeth clenched, while you go for me!'

'But don't you?' she insisted.

He avoided the question. 'All the darned women are like that,' he said. 'Either they don't go off at all, as if they were dead in there . . . or else they wait till a chap's really done, and then they start in to bring themselves off, and a chap's got to hang on. I never had a woman yet who went off just at the same moment as I did.'

Connie only half heard this piece of novel, masculine information. She was only stunned by his feeling against her . . . his incomprehensible brutality. She felt so innocent.

'But you want me to have my satisfaction too, don't you?' she repeated.

'Oh, all right! I'm quite willing. But I'm darned if hanging on waiting for a woman to go off is much of a game for a man . . .'

This speech was one of the crucial blows of Connie's life. It killed something in her. She had not been so very keen on Michaelis; till he started it, she did not want him. It was as if she never positively wanted him. But once he had started her, it seemed only natural for her to come to her own crisis with him. Almost she had loved him for it . . . almost that night she loved him, and wanted to marry him.

Perhaps instinctively he knew it, and that was why he had to bring down the whole show with a smash; the house of cards. Her whole sexual feeling for him, or for any man, collapsed that night. Her life fell apart from his as completely as if he had never existed.

And she went through the days drearily. There was nothing now but this empty treadmill of what Clifford called the integrated life, the long living together of two people, who are in the habit of being in the same house with one another.

Nothingness! To accept the great nothingness of life seemed to be the one end of living. All the many busy and important little things that make up the grand sum-total of nothingness!

6

'Why don't men and women really like one another nowadays?' Connie asked Tommy Dukes, who was more or less her oracle.

'Oh, but they do! I don't think since the human species was invented, there has ever been a time when men and women have liked one another as much as they do today. Genuine liking! Take myself . . . I really *like* women better than men; they are braver, one can be more frank with them.'

Connie pondered this.

'Ah, yes, but you never have anything to do with them!' she said.

'I? What am I doing but talking perfectly sincerely to a woman at this moment?'

'Yes, talking . . .'

'And what more could I do if you were a man, than talk perfectly sincerely to you?'

'Nothing perhaps. But a woman . . .'

'A woman wants you to like her and talk to her, and at the same time love her and desire her; and it seems to me the two things are mutually exclusive.'

'But they shouldn't be!'

'No doubt water ought not to be so wet as it is; it overdoes it in wetness. But there it is! I like women and talk to them, and therefore I don't love them and desire them. The two things don't happen at the same time in me.'

'I think they ought to.'

'All right. The fact that things ought to be something else than what they are, is not my department.'

Connie considered this, 'It isn't true,' she said. 'Men can love women and talk to them. I don't see how they can love them *without* talking, and being friendly and intimate. How can they?'

'Well,' he said. 'I don't know. What's the use of my generalizing? I only know my own case. I like women, but I don't desire them. I like talking to them; but talking to them, though it makes me intimate in one direction, sets me poles apart from them as far as kissing is concerned. So there you are! But don't take me as a general example, probably I'm just a special case: one of the men who like women, but don't love women, and even hate them if they force me into a pretence of love, or an entangled appearance.'

'But doesn't it make you sad?'

'Why should it? Not a bit! I look at Charlie May, and the rest of the men who have affairs . . . No, I don't envy them a bit! If fate sent me a woman I wanted, well and good. Since I don't know any woman I want, and never see one . . . why, I presume I'm cold, and really *like* some women very much.'

'Do you like me?'

'Very much! And you see there's no question of kissing between us, is there?'

'None at all!' said Connie. 'But oughtn't there to be?'

'*Why*, in God's name? I like Clifford, but what would you say if I went and kissed him?'

'But isn't there a difference?'

'Where does it lie, as far as we're concerned? We're all intelligent human beings, and the male and female business is in abeyance. Just in abeyance. How would you like me to start acting up like a continental male at this moment, and parading the sex thing?'

'I should hate it.'

'Well then! I tell you, if I'm really a male thing at all, I never run across the female of my species. And I don't miss her, I just *like* women. Who's going to force me into loving or pretending to love them, working up the sex game?'

'No, I'm not. But isn't something wrong?'

'You may feel it, I don't.'

'Yes, I feel something is wrong between men and women. A woman has no glamour for a man any more.'

'Has a man for a woman?'

She pondered the other side of the question.

'Not much,' she said truthfully.

'Then let's leave it all alone, and just be decent and simple, like proper human beings with one another. Be damned to the artificial sex-compulsion! I refuse it!'

Connie knew he was right, really. Yet it left her feeling so forlorn, so forlorn and stray. Like a chip on a dreary pond, she felt. What was the point, of her or anything?

It was her youth which rebelled. These men seemed so old and cold. Everything seemed old and cold. And Michaelis let one down so; he was no good. The men didn't want one; they just didn't really want a woman, even Michaelis didn't.

And the bounders who pretended they did, and started working the sex game, they were worse than ever.

It was just dismal, and one had to put up with it. It was quite true, men had no real glamour for a woman: if you could fool yourself into thinking they had, even as she had fooled herself over Michaelis, that was the best you could do. Meanwhile you just lived on and there was nothing to it. She understood perfectly well why people had cocktail parties, and jazzed, and Charlestoned till they were ready to drop. You had to take it out some way or other, your youth, or it ate you up. But what a ghastly thing, this youth! You felt as old as Methuselah, and yet the thing fizzed somehow, and didn't let you be comfortable. A mean sort of life! And no prospect! She almost wished she had gone off with Mick, and made her life one long cocktail party, and jazz evening. Anyhow that was better than just mooning yourself into the grave.

On one of her bad days she went out alone to walk in the wood, ponderously, heeding nothing, not even noticing where she was. The report of a gun not far off startled and angered her.

Then, as she went, she heard voices, and recoiled. People! She didn't want people. But her quick ear caught another sound, and she roused; it was a child sobbing. At once she attended; someone was ill-treating a child. She strode swinging down the wet drive, her sullen resentment uppermost. She felt just prepared to make a scene.

Turning the corner, she saw two figures in the drive beyond her, the keeper, and a little girl in a purple coat and moleskin cap, crying.

'Ah, shut it up, tha false little bitch!' came the man's angry voice, and the child sobbed louder.

Constance strode nearer, with blazing eyes. The man turned and looked at her, saluting coolly, but he was pale with anger.

'What's the matter? Why is she crying?' demanded Constance, peremptory but a little breathless.

A faint smile like a sneer came on the man's face. 'Nay, yo' mun ax 'er,' he replied callously, in broad vernacular.

Connie felt as if he had hit her in the face, and she changed colour. Then she gathered her defiance, and looked at him, her dark blue eyes blazing rather vaguely.

'I asked *you*,' she panted.

He gave a queer little bow, lifting his hat. 'You did, your Ladyship,' he said; then, with a return to the vernacular: 'but I canna tell yer.' And he became a soldier, inscrutable, only pale with annoyance.

Connie turned to the child, a ruddy, black-haired thing of nine or ten. 'What is it, dear? Tell me why you're crying!' she said, with the conventionalized sweetness suitable. More violent sobs, self-conscious. Still more sweetness on Connie's part.

'There, there, don't you cry! Tell me what they've done to you!' ... an intense tenderness of tone. At the same time she felt in the pocket of her knitted jacket, and luckily found a sixpence.

'Don't you cry then!' she said, bending in front of the child. 'See what I've got for you!'

Sobs, snuffles, a fist taken from a blubbered face, and a black shrewd eye cast for a second on the sixpence. Then more sobs, but subduing. 'There, tell me what's the matter, tell me!' said Connie, putting the coin into the child's chubby hand, which closed over it.

'It's the . . . it's the . . . pussy!'

Shudders of subsiding sobs.

'What pussy, dear?'

After a silence the shy fist, clenching on sixpence, pointed into the bramble brake.

'There!'

Connie looked, and there, sure enough, was a big black cat, stretched out grimly, with a bit of blood on it.

'Oh!' she said in repulsion.

'A poacher, your Ladyship,' said the man satirically.

She glanced at him angrily. 'No wonder the child cried,' she said, 'if you shot it when she was there. No wonder she cried!'

He looked into Connie's eyes, laconic, contemptuous, not hiding his feelings. And again Connie flushed; she felt she had been making a scene, the man did not respect her.

'What is your name?' she said playfully to the child. 'Won't you tell me your name?'

Sniffs; then very affectedly in a piping voice: 'Connie Mellors!'

'Connie Mellors! Well, that's a nice name! And did you come out with your Daddy, and he shot a pussy? But it was a bad pussy!'

The child looked at her, with bold, dark eyes of scrutiny, sizing her up, and her condolence.

'I wanted to stop with my Gran,' said the little girl.

'Did you? But where is your Gran?'

The child lifted an arm, pointing down the drive. 'At th' cottidge.'

'At the cottage! And would you like to go back to her?'

Sudden, shuddering quivers of reminiscent sobs. 'Yes!'

'Come then, shall I take you? Shall I take you to your Gran? Then your Daddy can do what he has to do.' She turned to the man. 'It is your little girl, isn't it?'

He saluted, and made a slight movement of the head in affirmation.

'I suppose I can take her to the cottage?' asked Connie.

'If your Ladyship wishes.'

Again he looked into her eyes, with that calm, searching detached glance. A man very much alone, and on his own.

'Would you like to come with me to the cottage, to your Gran, dear?'

The child peeped up again. 'Yes!' she simpered.

Connie disliked her; the spoilt, false little female. Nevertheless she wiped her face and took her hand. The keeper saluted in silence.

'Good morning!' said Connie.

It was nearly a mile to the cottage, and Connie senior was well bored by Connie junior by the time the game-keeper's picturesque little home was in sight. The child was already as full to the brim with tricks as a little monkey, and so self-assured.

At the cottage the door stood open, and there was a rattling heard inside. Connie lingered, the child slipped her hand, and ran indoors.

'Gran! Gran!'

'Why, are yer back a'ready!'

The grandmother had been blackleading the stove, it was Saturday morning. She came to the door in her sacking apron, a blacklead-brush in her hand, and a black smudge on her nose. She was a little, rather dry woman.

'Why, whatever?' she said, hastily wiping her arm across her face as she saw Connie standing outside.

'Good morning!' said Connie. 'She was crying, so I just brought her home.'

The grandmother looked around swiftly at the child:

'Why, wheer was yer Dad?'

The little girl clung to her grandmother's skirts and simpered.

'He was there,' said Connie, 'but he'd shot a poaching cat, and the child was upset.'

Oh, you'd no right t'ave bothered, Lady Chatterley, I'm sure! I'm sure it was very good of you, but you shouldn't 'ave bothered. Why, did ever you see!'–and the old woman turned to the child: 'Fancy Lady Chatterley takin' all that trouble over yer! Why, she shouldn't 'ave bothered!'

'It was no bother, just a walk,' said Connie smiling.

'Why, I'm sure 'twas very kind of you, I must say! So she was crying! I knew there'd be something afore they got far. She's frightened of 'im, that's wheer it is. Seems 'e's almost a stranger to 'er, fair a stranger, and I don't think they're two as'd hit it off very easy. He's got funny ways.'

Connie didn't know what to say.

'Look, Gran!' simpered the child.

The old woman looked down at the sixpence in the little girl's hand.

'An' sixpence an' all! Oh, your Ladyship, you shouldn't, you shouldn't. Why, isn't Lady Chatterley good to yer! My word, you're a lucky girl this morning!'

She pronounced the name, as all the people did: Chat'ley.–'Isn't Lady Chat'ley *good* to you!'–Connie couldn't help looking at the old woman's nose, and the latter again vaguely wiped her face with the back of her wrist, but missed the smudge.

Connie was moving away . . . 'Well, thank you ever so much, Lady Chat'ley, I'm sure. Say thank you to Lady Chat'ley!'–this last to the child.

'Thank you,' piped the child.

'There's a dear!' laughed Connie, and she moved away, saying 'Good morning', heartily relieved to get away from the contact. Curious, she thought, that that thin, proud man should have that little, sharp woman for a mother!

And the old woman, as soon as Connie had gone, rushed to the bit of mirror in the scullery, and looked at her face. Seeing it, she stamped her foot with impatience. 'Of *course* she had to catch me in my coarse apron, and a dirty face! Nice idea she'd get of me!'

Connie went slowly home to Wragby. 'Home!' . . . it was a warm word to use for that great, weary warren. But then it was a word that had had its day. It was somehow cancelled. All the great words, it seemed to Connie, were cancelled for her generation: love, joy, happiness, home, mother, father, husband, all these great, dynamic words were half dead now, and dying from day to day. Home was a place you lived in, love was a thing you didn't fool yourself about, joy was a word you applied to a good Charleston, happiness was a term of hypocrisy used to bluff other people, a father was an individual who enjoyed his own existence, a husband was a man you lived with and kept going in spirits. As for sex, the last of the great words, it was just a cocktail term for an excitement that bucked you up for a while, then left you more raggy than ever. Frayed! It was as if the very material you were made of was cheap stuff, and was fraying out to nothing.

All that really remained was a stubborn stoicism: and in that there was a certain pleasure. In the very experience of the nothingness of life, phase after phase, *étape* after *étape*, there was a certain grisly satisfaction. So that's *that*! Always this was the last utterance: home, love, marriage, Michaelis: So that's *that*! And when one died, the last words to life would be: So that's *that*! Money? Perhaps one couldn't say the same there. Money one always wanted. Money, Success, the bitch-goddess, as Tommy Dukes persisted in calling it, after Henry James, that was a permanent necessity. You couldn't spend your last sou, and say finally: So that's *that*! No, if you lived even another ten minutes, you wanted a few more sous for something or other. Just to keep the business mechanically going, you needed money. You had to have it. Money you *have* to have. You needn't really have anything else. So that's that!

Since, of course, it's not your own fault you are alive. Once you are alive, money is a necessity, and the only absolute necessity. All the rest you can get along without, at a pinch. But not money. Emphatically, that's *that*!

She thought of Michaelis, and the money she might have had with him; and even that she didn't want. She preferred the lesser amount which she helped Clifford to make by his writing. That she actually helped to make.–'Clifford and I together, we make twelve hundred a year out of writing'; so she put it to herself. Make money! Make it! Out of nowhere. Wring it out of the thin air! The last feat to be humanly proud of! The rest all-my-eye-Betty-Martin.

So she plodded home to Clifford, to join forces with him again, to make another story out of nothingness: and a story meant money. Clifford seemed to care very much whether his stories were considered first-class literature or not. Strictly, she didn't care. Nothing in it! said her father. Twelve hundred pounds last year! was the retort simple and final.

If you were young, you just set your teeth, and bit on and held on, till the money began to flow from the invisible; it was a question of power. It was a question of will; a subtle, subtle, powerful emanation of will out of yourself brought back to you the mysterious nothingness of money; a word on a bit of paper. It was a sort of magic, certainly it was triumph. The bitch-goddess! Well, if one had to prostitute oneself, let it be to a bitch-goddess! One could always despise her even while one prostituted oneself to her, which was good.

Clifford, of course, had still many childish taboos and fetishes. He wanted to be thought 'really good', which was all cock-a-hoopy nonsense. What was really good was what actually caught on. It was no good being really good and getting left with it. It seemed as if most of the 'really good' men just missed the bus. After all you only lived one life, and if you missed the bus, you were just left on the pavement, along with the rest of the failures.

Connie was contemplating a winter in London with Clifford, next winter. He and she had caught the bus all right, so they might as well ride on top for a bit and show it.

The worst of it was, Clifford tended to become vague, absent, and to fall into fits of vacant depression. It was the wound to his psyche coming out. But it made Connie want to scream. Oh God, if the mechanism of the consciousness itself was going to go wrong, then what was one to do? Hang it all, one did one's bit! Was one to be let down *absolutely*?

Sometimes she wept bitterly, but even as she wept she was saying to herself: Silly fool, wetting hankies! As if that would get you anywhere!

Since Michaelis, she had made up her mind she wanted nothing. That seemed the simplest solution of the otherwise insoluble. She wanted nothing more than what she'd got; only she wanted to get ahead with what she'd got: Clifford, the stories, Wragby, the Lady-Chatterley business, money and fame, such as it was . . . she wanted to go ahead with it all. Love, sex, all that sort of stuff, just water-ices! Lick it up and forget it. If you don't hang on to it in your mind, it's nothing. Sex especially . . . nothing! Make up your mind to it, and you've solved the problem. Sex and a cocktail: they both lasted about as long, had the same effect, and amounted to about the same thing.

But a child, a baby! That was still one of the sensations. She would venture very gingerly on that experiment. There was the man to consider, and it was curious, there wasn't a man in the world whose children you wanted. Mick's children! Repulsive thought! As lief have a child to a rabbit! Tommy Dukes? . . . he was very nice, but somehow you couldn't associate him with a baby, another generation. He ended in himself. And out of all the rest of Clifford's pretty wide acquaintance, there was not a man who did not rouse her contempt, when she thought of having a child by him. There were several who would have been quite possible as lovers, even Mick. But to let them breed a child on you! Ugh! Humiliation and abomination.

So that was that!

Nevertheless, Connie had the child at the back of her mind. Wait! wait! She would sift the generations of men through her sieve, and see if she couldn't find one who would do. – 'Go ye into the streets and byways of Jerusalem, and see if ye can find a *man*.' It had been impossible to find a man in the Jerusalem of the prophet, though there were thousands of male humans. But a *man*! *C'est une autre chose!*

She had an idea that he would have to be a foreigner: not an Englishman, still less an Irishman. A real foreigner.

But wait! wait! Next winter she would get Clifford to London; the following winter she would get him abroad to the South of France, Italy. Wait! She was in no hurry about the child. That was her own private affair, and the one point on which, in her own queer, female way, she was serious to the bottom of her soul. She was not going to risk any chance comer, not she! One might take a lover almost at any moment, but a man who should beget a child on one . . . wait! wait! it's a very different matter. – 'Go ye into the streets and byways of Jerusalem . . .' It was not a question of love; it was a question of a *man*. Why, one might even rather hate him, personally. Yet if he was the man, what would one's personal hate matter? This business concerned another part of oneself.

It had rained as usual, and the paths were too sodden for Clifford's chair, but Connie would go out. She went out alone every day now, mostly in the wood, where she was really alone. She saw nobody there.

This day, however, Clifford wanted to send a message to the keeper, and as the boy was laid up with influenza, somebody always seemed to have influenza at Wragby, Connie said she would call at the cottage.

The air was soft and dead, as if all the world were slowly dying. Grey and clammy and silent, even from the shuffling of the collieries, for the pits were working short time, and today they were stopped altogether. The end of all things!

In the wood all was utterly inert and motionless, only great drops fell from the bare boughs, with a hollow little crash. For the rest, among the old trees was depth within depth of grey, hopeless inertia, silence, nothingness.

Connie walked dimly on. From the old wood came an ancient melancholy, somehow soothing to her, better than the harsh insentence of the outer world. She liked the *inwardness* of the remnant of forest, the unspeaking reticence of the old trees. They seemed a very power of silence, and yet a vital presence. They, too, were waiting: obstinately, stoically waiting, and giving off a potency of silence. Perhaps they were only waiting for the end; to be cut down, cleared away, the end of the forest, for them the end of all things. But perhaps their strong and aristocratic silence, the silence of strong trees, meant something else.

As she came out of the wood on the north side, the keeper's cottage, a rather dark, brown stone cottage, with gables and a handsome chimney, looked uninhabited, it was so silent and alone. But a thread of smoke rose from the chimney, and the little railed-in garden in the front of the house was dug and kept very tidy. The door was shut.

Now she was here she felt a little shy of the man, with his curious far-seeing eyes. She did not like bringing him orders, and felt like going away again. She knocked softly, no one came. She knocked again, but still not loudly. There was no answer. She peeped through the window, and saw the dark little room, with its almost sinister privacy, not wanting to be invaded.

She stood and listened, and it seemed to her she heard sounds from the back of the cottage. Having failed to make herself heard, her mettle was roused, she would not be defeated.

So she went round the side of the house. At the back of the cottage the land rose steeply, so the back yard was sunken, and enclosed by a low stone wall. She turned the corner of the house and stopped. In the little yard two paces beyond her, the man was washing himself, utterly unaware. He was naked to the hips, his velveteen breeches slipping down over his slender loins. And his white slim back was curved over a big bowl of soapy water, in which he ducked his head, shaking his head with a queer, quick little motion, lifting his slender white arms, and pressing the soapy water from his ears, quick, subtle as a weasel playing with water, and utterly alone. Connie backed away round the corner of the house, and hurried away to the wood. In spite of herself, she had had a shock. After all, merely a man washing himself; commonplace enough, Heaven knows!

Yet in some curious way it was a visionary experience: it had hit her in the middle of the body. She saw the clumsy breeches slipping down over the pure, delicate, white loins, the bones showing a little, and the sense of aloneness, of a creature purely alone, overwhelmed her. Perfect, white solitary nudity of a creature that lives alone, and inwardly alone. And beyond that, a certain beauty of a pure creature. Not the stuff of beauty, not even the body of beauty, but a lambency, the warm, white flame of a single life, revealing itself in contours that one might touch: a body!

Connie had received the shock of vision in her womb, and she knew it; it lay inside her. But with her mind she was inclined to ridicule. A man washing himself in a backyard! No doubt with evil-smelling yellow soap! She was rather annoyed; why should she be made to stumble on these vulgar privacies?

So she walked away from herself, but after a while she sat down on a stump. She was too confused to think. But in the coil of her confusion, she was determined to deliver her message to the fellow. She would not be balked. She must give him time to dress himself, but not time to go out. He was probably preparing to go out somewhere.

So she sauntered slowly back, listening. As she came near, the cottage looked just the same. A dog barked, and she knocked at the door, her heart beating in spite of herself.

She heard the man coming lightly downstairs. He opened the door quickly, and startled her. He looked uneasy himself, but instantly a laugh came on his face.

'Lady Chatterley!' he said. 'Will you come in?'

His manner was so perfectly easy and good, she stepped over the threshold into the rather dreary little room.

'I only called with a message from Sir Clifford,' she said in her soft, rather breathless voice.

The man was looking at her with those blue, all-seeing eyes of his, which made her turn her face aside a little. He thought her comely, almost beautiful, in her shyness, and he took command of the situation himself at once.

'Would you care to sit down?' he asked, presuming she would not. The door stood open.

'No thanks! Sir Clifford wondered if you would . . .' and she delivered her message, looking unconsciously into his eyes again. And now his eyes looked warm and kind, particularly to a woman, wonderfully warm, and kind, and at ease.

'Very good, your Ladyship. I will see to it at once.'

Taking an order, his whole self had changed, glazed over with a sort of hardness and distance. Connie hesitated, she ought to go. But she looked round the clean, tidy, rather dreary little sitting-room with something like dismay.

'Do you live here quite alone?' she asked.

'Quite alone, your Ladyship.'

'But your mother . . . ?'

'She lives in her own cottage in the village.'

'With the child?' asked Connie.

'With the child!'

And his plain, rather worn face took on an indefinable look of derision. It was a face that changed all the time, baffling.

'No,' he said, seeing Connie stand at a loss, 'my mother comes and cleans up for me on Saturdays; I do the rest myself.'

Again Connie looked at him. His eyes were smiling again, a little mockingly, but warm and blue, and somehow kind. She wondered at him. He was in trousers and flannel shirt and a grey tie, his hair soft and damp, his face rather pale and worn-looking. When the eyes ceased to laugh they looked as if they had suffered a great deal, still without losing their warmth. But a pallor of isolation came over him, she was not really there for him.

She wanted to say so many things, and she said nothing. Only she looked up at him again, and remarked:

'I hope I didn't disturb you?'

The faint smile of mockery narrowed his eyes.

'Only combing my hair, if you don't mind. I'm sorry I hadn't a coat on, but then I had no idea who was knocking. Nobody knocks here, and the unexpected sounds ominous.'

He went in front of her down the garden path to hold the gate. In his shirt, without the clumsy velveteen coat, she saw again how slender he was, thin, stooping a little. Yet, as she passed him, there was something young and bright in his fair hair, and his quick eyes. He would be a man about thirty-seven or eight.

She plodded on into the wood, knowing he was looking after her; he upset her so much, in spite of herself.

And he, as he went indoors, was thinking: 'She's nice, she's real! She's nicer than she knows.'

She wondered very much about him; he seemed so unlike a game-keeper, so unlike a working-man anyhow; although he had something in common with the local people. But also something very uncommon.

'The game-keeper, Mellors, is a curious kind of person,' she said to Clifford; 'he might almost be a gentleman.'

'Might he?' said Clifford. 'I hadn't noticed.'

'But isn't there something special about him?' Connie insisted.

'I think he's quite a nice fellow, but I know very little about him. He only came out of the army last year, less than a year ago. From India, I rather think. He may have picked up certain tricks out there, perhaps he was an officer's servant, and improved on his position. Some of the men were like that. But it does them no good, they have to fall back into their old places when they get home again.'

Connie gazed at Clifford contemplatively. She saw in him the peculiar tight rebuff against anyone of the lower classes who might be really climbing up, which she knew was characteristic of his breed.

'But don't you think there is something special about him?' she asked.

'Frankly, no! Nothing I had noticed.'

He looked at her curiously, uneasily, half-suspiciously. And she felt he wasn't telling her the real truth; he wasn't telling himself the real truth, that was it. He disliked any suggestion of a really exceptional human being. People must be more or less at his level, or below it.

Connie felt again the tightness, niggardliness of the men of her generation. They were so tight, so scared of life!

7

When Connie went up to her bedroom she did what she had not done for a long time: took off all her clothes, and looked at herself naked in the huge mirror. She did not know what she was looking for, or at, very definitely, yet she moved the lamp till it shone full on her.

And she thought, as she had thought so often, what a frail, easily hurt, rather pathetic thing a human body is, naked; somehow a little unfinished, incomplete!

She had been supposed to have rather a good figure, but now she was out of fashion: a little too female, not enough like an adolescent boy. She was not very tall, a bit Scottish and short; but she had a certain fluent, down-slipping grace that might have been beauty. Her skin was faintly tawny, her limbs had a certain stillness, her body should have had a full, down-slipping richness; but it lacked something.

Instead of ripening its firm, down-running curves, her body was flattening and going a little harsh. It was as if it had not had enough sun and warmth; it was a little greyish and sapless.

Disappointed of its real womanhood, it had not succeeded in becoming boyish, and unsubstantial, and transparent; instead it had gone opaque.

Her breasts were rather small, and dropping pear-shaped. But they were unripe, a little bitter, without meaning hanging there. And her belly had lost the fresh, round gleam it had had when she was young, in the days of her German boy, who really loved her physically. Then it was young and expectant, with a real look of its own. Now it was going slack, and a little flat, thinner, but with a slack thinness. Her thighs, too, that used to look so quick and glimpsy in their female roundness, somehow they too were going flat, slack, meaningless.

Her body was going meaningless, going dull and opaque, so much insignificant substance. It made her feel immensely depressed and hopeless. What hope was there? She was old, old at twenty-seven, with no gleam and sparkle in the flesh. Old through neglect and denial, yes, denial. Fashionable women kept their bodies bright like delicate porcelain, by external attention. There was nothing inside the porcelain; but she was not even as bright as that. The mental life! Suddenly she hated it with a rushing fury, the swindle!

She looked in the other mirror's reflection at her back, her waist, her loins. She was getting thinner, but to her it was not becoming. The crumple of her waist at the back, as she bent back to look, was a little weary; and it used to be so gay-looking. And the longish slope of her haunches and her buttocks had lost its gleam and its sense of richness. Gone! Only the German boy had loved it, and he was ten years dead, very nearly. How time went by! Ten years dead, and she was only twenty-seven. The healthy boy with his fresh, clumsy sensuality that she had then been so scornful of! Where would she find it now? It was gone out of men. They had their pathetic, two-seconds spasms like Michaelis; but no healthy human sensuality, that warms the blood and freshens the whole being.

Still she thought the most beautiful part of her was the long-sloping fall of the haunches from the socket of the back, and the slumberous, round stillness of the buttocks. Like hillocks of sand, the Arabs say, soft and downward-slipping with a long slope. Here the life still lingered hoping. But here too she was thinner, and going unripe, astringent.

But the front of her body made her miserable. It was already beginning to slacken, with a slack sort of thinness, almost withered, going old before it had ever really lived. She thought of the child she might somehow bear. Was she fit, anyhow?

She slipped into her nightdress, and went to bed, where she sobbed bitterly. And in her bitterness burned a cold indignation against Clifford, and his writings and his talk: against all the men of his sort who defrauded a woman even of her own body.

Unjust! Unjust! The sense of deep physical injustice burned to her very soul.

But in the morning, all the same she was up at seven, and going downstairs to Clifford. She had to help him in all the intimate things, for he had no man, and refused a woman-servant. The housekeeper's husband, who had known him as a boy, helped him, and did any heavy lifting; but Connie did the personal things, and she did them willingly. It was a demand on her, but she had wanted to do what she could.

So she hardly ever went away from Wragby, and never for more than a day or two; when Mrs Betts, the housekeeper, attended to Clifford. He, as was inevitable in the course of time, took all the service for granted. It was natural he should.

And yet, deep inside herself, a sense of injustice, of being defrauded, begun to burn in Connie. The physical sense of injustice is a dangerous feeling, once it is awakened. It must have outlet, or it eats away the one in whom it is aroused.

Poor Clifford, he was not to blame. His was the greater misfortune. It was all part of the general catastrophe.

And yet was he not in a way to blame? This lack of warmth, this lack of the simple, warm, physical contact, was he not to blame for that? He was never really warm, nor even kind, only thoughtful, considerate, in a well-bred, cold sort of way! But never warm as a man can be warm to a woman, as even Connie's father could be warm to her, with the warmth of a man who did himself well, and intended to, but who still could comfort a woman with a bit of his masculine glow.

But Clifford was not like that. His whole race was not like that. They were all inwardly hard and separate, and warmth to them was just bad taste. You had to get on without it, and hold your own; which was all very well if you were of the same class and race. Then you could keep yourself cold and be very estimable, and hold your own, and enjoy the satisfaction of holding it. But if you were of another class and another race it wouldn't do; there was no fun merely holding your own, and feeling you belonged to the ruling class. What was the point, when even the smartest aristocrats had really nothing positive of their own to hold, and their rule was really a farce, not rule at all? What was the point? It was all cold nonsense.

A sense of rebellion smouldered in Connie. What was the good of it all? What was the good of her sacrifice, her devoting her life to Clifford? What was she serving, after all? A cold spirit of vanity, that had no warm human contacts, and that was as corrupt as any low-born Jew, in craving for prostitution to the bitch-goddess, Success. Even Clifford's cool and contactless assurance that he belonged to the ruling class didn't prevent his tongue lolling out of his mouth, as he panted after the bitch-goddess. After all, Michaelis was really more dig-nified in the matter, and far, far more successful. Really, if you looked closely at Clifford, he was a buffoon, and a buffoon is more humiliating than a bounder.

As between the two men, Michaelis really had far more use for her than Clifford had. He had even more need of her. Any good nurse can attend to crippled legs! And as for the heroic effort, Michaelis was a heroic rat, and Clifford was very much of a poodle showing off.

There were people staying in the house, among them Clifford's Aunt Eva, Lady Bennerley. She was a thin woman of sixty, with a red nose, a widow, and still something of a *grande dame*. She belonged to one of the best families, and had the character to carry it off. Connie liked her, she was so perfectly simple and frank, as far as she intended to be frank, and superficially kind. Inside herself she was a past-mistress in holding her own, and holding other people a little lower. She was not at all a snob: far too sure of herself. She was perfect at the social sport of coolly holding her own, and making other people defer to her.

She was kind to Connie, and tried to worm into her woman's soul with the sharp gimlet of her well-born observations.

'You're quite wonderful, in my opinion,' she said to Connie. 'You've done wonders for Clifford. I never saw any budding genius myself, and there he is, all the rage.' Aunt Eva was quite complacently proud of Clifford's success. Another feather in the family cap! She didn't care a straw about his books, but why should she?

'Oh, I don't think it's my doing,' said Connie.

'It must be! Can't be anybody else's. And it seems to me you don't get enough out of it.'

'How?'

'Look at the way you are shut up here. I said to Clifford: If that child rebels one day you'll have yourself to thank!'

'But Clifford never denies me anything,' said Connie.

'Look here, my dear child'–and Lady Bennerley laid her thin hand on Connie's arm. 'A woman has to live her life, or live to repent not having lived it. Believe me!' And she took another sip of brandy, which maybe was her form of repentance.

'But I do live my life, don't I?'

'Not in my idea! Clifford should bring you to London, and let you go about. His sort of friends are all right for him, but what are they for you? If I were you I should think it wasn't good enough. You'll let your youth slip by, and you'll spend your old age, and your middle age too, repenting it.'

Her ladyship lapsed into contemplative silence, soothed by the brandy.

But Connie was not keen on going to London, and being steered into the smart world by Lady Bennerley. She didn't feel really smart, it wasn't interesting. And she did feel the peculiar, withering coldness under it all; like the soil of Labrador, which has gay little flowers on its surface, and a foot down is frozen.

Tommy Dukes was at Wragby, and another man, Harry Winterslow, and Jack Strangeways with his wife Olive. The talk was much more desultory than when only the cronies were there, and everybody was a bit bored, for the weather was bad, and there was only billiards, and the pianola to dance to.

Olive was reading a book about the future, when babies would be bred in bottles, and women would be 'immunized'.

'Jolly good thing too!' she said. 'Then a woman can live her own life.' Strangeways wanted children, and she didn't.

'How'd you like to be immunized?' Winterslow asked her, with an ugly smile.

'I hope I am; naturally,' she said. 'Anyhow the future's going to have more sense, and a woman needn't be dragged down by her *functions.* '

'Perhaps she'll float off into space altogether,' said Dukes.

'I do think sufficient civilization ought to eliminate a lot of the physical disabilities,' said Clifford. 'All the love-business for example, it might just as well go. I suppose it would if we could breed babies in bottles.'

'No!' cried Olive. 'That might leave all the more room for fun.'

'I suppose,' said Lady Bennerley, contemplatively, 'if the love-business went, something else would take its place. Morphia, perhaps. A little morphine in all the air. It would be wonderfully refreshing for everybody.'

'The government releasing ether into the air on Saturdays, for a cheerful weekend!' said Jack. 'Sounds all right, but where should we be by Wednesday?'

'So long as you can forget your body you are happy,' said Lady Bennerley. 'And the moment you begin to be aware of your body, you are wretched. So, if civilization is any good, it has to help us to forget our bodies, and then time passes happily without our knowing it.'

'Help us to get rid of our bodies altogether,' said Winterslow. 'It's quite time man began to improve on his own nature, especially the physical side of it.'

'Imagine if we floated like tobacco smoke,' said Connie.

'It won't happen,' said Dukes. 'Our old show will come flop; our civilization is going to fall. It's going down the bottomless pit, down the chasm. And believe me, the only bridge across the chasm will be the phallus!'

'Oh do! *do* be impossible, General!' cried Olive.

'I believe our civilization is going to collapse,' said Aunt Eva.

'And what will come after it?' asked Clifford.

'I haven't the faintest idea, but something, I suppose,' said the elderly lady.

'Connie says people like wisps of smoke, and Olive says immunized women, and babies in bottles, and Dukes says the phallus is the bridge to what comes next. I wonder what it will really be?' said Clifford.

'Oh, don't bother! let's get on with today,' said Olive. 'Only hurry up with the breeding bottle, and let us poor women off.'

'There might even be real men, in the next phase,' said Tommy. 'Real, intelligent, wholesome men, and wholesome nice women! Wouldn't that be a change, an enormous change from us? *We're* not men, and the women aren't women. We're only cerebrating make-shifts, mechanical and intellectual experiments. There may even come a civilization of genuine men and women, instead of our little lot of clever-jacks, all at the intelligence-age of seven. It would be even more amazing than men of smoke or babies in bottles.'

'Oh, when people begin to talk about real women, I give up,' said Olive.

'Certainly nothing but the spirit in us is worth having,' said Winterslow.

'Spirits!' said Jack, drinking his whisky and soda.

'Think so? Give me the resurrection of the body!' said Dukes. 'But it'll come, in time, when we've shoved the cerebral stone away a bit, the money and the rest. Then we'll get a democracy of touch, instead of a democracy of pocket.'

Something echoed inside Connie: 'Give me the democracy of touch, the resurrection of the body!' She didn't at all know what it meant, but it comforted her, as meaningless things may do.

Anyhow everything was terribly silly, and she was exasperatedly bored by it all, by Clifford, by Aunt Eva, by Olive and Jack, and Winterslow, and even by Dukes. Talk, talk, talk! What hell it was, the continual rattle of it!

Then, when all the people went, it was no better. She continued plodding on, but exasperation and irritation had got hold of her lower body, she couldn't escape. The days seemed to grind by, with curious painfulness, yet nothing happened. Only she was getting thinner; even the housekeeper noticed it, and asked her about herself. Even Tommy Dukes insisted she was not well, though she said she was all right. Only she began to be afraid of the ghastly white tombstones, that peculiar loathsome whiteness of Carrara marble, detestable as false teeth, which stuck up on the hillside, under Tevershall church, and which she saw with such grim painfulness from the park. The bristling of the hideous false teeth of tombstones on the hill affected her with a grisly kind of horror. She felt the time not far off when she would be buried there, added to the ghastly host under the tombstones and the monuments, in these filthy Midlands.

She needed help, and she knew it: so she wrote a little *cri du cœur* to her sister, Hilda. 'I'm not well lately, and I don't know what's the matter with me.'

Down posted Hilda from Scotland, where she had taken up her abode. She came in March, alone, driving herself in a nimble two-seater. Up the drive she came, tooting up the incline, then sweeping round the oval of grass, where the two great wild beech-trees stood, on the flat in front of the house.

Connie had run out to the steps. Hilda pulled up her car, got out, and kissed her sister.

'But Connie!' she cried. 'Whatever is the matter?'

'Nothing!' said Connie, rather shamefacedly; but she knew how she had suffered in contrast to Hilda. Both sisters had the same rather golden, glowing skin, and soft brown hair, and naturally strong, warm physique. But now Connie was thin and earthy-looking, with a scraggy, yellowish neck, that stuck out of her jumper.

'But you're ill, child!' said Hilda, in the soft, rather breathless voice that both sisters had alike. Hilda was nearly, but not quite, two years older than Connie.

'No, not ill. Perhaps I'm bored,' said Connie a little pathetically.

The light of battle glowed in Hilda's face; she was a woman, soft and still as she seemed, of the old amazon sort, not made to fit with men.

'This wretched place!' she said softly, looking at poor, old, lumbering Wragby with real hate. She looked soft and warm herself, as a ripe pear, and she was an amazon of the real old breed.

She went quietly in to Clifford. He thought how handsome she looked, but also he shrank from her. His wife's family did not have his sort of manners, or his sort of etiquette. He considered them rather outsiders, but once they got inside they made him jump through the hoop.

He sat square and well-groomed in his chair, his hair sleek and blond, and his face fresh, his blue eyes pale, and a little prominent, his expression inscrutable, but well-bred. Hilda thought it sulky and stupid, and he waited. He had an air of aplomb, but Hilda didn't care what he had an air of; she was up in arms, and if he'd been Pope or Emperor it would have been just the same.

'Connie's looking awfully unwell,' she said in her soft voice, fixing him with her beautiful, glowering grey eyes. She looked so maidenly, so did Connie; but he well knew the tone of Scottish obstinacy underneath.

'She's a little thinner,' he said.

'Haven't you done anything about it?'

'Do you think it necessary?' he asked, with his suavest English stiffness, for the two things often go together.

Hilda only glowered at him without replying; repartee was not her forte, nor Connie's; so she glowered, and he was much more uncomfortable than if she had said things.

'I'll take her to a doctor,' said Hilda at length. 'Can you suggest a good one round here?'

'I'm afraid I can't.'

'Then I'll take her to London, where we have a doctor we trust.'

Though boiling with rage, Clifford said nothing.

'I suppose I may as well stay the night,' said Hilda, pulling off her gloves, 'and I'll drive her to town tomorrow.'

Clifford was yellow at the gills with anger, and at evening the whites of his eyes were a little yellow too. He ran to liver. But Hilda was consistently modest and maidenly.

'You must have a nurse or somebody, to look after you personally. You should really have a man-servant,' said Hilda as they sat, with apparent calmness, at coffee after dinner. She spoke in her soft, seemingly gentle way, but Clifford felt she was hitting him on the head with a bludgeon.

'You think so?' he said coldly.

'I'm sure! It's necessary. Either that, or Father and I must take Connie away for some months. This can't go on.'

'What can't go on?'

'Haven't you looked at the child!' asked Hilda, gazing at him full stare. He looked rather like a huge, boiled crayfish at the moment, or so she thought.

'Connie and I will discuss it,' he said.

'I've already discussed it with her,' said Hilda.

Clifford had been long enough in the hands of nurses; he hated them, because they left him no real privacy. And a man-servant! . . . he couldn't stand a man hanging around him. Almost better any woman. But why not Connie?

The two sisters drove off in the morning, Connie looking rather like an Easter lamb, rather small beside Hilda, who held the wheel. Sir Malcolm was away, but the Kensington house was open.

The doctor examined Connie carefully, and asked her all about her life. 'I see your photograph, and Sir Clifford's, in the illustrated papers sometimes. Almost notorieties, aren't you? That's how the quiet little girls grow up, though you're only a quiet little girl even now, in spite of the illustrated papers. No, no! There's nothing organically wrong, but it won't do! It won't do! Tell Sir Clifford he's got to bring you to town, or to take you abroad, and amuse you. You've got to be amused, got to! Your vitality is much too low; no reserves, no reserves. The nerves of the heart a bit queer already: oh, yes! Nothing but nerves; I'd put you right in a month at Cannes or Biarritz. But it mustn't go on, *mustn't*, I tell you, or I won't be answerable for consequences. You're spending your life without renewing it. You've got to be amused, properly, healthily amused. You're spending your vitality without making any. Can't go on, you know. Depression! Avoid depression!'

Hilda set her jaw, and that meant something.

Michaelis heard they were in town, and came running with roses. 'Why, whatever's wrong?' he cried. 'You're a shadow of yourself. Why, I never saw such a change! Why ever didn't you let me know? Come to Nice with me! Come down to Sicily! Go on, come to Sicily with me. It's lovely there just now. You want sun! You want life! Why, you're wasting away! Come away with me! Come to Africa! Oh, hang Sir Clifford! Chuck him, and come along with me. I'll marry you the minute he divorces you. Come along and try a life! God's love! That place Wragby would kill anybody. Beastly place! Foul place! Kill anybody! Come away with me into the sun! It's the sun you want, of course, and a bit of normal life.'

But Connie's heart simply stood still at the thought of abandoning Clifford there and then. She couldn't do it. No . . . no! She just couldn't. She had to go back to Wragby.

Michaelis was disgusted. Hilda didn't like Michaelis, but she *almost* preferred him to Clifford. Back went the sisters to the Midlands.

Hilda talked to Clifford, who still had yellow eyeballs when they got back. He, too, in his way, was overwrought; but he had to listen to all Hilda said, to all the doctor had said, not what Michaelis had said, of course, and he sat mum through the ultimatum.

'Here is the address of a good man-servant, who was with an invalid patient of the doctor's till he died last month. He is really a good man, and fairly sure to come.'

'But I'm *not* an invalid, and I will *not* have a man-servant,' said Clifford, poor devil.

'And here are the addresses of two women; I saw one of them, she would do very well; a woman of about fifty, quiet, strong, kind, and in her way cultured . . .'

Clifford only sulked, and would not answer.

'Very well, Clifford. If we don't settle something by tomorrow, I shall telegraph to Father, and we shall take Connie away.'

'Will Connie go?' asked Clifford.

'She doesn't want to, but she knows she must. Mother died of cancer, brought on by fretting. We're not running any risks.'

So next day Clifford suggested Mrs Bolton, Tevershall parish nurse. Apparently Mrs Betts had thought of her. Mrs Bolton was just retiring from her parish duties to take up private nursing jobs. Clifford had a queer dread of delivering himself into the hands of a stranger, but this Mrs Bolton had once nursed him through scarlet fever, and he knew her.

The two sisters at once called on Mrs Bolton, in a newish house in a row, quite select for Tevershall. They found a rather good-looking woman of forty-odd, in a nurse's uniform, with a white collar and apron, just making herself tea in a small crowded sitting-room.

Mrs Bolton was most attentive and polite, seemed quite nice, spoke with a bit of a broad slur, but in heavily correct English, and from having bossed the sick colliers for a good many years, had a very good opinion of herself, and a fair amount of assurance. In short, in her tiny way, one of the governing class in the village, very much respected.

'Yes, Lady Chatterley's not looking at all well! Why, she used to be that bonny, didn't she now? But she's been failing all winter! Oh, it's hard, it is. Poor Sir Clifford! Eh, that war, it's a lot to answer for.'

And Mrs Bolton would come to Wragby at once, if Dr Shardlow would let her off. She had another fortnight's parish nursing to do, by rights, but they might get a substitute, you know.

Hilda posted off to Dr Shardlow, and on the following Sunday Mrs Bolton drove up in Leiver's cab to Wragby with two trunks. Hilda had talks with her; Mrs Bolton was ready at any moment to talk. And she seemed so young! The way the passion would flush in her rather pale cheek. She was forty-seven.

Her husband, Ted Bolton, had been killed in the pit, twenty-two years ago, twenty-two years last Christmas, just at Christmas time, leaving her with two children, one a baby in arms. Oh, the baby was married now, Edith, to a young man in Boots Cash Chemists in Sheffield. The other one was a school-teacher in Chesterfield; she came home weekends, when she wasn't asked out somewhere. Young folks enjoyed themselves nowadays, not like when she, Ivy Bolton, was young.

Ted Bolton was twenty-eight when he was killed in an explosion down th' pit. The butty in front shouted to them all to lie down quick, there were four of them. And they all lay down in time, only Ted, and it killed him. Then at the inquiry, on the masters' side they said Ted had been frightened, and trying to run away, and not obeying orders, so it was like his fault really. So the compensation was only three hundred pounds, and they made out as if it was more of a gift than legal compensation, because it was really the man's own fault. And they wouldn't let her have the money down; she wanted to have a little shop. But they said she'd no doubt squander it, perhaps in drink! So she had to draw it thirty shillings a week. Yes, she had to go every Monday morning down to the offices, and stand there a couple of hours waiting her turn; yes, for almost four years she went every Monday. And what could she do with two little children on her hands? But Ted's mother was very good to her. When the baby could toddle she'd keep both the children for the day, while she, Ivy Bolton, went to Sheffied, and attended classes in ambulance, and then the fourth year she even took a nursing course and got qualified. She was determined to be independent and keep her children. So she was assistant at Uthwaite hospital, just a little place, for a while. But when the Company, the Tengshall Colliery Company, really Sir Geoffrey, saw that she could get on by herself, they were very good to her, gave her the parish nursing, and stood by her, she would say that for them. And she'd done it ever since, till now it was getting a bit much for her; she needed something a bit lighter, there was such a lot of traipsing around if you were a district nurse.

'Yes, the Company's been very good to *me*, I always say it. But I should never forget what they said about Ted, for he was as steady and fearless a chap as ever set foot on the cage, and it was as good as branding him a coward. But there, he was dead, and could say nothing to none of 'em.'

It was a queer mixture of feelings the woman showed as she talked. She liked the colliers, whom she had nursed for so long; but she felt very superior to them. She felt almost upper class; and at the same time a resentment against the ruling class smouldered in her. The masters! In a dispute between masters and men, she was always for the men. But when there was no question of contest, she was pining to be superior, to be one of the upper class. The upper classes fascinated her, appealing to her peculiar English passion for superiority. She was thrilled to come to Wragby; thrilled to talk to Lady Chatterley, my word, different from the common colliers' wives! She said so in so many words. Yet one could see a grudge against the Chatterleys peep out in her; the grudge against the masters.

'Why, yes, of course, it would wear Lady Chatterley out! It's a mercy she had a sister to come and help her. Men don't think, high and low alike, they take what a woman does for them as granted. Oh, I've told the colliers off about it many a time. But it's very hard for Sir Clifford, you know, crippled like that. They were always a haughty family, stand-offish in a way, as they've a right to be. But then to be brought down like that! And it's very hard on Lady Chatterley, perhaps harder on her. What she misses! I only had Ted three years, but my word, while I had him I had a husband I could never forget. He was one in a thousand, and jolly as the day. Who'd ever have thought he'd get killed? I don't believe it to this day somehow, I've never believed it, though I washed him with my own hands. But he was never dead for me, he never was. I never took it in.'

This was a new voice in Wragby, very new for Connie to hear; it roused a new ear in her.

For the first week or so, Mrs Bolton, however, was very quiet at Wragby; her assured, bossy manner left her, and she was nervous. With Clifford she was shy, almost frightened, and silent. He liked that, and soon recovered his self-possession, letting her do things for him without even noticing her.

'She's a useful nonentity!' he said. Connie opened her eyes in wonder, but she did not contradict him. So different are impressions on two different people!

And he soon became rather superb, somewhat lordly with the nurse. She had rather expected it, and he played up without knowing. So susceptible we are to what is expected of us! The colliers had been so like children, talking to her, and telling her what hurt them, while she bandaged them, or nursed them. They had always made her feel so grand, almost super-human in her administrations. Now Clifford made her feel small, and like a servant, and she accepted it without a word, adjusting herself to the upper classes.

She came very mute, with her long, handsome face, and downcast eyes, to administer to him. And she said very humbly: 'Shall I do this now, Sir Clifford? Shall I do that?'

'No, leave it for a time, I'll have it done later.'

'Very well, Sir Clifford.'

'Come in again in half an hour.'

'Very well, Sir Clifford.'

'And just take those old papers out, will you?'

'Very well, Sir Clifford.'

She went softly, and in half an hour she came softly again. She was bullied, but she didn't mind. She was experiencing the upper classes. She neither resented nor disliked Clifford; he was just part of a phenomenon, the phenomenon of the high-class folks, so far unknown to her, but now to be known. She felt more at home with Lady Chatterley, and after all it's the mistress of the house matters most.

Mrs Bolton helped Clifford to bed at night, and slept across the passage from his room, and came if he rang for her in the night. She also helped him in the morning, and soon valeted him completely, even shaving him, in her soft, tentative woman's way. She was very good and competent, and she soon knew how to have him in her power. He wasn't so very different from the colliers after all, when you lathered his chin, and softly rubbed the bristles. The stand-offishness and the lack of frankness didn't bother her; she was having a new experience.

Clifford, however, inside himself, never quite forgave Connie for giving up her personal care of him to a strange hired woman. It killed, he said to himself, the real flower of the intimacy between him and her. But Connie didn't mind that. The fine flower of their intimacy was to her rather like an orchid, a bulb stuck parasitic on her tree of life, and producing, to her eyes, a rather shabby flower.

Now she had more time to herself she could softly play the piano, up in her room, and sing: 'Touch not the nettle . . . for the bonds of love are ill to loose.' She had not realized till lately how ill to loose they were, these bonds of love. But thank Heaven she had loosened them! She was so glad to be alone, not always to have to talk to him. When he was alone he tapped-tapped-tapped on a typewriter, to infinity. But when he was not 'working', and she was there, he talked, always talked; infinite small analysis of people and motives, and results, characters and personalities, till now she had had enough. For years she had loved it, until she had enough, and then suddenly it was too much. She was thankful to be alone.

It was as if thousands and thousands of little roots and threads of consciousness in him and her had grown together into a tangled mass, till they could crowd no more, and the plant was dying. Now quietly, subtly, she was unravelling the tangle of his consciousness and hers, breaking the threads gently, one by one, with patience and impatience to get clear. But the bonds of such love are more ill to loose even than most bonds; though Mrs Bolton's coming had been a great help.

But he still wanted the old intimate evenings of talk with Connie: talk or reading aloud. But now she could arrange that Mrs Bolton should come at ten to disturb them. At ten o'clock Connie could go upstairs and be alone. Clifford was in good hands with Mrs Bolton.

Mrs Bolton ate with Mrs Betts in the housekeeper's room, since they were all agreeable. And it was curious how much closer the servants' quarters seemed to have come; right up to the doors of Clifford's study, when before they were so remote. For Mrs Betts would sometimes sit in Mrs Bolton's room, and Connie heard their lowered voices, and felt somehow the strong, other vibration of the working people almost invading the sitting-room, when she and Clifford were alone. So changed was Wragby merely by Mrs Bolton's coming.

And Connie felt herself released, in another world, she felt she breathed differently. But still she was afraid of how many of her roots, perhaps mortal ones, were tangled with Clifford's. Yet still, she breathed freer, a new phase was going to begin in her life.

8

Mrs Bolton also kept a cherishing eye on Connie, feeling she must extend to her her female and professional protection. She was always urging her ladyship to walk out, to drive to Uthwaite, to be in the air. For Connie had got into the habit of sitting still by the fire, pretending to read; or to sew feebly, and hardly going out at all.

It was a blowy day soon after Hilda had gone, that Mrs Bolton said: 'Now why don't you go for a walk through the wood, and look at the daffs behind the keeper's cottage? They're the prettiest sight you'd see in a day's march. And you could put some in your room; wild daffs are always so cheerful-looking, aren't they?'

Connie took it in good part, even daffs for daffodils. Wild daffodils! After all, one could not stew in one's own juice. The spring came back . . . 'Seasons return, but not to me returns Day, or the sweet approach of Ev'n or Morn.'

And the keeper, his thin, white body, like a lonely pistil of an invisible flower! She had forgotten him in her unspeakable depression. But now something roused . . . 'Pale beyond porch and portal' . . . the thing to do was to pass the porches and the portals.

She was stronger, she could walk better, and in the wood the wind would not be so tiring as it was across the park, flattening against her. She wanted to forget, to forget the world, and all the dreadful, carrion-bodied people. 'Ye must be born again! I believe in the resurrection of the body! Except a grain of wheat fall into the earth and die, it shall by no means bring forth. When the crocus cometh forth I too will emerge and see the sun!' In the wind of March endless phrases swept through her consciousness.

Little gusts of sunshine blew, strangely bright, and lit up the celandines at the wood's edge, under the hazel-rods, they spangled out bright and yellow. And the wood was still, stiller, but yet gusty with crossing sun. The first wind-flowers were out, and all the wood seemed pale with the pallor of endless little anemones, sprinkling the shaken floor. 'The world has grown pale with thy breath.' But it was the breath of Persephone, this time; she was out of hell on a cold morning. Cold breaths of wind came, and overhead there was an anger of entangled wind caught among the twigs. It, too, was caught and trying to tear itself free, the wind, like Absalom. How cold the anemones looked, bobbing their naked white shoulders over crinoline skirts of green. But they stood it. A few first bleached little primroses too, by the path, and yellow buds unfolding themselves.

The roaring and swaying was overhead, only cold currents came down below. Connie was strangely excited in the wood, and the colour flew in her cheeks, and burned blue in her eyes. She walked ploddingly, picking a few primroses and the first violets, that smelled sweet and cold, sweet and cold. And she drifted on without knowing where she was.

Till she came to the clearing, at the end of the wood, and saw the green-stained stone cottage, looking almost rosy, like the flesh underneath a mushroom, its stone warmed in a burst of sun. And there was a sparkle of yellow jasmine by the door; the closed door. But no sound; no smoke from the chimney; no dog barking.

She went quietly round to the back, where the bank rose up; she had an excuse, to see the daffodils.

And they were there, the short-stemmed flowers, rustling and fluttering and shivering, so bright and alive, but with nowhere to hide their faces, as they turned them away from the wind.

They shook their bright, sunny little rags in bouts of distress. But perhaps they liked it really; perhaps they really liked the tossing.

Constance sat down with her back to a young pine-tree, that swayed against her with curious life, elastic, and powerful, rising up. The erect, alive thing, with its top in the sun! And she watched the daffodils turn golden, in a burst of sun that was warm on her hands and lap. Even she caught the faint, tarry scent of the flowers. And then, being so still and alone, she seemed to get into the current of her own proper destiny. She had been fastened by a rope, and jagging and snarring like a boat at its moorings; now she was loose and adrift.

The sunshine gave way to chill; the daffodils were in shadow, dipping silently. So they would dip through the day and the long cold night. So strong in their frailty!

She rose, a little stiff, took a few daffodils, and went down. She hated breaking the flowers, but she wanted just one or two to go with her. She would have to go back to Wragby and its walls, and now she hated it, especially its thick walls. Walls! Always walls! Yet one needed them in this wind.

When she got home Clifford asked her:

'Where did you go?'

'Right across the wood! Look, aren't the little daffodils adorable? To think they should come out of the earth!'

'Just as much out of air and sunshine,' he said.

'But modelled in the earth,' she retorted, with a prompt contradiction, that surprised her a little.

The next afternoon she went to the wood again. She followed the broad riding that swerved round and up through the larches to a spring called John's Well. It was cold on this hillside, and not a flower in the darkness of larches. But the icy little spring softly pressed upwards from its tiny well-bed of pure, reddish-white pebbles. How icy and clear it was! Brilliant! The new keeper had no doubt put in fresh pebbles. She heard the faint tinkle of water, as the tiny overflow trickled over and downhill. Even above the hissing boom of the larch-wood, that spread its bristling, leafless, wolfish darkness on the down-slope, she heard the tinkle as of tiny water-bells.

This place was a little sinister, cold, damp. Yet the well must have been a drinking-place for hundreds of years. Now no more. Its tiny cleared space was lush and cold and dismal.

She rose and went slowly towards home. As she went she heard a faint tapping away on the right, and stood still to listen. Was it hammering, or a woodpecker? It was surely hammering.

She walked on, listening. And then she noticed a narrow track between young fir-trees, a track that seemed to lead nowhere. But she felt it had been used. She turned down it adventurously, between the thick young firs, which gave way soon to the old oak wood. She followed the track, and the hammering grew nearer, in the silence of the windy wood, for trees make a silence even in their noise of wind.

She saw a secret little clearing, and a secret little hut made of rustic poles. And she had never been here before! She realized it was the quiet place where the growing pheasants were reared; the keeper in his shirt-sleeves was kneeling, hammering. The dog trotted forward with a short, sharp bark, and the keeper lifted his face suddenly and saw her. He had a startled look in his eyes.

He straightened himself and saluted, watching her in silence, as she came forward with weakening limbs. He resented the intrusion; he cherished his solitude as his only and last freedom in life.

'I wondered what the hammering was,' she said, feeling weak and breathless, and a little afraid of him, as he looked so straight at her.

'Ah'm gettin' th' coops ready for th' young bods,' he said, in broad vernacular.

She did not know what to say, and she felt weak.

'I should like to sit down a bit,' she said.

'Come and sit 'ere i' th' 'ut,' he said, going in front of her to the hut, pushing aside some timber and stuff, and drawing out a rustic chair, made of hazel sticks.

'Am Ah t' light yer a little fire?' he asked, with the curious naïveté of the dialect.

'Oh, don't bother,' she replied.

But he looked at her hands; they were rather blue. So he quickly took some larch twigs to the little brick fire-place in the corner, and in a moment the yellow flame was running up the chimney. He made a place by the brick hearth.

'Sit 'ere then a bit, and warm yer,' he said.

She obeyed him. He had that curious kind of protective authority she obeyed at once. So she sat and warmed her hands at the blaze, and dropped logs on the fire, whilst outside he was hammering again. She did not really want to sit, poked in a corner by the fire; she would rather have watched from the door, but she was being looked after, so she had to submit.

The hut was quite cosy, panelled with unvarnished deal, having a little rustic table and stool beside her chair, and a carpenter's bench, then a big box, tools, new boards, nails; and many things hung from pegs: axe, hatchet, traps, things in sacks, his coat. It had no window, the light came in through the open door. It was a jumble, but also it was a sort of little sanctuary.

She listened to the tapping of the man's hammer; it was not so happy. He was oppressed. Here was a trespass on his privacy, and a dangerous one! A woman! He had reached the point where all he wanted on earth was to be alone. And yet he was powerless to preserve his privacy; he was a hired man, and these people were his masters.

Especially he did not want to come into contact with a woman again. He feared it; for he had a big wound from old contacts. He felt if he could not be alone, and if he could not be left alone, he would die. His recoil away from the outer world was complete; his last refuge was this wood; to hide himself there!

Connie grew warm by the fire, which she had made too big: then she grew hot. She went and sat on the stool in the doorway, watching the man at work. He seemed not to notice her, but he knew. Yet he worked on, as if absorbedly, and his brown dog sat on her tail near him, and surveyed the untrustworthy world.

Slender, quiet and quick, the man finished the coop he was making, turned it over, tried the sliding door, then set it aside. Then he rose, went for an old coop, and took it to the chopping-log where he was working. Crouching, he tried the bars; some broke in his hands; he began to draw the nails. Then he turned the coop over and deliberated, and he gave absolutely no sign of awareness of the woman's presence.

So Connie watched him fixedly. And the same solitary aloneness she had seen in him naked, she now saw in him clothed: solitary, and intent, like an animal that works alone, but also brooding, like a soul that recoils away, away from all human contact. Silently, patiently, he was recoiling away from her even now. It was the stillness, and the timeless sort of patience, in a man impatient and passionate, that touched Connie's womb. She saw it in his bent head, the quick quiet hands, the crouching of his slender, sensitive loins; something patient and withdrawn. She felt his experience had been deeper and wider than her own; much deeper and wider, and perhaps more deadly. And this relieved her of herself; she felt almost irresponsible.

So she sat in the doorway of the hut in a dream, utterly unaware of time and of particular circumstances. She was so drifted away that he glanced up at her quickly, and saw the utterly still, waiting look on her face. To him it was a look of waiting. And a little thin tongue of fire suddenly flickered in his loins, at the root of his back, and he groaned in spirit. He dreaded with a repulsion almost of death, any further close human contact. He wished above all things she would go away, and leave him to his own privacy. He dreaded her will, her female will, and her modern female insistency. And above all he dreaded her cool, upper-class impudence of having her own way. For after all he was only a hired man. He hated her presence there.

Connie came to herself with sudden uneasiness. She rose. The afternoon was turning to evening, yet she could not go away. She went over to the man, who stood up at attention, his worn face stiff and blank, his eyes watching her.

'It is so nice here, so restful,' she said. 'I have never been here before.'

'No?'

'I think I shall come and sit here sometimes.'

'Yes?'

'Do you lock the hut when you're not here?'

'Yes, your Ladyship.'

'Do you think I could have a key too, so that I could sit here sometimes? Are there two keys?'

'Not as Ah know on, ther' isna.'

He lapsed into the vernacular. Connie hesitated; he was putting up an opposition. Was it his hut, after all?

'Couldn't we get another key?' she asked in her soft voice, that underneath had the ring of a woman determined to get her way.

'Another!' he said, glancing at her with a flash of anger, touched with derision.

'Yes, a duplicate,' she said, flushing.

''Appen Sir Clifford 'ud know,' he said, putting her off.

'Yes!' she said, 'he might have another. Otherwise we could have one made from the one you have. It would only take a day or so, I suppose. You could spare your key for so long.'

'Ah canna tell yer, m'Lady!' Ah know nob'dy as ma'es keys round 'ere.'

Connie suddenly flushed with anger.

'Very well!' she said. 'I'll see to it.'

'All right, your Ladyship.'

Their eyes met. His had a cold, ugly look of dislike and contempt, and indifference to what would happen. Hers were hot with rebuff.

But her heart sank, she saw how utterly he disliked her, when she went against him. And she saw him in a sort of desperation.

'Good afternoon!'

'Afternoon, my Lady!' He saluted and turned abruptly away. She had wakened the sleeping dogs of old voracious anger in him, anger against the self-willed female. And he was powerless, powerless. He knew it!

And she was angry against the self-willed male. A servant too! She walked sullenly home.

She found Mrs Bolton under the great beech-tree on the knoll, looking for her.

'I just wondered if you'd be coming, my Lady,' the woman said brightly.

'Am I late?' asked Connie.

'Oh . . . only Sir Clifford was waiting for his tea.'

'Why didn't *you* make it then?'

'Oh, I don't think it's hardly my place. I don't think Sir Clifford would like it at all, my Lady.'

'I don't see why not,' said Connie.

She went indoors to Clifford's study, where the old brass kettle was simmering on the tray.

'Am I late, Clifford?' she said, putting down the few flowers and taking up the tea-caddy, as she stood before the tray in her hat and scarf. 'I'm sorry! Why didn't you let Mrs Bolton make the tea?'

'I didn't think of it,' he said ironically. 'I don't quite see her presiding at the tea-table.'

'Oh, there's nothing sacrosanct about a silver tea-pot,' said Connie.

He glanced up at her curiously.

'What did you do all afternoon?' he said.

'Walked and sat in a sheltered place. Do you know there are still berries on the big holly-tree?'

She took off her scarf, but not her hat, and sat down to make tea. The toast would certainly be leathery. She put the tea-cosy over the tea-pot, and rose to get a little glass for her violets. The poor flowers hung over, limp on their stalks.

'They'll revive again!' she said, putting them before him in their glass for him to smell.

'Sweeter than the lids of Juno's eyes,' he quoted.

'I don't see a bit of connexion with the actual violets,' she said. 'The Elizabethans are rather upholstered.'

She poured him his tea.

Lady Chatterley's Lover

'Do you think there is a second key to that little hut not far from John's Well, where the pheasants are reared?' she said.

'There may be. Why?'

'I happened to find it today–and I'd never seen it before. I think it's a darling place. I could sit there sometimes, couldn't I?'

'Was Mellors there?'

'Yes! That's how I found it: his hammering. He didn't seem to like my intruding at all. In fact he was almost rude when I asked him about a second key.'

'What did he say?'

'Oh, nothing: just his manner; and he said he knew nothing about keys.'

'There may be one in Father's study. Betts knows them all, they're all there. I'll get him to look.'

'Oh do!' she said.

'So Mellors was almost rude?'

'Oh, nothing, really! But I don't think he wanted me to have the freedom of the castle, quite.'

'I don't suppose he did.'

'Still, I don't see why he should mind. It's not his home, after all! It's not his private abode. I don't see why I shouldn't sit there if I want to.'

'Quite!' said Clifford. 'He thinks too much of himself, that man.'

'Do you think he does?'

'Oh, decidedly! He thinks he's something exceptional. You know he had a wife he didn't get on with, so he joined up in 1915 and was sent to India, I believe. Anyhow he was blacksmith to the cavalry in Egypt for a time; always was connected with horses, a clever fellow that way. Then some Indian colonel took a fancy to him, and he was made a lieutenant. Yes, they gave him a commission. I believe he went back to India with his colonel, and up to the north-west frontier. He was ill; he has a pension. He didn't come out of the army till last year, I believe, and then, naturally, it isn't easy for a man like that to get back to his own level. He's bound to flounder. But he does his duty all right, as far as I'm concerned. Only I'm not having any of the Lieutenant Mellors touch.'

'How could they make him an officer when he speaks broad Derbyshire?'

'He doesn't . . . except by fits and starts. He can speak perfectly well, for him. I suppose he has an idea if he's come down to the ranks again, he'd better speak as the ranks speak.'

'Why didn't you tell me about him before?'

'Oh, I've no patience with these romances. They're the ruin of all order. It's a thousand pities they ever happened.'

Connie was inclined to agree. What was the good of discontented people who fitted in nowhere?

In the spell of fine weather Clifford, too, decided to go to the wood. The wind was cold, but not so tiresome, and the sunshine was like life itself, warm and full.

'It's amazing,' said Connie, 'how different one feels when there's a really fresh fine day. Usually one feels the very air is half dead. People are killing the very air.'

'Do you think people are doing it?' he asked.

'I do. The steam of so much boredom, and discontent and anger out of all the people, just kills the vitality in the air. I'm sure of it.'

'Perhaps some condition of the atmosphere lowers the vitality of the people?' he said.

'No, it's man that poisons the universe,' she asserted.

'Fouls his own nest,' remarked Clifford.

The chair puffed on. In the hazel copse catkins were hanging pale gold, and in sunny places the wood-anemones were wide open, as if exclaiming with the joy of life, just as good as in past days, when people could exclaim along with them. They had a faint scent of apple-blossom. Connie gathered a few for Clifford.

He took them and looked at them curiously.

'Thou still unravished bride of quietness,' he quoted. 'It seems to fit flowers so much better than Greek vases.'

'Ravished is such a horrid word!' she said. 'It's only people who ravish things.'

'Oh, I don't know . . . snails and things,' he said.

'Even snails only eat them, and bees don't ravish.'

She was angry with him, turning everything into words. Violets were Juno's eyelids, and windflowers were unravished brides. How she hated words, always coming between her and life; they did the ravishing, if anything did: ready-made words and phrases, sucking all the life-sap out of living things.

The walk with Clifford was not quite a success. Between him and Connie there was a tension that each pretended not to notice, but there it was. Suddenly, with all the force of her female instinct, she was shoving him off. She wanted to be clear of him, and especially of his consciousness, his words, his obsession with himself, his endless treadmill obsession with himself, and his own words.

The weather came rainy again. But after a day or two she went out in the rain, and she went to the wood. And once there, she went towards the hut. It was raining, but not so cold, and the wood felt so silent and remote, inaccessible in the dusk of rain.

She came to the clearing. No one there! The hut was locked. But she sat on the log doorstep, under the rustic porch, and snuggled into her own warmth. So she sat, looking at the rain, listening to the many noiseless noises of it, and to the strange soughings of wind in upper branches, when there seemed to be no wind. Old oak-trees stood around, grey, powerful trunks, rain-blackened, round and vital, throwing off reckless limbs. The ground was fairly free of undergrowth, the anemones sprinkled, there was a bush or two, elder, or guelder-rose, and a purplish tangle of bramble: the old russet of bracken almost vanished under green anemone ruffs. Perhaps this was one of the unravished places. Unravished! The whole world was ravished.

Some things can't be ravished. You can't ravish a tin of sardines. And so many women are like that; and men. But the earth . . . !

The rain was abating. It was hardly making darkness among the oaks any more. Connie wanted to go; yet she sat on. But she was getting cold; yet the overwhelming inertia of her inner resentment kept her there as if paralysed.

Ravished! How ravished one could be without ever being touched. Ravished by dead words become obscene, and dead ideas become obsessions.

A wet brown dog came running and did not bark, lifting a wet feather of a tail. The man followed in a wet black oilskin jacket, like a chauffeur, and face flushed a little. She felt him recoil in his quick walk, when he saw her. She stood up in the handbreadth of dryness under the rustic porch. He saluted without speaking, coming slowly near. She began to withdraw.

'I'm just going,' she said.

'Was yer waitin' to get in?' he asked, looking at the hut, not at her.

'No, I only sat a few minutes in the shelter,' she said, with quiet dignity.

He looked at her. She looked cold.

'Sir Clifford 'adn't got no other key then?' he asked.

'No, but it doesn't matter. I can sit perfectly dry under this porch. Good afternoon!' She hated the excess of vernacular in his speech.

He watched her closely, as she was moving away. Then he hitched up his jacket, and put his hand in his breeches pocket, taking out the key of the hut.

''Appen yer'd better 'ave this key, an' Ah min fend for t' bods some other road.'

She looked at him.

'What do you mean?' she asked.

'I mean as 'appen Ah can find anuther pleece as'll du for rearin' th' pheasants. If yer want ter be 'ere, yo'll non want me messin' abaht a' th' time.'

She looked at him, getting his meaning through the fog of the dialect.

'Why don't you speak ordinary English?' she said coldly.

'Me! Ah thowt it *wor* ordinary.'

She was silent for a few moments in anger.

'So if yer want t' key, yer'd better ta'e it. Or 'appen Ah'd better gi'e 't yer termorrer, an' clear all t' stuff aht fust. Would that du for yer?'

She became more angry.

'I didn't want your key,' she said. 'I don't want you to clear anything out at all. I don't in the least want to turn you out of that hut, thank you! I only wanted to be able to sit here sometimes, like today. But I can sit perfectly well under the porch, so please say no more about it.'

He looked at her again, with his wicked blue eyes.

'Why,' he began, in the broad slow dialect. 'Your Ladyship's as welcome as Christmas ter th' hut an' th' key an' iverythink as is. On'y this time o' th' year ther's bods ter set, an' Ah've got ter be potterin' abaht a good bit, seein' after 'em, an a'. Winter time Ah ned 'ardly come nigh th' pleece. But what wi' spring, an' Sir Clifford wantin' ter start th' pheasants . . . An' your Ladyship'd non want me tinkerin' around an' about when she was 'ere, all the time.'

She listened with a dim kind of amazement.

'Why should I mind your being here?' she asked.

He looked at her curiously.

'T'nuisance on me!' he said briefly, but significantly. She flushed. 'Very well!' she said finally. 'I won't trouble you. But I don't think I should have minded at all sitting and seeing you look after the birds. I should have liked it. But since you think it interferes with you, I won't disturb you, don't be afraid. You are Sir Clifford's keeper, not mine.'

The phrase sounded queer, she didn't know why. But she let it pass.

'Nay, your Ladyship. It's your Ladyship's own 'ut. It's as your Ladyship likes an' pleases, every time. Yer can turn me off at a wik's notice. It wor only . . .'

'Only what?' she asked, baffled.

He pushed back his hat in an odd comic way.

'On'y as 'appen yo'd like the place ter yersen, when yer did come, an' not me messin' abaht.'

'But why?' she said, angry. 'Aren't you a civilized human being? Do you think I ought to be afraid of you? Why should I take any notice of you and your being here or not? Why is it important?'

He looked at her, all his face glimmering with wicked laughter.

'It's not, your Ladyship. Not in the very least,' he said.

'Well, why then?' she asked.

'Shall I get your Ladyship another key then?'

'No thank you! I don't want it.'

'Ah'll get it anyhow. We'd best 'ave two keys ter th' place.'

'And I consider you are insolent,' said Connie, with her colour up, panting a little.

'Nay, nay!' he said quickly. 'Dunna yer say that! Nay, nay! I niver meant nuthink. Ah on'y thought as if yo' come 'ere, Ah s'd 'ave ter clear out, an' it'd mean a lot of work, settin' up somewheres else. But if your Ladyship isn't going ter take no notice o' me, then . . . it's Sir Clifford's 'ut, an' everythink is as your Ladyship likes, everythink is as your Ladyship likes an' pleases, barrin' yer take no notice o' me, doin' th' bits of jobs as Ah've got ter do.'

Connie went away completely bewildered. She was not sure whether she had been insulted and mortally offended, or not. Perhaps the man really only meant what he said; that he thought she would expect him to keep away. As if she would dream of it! And as if he could possibly be so important, he and his stupid presence.

She went home in confusion, not knowing what she thought or felt.

9

Connie was surprised at her own feeling of aversion from Clifford. What is more, she felt she had always really disliked him. Not hate: there was no passion in it. But a profound physical dislike. Almost, it seemed to her, she had married him because she disliked him, in a secret, physical sort of way. But of course, she had married him really because in a mental way he attracted her and excited her. He had seemed, in some way, her master, beyond her.

Now the mental excitement had worn itself out and collapsed, and she was aware only of the physical aversion. It rose up in her from her depths: and she realized how it had been eating her life away.

She felt weak and utterly forlorn. She wished some help would come from outside. But in the whole world there was no help. Society was terrible because it was insane. Civilized society is insane. Money and so-called love are its two great manias; money a long way first. The individual asserts himself in his disconnected insanity in these two modes: money and love. Look at Michaelis! His life and activity were just insanity. His love was a sort of insanity.

And Clifford the same. All that talk! All that writing! All that wild struggling to push himself forwards! It was just insanity. And it was getting worse, really maniacal.

Connie felt washed-out with fear. But at least, Clifford was shifting his grip from her to Mrs Bolton. He did not know it. Like many insane people, his insanity might be measured by the things he was *not* aware of; the great desert tracts in his consciousness.

Mrs Bolton was admirable in many ways. But she had that queer sort of bossiness, endless assertion of her own will, which is one of the signs of insanity in modern woman. She *thought* she was utterly subservient and living for others. Clifford fascinated her because he always, or so often, frustrated her will, as if by a finer instinct. He had a finer, subtler will of self-assertion than herself. This was his charm for her.

Perhaps that had been his charm, too, for Connie.

'It's a lovely day, today!' Mrs Bolton would say in her caressive, persuasive voice. 'I should think you'd enjoy a little run in your chair today, the sun's just lovely.'

'Yes? Will you give me that book—there, that yellow one. And I think I'll have those hyacinths taken out.'

'Why they're so beautiful!' She pronounced it with the 'y' sound: be-yutiful! 'And the scent is simply gorgeous.'

'The scent is what I object to,' he said. 'It's a little funereal.'

'Do you think so!' she exclaimed in surprise, just a little offended, but impressed. And she carried the hyacinths out of the room, impressed by his higher fastidiousness.

'Shall I shave you this morning, or would you rather do it yourself?' Always the same soft, caressive, subservient, yet managing voice.

'I don't know. Do you mind waiting a while. I'll ring when I'm ready.'

'Very good, Sir Clifford!' she replied, so soft and submissive, withdrawing quietly. But every rebuff stored up new energy of will in her.

When he rang, after a time, she would appear at once. And then he would say: 'I think I'd rather you shaved me this morning.'

Her heart gave a little thrill, and she replied with extra softness:

'Very good, Sir Clifford!'

She was very deft, with a soft, lingering touch, a little slow. At first he had resented the infinitely soft touch of her fingers on his face. But now he liked it, with a growing voluptuousness. He let her shave him nearly every day: her face near his, her eyes so very concentrated, watching that she did it right. And gradually her fingertips knew his cheeks and lips, his jaw and chin and throat perfectly. He was well-fed and well-liking, his face and throat were handsome enough and he was a gentleman.

She was handsome too, pale, her face rather long and absolutely still, her eyes bright, but revealing nothing. Gradually, with infinite softness, almost with love, she was getting him by the throat, and he was yielding to her.

She now did almost everything for him, and he felt more at home with her, less ashamed of accepting her menial offices, than with Connie. She liked handling him. She loved having his body in her charge, absolutely, to the last menial offices. She said to Connie one day: 'All men are babies, when you come to the bottom of them. Why, I've handled some of the toughest customers as ever went down Tevershall pit. But let anything ail them so that you have to do for them, and they're babies, just big babies. Oh, there's not much difference in men!'

At first Mrs Bolton had thought there really was something different in a gentleman, a *real* gentleman, like Sir Clifford. So Clifford had got a good start of her. But gradually, as she came to the bottom of him, to use her own term, she found he was like the rest, a baby grown to man's proportions: but a baby with a queer temper and a fine manner and power in its control, and all sorts of odd knowledge that she had never dreamed of, with which he could still bully her. Connie was sometimes tempted to say to him:

'For God's sake, don't sink so horribly into the hands of that woman!' But she found she didn't care for him enough to say it, in the long run.

It was still their habit to spend the evening together, till ten o'clock. Then they would talk, or read together, or go over his manuscript. But the thrill had gone out of it. She was bored by his manuscripts. But she still dutifully typed them out for him. But in time Mrs Bolton would even do that.

For Connie had suggested to Mrs Bolton that she should learn to use a typewriter. And Mrs Bolton, always ready, had begun at once, and practised assiduously. So now Clifford would sometimes dictate a letter to her, and she would take it down rather slowly, but correctly. And he was very patient, spelling for her the difficult words, or the occasional phrases in French. She was so thrilled, it was almost a pleasure to instruct her.

Now Connie would sometimes plead a headache as an excuse for going up to her room after dinner.

'Perhaps Mrs Bolton will play piquet with you,' she said to Clifford.

'Oh, I shall be perfectly all right. You go to your own room and rest, darling.'

But no sooner had she gone, than he rang for Mrs Bolton, and asked her to take a hand at piquet or bezique, or even chess. He had taught her all these games. And Connie found it curiously objectionable to see Mrs Bolton, flushed and tremulous like a little girl, touching her queen or her knight with uncertain fingers, then drawing away again. And Clifford, faintly smiling with a half-teasing superiority, saying to her:

'You must say j'adoube!'

She looked up at him with bright, startled eyes, then murmured shyly, obediently:

'J'adoube!'

Yes, he was educating her. And he enjoyed it, it gave him a sense of power. And she was thrilled. She was coming bit by bit into possession of all that the gentry knew, all that made them upper class: apart from the money. That thrilled her. And at the same time, she was making him want to have her there with him. It was a subtle deep flattery to him, her genuine thrill.

To Connie, Clifford seemed to be coming out in his true colours: a little vulgar, a little common, and uninspired; rather fat. Ivy Bolton's tricks and humble bossiness were also only too transparent. But Connie did wonder at the genuine thrill which the woman got out of Clifford. To say she was in love with him would be putting it wrongly. She was thrilled by her contact with a man of the upper class, this titled gentleman, this author who could write books and poems, and whose photograph appeared in the illustrated newspapers. She was thrilled to a weird passion. And his 'educating' her roused in her a passion of excitement and response much deeper than any love affair could have done. In truth, the very fact that there could *be* no love affair left her free to thrill to her very marrow with this other passion, the peculiar passion of *knowing*, knowing as he knew.

There was no mistake that the woman was in some way in love with him: whatever force we give to the word love. She looked so handsome and so young, and her grey eyes were sometimes marvellous. At the same time, there was a lurking soft satisfaction about her, even of triumph, and private satisfaction. Ugh, that private satisfaction! How Connie loathed it!

But no wonder Clifford was caught by the woman! She absolutely adored him, in her persistent fashion, and put herself absolutely at his service, for him to use as he liked. No wonder he was flattered!

Connie heard long conversations going on between the two. Or rather, it was mostly Mrs Bolton talking. She had unloosed to him the stream of gossip about Tevershall village. It was more than gossip. It was Mrs Gaskell and George Eliot and Miss Mitford all rolled into one, with a great deal more, that these women left out. Once started, Mrs Bolton was better than any book, about the lives of the people. She knew them all so intimately, and had such a peculiar, flamey zest in all their affairs, it was wonderful, if just a *trifle* humiliating to listen to her. At first she had not ventured to 'talk Tevershall', as she called it, to Clifford. But once started, it went on. Clifford was listening for 'material', and he found it in plenty. Connie realized that his so-called genius was just this: a perspicuous talent for personal gossip, clever and apparently detached. Mrs Bolton, of course, was very warm when she 'talked Tevershall'. Carried away, in fact. And it was marvellous, the things that happened and that she knew about. She would have run to dozens of volumes.

Connie was fascinated, listening to her. But afterwards always a little ashamed. She ought not to listen with this queer rabid curiosity. After all, one may hear the most private affairs of other people, but only in a spirit of respect for the struggling, battered thing which any human soul is, and in a spirit of fine, discriminative sympathy. For even satire is a form of sympathy. It is the way our sympathy flows and recoils that really determines our lives. And here lies the vast importance of the novel, properly handled. It can inform and lead into new places the flow of our sympathetic consciousness, and it can lead our sympathy away in recoil from things gone dead. Therefore, the novel, properly handled, can reveal the most secret places of life: for it is in the *passional* secret places of life, above all, that the tide of sensitive awareness needs to ebb and flow, cleansing and freshening.

But the novel, like gossip, can also excite spurious sympathies and recoils, mechanical and deadening to the psyche. The novel can glorify the most corrupt feelings, so long as they are *conventionally* 'pure'. Then the novel, like gossip, becomes at last vicious, and, like gossip, all the more vicious because it is always ostensibly on the side of the angels. Mrs Bolton's gossip was always on the side of the angels. 'And he was such a *bad* fellow, and she was such a *nice* woman.' Whereas, as Connie could see even from Mrs Bolton's gossip, the woman had been merely a mealy-mouthed sort, and the man angrily honest. But angry honesty made a 'bad man' of him, and mealy-mouthedness made a 'nice woman' of her, in the vicious, conventional channelling of sympathy by Mrs Bolton.

For this reason, the gossip was humiliating. And for the same reason, most novels, especially popular ones, are humiliating too. The public responds now only to an appeal to its vices.

Nevertheless, one got a new vision of Tevershall village from Mrs Bolton's talk. A terrible, seething welter of ugly life it seemed: not at all the flat drabness it looked from outside. Clifford of course knew by sight most of the people mentioned, Connie knew only one or two. But it sounded really more like a Central African jungle than an English village.

'I suppose you heard as Miss Allsopp was married last week! Would you ever! Miss Allsopp, old James' daughter, the boot-and-shoe Allsopp. You know they built a house up at Pye Croft. The old man died last year from a fall; eighty-three, he was, an' nimble as a lad. An' then he slipped on Bestwood Hill, on a slide as the lads 'ad made last winter, an' broke his thigh, and that finished him, poor old man, it did seem a shame. Well, he left all his money to Tattie: didn't leave the boys a penny. An' Tattie, I know is five years—yes, she's fifty-three last autumn. And you know they were such Chapel people, my word! She taught Sunday school for thirty years, till her father died. And then she started carrying on with a fellow from Kinbrook, I don't know if you know him, an oldish fellow with a red nose, rather dandified, Willcock, as works in Harrison's woodyard. Well he's sixty-five, if he's a day, yet you'd have thought they were a pair of young turtle-doves, to see them, arm in arm, and kissing at the gate: yes, an' she sitting on his knee right in the bay window on Pye Croft Road, for anybody to see. And he's got sons over forty: only lost his wife two years ago. If old James Allsopp hasn't risen from his grave, it's because there is no rising: for he kept her that strict! Now they're married and gone to live down at Kinbrook, and they say she goes round in a dressing-gown from morning to night, a veritable sight. I'm sure it's awful, the way the old ones go on! Why they're a lot worse than the young, and a sight more disgusting. I lay it down to the pictures, myself. But you can't keep them away. I was always saying: go to a good instructive film, but do for goodness' sake keep away from these melodramas and love films. Anyhow keep the children away! But there you are, grown-ups are worse than the children: and the old ones beat the band. Talk about morality! Nobody cares a thing. Folks does as they like, and much better off they are for it, I must say. But they're having to draw their horns in nowadays, now th' pits are working so bad, and they haven't got the money. And the grumbling they do, it's awful, especially the women. The men are so good and patient! What can they do, poor chaps! But the women, oh, they do carry on! They go and show off, giving contributions for a wedding present for Princess Mary, and then when they see all the grand things that's been given, they simply rave: who's she, any better than anybody else! Why doesn't Swan & Edgar give me *one* fur coat, instead of giving her six. I wish I'd kept my ten shillings! What's she going to give *me*, I should like to know? Here I can't get a new spring coat, my dad's working that bad, and she gets van-loads. It's time as poor folks had some money to spend, rich ones 'as 'ad it long enough. I want a new spring coat, I do, an' wheer am I going to get it? I say to them, be thankful you're well fed and well clothed, without all the new finery you want! And they fly back at me: "Why isn't Princess Mary thankful to go about in her old rags, then, an' have nothing! Folks like *her* get van-loads, an' I can't have a new spring coat. It's a damned shame. Princess! Bloomin' rot about Princess! It's munney as matters, an' cos she's got lots, they give her more! Nobody's givin' me any, an' I've as much right as anybody else. Don't talk to me about education. It's munney as matters. I want a new spring coat, I do, an' I shan't get it, cos there's no munney . . ." That's all they care about, clothes. They think nothing of giving seven or eight guineas for a winter coat—colliers' daughters, mind you—and two guineas for a child's summer hat. And then they go to the Primitive Chapel in their two-guinea hat, girls as would have been proud of a three-and-sixpenny one in my day. I heard that at the Primitive Methodist anniversary this year, when they have a built-up platform for the Sunday School children, like a grandstand going almost up to th' ceiling, I heard Miss Thompson, who has the first class of girls in the Sunday School, say there'd be over a thousand pounds in new Sunday clothes sitting on that platform! And times are what they are! But you can't stop them. They're mad for clothes. And boys the same. The lads spend every penny on themselves, clothes, smoking, drinking in the Miners' Welfare, jaunting off to Sheffield two or three times a week. Why, it's another world. And they fear nothing, and they respect nothing, the young don't. The older men are that patient and good, really, they let the women take everything. And this is what it leads to. The women are positive demons. But the lads aren't like their dads. They're sacrificing nothing, they aren't: they're all for self. If you tell them they ought to be putting a bit by, for a home, they say: That'll keep, that will, I'm goin' t' enjoy mysen while I can. Owt else'll keep! Oh, they're rough an' selfish, if you like. Everything falls on the older men, an' it's a bad outlook all round.'

Clifford began to get a new idea of his own village. The place had always frightened him, but he had thought it more or less stable. Now–?

'Is there much Socialism, Bolshevism, among the people?' he asked.

'Oh!' said Mrs Bolton, 'you hear a few loud-mouthed ones. But they're mostly women who've got into debt. The men take no notice. I don't believe you'll ever turn our Tevershall men into reds. They're too decent for that. But the young ones blether sometimes. Not that they care for it really. They only want a bit of money in their pocket, to spend at the Welfare, or go gadding to Sheffield. That's all they care. When they've got no money, they'll listen to the reds spouting. But nobody believes in it, really.'

'So you think there's no danger?'

'Oh no! Not if trade was good, there wouldn't be. But if things were bad for a long spell, the young ones might go funny. I tell you, they're a selfish, spoilt lot. But I don't see how they'd ever do anything. They aren't ever serious about anything, except showing off on motor-bikes and dancing at the Palais-de-danse in Sheffield. You can't *make* them serious. The serious ones dress up in evening clothes and go off to the Pally to show off before a lot of girls and dance these new Charlestons and what not. I'm sure sometimes the bus'll be full of young fellows in evening suits, collier lads, off to the Pally: let alone those that have gone with their girls in motors or on motor-bikes. They don't give a serious thought to a thing–save Doncaster races, and the Derby: for they all of them bet on every race. And football! But even football's not what it was, not by a long chalk. It's too much like hard work, they say. No, they'd rather be off on motor-bikes to Sheffield or Nottingham, Saturday afternoons.'

'But what do they do when they get there?'

'Oh, hang around–and have tea in some fine tea-place like the Mikado–and go to the Pally or the pictures or the Empire, with some girl. The girls are as free as the lads. They do just what they like.'

'And what do they do when they haven't the money for these things?'

'They seem to get it, somehow. And they begin talking nasty then. But I don't see how you're going to get bolshevism, when all the lads want is just money to enjoy themselves, and the girls the same, with fine clothes: and they don't care about another thing. They haven't the brains to be socialists. They haven't enough seriousness to take anything really serious, and they never will have.'

Connie thought, how extremely like all the rest of the classes the lower classes sounded. Just the same thing over again, Tevershall or Mayfair or Kensington. There was only one class nowadays: moneyboys. The moneyboy and the moneygirl, the only difference was how much you'd got, and how much you wanted.

Under Mrs Bolton's influence, Clifford began to take a new interest in the mines. He began to feel he belonged. A new sort of self-assertion came into him. After all, he was the real boss in Tevershall, he was really the pits. It was a new sense of power, something he had till now shrunk from with dread.

Tevershall pits were running thin. There were only two collieries: Tevershall itself, and New London. Tevershall had once been a famous mine, and had made famous money. But its best days were over. New London was never very rich, and in ordinary times just got along decently. But now times were bad, and it was pits like New London that got left.

'There's a lot of Tevershall men left and gone to Stacks Gate and Whiteover,' said Mrs Bolton. 'You've not seen the new works at Stacks Gate, opened after the war, have you, Sir Clifford? Oh, you must go one day, they're something quite new: great big chemical works at the pit-head, doesn't look a bit like a colliery. They say they get more money out of the chemical by-products than out of the coal—I forget what it is. And the grand new houses for the men, fair mansions! Of course it's brought a lot of riff-raff from all over the country. But a lot of Tevershall men got on there, and doin' well, a lot better than our own men. They say Tevershall's done, finished: only a question of a few more years, and it'll have to shut down. And New London'll go first. My word, won't it be funny when there's no Tevershall pit working. It's bad enough during a strike, but my word, if it closes for good, it'll be like the end of the world. Even when I was a girl it was the best pit in the country, and a man counted himself lucky if he could on here. Oh, there's been some money made in Tevershall. And now the men say it's a sinking ship, and it's time they all got out. Doesn't it sound awful! But of course there's a lot as'll never go till they have to. They don't like these new fangled mines, such a depth, and all machinery to work them. Some of them simply dreads those iron men, as they call them, those machines for hewing the coal, where men always did it before. And they say it's wasteful as well. But what goes in waste is saved in wages, and a lot more. It seems soon there'll be no use for men on the face of the earth, it'll be all machines. But they say that's what folks said when they had to give up the old stocking frames. I can remember one or two. But my word, the more machines, the more people, that's what it looks like! They say you can't get the same chemicals out of Tevershall coal as you can out of Stacks Gate, and that's funny, they're not three miles apart. But they say so. But everybody says it's a shame something can't be started, to keep the men going a bit better, and employ the girls. All the girls traipsing off to Sheffield every day! My word, it would be something to talk about if Tevershall Collieries took a new lease of life, after everybody saying they're finished, and a sinking ship, and the men ought to leave them like rats leave a sinking ship. But folks talk so much. Of course there was a boom during the war. When Sir Geoffrey made a trust of himself and got the money safe for ever, somehow. So they say! But they say even the masters and the owners don't get much out of it now. You can hardly believe it, can you! Why I always thought the pits would go on for ever and ever. Who'd have thought, when I was a girl! But New England's shut down, so is Colwick Wood; yes, it's fair haunting to go through that coppy and see Colwick Wood standing there deserted among the trees, and bushes growing up all over the pit-head, and the lines red rusty. It's like death itself, a dead colliery. Why, whatever we should do if Tevershall shut down—? It doesn't bear thinking of. Always that throng it's been, except at strikes, and even then the fan-wheels didn't stand, except when they fetched the ponies up. I'm sure it's a funny world, you don't know where you are from year to year, you really don't.

It was Mrs Bolton's talk that really put a new fight into Clifford. His income, as she pointed out to him, was secure, from his father's trust, even though it was not large. The pits did not really concern him. It was the other world he wanted to capture, the world of literature and fame; the popular world, not the working world.

Now he realized the distinction between popular success and working success: the populace of pleasure and the populace of work. He, as a private individual, had been catering with his stories for the populace of pleasure. And he had caught on. But beneath the populace of pleasure lay the populace of work, grim, grimy, and rather terrible. They too had to have their providers. And it was a much grimmer business, providing for the populace of work, than for the populace of pleasure. While he was doing his stories, and 'getting on' in the world, Tevershall was going to the wall.

He realized now that the bitch-goddess of Success had two main appetites: one for flattery, adulation, stroking and tickling such as writers and artists gave her; but the other a grimmer appetite for meat and bones. And the meat and bones for the bitch-goddess were provided by the men who made money in industry.

Yes, there were two great groups of dogs wrangling for the bitch-goddess: the group of the flatterers, those who offered her amusement, stories, films, plays: and the other, much less showy, much more savage breed, those who gave her meat, the real substance of money. The well-groomed showy dogs of amusement wrangled and snarled among themselves for the favours of the bitch-goddess. But it was nothing to the silent fight-to-the-death that went on among the indispensables, the bone-bringers.

But under Mrs Bolton's influence, Clifford was tempted to enter this other fight, to capture the bitch-goddess by brute means of industrial production. Somehow, he got his pecker up. In one way, Mrs Bolton made a man of him, as Connie never did. Connie kept him apart, and made him sensitive and conscious of himself and his own states. Mrs Bolton made him aware only of outside things. Inwardly he began to go soft as pulp. But outwardly he began to be effective.

He even roused himself to go to the mines once more: and when he was there, he went down in a tub, and in a tub he was hauled out into the workings. Things he had learned before the war, and seemed utterly to have forgotten, now came back to him. He sat there, crippled, in a tub, with the underground manager showing him the seam with a powerful torch. And he said little. But his mind began to work.

He began to read again his technical works on the coal-mining industry, he studied the government reports, and he read with care the latest things on mining and the chemistry of coal and of shale which were written in German. Of course the most valuable discoveries were kept secret as far as possible. But once you started a sort of research in the field of coal-mining, a study of methods and means, a study of by-products and the chemical possibilities of coal, it was astounding the ingenuity and the almost uncanny cleverness of the modern technical mind, as if really the devil himself had lent fiend's wits to the technical scientists of industry. It was far more interesting than art, than literature, poor emotional half-witted stuff, was this technical science of industry. In this field, men were like gods, or demons, inspired to discoveries, and fighting to carry them out. In this activity, men were beyond any mental age calculable. But Clifford knew that when it did come to the emotional and human life, these self-made men were of a mental age of about thirteen, feeble boys. The discrepancy was enormous and appalling.

But let that be. Let man slide down to general idiocy in the emotional and 'human' mind, Clifford did not care. Let all that go hang. He was interested in the technicalities of modern coal-mining, and in pulling Tevershall out of the hole.

He went down to the pit day after day, he studied, he put the general manager, and the overhead manager, and the underground manager, and the engineers through a mill they had never dreamed of. Power! He felt a new sense of power flowing through him: power over all these men, over the hundreds and hundreds of colliers. He was finding out: and he was getting things into his grip.

And he seemed verily to be re-born. *Now* life came into him! He had been gradually dying, with Connie, in the isolated private life of the artist and the conscious being. Now let all that go. Let it sleep. He simply felt life rush into him out of the coal, out of the pit. The very stale air of the colliery was better than oxygen to him. It gave him a sense of power, power. He was doing something: and he was *going* to do something. He was going to win, to win: not as he had won with his stories, mere publicity, amid a whole sapping of energy and malice. But a man's victory.

At first he thought the solution lay in electricity: convert the coal into electric power. Then a new idea came. The Germans invented a new locomotive engine with a self feeder, that did not need a fireman. And it was to be fed with a new fuel, that burnt in small quantities, at a great heat, under peculiar conditions.

The idea of a new concentrated fuel that burnt with a hard slowness at a fierce heat was what first attracted Clifford. There must be some sort of external stimulus to the burning of such fuel, not merely air supply. He began to experiment, and got a clever young fellow, who had proved brilliant in chemistry, to help him.

And he felt triumphant. He had at last got out of himself. He had fulfilled his life-long secret yearning to get out of himself. Art had not done it for him. Art had only made it worse. But now, now he had done it.

He was not aware how much Mrs Bolton was behind him. He did not know how much he depended on her. But for all that, it was evident that when he was with her his voice dropped to an easy rhythm of intimacy, almost a trifle vulgar.

With Connie, he was a little stiff. He felt he owed her everything, everything, and he showed her the utmost respect and consideration, so long as she gave him mere outward respect. But it was obvious he had a secret dread of her. The new Achilles in him had a heel, and in this heel the woman, the woman like Connie, his wife, could lame him fatally. He went in a certain half-subservient dread of her, and was extremely nice to her. But his voice was a little tense when he spoke to her, and he began to be silent whenever she was present.

Only when he was alone with Mrs Bolton did he really feel a lord and a master, and his voice ran on with her almost as easily and garrulously as her own could run. And he let her shave him or sponge all his body as if he were a child, really as if he were a child.

10

Connie was a good deal alone now, fewer people came to Wragby. Clifford no longer wanted them. He had turned against even the cronies. He was queer. He preferred the radio, which he had installed at some expense, with a good deal of success at last. He could sometimes get Madrid or Frankfurt, even there in the uneasy Midlands.

And he would sit alone for hours listening to the loud-speaker bellowing forth. It amazed and stunned Connie. But there he would sit, with a blank entranced expression on his face, like a person losing his mind, and listen, or seem to listen, to the unspeakable thing.

Was he really listening? Or was it a sort of soporific he took, whilst something else worked on underneath in him? Connie did not know. She fled up to her room, or out of doors to the wood. A kind of terror filled her sometimes, a terror of the incipient insanity of the whole civilized species.

But now that Clifford was drifting off to this other weirdness of industrial activity, becoming almost a *creature*, with a hard, efficient shell of an exterior and a pulpy interior, one of the amazing crabs and lobsters of the modern, industrial and financial world, invertebrates of the crustacean order, with shells of steel, like machines, and inner bodies of soft pulp, Connie herself was really completely stranded.

She was not even free, for Clifford must have her there. He seemed to have a nervous terror that she should leave him. The curious pulpy part of him, the emotional and humanly-individual part, depended on her with terror, like a child, almost like an idiot. She must be there, there at Wragby, a Lady Chatterley, his wife. Otherwise he would be lost like an idiot on a moor.

This amazing dependence Connie realized with a sort of horror. She heard him with his pit managers, with the members of his Board, with young scientists, and she was amazed at his shrewd insight into things, his power, his uncanny material power over what is called practical men. He had become a practical man himself, and an amazingly astute and powerful one, a master. Connie attributed it to Mrs Bolton's influence upon him, just at the crisis in his life.

But this astute and practical man was almost an idiot when left alone to his own emotional life. He worshipped Connie. She was his wife, a higher being, and he worshipped her with a queer, craven idolatry, like a savage, a worship based on enormous fear, and even hate of the power of the idol, the dread idol. All he wanted was for Connie to swear, to swear not to leave him, not to give him away.

'Clifford,' she said to him—but this was after she had the key to the hut—'Would you really like me to have a child one day?'

He looked at her with a furtive apprehension in his rather prominent pale eyes.

'I shouldn't mind, if it made no difference between us,' he said.

'No difference to what?' she asked.

'To you and me; to our love for one another. If it's going to affect that, then I'm all against it. Why, I might even one day have a child of my own!'

She looked at him in amazement.

'I mean, it might come back to me one of these days.'

She still stared in amazement, and he was uncomfortable.

'So you would not like it if I had a child?' she said.

'I tell you,' he replied quickly, like a cornered dog, 'I am quite willing, provided it doesn't touch your love for me. If it would touch that, I am dead against it.'

Connie could only be silent in cold fear and contempt. Such talk was really the gabbling of an idiot. He no longer knew what he was talking about.

'Oh, it wouldn't make any difference to my feeling for you,' she said, with a certain sarcasm.

'There!' he said. 'That is the point! In that case I don't mind in the least. I mean it would be awfully nice to have a child running about the house, and feel one was building up a future for it. I should have something to strive for then, and I should know it was your child, shouldn't I, dear? And it would seem just the same as my own. Because it is you who count in these matters. You know that, don't you, dear? I don't enter, I am a cypher. You are the great I-am! as far as life goes. You know that, don't you? I mean, as far as I am concerned. I mean, but for you I am absolutely nothing. I live for your sake and your future. I am nothing to myself.'

Connie heard it all with deepening dismay and repulsion. It was one of the ghastly half-truths that poison human existence. What man in his senses would say such things to a woman! But men aren't in their senses. What man with a spark of honour would put this ghastly burden of life-responsibility upon a woman, and leave her there, in the void?

Moreover, in half an hour's time, Connie heard Clifford talking to Mrs Bolton, in a hot, impulsive voice, revealing himself in a sort of passionless passion to the woman, as if she were half mistress, half foster-mother to him. And Mrs Bolton was carefully dressing him in evening clothes, for there were important business guests in the house.

Connie really sometimes felt she would die at this time. She felt she was being crushed to death by weird lies, and by the amazing cruelty of idiocy. Clifford's strange business efficiency in a way over-awed her, and his declaration of private worship put her into a panic. There was nothing between them. She never even touched him nowadays, and he never touched her. He never even took her hand and held it kindly. No, and because they were so utterly out of touch, he tortured her with his declaration of idolatry. It was the cruelty of utter impotence. And she felt her reason would give way, or she would die.

She fled as much as possible to the wood. One afternoon, as she sat brooding, watching the water bubbling coldly in John's Well, the keeper had strode up to her.

'I got you a key made, my Lady!' he said, saluting, and he offered her the key.

'Thank you so much!' she said, startled.

'The hut's not very tidy, if you don't mind,' he said. 'I cleared it what I could.'

'But I didn't want you to trouble!' she said.

'Oh, it wasn't any trouble. I am setting the hens in about a week. But they won't be scared of you. I s'll have to see to them morning and night, but I shan't bother you any more than I can help.'

'But you wouldn't bother me,' she pleaded' 'I'd rather not go to the hut at all, if I am going to be in the way.'

He looked at her with his keen blue eyes. He seemed kindly, but distant. But at least he was sane, and wholesome, if even he looked thin and ill. A cough troubled him.

'You have a cough,' she said.

'Nothin—a cold! The last pneumonia left me with a cough, but it's nothing.'

He kept distant from her, and would not come any nearer.

She went fairly often to the hut, in the morning or in the afternoon, but he was never there. No doubt he avoided her on purpose. He wanted to keep his own privacy.

He had made the hut tidy, put the little table and chair near the fireplace, left a little pile of kindling and small logs, and put the tools and traps away as far as possible, effacing himself. Outside, by the clearing, he had built a low little roof of boughs and straw, a shelter for the birds, and under it stood the five coops. And, one day when she came, she found two brown hens sitting alert and fierce in the coops, sitting on pheasants' eggs, and fluffed out so proud and deep in all the heat of the pondering female blood. This almost broke Connie's heart. She, herself, was so forlorn and unused, not a female at all, just a mere thing of terrors.

Then all five coops were occupied by hens, three brown and a grey and a black. All alike, they clustered themselves down on the eggs in the soft nestling ponderosity of the female urge, the female nature, fluffing out their feathers. And with brilliant eyes they watched Connie, as she crouched before them, and they gave short sharp clucks of anger and alarm, but chiefly of female anger at being approached.

Connie found corn in the corn-bin in the hut. She offered it to the hens in her hand. They would not eat it. Only one hen pecked at her hand with a fierce little jab, so Connie was frightened. But she was pining to give them something, the brooding mothers who neither fed themselves nor drank. She brought water in a little tin, and was delighted when one of the hens drank.

Now she came every day to the hens, they were the only things in the world that warmed her heart. Clifford's protestations made her go cold from head to foot. Mrs Bolton's voice made her go cold, and the sound of the business men who came. An occasional letter from Michaelis affected her with the same sense of chill. She felt she would surely die if it lasted much longer.

Yet it was spring, and the bluebells were coming in the wood, and the leaf-buds on the hazels were opening like the spatter of green rain. How terrible it was that it should be spring, and everything cold-hearted, cold-hearted. Only the hens, fluffed so wonderfully on the eggs, were warm with their hot, brooding female bodies! Connie felt herself living on the brink of fainting all the time.

Then one day, a lovely sunny day with great tufts of primroses under the hazels, and many violets dotting the paths, she came in the afternoon to the coops and there was one tiny, tiny perky chicken tinily prancing round in front of a coop, and the mother hen clucking in terror. The slim little chick was greyish brown with dark markings, and it was the most alive little spark of a creature in seven kingdoms at that moment. Connie crouched to watch in a sort of ecstasy. Life, life! Pure, sparky, fearless new life! New life! So tiny and so utterly without fear! Even when it scampered a little, scrambling into the coop again, and disappeared under the hen's feathers in answer to the mother hen's wild alarm-cries, it was not really frightened, it took it as a game, the game of living. For in a moment a tiny sharp head was poking through the gold-brown feathers of the hen, and eyeing the Cosmos.

Connie was fascinated. And at the same time, never had she felt so acutely the agony of her own female forlornness. It was becoming unbearable.

She had only one desire now, to go to the clearing in the wood. The rest was a kind of painful dream. But sometimes she was kept all day at Wragby, by her duties as hostess. And then she felt as if she too were going blank, just blank and insane.

One evening, guests or no guests, she escaped after tea. It was late, and she fled across the park like one who fears to be called back. The sun was setting rosy as she entered the wood, but she pressed on among the flowers. The light would last long overhead.

She arrived at the clearing flushed and semi-conscious. The keeper was there, in his shirt-sleeves, just closing up the coops for the night, so the little occupants would be safe. But still one little trio was pattering about on tiny feet, alert drab mites, under the straw shelter, refusing to be called in by the anxious mother.

'I had to come and see the chickens!' she said, panting, glancing shyly at the keeper, almost unaware of him. 'Are there any more?'

'Thirty-six so far!' he said. 'Not bad!'

He too took a curious pleasure in watching the young things come out.

Connie crouched in front of the last coop. The three chicks had run in. But still their cheeky heads came poking sharply through the yellow feathers, then withdrawing, then only one beady little head eying forth from the vast mother-body.

'I'd love to touch them,' she said, putting her fingers gingerly through the bars of the coop. But the mother-hen pecked at her hand fiercely, and Connie drew back startled and frightened.

'How she pecks at me! She hates me!' she said in a wondering voice. 'But I wouldn't hurt them!'

The man standing above her laughed, and crouched down beside her, knees apart, and put his hand with quiet confidence slowly into the coop. The old hen pecked at him, but not so savagely. And slowly, softly, with sure gentle fingers, he felt among the old bird's feathers and drew out a faintly-peeping chick in his closed hand.

'There!' he said, holding out his hand to her. She took the little drab thing between her hands, and there it stood, on its impossible little stalks of legs, its atom of balancing life trembling through its almost weightless feet into Connie's hands. But it lifted its handsome, clean-shaped little head boldly, and looked sharply round, and gave a little 'peep'. 'So adorable! So cheeky!' she said softly.

The keeper, squatting beside her, was also watching with an amused face the bold little bird in her hands. Suddenly he saw a tear fall on to her wrist.

And he stood up, and stood away, moving to the other coop. For suddenly he was aware of the old flame shooting and leaping up in his loins, that he had hoped was quiescent for ever. He fought against it, turning his back to her. But it leapt, and leapt downwards, circling in his knees.

He turned again to look at her. 'She was kneeling and holding her two hands slowly forward, blindly, so that the chicken should run into the mother-hen again. And there was something so mute and forlorn in her, compassion flamed in his bowels for her.

Without knowing, he came quickly towards her and crouched beside her again, taking the chick from her hands, because she was afraid of the hen, and putting it back in the coop. At the back of his loins the fire suddenly darted stronger.

He glanced apprehensively at her. Her face was averted, and she was crying blindly, in all the anguish of her generation's forlornness. His heart melted suddenly, like a drop of fire, and he put out his hand and laid his fingers on her knee.

'You shouldn't cry,' he said softly.

But then she put her hands over her face and felt that really her heart was broken and nothing mattered any more.

He laid his hand on her shoulder, and softly, gently, it began to travel down the curve of her back, blindly, with a blind stroking motion, to the curve of her crouching loins. And there his hand softly, softly, stroked the curve of her flank, in the blind instinctive caress.

She had found her scrap of handkerchief and was blindly trying to dry her face.

'Shall you come to the hut?' he said, in a quiet, neutral voice.

And closing his hand softly on her upper arm, he drew her up and led her slowly to the hut, not letting go of her till she was inside. Then he cleared aside the chair and table, and took a brown, soldier's blanket from the tool chest, spreading it slowly. She glanced at his face, as she stood motionless.

His face was pale and without expression, like that of a man submitting to fate.

'You lie there,' he said softly, and he shut the door, so that it was dark, quite dark.

With a queer obedience, she lay down on the blanket. Then she felt the soft, groping helplessly desirous hand touching her body, feeling for her face. The hand stroked her face softly, softly, with infinite soothing and assurance, and at last there was the soft touch of a kiss on her cheek.

She lay quite still, in a sort of sleep, in a sort of dream. Then she quivered as she felt his hand groping softly, yet with queer thwarted clumsiness, among her clothing. Yet the hand knew, too, how to unclothe her where it wanted. He drew down the thin silk sheath, slowly, carefully, right down and over her feet. Then with a quiver of exquisite pleasure he touched the warm soft body, and touched her navel for a moment in a kiss. And he had to come in to her at once, to enter the peace on earth of her soft, quiescent body. It was the moment of pure peace for him, the entry into the body of the woman.

She lay still, in a kind of sleep, always in a kind of sleep. The activity, the orgasm was his, all his; she could strive for herself no more. Even the tightness of his arms around her, even the intense movement of his body, and the springing of his seed in her, was a kind of sleep, from which she did not begin to rouse till he had finished and lay softly panting against her breast.

Then she wondered, just dimly wondered, why? Why was this necessary? Why had it lifted a great cloud from her and given her peace? Was it real? Was it real?

Her tormented modern-woman's brain still had no rest. Was it real? And she knew, if she gave herself to the man, it was real. But if she kept herself for herself, it was nothing. She was old; millions of years old, she felt. And at last, she could bear the burden of herself no more. She was to be had for the taking. To be had for the taking.

The man lay in a mysterious stillness. What was he feeling? What was he thinking? She did not know. He was a strange man to her, she did not know him. She must only wait, for she did not dare to break his mysterious stillness. He lay there with his arms round her, his body on hers, his wet body touching hers, so close. And completely unknown. Yet not unpeaceful. His very stillness was peaceful.

She knew that, when at last he roused and drew away from her. It was like an abandonment. He drew her dress in the darkness down over her knees and stood a few moments, apparently adjusting his own clothing. Then he quietly opened the door and went out.

She saw a very brilliant little moon shining above the afterglow over the oaks. Quickly she got up and arranged herself; she was tidy. Then she went to the door of the hut.

All the lower wood was in shadow, almost darkness. Yet the sky overhead was crystal. But it shed hardly any light. He came through the lower shadow towards her, his face lifted like a pale blotch.

'Shall we go then?' he said.

'Where?'

'I'll go with you to the gate.'

He arranged things his own way. He locked the door of the hut and came after her.

'You aren't sorry, are you?' he asked, as he went at her side.

'No! No! Are you?' she said.

'For that! No!' he said. Then after a while he added: 'But there's the rest of things.'

'What rest of things?' she said.

'Sir Clifford. Other folks. All the complications.'

'Why complications?' she said, disappointed.

'It's always so. For you as well as for me. There's always complications.' He walked on steadily in the dark.

'And are you sorry?' she said.

'In a way!' he replied, looking up at the sky. 'I thought I'd done with it all. Now I've begun again.'

'Begun what?'

'Life.'

'Life!' she re-echoed, with a queer thrill.

'It's life,' he said. 'There's no keeping clear. And if you do keep clear you might almost as well die. So if I've got to be broken open again, I have.'

She did not quite see it that way, but still . . .

'It's just love,' she said cheerfully.

'Whatever that may be,' he replied.

They went on through the darkening wood in silence, till they were almost at the gate.

'But you don't hate me, do you?' she said wistfully.

'Nay, nay,' he replied. And suddenly he held her fast against his breast again, with the old connecting passion. 'Nay, for me it was good, it was good. Was it for you?'

'Yes, for me too,' she answered, a little untruthfully, for she had not been conscious of much.

He kissed her softly, softly, with the kisses of warmth.

'If only there weren't so many other people in the world,' he said lugubriously.

She laughed. They were at the gate to the park. He opened it for her.

'I won't come any further,' he said.

'No!' And she held out her hand, as if to shake hands. But he took it in both his.

'Shall I come again?' she asked wistfully.

'Yes! Yes!'

She left him and went across the park.

He stood back and watched her going into the dark, against the pallor of the horizon. Almost with bitterness he watched her go. She had connected him up again, when he had wanted to be alone. She had cost him that bitter privacy of a man who at last wants only to be alone.

He turned into the dark of the wood. All was still, the moon had set. But he was aware of the noises of the night, the engines at Stacks Gate, the traffic on the main road. Slowly he climbed the denuded knoll. And from the top he could see the country, bright rows of lights at Stacks Gate, smaller lights at Tevershall pit, the yellow lights of Tevershall and lights everywhere, here and there, on the dark country, with the distant blush of furnaces, faint and rosy, since the night was clear, the rosiness of the outpouring of white-hot metal. Sharp, wicked electric lights at Stacks Gate! An undefinable quick of evil in them! And all the unease, the ever-shifting dread of the industrial night in the Midlands. He could hear the winding-engines at Stacks Gate turning down the seven-o'clock miners. The pit worked three shifts.

He went down again into the darkness and seclusion of the wood. But he knew that the seclusion of the wood was illusory. The industrial noises broke the solitude, the sharp lights, though unseen, mocked it. A man could no longer be private and withdrawn. The world allows no hermits. And now he had taken the woman, and brought on himself a new cycle of pain and doom. For he knew by experience what it meant.

It was not the woman's fault, not even love's fault, nor the fault of sex. The fault lay there, out there, in those evil electric lights and diabolical rattlings of engines. There, in the world of the mechanical greedy, greedy mechanism and mechanized greed, sparkling with lights and gushing hot metal and roaring with traffic, there lay the vast evil thing, ready to destroy whatever did not conform. Soon it would destroy the wood, and bluebells would spring no more. All vulnerable things must perish under the rolling and running of iron.

He thought with infinite tenderness of the woman. Poor forlorn thing, she was nicer than she knew, and oh! so much too nice for the tough lot she was in contact with. Poor thing, she too had some of the vulnerability of the wild hyacinths, she wasn't all tough rubber-goods and platinum, like the modern girl. And they would do her in! As sure as life, they would do her in, as they do in all naturally tender life. Tender! Somewhere she was tender, tender with a tenderness of the growing hyacinths, something that has gone out of the celluloid women of today. But he would protect her with his heart for a little while. For a little while, before the insentient iron world and the Mammon of mechanized greed did them both in, her as well as him.

He went home with his gun and his dog, to the dark cottage, lit the lamp, started the fire, and ate his supper of bread and cheese, young onions and beer. He was alone, in a silence he loved. His room was clean and tidy, but rather stark. Yet the fire was bright, the hearth white, the petroleum lamp hung bright over the table, with its white oil-cloth. He tried to read a book about India, but tonight he could not read. He sat by the fire in his shirt-sleeves, not smoking, but with a mug of beer in reach. And he thought about Connie.

To tell the truth, he was sorry for what had happened, perhaps most for her sake. He had a sense of foreboding. No sense of wrong or sin; he was troubled by no conscience in that respect. He knew that conscience was chiefly fear of society, or fear of oneself. He was not afraid of himself. But he was quite consciously afraid of society, which he knew by instinct to be a malevolent, partly-insane beast.

The woman! If she could be there with him, and there were nobody else in the world! The desire rose again, his penis began to stir like a live bird. At the same time an oppression, a dread of exposing himself and her to that outside Thing that sparkled viciously in the electric lights, weighed down his shoulders. She, poor young thing, was just a young female creature to him; but a young female creature whom he had gone into and whom he desired again.

Stretching with the curious yawn of desire, for he had been alone and apart from man or woman for four years, he rose and took his coat again, and his gun, lowered the lamp and went out into the starry night, with the dog. Driven by desire and by dread of the malevolent Thing outside, he made his round in the wood, slowly, softly. He loved the darkness and folded himself into it. It fitted the turgidity of his desire which, in spite of all, was like a riches; the stirring restlessness of his penis, the stirring fire in his loins! Oh, if only there were other men to be with, to fight that sparkling electric Thing outside there, to preserve the tenderness of life, the tenderness of women, and the natural riches of desire. If only there were men to fight side by side with! But the men were all outside there, glorying in the Thing, triumphing or being trodden down in the rush of mechanized greed or of greedy mechanism.

Constance, for her part, had hurried across the park, home, almost without thinking. As yet she had no afterthought. She would be in time for dinner.

She was annoyed to find the doors fastened, however, so that she had to ring. Mrs Bolton opened.

'Why there you are, your Ladyship! I was beginning to wonder if you'd gone lost!' she said a little roguishly. 'Sir Clifford hasn't asked for you, though; he's got Mr Linley in with him, talking over something. It looks as if he'd stay to dinner, doesn't it, my Lady?'

'It does rather,' said Connie.

'Shall I put dinner back a quarter of an hour? That would give you time to dress in comfort.'

'Perhaps you'd better.'

Mr Linley was the general manager of the collieries, an elderly man from the north, with not quite enough punch to suit Clifford; not up to post-war conditions, nor post-war colliers either, with their 'ca' canny' creed. But Connie liked Mr Linley, though she was glad to be spared the toadying of his wife.

Linley stayed to dinner, and Connie was the hostess men liked so much, so modest, yet so attentive and aware, with big, wide blue eyes and a soft repose that sufficiently hid what she was really thinking. Connie had played this woman so much, it was almost second nature to her; but still, decidedly second. Yet it was curious how everything disappeared from her consciousness while she played it.

She waited patiently till she could go upstairs and think her own thoughts. She was always waiting, it seemed to be her *forte.*

Once in her room, however, she felt still vague and confused. She didn't know what to think. What sort of a man was he, really? Did he really like her? Not much, she felt. Yet he was kind. There was something, a sort of warm naïve kindness, curious and sudden, that almost opened her womb to him. But she felt he might be kind like that to any woman. Though even so, it was curiously soothing, comforting. And he was a passionate man, wholesome and passionate. But perhaps he wasn't quite individual enough; he might be the same with any woman as he had been with her. It really wasn't personal. She was only really a female to him.

But perhaps that was better. And after all, he was kind to the female in her, which no man had ever been. Men were very kind to the *person* she was, but rather cruel to the female, despising her or ignoring her altogether. Men were awfully kind to Constance Reid or to Lady Chatterley; but not to her womb they weren't kind. And he took notice of Constance or of Lady Chatterley; he just softly stroked her loins or her breasts.

She went to the wood next day. It was a grey, still afternoon, with the dark-green dog's-mercury spreading under the hazel copse, and all the trees making a silent effort to open their buds. Today she could almost feel it in her own body, the huge heave of the sap in the massive trees, upwards, up, up to the bud-tips, there to push into little flamey oak-leaves, bronze as blood. It was like a tide running turgid upward, and spreading on the sky.

She came to the clearing, but he was not there. She had only half expected him. The pheasant chicks were running lightly abroad, light as insects, from the coops where the fellow hens clucked anxiously. Connie sat and watched them, and waited. She only waited. Even the chicks she hardly saw. She waited.

The time passed with dream-like slowness, and he did not come. She had only half expected him. He never came in the afternoon. She must go home to tea. But she had to force herself to leave.

As she went home, a fine drizzle of rain fell.

'Is it raining again?' said Clifford, seeing her shake her hat.

'Just drizzle.'

She poured tea in silence, absorbed in a sort of obstinacy. She did want to see the keeper today, to see if it were really real. If it were really real.

'Shall I read a little to you afterwards?' said Clifford.

She looked at him. Had he sensed something?

'The spring makes me feel queer—I thought I might rest a little,' she said.

'Just as you like. Not feeling really unwell, are you?'

'No! Only rather tired—with the spring. Will you have Mrs Bolton to play something with you?'

'No! I think I'll listen in.'

She heard the curious satisfaction in his voice. She went upstairs to her bedroom. There she heard the loud-speaker begin to bellow, in an idiotically velveteen-genteel sort of voice, something about a series of street-cries, the very cream of genteel affection imitating old criers. She pulled on her old violet-coloured mackintosh, and slipped out of the house at the side door.

The drizzle of rain was like a veil over the world, mysterious, hushed, not cold. She got very warm as she hurried across the park. She had to open her light waterproof.

The wood was silent, still and secret in the evening drizzle of rain, full of the mystery of eggs and half-open buds, half-unsheathed flowers. In the dimness of it all trees glistened naked and dark as if they had unclothed themselves, and the green things on earth seemed to hum with greenness.

There was still no one at the clearing. The chicks had nearly all gone under the mother-hens, only one or two last adventurous ones still dibbed about in the dryness under the straw roof-shelter. And they were doubtful of themselves.

So! He still had not been. He was staying away on purpose. Or perhaps something was wrong. Perhaps she should go to the cottage and see.

But she was born to wait. She opened the hut with her key. It was all tidy, the corn put in the bin, the blankets folded on the shelf, the straw neat in a corner; a new bundle of straw. The hurricane lamp hung on a nail. The table and chair had been put back where she had lain.

She sat down on a stool in the doorway. How still everything was! The fine rain blew very softly, filmily, but the wind made no noise. Nothing made any sound. The trees stood like powerful beings, dim, twilit, silent and alive. How alive everthing was!

Night was drawing near again; she would have to go. He was avoiding her.

But suddenly he came striding into the clearing, in his black oilskin jacket a chauffeur, shining with wet. He glanced quickly at the hut, half-saluted, then veered aside and went on to the coops. There he crouched in silence, looking carefully at everything, then carefully shutting the hens and chicks up safe against the night.

At last he came slowly towards her. She still sat on her stool. He stood before her under the porch.

'You come then,' he said, using the intonation of the dialect.

'Yes,' she said, looking up at him. 'You're late!''

'Ay!' he replied, looking away into the wood.

She rose slowly, drawing aside her stool.

'Did you want to come in?' she asked.

He looked down at her shrewdly.

'Won't folks be thinkin' somethink, you comin' here every night?' he said.

'Why?' She looked up at him, at a loss. 'I said I'd come. Nobody knows.'

'They soon will, though,' he replied. 'An' what then?'

She was at a loss for an answer.

'Why should they know?' she said.

'Folks always does,' he said fatally.

Her lip quivered a little.

'Well I can't help it,' she faltered.

'Nay,' he said. 'You can help it by not comin'–if yer want to,' he added, in a lower tone.

'But I don't want to,' she murmured.

He looked away into the wood, and was silent.

'But what when folks find out?' he asked at last. 'Think about it! Think how lowered you'll feel, one of your husband's servants.'

She looked up at his averted face.

'Is it,' she stammered, 'is it that you don't want me?'

'Think!' he said. 'Think what if folks find out–Sir Clifford an' a'–an' everybody talkin'–'

'Well, I can go away.'

'Where to?'

'Anywhere! I've got money of my own. My mother left me twenty thousand pounds in trust, and I know Clifford can't touch it. I can go away.'

'But 'appen you don't want to go away.'

'Yes, yes! I don't care what happens to me.'

'Ay, you think that! But you'll care! You'll have to care, everybody has. You've got to remember your Ladyship is carrying on with a game-keeper. It's not as if I was a gentleman. Yes, you'd care. You'd care.'

'I shouldn't. What do I care about my ladyship! I hate it really. I feel people are jeering every time they say it. And they are, they are! Even you jeer when you say it.'

'Me!'

For the first time he looked straight at her, and into her eyes.

'I don't jeer at you,' he said.

As he looked into her eyes she saw his own eyes go dark, quite dark, the pupils dilating.

'Don't you care about a' the risk?' he asked in a husky voice. 'You should care. Don't care when it's too late!'

There was a curious warning pleading in his voice.

'But I've nothing to lose,' she said fretfully. 'If you knew what it is, you'd think I'd be glad to lose it. But are you afraid for yourself?'

'Ay!' he said briefly. 'I am. I'm afraid. I'm afraid o' things.'

'What things?' she asked.

He gave a curious backward jerk of his head, indicating the outer world.

'Things! Everybody! The lot of 'em.'

Then he bent down and suddenly kissed her unhappy face.

'Nay, I don't care,' he said. 'Let's have it, an' damn the rest. But if you was to feel sorry you'd ever done it–!'

'Don't put me off,' she pleaded.

He put his fingers to her cheek and kissed her again suddenly.

'Let me come in then,' he said softly. 'An' take off your mackintosh.'

He hung up his gun, slipped out of his wet leather jacket, and reached for the blankets.

'I brought another blanket,' he said, 'so we can put one over us if you like.'

'I can't stay long,' she said. 'Dinner is half past seven.'

He looked at her swiftly, then at his watch.

'All right,' he said.

He shut the door, and lit a tiny light in the hanging hurricane lamp.

'One time we'll have a long time,' he said.

He put the blankets down carefully, one folded for her head. Then he sat down a moment on the stool, and drew her to him, holding her close with one arm, feeling for her body with his free hand. She heard the catch of his intaken breath as he found her. Under her frail petticoat she was naked.

'Eh! what it is to touch thee!' he said, as his finger caressed the delicate, warm, secret skin of her waist and hips. He put his face down and rubbed his cheek against her belly and against her thighs again and again. And again she wondered a little over the sort of rapture it was to him. She did not understand the beauty he found in her, through touch upon her living secret body, almost the ecstasy of beauty. For passion alone is awake to it. And when passion is dead, or absent, then the magnificent throb of beauty is incomprehensible and even a little despicable; warm, live beauty of contact, so much deeper than the beauty of vision. She felt the glide of his cheek on her thighs and belly and buttocks, and the close brushing of his moustache and his soft thick hair, and her knees began to quiver. Far down in her she felt a new stirring, a new nakedness emerging. And she was half afraid. Half she wished he would not caress her so. He was encompassing her somehow. Yet she was waiting, waiting.

And when he came into her, with an intensification of relief and consummation that was pure peace to him, still she was waiting. She felt herself a little left out. And she knew, partly it was her own fault. She will herself into this separateness. Now perhaps she was condemned to it. She lay still, feeling his motion within her, his deep-sunk intentness, the sudden quiver of him at the springing of his seed, then the slow-subsiding thrust. That thrust of the buttocks, surely it was a little ridiculous. If you were a woman, and a part in all the business, surely that thrusting of the man's buttocks was supremely ridiculous. Surely the man was intensely ridiculous in this posture and this act!

But she lay still, without recoil. Even when he had finished, she did not rouse herself to get a grip on her own satisfaction, as she had done with Michaelis; she lay still, and the tears slowly filled and ran from her eyes.

He lay still, too. But he held her close and tried to cover her poor naked legs with his legs, to keep them warm. He lay on her with a close, undoubting warmth.

'Are yer cold?' he asked, in a soft, small voice, as if she were close, so close. Whereas she was left out, distant.

'No! But I must go,' she said gently.

He sighed, held her closer, then relaxed to rest again.

He had not guessed her tears. He thought she was there with him.

'I must go,' she repeated.

He lifted himself, kneeled beside her a moment, kissed the inner side of her thighs, then drew down her skirts, buttoning his own clothes unthinking, not even turning aside, in the faint, faint light from the lantern.

'Tha mun come ter th' cottage one time,' he said, looking down at her with a warm, sure, easy face.

But she lay there inert, and was gazing up at him thinking: Stranger! Stranger! She even resented him a little.

He put on his coat and looked for his hat, which had fallen, then slung on his gun.

'Come then!' he said, looking down at her with those warm, peaceful sort of eyes.

She rose slowly. She didn't want to go. She also rather resented staying. He helped her with her thin waterproof, and saw she was tidy.

Then he opened the door. The outside was quite dark. The faithful dog under the porch stood up with pleasure seeing him. The drizzle of rain drifted greyly past upon the darkness. It was quite dark.

'Ah mun ta'e th' lantern,' he said. The'll be nob'dy.'

He walked just before her in the narrow path, swinging the hurricane lamp low, revealing the wet grass, the black shiny tree-roots like snakes, wan flowers. For the rest, all was grey rain-mist and complete darkness.

'Tha mun com to the cottage one time,' he said, 'shall ta? We might as well be hung for a sheep as for a lamb.'

It puzzled her, his queer, persistent wanting her, when there was nothing between them, when he never really spoke to her, and in spite of herself she resented the dialect. His 'tha mun come' seemed not addressed to her, but some common woman. She recognized the foxglove leaves of the riding and knew, more or less, where they were.

'It's quarter past seven,' he said, 'you'll do it.' He had changed his voice, seemed to feel her distance. As they turned the last bend in the riding towards the hazel wall and the gate, he blew out the light. 'We'll see from here,' he said, taking her gently by the arm.

But it was difficult, the earth under their feet was a mystery, but he felt his way by tread: he was used to it. At the gate he gave her his electric torch. 'It's a bit lighter in the park,' he said; 'but take it for fear you get off the' path.'

It was true, there seemed a ghost-glimmer of greyness in the open space of the park. He suddenly drew her to him and whipped his hand under her dress again, feeling her warm body with his wet, chill hand.

'I could die for the touch of a woman like thee,' he said in his throat. 'If tha' would stop another minute.'

She felt the sudden force of his wanting her again.

'No, I must run,' she said, a little wildly.

'Ay,' he replied, suddenly changed, letting her go.

She turned away, and on the instant she turned back to him saying: 'Kiss me.'

He bent over her indistinguishable and kissed her on the left eye. She held her mouth and he softly kissed it, but at once drew away. He hated mouth kisses.

'I'll come tomorrow,' she said, drawing away; 'if I can,' she added.

'Ay! not so late,' he replied out of the darkness. Already she could not see him at all.

'Goodnight,' she said.

'Goodnight, your Ladyship,' his voice.

She stopped and looked back into the wet dark. She could just see the bulk of him. 'Why did you say that?' she said.

'Nay,' he replied. 'Goodnight then, run!'

She plunged on in the dark-grey tangible night. She found the side door open, and slipped into her room unseen. As she closed the door the gong sounded, but she would take her bath all the same–she must take her bath. 'But I won't be late any more,' she said to herself; 'it's too annoying.'

The next day she did not go to the wood. She went instead with Clifford to Uthwaite. He could occasionally go out now in the car, and had got a strong young man as chauffeur, who could help him out of the car if need be. He particularly wanted to see his godfather, Leslie Winter, who lived at Shipley Hall, not far from Uthwaite. Winter was an elderly gentleman now, wealthy, one of the wealthy coal-owners who had had their hey-day in King Edward's time. King Edward had stayed more than once at Shipley, for the shooting. It was a handsome old stucco hall, very elegantly appointed, for Winter was a bachelor and prided himself on his style; but the place was beset by collieries. Leslie Winter was attached to Clifford, but personally did not entertain a great respect for him, because of the photographs in illustrated papers and the literature. The old man was a buck of the King Edward school, who thought life was life and the scribbling fellows were something else. Towards Connie the Squire was always rather gallant; he thought her an attractive demure maiden and rather wasted on Clifford, and it was a thousand pities she stood no chance of bringing forth an heir to Wragby. He himself had no heir.

Connie wondered what he would say if he knew that Clifford's game-keeper had been having intercourse with her, and saying to her 'tha mun come to th' cottage one time.' He would detest and despise her, for he had come almost to hate the shoving forward of the working classes. A man of her own class he would not mind, for Connie was gifted from nature with this appearance of demure, submissive maidenliness, and perhaps it was part of her nature. Winter called her 'dear child' and gave her a rather lovely miniature of an eighteenth-century lady, rather against her will.

But Connie was preoccupied with her affair with the keeper. After all, Mr Winter, who was really a gentleman and a man of the world, treated her as a person and a discriminating individual; he did not lump her together with all the rest of his female womanhood in his 'thee' and 'tha'.

She did not go to the wood that day nor the next, nor the day following. She did not go so long as she felt, or imagined she felt, the man waiting for her, wanting her. But the fourth day she was terribly unsettled and uneasy. She still refused to go to the wood and open her thighs once more to the man. She thought of all the things she might do—drive to Sheffield, pay visits, and the thought of all these things was repellent. At last she decided to take a walk, not towards the wood, but in the opposite direction; she would go to Marehay, through the little iron gate in the other side of the park fence. It was a quiet grey day of spring, almost warm. She walked on unheeding, absorbed in thoughts she was not even conscious of. She was not really aware of anything outside her, till she was startled by the loud barking of the dog at Marehay Farm. Marehay Farm! Its pastures ran up to Wragby park fence, so they were neighbours, but it was some time since Connie had called.

'Bell!' she said to the big white bull-terrier. 'Bell! have you forgotten me? Don't you know me?' She was afraid of dogs, and Bell stood back and bellowed, and she wanted to pass through the farmyard on to the warren path.

Mrs Flint appeared. She was a woman of Constance's own age, had been a school-teacher, but Connie suspected her of being rather a false little thing.

'Why, it's Lady Chatterley! Why!' And Mrs Flint's eyes glowed again, and she flushed like a young girl. 'Bell, Bell. Why! barking at Lady Chatterley! Bell! Be quiet!' She darted forward and slashed at the dog with a white cloth she held in her hand, then came forward to Connie.

'She used to know me,' said Connie, shaking hands. The Flints were Chatterley tenants.

'Of course she knows your Ladyship! She's just showing off,' said Mrs Flint, glowing and looking up with a sort of flushed confusion, 'but it's so long since she's seen you. I do hope you are better.'

'Yes thanks, I'm all right.'

'We've hardly seen you all winter. Will you come in and look at the baby?'

'Well!' Connie hesitated. 'Just for a minute.'

Mrs Flint flew wildly in to tidy up, and Connie came slowly after her, hesitating in the rather dark kitchen where the kettle was boiling by the fire. Back came Mrs Flint.

'I do hope you'll excuse me,' she said 'Will you come in here?'

They went into the living-room, where a baby was sitting on the rag hearthrug, and the table was roughly set for tea. A young servant-girl backed down the passage, shy and awkward.

The baby was a perky little thing of about a year, with red hair like its father, and cheeky pale-blue eyes. It was a girl, and not to be daunted. It sat among cushions and was surrounded with rag dolls and other toys in modern excess.

'Why, what a dear she is!' said Connie, 'and how she's grown! A big girl! A big girl!'

She had given it a shawl when it was born, and celluloid ducks for Christmas.

'There, Josephine! Who's that come to see you? Who's this, Josephine? Lady Chatterley–you know Lady Chatterley, don't you?'

The queer pert little mite gazed cheekily at Connie. Ladyships were still all the same to her.

'Come! Will you come to me?' said Connie to the baby.

The baby didn't care one way or another, so Connie picked her up and held her in her lap. How warm and lovely it was to hold a child in one's lap, and the soft little arms, the unconscious cheeky little legs.

'I was just having a rough cup of tea all by myself. Luke's gone to market, so I can have it when I like. Would you care for a cup, Lady Chatterley? I don't suppose it's what you're used to, but if you would . . .'

Connie would, though she didn't want to be reminded of what she was used to. There was a great relaying of the table, and the best cups brought and the best tea-pot.

'If only you wouldn't take any trouble,' said Connie.

But if Mrs Flint took no trouble, where was the fun! So Connie played with the child and was amused by its little female dauntlessness, and got a deep voluptuous pleasure out of its soft young warmth. Young life! And so fearless! So fearless, because so defenceless. All the other people, so narrow with fear!

She had a cup of tea, which was rather strong, and very good bread and butter, and bottled damsons. Mrs Flint flushed and glowed and bridled with excitement, as if Connie were some gallant knight. And they had a real female chat, and both of them enjoyed it.

'It's a poor little tea, though,' said Mrs Flint.

'It's much nicer than at home,' said Connie truthfully.

'Oh-h!' said Mrs Flint, not believing, of course.

But at last Connie rose.

'I must go,' she said. 'My husband has no idea where I am. He'll be wondering all kinds of things.'

'He'll never think you're here,' laughed Mrs Flint excitedly. 'He'll be sending the crier round.'

'Goodbye, Josephine,' said Connie, kissing the baby and ruffling its red, wispy hair.

Mrs Flint insisted on opening the locked and barred front door. Connie emerged in the farm's little front garden, shut in by a privet hedge. There were two rows of auriculas by the path, very velvety and rich.

'Lovely auriculas,' said Connie.

'Recklesses, as Luke calls them,' laughed Mrs Flint. 'Have some.'

And eagerly she picked the velvet and primrose flowers.

'Enough! Enough!' said Connie.

They came to the little garden gate.

'Which way were you going?' asked Mrs Flint.

'By the warren.'

'Let me see! Oh yes, the cows are in the gin close. But they're not up yet. But the gate's locked, you'll have to climb.'

'I can climb,' said Connie.

'Perhaps I can just go down the close with you.'

They went down the poor, rabbit-bitten pasture. Birds were whistling in wild evening triumph in the wood. A man was calling up the last cows, which trailed slowly over the path-worn pasture.

'They're late milking, tonight,' said Mrs Flint severely. 'They know Luke won't be back till after dark.'

They came to the fence, beyond which the young fir-wood bristled dense. There was a little gate, but it was locked. In the grass on the inside stood a bottle, empty.

'There's the keeper's empty bottle for his milk,' explained Mrs Flint. 'We bring it as far as here for him, and then he fetches it himself.'

'When?' said Connie.

'Oh, any time he's around. Often in the morning. Well, goodbye Lady Chatterley! And do come again. It was so lovely having you.'

Connie climbed the fence into the narrow path between the dense, bristling young firs. Mrs Flint went running back across the pasture, in a sun-bonnet, because she was really a school-teacher. Constance didn't like this dense new part of the wood; it seemed gruesome and choking. She hurried on with her head down, thinking of the Flints' baby. It was a dear little thing, but it would be a bit bow-legged like its father. It showed already, but perhaps it would grow out of it. How warm and fulfilling somehow to have a baby, and how Mrs Flint had showed it off! She had something anyhow that Connie hadn't got, and apparently couldn't have. Yes, Mrs Flint had flaunted her motherhood. And Connie had been just a bit, just a little bit jealous. She couldn't help it.

She started out of her muse, and gave a little cry of fear. A man was there. It was the keeper. He stood in the path like Balaam's ass, barring her way.

'How's this?' he said in surprise.

'How did you come?' she panted.

'How did you? Have you been to the hut?'

'No! No! I went to Marehay.'

He looked at her curiously, searchingly, and she hung her head a little guiltily.

'And were you going to the hut now?' he asked rather sternly.

'No! I mustn't. I stayed at Marehay. No one knows where I am. I'm late. I've got to run.'

'Giving me the slip, like?' he said, with a faint ironic smile.

'No! No. Not that. Only—'

'Why, what else?' he said. And he stepped up to her and put his arms around her. She felt the front of his body terribly near to her, and alive.

'Oh, not now, not now,' she cried, trying to push him away.

'Why not? It's only six o'clock. You've got half an hour. Nay! Nay! I want you.'

He held her fast and she felt his urgency. Her old instinct was to fight for her freedom. But something else in her was strange and inert and heavy. His body was urgent against her, and she hadn't the heart any more to fight.

He looked around.

'Come—come here! Through here,' he said, looking penetratingly into the dense fir-trees, that were young and not more than half-grown.

He looked back at her. She saw his eyes, tense and brilliant, fierce, not loving. But her will had left her. A strange weight was on her limbs. She was giving way. She was giving up.

He led her through the wall of prickly trees, that were difficult to come through, to a place where was a little space and a pile of dead boughs. He threw one or two dry ones down, put his coat and waistcoat over them, and she had to lie down there under the boughs of the tree, like an animal, while he waited, standing there in his shirt and breeches, watching her with haunted eyes. But still he was provident—he made her lie properly, properly. Yet he broke the band of her underclothes, for she did not help him, only lay inert.

He too had bared the front part of his body and she felt his naked flesh against her as he came into her. For a moment he was still inside her, turgid there and quivering. Then as he began to move, in the sudden helpless orgasm, there awoke in her new strange thrills rippling inside her. Rippling, rippling, rippling, like a flapping overlapping of soft flames, soft as feathers, running to points of brilliance, exquisite, exquisite and melting her all molten inside. It was like bells rippling up and up to a culmination. She lay unconscious of the wild little cries she uttered at the last. But it was over too soon, too soon, and she could no longer force her own conclusion with her own activity. This was different, different. She could do nothing. She could no longer harden and grip for her own satisfaction upon him. She could only wait, wait and moan in spirit as she felt him withdrawing, withdrawing and contracting, coming to the terrible moment when he would slip out of her and be gone. Whilst all her womb was open and soft, and softly clamouring, like a sea-anemone under the tide, clamouring for him to come in again and make a fulfilment for her. She clung to him unconscious in passion, and he never quite slipped from her, and she felt the soft bud of him within her stirring, and strange rhythms flushing up into her with a strange rhythmic growing motion, swelling and swelling till it filled all her cleaving consciousness, and then began again the unspeakable motion that was not really motion, but pure deepening whirlpools of sensation swirling deeper and deeper through all her tissue and consciousness, till she was one perfect concentric fluid of feeling, and she lay there crying in unconscious inarticulate cries. The voice out of the uttermost night, the life! The man heard it beneath him with a kind of awe, as his life sprang out into her. And as it subsided, he subsided too and lay utterly still, unknowing, while her grip on him slowly relaxed, and she lay inert. And they lay and knew nothing, not even of each other, both lost. Till at last he began to rouse and become aware of his defenceless nakedness, and she was aware that his body was loosening its clasp on her. He was coming apart; but in her breast she felt she could not bear him to leave her uncovered. He must cover her now for ever.

But he drew away at last, and kissed her and covered her over, and began to cover himself. She lay looking up to the boughs of the tree, unable as yet to move. He stood and fastened up his breeches, looking around. All was dense and silent, save for the awed dog that lay with its paws against its nose. He sat down again on the brushwood and took Connie's hand in silence.

She turned and looked at him. 'We came off together that time,' he said.

She did not answer.

'It's good when it's like that. Most folks live their lives through and they never know it,' he said, speaking rather dreamily.

She looked into his brooding face.

'Do they?' she said. 'Are you glad?'

He looked back into her eyes. 'Glad,' he said, 'Ay, but never mind.' He did not want her to talk. And he bent over her and kissed her, and she felt, so he must kiss her for ever.

At last she sat up.

'Don't people often come off together?' she asked with naïve curiosity.

'A good many of them never. You can see by the raw look of them.' He spoke unwittingly, regretting he had begun.

'Have you come off like that with other women?'

He looked at her amused.

'I don't know,' he said, 'I don't know.'

And she knew he would never tell her anything he didn't want to tell her. She watched his face, and the passion for him moved in her bowels. She resisted it as far as she could, for it was the loss of herself to herself.

He put on his waistcoat and his coat, and pushed a way through to the path again.

The last level rays of the sun touched the wood. 'I won't come with you,' he said; 'better not.'

She looked at him wistfully before she turned. His dog was waiting so anxiously for him to go, and he seemed to have nothing whatever to say. Nothing left.

Connie went slowly home, realizing the depth of the other thing in her. Another self was alive in her, burning molten and soft in her womb and bowels, and with this self she adored him. She adored him till her knees were weak as she walked. In her womb and bowels she was flowing and alive now and vulnerable, and helpless in adoration of him as the most naïve woman. It feels like a child, she said to herself; it feels like a child in me. And so it did, as if her womb, that had always been shut, had opened and filled with new life, almost a burden, yet lovely.

'If I had a child!' she thought to herself; 'if I had him inside me as a child!'—and her limbs turned molten at the thought, and she realized the immense difference between having a child to oneself, and having a child to a man whom one's bowels yearned towards. The former seemed in a sense ordinary: but to have a child to a man whom one adored in one's bowels and one's womb, it made her feel she was very different from her old self, and as if she was sinking deep, deep to the centre of all womanhood and the sleep of creation.

It was not the passion that was new to her, it was the yearning adoration. She knew she had always feared it, for it left her helpless; she feared it still, lest if she adored him too much, then she would lose herself, become effaced, and she did not want to be effaced, a slave, like a savage woman. She must not become a slave. She feared her adoration, yet she would not at once fight against it. She knew she could fight it. She had a devil of self-will in her breast that could have fought the full soft heaving adoration of her womb and crushed it. She could even now do it, or she thought so, and she could then take up her passion with her own will.

Ah yes, to be passionate like a Bacchante, like a Bacchanal fleeing through the woods, to call on Iacchos, the bright phallos that had no independent personality behind it, but was pure god-servant to the woman! The man, the individual, let him not dare intrude. He was but a temple-servant, the bearer and keeper of the bright phallos, her own.

So, in the flux of new awakening, the old hard passion flamed in her for a time, and the man dwindled to a contemptible object, the mere phallos-bearer, to be torn to pieces when his service was performed. She felt the force of the Bacchae in her limbs and her body, the woman gleaming and rapid, beating down the male; but while she felt this, her heart was heavy. She did not want it, it was known and barren, birthless; the adoration was her treasure. It was so fathomless, so soft, so deep and so unknown. No, no, she would give up her hard bright female power; she was weary of it, stiffened with it; she would sink in the new bath of life, in the depths of her womb and her bowels that sang the voiceless song of adoration. It was early yet to begin to fear the man.

'I walked over by Marehay, and I had tea with Mrs Flint,' she said to Clifford. 'I wanted to see the baby. It's so adorable, with hair like red cobwebs. Such a dear! Mr Flint had gone to market, so she and I and the baby had tea together. Did you wonder where I was?'

'Well, I wondered, but I guessed you had dropped in somewhere to tea,' said Clifford jealously. With a sort of second sight he sensed something new in her, something to him quite incomprehensible, but he ascribed it to the baby. He thought that all that ailed Connie was that she did not have a baby, automatically bring one forth, so to speak.

'I saw you go across the park to the iron gate, my Lady,' said Mrs Bolton; 'so I thought perhaps you'd called at the Rectory.'

'I nearly did, then I turned towards Marehay instead.'

The eyes of the two women met: Mrs Bolton's grey and bright and searching; Connie's blue and veiled and strangely beautiful. Mrs Bolton was almost sure she had a lover, yet how could it be, and who could it be? Where was there a man?

'Oh, it's so good for you, if you go out and see a bit of company sometimes,' said Mrs Bolton. 'I was saying to Sir Clifford, it would do her ladyship a world of good if she'd go out among people more.'

'Yes, I'm glad I went, and such a quaint dear cheeky baby, Clifford,' said Connie. 'It's got hair just like spider-webs, and bright orange, and the oddest, cheekiest, pale-blue china eyes. Of course it's a girl, or it wouldn't be so bold, bolder than any little Sir Francis Drake.'

'You're right, my Lady–a regular little Flint. They were always a forward sandy-headed family, said Mrs Bolton.

'Wouldn't you like to see it, Clifford? I've asked them to tea for you to see it.'

'Who?' he asked, looking at Connie in great uneasiness.

'Mrs Flint and the baby, next Monday.'

'You can have them to tea up in your room,' he said.

'Why, don't you want to see the baby?' she cried.

'Oh, I'll see it, but I don't want to sit through a tea-time with them.'

'Oh,' cried Connie, looking at him with wide veiled eyes.

She did not really see him, he was somebody else.

'You can have a nice cosy tea in your room, my Lady, and Mrs Flint will be more comfortable than if Sir Clifford was there,' said Mrs Bolton.

She was sure Connie had a lover, and something in her soul exulted. But who was he? Who was he? Perhaps Mrs Flint would provide a clue.

Connie would not take her bath this evening. The sense of his flesh touching her, his very stickiness upon her, was dear to her, and in a sense holy.

Clifford was very uneasy. He would not let her go after dinner, and she had wanted so much to be alone. She looked at him, but was curiously submissive.

'Shall we play a game, or shall I read to you, or what shall it be?' he asked uneasily.

'You read to me,' said Connie.

'What shall I read—verse or prose? Or drama?

'Read Racine,' she said.

It had been one of his stunts in the past, to read Racine in the real French grand manner, but he was rusty now, and a little self-conscious; he really preferred the loud-speaker. But Connie was sewing, sewing a little frock of primrose silk, cut out of one of her dresses, for Mrs Flint's baby. Between coming home and dinner she had cut it out, and she sat in the soft quiescent rapture of herself, sewing, while the noise of the reading went on.

Inside herself she could feel the humming of passion, like the after-humming of deep bells.

Clifford said something to her about the Racine. She caught the sense after the words had gone.

'Yes! Yes!' she said, looking up at him 'It *is* splendid.'

Again he was frightened at the deep blue blaze of her eyes, and of her soft stillness, sitting there. She had never been so utterly soft and still. She fascinated him helplessly, as if some perfume about her intoxicated him. So he went on helplessly with his reading, and the throaty sound of the French was like the wind in the chimneys to her. Of the Racine she heard not one syllable.

She was gone in her own soft rapture, like a forest soughing with the dim, glad moan of spring, moving into bud. She could feel in the same world with her the man, the nameless man, moving on beautiful feet, beautiful in the phallic mystery. And in herself, in all her veins, she felt him and his child. His child was in all her veins, like a twilight.

'For hands she hath none, nor eyes, nor feet, nor golden Treasure of hair . . .'

She was like a forest, like the dark interlacing of the oak-wood, humming inaudibly with myriad unfolding buds. Meanwhile the birds of desire were asleep in the vast interlaced intricacy of her body.

But Clifford's voice went on, clapping and gurgling with unusual sounds. How extraordinary it was! How extraordinary he was, bent there over the book, queer and rapacious and civilized, with broad shoulders and no real legs! What a strange creature, with the sharp, cold inflexible will of some bird, and no warmth, no warmth at all! One of those creatures of the afterwards, that have no soul, but an extra-alert will, cold will. She shuddered a little, afraid of him. But then, the soft warm flame of life was stronger than he, and the real things were hidden from him.

The reading finished. She was startled. She looked up, and was more startled still to see Clifford watching her with pale, uncanny eyes, like hate.

'Thank you *so* much! You do read Racine beautifully!' she said softly.

'Almost as beautifully as you listen to him,' he said cruelly. 'What are you making?' he asked.

'I'm making a child's dress, for Mrs Flint's baby.'

He turned away. A child! A child! That was all her obsession.

'After all,' he said in a declamatory voice, 'one gets all one wants out of Racine. Emotions that are ordered and given shape are more important than disorderly emotions.'

She watched him with wide, vague, veiled eyes.

'Yes, I'm sure they are,' she said.

'The modern world has only vulgarized emotion by letting it loose. What we need is classic control.'

'Yes,' she said slowly, thinking of him listening with vacant face to the emotional idiocy of the radio. 'People pretend to have emotions, and they really feel nothing. I suppose that is being romantic.'

'Exactly!' he said.

As a matter of fact, he was tired. This evening had tired him. He would rather have been with his technical books, or his pit-manager, or listening-in to the radio.

Mrs Bolton came in with two glasses of malted milk: for Clifford, to make him sleep, and for Connie, to fatten her again. It was a regular night-cap she had introduced.

Connie was glad to go, when she had drunk her glass, and thankful she needn't help Clifford to bed. She took his glass and put it on the tray, then took the tray, to leave it outside.

'Goodnight Clifford! *Do* sleep well! The Racine gets into one like a dream. Goodnight!'

She had drifted to the door. She was going without kissing him goodnight. He watched her with sharp, cold eyes. So! She did not even kiss him goodnight, after he had spent an evening reading to her. Such depths of callousness in her! Even if the kiss was but a formality, it was on such formalities that life depends. She was a Bolshevik, really. Her instincts were Bolshevistic! He gazed coldly and angrily at the door whence she had gone. Anger!

And again the dread of the night came on him. He was a network of nerves, and when he was not braced up to work, and so full of energy: or when he was not listening-in, and so utterly neuter: then he was haunted by anxiety and a sense of dangerous impending void. He was afraid. And Connie could keep the fear off him, if she would. But it was obvious she wouldn't, she wouldn't. She was callous, cold and callous to all that he did for her. He gave up his life for her, and she was callous to him. She only wanted her own way. 'The lady loves her will.'

Now it was a baby she was obsessed by. Just so that it should be her own, all her own, and not his!

Clifford was so healthy, considering. He looked so well and ruddy in the face, his shoulders were broad and strong, his chest deep, he had put on flesh. And yet, at the same time, he was afraid of death. A terrible hollow seemed to menace him somewhere, somehow, a void, and into this void his energy would collapse. Energyless, he felt at times he was dead, really dead.

So his rather prominent pale eyes had a queer look, furtive, and yet a little cruel, so cold: and at the same time, almost impudent. It was a very odd look, this look of impudence: as if he were triumphing over life in spite of life. 'Who knoweth the mysteries of the will—for it can triumph even against the angels—'

But his dread was the nights when he could not sleep. Then it was awful indeed, when annihilation pressed in on him on every side. Then it was ghastly, to exist without having any life: lifeless, in the night, to exist.

But now he could ring for Mrs Bolton. And she would always come. That was a great comfort. She would come in her dressing-gown, with her hair in a plait down her back, curiously girlish and dim, though the brown plait was streaked with grey. And she would make him coffee or camomile tea, and she would play chess or piquet with him. She had a woman's queer faculty of playing even chess well enough, when she was three parts asleep, well enough to make her worth beating. So, in the silent intimacy of the night, they sat, or she sat and he lay on the bed, with the reading-lamp shedding its solitary light on them, she almost gone in sleep, he almost gone in a sort of fear, and they played, played together—then they had a cup of coffee and a biscuit together, hardly speaking, in the silence of night, but being a reassurance to one another.

And this night she was wondering who Lady Chatterley's lover was. And she was thinking of her own Ted, so long dead, yet for her never quite dead. And when she thought of him, the old, old grudge against the world rose up, but especially against the masters, that they had killed him. They had not really killed him. Yet, to her, emotionally, they had. And somewhere deep in herself, because of it, she was a nihilist, and really anarchic.

In her half-sleep, thoughts of her Ted and thoughts of Lady Chatterley's unknown lover commingled, and then she felt she shared with the other woman a great grudge against Sir Clifford and all he stood for. At the same time she was playing piquet with him, and they were gambling sixpences. And it was a source of satisfaction to be playing piquet with a baronet, and even losing sixpences to him.

When they played cards, they always gambled. It made him forget himself. And he usually won. Tonight too he was winning. So he would not go to sleep till the first dawn appeared. Luckily it began to appear at half past four or thereabouts.

Connie was in bed, and fast asleep all this time. But the keeper, too, could not rest. He had closed the coops and made his round of the wood, then gone home and eaten supper. But he did not go to bed. Instead he sat by the fire and thought.

He thought of his boyhood in Tevershall, and of his five or six years of married life. He thought of his wife, and always bitterly. She had seemed so brutal. But he had not seen her now since 1915, in the spring when he joined up. Yet there she was, not three miles away, and more brutal than ever. He hoped never to see her again while he lived.

He thought of his life abroad, as a soldier. India, Egypt, then India again: the blind, thoughtless life with the horses: the colonel who had loved him and whom he had loved: the several years that he had been an officer, a lieutenant with a very fair chance of being a captain. Then the death of the colonel from pneumonia, and his own narrow escape from death: his damaged health: his deep restlessness: his leaving the army and coming back to England to be a working man again.

He was temporizing with life. He had thought he would be safe, at least for a time, in this wood. There was no shooting as yet: he had to rear the pheasants. He would have no guns to serve. He would be alone, and apart from life, which was all he wanted. He had to have some sort of a background. And this was his native place. There was even his mother, though she had never meant very much to him. And he could go on in life, existing from day to day, without connexion and without hope. For he did not know what to do with himself.

He did not know what to do with himself. Since he had been an officer for some years, and had mixed among the other officers and civil servants, with their wives and families, he had lost all ambition to 'get on'. There was a toughness, a curious rubber-necked toughness and unlivingness about the middle and upper classes, as he had known them, which just left him feeling cold and different from them.

So, he had come back to his own class. To find there, what he had forgotten during his absence of years, a pettiness and a vulgarity of manner extremely distasteful. He admitted now at last, how important manner was. He admitted, also, how important it was even *to pretend* not to care about the half-pence and the small things of life. But among the common people there was no pretence. A penny more or less on the bacon was worse than a change in the Gospel. He could not stand it.

And again, there was the wage-squabble. Having lived among the owning classes, he knew the utter futility of expecting any solution of the wage-squabble. There was no solution, short of death. The only thing was not to care, not to care about the wages.

Yet, if you were poor and wretched you *had* to care. Anyhow, it was becoming the only thing they did care about. The *care* about money was like a great cancer, eating away the individuals of all classes. He refused to *care* about money.

And what then? What did life offer apart from the care of money? Nothing. Yet he could live alone, in the wan satisfaction of being alone, and raise pheasants to be shot ultimately by fat men after breakfast. It was futility, futility to the *n*th power.

But why care, why bother? And he had not cared nor bothered till now, when this woman had come into his life. He was nearly ten years older than she. And he was a thousand years older in experience, starting from the bottom. The connexion between them was growing closer. He could see the day when it would clinch up and they would have to make a life together. 'For the bonds of love are ill to loose!'

And what then? What then? Must he start again, with nothing to start on? Must he entangle this woman? Must he have the horrible broil with her lame husband? And also some sort of horrible broil with his own brutal wife, who hated him? Misery! Lots of misery! And he was no longer young and merely buoyant. Neither was he the insouciant sort. Every bitterness and every ugliness would hurt him: and the woman!

But even if they got clear of Sir Clifford and of his wife, even if they got clear, what were they going to do? What was he, himself, going to do? What was he going to do with his life? For he must do something. He couldn't be a mere hanger-on, on her money and his own very small pension.

It was the insoluble. He could only think of going to America, to try a new air. He disbelieved in the dollar utterly. But perhaps, perhaps there was something else.

He could not rest nor even go to bed. After sitting in a stupor of bitter thoughts until midnight, he got suddenly from his chair and reached for his coat and gun.

'Come on, lass,' he said to the dog. 'We're best outside.'

It was a starry night, but moonless. He went on a slow, scrupulous, soft-stepping and stealthy round. The only thing he had to contend with was the colliers setting snares for rabbits, particularly the Stacks Gate colliers, on the Marehay side. But it was breeding season, and even colliers respected it a little. Nevertheless the stealthy beating of the round in search of poachers soothed his nerves and took his mind off his thoughts.

But when he had done his slow, cautious beating of his bounds–it was nearly a five-mile walk–he was tired. He went to the top of the knoll and looked out. There was no sound save the noise, the faint shuffling noise from Stacks Gate colliery, that never ceased working: and there were hardly any lights, save the brilliant electric rows at the works. The world lay darkly and fumily sleeping. It was half past two. But even in its sleep it was an uneasy, cruel world, stirring with the noise of a train or some great lorry on the road, and flashing with some rosy lightning-flash from the furnaces. It was a world of iron and coal, the cruelty of iron and the smoke of coal, and the endless greed that drove it all. Only greed, greed stirring in its sleep.

It was cold, and he was coughing. A fine cold draught blew over the knoll. He thought of the woman. Now he would have given all he had or ever might have to hold her warm in his arms, both of them wrapped in one blanket, and sleep. All hopes of eternity and all gain from the past he would have given to have her there, to be wrapped warm with him in one blanket, and sleep, only sleep. It seemed the sleep with the woman in his arms was the only necessity.

He went to the hut, and wrapped himself in the blanket and lay on the floor to sleep. But he could not, he was cold. And besides, he felt cruelly his own unfinished nature. He felt his own unfinished condition of aloneness cruelly. He wanted her, to touch her, to hold her fast against him in one moment of completeness and sleep.

He got up and went out, towards the park gates this time: then slowly along the path towards the house. It was nearly four o'clock, still clear and cold, but no sign of dawn. He was used to the dark, he could see well.

Slowly, slowly the great house drew him, as a magnet. He wanted to be near her. It was not desire, not that. It was the cruel sense of unfinished aloneness, that needed a silent woman folded in his arms. Perhaps he could find her. Perhaps he could even call her out to him: or find some way in to her. For the need was imperious.

He slowly, silently climbed the incline to the hall. Then he came round the great trees at the top of the knoll, on to the drive, which made a grand sweep round a lozenge of grass in front of the entrance. He could already see the two magnificent beeches which stood in this big level lozenge in front of the house, detaching themselves darkly in the dark air.

There was the house, low and long and obscure, with one light burning downstairs, in Sir Clifford's room. But which room she was in, the woman who held the other end of the frail thread which drew him so mercilessly, that he did not know.

He went a little nearer, gun in hand, and stood motionless on the drive, watching the house. Perhaps even now he could find her, come at her in some way. The house was not impregnable: he was as clever as burglars are. Why not come to her?

He stood motionless, waiting, while the dawn faintly and imperceptibly paled behind him. He saw the light in the house go out. But he did not see Mrs Bolton come to the window and draw back the old curtain of dark-blue silk, and stand herself in the dark room, looking out on the half-dark of the approaching day, looking for the longed-for dawn, waiting, waiting for Clifford to be reassured that it was daybreak. For when he was sure of daybreak, he would sleep almost at once.

She stood blind with sleep at the window, waiting. And as she stood, she started, and almost cried out. For there was a man out there on the drive, a black figure in the twilight. She woke up greyly, and watched, but without making a sound to disturb Sir Clifford.

The daylight began to rustle into the world, and the dark figure seemed to go smaller and more defined. She made out the gun and gaiters and baggy jacket—it would be Oliver Mellors, the keeper. Yes, for there was the dog nosing around like a shadow, and waiting for him!

And what did the man want? Did he want to rouse the house? What was he standing there for, transfixed, looking up at the house like a love-sick male dog outside the house where the bitch is?

Goodness! The knowledge went through Mrs Bolton like a shot. He was Lady Chatterley's lover! He! He!

To think of it! Why, she, Ivy Bolton, had once been a tiny bit in love with him herself. When he was a lad of sixteen and she a woman of twenty-six. It was when she was studying, and he had helped her a lot with the anatomy and things she had had to learn. He'd been a clever boy, had a scholarship for Sheffield Grammar School, and learned French and things: and then after all had become an overhead blacksmith shoeing horses, because he was fond of horses, he said: but really because he was frightened to go out and face the world, only he'd never admit it.

But he'd been a nice lad, a nice lad, had helped her a lot, so clever at making things clear to you. He was quite as clever as Sir Clifford: and always one for the women. More with women than men, they said.

Till he'd gone and married that Bertha Coutts, as if to spite himself. Some people do marry to spite themselves, because they're disappointed of something. And no wonder it had been a failure.—For years he was gone, all the time of the war: and a lieutenant and all: quite the gentleman, really quite the gentleman!—Then to come back to Tevershall and go as a game-keeper! Really, some people can't take their chances when they've got them! And talking broad Derbyshire again like the worst, when she, Ivy Bolton, knew he spoke like any gentleman, *really*.

Well, well! So her ladyship had fallen for him! Well—her ladyship wasn't the first: there was something about him. But fancy! A Tevershall lad born and bred, and she her ladyship in Wragby Hall! My word, that was a slap back at the high-and-mighty Chatterleys!

But he, the keeper, as the day grew, had realized: it's no good! It's no good trying to get rid of your own aloneness. You've got to stick to it all your life. Only at times, at times, the gap will be filled in. At times! But you have to wait for the times. Accept your own aloneness and stick to it, all your life. And then accept the times when the gap is filled in, when they come. But they've got to come. You can't force them.

With a sudden snap the bleeding desire that had drawn him after her broke. He had broken it, because it must be so. There must be a coming together on both sides. And if she wasn't coming to him, he wouldn't track her down. He mustn't. He must go away, till she came.

He turned slowly, ponderingly, accepting again the isolation. He knew it was better so. She must come to him: it was no use his trailing after her. No use!

Mrs Bolton saw him disappear, saw his dog run after him.

'Well, well!' she said. 'He's the one man I never thought of; and the one man I might have thought of. He was nice to me when he was a lad, after I lost Ted. Well, well! Whatever would *he* say if he knew!'

And she glanced triumphantly at the already sleeping Clifford, as she stepped softly from the room.

II

Connie was sorting out one of the Wragby lumber rooms. There were several: the house was a warren, and the family never sold anything. Sir Geoffrey's father had liked pictures and Sir Geoffrey's mother had liked *cinquecento* furniture. Sir Geoffrey himself had liked old carved oak chests, vestry chests. So it went on through the generations. Clifford collected very modern pictures, at very moderate prices.

So in the lumber room there were bad Sir Edwin Landseers and pathetic William Henry Hunt birds' nests: and other Academy stuff, enough to frighten the daughter of an R.A. She determined to look through it one day, and clear it all. And the grotesque furniture interested her.

Wrapped up carefully to preserve it from damage and dry-rot was the old family cradle, of rosewood. She had to unwrap it, to look at it. It had a certain charm: she looked at it a long time.

'It's thousand pities it won't be called for,' sighed Mrs Bolton, who was helping. 'Though cradles like that are out of date nowadays.'

'It might be called for. I might have a child,' said Connie casually, as if saying she might have a new hat.

'You mean if anything happened to Sir Clifford!' stammered Mrs Bolton.

'No! I mean as things are. It's only muscular paralysis with Sir Clifford—it doesn't affect *him*,' said Connie lying as naturally as breathing.

Clifford had put the idea into her head. He had said: 'Of course *I* may have a child yet. I'm not really mutilated at all. The potency may easily come back, even if the muscles of the hips and legs are paralysed. And then the seed may be transferred.'

He really felt, when he had his periods of energy and worked so hard at the question of the mines, as if his sexual potency were returning. Connie had looked at him in terror. But she was quite quick-witted enough to use his suggestion for her own preservation. For she would have a child if she could: but not his.

Mrs Bolton was for a moment breathless, flabbergasted. Then she didn't believe it: she saw in it a ruse. Yet doctors could do such things nowadays. They might sort of graft seed.

'Well, my Lady, I only hope and pray you may. It would be lovely for you: and for everybody. My word, a child in Wragby, what a difference it would make!'

'Wouldn't it!' said Connie.

And she chose three R.A. pictures of sixty years ago, to send to the Duchess of Shortlands for that lady's next charitable bazaar. She was called 'the bazaar duchess', and she always asked all the county to send things for her to sell. She would be delighted with three framed R.A.s. She might even call, on the strength of them. How furious Clifford was when she called!

But oh my dear! Mrs Bolton was thinking to herself. Is it Oliver Mellors' child you're preparing us for? Oh my dear, that *would* be a Tevershall baby in the Wragby cradle, my word! Wouldn't shame it, neither!

Among other monstrosities in this lumber room was a largish black japanned box, excellently and ingeniously made some sixty or seventy years ago, and fitted with every imaginable object. On top was a concentrated toilet set: brushes, bottles, mirrors, combs, boxes, even three beautiful little razors in safety sheaths, shaving bowl and all. Underneath came a sort of *escritoire* outfit: blotters, pens, ink-bottles, paper, envelopes, memorandum books: and then a perfect sewing-outfit, with three different-sized scissors, thimbles, needles, silks and cottons, darning egg, all of the very best quality and perfectly finished. Then there was a little medicine store, with bottles labelled Laudanum, Tincture of Myrrh, Ess. Cloves and so on: but empty. Everything was perfectly new, and the whole thing, when shut up, was as big as a small, but fat weekend bag. And inside, it fitted together like a puzzle. The bottles could not possibly have spilled: there wasn't room.

The thing was wonderfully made and contrived, excellent craftsmanship of the Victorian order. But somehow it was monstrous. Some Chatterley must have felt for it, for the thing had never been used. It had a peculiar soullessness.

Yet Mrs Bolton was thrilled.

'Look what beautiful brushes, so expensive, even the shaving brushes, three perfect ones! No! and those scissors! They're the best that money could buy. Oh, I call it lovely!'

'Do you?' said Connie. 'Then you have it.'

'Oh no, my Lady!'

'Of course! It will only lie here till Doomsday. If you won't have it, I'll send it to the Duchess as well as the pictures, and she doesn't deserve them so much. Do have it!'

'Oh your Ladyship! Why, I shall never be able to thank you.'

'You needn't try,' laughed Connie.

And Mrs Bolton sailed down with the huge and very black box in her arms, flushing bright pink in her excitement.

Mr Betts drove her in the trap to her house in the village, with the box. And she *had* to have a few friends in, to show it: the school-mistress, the chemist's wife, Mrs Weedon the under-cashier's wife. They thought it marvellous. And then started the whisper of Lady Chatterley's child.

'Wonders'll never cease!' said Mrs Weedon.

But Mrs Bolton was *convinced*, if it did come, it would be Sir Clifford's child. So there!

Not long after, the rector said gently to Clifford:

'And may we really hope for an heir to Wragby? Ah, that would be the hand of God in mercy, indeed!'

'Well! We may *hope*,' said Clifford, with a faint irony, and at the same time, a certain conviction. He had begun to believe it really possible it might even be *his* child.

Then one afternoon came Leslie Winter, Squire Winter, as everybody called him: lean, immaculate, and seventy: and every inch a gentleman, as Mrs Bolton said to Mrs Betts. Every millimetre indeed! And with his old-fashioned, rather haw-haw! manner of speaking, he seemed more out of date than bag wigs. Time, in her flight, drops these fine old feathers.

They discussed the collieries. Clifford's idea was, that his coal, even the poor sort, could be made into hard concentrated fuel that would burn at great heat if fed with certain damp, acidulated air at a fairly strong pressure. It had long been observed that in a particularly strong, wet wind the pit-bank burned very vivid, gave off hardly any fumes, and left a fine powder of ash, instead of the slow pink gravel.

'But where will you find the proper engines for burning your fuel?' asked Winter.

'I'll make them myself. And I'll use my fuel myself. And I'll sell electric power. I'm certain I could do it.'

'If you can do it, then splendid, splendid, my dear boy. Haw! Splendid! If I can be of any help, I shall be delighted. I'm afraid I am a little out of date, and my collieries are like me. But who knows, when I'm gone, there may be men like you. Splendid! It will employ all the men again, and you won't have to sell your coal, or fail to sell it. A splendid idea, and I hope it will be a success. If I had sons of my own, no doubt they would have up-to-date ideas for Shipley: no doubt! By the way, dear boy, is there any foundation to the rumour that we may entertain hopes of an heir to Wragby?'

'Is there any rumour?' asked Clifford.

'Well, my dear boy, Marshall from Fillingwood asked *me*, that's all I can say about a rumour. Of course I wouldn't repeat it for the world, if there were no foundation.'

'Well, Sir,' said Clifford uneasily, but with strange bright eyes. 'There is a hope. There is a hope.'

Winter came across the room and wrung Clifford's hand.

'My dear boy, my dear lad, can you believe what it means to me, to hear that! And to hear you are working in the hopes of a son: and that you may again employ every man at Tevershall. Ah, my boy! to keep up the level of the race, and to have work waiting for any man who cares to work!–'

The old man was really moved.

Next day Connie was arranging tall yellow tulips in a glass vase.

'Connie,' said Clifford, 'did you know there was a rumour that you are going to supply Wragby with a son and heir?'

Connie felt dim with terror, yet she stood quite still, touching the flowers.

'No!' she said. 'Is it a joke? Or malice?'

He paused before he answered:

'Neither, I hope. I hope it may be a prophecy.'

Connie went on with her flowers.

'I had a letter from Father this morning,' she said. 'He wants to know if I am aware he has accepted Sir Alexander Cooper's invitation for me for July and August, to the Villa Esmeralda in Venice.'

'July *and* August?' said Clifford.

'Oh, I wouldn't stay all that time. Are you sure you wouldn't come?'

'I won't travel abroad,' said Clifford promptly.

She took her flowers to the window.

'Do you mind if I go?' she said. 'You know it was promised, for this summer.'

'For how long would you go?'

'Perhaps three weeks.'

There was silence for a time.

'Well,' said Clifford slowly, and a little gloomily. 'I suppose I could stand it for three weeks: if I were absolutely sure you'd want to come back.'

'I should want to come back,' she said, with a quiet simplicity, heavy with conviction. She was thinking of the other man.

Clifford felt her conviction, and somehow he believed her, he believed it was for him. He felt immensely relieved, joyful at once.

'In that case,' he said, 'I think it would be all right, don't you?'

'I think so,' she said.

'You'd enjoy the change?'

She looked up at him with strange blue eyes.

'I should like to see Venice again,' she said, 'and to bathe from one of the shingle islands across the lagoon. But you know I loathe the Lido! And I don't fancy I shall like Sir Alexander Cooper and Lady Cooper. But if Hilda is there, and we have a gondola of our own: yes, it will be rather lovely. I *do* wish you'd come.'

She said it sincerely. She would so love to make him happy, in these ways.

'Ah, but think of me, though, at the Gare du Nord: at Calais quay!'

'But why not? I see other men carried in litter-chairs, who have been wounded in the war. Besides, we'd motor all the way.'

'We should need to take two men.'

'Oh no! We'd manage with Field. There would always be another man there.'

But Clifford shook his head.

'Not this year, dear! Not this year! Next year probably I'll try.'

She went away gloomily. Next year! What would next year bring? She herself did not really want to go to Venice: not now, now there was the other man. But she was going as a sort of discipline: and also because, if she had a child, Clifford could think she had a lover in Venice.

It was already May, and in June they were supposed to start. Always these arrangements! Always one's life arranged for one! Wheels that worked one and drove one, and over which one had no real control!

It was May, but cold and wet again. A cold wet May, good for corn and hay! Much the corn and hay matter nowadays! Connie had to go into Uthwaite, which was their little town, where the Chatterleys were still *the* Chatterleys. She went alone, Field driving her.

In spite of May and a new greenness, the country was dismal. It was rather chilly, and there was smoke on the rain, and a certain sense of exhaust vapour in the air. One just had to live from one's resistance. No wonder these people were ugly and tough.

The car ploughed uphill through the long squalid straggle of Tevershall, the blackened brick dwellings, the black slate roofs glistening their sharp edges, the mud black with coal-dust, the pavements wet and black. It was as if dismalness had soaked through and through everything. The utter negation of natural beauty, the utter negation of the gladness of life, the utter absence of the instinct for shapely beauty which every bird and beast has, the utter death of the human intuitive faculty was appalling. The stacks of soap in the grocers'shops, the rhubarb and lemons in the greengrocers! the awful hats in the milliners! all went by ugly, ugly, ugly, followed by the plaster-and-gilt horror of the cinema with its wet picture announcements, 'A Woman's Love!', and the new big Primitive chapel, primitive enough in its stark brick and big panes of greenish and raspberry glass in the windows. The Wesleyan chapel, higher up, was of blackened brick and stood behind iron railings and blackened shrubs. The Congregational chapel, which thought itself superior, was built of rusticated sandstone and had a steeple, but not a very high one. Just beyond were the new school buildings, expensive pink brick, and gravelled playground inside iron railings, all very imposing, and mixing the suggestion of a chapel and a prison. Standard Five girls were having a singing lesson, just finishing the la-me-doh-la exercises and beginning a 'sweet children's song'. Anything more unlike song, spontaneous song, would be impossible to imagine: a strange bawling yell that followed the outlines of a tune. It was not like savages: savages have subtle rhythms. It was not like animals: animals *mean* something when they yell. It was like nothing on earth, and it was called singing. Connie sat and listened with her heart in her boots, as Field was filling petrol. What could possibly become of such a people, a people in whom the living intuitive faculty was dead as nails, and only queer mechanical yells and uncanny will-power remained?

A coal-cart was coming downhill, clanking in the rain. Field started upwards, past the big but weary-looking drapers and clothing shops, the post-office, into the little market-place of forlorn space, where Sam Black was peering out of the door of the Sun, that called itself an inn, not a pub, and where the commercial travellers stayed, and was bowing to Lady Chatterley's car.

The church was away to the left among black trees. The car slid on downhill, past the Miners' Arms. It had already passed the Wellington, the Nelson, the Three Tuns, and the Sun, now it passed the Miners' Arms, then the Mechanics' Hall, then the new and almost gaudy Miners' Welfare and so, past a few new 'villas', out into the blackened road between dark hedges and dark green fields, towards Stacks Gate.

Tevershall! That was Tevershall! Merrie England! Shakespeare's England! No, but the England of today, as Connie had realized since she had come to live in it. It was producing a new race of mankind, over-conscious in the money and social and political side, on the spontaneous, intuitive side dead, but dead. Half-corpses, all of them: but with a terrible insistent consciousness in the other half. There was something uncanny and underground about it all. It was an under-world. And quite incalculable. How shall we understand the reactions in half-corpses? When Connie saw the great lorries full of steel-workers from Sheffield, weird, distorted smallish beings like men, off for an excursion to Matlock, her bowels fainted and she thought: Ah God, what has man done to man? What have the leaders of men been doing to their fellow men? They have reduced them to less than humanness; and now there can be no fellowship any more! It is just a nightmare.

She felt again in a wave of terror the grey, gritty hopelessness of it all. With such creatures for the industrial masses, and the upper classes as she knew them, there was no hope, no hope any more. Yet she was wanting a baby, and an heir to Wragby! An heir to Wragby! She shuddered with dread.

Yet Mellors had come out of all this!–Yes, but he was as apart from it all as she was. Even in him there was no fellowship left. It was dead. The fellowship was dead. There was only apartness and hopelessness, as far as all this was concerned. And this was England, the vast bulk of England: as Connie knew, since she had motored from the centre of it.

The car was rising towards Stacks Gate. The rain was holding off, and in the air came a queer pellucid gleam of May. The country rolled away in long undulations, south towards the Peak, east towards Mansfield and Nottingham. Connie was travelling South.

As she rose on to the high country, she could see on her left, on a height above the rolling land, the shadowy, powerful bulk of Warsop Castle, dark grey, with below it the reddish plastering of miners' dwellings, newish, and below those the plumes of dark smoke and white steam from the great colliery which put so many thousand pounds per annum into the pockets of the Duke and the other shareholders. The powerful old castle was a ruin, yet it hung its bulk on the low sky-line, over the black plumes and the white that waved on the damp air below.

A turn, and they ran on the high level to Stacks Gate. Stacks Gate, as seen from the highroad, was just a huge and gorgeous new hotel, the Coningsby Arms, standing red and white and gilt in barbarous isolation off the road. But if you looked, you saw on the left rows of handsome 'modern' dwellings, set down like a game of dominoes, with spaces and gardens, a queer game of dominoes that some weird 'masters' were playing on the surprised earth. And beyond these blocks of dwellings, at the back, rose all the astonishing and frightening overhead erections of a really modern mine, chemical works and long galleries, enormous, and of shapes not before known to man. The head-stock and pit-bank of the mine itself were insignificant among the huge new installations. And in front of this, the game of dominoes stood forever in a sort of surprise, waiting to be played.

This was Stacks Gate, new on the face of the earth, since the war. But as a matter of fact, though even Connie did not know it, downhill half a mile below the 'hotel' was old Stacks Gate, with a little old colliery and blackish old brick dwellings, and a chapel or two and a shop or two and a little pub or two.

But that didn't count any more. The vast plumes of smoke and vapour rose from the new works up above, and this was now Stacks Gate; no chapels, no pubs, even no shops. Only the great 'works', which are the modern Olympia with temples to all the gods; then the model dwellings: then the hotel. The hotel in actuality was nothing but a miners' pub though it looked first-classy.

Even since Connie's arrival at Wragby this new place had arisen on the face of the earth, and the model dwellings had filled with riff-raff drifting in from anywhere, to poach Clifford's rabbits among other occupations.

The car ran on along the uplands, seeing the rolling county spread out. The county! It had once been a proud and lordly county. In front, looming again and hanging on the brow of the sky-line, was the huge and splendid bulk of Chadwick Hall, more window than wall, one of the most famous Elizabethan houses. Noble it stood alone above a great park, but out of date, passed over. It was still kept up, but as a show place. 'Look how our ancestors lorded it!'

That was the past. The present lay below. God alone knows where the future lies. The car was already turning, between little old blackened miners' cottages, to descend to Uthwaite. And Uthwaite, on a damp day, was sending up a whole array of smoke plumes and steam, to whatever gods there be. Uthwaite down in the valley, with all the steel threads of the railways to Sheffield drawn through it, and the coal-mines and the steel-works sending up smoke and glare from long tubes, and the pathetic little corkscrew spire of the church, that is going to tumble down, still pricking the fumes, always affected Connie strangely. It was an old market-town, centre of the dales. One of the chief inns was the Chatterley Arms. There, in Uthwaite, Wragby was known as Wragby, as if it were a whole place, not just a house, as it was to outsiders: Wragby Hall, near Tevershall: Wragby, a 'seat'.

The miners' cottages, blackened, stood flush on the pavement, with that intimacy and smallness of colliers' dwellings over a hundred years old. They lined all the way. The road had become a street, and as you sank, you forgot instantly the open, rolling country where the castles and big houses still dominated, but like ghosts. Now you were just above the tangle of naked railway-lines, and foundries and other 'works' rose about you, so big you were only aware of walls. And iron clanked with a huge reverberating clank, and huge lorries shook the earth, and whistles screamed.

Yet again, once you had got right down and into the twisted and crooked heart of the town, behind the church, you were in the world of two centuries ago, in the crooked streets where the Chatterley Arms stood, and the old pharmacy, streets which used to lead out to the wild open world of the castles and stately couchant houses.

But at the corner a policeman held up his hand as three lorries loaded with iron rolled past, shaking the poor old church. And not till the lorries were past could he salute her ladyship.

So it was. Upon the old crooked burgess streets hordes of oldish blackened miners' dwellings crowded, lining the roads out. And immediately after these came the newer, pinker rows of rather larger houses, plastering the valley: the homes of more modern workmen. And beyond that again, in the wide rolling regions of the castles, smoke waved against steam, and patch after patch of raw reddish brick showed the newer mining settlements, sometimes in the hollows, sometimes gruesomely ugly along the sky-line of the slopes. And between, in between, were the tattered remnants of the old coaching and cottage England, even the England of Robin Hood, where the miners prowled with the dismalness of suppressed sporting instincts, when they were not at work.

England, my England! But which is *my* England? The stately homes of England make good photographs, and create the illusion of a connexion with the Elizabethans. The handsome old halls are there, from the days of Good Queen Anne and Tom Jones. But smuts fall and blacken on the drab stucco, that has long ceased to be golden. And one by one, like the stately homes, they were abandoned. Now they are being pulled down. As for the cottages of England—there they are—great plasterings of brick dwellings on the hopeless countryside.

Now they are pulling down the stately homes, the Georgian halls are going. Fritchley, a perfect old Georgian mansion, was even now, as Connie passed in the car, being demolished. It was in perfect repair: till the war the Weatherleys had lived in style there. But now it was too big, too expensive, and the country had become too uncongenial. The gentry were departing to pleasanter places, where they could spend their money without having to see how it was made.

This is history. One England blots out another. The mines had made the halls wealthy. Now they were blotting them out, as they had already blotted out the cottages. The industrial England blots out the agricultural England. One meaning blots out another. The new England blots out the old England. And the continuity is not organic, but mechanical.

Connie, belonging to the leisured classes, had clung to the remnants of the old England. It had taken her years to realize that it was really blotted out by this terrifying new and gruesome England, and that the blotting out would go on till it was complete. Fritchley was gone, Eastwood was gone, Shipley was going: Squire Winter's beloved Shipley.

Connie called for a moment at Shipley. The park gates, at the back, opened just near the level crossing of the colliery railway; the Shipley colliery itself stood just beyond the trees. The gates stood open, because through the park was a right-of-way that the colliers used. They hung around the park.

The car passed the ornamental ponds, in which the colliers threw their newspapers, and took the private drive to the house. It stood above, aside, a very pleasant stucco building from the middle of the eighteenth century. It had a beautiful alley of yew trees, that had approached an older house, and the hall stood serenely spread out, winking its Georgian panes as if cheerfully. Behind, there were really beautiful gardens.

Connie liked the interior much better than Wragby. It was much lighter, more alive, shapen and elegant. The rooms were panelled with creamy-painted panelling, the ceilings were touched with gilt, and everything was kept in exquisite order, all the appointments were perfect, regardless of expense. Even the corridors managed to be ample and lovely, softly curved and full of life.

But Leslie Winter was alone. He had adored his house. But his park was bordered by three of his own collieries. He had been a generous man in his ideas. He had almost welcomed the colliers in his park. Had the miners not made him rich! So, when he saw the gangs of unshapely men lounging by his ornamental waters – not in the *private* part of the park, no, he drew the line there – he would say: 'the miners are perhaps not so ornamental as deer, but they are far more profitable.'

But that was in the golden – monetarily – latter half of Queen Victoria's reign. Miners were then 'good working men'.

Winter had made this speech, half apologetic, to his guest, the then Prince of Wales. And the Prince had replied, in his rather guttural English:

'You are quite right. If there were coal under Sandringham, I would open a mine on the lawns, and think it first-rate landscape gardening. Oh, I am quite willing to exchange roe-deer for colliers, at the price. Your men are good men too, I hear.'

But then, the Prince had perhaps an exaggerated idea of the beauty of money, and the blessings of industrialism.

However, the Prince had been a King, and the King had died, and now there was another King, whose chief function seemed to be to open soup-kitchens.

And the good working men were somehow hemming Shipley in. New mining villages crowded on the park, and the squire felt somehow that the population was alien. He used to feel, in a good-natured but quite grand way, lord of his own domain and of his own colliers. Now, by a subtle pervasion of the new spirit, he had somehow been pushed out. It was he who did not belong any more. There was no mistaking it. The mines, the industry, had a will of its own, and this will was against the gentleman-owner. All the colliers took part in the will, and it was hard to live up against it. It either shoved you out of the place, or out of life altogether.

Squire Winter, a soldier, had stood it out. But he no longer cared to walk in the park after dinner. He almost hid, indoors. Once he had walked, bare-headed, and in his patent-leather shoes and purple silk socks, with Connie down to the gate, talking to her in his well-bred rather haw-haw fashion. But when it came to passing the little gangs of colliers who stood and stared without either salute or anything else, Connie felt how the lean, well-bred old man winced, winced as an elegant antelope stag in a cage winces from the vulgar stare. The colliers were not *personally* hostile: not at all. But their spirit was cold, and shoving him out. And, deep down, there was a profound grudge. They 'worked for him'. And in their ugliness, they resented his elegant, well-groomed, well-bred existence. 'Who's he!' It was the *difference* they resented.

And somewhere, in his secret English heart, being a good deal of a soldier, he believed they were right to resent the difference. He felt himself a little in the wrong, for having all the advantages. Nevertheless he represented a system, and he would not be shoved out.

Except by death. Which came on him soon after Connie's call, suddenly. And he remembered Clifford handsomely in his will.

The heirs at once gave out the order for the demolishing of Shipley. It cost too much to keep up. No one would live there. So it was broken up. The avenue of yews was cut down. The park was denuded of its timber, and divided into lots. It was near enough to Uthwaite. In the strange, bald desert of this still-one-more no-man's-land, new little streets of semi-detacheds were run up, very desirable! The Shipley Hall Estate!

Within a year of Connie's last call, it had happened. There stood Shipley Hall Estate, an array of red-brick semi-detached 'villas' in new streets. No one would have dreamed that the stucco hall had stood there twelve months before.

But this is a later stage of King Edward's landscape gardening, the sort that has an ornamental coal-mine on the lawn.

One England blots out another. The England of the Squire Winters and the Wragby Halls was gone, dead. The blotting out was only not yet complete.

What would come after? Connie could not imagine. She could only see the new brick streets spreading into the fields, the new erections rising at the collieries, the new girls in their silk stockings, the new collier lads lounging into the Pally or the Welfare. The younger generation were utterly unconscious of the old England. There was a gap in the continuity of consciousness, almost American: but industrial really. What next?

Connie always felt there was no next. She wanted to hide her head in the sand: or, at least, in the bosom of a living man.

The world was so complicated and weird and gruesome! The common people were so many, and really so terrible. So she thought as she was going home, and saw the colliers trailing from the pits, grey-black, distorted, one shoulder higher than the other, slurring their heavy ironshod boots. Underground grey faces, whites of eyes rolling, necks cringing from the pit roof, shoulders out of shape. Men! Men! Alas, in some ways patient and good men. In other ways, non-existent. Something that men *should* have was bred and killed out of them. Yet they were men. They begot children. One might bear a child to them. Terrible, terrible thought! They were good and kindly. But they were only half, only the grey half of a human being. As yet, they were 'good'. But even that was the goodness of their halfness. Supposing the dead in them ever rose up! But no, it was too terrible to think of. Connie was absolutely afraid of the industrial masses. They seemed so *weird* to her. A life with utterly no beauty in it, no intuition, always 'in the pit'.

Children from such men! Oh God, oh God!

Yet Mellors had come from such a father. Not quite. Forty years had made a difference, an appalling difference in manhood. The iron and the coal had eaten deep into the bodies and souls of the men.

Incarnate ugliness, and yet alive! What would become of them all? Perhaps with the passing of the coal they would disappear again, off the face of the earth. They had appeared out of nowhere in their thousands, when the coal had called for them. Perhaps they were only weird fauna of the coal-seams. Creatures of another reality, there were elementals, serving the elements of coal, as the metal-workers were elementals, serving the element of iron. Men not men, but animas of coal and iron and clay. Fauna of the elements, carbon, iron, silicon: elementals. They had perhaps some of the weird, inhuman beauty of minerals, the lustre of coal, the weight and blueness and resistance of iron, the transparency of glass. Elemental creatures, weird and distorted, of the mineral world! They belonged to the coal, the iron, the clay, as fish belong to the sea and worms to dead wood. The anima of mineral disintegration!

Connie was glad to be home, to bury her head in the sand. She was glad even to babble to Clifford. For her fear of the mining and iron Midlands affected her with a queer feeling that went all over her, like influenza.

'Of course I had to have tea in Miss Bentley's shop,' she said.

'Really! Winter would have given you tea.'

'Oh yes, but I daren't disappoint Miss Bentley.'

Miss Bentley was a shallow old maid with a rather large nose and romantic disposition who served tea with a careful intensity worthy of a sacrament.

'Did she ask after me?' said Clifford.

'Of course!–*May* I ask your Ladyship how Sir Clifford is!–I believe she ranks you even higher than Nurse Cavell!'

'And I suppose you said I was blooming.'

'Yes! And she looked as rapt as if I had said the heavens had opened to you. I said if she ever came to Tevershall she was to come to see you.'

'Me! Whatever for! See me!'

'Why yes, Clifford. You can't be so adored without making some slight return. Saint George of Cappadocia was nothing to you, in her eyes.'

'And do you think she'll come?'

'Oh, she blushed! and looked quite beautiful for a moment, poor thing! Why don't men marry the women who would really adore them?'

'The women start adoring too late. But did she say she'd come?'

'Oh!' Connie imitated the breathless Miss Bentley, 'your Ladyship, if ever I should dare to presume!'

'Dare to presume! how absurd! But I hope to God she won't turn up. And how was her tea?'

'Oh, Lipton's and *very* strong. But Clifford, do you realize you are the *Roman de la rose* of Miss Bentley and lots like her?'

'I'm not flattered, even then.'

'They treasure up every one of your pictures in the illustrated papers, and probably pray for you every night. It's rather wonderful.'

She went upstairs to change.

That evening he said to her:

'You do think, don't you, that there is something eternal in marriage?'

She looked at him.

'But Clifford, you make eternity sound like a lid or a long, long chain that trailed after one, no matter how far one went.'

He looked at her, annoyed.

'What I mean,' he said, 'is that if you go to Venice, you won't go in the hopes of some love affair that you can take *au grand sérieux*, will you?'

'A love affair in Venice *au grand sérieux?* No. I assure you! No, I'd never take a love affair in Venice more than *au très petit sérieux.*'

She spoke with a queer kind of contempt. He knitted his brows, looking at her.

Coming downstairs in the morning, she found the keeper's dog Flossie sitting in the corridor outside Clifford's room, and whimpering very faintly. 'Why, Flossie!' she said softly. 'What are you doing here?'

And she quietly opened Clifford's door. Clifford was sitting up in bed, with the bed-table and typewriter pushed aside, and the keeper was standing at attention at the foot of the bed. Flossie ran in. With a faint gesture of head and eyes, Mellors ordered her to the door again, and she slunk out.

'Oh, good morning, Clifford!' Connie said. 'I didn't know you were busy.' Then she looked at the keeper, saying good morning to him. He murmured his reply, looking at her as if vaguely. But she felt a whiff of passion touch her, from his mere presence.

'Did I interrupt you, Clifford? I'm sorry.'

'No, it's nothing of any importance.'

She slipped out of the room again, and up to the blue boudoir on the first floor. She sat in the window, and saw him go down the drive, with his curious, silent motion, effaced. He had a natural sort of quiet distinction, an aloof pride, and also a certain look of frailty. A hireling! One of Clifford's hirelings! 'The fault, dear Brutus, is not in our stars, but in ourselves, that we are underlings.'

Was he an underling? Was he? What did he think of *her*?

It was a sunny day, and Connie was working in the garden, and Mrs Bolton was helping her. For some reason, the two women had drawn together, in one of the unaccountable flows and ebbs of sympathy that exist between people. They were pegging down carnations, and putting in small plants for the summer. It was work they both liked. Connie especially felt a delight in putting the soft roots of young plants into a soft black puddle, and cradling them down. On this spring morning she felt a quiver in her womb too, as if the sunshine had touched it and made it happy.

'It is many years since you lost your husband?' she said to Mrs Bolton as she took up another little plant and laid it in its hole.

'Twenty-three!' said Mrs Bolton, as she carefully separated the young columbines into single plants. 'Twenty-three years since they brought him home.'

Connie's heart gave a lurch, at the terrible finality of it. 'Brought him home!'

'Why did he get killed, do you think?' she asked. 'He was happy with you?'

It was a woman's question to a woman. Mrs Bolton put aside a strand of hair from her face, with the back of her hand.

'I don't know, my Lady! He sort of wouldn't give in to things: he wouldn't really go with the rest. And then he hated ducking his head for anything on earth. A sort of obstinacy, that *gets* itself killed. You see he didn't really care. I lay it down to the pit. He ought never to have been down pit. But his dad made him go down, as a lad; and then, when you're over twenty, it's not very easy to come out.'

'Did he say he hated it?'

'Oh no! Never! He never said he hated anything. He just made a funny face. He was one of those who wouldn't take care: like some of the first lads as went off so blithe to the war and got killed right away. He wasn't really wezzle-brained. But he wouldn't care. I used to say to him: 'You care for nought nor anybody!' But he did! The way he sat when my first baby was born, motionless, and the sort of fatal eyes he looked at me with, when it was over! I had a bad time, but I had to comfort *him*. ''It's all right, lad, it's all right!'' I said to him. And he gave me a look, and that funny sort of smile. He never said anything. But I don't believe he had any right pleasure with me at nights after; he'd never really let himself go. I used to say to him: Oh, let thysen go, lad!–I'd talk broad to him sometimes. And he said nothing. But he wouldn't let himself go, or he couldn't. He didn't want me to have any more children. I always blamed his mother, for letting him in th' room. He'd no right t'ave been there. Men makes so much more of things than they should, once they start brooding.'

'Did he mind so much?' said Connie in wonder.

'Yes, he sort of couldn't take it for natural, all that pain. And it spoilt his pleasure in his bit of married love. I said to him: If I don't care, why should you? It's my look-out!–But all he'd ever say was: It's not right!'

'Perhaps he was too sensitive,' said Connie.

'That's it! When you come to know men, that's how they are: too sensitive in the wrong place. And I believe, unbeknown to himself, he hated the pit, just hated it. He looked so quiet when he was dead, as if he'd got free. He was such a nice-looking lad. It just broke my heart to see him, so still and pure looking, as if he'd *wanted* to die. Oh, it broke my heart, that did. But it was the pit.'

She wept a few bitter tears, and Connie wept more. It was a warm spring day, with a perfume of earth and of yellow flowers, many things rising to bud, and the garden still with the very sap of sunshine.

'It must have been terrible for you!' said Connie.

'Oh, my Lady! I never realized at first. I could only say: Oh my lad, what did you want to leave me for!–That was all my cry. But somehow I felt he'd come back.'

'But he *didn't* want to leave you,' said Connie.

'Oh no, my Lady! That was only my silly cry. And I kept expecting him back. Especially at nights. I kept waking up thinking: Why he's not in bed with me!–It was as if my *feelings* wouldn't believe he'd gone. I just felt he'd *have* to come back and lie against me, so I could feel him with me. That was all I wanted, to feel him there with me, warm. And it took me a thousand shocks before I knew he wouldn't come back, it took me years.'

'The touch of him,' said Connie.

'That's it, my Lady, the touch of him! I've never got over it to this day, and never shall. And if there's a heaven above, he'll be there, and will lie up against me so I can sleep.'

Connie glanced at the handsome, brooding face in fear. Another passionate one out of Tevershall! The touch of him! For the bonds of love are ill to loose!

'Its terrible, once you've got a man into your blood!' she said.

'Oh, my Lady! And that's what makes you feel so bitter. You feel folks *wanted* him killed. You feel the pit fair *wanted* to kill him. Oh, I felt, if it hadn't been for the pit, an' them as runs the pit, there'd have been no leaving me. But they all *want* to separate a woman and a man, if they're together.'

'If they're physically together,' said Connie.

'That's right, my Lady! There's a lot of hard-hearted folks in the world. And every morning when he got up and went to th' pit, I felt it was wrong, wrong. But what else could he do? What can a man do?'

A queer hate flared in the woman.

'But can a touch last so long?' Connie asked suddenly. 'That you could feel him so long?'

'Oh my Lady, what else is there to last? Children grows away from you. But the man, well! But even *that* they'd like to kill in you, the very thought of the touch of him. Even your own children! Ah well! We might have drifted apart, who knows. But the feeling's something different. It's 'appen better never to care. But there, when I look at women who's never really been warmed through by a man, well, they seem to me poor dool-owls after all, no matter how they may dress up and gad. No, I'll abide by my own. I've not much respect for people.'

12

Connie went to the wood directly after lunch. It was really a lovely day, the first dandelions making suns, the first daisies so white. The hazel thicket was a lace-work, of half-open leaves, and the last dusty perpendicular of the catkins. Yellow celandines now were in crowds, flat open, pressed back in urgency, and the yellow glitter of themselves. It was the yellow, the powerful yellow of early summer. And primroses were broad, and full of pale abandon, thick-clustered primroses no longer shy. The lush, dark green of hyacinths was a sea, with buds rising like pale corn, while in the riding the forget-me-nots were fluffing up, and columbines were unfolding their ink-purple ruches, and there were bits of blue bird's eggshell under a bush. Everywhere the bud-knots and the leap of life!

The keeper was not at the hut. Everything was serene, brown chickens running lustily. Connie walked on towards the cottage, because she wanted to find him.

The cottage stood in the sun, off the wood's edge. In the little garden the double daffodils rose in tufts, near the wide-open door, and red double daisies made a border to the path. There was the bark of a dog, and Flossie came running.

The wide-open door! so he was at home. And the sunlight falling on the red-brick floor! As she went up the path, she saw him through the window, sitting at the table in his shirt-sleeves, eating. The dog wuffed softly, slowly wagging her tail.

He rose, and came to the door, wiping his mouth with a red handkerchief, still chewing.

'May I come in?' she said.

'Come in!'

The sun shone into the bare room, which still smelled of a mutton chop, done in a dutch oven before the fire, because the dutch oven still stood on the fender, with the black potato-saucepan on a piece of paper, beside it on the white hearth. The fire was red, rather low, the bar dropped, the kettle singing.

On the table was his plate, with potatoes and the remains of the chop; also bread in a basket, salt, and a blue mug with beer. The table-cloth was white oil-cloth, he stood in the shade.

'You are very late,' she said. 'Do go on eating!'

She sat down on a wooden chair, in the sunlight by the door.

'I had to go to Uthwaite,' he said, sitting down at the table but not eating.

'Do eat,' she said.

But he did not touch the food.

'Shall y'ave something?' he asked her. 'Shall y'ave a cup of tea? t'kettle's on t' boil'—he half rose again from his chair.

'If you'll let me make it myself,' she said, rising. He seemed sad, and she felt she was bothering him.

'Well, tea-pot's in there'—he pointed to a little, drab corner cupboard; 'an' cups. An' tea's on t' mantel ower yer 'ead.'

She got the black tea-pot, and the tin of tea from the mantelshelf. She rinsed the tea-pot with hot water, and stood a moment wondering where to empty it.

'Throw it out,' he said, aware of her. 'It's clean.'

She went to the door and threw the drop of water down the path. How lovely it was here, so still, so really woodland. The oaks were putting out ochre yellow leaves: in the garden the red daisies were like red plush buttons. She glanced at the big, hollow sandstone slab of the threshold, now crossed by so few feet.

'But it's lovely here,' she said. 'Such a beautiful stillness, everything alive and still.'

He was eating again, rather slowly and unwillingly, and she could feel he was discouraged. She made the tea in silence, and set the tea-pot on the hob, as she knew the people did. He pushed his plate aside and went to the back place; she heard a latch click, then he came back with cheese on a plate, and butter.

She set the two cups on the table; there were only two.

'Will you have a cup of tea?' she said.

'If you like. Sugar's in th' cupboard, an' there's a little cream-jug. Milk's in a jug in th' pantry.'

'Shall I take your plate away?' she asked him. He looked up at her with a faint ironical smile.

'Why . . . if you like,' he said, slowly eating bread and cheese. She went to the back, into the pent-house scullery, where the pump was. On the left was a door, no doubt the pantry door. She unlatched it, and almost smiled at the place he called a pantry; a long narrow white-washed slip of a cupboard. But it managed to contain a little barrel of beer, as well as a few dishes and bits of food. She took a little milk from the yellow jug.

'How do you get your milk?' she asked him, when she came back to the table.

'Flints! They leave me a bottle at the warren end. You know, where I met you!'

But he was discouraged.

She poured out the tea, poising the cream-jug.

'No milk,' he said; then he seemed to hear a noise, and looked keenly through the doorway.

' 'Appen we'd better shut,' he said.

'It seems a pity,' she replied. 'Nobody will come, will they?'

'Not unless it's one time in a thousand, but you never know.'

'And even then it's no matter,' she said. 'It's only a cup of tea. Where are the spoons?'

He reached over, and pulled open the table drawer. Connie sat at the table in the sunshine of the doorway.

'Flossie!' he said to the dog, who was lying on a little mat at the stair foot. 'Go an' hark, hark!'

He lifted his finger, and his 'hark!' was very vivid. The dog trotted out to reconnoitre.

'Are you sad today?' she asked him.

He turned his blue eyes quickly, and gazed direct on her.

'Sad! no, bored! I had to go getting summonses for two poachers I caught, and, oh well, I don't like people.'

He spoke cold, good English, and there was anger in his voice.

'Do you hate being a game-keeper?' she asked.

'Being a game-keeper, no! So long as I'm left alone. But when I have to go messing around at the police-station, and various other places, and waiting for a lot of fools to attend to me . . . oh well, I get mad . . .' and he smiled, with a certain faint humour.

'Couldn't you be really independent?' she asked.

'Me? I suppose I could, if you mean manage to exist on my pension. I could! But I've got to work, or I should die. That is, I've got to have something that keeps me occupied. And I'm not in a good enough temper to work for myself. It's got to be a sort of job for somebody else, or I should throw it up in a month, out of bad temper. So altogether I'm very well off here, especially lately . . .'

He laughed at her again, with mocking humour.

'But why are you in a bad temper?' she asked. 'Do you mean you are *always* in a bad temper?'

'Pretty well,' he said, laughing. 'I don't quite digest my bile.'

'But what bile?' she said.

'Bile!' he said. 'Don't you know what that is?' She was silent, and disappointed. He was taking no notice of her.

'I'm going away for a while next month,' she said.

'You are! Where to?'

'Venice.'

'Venice! With Sir Clifford. For how long?'

'For a month or so,' she replied. 'Clifford won't go.'

'He'll stay here?' he asked.

'Yes! He hates to travel as he is.'

'Ay, poor devil!' he said, with sympathy.

There was a pause.

'You won't forget me when I'm gone, will you?' she asked. Again he lifted his eyes and looked full at her.

'Forget?' he said. 'You know nobody forgets. It's not a question of memory.'

She wanted to say: 'What then?' but she didn't. Instead, she said in a mute kind of voice: 'I told Clifford I might have a child.'

Now he really looked at her, intense and searching.

'You did?' he said at last. 'And what did he say?'

'Oh, he wouldn't mind. He'd be glad, really, so long as it seemed to be his.' She dared not look up at him.

He was silent a long time, then he gazed again on her face.

'No mention of *me*, of course?' he said.

'No. No mention of you,' she said.

'No, he'd hardly swallow me as a substitute breeder. – Then where are you supposed to be getting the child?'

'I might have a love-affair in Venice,' she said.

'You might,' he replied slowly. 'So that's why you're going?'

'Not to have the love-affair,' she said, looking up at him, pleading.

'Just the appearance of one,' he said.

There was silence. He sat staring out the window, with a faint grin, half mockery, half bitterness, on his face. She hated his grin.

'You've not taken any precautions against having a child then?' he asked her suddenly. 'Because I haven't.'

'No,' she said faintly. 'I should hate that.'

He looked at her, then again with the peculiar subtle grin out of the window There was a tense silence.

At last he turned his head and said satirically:

'That was why you wanted me, then, to get a child?'

She hung her head.

'No. Not really,' she said.

'What then, *really*?' he asked rather bitingly.

She looked up at him reproachfully, saying: 'I don't know.'

He broke into a laugh.

'Then I'm damned if I do,' he said.

There was a long pause of silence, a cold silence.

'Well,' he said at last. 'It's as your Ladyship likes. If you get the baby, Sir Clifford's welcome to it. I shan't have lost anything. On the contrary, I've had a very nice experience, very nice indeed!'—and he stretched in a half-suppressed sort of yawn. 'If you've made use of me,' he said, 'it's not the first time I've been made use of; and I don't suppose it's ever been as pleasant as this time; though of course one can't feel tremendously dignified about it.'—He stretched again, curiously, his muscles quivering, and his jaw oddly set.

'But I didn't make use of you,' she said, pleading.

'At your Ladyship's service,' he replied.

'No,' she said. 'I liked your body.'

'Did you?' he replied, and he laughed. 'Well, then, we're quits, because I liked yours.'

He looked at her with queer darkened eyes.

'Would you like to go upstairs now?' he asked her, in a strangled sort of voice.

'No, not here. Not now!' she said heavily, though if he had used any power over her, she would have gone, for she had no strength against him.

He turned his face away again, and seemed to forget her.

'I want to touch you like you touch me,' she said. 'I've never really touched your body.'

He looked at her, and smiled again. 'Now?' he said.

'No! No! Not here! At the hut. Would you mind?'

'How do I touch you?' he asked.

'When you feel me.'

He looked at her, and met her heavy, anxious eyes.

'And do you like it when I feel you?' he asked, laughing at her still.

'Yes, do you?' she said.

'Oh me!' Then he changed his tone. 'Yes,' he said. 'You know without asking.' Which was true.

She rose and picked up her hat. 'I must go,' she said.

'Will you go?' he replied politely.

She wanted him to touch her, to say something to her, but he said nothing, only waited politely.

'Thank you for the tea,' she said.

'I haven't thanked your Ladyship for doing me the honours of my tea-pot,' he said.

She went down the path, and he stood in the doorway, faintly grinning. Flossie came running with her tail lifted. And Connie had to plod dumbly across into the wood, knowing he was standing there watching her, with that incomprehensible grin on his face.

She walked home very much downcast and annoyed. She didn't at all like his saying he had been made use of; because, in a sense, it was true. But he oughtn't to have said it. Therefore, again, she was divided between two feelings: resentment against him, and a desire to make it up with him.

She passed a very uneasy and irritated tea-time, and at once went up to her room. But when she was there it was no good; she could neither sit nor stand. She would have to do something about it. She would have to go back to the hut; if he was not there, well and good.

She slipped out of the side door, and took her way direct and a little sullen. When she came to the clearing she was terribly uneasy. But there he was again, in his shirt-sleeves, stooping, letting the hens out of the coops, among the chicks that were now growing a little gawky, but were much more trim then hen-chickens.

She went straight across to him.

'You see I've come!' she said.

'Ay, I see it!' he said, straightening his back, and looking at her with a faint amusement.

'Do you let the hens out now?' she asked.

'Yes, they've sat themselves to skin and bone,' he said. 'An' now they're not all that anxious to come out an' feed. There's no self in a sitting hen; she's all in the eggs or the chicks.'

The poor mother-hens; such blind devotion! even to eggs not their own! Connie looked at them in compassion. A helpless silence fell between the man and the woman.

'Shall us go i' th' 'ut?' he asked.

'Do you want me?' she asked, in a sort of mistrust.

'Ay, if you want to come.'

She was silent.

'Come then!' he said.

And she went with him to the hut. It was quite dark when he had shut the door, so he made a small light in the lantern, as before.

'Have you left your underthings off?' he asked her.

'Yes!'

'Ay, well, then I'll take my things off too.'

He spread the blankets, putting one at the side for a coverlet. She took off her hat, and shook her hair. He sat down, taking off his shoes and gaiters, and undoing his cord breeches.

'Lie down then!' he said, when he stood in his shirt. She obeyed in silence, and he lay beside her, and pulled the blanket over them both.

'There!' he said.

And he lifted her dress right back, till he came even to her breasts. He kissed them softly, taking the nipples in his lips in tiny caresses.

'Eh, but tha'rt nice, tha'rt nice!' he said, suddenly rubbing his face with a snuggling movement against her warm belly.

And she put her arms round him under his shirt, but she was afraid, afraid of his thin, smooth, naked body, that seemed so powerful, afraid of the violent muscles. She shrank, afraid.

And when he said, with a sort of little sigh: 'Eh, tha'rt nice!' something in her quivered, and something in her spirit stiffened in resistance: stiffened from the terribly physical intimacy, and from the peculiar haste of his possession. And this time the sharp ecstasy of her own passion did not overcome her; she lay with her hands inert on his striving body, and do what she might, her spirit seemed to look on from the top of her head, and the butting of his haunches seemed ridiculous to her, and the sort of anxiety of his penis to come to its little evacuating crisis seemed farcical. Yes, this was love, this ridiculous bouncing of the buttocks, and the wilting of the poor, insignificant, moist little penis. This was the divine love! After all, the moderns were right when they felt contempt for the performance; for it was a performance. It was quite true, as some poets said, that the God who created man must have had a sinister sense of humour, creating him a reasonable being, yet forcing him to take this ridiculous posture, and driving him with blind craving for this ridiculous performance. Even a Maupassant found it a humiliating anti-climax. Men despised the intercourse act, and yet did it.

Cold and derisive her queer female mind stood apart, and though she lay perfectly still, her impulse was to heave her loins, and throw the man out, escape his ugly grip, and the butting over-riding of his absurd haunches. His body was a foolish, impudent, imperfect thing, a little disgusting in its unfinished clumsiness. For surely a complete evolution would eliminate this performance, this 'function'.

And yet when he had finished, soon over, and lay very very still, receding into silence, and a strange motionless distance, far, farther than the horizon of her awareness, her heart began to weep. She could feel him ebbing away, ebbing away, leaving her there like a stone on a shore. He was withdrawing, his spirit was leaving her. He knew.

And in real grief, tormented by her own double consciousness and reaction, she began to weep. He took no notice, or did not even know. The storm of weeping swelled and shook her, and shook him.

'Ay!' he said. 'It was no good that time. You wasn't there.'—So he knew! Her sobs became violent.

'But what's amiss?' he said. 'It's once in a while that way.'

'I . . . I can't love you,' she sobbed, suddenly feeling her heart breaking.

'Canna ter? Well, dunna fret! There's no law says as tha's got to. Ta'e it for what it is.'

He still lay with his hand on her breast. But she had drawn both her hands from him.

His words were small comfort. She sobbed aloud.

'Nay, nay!' he said. 'Ta'e the thick wi' th' thin. This wor a bit o' thin for once.'

She wept bitterly, sobbing. 'But I want to love you, and I can't. It only seems horrid.'

He laughed a little, half bitter, half amused.

'It isna horrid,' he said, 'even if tha thinks it is. An' tha canna ma'e it horrid. Dunna fret thysen about lovin' me. Tha'lt niver force thysen to 't. There's sure to be a bad nut in a basketful. Tha mun ta'e th' rough wi' th' smooth.'

He took his hand away from her breast, not touching her. And now she was untouched she took an almost perverse satisfaction in it. She hated the dialect: the *thee* and the *tha* and the *thysen*. He could get up if he liked, and stand there, above her, buttoning down those absurd corduroy breeches, straight in front of her. After all, Michaelis had had the decency to turn away. This man was so assured in himself, he didn't know what a clown other people found him, a half-bred fellow.

Yet, as he was drawing away, to rise silently and leave her, she clung to him in terror.

'Don't! Don't go! Don't leave me! Don't be cross with me! Hold me! Hold me fast!' she whispered in blind frenzy, not even knowing what she said, and clinging to him with uncanny force. It was from herself she wanted to be saved, from her own inward anger and resistance. Yet how powerful was that inward resistance that possessed her!

He took her in his arms again and drew her to him, and suddenly she became small in his arms, small and nestling. It was gone, the resistance was gone, and she began to melt in a marvellous peace. And as she melted small and wonderful in his arms, she became infinitely desirable to him, all his blood-vessels seemed to scald with intense yet tender desire, for her, for her softness, for the penetrating beauty of her in his arms, passing into his blood. And softly, with that marvellous swoon-like caress of his hand in pure soft desire, softly he stroked the silky slope of her loins, down, down between her soft warm buttocks, coming nearer and nearer to the very quick of her. And she felt him like a flame of desire, yet tender, and she felt herself melting in the flame. She let herself go. She felt his penis risen against her with silent amazing force and assertion and she let herself go to him. She yielded with a quiver that was like death, she went all open to him. And oh, if he were not tender to her now, how cruel, for she was all open to him and helpless!

She quivered again at the potent inexorable entry inside her, so strange and terrible. It might come with the thrust of a sword in her softly-opened body, and that would be death. She clung in a sudden anguish of terror. But it came with a strange slow thrust of peace, the dark thrust of peace and a ponderous, primordial tenderness, such as made the world in the beginning. And her terror subsided in her breast, her breast dared to be gone in peace, she held nothing. She dared to let go everything, all herself, and be gone in the flood.

And it seemed she was like the sea, nothing but dark waves rising and heaving, heaving with a great swell, so that slowly her whole darkness was in motion, and she was the ocean rolling its dark, dumb mass. Oh, and far down inside her the deeps parted and rolled asunder, in long, far-travelling billows, and ever, at the quick of her, the depths parted and rolled asunder, from the centre of soft plunging, as the plunger went deeper and deeper, touching lower, and she was deeper and deeper and deeper disclosed, the heavier the billows of her rolled away to some shore, uncovering her, and closer and closer plunged the palpable unknown, and further and further rolled the waves of herself away from herself, leaving her, till suddenly, in a soft, shuddering convulsion, the quick of all her plasm was touched, she knew herself touched, the consummation was upon her, and she was gone. She was gone, she was not, and she was born: a woman.

Ah, too lovely, too lovely! In the ebbing she realized all the loveliness. Now all her body clung with tender love to the unknown man, and blindly to the wilting penis, as it so tenderly, frailly, unknowingly withdrew, after the fierce thrust of its potency. As it drew out and left her body, the secret, sensitive thing, she gave an unconscious cry of pure loss, and she tried to put it back. It had been so perfect! And she loved it so!

And only now she became aware of the small, bud-like reticence and tenderness of the penis, and a little cry of wonder and poignancy escaped her again, her woman's heart crying out over the tender frailty of that which had been the power.

'It was so lovely!' she moaned. 'It was so lovely!' But he said nothing, only softly kissed her, lying still above her. And she moaned with a sort of bliss, as a sacrifice, and a newborn thing.

And now in her heart the queer wonder of him was awakened. A man! The strange potency of manhood upon her! Her hands strayed over him, still a little afraid. Afraid of that strange, hostile, slightly repulsive thing that he had been to her, a man. And now she touched him, and it was the sons of god with the daughters of men. How beautiful he felt, how pure in tissue! How lovely, how lovely, strong, and yet pure and delicate, such stillness of the sensitive body! Such utter stillness of potency and delicate flesh. How beautiful! How beautiful! Her hands came timorously down his back, to the soft, smallish globes of the buttocks. Beauty! What beauty! a sudden little flame of new awareness went through her. How was it possible, this beauty here, where she had previously only been repelled? The unspeakable beauty to the touch of the warm, living buttocks! The life within life, the sheer warm, potent loveliness. And the strange weight of the balls between his legs! What a mystery! What a strange heavy weight of mystery, that could lie soft and heavy in one's hand! The roots, root of all that is lovely, the primeval root of all full beauty.

She clung to him, with a hiss of wonder that was almost awe, terror. He held her close, but he said nothing. He would never say anything. She crept nearer to him, nearer, only to be near to the sensual wonder of him. And out of his utter, incomprehensible stillness, she felt again the slow, momentous surging rise of the phallus again, the other power. And her heart melted out with a kind of awe.

And this time his being within her was all soft and iridescent, purely soft and iridescent, such as no consciousness could seize. Her whole self quivered unconscious and alive, like plasm. She could not know what it was. She could not remember what it had been. Only that it had been more lovely than anything ever could be. Only that. And afterwards she was utterly still, utterly unknowing, she was not aware for how long. And he was still with her, in an unfathomable silence along with her. And of this, they would never speak.

When awareness of the outside began to come back, she clung to his breast, murmuring 'My love! My love!' And he held her silently. And she curled on his breast, perfect.

But his silence was fathomless. His hands held her like flowers, so still and strange. 'Where are you?' she whispered to him. 'Where are you? Speak to me! Say something to me!'

He kissed her softly, murmuring: 'Ay, my lass!'

But she did not know what he meant, she did not know where he was. In his silence he seemed lost to her.

'You love me, don't you?' she murmured.

'Ay, tha knows!' he said.

'But tell me!' she pleaded.

'Ay! Ay 'asn't ter felt it?' he said dimly, but softly and surely. And she clung close to him, closer. He was so much more peaceful in love than she was, and she wanted him to reassure her.

'You do love me!' she whispered, assertive. And his hands stroked her softly, as if she were a flower, without the quiver of desire, but with delicate nearness. And still there haunted her a restless necessity to get a grip on love.

'Say you'll always love me!' she pleaded.

'Ay!' he said, abstractedly. And she felt her questions driving him away from her.

'Mustn't we get up?' he said at last.

'No!' she said.

But she could feel his consciousness straying, listening to the noises outside. 'It'll be nearly dark,' he said. And she heard the pressure of circumstances in his voice. She kissed him, with a woman's grief at yielding up her hour.

He rose, and turned up the lantern, then began to pull on his clothes, quickly disappearing inside them. Then he stood there, above her, fastening his breeches and looking down at her with dark, wide eyes, his face a little flushed and his hair ruffled, curiously warm and still and beautiful in the dim light of the lantern, so beautiful, she would never tell him how beautiful. It made her want to cling fast to him, to hold him, for there was a warm, half-sleepy remoteness in his beauty that made her want to cry out and clutch him, to have him. She would never have him. So she lay on the blanket with curved, soft naked haunches, and he had no idea what she was thinking, but to him too she was beautiful, the soft, marvellous thing he could go into, beyond everything.

'I love thee that I can go into thee,' he said.

'Do you like me?' she said, her heart beating.

'It heals it all up, that I can go into thee. I love thee that tha opened to me. I love thee that I came into thee like that.'

He bent down and kissed her soft flank, rubbed his cheek against it, then covered it up.

'And will you never leave me?' she said.

'Dunna ask them things,' he said.

'But you do believe I love you?' she said.

'Tha loved me just now, wider than iver tha thout tha would. But who knows what'll 'appen, once tha starts thinkin' about it!'

'No, don't say those things!–And you don't really think that I wanted to make use of you, do you?'

'How?'

'To have a child–?'

'Now anybody can 'ave any childt i' th' world,' he said, as he sat down fastening on his leggings.

'Ah no!' she cried. 'You don't mean it?'

'Eh well!' he said, looking at her under his brows. 'This wor t' best.'

She lay still. He softly opened the door. The sky was dark blue, with crystalline, turquoise rim. He went out, to shut up the hens, speaking softly to his dog. And she lay and wondered at the wonder of life, and of being.

When he came back she was still lying there, glowing like a gipsy. He sat on the stool by her.

'Tha mun come one naight ter th' cottage, afore tha goos; sholl ter?' he asked, lifting his eyebrows as he looked at her, his hands dangling between his knees.

'Sholl ter?' she echoed, teasing.

He smiled.

'Ay, sholl ter?' he repeated.

'Ay!' she said, imitating the dialect sound.

'Yi!' he said.

'Yi!' she repeated.

'An' slaip wi' me,' he said. 'It needs that. When sholt come?'

'When sholl I?' she said.

'Nay,' he said, 'tha canna do't. When sholt come then?'

''Appen Sunday,' she said.

' 'Appen a' Sunday! Ay!'
He laughed at her quickly.
'Nay, tha canna,' he protested.
'Why canna I?' she said.
He laughed. Her attempts at the dialect were so ludicrous, somehow.
'Coom then, tha mun goo!' he said.
'Mun I?' she said.
'Maun Ah!' he corrected.
'Why should I say *maun* when you said *mun?*' she protested. 'You're not playing fair.'
'Arena Ah!' he said, leaning forward and softly stroking her face.
'Th'art good cunt, though, aren't ter? Best bit o' cunt left on earth. When ter likes! When tha'rt willing'!'
'What is cunt?' she said.
'An' doesn't ter know? Cunt! It's thee down theer; an' what I get when I'm i'side thee, and what tha gets when I'm i'side thee; it's a' as it is, all on't.'
'All on't,' she teased. 'Cunt! It's like fuck then.'
'Nay nay! Fuck's only what you do. Animals fuck. But cunt's a lot more than that. It's thee, dost see: an' tha'rt a lot besides an animal, aren't ter?–even ter fuck? Cunt! Eh, that's the beauty o' thee, lass!'
She got up and kissed him between the eyes, that looked at her so dark and soft and unspeakably warm, so unbearably beautiful.
'Is it?' she said. 'And do you care for me?'
He kissed her without answering.
'Tha mun goo, let me dust thee,' he said.
His hand passed over the curves of her body, firmly, without desire, but with soft, intimate knowledge.
As she ran home in the twilight the world seemed a dream; the trees in the park seemed bulging and surging at anchor on a tide, and the heave of the slope to the house was alive.

13

On Sunday Clifford wanted to go into the wood. It was a lovely morning, the pear-blossom and plum had suddenly appeared in the world in a wonder of white here and there.
It was cruel for Clifford, while the world bloomed, to have to be helped from chair to bath-chair. But he had forgotten, and even seemed to have a certain conceit of himself in his lameness. Connie still suffered, having to lift his inert legs into place. Mrs Bolton did it now, or Field.
She waited for him at the top of the drive, at the edge of the screen of beeches. His chair came puffing along with a sort of valetudinarian slow importance. As he joined his wife he said:
'Sir Clifford on his foaming steed!'
'Snorting, at least!' she laughed.
He stopped and looked round at the façade of the long, low old brown house.

'Wragby doesn't wink an eyelid!' he said. 'But then why should it! I ride upon the achievements of the mind of man, and that beats a horse.'

'I suppose it does. And the souls in Plato riding up to heaven in a two-horse chariot would go in a Ford car now,' she said.

'Or a Rolls-Royce: Plato was an aristocrat!'

'Quite! No more black horse to thrash and maltreat. Plato never thought we'd go one better than his black steed and his white steed, and have no steeds at all, only an engine!'

'Only an engine and gas!' said Clifford.

'I hope I can have some repairs done to the old place next year. I think I shall have about a thousand to spare for that: but work costs so much!' he added.

'Oh, good!' said Connie. 'If only there aren't more strikes!'

'What would be the use of their striking again! Merely ruin the industry, what's left of it: and surely the owls are beginning to see it!'

'Perhaps they don't mind ruining the industry,' said Connie.

'Ah, don't talk like a woman! The industry fills their bellies, even if it can't keep their pockets quite so flush,' he said, using turns of speech that oddly had a twang of Mrs Bolton.

'But didn't you say the other day that you were a conservative-anarchist,' she asked innocently.

'And did you understand what I meant?' he retorted. 'All I meant is, people can be what they like and feel what they like and do what they like, strictly privately, so long as they keep the *form* of life intact, and the apparatus.'

Connie walked on in silence a few paces. Then she said, obstinately:

'It sounds like saying an egg may go as addled as it likes, so long as it keeps its shell on whole. But addled eggs do break of themselves.'

'I don't think people are eggs,' he said. 'Not even angels' eggs, my dear little evangelist.'

He was in rather high feather this bright morning. The larks were trilling away over the park, the distant pit in the hollow was fuming silent steam. It was almost like old days, before the war. Connie didn't really want to argue. But then she did not really want to go to the wood with Clifford either. So she walked beside his chair in a certain obstinacy of spirit.

'No,' he said. 'There will be no more strikes, if the thing is properly managed.'

'Why not?'

'Because strikes will be made as good as impossible.'

'But will the men let you?' she asked.

'We shan't ask them. We shall do it while they aren't looking: for their own good, to save the industry.'

'For your own good too,' she said.

'Naturally! For the good of everybody. But for their good even more than mine. I can live without the pits. They can't. They'll starve if there are no pits. I've got other provision.'

They looked up the shallow valley at the mine, and beyond it, at the black-lidded houses of Tevershall crawling like some serpent up the hill. From the old brown church the bells were ringing: Sunday, Sunday, Sunday!

'But will the men let you dictate terms?' she said.

'My dear, they will have to: if one does it gently.'

'But mightn't there be a mutual understanding?'

'Absolutely: when they realize that the industry comes before the individual.'

'But must you own the industry?' she said.

'I don't. But to the extent I do own it, yes, most decidedly. The ownership of property has now become a religious question: as it has been since Jesus and St Francis. The point is *not*: take all thou hast and give to the poor, but use all thou hast to encourage the industry and give work to the poor. It's the only way to feed all the mouths and clothe all the bodies. Giving away all we have to the poor spells starvation for the poor just as much as for us. And universal starvation is no high aim. Even general poverty is no lovely thing. Poverty is ugly.'

'But the disparity?'

'That is fate. Why is the star Jupiter bigger than the star Neptune? You can't start altering the make-up of things!'

'But when this envy and jealousy and discontent has once started,' she began.

'Do your best to stop it. Somebody's *got* to be boss of the show.'

'But who is boss of the show?' she asked.

'The men who own and run the industries.'

There was a long silence.

'It seems to me they're a bad boss,' she said.

'Then you suggest what they should do.'

'They don't take their boss-ship seriously enough,' she said.

'They take it far more seriously than you take your ladyship,' he said.

'That's thrust upon me. I don't really want it,' she blurted out. He stopped the chair and looked at her.

'Who's shirking their responsibility now!' he said. 'Who is trying to get away *now* from the responsibility of their own boss-ship, as you call it?'

'But I don't want any boss-ship,' she protested.

'Ah! But that is funk. You've got it: fated to it. And you should live up to it. Who has given the colliers all they have that's worth having: all their political liberty, and their education, such as it is, their sanitation, their health-conditions, their books, their music, everything. Who has given it them? Have colliers given it to colliers? No! All the Wragbys and Shipleys in England have given their part, and must go on giving. There's your responsibility.'

Connie listened, and flushed very red.

'I'd like to give something,' she said. 'But I'm not allowed. Everything is to be sold and paid for now; and all the things you mention now, Wragby and Shipley *sells* them to the people, at a good profit. Everything is sold. You don't give one heart-beat of real sympathy. And besides, who has taken away from the people their natural life and manhood, and given them this industrial horror? Who has done that?'

'And what must I do?' he asked, green. 'Ask them to come and pillage me?'

'Why is Tevershall so ugly, so hideous? Why are their lives so hopeless?'

'They built their own Tevershall, that's part of their display of freedom. They built themselves their pretty Tevershall, and they live their own pretty lives. I can't live their lives for them. Every beetle must live its own life.'

'But you make them work for you. They live the life of your coal-mine.'

'Not at all. Every beetle finds its own food. Not one man is forced to work for me.'

'Their lives are industrialized and hopeless, and so are ours,' she cried.

'I don't think they are. That's just a romantic figure of speech, a relic of the swooning and die-away romanticism. You don't look at all a hopeless figure standing there, Connie my dear.'

Which was true. For her dark-blue eyes were flashing, her colour was hot in her cheeks, she looked full of a rebellious passion far from the dejection of hopelessness. She noticed, in the tussocky places of the grass, cottony young cowslips standing up still bleared in their down. And she wondered with rage, why it was she felt Clifford was so *wrong*, yet she couldn't say it to him, she could not say exactly *where* he was wrong.

'No wonder the men hate you,' she said.

'They don't!' he replied. 'And don't fall into errors: in your sense of the word, they are *not* men. They are animals you don't understand, and never could. Don't thrust your illusions on other people. The masses were always the same, and will always be the same. Nero's slaves were extremely little different from our colliers or the Ford motor-car workmen. I mean Nero's mine slaves and his field slaves. It is the masses: they are the unchangeable. An individual may emerge from the masses. But the emergence doesn't alter the mass. The masses are unalterable. It is one of the most momentous facts of social science. *Panem et circenses!* Only today education is one of the bad substitutes for a circus. What is wrong today is that we've made a profound hash of the circuses part of the programme, and poisoned our masses with a little education.'

When Clifford became really roused in his feelings about the common people, Connie was frightened. There was something devastatingly true in what he said. But it was a truth that killed.

Seeing her pale and silent, Clifford started the chair again, and no more was said till he halted again at the wood gate, which she opened.

'And what we need to take up now,' he said, 'is whips, not swords. The masses have been ruled since time began, and till time ends, ruled they will have to be. It is sheer hypocrisy and farce to say they can rule themselves.'

'But can you rule them?' she asked.

'I? Oh yes! Neither my mind nor my will is crippled, and I don't rule with my legs. I can do my share of ruling: absolutely, my share; and give me a son, and he will be able to rule his portion after me.'

'But he wouldn't be your own son, of your own ruling class; or perhaps not,' she stammered.

'I don't care who his father may be, so long as he is a healthy man not below normal intelligence. Give me the child of any healthy, normally intelligent man, and I will make a perfectly competent Chatterley of him. It is not who begets us, that matters, but where fate places us. Place any child among the ruling classes, and he will grow up, to his own extent, a ruler. Put kings' and dukes' children among the masses, and they'll be little plebeians, mass products. It is the overwhelming pressure of environment.'

'Then the common people aren't a race, and the aristocrats aren't blood,' she said.

'No, my child! All that is romantic illusion. Aristocracy is a function, a part of fate. And the masses are a functioning of another part of fate. The individual hardly matters. It is a question of which function you are brought up to and adapted to. It is not the individuals that make an aristocracy: it is the functioning of the aristocratic whole. And it is the functioning of the whole mass that makes the common man what he is.'

'Then there is no common humanity between us all!'

'Just as you like. We all need to fill our bellies. But when it comes to expressive or executive functioning, I believe there is a gulf, and an absolute one, between the ruling and the serving classes. The two functions are opposed.

And the function determines the individual.'

Connie looked at him with dazed eyes.

'Won't you come on?' she said.

And he started his chair. He had said his say. Now he lapsed into his peculiar and rather vacant apathy, that Connie found so trying. In the wood, anyhow, she was determined not to argue.

In front of them ran the open cleft of the riding, between the hazel walls and the gay grey trees. The chair puffed slowly on, slowly surging into the forget-me-nots that rose up in the drive like milk froth, beyond the hazel shadows. Clifford steered the middle course, where feet passing had kept a channel through the flowers. But Connie, walking behind, had watched the wheels jolt over the wood-ruff and the bugle, and squash the little yellow cups of the creeping-jenny. Now they made a wake through the forget-me-nots.

All the flowers were there, the first bluebells in blue pools, like standing water.

'You are quite right about its being beautiful,' said Clifford. 'It is so amazingly. What is *quite* so lovely as an English spring!'

Connie thought it sounded as if even the spring bloomed by Act of Parliament. An English spring! Why not an Irish one? or Jewish? The chair moved slowly ahead, past tufts of sturdy bluebells that stood up like wheat and over grey burdock leaves. When they came to the open place where the trees had been felled, the light flooded in rather stark. And the bluebells made sheets of bright blue colour, here and there, sheering off into lilac and purple. And between, the bracken was lifting its brown curled heads, like legions of young snakes with a new secret to whisper to Eve.

Clifford kept the chair going till he came to the brow of the hill; Connie followed slowly behind. The oak-buds were opening soft and brown. Everything came tenderly out of the old hardness. Even the snaggy craggy oak-trees put out the softest young leaves, spreading thin, brown little wings like young bat-wings in the light. Why had men never any newness in them, any freshness to come forth with! Stale men!

Clifford stopped the chair at the top of the rise and looked down. The bluebells washed blue like flood-water over the broad riding, and lit up the downhill with a warm blueness.

'It's a very fine colour in itself,' said Clifford, 'but useless for making a painting.'

'Quite!' said Connie, completely uninterested.

'Shall I venture as far as the spring?' said Clifford.

'Will the chair get up again?' she said.

'We'll try; nothing venture, nothing win!'

And the chair began to advance slowly, joltingly down the beautiful broad riding washed over with blue encroaching hyacinths. O last of all ships, through the hyacinthian shallows! O pinnace on the last wild waters, sailing in the last voyage of our civilization! Whither, O weird wheeled ship, your slow course steering. Quiet and complacent, Clifford sat at the wheel of adventure: in his old black hat and tweed jacket, motionless and cautious. O Captain, my Captain, our splendid trip is done! Not yet though! Downhill, in the wake, came Constance in her grey dress, watching the chair jolt downwards.

They passed the narrow track to the hut. Thank heaven it was not wide enough for the chair: hardly wide enough for one person. The chair reached the bottom of the slope, and swerved round, to disappear. And Connie heard a low whistle behind her. She glanced sharply round: the keeper was striding downhill towards her, his dog keeping behind him.

'Is Sir Clifford going to the cottage?' he asked, looking into her eyes.

'No, only to the well.'

'Ah! Good! Then I can keep out of sight. But I shall see you tonight. I shall wait for you at the park gate about ten.'

He looked again direct into her eyes.

'Yes,' she faltered.

They heard the Papp! Papp! of Clifford's horn, tooting for Connie. She 'Coo-eed!' in reply. The keeper's face flickered with a little grimace, and with his hand he softly brushed her breast upwards, from underneath. She looked at him, frightened, and started running down the hill, calling Coo-ee! again to Clifford. The man above watched her, then turned, grinning faintly, back into his path.

She found Clifford slowly mounting to the spring, which was halfway up the slope of the dark larch-wood. He was there by the time she caught him up.

'She did that all right,' he said, referring to the chair.

Connie looked at the great grey leaves of burdock that grew out ghostly from the edge of the larch-wood. The people call it Robin Hood's Rhubarb. How silent and gloomy it seemed by the well! Yet the water bubbled so bright, wonderful! And there were bits of eye-bright and strong blue bugle . . . And there, under the bank, the yellow earth was moving. A mole! It emerged, rowing its pink hands, and waving its blind gimlet of a face, with the tiny pink nose-tip uplifted.

'It seems to see with the end of its nose,' said Connie.

'Better than with its eyes!' he said. 'Will you drink?'

'Will you?'

She took an enamel mug from a twig on a tree, and stooped to fill it for him. He drank in sips. Then she stooped again, and drank a little herself.

'So icy!' she said gasping.

'Good, isn't it! Did you wish?'

'Did you?'

'Yes, I wished. But I won't tell.'

She was aware of the rapping of a woodpecker, then of the wind, soft and eerie through the larches. She looked up. White clouds were crossing the blue.

'Clouds!' she said.

'White lambs only,' he replied.

A shadow crossed the little clearing. The mole had swum out on to the soft yellow earth.

'Unpleasant little beast, we ought to kill him,' said Clifford.

'Look! he's like a parson in a pulpit,' she said.

She gathered some sprigs of woodruff and brought them to him.

'New-mown hay!' he said. 'Doesn't it smell like the romantic ladies of the last century, who had their heads screwed on the right way after all!'

She was looking at the white clouds.

'I wonder if it will rain,' she said.

'Rain! Why! Do you want it to?'

They started on the return journey, Clifford jolting cautiously downhill. They came to the dark bottom of the hollow, turned to the right, and after a hundred yards swerved up the foot of the long slope, where bluebells stood in the light.

'Now, old girl!' said Clifford, putting the chair to it.

It was a steep and jolty climb. The chair pugged slowly, in a struggling unwilling fashion. Still, she nosed her way up unevenly, till she came to where the hyacinths were all around her, then she balked, struggled, jerked a little way out of the flowers, then stopped.

'We'd better sound the horn and see if the keeper will come,' said Connie. 'He could push her a bit. For that matter, I will push. It helps.'

'We'll let her breathe,' said Clifford. 'Do you mind putting a scotch under the wheel?'

Connie found a stone, and they waited. After a while Clifford started his motor again, then set the chair in motion. It struggled and faltered like a sick thing, with curious noises.

'Let me push!' said Connie, coming up behind.

'No! Don't push!' he said angrily. 'What's the good of the damned thing, if it has to be pushed! Put the stone under!'

There was another pause, then another start; but more ineffectual than before.

'You *must* let me push,' said she. 'Or sound the horn for the keeper.'

'Wait!'

She waited; and he had another try, doing more harm than good.

'Sound the horn then, if you won't let me push,' she said.

'Hell! Be quiet a moment!'

She was quiet a moment: he made shattering efforts with the little motor.

'You'll only break the thing down altogether, Clifford,' she remonstrated; 'besides wasting your nervous energy.'

'If I could only get out and look at the damned thing!' he said, exasperated. And he sounded the horn stridently. 'Perhaps Mellors can see what's wrong.'

They waited, among the mashed flowers under a sky softly curdling with cloud. In the silence a wood-pigeon began to coo roo-hoo hoo! roo-hoo hoo! Clifford shut her up with a blast on the horn.

The keeper appeared directly, striding inquiringly round the corner. He saluted.

'Do you know anything about motors?' asked Clifford sharply.

'I am afraid I don't. Has she gone wrong?'

'Apparently!' snapped Clifford.

The man crouched solicitiously by the wheel, and peered at the little engine.

'I'm afraid I know nothing at all about these mechanical things, Sir Clifford,' he said calmly. 'If she has enough petrol and oil—'

'Just look carefully and see if you can see anything broken,' snapped Clifford.

The man laid his gun against a tree, took off his coat, and threw it beside it. The brown dog sat guard. Then he sat down on his heels and peered under the chair, poking with his finger at the greasy little engine, and resenting the grease-marks on his clean Sunday shirt.

'Doesn't seem anything broken,' he said. And he stood up, pushing back his hat from his forehead, rubbing his brow and apparently studying.

'Have you looked at the rods underneath?' asked Clifford. 'See if they are all right!'

The man lay flat on his stomach on the floor, his neck pressed back, wriggling under the engine and poking with his finger. Connie thought what a pathetic sort of thing a man was, feeble and small-looking, when he was lying on his belly on the big earth.

'Seems all right as far as I can see,' came his muffled voice.

'I don't suppose you can do anything,' said Clifford.

'Seems as if I can't!' And he scrambled up and sat on his heels, collier fashion. 'There's certainly nothing obviously broken.'

Clifford started his engine, then put her in gear. She would not move.

'Run her a bit hard, like,' suggested the keeper.

Clifford resented the interference: but he made his engine buzz like a blue-bottle. Then she coughed and snarled and seemed to go better.

'Sounds as if she'd come clear,' said Mellors.

But Clifford had already jerked her into gear. She gave a sick lurch and ebbed weakly forwards.

'If I give her a push, she'll do it,' said the keeper, going behind.

'Keep off!' snapped Clifford. 'She'll do it by herself.'

'But Clifford!' put in Connie from the bank, 'you know it's too much for her. Why are you so obstinate!'

Clifford was pale with anger. He jabbed at his levers. The chair gave a sort of scurry, reeled on a few more yards, and came to her end amid a particularly promising patch of bluebells.

'She's done!' said the keeper. 'Not power enough.'

'She's been up here before,' said Clifford coldly.

'She won't do it this time,' said the keeper.

Clifford did not reply. He began doing things with his engine, running her fast and slow as if to get some sort of tune out of her. The wood re-echoed with weird noises. Then he put her in gear with a jerk, having jerked off his brake.

'You'll rip her inside out,' murmured the keeper.

The chair charged in a sick lurch sideways at the ditch.

'Clifford!' cried Connie, rushing forward.

But the keeper had got the chair by the rail. Clifford, however, putting on all his pressure, managed to steer into the riding, and with a strange noise the chair was fighting the hill. Mellors pushed steadily behind, and up she went, as if to retrieve herself.

'You see, she's doing it!' said Clifford, victorious, glancing over his shoulder. There he saw the keeper's face.

'Are you pushing her?'

'She won't do it without.'

'Leave her alone. I asked you not.'

'She won't do it.'

'*Let her try!*' snarled Clifford, with all his emphasis.

The keeper stood back: then turned to fetch his coat and gun. The chair seemed to strangle immediately. She stood inert. Clifford, seated a prisoner, was white with vexation. He jerked at the levers with his hand, his feet were no good. He got queer noises out of her. In savage impatience he moved little handles and got more noises out of her. But she would not budge. No, she would not budge. He stopped the engine and sat rigid with anger.

Constance sat on the bank and looked at the wretched and trampled bluebells. 'Nothing quite so lovely as an English spring.' 'I can do my share of ruling.' 'What we need to take up now is whips, not swords.' 'The ruling classes!'

The keeper strode up with his coat and gun, Flossie cautiously at his heels.

Clifford asked the man to do something or other to the engine. Connie, who understood nothing at all of the technicalities of motors, and who had had experience of break-downs, sat patiently on the bank as if she were a cipher. The keeper lay on his stomach again. The ruling classes and the serving classes!

He got to his feet and said patiently:

'Try her again, then.'

He spoke in a quiet voice, almost as if to a child.

Clifford tried her, and Mellors stepped quickly behind and began to push. She was going, the engine doing about half the work, the man the rest.

Clifford glanced round, yellow with anger.

'Will you get off there!'

The keeper dropped his hold at once, and Clifford added: 'How shall I know what she is doing!'

The man put his gun down and began to pull on his coat. He'd done.

The chair began slowly to run backwards.

'Clifford, your brake!' cried Connie.

She, Mellors, and Clifford moved at once, Connie and the keeper jostling lightly. The chair stood. There was a moment of dead silence.

'It's obvious I'm at everybody's mercy!' said Clifford. He was yellow with anger.

No one answered. Mellors was slinging his gun over his shoulder, his face queer and expressionless, save for an abstracted look of patience. The dog Flossie, standing on guard almost between her master's legs, moved uneasily, eyeing the chair with great suspicion and dislike, and very much perplexed between the three human beings. The *tableau vivant* remained set among the squashed bluebells, nobody proffering a word.

'I expect she'll have to be pushed,' said Clifford at last, with an affectation of *sang froid*.

No answer. Mellors's abstracted face looked as if he had heard nothing. Connie glanced anxiously at him. Clifford too glanced round.

'Do you mind pushing her home, Mellors!' he said in a cool superior tone. 'I hope I have said nothing to offend you,' he added, in a tone of dislike.

'Nothing at all, Sir Clifford! Do you want me to push that chair?'

'If you please.'

The man stepped up to it: but this time it was without effect. The brake was jammed. They poked and pulled, and the keeper took off his gun and his coat once more. And now Clifford said never a word. At last the keeper heaved the back of the chair off the ground and, with an instantaneous push of his foot, tried to loosen the wheels. He failed, the chair sank. Clifford was clutching the sides. The man gasped with the weight.

'Don't do it!' cried Connie to him.

'If you'll pull the wheel that way, so!' he said to her, showing her how.

'No! You mustn't lift it! You'll strain yourself,' she said, flushed now with anger.

But he looked into her eyes and nodded. And she had to go and take hold of the wheel, ready. He heaved and she tugged, and the chair reeled.

'For God's sake!' cried Clifford in terror.

But it was all right, and the brake was off. The keeper put a stone under the wheel, and went to sit on the bank, his heart beating and his face white with the effort, semi-conscious. Connie looked at him, and almost cried with anger.

There was a pause and a dead silence. She saw his hands trembling on his thighs.

'Have you hurt yourself?' she asked, going to him.

'No. No!' He turned away almost angrily.

There was dead silence. The back of Clifford's fair head did not move. Even the dog stood motionless. The sky had clouded over.

At last he sighed, and blew his nose on his red handkerchief.

'That pneumonia took a lot out of me,' he said.

No one answered. Connie calculated the amount of strength it must have taken to heave up that chair and the bulky Clifford: too much, far too much! If it hadn't killed him!

He rose, and again picked up his coat, slinging it through the handle of the chair.

'Are you ready, then, Sir Clifford?'

'When you are!'

He stooped and took out the scotch, then put his weight against the chair. He was paler than Connie had ever seen him: and more absent. Clifford was a heavy man: and the hill was steep. Connie stepped to the keeper's side.

'I'm going to push too!' she said.

And she began to shove with a woman's turbulent energy of anger. The chair went faster. Clifford looked round.

'Is that necessary?' he said.

'Very! Do you want to kill the man! If you'd let the motor work while it would–'

But she did not finish. She was already panting. She slackened off a little, for it was surprisingly hard work.

'Ay! slower!' said the man at her side, with a faint smile of his eyes.

'Are you sure you've not hurt yourself?' she said fiercely.

He shook his head. She looked at his smallish, short, alive hand, browned by the weather. It was the hand that caressed her. She had never even looked at it before. It seemed so still, like him, with a curious inward stillness that made her want to clutch it, as if she could not reach it. All her soul suddenly swept towards him: he was so silent, and out of reach! And he felt his limbs revive. Shoving with his left hand, he laid his right on her round white wrist, softly enfolding her wrist, with a caress. And the flame of strength went down his back and his loins, reviving him. And she bent suddenly and kissed his hand. Meanwhile the back of Clifford's head was held sleek and motionless, just in front of them.

At the top of the hill they rested, and Connie was glad to let go. She had had fugitive dreams of friendship between these two men: one her husband, the other the father of her child. Now she saw the screaming absurdity of her dreams. The two males were as hostile as fire and water. They mutually exterminated one another. And she realized for the first time what a queer subtle thing hate is. For the first time, she had consciously and definitely hated Clifford, with vivid hate: as if he ought to be obliterated from the face of the earth. And it was strange, how free and full of life it made her feel, to hate him and to admit it fully to herself–'Now I've hated him, I shall never be able to go on living with him,' came the thought into her mind.

On the level the keeper could push the chair alone. Clifford made a little conversation with her, to show his complete composure: about Aunt Eva, who was at Dieppe, and about Sir Malcolm, who had written to ask would Connie drive with him in his small car, to Venice, or would she and Hilda go by train.

'I'd much rather go by train,' said Connie. 'I don't like long motor drives, especially when there's dust. But I shall see what Hilda wants.'

'She will want to drive her own car, and take you with her,' he said.

'Probably!–I must help up here. You've no idea how heavy this chair is.'

She went to the back of the chair, and plodded side by side with the keeper, shoving up the pink path. She did not care who saw.

'Why not let me wait, and fetch Field? He is strong enough for the job,' said Clifford.

'It's so near,' she panted.

But both she and Mellors wiped the sweat from their faces when they came to the top. It was curious, but this bit of work together had brought them much closer than they had been before.

'Thanks so much, Mellors,' said Clifford, when they were at the house door. 'I must get a different sort of motor, that's all. Won't you go to the kitchen and have a meal? It must be about time.'

'Thank you, Sir Clifford. I was going to my mother for dinner today, Sunday.'

'As you like.'

Mellors slung into his coat, looked at Connie, saluted, and was gone. Connie, furious, went upstairs.

At lunch she could not contain her feeling.

'Why are you so abominably inconsiderate, Clifford?' she said to him.

'Of whom?'

'Of the keeper! If that is what you call ruling classes, I'm sorry for you.'

'Why?'

'A man who's been ill, and isn't strong! My word, if I were the serving classes, I'd let you wait for service. I'd let you whistle.'

'I quite believe it.'

'If he'd been sitting in a chair with paralysed legs, and behaved as you behaved, what would you have done for *him*?'

'My dear evangelist, this confusing of persons and personalities is in bad taste.'

'And your nasty, sterile want of common sympathy is in the worst taste imaginable. *Noblesse oblige!* You and your ruling class!'

'And to what should it oblige me? To have a lot of unnecessary emotions about my game-keeper? I refuse. I leave it all to my evangelist.'

'As if he weren't a man as much as you are, my word!'

'My game-keeper to boot, and I pay him two pounds a week and give him a house.'

'Pay him! What do you think you pay for, with two pounds a week and a house?'

'His services.'

'Bah! I would tell you to keep your two pounds a week and your house.'

'Probably he would like to: but can't afford the luxury!'

'You, and *rule*!' she said. 'You don't rule, don't flatter yourself. You have only got more than your share of the money, and make people work for you for two pounds a week, or threaten them with starvation. Rule! What do you give forth of rule? Why, you're dried up! You only bully with your money, like any Jew or any Schieber!'

'You are very elegant in your speech, Lady Chatterley!'

'I assure you, you were very elegant altogether out there in the wood. I was utterly ashamed of you. Why, my father is ten times the human being you are: you *gentleman*!'

He reached and rang for Mrs Bolton. But he was yellow at the gills.

She went up to her room, furious, saying to herself: 'Him and buying people! Well, he doesn't buy me, and therefore there's no need for me to stay with him. Dead fish of a gentleman, with his celluloid soul! And how they take one in, with their manners and their mock wistfulness and gentleness. They've got about as much feeling as celluloid has.'

She made her plans for the night, and determined to get Clifford off her mind. She didn't want to hate him. She didn't want to be mixed up very intimately with him in any sort of feeling. She wanted him not to know anything at all about herself: and especially, not to know anything about her feeling for the keeper. This squabble of her attitude to the servants was an old one. He found her too familiar, she found him stupidly insentient, tough and indiarubbery where other people were concerned.

She went downstairs calmly, with her old demure bearing, at dinner-time. He was still yellow at the gills: in for one of his liver bouts, when he was really very queer. – He was reading a French book.

'Have you ever read Proust?' he asked her.

'I've tried, but he bores me.'

'He's really very extraordinary.'

'Possibly! But he bores me: all that sophistication! He doesn't have feelings, he only has streams of words about feelings. I'm tired of self-important mentalities.'

'Would you prefer self-important animalities?'

'Perhaps! But one might possibly get something that wasn't self-important.'

'Well, I like Proust's subtlety and his well-bred anarchy.'

'It makes you very dead, really.'

'There speaks my evangelical little wife.'

They were at it again, at it again! But she couldn't help fighting him. He seemed to sit there like a skeleton, sending out a skeleton's cold grizzly *will* against her. Almost she could feel the skeleton clutching her and pressing her to its cage or ribs. He too was really up in arms: and she was a little afraid of him.

She went upstairs as soon as possible, and went to bed quite early. But at half past nine she got up, and went outside to listen. There was no sound. She slipped on a dressing-gown and went downstairs. Clifford and Mrs Bolton were playing cards, gambling. They would probably go on until midnight.

Connie returned to her room, threw her pyjamas on the tossed bed, put on a thin tennis-dress and over that a woollen day-dress, put on rubber tennis-shoes, and then a light coat. And she was ready. If she met anybody, she was just going out for a few minutes. And in the morning, when she came in again, she would just have been for a little walk in the dew, as she fairly often did before breakfast. For the rest, the only danger was that someone should go into her room during the night. But that was most unlikely: not one chance in a hundred.

Betts had not locked up. He fastened up the house at ten o'clock, and unfastened it again at seven in the morning. She slipped out silently and unseen. There was a half-moon shining, enough to make a little light in the world, not enough to show her up in her dark-grey coat. She walked quickly across the park, not really in the thrill of the assignation, but with a certain anger and rebellion burning in her heart. It was not the right sort of heart to take to a love-meeting. But *à la guerre comme à la guerre*!

14

When she got near the park-gate, she heard the click of the latch. He was there, then, in the darkness of the wood, and had seen her!

'You are good and early,' he said out of the dark. 'Was everything all right?'

'Perfectly easy.'

He shut the gate quietly after her, and made a spot of light on the dark ground, showing the pallid flowers still standing there open in the night. They went on apart, in silence.

'Are you sure you didn't hurt yourself this morning with that chair?' she asked.

'No, no!'

'When you had that pneumonia, what did it do to you?'

'Oh nothing! it left my heart not so strong and the lungs not so elastic. But it always does that.'

'And you ought not to make violent physical efforts?'

'Not often.'

She plodded on in an angry silence.

'Did you hate Clifford?' she said at last.

'Hate him, no! I've met too many like him to upset myself hating him. I know beforehand I don't care for his sort, and I let it go at that.'

'What is his sort?'

'Nay, you know better than I do. The sort of youngish gentleman a bit like a lady, and no balls.'

'What balls?'

'Balls! A man's balls!'

She pondered this.

'But is it a question of that?' she said, a little annoyed.

'You say a man's got no brain, when he's a fool: and no heart, when he's mean; and no stomach when he's a funker. And when he's got none of that spunky wild bit of a man in him, you say he's got no balls. When he's sort of tame.'

She pondered this.

'And is Clifford tame?' she asked.

'Tame, and nasty with it: like most such fellows, when you come up against 'em.'

'And do you think you're not tame?'

'Maybe not quite!'

At length she saw in the distance a yellow light.

She stood still.

'There is a light!' she said.

'I always leave a light in the house,' he said.

She went on again at his side, but not touching him, wondering why she was going with him at all.

He unlocked, and they went in, he bolting the door behind them. As if it were a prison, she thought! The kettle was singing by the red fire, there were cups on the table.

She sat in the wooden arm-chair by the fire. It was warm after the chill outside.

'I'll take off my shoes, they are wet,' she said.

She sat with her stockinged feet on the bright steel fender. He went to the pantry, bringing food: bread and butter and pressed tongue. She was warm: she took off her coat. He hung it on the door.

'Shall you have cocoa or tea or coffee to drink?' he asked.

'I don't think I want anything,' she said, looking at the table. 'But you eat.'

'Nay, I don't care about it. I'll just feed the dog.'

He tramped with a quiet inevitability over the brick floor, putting food for the dog in a brown bowl. The spaniel looked up at him anxiously.

'Ay, this is thy supper, tha nedna look as if tha wouldna get it!' he said.

He set the bowl on the stairfoot mat, and sat himself on a chair by the wall, to take off his leggings and boots. The dog instead of eating, came to him again, and sat looking up at him, troubled.

He slowly unbuckled his leggings. The dog edged a little nearer.

'What's amiss wi' thee then? Art upset because there's somebody else here? Tha'rt a female, tha art! Go an' eat thy supper.'

He put his hand on her head, and the bitch leaned her head sideways against him. He slowly, softly pulled the long silky ear.

'There!' he said. 'There! Go an' eat thy supper! Go!'

He tilted his chair towards the pot on the mat, and the dog meekly went, and fell to eating.

'Do you like dogs?' Connie asked him.

'No, not really. They're too tame and clinging.'

He had taken off his leggings and was unlacing his heavy boots. Connie had turned from the fire. How bare the little room was! Yet over his head on the wall hung a hideous enlarged photograph of a young married couple, apparently him and a bold-faced young woman, no doubt his wife.

'Is that you?' Connie asked him.

He twisted and looked at the enlargement above his head.

'Ay! Taken just afore we was married, when I was twenty-one.' He looked at it impassively.

'Do you like it?' Connie asked him.

'Like it? No! I never liked the thing. But she fixed it all up to have it done, like.'

He returned to pulling off his boots.

'If you don't like it, why do you keep it hanging there? Perhaps your wife would like to have it,' she said.

He looked up at her with a sudden grin.

'She carted off iverything as was worth taking from th' 'ouse,' he said. 'But she left *that*!'

'Then why do you keep it? For sentimental reasons?'

'Nay, I niver look at it. I hardly knowed it wor theer. It's bin theer sin' we come to this place.'

'Why don't you burn it?' she said.

He twisted round again and looked at the enlarged photograph. It was framed in a brown-and-gilt frame, hideous. It showed a clean-shaven, alert, very young-looking man in a rather high collar, and a somewhat plump, bold young woman with hair fluffed out and crimped, and wearing a dark satin blouse.

'It wouldn't be a bad idea, would it?' he said.

He had pulled off his boots, and put on a pair of slippers. He stood up on the chair, and lifted down the photograph. It left a big pale place on the greenish wall-paper.

'No use dusting it now,' he said, setting the thing against the wall.

He went to the scullery, and returned with hammer and pincers. Sitting where he had sat before, he started to tear off the back-paper from the big frame, and to pull out the sprigs that held the backboard in position, working with the immediate quiet absorption that was characteristic of him.

He soon had the nails out: then he pulled out the backboards, then the enlargement itself, in its solid white mount. He looked at the photograph with amusement.

'Shows me for what I was, a young curate, and her for what she was, a bully,' he said. 'The prig and the bully!'

'Let me look!' said Connie.

He did look indeed very clean-shaven and very clean altogether, one of the clean young men of twenty years ago. But even in the photograph his eyes were alert and dauntless. And the woman was not altogether a bully, though her jowl was heavy. There was a touch of appeal in her.

'One never should keep these things,' said Connie.

'That one shouldn't! One should never have them made!'

He broke the cardboard photograph and mount over his knee, and when it was small enough, put it on the fire.

'It'll spoil the fire though,' he said.

The glass and the backboard he carefully took upstairs.

The frame he knocked asunder with a few blows of the hammer, making the stucco fly. Then he took the pieces into the scullery.

'We'll burn that tomorrow,' he said. 'There's too much plaster-moulding on it.'

Having cleared away, he sat down.

'Did you love your wife?' she asked him.

'Love?' he said. 'Did you love Sir Clifford?'

But she was not going to be put off.

'But you cared for her?' she insisted.

'Cared?' He grinned.

'Perhaps you care for her now,' she said.

'Me!' His eyes widened. 'Ah no, I can't think of her,' he said quietly.

'Why?'

But he shook his head.

'Then why don't you get a divorce? She'll come back to you one day,' said Connie.

He looked up at her sharply.

'She wouldn't come within a mile of me. She hates me a lot worse than I hate her.'

'You'll see she'll come back to you.'

'That she never will. That's done! It would make me sick to see her.'

'You will see her. And you're not even legally separated, are you?'

'No.'

'Ah well, then she'll come back, and you'll have to take her in.'

He gazed at Connie fixedly. Then he gave the queer toss of his head.

'You might be right. I was a fool ever to come back here. But I felt stranded and had to go somewhere. A man's a poor bit of a wastrel blown about. But you're right. I'll get a divorce and get clear. I hate those things like death, officials and courts and judges. But I've got to get through with it. I'll get a divorce.'

And she saw his jaw set. Inwardly she exulted.

'I think I will have a cup of tea now,' she said.

He rose to make it. But his face was set.

As they sat at table she asked him:

'Why did you marry her? She was commoner than yourself. Mrs Bolton told me about her. She could never understand why you married her.'

He looked at her fixedly.

'I'll tell you,' he said. 'The first girl I had, I began with when I was sixteen. She was a school-master's daughter over at Ollerton, pretty, beautiful really. I was supposed to be a clever sort of young fellow from Sheffield Grammar School, with a bit of French and German, very much up aloft. She was the romantic sort that hated commonness. She egged me on to poetry and reading: in a way, she made a man of me. I read and I thought like a house on fire, for her. And I was a clerk in Butterley Offices, thin, white-faced fellow fuming with all the things I read. And about *everything* I talked to her: but everything. We talked ourselves into Persepolis and Timbuctoo. We were the most literary-cultured couple in ten counties. I held forth with rapture to her, positively with rapture. I simply went up in smoke. And she adored me. The serpent in the grass was sex. She somehow didn't have any; at least, not where it's supposed to be. I got thinner and crazier. Then I said we'd got to be lovers. I talked her into it, as usual. So she let me. I was excited, and she never wanted it. She just didn't want it. She adored me, she loved me to talk to her and kiss her: in that way she had a passion for me. But the other, she just didn't want. And there are lots of women like her. And it was just the other that I *did* want. So there we split. I was cruel, and left her. Then I took on with another girl, a teacher, who had made a scandal by carrying on with a married man and driving him nearly out of his mind. She was a soft, white-skinned, soft sort of a woman, older than me, and played the fiddle. And she was a demon. She loved everything about love, except the sex. Clinging, caressing, creeping into you in every way: but if you forced her to the sex itself, she just ground her teeth and sent out hate. I forced her to it, and she could simply numb me with hate because of it. So I was balked again. I loathed all that. I wanted a woman who wanted me, and wanted *it*.

'Then came Bertha Coutts. They'd lived next door to us when I was a little lad, so I knew 'em all right. And they were common. Well, Bertha went away to some place or other in Birmingham; she said, as a lady's companion; everybody else said, as a waitress or something in a hotel. Anyhow just when I was more than fed up with that other girl, when I was twenty-one, back comes Bertha, with airs and graces and smart clothes and a sort of bloom on her: a sort of sensual bloom that you'd see sometimes on a woman, or on a trolly. Well, I was in a state of murder. I chucked up my job at Butterley because I thought I was a weed, clerking there: and I got on as overhead blacksmith at Tevershall:

shoeing horses mostly. It had been my dad's job, and I'd always been with him. It was a job I liked: handling horses: and it came natural to me. So I stopped talking "fine", as they call it, talking proper English, and went back to talking broad. I still read books, at home: but I blacksmithed and had a pony-trap of my own, and was My Lord Duckfoot. My dad left me three hundred pounds when he died. So I took on with Bertha, and I was glad she was common. I wanted her to be common. I wanted to be common myself. Well, I married her, and she wasn't bad. Those other "pure" women had nearly taken all the balls out of me, but she was all right that way. She wanted me, and made no bones about it. And I was as pleased as punch. That was what I wanted: a woman who *wanted* me to fuck her. So I fucked her like a good un. And I think she despised me a bit, for being so pleased about it, and bringin' her her breakfast in bed sometimes. She sort of let things go, didn't get me a proper dinner when I came home from work, and if I said anything, flew out at me. And I flew back, hammer and tongs. She flung a cup at me and I took her by the scruff of the neck and squeezed the life out of her. That sort of thing! But she treated me with insolence. And she got so's she'd never have me when I wanted her: never. Always put me off, brutal as you like. And then when she'd put me right off, and I didn't want her, she'd come all lovey-dovey, and get me. And I always went. But when I had her, she'd never come off when I did. Never! She'd just wait. If I kept back for half an hour, she'd keep back longer. And when I'd come and really finished, then she'd start on her own account, and I had to stop inside her till she brought herself off, wriggling and shouting, she'd clutch clutch with herself down there, an' then she'd come off, fair in ecstasy. And then she'd say: That was lovely! Gradually I got sick of it: and she got worse. She sort of got harder and harder to bring off, and she'd sort of tear at me down there, as if it was a beak tearing at me. By God, you think a woman's soft down there, like a fig. But I tell you the old rampers have beaks between their legs, and they tear at you with it till you're sick. Self! Self! Self! all self! tearing and shouting! They talk about men's selfishness, but I doubt if it can ever touch a woman's blind beakishness, once she's gone that way. Like an old trull! And she couldn't help it. I told her about it, I told her how I hated it. And she'd even try. She'd try to lie still and let *me* work the business. She'd try. But it was no good. She got no feeling off it, from my working. She had to work the thing herself, grind her own coffee. And it came back on her like a raving necessity, she had to let herself go, and tear, tear, tear, as if she had no sensation in her except in the top of her beak, the very outside top tip, that rubbed and tore. That's how old whores used to be, so men used to say. It was a low kind of self-will in her, a raving sort of self-will: like in a woman who drinks. Well in the end I couldn't stand it. We slept apart. She herself had started it, in her bouts when she wanted to be clear of me, when she said I bossed her. She had started having a room for herself. But the time came when I wouldn't have her coming to my room. I wouldn't.

'I hated it. And she hated me. My God, how she hated me before that child was born! I often think she conceived it out of hate. Anyhow, after the child was born I left her alone. And then came the war, and I joined up. And I didn't come back till I knew she was with that fellow at Stacks Gate.'

He broke off, pale in the face.

'And what is the man at Stacks Gate like?' asked Connie.

'A big baby sort of fellow, very low-mouthed. She bullies him, and they both drink.'

'My word, if she came back!'

'My God, yes! I should just go, disappear again.'

There was a silence. The pasteboard in the fire had turned to grey ash.

'So when you did get a woman who wanted you,' said Connie, 'you got a bit too much of a good thing.'

'Ay! Seems so! Yet even then I'd rather have her than the never-never ones: the white love of my youth, and that other poison-smelling lily, and the rest.'

'What about the rest?' said Connie.

'The rest? There is no rest. Only to my experience the mass of women are like this: most of them want a man, but don't want the sex, but they put up with it, as part of the bargain. The more old-fashioned sort just lie there like nothing and let you go ahead. They don't mind afterwards: then they like you. But the actual thing itself is nothing to them, a bit distasteful. And most men like it that way. I hate it. But the sly sort of women who are like that pretend they're not. They pretend they're passionate and have thrills. But it's all cockaloopy. They make it up.—Then there's the ones that love everything, every kind of feeling and cuddling and going off, every kind except the natural one. They always make you go off when you're *not* in the only place you should be, when you go off.—Then there's the hard sort, that are the devil to bring off at all, and bring themselves off, like my wife. They want to be the active party.—Then there's the sort that's just dead inside: but dead: and they know it. Then there's the sort that puts you out before you really "come", and go on writhing their loins till they bring themselves off against your thighs. But they're mostly the Lesbian sort. It's astonishing how Lesbian women are, consciously or unconsciously. Seems to me they're nearly all Lesbian.'

'And do you mind?' asked Connie.

'I could kill them. When I'm with a woman who's really Lesbian, I fairly howl in my soul, wanting to kill her.'

'And what do you do?'

'Just go away as fast as I can.'

'But do you think Lesbian women any worse than homosexual men?'

'*I* do! Because I've suffered more from them. In the abstract, I've no idea. When I get with a Lesbian woman, whether she knows she's one or not, I see red. No, no! But I wanted to have nothing to do with any woman any more. I wanted to keep to myself: keep my privacy and my decency.'

He looked pale, and his brows were sombre.

'And were you sorry when I came along?' she asked.

'I was sorry and I was glad.'

'And what are you now?'

'I'm sorry, from the outside: all the complications and the ugliness and recrimination that's bound to come, sooner or later. That's when my blood sinks, and I'm low. But when my blood comes up, I'm glad. I'm even triumphant. I was really getting bitter. I thought there was no real sex left: never a woman who'd really "come" naturally with a man: except black women, and somehow, well, we're white men: and they're a bit like mud.'

'And now, are you glad of me?' she asked.

'Yes! When I can forget the rest. When I can't forget the rest, I want to get under the table and die.'

'Why under the table?'

'Why?' he laughed. 'Hide, I suppose. Baby!'

'You do seem to have had awful experiences of women,' she said.

'You see, I couldn't fool myself. That's where most men manage. They take an attitude, and accept a lie. I could never fool myself. I knew what I wanted with a woman, and I could never say I'd got it when I hadn't.'

'But have you got it now?'

'Looks as if I might have.'

'Then why are you so pale and gloomy?'

'Bellyful of remembering: and perhaps afraid of myself.'

She sat in silence. It was growing late.

'And do you think it's important, a man and a woman?' she asked him.

'For me it is. For me it's the core of my life: if I have a right relation with a woman.'

'And if you didn't get it?'

'Then I'd have to do without.'

Again she pondered, before she asked: ·

'And do you think you've always been right with women?'

'God, no! I let my wife get to what she was: my fault a good deal. I spoilt her. And I'm very mistrustful. You'll have to expect it. It takes a lot to make me trust anybody, inwardly. So perhaps I'm a fraud too. I mistrust. And tenderness is not to be mistaken.'

She looked at him.

'You don't mistrust with your body, when your blood comes up,' she said. 'You don't mistrust then, do you?'

'No, alas! That's how I've got into all the trouble. And that's why my mind mistrusts so thoroughly.'

'Let your mind mistrust. What does it matter!'

The dog sighed with discomfort on the mat. The ash-clogged fire sank.

'We *are* a couple of battered warriors,' said Connie.

'Are you battered too?' he laughed. 'And here we are returning to the fray!'

'Yes! I feel really frightened.'

'Ay!'

He got up, and put her shoes to dry, and wiped his own and set them near the fire. In the morning he would grease them. He poked the ash of pasteboard as much as possible out of the fire. 'Even burnt, it's filthy,' he said. Then he brought sticks and put them on the hob for the morning. Then he went out awhile with the dog.

When he came back, Connie said:

'I want to go out too, for a minute.'

She went alone into the darkness. There were stars overhead. She could smell flowers on the night air. And she could feel her wet shoes getting wetter again. But she felt like going away, right away from him and everybody.

It was chilly. She shuddered, and returned to the house. He was sitting in front of the low fire.

'Ugh! Cold!' she shuddered.

He put the sticks on the fire, and fetch more, till they had a good crackling chimneyful of blaze. The rippling running yellow flame made them both happy, warmed their faces and their souls.

'Never mind!' she said, taking his hand as he sat silent and remote. 'One does one's best.'

'Ay!'—He sighed, with a twist of a smile.

She slipped over to him, and into his arms, as he sat there before the fire.

'Forget then!' she whispered. 'Forget!'

He held her close, in the running warmth of the fire. The flame itself was like a forgetting. And her soft, warm, ripe weight! Slowly his blood turned, and began to ebb back into strength and reckless vigour again.

'And perhaps the women *really* wanted to be there and love you properly, only perhaps they couldn't. Perhaps it wasn't all their fault,' she said.

'I know it. Do you think I don't know what a broken-backed snake that's been trodden on I was myself!'

She clung to him suddenly. She had not wanted to start all this again. Yet some perversity had made her.

'But you're not now,' she said. 'You're not that now: a broken-backed snake that's been trodden on.'

'I don't know what I am. There's black days ahead.'

'No!' she protested, clinging to him. 'Why? Why?'

'There's black days coming for us all and for everybody,' he repeated with a prophetic gloom.

'No! You're not to say it!'

He was silent. But she could feel the black void of despair inside him. That was the death of all desire, the death of all love: this despair that was like the dark cave inside the men, in which their spirit was lost.

'And you talk so coldly about sex,' she said. 'You talk as if you had only wanted your own pleasure and satisfaction.'

She was protesting nervously against him.

'Nay!' he said. 'I wanted to have my pleasure and satisfaction of a woman, and I never got it: because I could never get my pleasure and satisfaction of *her* unless she got hers of me at the same time. And it never happened. It takes two.'

'But you never believed in your women. You don't even believe really in me,' she said.

'I don't know what believing in a woman means.'

'That's it, you see!'

She still was curled on his lap. But his spirit was grey and absent, he was not there for her. And everything she said drove him further.

'But what *do* you believe in?' she insisted.

'I don't know.'

'Nothing, like all the men I've ever known,' she said.

They were both silent. Then he roused himself and said:

'Yes, I do believe in something. I believe in being warm-hearted. I believe especially in being warm-hearted in love, in fucking with a warm heart. I believe if men could fuck with warm hearts, and the women take it warm-heartedly, everything would come all right. It's all this cold-hearted fucking that is death and idiocy.'

'But you don't fuck me cold-heartedly,' she protested.

'I don't want to fuck you at all. My heart's as cold as cold potatoes just now.'

'Oh!' she said, kissing him mockingly. 'Let's have them *sautées*.' He laughed, and sat erect.

'It's a fact!' he said. 'Anything for a bit of warm-heartedness. But the women don't like it. Even you don't really like it. You like good, sharp, piercing cold-hearted fucking, and then pretending it's all sugar. Where's your tenderness for me? You're as suspicious of me as a cat is of a dog. I tell you it take two even to be tender and warm-hearted. You love fucking all right: but you want it to be called something grand and mysterious, just to flatter your own self-importance. Your own self-importance is more to you, fifty times more, than any man, or being together with a man.'

'But that's what I'd say of you. Your own self-importance is everything to you.'

'Ay! Very well then!' he said, moving as if he wanted to rise. 'Let's keep apart then. I'd rather die than do any more cold-hearted fucking.'

She slid away from him, and he stood up.

'And do you think *I* want it?' she said.

'I hope you don't,' he replied. 'But anyhow, you go to bed an' I'll sleep down here.'

She looked at him. He was pale, his brows were sullen, he was as distant in recoil as the cold pole. Men were all alike.

'I can't go home till morning,' she said.

'No! Go to bed. It's a quarter to one.'

'I certainly won't,' she said.

He went across and picked up his boots.

'Then I'll go out!' he said.

He began to put on his boots. She stared at him.

'Wait!' she faltered. 'Wait! What's come between us?'

He was bent over, lacing his boot, and did not reply. The moments passed. A dimness came over her, like a swoon. All her consciousness died, and she stood there wide-eyed, looking at him from the unknown, knowing nothing any more.

He looked up, because of the silence, and saw her wide-eyed and lost. And as if a wind tossed him he got up and hobbled over to her, one shoe off and one shoe on, and took her in his arms, pressing her against his body, which somehow felt hurt right through. And there he held her, and there she remained.

Till his hands reached blindly down and felt for her, and felt under the clothing to where she was smooth and warm.

'Ma lass!' he murmured. 'Ma little lass! Dunna let's fight! Dunna let's niver fight! I love thee an' th' touch on thee. Dunna argue wi' me! Dunna! Dunna! Dunna! Let's be together.'

She lifted her face and looked at him.

'Don't be upset,' she said steadily. 'It's no good being upset. Do you really want to be together with me?'

She looked with wide, steady eyes into his face. He stopped, and went suddenly still, turning his face aside. All his body went perfectly still, but did not withdraw.

Then he lifted his head and looked into her eyes, with his odd, faintly mocking grin, saying: 'Ay-ay! Let's be together on oath.'

'But really?' she said, her eyes filling with tears.

'Ay really! Heart an' belly an' cock.'

He still smiled faintly down at her, with the flicker of irony in his eyes, and a touch of bitterness.

She was silently weeping, and he lay with her and went into her there on the hearthrug, and so they gained a measure of equanimity. And then they went quickly to bed, for it was growing chill, and they had tired each other out. And she nestled up to him, feeling small and enfolded, and they both went to sleep at once, fast in one sleep. And so they lay and never moved, till the sun rose over the wood and day was beginning.

Then he woke up and looked at the light. The curtains were drawn. He listened to the loud wild calling of blackbirds and thrushes in the wood. It would be a brilliant morning, about half past five, his hour for rising. He had slept so fast! It was such a new day! The woman was still curled asleep and tender. His hand moved on her, and she opened her blue wondering eyes, smiling unconsciously into his face.

'Are you awake?' she said to him.

He was looking into her eyes. He smiled, and kissed her. And suddenly she roused and sat up.

'Fancy that I am here!' she said.

She looked round the whitewashed little bedroom with its sloping ceiling and gable window where the white curtains were closed. The room was bare save for a little yellow-painted chest of drawers, and a chair: and the smallish white bed in which she lay with him.

'Fancy that we are here!' she said, looking down at him. He was lying watching her, stroking her breasts with his fingers, under the thin nightdress. When he was warm and smoothed out, he looked young and handsome. His eyes could look so warm. And she was fresh and young like a flower.

'I want to take this off!' she said, gathering the thin batiste nightdress and pulling it over her head. She sat there with bare shoulders and longish breasts faintly golden. He loved to make her breasts swing softly, like bells.

'You must take off your pyjamas too,' she said.

'Eh, nay!'

'Yes! Yes!' she commanded.

And he took off his old cotton pyjama-jacket, and pushed down the trousers. Save for his hands and wrists and face and neck he was white as milk, with fine slender muscular flesh. To Connie he was suddenly piercingly beautiful again, as when she had seen him that afternoon washing himself.

Gold of sunshine touched the closed white curtain. She felt it wanted to come in.

'Oh, do let's draw the curtains! The birds are singing so! Do let the sun in,' she said.

He slipped out of bed with his back to her, naked and white and thin, and went to the window, stooping a little, drawing the curtains and looking out for a moment. The back was white and fine, the small buttocks beautiful with an exquisite, delicate manliness, the back of the neck ruddy and delicate and yet strong.

There was an inward, not an outward strength in the delicate fine body.

'But you are beautiful!' she said. 'So pure and fine! Come!' She held her arms out.

He was ashamed to turn to her, because of his aroused nakedness.

He caught his shirt off the floor, and held it to him, coming to her.

'No!' she said still holding out her beautiful slim arms from her dropping breasts. 'Let me see you!'

He dropped the shirt and stood still looking towards her. The sun through the low window sent in a beam that lit up his thighs and slim belly and the erect phallos rising darkish and hot-looking from the little cloud of vivid gold-red hair. She was startled and afraid.

'How strange!' she said slowly. 'How strange he stands there! So big! and so dark and cock-sure! Is he like that?'

The man looked down the front of his slender white body, and laughed. Between the slim breasts the hair was dark, almost black. But at the root of the belly, where the phallos rose thick and arching, it was gold-red, vivid in a little cloud.

'So proud!' she murmured, uneasy. 'And so lordly! Now I know why men are so overbearing! But he's lovely, *really.* Like another being! A bit terrifying! But lovely really! And he come to *me*!–' She caught her lower lip between her teeth, in fear and excitement.

The man looked down in silence at the tense phallos, that did not change.–'Ay!' he said at last, in a little voice. 'Ay ma lad! tha're theer right enough. Yi, tha mun rear thy head! Theer on thy own, eh? an' ta'es no count o' nob'dy! Tha ma'es nowt o' me, John Thomas. Art boss? of me? Eh well, tha're more cocky than me, an' tha says less. John Thomas! Dost want *her*? Dost want my lady Jane? Tha's dipped me in again, tha hast. Ay, an' tha comes up smilin'.–Ax 'er then! Ax lady Jane! Say: Lift up your heads o' ye gates, that the king of glory may come in. Ay, th' cheek on thee! Cunt, that's what tha're after. Tell lady Jane tha wants cunt. John Thomas, an' th' cunt o' lady Jane!–'

'Oh, don't tease him,' said Connie, crawling on her knees on the bed towards him and putting her arms round his white slender loins, and drawing him to her so that her hanging swinging breasts touched the tip of the stirring, erect phallos, and caught the drop of moisture. She held the man fast.

'Lie down!' he said. 'Lie down! Let me come!'

He was in a hurry now.

And afterwards, when they had been quite still, the woman had to uncover the man again, to look at the mystery of the phallos.

'And now he's tiny, and soft like a little bud of life!' she said, taking the soft small penis in her hand. 'Isn't he somehow lovely! so on his own, so strange! And so innocent! And he comes so far into me! You must *never* insult him, you know. He's mine too. He's not only yours. He's mine! And so lovely and innocent!' And she held the penis soft in her hand.

He laughed.

'Blest be the tie that binds our hearts in kindred love,' he said.

'Of course!' she said. 'Even when he's soft and little I feel my heart simply tied to him. And how lovely your hair is here! quite, quite different!'

'That's John Thomas's hair, not mine!' he said.

'John Thomas! John Thomas!' and she quickly kissed the soft penis, that was beginning to stir again.

'Ay!' said the man, stretching his body almost painfully. 'He's got his root in my soul, has that gentleman! An' sometimes I don' know what ter do wi' him. Ay, he's got a will of his own, an' it's hard to suit him. Yet I wouldn't have him killed.'

'No wonder men have always been afraid of him!' she said. 'He's rather terrible.'

The quiver was going through the man's body, as the stream of consciousness again changed its direction, turning downwards. And he was helpless, as the penis in slow soft undulations filled and surged and rose up, and grew hard, standing there hard and overweening, in its curious towering fashion. The woman too trembled a little as she watched.

'There! Take him then! He's thine,' said the man.

And she quivered, and her own mind melted out. Sharp soft waves of unspeakable pleasure washed over her as he entered her, and started the curious molten thrilling that spread and spread till she was carried away with the last, blind flush of extremity.

He heard the distant hooters of Stacks Gate for seven o'clock. It was Monday morning. He shivered a little, and with his face between her breasts pressed her soft breasts up over his ears, to deafen him.

She had not even heard the hooters. She lay perfectly still, her soul washed transparent.

'You must get up, mustn't you?' he muttered.

'What time?' came her colourless voice.

'Seven-o'clock blowers a bit sin'.'

'I suppose I must.'

She was resenting as she always did, the compulsion from outside.

He sat up and looked blankly out of the window.

'You do love me, don't you?' she asked calmly.

He looked down at her.

'Tha knows what tha knows. What dost ax for!' he said a little fretfully.

'I want you to keep me, not to let me go,' she said.

His eyes seemed full of a warm, soft darkness that could not think.

'When? Now?'

'Now in your heart. Then I want to come and live with you always, soon.'

He sat naked on the bed, with his head dropped, unable to think.

'Don't you want it?' she asked.

'Ay!' he said.

Then with the same eyes darkened with another flame of consciousness, almost like sleep, he looked at her.

'Dunna ax me nowt now,' he said. 'Let me be. I like thee. I luv thee when tha lies theer. A woman's a lovely thing when 'er's deep ter fuck, and cunt's good. Ah luv thee, thy legs, an' th' shape on thee, an' th' womanness on thee. Ah luv th' womanness on thee. Ah luv thee wi' my ba's an' wi' my heart. But dunna ax me nowt. Dunna ma'e me say nowt. Let me stop as I am while I can. Tha can ax me iverything after. Now let me be, let me be!'

And softly, he laid his hand over her mound of Venus, on the soft brown maiden-hair, and himself sat still and naked on the bed, his face motionless in physical abstraction, almost like the face of Buddha. Motionless, and in the invisible flame of another consciousness, he sat with his hand on her, and waited for the turn.

After a while, he reached for his shirt and put it on, dressed himself swiftly in silence, looked at her once as she still lay naked and faintly golden like a Gloire de Dijon rose on the bed, and was gone. She heard him downstairs opening the door.

And still she lay musing, musing. It was very hard to go: to go out of his arms. He called from the foot of the stairs: 'Half past seven!' She sighed, and got out of bed. The bare little room! Nothing in it at all but the small chest of drawers and the smallish bed. But the board floor was scrubbed clean. And in the corner by the window gable was a shelf with some books, and some from a circulating library. She looked. There were books about Bolshevist Russia, books of travel, a volume about the atom and the electron, another about the composition on the earth's core, and the causes of earthquakes: then a few novels: then three books on India. So! He was a reader after all.

The sun fell on her naked limbs through the gable window. Outside she saw the dog Flossie roaming round. The hazel-brake was misted with green, and dark-green dogs-mercury under. It was a clear clean morning with birds flying and triumphantly singing. If only she could stay! If only there weren't the other ghastly world of smoke and iron! If only *he* would make her a world.

She came downstairs, down the steep, narrow wooden stairs. Still she would be content with this little house, if only it were in a world of its own.

He was washed and fresh, and the fire was burning.

'Will you eat anything?' he said.

'No! Only lend me a comb.'

She followed him into the scullery, and combed her hair before the handbreadth of mirror by the back door. Then she was ready to go.

She stood in the little front garden, looking at the dewy flowers, the grey bed of pinks in bud already.

'I would like to have all the rest of the world disappear,' she said, 'and live with you here.'

'It won't disappear,' he said.

They went almost in silence through the lovely dewy wood. But they were together in a world of their own.

It was bitter to her to go on to Wragby.

'I want soon to come and live with you altogether,' she said as she left him.

He smiled, unanswering.

She got home quietly and unremarked, and went up to her room.

15

There was a letter from Hilda on the breakfast-tray. 'Father is going to London this week, and I shall call for you on Thursday week, June 17th. You must be ready so that we can go at once. I don't want to waste time at Wragby, it's an awful place. I shall probably stay the night at Retford with the Colemans, so I should be with you for lunch, Thursday. Then we could start at tea-time, and sleep perhaps in Grantham. It is no use our spending an evening with Clifford. If he hates your going, it would be no pleasure to him.'

So! She was being pushed round on the chess-board again.

Clifford hated her going, but it was only because he didn't feel *safe* in her absence. Her presence, for some reason, made him feel safe, and free to do the things he was occupied with. He was a great deal at the pits, and wrestling in spirit with the almost hopeless problems of getting out his coal in the most economical fashion and then selling it when he'd got it out. He knew he ought to find some way of *using* it, or converting it, so that he needn't sell it, or needn't have the chagrin of failing to sell it. But if he made electric power, could he sell that or use it? And to convert into oil was as yet too costly and too elaborate. To keep industry alive there must be more industry, like a madness.

It was a madness, and it required a madman to succeed in it. Well, he was a little mad. Connie thought so. His very intensity and acumen in the affairs of the pits seemed like a manifestation of madness to her, his very inspirations were the inspirations of insanity.

He talked to her of all his serious schemes, and she listened in a kind of wonder, and let him talk. Then the flow ceased, and he turned on the loud-speaker, and became a blank, while apparently his schemes coiled on inside him like a kind of dream.

And every night now he played pontoon, that game of the Tommies, with Mrs Bolton, gambling with sixpences. And again, in the gambling he was gone in a kind of unconsciousness, or blank intoxication, or intoxication of blankness, whatever it was. Connie could not bear to see him. But when she had gone to bed, he and Mrs Bolton would gamble on till two and three in the morning, safely, and with strange lust. Mrs Bolton was caught in the lust as much as Clifford: the more so, as she nearly always lost.

She told Connie one day: 'I lost twenty-three shillings to Sir Clifford last night.'

'And did he take the money from you?' asked Connie aghast.

'Why of course, my Lady! Debt of honour!'

Connie expostulated roundly, and was angry with both of them. The upshot was, Sir Clifford raised Mrs Bolton's wages a hundred a year, and she could gamble on that. Meanwhile, it seemed to Connie, Clifford was really going deader.

She told him at length she was leaving on the seventeenth.

'Seventeenth!' he said. 'And when will you be back?'

'By the twentieth of July at the latest.'

'Yes! the twentieth of July.'

Strangely and blankly he looked at her, with the vagueness of a child, but with the queer blank cunning of an old man.

'You won't let me down, now, will you?' he said.

'How?'

'While you're away, I mean, you're sure to come back?'

'I'm as sure as I can be of anything, that I shall come back.'

'Yes! Well! Twentieth of July!'

He looked at her so strangely.

Yet he really wanted her to go. That was so curious. He wanted her to go, positively, to have her little adventures and perhaps come home pregnant, and all that. At the same time, he was afraid of her going.

She was quivering, watching her real opportunity for leaving him altogether, waiting till the time, herself, himself, should be ripe.

She sat and talked to the keeper of her going abroad.

'And then when I come back,' she said, 'I can tell Clifford I must leave him. And you and I can go away. They never need even know it is you. We can go to another country, shall we? To Africa or Australia. Shall we?'

She was quite thrilled by her plan.

'You've never been to the Colonies, have you?' he asked her.

'No! Have you?'

'I've been in India, and South Africa, and Egypt.'

'Why shouldn't we go to South Africa?'

'We might!' he said slowly.

'Or don't you want to?' she asked.

'I don't care. I don't much care what I do.'

'Doesn't it make you happy? Why not? We shan't be poor. I have about six hundred a year, I wrote and asked. It's not much, but it's enough, isn't it?'

'It's riches to me.'

'Oh, how lovely it will be!'

'But I ought to get divorced, and so ought you, unless we're going to have complications.'

There was plenty to think about.

Another day she asked him about himself. They were in the hut, and there was a thunderstorm.

'And weren't you happy, when you were a lieutenant and an officer and a gentleman?'

'Happy? All right. I liked my Colonel.'

'Did you love him?'

'Yes! I loved him.'

'And did he love you?'

'Yes! In a way, he loved me.'

'Tell me about him.'

'What is there to tell? He had risen from the ranks. He loved the army. And he had never married. He was twenty years older than me. He was a very intelligent man: and alone in the army, as such a man is: a passionate man in his way: and a very clever officer. I lived under his spell while I was with him. I sort of let him run my life. And I never regret it.'

'And did you mind very much when he died?'

'I was as near death myself. But when I came to, I knew another part of me was finished. But then I had always known it would finish in death. All things do, as far as that goes.'

She sat and ruminated. The thunder crashed outside. It was like being in a little ark in the Flood.

'You seem to have such a lot *behind* you,' she said.

'Do I? It seems to me I've died once or twice already. Yet here I am, pegging on, and in for more trouble.'

She was thinking hard, yet listening to the storm.

'And weren't you happy as an officer and a gentleman, when your Colonel was dead?'

'No! They were a mingy lot.' He laughed suddenly. 'The Colonel used to say: Lad, the English middle classes have to chew every mouthful thirty times because their guts are so narrow, a bit as big as a pea would give them a stoppage. They're the mingiest set of ladylike snipe ever invented: full of conceit of themselves, frightened even if their boot-laces aren't correct, rotten as high game, and always in the right. That's what finishes me up. Kow-tow, kow-tow, arse-licking till their tongues are tough: yet they're always in the right. Prigs on top of everything. Prigs! A generation of ladylike prigs with half a ball each–'

Connie laughed. The rain was rushing down.

'He hated them!'

'No,' said he. 'He didn't bother. He just disliked them. There's a difference. Because, as he said, the Tommies are getting just as priggish and half-balled and narrow-gutted. It's the fate of mankind, to go that way.'

'The common people too, the working people?'

'All the lot. Their spunk is gone dead. Motor-cars and cinemas and aeroplanes suck that last bit out of them. I tell you, every generation breeds a more rabbity generation, with indiarubber tubing for guts and tin legs and tin faces. Tin people! It's all a steady sort of bolshevism just as killing off the human thing, and worshipping the mechanical thing. Money, money, money! All the modern lot get their real kick out of killing the old human feeling out of man, making mincemeat of the old Adam and the old Eve. They're all alike. The world is all alike: kill off the human reality, a quid for every foreskin, two quid for each pair of balls. What is cunt but machine-fucking!– It's all alike.

Pay 'em money to cut off the world's cock. Pay money, money, money to them that will take spunk out of mankind, and leave 'em all little twiddling machines.'

He sat there in the hut, his face pulled to mocking irony. Yet even then, he had one ear set backwards, listening to the storm over the wood. It made him feel so alone.

'But won't it ever come to an end?' she said.

'Ay, it will. It'll achieve its own salvation. When the last real man is killed, and they're *all* tame: white, black, yellow, all colours of tame ones: then they'll *all* be insane. Because the root of sanity is in the balls. Then they'll all be *insane*, and they'll make their grand *auto da fe*. You know *auto da fe* means *act of faith*? Ay, well, they'll make their own grand little act of faith. They'll offer one another up.'

'You mean kill one another?'

'I do, duckie! If we go on at our present rate then in a hundred years' time there won't be ten thousand people in this island: there may not be ten. They'll have lovingly wiped each other out.' The thunder was rolling further away.

'How nice!' she said.

'Quite nice! To contemplate the extermination of the human species and the long pause that follows before some other species crops up, it calms you more than anything else. And if we go on in this way, with everybody, intellectuals, artists, government, industrialists and workers all frantically killing off the last human feeling, the last bit of their intuition, the last healthy instinct; if it goes on in algebraical progression, as it is going on: then ta-tah! to the human species! Goodbye! darling! the serpent swallows itself and leaves a void, considerably messed up, but not hopeless. Very nice! When savage wild dogs bark in Wragby, and savage wild pit-ponies stamp on Tevershall pit-bank! *te deum laudamus*!'

Connie laughed, but not very happily.

'Then you ought to be pleased that they are all bolshevists,' she said. 'You ought to be pleased that they hurry on towards the end.'

'So I am. I don't stop 'em. Because I couldn't if I would.'

'Then why are you so bitter?'

'I'm not! If my cock gives its last crow, I don't mind.'

'But if you have a child?' she said.

He dropped his head.

'Why,' he said at last. 'It seems to me a wrong and bitter thing to do, to bring a child into this world.'

'No! Don't say it! Don't say it!' she pleaded. 'I think I'm going to have one. Say you'll be pleased.' She laid her hand on his.

'I'm pleased for you to be pleased,' he said. 'But for me it seems a ghastly treachery to the unborn creature.'

'Ah no!' she said, shocked. 'Then you *can't* ever really want me! You *can't* want me, if you feel that!'

Again he was silent, his face sullen. Outside there was only the threshing of the rain.

'It's not quite true!' she whispered. 'It's not quite true! There's another truth.' She felt he was bitter now partly because she was leaving him, deliberately going away to Venice. And this half pleased her.

She pulled open his clothing and uncovered his belly, and kissed his navel. Then she laid her cheek on his belly and pressed her arm round his warm, silent loins. They were alone in the flood.

'Tell me you want a child, in hope!' she murmured, pressing her face against his belly. 'Tell me you do!'

'Why!' he said at last: and she felt the curious quiver of changing consciousness and relaxation going through his body. 'Why I've thought sometimes if one but tried, here among th' colliers even! They're workin' bad now, an' not earnin' much. If a man could say to 'em: Dunna think o' nowt but th' money. When it comes ter *wants*, we want but little. Let's not live for money–'

She softly rubbed her cheek on his belly, and gathered his balls in her hand. The penis stirred softly, with strange life, but it did not rise up. The rain beat bruisingly outside.

'Let's live for summat else. Let's not live ter make money, neither for us-selves nor for anybody else. Now we're forced to. We're forced to make a bit for us-selves, an' a fair lot for th' bosses. Let's stop it! Bit by bit, let's stop it. We needn't rant an' rave. Bit by bit, let's drop the whole industrial life an' go back. The least little bit o' money'll do. For everybody, me an' you, bosses an' masters, even th' king. The least little bit o' money'll really do. Just make up your mind to it, an' you've got out o' th' mess.' He paused, then went on:

'An' I'd tell 'em: Look! Look at Joe! He moves lovely! Look how he moves, alive and aware. He's beautiful! An' look at Jonah! He's clumsy, he's ugly, because he's niver willin' to rouse himself. I'd tell 'em: Look! look at yourselves! one shoulder higher than t'other, legs twisted, feet all lumps! What have yer done ter yerselves, wi' the blasted work? Spoilt yerselves. No need to work that much. Take yer clothes off an look at yourselves. Yer ought ter be alive an' beautiful, an' yer ugly an' half dead. So I'd tell 'em. An' I'd get my men to wear different clothes: 'appen close red trousers, bright red, an' little short white jackets. Why, if men had red, fine legs, that alone would change them in a month. They'd begin to be men again, to be men! An' the women could dress as they liked. Because if once the men walked with legs close bright scarlet, and buttocks nice and showing scarlet under a little white jacket: then the women 'ud begin to be women. It's because th' men *aren't* men, that th' women have to be.–An' in time pull down Tevershall and build a few beautiful buildings, that would hold us all. An' clean the country up again. An' not have many children, because the world is overcrowded.

'But I wouldn't preach to the men: only strip 'em an' say: Look at yourselves! That's working' for money!–Hark at yourselves! That's working for money. You've been working for money! Look at Tevershall! It's horrible. That's because it was built while you was working for money. Look at your girls! They don't care about you, you don't care about them. It's because you've spent your time working an' caring for money. You can't talk nor move nor live, you can't properly be with a woman. You're not alive. Look at yourselves!'

There fell a complete silence. Connie was half listening, and threading in the hair at the root of his belly a few forget-me-nots that she had gathered on the way to the hut. Outside, the world had gone still, and a little icy.

'You've got four kinds of hair,' she said to him. 'On your chest it's nearly black, and your hair isn't dark on your head: but your moustache is hard and dark red, and your hair here, your love-hair, is like a little brush of bright red-gold mistletoe. It's the loveliest of all!'

He looked down and saw the milky bits of forget-me-nots in the hair on his groin.

'Ay! That's where to put forget-me-nots, in the man-hair, or the maiden-hair. But don't you care about the future?'

She looked up at him.

'Oh, I do, terribly!' she said.

'Because when I feel the human world is doomed, has doomed itself by its own mingy beastliness, then I feel the Colonies aren't far enough. The moon wouldn't be far enough, because even there you could look back and see the earth, dirty, beastly, unsavoury among all the stars: made foul by men. Then I feel I've swallowed gall, and it's eating my inside out, and nowhere's far enough away to get away. But when I get a turn, I forget it all again. Though it's a shame, what's been done to people these last hundred years: men turned into nothing but labour-insects, and all their manhood taken away, and all their real life. I'd wipe the machines off the face of the earth again, and end the industrial epoch absolutely, like a black mistake. But since I can't, an' nobody can, I'd better hold my peace, an' try an' live my own life: if I've got one to live, which I rather doubt.'

The thunder had ceased outside, but the rain which had abated, suddenly came striking down, with a last blench of lightning and mutter of departing storm. Connie was uneasy. He had talked so long now, and he was really talking to himself, not to her. Despair seemed to come down on him completely, and she was feeling happy, she hated despair. She knew her leaving him, which he had only just realized inside himself, had plunged him back into this mood. And she triumphed a little.

She opened the door and looked at the straight heavy rain, like a steel curtain, and had a sudden desire to rush out into it, to rush away. She got up, and began swiftly pulling off her stockings, then her dress and underclothing, and he held his breath. Her pointed keen animal breasts tipped and stirred as she moved. She was ivory-coloured in the greenish light. She slipped on her rubber shoes again and ran out with a wild little laugh, holding up her breasts to the heavy rain and spreading her arms, and running blurred in the rain with the eurhythmic dance-movements she had learned so long ago in Dresden. It was a strange pallid figure lifting and falling, bending so the rain beat and glistened on the full haunches, swaying up again and coming belly-forward through the rain, then stooping again so that only the full loins and buttocks were offered in a kind of homage towards him, repeating a wild obeisance.

He laughed wryly, and threw off his clothes. It was too much. He jumped out, naked and white, with a little shiver, into the hard slanting rain. Flossie sprang before him with a frantic little bark. Connie, her hair all wet and sticking to her head, turned her hot face and saw him. Her blue eyes blazed with excitement as she turned and ran fast, with a strange charging movement, out of the clearing and down the path, the wet boughs whipping her. She ran, and he saw nothing but the round wet head, the wet back leaning forward in flight, the rounded buttocks twinkling: a wonderful cowering female nakedness in flight.

She was nearly at the wide riding when he came up and flung his naked arm round her soft, naked-wet middle. She gave a shriek and straightened herself, and the heap of her soft, chill flesh came up against his body. He pressed it all up against him, madly, the heap of soft, chilled female flesh that became quickly warm as flame, in contact. The rain streamed on them till they smoked. He gathered her lovely, heavy posteriors one in each hand and pressed them in towards him in a frenzy, quivering motionless in the rain. Then suddenly he tipped her up and fell with her on the path, in the roaring silence of the rain, and short and sharp, he took her, short and sharp and finished, like an animal.

He got up in an instant, wiping the rain from his eyes.

'Come in,' he said, and they started running back to the hut. He ran straight and swift: he didn't like the rain. But she came slower, gathering forget-me-nots and campion and bluebells, running a few steps and watching him fleeing away from her.

When she came with her flowers, panting to the hut, he had already started a fire, and the twigs were crackling. Her sharp breasts rose and fell, her hair was plastered down with rain, her face was flushed ruddy and her body glistened and trickled. Wide-eyed and breathless, with a small wet head and full, trickling, naïve haunches, she looked another creature.

He took the old sheet and rubbed her down, she standing like a child. Then he rubbed himself, having shut the door of the hut. The fire was blazing up. She ducked her head in the other end of the sheet, and rubbed her wet hair.

'We're drying ourselves together on the same towel, we shall quarrel!' he said.

She looked up for a moment, her hair all odds and ends.

'No!' she said, her eyes wide. 'It's not a towel, it's a sheet.'

And she went on busily rubbing her head, while he busily rubbed his.

Still panting with their exertions, each wrapped in an army blanket, but the front of the body open to the fire, they sat on a log side by side before the blaze, to get quiet. Connie hated the feel of the blanket against her skin. But now the sheet was all wet.

She dropped her blanket and kneeled on the clay hearth, holding her head to the fire, and shaking her hair to dry it. He watched the beautiful curving drop of her haunches. That fascinated him today. How it sloped with a rich down-slope to the heavy roundness of her buttocks! And in between, folded in the secret warmth, the secret entrances!

He stroked her tail with his hand, long and subtly taking in the curves and the globe-fullness.

'Tha's got such a nice tail on thee,' he said, in the throaty caressive dialect. 'Tha's got the nicest arse of anybody. It's the nicest, nicest woman's arse as is! An' ivery bit of it is woman, woman sure as nuts. Tha'rt not one o' them button-arsed lasses as should be lads, are ter! Tha's got a real soft sloping bottom on thee, as a man loves in 'is guts. It's a bottom as could hold the world up, it is!'

All the while he spoke he exquisitely stroked the rounded tail, till it seemed as if a slippery sort of fire came from it into his hands. And his finger-tips touched the two secret openings to her body, time after time, with a soft little brush of fire.

'An' if tha shits an' if tha pisses, I'm glad. I don't want a woman as couldna shit nor piss.'

Connie could not help a sudden snort of astonished laughter, but he went on unmoved.

'Tha'rt real, tha art! Tha'rt real, even a bit of a bitch. Here tha shits an' here tha' pisses: an' I lay my hand on 'em both an' like thee for it. I like thee for it. Tha's got a proper, woman's arse, proud of itself. It's none ashamed of itself, this isna.'

He laid his hand close and firm over her secret places, in a kind of close greeting.

'I like it,' he said. 'I like it! An' if I only lived ten minutes, an' stroked thy arse an' got to know it, I should reckon I'd lived *one* life, see ter! Industrial system or not! Here's one o' my lifetimes.'

She turned round and climbed into his lap, clinging to him. 'Kiss me!' she whispered.

And she knew the thought of their separation was latent in both their minds, and at last she was sad.

She sat on his thighs, her head against his breast, and her ivory-gleaming legs loosely apart, the fire glowing unequally upon them. Sitting with his head dropped, he looked at the folds of her body in the fire-glow, and at the fleece of soft brown hair that hung down to a point between her open thighs. He reached to the table behind, and took up her bunch of flowers, still so wet that drops of rain fell on to her.

'Flowers stop out of doors all weathers,' he said. 'They have no houses.'

'Not even a hut!' she murmured.

With quiet fingers he threaded a few forget-me-not flowers in the fine brown fleece of the mound of Venus.

'There!' he said. 'There's forget-me-nots in the right place!'

She looked down at the milky odd little flowers among the brown maiden-hair at the lower tip of her body.

'Doesn't it look pretty!' she said.

'Pretty as life,' he replied.

And he stuck a pink campion-bud among the hair.

'There! That's me where you won't forget me! That's Moses in the bull-rushes.'

'You don't mind, do you, that I'm going away?' she asked wistfully, looking up into his face.

But his face was inscrutable, under the heavy brows. He kept it quite blank.

'You do as you wish,' he said.

And he spoke in good English.

'But I won't go if you don't wish it,' she said, clinging to him.

There was silence. He leaned and put another piece of wood on the fire. The flame glowed on his silent, abstracted face. She waited, but he said nothing.

'Only I thought it would be a good way to begin a break with Clifford. I do want a child. And it would give me a chance to, to–,' she resumed.

'To let them think a few lies,' he said.

'Yes, that among other things. Do you want them to think the truth?'

'I don't care what they think.'

'I do! I don't want them handling me with their unpleasant cold minds, not while I'm still at Wragby. They can think what they like when I'm finally gone.'

He was silent.

'But Sir Clifford expects you to come back to him?'

'Oh, I must come back,' she said: and there was silence.

'And would you have a child in Wragby?' he asked.

She closed her arm round his neck.

'If you wouldn't take me away, I should have to,' she said.

'Take you where to?'

'Anywhere! away! But right away from Wragby.'

'When?'

'Why, when I come back.'

'But what's the good of coming back, doing the thing twice, if you're once gone?' he said.

'Oh, I must come back. I've promised! I've promised so faithfully. Besides, I come back to you, really.'

'To your husband's game-keeper?'

'I don't see that that matters,' she said.

'No?' he mused a while. 'And when would you think of going away again, then; finally? When exactly?'

'Oh, I don't know. I'd come back from Venice. And then we'd prepare everything.'

'How prepare?'

'Oh, I'd tell Clifford. I'd have to tell him.'

'Would you!'

He remained silent. She put her arms round his neck.

'Don't make it difficult for me,' she pleaded.

'Make what difficult?'

'For me to go to Venice and arrange things.'

A little smile, half a grin, flickered on his face.

'I don't make it difficult,' he said. 'I only want to find out just what you are after. But you don't really know yourself. You want to take time: get away and look at it. I don't blame you. I think you're wise. You may prefer to stay mistress of Wragby. I don't blame you. I've no Wragbys to offer. In fact, you know what you'll get out of me. No, no, I think you're right! I really do! And I'm not keen on coming to live on you, being kept by you. There's that too.'

She felt somehow as if he were giving her tit for tat.

'But you want me, don't you?' she asked.

'Do you want me?'

'You know I do. *That's* evident.'

'Quite! And *when* do you want me?'

'You know we can arrange it all when I come back. Now I'm out of breath with you. I must get calm and clear.'

'Quite! Get calm and clear!'

She was a little offended.

'But you trust me, don't you?' she said.

'Oh, absolutely!'

She heard the mockery in his tone.

'Tell me then,' she said flatly; 'do you think it would be better if I *don't* go to Venice?'

'I'm sure it's better if you *do* go to Venice,' he replied in the cool, slightly mocking voice.

'You know it's next Thursday?' she said.

'Yes!'

She now began to muse. At last she said:

'And we *shall* know better where we are when I come back, shan't we?'

'Oh surely!'

The curious gulf of silence between them!

'I've been to the lawyer about my divorce,' he said, a little constrainedly.

She gave a slight shudder.

'Have you!' she said. 'And what did he say?'

'He said I ought to have done it before; that may be a difficulty. But since I was in the army, he thinks it will go through all right. If only it doesn't bring *her* down on my head!'

'Will she have to know?'

'Yes! she is served with a notice: so is the man she lives with, the co-respondent.'

'Isn't it hateful, all the performances! I suppose I'd have to go through it with Clifford.'

There was a silence.

'And of course,' he said. 'I have to live an exemplary life for the next six or eight months. So if you go to Venice, there's temptation removed for a week or two, at least.'

'Am I temptation!' she said, stroking his face. 'I'm so glad I'm temptation to you! Don't let's think about it! You frighten me when you start thinking: you roll me out flat. Don't let's think about it. We can think so much when we are apart. That's the whole point! I've been thinking, I *must* come to you for another night before I go. I must come once more to the cottage. Shall I come on Thursday night?'

'Isn't that when your sister will be there?'

'Yes! But she said we would start at tea-time. So we could start at tea-time. But she could sleep somewhere else and I could sleep with you.'

'But then she'd have to know.'

'Oh, I shall tell her. I've more or less told her already. I must talk it all over with Hilda. She's a great help, so sensible.'

He was thinking of her plan.

'So you'd start off from Wragby at tea-time, as if you were going to London? Which way were you going?'

'By Nottingham and Grantham.'

'And then your sister would drop you somewhere and you'd walk or drive back here? Sounds very risky, to me.'

'Does it? Well, then, Hilda could bring me back. She could sleep at Mansfield, and bring me back here in the evening, and fetch me again in the morning. It's quite easy.'

'And the people who see you?'

'I'll wear goggles and a veil.'

He pondered for some time.

'Well,' he said. 'You please yourself, as usual.'

'But wouldn't it please you?'

'Oh yes! It'd please me all right,' he said a little grimly. 'I might as well smite while the iron's hot.'

'Do you know what I thought?' she said suddenly. 'It suddenly came to me. You are the "Knight of the Burning Pestle"!'

'Ay! And you? Are you the Lady of the Red-Hot Mortar?'

'Yes!' she said. 'Yes! You're Sir Pestle and I'm Lady Mortar.'

'All right, then I'm knighted. John Thomas is Sir John, to your Lady Jane.'

'Yes! John Thomas is knighted! I'm my-lady-maiden-hair, and you must have flowers too. Yes!'

She threaded two pink campions in the bush of red-gold hair above his penis.

'There!' she said. 'Charming! Charming! Sir John!'

And she pushed a bit of forget-me-not in the dark hair of his breast.

'And you won't forget me *there*, will you?' She kissed him on the breast, and made two bits of forget-me-not lodge one over each nipple, kissing him again.

'Make a calender of me!' he said. He laughed, and the flowers shook from his breast.

'Wait a bit!' he said.

He rose, and opened the door of the hut. Flossie, lying in the porch, got up and looked at him.

'Ay, it's me!' he said.

The rain had ceased. There was a wet, heavy, perfumed stillness. Evening was approaching.

He went out and down the little path in the opposite direction from the riding. Connie watched his thin, white figure, and it looked to her like a ghost, an apparition moving away from her.

When she could see it no more, her heart sank. She stood in the door of the hut, with a blanket round her, looking into the drenched, motionless silence.

But he was coming back, trotting strangely, and carrying flowers. She was a little afraid of him, as if he were not quite human. And when he came near, his eyes looked into hers, but she could not understand the meaning.

He had brought columbines and campions, and new-mown hay, and oak-tufts and honeysuckle in small bud. He fastened fluffy young oak-sprays round her breasts, sticking in tufts of bluebells and campion: and in her navel he poised a pink campion flower, and in her maiden-hair were forget-me-nots and wood-ruff.

'That's you in all your glory!' he said. 'Lady Jane, at her wedding with John Thomas.'

And he stuck flowers in the hair of his own body, and wound a bit of creeping-jenny round his penis, and stuck a single bell of a hyacinth in his navel. She watched him with amusement, his odd intentness. And she pushed a campion flower in his moustache, where it stuck, dangling under his nose.

'This is John Thomas marryin' Lady Jane,' he said. 'An' we mun let Constance an' Oliver go their ways. Maybe—'

He spread out his hand with a gesture, and then he sneezed, sneezing away the flowers from his nose and his navel. He sneezed again.

'Maybe what?' she said, waiting for him to go on.

He looked at her a little bewildered.

'Eh?' he said.

'Maybe what? Go on with what you were going to say,' she insisted.

'Ay what *was* I going to say?'

He had forgotten. And it was one of the disappointments of her life, that he never finished.

A yellow ray of sun shone over the trees.

'Sun!' he said. 'And time you went. Time, my Lady, time! What's that as flies without wings, your Ladyship! Time! Time!'

He reached for his shirt.

'Say goodnight! to John Thomas,' he said, looking down at his penis. 'He's safe in the arms of creeping-jenny! Not much burning pestle about him just now.'

And he put his flannel shirt over his head.

'A man's most dangerous moment,' he said, when his head had emerged, 'is when he's getting into his shirt. Then he puts his head in a bag. That's why I prefer those American shirts, that you put on like a jacket,' She still stood watching him. He stepped into his short drawers, and buttoned them round the waist.

'Look at Jane!' he said. 'In all her blossoms! Who'll put blossoms on you next year, Jinny? Me, or somebody else? "Good-bye, my bluebell, farewell to you!" I hate that song, it's early war days.' He then sat down, and was pulling on his stockings. She still stood unmoving. He laid his hand on the slope of her buttocks. 'Pretty little Lady Jane!' he said. 'Perhaps in Venice you'll find a man who'll put jasmine in your maiden-hair, and a pomegranate flower in your navel. Poor little Lady Jane!'

'Don't say those things!' she said. 'You only say them to hurt me.'

He dropped his head. Then he said, in dialect:

'Ay, maybe I do, maybe I do! Well then, I'll say nowt, an' ha' done wi't. But tha mun dress thysen, an' go back to thy stately homes of England, how beautiful they stand. Time's up! Time's up for Sir John, an' for little Lady Jane! Put thy shimmy on, Lady Chatterley! Tha might be anybody, standin' there be-out even a shimmy, an' a few rags o' flowers. There then, there then, I'll undress thee, tha bob-tailed young throstle.' And he took the leaves from her hair, kissing her damp hair, and the flowers from her breasts, and kissed her breasts, and kissed her navel, and kissed her maiden-hair, where he left the flowers threaded. 'They mun stop while they will,' he said. 'So! There tha'rt bare again, nowt but a bare-arsed lass an' a bit of a Lady Jane! Now put thy shimmy on, for tha mun go, or else Lady Chatterley's goin' to be late for dinner, an' where 'ave yer been to my pretty maid!'

She never knew how to answer him when he was in this condition of the vernacular. So she dressed herself and prepared to go a little ignominiously home to Wragby. Or so she felt it: a little ignominiously home.

He would accompany her to the broad riding. His young pheasants were all right under the shelter.

When he and she came out on to the riding, there was Mrs Bolton falteringly palely towards them.

'Oh, my Lady, we wondered if anything had happened!'

'No! Nothing has happened.'

Mrs Bolton looked into the man's face, that was smooth and new-looking with love. She met his half-laughing, half-mocking eyes. He always laughed at mischance. But he looked at her kindly.

'Evening, Mrs Bolton! Your Ladyship will be all right now, so I can leave you. Good-night to your Ladyship! Good-night, Mrs Bolton!'

He saluted and turned away.

16

Connie arrived home to an ordeal of cross-questioning. Clifford had been out at tea-time, had come in just before the storm, and where was her ladyship? Nobody knew, only Mrs Bolton suggested she had gone for a walk into the wood. Into the wood, in such a storm! Clifford for once let himself get into a state of nervous frenzy. He started at every flash of lightning, and blenched at every roll of thunder. He looked at the icy thunder-rain as if it were the end of the world. He got more and more worked up.

Mrs Bolton tried to soothe him.

'She'll be sheltering in the hut, till it's over. Don't worry, her Ladyship is all right.'

'I don't like her being in the wood in a storm like this! I don't like her being in the wood at all! She's been gone now more than two hours. When did she go out?'

'A little while before you came in.'

'I didn't see her in the park. God knows where she is and what has happened to her.'

'Oh, nothing's happened to her. You'll see, she'll be home directly after the rain stops. It's just the rain that's keeping her.'

But her ladyship did not come home directly the rain stopped. In fact time went by, the sun came out for his last yellow glimpse, and there still was no sign of her. The sun was set, it was growing dark, and the first dinner-gong had rung.

'It's no good!' said Clifford in a frenzy. 'I'm going to send out Field and Betts to find her.'

'Oh don't do that!' cried Mrs Bolton. 'They'll think there's a suicide or something. Oh don't start a lot of talk going. Let me slip over to the hut and see if she's not there. I'll find her all right.'

So, after some persuasion, Clifford allowed her to go.

And so Connie had come upon her in the drive, alone and palely loitering.

'You mustn't mind me coming to look for you, my Lady! But Sir Clifford worked himself up into such a state. He made sure you were struck by lightning, or killed by a falling tree. And he was determined to send Field and Betts to the wood to find the body. So I thought I'd better come, rather than set all the servants agog.'

She spoke nervously. She could still see on Connie's face the smoothness and the half-dream of passion, and she could feel the irritation against herself.

'Quite!' said Connie. And she could say no more.

The two women plodded on through the wet world, in silence, while great drops splashed like exposions in the wood. When they came to the park, Connie strode ahead, and Mrs Bolton panted a little. She was getting plumper.

'How foolish of Clifford to make a fuss!' said Connie at length, angrily, really speaking to herself.

'Oh, you know what men are! They like working themselves up. But he'll be all right as soon as he sees your Ladyship.'

Connie was very angry that Mrs Bolton knew her secret: for certainly she knew it.

Suddenly Constance stood still on the path.

'It's monstrous that I should have to be followed!' she said, her eyes flashing.

'Oh! your Ladyship, don't say that! He'd certainly have sent the two men, and they'd have come straight to the hut. I didn't know where it was, really.'

Connie flushed darker with rage, at the suggestion. Yet, while her passion was on her, she could not lie. She could not even pretend there was nothing between herself and the keeper. She looked at the other woman, who stood so sly, with her head dropped: yet somehow, in her femaleness, an ally.

'Oh well!' she said. 'If it is so it is so. I don't mind!'

'Why, you're all right, my Lady! You've only been sheltering in the hut. It's absolutely nothing.'

They went on to the house. Connie marched in to Clifford's room, furious with him, furious with his pale, over-wrought face and prominent eyes.

'I must say, I don't think you need send the servants after me' she burst out.

'My God!' he exploded. 'Where have you been, woman? You've been gone hours, hours, and in a storm like this! What the hell do you go to that bloody wood for? What have you been up to? It's hours even since the rain stopped, hours! Do you know what time it is? You're enough to drive anybody mad. Where have you been? What in the name of hell have you been doing?'

'And what if I don't choose to tell you?' She pulled her hat from her head and shook her hair.

He looked at her with his eyes bulging, and yellow coming into the whites. It was very bad for him to get into these rages: Mrs Bolton had a weary time with him for days after. Connie felt a sudden qualm.

'But really!' she said, milder. 'Anyone would think I'd been I don't know where! I just sat in the hut during all the storm, and made myself a little fire, and was happy!'

She spoke now easily. After all, why work him up any more! He looked at her suspiciously.

'And look at your hair!' he said; 'look at yourself!'

'Yes!' she replied calmly. 'I ran out in the rain with no clothes on.'

He stared at her speechless.

'You must be mad!' he said.

'Why? To like a shower-bath from the rain?'

'And how did you dry yourself?'

'On an old towel and at the fire.'

He still stared at her in a dumbfounded way.

'And supposing anybody came,' he said.

'Who would come?'

'Who? Why, anybody! And Mellors. Does he come? He must come in the evenings.'

'Yes, he came later, when it had cleared up, to feed the pheasants with corn.'

She spoke with amazing nonchalance. Mrs Bolton, who was listening in the next room, heard in sheer admiration. To think a woman could carry it off so naturally!

'And suppose he'd come while you were running about in the rain with nothing on, like a maniac?'

'I suppose he'd have had the fright of his life, and cleared out as fast as he could.'

Clifford still stared at her transfixed. What he thought in his under-consciousness he would never know. And he was too much taken aback to form one clear thought in his upper consciousness. He just simply accepted what she said, in a sort of blank. And he admired her. He could not help admiring her. She looked so flushed and handsome and smooth: love smooth.

'At least,' he said, subsiding, 'you'll be lucky if you've got off without a severe cold.'

'Oh, I haven't got a cold,' she replied. She was thinking to herself of the other man's words: Tha's got the nicest woman's arse of anybody! She wished, she dearly wished she could tell Clifford that this had been said to her, during the famous thunderstorm. However! She bore herself rather like an offended queen, and went upstairs to change.

That evening, Clifford wanted to be nice to her. He was reading one of the latest scientific-religious books: he had a streak of a spurious sort of religion in him, and was egocentrically concerned with the future of his own ego. It was like his habit to make conversation to Connie about some book, since the conversation between them had to be made, almost chemically. They had almost chemically to concoct it in their heads.

'What do you think of this, by the way?' he said, reaching for his book. 'You'd have no need to cool your ardent body by running out in the rain, if only we have a few more aeons of evolution behind us. Ah, here it is!–"The universe shows us two aspects: on one side it is physically wasting, on the other it is spiritually ascending."'

Connie listened, expecting more. But Clifford was waiting. She looked at him in surprise.

'And if it spiritually ascends,' she said, 'what does it leave down below, in the place where its tail used to be?'

'Ah!' he said. 'Take the man for what he means. *Ascending* is the opposite of his *wasting*, I presume.'

'Spiritually blown out, so to speak!'

'No, but seriously, without joking: do you think there is anything in it?'

She looked at him again.

'Physically wasting?' she said. 'I see you getting fatter, and I'm not wasting myself. Do you think the sun is smaller than he used to be? He's not to me. And I suppose the apple Adam offered Eve wasn't really much bigger, if any, than one of our orange pippins. Do you think it was?'

'Well, hear how he goes on: "It is thus slowly passing, with a slowness inconceivable in our measures of time, to new creative conditions, amid which the physical world, as we at present know it, will be represented by a ripple barely to be distinguished from nonentity."'

She listened with a glisten of amusement. All sorts of improper things suggested themselves. But she only said:

'What silly hocus-pocus! As if his little conceited consciousness could know what was happening as slowly as all that! It only means *he*'s a physical failure on the earth, so he wants to make the whole universe a physical failure. Priggish little impertinence!'

'Oh, but listen! Don't interrupt the great man's solemn words!–"The present type of order in the world has risen from an unimaginable past, and will find its grave in an unimaginable future. There remains the inexhaustive realm of abstract forms, and creativity with its shifting character ever determined afresh by its own creatures, and God, upon whose wisdom all forms of order depend."–There, that's how he winds up!'

Connie sat listening contemptuously.

'He's spiritually blown out,' she said. 'What a lot of stuff! Unimaginables, and types of order in graves, and realms of abstract forms, and creativity with a shifty character, and God mixed up with forms of order! Why, it's idiotic!'

'I must say, it is a little vaguely conglomerate, a mixture of gases, so to speak,' said Clifford. 'Still, I think there is something in the idea that the universe is physically wasting and spiritually ascending.'

'Do you? Then let it ascend, so long as it leaves me safely and solidly physically here below.'

'Do you like your physique?' he asked.

'I love it!' And through her mind went the words: It's the nicest, nicest woman's arse as is!

'But that is really rather extraordinary, because there's no denying it's an encumbrance. But then I suppose a woman doesn't take a supreme pleasure in the life of the mind.'

'Supreme pleasure?' she said, looking up at him. 'Is that sort of idiocy the supreme pleasure of the life of the mind? No thank you! Give me the body. I believe the life of the body is a greater reality than the life of the mind: when the body is really wakened to life. But so many people, like your famous wind-machine, have only got minds tacked on to their physical corpses.'

He looked at her in wonder.

'The life of the body,' he said, 'is just the life of the animals.'

'And that's better than the life of professional corpses. But it's not true! The human body is only just coming to real life. With the Greeks it gave a lovely flicker, then Plato and Aristotle killed it, and Jesus finished it off. But now the body is coming really to life, it is really rising from the tomb. And it will be a lovely, lovely life in the lovely universe, the life of the human body.'

'My dear, you speak as if you were ushering it all in! True, you are going away on a holiday: but don't please be quite so indecently elated about it. Believe me, whatever God there is is slowly eliminating the guts and alimentary system from the human being, to evolve a higher, more spiritual being.'

'Why should I believe you, Clifford, when I feel that whatever God there is has at last wakened up in my guts, as you call them, and is rippling so happily there, like dawn. Why should I believe you, when I feel so very much the contrary?'

'Oh, exactly! And what has caused this extraordinary change in you? running out stark naked in the rain, and playing Bacchante? desire for sensation, or the anticipation of going to Venice?'

'Both! Do you think it is horrid of me to be so thrilled at going off?' she said.

'Rather horrid to show it so plainly.'

'Then I'll hide it.'

'Oh, don't trouble! You almost communicate a thrill to me. I almost feel that it is *I* who am going off.'

'Well, why don't you come?'

'We've gone over all that. And as a matter of fact, I suppose your greatest thrill comes from being able to say a temporary farewell to all this. Nothing so thrilling, for the moment, as Good-bye-to-it-all!–But every parting means a meeting elsewhere. And every meeting is a new bondage.'

'I'm not going to enter any new bondages.'

'Don't boast, while the gods are listening,' he said.

She pulled up short.

'No! I won't boast!' she said.

But she was thrilled, none the less, to be going off: to feel bonds snap. She couldn't help it.

Clifford, who couldn't sleep, gambled all night with Mrs Bolton, till she was too sleepy almost to live.

And the day came round for Hilda to arrive. Connie had arranged with Mellors that if everything promised well for their night together, she would hang a green shawl out of the window. If there were frustration, a red one.

Mrs Bolton helped Connie to pack.

'It will be so good for your Ladyship to have a change.'

'I think it will. You don't mind having Sir Clifford on your hands alone for a time, do you?'

'Oh no! I can manage him quite all right. I mean, I can do all he needs me to do. Don't you think he's better than he used to be?'

'Oh much! You do wonders with him.'

'Do I though! But men are all alike: just babies, and you have to flatter them and wheedle them and let them think they're having their own way. Don't you find it so, my Lady?'

'I'm afraid I haven't much experience.'

Connie paused in her occupation.

'Even your husband, did you have to manage him, and wheedle him like a baby?' she asked, looking at the other woman.

Mrs Bolton paused too.

'Well!' she said. 'I had to do a good bit of coaxing, with him too. But he always knew what I was after, I must say that. But he generally gave in to me.'

'He was never the lord and master thing?'

'No! At least there'd be a look in his eyes sometimes, and then I knew *I'd* got to give in. But usually he gave in to me. No, he was never lord and master. But neither was I. I knew when I could go no further with him, and then I gave in: though it cost me a good bit, sometimes.'

'And what if you had held out against him?'

'Oh, I don't know, I never did. Even when he was in the wrong, if he was fixed, I gave in. You see, I never wanted to break what was between us. And if you really set your will against a man, that finishes it. If you care for a man, you have to give in to him once he's really determined; whether you're in the right or not, you have to give in. Else you break something. But I must say, Ted 'ud give in to me sometimes, when I was set on a thing, and in the wrong. So I suppose it cuts both ways.'

'And that's how you are with all your patients?' asked Connie.

'Oh, that's different. I don't care at all, in the same way. I know what's good for them, or I try to, and then I just contrive to manage them for their own good. It's not like anybody as you're really fond of. It's quite different. Once you've been really fond of a man, you can be affectionate to almost any man, if he needs you at all. But it's not the same thing. You don't really *care*. I doubt, once you've *really* cared, if you can ever really care again.'

These words frightened Connie.

'Do you think one can only care once?' she asked.

'Oh never. Most women never care, never begin to. They don't know what it means. Nor men either. But when I see a woman as cares, my heart stands still for her.'

'And do you think men easily take offence?'

'Yes! If you wound them on their pride. But aren't women the same? Only our two prides are a bit different.'

Connie pondered this. She began again to have some misgiving about her going away. After all, was she not giving her man the go-by, if only for a short time? And he knew it. That's why he was so queer and sarcastic.

Still! the human existence is a good deal controlled by the machine of external circumstance. She was in the power of this machine. She couldn't extricate herself all in five minutes. She didn't even want to.

Hilda arrived in good time on Thursday morning, in a nimble two-seater car, with her suit-case strapped firmly behind. She looked as demure and maidenly as ever, but she had the same will of her own. She had the very hell of a will of her own, as her husband had found out. But the husband was now divorcing her. Yes, she even made it easy for him to do that, though she had no lover. For the time being, she was 'off' men. She was very well content to be quite her own mistress: and mistress of her two children, whom she was going to bring up 'properly', whatever that may mean.

Connie was only allowed a suit-case, also. But she had sent on a trunk to her father, who was going by train. No use taking a car to Venice. And Italy much too hot to motor in, in July. He was going comfortably by train. He had just come down from Scotland.

So, like a demure arcadian field-marshal, Hilda arranged the material part of the journey. She and Connie sat in the upstairs room, chatting.

'But Hilda!' said Connie, a little frightened. 'I want to stay near here tonight. Not here: near here!'

Hilda fixed her sister with grey, inscrutable eyes. She seemed so calm: and she was so often furious.

'Where, near here?' she asked softly.

'Well, you know I love somebody, don't you?'

'I gathered there was something.'

'Well he lives near here, and I want to spend this last night with him. I must! I've promised.'

Connie became insistent.

Hilda bent her Minerva-like head in silence. Then she looked up.

'Do you want to tell me who he is?' she said.

'He's our game-keeper,' faltered Connie, and she flushed vividly, like a shamed child.

'Connie!' said Hilda, lifting her nose slightly with disgust: a motion she had from her mother.

'I know: but he's lovely really. He really understands tenderness,' said Connie, trying to apologize for him.

Hilda, like a ruddy, rich-coloured Athena, bowed her head and pondered. She was really violently angry. But she dared not show it, because Connie, taking after her father, would straightway become obstreperous and unmanageable.

It was true, Hilda did not like Clifford: his cool assurance that he was somebody! She thought he made use of Connie shamefully and impudently. She had hoped her sister *would* leave him. But, being solid Scotch middle class, she loathed any 'lowering' of oneself, or the family. She looked up at last.

'You'll regret it,' she said.

'I shan't,' cried Connie, flushed red. 'He's quite the exception. I *really* love him. He's lovely as a lover.'

Hilda still pondered.

'You'll get over him quite soon,' she said, 'and live to be ashamed of yourself because of him.'

'I shan't! I hope I'm going to have a child of his.'

'*Connie!*' said Hilda, hard as a hammer-stroke, and pale with anger.

'I shall if I possibly can. I should be fearfully proud if I had a child by him.'

It was no use talking to her. Hilda pondered.

'And doesn't Clifford suspect?' she said.

'Oh no! Why should he?'

'I've no doubt you've given him plenty of occasion for suspicion,' said Hilda.

'Not at all.'

'And tonight's business seems quite gratuitous folly. Where does the man live?'

'In the cottage at the other end of the wood.'

'Is he a bachelor?'

'No! His wife left him.'

'How old?'

'I don't know. Older than me.'

Hilda became more angry at every reply, angry as her mother used to be, in a kind of paroxysm. But still she hid it.

'I would give up tonight's escapade if I were you,' she advised calmly.

'I can't! I *must* stay with him tonight, or I can't go to Venice at all. I just can't.'

Hilda heard her father over again, and she gave way, out of mere diplomacy. And she consented to drive to Mansfield, both of them to dinner, to bring Connie back to the lane-end after dark, and to fetch her from the lane-end the next morning, herself sleeping in Mansfield, only half an hour away, good going. But she was furious. She stored it up against her sister, this balk in her plans.

Connie flung an emerald-green shawl over her window-sill.

On the strength of her anger, Hilda warmed towards Clifford. After all, he had a mind. And if he had no sex, functionally, all the better: so much the less to quarrel about! Hilda wanted no more of that sex business, where men became nasty, selfish little horrors. Connie really had less to put up with than many women, if she did but know it.

And Clifford decided that Hilda, after all, was a decidedly intelligent woman, and would make a man a first-rate help-mate, if he were going in for politics for example. Yes, she had none of Connie's silliness, Connie was more a child: you had to make excuses for her, because she was not altogether dependable.

There was an early cup of tea in the hall, where doors were open to let in the sun. Everybody seemed to be panting a little.

'Good-bye, Connie girl! Come back to me safely.'

'Good-bye, Clifford! Yes, I shan't be long.' Connie was almost tender.

'Good-bye, Hilda! You will keep an eye on her, won't you?'

'I'll even keep two!' said Hilda. 'She shan't go very far astray.'

'It's a promise!'

'Good-bye, Mrs Bolton! I know you'll look after Sir Clifford nobly.'

'I'll do what I can, your Ladyship.'

'And write to me if there is any news, and tell me about Sir Clifford, how he is.'

'Very good, your Ladyship, I will. And have a good time, and come back and cheer us up.'

Everybody waved. The car went off. Connie looked back and saw Clifford, sitting at the top of the steps in his house-chair. After all, he was her husband: Wragby was her home: circumstance had done it.

Mrs Chambers held the gate and wished her ladyship a happy holiday. The car slipped out of the dark spinney that masked the park, on to the highroad where the colliers were trailing home. Hilda turned to the Crosshill Road, that was not a main road, but ran to Mansfield. Connie put on goggles. They ran beside the railway, which was in a cutting below them. Then they crossed the cutting on a bridge.

'That's the lane to the cottage!' said Connie.

Hilda glanced at it impatiently.

'It's a frightful pity we can't go straight off!' she said. 'We could have been in Pall Mall by nine o'clock.'

'I'm sorry for your sake,' said Connie, from behind her goggles.

They were soon at Mansfield, that once-romantic, now utterly disheartening colliery town. Hilda stopped at the hotel named in the motor-car book, and took a room. The whole thing was utterly uninteresting, and she was almost too angry to talk. However, Connie *had* to tell her something of the man's history.

'*He! He!* What name do you call him by? You only say *he*,' said Hilda.

'I've never called him by any name: nor he me: which is curious, when you come to think of it. Unless we say Lady Jane and John Thomas. But his name is Oliver Mellors.'

'And how would you like to be Mrs Oliver Mellors, instead of Lady Chatterley?'

'I'd love it.'

There was nothing to be done with Connie. And anyhow, if the man had been a lieutenant in the army in India for four or five years, he must be more or less presentable. Apparently he had character. Hilda began to relent a little.

'But you'll be through with him in a while,' she said, 'and then you'll be ashamed of having been connected with him. One *can't* mix up with the working people.'

'But you are such a socialist! you're always on the side of the working classes.'

'I may be on their side in a political crisis, but being on their side makes me know how impossible it is to mix one's life with theirs. Not out of snobbery, but just because the whole rhythm is different.'

Hilda had lived among the real political intellectuals, so she was disastrously unanswerable.

The nondescript evening in the hotel dragged out, and at last they had a nondescript dinner. Then Connie slipped a few things into a little silk bag, and combed her hair once more.

'After all, Hilda,' she said, 'love can be wonderful; when you feel you *live*, an are in the middle of creation.' It was almost like bragging on her part.

'I suppose every mosquito feels the same,' said Hilda.

'Do you think it does? How nice for it!'

The evening was wonderfully clear and long-lingering, even in the small town. It would be half-light all night. With a face like a mask, from resentment, Hilda started her car again, and the two sped back on their traces, taking the other road, through Bolsover.

Connie wore her goggles and disguising cap, and she sat in silence. Because of Hilda's opposition, she was fiercely on the side of the man, she would stand by him through thick and thin.

They had their head-lights on, by the time they passed Crosshill, and the small lit-up train that chuffed past in the cutting made it seem like real night. Hilda had calculated the turn into the lane at the bridge-end. She slowed up rather suddenly and swerved off the road, the lights glaring white into the grassy, overgrown lane. Connie looked out. She saw a shadowy figure, and she opened the door.

'Here we are!' she said softly.

But Hilda had switched off the lights, and was absorbed backing, making the turn.

'Nothing on the bridge?' she asked shortly.

'You're all right,' said the man's voice.

She backed on to the bridge, reversed, let the car run forwards a few yards along the road, then backed into the lane, under a wych-elm tree, crushing the grass and bracken. Then all the lights went out. Connie stepped down. The man stood under the trees.

'Did you wait long?' Connie asked.

'Not so very,' he replied.

They both waited for Hilda to get out. But Hilda shut the door of the car and sat tight.

'This is my sister Hilda. Won't you come and speak to her? Hilda! This is Mr Mellors.'

The keeper lifted his hat, but went no nearer.

'Do walk down to the cottage with us, Hilda,' Connie pleaded. 'It's not far.'

'What about the car?'

'People do leave them on the lanes. You have the key.'

Hilda was silent, deliberating. Then she looked backwards down the lane.

'Can I back round the bush?' she said.

'Oh yes!' said the keeper.

She backed slowly round the curve, out of sight of the road, locked the car, and got down. It was night, but luminous dark. The hedges rose high and wild, by the unused lane, and very dark seeming. There was a fresh sweet scent on the air. The keeper went ahead, then came Connie, then Hilda, and in silence. He lit up the difficult places with a flash-light torch, and they went on again, while an owl softly hooted over the oaks, and Flossie padded silently around. Nobody could speak. There was nothing to say.

At length Connie saw the yellow light of the house, and her heart beat fast. She was a little frightened. They trailed on, still in Indian file.

He unlocked the door and preceded them into the warm but bare little room. The fire burned low and red in the grate. The table was set with two plates and two glasses on a proper white table-cloth for once. Hilda shook her hair and looked round the bare, cheerless room. Then she summoned her courage and looked at the man.

He was moderately tall, and thin, and she thought him good-looking. He kept a quiet distance of his own, and seemed absolutely unwilling to speak.

'Do sit down, Hilda,' said Connie.

'Do!' he said. 'Can I make you tea or anything, or will you drink a glass of beer? It's moderately cool.'

'Beer!' said Connie.

'Beer for me, please!' said Hilda, with a mock sort of shyness. He looked at her and blinked.

He took a blue jug and tramped to the scullery. When he came back with the beer, his face had changed again.

Connie sat down by the door, and Hilda sat in his seat, with the back to the wall, against the window corner.

'That is his chair,' said Connie softly. And Hilda rose as if it had burnt her.

'Sit yer still, sit yer still! Ta's ony cheer as yo'n a mind to, none of us is th' big bear,' he said, with complete equanimity.

And he brought Hilda a glass, and poured her beer first from the blue jug.

'As for cigarettes,' he said, 'I've got none, but 'appen you've got your own. I dunna smoke, mysen. Shall y' eat summat?' He turned direct to Connie. 'Shall t'eat a smite o' summat, if I bring it thee? Tha can usually do wi' a bite.' He spoke the vernacular with a curious calm assurance, as if he were the landlord of the inn.

'What is there?' asked Connie, flushing.

'Boiled ham, cheese, pickled wa'nuts, if yer like.–Nowt much.'

'Yes,' said Connie. 'Won't you, Hilda?'

Hilda looked up at him.

'Why do you speak Yorkshire?' she said softly.

'That! That's non Yorkshire, that's Derby.'

He looked back at her with that faint, distant grin.

'Derby, then! Why do you speak Derby? You spoke natural English at first.'

'Did Ah though? An' canna Ah change if Ah'm a mind to 't? Nay, nay, let me talk Derby if it suits me. If yo'n nowt against it.'

'It sounds a little affected,' said Hilda.

'Ay, 'appen so! An' up i' Tevershall yo'd sound affected.' He looked again at her, with a queer calculating distance, along his cheek-bone: as if to say: Yi, an' who are you?

He tramped away to the pantry for the food.

The sisters sat in silence. He brought another plate, and knife and fork. Then he said:

'An' if it's the same to you, I s'll ta'e my coat off, like I allers do.'

And he took off his coat, and hung it on the peg, then sat down to table in his shirt-sleeves: a shirt of thin, cream-coloured flannel.

''Elp yerselves!' he said. ''Elp yerselves! Dunna wait f'r axin'!'

He cut the bread, then sat motionless. Hilda felt, as Connie once used to, his power of silence and distance. She saw his smallish, sensitive, loose hand on the table. He was no simple working man, not he: he was acting! acting!

'Still!' she said, as she took a little cheese. 'It would be more natural if you spoke to us in normal English, not in vernacular.'

He looked at her, feeling her devil of a will.

'Would it?' he said in the normal English. 'Would it? Would anything that was said between you and me be quite natural, unless you said you wished me to hell before your sister ever saw me again: and unless I said something almost as unpleasant back again? Would anything else be natural?'

'Oh yes!' said Hilda. 'Just good manners would be quite natural.'

'Second nature, so to speak!' he said: then he began to laugh. 'Nay,' he said. 'I'm weary o' manners. Let me be!'

Hilda was frankly baffled and furiously annoyed. After all, he might show that he realized he was being honoured. Instead of which, with his play-acting and lordly airs, he seemed to think it was he who was conferring the honour. Just impudence! Poor misguided Connie, in the man's clutches!

The three ate in silence. Hilda looked to see what his table-manners were like. She could not help realizing that he was instinctively much more delicate and well-bred than herself. She had a certain Scottish clumsiness. And moreover, he had all the quiet self-contained assurance of the English, no loose edges. It would be very difficult to get the better of him.

But neither would he get the better of her.

'And do you really think,' she said, a little more humanly, 'it's worth the risk.'

'Is what worth what risk?'

'This escapade with my sister.'

He flickered his irritating grin.

'Yo' maun ax 'er!'

Then he looked at Connie.

'Tha comes o' thine own accord, lass, doesn't ter? It's non me as forces thee?'

Connie looked at Hilda.

'I wish you wouldn't cavil, Hilda.'

'Naturally I don't want to. But someone has to think about things. You've got to have some sort of continuity in your life. You can't just go making a mess.'

There was a moment's pause.

'Eh, continuity!' he said. 'An' what by that? What continuity ave yer got i' *your* life? I thought you was gettin' divorced. What continuity's that? Continuity o' yer own stubbornness. I can see that much. An' what good's it goin' to do yer? Yo'll be sick o' yer continuity afore yer a fat sight older. A stubborn woman an' 'er own self-will: ay, they make a fast continuity, they do. Thank heaven, it isn't me as 'as got th' 'andlin' of yer!'

'What right have you to speak like that to me?' said Hilda.

'Right! What right ha' yo' ter start harnessin' other folks i' your continuity? Leave folks to their own continuities.'

'My dear man, do you think I am concerned with you?' said Hilda softly.

'Ay,' he said. 'Yo' are. For it's a force-put. Yo' more or less my sister-in-law.'

'Still far from it, I assure you.'

'Not a' that far, I assure *you.* I've got my own sort o' continuity, back your life! Good as yours, any day. An' if your sister there comes ter me for a bit o' cunt an' tenderness, she knows what she's after. She's been in my bed afore: which you 'aven't, thank the Lord, with your continuity.' There was a dead pause, before he added: '–Eh, I don't wear me breeches arse-forrards. An' if I get a windfall, I thank my stars. A man gets a lot of enjoyment out o' that lass theer, which is more than anybody gets out o' th' likes o' you. Which is a pity, for you might 'appen a' bin a good apple, 'stead of a handsome crab. Women like you needs proper graftin'.'

He was looking at her with an odd, flickering smile, faintly sensual and appreciative.

'And men like you,' she said, 'ought to be segregated: justifying their own vulgarity and selfish lust.'

'Ay, ma'am! It's a mercy there's a few men left like me. But you deserve what you get: to be left severely alone.'

Hilda had risen and gone to the door. He rose and took his coat from the peg.

'I can find my way quite well alone,' she said.

'I doubt you can't,' he replied easily.

They tramped in ridiculous file down the lane again, in silence. An owl still hooted. He knew he ought to shoot it.

The car stood untouched, a little dewy. Hilda got in and started the engine. The other two waited.

'All I mean,' she said from her entrenchment, 'is that I doubt if you'll find it's been worth it, either of you!'

'One man's meat is another man's poison,' he said, out of the darkness. 'But it's meat an' drink to me.'

The lights flared out.

'Don't make me wait in the morning, Connie.'

'No, I won't. Goodnight!'

The car rose slowly on to the highroad, then slid swiftly away, leaving the night silent.

Connie timidly took his arm, and they went down the lane. He did not speak. At length she drew him to a standstill.

'Kiss me!' she murmured.

'Nay, wait a bit! Let me simmer down,' he said.

That amused her. She still kept hold of his arm, and they went quickly down the lane, in silence. She was so glad to be with him, just now. She shivered, knowing that Hilda might have snatched her away. He was inscrutably silent.

When they were in the cottage again, she almost jumped with pleasure, that she should be free of her sister.

'But you were horrid to Hilda,' she said to him.

'She should ha' been slapped in time.'

'But why? and she's *so* nice.'

He didn't answer, went round doing the evening chores, with a quiet, inevitable sort of motion. He was outwardly angry, but not with her. So Connie felt. And his anger gave him a peculiar handsomeness, an inwardness and glisten that thrilled her and made her limbs go molten.

Still he took no notice of her.

Till he sat down and began to unlace his boots. Then he looked up at her from under his brows, on which the anger still sat firm.

'Shan't you go up?' he said. 'There's a candle!'

He jerked his head swiftly to indicate the candle burning on the table. She took it obediently, and he watched the full curve of her hips as she went up the first stairs.

It was a night of sensual passion, in which she was a little startled and almost unwilling: yet pierced again with piercing thrills of sensuality, different, sharper, more terrible than the thrills of tenderness, but, at the moment, more desirable. Though a little frightened, she let him have his way, and the reckless, shameless sensuality shook her to her foundations, stripped her to the very last, and made a different woman of her. It was not really love. It was not voluptuousness. It was sensuality sharp and searing as fire, burning the soul to tinder.

Burning out the shames, the deepest, oldest shames, in the most secret places. It cost her an effort to let him have his way and his will of her. She had to be a passive, consenting thing, like a slave, a physical slave. Yet the passion licked round her, consuming, and when the sensual flame of it pressed through her bowels and breast, she really thought she was dying: yet a poignant, marvellous death.

She had often wondered what Abélard meant, when he said that in their year of love he and Héloïse had passed through all the stages and refinements of passion. The same thing, a thousand years ago: ten thousand years ago! The same on the Greek vases, everywhere! The refinements of passion, the extravagances of sensuality! And necessary, forever necessary, to burn out false shames and smelt out the heaviest ore of the body into purity. With the fire of sheer sensuality.

In the short summer night she learnt so much. She would have thought a woman would have died of shame. Instead of which, the shame died. Shame, which is fear: the deep organic shame, the old, old physical fear which crouches in the bodily roots of us, and can only be chased away by the sensual fire, at last it was roused up and routed by the phallic hunt of the man, and she came to the very heart of the jungle of herself. She felt, now, she had come to the real bed-rock of her nature, and was essentially shameless. She was her sensual self, naked and unashamed. She felt a triumph, almost a vainglory. So! That was how it was! That was life! That was how oneself really was! There was nothing left to disguise or be ashamed of. She shared her ultimate nakedness with a man, another being.

And what a reckless devil the man was! really like a devil! One had to be strong to bear him. But it took some getting at, the core of the physical jungle, the last and deepest recess of organic shame. The phallos alone could explore it. And how he had pressed in on her!

And how, in fear, she had hated it. But how she had really wanted it! She knew now. At the bottom of her soul, fundamentally, she had needed this phallic hunting out, she had secretly wanted it, and she had believed that she would never get it. Now suddenly there it was, and a man was sharing her last and final nakedness, she was shameless.

What liars poets and everybody were! They make one think one wanted sentiment. When what one supremely wanted was this piercing, consuming, rather awful sensuality. To find a man who dared do it, without shame or sin or final misgiving! If he had been ashamed afterwards, and made one feel ashamed, how awful! What a pity most men are so doggy, a bit shameful, like Clifford! Like Michaelis even! Both sensually a bit doggy and humiliating. The supreme pleasure of the mind! And what is that to a woman? What is it, really, to the man either! He becomes merely messy and doggy, even in his mind. It needs sheer sensuality even to purify and quicken the mind. Sheer fiery sensuality, not messiness.

Ah, God, how rare a thing a man is! They are all dogs that trot and sniff and copulate. To have found a man who was not afraid and not ashamed! She looked at him now, sleeping so like a wild animal asleep, gone, gone in the remoteness of it. She nestled down, not to be away from him.

Till his rousing waked her completely. He was sitting up in bed, looking down at her. She saw her own nakedness in his eyes, immediate knowledge of her. And the fluid, male knowledge of herself seemed to flow to her from his eyes and wrap her voluptuously. Oh, how voluptuous and lovely it was to have limbs and body half-asleep, heavy and suffused with passion.

'Is it time to wake up?' she said.

'Half past six.'

She had to be at the lane-end at eight. Always, always, always this compulsion on one!

'I might make the breakfast and bring it up here; should I?' he said.

'Oh yes!'

Flossie whimpered gently below. He got up and threw off his pyjamas, and rubbed himself with a towel. When the human being is full of courage and full of life, how beautiful it is! So she thought, as she watched him in silence.

'Draw the curtain, will you?'

The sun was shining already on the tender green leaves of morning, and the wood stood bluey-fresh, in the nearness. She sat up in bed, looking dreamily out through the dormer window, her naked arms pushing her naked breasts together. He was dressing himself. She was half-dreaming of life, a life together with him: just a life.

He was going, fleeing from her dangerous, crouching nakedness.

'Have I lost my nightie altogether?' she said.

He pushed his hand down in the bed, and pulled out the bit of flimsy silk.

'I knowed I felt silk at my ankles,' he said.

But the nightdress was slit almost in two.

'Never mind!' she said. 'It belongs here, really. I'll leave it.'

'Ay, leave it, I can put it between my legs at night, for company. There's no name nor mark on it, is there?'

She slipped on the torn thing, and sat dreamily looking out of the window. The window was open, the air of morning drifted in, and the sound of birds. Birds flew continuously past. Then she saw Flossie roaming out. It was morning.

Downstairs she heard him making the fire, pumping water, going out at the back door. By and by came the smell of bacon, and at length he came upstairs with a huge black tray that would only just go through the door. He set the tray on the bed, and poured out the tea. Connie squatted in her torn nightdress, and fell on her food hungrily. He sat on the one chair, with his plate on his knees.

'How good it is!' she said. 'How nice to have breakfast together.'

He ate in silence, his mind on the time that was quickly passing. That made her remember.

'Oh, how I wish I could stay here with you, and Wragby were a million miles away! It's Wragby I'm going away from really. You know that, don't you?'

'Ay!'

'And you promise we will live together and have a life together, you and me! You promise me, don't you?'

'Ay! When we can.'

'Yes! And we *will* we *will*, won't we?' she leaned over, making the tea spill, catching his wrist.

'Ay!' he said, tidying up the tea.

'We can't possibly *not* live together now, can we?' she said appealingly.

He looked up at her with his flickering grin.

'No!' he said. 'Only you've got to start in twenty-five minutes.'

'Have I?' she cried. Suddenly he held up a warning finger, and rose to his feet.

Flossie had given a short bark, then three loud sharp yaps of warning.

Silent, he put his plate on the tray and went downstairs. Constance heard him go down the garden path. A bicycle bell tinkled outside there.

'Morning, Mr Mellors! Registered letter!'

'Oh ay! Got a pencil?'

'Here y'are!'

There was a pause.

'Canada!' said the stranger's voice.

'Ay! That's a mate o' mine out there in British Columbia. Dunno what he's got to register.'

' 'Appen sent y'a fortune, like.'

'More like want summat.'

Pause.

'Well! Lovely day again!'

'Ay!'

'Morning!'

'Morning!'

After a time he came upstairs again, looking a little angry.

'Postman,' he said.

'Very early!' she replied.

'Rural round; he's mostly here by seven, when he does come.'

'Did your mate send you a fortune?'

'No! Only some photographs and papers about a place out there in British Columbia.'

'Would you go there?'

'I thought perhaps we might.'

'Oh yes! I believe it's lovely!'

But he was put out by the postman's coming.

'Them damn bikes, they're on you afore you know where you are. I hope he twigged nothing.'

'After all, what could he twig!'

'You must get up now, and get ready. I'm just goin' ter look round outside.'

She saw him go reconnoitring into the lane, with dog and gun. She went downstairs and washed, and was ready by the time he came back, with the few things in the little silk bag.

He locked up, and they set off, but through the wood, not down the lane. He was being wary.

'Don't you think one lives for times like last night?' she said to him.

'Ay! But there's the rest o' times to think on,' he replied, rather short.

They plodded on down the overgrown path, he in front, in silence.

'And we *will* live together and make a life together, won't we?' she pleaded.

'Ay!' he replied, striding on without looking round. 'When t' time comes! Just now you're off to Venice or somewhere.'

She followed him dumbly, with sinking heart. Oh, now she was *wae* to go! At last he stopped.

'I'll just strike across here,' he said, pointing to the right.

But she flung her arms round his neck, and clung to him.

'But you'll keep the tenderness for me, won't you?' she whispered. 'I loved last night. But you'll keep the tenderness for me, won't you?'

He kissed her and held her close for a moment. Then he sighed, and kissed her again.

'I must go an' look if th' car's there.'

He strode over the low brambles and bracken, leaving a trail through the fern. For a minute or two he was gone. Then he came striding back.

'Car's not there yet,' he said. 'But there's the baker's cart on t' road.'

He seemed anxious and troubled.

'Hark!'

They heard a car softly hoot as it came nearer. It slowed up on the bridge.

She plunged with utter mournfulness in his track through the fern, and came to a huge holly hedge. He was just behind her.

'Here! Go through there!' he said, pointing to a gap. 'I shan't come out.'

She looked at him in despair. But he kissed her and made her go. She crept in sheer misery through the holly and through the wooden fence, stumbled down the little ditch and up into the lane, where Hilda was just getting out of the car in vexation.

'Why you're there!' said Hilda. 'Where's *he*?'

'He's not coming.'

Connie's face was running with tears as she got into the car with her little bag. Hilda snatched up the motoring helmet with the disfiguring goggles. 'Put it on!' she said. And Connie pulled on the disguise, then the long motoring coat, and she sat down, a goggling inhuman, unrecognizable creature. Hilda started the car with a business-like motion. They heaved out of the lane, and were away down the road. Connie had looked round, but there was no sight of him. Away! Away! She sat in bitter tears. The parting had come so suddenly, so unexpectedly. It was like death.

'Thank goodness you'll be away from him for some time!' said Hilda, turning to avoid Crosshill village.

17

'You see, Hilda,' said Connie after lunch, when they were nearing London, 'you have never known either real tenderness or real sensuality: and if you do know them, with the same person, it makes a great difference.'

'For mercy's sake don't brag about your experiences!' said Hilda. 'I've never met the man yet who was capable of intimacy with a woman, giving himself up to her. That was what I wanted. I'm not keen on their self-satisfied tenderness, and their sensuality. I'm not content to be any man's little petsy-wetsy, nor his *chair à plaisir* either. I wanted a complete intimacy, and I didn't get it. That's enough for me.'

Connie pondered this. Complete intimacy! She supposed that meant revealing everything concerning yourself to the other person, and his revealing everything concerning himself. But that was a bore. And all that weary self-consciousness between a man and a woman! a disease!

'I think you're too conscious of yourself all the time, with everybody,' she said to her sister.

'I hope at least I haven't a slave nature,' said Hilda.

'But perhaps you have! Perhaps you are a slave to your own idea of yourself.'

Hilda drove in silence for some time after this piece of unheard-of insolence from that chit Connie.

'At least I'm not a slave to somebody's else's idea of me: and the somebody else a servant of my husband's,' she retorted at last, in crude anger.

'You see, it's not so,' said Connie calmly.

She had always let herself be dominated by her elder sister. Now, though somewhere inside herself she was weeping, she was free of the dominion of *other women*. Ah! that in itself was a relief, like being given another life: to be free of the strange dominion and obsession of *other women*. How awful they were, women!

She was glad to be with her father, whose favourite she had always been. She and Hilda stayed in a little hotel off Pall Mall, and Sir Malcolm was in his club. But he took his daughters out in the evening, and they liked going with him.

He was still handsome and robust, though just a little afraid of the new world that had sprung up around him. He had got a second wife in Scotland, younger than himself, and richer. But he had as many holidays away from her as possible: just as with his first wife.

Connie sat next to him at the opera. He was moderately stout, and had stout thighs, but they were still strong and well-knit, the thighs of a healthy man who had taken his pleasure in life. His good-humoured selfishness, his dogged sort of independence, his unrepenting sensuality, it seemed to Connie she could see them all in his well-knit straight thighs. Just a man! And now becoming an old man, which is sad. Because in his strong, thick male legs there was none of the alert sensitiveness and power of tenderness which is the very essence of youth, that which never dies, once it is there.

Connie woke up to the existence of legs. They became more important to her than faces, which are no longer very real. How few people had live, alert legs! She looked at the men in the stalls. Great puddingy thighs in black pudding-cloth, or lean wooden sticks in black funeral stuff, or well-shaped young legs without any meaning whatever, either sensuality or tenderness or sensitiveness, just mere leggy ordinariness that pranced around. Not even any sensuality like her father's. They were all daunted, daunted out of existence.

But the women were not daunted. The awful mill-posts of most females! really shocking, really enough to justify murder! Or the poor thin pegs! or the trim things in silk stockings, without the slightest look of life! Awful, the millions of meaningless legs prancing meaninglessly around!

But she was not happy in London. The people seemed so spectral and blank. They had no alive happiness, no matter how brisk and good-looking they were. It was all barren. And Connie had a woman's blind craving for happiness, to be assured of happiness.

In Paris at any rate she felt a bit of sensuality still. But what a weary, tired, worn-out sensuality. Worn-out for lack of tenderness. Oh! Paris was sad. One of the saddest towns: weary of its now-mechanical sensuality, weary of the tension of money, money, money, weary even of resentment and conceit, just weary to death, and still not sufficiently Americanized or Londonized to hide the weariness under a mechanical jig-jig-jig! Ah, these manly he-men, these *flâneurs*, the oglers, these eaters of good dinners! How weary they were! weary, worn-out for lack of a little tenderness, given and taken. The efficient, sometimes charming women knew a thing or two about the sensual realities: they had that pull over their jigging English sisters. But they knew even less of tenderness. Dry, with the endless dry tension of will, they too were wearing out. The human world was just getting worn out. Perhaps it would turn fiercely destructive. A sort of anarchy! Clifford and his conservative anarchy! Perhaps it wouldn't be conservative much longer. Perhaps it would develop into a very radical anarchy.

Connie found herself shrinking and afraid of the world. Sometimes she was happy for a little while in the Boulevards or in the Bois or the Luxembourg Gardens. But already Paris was full of Americans and English, strange Americans in the oddest uniforms, and the usual dreary English that are so hopeless abroad.

She was glad to drive on. It was suddenly hot weather, so Hilda was going through Switzerland and over the Brenner, then through the Dolomites down to Venice. Hilda loved all the managing and the driving and being mistress of the show. Connie was quite content to keep quiet.

And the trip was really quite nice. Only Connie kept saying to herself: Why don't I really care! Why am I never really thrilled? How awful, that I don't really care about the landscape any more! But I don't. It's rather awful. I'm like Saint Bernard, who could sail down the lake of Lucerne without ever noticing that there were even mountain and green water. I just don't care for landscape any more. Why should one stare at it? Why should one? I refuse to.

No, she found nothing vital in France or Switzerland or the Tyrol or Italy. She just was carted through it all. And it was all less real than Wragby. Less real than the awful Wragby! She felt she didn't care if she never saw France or Switzerland or Italy again. They'd keep. Wragby was more real.

As for people! people were all alike, with very little difference. They all wanted to get money out of you: or, if they were travellers, they wanted to get enjoyment, perforce, like squeezing blood out of a stone. Poor mountains! poor landscape! it all had to be squeezed and squeezed and squeezed again, to provide a thrill, to provide enjoyment. What did people mean, with their simply determined enjoying of themselves?

No! said Connie to herself. I'd rather be at Wragby, where I can go about and be still, and not stare at anything or do any performing of any sort. This tourist performance of enjoying oneself is too hopelessly humiliating: it's such a failure.

She wanted to go back to Wragby, even to Clifford, even to poor crippled Clifford. He wasn't such a fool as this swarming holidaying lot, anyhow.

But in her inner consciousness she was keeping touch with the other man. She mustn't let her connexion with him go: oh, she mustn't let it go, or she was lost, lost utterly in this world of riff-raffy expensive people and joy-hogs. Oh, the joy-hogs! Oh 'enjoying oneself'! Another modern form of sickness.

They left the car in Mestre, in a garage, and took the regular steamer over to Venice. It was a lovely summer afternoon, the shallow lagoon rippled, the full sunshine made Venice, turning its back to them across the water, look dim.

At the station quay they changed to a gondola, giving the man the address. He was a regular gondolier in a white-and-blue blouse, not very good-looking, not at all impressive.

'Yes! The Villa Esmeralda! Yes! I know it! I have been the gondolier for a gentleman there. But a fair distance out!'

He seemed a rather childish, impetuous fellow. He rowed with a certain exaggerated impetuosity, through the dark side-canals with the horrible, slimy green walls, the canals that go through the poorer quarters, where the washing hangs high up on ropes, and there is a slight, or strong, odour of sewage.

But at last he came to one of the open canals with pavement on either side, and looping bridges, that run straight, at right-angles to the Grand Canal. The two women sat under the little awning, the man was perched above, behind them.

'Are the signorine staying long at the Villa Esmeralda?' he asked, rowing easy, and wiping his perspiring face with a white-and-blue handkerchief.

'Some twenty days: we are both married ladies,' said Hilda, in her curious hushed voice, that made her Italian sound so foreign.

'Ah! Twenty days!' said the man. There was a pause. After which he asked: 'Do the signore want a gondolier for the twenty days or so that they will stay at the Villa Esmeralda? Or by the day, or by the week?'

Connie and Hilda considered. In Venice, it is always preferable to have one's own gondola, as it is preferable to have one's own car on land.

'What is there at the Villa? what boats?'

'There is a motor-launch, also a gondola. But–' The *but* meant: they won't be your property.

'How much do you charge?'

It was about thirty shillings a day, or ten pounds a week.

'Is that the regular price?' asked Hilda.

'Less, Signora, less. The regular price–'

The sisters considered.

'Well,' said Hilda, 'come tomorrow morning, and we will arrange it. What is your name?'

His name was Giovanni, and he wanted to know at what time he should come, and then for whom should he say he was waiting. Hilda had no card. Connie gave him one of hers. He glanced at it swiftly, with his hot, southern blue eyes, then glanced again.

'Ah!' he said, lighting up. 'Milady! Milady, isn't it?'

'Milady Costanza!' said Connie.

He nodded, repeating: 'Milady Costanza!' and putting the card carefully away in his blouse.

The Villa Esmeralda was quite a long way out, on the edge of the lagoon looking towards Chioggia. It was not a very old house, and pleasant, with the terraces looking seawards, and below, quite a big garden with dark trees, walled in from the lagoon.

Their host was a heavy, rather coarse Scotchman who had made a good fortune in Italy before the war, and had been knighted for his ultrapatriotism during the war. His wife was a thin, pale, sharp kind of person with no fortune of her own, and the misfortune of having to regulate her husband's rather sordid amorous exploits. He was terribly tiresome with the servants. But having had a slight stroke during the winter, he was now more manageable.

The house was pretty full. Besides Sir Malcolm and his two daughters, there were seven more people, a Scotch couple, again with two daughters; a young Italian Contessa, a widow; a young Georgian prince, and a youngish English clergyman who had had pneumonia and was being chaplain to Sir Alexander for his health's sake. The prince was penniless, good-looking, would make an excellent chauffeur, with the necessary impudence, and basta! The Contessa was a quiet little puss with a game on somewhere. The clergyman was a raw simple fellow from a Bucks vicarage: luckily he had left his wife and two children at home. And the Guthries, the family of four, were good solid Edinburgh middle class, enjoying everything in a solid fashion, and daring everything while risking nothing.

Connie and Hilda ruled out the prince at once. The Guthries were more or less their own sort, substantial, but boring: and the girls wanted husbands. The chaplain was not a bad fellow, but too deferential. Sir Alexander, after his slight stroke, had a terrible heaviness in his joviality, but he was still thrilled at the presence of so many handsome young women. Lady Cooper was a quiet, catty person who had a thin time of it, poor thing, and who watched every other woman with a cold watchfulness that had become her second nature, and who said cold, nasty things which showed what an utterly low opinion she had of all human nature. She was also quite venomously overbearing with the servants, Connie found: but in a quiet way. And she skilfully behaved so that Sir Alexander should think that *he* was lord and monarch of the whole caboosh, with his stout, would-be-genial paunch, and his utterly boring jokes, his humourosity, as Hilda called it.

Sir Malcolm was painting. Yes, he still would do a Venetian lagoonscape, now and then, in contrast to his Scottish landscapes. So in the morning he was rowed off with a huge canvas, to his 'site'. A little later, Lady Cooper would be rowed off into the heart of the city, with sketching-block and colours. She was an inveterate watercolour painter, and the house was full of rose-coloured palaces, dark canals, swaying bridges, medieval façades, and so on. A little later the Guthries, the prince, the countess, Sir Alexander, and sometimes Mr Lind, the chaplain, would go off to the Lido, where they would bathe; coming home to a late lunch at half past one.

The house-party, as a house-party, was distinctly boring. But this did not trouble the sisters. They were out all the time. Their father took them to the exhibition, miles and miles of weary paintings. He took them to all the cronies of his in the Villa Lucchese, he sat with them on warm evenings in the piazza, having got a table at Florian's: he took them to the theatre, to the Goldoni plays. There were illuminated water-fêtes, there were dances. This was a holiday-place of all holiday-places. The Lido, with its acres of sun-pinked or pyjamaed bodies, was like a strand with an endless heap of seals come up for mating. Too many people in the piazza, too many limbs and trunks of humanity on the Lido, too many gondolas, too many motor-launches, too many steamers, too many pigeons, too many ices, too many cocktails, too many menservants wanting tips, too many languages rattling, too much, too much sun, too much smell of Venice, too many cargoes of strawberries, too many silk shawls, too many huge, raw-beef slices of water-melon on stalls: too much enjoyment, altogether far too much enjoyment!

Connie and Hilda went around in their sunny frocks. There were dozens of people they knew, dozens of people knew them. Michaelis turned up like a bad penny. 'Hullo! Where you staying? Come and have an ice-cream or something! Come with me somewhere in my gondola.' Even Michaelis *almost* sun-burned: though sun-cooked is more appropriate to the look of the mass of human flesh.

It was pleasant in a way. It was *almost* enjoyment. But anyhow, with all the cocktails, all the lying in warmish water and sun-bathing on hot sand in hot sun, jazzing with your stomach up against some fellow in the warm nights, cooling off with ices, it was a complete narcotic. And that was what they all wanted, a drug: the slow water, a drug; the sun, a drug; jazz, a drug; cigarettes, cocktails, ices, vermouth. To be drugged! Enjoyment! Enjoyment!

Hilda half liked being drugged. She liked looking at all the women, speculating about them. The women were absorbingly interested in the women. How does she look! what man has she captured? what fun is she getting out of it?–The men were like great dogs in white flannel trousers, waiting to be patted, waiting to wallow, waiting to plaster some woman's stomach against their own, in jazz.

Hilda liked jazz, because she could plaster her stomach against the stomach of some so-called man, and let him control her movement from the visceral centre, here and there across the floor, and then she could break loose and ignore 'the creature'. He had been merely made use of. Poor Connie was rather unhappy. She wouldn't jazz, because she simply couldn't plaster her stomach against some 'creature's' stomach. She hated the conglomerate mass of nearly nude flesh on the Lido: there was hardly enough water to wet them all. She disliked Sir Alexander and Lady Cooper. She did not want Michaelis or anybody else trailing her.

The happiest times were when she got Hilda to go with her away across the lagoon, far across to some lonely shingle-bank, where they could bathe quite alone, the gondola remaining on the inner side of the reef.

Then Giovanni got another gondolier to help him, because it was a long way and he sweated terrifically in the sun. Giovanni was very nice: affectionate, as the Italians are, and quite passionless. The Italians are not passionate: passion has deep reserves. They are easily moved, and often affectionate, but they rarely have any abiding passion of any sort.

So Giovanni was already devoted to his ladies, as he had been devoted to cargoes of ladies in the past. He was perfectly ready to prostitute himself to them, if they wanted him: he secretly hoped they would want him. They would give him a handsome present, and it would come in very handy, as he was just going to be married. He told them about his marriage, and they were suitably interested.

He thought this trip to some lonely bank across the lagoon probably meant business: business being *l'amore*, love. So he got a mate to help him, for it *was* a long way; and after all, they were two ladies. Two ladies, two mackerels! Good arithmetic! Beautiful ladies, too! He was justly proud of them. And though it was the Signora who paid him and gave him orders, he rather hoped it would be the young milady who would select him for *l'amore*. She would give more money too.

The mate he brought was called Daniele. He was not a regular gondolier, so he had none of the cadger and prostitute about him. He was a sandola man, a sandola being a big boat that brings in fruit and produce from the islands.

Daniele was beautiful, tall and well-shapen, with a light round head of little, close-pale-blond curls, and a good-looking man's face, a little like a lion, and long-distance blue eyes. He was not effusive, loquacious, and bibulous like Giovanni. He was silent—and he rowed with a strength and ease as if he were alone on the water. The ladies were ladies, remote from him. He did not even look at them. He looked ahead.

He was a real man, a little angry when Giovanni drank too much wine and rowed awkwardly, with effusive shoves of the great oar. He was a man as a Mellors was a man, unprostituted. Connie pitied the wife of the easily-overflowing Giovanni. But Daniele's wife would be one of those sweet Venetian women of the people whom one still sees, modest and flower-like in the back of that labyrinth of a town.

Ah, how sad that man first prostitutes woman, then woman prostitutes man. Giovanni was pining to prostitute himself, dribbling like a dog, wanting to give himself to a woman. And for money!

Connie looked at Venice far off, low and rose-coloured upon the water. Built of money, blossomed of money, and dead.with money. The money-deadness! Money, money, money, prostitution and deadness.

Yet Daniele was still a man capable of a man's free allegiance. He did not wear the gondolier's blouse: only the knitted blue jersey. He was a little wild, uncouth and proud. So he was hireling to the rather doggy Giovanni who was hireling again to two women. So it is! When Jesus refused the devil's money, he left the devil like a Jewish banker, master of the whole situation.

Connie would come home from the blazing light of the lagoon in a kind of stupor, to find letters from home. Clifford wrote regularly. He wrote very good letters: they might all have been printed in a book. And for this reason Connie found them not very interesting.

She lived in the stupor of the light of the lagoon, the lapping saltiness of the water, the space, the emptiness, the nothingness: but health, health, complete stupor of health. It was gratifying, and she was lulled away in it, not caring for anything. Besides, she was pregnant. She knew now. So the stupor of sunlight and lagoon salt and sea-bathing and lying on shingle and finding shells and drifting away, away in a gondola, was completed by the pregnancy inside her, another fullness of health, satisfying and stupefying.

She had been at Venice a fortnight, and she was to stay another ten days or a fortnight. The sunshine blazed over any count of time, and the fullness of physical health made forgetfulness complete. She was in a sort of stupor of well-being.

From which a letter of Clifford roused her.

We too have had our mild local excitement. It appears the truant wife of Mellors, the keeper, turned up at the cottage and found herself unwelcome. He packed her off, and locked the door. Report has it, however, that when he returned from the wood he found the no longer fair lady firmly established in his bed, in *puris naturalibus*; or one should say, in *impuris naturalibus*. She had broken a window and got in that way. Unable to evict the somewhat man-handled Venus from his couch, he beat a retreat and retired, it is said, to his mother's house in Tevershall. Meanwhile the Venus of Stacks Gate is established in the cottage, which she claims is her home, and Apollo, apparently, is domiciled in Tevershall.

I repeat this from hearsay, as Mellors has not come to me personally. I had this particular bit of local garbage from our garbage bird, our ibis, our scavenging turkey-buzzard, Mrs Bolton. I would not have repeated it had she not exclaimed: her Ladyship will go no more to the wood if *that* woman's going to be about!

I like your picture of Sir Malcolm striding into the sea with white hair blowing and pink flesh glowing. I envy you that sun. Here it rains. But I don't envy Sir Malcolm his inveterate mortal carnality. However, it suits his age. Apparently one grows more carnal and more mortal as one grows older. Only youth has a taste of immortality—

This news affected Connie in her state of semi-stupefied well-being with vexation amounting to exasperation. Now she had got to be bothered by that beast of a woman! Now she must start and fret! She had no letter from Mellors. They had agreed not to write at all, but now she wanted to hear from him personally. After all, he was the father of the child that was coming. Let him write!

But how hateful! Now everything was messed up. How foul those low people were! How nice it was here, in the sunshine and the indolence, compared to that dismal mess of that English Midlands! After all, a clear sky was almost the most important thing in life.

She did not mention the fact of her pregnancy, even to Hilda. She wrote to Mrs Bolton for exact information.

Duncan Forbes, an artist friend of theirs, had arrived at the Villa Esmeralda, coming north from Rome. Now he made a third in the gondola, and he bathed with them across the lagoon, and was their escort: a quiet, almost taciturn young man, very advanced in his art.

She had a letter from Mrs Bolton:

You will be pleased, I am sure, my Lady, when you see Sir Clifford. He's looking quite blooming and working very hard, and very hopeful. Of course he is looking forward to seeing you among us again. It is a dull house without my Lady, and we shall all welcome her presence among us once more.

About Mr Mellors, I don't know how much Sir Clifford told you. It seems his wife came back all of a sudden one afternoon, and he found her sitting on the doorstep when he came in from the wood. She said she was come back to him and wanted to live with him again, as she was his legal wife, and he wasn't going to divorce her. But he wouldn't have anything to do with her, and wouldn't let her in the house, and did not go in himself; he went back into the wood without ever opening the door.

But when he came back after dark, he found the house broken into, so he went upstairs to see what she'd done, and he found her in bed without a rag on her. He offered her money, but she said she was his wife and he must take her back. I don't know what sort of a scene they had. His mother told me about it, she's terribly upset. Well, he told her he'd die rather than ever live with her again, so he took his things and went straight to his mother's on Tevershall hill. He stopped the night and went to the wood next day through the park, never going near the cottage. It seems he never saw his wife that day. But the day after she was at his brother Dan's at Beggarlee, swearing and carrying on, saying she was his legal wife, and that he'd been having women at the cottage, because she'd found a scent-bottle in his drawer, and gold-tipped cigarette-ends on the ash-heap, and I don't know what all. Then it seems the postman Fred Kirk says he heard somebody talking in Mr Mellors' bedroom early one morning, and a motor-car had been in the lane.

Mr Mellors stayed on with his mother, and went to the wood through the park, and it seems she stayed on at the cottage. Well, there was no end of talk. So at last Mr Mellors and Tom Phillips went to the cottage and fetched away most of the furniture and bedding, and unscrewed the handle of the pump, so she was forced to go. But instead of going back to Stacks Gate she went and lodged with that Mrs Swain at Beggarlee, because her brother Dan's wife wouldn't have her. And she kept going to old Mrs Mellors' house, to catch him, and she began swearing he'd got in bed with her in the cottage, and she went to a lawyer to make him pay her an allowance. She's grown heavy, and more common than ever, and as strong as a bull. And she goes about saying the most awful things about him, how he has women at the cottage, and how he behaved to her when they were married, the low, beastly things he did to her, and I don't know what all. I'm sure it's awful, the mischief a woman can do, once she starts talking. And no matter how low she may be, there'll be some as will believe her, and some of the dirt will stick. I'm sure the way she makes out that Mr Mellors was one of those low, beastly men with women, is simply shocking. And people are only too ready to believe things against anybody, especially things like that. She declares she'll never leave him alone while he lives. Though what I say is, if he was so beastly to her, why is she so anxious to go back to him? But of course she's coming near her change of life, for she's years older than he is. And these common, violent women always go partly insane when the change of life comes upon them—

This was a nasty blow to Connie. Here she was, sure as life, coming in for her share of the lowness and dirt. She felt angry with him for not having got clear of a Bertha Coutts: nay, for ever having married her. Perhaps he had a certain hankering after lowness. Connie remembered the last night she had spent with him, and shivered. He had known all that sensuality, even with a Bertha Coutts! It was really rather disgusting. It would be well to be rid of him; clear of him altogether. He was perhaps really common, really low.

She had a revulsion against the whole affair, and almost envied the Guthrie girls their gawky inexperience and crude maidenliness. And she now dreaded the thought that anybody would know about herself and the keeper. How unspeakably humiliating! She was weary, afraid, and felt a craving for utter respectability, even for the vulgar and deadening respectability of the Guthrie girls. If Clifford knew about her affair, how unspeakably humiliating! She was afraid, terrified of society and its unclean bite. She almost wished she could get rid of the child, and be quite clear. In short, she fell into a state of funk.

As for the scent-bottle, that was her own folly. She had not been able to refrain from perfuming his one or two handkerchiefs and his shirts in the drawer, just out of childishness, and she had left a little bottle of Coty's Wood-violet perfume, half empty, among his things. She wanted him to remember her in the perfume. As for the cigarette-ends, they were Hilda's.

She could not help confiding a little in Duncan Forbes. She didn't say she had been the keeper's lover, she only said she liked him, and told Forbes the history of the man.

'Oh,' said Forbes, 'you'll see, they'll never rest till they've pulled the man down and done him in. If he has refused to creep up into the middle classes, when he had a chance; and if he's a man who stands up for his own sex, then they'll do him in. It's the one thing they won't let you be, straight and open in your sex. You can be as dirty as you like. In fact the more dirt you do on sex the better they like it. But if you believe in your own sex, and won't have it done dirt to: they'll down you. It's the one insane taboo left: sex as a natural and vital thing. They won't have it, and they'll kill you before they'll let you have it. You'll see, they'll hound that man down. And what's he done, after all? If he's made love to his wife all ends on, hasn't he a right to? She ought to be proud of it. But you see, even a low bitch like that turns on him, and uses the hyena instinct of the mob against sex, to pull him down. You have a snivel and feel sinful or awful about your sex, before you're allowed to have any. Oh, they'll hound the poor devil down.'

Connie had a revulsion in the opposite direction now. What had he done, after all? what had he done to herself, Connie, but give her an exquisite pleasure and a sense of freedom and life? He had released her warm, natural sexual flow. And for that they would hound him down.

No no, it should not be. She saw the image of him, naked white with tanned face and hands, looking down and addressing his erect penis as if it were another being, the odd grin flickering on his face. And she heard his voice again: Tha's got the nicest woman's arse of anybody! And she felt his hand warmly and softly closing over her tail again, over her secret places, like a benediction. And the warmth ran through her womb, and the little flames flickered in her knees, and she said: Oh, no! I mustn't go back on it! I must not go back on him. I must stick to him and to what I had of him, through everything. I had no warm, flamy life till he gave it me. And I won't go back on it.

She did a rash thing. She sent a letter to Ivy Bolton, enclosing a note to the keeper, and asking Mrs Bolton to give it him. And she wrote to him:

I am very much distressed to hear of all the trouble your wife is making for you, but don't mind it, it is only a sort of hysteria. It will all blow over as suddenly as it came. But I'm awfully sorry about it, and I do hope you are not minding very much. After all, it isn't worth it. She is only a hysterical woman who wants to hurt you. I shall be home in ten days' time, and I do hope everything will be all right.

A few days later came a letter from Clifford. He was evidently upset.

I am delighted to hear you are prepared to leave Venice on the sixteenth. But if you are enjoying it, don't hurry home. We miss you, Wragby misses you. But it is essential that you should get your full amount of sunshine, sunshine and pyjamas, as the advertisements of the Lido say. So please do stay on a little longer, if it is cheering you up and preparing you for our sufficiently awful winter. Even today, it rains.

I am assiduously, admirably looked after by Mrs Bolton. She is a queer specimen. The more I live, the more I realize what strange creatures human beings are. Some of them might just as well have a hundred legs, like a centipede, or six, like a lobster. The human consistency and dignity one has been led to expect from one's fellow-men seem actually non-existent. One doubts if they exist to any startling degree even in oneself.

The scandal of the keeper continues and gets bigger like a snowball. Mrs Bolton keeps me informed. She reminds me of a fish which, though dumb, seems to be breathing silent gossip through its gills, while ever it lives. All goes through the sieve of her gills, and nothing surprises her. It is as if the events of other people's lives were the necessary oxygen of her own.

She is preoccupied with the Mellors scandal, and if I will let her begin, she takes me down to the depths. Her great indignation, which even then is like the indignation of an actress playing a role, is against the wife of Mellors, whom she persists in calling Bertha Coutts. I have been to the depths of the muddy lives of the Bertha Couttses of this world, and when, released from the current of gossip, I slowly rise to the surface again, I look at the daylight in wonder that it ever should be.

It seems to me absolutely true, that our world, which appears to us the surface of all things, is really the *bottom* of a deep ocean: all our trees are submarine growths, and we are weird, scaly-clad submarine fauna, feeding ourselves on offal like shrimps. Only occasionally the soul rises gasping through the fathomless fathoms under which we live, far up to the surface of the ether, where there is true air. I am convinced that the air we normally breathe is a kind of water, and men and women are a species of fish.

But sometimes the soul does come up, shoots like a kittiwake into the light, with ecstasy, after having preyed on the submarine depths. It is our mortal destiny, I suppose, to prey upon the ghastly subaqueous life of our fellow-men, in the submarine jungle of mankind. But our immortal destiny is to escape, once we have swallowed our swimmy catch, up again into the bright ether, bursting out from the surface of Old Ocean into real light. Then one realizes one's eternal nature.

When I hear Mrs Bolton talk, I feel myself plunging down, down, to the depths where the fish of human secrets wriggle and swim. Carnal appetite makes one seize a beakful of prey: then up, up again, out of the dense into the ethereal, from the wet into the dry. To you I can tell the whole process. But with Mrs Bolton I only feel the downward plunge, down, horribly, among the seaweeds and the pallid monsters of the very bottom.

I am afraid we are going to lose our game-keeper. The scandal of the truant wife, instead of dying down, has reverberated to greater and greater dimensions. He is accused of all unspeakable things and curiously enough, the woman has managed to get the bulk of the colliers' wives behind her, gruesome fish, and the village is putrescent with talk.

I hear this Bertha Coutts besieges Mellors in his mother's house, having ransacked the cottage and the hut. She seized one day upon her own daughter, as that chip of the female block was returning from school; but the little one, instead of kissing the loving mother's hand, bit it firmly, and so received from the other hand a smack in the face which sent her reeling into the gutter: whence she was rescued by an indignant and harassed grandmother.

The woman has blown off an amazing quantity of poison-gas. She has aired in detail all those incidents of her conjugal life which are usually buried down in the deepest grave of matrimonial silence, between married couples. Having chosen to exhume them, after ten years of burial, she has a weird array. I hear these details from Linley and the doctor: the latter being amused. Of course there is really nothing in it. Humanity has always had a strange avidity for unusual sexual postures, and if a man likes to use his wife, as Benvenuto Cellini says, 'in the Italian way', well that is a matter of taste. But I had hardly expected our game-keeper to be up to so many tricks. No doubt Bertha Coutts herself first put him up to them. In any case, it is a matter of their own personal squalor, and nothing to do with anybody else.

However, everybody listens: as I do myself. A dozen years ago, common decency would have hushed the thing. But common decency no longer exists, and the colliers' wives are all up in arms and unabashed in voice. One would think every child in Tevershall, for the last fifty years, had been an immaculate conception, and every one of our non-conformist females was a shining Joan of Arc. That our estimable game-keeper should have about him a touch of Rabelais seems to make him more monstrous and shocking than a murderer like Crippen. Yet these people in Tevershall are a loose lot, if one is to believe all accounts.

The trouble is, however, the execrable Bertha Coutts has not confined herself to her own experiences and sufferings. She has discovered, at the top of her voice, that her husband has been 'keeping' women down at the cottage, and has made a few random shots at naming the women. This has brought a few decent names trailing through the mud, and the thing has gone quite considerably too far. An injunction has been taken out against the woman.

I have had to interview Mellors about the business, as it was impossible to keep the woman away from the wood. He goes about as usual, with his Miller-of-the-Dee air, I care for nobody, no not I, if nobody care for me! Nevertheless, I shrewdly suspects he feels like a dog with a tin can tied to its tail: though he makes a very good show of pretending the tin can isn't there. But I hear that in the village the women call away their children if he is passing, as if he were the Marquis de Sade in person. He goes on with a certain impudence, but I am afraid the tin can is firmly tied to his tail, and that inwardly he repeats, like Don Rodrigo in the Spanish ballad: 'Ah, now it bites me where I most have sinned!'

I asked him if he thought he would be able to attend to his duty in the wood, and he said he did not think he had neglected it. I told him it was a nuisance to have the woman trespassing: to which he replied that he had no power to arrest her. Then I hinted at the scandal and its unpleasant course. 'Ay,' he said. 'Folks should do their own fuckin', then they wouldn't want to listen to a lot of clatfart about another man's.'

He said it with some bitterness, and no doubt it contains the real germ of truth. The mode of putting it, however, is neither delicate nor respectful. I hinted as much, and then I heard the tin can rattle again. 'It's not for a man i' the shape you're in, Sir Clifford, to twit me for havin' a cod atween my legs.'

These things, said indiscriminately to all and sundry, of course do not help him at all, and the rector, and Finley, and Burroughs all think it would be as well if the man left the place.

I asked him if it was true he entertained ladies down at the cottage, and all he said was: 'Why, what's that to you, Sir Clifford?' I told him I intended to have decency observed on my estate, to which he replied: 'Then you mun button the mouths o' a' th' women.'—When I pressed him about his manner of life at the cottage, he said: 'Surely you might ma'e a scandal out o' me an' my bitch Flossie. You've missed summat there.' As a matter of fact, for an example of impertinence he'd be hard to beat.

I asked him if it would be easy for him to find another job. He said: 'If you're hintin' that you'd like to shunt me out of this job, it'd be easy as wink.' So he made no trouble at all about leaving at the end of next week, and apparently is willing to initiate a young fellow, Joe Chambers, into as many mysteries of the craft as possible. I told him I would give him a month's wages extra, when he left. He said he'd rather I kept my money, as I'd no occasion to ease my conscience. I asked him what he meant, and he said: 'You don't owe me nothing extra, Sir Clifford, so don't pay me nothing extra. If you think you see my shirt hanging out, just tell me.'

Well, there is the end of it for the time being. The woman has gone away: we don't know where to: but she is liable to arrest if she shows her face in Tevershall. And I hear she is mortally afraid of gaol, because she merits it so well. Mellors will depart on Saturday week, and the place will soon become normal again.

Meanwhile, my dear Connie, if you would enjoy to stay in Venice or in Switzerland till the beginning of August, I should be glad to think you were out of all this buzz of nastiness, which will have died quite away by the end of the month.

So you see, we are deep-sea monsters, and when the lobster walks on mud, he stirs it up for everybody. We must perforce take it philosophically.

The irritation, and the lack of any sympathy in any direction, of Clifford's letter, had a bad effect on Connie. But she understood it better when she received the following from Mellors:

The cat is out of the bag, along with various other pussies. You have heard that my wife Bertha came back to my unloving arms, and took up her abode in the cottage: where, to speak disrespectfully, she smelled a rat, in the shape of a little bottle of Coty. Other evidence she did not find, at least for some days, when she began to howl about the burnt photograph. She noticed the glass and the back-board in the square bedroom. Unfortunately, on the back-board somebody had scribbled little sketches, and the initials, several times repeated: C. S. R. This, however, afforded no clue until she broke into the hut, and found one of your books, an autobiography of the actress Judith, with your name, Constance Stewart Reid, on the front page. After this, for some days she went round loudly saying that my paramour was no less a person than Lady Chatterley herself. The news came at last to the rector, Mr Burroughs, and to Sir Clifford. They then proceeded to take legal steps against my liege lady, who for her part disappeared, having always had a mortal fear of the police.

Sir Clifford asked to see me, so I went to him. He talked around things and seemed annoyed with me. Then he asked if I knew that even her ladyship's name had been mentioned. I said I never listened to scandal, and was surprised to hear this bit from Sir Clifford himself. He said, of course it was a great insult, and I told him there was Queen Mary on a calendar in the scullery, no doubt because Her Majesty formed part of my harem. But he didn't appreciate the sarcasm. He as good as told me I was a disreputable character who walked about with my breeches' buttons undone, and I as good as told him he'd nothing to unbutton anyhow, so he gave me the sack, and I leave on Saturday week, and the place thereof shall know me no more.

I shall go to London, and my old landlady, Mrs Inger, 17 Coburg Square, will either give me a room or will find one for me.

Be sure your sins will find you out, especially if you're married and her name's Bertha—

There was not a word about herself, or to her. Connie resented this. He might have said some few words of consolation or reassurance. But she knew he was leaving her free, free to go back to Wragby and to Clifford. She resented that too. He need not be so falsely chivalrous. She wished he had said to Clifford: 'Yes, she is my lover and my mistress and I am proud of it!' But his courage wouldn't carry him so far.

So her name was coupled with his in Tevershall! It was a mess. But that would soon die down.

She was angry, with the complicated and confused anger that made her inert. She did not know what to do nor what to say, so she said and did nothing. She went on at Venice just the same, rowing out in the gondola with Duncan Forbes, bathing, letting the days slip by. Duncan, who had been rather depressingly in love with her ten years ago, was in love with her again. But she said to him: 'I only want one thing of men, and that is, that they should leave me alone.'

So Duncan left her alone: really quite pleased to be able to. All the same, he offered her a soft stream of a queer, inverted sort of love. He wanted to be *with* her.

'Have you ever thought,' he said to her one day, 'how very little people are connected with one another. Look at Daniele! He is handsome as a son of the sun. But see how alone he looks in his handsomeness. Yet I bet he has a wife and family, and couldn't possibly go away from them.'

'Ask him,' said Connie.

Duncan did so. Daniele said he was married, and had two children, both male, aged seven and nine. But he betrayed no emotion over the fact.

'Perhaps only people who are capable of real togetherness have that look of being alone in the universe,' said Connie. 'The others have a certain stickiness, they stick to the mass, like Giovanni.' 'And,' she thought to herself, 'like you, Duncan.'

18

She had to make up her mind what to do. She would leave Venice on the Saturday that he was leaving Wragby: in six days' time. This would bring her to London on the Monday following, and she would then see him. She wrote to him to the London address, asking him to send her a letter to Harland's Hotel, and to call for her on the Monday evening at seven.

Inside herself, she was curiously and complicatedly angry, and all her responses were numb. She refused to confide even in Hilda, and Hilda, offended by her steady silence, had become rather intimate with a Dutch woman. Connie hated these rather stifling intimacies between women, intimacy into which Hilda always entered ponderously.

Sir Malcolm decided to travel with Connie, and Duncan could come on with Hilda. The old artist always did himself well: he took berths on the Orient Express, in spite of Connie's dislike of *trains de luxe*, the atmosphere of vulgar depravity there is aboard them nowadays. However, it would make the journey to Paris shorter.

Sir Malcolm was always uneasy going back to his wife. It was habit carried over from the first wife. But there would be a house-party for the grouse, and he wanted to be well ahead. Connie, sunburnt and handsome, sat in silence, forgetting all about the landscape.

'A little dull for you, going back to Wragby,' said her father, noticing her glumness.

'I'm not sure I shall go back to Wragby,' she said, with startling abruptness, looking into his eyes with her big blue eyes. His big blue eyes took on the frightened look of a man whose social conscience is not quite clear.

'You mean you'll stay on in Paris a while?'

'No! I mean never go back to Wragby.'

He was bothered by his own little problems, and sincerely hoped he was getting none of hers to shoulder.

'How's that, all at once?' he asked.

'I'm going to have a child.'

It was the first time she had uttered the words to any living soul, and it seemed to mark a cleavage in her life.

'How do you know?' said her father.

She smiled.

'How *should* I know?'

'But not Clifford's child, of course?'

'No! Another man's.'

She rather enjoyed tormenting him.

'Do I know the man?' asked Sir Malcolm.

'No! You've never seen him.'

There was a long pause.

'And what are your plans?'

'I don't know. That's the point.'

'No patching it up with Clifford?'

'I suppose Clifford would take it,' said Connie. 'He told me, after last time you talked to him, he wouldn't mind if I had a child, so long as I went about it discreetly.'

'Only sensible thing he could say, under the circumstances. Then I suppose it'll be all right.'

'In what way?' said Connie, looking into her father's eyes. They were big blue eyes rather like her own, but with a certain uneasiness in them, a look sometimes of an uneasy little boy, sometimes a look of sullen selfishness, usually good-humoured and wary.

'You can present Clifford with an heir to all the Chatterleys, and put another baronet in Wragby.'

Sir Malcolm's face smiled with a half-sensual smile.

'But I don't think I want to,' she said.

'Why not? Feeling entangled with the other man? Well! If you want the truth from me, my child, it's this. The world goes on. Wragby stands and will go on standing. The world is more or less a fixed thing and, externally, we have to adapt ourselves to it. Privately, in my private opinion, we can please ourselves. Emotions change. You may like one man this year and another next. But Wragby still stands. Stick by Wragby as far as Wragby sticks by you. Then please yourself. But you'll get very little out of making a break. You can make a break if you wish. You have an independent income, the only thing that never lets you down. But you won't get much out of it. Put a little baronet in Wragby. It's an amusing thing to do.'

And Sir Malcolm sat back and smiled again. Connie did not answer.

'I hope you had a real man at last,' he said to her after a while, sensually alert.

'I did. That's the trouble. There aren't many of them about,' she said.

'No, by God!' he mused. 'There aren't! Well, my dear, to look at you, he was a lucky man. Surely he wouldn't make trouble for you?'

'Oh no! He leaves me my own mistress entirely.'

'Quite! Quite! A genuine man would.'

Sir Malcolm was pleased. Connie was his favourite daughter, he had always liked the female in her. Not so much of her mother in her as in Hilda. And he had always disliked Clifford. So he was pleased, and very tender with his daughter, as if the unborn child were his child.

He drove with her to Hartland's Hotel, and saw her installed: then went round to his club. She had refused his company for the evening.

She found a letter from Mellors.

I won't come round to your hotel, but I'll wait for you outside the Golden Cock in Adam Street at seven.

There he stood, tall and slender, and so different, in a formal suit of thin dark cloth. He had a natural distinction, but he had not the cut-to-pattern look of her class. Yet, she saw at once, he could go anywhere. He had a native breeding which was really much nicer than the cut-to-pattern class thing.

'Ah, there you are! How well you look!'

'Yes! But not you.'

She looked in his face anxiously. It was thin, and the cheekbones showed. But his eyes smiled at her, and she felt at home with him. There it was: suddenly, the tension of keeping up her appearances fell from her. Something flowed out of him physically, that made her feel inwardly at ease and happy, at home. With a woman's now alert instinct for happiness, she registered it at once. 'I'm happy when he's there!' Not all the sunshine of Venice had given her this inward expansion and warmth.

'Was it horrid for you?' she asked as she sat opposite him at table. He was too thin; she saw it now. His hand lay as she knew it, with the curious loose forgottenness of a sleeping animal. She wanted so much to take it and kiss it. But she did not quite dare.

'People are always horrid,' he said.

'And did you mind very much?'

'I minded, as I always shall mind. And I knew I was a fool to mind.'

'Did you feel like a dog with a tin can tied to its tail? Clifford said you felt like that.'

He looked at her. It was cruel of her at that moment: for his pride had suffered bitterly.

'I suppose I did,' he said.

She never knew the fierce bitterness with which he resented insult.

There was a long pause.

'And did you miss me?' she asked.

'I was glad you were out of it.'

Again there was a pause.

'But did people *believe* about you and me?' she asked.

'No! I don't think so for a moment.'

'Did Clifford?'

'I should say not. He put it off without thinking about it. But naturally it made him want to see the last of me.'

'I'm going to have a child.'

The expression died utterly out of his face, out of his whole body. He looked at her with darkened eyes, whose look she could not understand at all: like some dark-flamed spirit looking at her.

'Say you're glad!' she pleaded, groping for his hand. And she saw a certain exultance spring up in him. But it was netted down by things she could not understand.

'It's the future,' he said.

'But aren't you glad?' she persisted.

'I have such a terrible mistrust of the future.'

'But you needn't be troubled by any responsibility. Clifford would have it as his own, he'd be glad.'

She saw him go pale, and recoil under this. He did not answer.

'Shall I go back to Clifford and put a little baronet into Wragby?' she asked.

He looked at her, pale and very remote. The ugly little grin flickered on his face.

'You wouldn't have to tell him who the father was?'

'Oh!' she said; 'he'd take it even then, if I wanted him to.'

He thought for a time.

'Ay!' he said at last, to himself. 'I suppose he would.'

There was silence. A big gulf was between them.

'But you don't want me to go back to Clifford, do you?' she asked him.

'What do you want yourself?' he replied.

'I want to live with you,' she said simply.

In spite of himself, little flames ran over his belly as he heard her say it, and he dropped his head. Then he looked up at her again, with those haunted eyes.

'If it's worth it to you,' he said. 'I've got nothing.'

'You've got more than most men. Come, you know it,' she said.

'In one way, I know it.' He was silent for a time, thinking. Then he resumed: 'They used to say I had too much of the woman in me. But it's not that. I'm not a woman not because I don't want to shoot birds, neither because I don't want to make money, or get on. I could have got on in the army, easily, but I didn't like the army. Though I could manage the men all right: they liked me and they had a bit of a holy fear of me when I got mad. No, it was stupid, dead-handed higher authority that made the army dead: absolutely fool-dead. I like men, and men like me. But I can't stand the twaddling bossy impudence of the people who run this world. That's why I can't get on. I hate the impudence of money, and I hate the impudence of class. So in the world as it is, what have I to offer a woman?'

'But why offer anything? It's not a bargain. It's just that we love one another,' she said.

'Nay, nay! It's more than that. Living is moving and moving on. My life won't go down the proper gutters, it just won't. So I'm a bit of a waste ticket by myself. And I've no business to take a woman into my life, unless my life does something and gets somewhere, inwardly at least, to keep us both fresh. A man must offer a woman *some* meaning in his life, if it's going to be an isolated life, and if she's a genuine woman. I can't be just your male concubine.'

'Why not?' she said.

'Why, because I can't. And you would soon hate it.'

'As if you couldn't trust me,' she said.

The grin flickered on his face.

'The money is yours, the position is yours, the decisions will lie with you. I'm not just my Lady's fucker, after all.'

'What else are you?'

'You may well ask. It no doubt is invisible. Yet I'm something to myself at least. I can see the point of my own existence, though I can quite understand nobody else's seeing it.'

'And will your existence have less point, if you live with me?'

He paused a long time before replying:

'It might.'

She too stayed to think about it.

'And what is the point of your existence?'

'I tell you, it's invisible. I don't believe in the world, nor in money, nor in advancement, nor in the future of our civilization. If there's got to be a future for humanity, there'll have to be a very big change from what now is.'

'And what will the real future have to be like?'

'God knows! I can feel something inside me, all mixed up with a lot of rage. But what it really amounts to, I don't know.'

'Shall I tell you?' she said, looking into his face. 'Shall I tell you what you have that other men don't have, and that will make the future? Shall I tell you?'

'Tell me then,' he replied.

'It's the courage of your own tenderness, that's what it is: like when you put your hand on my tail and say I've got a pretty tail.'

The grin came flickering on his face.

'That!' he said.

Then he sat thinking.

'Ay!' he said. 'You're right. It's that really. It's that all the way through. I knew it with the men. I had to be in touch with them, physically, and not go back on it. I had to be bodily aware of them and a bit tender to them, even if I put 'em through hell. It's a question of awareness, as Buddha said. But even he fought shy of the bodily awareness, and that natural physical tenderness, which is the best, even between men; in a proper manly way. Makes 'em really manly, not so monkeyish. Ay! it's tenderness, really; it's cunt-awareness. Sex is really only touch, the closest of all touch. And it's touch we're afraid of. We're only half-conscious, and half alive. We've got to come alive and aware. Especially the English have got to get into touch with one another, a bit delicate and a bit tender. It's our crying need.'

She looked at him.

'Then why are you afraid of me?' she said.

He looked at her a long time before he answered.

'It's the money, really, and the position. It's the world in you.'

'But isn't there tenderness in me?' she said wistfully.

He looked down at her, with darkened, abstract eyes.

'Ay! It comes an' goes, like in me.'

'But can't you trust it between you and me?' she asked, gazing anxiously at him.

She saw his face all softening down, losing its armour.

'Maybe!' he said.

They were both silent.

'I want you to hold me in your arms,' she said. 'I want you to tell me you are glad we are having a child.'

She looked so lovely and warm and wistful, his bowels stirred towards her.

'I suppose we can go to my room,' he said. 'Though it's scandalous again.'

But she saw the forgetfulness of the world coming over him again, his face taking the soft, pure look of tender passion.

They walked by the remoter streets to Coburg Square, where he had a room at the top of the house, an attic room where he cooked for himself on a gas ring. It was small, but decent and tidy.

She took off her things, and made him do the same. She was lovely in the soft first flush of her pregnancy.

'I ought to leave you alone,' he said.

'No!' she said. 'Love me! Love me, and say you'll keep me. Say you'll keep me! Say you'll never let me go, to the world nor to anybody.'

She crept close against him, clinging fast to his thin, strong naked body, the only home she had ever known.

'Then I'll keep thee,' he said. 'If tha wants it, then I'll keep thee.'

He held her round and fast.

'And say you're glad about the child,' she repeated. 'Kiss it! Kiss my womb and say you're glad it's there.'

But that was more difficult for him.

'I've a dread of puttin' children i' th' world,' he said. 'I've such a dread o' th' future for 'em.'

'But you've put it into me. Be tender to it, and that will be its future already. Kiss it!'

He quivered, because it was true. 'Be tender to it, and that will be its future.'—At that moment he felt a sheer love for the woman. He kissed her belly and her mound of Venus, to kiss close to the womb and the foetus within the womb.

'Oh, you love me! You love me!' she said, in a little cry like one of her blind, inarticulate love cries. And he went in to her softly, feeling the stream of tenderness flowing in release from his bowels to hers, the bowels of compassion kindled between them.

And he realized as he went into her that this was the thing he had to do, to come into tender touch, without losing his pride or his dignity or his integrity as a man. After all, if she had money and means, and he had none, he should be too proud and honourable to hold back his tenderness from her on that account. 'I stand for the touch of bodily awareness between human beings,' he said to himself, 'and the touch of tenderness. And she is my mate. And it is a battle against the money, and the machine, and the insentient ideal monkeyishness of the world. And she will stand behind me there. Thank God I've got a woman! Thank God I've got a woman who is with me, and tender and aware of me. Thank God she's not a bully, nor a fool. Thank God she's a tender, aware woman.' And as his seed sprang in her, his soul sprang towards her too, in the creative act that is far more than procreative.

She was quite determined now that there should be no parting between him and her. But the ways and means were still to settle.

'Did you hate Bertha Coutts?' she asked him.

'Don't talk to me about her.'

'Yes! You must let me. Because once you liked her. And once you were as intimate with her as you are with me. So you have to tell me. Isn't it rather terrible, when you've been intimate with her, to hate her so? Why is it?'

'I don't know. She sort of kept her will ready against me, always, always: her ghastly female will: her freedom! A woman's ghastly freedom that ends in the most beastly bullying! Oh, she always kept her freedom against me, like vitriol in my face.'

'But she's not free of you even now. Does she still love you?'

'No, no! If she's not free of me, it's because she's got that mad rage, she must try to bully me.'

'But she must have loved you.'

'No! Well, in specks she did. She was drawn to me. And I think even that she hated. She loved me in moments. But she always took it back, and started bullying. Her deepest desire was to bully me, and there was no altering her. Her *will* was wrong, from the first.'

'But perhaps she felt you didn't really love her, and she wanted to make you.'

'My God, it was bloody making.'

'But you didn't really love her, did you? You did her that wrong.'

'How could I? I began to. I began to love her. But somehow, she always ripped me up. No, don't let's talk of it. It was a doom, that was. And she was a doomed woman. This last time, I'd have shot her like I shoot a stoat, if I'd but been allowed: a raving, doomed thing in the shape of a woman! If only I could have shot her, and ended the whole misery! It ought to be allowed. When a woman gets absolutely possessed by her own will, her own will set against everything, then it's fearful, and she should be shot at last.'

'And shouldn't men be shot at last, if they get possessed by their own will?'

'Ay!–the same! But I must get free of her, or she'll be at me again. I wanted to tell you. I must get a divorce if I possibly can. So we must be careful. We mustn't really be seen together, you and I. I never, *never* could stand it if she came down on me and you.'

Connie pondered this.

'Then we can't be together?' she said.

'Not for six months or so. But I think my divorce will go through in September; then till March.'

'But the baby will probably be born at the end of February,' she said.

He was silent.

'I could wish the Cliffords and Berthas all dead,' he said.

'It's not being very tender to them,' she said.

'Tender to them? Yea, even then the tenderest thing you could do for them, perhaps, would be to give them death. They can't live! They only frustrate life. Their souls are awful inside them. Death ought to be sweet to them. And I ought to be allowed to shoot them.'

'But you wouldn't do it,' she said.

'I would though! and with less qualms than I shoot a weasel. It anyhow has a prettiness and a loneliness. But they are legion. Oh, I'd shoot them.'

'Then perhaps it is just as well you daren't.'

'Well.'

Connie had now plenty to think of. It was evident he wanted absolutely to be free of Bertha Coutts. And she felt he was right. The last attack had been too grim.–This meant her living alone, till spring. Perhaps she could get divorced from Clifford. But how? If Mellors were named, then there was an end to *his* divorce. How loathsome! Couldn't one go right away, to the far ends of the earth, and be free from it all?

One could not. The far ends of the world are not five minutes from Charing Cross, nowadays. While the wireless is active, there are no far ends of the earth. Kings of Dahomey and Lamas of Tibet listen in to London and New York.

Patience! Patience! The world is a vast and ghastly intricacy of mechanism, and one has to be very wary, not to get mangled by it.

Connie confided in her father.

'You see, Father, he was Clifford's game-keeper: but he was an officer in the army in India. Only he is like Colonel C. E. Florence, who preferred to become a private soldier again.'

Sir Malcolm, however, had no sympathy with the unsatisfactory mysticism of the famous C. E. Florence. He saw too much advertisement behind all the humility. It looked just like the sort of conceit the knight most loathed, the conceit of self-abasement.

'Where did your game-keeper spring from?' asked Sir Malcolm irritably.

'He was a collier's son in Tevershall. But he's absolutely presentable.'

The knighted artist became more angry.

'Looks to me like a gold-digger,' he said. 'And you're a pretty easy gold-mine, apparently.'

'No, Father, it's not like that. You'd know if you saw him. He's a man. Clifford always detested him for not being humble.'

'Apparently he had a good instinct, for once.'

What Sir Malcolm could not bear was the scandal of his daughter's having an intrigue with a game-keeper. He did not mind the intrigue: he minded the scandal.

'I care nothing about the fellow. He's evidently been able to get round you all right. But, by God, think of all the talk. Think of your step-mother, how she'll take it!'

'I know,' said Connie. 'Talk is beastly: especially if you live in society. And he wants so much to get his own divorce. I thought we might perhaps say it was another man's child, and not mention Mellors' name at all.'

'Another man's! What other man's?'

'Perhaps Duncan Forbes. He has been our friend all his life. And he's a fairly well-known artist. And he's fond of me.'

'Well I'm damned! Poor Duncan! And what's he going to get out of it?'

'I don't know. But he might rather like it, even.'

'He might, might he? Well, he's a funny man if he does. Why, you've never even had an affair with him, have you?'

'No! But he doesn't really want it. He only loves me to be near him, but not to touch him.'

'My God, what a generation!'

'He would like me most of all to be a model for him to paint from. Only I never wanted to.'

'God help him! But he looks down-trodden enough for anything.'

'Still, you wouldn't mind so much the talk about him?'

'My God, Connie, all the bloody contriving!'

'I know! It's sickening! But what can I do?'

'Contriving, conniving; conniving, contriving! Makes a man think he's lived too long.'

'Come, Father, if you haven't done a good deal of contriving and conniving in your time, you may talk.'

'But it was different, I assure you.'

'It's *always* different.'

Hilda arrived, also furious when she heard of the new developments. And she also simply could not stand the thought of a public scandal about her sister and a game-keeper. Too, too humiliating!

'Why should we not just disappear, separately, to British Columbia, and have no scandal?' said Connie.

But that was no good. The scandal would come out just the same. And if Connie was going with the man, she'd better be able to marry him. This was Hilda's opinion. Sir Malcolm wasn't sure. The affair might still blow over.

'But will you see him, Father?'

Poor Sir Malcolm! he was by no means keen on it. And poor Mellors, he was still less keen. Yet the meeting took place: a lunch in a private room at the club, the two men alone, looking one another up and down.

Sir Malcolm drank a fair amount of whisky, Mellors also drank. And they talked all the while about India, on which the young man was well informed. This lasted during the meal. Only when coffee was served, and the waiter had gone, Sir Malcolm lit a cigar and said, heartily:

'Well, young man, and what about my daughter?'

The grin flickered on Mellors's face.

'Well, Sir, and what about her?'

'You've got a baby in her all right.'

'I have that honour!' grinned Mellors.

'Honour, by God!' Sir Malcolm gave a little squirting laugh, and became Scotch and lewd. 'Honour! How was the going, eh? Good, my boy, what?'

'Good!'

'I'll bet it was! Ha-ha! My daughter, chip of the old block, what! I never went back on a good bit of fucking, myself. Though her mother, oh, holy saints!' He rolled his eyes to heaven. 'But you warmed her up, oh, you warmed her up, I can see that. Ha-ha! My blood in her! You set fire to her haystack all right. Ha-ha-ha! I was jolly glad of it, I can tell you. She needed it. Oh, she's a nice girl, she's a nice girl, and I knew she'd be good going, if only some damned man would set her stack on fire! Ha-ha-ha! A game-keeper, eh, my boy! Bloody good poacher, if you ask me. Ha-ha! But now, look here, speaking seriously, what are we going to do about it? Speaking seriously, you know!'

Speaking seriously, they didn't get very far. Mellors, though a little tipsy, was much the soberer of the two. He kept the conversation as intelligent as possible: which isn't saying much.

'So you're a game-keeper! Oh, you're quite right! That sort of game is worth a man's while, eh, what? The test of a woman is when you pinch her bottom. You can tell just by the feel of her bottom if she's going to come up all right. Ha-ha! I envy you, my boy. How old are you?'

'Thirty-nine.'

The knight lifted his eyebrows.

'As much as that! Well, you've another good twenty years, by the look of you. Oh, game-keeper or not, you're a good cock. I can see that with one eye shut. Not like that blasted Clifford! A lily-livered hound with never a fuck in him, never had. I like you, my boy, I'll bet you've a good cod on you; ho, you're a bantam, I can see that. You're a fighter. Game-keeper! Ha-ha, by crikey, I wouldn't trust my game to you! But look here, seriously, what are we going to do about it? The world's full of blasted old women.'

Seriously, they didn't do anything about it, except establish the old free-masonry of male sensuality between them.

'And look here, my boy, if ever I can do anything for you, you can rely on me. Game-keeper! Christ, but it's rich! I like it! Oh, I like it! Shows the girl's got spunk. What? After all, you know, she has her own income, moderate, moderate, but above starvation. And I'll leave her what I've got. By God, I will. She deserves it, for showing spunk, in a world of old women. I've been struggling to get myself clear of the skirts of old women for seventy years, and haven't managed it yet. But you're the man, I can see that.'

'I'm glad you think so. They usually tell me, in a sideways fashion, that I'm the monkey.'

'Oh they would! My dear fellow, what could you be but a monkey, to all the old women?'

They parted most genially, and Mellors laughed inwardly all the time for the rest of the day.

The following day he had lunch with Connie and Hilda, at some discreet place.

'It's a very great pity it's such an ugly situation all round,' said Hilda.

'I had a lot o' fun out of it,' said he.

'I think you might have avoided putting children into the world until you were both free to marry and have children.'

'The Lord blew a bit too soon on the spark,' said he.

'I think the Lord had nothing to do with it. Of course, Connie has enough money to keep you both, but the situation is unbearable.'

'But then you don't have to bear more than a small corner of it, do you?' said he.

'If you'd been in her own class.'

'Or if I'd been in a cage at the Zoo.'

There was silence.

'I think,' said Hilda, 'it will be best if she names quite another man as co-respondent, and you stay out of it altogether.'

'But I thought I'd put my foot right in.'

'I mean in the divorce proceedings.'

He gazed at her in wonder. Connie had not dared mention the Duncan scheme to him.

'I don't follow,' he said.

'We have a friend who would probably agree to be named as co-respondent, so that your name need not appear,' said Hilda.

'You mean a man?'

'Of course!'

'But she's got no other?'

He looked in wonder at Connie.

'No, no!' she said hastily. 'Only that old friendship, quite simple, no love.'

'Then why should the fellow take the blame? If he's had nothing out of you?'

'Some men are chivalrous and don't only count what they get out of a woman,' said Hilda.

'One for me, eh? But who's the johnny?'

'A friend whom we've known since we were children in Scotland, an artist.'

'Duncan Forbes!' he said at once, for Connie had talked to him. 'And how would you shift the blame on to him?'

'They would stay together in some hotel, or she could even stay in his apartment.'

'Seems to me like a lot of fuss for nothing,' he said.

'What else do you suggest?' said Hilda. 'If your name appears, you will get no divorce from your wife, who is apparently quite an impossible person to be mixed up with.'

'All that!' he said grimly.

There was a long silence.

'We could go right away,' he said.

'There is no right away for Connie,' said Hilda. 'Clifford is too well known.'

Again the silence of pure frustration.

'The world is what it is. If you want to live together without being persecuted, you will have to marry. To marry, you both have to be divorced. So how are you both going about it?'

He was silent for a long time.

'How are *you* going about it for us?' he said.

'We will see if Duncan will consent to figure as co-respondent: then we must get Clifford to divorce Connie: and you must go on with your divorce, and you must both keep apart till you are free.'

'Sounds like a lunatic asylum.'

'Possibly! And the world would look on you as lunatics: or worse.'

'What is worse?'

'Criminals, I suppose.'

'Hope I can plunge in the dagger a few more times yet,' he said, grinning. Then he was silent, and angry.

'Well!' he said at last. 'I agree to anything. The world is a raving idiot. and no man can kill it: though I'll do my best. But you're right. We must rescue ourselves as best we can.'

He looked in humiliation, anger, weariness and misery at Connie.

'Ma lass!' he said. 'The world's goin' to put salt on thy tail.'

'Not if we don't let it,' she said.

She minded this conniving against the world less than he did.

Duncan, when approached, also insisted on seeing the delinquent game-keeper, so there was a dinner, this time in his flat: the four of them. Duncan was a rather short, broad, dark-skinned, taciturn Hamlet of a fellow with straight black hair and a weird Celtic conceit of himself. His art was all tubes and valves and spirals and strange colours, ultra-modern, yet with a certain power, even a certain purity of form and tone: only Mellors thought it cruel and repellent. He did not venture to say so, for Duncan was almost insane on the point of his art: it was a personal cult, a personal religion with him.

They were looking at the pictures in the studio, and Duncan kept his smallish brown eyes on the other man. He wanted to hear what the game-keeper would say. He knew already Connie's and Hilda's opinions.

'It is like a pure bit of murder,' said Mellors at last; a speech Duncan by no means expected from a game-keeper.

'And who is murdered?' asked Hilda, rather coldly and sneeringly.

'Me! It murders all the bowels of compassion in a man.'

A wave of pure hate came out of the artist. He heard the note of dislike in the other man's voice, and the note of contempt. And he himself loathed the mention of bowels of compassion. Sickly sentiment!

Mellors stood rather tall and thin, worn-looking, gazing with flickering detachment that was something like the dancing of a moth on the wing, at the pictures.

'Perhaps stupidity is murdered; sentimental stupidity,' sneered the artist.

'Do you think so? I think all these tubes and corrugated vibrations are stupid enough for anything, and pretty sentimental. They show a lot of self-pity and an awful lot of nervous self-opinion, seems to me.'

In another wave of hate the artist's face looked yellow. But with a sort of silent *hauteur* he turned the pictures to the wall.

'I think we may go to the dining-room,' he said.

And they trailed off, dismally.

After coffee, Duncan said:

'I don't at all mind posing as the father of Connie's child. But only on the condition that she'll come and pose as a model for me. I've wanted her for years, and she's always refused.' He uttered it with the dark finality of an inquisitor announcing an *auto da fe*.

'Ah!' said Mellors. 'You only do it on condition, then?'

'Quite! I only do it on that condition.' The artist tried to put the utmost contempt of the other person into his speech. He put a little too much.

'Better have me as a model at the same time,' said Mellors. 'Better do us in a group, Vulcan and Venus under the net of art. I used to be a blacksmith, before I was a game-keeper.'

'Thank you,' said the artist. 'I don't think Vulcan has a figure that interests me.'

'Not even if it was tubified and titivated up?'

There was no answer. The artist was too haughty for further words.

It was a dismal party, in which the artist henceforth steadily ignored the presence of the other man, and talked only briefly, as if the words were wrung out of the depths of his gloomy portentousness, to the women.

'You didn't like him, but he's better than that, really. He's really kind,' Connie explained as they left.

'He's a little black pup with a corrugated distemper,' said Mellors.

'No, he wasn't nice today.'

'And will you go and be a model to him?'

'Oh, I don't really mind any more. He won't touch me. And I don't mind anything, if it paves the way to a life together for you and me.'

'But he'll only shit on you on canvas.'

'I don't care. He'll only be painting his own feelings for me, and I don't mind if he does that. I wouldn't have him touch me, not for anything. But if he thinks he can do anything with his owlish arty staring, let him stare. He can make as many empty tubes and corrugations out of me as he likes. It's his funeral. He hated you for what you said: that his tubified art is sentimental and self-important. But of course it's true.'

19

Dear Clifford, I am afraid what you foresaw has happened. I am really in love with another man, and do hope you will divorce me. I am staying at present with Duncan in his flat. I told you he was at Venice with us. I'm awfully unhappy for your sake: but do try to take it quietly. You don't really need me any more, and I can't bear to come back to Wragby. I'm awfully sorry. But do try to forgive me, and divorce me and find someone better. I'm not really the right person for you, I am too impatient and selfish, I suppose. But I can't ever come back to live with you again. And I feel so frightfully sorry about it all, for your sake. But if you don't let yourself get worked up, you'll see you won't mind so frightfully. You didn't really care about me personally. So do forgive me and get rid of me.

Clifford was not *inwardly* surprised to get this letter. Inwardly, he had known for a long time she was leaving him. But he had absolutely refused any outward admission of it. Therefore, outwardly, it came as the most terrible blow and shock to him. He had kept the surface of his confidence in her quite serene.

And that is how we are. By strength of will we cut off our inner intuitive knowledge from admitted consciousness. This causes a state of dread, or apprehension, which makes the blow ten times worse when it does fall.

Clifford was like a hysterical child. He gave Mrs Bolton a terrible shock, sitting up in bed ghastly and blank.

'Why, Sir Clifford, whatever's the matter?'

No answer! She was terrified lest he had had a stroke. She hurried and felt his face, took his pulse.

'Is there a pain? Do try and tell me where it hurts you. Do tell me!'

No answer!

'Oh dear, oh dear! Then I'll telephone to Sheffield for Dr Carrington, and Dr Lecky may as well run round straight away.'

She was moving to the door, when he said in a hollow tone: 'No!'

She stopped and gazed at him. His face was yellow, blank, and like the face of an idiot.

'Do you mean you'd rather I didn't fetch the doctor?'

'Yes! I don't want him,' came the sepulchral voice.

'Oh, but Sir Clifford, you're ill, and I daren't take the responsibility. I *must* send for the doctor, or *I* shall be blamed.'

A pause: then the hollow voice said:

'I'm not ill. My wife isn't coming back.'—It was as if an image spoke.

'Not coming back? you mean her ladyship?' Mrs Bolton moved a little nearer to the bed. 'Oh, don't you believe it. You can trust her ladyship to come back.'

The image in the bed did not change, but it pushed a letter over the counterpane.

'Read it!' said the sepulchral voice.

'Why, if it's a letter from her ladyship, I'm sure her ladyship wouldn't want me to read her letter to you, Sir Clifford. You can tell me what she says, if you wish.'

'Read it!' repeated the voice.

'Why, if I must, I do it to obey you, Sir Clifford,' she said.

And she read the letter.

'Well, I *am* surprised at her ladyship,' she said. 'She promised so faithfully she'd come back!'

The face in the bed seemed to deepen its expression of wild, but motionless distraction. Mrs Bolton looked at it and was worried. She knew what she was up against: male hysteria. She had not nursed soldiers without learning something about that very unpleasant disease.

She was a little impatient of Sir Clifford. Any man in his senses must have *known* his wife was in love with somebody else, and was going to leave. Even, she was sure, Sir Clifford was inwardly absolutely aware of it, only he wouldn't admit it to himself. If he would have admitted it, and prepared himself for it: or if he would have admitted it, and actively struggled with his wife against it: that would have been acting like a man. But no! he knew it, and all the time tried to kid himself it wasn't so. He felt the devil twisting his tail, and pretended it was the angels smiling on him. This state of falsity had now brought on that crisis of falsity and dislocation, hysteria, which is a form of insanity. 'It comes,' she thought to herself, hating him a little, 'because he always thinks of himself. He's so wrapped up in his own immortal self, that when he does get a shock he's like a mummy tangled in its own bandages. Look at him!'

But hysteria is dangerous: and she was a nurse, it was her duty to pull him out. Any attempt to rouse his manhood and his pride would only make him worse: for his manhood was dead, temporarily if not finally. He would only squirm softer and softer, like a worm, and become more dislocated.

The only thing was to release his self-pity. Like the lady in Tennyson, he must weep or he must die.

So Mrs Bolton began to weep first. She covered her face with her hand and burst into little wild sobs. 'I would never have believed it of her ladyship, I wouldn't!' she wept, suddenly summoning up all her old grief and sense of woe, and weeping the tears of her own bitter chagrin. Once she started, her weeping was genuine enough, for she had had something to weep for.

Clifford thought of the way he had been betrayed by the woman Connie, and in a contagion of grief, tears filled his eyes and began to run down his cheeks. He was weeping for himself. Mrs Bolton, as soon as she saw the tears running over his blank face, hastily wiped her own wet cheeks on her little handkerchief, and leaned towards him.

'Now, don't you fret, Sir Clifford!' she said, in a luxury of emotion. 'Now, don't you fret, don't, you'll only do yourself an injury!'

His body shivered suddenly in an indrawn breath of silent sobbing, and the tears ran quicker down his face. She laid her hand on his arm, and her own tears fell again. Again the shiver went through him, like a convulsion, and she laid her arm round his shoulder. 'There, there! There, there! Don't you fret, then, don't you! Don't you fret!' she moaned to him, while her own tears fell. And she drew him to her, and held her arms round his great shoulders, while he laid his face on her bosom and sobbed, shaking and hulking his huge shoulders, whilst she softly stroked his dusky-blond hair and said: 'There! There! There! There then! There then! Never you mind! Never you mind, then!'

And he put his arms round her and clung to her like a child, wetting the bib of her starched white apron, and the bosom of her pale-blue cotton dress, with his tears. He had let himself go altogether, at last.

So at length she kissed him, and rocked him on her bosom, and in her heart she said to herself: 'Oh, Sir Clifford! Oh, high and mighty Chatterleys! Is this what you've come down to!' And finally he even went to sleep, like a child. And she felt worn out, and went to her own room, where she laughed and cried at once, with a hysteria of her own. It was so ridiculous! It was so awful! Such a come-down! So shameful! And it *was* so upsetting as well.

After this, Clifford became like a child with Mrs Bolton. He would hold her hand, and rest his head on her breast, and when she once lightly kissed him, he said: 'Yes! Do kiss me! Do kiss me!' And when she sponged his great blond body, he would say the same: 'Do kiss me!' and she would lightly kiss his body, anywhere, half in mockery.

And he lay with a queer, blank face like a child, with a bit of the wonderment of a child. And he would gaze on her with wide, childish eyes, in a relaxation of madonna-worship. It was sheer relaxation on his part, letting go all his manhood, and sinking back to a childish position that was really perverse. And then he would put his hand into her bosom and feel her breasts, and kiss them in exultation, the exultation of perversity, of being a child when he was a man.

Mrs Bolton was both thrilled and ashamed, she both loved and hated it. Yet she never rebuffed nor rebuked him. And they drew into a closer physical intimacy, an intimacy of perversity, when he was a child stricken with an apparent candour and an apparent wonderment, that looked almost like a religious exaltation: the perverse and literal rendering of: 'except ye become again as a little child.'–While she was the Magna Mater, full of power and potency, having the great blond child-man under her will and her stroke entirely.

The curious thing was that when this child-man, which Clifford was now and which he had been becoming for years, emerged into the world, it was much sharper and keener than the real man he used to be. This perverted child-man was now a *real* business-man; when it was a question of affairs, he was an absolute he-man, sharp as a needle, and impervious as a bit of steel. When he was out among men, seeking his own ends, and 'making good' his colliery workings, he had an almost uncanny shrewdness, hardness, and a straight sharp punch. It was as if his very passivity and prostitution to the Magna Mater gave him insight into material business affairs, and lent him a certain remarkable inhuman force. The wallowing in private emotion, the utter abasement of his manly self, seemed to lend him a second nature, cold, almost visionary, business-clever. In business he was quite inhuman.

And in this Mrs Bolton triumphed. 'How he's getting on!' she would say to herself in pride. 'And that's my doing! My word, he'd never have got on like this with Lady Chatterley. She was not the one to put a man forward. She wanted too much for herself.'

At the same time, in some corner of her weird female soul, how she despised him and hated him! He was to her the fallen beast, the squirming monster. And while she aided and abetted him all she could, away in the remotest corner of her ancient healthy womanhood she despised him with a savage contempt that knew no bounds. The merest tramp was better than he.

His behaviour with regard to Connie was curious. He insisted on seeing her again. He insisted, moreover, on her coming to Wragby. On this point he was finally and absolutely fixed. Connie had promised to come back to Wragby, faithfully.

'But is it any use?' said Mrs Bolton. 'Can't you let her go, and be rid of her?'

'No! She said she was coming back, and she's got to come.'

Mrs Bolton opposed him no more. She knew what she was dealing with.

I needn't tell you what effect your letter has had on me [he wrote to Connie to London]. Perhaps you can imagine it if you try, though no doubt you won't trouble to use your imagination on my behalf.

I can only say one thing in answer: I must see you personally, here at Wragby, before I can do anything. You promised faithfully to come back to Wragby, and I hold you to the promise. I don't believe anything nor understand anything until I see you personally, here under normal circumstances. I needn't tell you that nobody here suspects anything, so your return would be quite normal. Then if you feel, after we have talked things over, that you still remain in the same mind, no doubt we can come to terms.

Connie showed this letter to Mellors.

'He wants to begin his revenge on you,' he said, handing the letter back.

Connie was silent. She was somewhat surprised to find that she was afraid of Clifford. She was afraid to go near him. She was afraid of him as if he were evil and dangerous.

'What shall I do?' she said.

'Nothing, if you don't want to do anything.'

She replied, trying to put Clifford off. He answered:

If you don't come back to Wragby now, I shall consider that you are coming back one day, and act accordingly. I shall just go on the same, and wait for you here, if I wait for fifty years.

She was frightened. This was bullying of an insidious sort. She had no doubt he meant what he said. He would not divorce her, and the child would be his, unless she could find some means of establishing its illegitimacy.

After a time of worry and harassment, she decided to go to Wragby. Hilda would go with her. She wrote this to Clifford. He replied:

I shall not welcome your sister, but I shall not deny her the door. I have no doubt she has connived at your desertion of your duties and responsibilities, so do not expect me to show pleasure in seeing her.

They went to Wragby. Clifford was away when they arrived. Mrs Bolton received them.

'Oh, your Ladyship, it isn't the happy home-coming we hoped for, is it!' she said.

'Isn't it?' said Connie.

So this woman knew! How much did the rest of the servants know or suspect?

She entered the house, which now she hated with every fibre in her body. The great, rambling mass of a place seemed evil to her, just a menace over her. She was no longer its mistress, she was its victim.

'I can't stay long here,' she whispered to Hilda, terrified.

And she suffered going into her own bedroom, re-entering into possession as if nothing had happened. She hated every minute inside the Wragby walls.

They did not meet Clifford till they went down to dinner. He was dressed, and with a black tie: rather reserved, and very much the superior gentleman. He behaved perfectly politely during the meal, and kept a polite sort of conversation going: but it seemed all touched with insanity.

'How much do the servants know?' asked Connie, when the woman was out of the room.

'Of your intentions? Nothing whatsoever.'

'Mrs Bolton knows.'

He changed colour.

'Mrs Bolton is not exactly one of the servants,' he said.

'Oh, I don't mind.'

There was tension till after coffee, when Hilda said she would go up to her room.

Clifford and Connie sat in silence when she had gone. Neither would begin to speak. Connie was so glad that he wasn't taking the pathetic line, she kept him up to as much haughtiness as possible. She just sat silent and looked down at her hands.

'I suppose you don't at all mind having gone back on your word?' he said at last.

'I can't help it,' she murmured.

'But if you can't, who can?'

'I suppose nobody.'

He looked at her with curious cold rage. He was used to her. She was as it were embedded in his will. How dared she now go back on him, and destroy the fabric of his daily existence? How dared she try to cause this derangement of his personality?

'And for *what* do you want to go back on everything?' he insisted.

'Love!' she said. It was best to be hackneyed.

'Love of Duncan Forbes? But you didn't think that worth having, when you met me. Do you mean to say you now love him better than anything else in life?'

'One changes,' she said.

'Possibly! Possibly you may have whims. But you still have to convince me of the importance of the change. I merely don't believe in your love of Duncan Forbes.'

'But why *should* you believe in it? You have only to divorce me, not to believe in my feelings.'

'And why should I divorce you?'

'Because I don't want to live here any more. And you really don't want me.'

'Pardon me! I don't change. For my part, since you are my wife, I should prefer that you should stay under my roof in dignity and quiet. Leaving aside personal feelings, and I assure you, on my part it is leaving aside a great deal, it is bitter as death to me to have this order of life broken up, here in Wragby, and the decent round of daily life smashed, just for some whim of yours.'

After a time of silence she said:

'I can't help it. I've got to go. I expect I shall have a child.'

He too was silent for a time.

'And is it for the child's sake you must go?' he asked at length.

She nodded.

'And why? Is Duncan Forbes so keen on his spawn?'

'Surely keener than you would be,' she said.

'But really? I want my wife, and I see no reason for letting her go. If she likes to bear a child under my roof, she is welcome, and the child is welcome: provided that the decency and order of life is preserved. Do you mean to tell me that Duncan Forbes has a greater hold over you? I don't believe it.'

There was a pause.

'But don't you see,' said Connie. 'I *must* go away from you, and I *must* live with the man I love.'

'No, I don't see it! I don't give tuppence for your love, nor for the man you love. I don't believe in that sort of cant.'

'But you see, I do.'

'Do you? My dear Madam, you are too intelligent, I assure you, to believe in your own love for Duncan Forbes. Believe me, even now you really care more for me. So why should I give in to such nonsense!'

She felt he was right there. And she felt she could keep silent no longer.

'Because it isn't Duncan that I *do* love,' she said, looking up at him. 'We only said it was Duncan, to spare your feelings.'

'To spare my feelings?'

'Yes! Because who I really love, and it'll make you hate me, is Mr Mellors, who was our game-keeper here.'

If he could have sprung out of his chair, he would have done so. His face went yellow, and his eyes bulged with disaster as he glared at her.

Then he dropped back in the chair, gasping and looking up at the ceiling.

At length he sat up.

'Do you mean to say you're telling me the truth?' he asked, looking gruesome.

'Yes! You know I am.'

'And when did you begin with him?'

'In the spring.'

He was silent like some beast in a trap.

'And it *was* you, then, in the bedroom at the cottage?'

So he had really inwardly known all the time.

'Yes!'

He still leaned forward in his chair, gazing at her like a cornered beast.

'My God, you ought to be wiped off the face of the earth!'

'Why?' she ejaculated faintly.

But he seemed not to hear.

'That scum! That bumptious lout! That miserable cad! And carrying on with him all the time, while you were here and he was one of my servants! My God, my God, is there any end to the beastly lowness of women!'

He was beside himself with rage, as she knew he would be.

'And you mean to say you want to have a child to a cad like that?'

'Yes! I'm going to.'

'You're going to! You mean you're sure! How long have you been sure?'

'Since June.'

He was speechless, and the queer blank look of a child came over him again.

'You'd wonder,' he said at last, 'that such beings were ever allowed to be born.'

'What beings?' she asked.

He looked at her weirdly, without an answer. It was obvious he couldn't even accept the fact of the existence of Mellors, in any connexion with his own life. It was sheer, unspeakable, impotent hate.

'And do you mean to say you'd marry him?—and bear his foul name?' he asked at length.

'Yes, that's what I want.'

He was again as if dumbfounded.

'Yes!' he said at last. 'That proves that what I've always thought about you is correct: you're not normal, you're not in your right senses. You're one of those half-insane, perverted women who must run after depravity, the *nostalgie de la boue.*'

Suddenly he had become almost wistfully moral, seeing himself the incarnation of good, and people like Mellors and Connie the incarnation of mud, of evil. He seemed to be growing vague, inside a nimbus.

'So don't you think you'd better divorce me and have done with it?' she said.

'No! You can go where you like, but I shan't divorce you,' he said idiotically.

'Why not?'

He was silent, in the silence of imbecile obstinacy.

'Would you even let the child be legally yours, and your heir?' she said.

'I care nothing about the child.'

'But if it's a boy it will be legally your son, and it will inherit your title, and have Wragby.'

'I care nothing about that,' he said.

'But you *must*! I shall prevent the child from being legally yours, if I can. I'd so much rather it were illegitimate, and mine: if it can't be Mellors'.'

'Do as you like about that.'

He was immovable.

'And won't you divorce me?' she said. 'You can use Duncan as a pretext! There'd be no need to bring in the real name. Duncan doesn't mind.'

'*I* shall never divorce you,' he said, as if a nail had been driven in.

'But why? Because I want you to?'

'Because I follow my own inclination, and I'm not inclined to.'

It was useless. She went upstairs and told Hilda the upshot.

'Better get away tomorrow,' said Hilda, 'and let him come to his senses.'
So Connie spent half the night packing her really private and personal
effects. In the morning she had her trunks sent to the station, without telling
Clifford. She decided to see him only to say good-bye, before lunch.

But she spoke to Mrs Bolton.

'I must say good-bye to you, Mrs Bolton, you know why. But I can trust you
not to talk.'

'Oh, you can trust me, your Ladyship, though it's a sad blow for us here,
indeed. But I hope you'll be happy with the other gentleman.'

'The other gentleman! It's Mr Mellors, and I care for him. Sir Clifford
knows. But don't say anything to anybody. And if one day you think Sir
Clifford may be willing to divorce me, let me know, will you? I should like to be
properly married to the man I care for.'

'I'm sure you would, my Lady. Oh, you can trust me. I'll be faithful to Sir
Clifford, and I'll be faithful to you, for I can see you're both right in your own
ways.'

'Thank you! And look! I want to give you this—may I?' So Connie left
Wragby once more, and went on with Hilda to Scotland. Mellors went into the
country and got work on a farm. The idea was, he should get his divorce, if
possible, whether Connie got hers or not. And for six months he should work at
farming, so that eventually he and Connie could have some small farm of their
own, into which he could put his energy. For he would have to have some work,
even hard work, to do, and he would have to make his own living, even if her
capital started him.

So they would have to wait till spring was in, till the baby was born, till the
early summer came round again.

The Grange Farm   *Old Heanor*   *29 September*

I got on here with a bit of contriving, because I knew Richards, the company engineer, in the
army. It is a farm belonging to Butler and Smitham Colliery Company, they use it for raising hay
and oats for the pit-ponies; not a private concern. But they've got cows and pigs and all the rest of it,
and I get thirty shillings a week as labourer. Rowley, the farmer, puts me on to as many jobs as he
can, so that I can learn as much as possible between now and next Easter. I've not heard a thing
about Bertha. I've no idea why she didn't show up at the divorce, nor where she is nor what she's up
to. But if I keep quiet till March I suppose I shall be free. And don't you bother about Sir Clifford.
He'll want to get rid of you one of these days. If he leaves you alone, it's a lot.

I've got lodging in a bit of an old cottage in Engine Row, very decent. The man is engine-driver at
High Park, tall, with a beard, and very chapel. The woman is a birdy bit of a thing who loves
anything superior, King's English and allow-me! all the time. But they lost their only son in the
war, and it's sort of knocked a hole in them. There's a long gawky lass of a daughter training for a
school-teacher, and I help her with her lessons sometimes, so we're quite the family. But they're
very decent people, and only too kind to me. I expect I'm more coddled than you are.

I like farming all right. It's not inspiring, but then I don't ask to be inspired. I'm used to horses,
and cows, though they are very female, have a soothing effect on me. When I sit with my head in her
side, milking, I feel very solaced. They have six rather fine Herefords. Oat-harvest is just over and I
enjoyed it, in spite of sore hands and a lot of rain. I don't take much notice of people, but get on with
them all right. Most things one just ignores.

The pits are working badly; this is a colliery district like Tevershall, only prettier. I sometimes sit
in the Wellington and talk to the men. They grumble a lot, but they're not going to alter anything.
As everybody says, the Notts–Derby miners have got their hearts in the right place. But the rest of
their anatomy must be in the wrong place, in a world that has no use for them. I like them, but they
don't cheer me much: not enough of the old fighting-cock in them. They talk a lot about
nationalization, nationalization of royalties, nationalization of the whole industry. But you can't
nationalize coal and leave all the other industries as they are. They talk about putting coal to new
uses, like Sir Clifford is trying to do. It may work here and there, but not as a general thing, I doubt.

Whatever you make you've got to sell it. The men are very apathetic. They feel the whole damned thing is doomed, and I believe it is. And they are doomed along with it. Some of the young ones spout about a Soviet, but there's not much conviction in them. There's no sort of conviction about anything, except that it's all a muddle and a hole. Even under a Soviet you've still got to sell coal: and that's the difficulty.

We've got this great industrial population, and they've got to be fed, so the damn show has to be kept going somehow. The women talk a lot more than the men, nowadays, and they are a sight more cock-sure. The men are limp, they feel a doom somewhere, and they go about as if there was nothing to be done. Anyhow, nobody knows what should be done, in spite of all the talk. The young ones get mad because they've no money to spend. Their whole life depends on spending money, and now they've got none to spend. That's our civilization and our education: bring up the masses to depend entirely on spending money, and then the money gives out. The pits are working two days, two and a half days a week, and there's no sign of betterment even for the winter. It means a man bringing up a family on twenty-five and thirty shillings. The women are the maddest of all. But then they're the maddest for spending, nowadays.

If you could only tell them that living and spending isn't the same thing! But it's no good. If only they were educated to *live* instead of earn and spend, they could manage very happily on twenty-five shillings. If the men wore scarlet trousers as I said, they wouldn't think so much of money: if they could dance and hop and skip, and sing and swagger and be handsome, they could do with very little cash. And amuse the women themselves, and be amused by the women. They ought to learn to be naked and handsome, and to sing in a mass and dance the old group dances, and carve the stools they sit on, and embroider their own emblems. Then they wouldn't need money. And that's the only way to solve the industrial problem: train the people to be able to live and live in handsomeness, without needing to spend. But you can't do it. They're all one-track minds nowadays. Whereas the mass of people oughtn't even to try to think, because they can't. They should be alive and frisky, and acknowledge the great god Pan. He's the only god for the masses, forever. The few can go in for higher cults if they like. But let the mass be forever pagan.

But the colliers aren't pagan, far from it. They're a sad lot, a deadened lot of men: dead to their women, dead to life. The young ones scoot about on motor-bikes with girls, and jazz when they get a chance. But they're very dead. And it needs money. Money poisons you when you've got it, and starves you when you haven't.

I'm sure you're sick of all this. But I don't want to harp on myself, and I've nothing happening to me. I don't like to think too much about you, in my head, that only makes a mess of us both. But, of course, what I live for now is for you and me to live together. I'm frightened, really. I feel the devil in the air, and he'll try to get us. Or not the devil, Mammon: which I think, after all, is only the mass-will of people, wanting money and hating life. Anyhow, I feel grasping white hands in the air, wanting to get hold of the throat of anybody who tries to live, to live beyond money, and squeeze the life out. There's a bad time coming. There's a bad time coming, boys, there's a bad time coming! If things go on as they are, there's nothing lies in the future but death and destruction, for these industrial masses. I feel my inside turn to water sometimes, and there you are, going to have a child by me. But never mind. All the bad times that ever have been, haven't been able to blow the crocus out: not even the love of women. So they won't be able to blow out my wanting you, nor the little glow there is between you and me. We'll be together next year. And though I'm frightened, I believe in your being with me. A man has to fend and fettle for the best, and then trust in something beyond himself. You can't insure against the future, except by really believing in the best bit of you, and in the power beyond it. So I believe in the little flame between us. For me now, it's the only thing in the world. I've got no friends, not inward friends. Only you. And now the little flame is all I care about in my life. There's the baby, but that is a side issue. It's my Pentecost, the forked flame between me and you. The old Pentecost isn't quite right. Me and God is a bit uppish, somehow. But the little forked flame between me and you: there you are! That's what I abide by, and will abide by, Cliffords and Berthas, collier companies and governments and the money-mass of people all notwithstanding.

That's why I don't like to start thinking about you actually. It only tortures me, and does you no good. I don't want you to be away from me. But if I start fretting it wastes something. Patience, always patience. This is my fortieth winter. And I can't help all the winters that have been. But this winter I'll stick to my little Pentecost flame, and have some peace. And I won't let the breath of people blow it out. I believe in a higher mystery, that doesn't let even the crocus be blown out. And if you're in Scotland and I'm in the Midlands, and I can't put my arms round you, and wrap my legs round you, yet I've got something of you. My soul softly flaps in the little Pentecost flame with you, like the peace of fucking. We fucked a flame into being. Even the flowers are fucked into being between the sun and the earth. But it's a delicate thing, and takes patience and the long pause.

So I love chastity now, because it is the peace that comes of fucking. I love being chaste now. I love it as snowdrops love the snow. I love this chastity, which is the pause of peace of our fucking, between us now like a snowdrop of forked white fire. And when the real spring comes, when the drawing together comes, then we can fuck the little flame brilliant and yellow, brilliant. But not now, not yet! Now is the time to be chaste, it is so good to be chaste, like a river of cool water in my soul. I love the chastity now that it flows between us. It is like fresh water and rain. How can men want wearisomely to philander. What a misery to be like Don Juan, and impotent ever to fuck oneself into peace, and the little flame alight, impotent and unable to be chaste in the cool betweenwhiles, as by a river.

Well, so many words, because I can't touch you. If I could sleep with my arms round you, the ink could stay in the bottle. We could be chaste together just as we can fuck together. But we have to be separate for a while, and I suppose it is really the wiser way. If only one were sure.

Never mind, never mind, we won't get worked up. We really trust in the little flame, and in the unnamed god that shields it from being blown out. There's so much of you here with me, really, that it's a pity you aren't all here.

Never mind about Sir Clifford. If you don't hear anything from him, never mind. He can't really do anything to you. Wait, he will want to get rid of you at last, to cast you out. And if he doesn't, we'll manage to keep clear of him. But he will. In the end he will want to spew you out as the abominable thing.

Now I can't even leave off writing to you.

But a great deal of us is together, and we can but abide by it, and steer our courses to meet soon. John Thomas says good-night to Lady Jane, a little droopingly, but with a hopeful heart.